THE SIX GREATEST NOVELS OF
ANATOLE FRANCE

*Évariste walked beside Élodie, smilingly recalling memories
of their first meetings.*

THE SIX GREATEST NOVELS
OF
ANATOLE FRANCE

Penguin Island · The Crime of Sylvestre
Bonnard · The Revolt of the Angels
The Gods Are Athirst · Thaïs
The Red Lily

Decorations by
FRANK C. PAPÉ, JOHN AUSTEN
DONIA NACHSHEN

WILDSIDE PRESS

CONTENTS

PENGUIN ISLAND

BOOK I: THE BEGINNINGS

I

LIFE OF SAINT MAËL

MAËL, a scion of a royal family of Cambria, was sent in his ninth year to the Abbey of Yvern so that he might there study both sacred and profane learning. At the age of fourteen he renounced his patrimony and took a vow to serve the Lord. His time was divided, according to the rule, between the singing of hymns, the study of grammar, and the meditation of eternal truths.

A celestial perfume soon disclosed the virtues of the monk throughout the cloister, and when the blessed Gal, the Abbot of Yvern, departed from this world into the next, young Maël succeeded him in the government of the monastery. He established therein a school, an infirmary, a guest-house, a forge, work-shops of all kinds, and sheds for building ships, and he compelled the monks to till the lands in the neighbourhood. With his own hands he cultivated the garden of the Abbey, he worked in metals, he instructed the novices, and his life was gently gliding along like a stream that reflects the heaven and fertilizes the fields.

At the close of the day this servant of God was accustomed to seat himself on the cliff, in the place that is to-day still called St. Maël's chair. At his feet the rocks bristling with green seaweed and tawny wrack seemed like black dragons as they faced the foam of the waves with their monstrous breasts. He watched the sun descending into the ocean like a red Host whose glorious blood gave a purple tone to the clouds and to the summits of the waves. And the holy man saw in this the image of the mystery of the Cross, by which the divine blood has clothed the earth with a royal purple. In the offing a line of dark blue marked the shores of the island of Gad where St. Bridget, who had been given the veil by St. Malo, ruled over a convent of women.

Now Bridget, knowing the merits of the venerable Maël, begged from him some work of his hands as a rich present. Maël cast a hand-bell of bronze for her and, when it was finished he blessed it and threw it into the sea. And the bell went ringing towards the coast of Gad, where St. Bridget, warned by the sound of the bell upon the waves, received it piously, and carried it in solemn procession with singing of psalms into the chapel of the convent.

Thus the holy Maël advanced from virtue to virtue. He had already passed through two-thirds of the way of life, and he hoped peacefully to reach his terrestrial end in the midst of his spiritual brethren, when he knew by a certain sign that the Divine wisdom had decided otherwise, and that the Lord was calling him to less peaceful but not less meritorious labours.

II

THE APOSTOLICAL VOCATION OF SAINT MAËL

ONE day as he walked in meditation to the furthest point of a tranquil beach, for which rocks jutting out into the sea formed a rugged dam, he saw a trough of stone which floated like a boat upon the waters.

It was in a vessel similar to this that St. Guirec, the great St. Columba, and so many holy men from Scotland and from Ireland had gone forth to evangelize Armorica. More recently still, St. Avoye having come from England, ascended the river Auray in a mortar made of rose-coloured granite into which children were afterwards placed in order to make them strong; St. Vouga passed from Hibernia to Cornwall on a rock whose fragments preserved at Penmarch, will cure of fever such pilgrims as place these splinters on their heads. St. Samson entered the Bay of St. Michael's Mount in a granite vessel which will one day be called St. Samson's basin. It is because of these facts that when he saw the stone trough the holy Maël understood that the Lord intended him for the apostolate of the pagans who still peopled the coast and the Breton islands.

He handed his ashen staff to the holy Budoc, thus investing him with the government of the monastery. Then, furnished with bread, a barrel of fresh water, and the book of the Holy Gospels, he entered the stone trough which carried him gently to the island of Hœdic.

This island is perpetually buffeted by the winds. In it some poor men fished among the clefts of the rocks and laboriously cultivated vegetables in gardens full of sand and pebbles that were sheltered from the wind by walls of barren stone and hedges of tamarisk. A

I

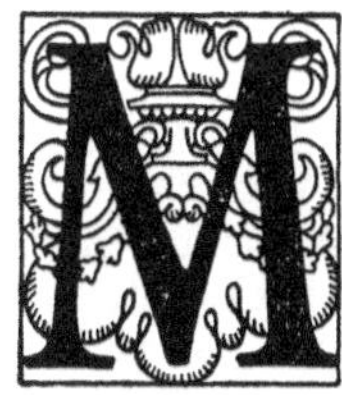

beautiful fig-tree raised itself in a hollow of the island and thrust forth its branches far and wide. The inhabitants of the island used to worship it.

And the holy Maël said to them: "You worship this tree because it is beautiful. Therefore you are capable of feeling beauty. Now I come to reveal to you the hidden beauty." And he taught them the Gospel. And after having instructed them, he baptized them with salt and water.

The islands of Morbihan were more numerous in those times than they are to-day. For since then many have been swallowed up by the sea. St. Maël evangelized sixty of them. Then in his granite trough he ascended the river Auray. And after sailing for three hours he landed before a Roman house. A thin column of smoke went up from the roof. The holy man crossed the threshold on which there was a mosaic representing a dog with its hind legs outstretched and its lips drawn back. He was welcomed by an old couple, Marcus Combabus and Valeria Moerens, who lived there on the products of their lands. There was a portico round the interior court the columns of which were painted red, half their height upwards from the base. A fountain made of shells stood against the wall and under the portico there rose an altar with a niche in which the master of the house had placed some little idols made of baked earth and whitened with whitewash. Some represented winged children, others Apollo or Mercury, and several were in the form of a naked woman twisting her hair. But the holy Maël, observing those figures, discovered among them the image of a young mother holding a child upon her knees.

Immediately pointing to that image he said:

"That is the Virgin, the mother of God. The poet Virgil foretold her in Sibylline verses before she was born and, in angelical tones he sang *Jam redit et virgo*. Throughout heathendom prophetic figures of her have been made, like that which you, O Marcus, have placed upon this altar. And without doubt it is she who has protected your modest household. Thus it is that those who faithfully observe the natural law prepare themselves for the knowledge of revealed truths."

Marcus Combabus and Valeria Moerens, having been instructed by this speech, were converted to the Christian faith. They received baptism together with their young freedwoman, Caelia Avitella, who was dearer to them than the light of their eyes. All their tenants renounced paganism and were baptized on the same day.

Marcus Combabus, Valeria Moerens, and Caelia Avitella led thenceforth a life full of merit. They died in the Lord and were admitted into the canon of the saints.

For thirty-seven years longer the blessed Maël evangelized the pagans of the inner lands. He built two hundred and eighteen chapels and seventy-four abbeys.

Now on a certain day in the city of Vannes, where he was preaching the Gospel, he learned that the monks of Yvern had in his absence declined from the rule of St. Gal. Immediately, with the zeal of a hen who gathers her brood, he repaired to his erring children. He was then towards the end of his ninety-seventh year; his figure was bent, but his arms were still strong, and his speech was poured forth abundantly like winter snow in the depths of the valleys.

Abbot Budoc restored the ashen staff to St. Maël and informed him of the unhappy state into which the Abbey had fallen. The monks were in disagreement as to the date on which the festival of Easter ought to be celebrated. Some held for the Roman calendar, others for the Greek calendar, and the horrors of a chronological schism distracted the monastery.

There also prevailed another cause of disorder. The nuns of the island of Gad, sadly fallen from their former virtue, continually came in boats to the coast of Yvern. The monks received them in the guest-house and from this there arose scandals which filled pious souls with desolation.

Having finished his faithful report, Abbot Budoc concluded in these terms:

"Since the coming of these nuns the innocence and peace of the monks are at an end."

"I readily believe it," answered the blessed Maël. "For woman is a cleverly constructed snare by which we are taken even before we suspect the trap. Alas! the delightful attraction of these creatures is exerted with even greater force from a distance than when they are close at hand. The less they satisfy desire the more they inspire it. This is the reason why a poet wrote this verse to one of them:

> When present I avoid thee, but when away I find thee.

Thus we see, my son, that the blandishments of carnal love have more power over hermits and monks than over men who live in the world. All through my life the demon of lust has tempted me in various ways, but his strongest temptations did not come to me from meeting a woman, however beautiful and fragrant she was. They came to me from the image of an absent woman. Even now, though full of days and approaching my ninety-eighth year, I am often led by the Enemy to sin against chastity at least in thought. At night when I am cold in my bed and my frozen old bones rattle together with a dull sound I hear voices reciting the second verse of the third Book of the Kings: 'Wherefore his servants said unto him, Let there be sought for my lord the king a young virgin: and let her stand before the king, and let her cherish him, and let her lie in thy bosom, that my lord the king may get heat,' and the devil shows me a girl in the bloom of youth who says to me: 'I am thy Abishag; I am thy Shunamite. Make, O my lord, room for me in thy couch.'

"Believe me," added the old man, "it is only by the special aid of Heaven that a monk can keep his chastity in act and in intention."

Applying himself immediately to restore innocence and peace to the monastery, he corrected the calendar according to the calculations of chronology and astronomy and he compelled all the monks to accept his decision; he sent the women who had declined from St. Bridget's rule back to their convent; but far from driving them away brutally, he caused them to be led to their boat with singing of psalms and litanies.

"Let us respect in them," he said, "the daughters of Bridget and the betrothed of the Lord. Let us beware lest we imitate the Pharisees who affect to despise sinners. The sin of these women and not their persons should be abased, and they should be made ashamed of what they have done and not of what they are, for they are all creatures of God."

And the holy man exhorted his monks to obey faithfully the rule of their order.

"When it does not yield to the rudder," said he to them, "the ship yields to the rock."

III

THE TEMPTATION OF SAINT MAËL

THE blessed Maël had scarcely restored order in the Abbey of Yvern before he learned that the inhabitants of the island of Hœdic, his first catechumens and the dearest of all to his heart, had returned to paganism, and that they were hanging crowns of flowers and fillets of wool to the branches of the sacred fig-tree.

The boatman who brought this sad news expressed a fear that soon those misguided men might violently destroy the chapel that had been built on the shore of their island.

The holy man resolved forthwith to visit his faithless children, so that he might lead them back to the faith and prevent them from yielding to such sacrilege. As he went down to the bay where his stone trough was moored, he turned his eyes to the sheds, then filled with the noise of saws and of hammers, which, thirty years before, he had erected on the fringe of that bay for the purpose of building ships.

At that moment, the Devil, who never tires, went out from the sheds and, under the appearance of a monk called Samson, he approached the holy man and tempted him thus:

"Father, the inhabitants of the island of Hœdic commit sins unceasingly. Every moment that passes removes them farther from God. They are soon going to use violence towards the chapel that you have raised with your own venerable hands on the shore of their island. Time is pressing. Do you not think that your stone trough would carry you more quickly towards them if it were rigged like a boat and furnished with a rudder, a mast, and a sail, for then you would be driven by the wind? Your arms are still strong and able to steer a small craft. It would be a good thing, too, to put a sharp stem in front of your apostolic trough. You are much too clear-sighted not to have thought of it already."

"Truly time is pressing," answered the holy man. "But to do as you say, Samson, my son, would it not be to make myself like those men of little faith who do not trust the Lord? Would it not be to despise the gifts of Him who has sent me this stone vessel without rigging or sail?"

This question, the Devil, who is a great theologian, answered by another.

"Father, is it praiseworthy to wait, with our arms folded, until help comes from on high, and to ask everything from Him who can do all things, instead of acting by human prudence and helping ourselves?"

"It certainly is not," answered the holy Maël, "and to neglect to act by human prudence is tempting God."

"Well," urged the Devil, "is it not prudence in this case to rig the vessel?"

"It would be prudence if we could not attain our end in any other way."

"Is your vessel then so very speedy?"

"It is as speedy as God pleases."

"What do you know about it? It goes like Abbot Budoc's mule. It is a regular old tub. Are you forbidden to make it speedier?"

"My son, clearness adorns your words, but they are unduly over-confident. Remember that this vessel is miraculous."

"It is, father. A granite trough that floats on the water like a cork is a miraculous trough. There is not the slightest doubt about it. What conclusion do you draw from that?"

"I am greatly perplexed. Is it right to perfect so miraculous a machine by human and natural means?"

"Father, if you lost your right foot and God restored it to you, would not that foot be miraculous?"

"Without doubt, my son."

"Would you put a shoe on it?"

"Assuredly."

"Well, then, if you believe that one may cover a miraculous foot with a natural shoe, you should also believe that we can put natural rigging on a miraculous boat. That is clear. Alas! Why must the holiest persons have their moments of weakness and despondency? The most illustrious of the apostles of Brittany could accomplish works worthy of eternal glory . . . But his spirit is tardy and his hand is slothful. Farewell then, father! Travel by short and slow stages and when at last you approach the coast of Hœdic you will see the smoking ruins of the chapel that was built and consecrated by your own hands. The pagans will have burned it and with it the deacon you left there. He will be as thoroughly roasted as a black pudding."

"My trouble is extreme," said the servant of God, drying with his sleeve the sweat that gathered upon his brow. "But tell me, Samson, my son, would not rigging this stone trough be a difficult piece of work? And if we undertook it might we not lose time instead of gaining it?"

"Ah! father," exclaimed the Devil, "in one turning of the hour-glass the thing would be done. We shall find the necessary rigging in this shed that you have formerly built here on the coast and in those store-houses abundantly stocked through your care. I will myself regulate all the ship's fittings. Before being a monk I was a sailor and a carpenter and I have worked at many other trades as well. Let us to work."

Immediately he drew the holy man into an out-house filled with all things needful for fitting out a boat.

"That for you, father!"

And he placed on his shoulders the sail, the mast, the gaff, and the boom.

Then, himself bearing a stem and a rudder with its screw and tiller, and seizing a carpenter's bag full of tools, he ran to the shore, dragging the holy man after him by his habit. The latter was bent, sweating, and breathless, under the burden of canvas and wood.

IV

ST. MAËL'S NAVIGATION ON THE OCEAN OF ICE

THE Devil, having tucked his clothes up to his armpits, dragged the trough on the sand, and fitted the rigging in less than an hour.

As soon as the holy Maël had embarked, the vessel, with all its sails set, cleft through the waters with such speed that the coast was almost immediately out of sight. The old man steered to the south so as to double the Land's End, but an irresistible current carried him to the south-west. He went along the southern coast of Ireland and turned sharply towards the north. In the evening the wind freshened. In vain did Maël attempt to furl the sail. The vessel flew distractedly towards the fabulous seas.

By the light of the moon the immodest sirens of the North came around him with their hempen-coloured hair, raising their white throats and their rose-tinted limbs out of the sea; and beating the water into foam with their emerald tails, they sang in cadence:

> Whither go'st thou, gentle Maël,
> In thy trough distracted?
> All distended is thy sail
> Like the breast of Juno
> When from it gushed the Milky Way.

For a moment their harmonious laughter followed him beneath the stars, but the vessel fled on, a hundred times more swiftly than the red ship of a Viking. And the petrels, surprised in their flight, clung with their feet to the hair of the holy man.

Soon a tempest arose full of darkness and groanings, and the trough, driven by a furious wind, flew like a sea-mew through the mist and the surge.

After a night of three times twenty-four hours the darkness was suddenly rent and the holy man discovered on the horizon a shore more dazzling than diamond. The coast rapidly grew larger, and soon by the glacial light of a torpid and sunken sun, Maël saw, rising above the waves, the silent streets of a white city, which, vaster than Thebes with its hundred gates, extended as far as the eye could see the ruins of its forum built of snow, its palaces of frost, its crystal arches, and its iridescent obelisks.

The ocean was covered with floating ice-bergs around which swam men of the sea of a wild yet gentle appearance. And Leviathan passed by hurling a column of water up to the clouds.

Moreover, on a block of ice which floated at the same rate as the stone trough there was seated a white bear holding her little one in her arms, and Maël heard her murmuring in a low voice this verse of Virgil, *Incipe parve puer.*

And full of sadness and trouble, the old man wept.

The fresh water had frozen and burst the barrel that contained it. And Maël was sucking pieces of ice to quench his thirst, and his food was bread dipped in dirty water. His beard and his hair were broken like glass. His habit was covered with a layer of ice and cut into him at every movement of his limbs. Huge waves rose up and opened their foaming jaws at the old man. Twenty times the boat was filled by masses of sea. And the ocean swallowed up the book of the Holy Gospels which the apostle guarded with extreme care in a purple cover marked with a golden cross.

Now on the thirtieth day the sea calmed. And lo! with a frightful clamour of sky and waters a mountain of dazzling whiteness advanced towards the stone vessel. Maël steered to avoid it, but the tiller broke in his hands. To lessen the speed of his progress towards the rock he attempted to reef the sails, but when he tried to knot the reef-points the wind pulled them away from him and the rope seared his hands. He saw three demons with wings of black skin having hooks at their ends, who, hanging from the rigging, were puffing with their breath against the sails.

Understanding from this sight that the Enemy had governed him in all these things, he guarded himself by making the sign of the Cross. Immediately a furious gust of wind filled with the noise of sobs and howls struck the stone trough, carried off the mast with all the sails, and tore away the rudder and the stem.

The trough was drifting on the sea, which had now grown calm. The holy man knelt and gave thanks to the Lord who had delivered him from the snares of the demon. Then he recognised, sitting on a block of ice, the mother bear who had spoken during the storm. She pressed her beloved child to her bosom, and in her hand she held a purple book marked with a golden cross. Hailing the granite trough, she saluted the holy man with these words:

"Pax tibi Maël"

And she held out the book to him.

The holy man recognised his evangelistary, and, full of astonishment, he sang in the tepid air a hymn to the Creator and His creation.

V

THE BAPTISM OF THE PENGUINS

AFTER having drifted for an hour the holy man approached a narrow strand, shut in by steep mountains. He went along the coast for a whole day and a night, passing around the reef which formed an insuperable barrier. He discovered in this way that it was a round island in the middle of which rose a mountain crowned with clouds. He joyfully breathed the fresh breath of the moist air. Rain fell, and this was so pleasant that the holy man said to the Lord:

"Lord, this is the island of tears, the island of contrition."

The strand was deserted. Worn out with fatigue and hunger, he sat down on a rock in the hollow of which there lay some yellow eggs, marked with black spots, and about as large as those of a swan. But he did not touch them, saying:

"Birds are the living praises of God. I should not like a single one of these praises to be lacking through me."

And he munched the lichens which he tore from the crannies of the rocks.

The holy man had gone almost entirely round the island without meeting any inhabitants, when he came to a vast amphitheatre formed of black and red rocks whose summits became tinged with blue as they rose towards the clouds, and they were filled with sonorous cascades.

The reflection from the polar ice had hurt the old man's eyes, but a feeble gleam of light still shone through his swollen eyelids. He distinguished animated forms which filled the rocks, in stages, like a crowd of men on the tiers of an amphitheatre. And at the same time, his ears, deafened by the continual noises of the sea, heard a feeble sound of voices. Thinking that what he saw were men living under the natural law, and that the Lord had sent him to teach them the Divine law, he preached the gospel to them.

Mounted on a lofty stone in the midst of the wild circus:

"Inhabitants of this island," said he, "although you be of small stature, you look less like a band of fishermen and mariners than like the senate of a judicious republic. By your gravity, your silence, your tranquil deportment, you form on this wild rock an assembly comparable to the Conscript Fathers at Rome deliberat-

ing in the temple of Victory, or rather, to the philosophers of
Athens disputing on the benches of the Areopagus. Doubtless you
possess neither their science nor their genius, but perhaps in the
sight of God you are their superiors. I believe that you are simple
and good. As I went round your island I saw no image of murder, no sign of carnage, no enemies' heads or scalps hung from a
lofty pole or nailed to the doors of your villages. You appear to me
to have no arts and not to work in metals. But your hearts are
pure and your hands are innocent, and the truth will easily enter
into your souls."

Now what he had taken for men of small stature but of grave
bearing were penguins whom the spring had gathered together, and
who were ranged in couples on the natural steps of the rock, erect
in the majesty of their large white bellies. From moment to moment they moved their winglets like arms, and uttered peaceful
cries. They did not fear men, for they did not know them, and had
never received any harm from them; and there was in the monk
a certain gentleness that reassured the most timid animals and
that pleased these penguins extremely. With a friendly curiosity
they turned towards him their little round eyes lengthened in front
by a white oval spot that gave something odd and human to their
appearance.

Touched by their attention, the holy man taught them the Gospel.

"Inhabitants of this island, the early day that has just risen over
your rocks is the image of the heavenly day that rises in your
souls. For I bring you the inner light; I bring you the light and
heat of the soul. Just as the sun melts the ice of your mountains
so Jesus Christ will melt the ice of your hearts."

Thus the old man spoke. As everywhere throughout nature voice
calls to voice, as all which breathes in the light of day loves alter-
nate strains, these penguins answered the old man by the sounds
of their throats. And their voices were soft, for it was the season
of their loves.

The holy man, persuaded that they belonged to some idolatrous
people and that in their own language they gave adherence to the
Christian faith, invited them to receive baptism.

"I think," said he to them, "that you bathe often, for all the hollows of the rocks are full of pure water, and as I came to your
assembly I saw several of you plunging into these natural baths.
Now purity of body is the image of spiritual purity."

And he taught them the origin, the nature, and the effects of
baptism.

"Baptism," said he to them, "is Adoption, New Birth, Regeneration, Illumination."

And he explained each of these points to them in succession.

Then, having previously blessed the water that fell from the cascades and recited the exorcisms, he baptized those whom he had just taught, pouring on each of their heads a drop of pure water and pronouncing the sacred words.

And thus for three days and three nights he baptized the birds.

VI

AN ASSEMBLY IN PARADISE

WHEN the baptism of the penguins was known in Paradise, it caused neither joy nor sorrow, but an extreme surprise. The Lord himself was embarrassed. He gathered an assembly of clerics and doctors, and asked them whether they regarded the baptism as valid.

"It is void," said St. Patrick.

"Why is it void?" asked St. Gal, who had evangelized the people of Cornwall and had trained the holy Maël for his apostolical labours.

"The sacrament of baptism," answered St. Patrick, "is void when it is given to birds, just as the sacrament of marriage is void when it is given to a eunuch."

But St. Gal replied:

"What relation do you claim to establish between the baptism of a bird and the marriage of a eunuch? There is none at all. Marriage is, if I may say so, a conditional, a contingent sacrament. The priest blesses an event beforehand; it is evident that if the act is not consummated the benediction remains without effect. That is obvious. I have known on earth, in the town of Antrim, a rich man named Sadoc, who, living in concubinage with a woman, caused her to be the mother of nine children. In his old age, yielding to my reproofs, he consented to marry her, and I blessed their union. Unfortunately Sadoc's great age prevented him from consummating the marriage. A short time afterwards he lost all his property, and Germaine (that was the name of the woman), not feeling herself able to endure poverty, asked for the annulment of a marriage which was no reality. The Pope granted her request, for it was just. So much for marriage. But baptism is conferred without restrictions or reserves of any kind. There is no doubt about it, what the penguins have received is a sacrament."

Called to give his opinion, Pope St. Damasus expressed himself in these terms:

"In order to know if a baptism is valid and will produce its result, that is to say, sanctification, it is necessary to consider who gives it and not who receives it. In truth, the sanctifying virtue of this sacrament results from the exterior act by which it is conferred, without the baptized person co-operating in his own sanctification by any personal act; if it were otherwise it would not be administered to the newly born. And there is no need, in order to baptize, to fulfill any special condition; it is not necessary to be in a state of grace; it is sufficient to have the intention of doing what the Church does, to pronounce the consecrated words and to observe the prescribed forms. Now we cannot doubt that the venerable Maël has observed these conditions. Therefore the penguins are baptized."

"Do you think so?" asked St. Guénolé. "And what then do you believe that baptism really is? Baptism is the process of regeneration by which man is born of water and of the spirit, for having entered the water covered with crimes, he goes out of it a neophyte, a new creature, abounding in the fruits of righteousness; baptism is the seed of immortality; baptism is the pledge of the resurrection; baptism is the burying with Christ in His death and participation in His departure from the sepulchre. That is not a gift to bestow upon birds. Reverend Fathers, let us consider. Baptism washes away original sin; now the penguins were not conceived in sin. It removes the penalty of sin; now the penguins have not sinned. It produces grace and the gift of virtues, uniting Christians to Jesus Christ, as the members to the body, and it is obvious to the senses that penguins cannot acquire the virtues of confessors, of virgins, and of widows, or receive grace and be united to——"

St. Damasus did not allow him to finish.

"That proves," said he warmly, "that the baptism was useless; it does not prove that it was not effective."

"But by this reasoning," said St. Guénolé, "one might baptize in the name of the Father, of the Son, and of the Holy Ghost, by aspersion or immersion, not only a bird or a quadruped, but also an inanimate object, a statue, a table, a chair, etc. That animal would be Christian, that idol, that table would be Christian! It is absurd!"

St. Augustine began to speak. There was a great silence.

"I am going," said the ardent bishop of Hippo, "to show you, by an example, the power of formulas. It deals, it is true, with a diabolical operation. But if it be established that formulas taught by the Devil have effect upon unintelligent animals or even on inanimate objects, how can we longer doubt that the effect of the sacramental formulas extends to the minds of beasts and even to inert matter?

"This is the example. There was during my lifetime in the town of Madaura, the birthplace of the philosopher Apuleius, a witch who was able to attract men to her chamber by burning a few of their hairs along with certain herbs upon her tripod, pronouncing at the same time certain words. Now one day when she wished by this means to gain the love of a young man, she was deceived by her maid, and instead of the young man's hairs, she burned some hairs pulled from a leather bottle, made out of a goatskin that hung in a tavern. During the night the leather bottle, full of wine, capered through the town up to the witch's door. This fact is undoubted. And in sacraments as in enchantments it is the form which operates. The effect of a divine formula cannot be less in power and extent than the effect of an infernal formula."

Having spoken in this fashion the great St. Augustine sat down amidst applause.

One of the blessed, of an advanced age and having a melancholy appearance, asked permission to speak. No one knew him. His name was Probus, and he was not enrolled in the canon of the saints.

"I beg the company's pardon," said he, "I have no halo, and I gained eternal blessedness without any eminent distinction. But after what the great St. Augustine has just told you I believe it right to impart a cruel experience, which I had, relative to the conditions necessary for the validity of a sacrament. The bishop of Hippo is indeed right in what he said. A sacrament depends on the form; its virtue is in its form; its vice is in its form. Listen, confessors and pontiffs, to my woeful story. I was a priest in Rome under the rule of the Emperor Gordianus. Without desiring to recommend myself to you for any special merit, I may say that I exercised my priesthood with piety and zeal. For forty years I served the church of St. Modestus-beyond-the-Walls. My habits were regular. Every Saturday I went to a tavern-keeper called Barjas, who dwelt with his wine-jars under the Porta Capena, and from him I bought the wine that I consecrated daily throughout the week. During that long space of time I never failed for a single morning to consecrate the holy sacrifice of the mass. However, I had no joy, and it was with a heart oppressed by sorrow that, on the steps of the altar I used to ask, 'Why art thou so heavy, O my soul, and why art thou so disquieted within me?' The faithful whom I invited to the holy table gave me cause for affliction, for having, so to speak, the Host that I administered still upon their tongues, they fell again into sin just as if the sacrament had been without power or efficacy. At last I reached the end of my earthly trials, and falling asleep in the Lord, I awoke in this abode of the elect. I learned then from the mouth of the angel who brought me here, that Barjas, the tavern-keeper of the Porta Capena, had sold for wine a decoction of roots and barks in which there was not a single drop of the juice of the grape. I had been unable to transmute this vile brew into blood, for it was not wine, and wine alone is changed into the blood of Jesus Christ. Therefore all my consecrations were invalid, and unknown to us, my faithful and myself had for forty years been deprived of the sacrament and were in fact in a state of excommunication. This revelation threw me

into a stupor which overwhelms me even to-day in this abode of
bliss. I go all through Paradise without ever meeting a single one
of those Christians whom formerly I admitted to the holy table
in the basilica of the blessed Modestus. Deprived of the bread of
angels, they easily gave way to the most abominable vices, and
they have all gone to hell. It gives me some satisfaction to think
that Barjas, the tavern-keeper, is damned. There is in these things
a logic worthy of the author of all logic. Nevertheless my unhappy
example proves that it is sometimes inconvenient that form should
prevail over essence in the sacraments, and I humbly ask, Could not
eternal wisdom remedy this?"

"No," answered the Lord. "The remedy would be worse than the
disease. It would be the ruin of the priesthood if essence prevailed
over form in the laws of salvation."

"Alas! Lord," sighed the humble Probus. "Be persuaded by my
humble experience; as long as you reduce your sacraments to formulas your justice will meet with terrible obstacles."

"I know that better than you do," replied the Lord. "I see in a
single glance both the actual problems which are difficult, and the
future problems which will not be less difficult. Thus I can foretell
that when the sun will have turned round the earth two hundred
and forty times more. . . ."

"Sublime language," exclaimed the angels.

"And worthy of the creator of the world," answered the pontiffs.

"It is," resumed the Lord, "a manner of speaking in accordance
with my old cosmogony and one which I cannot give up without
losing my immutability. . . .

"After the sun, then, will have turned another two hundred and
forty times round the earth, there will not be a single cleric left in
.Rome who knows Latin. When they sing their litanies in the
churches people will invoke Orichel, Roguel, and Totichel, and, as
you know, these are devils and not angels. Many robbers desiring
to make their communions, but fearing that before obtaining pardon they would be forced to give up the things they had robbed
to the Church, will make their confessions to travelling priests,
who, ignorant of both Italian and Latin, and only speaking the
patois of their village, will go through cities and towns selling the
remission of sins for a base price, often for a bottle of wine. Probably we shall not be inconvenienced by those absolutions as they
will want contrition to make them valid, but it may be that their
baptisms will cause us some embarrassment. The priests will become so ignorant that they will baptize children *in nomine patria
et filia et spirita sancta,* as Louis de Potter will take a pleasure in
relating in the third volume of his 'Philosophical, Political, and
Critical History of Christianity.' It will be an arduous question to
decide on the validity of such baptisms; for even if in my sacred
writings I tolerate a Greek less elegant than Plato's and a scarcely

Ciceronian Latin, I cannot possibly admit a piece of pure *patois* as a liturgical formula. And one shudders when one thinks that millions of new-born babes will be baptized by this method. But let us return to our penguins."

"Your divine words, Lord, have already led us back to them," said St. Gal. "In the signs of religion and the laws of salvation form necessarily prevails over essence, and the validity of a sacrament solely depends upon its form. The whole question is whether the penguins have been baptized with the proper forms. Now there is no doubt about the answer."

The fathers and the doctors agreed, and their perplexity became only the more cruel.

"The Christian state," said St. Cornelius, "is not without serious inconveniences for a penguin. In it the birds are obliged to work out their own salvation. How can they succeed? The habits of birds are, in many points, contrary to the commandments of the Church, and the penguins have no reason for changing theirs. I mean that they are not intelligent enough to give up their present habits and assume better."

"They cannot," said the Lord; "my decrees prevent them."

"Nevertheless," resumed St. Cornelius, "in virtue of their baptism their actions no longer remain indifferent. Henceforth they will be good or bad, susceptible of merit or of demerit."

"That is precisely the question we have to deal with," said the Lord.

"I see only one solution," said St. Augustine. "The penguins will go to hell."

"But they have no soul," observed St. Irenaeus.

"It is a pity," sighed Tertullian.

"It is indeed," resumed St. Gal. "And I admit that my disciple, the holy Maël, has, in his mind zeal, created great theological difficulties for the Holy Spirit and introduced disorder into the economy of mysteries."

"He is an old blunderer," cried St. Adjutor of Alsace, shrugging his shoulders.

But the Lord cast a reproachful look on Adjutor.

"Allow me to speak," said he; "the holy Maël has not intuitive knowledge like you, my blessed ones. He does not see me. He is an old man burdened by infirmities; he is half deaf and three parts blind. You are too severe on him. However, I recognise that the situation is an embarrassing one."

"Luckily it is but a passing disorder," said St. Irenaeus. "The penguins are baptized, but their eggs are not, and the evil will stop with the present generation."

"Do not speak thus, Irenaeus my son," said the Lord. "There are exceptions to the laws that men of science lay down on the earth because they are imperfect and have not an exact application to nature. But the laws that I establish are perfect and suffer no exception. We must decide the fate of the baptized penguins without violating any divine law, and in a manner conformable to the decalogue as well as to the commandments of my Church."

"Lord," said St. Gregory Nazianzen, "give them an immortal soul."

"Alas! Lord, what would they do with it," sighed Lactantius. "They have not tuneful voices to sing your praises. They would not be able to celebrate your mysteries."

"Without doubt," said St. Augustine, "they would not observe the divine law."

"They could not," said the Lord.

"They could not," continued St. Augustine. "And if, Lord, in your wisdom, you pour an immortal soul into them, they will burn eternally in hell in virtue of your adorable decrees. Thus will the transcendent order, that this old Welshman has disturbed, be reestablished."

"You propose a correct solution to me, son of Monica," said the Lord, "and one that accords with my wisdom. But it does not satisfy my mercy. And, although in my essence I am immutable, the longer I endure, the more I incline to mildness. This change of character is evident to anyone who reads my two Testaments."

As the discussion continued without much light being thrown upon the matter and as the blessed showed a disposition to keep repeating the same thing, it was decided to consult St. Catherine of Alexandria. This is what was usually done in such cases. St. Catherine while on earth had confounded fifty very learned doctors. She knew Plato's philosophy in addition to the Holy Scriptures, and she also possessed a knowledge of rhetoric.

VII

AN ASSEMBLY IN PARADISE

(*Continuation and End*)

ST. CATHERINE entered the assembly, her head encircled by a crown of emeralds, sapphires, and pearls, and she was clad in a robe of cloth of gold. She carried at her side a blazing wheel, the image of the one whose fragments had struck her persecutors.

The Lord having invited her to speak, she expressed herself in these terms:

"Lord, in order to solve the problem you deign to submit to me I shall not study the habits of animals in general nor those of birds in particular. I shall only remark to the doctors, confessors, and pontiffs gathered in this assembly that the separation between man and animal is not complete since there are monsters who proceed from both. Such are chimeras—half nymphs and half serpents; such are the three Gorgons and the Capripeds; such are the Scyllas and the Sirens who sing in the sea. These have a woman's breast and a fish's tail. Such also are the Centaurs, men down to the waist and the remainder horses. They are a noble race of monsters. One of them, as you know, was able, guided by the light of reason alone, to direct his steps towards eternal blessedness, and you sometimes see his heroic bosom prancing on the clouds. Chiron, the Centaur, deserved for his works on the earth to share the abode of the blessed; he it was who gave Achilles his education; and that young hero, when he left the Centaur's hands, lived for two years, dressed as a young girl, among the daughters of King Lycomedes. He shared their games and their bed without allowing any suspicion to arise that he was not a young virgin like them. Chiron, who taught him such good morals, is, with the Emperor Trajan, the only righteous man who obtained celestial glory by following the law of nature. And yet he was but half human.

"I think I have proved by this example that, to reach eternal blessedness, it is enough to possess some parts of humanity, always on the condition that they are noble. And what Chiron, the Centaur, could obtain without having been regenerated by baptism, would not the penguins deserve too if they became half penguins and half men? That is why, Lord, I entreat you to give old Maël's penguins a human head and breast so that they can praise you worthily. And grant them also an immortal soul—but one of small size."

Thus Catherine spoke, and the fathers, doctors, confessors, and pontiffs heard her with a murmur of approbation.

But St. Anthony, the Hermit, arose and stretching two red and knotty arms towards the Most High:

"Do not so, O Lord God," he cried, "in the name of your holy Paraclete, do not so!"

He spoke with such vehemence that his long white beard shook on his chin like the empty nose-bag of a hungry horse.

"Lord, do not so. Birds with human heads exist already. St. Catherine has told us nothing new."

"The imagination groups and compares; it never creates," replied St. Catherine drily.

"They exist already," continued St. Anthony, who would listen to nothing. "They are called harpies, and they are the most obscene animals in creation. One day as I was having supper in the desert with the Abbot St. Paul, I placed the table outside my cabin under an old sycamore tree. The harpies came and sat in its branches; they deafened us with their shrill cries and cast their excrement over all our food. The clamour of the monsters prevented me from listening to the teaching of the Abbot St. Paul, and we ate birds' dung with our bread and lettuces. Lord, it is impossible to believe that harpies could give thee worthy praise.

"Truly in my temptations I have seen many hybrid beings, not only women-serpents and women-fishes, but beings still more confusedly formed such as men whose bodies were made out of a pot, a bell, a clock, a cupboard full of food and crockery, or even out of a house with doors and windows through which people engaged in their domestic tasks could be seen. Eternity would not suffice were I to describe all the monsters that assailed me in my solitude, from whales rigged like ships to a shower of red insects which changed the water of my fountain into blood. But none were as disgusting as the harpies whose offal polluted the leaves of my sycamore."

"Harpies," observed Lactantius, "are female monsters with birds' bodies. They have a woman's head and breast. Their forwardness, their shamelessness, and their obscenity proceed from their female nature as the poet Virgil demonstrated in his 'Æneid.' They share the curse of Eve."

"Let us not speak of the curse of Eve," said the Lord. "The second Eve has redeemed the first."

Paul Orosius, the author of a universal history that Bossuet was to imitate in later years, arose and prayed to the Lord:

"Lord, hear my prayer and Anthony's. Do not make any more monsters like the Centaurs, Sirens, and Fauns, whom the Greeks, those collectors of fables, loved. You will derive no satisfaction from them. Those species of monsters have pagan inclinations and their double nature does not dispose them to purity of morals."

The bland Lactantius replied in these terms:

"He who has just spoken is assuredly the best historian in Paradise, for Herodotus, Thucydides, Polybius, Livy, Velleius Paterculus, Cornelius Nepos, Suetonius, Manetho, Diodorus Siculus, Dion Cassius, and Lampridius are deprived of the sight of God, and Tacitus suffers in hell the torments that are reserved for blasphemers. But Paul Orosius does not know heaven as well as he knows the earth, for he does not seem to bear in mind that the angels, who proceed from man and bird, are purity itself."

"We are wandering," said the Eternal. "What have we to do with all those centaurs, harpies, and angels? We have to deal with penguins."

"You have spoken to the point, Lord," said the chief of the fifty doctors, who, during their mortal life had been confounded by the Virgin of Alexandria, "and I dare express the opinion that, in order to put an end to the scandal by which heaven is now stirred, old Maël's penguins should, as St. Catherine who confounded us has proposed, be given half of a human body with an eternal soul proportioned to that half."

At this speech there arose in the assembly a great noise of private conversations and disputes of the doctors. The Greek fathers argued with the Latins concerning the substance, nature, and dimensions of the soul that should be given to the penguins.

"Confessors and pontiffs," exclaimed the Lord, "do not imitate the conclaves and synods of the earth. And do not bring into the Church Triumphant those violences that trouble the Church Militant. For it is but too true that in all the councils held under the inspiration of my spirit, in Europe, in Asia, and in Africa, fathers have torn the beards and scratched the eyes of other fathers. Nevertheless they were infallible, for I was with them."

Order being restored, old Hermas arose and slowly uttered these words:

"I will praise you, Lord, for that you caused my mother, Saphira, to be born amidst your people, in the days when the dew of heaven refreshed the earth which was in travail with its Saviour. And I will praise you, Lord, for having granted to me to see with my mortal eyes the Apostles of your divine Son. And I will speak in this illustrious assembly because you have willed that truth should proceed out of the mouths of the humble, and I will say: 'Change these penguins to men. It is the only determination conformable to your justice and your mercy.'"

Several doctors asked permission to speak, others began to do so. No one listened, and all the confessors were tumultuously shaking their palms and their crowns.

The Lord, by a gesture of his right hand, appeased the quarrels of his elect.

"Let us not deliberate any longer," said he. "The opinion broached by gentle old Hermas is the only one conformable to my eternal designs. These birds will be changed into men. I foresee in this several disadvantages. Many of those men will commit sins they would not have committed as penguins. Truly their fate through this change will be far less enviable than if they had been without this baptism and this incorporation into the family of Abraham. But my foreknowledge must not encroach upon their free will.

"In order not to impair human liberty, I will be ignorant of what I know, I will thicken upon my eyes the veils I have pierced, and in my blind clearsightedness I will let myself by surprised by what I have foreseen."

And immediately calling the archangel Raphael:

"Go and find the holy Maël," said he to him; "inform him of his mistake and tell him, armed with my Name, to change these penguins into men."

VIII

METAMORPHOSIS OF THE PENGUINS

HE archangel, having gone down into the Island of the Penguins, found the holy man asleep in the hollow of a rock surrounded by his new disciples. He laid his hand on his shoulder and, having waked him, said in a gentle voice:

"Maël, fear not!"

The holy man, dazzled by a vivid light, inebriated by a delicious odour, recognised the angel of the Lord, and prostrated himself with his forehead on the ground.

The angel continued:

"Maël, know thy error, believing that thou wert baptizing children of Adam thou hast baptized birds; and it is through thee that penguins have entered into the Church of God."

At these words the old man remained stupefied.

And the angel resumed:

"Arise, Maël, arm thyself with the mighty Name of the Lord, and say to these birds, 'Be ye men!' "

And the holy Maël, having wept and prayed, armed himself with the mighty Name of the Lord and said to the birds:

"Be ye men!"

Immediately the penguins were transformed. Their foreheads enlarged and their heads grew round like the dome of St. Maria Rotunda in Rome. Their oval eyes opened more widely on the universe; a fleshy nose clothed the two clefts of their nostrils; their beaks were changed into mouths, and from their mouths went forth speech; their necks grew short and thick; their wings became arms and their claws legs; a restless soul dwelt within the breast of each of them.

However, there remained with them some traces of their first nature. They were inclined to look sideways; they balanced themselves on their short thighs; their bodies were covered with fine down.

And Maël gave thanks to the Lord, because he had incorporated these penguins into the family of Abraham.

But he grieved at the thought that he would soon leave the island to come back no more, and that perhaps when he was far away the faith of the penguins would perish for want of care like a young and tender plant.

And he formed the idea of transporting their island to the coasts of Armorica.

"I know not the designs of eternal Wisdom," said he to himself.

"But if God wills that this island be transported, who could prevent it?"

And the holy man made a very fine cord about forty feet long out of the flax of his stole. He fastened one end of the cord round a point of rock that jutted up through the sand of the shore and, holding the other end of the cord in his hand, he entered the stone trough.

The trough glided over the sea and towed Penguin Island behind it; after nine days' sailing it approached the Breton coast, bringing the island with it.

BOOK II: THE ANCIENT TIMES

I

THE FIRST CLOTHES

NE day St. Maël was sitting by the seashore on a warm stone that he found. He thought it had been warmed by the sun and he gave thanks to God for it, not knowing that the Devil had been resting on it.

The apostle was waiting for the monks of Yvern who had been commissioned to bring a freight of skins and fabrics to clothe the inhabitants of the island of Alca.

Soon he saw a monk called Magis coming ashore and carrying a chest upon his back. This monk enjoyed a great reputation for holiness.

When he had drawn near to the old man he laid the chest on the ground and wiping his forehead with the back of his sleeve, he said:

"Well, father, you wish then to clothe these penguins?"

"Nothing is more needful, my son," said the old man. "Since they have been incorporated into the family of Abraham these penguins share the curse of Eve, and they know that they are naked, a thing of which they were ignorant before. And it is high time to clothe them, for they are losing the down that remained on them after their metamorphosis."

"It is true," said Magis as he cast his eyes over the coast where the penguins were to be seen looking for shrimps, gathering mussels, singing, or sleeping, "they are naked. But do you not think, father, that it would be better to leave them naked? Why clothe them? When they wear clothes and are under the moral law they will assume an immense pride, a vile hypocrisy, and an excessive cruelty."

"Is it possible, my son," sighed the old man, "that you understand so badly the effects of the moral law to which even the heathen submit?"

"The moral law," answered Magis, "forces men who are beasts to live otherwise than beasts, a thing that doubtless puts a constraint upon them, but that also flatters and reassures them; and as they are proud, cowardly, and covetous of pleasure, they willingly submit to restraints that tickle their vanity and on which they found both their present security and the hope of their future happiness. That is the principle of all morality. . . . But let us not mislead ourselves. My companions are unloading their cargo of stuffs and skins on the island. Think, father, while there is still time! To clothe the penguins is a very serious business. At present when a penguin desires a penguin he knows precisely what he desires and his lust is limited by an exact knowledge of its object. At this moment two or three couples of penguins are making love on the beach. See with what simplicity! No one pays any attention and the actors themselves do not seem to be greatly preoccupied. But when the female penguins are clothed, the male penguin will not form so exact a notion of what it is that attracts him to them. His indeterminate desires will fly out into all sorts of dreams and illusions; in short, father, he will know love and its mad torments. And all the time the female penguins will cast down their eyes and bite their lips, and take on airs as if they kept a treasure under their clothes! . . . what a pity!

"The evil will be endurable as long as these people remain rude and poor; but only wait for a thousand years and you will see, father, with what powerful weapons you have endowed the daughters of Alca. If you will allow me, I can give you some idea of it beforehand. I have some old clothes in this chest. Let us take at hazard one of these female penguins to whom the male penguins give such little thought, and let us dress her as well as we can.

"Here is one coming towards us. She is neither more beautiful nor uglier than the others; she is young. No one looks at her. She strolls indolently along the shore, scratching her back and with her finger at her nose as she walks. You cannot help seeing, father, that she has narrow shoulders, clumsy breasts, a stout figure, and short legs. Her reddish knees pucker at every step she takes, and there is, at each of her joints, what looks like a little monkey's head. Her broad and sinewy feet cling to the rock with their four crooked toes, while the great toes stick up like the heads of two cunning serpents. She begins to walk, all her muscles are engaged in the task, and, when we see them working, we think of her as a machine intended for walking rather than as a machine intended for making love, although visibly she is both, and contains within herself several other pieces of machinery besides. Well, venerable apostle, you will see what I am going to make of her."

With these words the monk, Magis, reached the female penguin in three bounds, lifted her up, carried her in his arms with her hair trailing behind her, and threw her, overcome with fright, at the feet of the holy Maël.

, And whilst she wept and begged him to do her no harm, he took a pair of sandals out of his chest and commanded her to put them on.

"Her feet," observed the old man, "will appear smaller when squeezed in by the woollen cords. The soles, being two fingers high, will give an elegant length to her legs and the weight they bear will seem magnified."

As the penguin tied on her sandals she threw a curious look towards the open coffer, and seeing that it was full of jewels and finery, she smiled through her tears.

The monk twisted her hair on the back of her head and covered it with a chaplet of flowers. He encircled her wrist with golden bracelets and making her stand upright, he passed a large linen band beneath her breasts, alleging that her bosom would thereby derive a new dignity and that her sides would be compressed to the greater glory of her hips.

He fixed this band with pins, taking them one by one out of his mouth.

"You can tighten it still more," said the penguin.

When he had, with much care and study, enclosed the soft parts of her bust in this way, he covered her whole body with a rose-coloured tunic which gently followed the lines of her figure.

"Does it hang well?" asked the penguin.

And bending forward with her head on one side and her chin on her shoulder, she kept looking attentively at the appearance of her toilet.

Magis asked her if she did not think the dress a little long, but she answered with assurance that it was not—she would hold it up.

Immediately, taking the back of her skirt in her left hand, she drew it obliquely across her hips, taking care to disclose a glimpse of her heels. Then she went away, walking with short steps and swinging her hips.

She did not turn her head, but as she passed near a stream she glanced out of the corner of her eye at her own reflection.

A male penguin, who met her by chance, stopped in surprise, and retracing his steps began to follow her. As she went along the shore, others coming back from fishing, went up to her, and after looking at her, walked behind her. Those who were lying on the sand got up and joined the rest.

Unceasingly, as she advanced, fresh penguins, descending from the paths of the mountain, coming out of clefts of the rocks, and emerging from the water, added to the size of her retinue.

And all of them, men of ripe age with vigorous shoulders and hairy breasts, agile youths, old men shaking the multitudinous wrinkles of their rosy, and white-haired skins, or dragging their legs thinner and drier than the juniper staff that served them as a third leg, hurried on, panting and emitting an acrid odour and hoarse gasps. Yet she went on peacefully and seemed to see nothing.

"Father," cried Magis, "notice how each one advances with his nose pointed towards the centre of gravity of that young damsel now that the centre is covered by a garment. The sphere inspires the meditations of geometers by the number of its properties. When it proceeds from a physical and living nature it acquires new qualities, and in order that the interest of that figure might be fully revealed to the penguins it was necessary that, ceasing to see it distinctly with their eyes, they should be led to represent it to themselves in their minds. I myself feel at this moment irresistibly attracted towards that penguin. Whether it be because her skirt gives more importance to her hips, and that in its simple magnificence it invests them with a synthetic and general character and allows only the pure idea, the divine principle, of them to be seen, whether this be the cause I cannot say, but I feel that if I embraced her I would hold in my hands the heaven of human pleasure. It is certain that modesty communicates an invincible attraction to women. My uneasiness is so great that it would be vain for me to try to conceal it."

He spoke, and, gathering up his habit, he rushed among the crowd of penguins, pushing, jostling, trampling, and crushing, until he reached the daughter of Alca, whom he seized and suddenly carried in his arms into a cave that had been hollowed out by the sea.

Then the penguins felt as if the sun had gone out. And the holy Maël knew that the Devil had taken the features of the monk, Magis, in order that he might give clothes to the daughter of Alca. He was troubled in spirit, and his soul was sad. As with slow steps he went towards his hermitage he saw the little penguins of six and seven years of age tightening their waists with belts made of seaweed and walking along the shore to see if anybody would follow them.

II

THE FIRST CLOTHES

(Continuation and End)

THE holy Maël felt a profound sadness that the first clothes put upon a daughter of Alca should have betrayed the penguin modesty instead of helping it. He persisted, none the less, in his design of giving clothes to the inhabitants of the miraculous island. Assembling them on the shore, he distributed to them the garments that the monks of Yvern had brought. The male penguins received short tunics and breeches, the female penguins long robes. But these robes were far from creating the effect that the former one had produced.

They were not so beautiful, their shape was uncouth and without art, and no attention was paid to them since every woman had one. As they prepared the meals and worked in the fields they soon had nothing but slovenly bodices and soiled petticoats.

The male penguins loaded their unfortunate consorts with work until they looked like beasts of burden. They knew nothing of the troubles of the heart and the disorders of passion. Their habits were innocent. Incest, though frequent, was a sign of rustic simplicity and if drunkenness led a youth to commit some such crime he thought nothing more about it the day afterwards.

III

SETTING BOUNDS TO THE FIELDS AND THE ORIGIN OF PROPERTY

THE island did not preserve the rugged appearance that it had formerly, when in the midst of floating icebergs it sheltered a population of birds within its rock amphitheatre. Its snow-clad peak had sunk down into a hill from the summit of which one could see the coasts of Armorica eternally covered with mist, and the ocean strewn with sullen reefs like monsters half raised out of its depths.

Its coasts were now very extensive and clearly defined and its shape reminded one of a mulberry leaf. It was suddenly covered with coarse grass, pleasing to the flocks, and with willows, ancient fig-trees, and mighty oaks. This fact is attested by the venerable Bede and several other authors worthy of credence.

To the north the shore formed a deep bay that in after years became one of the most famous ports in the universe. To the east, along a rocky coast beaten by a foaming sea, there stretched a deserted and fragrant heath. It was the Beach of Shadows, and the inhabitants of the island never ventured on it for fear of the serpents that lodged in the hollows of the rocks and lest they might encounter the souls of the dead who resembled livid flames. To the south, orchards and woods bounded the languid Bay of Divers. On this fortunate shore old Maël built a wooden church and a monastery. To the west, two streams, the Clange and the Surelle, watered the fertile valleys of Dalles and Dombes.

Now one autumn morning, as the blessed Maël was walking in the valley of Clange in company with a monk of Yvern called Bulloch, he saw bands of fierce-looking men loaded with stones passing along the roads. At the same time he heard in all directions cries and complaints mounting up from the valley towards the tranquil sky.

And he said to Bulloch:

"I notice with sadness, my son; that since they became men the inhabitants of this island act with less wisdom than formerly. When they were birds they only quarrelled during the season of their love affairs. But now they dispute all the time; they pick quarrels with each other in summer as well as in winter. How greatly have they fallen from that peaceful majesty which made the assembly of the penguins look like the Senate of a wise republic!

"Look towards Surelle, Bulloch, my son. In yonder pleasant valley a dozen men penguins are busy knocking each other down with the spades and picks that they might employ better in tilling the ground. The women, still more cruel than the men, are tearing their opponents' faces with their nails. Alas! Bulloch, my son, why are they murdering each other in this way?"

"From a spirit of fellowship, father, and through forethought for the future," answered Bulloch. "For man is essentially provident and sociable. Such is his character and it is impossible to imagine it apart from a certain appropriation of things. Those penguins whom you see are dividing the ground among themselves."

"Could they not divide it with less violence?" asked the aged man. "As they fight they exchange invectives and threats. I do not distinguish their words, but they are angry ones, judging from the tone."

"They are accusing one another of theft and encroachment," answered Bulloch. "That is the general sense of their speech."

At that moment the holy Maël clasped his hands and sighed deeply.

"Do you see, my son," he exclaimed, "that madman who with his teeth is biting the nose of the adversary he has overthrown and that other one who is pounding a woman's head with a huge stone?"

"I see them," said Bulloch. "They are creating law; they are founding property; they are establishing the principles of civilization, the basis of society, and the foundations of the State."

"How is that?" asked old Maël.

"By setting bounds to their fields. That is the origin of all government. Your penguins, O Master, are performing the most august of functions. Throughout the ages their work will be consecrated by lawyers, and magistrates will confirm it."

Whilst the monk, Bulloch, was pronouncing these words a big penguin with a fair skin and red hair went down into the valley carrying a trunk of a tree upon his shoulder. He went up to a little penguin who was watering his vegetables in the heat of the sun, and shouted to him:

"Your field is mine!"

And having delivered himself of this stout utterance he brought down his club on the head of the little penguin, who fell dead upon the field that his own hands had tilled.

At this sight the holy Maël shuddered through his whole body and poured forth a flood of tears.

And in a voice stifled by horror and fear he addressed this prayer to heaven:

"O Lord, my God, O thou who didst receive young Abel's sacrifices, thou who didst curse Cain, avenge, O Lord, this innocent penguin sacrificed upon his own field and make the murderer feel the weight of thy arm. Is there a more odious crime, is there a graver offence against thy justice, O Lord, than this murder and this robbery?"

"Take care, father," said Bulloch gently, "that what you call murder and robbery may not really be war and conquest, those sacred foundations of empires, those sources of all human virtues and all human greatness. Reflect, above all, that in blaming the big penguin you are attacking property in its origin and in its source. I shall have no trouble in showing you how. To till the land is one thing, to possess it is another, and these two things must not be confused; as regards ownership the right of the first occupier is uncertain and badly founded. The right of conquest, on the other hand, rests on more solid foundations. It is the only right that receives respect since it is the only one that makes itself respected. The sole and proud origin of property is force. It is born and preserved by force. In that it is august and yields only to a greater force. This is why it is correct to say that he who possesses is noble. And that big red man, when he knocked down a labourer to get possession of his field, founded at that moment a very noble house upon this earth. I congratulate him upon it."

Having thus spoken, Bulloch approached the big penguin, who was leaning upon his club as he stood in the blood-stained furrow:

"Lord Greatauk, dreaded Prince," said he, bowing to the ground, "I come to pay you the homage due to the founder of legitimate power and hereditary wealth. The skull of the vile Penguin you have overthrown will, buried in your field, attest for ever the sacred rights of your posterity over this soil that you have ennobled. Blessed be your sons and your sons' sons! They shall be Greatauks, Dukes of Skull, and they shall rule over this island of Alca."

Then raising his voice and turning towards the holy Maël:

"Bless Greatauk, father, for all power comes from God."

Maël remained silent and motionless, with his eyes raised towards heaven; he felt a painful uncertainty in judging the monk Bulloch's doctrine. It was, however, the doctrine destined to prevail in epochs of advanced civilization. Bulloch can be considered as the creator of civil law in Penguinia.

IV

THE FIRST ASSEMBLY OF THE ESTATES
OF PENGUINIA

ULLOCH, my son," said old Maël, "we ought to make a census of the Penguins and inscribe each of their names in a book."

"It is a most urgent matter," answered Bulloch, "there can be no good government without it."

Forthwith, the apostle, with the help of twelve monks, proceeded to make a census of the people.

And old Maël then said:

"Now that we keep a register of all the inhabitants, we ought, Bulloch, my son, to levy a just tax so as to provide for public expenses and the maintenance of the Abbey. Each ought to contribute according to his means. For this reason, my son, call together the Elders of Alca, and in agreement with them we shall establish the tax."

The Elders, being called together, assembled to the number of thirty under the great sycamore in the courtyard of the wooden monastery. They were the first Estates of Penguinia. Three-fourths of them were substantial peasants of Surelle and Clange. Greatauk, as the noblest of the Penguins, sat upon the highest stone.

The venerable Maël took his place in the midst of his monks and uttered these words:

"Children, the Lord when he pleases grants riches to men and he takes them away from them. Now I have called you together to levy contributions from the people so as to provide for public expenses and the maintenance of the monks. I consider that these contributions ought to be in proportion to the wealth of each. Therefore he who has a hundred oxen will give ten; he who has ten will give one."

When the holy man had spoken, Morio, a labourer at Anis-on-the-Clange, one of the richest of the Penguins, rose up and said:

"O Father Maël, I think it right that each should contribute to the public expenses and to the support of the Church. For my part I am ready to give up all that I possess in the interest of my brother Penguins, and if it were necessary I would even cheerfully part with my shirt. All the elders of the people are ready, like me, to sacrifice their goods, and no one can doubt their absolute devotion to their country and their creed. We have, then, only to consider the public interest and to do what it requires. Now, Father, what it requires, what it demands, is not to ask much from those who possess much, for then the rich would be less rich and the poor still poorer. The poor live on the wealth of the rich and that is the reason why that wealth is sacred. Do not touch it, to do so would be an uncalled for evil. You will get no great profit by taking from the rich, for they are very few in number; on the contrary you will strip yourself of all your resources and plunge the country into misery. Whereas if you ask a little from each inhabitant without regard to his wealth, you will collect enough for the public necessities and you will have no need to enquire into each citizen's resources, a thing that would be regarded by all as a most vexatious measure. By taxing all equally and easily you will spare the poor, for you will leave them the wealth of the rich. And how could you possibly proportion taxes to wealth? Yesterday I had two hundred oxen, to-day I have sixty, to-morrow I shall have a hundred. Clunic has three cows, but they are thin; Nicclu has only two, but they are fat. Which is the richer, Clunic or Nicclu? The signs of opulence are deceitful. What is certain is that everyone eats and drinks. Tax people according to what they consume. That would be wisdom and it would be justice."

Thus spoke Morio amid the applause of the Elders.

"I ask that this speech be graven on bronze," cried the monk, Bulloch. "It is spoken for the future; in fifteen hundred years the best of the Penguins will not speak otherwise."

The Elders were still applauding when Greatauk, his hand on the pommel of his sword, made this brief declaration:

"Being noble, I shall not contribute; for to contribute is ignoble. It is for the rabble to pay."

After this warning the Elders separated in silence.

As in Rome, a new census was taken every five years; and by this means it was observed that the population increased rapidly. Although children died in marvellous abundance and plagues and famines came with perfect regularity to devastate entire villages, new Penguins, in continually greater numbers, contributed by their private misery to the public prosperity.

V

THE MARRIAGE OF KRAKEN AND ORBEROSIA

URING these times there lived in the island of Alca a Penguin whose arm was strong and whose mind was subtle. He was called Kraken, and had his dwelling on the Beach of Shadows whither the inhabitants never ventured for fear of serpents that lodged in the hollows of the rocks and lest they might encounter the souls of Penguins that had died without baptism. These, in appearance like livid flames, and uttering doleful groans, wandered night and day along the deserted beach. For it was generally believed, though without proof, that among the Penguins that had been changed into men at the blessed Maël's prayer, several had not received baptism and returned after their death to lament amid the tempests. Kraken dwelt on this savage coast in an inaccessible cavern. The only way to it was through a natural tunnel a hundred feet long, the entrance of which was concealed by a thick wood. One evening as Kraken was walking through this deserted plain he happened to meet a young and charming woman Penguin. She was the one that the monk Magis had clothed with his own hands and thus was the first to have worn the garments of chastity. In remembrance of the day when the astonished crowd of Penguins had seen her moving gloriously in her robe tinted like the dawn, this maiden had received the name of Orberosia.*

At the sight of Kraken she uttered a cry of alarm and darted forward to escape from him. But the hero seized her by the garments that floated behind her, and addressed her in these words:

"Damsel, tell me thy name, thy family and thy country."

But Orberosia kept looking at Kraken with alarm.

"Is it you, I see, sir," she asked him, trembling, "or is it not rather your troubled spirit?"

She spoke in this way because the inhabitants of Alca, having no news of Kraken since he went to live on the Beach of Shadows, believed that he had died and descended among the demons of night.

"Cease to fear, daughter of Alca," answered Kraken. "He who speaks to thee is not a wandering spirit, but a man full of strength and might. I shall soon possess great riches."

And young Orberosia asked:

"How dost thou think of acquiring great riches, O Kraken, since thou art a child of the Penguins?"

"By my intelligence," answered Kraken.

*"Orb, poetically, a globe when speaking of the heavenly bodies. By extension any species of globular body."—*Littre.*

"I know," said Orberosia, "that in the time that thou dwelt among us thou wert renowned for thy skill in hunting and fishing. No one equalled thee in taking fishes in a net or in piercing with thy arrows the swift-flying birds."

"It was but a vulgar and laborious industry, O maiden. I have found a means of gaining much wealth for myself without fatigue. But tell me who thou art?"

"I am called Orberosia," answered the young girl.

"Why art thou so far away from thy dwelling and in the night?"

"Kraken, it was not without the will of Heaven."

"What meanest thou, Orberosia?"

"That Heaven, O Kraken, placed me in thy path, for what reason I know not."

Kraken beheld her for a long time in silence.

Then he said with gentleness:

"Orberosia, come into my house; it is that of the bravest and most ingenious of the sons of the Penguins. If thou art willing to follow me, I will make thee my companion."

Then casting down her eyes, she murmured:

"I will follow thee, master."

It is thus that the fair Orberosia became the consort of the hero Kraken. This marriage was not celebrated with songs and torches because Kraken did not consent to show himself to the people of the Penguins; but hidden in his cave he planned great designs.

<h2 style="text-align:center">VI</h2>

<h2 style="text-align:center">THE DRAGON OF ALCA</h2>

> "We afterwards went to visit the cabinet of natural history. . . . The caretaker showed us a sort of packet bound in straw that he told us contained the skeleton of a dragon; a proof, added he, that the dragon is not a fabulous animal."
> —*Memoirs of Jacques Casanova,* Paris, 1843. Vol. IV., pp. 404, 405.

IN the meantime the inhabitants of Alca practised the labours of peace. Those of the northern coast went in boats to fish or to search for shellfish. The labourers of Dombes cultivated oats, rye, and wheat. The rich Penguins of the valley of Dalles reared domestic animals, while those of the Bay of Divers cultivated their orchards. Merchants of Port-Alca carried on a trade in salt fish with Armorica and the gold of the two Britains, which began to be introduced into the island, facilitated exchange. The Penguin people were enjoying the fruit of their labours in perfect tranquillity when suddenly a sinister rumour ran from village to village. It was said everywhere that a frightful dragon had ravaged two farms in the Bay of Divers.

A few days before, the maiden Orberosia had disappeared. Her absence had at first caused no uneasiness because on several occasions she had been carried off by violent men who were consumed with love. And thoughtful people were not astonished at this, reflecting that the maiden was the most beautiful of the Penguins. It was even remarked that she sometimes went to meet her ravishers, for none of us can escape his destiny. But this time, as she did not return, it was feared that the dragon had devoured her. The more so as the inhabitants of the valley of Dalles soon knew that the dragon was not a fable told by the women around the fountains. For one night the monster devoured out of the village of Anis six hens, a sheep, and a young orphan child called little Elo. The next morning nothing was to be found either of the animals or of the child.

Immediately the Elders of the village assembled in the public place and seated themselves on the stone bench to take counsel concerning what it was expedient to do in these terrible circumstances.

Having called all those Penguins who had seen the dragon during the disastrous night, they asked them:

"Have you not noticed his form and his behaviour?"

And each answered in his turn:

"He has the claws of a lion, the wings of an eagle, and the tail of a serpent."

"His back bristles with thorny crests."

"His whole body is covered with yellow scales."

"His look fascinates and confounds. He vomits flames."

"He poisons the air with his breath."

"He has the head of a dragon, the claws of a lion, and the tail of a fish."

And a woman of Anis, who was regarded as intelligent and of sound judgment and from whom the dragon had taken three hens, deposed as follows:

"He is formed like a man. The proof is that I thought he was my husband, and I said to him, 'Come to bed, you old fool.'"

Others said:

"He is formed like a cloud."

"He looks like a mountain."

And a little child came and said:

"I saw the dragon taking off his head in the barn so that he might give a kiss to my sister Minnie."

And the Elders also asked the inhabitants:

"How big is the dragon?"

And it was answered:

"As big as an ox."

"Like the big merchant ships of the Bretons."

"He is the height of a man."

"He is higher than the fig-tree under which you are sitting."

"He is as large as a dog."

Questioned finally on his colour, the inhabitants said:

"Red."

"Green."

"Blue."

"Yellow."

"His head is bright green, his wings are brilliant orange tinged with pink, his limbs are silver grey, his hind-quarters and his tail are striped with brown and pink bands, his belly bright yellow spotted with black."

"His colour? He has no colour."

"He is the colour of a dragon."

After hearing this evidence the Elders remained uncertain as to what should be done. Some advised to watch for him, to surprise him and overthrow him by a multitude of arrows. Others, thinking it vain to oppose so powerful a monster by force, counselled that he should be appeased by offerings.

"Pay him tribute," said one of them who passed for a wise man. "We can render him propitious to us by giving him agreeable presents, fruits, wine, lambs, a young virgin."

Others held for poisoning the fountains where he was accustomed to drink or for smoking him out of his cavern.

But none of these counsels prevailed. The dispute was lengthy and the Elders dispersed without coming to any resolution.

VII

THE DRAGON OF ALCA

(Continuation)

URING all the month dedicated by the Romans to their false god Mars or Mavors, the dragon ravaged the farms of Dalles and Dombes. He carried off fifty sheep, twelve pigs, and three young boys. Every family was in mourning and the island was full of lamentations. In order to remove the scourge, the Elders of the unfortunate villages watered by the Clange and the Survelle resolved to assemble and together go and ask the help of the blessed Maël.

On the fifth day of the month whose name among the Latins signifies opening, because it opens the year, they went in procession to the wooden monastery that had been built on the southern coast of the island. When they were introduced into the cloister they filled it with their sobs and groans. Moved by their lamentations, old Maël left the room in which he devoted himself to the study of astronomy and the meditation of the Scriptures, and went down to them, leaning on his pastoral staff. At his approach, the Elders, prostrating themselves, held out to him green branches of trees and some of them burnt aromatic herbs.

And the holy man, seating himself beside the cloistral fountain under an ancient fig-tree, uttered these words:

"O my sons, offspring of the Penguins, why do you weep and groan? Why do you hold out those suppliant boughs towards me? Why do you raise towards heaven the smoke of those herbs? What calamity do you expect that I can avert from your heads? Why do you beseech me? I am ready to give my life for you. Only tell your father what it is you hope from him."

To these questions the chief of the Elders answered:

"O Maël, father of the sons of Alca, I will speak for all. A horrible dragon is laying waste our lands, depopulating our cattle-sheds, and carrying off the flower of our youth. He has devoured the child Elo and seven young boys; he has mangled the maiden Orberosia, the fairest of the Penguins, with his teeth. There is not a village in which he does not emit his poisoned breath and which he has not filled with desolation. A prey to this terrible scourge, we come, O Maël, to pray thee, as the wisest, to advise us concerning the safety of the inhabitants of this island lest the ancient race of Penguins be extinguished."

"O chief of the Elders of Alca," replied Maël, "thy words fill me with profound grief, and I groan at the thought that this island is the prey of a terrible dragon. But such an occurrence is not unique, for we find in books several tales of very fierce dragons. The monsters are oftenest found in caverns, by the brinks of waters, and, in preference, among pagan peoples. Perhaps there are some among you who, although they have received holy baptism and been incorporated into the family of Abraham, have yet worshipped idols, like the ancient Romans, or hung up images, votive tablets, fillets of wool, and garlands of flowers on the branches of some sacred tree. Or perhaps some of the women Penguins have danced round a magic stone and drunk water from the fountains where the nymphs dwell. If it be so, I believe, O Penguins, that the Lord has sent this dragon to punish all for the crimes of some, and to lead you, O children of the Penguins, to exterminate blasphemy, superstition, and impiety from amongst you. For this reason I advise, as a remedy against the great evil from which you suffer, that you carefully search your dwellings for idolatry, and extirpate it from them. I think it would be also efficacious to pray and do penance."

Thus spoke the holy Maël. And the Elders of the Penguin people kissed his feet and returned to their villages with renewed hope.

VIII

THE DRAGON OF ALCA
(*Continuation*)

OLLOWING the counsel of the holy Maël the inhabitants of Alca endeavoured to uproot the superstitions that had sprung up amongst them. They took care to prevent the girls from dancing with incantations round the fairy tree. Young mothers were sternly forbidden to rub their children against the stones that stood upright in the fields so as to make them strong. An old man of Dombes who foretold the future by shaking grains of barley on a sieve, was thrown into a well.

However, each night the monster still raided the poultry-yards and the cattle-sheds. The frightened peasants barricaded themselves in their houses. A woman with child who saw the shadow of a dragon on the road through a window in the moonlight, was so terrified that she was brought to bed before her time.

In those days of trial, the holy Maël meditated unceasingly on the nature of dragons and the means of combating them. After six months of study and prayer he thought he had found what he sought. One evening as he was walking by the sea with a young monk called Samuel, he expressed his thought to him in these terms:

"I have studied at length the history and habits of dragons, not to satisfy a vain curiosity, but to discover examples to follow in the present circumstances. For such, Samuel, my son, is the use of history.

"It is an invariable fact that dragons are extremely vigilant. They never sleep, and for this reason we often find them employed in guarding treasures. A dragon guarded at Colchis the golden fleece that Jason conquered from him. A dragon watched over the golden apples in the garden of the Hesperides. He was killed by Hercules and transformed into a star by Juno. This fact is related in some books, and if it be true, it was done by magic, for the gods of the pagans are in reality demons. A dragon prevented barbarous and ignorant men from drinking at the fountain of Castalia. We must also remember the dragon of Andromeda, which was slain by Perseus. But let us turn from these pagan fables, in which error is always mixed with truth. We meet dragons in the histories of the glorious archangel Michael, of St. George, St. Philip, St. James the Great, St. Patrick, St. Martha, and St. Margaret. And it is in such writings, since they are worthy of full credence, that we ought to look for comfort and counsel.

"The story of the dragon of Silena affords us particularly precious examples. You must know, my son, that on the banks of a vast pool close to that town there dwelt a dragon who sometimes approached the walls and poisoned with his breath all who dwelt in the suburbs. And that they might not be devoured by the monster, the inhabitants of Silena delivered up to him one of their number every morning. The victim was chosen by lot, and after a hundred others, the lot fell upon the king's daughter.

"Now St. George, who was a military tribune, as he passed through the town of Silena, learned that the king's daughter had just been given to the fierce beast. He immediately mounted his horse, and, armed with his lance, rushed to encounter the dragon, whom he reached just as the monster was about to devour the royal virgin. And when St. George had overthrown the dragon, the king's daughter fastened her girdle round the beast's neck and he followed her like a dog led on a leash.

"That is an example for us of the power of virgins over dragons. The history of St. Martha furnishes us with a still more certain proof. Do you know the story, Samuel, my son?"

"Yes, father," answered Samuel.

And the blessed Maël went on:

"There was in a forest on the banks of the Rhone, between Arles and Avignon, a dragon half quadruped and half fish, larger than an ox, with sharp teeth like horns and huge wings at his shoulders. He sank the boats and devoured their passengers. Now St. Martha, at the entreaty of the people, approached this dragon, whom she found devouring a man. She put her girdle round his neck and led him easily into the town.

"These two examples lead me to think that we should have recourse to the power of some virgin so as to conquer the dragon who scatters terror and death through the island of Alca.

"For this reason, Samuel my son, gird up thy loins and go, I pray thee, with two of thy companions, into all the villages of this island, and proclaim everywhere that a virgin alone shall be able to deliver the island from the monster that devastates it.

"Thou shalt sing psalms and canticles and thou shalt say:

" 'O sons of the Penguins, if there be among you a pure virgin, let her arise and go, armed with the sign of the cross, to combat the dragon!' "

Thus the old man spake, and Samuel promised to obey him. The next day he girded up his loins and set out with two of his companions to proclaim to the inhabitants of Alca that a virgin alone would be able to deliver the Penguins from the rage of the dragon.

IX

THE DRAGON OF ALCA
(*Continuation*)

RBEROSIA loved her husband, but she did not love him alone. At the hour when Venus lightens in the pale sky, whilst Kraken scattered terror through the villages, she used to visit in his moving hut, a young shepherd of Dalles called Marcel, whose pleasing form was invested with inexhaustible vigour. The fair Orberosia shared the shepherd's aromatic couch with delight, but far from making herself known to him, she took the name of Bridget, and said that she was the daughter of a gardener in the Bay of Divers. When regretfully she left his arms she walked across the smoking fields towards the Coast of Shadows, and if she happened to meet some belated peasant she immediately spread out her garments like great wings and cried:

"Passer by, lower your eyes, that you may not have to say, 'Alas! alas! woe is me, for I have seen the angel of the Lord.' "

The villagers tremblingly knelt with their faces to the ground. And several of them used to say that angels, whom it would be death to see, passed along the roads of the island in the night time.

Kraken did not know of the loves of Orberosia and Marcel, for he was a hero, and heroes never discover the secrets of their wives. But though he did not know of these loves, he reaped the benefit of them. Every night he found his companion more good-humoured and more beautiful, exhaling pleasure and perfuming the nuptial bed with a delicious odour of fennel and vervain. She loved Kraken with a love that never became importunate or anxious, because she did not rest its whole weight on him alone.

This lucky infidelity of Orberosia was destined soon to save the hero from a great peril and to assure his fortune and his glory for ever. For it happened that she saw passing in the twilight a neatherd from Belmont, who was goading on his oxen, and she fell more deeply in love with him than she had ever been with the shepherd Marcel. He was hunch-backed; his shoulders were higher than his ears; his body was supported by legs of different lengths; his rolling eyes flashed from beneath his matted hair. From his throat issued a hoarse voice and strident laughter; he smelt of the cowshed. However, to her he was beautiful. "A plant," as Gnatho says, "has been loved by one, a stream by another, a beast by a third."

Now, one day, as she was sighing within the neatherd's arms in a village barn, suddenly the blasts of a trumpet, with sounds and footsteps, fell upon her ears; she looked through the window and saw the inhabitants collected in the marketplace round a young monk, who, standing upon a rock, uttered these words in a distinct voice:

"Inhabitants of Belmont, Abbot Maël, our venerable father, informs you through my mouth that neither by strength nor skill in arms shall you prevail against the dragon; but the beast shall be overcome by a virgin. If, then, there be among you a perfectly pure virgin, let her arise and go towards the monster; and when she meets him let her tie her girdle round his neck and she shall lead him as easily as if he were a little dog."

And the young monk, replacing his hood upon his head, departed to carry the proclamation of the blessed Maël to other villages.

Orberosia sat in the amorous straw, resting her head in her hand and supporting her elbow upon her knee, meditating on what she had just heard.

Although, so far as Kraken was concerned, she feared the power of a virgin much less than the strength of armed men, she did not feel reassured by the proclamation of the blessed Maël. A vague but sure instinct ruled her mind and warned her that Kraken could not henceforth be a dragon with safety.

She said to the neatherd:

"My own heart, what do you think about the dragon?"

The rustic shook his head.

"It is certain that dragons laid waste the earth in ancient times and some have been seen as large as mountains. But they come no longer, and I believe that what has been taken for a dragon is not one at all, but pirates or merchants who have carried off the fair Orberosia and the best of the children of Alca in their ships. But if one of those brigands attempts to rob me of my oxen, I will either by force or craft find a way to prevent him from doing me any harm."

This remark of the neatherd increased Orberosia's apprehensions and added to her solicitude for the husband whom she loved.

X

THE DRAGON OF ALCA
(*Continuation*)

HE days passed by and no maiden arose in the island to combat the monster. And in the wooden monastery old Maël, seated on a bench in the shade of an old fig-tree, accompanied by a pious monk called Regimental, kept asking himself anxiously and sadly how it was that there was not in Alca a single virgin fit to overthrow the monster.

He sighed and brother Regimental sighed too. At that moment old Maël called young Samuel, who happened to pass through the garden, and said to him:

"I have meditated anew, my son, on the means of destroying the dragon who devours the flower of our youth, our flocks, and our harvests. In this respect the story of the dragons of St. Riok and of St. Pol de Leon seems to me particularly instructive. The dragon of St. Riok was six fathoms long; his head was derived from the cock and the basilisk, his body from the ox and the serpent; he ravaged the banks of the Elorn in the time of King Bristocus. St. Riok, then aged two years, led him by a leash to the sea, in which the monster drowned himself of his own accord. St. Pol's dragon was sixty feet long and not less terrible. The blessed apostle of Leon bound him with his stole and allowed a young noble of great purity of life to lead him. These examples prove that in the eyes of God a chaste young man is as agreeable as a chaste girl. Heaven makes no distinction between them. For this reason, my son, if you believe what I say, we will both go to the Coast of Shadows; when we reach the dragon's cavern we will call the monster in a loud voice, and when he comes forth I will tie my stole round his neck and you will lead him to the sea, where he will not fail to drown himself."

At the old man's words Samuel cast down his head and did not answer.

"You seem to hesitate, my son," said Maël.

Brother Regimental, contrary to his custom, spoke without being addressed.

"There is at least cause for some hesitation," said he. "St. Riok was only two years old when he overcame the dragon. Who says that nine or ten years later he could have done as much? Remember, father, that the dragon who is devastating our island has devoured little Elo and four or five other young boys. Brother Samuel is not so presumptuous as to believe that at nineteen years of age he is more innocent than they were at twelve and fourteen.

"Alas!" added the monk, with a groan, "who can boast of being chaste in this world, where everything gives the example and model of love, where all things in nature, animals, and plants, show us the caresses of love and advise us to share them? Animals are eager to unite in their own fashion, but the various marriages of quadrupeds, birds, fishes, and reptiles are far from equalling in lust the nuptials of the trees. The greater extremes of lewdness that the pagans have imagined in their fables are outstripped by the simple flowers of the field, and, if you knew the irregularities of lilies and roses you would take those chalices of impurity, those vases of scandal, away from your altars."

"Do not speak in this way, Brother Regimental," answered old Maël. "Since they are subject to the law of nature, animals and plants are always innocent. They have no souls to save, whilst man——"

"You are right," replied Brother Regimental, "it is quite a different thing. But do not send young Samuel to the dragon—the dragon might devour him. For the last five years Samuel is not in a state to show his innocence to monsters. In the year of the comet, the Devil in order to seduce him, put in his path a milkmaid, who was lifting up her petticoat to cross a ford. Samuel was tempted, but he overcame the temptation. The Devil, who never tires, sent him the image of that young girl in a dream. The shade did what the reality was unable to accomplish, and Samuel yielded. When he awoke he moistened his couch with his tears, but alas! repentance did not give him back his innocence."

As he listened to this story Samuel asked himself how his secret could be known, for he was ignorant that the Devil had borrowed the appearance of Brother Regimental, so as to trouble the hearts of the monks of Alca.

And old Maël remained deep in thought and kept asking himself in grief:

"Who will deliver us from the dragon's tooth? Who will preserve us from his breath? Who will save us from his look?"

However, the inhabitants of Alca began to take courage. The labourers of Dombes and the neatherds of Belmont swore that they themselves would be of more avail than a girl against the ferocious beast, and they exclaimed as they stroked the muscles on their arms, "Let the dragon come!" Many men and women had seen him. They did not agree about his form and his figure, but all now united in saying that he was not as big as they had thought, and that his height was not much greater than a man's. The defence was organised; towards nightfall watches were stationed at the entrances of the villages ready to give the alarm; and during the night companies armed with pitchforks and scythes protected the paddocks in which the animals were shut up. Indeed, once in the village of Anis some plucky labourers surprised him as he was scaling Morio's wall, and, as they had flails, scythes, and pitchforks, they fell upon him and pressed him hard. One of them, a very quick and courageous man, thought to have run him through with his pitchfork; but he slipped in a pool and so let him escape. The others would certainly have caught him had they not waited to pick up the rabbits and fowls that he dropped in his flight.

Those labourers declared to the Elders of the village that the monster's form and proportions appeared to them human enough except for his head and his tail, which were, in truth, terrifying.

XI

THE DRAGON OF ALCA
(*Continuation*)

N that day Kraken came back to his cavern sooner than usual. He took from his head his sealskin helmet with its two bull's horns and its visor trimmed with terrible hooks. He threw on the table his gloves that ended in horrible claws—they were the beaks of sea-birds. He unhooked his belt from which hung a long green tail twisted into many folds. Then he ordered his page, Elo, to help him off with his boots and, as the child did not succeed in doing this very quickly, he gave him a kick that sent him to the other end of the grotto.

Without looking at the fair Orberosia, who was spinning, he seated himself in front of the fireplace, on which a sheep was roasting, and he muttered:

"Ignoble Penguins. . . . There is no worse trade than a dragon's."

"What does my master say?" asked the fair Orberosia.

"They fear me no longer," continued Kraken. "Formerly everyone fled at my approach. I carried away hens and rabbits in my bag; I drove sheep and pigs, cows, and oxen before me. To-day these clod-hoppers keep a good guard; they sit up at night. Just now I was pursued in the village of Anis by doughty labourers armed with flails and scythes and pitchforks. I had to drop the hens and rabbits, put my tail under my arm, and run as fast as I could. Now I ask you, is it seemly for a dragon of Cappadocia to run away like a robber with his tail under his arm? Further, incommoded as I was by crests, horns, hooks, claws, and scales, I barely escaped a brute who ran half an inch of his pitchfork into my left thigh."

As he said this he carefully ran his hand over the insulted part, and, after giving himself up for a few moments to bitter meditation:

"What idiots those Penguins are! I am tired of blowing flames in the faces of such imbeciles. Orberosia, do you hear me?"

Having thus spoken the hero raised his terrible helmet in his hands and gazed at it for a long time in gloomy silence. Then he pronounced these rapid words:

"I have made this helmet with my own hands in the shape of a fish's head, covering it with the skin of a seal. To make it more terrible I have put on it the horns of a bull and I have given it a boar's jaws; I have hung from it a horse's tail dyed vermilion. When in the gloomy twilight I threw it over my shoulders no inhabitant of this island had courage to withstand its sight. Women and children, young men and old men fled distracted at its approach, and I carried terror among the whole race of Penguins. By what advice does that insolent people lose its earlier fears and dare to-day to behold these horrible jaws and to attack this terrible crest?"

And throwing his helmet on the rocky soil:

"Perish, deceitful helmet!" cried Kraken. "I swear by all the demons of Armor that I will never bear you upon my head again."

And having uttered this oath he stamped upon his helmet, his gloves, his boots, and upon his tail with its twisted folds.

"Kraken," said the fair Orberosia, "will you allow your servant to employ artifice to save your reputation and your goods? Do not despise a woman's help. You need it, for all men are imbeciles."

"Woman," asked Kraken, "what are your plans?"

And the fair Orberosia informed her husband that the monks were going through the villages teaching the inhabitants the best way of combating the dragon; that, according to their instructions, the beast would be overcome by a virgin, and that if a maid placed her girdle around the dragon's neck she could lead him as easily as if he were a little dog.

"How do you know that the monks teach this?" asked Kraken.

"My friend," answered Orberosia, "do not interrupt a serious subject by frivolous questions. . . . 'If, then,' added the monks, 'there be in Alca a pure virgin, let her arise!' Now, Kraken, I have determined to answer their call. I will go and find the holy Maël and I will say to him: 'I am the virgin destined by Heaven to overthrow the dragon.'"

At these words Kraken exclaimed: "How can you be that pure virgin? And why do you want to overthrow me, Orberosia? Have you lost your reason? Be sure that I will not allow myself to be conquered by you!"

"Can you not try and understand me before you get angry?" sighed the fair Orberosia with deep though gentle contempt.

And she explained the cunning designs that she had formed.

As he listened, the hero remained pensive. And when she ceased speaking:

"Orberosia, your cunning is deep," said he. "And if your plans are carried out according to your intentions I shall derive great advantages from them. But how can you be the virgin destined by heaven?"

"Don't bother about that," she replied, "and come to bed."

The next day in the grease-laden atmosphere of the cavern, Kraken plaited a deformed skeleton out of osier rods and covered it with bristling, scaly, and filthy skins. To one extremity of the skeleton Orberosia sewed the fierce crest and the hideous mask that Kraken used to wear in his plundering expeditions, and to its other end she fastened the tail with twisted folds which the hero was wont to trail behind him. And when the work was finished they showed little Elo and the other five children who waited on them how to get inside this machine, how to make it walk, how to blow horns and burn tow in it so as to send forth smoke and flames through the dragon's mouth.

XII

THE DRAGON OF ALCA

(Continuation)

RBEROSIA, having clothed herself in a robe made of coarse stuff and girt herself with a thick cord, went to the monastery and asked to speak to the blessed Maël. And because women were forbidden to enter the enclosure of the monastery the old man advanced outside the gates, holding his pastoral cross in his right hand and resting his left on the shoulder of Brother Samuel, the youngest of his disciples.

He asked:

"Woman, who art thou?"

"I am the maiden Orberosia."

At this reply Maël raised his trembling arms to heaven.

"Do you speak truth, woman? It is a certain fact that Orberosia was devoured by the dragon. And yet I see Orberosia and hear her. Did you not, O my daughter, while within the dragon's bowels arm yourself with the sign of the cross and come uninjured out of his throat? That is what seems to me the most credible explanation."

"You are not deceived, father," answered Orberosia. "That is precisely what happened to me. Immediately I came out of the creature's bowels I took refuge in a hermitage on the Coast of Shadows. I lived there in solitude, giving myself up to prayer and meditation, and performing unheard of austerities, until I learnt by a revelation from heaven that a maid alone could overcome the dragon, and that I was that maid."

"Show me a sign of your mission," said the old man.

"I myself am the sign," answered Orberosia.

"I am not ignorant of the power of those who have placed a seal upon their flesh," replied the apostle of the Penguins. "But are you indeed such as you say?"

"You will see by the result," answered Orberosia.

The monk Regimental drew near:

"That will," said he, "be the best proof. King Solomon has said: 'Three things are hard to understand and a fourth is impossible: they are the way of a serpent on the earth, the way of a bird in the air, the way of a ship in the sea, and the way of a man with a maid.' I regard such matrons as nothing less than presumptuous who claim to compare themselves in these matters with the wisest of kings. Father, if you are led by me you will not consult them in regard to the pious Orberosia. When they have given their opinion you will not be a bit farther on than before. Virginity is not less difficult to prove than to keep. Pliny tells us in his history that its signs are either imaginary or very uncertain.* One who bears upon her the fourteen signs of corruption may yet be pure in the eyes of the angels, and, on the contrary, another who has been pronounced pure by the matrons who inspected her may know that her good appearance is due to the artifices of a cunning perversity. As for the purity of this holy girl here, I would put my hand in the fire in witness of it."

He spoke thus because he was the Devil. But old Maël did not know it. He asked the pious Orberosia:

"My daughter, how would you proceed to conquer so fierce an animal as he who devoured you?"

The virgin answered:

"To-morrow at sunrise, O Maël, you will summon the people together on the hill in front of the desolate moor that extends to the Coast of Shadows, and you will take care that no man of the Penguins remains less than five hundred paces from those rocks so that he may not be poisoned by the monster's breath. And the dragon will come out of the rocks and I will put my girdle round his neck and lead him like an obedient dog."

"Ought you not to be accompanied by a courageous and pious man who will kill the dragon?" asked Maël.

"It will be as thou sayest, venerable father. I shall deliver the monster to Kraken, who will slay him with his flashing sword. For I tell thee that the noble Kraken, who was believed to be dead, will return among the Penguins and he shall slay the dragon. And from

*We have vainly sought for this phrase in Pliny's "Natural History."
—*Editor*.

the creature's belly will come forth the little children whom he has devoured."

"What you declare to me, O virgin," cried the apostle, "seems wonderful and beyond human power."

"It is," answered the virgin Orberosia. "But learn, O Maël, that I have had a revelation that as a reward for their deliverance, the Penguin people will pay to the knight Kraken an annual tribute of three hundred fowls, twelve sheep, two oxen, three pigs, one thousand eight hundred bushels of corn, and vegetables according to their season; and that, moreover, the children who will come out of the dragon's belly will be given and committed to the said Kraken to serve him and obey him in all things. If the Penguin people fail to keep their engagements a new dragon will come upon the island more terrible than the first. I have spoken."

<h2 style="text-align:center">XIII</h2>

<h1 style="text-align:center">THE DRAGON OF ALCA</h1>

(Continuation and End)

HE people of the Penguins were assembled by Maël and they spent the night on the Coast of Shadows within the bounds which the holy man had prescribed in order that none among the Penguins should be poisoned by the monster's breath.

The veil of night still covered the earth when, preceded by a hoarse bellowing, the dragon showed his indistinct and monstrous form upon the rocky coast. He crawled like a serpent and his writhing body seemed about fifteen feet long. At his appearance the crowd drew back in terror. But soon all eyes were turned towards the Virgin Orberosia, who, in the first light of the dawn, clothed in white, advanced over the purple heather. With an intrepid though modest gait she walked towards the beast, who, uttering awful bellowings, opened his flaming throat. An immense cry of terror and pity arose from the midst of the Penguins. But the virgin, unloosing her linen girdle, put it round the dragon's neck and led him on the leash like a faithful dog amid the acclamations of the spectators.

She had walked over a long stretch of the heath when Kraken appeared armed with a flashing sword. The people, who believed him dead, uttered cries of joy and surprise. The hero rushed towards the beast, turned him over on his back, and with his sword cut open his belly, from whence came forth in their shirts, with curling hair and folded hands, little Elo and the five other children whom the monster had devoured.

Immediately they threw themselves on their knees before the virgin Orberosia, who took them in her arms and whispered into their ears:

"You will go through the villages saying: 'We are the poor little children who were devoured by the dragon, and we came out of his belly in our shirts.' The inhabitants will give you abundance of all that you can desire. But if you say anything else you will get nothing but cuffs and whippings. Go!"

Several Penguins, seeing the dragon disembowelled, rushed forward to cut him to pieces, some from a feeling of rage and vengeance, others to get the magic stone called dragonite, that is engendered in his head. The mothers of the children who had come back to life ran to embrace their little ones. But the holy Maël kept them back, saying that none of them were holy enough to approach a dragon without dying.

And soon little Elo and the five other children came towards the people and said:

"We are the poor little children who were devoured by the dragon and we came out of his belly in our shirts."

And all who heard them kissed them and said:

"Blessed children, we will give you abundance of all that you can desire."

And the crowd of people dispersed, full of joy, singing hymns and canticles.

To commemorate this day on which Providence delivered the people from a cruel scourge, processions were established in which the effigy of a chained dragon was led about.

Kraken levied the tribute and became the richest and most powerful of the Penguins. As a sign of his victory and so as to inspire a salutary terror, he wore a dragon's crest upon his head and he had a habit of saying to the people:

"Now that the monster is dead I am the dragon."

For many years Orberosia bestowed her favours upon neatherds and shepherds, whom she thought equal to the gods. But when she was no longer beautiful she consecrated herself to the Lord.

At her death she became the object of public veneration, and was admitted into the calendar of the saints and adopted as the patron saint of Penguinia.

Kraken left a son, who, like his father, wore a dragon's crest, and he was for this reason surnamed Draco. He was the founder of the first royal dynasty of the Penguins.

BOOK III: THE MIDDLE AGES AND THE RENAISSANCE

I

BRIAN THE GOOD AND QUEEN GLAMORGAN

THE kings of Alca were descended from Draco, the son of Kraken, and they wore on their heads a terrible dragon's crest, as a sacred badge whose appearance alone inspired the people with veneration, terror, and love. They were perpetually in conflict either with their own vassals and subjects or with the princes of the adjoining islands and continents.

The most ancient of these kings has left but a name. We do not even know how to pronounce or write it. The first of the Draconides whose history is known was Brian the Good, renowned for his skill and courage in war and in the chase.

He was a Christian and loved learning. He also favoured men who had vowed themselves to the monastic life. In the hall of his palace where, under the sooty rafters, there hung the heads, pelts, and horns of wild beasts, he held feasts to which all the harpers of Alca and of the neighbouring islands were invited, and he himself used to join in singing the praises of the heroes. He was just and magnanimous, but inflamed by so ardent a love of glory that he could not restrain himself from putting to death those who had sung better than himself.

The monks of Yvern having been driven out by the pagans who ravaged Brittany, King Brian summoned them into his kingdom and built a wooden monastery for them near his palace. Every day he went with Queen Glamorgan, his wife, into the monastery chapel and was present at the religious ceremonies and joined in the hymns.

Now among these monks there was a brother called Oddoul, who, while still in the flower of his youth, had adorned himself with knowledge and virtue. The devil entertained a great grudge against him, and attempted several times to lead him into temptation. He took several shapes and appeared to him in turn as a war-horse, a young maiden, and a cup of mead. Then he rattled two dice in a dice-box and said to him:

"Will you play with me for the kingdoms of the world against one of the hairs of your head?"

But the man of the Lord, armed with the sign of the Cross, repulsed the enemy. Perceiving that he could not seduce him, the devil thought of an artful plan to ruin him. One summer night he approached the queen, who slept upon her couch, showed her an image of the young monk whom she saw every day in the wooden monastery, and upon this image he placed a spell. Forthwith, like a subtle poison, love flowed into Glamorgan's veins, and she burned with an ardent desire to do as she listed with Oddoul. She formed unceasing pretexts to have him near her. Several times she asked him to teach reading and singing to her children.

"I entrust them to you," said she to him. "And I will follow the lessons you will give them so that I myself may learn also. You will teach both mother and sons at the same time."

But the young monk kept making excuses. At times he would say that he was not a learned enough teacher, and on other occasions that his state forbade him all intercourse with women. This refusal inflamed Glamorgan's passion. One day as she lay pining upon her couch, her malady having become intolerable, she summoned Oddoul to her chamber. He came in obedience to her orders, but remained with his eyes cast down towards the threshold of the door. With impatience and grief she resented his not looking at her.

"See," said she to him, "I have no more strength, a shadow is on my eyes. My body is both burning and freezing."

And as he kept silence and made no movement, she called him in a voice of entreaty:

"Come to me, come!"

With outstretched arms to which passion gave more length, she endeavoured to seize him and draw him towards her.

But he fled away, reproaching her for her wantonness.

Then, incensed with rage and fearing that Oddoul might divulge the shame into which she had fallen, she determined to ruin him so that he might not ruin her.

In a voice of lamentation that resounded throughout all the palace she called for help, as if, in truth, she were in some great danger. Her servants rushed up and saw the young monk fleeing and the queen pulling back the sheets upon her couch. They all cried out together. And when King Brian, attracted by the noise, entered the chamber, Glamorgan, showing him her dishevelled hair, her eyes flooded with tears, and her bosom that in the fury of her love she had torn with her nails, said:

"My lord and husband, behold the traces of the insults I have undergone. Driven by an infamous desire Oddoul has approached me and attempted to do me violence."

When he heard these complaints and saw the blood, the king,

transported with fury, ordered his guards to seize the young monk and burn him alive before the palace under the queen's eyes.

Being told of the affair, the Abbot of Yvern went to the king and said to him:

"King Brian, know by this example the difference between a Christian woman and a pagan. Roman Lucretia was the most virtuous of idolatrous princesses, yet she had not the strength to defend herself against the attacks of an effeminate youth, and, ashamed of her weakness, she gave way to despair, whilst Glamorgan has successfully withstood the assaults of a criminal filled with rage, and possessed by the most terrible of demons." Meanwhile Oddoul, in the prison of the palace, was waiting for the moment when he should be burned alive. But God did not suffer an innocent to perish. He sent to him an angel, who, taking the form of one of the queen's servants called Gudrune, took him out of his prison and led him into the very room where the woman whose appearance he had taken dwelt.

And the angel said to young Oddoul:

"I love thee because thou art daring."

And young Oddoul, believing that it was Gudrune herself, answered with downcast looks:

"It is by the grace of the Lord that I have resisted the violence of the queen and braved the anger of that powerful woman."

And the angel asked:

"What? Hast thou not done what the queen accuses thee of?"

"In truth no, I have not done it," answered Oddoul, his hand on his heart.

"Thou hast not done it?"

"No, I have not done it. The very thought of such an action fills me with horror."

"Then," cried the angel, "what art thou doing here, thou impotent creature?"*

And she opened the door to facilitate the young man's escape. Oddoul felt himself pushed violently out. Scarcely had he gone down into the street than a chamber-pot was poured over his head; and he thought:

"Mysterious are thy designs, O Lord, and thy ways past finding out."

II

DRACO THE GREAT

(*Translation of the Relics of St. Orberosia*)

THE direct posterity of Brian the Good was extinguished about the year 900 in the person of Collic of the Short Nose. A cousin of that prince, Bosco the Magnanimous, succeeded him, and took care, in order to assure himself of the throne, to put to death all his relations. There issued from him a long line of powerful kings.

One of them, Draco the Great, attained great renown as a man of war. He was defeated more frequently than the others. It is by this constancy in defeat that great captains are recognized. In twenty years he burned down more than a hundred thousand hamlets, market towns, unwalled towns, villages, walled towns, cities, and universities. He set fire impartially to his enemies' territory and to his own domains. And he used to explain his conduct by saying:

"War without fire is like tripe without mustard: it is an insipid thing."

His justice was rigorous. When the peasants whom he made prisoners were unable to raise the money for their ransoms he had them hanged from a tree, and if any unhappy woman came to plead for her destitute husband he dragged her by the hair at his horse's tail. He lived like a soldier without effeminacy. It is satisfactory to relate that his manner of life was pure. Not only did he not allow his kingdom to decline from its hereditary glory, but, even in his reverses he valiantly supported the honour of the Penguin people.

Draco the Great caused the relics of St. Orberosia to be transferred to Alca.

The body of the blessed saint had been buried in a grotto on the Coast of Shadows at the end of a scented heath. The first pilgrims

---

*The Penguin chronicler who relates the fact employs the expression, *Species inductilis.* I have endeavoured to translate it literally.

who went to visit it were the boys and girls from the neighbouring villages. They used to go there in the evening, by preference in couples, as if their pious desires naturally sought satisfaction in darkness and solitude. They worshipped the saint with a fervent and discreet worship whose mystery they seemed jealously to guard, for they did not like to publish too openly the experiences they felt. But they were heard to murmur one to another words of love, delight, and rapture with which they mingled the name of Orberosia. Some would sigh that there they forgot the world; others would say that they came out of the grotto in peace and calm; the young girls among them used to recall to each other the joys with which they had been filled in it.

Such were the marvels that the virgin of Alca performed in the morning of her glorious eternity; they had the sweetness and indefiniteness of the dawn. Soon the mystery of the grotto spread like a perfume throughout the land; it was a ground of joy and edification for pious souls, and corrupt men endeavoured, though in vain, by falsehood and calumny, to divert the faithful from the springs of grace that flowed from the saint's tomb. The Church took measures so that these graces should not remain reserved for a few children, but should be diffused throughout all Penguin Christianity. Monks took up their quarters in the grotto, they built a monastery, a chapel, and a hostelry on the coast, and pilgrims began to flock thither.

As if strengthened by a longer sojourn in heaven, the blessed Orberosia now performed still greater miracles for those who came to lay their offerings on her tomb. She gave hopes to women who had been hitherto barren, she sent dreams to reassure jealous old men concerning the fidelity of the young wives whom they had suspected without cause, and she protected the country from plagues, murrains, famines, tempests, and dragons of Cappadocia.

But during the troubles that desolated the kingdom in the time of King Collic and his successors, the tomb of St. Orberosia was plundered of its wealth, the monastery burned down, and the monks dispersed. The road that had been so long trodden by devout pilgrims was overgrown with furze and heather, and the blue thistles of the sands. For a hundred years the miraculous tomb had been visited by none save vipers, weasels, and bats, when, one day the saint appeared to a peasant of the neighbourhood, Momordic by name.

"I am the virgin Orberosia," said she to him; "I have chosen thee to restore my sanctuary. Warn the inhabitants of the country that if they allow my memory to be blotted out, and leave my tomb without honour and wealth, a new dragon will come and devastate Penguinia."

Learned churchmen held an inquiry concerning this apparition, and pronounced it genuine, and not diabolical but truly heavenly, and in later years it was remarked that in France, in like circumstances, St. Foy and St. Catherine had acted in the same way and made use of similar language.

The monastery was restored and pilgrims flocked to it anew. The virgin Orberosia worked greater and greater miracles. She cured divers hurtful maladies, particularly club-foot, dropsy, paralysis, and St. Guy's disease. The monks who kept the tomb were enjoying an enviable opulence, when the saint, appearing to King Draco the Great, ordered him to recognise her as the heavenly patron of the kingdom and to transfer her precious remains to the cathedral of Alca.

In consequence, the odoriferous relics of that virgin were carried with great pomp to the metropolitan church and placed in the middle of the choir in a shrine made of gold and enamel and ornamented with precious stones.

The chapter kept a record of the miracles wrought by the blessed Orberosia.

Draco the Great, who had never ceased to defend and exalt the Christian faith, died fulfilled with the most pious sentiments and bequeathed his great possessions to the Church.

III

QUEEN CRUCHA

TERRIBLE disorders followed the death of Draco the Great. That prince's successors have often been accused of weakness, and it is true that none of them followed, even from afar, the example of their valiant ancestor.

His son, Chum, who was lame, failed to increase the territory of the Penguins. Bolo, the son of Chum, was assassinated by the palace guards at the age of nine, just as he was ascending the throne. His brother Gun succeeded him. He was only seven years old and allowed himself to be governed by his mother, Queen Crucha.

Crucha was beautiful, learned, and intelligent; but she was unable to curb her own passions.

These are the terms in which the venerable Talpa expresses himself in his chronicle regarding that illustrious queen:

"In beauty of face and symmetry of figure Queen Crucha yields neither to Semiramis of Babylon nor to Penthesilea, queen of the Amazons nor to Salome, the daughter of Herodias. But she offers in her person certain singularities that will appear beautiful or uncomely according to the contradictory opinions of men and the varying judgments of the world. She has on her forehead two small horns which she conceals in the abundant folds of her golden hair; one of her eyes is blue and one is black; her neck is bent towards the left side; and, like Alexander of Macedon, she has six fingers on her right hand, and a stain like a little monkey's head upon her skin.

"Her gait is majestic and her manner affable. She is magnificent in her expenses, but she is not always able to rule desire by reason.

"One day, having noticed in the palace stables, a young groom of great beauty, she immediately fell violently in love with him, and entrusted to him the command of her armies. What one must praise unreservedly in this great queen is the abundance of gifts that she makes to the churches, monasteries, and chapels in her kingdom, and especially to the holy house of Beargarden, where, by the grace of the Lord, I made my profession in my fourteenth year. She has founded masses for the repose of her soul in such great numbers that every priest in the Penguin Church is, so to speak, transformed into a taper lighted in the sight of heaven to draw down the divine mercy upon the august Crucha."

From these lines and from some others with which I have enriched my text the reader can judge of the historical and literary value of the "Gesta Penguinorum." Unhappily, that chronicle suddenly comes to an end at the third year of Draco the Simple, the successor of Gun the Weak. Having reached that point of my history, I deplore the loss of an agreeable and trustworthy guide.

During the two centuries that followed, the Penguins remained plunged in blood-stained disorder. All the arts perished. In the midst of the general ignorance, the monks in the shadow of their cloister devoted themselves to study, and copied the Holy Scriptures with indefatigable zeal. As parchment was scarce, they scraped the writing off old manuscripts in order to transcribe upon them the divine word. Thus throughout the breadth of Penguinia Bibles blossomed forth like roses on a bush.

A monk of the order of St. Benedict, Ermold the Penguin, had himself alone defaced four thousand Greek and Latin manuscripts so as to copy out the Gospel of St. John four thousand times. Thus the masterpieces of ancient poetry and eloquence were destroyed in great numbers. Historians are unanimous in recognising that the Penguin convents were the refuge of learning during the Middle Ages.

Unending wars between the Penguins and the Porpoises filled the close of this period. It is extremely difficult to know the truth concerning these wars, not because accounts are wanting, but because there are so many of them. The Porpoise Chronicles contradict the Penguin Chronicles at every point. And, moreover, the Penguins contradict each other as well as the Porpoises. I have discovered two chroniclers that are in agreement, but one has copied from the other. A single fact is certain, namely, that massacres, rapes, conflagrations, and plunder succeeded one another without interruption.

Under the unhappy prince Bosco IX. the kingdom was at the verge of ruin. On the news that the Porpoise fleet, composed of six hundred great ships, was in sight of Alca, the bishop ordered a solemn procession. The cathedral chapter, the elected magistrates, the members of Parliament, and the clerics of the University entered the Cathedral and, taking up St. Orberosia's shrine, led it in procession through the town, followed by the entire people singing hymns. The holy patron of Penguinia was not invoked in vain. Nevertheless, the Porpoises besieged the town both by land and sea, took it by assault, and for three days and three nights killed, plundered, violated, and burned, with all the indifference that habit produces.

Our astonishment cannot be too great at the fact that, during those iron ages, the faith was preserved intact among the Penguins. The splendour of the truth in those times illumined all souls that had not been corrupted by sophisms. This is the explanation of the unity of belief. A constant practice of the Church doubtless contributed also to maintain this happy communion of the faithful —every Penguin who thought differently from the others was immediately burned at the stake.

IV

LETTERS: JOHANNES TALPA

URING the minority of King Gun, Johannes Talpa, in the monastery of Beargarden, where at the age of fourteen he had made his profession and from which he never departed for a single day throughout his life, composed his celebrated Latin chronicle in twelve books called "De Gestis Penguinorum."

The monastery of Beargarden lifts its high walls on the summit of an inaccessible peak. One sees around it only the blue tops of mountains, divided by the clouds.

When he began to write his "Gesta Penguinorum," Johannes Talpa was already old. The good monk has taken care to tell us this in his book: "My head has long since lost," he says, "its adornment of fair hair, and my scalp resembles those convex mirrors of metal which the Penguin ladies consult with so much care and zeal. My stature, naturally small, has with years become diminished and bent. My white beard gives warmth to my breast."

With a charming simplicity, Talpa informs us of certain circum-

stances in his life and some features in his character. "Descended,"
he tells us, "from a noble family, and destined from childhood for
the ecclesiastical state, I was taught grammar and music. I learned
to read under the guidance of a master who was called Amicus,
and who would have been better named Inimicus. As I did not
easily attain to a knowledge of my letters, he beat me violently
with rods so that I can say that he printed the alphabet in strokes
upon my back."

In another passage Talpa confesses his natural inclination
towards pleasure. These are his expressive words: "In my youth
the ardour of my senses was such that in the shadow of the woods
I experienced a sensation of boiling in a pot rather than of breathing the fresh air. I fled from women, but in vain, for every object
recalled them to me."

While he was writing his chronicle, a terrible war, at once foreign and domestic, laid waste the Penguin land. The soldiers of
Crucha came to defend the monastery of Beargarden against the
Penguin barbarians and established themselves strongly within its
walls. In order to render it impregnable they pierced loop-holes
through the walls and they took the lead off the church roof to
make balls for their slings. At night they lighted huge fires in the
courts and cloisters and on them they roasted whole oxen which
they spitted upon the ancient pine-trees of the mountain. Sitting
around the flames, amid smoke filled with a mingled odour of resin
and fat, they broached huge casks of wine and beer. Their songs,
their blasphemies, and the noise of their quarrels drowned the
sound of the morning bells.

At last the Porpoises, having crossed the defiles, laid siege to the
monastery. They were warriors from the North, clad in copper
armour. They fastened ladders a hundred and fifty fathoms long to
the sides of the cliffs and sometimes in the darkness and storm
these broke beneath the weight of men and arms, and bunches of
the besiegers were hurled into the ravines and precipices. A prolonged wail would be heard going down into the darkness, and the
assault would begin again. The Penguins poured streams of burning wax upon their assailants, which made them blaze like torches.
Sixty times the enraged Porpoises attempted to scale the monastery
and sixty times they were repulsed.

For six months they had closely invested the monastery, when,
on the day of the Epiphany, a shepherd of the valley showed them
a hidden path by which they climbed the mountain, penetrated into
the vaults of the abbey, ran through the cloisters, the kitchens, the
church, the chapter halls, the library, the laundry, the cells, the re-
fectories, and the dormitories, and burned the buildings, killing and
violating without distinction of age or sex. The Penguins, awakened unexpectedly, ran to arms, but in the darkness and alarm they
struck at one another, whilst the Porpoises with blows of their axes

disputed the sacred vessels, the censers, the candlesticks, dalmatics, reliquaries, golden crosses, and precious stones.

The air was filled with an acrid odour of burnt flesh. Groans and death-cries arose in the midst of the flames, and on the edges of the crumbling roofs monks ran in thousands like ants, and fell into the valley. Yet Johannes Talpa kept on writing his Chronicle. The soldiers of Crucha retreated speedily and filled up all the issues from the monastery with pieces of rock so as to shut up the Porpoises in the burning buildings. And to crush the enemy beneath the ruin they employed the trunks of old oaks as battering-rams. The burning timbers fell in with a noise like thunder and the lofty arches of the naves crumbled beneath the shock of these giant trees when moved by six hundred men together. Soon there was left nothing of the rich and extensive abbey but the cell of Johannes Talpa, which, by a marvellous chance, hung from the ruin of a smoking gable. The old chronicler still kept writing.

This admirable intensity of thought may seem excessive in the case of an annalist who applies himself to relate the events of his own time. For, however abstracted and detached we may be from surrounding things, we nevertheless resent their influence. I have consulted the original manuscript of Johannes Talpa in the National Library, where it is preserved (*Monumenta Peng., K. L6.,* 12390 *four*). It is a parchment manuscript of 628 leaves. The writing is extremely confused, the letters instead of being in a straight line, stray in all directions and are mingled together in great disorder, or, more correctly speaking, in absolute confusion. They are so badly formed that for the most part it is impossible not merely to say what they are, but even to distinguish them from the splashes of ink with which they are plentifully interspersed. Those inestimable pages bear witness in this way to the troubles amid which they were written. To read them is difficult. On the other hand, the monk of Beargarden's style shows no trace of emotion. The tone of the "Gesta Penguinorum" never departs from simplicity. The narration is rapid and of a conciseness that sometimes approaches dryness. The reflections are rare and, as a rule, judicious.

V

THE ARTS: THE PRIMITIVES OF PENGUIN PAINTING

HE Penguin critics vie with one another in affirming that Penguin art has from its origin been distinguished by a powerful and pleasing originality, and that we may look elsewhere in vain for the qualities of grace and reason that characterise its earliest works. But the Porpoises claim that their artists were undoubtedly the instructors and masters of the Penguins. It is difficult to form an opinion on the matter, because the Penguins, before they began to admire their primitive painters, destroyed all their works.

We cannot be too sorry for this loss. For my own part I feel it cruelly, for I venerate the Penguin antiquities and I adore the primitives. They are delightful. I do not say they are all alike, for that would be untrue, but they have common characters that are found in all schools—I mean formulas from which they never depart—and there is besides something finished in their work, for what they know they know well. Luckily we can form a notion of the Penguin primitives from the Italian, Flemish, and Dutch primitives, and from the French primitives, who are superior to all the rest; as M. Gruyer tells us they are more logical, logic being a peculiarly French quality. Even if this is denied it must at least be admitted that to France belongs the credit of having kept primitives when the other nations knew them no longer. The Exhibition of French Primitives at the Pavilion Marsan in 1904 contained several little panels contemporary with the later Valois kings and with Henry IV.

I have made many journeys to see the pictures of the brothers Van Eyck, of Memling, of Roger van der Weyden, of the painter of the death of Mary, of Ambrogio Lorenzetti, and of the old Umbrian masters. It was, however, neither Bruges, nor Cologne, nor Sienna, nor Perugia, that completed my initiation; it was in the little town of Arezzo that I became a conscious adept in primitive painting. That was ten years ago or even longer. At that period of indigence and simplicity, the municipal museums, though usually kept shut, were always opened to foreigners. One evening, an old woman with a candle showed me, for half a lira, the sordid museum of Arezzo, and in it I discovered a painting by Margaritone, a "St. Francis," the pious sadness of which moved me to tears. I was deeply touched, and Margaritone of Arezzo became from that day my dearest primitive.

I picture to myself the Penguin primitives in conformity with the works of that master. It will not therefore be thought superfluous if in this place I consider his works with some attention, if not in detail, at least under their more general and, if I dare say so, most representative aspect.

We possess five or six pictures signed with his hand. His master-piece, preserved in the National Gallery of London, represents the Virgin seated on a throne and holding the infant Jesus in her arms. What strikes one first when one looks at this figure is the propor-tion. The body from the neck to the feet is only twice as long as the head, so that it appears extremely short and podgy. This work is not less remarkable for its painting than for its drawing. The great Margaritone had but a limited number of colours in his possession, and he used them in all their purity without ever modifying the tones. From this it follows that his colouring has more vivacity than harmony. The cheeks of the Virgin and those of the Child are of a bright vermilion which the old master, from a naïve preference for clear definitions, has placed on each face in two circumferences as exact as if they had been traced out by a pair of compasses.

A learned critic of the eighteenth century, the Abbé Lanzi, has treated Margaritone's works with profound disdain. "They are," he says, "merely crude daubs. In those unfortunate times people could neither draw nor paint." Such was the common opinion of the con-noisseurs of the days of powdered wigs. But the great Margaritone and his contemporaries were soon to be avenged for this cruel con-tempt. There was born in the nineteenth century, in the biblical villages and reformed cottages of pious England, a multitude of little Samuels and little St. Johns with hair curling like lambs, who, about 1840 and 1850, became spectacled professors and founded the cult of the primitives.

That eminent theorist of Pre-Raphaelitism, Sir James Tuckett, does not shrink from placing the Madonna of the National Gallery on a level with the masterpieces of Christian art. "By giving to the Virgin's head," says Sir James Tuckett, "a third of the total height of the figure, the old master attracts the spectator's attention and keeps it directed towards the more sublime parts of the human figure, and in particular the eyes, which we ordinarily describe as the spiritual organs. In this picture, colouring and design conspire to produce an ideal and mystical impression. The vermilion of the cheeks does not recall the natural appearance of the skin; it rather seems as if the old master has applied the roses of Paradise to the faces of the Mother and the Child."

We see, in such a criticism as this, a shining reflection, so to speak, of the work which it exalts; yet MacSilly, the seraphic æsthete of Edinburgh, has expressed in a still more moving and penetrating fashion the impression produced upon his mind by the sight of this primitive painting. "The Madonna of Margaritone," says the revered MacSilly, "attains the transcendent end of art. It inspires its beholders with feelings of innocence and purity; it makes them like little children. And so true is this, that at the age of sixty-six, after having had the joy of contemplating it closely for three hours, I felt myself suddenly transformed into a little child. While my cab was taking me through Trafalgar Square I kept laughing and prattling and shaking my spectacle-case as if it were a rattle. And when the maid in my boarding-house had served my meal I kept pouring spoonfuls of soup into my ear with all the artlessness of childhood."

"It is by such results," adds MacSilly, "that the excellence of a work of art is proved."

Margaritone, according to Vasari, died at the age of seventy-seven, "regretting that he had lived to see a new form of art arising and the new artists crowned with fame."

These lines, which I translate literally, have inspired Sir James Tuckett with what are perhaps the finest pages in his work. They form part of his "Breviary for Æsthetes"; all the Pre-Raphaelites know them by heart. I place them here as the most precious ornament of this book. You will agree that nothing more sublime has been written since the days of the Hebrew prophets.

MARGARITONE'S VISION

Margaritone, full of years and labours, went one day to visit the studio of a young painter who had lately settled in the town. He noticed in the studio a freshly painted Madonna, which, although severe and rigid, nevertheless, by a certain exactness in the proportions and a devilish mingling of light and shade, assumed an appearance of relief and life. At this sight the artless and sublime worker of Arezzo perceived with horror what the future of painting would be. With his brow clasped in his hands he exclaimed:

"What things of shame does not this figure show forth! I descern in it the end of that Christian art which paints the soul and inspires the beholder with an ardent desire for heaven. Future painters will not restrain themselves as does this one to portraying on the side of a wall or on a wooden panel the cursed matter of which our bodies are formed; they will celebrate and glorify it. They will clothe their figures with dangerous appearances of flesh, and these figures will seem like real persons. Their bodies will be seen; their forms will appear through their clothing. St. Magdalen will have a bosom. St. Martha a belly, St. Barbara hips, St. Agnes buttocks; St. Sebastian will unveil his youthful beauty, and St. George will display beneath his armour the muscular wealth of a robust virility; apostles, confessors, doctors, and God the Father himself will appear as ordinary beings like you and me; the angels will affect an equivocal, ambiguous, mysterious beauty which will trouble hearts. What desire for heaven will these representations impart? None; but from them you will learn to take pleasure in the forms of ter-

restrial life. Where will painters stop in their indiscreet inquiries?
They will stop nowhere. They will go so far as to show men and
women naked like the idols of the Romans. There will be a sacred
art and a profane art, and the sacred art will not be less profane
than the other.

"Get ye behind me, demons," exclaimed the old master. For in
prophetic vision he saw the righteous and the saints assuming the
appearance of melancholy athletes. He saw Apollos playing the
lute on a flowery hill, in the midst of the Muses wearing light tunics.
He saw Venuses lying under shady myrtles and the Danae exposing their charming sides to the golden rain. He saw pictures of
Jesus under the pillars of the temple amidst patricians, fair ladies,
musicians, pages, negroes, dogs, and parrots. He saw in an inextricable confusion of human limbs, outspread wings, and flying
draperies, crowds of tumultuous Nativities, opulent Holy Families,
emphatic Crucifixions. He saw St. Catherines, St. Barbaras, St.
Agneses humiliating patricians by the sumptuousness of their velvets,
their brocades, and their pearls, and by the splendour of their
breasts. He saw Auroras scattering roses, and a multitude of naked
Dianas and Nymphs surprised on the banks of retired streams. And
the great Margaritone died, strangled by so horrible a presentiment
of the Renaissance and the Bolognese School.

VI

MARBODIUS

W E possess a precious monument of the Penguin liter-
ature of the fifteenth century. It is a narrative of a
journey to hell undertaken by the monk Marbodius,
of the order of St. Benedict, who professed a fervent admiration for the poet Virgil. This narrative,
written in fairly good Latin, has been published by
M. du Clos des Lunes. It is here translated for the
first time. I believe that I am doing a service to my
fellow-countrymen in making them acquainted with these pages,
though doubtless they are far from forming a unique example of
this class of mediæval Latin literature. Among the fictions that
may be compared with them we may mention "The Voyage of St.
Brendan," "The Vision of Albericus," and "St. Patrick's Purgatory," imaginary descriptions, like Dante Alighieri's "Divine Comedy," of the supposed abode of the dead. The narrative of
Marbodius is one of the latest works dealing with this scheme, but
it is not the least singular.

THE DESCENT OF MARBODIUS INTO HELL

In the fourteen hundred and fifty-third year of the incarnation of the Son of God, a few days before the enemies of the Cross entered the city of Helena and the great Constantine, it was given to me, Brother Marbodius, an unworthy monk, to see and to hear what none had hitherto seen or heard. I have composed a faithful narrative of those things so that their memory may not perish with me, for man's time is short.

On the first day of May in the aforesaid year, at the hour of vespers, I was seated in the Abbey of Corrigan on a stone in the cloisters and, as my custom was, I read the verses of the poet whom I love best of all, Virgil, who has sung of the labours of the field, of shepherds, and of heroes. Evening was hanging its purple folds from the arches of the cloisters and in a voice of emotion I was murmuring the verses which describe how Dido, the Phœnician queen, wanders with her ever-bleeding wound beneath the myrtles of hell. At that moment Brother Hilary happened to pass by, followed by Brother Jacinth, the porter.

Brought up in the barbarous ages before the resurrection of the Muses, Brother Hilary has not been initiated into the wisdom of the ancients; nevertheless, the poetry of the Mantuan has, like a subtle torch, shed some gleams of light into his understanding.

"Brother Marbodius," he asked me, "do those verses that you utter with swelling breast and sparkling eyes—do they belong to that great 'Æneid' from which morning or evening your glances are never withheld?"

I answered that I was reading in Virgil how the son of Anchises perceived Dido like a moon behind the foliage.*

"Brother Marbodius," he replied, "I am certain that on all occasions Virgil gives expression to wise maxims and profound thoughts. But the songs that he modulates on his Syracusan flute hold such a lofty meaning and such exalted doctrine that I am continually puzzled by them."

"Take care, father," cried Brother Jacinth, in an agitated voice. "Virgil was a magician who wrought marvels by the help of demons. It is thus he pierced through a mountain near Naples and fashioned a bronze horse that had power to heal all the diseases of horses. He was a necromancer, and there is still shown, in a certain town in Italy, the mirror in which he made the dead appear. And yet a woman deceived this great sorcerer. A Neapolitan cour-

---

*The text runs

> . . . qualem primo qui surgere mense
> Aut videt aut vidisse putat per nubila lunam.

Brother Marbodius, by a strange misunderstanding, substitutes an entirely different image for the one created by the poet.

tesan invited him to hoist himself up to her window in the basket
that was used to bring the provisions, and she left him all night
suspended between two storeys."

Brother Hilary did not appear to hear these observations.

"Virgil is a prophet," he replied, "and a prophet who leaves far
behind him the sibyls with their sacred verses as well as the daughter of King Priam, and that great diviner of future things, Plato
of Athens. You will find in the fourth of his Syracusan cantos the
birth of our Lord foretold in a language that seems of heaven
rather than of earth.* In the time of my early studies, when I read
for the first time JAM REDIT ET VIRGO, I felt myself bathed in an infinite delight, but I immediately experienced intense grief at the
thought that, for ever deprived of the presence of God, the author
of this prophetic verse, the noblest that has come from human lips,
was pining among the heathen in eternal darkness. This cruel
thought did not leave me. It pursued me even in my studies, my
prayers, my meditations, and my ascetic labours. Thinking that
Virgil was deprived of the sight of God and that possibly he might
even be suffering the fate of the reprobate in hell, I could neither
enjoy peace nor rest, and I went so far as to exclaim several times
a day with my arms outstretched to heaven:

" 'Reveal to me, O Lord, the lot thou hast assigned to him who
sang on earth as the angels sing in heaven!'

"After some years my anguish ceased when I read in an old book
that the great Apostle St. Paul, who called the Gentiles into the
Church of Christ, went to Naples and sanctified with his tears the
tomb of the prince of poets.† This was some ground for believing
that Virgil, like the Emperor Trajan, was admitted to Paradise because even in error he had a presentiment of the truth. We are not
compelled to believe it, but I can easily persuade myself that it is
true."

Having thus spoken, old Hilary wished me the peace of a holy
night and went away with Brother Jacinth.

I resumed the delightful study of my poet. Book in hand, I meditated upon the way in which those whom Love destroys with its
cruel malady wander through the secret paths in the depth of the

---

*Three centuries before the epoch in which our Marbodius lived the
words—

        Maro, vates gentilium
        Da Christo testimonium

were sung in the churches on Christmas Day.

        †Ad maronis mausoleum
        Ductus, fudit super eum
        Piae rorem lacrymæ.

        Quem te, inquit, reddidissem,
        Si te vivum invenissem,
        Poetarum maxime!

myrtle forest, and, as I meditated, the quivering reflections of the stars came and mingled with those of the leafless eglantines in the waters of the cloister fountain. Suddenly the lights and the perfumes and the stillness of the sky were overwhelmed, a fierce Northwind charged with storm and darkness burst roaring upon me. It lifted me up and carried me like a wisp of straw over fields, cities, rivers, and mountains, and through the midst of thunderclouds, during a long night composed of a whole series of nights and days. And when, after this prolonged and cruel rage, the hurricane was at last stilled, I found myself far from my native land at the bottom of a valley bordered by cypress trees. Then a woman of wild beauty, trailing long garments behind her, approached me. She placed her left hand on my shoulder, and, pointing her right arm to an oak with thick foliage:

"Look!" said she to me.

Immediately I recognised the Sibyl who guards the sacred wood of Avernus, and I discerned the fair Proserpine's beautiful golden twig amongst the tufted boughs of the tree to which her finger pointed.

"O prophetic Virgin," I exclaimed, "thou hast comprehended my desire and thou hast satisfied it in this way. Thou has revealed to me the tree that bears the shining twig without which none can enter alive into the dwelling-place of the dead. And in truth, eagerly did I long to converse with the shade of Virgil."

Having said this, I snatched the golden branch from its ancient trunk and I advanced without fear into the smoking gulf that leads to the miry banks of the Styx, upon which the shades are tossed about like dead leaves. At sight of the branch dedicated to Proserpine, Charon took me in his bark, which groaned beneath my weight, and I alighted on the shores of the dead, and was greeted by the mute baying of the threefold Cerberus. I pretended to throw the shade of a stone at him, and the vain monster fled into his cave. There, amidst the rushes, wandered the souls of those children whose eyes had but opened and shut to the kindly light of day, and there in a gloomy cavern Minos judges men. I penetrated into the myrtle wood in which the victims of love wander languishing, Phædra, Procris, the sad Eriphyle, Evadne, Pasiphaë, Laodamia, and Cenis, and the Phœnician Dido. Then I went through the dusty plains reserved for famous warriors. Beyond them open two ways. That to the left leads to Tartarus, the abode of the wicked. I took that to the right, which leads to Elysium and to the dwellings of Dis. Having hung the sacred branch at the goddess's door, I reached pleasant fields flooded with purple light. The shades of philosophers and poets hold grave converse there. The Graces and the Muses formed sprightly choirs upon the grass. Old Homer sang, accompanying himself upon his rustic lyre. His eyes were closed, but divine images shone upon his lips. I saw Solon, Democritus, and

Pythagoras watching the games of the young men in the meadow, and, through the foliage of an ancient laurel, I perceived also Hesiod, Orpheus, the melancholy Euripides, and the masculine Sappho. I passed and recognised, as they sat on the bank of a fresh rivulet, the poet Horace, Varius, Gallus, and Lycoris. A little apart, leaning against the trunk of a dark holm-oak, Virgil was gazing pensively at the grove. Of lofty stature, though spare, he still preserved that swarthy complexion, that rustic air, that negligent bearing, and unpolished appearance which during his lifetime concealed his genius. I saluted him piously and remained for a long time without speech.

At last when my halting voice could proceed out of my throat:

"O thou, so dear to the Ausonian Muses, thou honour of the Latin name, Virgil," cried I, "it is through thee I have known what beauty is, it is through thee I have known what the tables of the gods and the beds of the goddesses are like. Suffer the praises of the humblest of thy adorers."

"Arise, stranger," answered the divine poet. "I perceive that thou art a living being among the shades, and that thy body treads down the grass in this eternal evening. Thou art not the first man who has descended before his death into these dwellings, although all intercourse between us and the living is difficult. But cease from praise; I do not like eulogies and the confused sounds of glory have always offended my ears. That is why I fled from Rome, where I was known to the idle and curious, and laboured in the solitude of my beloved Parthenope. And then I am not so convinced that the men of thy generation understand my verses that I should be gratified by thy praises. Who art thou?"

"I am called Marbodius of the Kingdom of Alca. I made my profession in the Abbey of Corrigan. I read thy poems by day and I read them by night. It is thee whom I have come to see in Hell; I was impatient to know what thy fate was. On earth the learned often dispute about it. Some hold it probable that, having lived under the power of demons, thou art now burning in inextinguishable flames; others, more cautious, pronounce no opinion, believing that all which is said concerning the dead is uncertain and full of lies; several, though not in truth the ablest, maintain that, because thou didst elevate the tone of the Sicilian Muses and foretell that a new progeny would descend from heaven, thou wert admitted, like the Emperor Trajan, to enjoy eternal blessedness in the Christian heaven."

"Thou seest that such is not the case," answered the shade, smiling.

"I meet thee in truth, O Virgil, among the heroes and sages in those Elysian fields which thou thyself hast described. Thus, contrary to what several on earth believe, no one has come to seek thee on the part of Him who reigns on high?"

After a rather long silence:

"I will conceal nought from thee. He sent for me; one of His messengers, a simple man, came to say that I was expected, and that, although I had not been initiated into their mysteries, in consideration of my prophetic verses a place had been reserved for me among those of the new sect. But I refused to accept that invitation; I had no desire to change my place. I did so not because I share the admiration of the Greeks for the Elysian fields, or because I taste here those joys which caused Proserpine to lose the remembrance of her mother. I never believed much myself in what I say about these things in the 'Æneid.' I was instructed by philosophers and men of science and I had a correct foreboding of the truth. Life in hell is extremely attenuated; we feel neither pleasure nor pain; we are as if we were not. The dead have no existence here except such as the living lend them. Nevertheless I prefer to remain here."

"But what reason didst thou give, O Virgil, for so strange a refusal?"

"I gave excellent ones. I said to the messenger of the god that I did not deserve the honour he brought me, and that a meaning had been given to my verses which they did not bear. In truth I have not in my fourth Eclogue betrayed the faith of my ancestors. Some ignorant Jews alone have interpreted in favour of a barbarian god a verse which celebrates the return of the golden age predicted by the Sibylline oracles. I excused myself then on the ground that I could not occupy a place which was destined for me in error and to which I recognised that I had no right. Then I alleged my disposition and my tastes, which do not accord with the customs of the new heavens.

" 'I am not unsociable,' said I to this man. 'I have shown in life a complaisant and easy disposition, although the extreme simplicity of my habits caused me to be suspected of avarice. I kept nothing for myself alone. My library was open to all and I have conformed my conduct to that fine saying of Euripides, "all ought to be common among friends." Those praises that seemed obtrusive when I myself received them became agreeable to me when addressed to Varius or to Macer. But at bottom I am rustic and uncultivated. I take pleasure in the society of animals; I was so zealous in observing them and took so much care of them that I was regarded, not altogether wrongly, as a good veterinary surgeon. I am told that the people of thy sect claim an immortal soul for themselves, but refuse one to the animals. That is a piece of nonsense that makes me doubt their judgment. Perhaps I love the flocks and the shepherds a little too much. That would not seem right amongst you. There is a maxim to which I endeavour to conform my actions, "Nothing too much." More even than my feeble health my philosophy teaches me to use things with measure. I am sober; a lettuce and some olives with a drop of Falernian wine form all my meals. I have, indeed, to some extent gone with strange women, but I have not delayed over long in taverns to watch the young Syrians dance to the sound of the *crotalum*.* But if I have restrained my desires it was for my own satisfaction and for the sake of good discipline. To fear pleasure and to fly from joy appears to me the worst insult that one can offer to nature, I am assured that during their lives certain of the elect of thy god abstained from food and avoided women through love of asceticism, and voluntarily exposed themselves to useless sufferings. I should be afraid of meeting those criminals whose frenzy horrifies me. A poet must not be asked to attach himself too strictly to any scientific or moral doctrine. Moreover, I am a Roman, and the Romans, unlike the Greeks, are unable to pursue profound speculations in a subtle manner. If they adopt a philosophy it is above all in order to derive some practical advantages from it. Siro, who enjoyed a great renown among us, taught me the system of Epicurus and thus freed me from vain terrors and turned me aside from the cruelties to which religion persuades ignorant men. I have embraced the views of Pythagoras concerning the souls of men and animals, both of which are of divine essence; this invites us to look upon ourselves without pride and without shame. I have learnt from the Alexandrines how the earth, at first soft and without form, hardened in proportion as Nereus withdrew himself from it to dig his humid dwellings; I have learned how things were formed insensibly; in what manner the rains, falling from the burdened clouds, nourished the silent forests, and by what progress a few animals at last began to wander over the nameless mountains. I could not accustom myself to your cosmogony either, for it seems to me fitter for a camel-driver on the Syrian sands than for a disciple of Aristarchus and Samos. And what would become of me in the abode of your beatitude if I did not find there my friends, my ancestors, my masters, and my gods, and if it is not given me to see Rhea's noble son, or Venus, mother of Æneas, with her winning smile, or Pan, or the young Dryads, or the Sylvans, or old Silenus, with his face stained by Ægle's purple mulberries.' These are the reasons which I begged that simple man to plead before the successor of Jupiter."

"And since then, O great shade, thou hast received no other messages?"

"I have received none."

"To console themselves for thy absence, O Virgil, they have three poets, Commodianus, Prudentius, and Fortunatus, who were all three born in those dark days when neither prosody nor grammar were known. But tell me, O Mantuan, hast thou never received

---

*This phrase seems to indicate that, if one is to believe Macrobius, the "Copa" is by Virgil.

other intelligence of the God whose company thou didst so deliberately refuse?"

"Never that I remember."

"Hast thou not told me that I am not the first who descended alive into these abodes and presented himself before thee?"

"Thou dost remind me of it. A century and a half ago, or so it seems to me (it is difficult to reckon days and years amid the shades), my profound peace was intruded upon by a strange visitor. As I was wandering beneath the gloomy foliage that borders the Styx, I saw rising before me a human form more opaque and darker than that of the inhabitants of these shores. I recognised a living person. He was of high stature, thin, with an aquiline nose, sharp chin, and hollow cheeks. His dark eyes shot forth fire; a red hood girt with a crown of laurels bound his lean brows. His bones pierced through the tight brown cloak that descended to his heels. He saluted me with deference, tempered by a sort of fierce pride, and addressed me in a speech more obscure and incorrect than that of those Gauls with whom the divine Julius filled both his legions and the Curia. At last I understood that he had been born near Fiesole, in an ancient Etruscan colony that Sulla had founded on the banks of the Arno, and which had prospered; that he had obtained municipal honours, but that he had thrown himself vehemently into the sanguinary quarrels which arose between the senate, the knights, and the people, that he had been defeated and banished, and now he wandered in exile throughout the world. He described Italy to me as distracted by more wars and discords than in the time of my youth, and as sighing anew for a second Augustus. I pitied his misfortunes, remembering what I myself had formerly endured.

"An audacious spirit unceasingly disquieted him, and his mind harboured great thoughts, but alas! his rudeness and ignorance displayed the triumph of barbarism. He knew neither poetry, nor science, nor even the tongue of the Greeks, and he was ignorant, too, of the ancient traditions concerning the origin of the world and the nature of the gods. He gravely repeated fables which in my time would have brought smiles to the little children who were not yet old enough to pay for admission at the baths. The vulgar easily believe in monsters. The Etruscans especially peopled hell with demons, hideous as a sick man's dreams. That they have not abandoned their childish imaginings after so many centuries is explained by the continuation and progress of ignorance and misery, but that one of their magistrates whose mind is raised above the common level should share these popular illusions and should be frightened by the hideous demons that the inhabitants of that country painted on the walls of their tombs in the time of Porsena —that is something which might sadden even a sage. My Etruscan visitor repeated verses to me which he had composed in a new dialect, called by him the vulgar tongue, the sense of which I could not understand. My ears were more surprised than charmed as I heard him repeat the same sound three or four times at regular intervals in his efforts to mark the rhythm. That artifice did not seem ingenious to me; but it is not for the dead to judge of novelties.

"But I do not reproach this colonist of Sulla, born in an unhappy time, for making inharmonious verses or for being, if it be possible, as bad a poet as Bavius or Maevius. I have grievances against him which touch me more closely. The thing is monstrous and scarcely credible, but when this man returned to earth he disseminated the most odious lies about me. He affirmed in several passages of his barbarous poems that I had served him as a guide in the modern Tartarus, a place I know nothing of. He insolently proclaimed that I had spoken of the gods of Rome as false and lying gods, and that I held as the true God the present successor of Jupiter. Friend, when thou art restored to the kindly light of day and beholdest again thy native land, contradict those abominable falsehoods. Say to thy people that the singer of the pious Æneas has never worshipped the god of the Jews. I am assured that his power is declining and that his approaching fall is manifested by undoubted indications. This news would give me some pleasure if one could rejoice in these abodes, where we feel neither fears nor desires."

He spoke, and with a gesture of farewell he went away. I beheld his shade gliding over the asphodels without bending their stalks. I saw that it became fainter and vaguer as it receded farther from me, and it vanished before it reached the wood of evergreen laurels. Then I understood the meaning of the words, "The dead have no life, but that which the living lend them," and I walked slowly through the pale meadow to the gate of horn.

I affirm that all in this writing is true.*

*There is in Marbodius's narrative a passage very worthy of notice, viz., that in which the monk of Corrigan describes Dante Alighieri such as we picture him to ourselves to-day. The miniatures in a very old manuscript of the "Divine Comedy," the "Codex Venetianus," represent the poet as a little fat man clad in a short tunic, the skirts of which fall above his knees. As for Virgil, he still wears the philosophical beard, in the wood-engravings of the sixteenth century.

One would not have thought either that Marbodius, or even Virgil, could have known the Etruscan tombs of Chiusi and Corneto, where, in fact, there are horrible and burlesque devils closely resembling those of Orcagna. Nevertheless, the authenticity of the "Descent of Marbodius into Hell" is indisputable. M. du Clos des Lunes has firmly established it. To doubt it would be to doubt palæography itself.

VII

SIGNS IN THE MOON

T THAT time, whilst Penguinia was still plunged in ignorance and barbarism, Giles Bird-catcher, a Franciscan monk, known by his writings under the name Ægidius Aucùpis, devoted himself with indefatigable zeal to the study of letters and the sciences. He gave his nights to mathematics and music, which he called the two adorable sisters, the harmonious daughters of Number and Imagination. He was versed in medicine and astrology. He was suspected of practising magic, and it seemed true that he wrought metamorphoses and discovered hidden things.

The monks of his convent, finding in his cell Greek books which they could not read, imagined them to be conjuring-books, and denounced their too learned brother as a wizard. Ægidius Aucupis fled, and reached the island of Ireland, where he lived for thirty studious years. He went from monastery to monastery, searching for and copying the Greek and Latin manuscripts which they contained. He also studied physics and alchemy. He acquired a universal knowledge and discovered notable secrets concerning animals, plants, and stones. He was found one day in the company of a very beautiful woman who sang to her own accompaniment on the lute, and who was afterwards discovered to be a machine which he had himself constructed.

He often crossed the Irish Sea to go into the land of Wales and to visit the libraries of the monasteries there. During one of these crossings, as he remained during the night on the bridge of the ship, he saw beneath the waters two sturgeons swimming side by side. He had very good hearing and he knew the languages of the fishes. Now he heard one of the sturgeons say to the other:

"The man in the moon, whom we have often seen carrying fagots on his shoulders, has fallen into the sea."

And the other sturgeon said in its turn:

"And in the silver disc there will be seen the image of two lovers kissing each other on the mouth."

Some years later, having returned to his native country, Ægidius Aucupis found that ancient learning had been restored. Manners had softened. Men no longer pursued the nymphs of the fountains, of the woods, and of the mountains with their insults. They placed images of the Muses and of the modest Graces in their gardens, and they rendered her former honours to the Goddess with ambrosial lips, the joy of men and gods. They were becoming reconciled to nature. They trampled vain terrors beneath their feet and raised their eyes to heaven without fearing, as they formerly did, to read signs of anger and threats of damnation in the skies.

At this spectacle Ægidius Aucupis remembered what the two sturgeons of the sea of Erin had foretold.

BOOK IV: MODERN TIMES: TRINCO

I

MOTHER ROUQUIN

EGIDIUS AUCUPIS, the Erasmus of the Penguins, was not mistaken; his age was an age of free inquiry. But that great man mistook the elegances of the humanists for softness of manners, and he did not foresee the effects that the awaking of intelligence would have amongst the Penguins. It brought about the religious Reformation; Catholics massacred Protestants and Protestants massacred Catholics. Such were the first results of liberty of thought. The Catholics prevailed in Penguinia. But the spirit of inquiry had penetrated among them without their knowing it. They joined reason to faith, and claimed that religion had been divested of the superstitious practices that dishonoured it, just as in later days the booths that the cobblers, hucksters, and dealers in old clothes had built against the walls of the cathedrals were cleared away. The word, legend, which at first indicated what the faithful ought to read, soon suggested the idea of pious fables and childish tales.

The saints had to suffer from this state of mind. An obscure canon called Princeteau, a very austere and crabbed man, designated so great a number of them as not worthy of having their days observed, that he was surnamed the exposer of the saints. He did not think, for instance, that if St. Margaret's prayer were applied as a poultice to a woman in travail that the pains of childbirth would be softened.

Even the venerable patron saint of Penguinia did not escape his rigid criticism. This is what he says of her in his "Antiquities of Alca":

"Nothing is more uncertain than the history, or even the existence, of St. Orberosia. An ancient anonymous annalist, a monk of Dombes, relates that a woman called Orberosia was possessed by the devil in a cavern where, even down to his own days, the little boys and girls of the village used to play at a sort of game repre-

75

senting the devil and the fair Orberosia. He adds that this woman
became the concubine of a horrible dragon, who ravaged the country. Such a statement is hardly credible, but the history of Orberosia, as it has since been related, seems hardly more worthy of belief. The life of that saint by the Abbot Simplicissimus is three
hundred years later than the pretended events which it relates and
that author shows himself excessively credulous and devoid of all
critical faculty."

Suspicion attacked even the supernatural origin of the Penguins.
The historian Ovidius Capito went so far as to deny the miracle of
their transformation. He thus begins his "Annals of Penguinia":

"A dense obscurity envelopes this history, and it would be no
exaggeration to say that it is a tissue of puerile fables and popular
tales. The Penguins claim that they are descended from birds who
were baptized by St. Maël and whom God changed into men at the
intercession of that glorious apostle. They hold that, situated at
first in the frozen ocean, their island, floating like Delos, was
brought to anchor in these heaven-favoured seas, of which it is to-
day the queen. I conclude that this myth is a reminiscence of the
ancient migrations of the Penguins."

In the following century, which was that of the philosophers,
scepticism became still more acute. No further evidence of it is
needed than the following celebrated passage from the "Moral
Essay."

"Arriving we know not from whence (for indeed their origins
are not very clear), and successively invaded and conquered by
four or five peoples from the north, south, east, and west, mis-
cegenated, inter-bred, amalgamated, and commingled, the Penguins boast of the purity of their race, and with justice, for they
have become a pure race. This mixture of all mankind, red, black,
yellow, and white, round-headed and long-headed, has formed in
the course of ages a fairly homogeneous human family, and one
which is recognisable by certain features due to a community of
life and customs.

"This idea that they belong to the best race in the world, and
that they are its finest family, inspires them with noble pride, indomitable courage, and a hatred for the human race.

"The life of a people is but a succession of miseries, crimes, and
follies. This is true of the Penguin nation, as of all other nations.
Save for this exception its history is admirable from beginning to
end."

The two classic ages of the Penguins are too well-known for me
to lay stress upon them. But what has not been sufficiently noticed
is the way in which the rationalist theologians such as Canon
Princeteau called into existence the unbelievers of the succeeding
age. The former employed their reason to destroy what did not
seem to them essential to their religion; they only left untouched

the most rigid article of faith. Their intellectual successors, being taught by them how to make use of science and reason, employed them against whatever beliefs remained. Thus rational theology engendered natural philosophy.

That is why (if I may turn from the Penguins of former days to the Sovereign Pontiff, who, to-day governs the universal Church) we cannot admire too greatly the wisdom of Pope Pius X. in condemning the study of exegesis as contrary to revealed truth, fatal to sound theological doctrine, and deadly to the faith. Those clerics who maintain the rights of science in opposition to him are pernicious doctors and pestilent teachers, and the faithful who approve of them are lacking in either mental or moral ballast.

At the end of the age of philosophers, the ancient kingdom of Penguinia was utterly destroyed, the king put to death, the privileges of the nobles abolished, and a Republic proclaimed in the midst of public misfortunes and while a terrible war was raging. The assembly which then governed Penguinia ordered all the metal articles contained in the churches to be melted down. The patriots even desecrated the tombs of the kings. It is said that when the tomb of Draco the Great was opened, that king presented an appearance as black as ebony and so majestic that those who profaned his corpse fled in terror. According to other accounts, these churlish men insulted him by putting a pipe in his mouth and derisively offering him a glass of wine.

On the seventeenth day of the month of Mayflowers, the shrine of St. Orberosia, which had for five hundred years been exposed to the veneration of the faithful in the Church of St. Maël, was transported into the town-hall and submitted to the examination of a jury of experts appointed by the municipality. It was made of gilded copper in shape like the nave of a church, entirely covered with enamels and decorated with precious stones, which latter were perceived to be false. The chapter in its foresight had removed the rubies, sapphires, emeralds, and great balls of rock-crystal, and had substituted pieces of glass in their place. It contained only a little dust and a piece of old linen, which were thrown into a great fire that had been lighted on the Place de Grève to burn the relics of the saints. The people danced around it singing patriotic songs.

From the threshold of their booth, which leant against the town-hall, a man called Rouquin and his wife were watching this group of madmen. Rouquin clipped dogs and gelded cats; he also frequented the inns. His wife was a ragpicker and a bawd, but she had plenty of shrewdness.

"You see, Rouquin," said she to her man, "they are committing a sacrilege. They will repent of it."

"You know nothing about it, wife," answered Rouquin; "they have become philosophers, and when one is once a philosopher he is a philosopher for ever."

"I tell you, Rouquin, that sooner or later they will regret what they are doing to-day. They ill-treat the saints because they have not helped them enough, but for all that the quails won't fall ready cooked into their mouths. They will soon find themselves as badly off as before, and when they have put out their tongues for enough they will become pious again. Sooner than people think the day will come when Penguinia will again begin to honour her blessed patron. Rouquin, it would be a good thing, in readiness for that day, if we kept a handful of ashes and some rags and bones in an old pot in our lodgings. We will say that they are the relics of St. Orberosia and that we have saved them from the flames at the peril of our lives. I am greatly mistaken if we don't get honour and profit out of them. That good action might be worth a place from the Curé to sell tapers and hire chairs in the chapel of St. Orberosia."

On that same day Mother Rouquin took home with her a little ashes and some bones, and put them in an old jam-pot in her cupboard.

II

TRINCO

THE sovereign Nation had taken possession of the lands of the nobility and clergy to sell them at a low price to the middle classes and the peasants. The middle classes and the peasants thought that the revolution was a good thing for acquiring lands and a bad one for retaining them.

The legislators of the Republic made terrible laws for the defence of property, and decreed death to anyone who should propose a division of wealth. But that did not avail the Republic. The peasants who had become proprietors bethought themselves that though it had made them rich, the Republic had nevertheless caused a disturbance to wealth, and they desired a system more respectful of private property and more capable of assuring the permanence of the new institutions.

They had not long to wait. The Republic, like Agrippina, bore her destroyer in her bosom.

Having great wars to carry on, it created military forces, and these were destined both to save it and to destroy it. Its legislators thought they could restrain their generals by the fear of punishment, but if they sometimes cut off the heads of unlucky soldiers they could not do the same to the fortunate soldiers who obtained over it the advantages of having saved its existence.

In the enthusiasm of victory the renovated Penguins delivered themselves up to a dragon, more terrible than that of their fables, who, like a stork amongst frogs, devoured them for fourteen years with his insatiable beak.

Half a century after the reign of the new dragon a young Maharajah of Malay, called Djambi, desirous, like the Scythian Anacharsis, of instructing himself by travel, visited Penguinia and wrote an interesting account of his travels. I transcribe the first page of his account:

ACCOUNT OF THE TRAVELS OF YOUNG DJAMBI IN PENGUINIA

After a voyage of ninety days I landed at the vast and deserted port of the Penguins and travelled over untilled fields to their ruined capital. Surrounded by ramparts and full of barracks and arsenals it had a martial though desolate appearance. Feeble and crippled men wandered proudly through the streets, wearing old uniforms and carrying rusty weapons.

"What do you want?" I was rudely asked at the gate of the city by a soldier whose moustaches pointed to the skies.

"Sir," I answered, "I come as an inquirer to visit this island."

"It is not an island," replied the soldier.

"What!" I exclaimed, "Penguin Island is not an island?"

"No, sir, it is an insula. It was formerly called an island, but for a century it has been decreed that it shall bear the name of insula. It is the only insula in the whole universe. Have you a passport?"

"Here it is."

"Go and get it signed at the Ministry of Foreign Affairs."

A lame guide who conducted me came to a pause in a vast square.

"The insula," said he, "has given birth, as you know, to Trinco, the greatest genius of the universe, whose statue you see before you. That obelisk standing to your right commemorates Trinco's birth; the column that rises to your left has Trinco crowned with a diadem upon its summit. You see here the triumphal arch dedicated to the glory of Trinco and his family."

"What extraordinary feat has Trinco performed?" I asked.

"War."

"That is nothing extraordinary. We Malayans make war constantly."

"That may be, but Trinco is the greatest warrior of all countries and all times. There never existed a greater conquerer than he. As you anchored in our port you saw to the east a volcanic island called Ampelophoria, shaped like a cone, and of small size, but renowned for its wines. And to the west a larger island which raises to the sky a long range of sharp teeth; for this reason it is called the Dog's Jaws. It is rich in copper mines. We possessed both before Trinco's reign and they were the boundaries of our empire.

Trinco extended the Penguin dominion over the Archipelago of the Turquoises and the Green Continent, subdued the gloomy Porpoises, and planted his flag amid the icebergs of the Pole and on the burning sands of the African deserts. He raised troops in all the countries he conquered, and when his armies marched past in the wake of our own light infantry, our island grenadiers, our hussars, our dragoons, our artillery, and our engineers there were to be seen yellow soldiers looking in their blue armour like crayfish standing on their tails; red men with parrots' plumes, tatooed with solar and Phallic emblems, and with quivers of poisoned arrows resounding on their backs; naked blacks armed only with their teeth and nails; pygmies riding on cranes; gorillas carrying trunks of trees and led by an old ape who wrote upon his hairy breast the cross of the Legion of Honour. And all those troops, led to Trinco's banner by the most ardent patriotism, flew on from victory to victory, and in thirty years of war Trinco conquered half the known world."

"What!" cried I, "you possess half of the world."

"Trinco conquered it for us, and Trinco lost it to us. As great in his defeats as in his victories he surrendered all that he had conquered. He even allowed those two islands we possessed before his time, Ampelophoria and the Dog's Jaws, to be taken from us. He left Penguinia impoverished and depopulated. The flower of the insula perished in his wars. At the time of his fall there were left in our country none but the hunchbacks and cripples from whom we are descended. But he gave us glory."

"He made you pay dearly for it!"

"Glory never costs too much," replied my guide.

III

THE JOURNEY OF DOCTOR OBNUBILE

FTER a succession of amazing vicissitudes, the memory of which is in great part lost by the wrongs of time and the bad style of historians, the Penguins established the government of the Penguins by themselves. They elected a diet or assembly, and invested it with the privilege of naming the Head of the State. The latter, chosen from among the simple Penguins, wore no formidable monster's crest upon his head and exercised no absolute authority over the people. He was himself subject to the laws of the nation. He was not given the title of king, and no ordinal number followed his name. He bore such names as Paturle, Janvion, Truffaldin, Coquenhot, and Bredouille. These magistrates did not make war. They were not suited for that.

The new state received the name of Public Thing or Republic. Its partisans were called republicanists or republicans. They were also named Thingmongers and sometimes Scamps, but this latter name was taken in ill part.

The Penguin democracy did not itself govern. It obeyed a financial oligarchy which formed opinion by means of the newspapers, and held in its hands the representatives, the ministers, and the president. It controlled the finances of the republic, and directed the foreign affairs of the country as if it were possessed of sovereign power.

Empires and kingdoms in those days kept up enormous fleets. Penguinia, compelled to do as they did, sank under the pressure of her armaments. Everybody deplored or pretended to deplore so grievous a necessity. However, the rich, and those engaged in business or affairs, submitted to it with a good heart through a spirit of patriotism, and because they counted on the soldiers and sailors to defend their goods at home and to acquire markets and territories abroad. The great manufacturers encouraged the making of cannons and ships through a zeal for the national defence and in order to obtain orders. Among the citizens of middle rank and of the liberal professions some resigned themselves to this state of affairs without complaining, believing that it would last for ever; others waited impatiently for its end and thought they might be able to lead the powers to a simultaneous disarmament.

The illustrious Professor Obnubile belonged to this latter class.

"War," said he, "is a barbarity to which the progress of civilization will put an end. The great democracies are pacific and will soon impose their will upon the aristocrats."

Professor Obnubile, who had for sixty years led a solitary and retired life in his laboratory, whither external noises did not penetrate, resolved to observe the spirit of the peoples for himself. He began his studies with the greatest of all democracies and set sail for New Atlantis.

After a voyage of fifteen days his steamer entered, during the night, the harbour of Titanport, where thousands of ships were anchored. An iron bridge thrown across the water and shining with lights, stretched between two piers so far apart that Professor Obnubile imagined he was sailing on the seas of Saturn and that he saw the marvellous ring which girds the planet of the Old Man. And this immense conduit bore upon it more than a quarter of the wealth of the world. The learned Penguin, having disembarked, was waited on by automatons in a hotel forty-eight stories high. Then he took the great railway that led to Gigantopolis, the capital of New Atlantis. In the train there were restaurants, gaming-rooms, athletic arenas, telegraphic, commercial, and financial

offices, a Protestant Church, and the printing-office of a great newspaper, which latter the doctor was unable to read, as he did not
know the language of the New Atlantans. The train passed along
the banks of great rivers, through manufacturing cities which concealed the sky with the smoke from their chimneys, towns black in
the day, towns red at night, full of noise by day and full of noise
also by night.

"Here," thought the doctor, "is a people far too much engaged
in industry and trade to make war. I am already certain that the
New Atlantans pursue a policy of peace. For it is an axiom admitted by all economists that peace without and peace within are
necessary for the progress of commerce and industry."

As he surveyed Gigantopolis, he was confirmed in this opinion.
People went through the streets so swiftly propelled by hurry that
they knocked down all who were in their way. Obnubile was thrown
down several times, but soon succeeded in learning how to demean
himself better; after an hour's walking he himself knocked down
an Atlantan.

Having reached a great square he saw the portico of a palace
in the classic style, whose Corinthian columns reared their capitals of arborescent acanthus seventy metres above the stylobate.

As he stood with his head thrown back admiring the building,
a man of modest appearance approached him and said in Penguin:

"I see by your dress that you are from Penguinia. I know your
language; I am a sworn interpreter. This is the Parliament palace.
At the present moment the representatives of the States are in deliberation. Would you like to be present at the sitting?"

The doctor was brought into the hall and cast his looks upon
the crowd of legislators who were sitting on cane chairs with their
feet upon their desks.

The president arose and, in the midst of general inattention, muttered rather than spoke the following formulas which the interpreter immediately translated to the doctor.

"The war for the opening of the Mongol markets being ended
to the satisfaction of the States, I propose that the accounts be
laid before the finance committee. . . ."

"Is there any opposition? . . ."

"The proposal is carried."

"The war for the opening of the markets of Third-Zealand being
ended to the satisfaction of the States, I propose that the accounts
be laid before the finance committee. . . ."

"Is there any opposition? . . ."

"The proposal is carried."

"Have I heard aright?" asked Professor Obnubile. "What? you
an industrial people and engaged in all these wars!"

"Certainly," answered the interpreter, "these are industrial wars.
Peoples who have neither commerce nor industry are not obliged

to make war, but a business people is forced to adopt a policy of conquest. The number of wars necessarily increases with our productive activity. As soon as one of our industries fails to find a market for its products a war is necessary to open new outlets. It is in this way we have had a coal war, a copper war, and a cotton war. In Third-Zealand we have killed two-thirds of the inhabitants in order to compel the remainder to buy our umbrellas and braces."

At that moment a fat man who was sitting in the middle of the assembly ascended the tribune.

"I claim," said he, "a war against the Emerald Republic, which insolently contends with our pigs for the hegemony of hams and sauces in all the markets of the universe."

"Who is that legislator?" asked Doctor Obnubile.

"He is a pig merchant."

"Is there any opposition?" said the President. "I put the proposition to the vote."

The war against the Emerald Republic was voted with uplifted hands by a very large majority.

"What?" said Obnubile to the interpreter; "you have voted a war with that rapidity and that indifference!"

"Oh! it is an unimportant war which will hardly cost eight million dollars."

"And men . . ."

"The men are included in the eight million dollars."

Then Doctor Obnubile bent his head in bitter reflection.

"Since wealth and civilization admit of as many causes of wars as poverty and barbarism, since the folly and wickedness of men are incurable, there remains but one good action to be done. The wise man will collect enough dynamite to blow up this planet. When its fragments fly through space an imperceptible amelioration will be accomplished in the universe and a satisfaction will be given to the universal conscience. Moreover, this universal conscience does not exist."

BOOK V: MODERN TIMES: CHATILLON

I

THE REVEREND FATHERS AGARIC AND CORNEMUSE

VERY system of government produces people who are dissatisfied. The Republic or Public Thing produced them at first from among the nobles who had been despoiled of their ancient privileges. These looked with regret and hope to Prince Crucho, the last of the Draconides, a prince adorned both with the grace of youth and the melancholy of exile. It also produced them from among the smaller traders, who, owing to profound economic causes, no longer gained a livelihood. They believed that this was the fault of the republic which they had at first adored and from which each day they were now becoming more detached. The financiers, both Christians and Jews, became by their insolence and their cupidity the scourge of the country, which they plundered and degraded, as well as the scandal of a government which they never troubled either to destroy or preserve, so confident were they that they could operate without hindrance under all governments. Nevertheless, their sympathies inclined to absolute power as the best protection against the socialists, their puny but ardent adversaries. And just as they imitated the habits of the aristocrats, so they imitated their political and religious sentiments. Their women, in particular, loved the Prince and had dreams of appearing one day at his Court.

However, the Republic retained some partisans and defenders. If it was not in a position to believe in the fidelity of its own officials it could at least still count on the devotion of the manual labourers, although it had never relieved their misery. These came forth in crowds from their quarries and their factories to defend it, and marched in long processions, gloomy, emaciated, and sinister. They would have died for it because it had given them hope.

Now, under the Presidency of Theodore Formose, there lived in a peaceable suburb of Alca a monk called Agaric, who kept a school and assisted in arranging marriages. In his school he taught fenc-

84

ing and riding to the sons of old families, illustrious by their birth, but now as destitute of wealth as of privilege. And as soon as they were old enough he married them to the daughters of the opulent and despised caste of financiers.

Tall, thin, and dark, Agaric used to walk in deep thought, with his breviary in his hand and his brow loaded with care, through the corridors of the school and the alleys of the garden. His care was not limited to inculcating in his pupils abstruse doctrines and mechanical precepts and to endowing them afterwards with legitimate and rich wives. He entertained political designs and pursued the realisation of a gigantic plan. His thought of thoughts and labour of labours was to overthrow the Republic. He was not moved to this by any personal interest. He believed that a democratic state was opposed to the holy society to which body and soul he belonged. And all the other monks, his brethren, thought the same. The Republic was perpetually at strife with the congregation of monks and the assembly of the faithful. True, to plot the death of the new government was a difficult and perilous enterprise. Still, Agaric was in a position to carry on a formidable conspiracy. At that epoch, when the clergy guided the superior classes of the Penguins, this monk exercised a tremendous influence over the aristocracy of Alca.

All the young men whom he had brought up waited only for a favourable moment to march against the popular power. The sons of the ancient families did not practise the arts or engage in business. They were almost all soldiers and served the Republic. They served it, but they did not love it; they regretted the dragon's crest. And the fair Jewesses shared in these regrets in order that they might be taken for Christians.

One July as he was walking in a suburban street which ended in some dusty fields, Agaric heard groans coming from a mossgrown well that had been abandoned by the gardeners. And almost immediately he was told by a cobbler of the neighbourhood that a ragged man who had shouted out "Hurrah for the Republic!" had been thrown into the well by some cavalry officers who were passing, and had sunk up to his ears in the mud. Agaric was quite ready to see a general significance in this particular fact. He inferred a great fermentation in the whole aristocratic and military caste, and concluded that it was the moment to act.

The next day he went to the end of the Wood of Conils to visit the good Father Cornemuse. He found the monk in his laboratory pouring a golden-coloured liquor into a still. He was a short, fat, little man, with vermilion-tinted cheeks and elaborately polished bald head. His eyes had ruby-coloured pupils like a guinea-pig's. He graciously saluted his visitor and offered him a glass of the St. Orberosian *liqueur,* which he manufactured, and from the sale of which he gained immense wealth.

Agaric made a gesture of refusal. Then, standing on his long feet and pressing his melancholy hat against his stomach, he remained silent.

"Take a seat," said Cornemuse to him.

Agaric sat down on a rickety stool, but continued mute.

Then the monk of Conils inquired:

"Tell me some news of your young pupils. Have the dear children sound views?"

"I am very satisfied with them," answered the teacher. "It is everything to be nurtured in sound principles. It is necessary to have sound views before having any views at all, for afterwards it is too late. . . . Yes, I have great grounds for comfort. But we live in a sad age."

"Alas!" sighed Cornemuse.

"We are passing through evil days. . . ."

"Times of trial."

"Yet, Cornemuse, the mind of the public is not so entirely corrupted as it seems."

"Perhaps you are right."

"The people are tired of a government that ruins them and does nothing for them. Every day fresh scandals spring up. The Republic is sunk in shame. It is ruined."

"May God grant it!"

"Cornemuse, what do you think of Prince Crucho?"

"He is an amiable young man and, I dare say, a worthy scion of an august stock. I pity him for having to endure the pains of exile at so early an age. Spring has no flowers for the exile, and autumn no fruits. Prince Crucho has sound views; he respects the clergy; he practises our religion; besides, he consumes a good deal of my little products."

"Cornemuse, in many homes, both rich and poor, his return is hoped for. Believe me, he will come back."

"May I live to throw my mantle beneath his feet!" sighed Cornemuse.

Seeing that he held these sentiments, Agaric depicted to him the state of people's minds such as he himself imagined them. He showed him the nobles and the rich exasperated against the popular government; the army refusing to endure fresh insults; the officials willing to betray their chiefs; the people discontented, riot ready to burst forth, and the enemies of the monks, the agents of the constituted authority, thrown into the wells of Alca. He concluded that it was the moment to strike a great blow.

"We can," he cried, "save the Penguin people, we can deliver it from its tyrants, deliver it from itself, restore the Dragon's crest, re-establish the ancient State, the good State, for the honour of the faith and the exaltation of the Church. We can do this if we will. We possess great wealth and we exert secret influences; by

our evangelistic and outspoken journals we communicate with all
the ecclesiastics in towns and country alike, and we inspire them
with our own eager enthusiasm and our own burning faith. They
will kindle their penitents and their congregations. I can dispose
of the chiefs of the army; I have an understanding with the men
of the people. Unknown to them I sway the minds of umbrella
sellers, publicans, shopmen, gutter merchants, newspaper boys,
women of the streets, and police agents. We have more people on
our side than we need. What are we waiting for? Let us act!"

"What do you think of doing?" asked Cornemuse.

"Of forming a vast conspiracy and overthrowing the Republic,
of re-establishing Crucho on the throne of the Draconides."

Cornemuse moistened his lips with his tongue several times.
Then he said with unction:

"Certainly the restoration of the Draconides is desirable; it is
eminently desirable; and for my part, I desire it with all my heart.
As for the Republic, you know what I think of it. . . . But would
it not be better to abandon it to its fate and let it die of the vices
of its own constitution? Doubtless, Agaric, what you propose is
noble and generous. It would be a fine thing to save this great and
unhappy country, to re-establish it in its ancient splendour. But
reflect on it, we are Christians before we are Penguins. And we
must take heed not to compromise religion in political enterprises."

Agaric replied eagerly:

"Fear nothing. We shall hold all the threads of the plot, but we
ourselves shall remain in the background. We shall not be seen."

"Like flies in milk," murmured the monk of Conils.

And turning his keen ruby-coloured eyes towards his brother
monk:

"Take care. Perhaps the Republic is stronger than it seems. Possibly, too, by dragging it out of the nerveless inertia in which it
now rests we may only consolidate its forces. Its malice is great;
if we attack it, it will defend itself. It makes bad laws which hardly
affect us; if it is frightened it will make terrible ones against us.
Let us not lightly engage in an adventure in which we may get
fleeced. You think the opportunity a good one. I don't, and I am
going to tell you why. The present government is not yet known
by everybody, that is to say, it is known by nobody. It proclaims
that it is the Public Thing, the common thing. The populace believes it and remains democratic and Republican. But patience!
This same people will one day demand that the public thing be the
people's thing. I need not tell you how insolent, unregulated, and
contrary to Scriptural polity such claims seem to me. But the people will make them, and enforce them, and then there will be an
end of the present government. The moment cannot now be far
distant; and it is then that we ought to act in the interests of our

august body. Let us wait. What hurries us? Our existence is not in peril. It has not been rendered absolutely intolerable to us. The Republic fails in respect and submission to us; it does not give the priests the honours it owes them. But it lets us live. And such is the excellence of our position that with us to live is to prosper. The Republic is hostile to us, but women revere us. President Formose does not assist at the celebration of our mysteries, but I have seen his wife and daughters at my feet. They buy my phials by the gross. I have no better clients even among the aristocracy. Let us say what there is to be said for it. There is no country in the world as good for priests and monks as Penguinia. In what other country would you find our virgin wax, our virile incense, our rosaries, our scapulars, our holy water, and our St. Orberosian liqueur sold in such great quantities? What other people would, like the Penguins, give a hundred golden crowns for a wave of our hands, a

sound from our mouths, a movement of our lips? For my part, I gain a thousand times more, in this pleasant, faithful, and docile Penguinia, by extracting the essence from a bundle of thyme, than I could make by tiring my lungs with preaching the remission of sins in the most populous States of Europe and America. Honestly, would Penguinia be better off if a police officer came to take me away from here and put me on a steamboat bound for the Islands of Night?"

Having thus spoken, the monk of Conils got up and led his guest into a huge shed where hundreds of orphans clothed in blue were packing bottles, nailing up cases, and gumming tickets. The ear was deafened by the noise of hammers mingled with the dull rumbling of bales being placed upon the rails.

"It is from here that consignments are forwarded," said Cornemuse. "I have obtained from the government a railway through the Wood and a station at my door. Every three days I fill a truck with my own products. You see that the Republic has not killed all beliefs."

Agaric made a last effort to engage the wise distiller in his enterprise. He pointed him to a prompt, certain, dazzling success.

"Don't you wish to share in it?" he added. "Don't you wish to bring back your king from exile?"

"Exile is pleasant to men of good will," answered the monk of Conils. "If you are guided by me, my dear Brother Agaric, you will give up your project for the present. For my own part I have no illusions. Whether or not I belong to your party, if you lose, I shall have to pay like you."

Father Agaric took leave of his friend and went back satisfied to his school. "Cornemuse," thought he, "not being able to prevent the plot, would like to make it succeed and he will give money." Agaric was not deceived. Such, indeed, was the solidarity among priests and monks that the acts of a single one bound them all. That was at once both their strength and their weakness.

II

PRINCE CRUCHO

GARIC resolved to proceed without delay to Prince Crucho, who honoured him with his familiarity. In the dusk of the evening he went out of his school by the side door, disguised as a cattle merchant and took passage on board the *St. Maël*.

The next day he landed in Porpoisia, for it was at Chitterlings Castle on this hospitable soil that Crucho ate the bitter bread of exile.

Agaric met the Prince on the road driving in a motor-car with two young ladies at the rate of a hundred miles an hour. When the monk saw him he shook his red umbrella and the prince stopped his car.

"Is it you, Agaric? Get in! There are already three of us, but we can make room for you. You can take one of these young ladies on your knee."

The pious Agaric got in.

"What news, worthy father?" asked the young prince.

"Great news," answered Agaric. "Can I speak?"

"You can. I have nothing secret from these two ladies."

"Sire, Penguinia claims you. You will not be deaf to her call."

Agaric described the state of feeling and outlined a vast plot.

"On my first signal," said he, "all your partisans will rise at once. With cross in hand and habits girded up, your venerable clergy will lead the armed crowd into Formose's palace. We shall carry terror and death among your enemies. For a reward of our efforts we only ask of you, Sire, that you will not render them useless. We entreat you to come and seat yourself on the throne that we shall prepare."

The prince returned a simple answer:

"I shall enter Alca on a green horse."

Agaric declared that he accepted this manly response. Although, contrary to his custom, he had a lady on his knee, he adjured the young prince, with a sublime loftiness of soul, to be faithful to his royal duties.

"Sire," he cried, with tears in his eyes, "you will live to remember the day on which you have been restored from exile, given back to your people, re-established on the throne of your ancestors by the hands of your monks, and crowned by them with the august crest of the Dragon. King Crucho, may you equal the glory of your ancestor Draco the Great!"

The young prince threw himself with emotion on his restorer and attempted to embrace him, but he was prevented from reaching

him by the girth of the two ladies, so tightly packed were they all
in that historic carriage.

"Worthy father," said he, "I would like all Penguinia to witness
this embrace."

"It would be a cheering spectacle," said Agaric.

In the mean time the motor-car rushed like a tornado through
hamlets and villages, crushing hens, geese, turkeys, ducks, guinea-
fowls, cats, dogs, pigs, children, labourers, and women beneath its
insatiable tyres. And the pious Agaric turned over his great designs in his mind. His voice, coming from behind one of the ladies,
expressed this thought:

"We must have money, a great deal of money."

"That is your business," answered the prince.

But already the park gates were opening to the formidable
motor-car.

The dinner was sumptuous. They toasted the Dragon's crest.
Everybody knows that a closed goblet is a sign of sovereignty; so
Prince Crucho and Princess Gudrune, his wife, drank out of goblets
that were covered over like ciboriums. The prince had his filled
several times with the wines of Penguinia, both white and red.

Crucho had received a truly princely education, and he excelled
in motoring, but was not ignorant of history either. He was said to
be well versed in the antiquities and famous deeds of his family;
and, indeed, he gave a notable proof of his knowledge in this respect. As they were speaking of the various remarkable peculiarities that had been noticed in famous women:

"It is perfectly true," said he, "that Queen Crucha, whose name
I bear, had the mark of a little monkey's head upon her body."

During the evening Agaric had a decisive interview with three of
the prince's oldest councillors. It was decided to ask for funds from
Crucho's father-in-law, as he was anxious to have a king for son-
in-law, from several Jewish ladies, who were impatient to become
ennobled, and, finally, from the Prince Regent of the Porpoises, who
had promised his aid to the Draconides, thinking that by Crucho's
restoration he would weaken the Penguins, the hereditary enemies
of his people. The three old councillors divided among themselves
the three chief offices of the Court, those of Chamberlain, Senes-
chal, and High Steward, and authorised the monk to distribute the
other places to the prince's best advantage.

"Devotion has to be rewarded," said the three old councillors.

"And treachery also," said Agaric.

"It is but too true," replied one of them, the Marquis of Seven-
wounds, who had experience of revolutions.

There was dancing, and after the ball Princess Gudrune tore up
her green robe to make cockades. With her own hands she sewed a
piece of it on the monk's breast, upon which he shed tears of sensibility and gratitude.

M. de Plume, the prince's equerry, set out the same evening to look for a green horse.

III

THE CABAL

AFTER his return to the capital of Penguinia, the Reverend Father Agaric disclosed his projects to Prince Adélestan des Boscénos, of whose Draconian sentiments he was well aware.

The Prince belonged to the highest nobility. The Torticol des Boscénos went back to Brian the Good, and under the Draconides had held the highest offices in the kingdom. In 1179, Philip Torticol, High Admiral of Penguinia, a brave, faithful, and generous, but vindictive man, delivered over the port of La Crique and the Penguin fleet to the enemies of the kingdom, because he suspected that Queen Crucha, whose lover he was, had been unfaithful to him and loved a stable-boy. It was that great queen who gave to the Boscénos the silver warming-pan which they bear in their arms. As for their motto, it only goes back to the sixteenth century. The story of its origin is as follows: One gala night, as he mingled with the crowd of courtiers who were watching the fire-works in the king's garden, Duke John des Boscénos approached the Duchess of Skull and put his hand under the petticoat of that lady, who made no complaint at the gesture. The king, happening to pass, surprised them and contented himself with saying, "And thus I find you." These four words became the motto of the Boscénos.

Prince Adélestan had not degenerated from his ancestors. He preserved an unalterable fidelity for the race of the Draconides and desired nothing so much as the restoration of Prince Crucho, an event which was in his eyes to be the fore-runner of the restoration of his own fortune. He therefore readily entered into the Reverend Father Agaric's plans. He joined himself at once to the monk's projects, and hastened to put him into communication with the most loyal Royalists of his acquaintance, Count Cléna, M. de la Trumelle, Viscount Olive, and M. Bigourd. They met together one night in the Duke of Ampoule's country house, six miles eastward of Alca, to consider ways and means.

M. de la Trumelle was in favor of legal action.

"We ought to keep within the law," said he in substance. "We are for order. It is by an untiring propaganda that we shall best pursue the realisation of our hopes. We must change the feeling of the country. Our cause will conquer because it is just."

The Prince des Boscénos expressed a contrary opinion. He thought that, in order to triumph, just causes need force quite as much and even more than unjust causes require it.

"In the present situation," said he tranquilly, "three methods of action present themselves; to hire the butcher boys, to corrupt the ministers, and to kidnap President Formose."

"It would be a mistake to kidnap Formose," objected M. de la Trumelle. "The President is on our side."

The attitude and sentiments of the President of the Republic are explained by the fact that one Dracophil proposed to seize Formose while another Dracophil regarded him as a friend. Formose showed himself favourable to the Royalists, whose habits he admired and imitated. If he smiled at the mention of the Dragon's crest it was at the thought of putting it on his own head. He was envious of sovereign power, not because he felt himself capable of exercising it, but because he loved to appear so. According to the expression of a Penguin chronicler, "he was a goose."

Prince des Boscénos maintained his proposal to march against Formose's palace and the House of Parliament.

Count Cléna was even still more energetic.

"Let us begin," said he, "by slaughtering, disembowelling, and braining the Republicans and all partisans of the government. Afterwards we shall see what more need be done."

M. de la Trumelle was a moderate, and moderates are always moderately opposed to violence. He recognised that Count Cléna's policy was inspired by a noble feeling and that it was high-minded, but he timidly objected that perhaps it was not conformable to principle, and that it presented certain dangers. At last he consented to discuss it.

"I propose," added he, "to draw up an appeal to the people. Let us show who we are. For my own part I can assure you that I shall not hide my flag in my pocket."

M. Bigourd began to speak.

"Gentlemen, the Penguins are dissatisfied with the new order because it exists, and it is natural for men to complain of their condition. But at the same time the Penguins are afraid to change their government because new things alarm them. They have not known the Dragon's crest and, although they sometimes say that they regret it, we must not believe them. It is easy to see that they speak in this way either without thought or because they are in an ill-temper. Let us not have any illusions about their feelings towards ourselves. They do not like us. They hate the aristocracy both from a base envy and from a generous love of equality. And these two united feelings are very strong in a people. Public opinion is not against us, because it knows nothing about us. But when it knows what we want it will not follow us. If we let it be seen that we wish to destroy democratic government and restore the Dragon's crest, who will be our partisans? Only the butcher-boys and the little shop-keepers of Alca. And could we even count on them to the end? They are dissatisfied, but at the bottom of their hearts they are Republicans. They are more anxious to sell their cursed wares than to see Crucho again. If we act openly we shall only cause alarm.

"To make people sympathise with us and follow us we must make them believe that we want, not to overthrow the Republic, but, on the contrary, to restore it, to cleanse, to purify, to embellish, to adorn, to beautify, and to ornament it, to render it, in a word, glorious and attractive. Therefore, we ought not to act openly ourselves. It is known that we are not favourable to the present order. We must have recourse to a friend of the Republic, and, if we are to do what is best, to a defender of this government. We have plenty to choose from. It would be well to prefer the most popular and, if I dare say so, the most republican of them. We shall win him over to us by flattery, by presents, and above all by prom-ises. Promises cost less than presents, and are worth more. No one gives as much as he who gives hopes. It is not necessary for the man we choose to be of brilliant intellect. I would even prefer him to be of no great ability. Stupid people show an inimitable grace in roguery. Be guided by me, gentlemen, and overthrow the Republic by the agency of a Republican. Let us be prudent. But prudence does not exclude energy. If you need me you will find me at your disposal."

This speech made a great impression upon those who heard it. The mind of the pious Agaric was particularly impressed. But each of them was anxious to appoint himself to a position of honour and profit. A secret government was organised of which all those pres-ent were elected active members. The Duke of Ampoule, who was the great financier of the party, was chosen treasurer and charged with organising funds for the propaganda.

The meeting was on the point of coming to an end when a rough voice was heard singing an old air:

> Boscénos est un gros cochon;
> On en va faire des andouilles
> Des saucisses et du jambon
> Pour le réveillon des pauv' bougres.

It had, for two hundred years, been a well-known song in the slums of Alca. Prince Boscénos did not like to hear it. He went down into the street, and, perceiving that the singer was a workman who was placing some slates on the roof of a church, he politely asked him to sing something else.

"I will sing what I like," answered the man.

"My friend, to please me. . . ."

"I don't want to please you."

Prince Boscénos was as a rule good-tempered, but he was easily angered and a man of great strength.

"Fellow, come down or I will go up to you," cried he, in a terrible voice.

As the workman, astride on his coping, showed no sign of budging, the prince climbed quickly up the staircase of the tower and attacked the singer. He gave him a blow that broke his jaw-bone and sent him rolling into a water-spout. At that moment seven or eight carpenters, who were working on the rafters, heard their companion's cry and looked through the window. Seeing the prince on the coping they climbed along a ladder that was leaning on the slates and reached him just as he was slipping into the tower. They sent him, head foremost, down the one hundred and thirty-seven steps of the spiral staircase.

IV

VISCOUNTESS OLIVE

HE Penguins had the finest army in the world. So had the Porpoises. And it was the same with the other nations of Europe. The smallest amount of thought will prevent any surprise at this. For all armies are the finest in the world. The second finest army, if one could exist, would be in a notoriously inferior position; it would be certain to be beaten. It ought to be disbanded at once. Therefore, all armies are the finest in the world. In France the illustrious Colonel Marchand understood this when, before the passage of the Yalou, being questioned by some journalists about the Russo-Japanese war, he did not hesitate to describe the Russian army as the finest in the world, and also the Japanese. And it should be noticed that even after suffering the most terrible reverses an army does not fall from its position of being the finest in the world. For if nations ascribe their victories to the ability of their generals and the courage of their soldiers, they always attribute their defeats to an inexplicable fatality. On the other hand, navies are classed according to the number of their ships. There is a first, a second, a third, and so on. So that there exists no doubt as to the result of naval wars.

The Penguins had the finest army and the second navy in the world. This navy was commanded by the famous Chatillon, who bore the title of Emiralbahr, and by abbreviation Emiral. It is the same word which, unfortunately in a corrupt form, is used to-day among several European nations to designate the highest grade in the naval service. But as there was but one Emiral among the Penguins, a singular prestige, if I dare say so, was attached to that rank.

The Emiral did not belong to the nobility. A child of the people, he was loved by the people. They were flattered to see a man who sprang from their own ranks holding a position of honour. Chatillon was good-looking and fortune favoured him. He was not over-addicted to thought. No event ever disturbed his serene outlook.

The Reverend Father Agaric, surrendering to M. Bigourd's reasons and recognising that the existing government could only be destroyed by one of its defenders, cast his eyes upon Emiral Chatillon. He asked a large sum of money from his friend, the Reverend Father Cornemuse, which the latter handed him with a sigh. And with this sum he hired six hundred butcher boys of Alca to run behind Chatillon's horse and shout, "Hurrah for the Emiral!" Henceforth Chatillon could not take a single step without being cheered.

Viscountess Olive asked him for a private interview. He received her at the Admiralty* in a room decorated with anchors, shells, and grenades.

She was discreetly dressed in greyish blue. A hat trimmed with roses covered her pretty, fair hair. Behind her veil her eyes shone like sapphires. Although she came of Jewish origin there was no more fashionable woman in the whole nobility. She was tall and well shaped; her form was that of the year, her figure that of the season.

"Emiral," said she, in a delightful voice, "I cannot conceal my emotion from you. . . . It is very natural . . . before a hero."

"You are too kind. But tell me, Viscountess, what brings me the honour of your visit."

"For a long time I have been anxious to see you, to speak to you. . . . So I very willingly undertook to convey a message to you."

"Please take a seat."

"How still it is here."

"Yes, it is quiet enough."

"You can hear the birds singing."

"Sit down, then, dear lady."

And he drew up an arm-chair for her.

She took a seat with her back to the light.

"Emiral, I came to bring you a very important message, a message . . ."

"Explain."

"Emiral, have you ever seen Prince Crucho?"

"Never."

She sighed.

"It is a great pity. He would be so delighted to see you! He esteems and appreciates you. He has your portrait on his desk besides his mother's. What a pity it is he is not better known! He is a

---

*Or better, *Emiralty*.

charming prince and so grateful for what is done for him! He will
be a great king. For he will be king without doubt. He will come
back and sooner than people think. . . . What I have to tell you,
the message with which I am entrusted, refers precisely to . . ."

The Emiral stood up.

"Not a word more, dear lady. I have the esteem, the confidence
of the Republic. I will not betray it. And why should I betray it? I
am loaded with honours and dignities."

"Allow me to tell you, my dear Emiral, that your honours and
dignities are far from equalling what you deserve. If your services
were properly rewarded, you would be Emiralissimo and Generalissimo, Commander-in-chief of the troops both on land and sea. The
Republic is very ungrateful to you."

"All governments are more or less ungrateful."

"Yes, but the Republicans are jealous of you. That class of person is always afraid of his superiors. They cannot endure the Services. Everything that has to do with the navy and the army is
odious to them. They are afraid of you."

"That is possible."

"They are wretches; they are ruining the country. Don't you wish
to save Penguinia?"

"In what way?"

"By sweeping away all the rascals of the Republic, all the Republicans."

"What a proposal to make to me, dear lady!"

"It is what will certainly be done, if not by you, then by some
one else. The Generalissimo, to mention him alone, is ready to throw
all the ministers, deputies, and senators into the sea, and to recall
Prince Crucho."

"Oh, the rascal, the scoundrel," exclaimed the Emiral.

"Do to him what he would do to you. The prince will know how to
recognise your services. He will give you the Constable's sword and
a magnificent grant. I am commissioned, in the meantime, to hand
you a pledge of his royal friendship."

As she said these words she drew a green cockade from her
bosom.

"What is that?" asked the Emiral.

"It is his colours which Crucho sends you."

"Be good enough to take them back."

"So that they may be offered to the Generalissimo who will accept
them! . . . No, Emiral, let me place them on your glorious breast."

Chatillon gently repelled the lady. But for some minutes he
thought her extremely pretty, and he felt this impression still more
when two bare arms and the rosy palms of two delicate hands
touched him lightly. He yielded almost immediately. Olive was slow
in fastening the ribbon. Then when it was done she made a low
courtesy and saluted Chatillon with the title of Constable.

"I have been ambitious like my comrades," answered the sailor, "I don't hide it, and perhaps I am so still; but upon my word of honour, when I look at you, the only desire I feel is for a cottage and a heart."

She turned upon him the charming sapphire glances that flashed from under her eyelids.

"That is to be had also . . . what are you doing, Emiral?"

"I am looking for the heart."

When she left the Admiralty, the Viscountess went immediately to the Reverend Father Agaric to give an account of her visit.

"You must go to him again, dear lady," said that austere monk.

V

THE PRINCE DES BOSCÉNOS

ORNING and evening the newspapers that had been bought by the Dracophils proclaimed Chatillon's praises and hurled shame and opprobrium upon the Ministers of the Republic. Chatillon's portrait was sold through the streets of Alca. Those young descendants of Remus who carry plaster figures on their heads, offered busts of Chatillon for sale upon the bridges.

Every evening Chatillon rode upon his white horse round the Queen's Meadow, a place frequented by the people of fashion. The Dracophils posted along the Emiral's route a crowd of needy Penguins who kept shouting: "It is Chatillon we want." The middle classes of Alca conceived a profound admiration for the Emiral. Shopwomen murmured: "He is good-looking." Women of fashion slackened the speed of their motor-cars and kissed hands to him as they passed, amidst the hurrahs of an enthusiastic populace.

One day, as he went into a tobacco shop, two Penguins who were putting letters in the box recognized Chatillon and cried at the top of their voices: "Hurrah for the Emiral! Down with the Republicans." All those who were passing stopped in front of the shop. Chatillon lighted his cigar before the eyes of a dense crowd of frenzied citizens who waved their hats and cheered. The crowd kept increasing, and the whole town, singing and marching behind its hero, went back with him to the Admiralty.

The Emiral had an old comrade in arms, Under-Emiral Vulcanmould, who had served with great distinction, a man as true as gold and as loyal as his sword. Vulcanmould plumed himself on his thoroughgoing independence and he went among the partisans of Crucho and the Minister of the Republic telling both parties what he thought of them. M. Bigourd maliciously declared that he told each party what the other party thought of it. In truth he had on several occasions been guilty of regrettable indiscretions, which were overlooked as being the freedoms of a soldier who knew nothing of intrigue. Every morning he went to see Chatillon, whom he treated with the cordial roughness of a brother in arms.

"Well, old buffer, so you are popular," said he to him. "Your phiz is sold on the heads of pipes and on liqueur bottles and every drunkard in Alca spits out your name as he rolls in the gutter. . . . Chatillon, the hero of the Penguins! Chatillon, defender of the Penguin glory! . . . Who would have said it? Who would have thought it?"

And he laughed with his harsh laugh. Then changing his tone:

"But, joking aside, are you not a bit surprised at what is happening to you?"

"No, indeed," answered Chatillon.

And out went the honest Vulcanmould, banging the door behind him.

In the meantime Chatillon had taken a little flat at number 18 Johannes-Talpa Street, so that he might receive Viscountess Olive. They met there every day. He was desperately in love with her. During his martial and neptunian life he had loved crowds of women, red, black, yellow, and white, and some of them had been very beautiful. But before he met the Viscountess he did not know what a woman really was. When the Viscountess Olive called him her darling, her dear darling, he felt in heaven and it seemed to him that the stars shone in her hair.

She would come a little late, and, as she put her bag on the table, she would ask pensively:

"Let me sit on your knee."

And then she would talk of subjects suggested by the pious Agaric, interrupting the conversation with sighs and kisses. She would ask him to dismiss such and such an officer, to give a command to another, to send the squadron here or there. And at the right moment she would exclaim:

"How young you are, my dear!"

And he did whatever she wished, for he was simple, he was anxious to wear the Constable's sword, and to receive a large grant; he did not dislike playing a double part, he had a vague idea of saving Penguinia, and he was in love.

This delightful woman induced him to remove the troops that were at La Cirque, the port where Crucho was to land. By this means it was made certain that there would be no obstacle to prevent the prince from entering Penguinia.

The pious Agaric organised public meetings so as to keep up the agitation. The Dracophils held one or two every day in some of the thirty-six districts of Alca, and preferably in the poorer quarters.

They desired to win over the poor, for they are the most numerous. On the fourth of May a particularly fine meeting was held in an old cattle-market, situated in the centre of a populous suburb filled with housewives sitting on the doorsteps and children playing in the gutters. There were present about two thousand people, in the opinion of the Republicans, and six thousand according to the reckoning of the Dracophils. In the audience was to be seen the flower of Penguin society, including Prince and Princess des Boscénos, Count Cléna, M. de La Trumelle, M. Bigourd, and several rich Jewish ladies.

The Generalissimo of the national army had come in uniform. He was cheered.

The committee had been carefully formed. A man of the people, a workman, but a man of sound principles, M. Rauchin, the secretary of the yellow syndicate, was asked to preside, supported by Count Cléna and M. Michaud, a butcher.

The government which Penguinia had freely given itself was called by such names as cesspool and drain in several eloquent speeches. But President Formose was spared and no mention was made of Crucho or the priests.

The meeting was not unanimous. A defender of the modern State and of the Republic, a manual labourer, stood up.

"Gentlemen," said M. Rauchin, the chairman, "we have told you that this meeting would not be unanimous. We are not like our opponents, we are honest men. I allow our opponent to speak. Heaven knows what you are going to hear. Gentlemen, I beg of you to restrain as long as you can the expression of your contempt, your disgust, and your indignation."

"Gentlemen," said the opponent. . . .

Immediately he was knocked down, trampled beneath the feet of the indignant crowd, and his unrecognisable remains thrown out of the hall.

The tumult was still resounding when Count Cléna ascended the tribune. Cheers took the place of groans and when silence was restored the orator uttered these words:

"Comrades, we are going to see whether you have blood in your veins. What we have got to do is to slaughter, disembowel, and brain all the Republicans."

This speech let loose such a thunder of applause that the old shed rocked with it, and a cloud of acrid and thick dust fell from its filthy walls and worm-eaten beams and enveloped the audience.

A resolution was carried vilifying the government and acclaiming Chatillon. And the audience departed singing the hymn of the liberator: "It is Chatillon we want."

The only way out of the old market was through a muddy alley shut in by omnibus stables and coal sheds. There was no moon and a cold drizzle was coming down. The police, who were assembled in great numbers, blocked the alley and compelled the Dracophils to disperse in little groups. These were the instructions they had received from their chief, who was anxious to check the enthusiasm of the excited crowd.

The Dracophils who were detained in the alley kept marking time and singing, "It is Chatillon we want." Soon, becoming impatient of the delay, the cause of which they did not know, they began to push those in front of them. This movement, propagated along the alley, threw those in front against the broad chests of the police. The latter had no hatred for the Dracophils. In the bottom of their hearts they liked Chatillon. But it is natural to resist aggression and strong men are inclined to make use of their strength. For these reasons the police kicked the Dracophils with their hob-nailed boots. As a result there were sudden rushes backwards and forwards. Threats and cries mingled with the songs.

"Murder! Murder! . . . It is Chatillon we want! Murder! Murder!"

And in the gloomy alley the more prudent kept saying, "Don't push." Among these latter, in the darkness, his lofty figure rising above the moving crowd, his broad shoulders and robust body noticeable among the trampled limbs and crushed sides of the rest, stood the Prince des Boscénos, calm, immovable and placid. Serenely and indulgently he waited. In the meantime, as the exit was opened at regular intervals between the ranks of the police, the pressure of elbows against the chests of those around the prince diminished and people began to breathe again.

"You see we shall soon be able to go out," said that kindly giant, with a pleasant smile. "Time and patience . . ."

He took a cigar from his case, raised it to his lips and struck a match. Suddenly, in the light of the match, he saw Princess Anne, his wife, clasped in Count Cléna's arms. At this sight he rushed towards them, striking both them and those around with his cane. He was disarmed, though not without difficulty, but he could not be separated from his opponent. And whilst the fainting princess was lifted from arm to arm to her carriage over the excited and curious crowd, the two men still fought furiously. Prince des Boscénos lost his hat, his eye-glass, his cigar, his necktie, and his portfolio full of private letters and political correspondence; he even lost the miraculous medals that he had received from the good Father Cornemuse. But he gave his opponent so terrible a kick in the stomach that the unfortunate Count was knocked through an iron grating and went, head foremost, through a glass door and into a coal shed.

Attracted by the struggle and the cries of those around, the police rushed towards the prince, who furiously resisted them. He stretched three of them gasping at his feet and put seven others to flight, with, respectively, a broken jaw, a split lip, a nose pouring blood, a fractured skull, a torn ear, a dislocated collar-bone, and broken ribs. He fell, however, and was dragged bleeding and disfigured, with his clothes in rags, to the nearest police-station, where, jumping about and bellowing, he spent the night.

Until daybreak groups of demonstrators went about the town singing, "It is Chatillon we want," and breaking the windows of the houses in which the Ministers of the Republic lived.

VI

THE EMIRAL'S FALL

THAT night marked the culmination of the Dracophil movement. The Royalists had no longer any doubt of its triumph. Their chiefs sent congratulations to Prince Crucho by wireless telegraphy. Their ladies embroidered scarves and slippers for him. M. de Plume had found the green horse.

The pious Agaric shared the common hope. But he still worked to win partisans for the Pretender. They ought, he said, to lay their foundations upon the bed-rock.

With this design he had an interview with three Trade Union workmen.

In these times the artisans no longer lived, as in the days of the Draconides, under the government of corporations. They were free, but they had no assured pay. After having remained isolated from each other for a long time, without help and without support, they had formed themselves into unions. The coffers of the unions were empty, as it was not the habit of the unionists to pay their subscriptions. There were unions numbering thirty thousand members, others with a thousand, five hundred, two hundred, and so forth. Several numbered two or three members only, or even a few less. But as the lists of adherents were not published, it was not easy to distinguish the great unions from the small ones.

After some dark and indirect steps the pious Agaric was put into communication in a room in the Moulin de la Galette, with comrades Dagobert, Tronc, and Balafille, the secretaries of three unions of which the first numbered fourteen members, the second twenty-four, and the third only one. Agaric showed extreme cleverness at this interview.

"Gentlemen," said he, "you and I have not, in most respects, the same political and social views, but there are points in which we may come to an understanding. We have a common enemy. The government exploits you and despises us. Help us to overthrow it;

we will supply you with the means so far as we are able, and you
can in addition count on our gratitude."

"Fork out the tin," said Dagobert.

The Reverend Father placed on the table a bag which the distiller
of Conils had given him with tears in his eyes.

"Done!" said the three companions.

Thus was the solemn compact sealed.

As soon as the monk had departed, carrying with him the joy of
having won over the masses to his cause, Dagobert, Tronc, and
Balafille whistled to their wives, Amelia, Queenie, and Matilda, who
were waiting in the street for the signal, and all six holding each
other's hands, danced around the bag, singing:

> J'ai du bon pognon;
> Tu n'l'auras pas Chatillon!
> Hou! Hou! la calotte!

And they ordered a salad-bowl of warm wine.

In the evening all six went through the street from stall to stall
singing their new song. The song became popular, for the detectives
reported that every day showed an increase of the number of work-
people who sang through the slums:

> J'ai du bon pognon;
> Tu n'l'auras pas Chatillon!
> Hou! Hou! la calotte!

The Dracophil agitation made no progress in the provinces. The
pious Agaric sought to find the cause of this, but was unable to discover it until old Cornemuse revealed it to him.

"I have proofs," sighed the monk of Conils, "that the Duke of
Ampoule, the treasurer of the Dracophils, has bought property in
Porpoisia with the funds that he received for the propaganda."

The party wanted money. Prince des Boscénos had lost his portfolio in a brawl and he was reduced to painful expedients which
were repugnant to his impetuous character. The Viscountess Olive
was expensive. Cornemuse advised that the monthly allowance of
that lady should be diminished.

"She is very useful to us," objected the pious Agaric.

"Undoubtedly," answered Cornemuse, "but she does us an injury
by ruining us."

A schism divided the Dracophils. Misunderstandings reigned in
their councils. Some wished that in accordance with the policy of
M. Bigourd and the pious Agaric, they should carry on the design
of reforming the Republic. Others, wearied by their long constraint,
had resolved to proclaim the Dragon's crest and swore to conquer
beneath that sign.

The latter urged the advantage of a clear situation and the impossibility of making a pretence much longer, and in truth, the public began to see whither the agitation was tending and that the

Emiral's partisans wanted to destroy the very foundations of the Republic.

A report was spread that the prince was to land at La Cirque and make his entry into Alca on a green horse.

These rumours excited the fanatical monks, delighted the poor nobles, satisfied the rich Jewish ladies, and put hope in the hearts of the small traders. But very few of them were inclined to purchase these benefits at the price of a social catastrophe and the overthrow of the public credit; and there were fewer still who would have risked their money, their peace, their liberty, or a single hour from their pleasures in the business. On the other hand, the workmen held themselves ready, as ever, to give a day's work to the Republic, and a strong resistance was being formed in the suburbs.

"The people are with us," the pious Agaric used to say.

However, men, women, and children, when leaving their factories, used to shout with one voice:

A bas Chatillon!
Hou! Hou! la calotte!

As for the government, it showed the weakness, indecision, flabbiness, and heedlessness common to all governments, and from which none has ever departed without falling into arbitrariness and violence. In three words it knew nothing, wanted nothing, and could do nothing. Formose, shut in his presidential palace, remained blind, dumb, deaf, huge, invisible, wrapped up in his pride as in an eider-down.

Count Olive advised the Dracophils to make a last appeal for funds and to attempt a great stroke while Alca was still in a ferment.

An executive committee, which he himself had chosen, decided to kidnap the members of the Chamber of Deputies, and considered ways and means.

The affair was fixed for the twenty-eighth of July. On that day the sun rose radiantly over the city. In front of the legislative palace women passed to market with their baskets; hawkers cried their peaches, pears, and grapes; cab horses with their noses in their bags munched their hay. Nobody expected anything, not because the secret had been kept but because it met with nothing but unbelievers. Nobody believed in a revolution, and from this fact we may conclude that nobody desired one. About two o'clock the deputies began to pass, few and unnoticed, through the side-door of the palace. At three o'clock a few groups of badly dressed men had formed. At half past three black masses coming from the adjacent streets spread over Revolution Square. This vast expanse was soon covered by an ocean of soft hats, and the crowd of demonstrators, continually increased by sight-seers, having crossed the bridge, struck its dark wave against the walls of the legislative enclosure.

Cries, murmurs, and songs went up to the impassive sky. "It is Chatillon we want!" "Down with the Deputies!" "Down with the Republicans!" "Death to the Republicans!" The devoted band of Dracophils, led by Prince des Boscénos, struck up the august canticle:

> Vive Crucho,
> Vaillant et sage,
> Plein de courage
> Dès le berceau!

Behind the wall silence alone replied.

This silence and the absence of guards encouraged and at the same time frightened the crowd. Suddenly a formidable voice cried out:

"Attack!"

And Prince des Boscénos was seen raising his gigantic form to the top of the wall, which was covered with barbs and iron spikes. Behind him rushed his companions, and the people followed. Some hammered against the wall to make holes in it; others endeavoured to tear down the spikes and to pull out the barbs. These defences had given way in places and some of the invaders had stripped the wall and were sitting astride on the top. Prince des Boscénos was waving an immense green flag. Suddenly the crowd wavered and from it came a long cry of terror. The police and the Republican carabineers issuing out of all the entrances of the palace formed themselves into a column beneath the wall and in a moment it was cleared of its besiegers. After a long moment of suspense the noise of arms was heard, and the police charged the crowd with fixed bayonets. An instant afterwards and on the deserted square strewn with hats and walking-sticks there reigned a sinister silence. Twice again the Dracophils attempted to form, twice they were repulsed. The rising was conquered. But Prince des Boscénos, standing on the wall of the hostile palace, his flag in his hand, still repelled the attack of a whole brigade. He knocked down all who approached him. At last he, too, was thrown down, and fell on an iron spike, to which he remained hooked, still clasping the standard of the Draconides.

On the following day the Ministers of the Republic and the Members of Parliament determined to take energetic measures. In vain this time, did President Formose attempt to evade his responsibilities. The government discussed the question of depriving Chatillon of his rank and dignities and of indicting him before the High Court as a conspirator, an enemy of the public good, a traitor, etc.

At this news the Emiral's old companions in arms, who the very evening before had beset him with their adulations, made no effort to conceal their joy. But Chatillon remained popular with the middle classes of Alca and one still heard the hymn of the liberator sounding in the streets, "It is Chatillon we want."

The Ministers were embarrassed. They intended to indict Chatillon before the High Court. But they knew nothing; they remained in that total ignorance reserved for those who govern men. They were incapable of advancing any grave charges against Chatillon. They could supply the prosecution with nothing but the ridiculous lies of their spies. Chatillon's share in the plot and his relations with Prince Crucho remained the secret of the thirty thousand Dracophils. The Ministers and the Deputies had suspicions and even certainties, but they had no proofs. The Public Prosecutor said to the Minister of Justice: "Very little is needed for a political prosecution! but I have nothing at all and that is not enough." The affair made no progress. The enemies of the Republic were triumphant.

On the eighteenth of September the news ran in Alca that Chatillon had taken flight. Everywhere there was surprise and astonishment. People doubted, for they could not understand.

This is what had happened: One day as the brave Under-Emiral Vulcanmould happened, as if by chance, to go into the office of M. Barbotan, the Minister of Foreign Affairs, he remarked with his usual frankness:

"M. Barbotan, your colleagues do not seem to me to be up to much; it is evident that they have never commanded a ship. That fool Chatillon gives them a deuced bad fit of the shivers."

The Minister, in sign of denial, waved his paper-knife in the air above his desk.

"Don't deny it," answered Vulcanmould. "You don't know how to get rid of Chatillon. You do not dare to indict him before the High Court because you are not sure of being able to bring forward a strong enough charge. Bigourd will defend him, and Bigourd is a clever advocate. . . . You are right, M. Barbotan, you are right. It would be a dangerous trial."

"Ah! my friend," said the Minister, in a careless tone, "if you knew how satisfied we are. . . . I receive the most reassuring news from my prefects. The good sense of the Penguins will do justice to the intrigues of this mutinous soldier. Can you suppose for a moment that a great people, an intelligent, laborious people, devoted to liberal institutions which . . ."

Vulcanmould interrupted with a great sigh:

"Ah! If I had time to do it I would relieve you of your difficulty. I would juggle away my Chatillon like a nutmeg out of a thimble. I would filip him off to Porpoisia."

The Minister paid close attention.

"It would not take long," continued the sailor. "I would rid you in a trice of the creature. . . . But just now I have other fish to fry. . . . I am in a bad hole. I must find a pretty big sum. But, deuce take it, honour before everything."

The Minister and the Under-Emiral looked at each other for a moment in silence. Then Barbotan said with authority:

"Under-Emiral Vulcanmould, get rid of this seditious soldier. You will render a great service to Penguinia, and the Minister of Home Affairs will see that your gambling debts are paid."

The same evening Vulcanmould called on Chatillon and looked at him for some time with an expression of grief and mystery.

"Why do you look like that?" answered the Emiral in an uneasy tone.

Vulcanmould said to him sadly:

"Old brother in arms, all is discovered. For the past half-hour the government knows everything."

At these words Chatillon sank down overwhelmed.

Vulcanmould continued:

"You may be arrested any moment. I advise you to make off."

And drawing out his watch:

"Not a minute to lose."

"Have I time to call on the Viscountess Olive?"

"It would be mad," said Vulcanmould, handing him a passport and a pair of blue spectacles, and telling him to have courage.

"I will," said Chatillon.

"Good-bye! old chum."

"Good-bye and thanks! You have saved my life."

"That is the least I could do."

A quarter of an hour later the brave Emiral had left the city of Alca.

He embarked at night on an old cutter at La Cirque and set sail for Porpoisia. But eight miles from the coast he was captured by a despatch-boat which was sailing without lights and which was under the flag of the Queen of the Black Islands. That Queen had for a long time nourished a fatal passion for Chatillon.

VII

CONCLUSION

UNC est bibendum. Delivered from its fears and pleased at having escaped from so great a danger, the government resolved to celebrate the anniversary of the Penguin regeneration and the establishment of the Republic by holding a general holiday.

President Formose, the Ministers, and the members of the Chamber and of the Senate were present at the ceremony.

The Generalissimo of the Penguin army was present in uniform. He was cheered.

Preceded by the black flag of misery and the red flag of revolt, deputations of workmen walked in the procession, their aspect one of grim protection.

President, Ministers, Deputies, officials, heads of the magistracy and of the army, each, in their own names and in the name of the sovereign people, renewed the ancient oath to live in freedom or to die. It was an alternative upon which they were resolutely determined. But they preferred to live in freedom. There were games, speeches, and songs.

After the departure of the representatives of the State the crowd of citizens separated slowly and peaceably, shouting out, "Hurrah for the Republic!" "Hurrah for liberty!" "Down with the shaven pates!"

The newspapers mentioned only one regrettable incident that happened on that wonderful day. Prince des Boscénos was quietly smoking a cigar in the Queen's Meadow when the State procession passed by. The prince approached the Minister's carriage and said in a loud voice: "Death to the Republicans!" He was immediately apprehended by the police, to whom he offered a most desperate resistance. He knocked them down in crowds, but he was conquered by numbers, and, bruised, scratched, swollen, and unrecognisable even to the eyes of his wife, he was dragged through the joyous streets into an obscure prison.

The magistrates carried on the case against Chatillon in a peculiar style. Letters were found at the Admiralty which revealed the complicity of the Reverend Father Agaric in the plot. Immediately public opinion was inflamed against the monks, and Parliament voted, one after the other, a dozen laws which restrained, diminished, limited, prescribed, suppressed, determined, and curtailed, their rights, immunities, exemptions, privileges, and benefits, and created many invalidating disqualifications against them.

The Reverend Father Agaric steadfastly endured the rigour of the laws which struck himself personally, as well as the terrible fall of the Emiral of which he was the chief cause. Far from yielding to evil fortune, he regarded it as but a bird of passage. He was planning new political designs more audacious than the first.

When his projects were sufficiently ripe he went one day to the Wood of Conils. A thrush sang in a tree and a little hedge-hog crossed the stony path in front of him with awkward steps. Agaric walked with great strides, muttering fragments of sentences to himself.

When he reached the door of the laboratory in which, for so many years, the pious manufacturer had distilled the golden liqueur of St. Orberosia, he found the place deserted and the door shut. Having walked around the building he saw in the backyard the venerable Cornemuse, who, with his habit pinned up, was climbing a ladder that leant against the wall.

"Is that you, my dear friend?" said he to him. "What are you doing there?"

"You can see for yourself," answered the monk of Conils in a feeble voice, turning a sorrowful look upon Agaric. "I am going into my house."

The red pupils of his eyes no longer imitated the triumph and brilliance of the ruby, they flashed mournful and troubled glances. His countenance had lost its happy fulness. His shining head was no longer pleasant to the sight; perspiration and inflamed blotches had altered its inestimable perfection.

"I don't understand," said Agaric.

"It is easy enough to understand. You see the consequences of your plot. Although a multitude of laws are directed against me I have managed to elude the greater number of them. Some, however, have struck me. These vindictive men have closed my laboratories and my shops, and confiscated my bottles, my stills, and my retorts. They have put seals on my doors and now I am compelled to go in through the window. I am barely able to extract in secret from time to time the juice of a few plants and that with an apparatus which the humblest labourer would despise."

"You suffer from the persecution," said Agaric. "It strikes us all."

The monk of Conils passed his hand over his afflicted brow:

"I told you so, Brother Agaric; I told you that your enterprise would turn against ourselves."

"Our defeat is only momentary," replied Agaric eagerly. "It is due to purely accidental causes; it results from mere contingencies. Chatillon was a fool; he has drowned himself in his own ineptitude. Listen to me, Brother Cornemuse. We have not a moment to lose. We must free the Penguin people, we must deliver them from their tyrants, save them from themselves, restore the Dragon's crest, re-establish the ancient State, the good State, for the honour of religion and the exaltation of the Catholic faith. Chatillon was a bad instrument; he broke in our hands. Let us take a better instrument to replace him. I have the man who will destroy this impious democracy. He is a civil official; his name is Gomoru. The Penguins worship him. He has already betrayed his party for a plate of rice. There's the man we want!"

At the beginning of this speech the monk of Conils had climbed into his window and pulled up the ladder.

"I foresee," answered he, with his nose through the sash, "that you will not stop until you have us all expelled from this pleasant, agreeable, and sweet land of Penguinia. Good night; God keep you!"

Agaric, standing before the wall, entreated his dearest brother to listen to him for a moment:

"Understand your own interest better, Cornemuse! Penguinia is ours. What do we need to conquer it? Just one effort more . . . one more little sacrifice of money and . . ."

But without listening further, the monk of Conils drew in his head and closed his window.

BOOK VI: MODERN TIMES

THE AFFAIR OF THE EIGHTY THOUSAND TRUSSES OF HAY

> Ζεῦ πάτερ ἀλλὰ σὺ ῥῦσαι ὑπ' ἠέρος υἶας Αχαιῶν,
> ποίησον δ'αἴθρην, δὸς δ'ὀφθαλμοῖ σιν ἰδέσθαι.
> ἐν δὲ φάιει ὄλεσσον ἐπει νύ τοι εὔαδεν οὕτως.*
>
> (Iliad xvii. 645 *et seq.*)

I

GENERAL GREATAUK, DUKE OF SKULL

 SHORT time after the flight of the Emiral, a middle-class Jew called Pyrot, desirous of associating with the aristocracy and wishing to serve his country, entered the Penguin army. The Minister of War, who at the time was Greatauk, Duke of Skull, could not endure him. He blamed him for his zeal, his hooked nose, his vanity, his fondness for study, his thick lips, his exemplary conduct. Every time the author of any misdeed was looked for, Greatauk used to say:

"It must be Pyrot!"

One morning General Panther, the Chief of the Staff, informed Greatauk of a serious matter. Eighty thousand trusses of hay intended for the cavalry had disappeared and not a trace of them was to be found.

Greatauk exclaimed at once:

"It must be Pyrot who has stolen them!"

He remained in thought for some time and said:

"The more I think of it the more I am convinced that Pyrot has stolen those eighty thousand trusses of hay. And I know it is by this: he stole them in order that he might sell them to our bitter enemies the Porpoises. What an infamous piece of treachery!"

*O Father Zeus, only save thou the sons of the Acheans from the darkness, and make clear sky and vouchsafe sight to our eyes, and then, so it be but light, slay us, since such is thy good pleasure.

"There is no doubt about it," answered Panther; "it only remains
to prove it."

The same day, as he passed by a cavalry barracks, Prince des
Boscénos heard the troopers as they were sweeping out the yard,
singing:

> Boscénos est un gros cochon;
> On en va faire des andouilles,
> Des saucisses et du jambon
> Pour le réveillon des pauv' bougres.

It seemed to him contrary to all discipline that soldiers should
sing this domestic and revolutionary refrain which on days of riot
had been uttered by the lips of jeering workmen. On this occasion
he deplored the moral degeneration of the army and thought with
a bitter smile that his old comrade Greatauk, the head of this degenerate army, basely exposed him to the malice of an unpatriotic
government. And he promised himself that he would make an improvement before long.

"That scoundrel Greatauk," said he to himself, "will not remain
long a Minister."

Prince des Boscénos was the most irreconcilable of the opponents
of modern democracy, free thought, and the government which the
Penguins had voluntarily given themselves. He had a vigorous and
undisguised hatred for the Jews, and he worked in public and in
private, night and day, for the restoration of the line of the Draconides. His ardent royalism was still further excited by the
thought of his private affairs, which were in a bad way and were
hourly growing worse. He had no hope of seeing an end to his pecuniary embarrassments until the heir of Draco the Great entered
the city of Alca.

When he returned to his house, the prince took out of his safe a
bundle of old letters consisting of a private correspondence of the
most secret nature, which he had obtained from a treacherous secretary. They proved that his old comrade Greatauk, the Duke of
Skull, had been guilty of jobbery regarding the military stores and
had received a present of no great value from a manufacturer called
Maloury. The very smallness of this present deprived the Minister
who had accepted it of all excuse.

The prince re-read the letters with a bitter satisfaction, put them
carefully back into his safe, and dashed to the Minister of War. He
was a man of resolute character. On being told that the Minister
could see no one he knocked down the ushers, swept aside the order-
lies, trampled under foot the civil and military clerks, burst through
the doors, and entered the room of the astonished Greatauk.

"I will not say much," said he to him, "but I will speak to the
point. You are a confounded cad. I have asked you to put a flea in
the ear of General Mouchin, the tool of those Republicans, and you

would not do it. I have asked you to give a command to General des
Clapiers, who works for the Dracophils, and who has obliged me
personally, and you would not do it. I have asked you to dismiss
General Tandem, the commander of Port Alca, who robbed me of
fifty louis at cards, and who had me handcuffed when I was brought
before the High Court as Emiral Chatillon's accomplice. You would
not do it. I asked you for the hay and bran stores. You would not
give them. I asked you to send me on a secret mission to Porpoisia.
You refused. And not satisfied with these repeated refusals you
have designated me to your Government colleagues as a dangerous
person, who ought to be watched, and it is owing to you that I have
been shadowed by the police. You old traitor! I ask nothing more
from you and I have but one word to say to you: Clear out; you
have bothered us too long. Besides, we will force the vile Republic
to replace you by one of our own party. You know that I am a man
of my word. If in twenty-four hours you have not handed in your
resignation I will publish the Maloury *dossier* in the newspapers."

But Greatauk calmly and serenely replied:

"Be quiet, you fool. I am just having a Jew transported. I am
handing over Pyrot to justice as guilty of having stolen eighty
thousand trusses of hay."

Prince Boscénos, whose anger vanished like a dream, smiled.

"Is that true?"

"You will see."

"My congratulations, Greatauk. But as one always needs to take
precautions with you I shall immediately publish the good news.
People will read this evening about Pyrot's arrest in every newspaper in Alca. . . ."

And he went away muttering:

"That Pyrot! I suspected he would come to a bad end."

A moment later General Panther appeared before Greatauk.

"Sir," said he, "I have just examined the business of the eighty
thousand trusses of hay. There is no evidence against Pyrot."

"Let it be found," answered Greatauk. "Justice requires it. Have
Pyrot arrested at once."

II

PYROT

LL Penguinia heard with horror of Pyrot's crime; at the same time there was a sort of satisfaction that this embezzlement combined with treachery and even bordering on sacrilege, had been committed by a Jew. In order to understand this feeling it is necessary to be acquainted with the state of the public opinion regarding the Jews both great and small. As we have had occasion to say in this history, the universally detested and all powerful financial caste was composed of Christians and of Jews. The Jews who formed part of it and on whom the people poured all their hatred were the upper-class Jews. They possessed immense riches and, it was said, held more than a fifth part of the total property of Penguinia. Outside this formidable caste there was a multitude of Jews of a mediocre condition, who were not more loved than the others and who were feared much less. In every ordered State, wealth is a sacred thing: in democracies it is the only sacred thing. Now the Penguin State was democratic. Three or four financial companies exercised a more extensive, and above all, more effective and continuous power, than that of the Ministers of the Republic. The latter were puppets whom the companies ruled in secret, whom they compelled by intimidation or corruption to favour themselves at the expense of the State, and whom they ruined by calumnies in the press if they remained honest. In spite of the secrecy of the Exchequer, enough appeared to make the country indignant, but the middle-class Penguins had, from the greatest to the last of them, been brought up to hold money in great reverence, and as they all had property, either much or little, they were strongly impressed with the solidarity of capital and understood that a small fortune is not safe unless a big one is protected. For these reasons they conceived a religious respect for the Jews' millions, and self-interest being stronger with them than aversion, they were as much afraid as they were of death to touch a single hair of one of the rich Jews whom they detested. Towards the poorer Jews they felt less ceremonious and when they saw any of them down they trampled on them. That is why the entire nation learnt with thorough satisfaction that the traitor was a Jew. They could take vengeance on all Israel in his person without any fear of compromising the public credit.

That Pyrot had stolen the eighty thousand trusses of hay nobody hesitated for a moment to believe. No one doubted because the general ignorance in which everybody was concerning the affair did not allow of doubt, for doubt is a thing that demands motives. People do not doubt without reasons in the same way that people believe without reasons. The thing was not doubted because it was repeated everywhere and, with the public, to repeat is to prove. It was not doubted because people wished to believe Pyrot guilty and one believes what one wishes to believe. Finally, it was not doubted because the faculty of doubt is rare amongst men; very few minds carry in them its germs and these are not developed without cultivation. Doubt is singular, exquisite, philosophic, immoral, transcendent, monstrous, full of malignity, injurious to persons and to property, contrary to the good order of governments, and to the prosperity of empires, fatal to humanity, destructive of the gods, held in horror by heaven and earth. The mass of the Penguins were ignorant of doubt: it believed in Pyrot's guilt and this conviction

immediately became one of its chief national beliefs and an essential truth in its patriotic creed.

Pyrot was tried secretly and condemned.

General Panther immediately went to the Minister of War to tell him the result.

"Luckily," said he, "the judges were certain, for they had no proofs."

"Proofs," muttered Greatauk, "proofs, what do they prove? There is only one certain, irrefragable proof—the confession of the guilty person. Has Pyrot confessed?"

"No, General."

"He will confess, he ought to. Panther, we must induce him; tell him it is to his interest. Promise him that, if he confesses, he will obtain favours, a reduction of his sentence, full pardon; promise him that if he confesses his innocence will be admitted, that he will be decorated. Appeal to his good feelings. Let him confess from patriotism, for the flag, for the sake of order, from respect for the hierarchy, at the special command of the Minister of War militarily. . . . But tell me, Panther, has he not confessed already? There are tacit confessions; silence is a confession."

"But, General, he is not silent; he keeps on squealing like a pig that he is innocent."

"Panther, the confessions of a guilty man sometimes result from the vehemence of his denials. To deny desperately is to confess. Pyrot has confessed; we must have witnesses of his confessions, justice requires them."

There was in Western Penguinia a seaport called La Cirque, formed of three small bays and formerly greatly frequented by ships, but now solitary and deserted. Gloomy lagoons stretched along its low coasts exhaling a pestilent odour, while fever hovered over its sleepy waters. Here, on the borders of the sea, there was built a high square tower, like the old Campanile at Venice, from the side of which, close to the summit, hung an open cage which was fastened by a chain to a transverse beam. In the times of the Draconides the Inquisitors of Alca used to put heretical clergy into this cage. It had been empty for three hundred years, but now Pyrot was imprisoned in it under the guard of sixty warders, who lived in the tower and did not lose sight of him night or day, spying on him for confessions that they might afterwards report to the Minister of War. For Greatauk, careful and prudent, desired confessions and still further confessions. Greatauk, who was looked upon as a fool, was in reality a man of great ability and full of rare foresight.

In the mean time Pyrot, burnt by the sun, eaten by mosquitoes, soaked in the rain, hail and snow, frozen by the cold, tossed about terribly by the wind, beset by the sinister croaking of the ravens that perched upon his cage, kept writing down his innocence on pieces torn off his shirt with a tooth-pick dipped in blood. These rags were lost in the sea or fell into the hands of the gaolers. Some of them, however, came under the eyes of the public. But Pyrot's protests moved nobody because his confessions had been published.

III

COUNT DE MAUBEC DE LA DENTDULYNX

THE morals of the Jews were not always pure; in most cases they were averse from none of the vices of Christian civilization, but they retained from the Patriarchal age a recognition of family ties and an attachment to the interest of the tribe. Pyrot's brothers, half-brothers, uncles, great-uncles, first, second, and third cousins, nephews and great-nephews, relations by blood and relations by marriage, and all who were related to him to the number of about seven hundred, were at first overwhelmed by the blow that had struck their relative, and they shut themselves up in their houses, covering themselves with ashes and blessing the hand that had chastised them. For forty days they kept a strict fast. Then they bathed themselves and resolved to search, without rest, at the cost of any toil and at the risk of every danger, for the demonstration of an innocence which they did not doubt. And how could they have doubted? Pyrot's innocence had been revealed to them in the same way that his guilt had been revealed to Christian Penguinia; for these things, being hidden, assume a mystic character and take on the authority of religious truths. The seven hundred Pyrotists set to work with as much zeal as prudence, and made the most thorough inquiries in secret. They were everywhere; they were seen nowhere. One would have said that, like the pilot of Ulysses, they wandered freely over the earth. They penetrated into the War Office and approached, under different disguises, the judges, the registrars, and the witnesses of the affair. Then Greatauk's cleverness was seen. The witnesses knew nothing; the judges and registrars knew nothing. Emissaries reached even Pyrot and anxiously questioned him in his cage amid the prolonged moanings of the sea and the hoarse croaks of the ravens. It was in vain; the prisoner knew nothing. The seven hundred Pyrotists could not subvert the proofs of the accusation because they could not know what they were, and they could not know what they were because there were none. Pyrot's guilt was indefeasible through its very nullity. And it was with a legitimate pride that Greatauk, expressing himself as a true artist, said one day to General Panther: "This case is a masterpiece: it is made out of nothing." The seven hundred Pyrotists despaired of ever clearing up this dark business, when suddenly they discovered, from a stolen letter, that the eighty thousand trusses of hay had never existed, that a most distinguished nobleman, Count de Maubec, had sold them to the State, that he had received the price but had never delivered them. Indeed seeing that he was descended from the richest land proprietors of ancient Penguinia, the heir of the Maubecs of Dentdulynx, once the possessors of four duchies, sixty counties, and six hundred and twelve marquisates, baronies, and viscounties, he did not possess as much land as he could cover with his hand, and would not have been able to cut a single day's mowing of forage off his own domains. As to his getting a single rush from a land-owner or a merchant, that would have been quite impossible, for everybody except the Ministers of State and the Government officials knew that it would be easier to get blood from a stone than a farthing from a Maubec.

The seven hundred Pyrotists made a minute inquiry concerning the Count Maubec de la Dentdulynx's financial resources, and they proved that that nobleman was chiefly supported by a house in which some generous ladies were ready to furnish all comers with the most lavish hospitality. They publicly proclaimed that he was guilty of the theft of the eighty thousand trusses of straw for which an innocent man had been condemned and was now imprisoned in the cage.

Maubec belonged to an illustrious family which was allied to the Draconides. There is nothing that a democracy esteems more highly than noble birth. Maubec had also served in the Penguin army, and since the Penguins were all soldiers, they loved their army to idolatry. Maubec, on the field of battle, had received the Cross, which is a sign of honour among the Penguins and which they valued even more highly than the embraces of their wives. All Penguinia declared for Maubec, and the voice of the people which began to assume a threatening tone, demanded severe punishments for the seven hundred calumniating Pyrotists.

Maubec was a nobleman; he challenged the seven hundred Pyrotists to combat with either sword, sabre, pistols, carabines, or sticks.

"Vile dogs," he wrote to them in a famous letter, "you have crucified my God and you want my life too; I warn you that I will not be such a duffer as He was and that I will cut off your fourteen hundred ears. Accept my boot on your seven hundred behinds."

The Chief of the Government at the time was a peasant called Robin Mielleux, a man pleasant to the rich and powerful, but hard towards the poor, a man of small courage and ignorant of his own interests. In a public declaration he guaranteed Maubec's innocence and honour, and presented the seven hundred Pyrotists to the criminal courts where they were condemned, as libellers, to imprisonment, to enormous fines, and to all the damages that were claimed by their innocent victim.

It seemed as if Pyrot was destined to remain for ever shut in the cage on which the ravens perched. But all the Penguins being anxious to know and prove that this Jew was guilty, all the proofs brought forward were found not to be good, while some of them were also contradictory. The officers of the Staff showed zeal but lacked prudence. Whilst Greatauk kept an admirable silence, General Panther made inexhaustible speeches and every morning demonstrated in the newspapers that the condemned man was guilty. He would have done better, perhaps, if he had said nothing. The guilt was evident and what is evident cannot be demonstrated. So much reasoning disturbed people's minds; their faith, though still alive, became less serene. The more proofs one gives a crowd the more they ask for.

Nevertheless the danger of proving too much would not have been great if there had not been in Penguinia, as there are, indeed, everywhere, minds framed for free inquiry, capable of studying a difficult question, and inclined to philosophic doubt. They were few; they were not all inclined to speak, and the public was by no means inclined to listen to them. Still, they did not always meet with deaf ears. The great Jews, all the Israelite millionaires of Alca, when spoken to of Pyrot, said: "We do not know the man"; but they thought of saving him. They preserved the prudence to which their wealth inclined them and wished that others would be less timid. Their wish was to be gratified.

IV

COLOMBAN

OME weeks after the conviction of the seven hundred Pyrotists, a little, gruff, hairy, short-sighted man left his house one morning with a paste-pot, a ladder, and a bundle of posters and went about the streets pasting placards to the walls on which might be read in large letters: *Pyrot is innocent, Maubec is guilty.* He was not a bill-poster; his name was Colomban, and as the author of sixty volumes on Penguin sociology he was numbered among the most laborious and respected writers in Alca. Having given sufficient thought to the matter and no longer doubting Pyrot's innocence, he proclaimed it in the manner which he thought would be most sensational. He met with no hindrance while posting his bills in the quiet streets, but when he came to the populous quarters, every time he mounted his ladder, inquisitive people crowded round him and, dumfounded with surprise and indignation, threw at him threatening looks which he received with the calm that comes from courage and short-sightedness. Whilst caretakers and tradespeople tore down the bills he had posted, he kept on zealously placarding, carrying his tools and followed by little boys who, with their baskets under their arms or their satchels on their backs, were in no hurry to reach school. To the mute indignation against him, protests and murmurs were now added. But Colomban did not condescend to see or hear anything. As, at the entrance to the Rue St. Orberosia, he was posting one of his squares of paper bearing the words: *Pyrot is innocent, Maubec is guilty,* the riotous crowd showed signs of the most violent anger. They called after him, "Traitor, thief, rascal, scoundrel." A woman opened a window and emptied a vessel full of filth over his head, a cabby sent his hat flying from one end of the street to the other by a blow of his whip amid the cheers of the crowd who now felt themselves avenged. A butcher's boy knocked Colomban with his paste-pot, his brush, and his posters, from the top of his ladder into the gutter, and the proud Penguins then felt the greatness of their country. Colomban stood up, covered with filth, lame, and with his elbow injured, but tranquil and resolute.

"Low brutes," he muttered, shrugging his shoulders.

Then he went down on all-fours in the gutter to look for his glasses which he had lost in his fall. It was then seen that his coat was split from the collar to the tails and that his trousers were in rags. The rancour of the crowd grew stronger.

On the other side of the street stretched the big St. Orberosian Stores. The patriots seized whatever they could lay their hands on from the shop front, and hurled at Colomban oranges, lemons, pots of jam, pieces of chocolate, bottles of liqueurs, boxes of sardines, pots of *foie gras,* hams, fowls, flasks of oil, and bags of haricots. Covered with the débris of the food, bruised, tattered, lame, and blind, he took to flight, followed by the shop-boys, bakers, loafers, citizens, and hooligans whose number increased each moment and who kept shouting: "Duck him! Death to the traitor! Duck him!" This torrent of vulgar humanity swept along the streets and rushed into the Rue St. Maël. The police did their duty. From all the adjacent streets constables proceeded and, holding their scabbards with their left hands, they went at full speed in front of the pursuers. They were on the point of grabbing Colomban in their huge hands when he suddenly escaped them by falling through an open manhole to the bottom of a sewer.

He spent the night there in the darkness, sitting close by the dirty water amidst the fat and slimy rats. He thought of his task, and his swelling heart filled with courage and pity. And when the dawn threw a pale ray of light into the air-hole he got up and said, speaking to himself:

"I see that the fight will be a stiff one."

Forthwith he composed a memorandum in which he clearly showed that Pyrot could not have stolen from the Ministry of War the eighty thousand trusses of hay which it had never received, for the reason that Maubec had never delivered them, though he had received the money. Colomban caused this statement to be distributed in the streets of Alca. The people refused to read it and tore it up in anger. The shop-keepers shook their fists at the distributers, who made off, chased by angry women armed with brooms. Feeling grew warm and the ferment lasted the whole day. In the evening bands of wild and ragged men went about the streets yelling: "Death to Colomban!" The patriots snatched whole bundles of the memorandum from the newsboys and burned them in the public squares, dancing wildly round these bon-fires with girls whose petticoats were tied up to their waists.

Some of the more enthusiastic among them went and broke the windows of the house in which Colomban had lived in perfect tranquillity during his forty years of work.

Parliament was roused and asked the Chief of the Government what measures he proposed to take in order to repel the odious attacks made by Colomban upon the honour of the National Army and the safety of Penguinia. Robin Mielleux denounced Colomban's impious audacity and proclaimed amid the cheers of the legislators that the man would be summoned before the Courts to answer for his infamous libel.

The Minister of War was called to the tribune and appeared in it transfigured. He had no longer the air, as in former days, of one of the sacred geese of the Penguin citadels. Now, bristling, with out-stretched neck and hooked beak, he seemed the symbolical vulture fastened to the livers of his country's enemies.

In the august silence of the assembly he pronounced these words only:

"I swear that Pyrot is a rascal."

This speech of Greatauk was reported all over Penguinia and satisfied the public conscience.

V

THE REVEREND FATHERS AGARIC AND CORNEMUSE

COLOMBAN bore with meekness and surprise the weight of the general reprobation. He could not go out without being stoned, so he did not go out. He remained in his study with a superb obstinacy, writing new memoranda in favour of the encaged innocent. In the mean time among the few readers that he found, some, about a dozen, were struck by his reasons and began to doubt Pyrot's guilt. They broached the subject to their friends and endeavoured to spread the light that had arisen in their minds. One of them was a friend of Robin Mielleux and confided to him his perplexities, with the result that he was no longer received by that Minister. Another demanded explanations in an open letter to the Minister of War. A third published a terrible pamphlet. The latter, whose name was Kerdanic, was a formidable controversialist. The public was unmoved. It was said that these defenders of the traitor had been bribed by the rich Jews; they were stigmatized by the name of Pyrotists and the patriots swore to exterminate them. There were only a thousand or twelve hundred Pyrotists in the whole vast Republic, but it was believed that they were everywhere. People were afraid of finding them in the promenades, at meetings, at receptions, in fashionable drawing-rooms, at the dinner-table, even in the conjugal couch. One half of the population was suspected by the other half. The discord set all Alca on fire.

In the mean time Father Agaric, who managed his big school for young nobles, followed events with anxious attention. The misfortunes of the Penguin Church had not disheartened him. He remained faithful to Prince Crucho and preserved the hope of restoring the heir of the Draconides to the Penguin throne. It appeared to him that the events that were happening or about to happen in the country, the state of mind of which they were at once the effect and the cause, and the troubles that necessarily resulted from them might—if they were directed, guided, and led by the profound wisdom of a monk—overthrow the Republic and incline the Penguins to restore Prince Crucho, from whose piety the faithful hoped for so much solace. Wearing his huge black hat, the brim of which looked like the wings of Night, he walked through the Wood of Conils towards the factory where his venerable friend, Father Cornemuse, distilled the hygienic St. Orberosian liqueur. The good monk's industry, so cruelly affected in the time of Emiral Chatillon, was being restored from its ruins. One heard goods trains rumbling through the Wood and one saw in the sheds hundreds of orphans clothed in blue, packing bottles and nailing up cases.

Agaric found the venerable Cornemuse standing before his stoves and surrounded by his retorts. The shining pupils of the old man's eyes had again become as bright as rubies, his skull shone with its former elaborate and careful polish.

Agaric first congratulated the pious distiller on the restored activity of his laboratories and workshops.

"Business is recovering. I thank God for it," answered the old man of Conils. "Alas! it had fallen into a bad state, Brother Agaric. You saw the desolation of this establishment. I need say no more."

Agaric turned away his head.

"The St. Orberosian liqueur," continued Cornemuse, "is making fresh conquests. But none the less my industry remains uncertain and precarious. The laws of ruin and desolation that struck it have not been abrogated, they have only been suspended."

And the monk of Conils lifted his ruby eyes to heaven.

Agaric put his hand on his shoulder.

"What a sight, Cornemuse, does unhappy Penguinia present to us! Everywhere disobedience, independence, liberty! We see the proud, the haughty, the men of revolt rising up. After having braved the Divine laws they now rear themselves against human laws, so true is it that in order to be a good citizen a man must be a good Christian. Colomban is trying to imitate Satan. Numerous criminals are following his fatal example. They want, in their rage, to put aside all checks, to throw off all yokes, to free themselves from the most sacred bonds, to escape from the most salutary restraints. They strike their country to make it obey them. But they will be overcome by the weight of public animadversion, vituperation, indignation, fury, execration, and abomination. That is the abyss to which they have been led by atheism, free thought, and the monstrous claim to judge for themselves and to form their own opinions."

"Doubtless, doubtless," replied Father Cornemuse, shaking his head, "but I confess that the care of distilling these simples has prevented me from following public affairs. I only know that people are talking a great deal about a man called Pyrot. Some maintain that he is guilty, others affirm that he is innocent, but I do not clearly understand the motives that drive both parties to mix themselves up in a business that concerns neither of them."

The pious Agaric asked eagerly:

"You do not doubt Pyrot's guilt?"

"I cannot doubt it, dear Agaric," answered the monk of Conils. "That would be contrary to the laws of my country which we ought to respect as long as they are not opposed to the Divine laws. Pyrot is guilty, for he has been convicted. As to saying more for or against his guilt, that would be to erect my own authority against that of the judges, a thing which I will take good care not to do. Besides, it is useless, for Pyrot has been convicted. If he has not been convicted because he is guilty, he is guilty because he has been convicted; it comes to the same thing. I believe in his guilt as every good citizen ought to believe in it; and I will believe in it as long as the established jurisdiction will order me to believe in it, for it is not for a private person but for a judge to proclaim the innocence of a convicted person. Human justice is venerable even in the errors inherent in its fallible and limited nature. These errors are never irreparable; if the judges do not repair them on earth, God will repair them in Heaven. Besides I have great confidence in General Greatauk, who, though he certainly does not look it, seems to me to be an abler man than all those who are attacking him."

"Dearest Cornemuse," cried the pious Agaric, "the Pyrot affair, if pushed to the point whither we can lead it by the help of God and the necessary funds, will produce the greatest benefits. It will lay bare the vices of this Anti-Christian Republic and will incline the Penguins to restore the throne of the Draconides and the prerogatives of the Church. But to do that it is necessary for the people to see the clergy in the front rank of its defenders. Let us march against the enemies of the army, against those who insult our heroes, and everybody will follow us."

"Everybody will be too many," murmured the monk of Conils, shaking his head. "I see that the Penguins want to quarrel. If we mix ourselves up in their quarrel they will become reconciled at our expense and we shall have to pay the cost of the war. That is why, if you are guided by me, dear Agaric, you will not engage the Church in this adventure."

"You know my energy; you know my prudence. I will compromise nothing. . . . Dear Cornemuse, I only want from you the funds necessary for us to begin the campaign."

For a long time Cornemuse refused to bear the expenses of what he thought was a fatal enterprise. Agaric was in turn pathetic and terrible. At last, yielding to his prayers and threats, Cornemuse, with hanging head and swinging arms, went to the austere cell that concealed his evangelical poverty. In the whitewashed wall under a branch of blessed box, there was fixed a safe. He opened it, and with a sigh took out a bundle of bills which, with hesitating hands, he gave to the pious Agaric.

"Do not doubt it, dear Cornemuse," said the latter, thrusting the papers into the pocket of his overcoat, "this Pyrot affair has been sent us by God for the glory and exaltation of the Church of Penguinia."

"I pray that you may be right!" sighed the monk of Conils.

And, left alone in his laboratory, he gazed, through his exquisite eyes, with an ineffable sadness at his stoves and his retorts.

VI

THE SEVEN HUNDRED PYROTISTS

HE seven hundred Pyrotists inspired the public with an increasing aversion. Every day two or three of them were beaten to death in the streets. One of them was publicly whipped, another thrown into the river, a third tarred and feathered and led through a laughing crowd, a fourth had his nose cut off by a captain of dragoons. They did not dare to show themselves at their clubs, at tennis, or at the races; they put on a disguise when they went to the Stock Exchange. In these circumstances the Prince des Boscénos thought it urgent to curb their audacity and repress their insolence. For this purpose he joined with Count Cléna, M. de La Trumelle, Viscount Olive, and M. Bigourd in founding a great anti-Pyrotist association to which citizens in hundreds of thousands, soldiers in companies, regiments, brigades, divisions, and army corps, towns, districts, and provinces, all gave their adhesion.

About this time the Minister of War happening to visit one day his Chief of Staff, saw with surprise that the large room where General Panther worked, which was formerly quite bare, had now along each wall from floor to ceiling in sets of deep pigeon-holes, triple and quadruple rows of paper bundles of every form and colour. These sudden and monstrous records had in a few days reached the dimensions of a pile of archives such as it takes centuries to accumulate.

"What is this?" asked the astonished minister.

"Proofs against Pyrot," answered General Panther with patriotic satisfaction. "We had not got them when we convicted him, but we have plenty of them now."

The door was open, and Greatauk saw coming up the stair-case a long file of porters who were unloading heavy bales of papers in the hall, and he saw the lift slowly rising heavily loaded with paper packets.

"What are those others?" said he.

"They are fresh proofs against Pyrot that are now reaching us," said Panther. "I have asked for them in every county of Penguinia, in every Staff Office and in every Court in Europe. I have ordered them in every town in America and in Australia, and in every factory in Africa, and I am expecting bales of them from Bremen and a ship-load from Melbourne."

And Panther turned towards the Minister of War the tranquil and radiant look of a hero. However, Greatauk, his eye-glass in his eye, was looking at the formidable pile of papers with less satisfaction than uneasiness.

"Very good," said he, "very good! but I am afraid that this Pyrot business may lose its beautiful simplicity. It was limpid; like a rock-crystal its value lay in its transparency. You could have searched it in vain with a magnifying-glass for a straw, a bend, a blot, for the least fault. When it left my hands it was as pure as the light. Indeed it was the light. I give you a pearl and you make a mountain out of it. To tell you the truth I am afraid that by wishing to do too well you have done less well. Proofs! of course it is good to have proofs, but perhaps it is better to have none at all. I have already told you, Panther, there is only one irrefutable proof, the confession of the guilty person (or if the innocent what matter!). The Pyrot affair, as I arranged it, left no room for criticism; there was no spot where it could be touched. It defied assault. It was invulnerable because it was invisible. Now it gives an enormous handle for discussion. I advise you, Panther, to use your paper packets with great reserve. I should be particularly grateful if you would be more sparing of your communications to journalists. You speak well, but you say too much. Tell me, Panther, are there any forged documents among these?"

"There are some adapted ones."

"That is what I meant. There are some adapted ones. So much the better. As proofs, forged documents, in general, are better than genuine ones, first of all because they have been expressly made to suit the needs of the case, to order and measure, and therefore they are fitting and exact. They are also preferable because they carry the mind into an ideal world and turn it aside from the reality which, alas! in this world is never without some alloy. . . . Nevertheless, I think I should have preferred, Panther, that we had no proofs at all."

The first act of the Anti-Pyrotist Association was to ask the Government immediately to summon the seven hundred Pyrotists and their accomplices before the High Court of Justice as guilty of high treason. Prince des Boscénos was charged to speak on behalf of the Association and presented himself before the Council which had assembled to hear him. He expressed a hope that the vigilance and firmness of the Government would rise to the height of the occasion. He shook hands with each of the ministers and as he passed General Greatauk he whispered in his ear:

"Behave properly, you ruffian, or I will publish the Maloury *dossier!*"

Some days later by a unanimous vote of both Houses, on a motion proposed by the Government, the Anti-Pyrotist Association was granted a charter recognising it as beneficial to the public interest.

The Association immediately sent a deputation to Chitterlings

Castle in Porpoisia, where Crucho was eating the bitter bread of exile, to assure the prince of the love and devotion of the Anti-Pyrotist members.

However, the Pyrotists grew in numbers, and now counted ten thousand. They had their regular cafés on the boulevards. The patriots had theirs also, richer and bigger, and every evening glasses of beer, saucers, match-stands, jugs, chairs, and tables were hurled from one to the other. Mirrors were smashed to bits, and the police ended the struggles by impartially trampling the combatants of both parties under their hob-nailed shoes.

On one of these glorious nights, as Prince des Boscénos was leaving a fashionable café in the company of some patriots, M. de La Trumelle pointed out to him a little, bearded man with glasses, hatless, and having only one sleeve to his coat, who was painfully dragging himself along the rubbish-strewn pavement.

"Look!" said he, "there is Colomban!"

The prince had gentleness as well as strength; he was exceedingly mild; but at the name of Colomban his blood boiled. He rushed at the little spectacled man, and knocked him down with one blow of his fist on the nose.

M. de La Trumelle then perceived that, misled by an undeserved resemblance, he had mistaken for Colomban, M. Bazile, a retired lawyer, the secretary of the Anti-Pyrotist Association, and an ardent and generous patriot. Prince des Boscénos was one of those antique souls who never bend. However, he knew how to recognise his faults.

"M. Bazile," said he, raising his hat, "if I have touched your face with my hand you will excuse me and you will understand me, you will approve of me, nay, you will compliment me, you will congratulate me and felicitate me, when you know the cause of that act. I took you for Colomban."

M. Bazile, wiping his bleeding nostrils with his handkerchief and displaying an elbow laid bare by the absence of his sleeve:

"No, sir," answered he drily, "I shall not felicitate you, I shall not congratulate you, I shall not compliment you, for your action was, at the very least, superfluous; it was, I will even say, supererogatory. Already this evening I have been three times mistaken for Colomban and received a sufficient amount of the treatment he deserves. The patriots have knocked in my ribs and broken my back, and, sir, I was of opinion that that was enough."

Scarcely had he finished this speech than a band of Pyrotists appeared, and misled in their turn by the insidious resemblance, they believed that the patriots were killing Colomban. They fell on Prince des Boscénos and his companions with loaded canes and leather thongs, and left them for dead. Then seizing Bazile they carried him in triumph, and in spite of his protests, along the boulevards, amid cries of: "Hurrah for Colomban! Hurrah for Pyrot!" At last the police, who had been sent after them, attacked and defeated them and dragged them ignominiously to the station, where Bazile, under the name of Colomban, was trampled on by an innumerable quantity of thick, hob-nailed shoes.

VII

BIDAULT–COQUILLE AND MANIFLORE, THE SOCIALISTS

HILST the wind of anger and hatred blew in Alca, Eugène Bidault-Coquille, poorest and happiest of astronomers, installed in an old steam-engine of the time of the Draconides, was observing the heavens through a bad telescope, and photographing the paths of the meteors upon some damaged photographic plates. His genius corrected the errors of his instruments and his love of science triumphed over the worthlessness of his apparatus. With an inextinguishable ardour he observed aerolites, meteors, and fire-balls, and all the glowing ruins and blazing sparks which pass through the terrestrial atmosphere with prodigious speed, and as a reward for his studious vigils he received the indifference of the public, the ingratitude of the State and the blame of the learned societies. Engulfed in the celestial spaces he knew not what occurred upon the surface of the earth. He never read the newspapers, and when he walked through the town his mind was occupied with the November asteroids, and more than once he found himself at the bottom of a pond in one of the public parks or beneath the wheels of a motor omnibus.

Elevated in stature as in thought he respected himself and others. This was shown by his cold politeness as well as by a very thin black frock coat and a tall hat which gave to his person an appearance at once emaciated and sublime. He took his meals in a little restaurant from which all customers less intellectual than himself had fled, and thenceforth his napkin bound by its wooden ring rested alone in the abandoned rack.

In this cook-shop his eyes fell one evening upon Colomban's memorandum in favour of Pyrot. He read it as he was cracking some bad nuts and suddenly, exalted with astonishment, admiration, horror, and pity, he forgot all about falling meteors and shooting stars and saw nothing but the innocent man hanging in his cage exposed to the winds of heaven and the ravens perching upon it.

That image did not leave him. For a week he had been obsessed by the innocent convict, when, as he was leaving his cook-shop, he saw a crowd of citizens entering a public-house in which a public meeting was going on. He went in. The meeting was disorderly; they were yelling, abusing one another and knocking one another down in the smoke-laden hall. The Pyrotists and the Anti-Pyrotists spoke in turn and were alternately cheered and hissed at. An obscure and confused enthusiasm moved the audience. With the audacity of a timid and retired man Bidault-Coquille leaped upon the platform and spoke for three-quarters of an hour. He spoke very quickly, without order, but with vehemence, and with all the conviction of a mathematical mystic. He was cheered. When he got down from the platform a big woman of uncertain age, dressed in red, and wearing an immense hat trimmed with heroic feathers, throwing herself into his arms, embraced him, and said to him:

"You are splendid!"

He thought in his simplicity that there was some truth in the statement.

She declared to him that henceforth she would live but for Pyrot's defence and Colomban's glory. He thought her sublime and beautiful. She was Maniflore, a poor old courtesan, now forgotten and discarded, who had suddenly become a vehement politician.

She never left him. They spent glorious hours together in doss-houses and in lodgings beautified by their love, in newspaper offices, in meeting-halls and in lecture-halls. As he was an idealist, he persisted in thinking her beautiful, although she gave him abundant opportunity of seeing that she had preserved no charm of any kind. From her past beauty she only retained a confidence in her capacity for pleasing and a lofty assurance in demanding homage. Still, it must be admitted that this Pyrot affair, so fruitful in prodigies, invested Maniflore with a sort of civic majesty, and transformed her, at public meetings, into an august symbol of justice and truth.

Bidault-Coquille and Maniflore did not kindle the least spark of irony or amusement in a single Anti-Pyrotist, a single defender of Greatauk, or a single supporter of the army. The gods, in their anger, had refused to those men the precious gift of humour. They gravely accused the courtesan and the astronomer of being spies, of treachery, and of plotting against their country. Bidault-Coquille and Maniflore grew visibly greater beneath insult, abuse, and calumny.

For long months Penguinia had been divided into two camps and, though at first sight it may appear strange, hitherto the socialists had taken no part in the contest. Their groups comprised almost all the manual workers in the country, necessarily scattered, confused, broken up, and divided, but formidable. The Pyrot affair threw the group leaders into a singular embarrassment. They did not wish to place themselves either on the side of the financiers or on the side of the army. They regarded the Jews, both great and small, as their uncompromising opponents. Their principles were not at stake, nor were their interests concerned in the affair. Still the greater number felt how difficult it was growing for them to remain aloof from struggles in which all Penguinia was engaged.

Their leaders called a sitting of their federation at the Rue de la Queue-du-diable-St. Maël, to take into consideration the conduct they ought to adopt in the present circumstances and in future eventualities.

Comrade Phœnix was the first to speak.

"A crime," said he, "the most odious and cowardly of crimes, a judicial crime, has been committed. Military judges, coerced or mis-led by their superior officers, have condemned an innocent man to an infamous and cruel punishment. Let us not say that the victim is not one of our own party, that he belongs to a caste which was, and always will be, our enemy. Our party is the party of social justice; it can look upon no iniquity with indifference.

"It would be a shame for us if we left it to Kerdanic, a radical, to Colomban, a member of the middle classes, and to a few moderate Republicans, alone to proceed against the crimes of the army. If the victim is not one of us, his executioners are our brothers' executioners, and before Greatauk struck down this soldier he shot our comrades who were on strike.

"Comrades, by an intellectual, moral and material effort you must rescue Pyrot from his torment, and in performing this generous act you are not turning aside from the liberating and revolutionary task you have undertaken, for Pyrot has become the symbol of the oppressed and of all the social iniquities that now exist; by destroying one you make all the others tremble."

When Phœnix ended, comrade Sapor spoke in these terms:

"You are advised to abandon your task in order to do something with which you have no concern. Why throw yourselves into a conflict where, on whatever side you turn, you will find none but your natural, uncompromising, even necessary opponents? Are the financiers to be less hated by us than the army? What inept and criminal generosity is it that hurries you to save those seven hundred Pyrotists whom you will always find confronting you in the social war?

"It is proposed that you act the part of the police for your enemies, and that you are to re-establish for them the order which their own crimes have disturbed. Magnanimity pushed to this degree changes its name.

"Comrades, there is a point at which infamy becomes fatal to a society. Penguin society is being strangled by its infamy, and you are requested to save it, to give it air that it can breathe. This is simply turning you into ridicule.

"Leave it to smother itself and let us gaze at its last convulsions with joyful contempt, only regretting that it has so entirely corrupted the soil on which it has been build that we shall find nothing but poisoned mud on which to lay the foundations of a new society."

When Sapor had ended his speech comrade Lapersonne pronounced these few words:

"Phœnix calls us to Pyrot's help for the reason that Pyrot is innocent. It seems to me that that is a very bad reason. If Pyrot is innocent he has behaved like a good soldier and has always conscientiously worked at his trade, which principally consists in shooting the people. That is not a motive to make the people brave all dangers in his defence. When it is demonstrated to me that Pyrot is guilty and that he stole the army hay, I shall be on his side."

Comrade Larrivée afterwards spoke.

"I am not of my friend, Phœnix's opinion but I am not with my friend Sapor either. I do not believe that the party is bound to embrace a cause as soon as we are told that that cause is just. That, I am afraid, is a grievous abuse of words and a dangerous equivocation. For social justice is not revolutionary justice. They are both in perpetual antagonism: to serve the one is to oppose the other. As for me, my choice is made. I am for revolutionary justice as against social justice. Still, in the present case I am against abstention. I say that when a lucky chance brings us an affair like this we should be fools not to profit by it.

"How? We are given an opportunity of striking terrible, perhaps fatal, blows against militarism. And am I to fold my arms? I tell you, comrades, I am not a fakir, I have never been a fakir, and if there are fakirs here let them not count on me. To sit in meditation is a policy without results and one which I shall never adopt.

"A party like ours ought to be continually asserting itself. It ought to prove its existence by continual action. We will intervene in the Pyrot affair but we will intervene in it in a revolutionary manner; we will adopt violent action. . . . Perhaps you think that violence is old-fashioned and superannuated, to be scrapped along with diligences, hand-presses and aerial telegraphy. You are mistaken. To-day as yesterday nothing is obtained except by violence; it is the one efficient instrument. The only thing necessary is to know how to use it. You ask what will our action be? I will tell you: it will be to stir up the governing classes against one another, to put the army in conflict with the capitalists, the government with the magistracy, the nobility and clergy with the Jews, and if possible to drive them all to destroy one another. To do this would be to carry on an agitation which would weaken government in the same way that fever wears out the sick.

"The Pyrot affair, little as we know how to turn it to advantage, will put forward by ten years the growth of the Socialist party and the emancipation of the proletariat, by disarmament, the general strike, and revolution."

The leaders of the party having each expressed a different opinion, the discussion was continued, not without vivacity. The orators, as always happens in such a case, reproduced the arguments they had already brought forward, though with less order and moderation than before. The dispute was prolonged and none changed his opinion. But these opinions, in the final analysis, were reduced to two, that of Sapor and Lapersonne who advised abstention, and that of Phœnix and Larrivée, who wanted intervention. Even these two contrary opinions were united in a common hatred of the heads of the army and of their justice, and in a common belief in Pyrot's innocence. So that public opinion was hardly mistaken in regarding all the Socialist leaders as pernicious Anti-Pyrotists.

As for the vast masses in whose name they spoke and whom they represented as far as speech can express the inexpressible— as for the proletarians whose thought is difficult to know and who do not know it themselves, it seemed that the Pyrot affair did not interest them. It was too literary for them, it was in too classical a style, and had an upper-middle-class and high-finance tone about it that did not please them much.

VIII

THE COLOMBAN TRIAL

WHEN the Colomban trial began, the Pyrotists were not many more than thirty thousand, but they were everywhere and might be found even among the priests and millionaires. What injured them most was the sympathy of the rich Jews. On the other hand they derived valuable advantages from their feeble number. In the first place there were among them fewer fools than among their opponents, who were over-burdened with them. Comprising but a feeble minority they co-operated easily, acted with harmony, and had no temptation to divide and thus counteract one another's efforts. Each of them felt the necessity of doing the best possible and was the more careful of his conduct as he found himself more in the public eye. Finally, they had every reason to hope that they would gain fresh adherents, while their opponents, having had everybody with them at the beginning, could only decrease.

Summoned before the judges at a public sitting, Colomban immediately perceived that his judges were not anxious to discover the truth. As soon as he opened his mouth the President ordered him to be silent in the superior interests of the State. For the same reason, which is the supreme reason, the witnesses for the defence were not heard. General Panther, the Chief of the Staff, appeared in the witness-box, in full uniform and decorated with all his orders. He deposed as follows:

"The infamous Colomban states that we have no proofs against Pyrot. He lies; we have them. I have in my archives seven hundred and thirty-two square yards of them which at five hundred pounds each make three hundred and sixty-six thousand pounds weight."

That superior officer afterwards gave, with elegance and ease, a summary of those proofs.

"They are of all colours and all shades," said he in substance, "they are of every form—pot, crown, sovereign, grape, dove-cot, grand eagle, etc. The smallest is less than the hundredth part of a square inch, the largest measures seventy yards long by ninety yards broad."

At this revelation the audience shuddered with horror.

Greatauk came to give evidence in his turn. Simpler, and perhaps greater, he wore a grey tunic and held his hands joined behind his back.

"I leave," said he calmly and in a slightly raised voice, "I leave to M. Colomban the responsibility for an act that has brought our country to the brink of ruin. The Pyrot affair is secret; it ought to remain secret. If it were divulged the cruelest ills, wars, pillages, depredations, fires, massacres, and epidemics would immediately burst upon Penguinia. I should consider myself guilty of high treason if I uttered another word."

Some persons known for their political experience, among others M. Bigourd, considered the evidence of the Minister of War as abler and of greater weight than that of his Chief of Staff.

The evidence of Colonel de Boisjoli made a great impression.

"One evening at the Ministry of War," said that officer, "the attaché of a neighbouring Power told me that while visiting his sovereign's stables he had once admired some soft and fragrant hay, of a pretty green colour, the finest hay he had ever seen! 'Where did it come from?' I asked him. He did not answer, but there seemed to me no doubt about its origin. It was the hay Pyrot had stolen. Those qualities of verdure, softness, and aroma, are those of our national hay. The forage of the neighbouring Power is grey and brittle; it sounds under the fork and smells of dust. One can draw one's own conclusions."

Lieutenant-Colonel Hastaing said in the witness-box, amid hisses, that he did not believe Pyrot guilty. He was immediately seized by the police and thrown into the bottom of a dungeon where, amid vipers, toads, and broken glass, he remained insensible both to promises and threats.

The usher called:

"Count Pierre Maubec de la Dentdulynx."

There was deep silence, and a stately but ill-dressed nobleman, whose moustaches pointed to the skies and whose dark eyes shot forth flashing glances, was seen advancing toward the witness-box.

He approached Colomban and casting upon him a look of ineffable disdain:

"My evidence," said he, "here it is: you excrement!"

At these words the entire hall burst into enthusiastic applause and jumped up, moved by one of those transports that stir men's hearts and rouse them to extraordinary actions. Without another word Count Maubec de la Dentdulynx withdrew.

All those present left the Court and formed a procession behind him. Prostrate at his feet, Princess des Boscénos held his legs in a close embrace, but he went on, stern and impassive, beneath a shower of handkerchiefs and flowers. Viscountess Olive, clinging to his neck, could not be removed, and the calm hero bore her along with him, floating on his breast like a light scarf.

When the court resumed its sitting, which it had been compelled to suspend, the President called the experts.

Vermillard, the famous expert in handwriting, gave the results of his researches.

"Having carefully studied," said he, "the papers found in Pyrot's house, in particular his account book and his laundry books, I noticed that, though apparently not out of the common, they formed an impenetrable cryptogram, the key to which, however, I discovered. The traitor's infamy is to be seen in every line. In this system of writing the words 'Three glasses of beer and twenty francs for Adèle,' mean 'I have delivered thirty thousand trusses of hay to a neighbouring Power.' From these documents I have even been able to establish the composition of the hay delivered by this officer. The words waistcoat, drawers, pocket handkerchief, collars, drink, tobacco, cigars, mean clover, meadow-grass, lucern, burnet, oats, rye-grass, vernal-grass, and common cat's tail grass. And these are precisely the constituents of the hay furnished by Count Maubec to the Penguin cavalry. In this way Pyrot mentioned his crimes in a language that he believed would always remain indecipherable. One is confounded by so much astuteness and so great a want of conscience."

Colomban, pronounced guilty without any extenuating circumstances, was condemned to the severest penalty. The judges immediately signed a warrant consigning him to solitary confinement.

In the Place du Palais on the sides of a river whose banks had during the course of twelve centuries seen so great a history, fifty thousand persons were tumultuously awaiting the result of the trial. Here were the heads of the Anti-Pyrotist Association, among whom might be seen Prince des Boscénos, Count Cléna, Viscount Olive, and M. de La Trumelle; here crowded the Reverend Father Agaric and the teachers of St. Maël College with their pupils; here the monk Douillard and General Caraguel, embracing each other, formed a sublime group. The market women and laundry women with spits, shovels, tongs, beetles, and kettles full of water might be seen running across the Pont-Vieux. On the steps in front of the bronze gates were assembled all the defenders of Pyrot in Alca, professors, publicists, workmen, some conservatives, others Radicals or Revolutionaries, and by their negligent dress and fierce aspect could be recognised comrades Phœnix, Larrivée, Lapersonne, Dagobert, and Varambille. Squeezed in his funereal frock-coat and wearing his hat of ceremony, Bidault-Coquille invoked the sentimental mathematics on behalf of Colomban and Colonel Hastaing. Maniflore shone smiling and resplendent on the topmost step, anxious, like Leæna, to deserve a glorious monument, or to be given, like Epicharis, the praises of history.

The seven hundred Pyrotists disguised as lemonade sellers, gutter-merchants, collectors of odds and ends, or as Anti-Pyrotists, wandered round the vast building.

When Colomban appeared, so great an uproar burst forth that, struck by the commotion of air and water, birds fell from the trees and fishes floated on the surface of the stream.

On all sides there were yells:

"Duck Colomban, duck him, duck him!"

There were some cries of "Justice and truth!" and a voice was even heard shouting:

"Down with the Army!"

This was the signal for a terrible struggle. The combatants fell in thousands, and their bodies formed howling and moving mounds on top of which fresh champions gripped each other by the throats. Women, eager, pale, and dishevelled, with clenched teeth and frantic nails, rushed on the man, in transports that, in the brilliant light of the public square, gave to their faces expressions unsurpassed even in the shade of curtains and in the hollows of pillows. They were going to seize Colomban, to bite him, to strangle, dismember and rend him, when Maniflore, tall and dignified in her red tunic, stood forth, serene and terrible, confronting these furies who recoiled from before her in terror. Colomban seemed to be saved; his partisans succeeded in clearing a passage for him through the Place du Palais and in putting him into a cab stationed at the corner of the Pont-Vieux. The horse was already in full trot when Prince des Boscénos, Count Cléna, and M. de La Trumelle knocked the driver off his seat. Then, making the animal back and pushing the spokes of the wheels, they ran the vehicle on to the parapet of the bridge, whence they overturned it into the river amid the cheers of the delirious crowd. With a resounding splash a jet of water rose upwards,

and then nothing but a slight eddy was to be seen on the surface of
the stream.

Almost immediately comrades Dagobert and Varambille, with the
help of the seven hundred disguised Pyrotists, sent Prince des
Boscénos head foremost into a river-laundry in which he was la-
mentably swallowed up.

Serene night descended over the Place du Palais and shed silence
and peace upon the frightful ruins with which it was strewed. In
the meantime, Colomban, three hundred yards down the stream,
cowering beside a lame old horse on a bridge, was meditating on
the ignorance and injustice of crowds.

"The business," said he to himself, "is even more troublesome
than I believed. I foresee fresh difficulties."

He got up and approached the unhappy animal.

"What have you, poor friend, done to them?" said he. "It is on
my account they have used you so cruelly."

He embraced the unfortunate beast and kissed the white star on
his forehead. Then he took him by the bridle and led him, both of
them limping, through the sleeping city to his house, where sleep
soon allowed them to forget mankind.

IX

FATHER DOUILLARD

N their minute gentleness and at the suggestion of
the common father of the faithful, the bishops,
canons, vicars, curates, abbots, and friars of Penguinia resolved to hold a solemn service in the
cathedral of Alca, and to pray that Divine mercy
would deign to put an end to the troubles that distracted one of the noblest countries in Christendom, and grant to repentant Penguinia pardon for
its crimes against God and against ministers of religion.

The ceremony took place on the fifteenth of June. General Caraguel, surrounded by his staff, occupied the churchwarden's pew.
The congregation was numerous and brilliant. According to M.
Bigourd's expression it was both crowded and select. In the front
rank was to be seen M. de la Bertheoseille, Chamberlain to his
Highness Prince Crucho. Near the pulpit, which was to be ascended
by the Reverend Father Douillard, of the Order of St. Francis, were
gathered, in an attitude of attention with their hands crossed upon
their wands of office, the great dignitaries of the Anti-Pyrotist association, Viscount Olive, M. de La Trumelle, Count Cléna, the Duke
d'Ampoule, and Prince des Boscénos. Father Agaric was in the apse

with the teachers and pupils of St. Maël College. The right-hand transept and aisle were reserved for officers and soldiers in uniform, this side being thought the more honourable, since the Lord leaned his head to the right when he died on the Cross. The ladies of the aristocracy, and among them Countess Cléna, Viscountess Olive, and Princess des Boscénos, occupied reserved seats. In the immense building and in the square outside were gathered twenty thousand clergy of all sorts, as well as thirty thousand of the laity.

After the expiatory and propitiatory ceremony the Reverend Father Douillard ascended the pulpit. The sermon had at first been entrusted to the Reverend Father Agaric, but, in spite of his merits, he was thought unequal to the occasion in zeal and doctrine, and the eloquent Capuchin friar, who for six months had gone through the barracks preaching against the enemies of God and authority, had been chosen in his place.

The Reverend Father Douillard, taking as his text, "He hath put down the mighty from their seat," established that all temporal power has God as its principle and its end, and that it is ruined and destroyed when it turns aside from the path that Providence has traced out for it and from the end to which He has directed it.

Applying these sacred rules to the government of Penguinia, he drew a terrible picture of the evils that the country's rulers had been unable either to prevent or to foresee.

"The first author of all these miseries and degradations, my brethren," said he, "is only too well known to you. He is a monster whose destiny is providentially proclaimed by his name, for it is derived from the Greek word, *pyros,* which means fire. Eternal wisdom warns us by this etymology that a Jew was to set ablaze the country that had welcomed him."

He depicted the country, persecuted by the persecutors of the Church, and crying in its agony:

"O woe! O glory! Those who have crucified my God are crucifying me!"

At these words a prolonged shudder passed through the assembly.

The powerful orator excited still greater indignation when he described the proud and crime-stained Colomban, plunged into the stream, all the waters of which could not cleanse him. He gathered up all the humiliations and all the perils of the Penguins in order to reproach the President of the Republic and his Prime Minister with them.

"That Minister," said he, "having been guilty of degrading cowardice in not exterminating the seven hundred Pyrotists with their allies and defenders, as Saul exterminated the Philistines at Gibeah, has rendered himself unworthy of exercising the power that God delegated to him, and every good citizen ought henceforth to insult his contemptible government. Heaven will look favourably on those who despise him. 'He hath put down the mighty from their seat.'

God will depose these pusillanimous chiefs and will put in their place strong men who will call upon Him. I tell you, gentlemen, I tell you officers, non-commissioned officers, and soldiers who listen to me, I tell you General of the Penguin armies, the hour has come! If you do not obey God's orders, if in His name you do not depose those now in authority, if you do not establish a religious and strong government in Penguinia, God will none the less destroy what He has condemned, He will none the less save His people. He will save them, but, if you are wanting, He will do so by means of a humble artisan or a simple corporal. Hasten! The hour will soon be past."

Excited by this ardent exhortation, the sixty thousand people present rose up trembling and shouting: "To arms! To arms! Death to the Pyrotists! Hurrah for Crucho!" and all of them, monks, women, soldiers, noblemen, citizens, and loafers, who were gathered beneath the superhuman arm uplifted in the pulpit, struck up the hymn, "Let us save Penguinia!" They rushed impetuously from the basilica and marched along the quays to the Chamber of Deputies.

Left alone in the deserted nave, the wise Cornemuse, lifting his arms to heaven, murmured in broken accents:

"Agnosco fortunam ecclesiæ penguicanæ! I see but too well whither this will lead us."

The attack which the crowd made upon the legislative palace was repulsed. Vigorously charged by the police and Alcan guards, the assailants were already fleeing in disorder, when the Socialists, running from the slums and led by comrades Phœnix, Dagobert, Lapersonne, and Varambille, threw themselves upon them and completed their discomfiture. MM. de La Trumelle and d'Ampoule were taken to the police station. Prince des Boscénos, after a valiant struggle, fell upon the bloody pavement with a fractured skull.

In the enthusiasm of victory, the comrades, mingled with an innumerable crowd of paper-sellers and gutter-merchants, ran through the boulevards all night, carrying Maniflore in triumph, and breaking the mirrors of the cafés and the glasses of the street lamps amid cries of "Down with Crucho! Hurrah for the Social Revolution!" The Anti-Pyrotists in their turn upset the newspaper kiosks and tore down the hoardings.

These were spectacles of which cool reason cannot approve and they were fit causes for grief to the municipal authorities, who desired to preserve the good order of the roads and streets. But what was sadder for a man of heart was the sight of the canting humbugs, who, from fear of blows, kept at an equal distance from the two camps, and who, although they allowed their selfishness and cowardice to be visible, claimed admiration for the generosity of their sentiments and the nobility of their souls. They rubbed their eyes with onions, gaped like whitings, blew violently into their handkerchiefs, and, bringing their voices out of the depth of their stomachs, groaned forth: "O Penguins, cease these fratricidal struggles; cease to rend your mother's bosom!" As if men could live in society without disputes and without quarrels, and as if civil discords were not the necessary conditions of national life and progress. They showed themselves hypocritical cowards by proposing a compromise between the just and the unjust, offending the just in his rectitude and the unjust in his courage. One of these creatures, the rich and powerful Machimel, a champion coward, rose upon the town like a colossus of grief; his tears formed poisonous lakes at his feet and his sighs capsized the boats of the fishermen.

During these stormy nights Bidault-Coquille at the top of his old steam-engine, under the serene sky, boasted in his heart, while the shooting stars registered themselves upon his photographic plates. He was fighting for justice. He loved and was loved with a sublime passion. Insult and calumny raised him to the clouds. A caricature of him in company with those of Colomban, Kerdanic, and Colonel Hastaing was to be seen in the newspaper kiosks. The Anti-Pyrotists proclaimed that he had received fifty thousand francs from the big Jewish financiers. The reporters of the militarist sheets held interviews regarding his scientific knowledge with official scholars, who declared he had no knowledge of the stars, disputed his most solid observations, denied his most certain discoveries, and condemned his most ingenious and most fruitful hypotheses. He exulted under these flattering blows of hatred and envy.

He contemplated the black immensity pierced by a multitude of lights, without giving a thought to all the heavy slumbers, cruel insomnias, vain dreams, spoilt pleasures, and infinitely diverse miseries that a great city contains.

"It is in this enormous city," said he to himself, "that the just and the unjust are joining battle."

And substituting a simple and magnificent poetry for the multiple and vulgar reality, he represented to himself the Pyrot affair as a struggle between good and bad angels. He awaited the eternal triumph of the Sons of Light and congratulated himself on being a Child of the Day confounding the Children of Night.

X

MR. JUSTICE CHAUSSEPIED

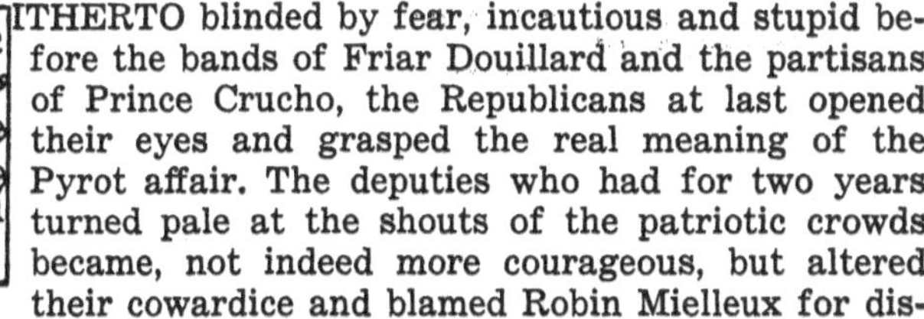ITHERTO blinded by fear, incautious and stupid before the bands of Friar Douillard and the partisans of Prince Crucho, the Republicans at last opened their eyes and grasped the real meaning of the Pyrot affair. The deputies who had for two years turned pale at the shouts of the patriotic crowds became, not indeed more courageous, but altered their cowardice and blamed Robin Mielleux for disorders which their own compliance had encouraged, and the instigators of which they had several times slavishly congratulated. They reproached him for having imperilled the Republic by a weakness which was really theirs and a timidity which they themselves had imposed upon him. Some of them began to doubt whether it was not to their interest to believe in Pyrot's innocence rather than in his guilt, and thenceforward they felt a bitter anguish at the thought that the unhappy man might have been wrongly convicted and that in his aerial cage he might be expiating another man's crimes. "I cannot sleep on account of it!" was what several members of Minister Guillaumette's majority used to say. But these were ambitious to replace their chief.

These generous legislators overthrew the cabinet, and the President of the Republic put in Robin Mielleux's place, a patriarchal Republican with a flowing beard, La Trinité by name, who, like most of the Penguins, understood nothing about the affair, but thought that too many monks were mixed up in it.

General Greatauk, before leaving the Ministry of War, gave his final advice to Panther, the Chief of the Staff.

"I go and you remain," said he, as he shook hands with him. "The Pyrot affair is my daughter; I confide her to you, she is worthy of your love and your care; she is beautiful. Do not forget that her beauty loves the shade, is pleased with mystery, and likes to remain veiled. Treat her modesty with gentleness. Too many indiscreet looks have already profaned her charms. . . . Panther, you desired proofs and you obtained them. You have many, perhaps too many, in your possession. I see that there will be many tiresome interventions and much dangerous curiosity. If I were in your place I would tear up all those documents. Believe me, the best of proofs is none at all. That is the only one which nobody discusses."

Alas! General Panther did not realise the wisdom of this advice. The future was only too thoroughly to justify Greatauk's perspicacity. La Trinité demanded the documents belonging to the Pyrot affair. Péniche, his Minister of War, refused them in the superior interests of the national defence, telling him that the documents under General Panther's care formed the hugest mass of archives in the world. La Trinité studied the case as well as he could, and, without penetrating to the bottom of the matter, suspected it of irregularity. Conformably to his rights and prerogatives he then ordered a fresh trial to be held. Immediately, Péniche, his Minister of War, accused him of insulting the army and betraying the country, and flung his portfolio at his head. He was replaced by a second, who did the same. To him succeeded a third, who imitated these examples, and those after him to the number of seventy acted like their predecessors, until the venerable La Trinité groaned beneath the weight of bellicose portfolios. The seventy-first Minister of War, van Julep, retained office. Not that he was in disagreement with so many and such noble colleagues, but he had been commissioned by them generously to betray his Prime Minister, to cover him with shame and opprobrium, and to convert the new trial to the glory of Greatauk, the satisfaction of the Anti-Pyrotists, the profit of the monks, and the restoration of Prince Crucho.

General van Julep, though endowed with high military virtues, was not intelligent enough to employ the subtle conduct and exquisite methods of Greatauk. He thought, like General Panther, that tangible proofs against Pyrot were necessary, that they could never have too many of them, that they could never have even enough. He expressed these sentiments to his Chief of Staff, who was only too inclined to agree with them.

"Panther," said he, "we are at the moment when we need abundant and superabundant proofs."

"You have said enough, General," answered Panther, "I will complete my piles of documents."

Six months later the proofs against Pyrot filled two stories of the Ministry of War. The ceiling fell in beneath the weight of the bundles, and the avalanche of falling documents crushed two head clerks, fourteen second clerks, and sixty copying clerks, who were at work upon the ground floor arranging a change in the fashion of the cavalry gaiters. The walls of the huge edifice had to be propped. Passers by saw with amazement enormous beams and monstrous stanchions which reared themselves obliquely against the noble front of the building now tottering and disjointed, and blocked up the streets, stopped the carriages, and presented to the motor-omnibuses an obstacle against which they dashed with their loads of passengers.

The judges who had condemned Pyrot were not, properly speaking, judges but soldiers. The judges who had condemned Colomban were real judges, but of inferior rank, wearing seedy black clothes like church vergers, unlucky wretches of judges, miserable judgelings. Above them were the superior judges who wore ermine robes over their black gowns. These, renowned for their knowledge and doctrine, formed a court whose terrible name expressed power. It was called the Court of Appeal (Cassation) so as to make it clear that it was the hammer suspended over the judgments and decrees of all other jurisdictions.

One of these superior red judges of the Supreme Court, called Chaussepied, led a modest and tranquil life in a suburb of Alca. His soul was pure, his heart honest, his spirit just. When he had finished studying his documents he used to play the violin and cultivate hyacinths. Every Sunday he dined with his neighbours the Mesdemoiselles Helbivore. His old age was cheerful and robust and his friends often praised the amenity of his character.

For some months, however, he had been irritable and touchy, and when he opened a newspaper his broad and ruddy face would become covered with dolorous wrinkles and darkened with an angry purple. Pyrot was the cause of it. Justice Chaussepied could not understand how an officer could have committed so black a crime as to hand over eighty thousand trusses of military hay to a neighbouring and hostile Power. And he could still less conceive how a scoundrel should have found official defenders in Penguinia. The thought that there existed in his country a Pyrot, a Colonel Hastaing, a Colomban, a Kerdanic, a Phœnix, spoilt his hyacinths, his violin, his heaven, and his earth, all nature, and even his dinner with the Mesdemoiselles Helbivore!

In the meantime the Pyrot case, having been presented to the Supreme Court by the Keeper of the Seals, it fell to Chaussepied to examine it and discover its defects, in case any existed. Although as upright and honest as a man can be, and trained by long habit to exercise his magistracy without fear or favour, he expected to find in the documents to be submitted to him proofs of certain guilt and of obvious criminality. After lengthened difficulties and repeated refusals on the part of General van Julep, Justice Chaussepied was allowed to examine the documents. Numbered and initialed they ran to the number of fourteen millions six hundred and twenty-six thousand three hundred and twelve. As he studied them the judge was at first surprised, then astonished, then stupefied, amazed, and, if I dare say so, flabbergasted. He found among the documents prospectuses of new fancy shops, newspapers, fashion-plates, paper bags, old business letters, exercise books, brown paper, green paper for rubbing parquet floors, playing cards, diagrams, six thousand copies of the "Key to Dreams," but not a single document in which any mention was made of Pyrot.

XI

CONCLUSION

HE appeal was allowed, and Pyrot was brought down from his cage. But the Anti-Pyrotists did not regard themselves as beaten. The military judges retried Pyrot. Greatauk, in this second affair, surpassed himself. He obtained a second conviction; he obtained it by declaring that the proofs communicated to the Supreme Court were worth nothing, and that great care had been taken to keep back the good ones, since they ought to remain secret. In the opinion of connoisseurs he had never shown so much address. On leaving the court, as he passed through the vestibule with a tranquil step, and his hands behind his back, amidst a crowd of sight-seers, a woman dressed in red and with her face covered by a black veil rushed at him, brandishing a kitchen knife.

"Die, scoundrel!" she cried. It was Maniflore. Before those present could understand what was happening, the general seized her by the wrist, and with apparent gentleness, squeezed it so forcibly that the knife fell from her aching hand.

Then he picked it up and handed it to Maniflore.

"Madam," said he with a bow, "you have dropped a household utensil."

He could not prevent the heroine from being taken to the police-station; but he had her immediately released and afterwards he employed all his influence to stop the prosecution.

The second conviction of Pyrot was Greatauk's last victory.

Justice Chaussepied, who had formerly liked soldiers so much, and esteemed their justice so highly, being now enraged with the military judges, squashed their judgments as a monkey cracks nuts. He rehabilitated Pyrot a second time; he would, if necessary, have rehabilitated him five hundred times.

Furious at having been cowards and at having allowed themselves to be deceived and made game of, the Republicans turned against the monks and clergy. The deputies passed laws of expulsion, separation, and spoliation against them. What Father Cornemuse had forseen took place. That good monk was driven from the Wood of Conils. Treasury officers confiscated his retorts and his stills, and the liquidators divided amongst them his bottles of St. Orberosian liqueur. The pious distiller lost the annual income of three million five hundred thousand francs that his products procured for him. Father Agaric went into exile, abandoning his school into the hands of laymen, who soon allowed it to fall into decay.

Separated from its foster-mother, the State, the Church of Penguinia withered like a plucked flower.

The victorious defenders of the innocent man now abused each other and overwhelmed each other reciprocally with insults and calumnies. The vehement Kerdanic hurled himself upon Phœnix as if ready to devour him. The wealthy Jews and the seven hundred Pyrotists turned away with disdain from the socialist comrades whose aid they had humbly implored in the past.

"We know you no longer," said they. "To the devil with you and your social justice. Social justice is the defence of property."

Having been elected a Deputy and chosen to be the leader of the new majority, comrade Larrivée was appointed by the Chamber and public opinion to the Premiership. He showed himself an energetic defender of the military tribunals that had condemned Pyrot. When his former socialist comrades claimed a little more justice and liberty for the employés of the State as well as for manual workers, he opposed their proposals in an eloquent speech.

"Liberty," said he, "is not licence. Between order and disorder my choice is made: revolution is impotence. Progress has no more formidable enemy than violence. Gentlemen, those who, as I am, are anxious for reform, ought to apply themselves before everything else to cure this agitation which enfeebles government just as fever exhausts those who are ill. It is time to reassure honest people."

This speech was received with applause. The government of the Republic remained in subjection to the great financial companies, the army was exclusively devoted to the defence of capital, while the fleet was designed solely to procure fresh orders for the mineowners. Since the rich refused to pay their just share of the taxes, the poor, as in the past, paid for them.

In the meantime from the height of his old steam-engine, beneath the crowded stars of night, Bidault-Coquille gazed sadly at the sleeping city. Maniflore had left him. Consumed with a desire for fresh devotions and fresh sacrifices, she had gone in company with a young Bulgarian to bear justice and vengeance to Sofia. He did not regret her, having perceived, after the Affair, that she was less beautiful in form and in thought than he had at first imagined. His impressions had been modified in the same direction concerning many other forms and many other thoughts. And what was cruelest of all to him, he regarded himself as not so great, not so splendid, as he had believed.

And he reflected:

"You considered yourself sublime when you had but candour and good-will. Of what were you proud, Bidault-Coquille? Of having been one of the first to know that Pyrot was innocent and Greatauk a scoundrel. But three-fourths of those who defended Greatauk against the attacks of the seven hundred Pyrotists knew that better than you. Of what then did you show yourself so proud? Of having dared to say what you thought? That is civic courage, and, like military courage, it is a mere result of imprudence. You have been imprudent. So far so good, but that is no reason for praising yourself beyond measure. Your imprudence was trifling; it exposed you to trifling perils; you did not risk your head by it. The Penguins have lost that cruel and sanguinary pride which formerly gave a tragic grandeur to their revolutions; it is the fatal result of the weakening of beliefs and characters. Ought one to look upon oneself as a superior spirit for having shown a little more clearsightedness than the vulgar? I am very much afraid, on the contrary, Bidault-Coquille, that you have given proof of a gross misunderstanding of the conditions of the moral and intellectual development of a people. You imagined that social injustices were threaded together like pearls and that it would be enough to pull off one in order to unfasten the whole necklace. That is a very ingenuous conception. You flattered yourself that at one stroke you were establishing justice in your own country and in the universe. You were a brave man, an honest idealist, though without much experimental philosophy. But go home to your own heart and you will recognise that you had in you a spice of malice and that your ingenuousness was not without cunning. You believed you were performing a fine moral action. You said to yourself: 'Here am I, just and courageous once for all. I can henceforth repose in the public esteem and the praise of historians.' And now that you have lost your illusions, now that you know how hard it is to redress wrongs, and that the task must ever be begun afresh, you are going back to your asteroids. You are right; but go back to them with modesty, Bidault-Coquille!"

BOOK VII: MODERN TIMES

"Only extreme things are tolerable."
Count Robert de Montesquiou.

I

MADAME CLARENCE'S DRAWING-ROOM

ADAME CLARENCE the widow of an exalted functionary of the Republic, loved to entertain. Every Thursday she collected together some friends of modest condition who took pleasure in conversation. The ladies who went to see her, very different in age and rank, were all without money and had all suffered much. There was a duchess who looked like a fortune-teller and a fortune-teller who looked like a duchess. Madame Clarence was pretty enough to maintain some old *liaisons,* but not to form new ones, and she generally inspired a quiet esteem. She had a very pretty daughter, who, since she had no dower, caused some alarm among the male guests; for the Penguins were as much afraid of portionless girls as they were of the devil himself. Eveline Clarence, noticing their reserve and perceiving its cause, used to hand them their tea with an air of disdain. Moreover, she seldom appeared at the parties and talked only to the ladies or the very young people. Her discreet and retiring presence put no restraint upon the conversation, since those who took part in it thought either that as she was a young girl she would not understand it, or that, being twenty-five years old, she might listen to everything.

One Thursday therefore, in Madame Clarence's drawing-room, the conversation turned upon love. The ladies spoke of it with pride, delicacy, and mystery, the men with discretion and fatuity; everyone took an interest in the conversation, for each one was interested in what he or she said. A great deal of wit flowed; brilliant apostrophes were launched forth and keen repartees were returned. But when Professor Haddock began to speak he overwhelmed everybody.

"It is the same with our ideas on love as with our ideas on everything else," said he, "they rest upon anterior habits whose very memory has been effaced. In morals, the limitations that have lost their grounds for existing, the most useless obligations, the cruelest and most injurious restraints, are because of their profound antiquity and the mystery of their origin, the least disputed and the least disputable as well as the most respected, and they are those that cannot be violated without incurring the most severe blame. All morality relative to the relations of the sexes is founded on this principle: that a woman once obtained belongs to the man, that she is his property like his horse or his weapons. And this having ceased to be true, absurdities result from it, such as the marriage or contract of sale of a woman to a man, with clauses restricting the right of ownership introduced as a consequence of the gradual diminution of the claims of the possessor.

"The obligation imposed on a girl that she should bring her virginity to her husband comes from the times when girls were married immediately they were of a marriageable age. It is ridiculous that a girl who marries at twenty-five or thirty should be subject to that obligation. You will, perhaps, say that it is a present with which her husband, if she gets one at last, will be gratified; but every moment we see men wooing married women and showing themselves perfectly satisfied to take them as they find them.

"Still, even in our own day, the duty of girls is determined in religious morality by the old belief that God, the most powerful of warriors, is polygamous, that he has reserved all maidens for himself, and that men can only take those whom he has left. This belief, although traces of it exist in several metaphors of mysticism, is abandoned to-day by most civilised peoples. However, it still dominates the education of girls not only among our believers, but even among our free-thinkers, who, as a rule, think freely for the reason that they do not think at all.

"Discretion means ability to separate and discern. We say that a girl is discreet when she knows nothing at all. We cultivate her ignorance. In spite of all our care the most discreet know something, for we cannot conceal from them their own nature and their own sensations. But they know badly, they know in a wrong way. That is all we obtain by our careful education. . . ."

"Sir," suddenly said Joseph Boutourlé, the High Treasurer of Alca, "believe me, there are innocent girls, perfectly innocent girls, and it is a great pity. I have known three. They married, and the result was tragical."

"I have noticed," Professor Haddock went on, "that Europeans in general and Penguins in particular occupy themselves, after sport and motoring, with nothing so much as with love. It is giving a great deal of importance to a matter that has very little weight."

"Then, Professor," exclaimed Madame Crémeur in a choking voice, "when a woman has completely surrendered herself to you, you think it is a matter of no importance?"

"No, Madam; it can have its importance," answered Professor Haddock, "but it is necessary to examine if when she surrenders herself to us she offers us a delicious fruit-garden or a plot of thistles and dandelions. And then, do we not misuse words? In love, a woman lends herself rather than gives herself. Look at the pretty Madame Pensée. . . ."

"She is my mother," said a tall, fair young man.

"Sir, I have the greatest respect for her," replied Professor Haddock; "do not be afraid that I intend to say anything in the least offensive about her. But allow me to tell you that, as a rule, the opinions of sons about their mothers are not to be relied on. They do not bear enough in mind that a mother is a mother only because she loved, and that she can still love. That, however, is the case, and it would be deplorable were it otherwise. I have noticed, on the contrary, that daughters do not deceive themselves about their mothers' faculty for loving or about the use they make of it; they are rivals; they have their eyes upon them."

The insupportable Professor spoke a great deal longer, adding indecorum to awkwardness, and impertinence to incivility, accumulating incongruities, despising what is respectable, respecting what is despicable; but no one listened to him further.

During this time in a room that was simple without grace, a room sad for the want of love, a room which, like all young girls' rooms, had something of the cold atmosphere of a place of waiting about it, Eveline Clarence turned over the pages of club annuals and prospectuses of charities in order to obtain from them some acquaintance with society. Being convinced that her mother, shut up in her own intellectual but poor world, could neither bring her out nor push her into prominence, she decided that she herself would seek the best means of winning a husband. At once calm and obstinate, without dreams or illusions, and regarding marriage as but a ticket of admission or a passport, she kept before her mind a clear notion of the hazards, difficulties, and chances of her enterprise. She had the art of pleasing and a coldness of temperament that enabled her to turn it to its fullest advantage. Her weakness lay in the fact that she was dazzled by anything that had an aristocratic air.

When she was alone with her mother she said: "Mamma, we will go to-morrow to Father Douillard's retreat."

II

THE CHARITY OF ST. ORBEROSIA

VERY Friday evening at nine o'clock the choicest of Alcan society assembled in the aristocratic church of St. Maël for the Reverend Father Douillard's retreat. Prince and Princess des Boscénos, Viscount and Viscountess Olive, M. and Madame Bigourd, Monsieur and Madame de La Trumelle were never absent. The flower of the aristocracy might be seen there, and fair Jewish baronesses also adorned it by their presence, for the Jewish baronesses of Alca were Christians.

This retreat, like all religious retreats, had for its object to procure for those living in the world opportunities for recollection so that they might think of their eternal salvation. It was also intended to draw down upon so many noble and illustrious families the benediction of St. Orberosia, who loves the Penguins. The Reverend Father Douillard strove for the completion of his task with a truly apostolical zeal. He hoped to restore the prerogatives of St. Orberosia as the patron saint of Penguinia and to dedicate to her a monumental church on one of the hills that dominate the city. His efforts had been crowned with great success, and for the accomplishing of this national enterprise he had already united more than a hundred thousand adherents and collected more than twenty millions of francs.

It was in the choir of St. Maël's that St. Orberosia's new shrine, shining with gold, sparkling with precious stones, and surrounded by tapers and flowers, had been erected.

The following account may be read in the "History of the Miracles of the Patron Saint of Alca" by the Abbé Plantain:

"The ancient shrine had been melted down during the Terror and the precious relics of the saint thrown into a fire that had been lit on the Place de Grève; but a poor woman of great piety, named Rouquin, went by night at the peril of her life to gather up the calcined bones and the ashes of the blessed saint. She preserved them in a jam-pot, and when religion was again restored, brought them to the venerable Curé of St. Maël's. The woman ended her days piously as a vendor of tapers and custodian of seats in the saint's chapel."

It is certain that in the time of Father Douillard, although faith was declining, the cult of St. Orberosia, which for three hundred years had fallen under the criticism of Canon Princeteau and the silence of the Doctors of the Church, recovered, and was surrounded with more pomp, more splendour, and more fervour than ever. The theologians did not now subtract a single iota from the legend. They held as certainly established all facts related by Abbot Simplicissimus, and in particular declared, on the testimony of that monk, that the devil, assuming a monk's form had carried off the saint to a cave and had there striven with her until she overcame him. Neither places nor dates caused them any embarrassment. They paid no heed to exegesis and took good care not to grant as much to science as Canon Princeteau had formerly conceded. They knew too well whither that would lead.

The church shone with lights and flowers. An operatic tenor sang the famous canticle of St. Orberosia

> Virgin of Paradise
> Come, come in the dusky night
> And on us shed
> Thy beams of light.

Mademoiselle Clarence sat beside her mother and in front of Viscount Cléna. She remained kneeling during a considerable time, for the attitude of prayer is natural to discreet virgins and it shows off their figures.

The Reverend Father Douillard ascended the pulpit. He was a powerful orator and could, at once melt, surprise, and rouse his hearers. Women complained only that he fulminated against vice with excessive harshness and in crude terms that made them blush. But they liked him none the less for it.

He treated in his sermon of the seventh trial of St. Orberosia, who was tempted by the dragon which she went forth to combat. But she did not yield, and she disarmed the monster.

The orator demonstrated without difficulty that we, also, by the aid of St. Orberosia, and strong in the virtue which she inspires, can in our turn overthrow the dragons that dart upon us and are waiting to devour us, the dragon of doubt, the dragon of impiety, the dragon of forgetfulness of religious duties. He proved that the charity of St. Orberosia was a work of social regeneration, and he concluded by an ardent appeal to the faithful "to become instruments of the Divine mercy, eager upholders and supporters of the charity of St. Orberosia, and to furnish it with all the means which it required to take its flight and bear its salutary fruits."*

After the ceremony, the Reverend Father Douillard remained in the sacristy at the disposal of those of the faithful who desired information concerning the charity, or who wished to bring their contributions. Mademoiselle Clarence wished to speak to Father Douillard, so did Viscount Cléna. The crowd was large, and a queue was formed. By chance Viscount Cléna and Mademoiselle Clarence were side by side and possibly they were squeezed a little closely to each other by the crowd. Eveline had noticed this fashionable

*Cf. J. Ernest Charles in the "Censeur," May–August, 1907, p. 562, col. 2.

young man, who was almost as well known as his father in the world of sport. Cléna had noticed her, and, as he thought her pretty, he bowed to her, then apologized and pretended to believe that he had been introduced to the ladies, but could not remember where. They pretended to believe it also.

He presented himself the following week at Madame Clarence's, thinking that her house was a bit fast—a thing not likely to displease him—and when he saw Eveline again he felt he had not been mistaken and that she was an extremely pretty girl.

Viscount Cléna had the finest motor-car in Europe. For three months he drove the Clarences every day over hills and plains, through woods and valleys; they visited famous sites and went over celebrated castles. He said to Eveline all that could be said and did all that could be done to overcome her resistance. She did not conceal from him that she loved him, that she would always love him,

and love no one but him. She remained grave and trembling by his side. To his devouring passion she opposed the invincible defence of a virtue conscious of its danger. At the end of three months, after having gone uphill and down hill, turned sharp corners and negotiated level crossings, and experienced innumerable breakdowns, he knew her as well as he knew the fly-wheel of his car, but not much better. He employed surprises, adventures, sudden stoppages in the depths of forests and before hotels, but he had advanced no farther. He said to himself that it was absurd; then, taking her again in his car he set off at fifty miles an hour quite prepared to upset her in a ditch or to smash himself and her against a tree.

One day, having come to take her on some excursion, he found her more charming than ever, and more provoking. He darted upon her as a storm falls upon the reeds that border a lake. She bent with adorable weakness beneath the breath of the storm and twenty times was almost carried away by its strength, but twenty times she arose, supple and bowing to the wind. After all these shocks one would have said that a light breeze had barely touched her charming stem; she smiled as if ready to be plucked by a bold hand. Then her unhappy aggressor, desperate, enraged, and three parts mad, fled so as not to kill her, mistook the door, went into the bedroom of Madame Clarence, whom he found putting on her hat in front of a wardrobe, seized her, flung her on the bed, and possessed her before she knew what had happened.

The same day Eveline, who had been making inquiries, learned that Viscount Cléna had nothing but debts, lived on money given him by an elderly lady, and promoted the sale of the latest models of a motor-car manufacturer. They separated with common accord and Eveline began again disdainfully to serve tea to her mother's guests.

III

HIPPOLYTE CÉRÈS

N Madame Clarence's drawing-room the conversation turned upon love, and many charming things were said about it.

"Love is a sacrifice," sighed Madame Crémeur.

"I agree with you," replied M. Boutourlé with animation.

But Professor Haddock soon displayed his fastidious insolence.

"It seems to me," said he, "that the Penguin ladies have made a great fuss since, through St. Maël's agency, they became viviparous.

But there is nothing to be particularly proud of in that, for it is a state they share in common with cows and pigs, and even with orange and lemon trees, for the seeds of these plants germinate in the pericarp."

"The self-importance which the Penguin ladies give themselves does not go so far back as that," answered M. Boutourlé. "It dates from the day when the holy apostle gave them clothes. But this self-importance was long kept in restraint, and displayed itself fully only with increased luxury of dress and in a small section of society. For go only two leagues from Alca into the country at harvest time, and you will see whether women are over-precise or self-important."

On that day M. Hippolyte Cérès paid his first call. He was a deputy of Alca, and one of the youngest members of the House. His father was said to have kept a dram shop, but he himself was a lawyer of robust physique, a good though prolix speaker, with a self-important air and a reputation for ability.

"M. Cérès," said the mistress of the house, "your constituency is one of the finest in Alca."

"And there are fresh improvements made in it every day, Madame."

"Unfortunately, it is impossible to take a stroll through it any longer," said M. Boutourlé.

"Why?" asked M. Cérès.

"On account of the motors, of course."

"Do not give them a bad name," answered the Deputy. "They are our great national industry."

"I know. The Penguins of to-day make me think of the ancient Egyptians. According to Clement of Alexandria, Taine tells us—though he misquotes the text—the Egyptians worshipped the crocodiles that devoured them. The Penguins to-day worship the motors that crush them. Without a doubt the future belongs to the metal beast. We are no more likely to go back to cabs than we are to go back to the diligence. And the long martyrdom of the horse will come to an end. The motor, which the frenzied cupidity of manufacturers hurls like a Juggernaut's car upon the bewildered people and of which the idle and fashionable make a foolish though fatal elegance, will soon begin to perform its true function, and putting its strength at the service of the entire people, will behave like a docile, toiling monster. But in order that the motor may cease to be injurious and become beneficent we must build roads suited to its speed, roads which it cannot tear up with its ferocious tyres, and from which it will send no clouds of poisonous dust into human lungs. We ought not to allow slower vehicles or mere animals to go upon those roads, and we should establish garages upon them and foot-bridges over them, and so create order and harmony among the means of communication of the future. That is the wish of every good citizen."

Madame Clarence led the conversation back to the improvements in M. Cérès' constituency. M. Cérès showed his enthusiasm for demolitions, tunnelings, constructions, reconstructions, and all other fruitful operations.

"We build to-day in an admirable style," said he; "everywhere majestic avenues are being reared. Was ever anything as fine as our arcaded bridges and our domed hotels!"

"You are forgetting that big palace surmounted by an immense melon-shaped dome," grumbled M. Daniset, an old art amateur, in a voice of restrained rage. "I am amazed at the degree of ugliness which a modern city can attain. Alca is becoming Americanised. Everywhere we are destroying all that is free, unexpected, measured, restrained, human, or traditional among the things that are left us. Everywhere we are destroying that charming object, a piece of an old wall that bears up the branches of a tree. Everywhere we are suppressing some fragment of light and air, some fragment of nature, some fragment of the associations that still remain with us, some fragment of our fathers, some fragment of ourselves. And we are putting up frightful, enormous, infamous houses, surmounted in Viennese style by ridiculous domes, or fashioned after the models of the 'new art' without mouldings, or having profiles with sinister corbels and burlesque pinnacles, and such monsters as these shamelessly peer over the surrounding buildings. We see bulbous protuberances stuck on the fronts of buildings and we are told they are 'new art' motives. I have seen the 'new art' in other countries, but it is not so ugly as with us; it has fancy and it has simplicity. It is only in our own country that by a sad privilege we may behold the newest and most diverse styles of architectural ugliness. What an enviable privilege!"

"Are you not afraid," asked M. Cérès severely, "are you not afraid that these bitter criticisms tend to keep out of our capital the foreigners who flow into it from all parts of the world and who leave millions behind them?"

"You may set your mind at rest about that," answered M. Daniset. "Foreigners do not come to admire our buildings; they come to see our courtesans, our dressmakers, and our dancing saloons."

"We have one bad habit," sighed M. Cérès, "it is that we calumniate ourselves."

Madame Clarence as an accomplished hostess thought it was time to return to the subject of love and asked M. Jumel his opinion of M. Léon Blum's recent book in which the author complained. . . .

". . . That an irrational custom," went on Professor Haddock, "prevents respectable young ladies from making love, a thing they would enjoy doing, whilst mercenary girls do it too much and without getting any enjoyment out of it. It is indeed deplorable. But M. Léon Blum need not fret too much. If the evil exists, as he says it does, in our middle-class society, I can assure him that everywhere else he would see a consoling spectacle. Among the people, the mass of the people through town and country, girls do not deny themselves that pleasure."

"It is depravity!" said Madame Crémeur.

And she praised the innocence of young girls in terms full of modesty and grace. It was charming to hear her.

Professor Haddock's views on the same subject were, on the contrary, painful to listen to.

"Respectable young girls," said he, "are guarded and watched over. Besides, men do not, as a rule, pursue them much, either through probity, or from a fear of grave responsibilities, or because the seduction of a young girl would not be to their credit. Even then we do not know what really takes place, for the reason that what is hidden is not seen. This is a condition necessary to the existence of all society. The scruples of respectable young girls could be more easily overcome than those of married women if the same pressure were brought to bear on them, and for this there are two reasons: they have more illusions, and their curiosity has not been satisfied. Women, for the most part, have been so disappointed by their husbands that they have not courage enough to begin again with somebody else. I myself have been met by this obstacle several times in my attempts at seduction."

At the moment when Professor Haddock ended his unpleasant remarks, Mademoiselle Eveline Clarence entered the drawing-room and listlessly handed about tea with that expression of boredom which gave an oriental charm to her beauty.

"For my part," said Hippolyte Cérès, looking at her, "I declare myself the young ladies' champion."

"He must be a fool," thought the girl.

Hippolyte Cérès, who had never set foot outside of his political world of electors and elected, thought Madame Clarence's drawing-room most select, its mistress exquisite, and her daughter amazingly beautiful. His visits became frequent and he paid court to both of them. Madame Clarence, who now liked attention, thought him agreeable. Eveline showed no friendliness towards him, and treated him with a hauteur and disdain that he took for aristocratic behaviour and fashionable manners, and he thought all the more of her on that account.

This busy man taxed his ingenuity to please them, and he sometimes succeeded. He got them cards for fashionable functions and boxes at the Opera. He furnished Mademoiselle Clarence with several opportunities of appearing to great advantage and in particular at a garden party which, although given by a Minister, was regarded as really fashionable, and gained its first success in society circles for the Republic.

At that party Eveline had been much noticed and had attracted the special attention of a young diplomat called Roger Lambilly

who, imagining that she belonged to a rather fast set, invited her
to his bachelor's flat. She thought him handsome and believed him
rich, and she accepted. A little moved, almost disquieted, she very
nearly became the victim of her daring, and only avoided defeat
by an offensive measure audaciously carried out. This was the most
foolish escapade in her unmarried life.

Being now on friendly terms with Ministers and with the President, Eveline continued to wear her aristocratic and pious affectations, and these won for her the sympathy of the chief personages
in the anti-clerical and democratic Republic. M. Hippolyte Cérès,
seeing that she was succeeding and doing him credit, liked her still
more. He even went so far as to fall madly in love with her.

Henceforth, in spite of everything, she began to observe him with
interest, being curious to see if his passion would increase. He appeared to her without elegance or grace, and not well bred, but
active, clear-sighted, full of resource, and not too great a bore. She
still made fun of him, but he had now won her interest.

One day she wished to test him. It was during the elections, when
members of Parliament were, as the phrase runs, requesting a renewal of their mandates. He had an opponent, who, though not
dangerous at first and not much of an orator, was rich and was
reported to be gaining votes every day. Hippolyte Cérès, banishing
both dull security and foolish alarm from his mind, redoubled his
care. His chief method of action was by public meetings at which he
spoke vehemently against the rival candidate. His committee held
huge meetings on Saturday evenings and at three o'clock on Sunday
afternoons. One Sunday, as he called on the Clarences, he found
Eveline alone in the drawing-room. He had been chatting for about
twenty or twenty-five minutes, when, taking out his watch, he saw
that it was a quarter to three. The young girl showed herself amiable, engaging, attractive, and full of promises. Cérès was fascinated,
but he stood up to go.

"Stay a little longer," said she in a pressing and agreeable voice
which made him promptly sit down again.

She was full of interest, of abandon, curiosity, and weakness. He
blushed, turned pale, and again got up.

Then, in order to keep him still longer, she looked at him out of
two grey and melting eyes, and though her bosom was heaving, she
did not say another word. He fell at her feet in distraction, but once
more looking at his watch, he jumped up with a terrible oath.

"D——! a quarter to four! I must be off."

And immediately he rushed down the stairs.

From that time onwards she had a certain amount of esteem for
him.

IV

A POLITICIAN'S MARRIAGE

HE was not quite in love with him, but she wished him to be in love with her. She was, moreover, very reserved with him, and that not solely from any want of inclination to be otherwise, since in affairs of love some things are due to indifference, to inattention, to a woman's instinct, to traditional custom and feeling, to a desire to try one's power, and to satisfaction at seeing its results. The reason of her prudence was that she knew him to be very much infatuated and capable of taking advantage of any familiarities she allowed as well as of reproaching her coarsely afterwards if she discontinued them.

As he was a professed anti-clerical and free-thinker, she thought it a good plan to affect an appearance of piety in his presence and to be seen with huge prayer-books bound in red morocco, such as Queen Marie Leczinska's or the Dauphiness Marie Josephine's "The Last Two Weeks of Lent." She lost no opportunity either, of showing him the subscriptions that she collected for the endowment of the national cult of St. Orberosia. Eveline did not act in this way because she wished to tease him. Nor did it spring from a young girl's archness, or a spirit of constraint, or even from snobbishness, though there was more than a suspicion of this latter in her behaviour. It was but her way of asserting herself, of stamping herself with a definite character, of increasing her value. To rouse the Deputy's courage she wrapped herself up in religion, just as Brunhild surrounded herself with flames so as to attract Sigard. Her audacity was successful. He thought her still more beautiful thus. Clericalism was in his eyes a sign of good form.

Cérès was re-elected by an enormous majority and returned to a House which showed itself more inclined to the Left, more advanced, and, as it seemed, more eager for reform than its predecessor. Perceiving at once that so much zeal was but intended to hide a fear of change, and a sincere desire to do nothing, he determined to adopt a policy that would satisfy these aspirations. At the beginning of the session he made a great speech, cleverly thought out and well arranged, dealing with the idea that all reform ought to be put off for a long time. He showed himself heated, even fervid; holding the principle that an orator should recommend moderation with extreme vehemence. He was applauded by the entire assembly. The Clarences listened to him from the President's box and Eveline trembled in spite of herself at the solemn sound of the applause.

On the same bench the fair Madame Pensée shivered at the intonations of his virile voice.

As soon as he descended from the tribune, Cérès, even while the audience were still clapping, went without a moment's delay to salute the Clarences in their box. Eveline saw in him the beauty of success, and as he leaned towards the ladies, wiping his neck with his handkerchief and receiving their congratulations with an air of modesty though not without a tinge of self-conceit, the young girl glanced towards Madame Pensée and saw her, palpitating and breathless, drinking in the hero's applause with her head thrown backwards. It seemed as if she were on the point of fainting. Eveline immediately smiled tenderly on M. Cérès.

The Alcan deputy's speech had a great vogue. In political "spheres" it was regarded as extremely able. "We have at last heard an honest pronouncement," said the chief Moderate journal. "It is a regular programme!" they said in the House. It was agreed that he was a man of immense talent.

Hippolyte Cérès had now established himself as leader of the radicals, socialists, and anti-clericals, and they appointed him President of their group, which was then the most considerable in the House. He thus found himself marked out for office in the next ministerial combination.

After a long hesitation Eveline Clarence accepted the idea of marrying M. Hippolyte Cérès. The great man was a little common for her taste. Nothing had yet proved that he would one day reach the point where politics bring in large sums of money. But she was entering her twenty-seventh year and knew enough of life to see that she must not be too fastidious or show herself too difficult to please.

Hippolyte Cérès was celebrated; Hippolyte Cérès was happy. He was no longer recognisable; the elegance of his clothes and deportment had increased tremendously. He wore an undue number of white gloves. Now that he was too much of a society man, Eveline began to doubt if it was not worse than being too little of one. Madame Clarence regarded the engagement with favour. She was reassured concerning her daughter's future and pleased to have flowers given her every Thursday for her drawing-room.

The celebration of the marriage raised some difficulties. Eveline was pious and wished to receive the benediction of the Church. Hippolyte Cérès, tolerant but a free-thinker, wanted only a civil marriage. There were many discussions and even some violent scenes upon the subject. The last took place in the young girl's room at the moment when the invitations were being written. Eveline declared that if she did not go to church she would not believe herself married. She spoke of breaking off the engagement, and of going abroad with her mother, or of retiring into a convent. Then she became tender, weak, suppliant. She sighed, and everything in her virginal chamber sighed in chorus, the holy-water font, the palm-branch above her white bed, the books of devotion on their little shelves, and the blue and white statuette of St. Orberosia chaining the dragon of Cappadocia, that stood upon the marble mantelpiece. Hippolyte Cérès was moved, softened, melted.

Beautiful in her grief, her eyes shining with tears, her wrists girt by a rosary of lapis lazuli and, so to speak, chained by her faith, she suddenly flung herself at Hippolyte's feet, and dishevelled, almost dying, she embraced his knees.

He nearly yielded.

"A religious marriage," he muttered, "a marriage in church, I could make my constituents stand that, but my committee would not swallow the matter so easily. . . . Still I'll explain it to them . . . toleration, social necessities. . . . They all send their daughters to Sunday school. . . . But as for office, my dear I am afraid we are going to drown all hope of that in your holy water."

At these words she stood up grave, generous, resigned, conquered also in her turn.

"My dear, I insist no longer."

"Then we won't have a religious marriage. It will be better, much better not."

"Very well, but be guided by me. I am going to try and arrange everything both to your satisfaction and mine."

She sought the Reverend Father Douillard and explained the situation. He showed himself even more accommodating and yielding than she had hoped.

"Your husband is an intelligent man, a man of order and reason; he will come over to us. You will sanctify him. It is not in vain that God has granted him the blessing of a Christian wife. The Church needs no pomp and ceremonial display for her benedictions. Now that she is persecuted, the shadow of the crypts and the recesses of the catacombs are in better accord with her festivals. Mademoiselle, when you have performed the civil formalities come here to my private chapel in walking costume with M. Cérès. I will marry you, and I will observe the most absolute discretion. I will obtain the necessary dispensations from the Archbishop as well as all facilities regarding the banns, confession-tickets, etc."

Hippolyte, although he thought the combination a little dangerous, agreed to it, a good deal flattered at bottom.

"I will go in a short coat," he said.

He went in a frock coat with white gloves and varnished shoes, and he genuflected.

"Politeness demands. . . ."

V

THE VISIRE CABINET

HE Cérès household was established with modest decency in a pretty flat situated in a new building. Cérès loved his wife in a calm and tranquil fashion. He was often kept late from home by the Commission on the Budget and he worked more than three nights a week at a report on the postal finances of which he hoped to make a masterpiece. Eveline thought she could twist him round her finger, and this did not displease him. The bad side of their situation was that they had not much money; in truth they had very little. The servants of the Republic do not grow rich in her service as easily as people think. Since the sovereign is no longer there to distribute favours, each of them takes what he can, and his depredations, limited by the depredations of all the others, are reduced to modest proportions. Hence that austerity of morals that is noticed in democratic leaders. They can only grow rich during periods of great business activity and then they find themselves exposed to the envy of their less favoured colleagues. Hippolyte Cérès had for a long time foreseen such a period. He was one of those who had made preparations for its arrival. Whilst waiting for it he endured his poverty with dignity, and Eveline shared that poverty without suffering as much as one might have thought. She was in close intimacy with the Reverend Father Douillard and frequented the chapel of St. Orberosia, where she met with serious society and people in a position to render her useful services. She knew how to choose among them and gave her confidence to none but those who deserved it. She had gained experience since her motor excursions with Viscount Cléna, and above all she had now acquired the value of a married woman.

The deputy was at first uneasy about these pious practices, which were ridiculed by the demagogic newspapers, but he was soon reassured, for he saw all around him democratic leaders joyfully becoming reconciled to the aristocracy and the Church.

They found that they had reached one of those periods (which often recur) when advance had been carried a little too far. Hippolyte Cérès gave a moderate support to this view. His policy was not a policy of persecution but a policy of tolerance. He had laid its foundations in his splendid speech on the preparations for reform. The Prime Minister was looked upon as too advanced. He proposed schemes which were admitted to be dangerous to capital, and the great financial companies were opposed to him. Of course it followed that the newspapers of all views supported the companies. Seeing the danger increasing, the Cabinet abandoned its schemes, its programme, and its opinions, but it was too late. A new administration was already ready. An insidious question by Paul Visire which was immediately made the subject of a resolution, and a fine speech by Hippolyte Cérès, overthrew the Cabinet.

The President of the Republic entrusted the formation of a new Cabinet to this same Paul Visire, who, though still very young, had been a Minister twice. He was a charming man, spending much of his time in the green-rooms of theatres, very artistic, a great society man, of amazing ability and industry. Paul Visire formed a temporary ministry intended to reassure public feeling which had taken alarm, and Hippolyte Cérès was invited to hold office in it.

The new ministry, belonging to all the groups in the majority, represented the most diverse and contrary opinions, but they were all moderate and convinced conservatives.* The Minister of Foreign Affairs was retained from the former cabinet. He was a little dark man called Crombile, who worked fourteen hours a day with the conviction that he dealt with tremendous questions. He refused to see even his own diplomatic agents, and was terribly uneasy, though he did not disturb anybody else, for the want of foresight of peoples is infinite and that of governments is just as great.

The office of Public Works was given to a Socialist, Fortuné Lapersonne. It was then a political custom and one of the most solemn, most severe, most rigorous, and if I may dare say so, the most terrible and cruel of all political customs, to include a member of the Socialist party in each ministry intended to oppose Socialism, so that the enemies of wealth and property should suffer the shame of being attacked by one of their own party, and so that they could not unite against these forces without turning to some one who might possibly attack themselves in the future. Nothing but a profound ignorance of the human heart would permit the belief that it was difficult to find a Socialist to occupy these functions. Citizen Fortuné Lapersonne entered the Visire cabinet of his own free will and without any constraint; and he found those who approved of his action even among his former friends, so great was the fascination that power exercised over the Penguins!

General Débonnaire went to the War Office. He was looked upon as one of the ablest generals in the army, but he was ruled by a woman, the Baroness Bildermann, who, though she had reached the age of intrigue, was still beautiful. She was in the pay of a neighbouring and hostile Power.

*As this ministry exercised considerable influence upon the destinies of the country and of the world, we think it well to give its composition: Minister of the Interior and Prime Minister, Paul Visire; Minister of Justice, Pierre Bouc; Foreign Affairs, Victor Crombile; Finance, Terrasson; Education, Labillette; Commerce, Posts and Telegraphs, Hippolyte Cérès; Agriculture, Aulac; Public Works, Lapersonne; War, General Débonnaire; Admiralty, Admiral Vivier des Murènes.

The new Minister of Marine, the worthy Admiral Vivier des Murènes, was generally regarded as an excellent seaman. He displayed a piety that would have seemed excessive in an anti-clerical minister, if the Republic had not recognised that religion was of great maritime utility. Acting on the instruction of his spiritual director, the Reverend Father Douillard, the worthy Admiral had dedicated his fleet to St. Orberosia and directed canticles in honour of the Alcan Virgin to be composed by Christian bards. These replaced the national hymn in the music played by the navy.

Prime Minister Visire declared himself to be distinctly anticlerical but ready to respect all creeds; he asserted that he was a sober-minded reformer. Paul Visire and his colleagues desired reforms, and it was in order not to compromise reform that they proposed none; for they were true politicians and knew that reforms are compromised the moment they are proposed. The government was well received, respectable people were reassured, and the funds rose.

The administration announced that four new ironclads would be put into commission, that prosecutions would be undertaken against the Socialists, and it formally declared its intention to have nothing to do with any inquisitorial income-tax. The choice of Terrasson as Minister of Finance was warmly approved by the press. Terrasson, an old minister famous for his financial operations, gave warrant to all the hopes of the financiers and shadowed forth a period of great business activity. Soon those three udders of modern nations, monopolies, bill discounting, and fraudulent speculation, were swollen with the milk of wealth. Already whispers were heard of distant enterprises, and of planting colonies, and the boldest put forward in the newspapers the project of a military and financial protectorate over Nigritia.

Without having yet shown what he was capable of, Hippolyte Cérès was considered a man of weight. Business people thought highly of him. He was congratulated on all sides for having broken with the extreme sections, the dangerous men, and for having realised the responsibilities of government.

Madame Cérès shone alone amid the Ministers' wives. Crombile withered away in bachelordom. Paul Visire had married money in the person of Mademoiselle Blampignon, an accomplished, estimable, and simple lady who was always ill, and whose feeble health compelled her to stay with her mother in the depths of a remote province. The other Ministers' wives were not born to charm the sight, and people smiled when they read that Madame Labillette had appeared at the Presidency Ball wearing a head-dress of birds of paradise. Madame Vivier des Murènes, a woman of good family, was stout rather than tall, had a face like a beef-steak and the voice of a newspaper-seller. Madame Débonnaire, tall, dry, and florid, was devoted to young officers. She ruined herself by her escapades and crimes and only regained consideration by dint of ugliness and insolence.

Madame Cérès was the charm of the Ministry and its title to consideration. Young, beautiful, and irreproachable, she charmed alike society and the masses by her combination of elegant costumes and pleasant smiles.

Her receptions were thronged by the great Jewish financiers. She gave the most fashionable garden parties in the Republic. The newspapers described her dresses and the milliners did not ask her to pay for them. She went to Mass; she protected the chapel of St. Orberosia from the ill-will of the people; and she aroused in aristocratic hearts the hope of a fresh Concordat.

With her golden hair, grey eyes, and supple and slight though rounded figure, she was indeed pretty. She enjoyed an excellent reputation and she was so adroit, and calm, so much mistress of herself, that she would have preserved it intact even if she had been discovered in the very act of ruining it.

The session ended with a victory for the cabinet which, amid the almost unanimous applause of the House, defeated a proposal for an inquisitorial tax, and with a triumph for Madame Cérès who gave parties in honour of three kings who were at the moment passing through Alca.

VI

THE SOFA OF THE FAVOURITE

THE Prime Minister invited Monsieur and Madame Cérès to spend a couple of weeks of the holidays in a little villa that he had taken in the mountains, and in which he lived alone. The deplorable health of Madame Paul Visire did not allow her to accompany her husband, and she remained with her relatives in one of the southern provinces.

The villa had belonged to the mistress of one of the last Kings of Alca: the drawing-room retained its old furniture, and in it was still to be found the Sofa of the Favourite. The country was charming; a pretty blue stream, the Aiselle, flowed at the foot of the hill that dominated the villa. Hippolyte Cérès loved fishing; when engaged at this monotonous occupation he often formed his best Parliamentary combinations, and his happiest oratorical inspirations. Trout swarmed in the Aiselle; he fished it from morning till evening in a boat that the Prime Minister readily placed at his disposal.

In the mean time, Eveline and Paul Visire sometimes took a turn together in the garden, or had a little chat in the drawing-room.

Eveline, although she recognised the attraction that Visire had for women, had hitherto displayed towards him only an intermittent and superficial coquetry, without any deep intentions or settled design. He was a connoisseur and saw that she was pretty. The House and the Opera had deprived him of all leisure, but, in a little villa, the grey eyes and rounded figure of Eveline took on a value in his eyes. One day as Hippolyte Cérès was fishing in the Aiselle, he made her sit beside him on the Sofa of the Favourite. Long rays of gold struck Eveline like arrows from a hidden Cupid through the chinks of the curtains which protected her from the heat and glare of a brilliant day. Beneath her white muslin dress her rounded yet slender form was outlined in its grace and youth. Her skin was cool and fresh, and had the fragrance of freshly mown hay. Paul Visire behaved as the occasion warranted, and for her part, she was opposed neither to the games of chance or of society. She believed it would be nothing or a trifle; she was mistaken.

"There was," says the famous German ballad, "on the sunny side of the town square, beside a wall whereon the creeper grew, a pretty little letter-box, as blue as the corn-flowers, smiling and tranquil.

"All day long there came to it, in their heavy shoes, small shop-keepers, rich farmers, citizens, the tax-collector and the policeman, and they put into it their business letters, their invoices, their summonses, their notices to pay taxes, the judges' returns, and orders for the recruits to assemble. It remained smiling and tranquil.

"With joy, or in anxiety, there advanced towards it workmen and farm servants, maids and nursemaids, accountants, clerks, and women carrying their little children in their arms; they put into it notifications of births, marriages, and deaths, letters between engaged couples, between husbands and wives, from mothers to their sons, and from sons to their mothers. It remained smiling and tranquil.

"At twilight, young lads and young girls slipped furtively to it, and put in love-letters, some moistened with tears that blotted the ink, others with a little circle to show the place to kiss, all of them very long. It remained smiling and tranquil.

"Rich merchants came themselves through excess of carefulness at the hour of daybreak, and put into it registered letters, and letters with five red seals, full of bank notes or cheques on the great financial establishments of the Empire. It remained smiling and tranquil.

"But one day, Gaspar, whom it had never seen, and whom it did not know from Adam, came to put in a letter, of which nothing is known but that it was folded like a little hat. Immediately the pretty letter-box fell into a swoon. Henceforth it remains no longer in its place; it runs through streets, fields, and woods, girdled with ivy, and crowned with roses. It keeps running up hill and down dale; the country policeman surprises it sometimes, amidst the corn, in Gaspar's arms kissing him upon the mouth."

Paul Visire had recovered all his customary nonchalance. Eveline remained stretched on the Divan of the Favourite in an attitude of delicious astonishment.

The Reverend Father Douillard, an excellent moral theologian, and a man who in the decadence of the Church has preserved his principles, was very right to teach, in conformity with the doctrine of the Fathers, that while a woman commits a great sin by giving herself for money, she commits a much greater one by giving herself for nothing. For, in the first case she acts to support her life, and that is sometimes not merely excuseable but pardonable, and even worthy of the Divine Grace, for God forbids suicide, and is unwilling that his creatures should destroy themselves. Besides, in giving herself in order to live, she remains humble, and derives no pleasure from it, a thing which diminishes the sin. But a woman who gives herself for nothing sins with pleasure and exults in her fault. The pride and delight with which she burdens her crime increase its load of moral guilt.

Madame Hippolyte Cérès' example shows the profundity of these moral truths. She perceived that she had senses. A second was enough to bring about this discovery, to change her soul, to alter her whole life. To have learned to know herself was at first a delight. The $\gamma\nu\hat{\omega}\theta\iota$ $\sigma\epsilon\alpha\nu\tau\grave{o}\nu$ of the ancient philosophy is not a precept the moral fulfilment of which procures any pleasure, since one enjoys little satisfaction from knowing one's soul. It is not the same with the flesh, for in it sources of pleasure may be revealed to us. Eveline immediately felt an obligation to her revealer equal to the benefit she had received, and she imagined that he who had discovered these heavenly depths was the sole possessor of the key to them. Was this an error, and might she not be able to find others who also had the golden key? It is difficult to decide; and Professor Haddock, when the facts were divulged (which happened without much delay as we shall see), treated the matter from an experimental point of view, in a scientific review, and concluded that the chances Madame C—— would have of finding the exact equivalent of M. V—— were in the proportion of 305 to 975008. This is as much as to say that she would never find it. Doubtless her instinct told her the same, for she attached herself distractedly to him.

I have related these facts with all the circumstances which seemed to me worthy of attracting the attention of mediative and philosophic minds. The Sofa of the Favourite is worthy of the majesty of history; on it were decided the destinies of a great people; nay, on it was accomplished an act whose renown was to extend over the neighbouring nations both friendly and hostile, and even over all humanity. Too often events of this nature escape the superficial minds and shallow spirits who inconsiderately assume the task of writing history. Thus the secret springs of events remain hidden from us. The fall of Empires and the transmission of dominions astonish us and remain incomprehensible to us, because we have not discovered the imperceptible point, or touched the secret spring which when put in movement has destroyed and overthrown everything. The author of this great history knows better than anyone else his faults and his weaknesses, but he can do himself this justice—that he has always kept the moderation, the seriousness, the austerity, which an account of affairs of State demands, and that he has never departed from the gravity which is suitable to a recital of human actions.

VII

THE FIRST CONSEQUENCES

WHEN Eveline confided to Paul Visire that she had never experienced anything similar, he did not believe her. He had had a good deal to do with women and knew that they readily say these things to men in order to make them more in love with them. Thus his experience, as sometimes happens, made him disregard the truth. Incredulous, but gratified all the same, he soon felt love and something more for her. This state at first seemed favourable to his intellectual faculties. Visire delivered in the chief town of his constituency a speech full of grace, brilliant and happy, which was considered to be a masterpiece.

The re-opening of Parliament was serene. A few isolated jealousies, a few timid ambitions raised their heads in the House, and that was all. A smile from the Prime Minister was enough to dissipate these shadows. She and he saw each other twice a day, and wrote to each other in the interval. He was accustomed to intimate relationships, was adroit, and knew how to dissimulate; but Eveline displayed a foolish imprudence: she made herself conspicuous with him in drawing-rooms, at the theatre, in the House, and at the Embassies; she wore her love upon her face, upon her whole person, in her moist glances, in the languishing smile of her lips, in the heaving of her breast, in all her heightened, agitated, and distracted beauty. Soon the entire country knew of their intimacy. Foreign Courts were informed of it. The President of the Republic and Eveline's husband alone remained in ignorance. The President became acquainted with it in the country, through a misplaced police report which found its way, it is not known how, into his portmanteau.

Hippolyte Cérès, without being either very subtle, or very perspicacious, noticed that there was something different in his home. Eveline, who quite lately had interested herself in his affairs, and shown, if not tenderness, at least affection, towards him, displayed henceforth nothing but indifference and repulsion. She had always had periods of absence, and made prolonged visits to the Charity of St. Orberosia; now, she went out in the morning, remained out all day, and sat down to dinner at nine o'clock in the evening with the face of a somnambulist. Her husband thought it absurd; however, he might perhaps have never known the reason for this; a profound ignorance of women, a crass confidence in his own merit, and in his own fortune, might perhaps have always hidden the truth from him, if the two lovers had not, so to speak, compelled him to discover it.

When Paul Visire went to Eveline's house and found her alone, they used to say, as they embraced each other; "Not here! not here!" and immediately they affected an extreme reserve. That was their invariable rule. Now, one day, Paul Visire went to the house of his colleague Cérès, with whom he had an engagement. It was Eveline who received him, the Minister of Commerce being delayed by a commission.

"Not here!" said the lovers, smiling.

They said it, mouth to mouth, embracing, and clasping each other. They were still saying it, when Hippolyte Cérès entered the drawing-room.

Paul Visire did not lose his presence of mind. He declared to Madame Cérès that he would give up his attempt to take the dust out of her eye. By this attitude he did not deceive the husband, but he was able to leave the room with some dignity.

Hippolyte Cérès was thunderstruck. Eveline's conduct appeared incomprehensible to him; he asked her what reasons she had for it.

"Why? why?" he kept repeating continually, "why?"

She denied everything, not to convince him, for he had seen them, but from expediency and good taste, and to avoid painful explanations. Hippolyte Cérès suffered all the tortures of jealousy. He admitted it to himself, he kept saying inwardly, "I am a strong man; I am clad in armour; but the wound is underneath, it is in my heart," and turning towards his wife, who looked beautiful in her guilt, he would say:

"It ought not to have been with him."

He was right—Eveline ought not to have loved in government circles.

He suffered so much that he took up his revolver, exclaiming: "I will go and kill him!" But he remembered that a Minister of Commerce cannot kill his own Prime Minister, and he put his revolver back into his drawer.

The weeks passed without calming his sufferings. Each morning he buckled his strong man's armour over his wound and sought in work and fame the peace that fled from him. Every Sunday he inaugurated busts, statues, fountains, artesian wells, hospitals, dispensaries, railways, canals, public markets, drainage systems, triumphal arches, and slaughter houses, and delivered moving speeches on each of these occasions. His fervid activity devoured whole piles of documents; he changed the colours of the postage stamps fourteen times in one week. Nevertheless, he gave vent to outbursts of grief and rage that drove him insane; for whole days his reason abandoned him. If he had been in the employment of a private administration this would have been noticed immediately, but it is much more difficult to discover insanity or frenzy in the conduct of affairs of State. At that moment the government employés were forming themselves into associations and federations amid a ferment that was giving alarm both to the Parliament and to public feeling. The postmen were especially prominent in their enthusiasm for trade unions.

Hippolyte Cérès informed them in a circular that their action was strictly legal. The following day he sent out a second circular forbidding all associations of government employés as illegal. He dismissed one hundred and eighty postmen, reinstated them, reprimanded them, and awarded them gratuities. At Cabinet councils he was always on the point of bursting forth. The presence of the Head of the State scarcely restrained him within the limits of the decencies, and as he did not dare to attack his rival he consoled himself by heaping invectives upon General Débonnaire, the respected Minister of War. The General did not hear them, for he was deaf and occupied himself in composing verses for the Baroness Bildermann. Hippolyte Cérès offered an indistinct opposition to everything the Prime Minister proposed. In a word, he was a madman. One faculty alone escaped the ruin of his intellect: he retained his Parliamentary sense, his consciousness of the temper of majorities, his thorough knowledge of groups, and his certainty of the direction in which affairs were moving.

VIII

FURTHER CONSEQUENCES

THE session ended calmly, and the Ministry saw no dangerous signs upon the benches where the majority sat. It was visible, however, from certain articles in the Moderate journals, that the demands of the Jewish and Christian financiers were increasing daily, that the patriotism of the banks required a civilizing expedition to Nigritia, and that the steel trusts, eager in the defence of our coasts and colonies, were crying out for armoured cruisers and still more armoured cruisers. Rumours of war began to be heard. Such rumours sprang up every year as regularly as the trade winds; serious people paid no heed to them and the government usually let them die away from their own weakness unless they grew stronger and spread. For in that case the country would be alarmed. The financiers only wanted colonial wars and the people did not want any wars at all. It loved to see its government proud and even insolent, but at the least suspicion that a European war was brewing, its violent emotion would quickly have reached the House. Paul Visire was not uneasy. The European situation was in his view completely reassuring. He was only irritated by the maniacal silence of his Minister of Foreign Affairs. That gnome went to the Cabinet meetings with a portfolio bigger than himself stuffed full of papers, said nothing, refused to answer all questions, even those asked him by the respected President of the Republic, and, exhausted by his obstinate labours, took a few moments' sleep in his arm-chair in which nothing but the top of his little black head was to be seen above the green tablecloth.

In the mean time Hippolyte Cérès became a strong man again. In company with his colleague Lapersonne he formed numerous intimacies with ladies of the theatre. They were both to be seen at night entering fashionable restaurants in the company of ladies whom they over-topped by their lofty stature and their new hats, and they were soon reckoned amongst the most sympathetic frequenters of the boulevards. Fortuné Lapersonne had his own wound beneath his armour. His wife, a young milliner whom he carried off from a marquis, had gone to live with a chauffeur. He loved her still, and could not console himself for her loss, so that very often in the private room of a restaurant, in the midst of a group of girls who laughed and ate crayfish, the two ministers exchanged a look full of their common sorrow and wiped away an unbidden tear.

Hippolyte Cérès, although wounded to the heart, did not allow himself to be beaten. He swore that he would be avenged.

Madame Paul Visire, whose deplorable health forced her to live with her relatives in a distant province, received an anonymous letter specifying that M. Paul Visire, who had not a half-penny when he married her, was spending her dowry on a married woman, E—— C——, that he gave this woman thirty-thousand-franc motor-cars, and pearl necklaces costing twenty-five thousand francs, and that he was going straight to dishonour and ruin. Madame Paul Visire read the letter, fell into hysterics, and handed it to her father.

"I am going to box your husband's ears," said M. Blampignon; "he is a blackguard who will land you in the workhouse unless we look out. He may be Prime Minister, but he won't frighten me."

When he stepped off the train M. Blampignon presented himself at the Ministry of the Interior, and was immediately received. He entered the Prime Minister's room in a fury.

"I have something to say to you, sir!" And he waved the anonymous letter.

Paul Visire welcomed him smiling.

"You are welcome, my dear father. I was going to write to you. . . . Yes, to tell you of your nomination to the rank of officer of the Legion of Honour. I signed the patent this morning."

M. Blampignon thanked his son-in-law warmly and threw the anonymous letter into the fire.

He returned to his provincial house and found his daughter fretting and agitated.

"Well! I saw your husband. He is a delightful fellow. But then, you don't understand how to deal with him."

About this time Hippolyte Cérès learned through a little scandalous newspaper (it is always through the newspapers that ministers are informed of the affairs of State) that the Prime Minister dined every evening with Mademoiselle Lysiane of the Folies Dramatiques, whose charm seemed to have made a great impression on him. Thenceforth Cérès took a gloomy joy in watching his wife. She came in every evening to dine or dress with an air of agreeable fatigue and the serenity that comes from enjoyment.

Thinking that she knew nothing, he sent her anonymous communications. She read them at the table before him and remained still listless and smiling.

He then persuaded himself that she gave no heed to these vague reports, and that in order to disturb her it would be necessary to enable her to verify her lover's infidelity and treason for herself. There were at the Ministry a number of trustworthy agents charged with secret inquiries regarding the national defence. They were then employed in watching the spies of a neighbouring and hostile Power who had succeeded in entering the Postal and Telegraphic service. M. Cérès ordered them to suspend their work for the present and to inquire where, when, and how the Minister of the Interior saw Mademoiselle Lysiane. The agents performed their missions faithfully and told the minister that they had several times seen the Prime Minister with a woman, but that she was not Mademoiselle Lysiane. Hippolyte Cérès asked them nothing further. He was right; the loves of Paul Visire and Lysiane were but an alibi invented by Paul Visire himself, with Eveline's approval, for his fame was rather inconvenient to her, and she sighed for secrecy and mystery.

They were not shadowed by the agents of the Ministry of Commerce alone. They were also followed by those of the Prefect of Police, and even by those of the Minister of the Interior, who disputed with each other the honour of protecting their chief. Then there were the emissaries of several royalist, imperialist, and clerical organisations, those of eight or ten blackmailers, several amateur detectives, a multitude of reporters, and a crowd of photographers, who all made their appearance wherever these two took refuge in their perambulating love affairs, at big hotels, small hotels, town houses, country houses, private apartments, villas, museums, palaces, hovels. They kept watch in the streets, from neighbouring houses, trees, walls, stair-cases, landings, roofs, adjoining rooms, and even chimneys. The Minister and his friend saw with alarm all round their bed room, gimlets boring through doors and shutters, and drills making holes in the walls. A photograph of Madame Cérès in night attire buttoning her boots was the utmost that had been obtained.

Paul Visire grew impatient and irritable, and often lost his good humour and agreeableness. He came to the cabinet meetings in a rage and he, too, poured invectives upon General Débonnaire—a brave man under fire but a lax disciplinarian—and launched his sarcasms against the venerable admiral Vivier des Murènes whose ships went to the bottom without any apparent reason.

Fortuné Lapersonne listened open-eyed, and grumbled scoffingly between his teeth:

"He is not satisfied with robbing Hippolyte Cérès of his wife, but he must go and rob him of his catch-words too."

These storms were made known by the indiscretion of some ministers and by the complaints of the two old warriors, who declared their intention of flinging their portfolios at the beggar's head, but who did nothing of the sort. These outbursts, far from injuring the lucky Prime Minister, had an excellent effect on Parliament and public opinion, who looked on them as signs of a keen solicitude for the welfare of the national army and navy. The Prime Minister was recipient of general approbation.

To the congratulations of the various groups and of notable per-

sonages, he replied with simple firmness: "Those are my principles!" and he had seven or eight Socialists put in prison.

The session ended, and Paul Visire, very exhausted, went to take
the waters. Hippolyte Cérès refused to leave his Ministry, where
the trade union of telephone girls was in tumultuous agitation. He
opposed it with an unheard of violence, for he had now become a
woman-hater. On Sundays he went into the suburbs to fish along
with his colleague Lapersonne, wearing the tall hat that never left
him since he had become a Minister. And both of them, forgetting
the fish, complained of the inconstancy of women and mingled their
griefs.

Hippolyte still loved Eveline and he still suffered. However, hope
had slipped into his heart. She was now separated from her lover,
and, thinking to win her back, he directed all his efforts to that
end. He put forth all his skill, showed himself sincere, adaptable,
affectionate, devoted, even discreet; his heart taught him the
delicacies of feeling. He said charming and touching things to the

faithless one, and, to soften her, he told her all that he had suffered.

Crossing the band of his trousers upon his stomach.

"See," said he, "how thin I have got."

He promised her everything he thought could gratify a woman, country parties, hats, jewels.

Sometimes he thought she would take pity on him. She no longer displayed an insolently happy countenance. Being separated from Paul, her sadness had an air of gentleness. But the moment he made a gesture to recover her she turned away fiercely and gloomily, girt with her fault as if with a golden girdle.

He did not give up, making himself humble, suppliant, lamentable.

One day he went to Lapersonne and said to him with tears in his eyes:

"Will you speak to her?"

Lapersonne excused himself, thinking that his intervention would be useless, but he gave some advice to his friend.

"Make her think that you don't care about her, that you love another, and she will come back to you."

Hippolyte, adopting this method, inserted in the newspapers that he was always to be found in the company of Mademoiselle Guinaud of the Opera. He came home late or did not come home at all, assumed in Eveline's presence an appearance of inward joy impossible to restrain, took out of his pocket, at dinner, a letter on scented paper which he pretended to read with delight, and his lips seemed as in a dream to kiss invisible lips. Nothing happened. Eveline did not even notice the change. Insensible to all around her, she only came out of her lethargy to ask for some louis from her husband, and if he did not give them she threw him a look of contempt, ready to upbraid him with the shame which she poured upon him in the sight of the whole world. Since she had loved she spent a great deal on dress. She needed money, and she had only her husband to secure it for her; she was so far faithful to him.

He lost patience, became furious, and threatened her with his revolver. He said one day before her to Madame Clarence:

"I congratulate you, Madame; you have brought up your daughter to be a wanton hussy."

"Take me away, Mamma," exclaimed Eveline. "I will get a divorce!"

He loved her more ardently than ever. In his jealous rage, suspecting her, not without probability, of sending and receiving letters, he swore that he would intercept them, re-established a censorship over the post, threw private correspondence into confusion, delayed stock-exchange quotations, prevented assignations, brought out bankruptcies, thwarted passions, and caused suicides. The independent press gave utterance to the complaints of the public and indignantly supported them. To justify these arbitrary measures, the ministerial journals spoke darkly of plots and public dangers, and promoted a belief in a monarchical conspiracy. The less well-informed sheets gave more precise information, told of the seizure of fifty thousand guns, and the landing of Prince Crucho. Feeling grew throughout the country, and the republican organs called for the immediate meeting of Parliament. Paul Visire returned to Paris, summoned his colleagues, held an important Cabinet Council, and proclaimed through his agencies that a plot had been actually formed against the national representation, but that the Prime Minister held the threads of it in his hand, and that a judicial inquiry was about to be opened.

He immediately ordered the arrest of thirty Socialists, and whilst the entire country was acclaiming him as its saviour, baffling the watchfulness of his six hundred detectives, he secretly took Eveline to a little house near the Northern railway station, where they remained until night. After their departure, the maid of their hotel, as she was putting their room in order, saw seven little crosses traced by a hairpin on the wall at the head of the bed.

That is all that Hippolyte Cérès obtained as a reward of his efforts.

IX

THE FINAL CONSEQUENCES

EALOUSY is a virtue of democracies which preserves them from tyrants. Deputies began to envy the Prime Minister his golden key. For a year his domination over the beauteous Madame Cérès had been known to the whole universe. The provinces, whither news and fashions only arrive after a complete revolution of the earth round the sun, were at last informed of the illegitimate loves of the Cabinet. The provinces preserve an austere morality; women are more virtuous there than they are in the capital. Various reasons have been alleged for this: Education, example, simplicity of life. Professor Haddock asserts that this virtue of provincial ladies is solely due to the fact that the heels of their shoes are low. "A woman," said he, in a learned article in the "Anthropological Review," "a woman attracts a civilized man in proportion as her feet make an angle with the ground. If this angle is as much as thirty-five degrees, the attraction becomes acute. For the position of the feet upon the ground determines the whole carriage of the body, and it results that provincial women, since they wear low heels, are not very attractive, and preserve their virtue with ease." These con-

clusions were not generally accepted. It was objected that under
the influence of English and American fashions, low heels had
been introduced generally without producing the results attributed
to them by the learned Professor; moreover, it was said that the
difference he pretended to establish between the morals of the me-
tropolis and those of the provinces is perhaps illusory, and that if
it exists, it is apparently due to the fact that great cities offer
more advantages and facilities for love than small towns provide.
However that may be, the provinces began to murmur against the
Prime Minister, and to raise a scandal. This was not yet a danger,
but there was a possibility that it might become one.

For the moment the peril was nowhere and yet everywhere. The
majority remained solid; but the leaders became stiff and exacting.
Perhaps Hippolyte Cérès would never have intentionally sacrificed
his interests to his vengeance. But thinking that he could henceforth, without compromising his own fortune, secretly damage that
of Paul Visire, he devoted himself to the skilful and careful prepa-
ration of difficulties and perils for the Head of the Government.
Though far from equalling his rival in talent, knowledge, and
authority, he greatly surpassed him in his skill as a lobbyist. The
most acute parliamentarians attributed the recent misfortunes of
the majority to his refusal to vote. At committees, by a calculated
imprudence, he favoured motions which he knew the Prime Minister could not accept. One day his intentional awkwardness provoked a sudden and violent conflict between the Minister of the
Interior, and his departmental Treasurer. Then Cérès became
frightened and went no further. It would have been dangerous for
him to overthrow the ministry too soon. His ingenious hatred found
an issue by circuitous paths. Paul Visire had a poor cousin of easy
morals who bore his name. Cérès, remembering this lady, Céline
Visire, brought her into prominence, arranged that she should become intimate with several foreigners, and procured her engagements in the music-halls. One summer night, on a stage in the
Champs Elysées before a tumultuous crowd, she performed risky
dances to the sounds of wild music which was audible in the gardens where the President of the Republic was entertaining Royalty.
The name of Visire, associated with these scandals, covered the
walls of the town, filled the newspapers, was repeated in the cafés
and at balls, and blazed forth in letters of fire upon the boulevards.

Nobody regarded the Prime Minister as responsible for the scandal of his relatives, but a bad idea of his family came into existence, and the influence of the statesman was diminished.

Almost immediately he was made to feel this in a pretty sharp
fashion. One day in the House, on a simple question, Labillette, the
Minister of Religion and Public Worship, who was suffering from
an attack of liver, and beginning to be exasperated by the inten-

tions and intrigues of the clergy, threatened to close the Chapel
of St. Orberosia, and spoke without respect of the National Virgin. The entire Right rose up in indignation; the Left appeared to
give but a half-hearted support to the rash Minister. The leaders
of the majority did not care to attack a popular cult which brought
thirty millions a year into the country. The most moderate of the
supporters of the Right, M. Bigourd, made the question the subject
of a resolution and endangered the Cabinet. Luckily, Fortuné
Lapersonne, the Minister of Public Works, always conscious of the
obligations of power, was able in the Prime Minister's absence to
repair the awkwardness and indecorum of his colleague, the Minister of Public Worship. He ascended the tribune and bore witness
to the respect in which the Government held the heavenly Patron
of the country, the consoler of so many ills which science admitted
its powerlessness to relieve.

When Paul Visire, snatched at last from Eveline's arms, appeared
in the House, the administration was saved; but the Prime Minister
saw himself compelled to grant important concessions to the upper
classes. He proposed in Parliament that six armoured cruisers
should be laid down, and thus won the sympathies of the Steel
Trust; he gave new assurances that the income tax would not be
imposed, and he had eighteen Socialists arrested.

He was soon to find himself opposed by more formidable obstacles. The Chancellor of the neighbouring Empire in an ingenious and profound speech upon the foreign relations of his sovereign,
made a sly allusion to the intrigues that inspired the policy of a
great country. This reference, which was received with smiles by
the Imperial Parliament, was certain to irritate a punctilious republic. It aroused the national susceptibility, which directed its
wrath against its amorous Minister. The Deputies seized upon a
frivolous pretext to show their dissatisfaction. A ridiculous incident, the fact that the wife of a sub-prefect had danced at the
Moulin Rouge, forced the minister to face a vote of censure, and
he was within a few votes of being defeated. According to general
opinion, Paul Visire had never been so weak, so vacillating, or so
spiritless, as on that occasion.

He understood that he could only keep himself in office by a
great political stroke, and he decided on the expedition to Nigritia.
This measure was demanded by the great financial and industrial
corporations and was one which would bring concessions of immense forests to the capitalists, a loan of eight millions to the
banking companies, as well as promotions and decorations to the
naval and military officers. A pretext presented itself; some insult
needed to be avenged, or some debt to be collected. Six battleships,
fourteen cruisers, and eighteen transports sailed up the mouth of
the river Hippopotamus. Six hundred canoes vainly opposed the
landing of the troops. Admiral Vivier des Murènes' cannons pro-

duced an appalling effect upon the blacks, who replied to them with flights of arrows, but in spite of their fanatical courage they were entirely defeated. Popular enthusiasm was kindled by the newspapers which the financiers subsidised, and burst into a blaze. Some Socialists alone protested against this barbarous, doubtful, and dangerous enterprise. They were at once arrested.

At that moment when the Minister, supported by wealth, and now beloved by the poor, seemed unconquerable, the light of hate showed Hippolyte Cérès alone the danger, and looking with a gloomy joy at his rival, he muttered between his teeth, "He is wrecked, the brigand!"

Whilst the country intoxicated itself with glory, the neighouring Empire protested against the occupation of Nigritia by a European power, and these protests following one another at shorter and shorter intervals became more and more vehement. The newspapers of the interested Republic concealed all causes for uneasiness; but Hippolyte Cérès heard the growing menace, and determined at last to risk everything, even the fate of the ministry, in order to ruin his enemy. He got men whom he could trust to write and insert articles in several of the official journals, which, seeming to express Paul Visire's precise views, attributed warlike intentions to the Head of the Government.

These articles roused a terrible echo abroad, and they alarmed the public opinion of a nation which, while fond of soldiers, was not fond of war. Questioned in the House on the foreign policy of his government, Paul Visire made a re-assuring statement, and promised to maintain a peace compatible with the dignity of a great nation. His Minister of Foreign Affairs, Crombile, read a declaration which was absolutely unintelligible, for the reason that it was couched in diplomatic language. The Minister obtained a large majority.

But the rumours of war did not cease, and in order to avoid a new and dangerous motion, the Prime Minister distributed eighty thousand acres of forests in Nigritia among the Deputies, and had fourteen Socialists arrested. Hippolyte Cérès went gloomily about the lobbies, confiding to the Deputies of his group that he was endeavouring to induce the Cabinet to adopt a pacific policy, and that he still hoped to succeed. Day by day the sinister rumours grew in volume, and penetrating amongst the public, spread uneasiness and disquiet. Paul Visire himself began to take alarm. What disturbed him most were the silence and absence of the Minister of Foreign Affairs. Crombile no longer came to the meetings of the Cabinet. Rising at five o'clock in the morning, he worked eighteen hours at his desk, and at last fell exhausted into his waste-paper basket, from whence the registrars removed him, together with the papers which they were going to sell to the military attachés of the neighbouring Empire.

General Débonnaire believed that a campaign was imminent, and prepared for it. Far from fearing war, he prayed for it, and confided his generous hopes to Baroness Bildermann, who informed the neighbouring nation, which, acting on her information, proceeded to a rapid mobilization.

The Minister of Finance unintentionally precipitated events. At the moment, he was speculating for a fall, and in order to bring about a panic on the Stock Exchange, he spread the rumour that war was now inevitable. The neighbouring Empire, deceived by this action, and expecting to see its territory invaded, mobilized its troops in all haste. The terrified Chamber overthrew the Visire ministry by an enormous majority (814 votes to 7, with 28 abstentions). It was too late. The very day of this fall the neighbouring and hostile nation recalled its ambassador and flung eight millions of men into Madame Cérès' country. War became universal, and the whole world was drowned in a torrent of blood.

THE ZENITH OF PENGUIN CIVILIZATION

ALF a century after the events we have just related, Madame Cérès died surrounded with respect and veneration, in the eighty-ninth year of her age. She had long been the widow of a statesman whose name she bore with dignity. Her modest and quiet funeral was followed by the orphans of the parish and the sisters of the Sacred Compassion.

The deceased left all her property to the Charity of St. Orberosia.

"Alas!" sighed M. Monnoyer, a canon of St. Maël, as he received the pious legacy, "it was high time for a generous benefactor to come to the relief of our necessities. Rich and poor, learned and ignorant are turning away from us. And when we try to lead back these misguided souls, neither threats nor promises, neither gentleness nor violence, nor anything else is now successful. The Penguin clergy pine in desolation; our country priests, reduced to following the humblest of trades, are shoeless, and compelled to live upon such scraps as they can pick up. In our ruined churches the rain of heaven falls upon the faithful, and during the holy offices they can hear the noise of stones falling from the arches. The tower of the cathedral is tottering and will soon fall. St. Orberosia is forgotten by the Penguins, her devotion abandoned, and her sanctuary deserted. On her shrine, bereft of its gold and precious stones, the spider silently weaves her web."

Hearing these lamentations, Pierre Mille, who at the age of ninety-eight years had lost nothing of his intellectual and moral

power, asked the canon if he did not think that St. Orberosia would
one day rise out of this wrongful oblivion.

"I hardly dare to hope so," sighed M. Monnoyer.

"It is a pity!" answered Pierre Mille. "Orberosia is a charming
figure and her legend is a beautiful one. I discovered the other day
by the merest chance, one of her most delightful miracles, the miracle of Jean Violle. Would you like to hear it, M. Monnoyer?"

"I should be very pleased, M. Mille."

"Here it is, then, just as I found it in a fifteenth-century manuscript:

"Cécile, the wife of Nicolas Gaubert, a jeweller on the Pont-au-
Change, after having led an honest and chaste life for many years,
and being now past her prime, became infatuated with Jean Violle,
the Countess de Maubec's page, who lived at the Hôtel du Paon on
the Place de Grève. He was not yet eighteen years old, and his face
and figure were attractive. Not being able to conquer her passion,
Cécile resolved to satisfy it. She attracted the page to her house,
loaded him with caresses, supplied him with sweetmeats and finally
did as she wished with him.

"Now one day, as they were together in the jeweller's bed, Master Nicolas came home sooner than he was expected. He found the
bolt drawn, and heard his wife on the other side of the door exclaiming, 'My heart! my angel! my love!' Then suspecting that she
was shut up with a gallant, he struck great blows upon the door
and began to shout: 'Slut! hussy! wanton! open so that I may cut
off your nose and ears!' In this peril, the jeweller's wife besought
St. Orberosia, and vowed her a large candle if she helped her and
the little page, who was dying of fear beside the bed, out of their
difficulty.

"The saint heard the prayer. She immediately changed Jean
Violle into a girl. Seeing this, Cécile was completely reassured, and
began to call out to her husband: 'Oh! you brutal villain, you jealous wretch! Speak gently if you want the door to be opened.' And
scolding in this way, she ran to the wardrobe and took out of it an
old hood, a pair of stays, and a long grey petticoat, in which she
hastily wrapped the transformed page. Then when this was done,
'Catherine, dear Catherine,' said she, loudly, 'open the door for your
uncle; he is more fool than knave, and won't do you any harm.' The
boy who had become a girl, obeyed. Master Nicolas entered the
room and found in it a young maid whom he did not know, and his
wife in bed. 'Big booby,' said the latter to him, 'don't stand gaping
at what you see. Just as I had come to bed because I had a stomach
ache, I received a visit from Catherine, the daughter of my sister
Jeanne de Palaiseau, with whom we quarrelled fifteen years ago.
Kiss your niece. She is well worth the trouble.' The jeweller gave
Violle a hug, and from that moment he wanted nothing so much as
to be alone with her a moment, so that he might embrace her as

much as he liked. For this reason he led her without any delay down to the kitchen, under the pretext of giving her some walnuts and wine, and he was no sooner there with her than he began to caress her very affectionately. He would not have stopped at that if St. Orberosia had not inspired his good wife with the idea of seeing what he was about. She found him with the pretended niece sitting on his knee. She called him a debauched creature, boxed his ears, and forced him to beg her pardon. The next day Violle resumed his previous form."

Having heard this story the venerable Canon Monnoyer thanked Pierre Mille for having told it, and, taking up his pen, began to write out a list of horses that would win at the next race meeting. For he was a book-maker's clerk.

In the mean time Penguinia gloried in its wealth. Those who produced the things necessary for life, wanted them; those who did not produce them had more than enough. "But these," as a member of the Institute said, "are necessary economic fatalities." The great Penguin people had no longer either traditions, intellectual culture, or arts. The progress of civilisation manifested itself among them by murderous industry, infamous speculation, and hideous luxury. Its capital assumed, as did all the great cities of the time, a cosmopolitan and financial character. An immense and regular ugliness reigned within it. The country enjoyed perfect tranquillity. It had reached its zenith.

BOOK VIII: FUTURE TIMES

THE ENDLESS HISTORY

Alca is becoming Americanised.—*M. Daniset.*

And he overthrew those cities, and all the plain, and all the inhabitants of the cities, and that which grew upon the ground.—*Genesis xix.* 25.

Τῇ Ἑλλάδι πενίη μέν ἀεὶ κοτε σύντροφός ἐστι, ἀρετὴ δὲ ἔπακτός ἐστι, ἀπό τε σοφίης κατεργασμένη καὶ νόμου ἰσχυρομ.*
(Herodotus, Histories, VII. cii.)

You have not seen angels then.—*Liber Terribilis.*

Bqsfttfusftpvtuse jufbmbb b up sjufef tspjtfucftfnqfsf-
vstbqsftbnpjsqsp dmbnfusojsjghjttdmjcfsufnbgsbodftftutpb-
njtfbeftdpnqb hojttgjobo—djfsftr—vjejtqpteoueftsjdiftfste-
vqbzt fuqbsmfn Pzfoevofqsf ttfbdifuffejsjhfboumpqjojno
Voufnpjoxfsiejrvf

We are now beginning to study a chemistry which will deal with effects produced by bodies containing a quantity of concentrated energy the like of which we have not yet had at our disposal.—*Sir William Ramsay.*

THE houses were never high enough to satisfy them; they kept on making them still higher and built them of thirty or forty storeys with offices, shops, banks, societies one above another; they dug cellars and tunnels ever deeper downwards.

Fifteen millions of men laboured in a giant town by the light of beacons which shed forth their glare both day and night. No light of heaven pierced through the smoke of the factories with which the town was girt, but sometimes the red disk of a rayless sun might be seen riding

*Poverty has ever been familiar to Greece, but virtue has been acquired, having been accomplished by wisdom and firm laws.
—Henry Cary's Translation.

in the black firmament through which iron bridges ploughed their way, and from which there descended a continual shower of soot and cinders. It was the most industrial of all the cities in the world and the richest. Its organisation seemed perfect. None of the ancient aristocratic or democratic forms remained; everything was subordinated to the interests of the trusts. This environment gave rise to what anthropologists called the multi-millionaire type. The men of this type were at once energetic and frail, capable of great activity in forming mental combinations and of prolonged labour in offices, but men whose nervous irritability suffered from hereditary troubles which increased as time went on.

Like all true aristocrats, like the patricians of republican Rome or the squires of old England, these powerful men affected a great severity in their habits and customs. They were the ascetics of wealth. At the meetings of the trusts an observer would have noticed their smooth and puffy faces, their lantern cheeks, their sunken eyes and wrinkled brows. With bodies more withered, complexions yellower, lips drier, and eyes filled with a more burning fanaticism than those of the old Spanish monks, these multi-millionaires gave themselves up with inextinguishable ardour to the austerities of banking and industry. Several, denying themselves all happiness, all pleasure, and all rest, spent their miserable lives in rooms without light or air, furnished only with electrical apparatus, living on eggs and milk, and sleeping on camp beds. By doing nothing except pressing nickel buttons with their fingers, these mystics heaped up riches of which they never even saw the signs, and acquired the vain possibility of gratifying desires that they never experienced.

The worship of wealth had its martyrs. One of these multi-millionaires, the famous Samuel Box, preferred to die rather than surrender the smallest atom of his property. One of his workmen, the victim of an accident while at work, being refused any indemnity by his employer, obtained a verdict in the courts, but repelled by innumerable obstacles of procedure, he fell into the direst poverty. Being thus reduced to despair, he succeeded by dint of cunning and audacity in confronting his employer with a loaded revolver in his hand, and threatened to blow out his brains if he did not give him some assistance. Samuel Box gave nothing, and let himself be killed for the sake of principle.

Examples that come from high quarters are followed. Those who possessed some small capital (and they were necessarily the greater number), affected the ideas and habits of the multi-millionaires, in order that they might be classed among them. All passions which injured the increase or the preservation of wealth, were regarded as dishonourable; neither indolence, nor idleness, nor the taste for disinterested study, nor love of the arts, nor, above all, extravagance, was ever forgiven; pity was condemned as a dangerous

weakness. Whilst every inclination to licentiousness excited public
reprobation, the violent and brutal satisfaction of an appetite was,
on the contrary, excused; violence, in truth, was regarded as less
injurious to morality, since it manifested a form of social energy.
The State was firmly based on two great public virtues: respect for
the rich and contempt for the poor. Feeble spirits who were still
moved by human suffering had no other resource than to take
refuge in a hypocrisy which it was impossible to blame, since it
contributed to the maintenance of order and the solidity of institutions.

Thus, among the rich, all were devoted to the social order, or
seemed to be so; all gave good examples, if all did not follow them.
Some felt the severity of their position cruelly; but they endured
it either from pride or from duty. Some attempted, in secret and by
subterfuge, to escape from it for a moment. One of these, Edward
Martin, the President of the Steel Trust, sometimes dressed himself
as a poor man, went forth to beg his bread, and allowed himself to
be jostled by the passers-by. One day, as he asked alms on a bridge,
he engaged in a quarrel with a real beggar, and filled with a fury of
envy, he strangled him.

As they devoted their whole intelligence to business, they sought
no intellectual pleasures. The theatre, which had formerly been very
flourishing among them, was now reduced to pantomimes and comic
dances. Even the pieces in which women acted were given up; the
taste for pretty forms and brilliant toilettes had been lost; the
somersaults of clowns and the music of negroes were preferred
above them, and what roused enthusiasm was the sight of women
upon the stage whose necks were bedizened with diamonds, or processions carrying golden bars in triumph. Ladies of wealth were as
much compelled as the men to lead a respectable life. According to
a tendency common to all civilizations, public feeling set them up as
symbols; they were, by their austere magnificence, to represent both
the splendour of wealth and its intangibility. The old habits of gallantry had been reformed, but fashionable lovers were now secretly
replaced by muscular labourers or stray grooms. Nevertheless,
scandals were rare, a foreign journey concealed nearly all of them,
and the Princesses of the Trusts remained objects of universal
esteem.

The rich formed only a small minority, but their collaborators,
who composed the entire people, had been completely won over or
completely subjugated by them. They formed two classes, the agents
of commerce or banking, and workers in the factories. The former
contributed an immense amount of work and received large salaries.
Some of them succeeded in founding establishments of their own;
for in the constant increase of the public wealth the more intelligent and audacious could hope for anything. Doubtless it would
have been possible to find a certain number of discontented and

rebellious persons among the immense crowd of engineers and accountants, but this powerful society had imprinted its firm discipline even on the minds of its opponents. The very anarchists were laborious and regular.

As for the workmen who toiled in the factories that surrounded the town, their decadence, both physical and moral, was terrible; they were examples of the type of poverty as it is set forth by anthropology. Although the development among them of certain muscles, due to the particular nature of their work, might give a false idea of their strength, they presented sure signs of morbid debility. Of low stature, with small heads and narrow chests, they were further distinguished from the comfortable classes by a multitude of physiological anomalies, and, in particular, by a common want of symmetry between the head and the limbs. And they were destined to a gradual and continuous degeneration, for the State made soldiers of the more robust among them, and the health of these did not long withstand the brothels and the drink-shops that sprang up around their barracks. The proletarians became more and more feeble in mind. The continued weakening of their intellectual faculties was not entirely due to their manner of life; it resulted also from a methodical selection carried out by the employers. The latter, fearing that workmen of too great ability might be inclined to put forward legitimate demands, took care to eliminate them by every possible means, and preferred to engage ignorant and stupid labourers, who were incapable of defending their rights, but were yet intelligent enough to perform their toils, which highly perfected machines rendered extremely simple. Thus the proletarians were unable to do anything to improve their lot. With difficulty did they succeed by means of strikes in maintaining the rate of their wages. Even this means began to fail them. The alternations of production inherent in the capitalist system caused such cessations of work that, in several branches of industry, as soon as a strike was declared, the accumulation of products allowed the employers to dispense with the strikers. In a word, these miserable employees were plunged in a gloomy apathy that nothing enlightened and nothing exasperated. They were necessary instruments for the social order and well adapted to their purpose.

Upon the whole, this social order seemed the most firmly established that had yet been seen, at least among mankind, for that of bees and ants is incomparably more stable. Nothing could foreshadow the ruin of a system founded on what is strongest in human nature, pride and cupidity. However, keen observers discovered several grounds for uneasiness. The most certain, although the least apparent, were of an economic order, and consisted in the continually increasing amount of over-production, which entailed long and cruel interruption of labour, though these were, it is true, utilized by the manufacturers as a means of breaking the power of the

workmen, by facing them with the prospect of a lock-out. A more
obvious peril resulted from the physiological state of almost the
entire population. "The health of the poor is what it must be," said
the experts in hygiene, "but that of the rich leaves much to be
desired." It was not difficult to find the causes of this. The supply
of oxygen necessary for life was insufficient in the city, and men
breathed in an artificial air. The food trusts, by means of the most
daring chemical syntheses, produced artificial wines, meat, milk,
fruit, and vegetables, and the diet thus imposed gave rise to stomach and brain troubles. The multi-millionaires were bald at the age
of eighteen; some showed from time to time a dangerous weakness
of mind. Over-strung and enfeebled, they gave enormous sums to
ignorant charlatans; and it was a common thing for some trumpery
bath-attendant or other who turned healer or prophet, to make a
rapid fortune by the practice of medicine or theology. The number
of lunatics increased continually; suicides multiplied in the world
of wealth, and many of them were accompanied by atrocious and
extraordinary circumstances, which bore witness to an unheard of
perversion of intelligence and sensibility.

Another fatal symptom created a strong impression upon average
minds. Terrible accidents, henceforth periodical and regular, entered into people's calculations, and kept mounting higher and
higher in statistical tables. Every day, machines burst into fragments, houses fell down, trains laden with merchandise fell on to
the streets, demolishing entire buildings and crushing hundreds of
passers-by. Through the ground, honey-combed with tunnels, two
or three storeys of work-shops would often crash, engulfing all
those who worked in them.

§ 2

In the southwestern district of the city, on an eminence which
had preserved its ancient name of Fort Saint-Michel, there stretched
a square where some old trees still spread their exhausted arms
above the greensward. Landscape gardeners had constructed a cascade, grottos, a torrent, a lake, and an island, on its northern slope.
From this side one could see the whole town with its streets, its
boulevards, its squares, the multitude of its roofs and domes, its
air-passages, and its crowds of men, covered with a veil of silence,
and seemingly enchanted by the distance. This square was the
healthiest place in the capital; here no smoke obscured the sky,
and children were brought here to play. In summer some employees
from the neighbouring offices and laboratories used to resort to it
for a moment after their luncheons, but they did not disturb its
solitude and peace.

It was owing to this custom that, one day in June, about midday, a telegraph clerk, Caroline Meslier, came and sat down on a

bench at the end of a terrace. In order to refresh her eyes by the sight of a little green, she turned her back to the town. Dark, with brown eyes, robust and placid, Caroline appeared to be from twenty-five to twenty-eight years of age. Almost immediately, a clerk in the Electricity Trust, George Clair, took his place beside her. Fair, thin, and supple, he had features of a feminine delicacy; he was scarcely older than she, and looked still younger. As they met almost every day in this place, a comradeship had sprung up between them, and they enjoyed chatting together. But their conversation had never been tender, affectionate, or even intimate. Caroline, although it had happened to her in the past to repent of her confidence, might perhaps have been less reserved had not George Clair always shown himself extremely restrained in his expressions and behaviour. He always gave a purely intellectual character to the conversation, keeping it within the realm of general ideas, and, moreover, expressing himself on all subjects with the greatest freedom. He spoke frequently of the organization of society, and the conditions of labour.

"Wealth," said he, "is one of the means of living happily; but people have made it the sole end of existence."

And this state of things seemed monstrous to both of them.

They returned continually to various scientific subjects with which they were both familiar.

On that day they discussed the evolution of chemistry.

"From the moment," said Clair, "that radium was seen to be transformed into helium, people ceased to affirm the immutability of simple bodies; in this way all those old laws about simple relations and about the indestructibility of matter were abolished."

"However," said she, "chemical laws exist."

For, being a woman, she had need of belief.

He resumed carelessly:

"Now that we can procure radium in sufficient quantities, science possesses incomparable means of analysis; even at present we get glimpses, within what are called simple bodies, of extremely diversified complex ones, and we discover energies in matter which seem to increase even by reason of its tenuity."

As they talked, they threw bits of bread to the birds, and some children played around them.

Passing from one subject to another:

"This hill, in the quaternary epoch," said Clair, "was inhabited by wild horses. Last year, as they were tunnelling for the water mains, they found a layer of the bones of primeval horses."

She was anxious to know whether, at that distant epoch, man had yet appeared.

He told her that man used to hunt the primeval horse long before he tried to domesticate him.

"Man," he added, "was at first a hunter, then he became a shepherd, a cultivator, a manufacturer . . . and these diverse civilizations succeeded each other at intervals of time that the mind cannot conceive."

He took out his watch.

Caroline asked if it was already time to go back to the office.

He said it was not, that it was scarcely half-past twelve.

A little girl was making mud pies at the foot of their bench; a little boy of seven or eight years was playing in front of them. Whilst his mother was sewing on an adjoining bench, he played all alone at being a run-away horse, and with that power of illusion, of which children are capable, he imagined that he was at the same time the horse, and those who ran after him, and those who fled in terror before him. He kept struggling with himself and shouting: "Stop him, Hi! Hi! This is an awful horse, he has got the bit between his teeth."

Caroline asked the question:

"Do you think that men were happy formerly?"

Her companion answered:

"They suffered less when they were younger. They acted like that little boy: they played; they played at arts, at virtues, at vices, at heroism, at beliefs, at pleasures; they had illusions; which entertained them; they made a noise, they amused themselves. But now. . . ."

He interrupted himself, and looked again at his watch.

The child, who was running, struck his foot against the little girl's pail, and fell his full length on the gravel. He remained a moment stretched out motionless, then raised himself up on the palms of his hands. His forehead puckered, his mouth opened, and he burst into tears. His mother ran up but Caroline had lifted him from the ground and was wiping his eyes and mouth with her handkerchief. The child kept on sobbing and Clair took him in his arms.

"Come, don't cry, my little man! I am going to tell you a story.

"A fisherman once threw his net into the sea and drew out a little, sealed, copper pot, which he opened with his knife. Smoke came out of it, and as it mounted up to the clouds the smoke grew thicker and thicker and became a giant who gave such a terrible yawn that the whole world was blown to dust. . . ."

Clair stopped himself, gave a dry laugh, and handed the child back to his mother. Then he took out his watch again, and kneeling on the bench with his elbows resting on its back he gazed at the town. As far as the eye could reach, the multitude of houses stood out in their tiny immensity.

Caroline turned her eyes in the same direction.

"What splendid weather it is!" said she. "The sun's rays change the smoke on the horizon into gold. The worst thing about civilization is that it deprives one of the light of day."

He did not answer; his looks remained fixed on a place in the town.

After some seconds of silence they saw about half a mile away, in the richer district on the other side of the river, a sort of tragic fog rearing itself upwards. A moment afterwards an explosion was heard even where they were sitting, and an immense tree of smoke mounted towards the pure sky. Little by little the air was filled with an imperceptible murmur caused by the shouts of thousands of men. Cries burst forth quite close to the square.

"What has been blown up?"

The bewilderment was great, for although accidents were common, such a violent explosion as this one had never been seen, and everybody perceived that something terribly strange had happened.

Attempts were made to locate the place of the accident; districts, streets, different buildings, clubs, theatres, and shops were mentioned. Information gradually became more precise and at last the truth was known.

"The Steel Trust has just been blown up."

Clair put his watch back into his pocket.

Caroline looked at him closely and her eyes filled with astonishment.

At last she whispered in his ear:

"Did you know it? Were you expecting it? Was it you . . ."

He answered very calmly:

"That town ought to be destroyed."

She replied in a gentle and thoughtful tone:

"I think so too."

And both of them returned quietly to their work.

§ 3

From that day onward, anarchist attempts followed one another every week without interruption. The victims were numerous, and almost all of them belonged to the poorer classes. These crimes roused public resentment. It was among domestic servants, hotel-keepers, and the employees of such small shops as the Trusts still allowed to exist, that indignation burst forth most vehemently. In popular districts women might be heard demanding unusual punishments for the dynamitards. (They were called by this old name, although it was hardly appropriate to them, since, to these unknown chemists, dynamite was an innocent material only fit to destroy ant-hills, and they considered it mere child's play to explode nitro-glycerine with a cartridge made of fulminate of mercury.) Business ceased suddenly, and those who were least rich were the first to feel the effects. They spoke of doing justice themselves to the anarchists. In the mean time the factory workers remained hostile or indifferent to violent action. They were threatened, as a result of the decline of business, with a likelihood of losing their work, or even a lock-out in all the factories. The Federation of Trade Unions proposed a general strike as the most powerful means of influencing the employers, and the best aid that could be given to the revolutionists, but all the trades with the exception of the gilders refused to cease work.

The police made numerous arrests. Troops summoned from all parts of the National Federation protected the offices of the Trusts, the houses of the multi-millionaires, the public halls, the banks, and the big shops. A fortnight passed without a single explosion, and it was concluded that the dynamitards, in all probability but a handful of persons, perhaps even still fewer, had all been killed or captured, or that they were in hiding, or had taken flight. Confidence returned; it returned at first among the poorer classes. Two or three hundred thousand soldiers, who had been lodged in the most closely populated districts, stimulated trade, and people began to cry out: "Hurrah for the army!"

The rich, who had not been so quick to take alarm, were reassured more slowly. But at the Stock Exchange a group of "bulls" spread optimistic rumours and by a powerful effort put a brake upon the fall in prices. Business improved. Newspapers with big circulations supported the movement. With patriotic eloquence they depicted capital as laughing in its impregnable position at the assaults of a few dastardly criminals, and public wealth maintaining its serene ascendency in spite of the vain threats made against it. They were sincere in their attitude, though at the same time they found it benefited them. Outrages were forgotten or their occurrence denied. On Sundays, at the race-meetings, the stands were adorned by women covered with pearls and diamonds. It was observed with joy that the capitalists had not suffered. Cheers were given for the multi-millionaires in the saddling rooms.

On the following day the Southern Railway Station, the Petroleum Trust, and the huge church built at the expense of Thomas Morcellet were all blown up. Thirty houses were in flames, and the beginning of a fire was discovered at the docks. The firemen showed amazing intrepidity and zeal. They managed their tall fire-escapes with automatic precision, and climbed as high as thirty storeys to rescue the luckless inhabitants from the flames. The soldiers performed their duties with spirit, and were given a double ration of coffee. But these fresh casualties started a panic. Millions of people, who wanted to take their money with them and leave the town at once, crowded the great banking houses. These establishments, after paying out money for three days, closed their doors amid mutterings of a riot. A crowd of fugitives, laden with their baggage, besieged the railway stations and took the town by storm. Many who were anxious to lay in a stock of provisions and take refuge in the cellars, attacked the grocery stores, although they were guarded by soldiers with fixed bayonets. The public authorities displayed energy. Numerous arrests were made and thousands of warrants issued against suspected persons.

During the three weeks that followed no outrage was committed. There was a rumour that bombs had been found in the Opera House, in the cellars of the Town Hall, and beside one of the pillars of the Stock Exchange. But it was soon known that these were boxes of sweets that had been put in those places by practical jokers or lunatics. One of the accused, when questioned by a magistrate, declared that he was the chief author of the explosions, and said that all his accomplices had lost their lives. These confessions were published by the newspapers and helped to reassure public opinion. It was only towards the close of the examination that the magistrates saw they had to deal with a pretender who was in no way connected with any of the crimes.

The experts chosen by the courts discovered nothing that enabled them to determine the engine employed in the work of destruction. According to their conjectures the new explosion emanated from a gas which radium evolves, and it was supposed that electric waves, produced by a special type of oscillator, were propagated through space and thus caused the explosion. But even the ablest chemist could say nothing precise or certain. At last two policemen, who were passing in front of the Hôtel Meyer, found on the pavement, close to a ventilator, an egg made of white metal and provided with a capsule at each end. They picked it up carefully, and, on the orders of their chief, carried it to the municipal laboratory. Scarcely had the experts assembled to examine it, than the egg burst and blew up the amphitheatre and the dome. All the experts perished, and with them Collin, the General of Artillery, and the famous Professor Tigre.

The capitalist society did not allow itself to be daunted by this fresh disaster. The great banks re-opened their doors, declaring that they would meet demands partly in bullion and partly in paper money guaranteed by the State. The Stock Exchange and the Trade Exchange, in spite of the complete cessation of business, decided not to suspend their sittings.

In the meantime the magisterial investigation into the case of those who had been first accused had come to an end. Perhaps the evidence brought against them might have appeared insufficient under other circumstances, but the zeal both of the magistrates and the public made up for this insufficiency. On the eve of the day fixed for the trial the Courts of Justice were blown up and eight hundred people were killed, the greater number of them being judges and lawyers. A furious crowd broke into the prison and lynched the prisoners. The troops sent to restore order were received with showers of stones and revolver shots; several soldiers being dragged from their horses and trampled underfoot. The sol-

diers fired on the mob and many persons were killed. At last the
public authorities succeeded in establishing tranquillity. Next day
the Bank was blown up.

From that time onwards unheard-of things took place. The factory workers, who had refused to strike, rushed in crowds into the
town and set fire to the houses. Entire regiments, led by their officers, joined the workmen, went with them through the town singing revolutionary hymns, and took barrels of petroleum from the
docks with which to feed the fires. Explosions were continual. One
morning a monstrous tree of smoke, like the ghost of a huge palm
tree half a mile in height, rose above the giant Telegraph Hall
which suddenly fell into a complete ruin.

Whilst half the town was in flames, the other half pursued its
accustomed life. In the mornings, milk pails could be heard jingling
in the dairy carts. In a deserted avenue some old navvy might be
seen seated against a wall slowly eating hunks of bread with perhaps a little meat. Almost all the presidents of the trusts remained
at their posts. Some of them performed their duty with heroic simplicity. Raphael Box, the son of a martyred multi-millionaire, was
blown up as he was presiding at the general meeting of the Sugar
Trust. He was given a magnificent funeral and the procession on
its way to the cemetery had to climb six times over piles of ruins
or cross upon planks over the uprooted roads.

The ordinary helpers of the rich, the clerks, employees, brokers,
and agents, preserved an unshaken fidelity. The surviving clerks of
the Bank that had been blown up, made their way along the ruined
streets through the midst of smoking houses to hand in their bills
of exchange, and several were swallowed up in the flames while
endeavouring to present their receipts.

Nevertheless, any illusion concerning the state of affairs was impossible. The enemy was master of the town. Instead of silence the
noise of explosions was now continuous and produced an insur-
mountable feeling of horror. The lighting apparatus having been
destroyed, the city was plunged in darkness all through the night,
and appalling crimes were committed. The populous districts alone,
having suffered the least, still preserved measures of protection.
They were paraded by patrols of volunteers who shot the robbers,
and at every street corner one stumbled over a body lying in a pool
of blood, the hands bound behind the back, a handkerchief over
the face, and a placard pinned upon the breast.

It became impossible to clear away the ruins or to bury the dead.
Soon the stench from the corpses became intolerable. Epidemics
raged and caused innumerable deaths, while they also rendered
the survivors feeble and listless. Famine carried off almost all who
were left. A hundred and one days after the first outrage, whilst
six army corps with field artillery and siege artillery were marching, at night, into the poorest quarter of the city, Caroline and

Clair, holding each other's hands, were watching from the roof a lofty house, the only one still left standing, but now surrounded by smoke and flame. Joyous songs ascended from the street, where the crowd was dancing in delirium.

"To-morrow it will be ended," said the man "and it will be better."

The young woman, her hair loosened and her face shining with the reflection of the flames, gazed with a pious joy at the circle of fire that was growing closer around them.

"It will be better," said she also.

And throwing herself into the destroyer's arms she pressed a passionate kiss upon his lips.

§ 4

The other towns of the federation also suffered from disturbances and outbreaks, and then order was restored. Reforms were introduced into institutions and great changes took place in habits and customs, but the country never recovered the loss of its capital, and never regained its former prosperity. Commerce and industry dwindled away, and civilization abandoned those countries which for so long it had preferred to all others. They became insalubrious and sterile; the territory that had supported so many millions of men became nothing more than a desert. On the hill of Fort St. Michel wild horses cropped the coarse grass.

Days flowed by like water from the fountains, and the centuries passed like drops falling from the ends of stalactites. Hunters came to chase the bears upon the hills that covered the forgotten city; shepherds led their flocks upon them; labourers turned up the soil with their ploughs; gardeners cultivated their lettuces and grafted their pear trees. They were not rich, and they had no arts. The walls of their cabins were covered with old vines and roses. A goat-skin clothed their tanned limbs, while their wives dressed themselves with the wool that they themselves had spun. The goat-herds moulded little figures of men and animals out of clay, or sang songs about the young girl who follows her lover through woods or among the browsing goats while the pine trees whisper together and the water utters its murmuring sound. The master of the house grew angry with the beetles who devoured his figs; he planned snares to protect his fowls from the velvet-tailed fox, and he poured out wine for his neighbours saying:

"Drink! The flies have not spoilt my vintage; the vines were dry before they came."

Then in the course of ages the wealth of the villages and the corn that filled the fields were pillaged by barbarian invaders. The country changed its masters several times. The conquerors built castles upon the hills; cultivation increased; mills, forges, tanneries, and looms were established; roads were opened through the woods and over the marshes; the river was covered with boats. The hamlets became large villages and joining together formed a town which protected itself by deep trenches and lofty walls. Later, becoming the capital of a great State, it found itself straitened within its now useless ramparts, and it converted them into grass-covered walks.

It grew very rich and large beyond measure. The houses were never high enough to satisfy the people; they kept on making them still higher and built them of thirty or forty storeys, with offices, shops, banks, societies one above another; they dug cellars and tunnels ever deeper downwards. Fifteen millions of men laboured in the giant town.

THE CRIME OF SYLVESTRE BONNARD

PART ONE: THE LOG

December 24, 1849.

HAD put on my slippers and my dressing-gown. I wiped away a tear with which the north wind blowing over the quay had obscured my vision. A bright fire was leaping in the chimney of my study. Ice-crystals, shaped like fern-leaves, were sprouting over the window-panes, and concealed from me the Seine with its bridges and the Louvre of the Valois.

I drew up my easy-chair to the hearth, and my *table-volante,* and took up so much of my place by the fire as Hamilcar deigned to allow me. Hamilcar was lying in front of the andirons, curled up on a cushion, with his nose between his paws. His thick fine fur rose and fell with his regular breathing. At my coming, he slowly slipped a glance of his agate eyes at me from between his half-opened lids, which he closed again almost at once, thinking to himself, "It is nothing; it is only my friend."

"Hamilcar," I said to him, as I stretched my legs—"Hamilcar, somnolent Prince of the City of Books—thou guardian nocturnal! Like that Divine Cat who combated the impious in Heliopolis—in the night of the great combat—thou dost defend from vile nibblers those books which the old savant acquired at the cost of his slender savings and indefatigable zeal. Sleep, Hamilcar, softly as a sultana, in this library, that shelters thy military virtues; for verily in thy person are united the formidable aspect of a Tartar warrior and the slumbrous grace of a woman of the Orient. Sleep, thou heroic and voluptuous Hamilcar, while awaiting that moonlight hour in which the mice will come forth to dance before the 'Acta Sanctorum' of the learned Bolandists!"

The beginning of this discourse pleased Hamilcar, who accompanied it with a throat-sound like the song of a kettle on the fire. But as my voice waxed louder, Hamilcar notified me by lowering his ears and by wrinkling the striped skin of his brow that it was bad taste on my part so to declaim.

"This old-book man," evidently thought Hamilcar, "talks to no purpose at all, while our housekeeper never utters a word which is

195

not full of good sense, full of significance—containing either the announcement of a meal or the promise of a whipping. One knows what she says. But this old man puts together a lot of sounds signifying nothing."

So thought Hamilcar to himself. Leaving him to his reflections, I opened a book, which I began to read with interest; for it was a catalogue of manuscripts. I do not know any reading more easy, more fascinating, more delightful than that of a catalogue. The one which I was reading—edited in 1824 by Mr. Thompson, librarian to Sir Thomas Raleigh—sins, it is true, by excess of brevity, and does not offer that character of exactitude which the archivists of my own generation were the first to introduce into works upon diplomatics and paleography. It leaves a good deal to be desired and to be divined. This is perhaps why I find myself aware, while reading it, of a state of mind which in a nature more imaginative than mine might be called reverie. I had allowed myself to drift away thus gently upon the current of my thoughts, when my housekeeper announced, in a tone of ill-humour, that Monsieur Coccoz desired to speak with me.

In fact, some one had slipped into the library after her. He was a little man—a poor little man of puny appearance, wearing a thin jacket. He approached me with a number of little bows and smiles. But he was very pale, and, although still young and alert, he looked ill. I thought, as I looked at him, of a wounded squirrel. He carried under his arm a green *toilette,* which he put upon a chair; then unfastening the four corners of the *toilette,* he uncovered a heap of little yellow books.

"Monsieur," he then said to me, "I have not the honour to be known to you. I am a book-agent, Monsieur. I represent the leading houses of the capital, and in the hope that you will kindly honour me with your confidence, I take the liberty to offer you a few novelties."

Kind gods! just gods! such novelties as the homunculus Coccoz showed me! The first volume that he put in my hand was "L'Histoire de la Tour de Nesle," with the amours of Marguerite de Bourgogne and the Captain Buridan.

"It is a historical book," he said to me, with a smile—"a book of real history."

"In that case," I replied, "it must be very tiresome; for all the historical books which contain no lies are extremely tedious. I write some authentic ones myself; and if you were unlucky enough to carry a copy of any of them from door to door you would run the risk of keeping it all your life in that green baize of yours, without ever finding ever a cook foolish enough to buy it from you."

"Certainly Monsieur," the little man answered, out of pure good-nature.

And, all smiling again, he offered me the "Amours d'Héloïse et d'Abeilard"; but I made him understand that, at my age, I had no use for love-stories.

Still smiling, he proposed me the "Règle des Jeux de la Société" —piquet, bezique, écarté, whist, dice, draughts, and chess.

"Alas!" I said to him, "if you want to make me remember the rules of bezique, give me back my old friend Bignan, with whom I used to play cards every evening before the Five Academies solemnly escorted him to the cemetery; or else bring down to the frivolous level of human amusements the grave intelligence of Hamilcar, whom you see on that cushion, for he is the sole companion of my evenings."

The little man's smile became vague and uneasy.

"Here," he said, "is a new collection of society amusements—jokes and puns—with a receipt for changing a red rose to a white rose."

I told him that I had fallen out with roses for a long time, and that, as to jokes, I was satisfied with those which I unconsciously permitted myself to make in the course of my scientific labours.

The homunculus offered me his last book, with his last smile. He said to me:

"Here is the 'Clef des Songes'—the 'Key of Dreams'—with the explanation of any dreams that anybody can have; dreams of gold, dreams of robbers, dreams of death, dreams of falling from the top of a tower. . . . It is exhaustive."

I had taken hold of the tongs, and, brandishing them energetically, I replied to my commercial visitor:

"Yes, my friend; but those dreams and a thousand others, joyous or tragic, are all summed up in one—the Dream of Life; is your little yellow book able to give me the key to that?"

"Yes, Monsieur," answered the homunculus; "the book is complete, and it is not dear—one franc twenty-five centimes, Monsieur."

I called my housekeeper—for there is no bell in my room—and said to her:

"Thérèse, Monsieur Coccoz—whom I am going to ask you to show out—has a book here which might interest you: the 'Key of Dreams.' I shall be very glad to buy it for you."

My housekeeper responded:

"Monsieur, when one has not even time to dream awake, one has still less time to dream asleep. Thank God, my days are just enough for my work and my work for my days, and I am able to say every night, 'Lord, bless Thou the rest which I am going to take.' I never dream, either on my feet or in bed; and I never mistake my eider-down coverlet for a devil, as my cousin did; and, if you will allow me to give my opinion about it, I think you have books enough here now. Monsieur has thousands and thousands of books, which simply turn his head; and as for me, I have just two, which are quite enough for all my wants and purposes—my Catholic prayer-book and my 'Cuisinière Bourgeoise.'"

And with these words my housekeeper helped the little man to fasten up his stock again within the green *toilette*.

The homunculus Coccoz had ceased to smile. His relaxed features took such an expression of suffering that I felt sorry to have made fun of so unhappy a man. I called him back, and told him that I had caught a glimpse of a copy of the "Histoire d'Estelle et de Némorin," which he had among his books; that I was very fond of shepherds and shepherdesses, and that I would be quite willing to purchase, at a reasonable price, the story of these two perfect lovers.

"I will sell you that book for one franc twenty-five centimes, Monsieur," replied Coccoz, whose face at once beamed with joy. "It is historical; and you will be pleased with it. I know now just what suits you. I see that you are a connoisseur. To-morrow I will bring you the 'Crimes des Papes.' It is a good book. I will bring you the *édition d'amateur,* with coloured plates."

I begged him not to do anything of the sort, and sent him away happy. When the green *toilette* and the agent had disappeared in the shadow of the corridor I asked my housekeeper whence this little man had dropped upon us.

"Dropped is the word," she answered; "he dropped on us from the roof, Monsieur, where he lives with his wife."

"You say he has a wife, Thérèse? That is marvellous! women are very strange creatures! This one must be a very unfortunate little woman."

"I don't really know what she is," answered Thérèse; "but every morning I see her trailing a silk dress covered with grease-spots over the stairs. She makes soft eyes at people. And, in the name of common sense! does it become a woman that has been received here out of charity to make eyes and to wear dresses like that? For they allowed the couple to occupy the attic during the time the roof was being repaired, in consideration of the fact that the husband is sick and the wife in an interesting condition. The concierge even says that the pains came on her this morning, and that she is now confined. They must have been very badly off for a child!"

"Thérèse," I replied, "they had no need of a child, doubtless. But Nature had decided they should bring one into the world; Nature made them fall into her snare. One must have exceptional prudence to defeat Nature's schemes. Let us be sorry for them, and not blame them! As for silk dresses, there is no young woman who does not like them. The daughters of Eve adore adornment. You yourself, Thérèse—who are so serious and sensible—what a fuss you make when you have no white apron to wait at table in! But, tell me, have they got everything necessary in their attic?"

"How could they have it, Monsieur," my housekeeper made answer. "The husband, whom you have just seen, used to be a jewellery-peddler—at least, so the concierge tells me—and nobody knows why he stopped selling watches. You have just seen that he is now selling almanacs. That is no way to make an honest living, and I never will believe that God's blessing can come to an almanac-peddler. Between ourselves, the wife looks to me for all the world like a good-for-nothing—a *Marie-couche toi-là*. I think she would be just as capable of bringing up a child as I should be of playing the guitar. Nobody seems to know where they came from; but I am sure they must have come by Misery's coach from the country of *Sans-souci*."

"Wherever they have come from, Thérèse, they are unfortunate; and their attic is cold."

"*Pardi!*—the roof is broken in several places, and the rain comes through in streams. They have neither furniture nor clothing. I don't think cabinet-makers and weavers work much for Christians of that sect!"

"That is very sad, Thérèse; a Christian woman much less well provided for than this pagan, Hamilcar here!—what does she have to say?"

"Monsieur, I never speak to those people; I don't know what she says or what she sings. But she sings all day long; I hear her from the stairway whenever I am going out or coming in."

"Well! the heir of the Coccoz family will be able to say, like the Egg in the village riddle: '*Ma mère me fit en chantant*.'* The like happened in the case of Henry IV. When Jeanne d'Albret felt herself about to be confined she began to sing an old Béarnaise canticle:

> " 'Notre-Dame du bout du pont,
> Venez à mon aide en cette heure!
> Priez le Dieu du ciel
> Qu'il me délivre vite,
> Qu'il me donne un garçon!'

"It is certainly unreasonable to bring little unfortunates into the world. But the thing is done every day, my dear Thérèse and all the philosophers on earth will never be able to reform the silly custom. Madame Coccoz has followed it, and she sings. That is creditable at all events! But, tell me, Thérèse, have you not put on the soup to boil to-day?"

"Yes, Monsieur; and it is time for me to go and skim it."

"Good! but don't forget, Thérèse, to take a good bowl of soup out of the pot and carry it to Madame Coccoz, our attic neighbour."

*"My mother sang when she brought me into the world."

My housekeeper was on the point of leaving the room when I
added, just in time:

"Thérèse, before you do anything else, please call your friend the
porter, and tell him to take a good bundle of wood out of our stock
and carry it up to the attic of those Coccoz folks. See, above all,
that he puts a first-class log in the lot—a real Christmas log. As for
the homunculus, if he comes back again, do not allow either himself or any of his yellow books to come in here."

Having taken all these little precautions with the refined egotism
of an old bachelor, I returned to my catalogue again.

With what surprise, with what emotion, with what anxiety did I
therein discover the following mention, which I cannot even now
copy without feeling my hand tremble:

"LA LEGENDE DORÉE DE JACQUES DE GENES
(Jacques de Voragine);—traduction française, petit in-4.

"This MS. of the fourteenth century contains, besides the tolerably
complete translation of the celebrated work of Jacques de Voragine,
1. The Legends of Saints Ferréol, Ferrution, Germain, Vincent, and Droctoveus; 2. A poem *On the Miraculous Burial of Monsieur Saint-Germain
of Auxerre*. This translation, as well as the legends and the poem, are
due to the Clerk Alexander.

"This MS. is written upon vellum. It contains a great number of illuminated letters, and two finely executed miniatures, in a rather imperfect
state of preservation:—one represents the Purification of the Virgin, and
the other the Coronation of Proserpine."

What a discovery! Perspiration moistened my forehead, and a
veil seemed to come before my eyes. I trembled; I flushed; and,
without being able to speak, I felt a sudden impulse to cry out at
the top of my voice.

What a treasure! For more than forty years I had been making
a special study of the history of Christian Gaul, and particularly of
that glorious Abbey of Saint-Germain-des-Prés, whence issued forth
those King-Monks who founded our national dynasty. Now, despite
the culpable insufficiency of the description given, it was evident
to me that the MS. of the Clerk Alexander must have come from
the great Abbey. Everything proved this fact. All the legends added
by the translator related to the pious foundation of the Abbey by
King Childebert. Then the legend of Saint-Droctoveus was particularly significant; being the legend of the first abbot of my dear
Abbey. The poem in French verse on the burial of Saint-Germain
led me actually into the nave of that venerable basilica which was
the *umbilicus* of Christian Gaul.

The "Golden Legend" is in itself a vast and gracious work.
Jacques de Voragine, Definitor of the Order of Saint-Dominic, and
Archbishop of Genoa, collected in the thirteenth century the vari-
ous legends of Catholic saints, and formed so rich a compilation

that from all the monasteries and castles of the time there arose
the cry: "This is the 'Golden Legend.'" The "Légende Dorée" was
especially opulent in Roman hagiography. Edited by an Italian
monk, it reveals its best merits in the treatment of matters relating to the terrestrial domains of Saint Peter. Voragine can only
perceive the greater saints of the Occident as through a cold mist.
For this reason the Aquitanian and Saxon translators of the good
legend-writer were careful to add to his recital the lives of their
own national saints.

I have read and collated a great many manuscripts of the
"Golden Legend." I know all those described by my learned colleague, M. Paulin Paris, in his handsome catalogue of the MSS. of
the Bibliothèque du Roi. There were two among them which especially drew my attention. One is of the fourteenth century and contains a translation by Jean Belet; the other, younger by a century,
presents the version of Jacques Vignay. Both come from the Col-
bert collection, and were placed on the shelves of that glorious Col-
bertine library by the Librarian Baluze—whose name I can never
pronounce without uncovering my head; for even in the century of
the giants of erudition, Baluze astounds by his greatness. I know

also a very curious codex in the Bigot collection; I know seventy-four printed editions of the work, commencing with the venerable ancestor of all—the Gothic of Strasburg, begun in 1471, and finished in 1475. But no one of those MSS., no one of those editions, contains the legends of Saints Ferréol, Ferrution, Germain, Vincent, and Droctoveus; no one bears the name of the Clerk Alexander; no one, in fine, came from the Abbey of Saint-Germain-des-Prés. Compared with the MS. described by Mr. Thompson, they are only as straw to gold. I have seen with my eyes, I have touched with my fingers, an incontrovertible testimony to the existence of this document. But the document itself—what has become of it? Sir Thomas Raleigh went to end his days by the shores of the Lake of Como, whither he carried with him a part of his literary wealth. Where did the books go after the death of that aristocratic collector? Where could the manuscript of the Clerk Alexander have gone?

"And why," I asked myself, "why should I have learned that this precious book exists, if I am never to possess it—never even to see it? I would go to seek it in the burning heart of Africa, or in the icy regions of the Pole if I knew it were there. But I do not know where it is. I do not know if it be guarded in a triple-locked iron case by some jealous biblomaniac. I do not know if it be growing mouldy in the attic of some ignoramus. I shudder at the thought that perhaps its torn-out leaves may have been used to cover the pickle-jars of some housekeeper."

August 30, 1850.

THE heavy heat compelled me to walk slowly. I kept close to the walls of the north quays; and, in the lukewarm shade, the shops of the dealers in old books, engravings, and antiquated furniture drew my eyes and appealed to my fancy. Rummaging and idling among these, I hastily enjoyed some verses spiritedly thrown off by a poet of the Pleiad. I examined an elegant Masquerade by Watteau. I felt, with my eye, the weight of a two-handed sword, a steel *gorgerin,* a morion. What a thick helmet! What a ponderous breastplate—*Seigneur!* A giant's garb? No—the carapace of an insect. The men of those days were cuirassed like beetles; their weakness was within them. Today, on the contrary, our strength is interior, and our armed souls dwell in feeble bodies.

. . . Here is a pastel-portrait of a lady of the old time—the face, vague like a shadow, smiles; and a hand, gloved with an openwork mitten, retains upon her satiny knees a lap-dog, with a ribbon about its neck. That picture fills me with a sort of charming melancholy. Let those who have no half-effaced pastels in their own hearts laugh at me! Like the horse that scents the stable, I hasten my pace as I near my lodgings. There it is—that great human hive, in which I have a cell, for the purpose of therein distilling the somewhat acrid honey of erudition. I climb the stairs with slow effort. Only a few steps more, and I shall be at my own door. But I divine, rather than see, a robe descending with a sound of rustling silk. I stop, and press myself against the balustrade to make room. The lady who is coming down is bareheaded; she is young; she sings; her eyes and teeth gleam in the shadow, for she laughs with lips and eyes at the same time. She is certainly a neighbour, and a very familiar one. She holds in her arms a pretty child, a little boy —quite naked, like the son of a goddess; he has a medal hung round his neck by a little silver chain. I see him sucking his thumbs and looking at me with those big eyes so newly opened on this old universe. The mother simultaneously looks at me in a sly, mysterious way; she stops—I think blushes a little—and holds out the little creature to me. The baby has a pretty wrinkle between wrist and arm, a pretty wrinkle about his neck, and all over him, from head to foot, the daintiest dimples laugh in his rosy flesh.

The mamma shows him to me with pride.

"Monsieur," she says, "don't you think he is very pretty—my little boy?"

She takes one tiny hand, lifts it to the child's own lips, and, drawing out the darling pink fingers again towards me, says,

"Baby, throw the gentleman a kiss."

Then, folding the little being in her arms, she flees away with the agility of a cat, and is lost to sight in a corridor which, judging by the odour, must lead to some kitchen.

I enter my own quarters.

"Thérèse, who can that young mother be whom I saw bareheaded on the stairs just now, with a pretty little boy?"

And Thérèse replies that it was Madame Coccoz.

I stare up at the ceiling, as if trying to obtain some further illumination. Thérèse then recalls to me the little book-peddler who tried to sell me almanacs last year, while his wife was lying in.

"And Coccoz himself?" I asked.

I was answered that I would never see him again. The poor little man had been laid away underground, without my knowledge, and, indeed, with the knowledge of very few people, only a short time after the happy delivery of Madame Coccoz. I learned that his wife had been able to console herself: I did likewise.

"But, Thérèse," I asked, "has Madame Coccoz got everything she needs in that attic of hers?"

"You would be a great dupe, Monsieur," replied my housekeeper, "if you should bother yourself about that creature. They gave her notice to quit the attic when the roof was repaired. But she stays there yet—in spite of the proprietor, the agent, the concierge, and the bailiffs. I think she has bewitched every one of them. She will leave that attic when she pleases, Monsieur; but she is going to leave in her own carriage. Let me tell you that!"

Thérèse reflected for a moment; and then uttered these words:
"A pretty face is a curse from Heaven."

"Then I ought to thank Heaven for having spared me that curse. But here! put my hat and cane away. I am going to amuse myself with a few pages of Moréri. If I can trust my old fox-nose, we are going to have a nicely flavoured pullet for dinner. Look after that estimable fowl, my girl, and spare your neighbours, so that you and your old master may be spared by them in turn."

Having thus spoken, I proceeded to follow out the tufted ramifications of a princely genealogy.

May 7, 1851.

I HAVE passed the winter according to the ideal of the sages, *in angello cum libello;* and now the swallows of the Quai Malaquais find me on their return about as when they left me. He who lives little, changes little; and it is scarcely living at all to use up one's days over old texts.

Yet I feel myself to-day a little more deeply impregnated than ever before with that vague melancholy which life distils. The economy of my intelligence (I dare scarcely confess it to myself!) has remained disturbed ever since that momentous hour in which the existence of the manuscript of the Clerk Alexander was first revealed to me.

It is strange that I should have lost my rest simply on account of a few old sheets of parchment; but it is unquestionably true. The poor man who has no desires possesses the greatest of riches; he possesses himself. The rich man who desires something is only a wretched slave. I am just such a slave. The sweetest pleasures— those of converse with some one of a delicate and well-balanced mind, or dining out with a friend—are insufficient to enable me to forget the manuscript which I know that I want, and have been wanting from the moment I knew of its existence. I feel the want of it by day and by night: I feel the want of it in all my joys and pains; I feel the want of it while at work or asleep.

I recall my desires as a child. How well I can now comprehend the intense wishes of my early years!

I can see once more, with astonishing vividness, a certain doll which, when I was eight years old, used to be displayed in the window of an ugly little shop of the Rue de Seine. I cannot tell how it happened that this doll attracted me. I was very proud of being a boy; I despised little girls; and I longed impatiently for the day (which, alas! has come) when a strong beard should bristle on my chin. I played at being a soldier; and, under the pretext of obtaining forage for my rocking-horse, I used to make sad havoc among the plants my poor mother delighted to keep on her window-sill. Manly amusements those, I should say! And, nevertheless, I was consumed with longing for a doll. Characters like Hercules have such weaknesses occasionally. Was the one I had fallen in love with at all beautiful? No. I can see her now. She had a splotch of vermilion on either cheek, short soft arms, horrible wooden hands, and long sprawling legs. Her flowered petticoat was fastened at the waist with two pins. Even now I can see the black heads of those two pins. It was a decidedly vulgar doll—smelt of the *faubourg*. I remember perfectly well that, child as I was then, before I had put on my first pair of trousers, I was quite conscious in my own way that this doll lacked grace and style—that she was gross, that she was coarse. But I loved her in spite of that; I loved her just for that; I loved her only; I wanted her. My soldiers and my drums had become as nothing in my eyes, I ceased to stick sprigs of heliotrope and veronica into the mouth of my rocking-horse. That doll was all the word to me. I invented ruses worthy of a savage to oblige Virginie, my nurse, to take me by the little shop in the Rue de Seine. I would press my nose against the window until my nurse had to take my arm and drag me away. "Monsieur Sylvestre, it is late, and your mamma will scold you." Monsieur Sylvestre in those days made very little of either scoldings or whippings. But his nurse lifted him up like a feather, and Monsieur Sylvestre yielded to force. In after-years, with age, he degenerated, and sometimes yielded to fear. But at that time he used to fear nothing.

I was unhappy. An unreasoning but irresistible shame prevented me from telling my mother about the object of my love. Thence all my sufferings. For many days that doll, incessantly present in fancy, danced before my eyes, stared at me fixedly, opened her arms to me, assuming in my imagination a sort of life which made her appear at once mysterious and weird, and thereby all the more charming and desirable.

Finally, one day—a day I shall never forget—my nurse took me to see my uncle, Captain Victor, who had invited me to lunch. I admired my uncle a great deal, as much because he had fired the last French cartridge at Waterloo, as because he used to prepare with his own hands, at my mother's table, certain *chapons-à-l'ail*,* which he afterwards put into the chicory salad. I thought that was very fine! My Uncle Victor also inspired me with much respect by his frogged coat, and still more by his way of turning the whole house upside down from the moment he came into it. Even now I cannot tell just how he managed it, but I can affirm that whenever my Uncle Victor found himself in any assembly of twenty persons, it was impossible to see or to hear anybody but him. My excellent father, I have reason to believe, never shared my admiration for Uncle Victor, who used to sicken him with his pipe, give him great thumps in the back by way of friendliness, and accuse him of lack-

---

*Crust on which garlic has been rubbed.

ing energy. My mother, though always showing a sister's indulgence to the Captain, sometimes advised him to fondle the brandy-bottle a little less frequently. But I had no part either in these repugnances or these reproaches, and Uncle Victor inspired me with the purest enthusiasm. It was therefore with a feeling of pride that I entered into the little lodging he occupied in the Rue Guénégaud. The entire lunch, served on a small table close to the fireplace, consisted of cold meats and confectionery.

The Captain stuffed me with cakes and undiluted wine. He told me of numberless injustices to which he had been a victim. He complained particularly of the Bourbons; and as he neglected to tell me who the Bourbons were, I got the idea—I can't tell how—that the Bourbons were horse-dealers established at Waterloo. The Captain, who never interrupted his talk except for the purpose of pouring out wine, furthermore made charges against a number of dirty scoundrels, blackguards, and good-for-nothings whom I did not know anything about, but whom I hated from the bottom of my heart. At dessert I thought I heard the Captain say my father was a man who could be led anywhere by the nose; but I am not quite sure that I understood him. I had a buzzing in my ears; and it seemed to me that the table was dancing.

My uncle put on his frogged coat, took his bell-shaped hat, and we descended to the street, which seemed to me singularly changed. It looked to me as if I had not been in it before for ever so long a time. Nevertheless, when we came to the Rue de Seine, the idea of my doll suddenly returned to my mind and excited me in an extraordinary way. My head was on fire. I resolved upon a desperate expedient. We were passing before the window. She was there, behind the glass—with her red cheeks, and her flowered petticoat, and her long legs.

"Uncle," I said, with a great effort, "will you buy that doll for me?"

And I waited.

"Buy a doll for a boy—*sacrebleu!*" cried my uncle, in a voice of thunder. "Do you wish to dishonour yourself? And it is that old Mag there that you want! Well, I must compliment you, my young fellow! If you grow up with such tastes as that, you will never have any pleasure in life; and your comrades will call you a precious ninny. If you asked me for a sword or a gun, my boy, I would buy them for you with the last silver crown of my pension. But to buy a doll for you—by all that's holy!—to disgrace you! Never in the world! Why, if I were ever to see you playing with a puppet rigged out like that, Monsieur, my sister's son, I would disown you for my nephew!"

On hearing these words, I felt my heart so wrung that nothing but pride—a diabolic pride—kept me from crying.

My uncle, suddenly calming down, returned to his ideas about the

Bourbons; but I, still smarting under the weight of his indignation, felt an unspeakable shame. My resolve was quickly made. I promised myself never to disgrace myself—I firmly and for ever renounced that red-cheeked doll.

I felt that day, for the first time, the austere sweetness of sacrifice.

Captain, though it be true that all your life you swore like a pagan, smoked like a beadle, and drank like a bell-ringer, be your memory nevertheless honoured—not merely because you were a brave soldier, but also because you revealed to your little nephew in petticoats the sentiment of heroism! Pride and laziness had made you almost insupportable, Uncle Victor!—but a great heart used to beat under those frogs upon your coat. You always used to wear, I now remember, a rose in your button-hole. That rose which you offered so readily to the shop-girls—that large, open-hearted flower, scattering its petals to all the winds, was the symbol of your glorious youth. You despised neither wine nor tobacco; but you despised life. Neither delicacy nor common sense could have been learned from you, Captain; but you taught me, even at an age when my nurse had to wipe my nose, a lesson of honour and self-abnegation that I shall never forget.

You have now been sleeping for many years in the Cemetery of Mont-Parnasse, under a plain slab bearing this epitaph:

CI–GIT

ARISTIDE VICTOR MALDENT,

CAPITAINE D'INFANTERIE,
CHEVALIER DE LA LEGION D'HONNEUR.

But such, Captain, was not the inscription devised by yourself to be placed above those old bones of yours—knocked about so long on fields of battle and in haunts of pleasure. Among your papers was found this proud and bitter epitaph, which, despite your last will, none could have ventured to put upon your tomb:

CI–GIT

UN BRIGAND DE LA LOIRE.

"Thérèse, we will get a wreath of immortelles to-morrow, and lay them on the tomb of the 'Brigand of the Loire.'" . . .

But Thérèse is not here. And how, indeed, could she be near me, seeing that I am at the *rondpoint* of the Champs-Élysées? There, at the termination of the avenue, the Arc de Triomphe, which bears under its vaults the names of Uncle Victor's companions-in-arms, opens its giant gate against the sky. The trees of the avenue are unfolding to the sun of spring their first leaves, still all pale and chilly. Beside me the carriages keep rolling by to the Bois de Boulogne. Unconsciously I have wandered into this fashionable avenue on my promenade, and halted, quite stupidly, in front of a booth stocked with gingerbread and decanters of liquorice-water, each topped by a lemon. A miserable little boy, covered with rags, which expose his chapped skin, stares with widely opened eyes at those sumptuous sweets which are not for such as he. With the shamelessness of innocence he betrays his longing. His round, fixed eyes contemplate a certain gingerbread man of lofty stature. It is a general, and it looks a little like Uncle Victor. I take it, I pay for it, and present it to the little pauper, who dares not extend his hand to receive it—for, by reason of precocious experience, he cannot believe in luck; he looks at me, in the same way that certain big dogs do, with the air of one saying, "You are cruel to make fun of me like that!"

"Come, little stupid," I say to him, in that rough tone I am accustomed to use, "take it—take it, and eat it; for you, happier than I was at your age, you can satisfy your tastes without disgracing yourself." . . . And you, Uncle Victor—you, whose manly figure has been recalled to me by that gingerbread general, come, glorious Shadow, help me to forget my new doll. We remain for ever children, and are always running after new toys.

Same day.

In the oddest way that Coccoz family has become associated in my mind with the Clerk Alexander.

"Thérèse," I said, as I threw myself into my easy-chair, "tell me if the little Coccoz is well, and whether he has got his first teeth yet—and bring me my slippers."

"He ought to have them by this time, Monsieur," replied Thérèse; "but I never saw them. The very first fine day of spring the mother disappeared with the child, leaving furniture and clothes and everything behind her. They found thirty-eight empty pomade-pots in the attic. It passes all belief! She had visitors latterly; and you may be quite sure she is not now in a convent of nuns. The niece of the concierge says she saw her driving about in a carriage on the boulevards. I always told you she would end badly."

"Thérèse," I replied, "that young woman has not ended either badly or well as yet. Wait until the term of her life is over before you judge her. And be careful not to talk too much with that concierge. It seemed to me—though I only saw her for a moment on the stairs—that Madame Coccoz was very fond of her child. For that mother's love at least, she deserves credit."

"As far as that goes, Monsieur, certainly the little one never wanted for anything. In all the Quarter one could not have found a child better kept, or better nourished, or more petted and coddled.

Every day that God makes she puts a clean bib on him, and sings to him to make him laugh from morning till night."

"Thérèse, a poet has said, 'That child whose mother has never smiled upon him is worthy neither of the table of the gods nor of the couch of the goddesses.' "

July 8, 1852.

HAVING been informed that the Chapel of the Virgin at Saint-Germain-des-Prés was being repaved, I entered the church with the hope of discovering some old inscriptions, possibly exposed by the labours of the workmen. I was not disappointed. The architect kindly showed me a stone which he had just had raised up against the wall. I knelt down to look at the inscription engraved upon that stone; and then, half aloud, I read in the shadow of the old apsis these words, which made my heart leap:

"Cy-gist Alexandre, moyne de ceste église, qui fist mettre en argent le menton de Saint-Vincent et de Saint-Amant et le pié des Innocens; qui toujours en son vivant fut preud'homme et vayllant. Priez pour l'âme de lui."

I wiped gently away with my handkerchief the dust covering that gravestone; I could have kissed it.

"It is he! it is Alexander!" I cried out; and from the height of the vaults the name fell back upon me with a clang, as if broken.

The silent severity of the beadle, whom I saw advancing towards me, made me ashamed of my enthusiasm; and I fled between the two holy-water sprinklers with which two rival *"rats d'église"* seemed desirous of barring my way.

At all events it was certainly my own Alexander! there could be no more doubt possible; the translator of the "Golden Legend," the author of the lives of Saints Germain, Vincent, Ferréol, Ferrution, and Droctoveus was, just as I had supposed, a monk of Saint-Germain-des-Prés. And what a monk, too—pious and generous! He had a silver chin, a silver head, and a silver foot made, that certain precious remains should be covered with an incorruptible envelope! But shall I never be able to view his handiwork? or is this new discovery only destined to increase my regrets?

August 20, 1859.

> "I, that please some, try all; both joy and terror
> Of good and bad; that make and unfold error—
> Now take upon me, in the name of Time
> To use my wings. Impute it not a crime
> To me or my swift passage, that I slide
> O'er years."

Who speaks thus? 'Tis an old man whom I know too well. It is Time.

Shakespeare, after having terminated the third act of the "Winter's Tale," pauses in order to leave time for little Perdita to grow up in wisdom and in beauty; and when he raises the curtain again he evokes the ancient Scythe-bearer upon the stage to render account to the audience of those many long days which have weighed down upon the head of the jealous Leontes.

Like Shakespeare in his play, I have left in this diary of mine a long interval to oblivion; and after the fashion of the poet, I make Time himself intervene to explain the omission of ten whole years. Ten whole years, indeed, have passed since I wrote one single line in this diary; and now that I take up the pen again, I have not the pleasure, alas! to describe a Perdita "now grown in grace." Youth and beauty are the faithful companions of poets; but those charming phantoms scarcely visit the rest of us, even for the space of a season. We do not know how to retain them with us. If the fair shade of some Perdita should ever, through some inconceivable whim, take a notion to traverse my brain, she would hurt herself horribly against heaps of dog-eared parchments. Happy the poets!—their white hairs never scare away the hovering shades of Helens, Francescas, Juliets, Julias, and Dorotheas! But the nose alone of Sylvestre Bonnard would put to flight the whole swarm of love's heroines.

Yet I, like others, have felt beauty; I have known that mysterious charm which Nature has lent to animate form; and the clay which lives has given to me that shudder of delight which makes the lover and the poet. But I have never known either how to love or how to sing. Now, in my memory—all encumbered as it is with the rubbish of old texts—I can discern again, like a miniature forgotten in some attic, a certain bright young face, with violet eyes. . . . Why, Bonnard, my friend, what an old fool you are becoming! Read that catalogue which a Florentine bookseller sent you this very morning. It is a catalogue of Manuscripts; and he promises you a description of several famous ones, long preserved by the collectors of Italy and Sicily. There is something better suited to you, something more in keeping with your present appearance.

I read; I cry out! Hamilcar, who has assumed with the approach of age an air of gravity that intimidates me, looks at me reproachfully, and seems to ask me whether there is any rest in this world, since he cannot enjoy it beside me, who am old also like himself.

In the sudden joy of my discovery, I need a confidant; and it is to the sceptic Hamilcar that I address myself with all the effusion of a happy man.

"No, Hamilcar! no," I said to him; "there is no rest in this world, and the quietude you long for is incompatible with the duties of life. And you say that we are old, indeed! Listen to what I read in this catalogue, and then tell me whether this is a time to be reposing:

"'LA LÉGENDE DORÉE DE JACQUES DE VORAGINE;—traduction
française du quatorzième siècle, par le Clerc Alexandre.

" 'Superb MS., ornamented with two miniatures, wonderfully executed,
and in a perfect state of preservation:—one representing the Purification of the Virgin; the other the Coronation of Proserpine.

" 'At the termination of the "Légende Dorée" .are the Legends of
Saints Ferréol, Ferrution, Germain, and Droctoveus (xxviij pp.) and the
Miraculous Sepulture of Monsieur Saint-Germain d'Auxerre (xij pp.).

" 'This rare manscript, which formed part of the collection of Sir
Thomas Raleigh, is now in the private study of Signor Michel-Angelo
Polizzi, of Girgenti.'

"You hear that, Hamilcar? The manuscript of the Clerk Alexander is in Sicily, at the house of Michel-Angelo Polizzi. Heaven grant
he may be a friend of learned men! I am going to write to him!"

Which I did forthwith. In my letter I requested Signor Polizzi to
allow me to examine the manuscript of Clerk Alexander, stating
on what grounds I ventured to consider myself worthy of so great
a favour. I offered at the same time to put at his disposal several
unpublished texts in my own possession, not devoid of interest. I
begged him to favour me with a prompt reply, and below my signature I wrote down all my honorary titles.

"Monsieur! Monsieur! where are you running like that?" cried
Thérèse, quite alarmed, coming down the stairs in pursuit of me,
four steps at a time, with my hat in her hand.

"I am going to post a letter, Thérèse."

"Good God! is that a way to run out in the street, bareheaded,
like a crazy man?"

"I am crazy, I know, Thérèse. But who is not? Give me my hat,
quick!"

"And your gloves, Monsieur! and your umbrella!"

I had reached the bottom of the stairs, but still heard her pro-
testing and lamenting.

October 10, 1859.

I AWAITED Signor Polizzi's reply with ill-contained impatience. I
could not even remain quiet; I would make sudden nervous gestures—open books and violently close them again. One day I happened to upset a book with my elbow—a volume of Moréri. Hamilcar, who was washing himself, suddenly stopped, and looked
angrily at me, with his paw over his ear. Was this the tumultuous
existence he must expect under my roof? Had there not been a
tacit understanding between us that we should live a peaceful life?
I had broken the covenant.

"My poor dear comrade," I made answer, "I am the victim of a
violent passion, which agitates and masters me. The passions are
enemies of peace and quiet, I acknowledge; but without them there

would be no arts or industries in the world. Everybody would sleep
naked on a dung-heap; and you would not be able, Hamilcar, to repose all day on a silken cushion, in the City of Books."

I expatiated no further to Hamilcar on the theory of the passions, however, because my housekeeper brought me a letter. It
bore the postmark of Naples, and read as follows:

"MOST ILLUSTRIOUS SIR,—I do indeed possess that incomparable manuscript of the 'Golden Legend' which could not escape your keen observation. All-important reasons, however, forbid me, imperiously, tyranni-
cally, to let the manuscript go out of my possession for a single day, for
even a single minute. It will be a joy and pride for me to have you examine it in my humble home at Girgenti, which will be embellished and
illuminated by your presence. It is with the most anxious expectation of
your visit that I presume to sign myself, Seigneur Academician,
"Your humble and devoted servant
"MICHEL-ANGELO POLIZZI,
"Wine-merchant and Archæologist at Girgenti, Sicily."

Well, then! I will go to Sicily:

"Extremum hunc, Arethusa, mihi concede laborem."

October 25, 1859.

MY resolve had been taken and my preparations made; it only
remained for me to notify my housekeeper. I must acknowledge it
was a long time before I could make up my mind to tell her I was
going away. I feared her remonstrances, her railleries, her objurga-
tions, her tears. "She is a good, kind girl," I said to myself; "she
is attached to me; she will want to prevent me from going; and the
Lord knows that when she has her mind set upon anything, gestures and cries cost her no effort. In this instance she will be sure
to call the concierge, the scrubber, the mattress-maker, and the
seven sons of the fruit-seller; they will all kneel down in a circle
around me; they will begin to cry, and then they will look so ugly
that I shall be obliged to yield, so as not to have the pain of seeing them any more."

Such were the awful images, the sick dreams, which fear mar-
shalled before my imagination. Yes, fear—"fecund Fear," as the
poet says—gave birth to these monstrosities in my brain. For—I
may as well make the confession in these private pages—I am
afraid of my housekeeper. I am aware that she knows I am weak;
and this fact alone is sufficient to dispel all my courage in any contest with her. Contests are of frequent occurrence; and I invariably
succumb.

But for all that, I had to announce my departure to Thérèse. She
came into the library with an armful of wood to make a little fire—
"une flambé," she said. For the mornings are chilly. I watched her

out of the corner of my eye while she crouched down at the hearth,
with her head in the opening of the fireplace. I do not know how
I then found the courage to speak, but I did so without much hesitation. I got up, and, walking up and down the room, observed in a

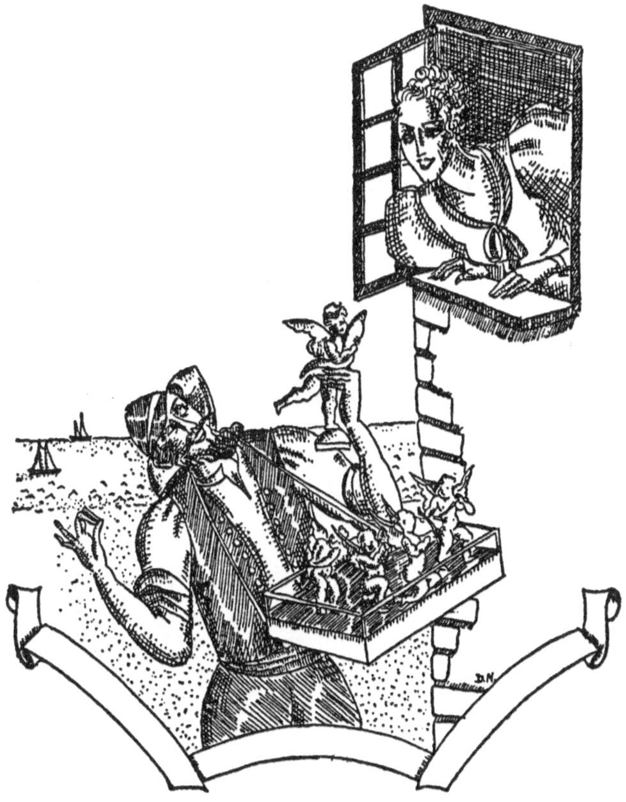

careless tone, with that swaggering manner characteristic of cowards,

"By the way, Thérèse, I am going to Sicily."

Having thus spoken, I awaited the consequence with great
anxiety. Thérèse did not reply. Her head and her vast cap remained
buried in the fireplace; and nothing in her person, which I closely
watched, betrayed the least emotion. She poked some paper under
the wood, and blew up the fire. That was all!

Finally I saw her face again;—it was calm—so calm that it made
me vexed. "Surely," I thought to myself, "this old maid has no
heart. She lets me go away without saying so much as '*Ah!*' Can
the absence of her old master really affect her so little?"

"Well, then go, Monsieur," she answered at last, "only be back here by six o'clock! There is a dish for dinner to-day which will not wait for anybody."

Naples, November 10, 1859.

"Co tra calle vive, magna, e lave a faccia."

I understand, my friend—for three centimes I can eat, drink, and wash my face, all by means of one of those slices of watermelon you display there on a little table. But Occidental prejudices would prevent me from enjoying that simple pleasure freely and frankly. And how could I suck a watermelon? I have enough to do merely to keep on my feet in this crowd. What a luminous, noisy night in the Strada di Porto! Mountains of fruit tower up in the shops, illuminated by multicoloured lanterns. Upon charcoal furnaces lighted in the open air water boils and streams, and ragouts are singing in frying-pans. The smell of fried fish and hot meats tickles my nose and makes me sneeze. At this moment I find that my handkerchief has left the pocket of my frock-coat. I am pushed, lifted up, and turned about in every direction by the gayest, the most talkative, the most animated and the most adroit populace possible to imagine; and suddenly a young woman of the people, while I am admiring her magnificent hair, with a single shock of her powerful elastic shoulder, pushes me staggering three paces back at least, without injury, into the arms of a maccaroni-eater, who receives me with a smile.

I am in Naples. How I ever managed to arrive here, with a few mutilated and shapeless remains of baggage, I cannot tell, because I am no longer myself. I have been travelling in a condition of perpetual fright; and I think that I must have looked awhile ago in this bright city like an owl bewildered by sunshine. To-night it is much worse! Wishing to obtain a glimpse of popular manners, I went to the Strada di Porto, where I now am. All about me animated throngs of people crowd and press before the eating-places; and I float like a waif among these living surges, which, even while they submerge you, still caress. For this Neapolitan people has, in its very vivacity, something indescribably gentle and polite. I am not roughly jostled, I am merely swayed about; and I think that by dint of thus rocking me to and fro, these good folks want to lull me asleep on my feet. I admire, as I tread the lava pavements by the *strada,* those porters and fishermen who move by me chatting, singing, smoking, gesticulating, quarrelling, and embracing each other the next moment with astonishing versatility of mood. They live through all their senses at the same time; and, being philosophers without knowing it, keep the measure of their desires in accordance with the brevity of life. I approach a much-patronised tavern, and see inscribed above the entrance this quatrain in Neapolitan patois:

"Amice, alliegre magnammo e bevimmo
Nfin che n'ce stace noglio a la lucerna:
Chi sa s'a l'autro munno n'ce vedimmo?
*Chi sa s'a l'autro munno n'ce taverna?"**

Even such counsels was Horace wont to give to his friends. You received them, Posthumus; you heard them also, Leuconoë, perverse beauty who wished to know the secrets of the future. That future is now the past, and we know it well. Of a truth you were foolish to worry yourselves about so small a matter; and your friend showed his good sense when he told you to take life wisely and to filter your Greek wines—*"Sapias, vina liques."* Even thus the sight of a fair land under a spotless sky urges to the pursuit of quiet pleasures. But there are souls for ever harassed by some sublime discontent; those are the noblest. You were of such, Leuconoë; and I, visiting for the first time, in my declining years, that city where your beauty was famed of old, I salute with deep respect your melancholy memory. Those souls of kin to your own who appeared in the age of Christianity were souls of saints; and the "Golden Legend" is full of the miracles they wrought. Your friend Horace left a less noble posterity, and I see one of his descendants in the person of that tavern poet, who at this moment is serving out wine in cups under the epicurean motto of his sign.

And yet life decides in favour of friend Flaccus, and his philosophy is the only one which adapts itself to the course of events. There is a fellow leaning against that trellis-work covered with vine-leaves, and eating an ice, while watching the stars. He would not stoop even to pick up the old manuscript I am going to seek with so much trouble and fatigue. And in truth man is made rather to eat ices than to pore over old texts.

I continued to wander about among the drinkers and the singers. There were lovers biting into beautiful fruit, each with an arm about the other's waist. Man must be naturally bad; for all this strange joy only evoked in me a feeling of uttermost despondency. That thronging populace displayed such artless delight in the simple act of living, that all the shynesses begotten by my old habits as an author awoke and intensified into something like fright. Furthermore, I found myself much discouraged by my inability to understand a word of all the storm of chatter about me. It was a humiliating experience for a philologist. Thus I had begun to feel quite sulky, when I was startled to hear some one just behind me observe:

"Dimitri, that old man is certainly a Frenchman. He looks so bewildered that I really feel sorry for him. Shall I speak to him?

---

*"Friends, let us merrily eat and drink as long as oil remains in the lamp. Who knows if we shall meet again in the other world? Who knows if in the other world there be a tavern?"

. . . He has such a good-natured look, with that round back of his
—do you not think so, Dimitri?"

It was said in French by a woman's voice. For the moment it
was disagreeable to hear myself spoken of as an old man. Is a man
old at sixty-two? Only the other day, on the Pont des Arts, my
colleague Perrot d'Avrignac complimented me on my youthful appearance; and I should think him a better authority about one's
age than that young chatterbox who has taken it on herself to
make remarks about my back. My back is round, she says. Ah! ah!
I had some suspicion myself to that effect, but I am not going now
to believe it at all, since it is the opinion of a giddy-headed young
woman. Certainly I will not turn my head round to see who it was
that spoke; but I am sure it was a pretty woman. Why? Because
she talks like a capricious person and like a spoiled child. Ugly
women may be naturally quite as capricious as pretty ones; but as
they are never petted and spoiled, and as no allowances are made
for them, they soon find themselves obliged either to suppress their
whims or to hide them. On the other hand, the pretty women can
be just as fantastical as they please. My neighbour is evidently one
of the latter. . . . But, after all, coming to think it over, she really
did nothing worse than to express, in her own way, a kindly
thought about me, for which I ought to feel grateful.

These reflections—including the last and decisive one—passed
through my mind in less than a second; and if I have taken a whole
minute to tell them, it is only because I am a bad writer, which
failing is characteristic of most philologists. In less than a second,
therefore, after the voice had ceased, I did turn round, and saw a
pretty little woman—a sprightly brunette.

"Madame," I said, with a bow, "excuse my involuntary indiscretion. I could not help overhearing what you have just said. You
would like to be of service to a poor old man. And the wish, Madame, has already been fulfilled—the mere sound of a French voice
has given me such pleasure that I must thank you."

I bowed again, and turned to go away; but my foot slipped upon
a melon-rind, and I should certainly have embraced the Partheno-
pean soil had not the young lady put out her hand and caught me.

There is a force in circumstances—even in the very smallest circumstances—against which resistance is vain. I resigned myself to
remain the *protégé* of the fair unknown.

"It is late," she said; "do you not wish to go back to your hotel,
which must be quite close to ours—unless it be the same one?"

"Madame," I replied, "I do not know what time it is, because
somebody has stolen my watch; but I think, as you say, that it
must be time to retire; and I shall be very glad to regain my hotel
in the company of such courteous compatriots."

So saying, I bowed once more to the young lady, and also saluted her companion, a silent colossus with a gentle and melancholy face.

After having gone a little way with them, I learned, among other matters, that my new acquaintances were the Prince and Princess Trépof, and that they were making a trip round the world for the purpose of finding match-boxes, of which they were making a collection.

We proceeded along a narrow, tortuous *vicoletto,* lighted only by a single lamp burning in the niche of a Madonna. The purity and transparency of the air gave a celestial softness and clearness to the very darkness itself; and one could find one's way without difficulty under such a limpid night. But in a little while we began to pass through a "venella," or, in Neapolitan parlance, a *sottoportico,* which led under so many archways and so many far-projecting balconies that no gleam of light from the sky could reach us. My young guide had made us take this route as a short cut, she assured us; but I think she did so quite as much simply in order to show that she felt at home in Naples, and knew the city thoroughly. Indeed, she needed to know it very thoroughly to venture by night into that labyrinth of subterranean alleys and flights of steps. If ever any man showed absolute docility in allowing himself to be guided, that man was myself. Dante never followed the steps of Beatrice with more confidence than I felt in following those of Princess Trépof.

The lady appeared to find some pleasure in my conversation, for she invited me to take a carriage-drive with her on the morrow to visit the grotto of Posilippo and the tomb of Virgil. She declared she had seen me somewhere before; but she could not remember if it had been at Stockholm or at Canton. In the former event I was a very celebrated professor of geology; in the latter, a provision-merchant whose courtesy and kindness had been much appreciated. One thing certain was that she had seen my back somewhere before.

"Excuse me," she added; "we are continually travelling, my husband and I, to collect match-boxes and to change our *ennui* by changing country. Perhaps it would be more reasonable to content ourselves with a single variety of *ennui.* But we have made all our preparations and arrangements for travelling: all our plans have been laid out in advance, and it gives us no trouble, whereas it would be very troublesome for us to stop anywhere in particular. I tell you all this so that you may not be surprised if my recollections have become a little mixed up. But from the moment I first saw you at a distance this evening, I felt—in fact I knew—that I had seen you before. Now the question is, 'Where was it that I saw you?' You are not, then, either the geologist or the provision-merchant?"

"No, Madame," I replied, "I am neither the one nor the other;

and I am sorry for it—since you have had reason to esteem them.
There is really nothing about me worthy of your interest. I have
spent all my life poring over books, and I have never travelled: you
might have known that from my bewilderment, which excited your
compassion. I am a member of the Institute."

"You are a member of the Institute! How nice! Will you not
write something for me in my album? Do you know Chinese? I
would like so much to have you write something in Chinese or
Persian in my album. I will introduce you to my friend, Miss Fer-
gusson, who travels everywhere to see all the famous people in the
world. She will be delighted. . . . Dimitri, did you hear that?—
this gentleman is a member of the Institute, and he has passed all
his life over books."

The prince nodded approval.

"Monsieur," I said, trying to engage him in our conversation, "it
is true that something can be learned from books; but a great deal
more can be learned by travelling, and I regret that I have not been
able to go round the world like you. I have lived in the same house
for thirty years and I scarcely ever go out."

"Lived in the same house for thirty years!" cried Madame Trépof; "is it possible?"

"Yes, Madame," I answered. "But you must know the house is
situated on the bank of the Seine, and in the very handsomest and
most famous part of the world. From my window I can see the
Tuileries and the Louvre, the Pont-Neuf, the towers of Notre-
Dame, the turrets of the Palais de Justice, and the spire of the
Sainte-Chapelle. All those stones speak to me; they tell me stories
about the days of Saint-Louis, of the Valois, of Henri IV., and of
Louis XIV. I understand them, and I love them all. It is only a very
small corner of the world, but honestly, Madame, where is there a
more glorious spot?"

At this moment we found ourselves upon a public square—a
largo steeped in the soft glow of the night. Madame Trépof looked
at me in an uneasy manner; her lifted eyebrows almost touched
the black curls about her forehead.

"Where do you live, then?" she demanded brusquely.

"On the Quai Malaquais, Madame, and my name is Bonnard. It is
not a name very widely known, but I am contented if my friends do
not forget it."

This revelation, unimportant as it was, produced an extraordinary effect upon Madame Trépof. She immediately turned her back
upon me and caught her husband's arm.

"Come, Dimitri!" she exclaimed, "do walk a little faster. I am
horribly tired, and you will not hurry yourself in the least. We
shall never get home. . . . As for you, monsieur, your way lies
over there!"

She made a vague gesture in the direction of some dark *vicolo*, pushed her husband the opposite way, and called to me, without even turning her head.

"Adieu, Monsieur! We shall not go to Posilippo to-morrow, nor the day after, either. I have a frightful headache! . . . Dimitri, you are unendurable! Will you not walk faster?"

I remained for the moment stupefied, vainly trying to think what I could have done to offend Madame Trépof. I had also lost my way, and seemed doomed to wander about all night. In order to ask my way, I would have to see somebody; and it did not seem likely that I should find a single human being who could understand me. In my despair I entered a street at random—a street, or rather a horrible alley that had the look of a murderous place. It proved so in fact, for I had not been two minutes in it before I saw two men fighting with knives. They were attacking each other even more fiercely with their tongues than with their weapons; and I concluded from the nature of the abuse they were showering upon each other that it was a love affair. I prudently made my way into a side alley while those two good fellows were still much too busy with their own affairs to think about mine. I wandered hopelessly about for a while, and at last sat down, completely discouraged, on a stone bench, inwardly cursing the strange caprices of Madame Trépof.

"How are you, Signor? Are you back from San Carlo? Did you hear the diva sing? It is only at Naples you can hear singing like hers."

I looked up, and recognised my host. I had seated myself with my back to the façade of my hotel, under the window of my own room.

Monte-Allegro, November 30, 1859.

WE were all resting—myself, my guides, and their mules—on the road from Sciacoa to Girgenti, at a tavern in the miserable village of Monte-Allegro, whose inhabitants, consumed by the *mal' aria,* continually shiver in the sun. But nevertheless they are Greeks, and their gaiety triumphs over all circumstances. A few gather about the tavern, full of smiling curiosity. One good story would have sufficed, had I known how to tell it to them, to make them forget all the woes of life. They had all a look of intelligence! and their women, although tanned and faded, wore their long black cloaks with much grace.

Before me I could see old ruins whitened by the sea-wind—ruins about which no grass ever grows. The dismal melancholy of deserts prevails over this arid land, whose cracked surface can barely nourish a few shrivelled mimosas, cacti, and dwarf palms. Twenty yards away, along the course of a ravine, stones were gleaming whitely like a long line of scattered bones. They told me that was the bed of a stream.

I had been about fifteen days in Sicily. On coming into the Bay of Palermo—which opens between the two mighty naked masses of the Pelligrino and the Catalfano, and extends inward along the "Golden Conch"—the view inspired me with such admiration that I resolved to travel a little in this island, so ennobled by historic memories, and rendered so beautiful by the outlines of its hills, which reveal the principles of Greek art. Old pilgrim though I was, grown hoary in the Gothic Occident—I dared to venture upon that classic soil; and, securing a guide, I went from Palermo to Trapani, from Trapani to Selinonte, from Selinonte to Sciacca—which I left this morning to go to Girgenti, where I am to find the MS. of Clerk Alexander. The beautiful things I have seen are still so vivid in my mind that I feel the task of writing them would be a useless fatigue. Why spoil my pleasure-trip by collecting notes? Lovers who love truly do not write down their happiness.

Wholly absorbed by the melancholy of the present and the poetry of the past, my thoughts peopled with beautiful shapes, and my eyes ever gratified by the pure and harmonious lines of the land-scape, I was resting in the tavern at Monte-Allegro, sipping a glass of heavy, fiery wine, when I saw two persons enter the waiting-room, whom, after a moment's hesitation, I recognised as the Prince and Princess Trépof.

This time I saw the princess in the light—and what a light! He who has known that of Sicily can better comprehend the words of Sophocles: *"Oh holy light! . . . Eye of the Golden Day!"* Madame Trépof, dressed in brown-holland and wearing a broad-brimmed straw hat, appeared to me a very pretty woman of about twenty-eight. Her eyes were luminous as a child's; but her slightly plump chin indicated the age of plenitude. She is, I must confess it, quite an attractive person. She is supple and changeful; her mood is like water itself—and, thank Heaven! I am no navigator. I thought I discerned in her manner a sort of ill-humour, which I attributed presently, by reason of some observations she uttered at random, to the fact that she had met no brigands upon her route.

"Such things only happen to us!" she exclaimed, with a gesture of discouragement.

She called for a glass of iced water, which the landlord presented to her with a gesture that recalled to me those scenes of funeral offerings painted upon Greek vases.

I was in no hurry to introduce myself to a lady who had so abruptly dropped my acquaintance in the public square at Naples; but she perceived me in my corner, and her frown notified me very plainly that our accidental meeting was disagreeable to her.

After she had sipped her ice-water for a few moments—whether because her whim had suddenly changed, or because my loneliness aroused her pity, I did not know—she walked directly to me.

"Good-day, Monsieur Bonnard," she said. "How do you do? What strange chance enables us to meet again in this frightful country?"

"This country is not frightful, Madame," I replied. "Beauty is so great and so august a quality that centuries of barbarism cannot efface it so completely that adorable vestiges of it will not always remain. The majesty of the antique Ceres still overshadows these arid valleys; and that Greek Muse who made Arethusa and Mænalus ring with her divine accents, still sings for my ears upon the barren mountain and in the place of the dried-up spring. Yes, Madame, when our globe, no longer inhabited, shall, like the moon, roll a wan corpse through space, the soil which bears the ruins of Selinonte will still keep the seal of beauty in the midst of universal death; and then, then, at least there will be no frivolous mouth to blaspheme the grandeur of these solitudes."

I knew well enough that my words were beyond the comprehension of the pretty little empty-head which heard them. But an old fellow like myself who has worn out his life over books does not know how to adapt his tone to circumstances. Besides, I wished to give Madame Trépof a lesson in politeness. She received it with so much submission, and with such an air of comprehension, that I hastened to add, as good-naturedly as possible,

"As to whether the chance which has enabled me to meet you again be lucky or unlucky, I cannot decide the question until I am sure that my presence be not disagreeable to you. You appeared to become weary of my company very suddenly at Naples the other day. I can only attribute that misfortune to my naturally unpleasant manner—since, on that occasion, I had had the honour of meeting you for the first time in my life."

These words seemed to cause her inexplicable joy. She smiled upon me in the most gracious, mischievous way, and said very earnestly, holding out her hand, which I touched with my lips,

"Monsieur Bonnard, do not refuse to accept a seat in my carriage. You can chat with me on the way about antiquity, and that will amuse me ever so much."

"My dear," exclaimed the prince, "you can do just as you please; but you ought to remember that one is horribly cramped in that carriage of yours; and I fear you are only offering Monsieur Bonnard the chance of getting a frightful attack of lumbago."

Madame Trépof simply shook her head by way of explaining that such considerations had no weight with her whatever; then she untied her hat. The darkness of her black curls descended over her eyes, and bathed them in velvety shadow. She remained a little while quite motionless, and her face assumed a surprising expression of reverie. But all of a sudden she darted at some oranges which the tavern-keeper had brought in a basket, and began to throw them, one by one, into a fold of her dress.

"These will be nice on the road," she said. "We are going just where you are going—to Girgenti. I must tell you all about it. You know that my husband is making a collection of match-boxes. We bought thirteen hundred match-boxes at Marseilles. But we heard there was a factory of them at Girgenti. According to what we were told, it is a very small factory, and its products—which are very ugly—never go outside the city and its suburbs. So we are going to Girgenti just to buy match-boxes. Dimitri has been a collector of all sorts of things; but the only kind of collection which can now interest him is a collection of match-boxes. He has already got five thousand two hundred and fourteen different kinds. Some of them gave us frightful trouble to find. For instance, we knew that at Naples boxes were once made with the portraits of Mazzini and Garibaldi on them; and that the police had seized the plates from which the portraits were printed, and put the manufacturer in gaol. Well, by dint of searching and inquiring for ever so long a while, we found one of those boxes at last for sale at one hundred francs, instead of two sous. It was not really too dear at that price; but we were denounced for buying it. We were taken for conspirators. All our baggage was searched; they could not find the box, because I had hidden it so well; but they found my jewels, and carried them off. They have them still. The incident made quite a sensation, and we were going to get arrested. But the king was displeased about it, and he ordered them to leave us alone. Up to that time, I used to think it was very stupid to collect match-boxes; but when I found that there were risks of losing liberty, and perhaps even life, by doing it, I began to feel a taste for it. Now I am an absolute fanatic on the subject. We are going to Sweden next summer to complete our series. . . . Are we not, Dimitri?"

I felt—must I confess it?—a thorough sympathy with these intrepid collectors. No doubt I would rather have found Monsieur and Madame Trépof engaged in collecting antique marbles or painted vases in Sicily. I should have liked to have found them interested in the ruins of Syracuse, or the poetical traditions of the Eryx. But at all events, they were making some sort of a collection—they belonged to the great confraternity—and I could not possibly make fun of them without making fun of myself. Besides, Madame Trépof had spoken of her collection with such an odd mingling of irony and enthusiasm that I could not help finding the idea a very good one.

We were getting ready to leave the tavern, when we noticed some people coming downstairs from the upper room, carrying carbines under their dark cloaks. To me they had the look of thorough bandits; and after they were gone I told Monsier Trépof my opinion of them. He answered me, very quietly, that he also thought they were regular bandits; and the guides begged us to apply for an escort of gendarmes, but Madame Trépof besought us not to do anything of the kind. She declared that we must not "spoil her journey."

Then, turning her persuasive eyes upon me, she asked,

"Do you not believe, Monsieur Bonnard, that there is nothing in life worth having except sensations?"

"Why, certainly, Madame," I answered; "but then we must take into consideration the nature of the sensations themselves. Those which a noble memory or a grand spectacle creates within us certainly represent what is best in human life; but those merely resulting from the menace of danger seem to me sensations which one should be very careful to avoid as much as possible. For example, would you think it a very pleasant thing, Madame, while travelling over the mountains at midnight, to find the muzzle of a carbine suddenly pressed against your forehead?"

"Oh, no!" she replied; "the comic-operas have made carbines absolutely ridiculous, and it would be a great misfortune to any young woman to find herself in danger from an absurd weapon. But it would be quite different with a knife—a very cold and very bright knife blade, which makes a cold shudder go right through one's heart."

She shuddered even as she spoke; closed her eyes, and threw her head back. Then she resumed:

"People like you are so happy! You can interest yourselves in all sorts of things!"

She gave a sidelong look at her husband, who was talking with the innkeeper. Then she leaned towards me, and murmured very low:

"You see, Dimitri and I, we are both suffering from *ennui!* We have still the match-boxes. But at last one gets tired even of match-boxes. Besides, our collection will soon be complete. And then what are we going to do?"

"Oh, Madame!" I exclaimed, touched by the moral unhappiness of this pretty person, "if you only had a son, then you would know what to do. You would then learn the purpose of your life, and your thoughts would become at once more serious and yet more cheerful."

"But I have a son," she replied. "He is a big boy; he is eleven years old, and he suffers from *ennui* like the rest of us. Yes, my George has *ennui,* too; he is tired of everything. It is very wretched."

She glanced again towards her husband, who was superintending the harnessing of the mules on the road outside—testing the condition of girths and straps. Then she asked me whether there had been many changes on the Quai Malaquais during the past ten years. She declared she never visited that neighbourhood because it was too far away.

"Too far from Monte-Allegro?" I queried.

"Why, no!" she replied. "Too far from the Avenue des Champs Élysées, where we live."

And she murmured over again, as if talking to herself, "Too far!
—too far!" in a tone of reverie which I could not possibly account
for. All at once she smiled again, and said to me,

"I like you, Monsieur Bonnard!—I like you very, very much!"

The mules had been harnessed. The young woman hastily picked
up a few oranges which had rolled off her lap; rose up; looked at
me, and burst out laughing.

"Oh!" she exclaimed, "how I should like to see you grappling
with the brigands! You would say such extraordinary things to
them! . . . Please take my hat, and hold my umbrella for me, Monsieur Bonnard."

"What a strange little mind!" I thought to myself, as I followed
her. "It could only have been in a moment of inexcusable thought-
lessness that Nature gave a child to such a giddy little woman!"

Girgenti. Same day.

HER manners had shocked me. I left her to arrange herself in her
lettica, and I made myself as comfortable as I could in my own.
These vehicles, which have no wheels, are carried by two mules—
one before and one behind. This kind of litter, or chaise, is of
ancient origin. I had often seen representations of similar ones in
the French MSS. of the fourteenth century. I had no idea then that
one of those vehicles would be at a future day placed at my own
disposal. We must never be too sure of anything.

For three hours the mules sounded their little bells, and thumped
the calcined ground with their hoofs. On either hand there slowly
defiled by us the barren monstrous shapes of a nature totally
African.

Half-way we made a halt to allow our animals to recover breath.

Madame Trépof came to me on the road, took my arm, and drew
me a little away from the party. Then, very suddenly, she said to
me in a tone of voice I had never heard before:

"Do not think that I am a wicked woman. My George knows that
I am a good mother."

We walked side by side for a moment in silence. She looked up,
and I saw that she was crying.

"Madame," I said to her, "look at this soil which has been burned
and cracked by five long months of fiery heat. A little white lily has
sprung up from it."

And I pointed with my cane to the frail stalk, tipped by a double
blossom.

"Your heart," I said, "however arid it be, bears also its white
lily; and that is reason enough why I do not believe that you are
what you say—a wicked woman."

"Yes, yes, yes!" she cried, with the obstinacy of a child—"I am a wicked woman. But I am ashamed to appear so before you who are so good—so very, very good."

"You do not know anything at all about it," I said to her.

"I know it! I know all about you, Monsieur Bonnard!" she declared, with a smile.

And she jumped back into her *lettica*.

Girgenti, November 30, 1859.

I AWOKE the following morning in the House of Gellias. Gellias was a rich citizen of ancient Agrigentum. He was equally celebrated for his generosity and for his wealth; and he endowed his native city with a great number of free inns. Gellias has been dead for thirteen hundred years; and nowadays there is no gratuitous hospitality among civilised peoples. But the name of Gellias has become that of a hotel in which, by reason of fatigue, I was able to obtain one good night's sleep.

The modern Girgenti lifts its high, narrow, solid streets, dominated by a sombre Spanish cathedral, upon the site of the acropolis of the antique Agrigentum. I can see from my windows, half-way on the hillside towards the sea, the white range of temples partially destroyed. The ruins alone have some aspect of coolness. All the rest is arid. Water and life have forsaken Agrigentum. Water—the divine Nestis of the Agrigentine Empedocles—is so necessary to animated beings that nothing can live far from the rivers and the springs. But the port of Girgenti, situated at a distance of three kilometres from the city, has a great commerce. "And it is in this dismal city," I said to myself, "upon this precipitous rock, that the manuscript of Clerk Alexander is to be found!" I asked my way to the house of Signor Michel-Angelo Polizzi, and proceeded thither.

I found Signor Polizzi, dressed all in white from head to feet, busy cooking sausages in a frying-pan. At the sight of me, he let go the handle of the frying-pan, threw up his arms in the air, and uttered shrieks of enthusiasm. He was a little man whose pimply features, aquiline nose, round eyes, and projecting chin formed a very expressive physiognomy.

He called me "Excellence," said he was going to mark the day with a white stone, and made me sit down. The hall in which we were represented the union of kitchen, reception-room, bedchamber, studio, and wine-cellar. There were charcoal furnaces visible, a bed, paintings, an easel, bottles, strings of onions, and a magnificent lustre of coloured glass pendants. I glanced at the paintings on the wall.

"The arts! the arts!" cried Signor Polizzi, throwing up his arms again to heaven—"the arts! What dignity! what consolation! Excellence, I am a painter!"

And he showed me an unfinished Saint-Francis, which indeed

could very well remain unfinished for ever without any loss to religion or to art. Next he showed me some old paintings of a better style, but apparently restored after a decidedly reckless manner.

"I repair," he said—"I repair old paintings. Oh, the Old Masters! What genius, what soul!"

"Why, then," I said to him, "you must be a painter, an archæologist, and a wine-merchant all in one?"

"At your service, Excellence," he answered. "I have a *zucco* here at this very moment—a *zucco* of which every single drop is a pearl of fire. I want your Lordship to taste of it."

"I esteem the wines of Sicily," I responded, "but it was not for the sake of your flagons that I came to see you, Signor Polizzi."

He: "Then you have come to see me about paintings. You are an amateur. It is an immense delight for me to receive amateurs. I am going to show you the *chef-d'œuvre* of Monrealese; yes, Excellence, his *chef-d'œuvre!* An Adoration of Shepherds! It is the pearl of the whole Sicilian school!"

I: "Later on I will be glad to see the *chef-d'œuvre;* but let us first talk about the business which brings me here."

His little quick bright eyes watched my face curiously; and I perceived, with anguish, that he had not the least suspicion of the purpose of my visit.

A cold sweat broke out over my forehead; and in the bewilderment of my anxiety I stammered out something to this effect:

"I have come from Paris expressly to look at a manuscript of the 'Légende Dorée,' which you informed me was in your possession."

At these words he threw up his arms, opened his mouth and eyes to the widest possible extent, and betrayed every sign of extreme nervousness.

"Oh! the manuscript of the 'Golden Legend!' A pearl, Excellence! a ruby, a diamond! Two miniatures so perfect that they give one the feeling of glimpses of Paradise! What suavity! Those colours ravished from the corollas of flowers make a honey for the eyes! Even a Sicilian could have done no better!"

"Let me see it, then," I asked; unable to conceal either my anxiety or my hope.

"Let you see it!" cried Polizzi. "But how can I, Excellence? I have not got it any longer! I have not got it!"

And he seemed determined to tear out his hair. He might indeed have pulled every hair in his head out of his hide before I should have tried to prevent him. But he stopped of his own accord, before he had done himself any grievous harm.

"What!" I cried out in anger—"what! you make me come all the way from Paris to Girgenti, by promising to show me a manuscript, and now, when I come, you tell me you have not got it! It is simply infamous, Monsieur! I shall leave your conduct to be judged by all honest men!"

Anybody who could have seen me at that moment would have been able to form a good idea of the aspect of a furious sheep.

"It is infamous! it is infamous!" I repeated, waving my arms, which trembled from anger.

Then Michel-Angelo Polizzi let himself fall into a chair in the attitude of a dying hero. I saw his eyes fill with tears, and his hair —until then flamboyant and erect upon his head—fall down in limp disorder over his brow.

"I am a father, Excellence! I am a father!" he groaned, wringing his hands.

He continued, sobbing:

"My son Rafael—the son of my poor wife, for whose death I have been mourning fifteen years—Rafael, Excellence, wanted to settle at Paris; he hired a shop in the Rue Lafitte for the sale of curiosities. I gave him everything precious which I had—I gave him my finest majolicas; my most beautiful Urbino ware; my masterpieces of art; what paintings, Signor! Even now they dazzle me when I see them only in imagination! And all of them signed! Finally, I gave him the manuscript of the 'Golden Legend'! I would have given him my flesh and my blood! An only son, Signor! the son of my poor saintly wife!"

"So," I said, "while I—relying upon your written word, Monsieur —was travelling to the very heart of Sicily to find the manuscript of the Clerk Alexander, the same manuscript was actually exposed for sale in a window in the Rue Lafitte, only fifteen hundred yards from my house?"

"Yes, it was there! that is positively true!" exclaimed Signor Polizzi, suddenly growing calm again; "and it is there still—at least I hope it is, Excellence."

He took a card from a shelf as he spoke, and offered it to me, saying,

"Here is the address of my son. Make it known to your friends, and you will oblige me. Faïence and enamelled wares; hangings; pictures. He has a complete stock of objects of art—all at the fairest possible prices—and everything authentic, I can vouch for it, upon my honour! Go and see him. He will show you the manuscript of the 'Golden Legend.' Two miniatures miraculously fresh in colour!"

I was feeble enough to take the card he held out to me.

The fellow was taking further advantage of my weakness to make me circulate the name of Rafael Polizzi among the Societies of the learned!

My hand was already on the door-knob, when the Sicilian caught me by the arm; he had a look as of sudden inspiration.

"Ah! Excellence!" he cried, "what a city is this city of ours! It gave birth to Empedocles! Empedocles! What a great man what a

great citizen! What audacity of thought! what virtue! what soul!
At the port over there is a statue of Empedocles, before which I
bare my head each time that I pass by! When Rafael, my son, was
going away to found an establishment of antiquities in the Rue
Lafitte, at Paris, I took him to the port, and there, at the foot of
that statue of Empedocles, I bestowed upon him my paternal benediction! 'Always remember Empedocles!' I said to him. Ah! Signor,
what our unhappy country needs to-day is a new Empedocles!
Would you not like me to show you the way to his statue, Excellence? I will be your guide among the ruins here. I will show you
the temple of Castor and Pollux, the temple of the Olympian Jupiter, the temple of the Lucinian Juno, the antique well, the tomb of
Theron, and the Gate of Gold! All the professional guides are asses;
but we—we shall make excavations, if you are willing—and we
shall discover treasures! I know the science of discovering hidden
treasures—the secret art of finding their whereabouts—a gift from
Heaven!"

I succeeded in tearing myself away from his grasp. But he ran
after me again, stopped me at the foot of the stairs, and said in my
ear,

"Listen, Excellence. I will conduct you about the city; I will introduce you to some Girgentines! What a race! what types! what
forms! Sicilian girls, Signor!—the antique beauty itself!"

"Go to the devil!" I cried at last, in anger, and rushed into the
street, leaving him still writhing in the loftiness of his enthusiasm.

When I had got out of his sight, I sank down upon a stone, and
began to think, with my face in my hands.

"And it was for this," I said to myself—"it was to hear such
propositions as this that I came to Sicily! That Polizzi is simply a
scoundrel, and his son another; and they made a plan together to
ruin me." But what was their scheme? I could not unravel it. Meanwhile, it may be imagined how discouraged and humiliated I felt.

A merry burst of laughter caused me to turn my head, and I saw
Madame Trépos running in advance of her husband, and holding up
something which I could not distinguish clearly.

She sat down beside me, and showed me—laughing more merrily
all the while—an abominable little paste-board box, on which was
printed a red and blue face, which the inscription declared to be the
face of Empedocles.

"Yes, Madame," I said, "but that abominable Polizzi, to whom I
advise you not to send Monsieur Trépof, has made me fall out for
ever with Empedocles; and this portrait is not at all of a nature
to make me feel more kindly to the ancient philosopher."

"Oh!" declared Madame Trépof, "it is ugly, but it is rare! These
boxes are not exported at all; you can buy them only where they
are made. Dimitri has six others just like this in his pocket. We got
them so as to exchange with other collectors. You understand? At

nine o'clock this morning we were at the factory. You see we did not waste our time."

"So I certainly perceive, Madame," I replied, bitterly; "but I have lost mine."

I then saw that she was naturally a good-hearted woman. All her merriment vanished.

"Poor Monsieur Bonnard! poor Monsieur Bonnard!" she murmured.

And, taking my hand in hers, she added:

"Tell me about your troubles."

I told her about them. My story was long; but she was evidently touched by it, for she asked me quite a number of circumstantial questions, which I took for proof of friendly interest. She wanted to know the exact title of the manuscript, its shape, its appearance, and its age; she asked me for the address of Signor Rafael Polizzi.

And I gave it to her; thus doing (O destiny!) precisely what the abominable Polizzi had told me to do.

It is sometimes difficult to check oneself. I recommenced my plaints and my imprecations. But this time Madame Trépof only burst out laughing.

"Why do you laugh?" I asked her.

"Because I am a wicked woman," she answered.

And she fled away, leaving me all disheartened on my stone.

Paris, December 8, 1859.

MY unpacked trunks still encumbered the hall. I was seated at a table covered with all those good things which the land of France produces for the delectation of *gourmets*. I was eating a *pâte le Chartres,* which is alone sufficient to make one love one's country. Thérèse, standing before me with her hands joined over her white apron, was looking at me with benignity, with anxiety, and with pity. Hamilcar was rubbing himself against my legs, wild with delight.

These words of an old poet came back to my memory:

"Happy is he who, like Ulysses, hath made a goodly journey."

. . . "Well," I thought to myself, "I travelled to no purpose; I have come back with empty hands; but, like Ulysses, I made a goodly journey."

And having taken my last sip of coffee, I asked Thérèse for my hat and cane, which she gave me not without dire suspicions: she feared I might be going upon another journey. But I reassured her by telling her to have dinner ready at six o'clock.

It had always been a keen pleasure for me to breathe the air in those Parisian streets whose every paving-slab and every stone I

love devotedly. But I had an end in view, and I took my way straight
to the Rue Lafitte. I was not long in finding the establishment of
Signor Rafael Polizzi. It was distinguishable by a great display of
old paintings which, although all bearing the signature of some
illustrious artist, had a certain family air of resemblance that
might have suggested some touching idea about the fraternity of
genius, had it not still more forcibly suggested the professional
tricks of Polizzi senior. Enriched by these doubtful works of art,
the shop was further rendered attractive by various petty curiosities: poniards, drinking-vessels, goblets, *figulines,* brass *gaudrons,*
and Hispano-Arabian wares of metallic lustre.

Upon a Portuguese arm-chair, decorated with an escutcheon, lay
a copy of the "Heures" of Simon Vostre, open at the page which has
an astrological figure on it; and an old Vitruvius, placed upon a
quaint chest, displayed its masterly engravings of caryatides and
telamones. This apparent disorder which only masked cunning arrangement, this factitious hazard which had placed the best objects
in the most favourable light, would have increased my distrust of
the place, but that the distrust which the mere name of Polizzi had
already inspired could not have been increased by any circumstances—being already infinite.

Signor Rafael, who sat there as the presiding genius of all these
vague and incongruous shapes, impressed me as a phlegmatic young
man, with a sort of English character. He betrayed no sign whatever of those transcendent faculties displayed by his father in the
arts of mimicry and declamation.

I told him what I had come for; he opened a cabinet and drew
from it a manuscript, which he placed on a table that I might examine it at my leisure.

Never in my life did I experience such an emotion—except, indeed, during some few brief months of my youth, months whose
memories, though I should live a hundred years, would remain as
fresh at my last hour as in the first day they came to me.

It was, indeed, the very manuscript described by the librarian of
Sir Thomas Raleigh; it was, indeed, the manuscript of the Clerk
Alexander which I saw, which I touched! The work of Voragine
himself had been perceptibly abridged; but that made little difference to me. All the inestimable additions of the monk of Saint-
Germain-des-Prés were there. That was the main point! I tried to
read the Legend of Saint Droctoveus; but I could not—all the lines
of the page quivered before my eyes, and there was a sound in my
ears like the noise of a windmill in the country at night. Nevertheless, I was able to see that the manuscript offered every evidence
of indubitable authenticity. The two drawings of the Purification of
the Virgin and the Coronation of Proserpine were meagre in design
and vulgar in violence of colouring. Considerably damaged in 1824,
as attested by the catalogue of Sir Thomas, they had obtained dur-

ing the interval a new aspect of freshness. But this miracle did not surprise me at all. And, besides, what did I care about the two miniatures? The legends and the poem of Alexander—those alone formed the treasure I desired. My eyes devoured as much of it as they had the power to absorb.

I affected indifference while asking Signor Polizzi the price of the manuscript; and, while awaiting his reply, I offered up a secret prayer that the price might not exceed the amount of ready money at my disposal—already much diminished by the cost of my expensive voyage. Signor Polizzi, however, informed me that he was not at liberty to dispose of the article, inasmuch as it did not belong to him, and was to be sold at auction shortly, at the Hôtel des Ventes, with a number of other MSS. and several *incunabula*.

This was a severe blow to me. I tried to preserve my calmness, notwithstanding, and replied somewhat to this effect:

"You surprise me, Monsieur! Your father, whom I talked with recently at Girgenti, told me positively the manuscript was yours. You cannot now attempt to make me discredit your father's word."

"I *did* own the manuscript, indeed," answered Signor Rafael with absolute frankness; "but I do not own it any longer. I sold that manuscript—the remarkable interest of which you have not failed to perceive—to an amateur whom I am forbidden to name, and who, for reasons which I am not at liberty to mention, finds himself obliged to sell his collection. I am honoured with the confidence of my customer, and was commissioned by him to draw up the catalogue and manage the sale, which takes place the 24th of December. Now, if you will be kind enough to give me your address, I shall have the pleasure of sending you the catalogue, which is already in the press. You will find the 'Légende Dorée' described in it as 'No. 42.'"

I gave my address, and left the shop.

The polite gravity of the son impressed me quite as disagreeably as the impudent buffoonery of the father. I hated, from the bottom of my heart, the tricks of the vile hagglers! It was perfectly evident that the two rascals had a secret understanding, and had only devised this auction-sale, with the aid of a professional appraiser, to force the bidding on the manuscript I wanted so much up to an outrageous figure. I was completely at their mercy. There is one evil in all passionate desires, even the noblest—namely, that they leave us subject to the will of others, and in so far dependent. This reflection made me suffer cruelly; but it did not conquer my longing to own the work of Clerk Alexander. While I was thus meditating, I heard a coachman swear. And I discovered it was I whom he was swearing at only when I felt the pole of a carriage poke me in the ribs. I started aside, barely in time to save myself from being run over; and whom did I perceive through the windows of the *coupé?* Madame Trépof, being taken by two beautiful horses, and a coach-

man all wrapped up in furs like a Russian *boyard,* into the very
street I had just left. She did not notice me; she was laughing to
herself with that artless grace of expression which still preserved
for her, at thirty years, all the charm of her early youth.

"Well, well!" I said to myself, "she is laughing! I suppose she
must have just found another match-box."

And I made my way back to the Ponts, feeling very miserable.

Nature, eternally indifferent, neither hastened nor hurried the
twenty-fourth day of December. I went to the Hôtel Bullion, and
took my place in *Salle* No. 4, immediately below the high desk at
which the auctioneer Boulouze and the expert Polizzi were to sit. I
saw the hall gradually fill with familiar faces. I shook hands with
several old booksellers of the quays; but that prudence which any
large interest inspires in even the most self-assured caused me to
keep silence in regard to the reason of my unaccustomed presence in
the halls of the Hôtel Bullion. On the other hand, I questioned those
gentlemen closely about the purpose of their attendance at the auction sale; and I had the satisfaction of finding them all interested
about matters in no wise related to my affair.

Little by little the hall became thronged with interested or merely
curious spectators; and, after half an hour's delay, the auctioneer
with his ivory hammer, the clerk with his bundle of memorandum-
papers, and the crier, carrying his collection-box fixed to the end
of a pole, all took their places on the platform in the most solemn
business manner. The attendants ranged themselves at the foot of
the desk. The presiding officer having declared the sale open, a par-
tial hush followed.

A commonplace series of *Preces diæ,* with miniatures, were first
sold off at mediocre prices. Needless to say, the illuminations of
these books were in perfect condition!

The lowness of the bids gave courage to the gathering of second-
hand booksellers present, who began to mingle with us, and become
familiar. The dealers in old brass and *bric-à-brac* pressed forward
in their turn, waiting for the doors of an adjoining room to be
opened; and the voice of the auctioneer was drowned by the jests
of the *Auvergnats.*

A magnificent codex of the "Guerre des Juifs" revived attention.
It was long disputed for. "Five thousand francs! five thousand!"
called the crier, while the *bric-à-brac* dealers remained silent with
admiration. Then seven or eight antiphonaries brought us back
again to low prices. A fat old woman, in a loose gown, bareheaded
—a dealer in second-hand goods—encouraged by the size of the
books and the low prices bidden, had one of the antiphonaries
knocked down to her for thirty francs.

At last the expert Polizzi announced No. 42: "The 'Golden
Legend'; French MS.; unpublished; two superb miniatures, with a
starting bid of three thousand francs."

"Three thousand! three thousand bid!" yelled the crier.

"Three thousand!" dryly repeated the auctioneer.

There was a buzzing in my head, and, as through a cloud, I saw a host of curious faces all turning towards the manuscript, which a boy was carrying open through the audience.

"Three thousand and fifty!" I said.

I was frightened by the sound of my own voice, and further confused by seeing, or thinking that I saw, all eyes turned upon me.

"Three thousand and fifty on the right!" called the crier, taking up my bid.

"Three thousand one hundred!" responded Signor Polizzi.

Then began a heroic duel between the expert and myself.

"Three thousand five hundred!"

"Six hundred!"

"Seven hundred!"

"Four thousand!"

"Four thousand five hundred."

Then, by a sudden bold stroke, Signor Polizzi raised the bid at once to six thousand.

Six thousand francs was all the money I could dispose of. It represented the possible. I risked the impossible.

"Six thousand one hundred!"

Alas! even the impossible did not suffice.

"Six thousand five hundred!" replied Signor Polizzi, with calm.

I bowed my head and sat there stupefied, unable to answer either yes or no to the crier, who called to me:

"Six thousand five hundred, by me—not by you on the right there!—it is my bid—no mistake! Six thousand five hundred!"

"Perfectly understood!" declared the auctioneer. "Six thousand five hundred. Perfectly clear; perfectly plain. . . . Any more bids? The last bid is six thousand five hundred francs."

A solemn silence prevailed. Suddenly I felt as if my head had burst open. It was the hammer of the officiant, who, with a loud blow on the platform, adjudged No. 42 irrevocably to Signor Polizzi. Forthwith the pen of the clerk, coursing over the *papier-timbré,* registered that great fact in a single line.

I was absolutely prostrated, and I felt the utmost need of rest and quiet. Nevertheless, I did not leave my seat. My powers of re-flection slowly returned. Hope is tenacious. I had one more hope. It occurred to me that the new owner of the "Légende Dorée" might be some intelligent and liberal bibliophile who would allow me to examine the MS., and perhaps even to publish the more important parts. And, with this idea, as soon as the sale was over I approached the expert as he was leaving the platform.

"Monsieur," I asked him, "did you buy in No. 42 on your own account, or on commission?"

"On commission. I was instructed not to let it go at any price."

"Can you tell me the name of the purchaser?"

"Monsieur, I regret that I cannot serve you in that respect. I have been strictly forbidden to mention the name."

I went home in despair.

December 30, 1859.

"Thérèse! don't you hear the bell? Somebody has been ringing at the door for the last quarter of an hour?"

Thérèse does not answer. She is chattering downstairs with the concierge, for sure. So that is the way you observe your old master's birthday? You desert me even on the eve of Saint-Sylvestre! Alas! if I am to hear any kind wishes to-day, they must come up from the ground; for all who love me have long been buried. I really don't know what I am still living for. There is the bell again! . . . I get up slowly from my seat at the fire, with my shoulders still bent from stooping over it, and go to the door myself. Whom do I see at the threshold? It is not a dripping love, and I am not an old Anacreon; but it is a very pretty little boy of about ten years old. He is alone; he raises his face to look at me. His cheeks are blushing; but his little pert nose gives one an idea of mischievous pleasantry. He has feathers in his cap, and a great lace-ruff on his jacket. The pretty little fellow! He holds in both arms a bundle as big as himself, and asks me if I am Monsieur Sylvestre Bonnard. I tell him yes; he gives me the bundle, tells me his mamma sent it to me, and then he runs downstairs.

I go down a few steps; I lean over the balustrade, and see the little cap whirling down the spiral of the stairway like a feather in the wind. "Good-bye, my little boy!" I should have liked so much to question him. But what, after all, could I have asked? It is not polite to question children. Besides, the package itself will probably give me more information than the messenger could.

It is a very big bundle, but not very heavy. I take it into my library, and there untie the ribbons and unfasten the paper wrappings; and I see—what? a log! a first-class log! a real Christmas log, but so light that I know it must be hollow. Then I find that it is indeed composed of two separate pieces, opening on hinges, and fastened with hooks. I slip the hooks back, and find myself inundated with violets! Violets! they pour over my table, over my knees, over the carpet. They tumble into my vest, into my sleeves. I am all perfumed with them.

"Thérèse! Thérèse! fill me some vases with water, and bring them here, quick! Here are violets sent to us I know not from what country nor by what hand; but it must be from a perfumed country, and by a very gracious hand. . . . Do you hear me, old crow?"

I have put all the violets on my table—now completely covered by the odorous mass. But there is still something in the log . . . a book—a manuscript. It is . . . I cannot believe it, and yet I cannot doubt it. . . . It is the "Légende Dorée"!—it is the manuscript of the Clerk Alexander! Here is the "Purification of the Virgin" and the "Coronation of Proserpine";—here is the legend of Saint Droctoveus. I contemplate this violet-perfumed relic. I turn the leaves of it—between which the dark rich blossoms have slipped in here and there; and, right opposite the legend of Saint-Cecilia, I find a card bearing this name:

"Princess Trépof."

Princess Trépof!—you who laughed and wept by turns so sweetly under the fair sky of Agrigentum!—you, whom a cross old man believed to be only a foolish little woman!—to-day I am convinced of your rare and beautiful folly; and the old fellow whom you now overwhelm with happiness will go to kiss your hand, and give you back, in another form, this precious manuscript, of which both he and science owe you an exact and sumptuous publication!

Thérèse entered my study just at that moment; she seemed to be very much excited.

"Monsieur!" she cried, "guess whom I saw just now in a carriage, with a coat-of-arms painted on it, that was stopping before the door?"

"Parbleu!—Madame Trépof," I exclaimed.

"I don't know anything about any Madame Trépof," answered my housekeeper. "The woman I saw just now was dressed like a duchess, and had a little boy with her, with lace-frills all along the seams of his clothes. And it was that same little Madame Coccoz you once sent a log to, when she was lying-in here about eleven years ago. I recognised her at once."

"What!" I exclaimed, "you mean to say it was Madame Coccoz, the widow of the almanac-peddler?"

"Herself, Monsieur! The carriage-door was open for a minute to let her little boy, who had just come from I don't know where, get in. She hasn't changed scarcely at all. Well, why should those women change?—they never worry themselves about anything. Only the Coccoz woman looks a little fatter than she used to be. And the idea of a woman that was taken in here out of pure charity coming to show off her velvets and diamonds in a carriage with a crest painted on it! Isn't it shameful!"

"Thérèse!" I cried, in a terrible voice, "if you ever speak to me again about that lady except in terms of the deepest respect, you and I will fall out! . . . Bring me the Sèvres vases to put those violets in, which now give the City of Books a charm it never had before."

While Thérèse went off with a sigh to get the Sèvres vases, I continued to contemplate those beautiful scattered violets, whose odour spread all about me like the perfume of some sweet presence, some charming soul; and I asked myself how it had been possible for me never to recognise Madame Coccoz in the person of the Princess Trépof. But that vision of the young widow, showing me her little child on the stairs, had been a very rapid one. I had much more reason to reproach myself for having passed by a gracious and lovely soul without knowing it.

"Bonnard," I said to myself, "thou knowest how to decipher old texts; but thou dost not know how to read in the Book of Life. That giddy little Madame Trépof, whom thou once believed to possess no more soul than a bird, has expended, in pure gratitude, more zeal and finer tact than thou didst ever show for anybody's sake. Right royally hath she repaid thee for the log-fire of her churching-day!

"Thérèse! Awhile ago you were a magpie; now you are becoming a tortoise! Come and give some water to these Parmese violets."

PART II: THE DAUGHTER OF CLÉMENTINE

I

THE FAIRY

HEN I left the train at the Melun station, night had already spread its peace over the silent country. The soil, heated through all the long day by a strong sun—by a *"gros soleil,"* as the harvesters of the Val de Vire say—still exhaled a warm heavy smell. Lush dense odours of grass passed over the level of the fields. I brushed away the dust of the railway carriage, and joyfully inhaled the pure air. My travelling-bag—filled by my housekeeper with linen and various small toilet articles, *munditiis,* seemed so light in my hand that I swung it about just as a schoolboy swings his strapped package of rudimentary books when the class is let out.

Would to Heaven that I were again a little urchin at school! But it is fully fifty years since my good dead mother made me some *tartines* of bread and preserves, and placed them in a basket of which she slipped the handle over my arm, and then led me, thus prepared, to the school kept by Monsieur Douloir, at a corner of the Passage du Commerce well known to the sparrows, between a court and a garden. The enormous Monsieur Douloir smiled upon us genially, and patted my cheek to show, no doubt, the affectionate interest which my first appearance had inspired. But when my mother had passed out of the court, startling the sparrows as she went, Monsieur Douloir ceased to smile—he showed no more affectionate interest; he appeared, on the contrary, to consider me as a very troublesome little fellow. I discovered, later on, that he entertained the same feelings towards all his pupils. He distributed whacks of his ferule with an agility no one could have expected on the part of so corpulent a person. But his first aspect of tender interest invariably reappeared when he spoke to any of our mothers in our presence; and always at such times, while warmly praising our remarkable aptitudes, he would cast down upon us a look of intense affection. Still, those were happy days which I passed on

the benches of Monsieur Douloir with my little playfellows, who,
like myself, cried and laughed by turns with all their might, from
morning till evening.

After a whole half-century these souvenirs float up again, fresh
and bright as ever, to the surface of memory, under this starry sky,
whose face has in no wise changed since then, and whose serene
and immutable lights will doubtless see many other schoolboys such
as I was slowly turn into grey-headed savants, afflicted with
catarrh.

Stars, who have shone down upon each wise or foolish head
among all my forgotten ancestors, it is under your soft light that I
now feel stir within me a certain poignant regret! I would that I
could have a son who might be able to see you when I shall see you
no more. How I should love him! Ah! such a son would—what am
I saying?—why, he would be now just twenty years old if you had
only been willing, Clémentine—you whose cheeks used to look so
ruddy under your pink hood! But you are married to that young
bank clerk, Noël Alexandre, who made so many millions afterwards!
I never met you again after your marriage, Clémentine, but I can
see you now, with your bright curls and your pink hood.

A looking-glass! a looking-glass! a looking-glass! Really, it would
be curious to see what I look like now, with my white hair, sighing
Clémentine's name to the stars! Still, it is not right to end with
sterile irony the thought begun in the spirit of faith and love. No,
Clémentine, if your name came to my lips by chance this beautiful
night, be it for ever blessed, your dear name! and may you ever, as
a happy mother, a happy grandmother, enjoy to the very end of life
with your rich husband the utmost degree of that happiness which
you had the right to believe you could not win with the poor young
scholar who loved you! If—though I cannot even now imagine it—
if your beautiful hair has become white, Clémentine, bear worthily
the bundle of keys confided to you by Noël Alexandre, and impart
to your grandchildren the knowledge of all domestic virtues!

Ah! beautiful Night! She rules, with such noble repose, over men
and animals alike, kindly loosed by her from the yoke of daily toil;
and even I feel her beneficent influence, although my habits of sixty
years have so changed me that I can feel most things only through
the signs which represent them. My world is wholly formed of
words—so much of a philologist I have become! Each one dreams
the dream of life in his own way. I have dreamed it in my library;
and when the hour shall come in which I must leave this world,
may it please God to take me from my ladder—from before my
shelves of books! . . .

"Well, well! it is really himself, *pardieu!* How are you, Monsieur
Sylvestre Bonnard? And where have you been travelling to all this
time, over the country, while I was waiting for you at the station
with my cabriolet? You missed me when the train came in, and I

was driving back, quite disappointed, to Lusance. Give me your valise, and get up here beside me in the carriage. Why, do you know it is fully seven kilometres from here to the château?"

Who addresses me thus, at the very top of his voice from the height of his cabriolet? Monsieur Paul de Gabry, nephew and heir of Monsieur Honoré de Gabry, peer of France in 1842, who recently died at Monaco. And it was precisely to Monsieur Paul de Gabry's house that I was going with that valise of mine, so carefully strapped by my housekeeper. This excellent young man has just inherited, conjointly with his two brothers-in-law, the property of his uncle, who, belonging to a very ancient family of distinguished lawyers, had accumulated in his château at Lusance a library rich in MSS., some dating back to the fourteenth century. It was for the purpose of making an inventory and a catalogue of these MSS. that I had come to Lusance at the urgent request of Monsieur Paul de Gabry, whose father, a perfect gentleman and distinguished bibliophile, had maintained the most pleasant relations with me during his lifetime. To tell the truth, Monsieur Paul has not inherited the fine tastes of his father. Monsieur Paul likes sporting; he is a great authority on horses and dogs; and I much fear that of all the sciences capable of satisfying or of duping the inexhaustible curiosity of mankind, those of the stable and the dog-kennel are the only ones thoroughly mastered by him.

I cannot say I was surprised to meet him, since we had made a rendezvous; but I acknowledge that I had become so preoccupied with my own thoughts that I had forgotten all about the Château de Lusance and its inhabitants, and that the voice of the gentleman calling out to me as I started to follow the country road winding away before me—*"un bon ruban de queue,"* as they say—had given me quite a start.

I fear my face must have betrayed my incongruous distraction by a certain stupid expression which it is apt to assume in most of my social transactions. My valise was pulled up into the carriage, and I followed my valise. My host pleased me by his straightforward simplicity.

"I don't know anything myself about your old parchments," he said; "but I think you will find some folks to talk to at the house. Beside the curé, who writes books himself, and the doctor, who is a very good fellow—although a radical—you will meet somebody able to keep your company. I mean my wife. She is not a very learned woman, but there are few things which she can't divine pretty well. Then I count upon being able to keep you with us long enough to make you acquainted with Mademoiselle Jeanne, who has the fingers of a magician and the soul of an angel."

"And is this delightfully gifted young lady one of your family?" I asked.

"Not at all," replied Monsieur Paul.

"Then she is just a friend of yours?" I persisted, rather stupidly.

"She has lost both her father and mother," answered Monsieur de Gabry, keeping his eyes fixed upon the ears of his horse, whose hoofs rang loudly over the road blue-tinted by the moonshine. "Her father managed to get us into some very serious trouble; and we did not get off with a fright either!"

Then he shook his head, and changed the subject. He gave me due warning of the ruinous condition in which I should find the château and the park; they had been absolutely deserted for thirty-two years.

I learned from him that Monsieur Honoré de Gabry, his uncle, had been on very bad terms with some poachers, whom he used to shoot at like rabbits. One of them, a vindictive peasant, who had received a whole charge of shot in his face, lay in wait for the Seigneur one evening behind the trees of the mall, and very nearly succeeded in killing him, for the ball took off the tip of his ear.

"My uncle," Monsieur Paul continued, "tried to discover who had fired the shot; but he could not see any one, and he walked back slowly to the house. The day after he called his steward, and ordered him to close up the manor and the park, and allow no living soul to enter. He expressly forbade that anything should be touched, or looked after, or any repairs made on the estate during his absence. He added, between his teeth, that he would return at Easter, or Trinity Sunday, as they say in the song; and, just as the song has it, Trinity Sunday passed without a sign of him. He died last year at Monaco; my brother-in-law and myself were the first to enter the château after it had been abandoned for thirty-two years. We found a chestnut-tree growing in the middle of the parlour. As for the park, it was useless trying to visit it, because there were no longer any paths or alleys."

My companion ceased to speak; and only the regular hoof-beat of the trotting horse, and the chirping of insects in the grass, broke the silence. On either hand, the sheaves standing in the fields took, in the vague moonlight, the appearance of tall white women kneeling down; and I abandoned myself awhile to those wonderful childish fancies which the charm of night always suggests. After driving under the heavy shadows of the mall, we turned to the right and rolled up a lordly avenue at the end of which the château suddenly rose into view—a black mass, with turrets *en poivrière*. We followed a sort of causeway, which gave access to the court-of-honour, and which, passing over a moat full of running water, doubtless replaced a long-vanished drawbridge. The loss of that drawbridge must have been, I think, the first of various humiliations to which the warlike manor had been subjected ere being reduced to that pacific aspect with which it received me. The stars reflected themselves with marvellous clearness in the dark water. Monsieur Paul, like a courteous host, escorted me to my chamber at the very top of the building, at the end of a long corridor; and then, excusing himself for not presenting me at once to his wife by reason of the lateness of the hour, bade me good-night.

My apartment, painted in white and hung with chintz, seemed to keep some traces of the elegant gallantry of the eighteenth century. A heap of still-glowing ashes—which testified to the pains taken to dispel humidity—filled the fireplace, whose marble mantelpiece supported a bust of Marie Antoinette in *biscuit*. Attached to the frame of the tarnished and discoloured mirror, two brass hooks, that had once doubtless served the ladies of old-fashioned days to hang their *chatelaines* on, seemed to offer a very opportune means of suspending my watch, which I took care to wind up beforehand; for, contrary to the opinion of the Thelemites, I hold that man is only master of time, which is Life itself, when he has divided it into hours, minutes and seconds—that is to say, into parts proportioned to the brevity of human existence.

And I thought to myself that life really seems short to us only because we measure it irrationally by our own mad hopes. We have all of us, like the old man in the fable, a new wing to add to our building. I want, for example, before I die, to finish my "History of the Abbots of Saint-Germain-des-Prés." The time God allots to each one of us is like a precious tissue which we embroider as we best know how. I had begun my woof with all sorts of philological illustrations. . . . So my thoughts wandered on; and at last, as I bound my *foulard* about my head, the notion of Time led me back to the past; and for the second time within the same round of the dial I thought of you, Clémentine—to bless you again in your prosperity, if you have any, before blowing out my candle and falling asleep amid the chanting of the frogs.

II

URING breakfast I had many opportunities to appreciate the good taste, tact, and intelligence of Madame de Gabry, who told me that the château had its ghosts, and was especially haunted by the "Lady-with-three-wrinkles-in-her-back," a poisoner during her lifetime, and thereafter a Soul-in-pain. I could never describe how much wit and animation she gave to this old nurse's tale. We took our coffee on the terrace, whose balusters, clasped and forcibly torn away from their stone coping by a vigorous growth of ivy, remained suspended in the grasp of the amorous plant like bewildered Athenian women in the arms of ravishing Centaurs.

The château, shaped something like a four-wheeled wagon, with a

turret at each of the four angles, had lost all original character by
reason of repeated remodellings. It was merely a fine spacious building, nothing more. It did not appear to me to have suffered much
damage during its abandonment of thirty-two years. But when
Madame de Gabry conducted me into the great salon of the ground-
floor, I saw that the planking was bulged in and out, the plinths
rotten, the wainscotings split apart, the paintings of the piers
turned black and hanging more than half out of their settings. A
chestnut-tree, after forcing up the planks of the floor, had grown
tall under the ceiling, and was reaching out its large-leaved
branches towards the glassless windows.

This spectacle was not devoid of charm; but I could not look at it
without anxiety, as I remembered that the rich library of Monsieur
Honoré de Gabry, in an adjoining apartment, must have been exposed for the same length of time to the same forces of decay. Yet,
as I looked at the young chestnut-tree in the salon, I could not but
admire the magnificent vigour of Nature, and that resistless power
which forces every germ to develop into life. On the other hand I
felt saddened to think that, whatever effort we scholars may make
to preserve dead things from passing away, we are labouring painfully in vain. Whatever has lived becomes the necessary food of
new existences. And the Arab who builds himself a hut out of the
marble fragments of a Palmyra temple is really more of a philosopher than all the guardians of museums at London, Munich, or
Paris.

August 11.

ALL day long I have been classifying MSS. . . . The sun came
in through the lofty uncurtained windows; and, during my reading,
often very interesting, I could hear the languid bumble-bees bump
heavily against the windows, and the flies, intoxicated with light
and heat, making their wings hum in circles around my head. So
loud became their humming about three o'clock that I looked up
from the document I was reading—a document containing very
precious materials for the history of Melun in the thirteenth century—to watch the concentric movements of those tiny creatures.
"Bestions," Lafontaine calls them: he found this form of the word
in the old popular speech, whence also the term, *tapisserie-à-
bestions,* applied to figured tapestry. I was compelled to confess
that the effect of heat upon the wings of a fly is totally different
from that it exerts upon the brain of a paleographical archivist;
for I found it very difficult to think, and a rather pleasant languor
weighing upon me, from which I could rouse myself only by a very
determined effort. The dinner-bell then startled me in the midst of
my labours; and I had barely time to put on my new dress-coat, so
as to make a respectable appearance before Madame de Gabry.

The repast, generously served, seemed to prolong itself for my benefit. I am more than a fair judge of wine; and my hostess, who discovered my knowledge in this regard, was friendly enough to open a certain bottle of Château-Margaux in my honour. With deep respect I drank of this famous and knightly old wine, which comes from the slopes of Bordeaux, and of which the flavour and exhilarating power are beyond all praise. The ardour of it spread gently through my veins, and filled me with an almost juvenile animation. Seated beside Madame de Gabry on the terrace, in the gloaming which gave a charming melancholy to the park, and lent to every object an air of mystery, I took pleasure in communicating my impressions of the scene to my hostess. I discoursed with a vivacity quite remarkable on the part of a man so devoid of imagination as I am. I described to her spontaneously, without quoting from any old texts, the caressing melancholy of the evening, and the beauty of that natal earth which feeds us, not only with bread and wine, but also with ideas, sentiments, beliefs, and which will at last take us all back to her maternal breast again, like so many tired little children at the close of a long day.

"Monsieur," said the kind lady, "you see these old towers, those trees, that sky; is it not quite natural that the personages of the popular tales and folk-songs should have been evoked by such scenes? Why, over there is the very path which Little Red Riding-hood followed when she went to the woods to pick nuts. Across this changeful and always vapoury sky the fairy chariots used to roll; and the north tower might have sheltered under its pointed roof that same old spinning woman whose distaff pricked the Sleeping Beauty in the Wood."

I continued to muse upon her pretty fancies, while Monsieur Paul related to me, as he puffed a very strong cigar, the history of some suit he had brought against the commune about a water-right. Madame de Gabry, feeling the chill night air, began to shiver under the shawl her husband had wrapped about her, and left us to go to her room. I then decided, instead of going to my own, to return to the library and continue my examination of the manuscripts. In spite of the protests of Monsieur Paul, I entered what I may call, in old-fashioned phrase, "the book-room," and started to work by the light of a lamp.

After having read fifteen pages, evidently written by some ignorant and careless scribe, for I could scarcely discern their meaning, I plunged my hand into the pocket of my coat to get my snuff-box; but this movement, usually so natural and almost instinctive, this time cost me some effort and even fatigue. Nevertheless, I got out the silver box, and took from it a pinch of the odorous powder, which, somehow or other, I managed to spill all over my shirt-bosom under my baffled nose. I am sure my nose must have expressed its disappointment, for it is a very expressive nose. More than once it has betrayed my secret thoughts, and especially upon a certain occasion at the public library of Coutances, where I discovered, right in front of my colleague Brioux, the "Cartulary of Notre-Dame-des-Anges."

What a delight! My little eyes remained as dull and expressionless as ever behind my spectacles. But at the mere sight of my thick pug-nose, which quivered with joy and pride, Brioux knew that I had found something. He noted the volume I was looking at, observed the place where I put it back, pounced upon it as soon as I turned my heel, copied it secretly, and published it in haste, for the sake of playing me a trick. But his edition swarms with errors, and I had the satisfaction of afterwards criticising some of the gross blunders he made.

But to come back to the point at which I left off: I began to suspect that I was getting very sleepy indeed. I was looking at a chart of which the interest may be divined from the fact that it contained mention of a hutch sold to Jehan d'Estonville, priest, in 1312. But although, even then, I could recognise the importance of the document, I did not give it that attention it so strongly invited. My eyes would keep turning, against my will, towards a certain corner of the table where there was nothing whatever interesting to a learned mind. There was only a big German book there, bound in pigskin, with brass studs on the sides, and very thick cording upon the back. It was a fine copy of a compilation which has little to recommend it except the wood engravings it contains, and which is well known as the "Cosmography of Munster." This volume, with its covers slightly open, was placed upon edge, with the back upwards.

I could not say for how long I had been staring causelessly at the sixteenth-century folio, when my eyes were captivated by a sight so extraordinary that even a person as devoid of imagination as I could not but have been greatly astonished by it.

I perceived, all of a sudden, without having noticed her coming into the room, a little creature seated on the back of the book, with one knee bent and one leg hanging down—somewhat in the attitude of the amazons of Hyde Park or the Bois de Boulogne on horseback. She was so small that her swinging foot did not reach the table, over which the trail of her dress extended in a serpentine line. But her face and figure were those of an adult. The fulness of her corsage and the roundness of her waist could leave no doubt of that, even for an old *savant* like myself. I will venture to add that she was very handsome, with a proud mien; for my iconographic studies have long accustomed me to recognise at once the perfection of a type and the character of a physiognomy. The countenance of this lady who had seated herself inopportunely on the back of a "Cosmography of Munster" expressed a mingling of haughtiness and mischievousness. She had the air of a queen, but a capricious queen; and I judged, from the mere expression of her eyes, that she was accustomed to wield great authority somewhere, in a very whimsical manner. Her mouth was imperious and mocking, and those blue eyes of hers seemed to laugh in a disquieting way under her finely arched black eyebrows. I have always heard that black eyebrows are very becoming to blondes; and this lady was very blonde. On the whole, the impression she gave me was one of greatness.

It may seem odd to say that a person who was no taller than a wine-bottle, and who might have been hidden in my coat pocket— but that it would have been very disrespectful to put her in it— gave me precisely an idea of greatness. But in the fine proportions of the lady seated upon the "Cosmography of Munster" there was such a proud elegance, such a harmonious majesty, and she maintained an attitude at once so easy and so noble, that she really seemed to me a very great person. Although my ink-bottle, which she examined with an expression of such mockery as appeared to indicate that she knew in advance every word that could ever come out of it at the end of my pen, was for her a deep basin in which she would have blackened her gold-clocked pink stockings up to the garter, I can assure you that she was great, and imposing even in her sprightliness.

Her costume, worthy of her face, was extremely magnificent; it consisted of a robe of gold-and-silver brocade, and a mantle of nacarat velvet, lined with vair. Her head-dress was a sort of *hennin,* with two high points; and pearls of splendid lustre made it bright and luminous as a crescent moon. Her little white hand held a wand. That wand drew my attention very strongly, because my archæological studies had taught me to recognise with certainty every sign by which the notable personages of legend and of history are distinguished. This knowledge came to my aid during various very queer conjectures with which I was labouring. I examined the wand, and saw that it appeared to have been cut from a branch of hazel.

"Then it is a fairy's wand," I said to myself; "consequently the lady who carries it is a fairy."

Happy at thus discovering what sort of a person was before me, I tried to collect my mind sufficiently to make her a graceful compliment. It would have given me much satisfaction, I confess, if I could have talked to her about the part taken by her people, not less in the life of the Saxon and Germanic races, than in that of the Latin Occident. Such a dissertation, it appeared to me, would have been an ingenious method of thanking the lady for having thus appeared to an old scholar, contrary to the invariable custom of her kindred, who never show themselves but to innocent children or ignorant village-folk.

Because one happens to be a fairy, one is none the less a woman, I said to myself; and since Madame Récamier, according to what I

heard J. J. Ampère say, used to blush with pleasure when the little
chimney-sweeps opened their eyes as wide as they could to look at
her, surely the supernatural lady seated upon the "Cosmography of
Munster" might feel flattered to hear an erudite man discourse
learnedly about her, as about a medal, a seal, a fibula, or a token.
But such an undertaking, which would have cost my timidity a
great deal, became totally out of the question when I observed the
Lady of the Cosmography suddenly take from an alms-purse hanging at her girdle the very smallest nuts I had ever seen, crack the
shells between her teeth, and throw them at my nose, while she nib-
bled the kernels with the gravity of a sucking child.

At this conjuncture, I did what the dignity of science demanded
of me—I remained silent. But the nut-shells caused such a painful tickling that I put up my hand to my nose, and found, to my
great surprise, that my spectacles were straddling the very end of
it—so that I was actually looking at the lady, not through my spectacles, but over them. This was incomprehensible, because my eyes,
worn out over old texts, cannot ordinarily distinguish anything
without glasses—could not tell a melon from a decanter, though
the two were placed close up to my nose.

That nose of mine, remarkable for its size, its shape, and its
coloration, legitimately attracted the attention of the fairy; for she
seized my goose-quill pen, which was sticking up from the ink-
bottle like a plume, and she began to pass the feather-end of that
pen over my nose. I had had more than once, in company, occasion
to suffer cheerfully from the innocent mischief of young ladies, who
made me join their games, and would offer me their cheeks to kiss
through the back of a chair, or invite me to blow out a candle
which they would lift suddenly above the range of my breath. But
until that moment no person of the fair sex had ever subjected me
to such a whimsical piece of familiarity as that of tickling my nose
with my own feather pen. Happily I remembered the maxim of my
late grandfather, who was accustomed to say that everything was
permissible on the part of ladies, and that whatever they do to us
is to be regarded as a grace and a favour. Therefore, as a grace
and a favour I received the nutshells and the titillations with my
own pen, and I tried to smile. Much more!—I even found speech.

"Madame," I said, with dignified politeness, "you accord the honour of a visit not to a silly child, nor to a boor, but to a bibliophile
who is very happy to make your acquaintance, and who knows that
long ago you used to make elf-knots in the manes of mares at the
crib, drink the milk from the skimming-pails, slip *graines-à-gratter*
down the backs of our great-grandmothers, make the hearth
sputter in the faces of the old folks, and, in short, fill the house
with disorder and gaiety. You can also boast of giving the nicest
frights in the world to lovers who stayed out in the woods too late
of evenings. But I thought you had vanished out of existence at

least three centuries ago. Can it really be, Madame, that you are still to be seen in this age of railways and telegraphs? My concierge, who used to be a nurse in her young days, does not know your story; and my little boy-neighbour, whose nose is still wiped for him by his *bonne,* declares that you do not exist."

"What do you yourself think about it?" she cried, in a silvery voice, straightening up her royal little figure in a very haughty fashion, and whipping the back of the "Cosmography of Munster" as though it were a hippogriff.

"I don't really know," I answered, rubbing my eyes.

This reply, indicating a deeply scientific scepticism, had the most deplorable effect upon my questioner.

"Monsieur Sylvestre Bonnard," she said to me, "you are nothing but an old pedant. I always suspected as much. The smallest little ragamuffin who goes along the road with his shirt-tail sticking out through a hole in his pantaloons knows more about me than all the old spectacled folks in your Institutes and your Academies. To know is nothing at all; to imagine is everything. Nothing exists except that which is imagined. I am imaginary. That is what it is to exist, I should think! I am dreamed of, and I appear. Everything is only dream; and as nobody ever dreams about you, Sylvestre Bonnard, it is *you* who do not exist. I charm the world; I am everywhere—on a moonbeam, in the trembling of a hidden spring, in the moving of leaves that murmur, in the white vapours that rise each morning from the hollow meadow, in the thickets of pink brier—everywhere! . . . I am seen; I am loved. There are sighs uttered, weird thrills of pleasure felt by those who follow the light print of my feet, as I make the dead leaves whisper. I make the little children smile; I give wit to the dullest-minded nurses. Leaning above the cradles, I play, I comfort, I lull to sleep—and you doubt whether I exist! Sylvestre Bonnard, your warm coat covers the hide of an ass!"

She ceased speaking; her delicate nostrils swelled with indignation; and while I admired, despite my vexation, the heroic anger of this little person, she pushed my pen about in the ink-bottle, backward and forward, like an oar, and then suddenly threw it at my nose, point first.

I rubbed my face, and felt it all covered with ink. She had disappeared. My lamp was extinguished. A ray of moonlight streamed down through a window and descended upon the "Cosmography of Munster." A strong cool wind, which had arisen very suddenly without my knowledge, was blowing my papers, pens, and wafers about. My table was all stained with ink. I had left my window open during the storm. What an imprudence!

III

WROTE to my housekeeper, as I promised, that I was safe and sound. But I took care not to tell her that I had caught cold from going to sleep in the library at night with the window open; for the good woman would have been as unsparing in her remonstrances to me as parliaments to kings. "At your age, Monsieur," she would have been sure to say, "one ought to have more sense." She is simple enough to believe that sense grows with age. I seem to her an exception to this rule.

Not having any similar motive for concealing my experiences from Madame de Gabry, I told her all about my vision, which she seemed to enjoy very much.

"Why, that was a charming dream of yours," she said; "and one must have real genius to dream such a dream."

"Then I am a real genius when I am asleep," I responded.

"When you dream," she replied; "and you are always dreaming."

I know that Madame de Gabry, in making this remark, only wished to please me; but that intention alone deserves my utmost gratitude; and it is therefore in a spirit of thankfulness and kindliest remembrance that I write down her words, which I will read over and over again until my dying day, and which will never be read by any one save myself.

I passed the next few days in completing the inventory of the manuscripts in the Lusance library. Certain confidential observations dropped by Monsieur Paul de Gabry, however, caused me some painful surprise, and made me decide to pursue the work after a different manner from that in which I had begun it. From those few words I learned that the fortune of Monsieur Honoré de Gabry, which had been badly managed for many years, and subsequently swept away to a large extent through the failure of a banker whose name I do not know, had been transmitted to the heirs of the old French nobleman only under the form of mortgaged real estate and irrecoverable assets.

Monsieur Paul, by agreement with his joint heirs, had decided to sell the library, and I was intrusted with the task of making arrangements to have the sale effected upon advantageous terms. But, totally ignorant as I was of all business methods and trade-customs, I thought it best to get the advice of a publisher who was one of my private friends. I wrote him at once to come and join me at Lusance; and while waiting for his arrival I took my hat and cane and made visits to the different churches of the diocese, in several of which I knew there were certain mortuary inscriptions to be found which had never been correctly copied.

So I left my hosts and departed on my pilgrimage. Exploring the churches and the cemeteries every day, visiting the parish priests and the village notaries, supping at the public inns with peddlers and cattle-dealers, sleeping at night between sheets scented with lavender, I passed one whole week in the quiet but profound enjoyment of observing the living engaged in their various daily occupations even while I was thinking of the dead. As for the purpose of my researches, I made only a few mediocre discoveries, which caused me only a mediocre joy, and one therefore salubrious and not at all fatiguing. I copied a few interesting epitaphs; and I added to this little collection a few recipes for cooking country dishes, which a certain good priest kindly gave me.

With these riches, I returned to Lusance; and I crossed the court-of-honour with such secret satisfaction as a *bourgeois* feels on entering his own home. This was the effect of the kindness of my hosts; and the impression I received on crossing their threshold proves, better than any reasoning could do, the excellence of their hospitality.

I entered the great parlour without meeting anybody; and the young chestnut-tree there spreading out its broad leaves seemed to me like an old friend. But the next thing which I saw—on the pier-table—caused me such a shock of surprise that I readjusted my glasses upon my nose with both hands at once, and then felt myself over so as to get at least some superficial proof of my own existence. In less than one second there thronged into my mind twenty different conjectures—the most rational of which was that I had suddenly become crazy. It seemed to me absolutely impossible that what I was looking at could exist; yet it was equally impossible for me not to see it as a thing actually existing. What caused my surprise was resting on the pier-table, above which rose a great dull speckled mirror.

I saw myself in that mirror; and I can say that I saw for once in my life the perfect image of stupefaction. But I made proper allowance for myself; I approved myself for being so stupefied by a really stupefying thing.

The object I was thus examining with a degree of astonishment that all my reasoning power failed to lessen, obtruded itself on my attention though quite motionless. The persistence and fixity of the phenomenon excluded any idea of hallucination. I am totally exempt from all nervous disorders capable of influencing the sense of sight. The cause of such visual disturbance is, I think, generally due to stomach trouble; and, thank God! I have an excellent stomach. Moreover, visual illusions are accompanied with special abnormal conditions which impress the victims of hallucination themselves, and inspire them with a sort of terror. Now, I felt nothing of this kind; the object which I saw, although seemingly impossible in itself, appeared to me under all the natural conditions of reality. I observed that it had three dimensions, and colours, and that it cast a shadow. Ah! how I stared at it! The water came into my eyes so that I had to wipe the glasses of my spectacles.

Finally I found myself obliged to yield to the evidence, and to affirm that I had really before my eyes the Fairy, the very same Fairy I had been dreaming of in the library a few evenings before. It was she, it was her very self, I assure you! She had the same air of child-queen, the same proud supple poise; she held the same hazel wand in her hand; she still wore her double-peaked head-dress, and the train of her long brocade robe undulated about her little feet. Same face, same figure. It was she indeed; and to prevent any possible doubt of it, she was seated on the back of a huge old-fashioned book strongly resembling the "Cosmography of Munster." Her immobility but half reassured me; I was really afraid that she was going to take some more nuts out of her alms-purse and throw the shells at my face.

I was standing there, waving my hands and gaping, when the musical and laughing voice of Madame de Gabry suddenly rang in my ears.

"So you are examining your fairy, Monsieur Bonnard!" said my hostess. "Well, do you think the resemblance good?"

It was very quickly said; but even while hearing it I had time to perceive that my fairy was a statuette in coloured wax, modelled with much taste and spirit by some novice hand. But the phenomenon, even thus reduced by a rational explanation, did not cease to excite my surprise. How, and by whom, had the Lady of the Cosmography been enabled to assume plastic existence? That was what remained for me to learn.

Turning towards Madame de Gabry, I perceived that she was not alone. A young girl dressed in black was standing beside her. She had large intelligent eyes, of a grey as sweet as that of the sky of the Isle of France, and at once artless and characteristic in their expression. At the extremities of her rather thin arms were fidgeting uneasily two slender hands, supple but slightly red, as it becomes the hands of young girls to be. Sheathed in her closely fitting merino robe, she had the slim grace of a young tree; and her large mouth bespoke frankness. I could not describe how much the child pleased me at first sight! She was not beautiful; but the three dimples of her cheeks and chin seemed to laugh, and her whole person, which revealed the awkwardness of innocence, had something in it indescribably good and sincere.

My gaze alternated from the statuette to the young girl; and I saw her blush—so frankly and fully!—the crimson passing over her face as by waves.

"Well," said my hostess, who had become sufficiently accustomed to my distracted moods to put the same question to me twice, "is that the very same lady who came in to see you through the window that you left open? She was very saucy, but then you were quite imprudent! Anyhow, do you recognise her?"

"It is her very self," I replied; "I see her now on that pier-table precisely as I saw her on the table in the library."

"Then, if that be so," replied Madame de Gabry, "you have to blame for it, in the first place, yourself, as a man who, although devoid of all imagination, to use your own words, knew how to depict your dream in such vivid colours; in the second place, me, who was able to remember and repeat faithfully all your dream; and, lastly, Mademoiselle Jeanne, whom I now introduce to you, for she herself modelled that wax figure precisely according to my instructions."

Madame de Gabry had taken the young girl's hand as she spoke; but the latter had suddenly broken away from her, and was already running through the park with the speed of a bird.

"Little crazy creature!" Madame de Gabry cried after her. "How can one be so shy? Come back here to be scolded and kissed!"

But it was all of no avail; the frightened child disappeared among the shrubbery. Madame de Gabry seated herself in the only chair remaining in the dilapidated parlour.

"I should be much surprised," she said, "if my husband had not already spoken to you of Jeanne. She is a sweet child, and we both love her very much. Tell me the plain truth; what do you think of her statuette?"

I replied that the work was full of good taste and spirit, but that it showed some want of study and practice on the author's part; otherwise I had been extremely touched to think that those young fingers should have thus embroidered an old man's rough sketch of fancy, and given form so brilliantly to the dreams of a dotard like myself.

"The reason I ask your opinion," replied Madame de Gabry, seriously, "is that Jeanne is a poor orphan. Do you think she could earn her living by modelling statuettes like this one?"

"As for that, no!" I replied; "and I think there is no reason to regret the fact. You say the girl is affectionate and sensitive; I can well believe you; I could believe it from her face alone. There are excitements in artist-life which impel generous hearts to act out of all rule and measure. This young creature is made to love; keep her for the domestic hearth. There only is real happiness."

"But she has no dowry!" replied Madame de Gabry.

Then, extending her hand to me, she continued:

"You are our friend; I can tell you everything. The father of this child was a banker, and one of our friends. He went into a colossal speculation, and it ruined him. He survived only a few months after his failure, in which, as Paul must have told you, three-fourths of my uncle's fortune were lost, and more than half of our own.

"We had made his acquaintance at Monaco, during the winter we passed there at my uncle's house. He had an adventurous disposition, but such an engaging manner! He deceived himself before ever he deceived others. After all, it is in the ability to deceive oneself that the greatest talent is shown, is it not? Well, we were captured —my husband, my uncle, and I; and we risked much more than a reasonable amount in a very hazardous undertaking. But, bah! as Paul says, since we have no children we need not worry about it. Besides, we have the satisfaction of knowing that the friend in whom we trusted was an honest man. . . . You must know his name, it was so often in the papers and on public placards—Noël Alexandre. His wife was a very sweet person. I knew her only when she was already past her prime, with traces of having once been very pretty, and a taste for fashionable style and display which seemed quite becoming to her. She was naturally fond of social excitement; but she showed a great deal of courage and dignity after the death of her husband. She died a year after him, leaving Jeanne alone in the world."

"Clémentine!" I cried out.

And on thus learning what I had never even imagined—the mere idea of which would have set all the forces of my soul in revolt— upon hearing that Clémentine was no longer in this world, something like a great silence came upon me; and the feeling which flooded my whole being was not a keen, strong pain, but a quiet and solemn sorrow. Yet I was conscious of some incomprehensible sense of alleviation, and my thought rose suddenly to heights before unknown.

"From wheresoever thou art at this moment, Clémentine," I said to myself, "look down upon this heart now indeed cooled by age, yet whose blood once boiled for thy sake, and say whether it is not reanimated by the mere thought of being able to love all that remains of thee on earth. Everything passes away since thou thyself hast passed away; but Life is immortal; it is that Life we must love in its forms eternally renewed. All the rest is child's play; and I myself, with all my books, am only like a child playing with marbles. The purpose of life—it is thou, Clémentine, who hast revealed it to me!" . . .

Madame de Gabry aroused me from my thoughts by murmuring,

"The child is poor."

"The daughter of Clémentine is poor!" I exclaimed aloud; "how fortunate that it is so! I would not wish that any one but myself should provide for her and dower her! No! the daughter of Clémentine must not have her dowry from any one but me."

And, approaching Madame de Gabry as she rose from her chair, I took her right hand; I kissed that hand, and placed it on my arm, and said:

"You will conduct me to the grave of the widow of Noël Alexandre."

And I heard Madame de Gabry asking me:

"Why are you crying?"

IV

THE LITTLE SAINT-GEORGE

April 16.

AINT DROCTOVEUS and the early abbots of Saint-Germain-des-Prés have been occupying me for the past forty years; but I do not know if I shall be able to write their history before I go to join them. It is already quite a long time since I became an old man. One day last year, on the Pont des Arts, one of my fellow members at the Institute was lamenting before me over the *ennui* of becoming old.

"Still," Saint-Beuve replied to him, "it is the only way that has yet been found of living a long time."

I have tried this way, and I know just what it is worth. The trouble of it is not that one lasts too long, but that one sees all about him pass away—mother, wife, friends, children. Nature makes and unmakes all these divine treasures with gloomy indifference, and at last we find that we have not loved, we have only been embracing shadows. But how sweet some shadows are! If ever creature glided like a shadow through the life of a man, it was certainly that young girl whom I fell in love with when—incredible though it now seems—I was myself a youth.

A Christian sarcophagus from the catacombs of Rome bears a formula of imprecation, the whole terrible meaning of which I only learned with time. It says: *"Whatsoever impious man violates this sepulchre, may he die the last of his own people!"* In my capacity of archæologist, I have opened tombs and disturbed ashes in order to collect the shreds of apparel, metal ornaments, or gems that were mingled with those ashes. But I did it only through that scientific curiosity which does not exclude the feelings of reverence and of piety. May that malediction graven by some one of the first followers of the apostles upon a martyr's tomb never fall upon me! I ought not to fear to survive my own people so long as there are men in the world; for there are always some whom one can love.

But the power of love itself weakens and gradually becomes lost with age, like all the other energies of man. Example proves it; and it is this which terrifies me. Am I sure that I have not myself already suffered this great loss? I should surely have felt it, but for the happy meeting which has rejuvenated me. Poets speak of the Fountain of Youth; it does exist; it gushes up from the earth at every step we take. And one passes by without drinking of it!

The young girl I loved, married of her own choice to a rival, passed, all grey-haired, into the eternal rest. I have found her daughter—so that my life, which before seemed to me without utility, now once more finds a purpose and a reason for being.

To-day I "take the sun," as they say in Provence; I take it on the terrace of the Luxembourg, at the foot of the statue of Marguerite de Navarre. It is a spring sun, intoxicating as young wine. I sit and dream. My thoughts escape from my head like the foam from a bottle of beer. They are light, and their fizzing amuses me. I dream; such a pastime is certainly permissible to an old fellow who has published thirty volumes of texts, and contributed to the *Journal des Savants* for twenty-six years. I have the satisfaction of feeling that I performed my task as well as it was possible for me to do, and that I utilised to their fullest extent those mediocre faculties with which Nature endowed me. My efforts were not all in vain, and I have contributed, in my own modest way, to that renaissance of historical labours which will remain the honour of this restless century. I shall certainly be counted among those ten or twelve who revealed to France her own literary antiquities. My publication of the poetical works of Gautier de Coincy inaugurated a judicious system and fixed a date. It is in the austere calm of old age that I decree to myself this deserved credit, and God, who sees my heart, knows whether pride or vanity have aught to do with this self-award of justice.

But I am tired; my eyes are dim; my hand trembles, and I see an image of myself in those old men of Homer, whose weakness excluded them from the battle, and who, seated upon the ramparts, lifted up their voices like crickets among the leaves.

So my thoughts were wandering when three young men seated themselves near me. I do not know whether each one of them had come in three boats, like the monkey of Lafontaine, but the three certainly displayed themselves over the space of twelve chairs. I took pleasure in watching them, not because they had anything very extraordinary about them, but because I discerned in them that brave joyous manner which is natural to youth. They were from the schools. I was less assured of it by the books they were carrying than by the character of their physiognomy. For all who busy themselves with the things of the mind can be at once recognised by an indescribable something which is common to all of them. I am very fond of young people; and these pleased me, in spite of a certain provoking wild manner which recalled to me my own college days with marvellous vividness. But they did not wear velvet doublets and long hair, as we used to do; they did not walk about, as we used to do, with a death's-head; they did not cry out, as we used to do, "Hell and malediction!" They were quite properly dressed, and neither their costume nor their language had anything suggestive of the Middle Ages. I must also add that they paid considerable attention to the women passing on the terrace, and expressed their admiration of some of them in very animated language. But their reflections, even on this subject, were not of a character to oblige me to flee from my seat. Besides, so long as youth is studious, I think it has a right to its gaieties.

One of them, having made some gallant pleasantry which I forget, the smallest and darkest of the three exclaimed, with a slight Gascon accent,

"What a thing to say! Only physiologists like us have any right to occupy ourselves about living matter. As for you, Gélis, who only live in the past—like all your fellow archivists and paleographers—you will do better to confine yourself to those stone women over there, who are your contemporaries."

And he pointed to the statues of the Ladies of Ancient France which towered up, all white, in a half-circle under the trees of the terrace. This joke, though in itself trifling, enabled me to know that the young man called Gélis was a student at the École des Chartes. From the conversation which followed I was able to learn that his neighbour, blond and wan almost to diaphaneity, taciturn and sarcastic, was Boulmier, a fellow student. Gélis and the future doctor (I hope he will become one some day) discoursed together with much fantasy and spirit. In the midst of the loftiest speculations they would play upon words, and make jokes after the peculiar fashion of really witty persons—that is to say, in a style of enormous absurdity. I need hardly say, I suppose, that they only deigned to maintain the most monstrous kind of paradoxes. They employed all their powers of imagination to make themselves as ludicrous as possible, and all their powers of reasoning to assert the contrary of common sense. All the better for them! I do not like to see young folks too rational.

The student of medicine, after glancing at the title of the book that Boulmier held in his hand, exclaimed,

"What!—you read Michelet—you?"

"Yes," replied Boulmier, very gravely. "I like novels."

Gélis, who dominated both by his fine stature, imperious gestures, and ready wit, took the book, turned over a few pages rapidly, and said,

"Michelet always had a great propensity to emotional tenderness. He wept sweet tears over Maillard, that nice little man who introduced *la paperasserie* into the September massacres. But as emotional tenderness leads to fury, he becomes all at once furious against the victims. There was no help for it. It is the sentimentality of the age. The assassin is pitied, but the victim is considered quite unpardonable. In his later manner Michelet is more Michelet than ever before. There is no common sense in it; it is simply wonderful! Neither art nor science, neither criticism nor narrative; only furies and fainting-spells and epileptic fits over matters which he never deigns to explain. Childish outcries—*envies de femme grosse!*—and a style, my friend!—not a single finished phrase! It is astounding!"

And he handed the book back to his comrade. "This is amusing madness," I thought to myself, "and not quite so devoid of common sense as it appears. This young man, though only playing, has sharply touched the defect in the cuirass."

But the Provençal student declared that history was a thoroughly despicable exercise of rhetoric. According to him, the only true history was the natural history of man. Michelet was in the right path when he came in contact with the fistula of Louis XIV., but he fell back into the old rut almost immediately afterwards.

After this judicious expression of opinion, the young physiologist went to join a party of passing friends. The two archivists, less well acquainted in the neighbourhood of a garden so far from the Rue Paradis-au-Marais, remained together, and began to chat about their studies. Gélis, who had completed his third class-year, was preparing a thesis on the subject of which he expatiated with youthful enthusiasm. Indeed, I thought the subject a very good one, particularly because I had recently thought myself called upon to treat a notable part of it. It was the *Monasticon Gallicanum.* The young erudite (I give him the name as a presage) wanted to describe all the engravings made about 1690 for the work which Dom Michel Germain would have had printed but for the one irremediable hindrance which is rarely foreseen and never avoided. Dom Michel Germain left his manuscript complete, however, and in good order when he died. Shall I be able to do as much with mine?—but that is not the present question. So far as I am able to understand, Monsieur Gélis intends to devote a brief archæological notice to each of the abbeys pictured by the humble engravers of Dom Michel Germain.

His friend asked him whether he was acquainted with all the manuscripts and printed documents relating to the subject. It was then that I pricked up my ears. They spoke at first of original sources; and I must confess they did so in a satisfactory manner, despite their innumerable and detestable puns. Then they began to speak about contemporary studies on the subject.

"Have you read," asked Boulmier, "the notice of Courajod?"

"Good!" I thought to myself.

"Yes," replied Gélis; "it is accurate."

"Have you read," said Boulmier, "the article by Tamisey de Larroque in the 'Revue des Questions Historiques'?"

"Good!" I thought to myself, for the second time.

"Yes," replied Gélis, "it is full of things." . . .

"Have you read," said Boulmier, "the 'Tableau des Abbayes Bénédictines en 1600,' by Sylvestre Bonnard?"

"Good!" I said to myself, for the third time.

"Mai foi! no!" replied Gélis. "Bonnard is an idiot!" Turning my head, I perceived that the shadow had reached the place where I was sitting. It was growing chilly, and I thought to myself what a fool I was to have remained sitting there, at the risk of getting the rheumatism, just to listen to the impertinence of those two young fellows!

"Well! well!" I said to myself as I got up. "Let this prattling fledgling write his thesis, and sustain it! He will find my colleague, Quicherat, or some other professor at the school, to show him what an ignoramus he is. I consider him neither more nor less than a rascal; and really, now that I come to think of it, what he said about Michelet awhile ago was quite insufferable, outrageous! To talk in that way about an old master replete with genius! It was simply abominable!"

April 17.

"THÉRÈSE, give me my new hat, my best frock-coat, and my silver-headed cane."

But Thérèse is deaf as a sack of charcoal and slow as Justice. Years have made her so. The worst is that she thinks she can hear well and move about well; and, proud of her sixty years of upright domesticity, she serves her old master with the most vigilant despotism.

"What did I tell you?" . . . And now she will not give me my silver-headed cane, for fear that I might lose it! It is true that I often forget umbrellas and walking-sticks in the omnibuses and booksellers' shops. But I have a special reason for wanting to take out with me to-day my old cane with the engraved silver head representing Don Quixote charging a windmill, lance in rest, while Sancho Panza, with uplifted arms, vainly conjures him to stop. That cane is all that came to me from the heritage of my uncle, Captain Victor, who in his lifetime resembled Don Quixote much more than Sancho Panza, and who loved blows quite as much as most people fear them.

For thirty years I have been in the habit of carrying this cane upon all memorable or solemn visits which I make; and those two figures of knight and squire give me inspiration and counsel. I imagine I can hear them speak. Don Quixote says,

"Think well about great things; and know that thought is the only reality in this world. Lift up Nature to thine own stature; and let the whole universe be for thee no more than the reflection of thine own heroic soul. Combat for honour's sake: that alone is worthy of a man! and if it should fall to thee to receive wounds, shed thy blood as a beneficent dew, and smile."

And Sancho Panza says to me in his turn,

"Remain just what heaven made thee, comrade! Prefer the bread-crust which has become dry in thy wallet to all the partridges that roast in the kitchens of lords. Obey thy master, whether he be a wise man or a fool, and do not cumber thy brain with too many useless things. Fear blows; 'tis verily tempting God to seek after danger!"

But if the incomparable knight and his matchless squire are imaged only upon this cane of mine, they are realities to my inner conscience. Within every one of us there lives both a Don Quixote and a Sancho Panza to whom we hearken by turns; and though Sancho most persuades us, it is Don Quixote that we find ourselves obliged to admire. . . . But a truce to this dotage!—and let us go to see Madame de Gabry about some matters more important than the everyday details of life. . . .

Same day.

I found Madame de Gabry dressed in black, just buttoning her gloves.

"I am ready," she said.

Ready!—so I have always found her upon any occasion of doing a kindness.

After some compliments about the good health of her husband, who was taking a walk at the time, we descended the stairs and got into the carriage.

I do not know what secret influence I feared to dissipate by breaking silence, but we followed the great deserted drives without speaking, looking at the crosses, the monumental columns, and the mortuary wreaths awaiting sad purchasers.

The vehicle at last halted at the extreme verge of the land of the living, before the gate upon which words of hope are graven.

"Follow me," said Madame de Gabry, whose tall stature I noticed then for the first time. She first walked down an alley of cypresses, and then took a very narrow path contrived between the tombs. Finally, halting before a plain slab, she said to me,

"It is here."

And she knelt down. I could not help noticing the beautiful easy manner in which this Christian woman fell upon her knees, leaving the folds of her robe to spread themselves at random about her. I had never before seen any lady kneel down with such frankness and such forgetfulness of self, except two fair Polish exiles, one evening long ago, in a deserted church in Paris.

This image passed like a flash; and I saw only the sloping stone on which was graven the name of Clémentine. What I then felt was something so deep and vague that only the sound of some rich music could convey any idea of it. I seemed to hear instruments of celestial sweetness make harmony in my old heart. With the solemn accords of a funeral chant there seemed to mingle the subdued melody of a song of love; for my soul blended into one feeling the grave sadness of the present with the familiar graces of the past.

I cannot tell whether we had remained a long time at the tomb of Clémentine before Madame de Gabry arose. We passed through the cemetery again without speaking to each other. Only when we found ourselves among the living once more did I feel able to speak.

"While following you there," I said to Madame de Gabry, "I could not help thinking of those angels with whom we are said to meet on the mysterious confines of life and death. That tomb you led me to, of which I knew nothing—as I know nothing, or scarcely anything, concerning her whom it covers—brought back to me emotions which were unique in my life, and which seem in the dulness of that life like some light gleaming upon a dark road. The light recedes farther and farther away as the journey lengthens; I have now almost reached the bottom of the last slope; and, nevertheless, each time I turn to look back I see the glow as bright as ever.

"You, Madame, who knew Clémentine as a wife and mother after her hair had become grey, you cannot imagine her as I see her still; a young fair girl, all pink and white. Since you have been so kind as to be my guide, dear Madame, I ought to tell you what feelings were awakened in me by the sight of that grave to which you led me. Memories throng back upon me. I feel myself like some old gnarled and mossy oak which awakens a nestling world of birds by the shaking of its branches. Unfortunately the song my birds sing is old as the world, and can amuse no one but myself."

"Tell me your souvenirs," said Madame de Gabry. "I cannot read your books, because they are written only for scholars; but I like very much to have you talk to me, because you know how to give interest to the most ordinary things in life. And talk to me just as you would talk to an old woman. This morning I found three grey threads in my hair."

"Let them come without regret, Madame," I replied. "Time deals gently only with those who take it gently. And when in some years more you will have a silvery fringe under your black fillet, you will be reclothed with a new beauty, less vivid but more touching than the first; and you will find your husband admiring your grey tresses as much as he did that black curl which you gave him when about to be married, and which he preserves in a locket as a thing sacred. . . . These boulevards are broad and very quiet. We can talk at our ease as we walk along. I will tell you, to begin with, how I first made the acquaintance of Clémentine's father. But you must not expect anything extraordinary, or anything even remarkable; you would be greatly deceived.

"Monsieur de Lessay used to live in the second storey of an old house in the Avenue de l'Observatoire, having a stuccoed front, ornamented with antique busts, and a large unkept garden attached to it. That façade and that garden were the first images my child-eyes perceived; and they will be the last, no doubt, which I shall still see through my closed eyelids when the Inevitable Day comes. For it was in that house that I was born; it was in that garden I first learned, while playing, to feel and know some particles of this old universe. Magical hours!—sacred hours!—when the soul, all fresh from the making, first discovers the world, which for its sake seems to assume such caressing brightness, such mysterious charm! And that, Madame, is indeed because the universe itself is only the reflection of our soul.

"My mother was a being very happily constituted. She rose with the sun, like the birds; and she herself resembled the birds by her domestic industry, by her maternal instinct, by her perpetual desire to sing, and by a sort of brusque grace, which I could feel the charm of very well even as a child. She was the soul of the house, which she filled with her systematic and joyous activity. My father was just as slow as she was brisk. I can recall very well that placid face of his, over which at times an ironical smile used to flit. He was fatigued with active life; and he loved his fatigue. Seated beside the fire in his big arm-chair, he used to read from morning till night; and it is from him that I inherit my love of books. I have in my library a Mably and a Raynal, which he annotated with his own hand from beginning to end. But it was utterly useless attempting to interest him in anything practical whatever. When my mother would try, by all kinds of gracious little ruses, to lure him out of his retirement, he would simply shake his head with that inexorable gentleness which is the force of weak characters. He used in this way greatly to worry the poor woman, who could not enter at all into his own sphere of meditative wisdom, and could understand nothing of life except its daily duties and the merry labour of each hour. She thought him sick, and feared he was going to become still more so. But his apathy had a different cause.

"My father, entering the Naval office under Monsieur Decrès, in 1801, gave early proof of high administrative talent. There was a great deal of activity in the marine department in those times; and in 1805 my father was appointed chief of the Second Adminis-trative Division. That same year, the Emperor, whose attention had been called to him by the Minister, ordered him to make a report upon the organisation of the English navy. This work, which re-flected a profoundly liberal and philosophic spirit, of which the edi-tor himself was unconscious, was only finished in 1807—about eighteen months after the defeat of Admiral Villeneuve at Trafal-gar. Napoleon, who, from that disastrous day, never wanted to hear the word ship mentioned in his presence, angrily glanced over a few pages of the memoir, and then threw it into the fire, vociferat-ing, 'Words!—words! I said once before that I hated ideologists.'

My father was told afterwards that the Emperor's anger was so intense at the moment that he stamped the manuscript down into the fire with his boot-heels. At all events, it was his habit, when very much irritated, to poke down the fire with his feet until he had scorched his boot-soles. My father never fully recovered from this disgrace; and the fruitlessness of all his efforts towards reform was certainly the cause of the apathy which came upon him at a later day. Nevertheless, Napoleon, after his return from Elba, sent for him, and ordered him to prepare some liberal and patriotic bulletins and proclamations for the fleet. After Waterloo, my father, whom the event had rather saddened than surprised, retired into private life, and was not interfered with—except that it was generally averred of him that he was a Jacobin, a *buveur-de-sang*— one of those men with whom no one could afford to be on intimate terms. My mother's eldest brother, Victor Maldent, an infantry captain—retired on half-pay in 1814, and disbanded in 1815—aggravated by his bad attitude the situation in which the fall of the Empire had placed my father. Captain Victor used to shout in the *cafés* and the public balls that the Bourbons had sold France to the Cossacks. He used to show everybody a tricoloured cockade hidden in the lining of his hat; and carried with much ostentation a walking-stick, the handle of which had been so carved that the shadow thrown by it made the silhouette of the Emperor.

"Unless you have seen certain lithographs by Charlet, Madame, you could form no idea of the physiognomy of my Uncle Victor, when he used to stride about the garden of the Tuileries with a fiercely elegant manner of his own—buttoned up in his frogged coat, with his cross-of-honour upon his breast, and a bouquet of violets in his buttonhole.

"Idleness and intemperance greatly intensified the vulgar recklessness of his political passions. He used to insult people whom he happened to see reading the *Quotidienne,* or the *Drapeau Blanc,* and compel them to fight with him. In this way he had the pain and the shame of wounding a boy of sixteen in a duel. In short, my Uncle Victor was the very reverse of a well-behaved person; and as he came to lunch and dine at our house every blessed day in the year, his bad reputation became attached to our family. My poor father suffered cruelly from some of his guest's pranks; but being very good-natured, he never made any remarks, and continued to give the freedom of his house to the captain, who only despised him for it.

"All this which I have told you, Madame, was explained to me afterwards. But at the time in question, my uncle the captain filled me with the very enthusiasm of admiration, and I promised myself to try to become some day as like him as possible. So one fine morning, in order to begin the likeness, I put my arms akimbo, and swore like a trooper. My excellent mother at once gave me such

a box on the ear that I remained half stupefied for some little
while before I could even burst out crying. I can still see the old
arm-chair, covered with yellow Utrecht velvet, behind which I wept
innumerable tears that day.

"I was a very little fellow then. One morning my father, lifting
me upon his knees, as he was in the habit of doing, smiled at me
with that slightly ironical smile which gave a certain piquancy to
his perpetual gentleness of manner. As I sat on his knee, playing
with his long white hair, he told me something which I did not
understand very well, but which interested me very much, for the
simple reason that it was mysterious to me. I think, but am not
quite sure, that he related to me that morning the story of the little King of Yvetot, according to the song. All of a sudden we heard
a great report; and the windows rattled. My father slipped me down
gently on the floor at his feet; he threw up his trembling arms,
with a strange gesture; his face became all inert and white, and
his eyes seemed enormous. He tried to speak, but his teeth were
chattering. At last he murmured, 'They have shot him!' I did not
know what he meant, and felt only a vague terror. I knew afterwards, however, that he was speaking of Marshal Ney, who fell on
the 7th of December, 1815, under the wall enclosing some waste
ground beside our house.

"About that time I used often to meet on the stairway an old
man (or, perhaps, not exactly an old man) with little black eyes
which flashed with extraordinary vivacity, and an impassive,
swarthy face. He did not seem to me alive—or at least he did not
seem to me alive in the same way that other men were alive. I had
once seen, at the residence of Monsieur Denon, where my father
had taken me with him on a visit, a mummy brought from Egypt;
and I believed in good faith that Monsieur Denon's mummy used to
get up when no one was looking, leave its gilded case, put on a
brown coat and powdered wig, and become transformed into Monsieur de Lessay. And even to-day dear Madame, while I reject that
opinion as being without foundation, I must confess that Monsieur
de Lessay bore a very strong resemblance to Monsieur Denon's
mummy. The fact is enough to explain why this person inspired me
with fantastic terror.

"In reality, Monsieur de Lessay was a small gentleman and a
great philosopher. As a disciple of Mably and Rousseau, he flattered
himself on being a man without any prejudices; and this preten-
sion itself is a very great prejudice.

"He professed to hate fanaticism, yet was himself a fanatic on
the topic of toleration. I am telling you, Madame, about a character
belonging to an age that is past. I fear I may not be able to make
you understand, and I am sure I shall not be able to interest you.
It was so long ago! But I will abridge as much as possible: besides,
I did not promise you anything interesting; and you could not have

expected to hear of remarkable adventures in the life of Sylvestre Bonnard."

Madame de Gabry encouraged me to proceed, and I resumed:

"Monsieur de Lessay was brusque with men and courteous to ladies. He used to kiss the hand of my mother, whom the customs of the Republic and the Empire had not habituated to such gallantry. In him, I touched the age of Louis XVI. Monsieur de Lessay was a geographer; and nobody, I believe, ever showed more pride than he in occupying himself with the face of the earth. Under the Old Régime he had attempted philosophical agriculture, and thus squandered his estates to the very last acre. When he had ceased to own one square foot of ground, he took possession of the whole globe, and prepared an extraordinary number of maps, based upon the narratives of travellers. But as he had been mentally nourished with the very marrow of the 'Encyclopédie,' he was not satisfied with merely parking off human beings within so many degrees, minutes, and seconds of latitude and longitude. He also occupied himself, alas! with the question of their happiness. It is worthy of remark, Madame, that those who have given themselves the most concern about the happiness of peoples have made their neighbours very miserable. Monsieur de Lessay, who was more of a geometrician than D'Alembert, and more of a philosopher than Jean Jacques, was also more of a royalist than Louis XVIII. But his love for the King was as nothing to his hate for the Emperor. He had joined the conspiracy of Georges against the First Consul; but in the framing of the indictment he was not included among the inculpated parties, having been either ignored or despised, and this injury he never could forgive Bonaparte, whom he called the Ogre of Corsica, and to whom he used to say he would never have confided even the command of a regiment, so pitiful a soldier he judged him to be.

"In 1820, Monsieur de Lessay, who had then been a widower for many years, married again, at the age of sixty, a very young woman, whom he pitilessly kept at work preparing maps for him, and who gave him a daughter some years after their marriage, and died in childbed. My mother had nursed her during her brief illness, and had taken care of the child. The name of that child was Clémentine.

"It was from the time of that birth and that death that the relations between our family and Monsieur de Lessay began. In the meanwhile I had been growing dull as I began to leave my true childhood behind me. I had lost the charming power of being able to see and feel; and things no longer caused me those delicious surprises which form the enchantment of the more tender age. For the same reason, perhaps, I have no distinct remembrance of the period following the birth of Clémentine; I only know that a few months afterwards I had a misfortune, the mere thought of which still wrings my heart. I lost my mother. A great silence, a great coldness, and a great darkness seemed all at once to fill the house.

"I fell into a sort of torpor. My father sent me to the *lycée,* but I could only arouse myself from my lethargy with the greatest effort.

"Still, I was not altogether a dullard, and my professors were able to teach me almost everything they wanted, namely, a little Greek and a great deal of Latin. My acquaintances were confined to the ancients. I learned to esteem Miltiades, and to admire Themistocles. I became familiar with Quintus Fabius, as far, at least, as it was possible to become familiar with so great a Consul. Proud of these lofty acquaintances, I scarcely ever condescended to notice little Clémentine and her old father, who, in any event, went away to Normandy one fine morning without my having deigned to give a moment's thought to their possible return.

"They came back, however, Madame, they came back! Influences of Heaven, forces of nature, all ye mysterious powers which vouchsafe to man the ability to love, you know how I again beheld Clémentine! They re-entered our melancholy home. Monsieur de Lessay no longer wore a wig. Bald, with a few grey locks about his ruddy temples, he had all the aspect of robust old age. But that divine being whom I saw all resplendent, as she leaned upon his arm—she whose presence illuminated the old faded parlour—she was not an apparition! It was Clémentine herself! I am speaking the simple truth: her violet eyes seemed to me in that moment supernatural, and even to-day I cannot imagine how those two living jewels could have endured the fatigues of life, or become subjected to the corruption of death.

"She betrayed a little shyness in greeting my father, whom she did not remember. Her complexion was slightly pink, and her half-open lips smiled with that smile which makes one think of the Infinite—perhaps because it betrays no particular thought, and expresses only the joy of living and the bliss of being beautiful. Under a pink hood her face shone like a gem in an open casket; she wore a cashmere scarf over a robe of white muslin plaited at the waist, from beneath which protruded the tip of a little Morocco shoe. . . . Oh! you must not make fun of me, dear Madame, that was the fashion of the time; and I do not know whether our new fashions have nearly so much simplicity, brightness, and decorous grace.

"Monsieur de Lessay informed us that, in consequence of having undertaken the publication of a historical atlas, he had come back to live in Paris, and that he would be pleased to occupy his former apartment, if it was still vacant. My father asked Mademoiselle de Lessay whether she was pleased to visit the capital. She appeared to be, for her smile blossomed out in reply. She smiled at the windows that looked out upon the green and luminous garden; she smiled at the bronze Marius seated among the ruins of Carthage above the dial of the clock; she smiled at the old yellow-velveted

arm-chairs, and at the poor student who was afraid to lift his eyes
to look at her. From that day—how I loved her!

"But here we are already at the Rue de Sèvres, and in a little
while we shall be in sight of your windows. I am a very bad story-
teller; and if I were—by some impossible chance—to take it into
my head to compose a novel, I know I should never succeed. I have
been drawing out to tiresome length a narrative which I must finish
briefly; for there is a certain delicacy, a certain grace of soul, which
an old man could not help offending by any complacent expatiation
upon the sentiments of even the purest love. Let us take a short
turn on this boulevard, lined with convents; and my recital will be
easily finished within the distance separating us from that little
spire you see over there. . . .

"Monsieur de Lessay, on finding that I had graduated at the
École des Chartes, judged me worthy to assist him in preparing his
historical atlas. The plan was to illustrate, by a series of maps,
what the old philosopher termed the Vicissitudes of Empires from
the time of Noah down to that of Charlemagne. Monsieur de Lessay
had stored up in his head all the errors of the eighteenth century
in regard to antiquity. I belonged, so far as my historical studies
were concerned, to the new school; and I was just at that age when
one does not know how to dissemble. The manner in which the old
man understood, or, rather, misunderstood, the epoch of the Barbarians—his obstinate determination to find in remote antiquity
only ambitious princes, hypocritical and avaricious prelates, virtuous citizens, poet-philosophers, and other personages who never
existed outside of the novels of Marmontel,—made me dreadfully
unhappy, and at first used to excite me into attempts at argument,
—rational enough, but perfectly useless and sometimes dangerous,
for Monsieur de Lessay was very irascible, and Clémentine was
very beautiful. Between her and him I passed many hours of torment and of delight. I was in love; I was a coward, and I granted
to him all that he demanded of me in regard to the political and
historical aspect which the Earth—that was at a later day to bear
Clémentine—presented in the time of Abraham, of Menes, and of
Deucalion.

"As fast as we drew our maps Mademoiselle de Lessay tinted
them in water-colours. Bending over the table, she held the brush
lightly between two fingers; the shadow of her eyelashes descended
upon her cheeks, and bathed her half-closed eyes in a delicious pe-
numbra. Sometimes she would lift her head, and I would see her
lips pout. There was so much expression in her beauty that she
could not breathe without seeming to sigh; and her most ordinary
poses used to throw me into the deepest ecstasies of admiration.
Whenever I gazed at her I fully agreed with Monsieur de Lessay
that Jupiter had once reigned as a despot-king over the mountainous
regions of Thessaly, and that Orpheus had committed the impru-

dence of leaving the teaching of philosophy to the clergy. I am not now quite sure whether I was a coward or a hero when I accorded all this to the obstinate old man.

"Mademoiselle de Lessay, I must acknowledge, paid very little attention to me. But this indifference seemed to me so just and so natural that I never even dreamed of thinking I had a right to complain about it; it made me unhappy, but without my knowing that I was unhappy at the time. I was hopeful;—we had then only got as far as the First Assyrian Empire.

"Monsieur de Lessay came every evening to take coffee with my father. I do not know how they became such friends; for it would have been difficult to find two characters more oppositely constituted. My father was a man who admired very few things, but was capable of excusing a great many. Still, as he grew older, he evinced more and more dislike of everything in the shape of exaggeration. He clothed his ideas with a thousand delicate shades of expression, and never pronounced an opinion without all sorts of reservations. These conversational habits, natural to a finely trained mind, used greatly to irritate the dry, terse old aristocrat, who was never in the least disarmed by the moderation of an adversary— quite the contrary! I always foresaw one danger. That danger was Bonaparte. My father had not himself retained any particular affection for his memory; but, having worked under his direction, he did not like to hear him abused, especially in favour of the Bourbons, against whom he had serious reason to feel resentment. Monsieur de Lessay, more of a Voltairean and a Legitimist than ever, now traced back to Bonaparte the origin of every social, political, and religious evil. Such being the situation, the idea of Uncle Victor made me feel particularly uneasy. This terrible uncle had become absolutely insufferable now that his sister was no longer there to calm him down. The harp of David was broken, and Saul was wholly delivered over to the spirit of madness. The fall of Charles X. had increased the audacity of the old Napoleonic veteran, who uttered all imaginable bravadoes. He no longer frequented our house, which had become too silent for him. But sometimes, at the dinner-hour, we would see him suddenly make his appearance, all covered with flowers, like a mausoleum. Ordinarily he would sit down to table with an oath, growled out from the very bottom of his chest, and brag, between every two mouthfuls, of his good fortune with the ladies as a *vieux brave*. Then, when the dinner was over, he would fold up his napkin in the shape of a bishop's mitre, gulp down half a decanter of brandy, and rush away with the hurried air of a man terrified at the mere idea of remaining for any length of time, without drinking, in conversation with an old philosopher and a young scholar. I felt perfectly sure that, if ever he and Monsieur de Lessay should come together, all would be lost. But that day came, Madame!

"The captain was almost hidden by flowers that day, and seemed so much like a monument commemorating the glories of the Empire that one would have liked to pass a garland of immortelles over each of his arms. He was in an extraordinarily good humour; and the first person to profit by that good humour was our cook—for he put his arm round her waist while she was placing the roast on the table.

"After dinner he pushed away the decanter presented to him, observing that he was going to burn some brandy in his coffee later on. I asked him tremblingly whether he would not prefer to have his coffee at once. He was very suspicious, and not at all dull of comprehension—my Uncle Victor. My precipitation seemed to him in very bad taste; for he looked at me in a peculiar way, and said,

" 'Patience! my nephew. It isn't the business of the baby of the regiment to sound the retreat! Devil take it! You must be in a great hurry, Master Pedant, to see if I've got spurs on my boots!'

"It was evident the captain had divined that I wanted him to go. And I knew him well enough to be sure that he was going to stay. He stayed. The least circumstances of that evening remain impressed on my memory. My uncle was extremely jovial. The mere idea of being in somebody's way was enough to keep him in good humour. He told us, in regular barrack style, *ma foi!* a certain story about a monk, a trumpet, and five bottles of Chambertin, which must have been much enjoyed in garrison society, but which I would not venture to repeat to you, Madame, even if I could remember it. When we passed into the parlour, the captain called attention to the bad condition of our andirons, and learnedly discoursed on the merits of rotten-stone as a brass-polisher. Not a word on the subject of politics. He was husbanding his forces. Eight o'clock sounded from the ruins of Carthage on the mantelpiece. It was Monsieur de Lessay's hour. A few moments later he entered the parlour with his daughter. The ordinary evening chat began. Clémentine sat down and began to work on some embroidery beside the lamp, whose shade left her pretty head in a soft shadow, and threw down upon her fingers a radiance that made them seem almost self-luminous. Monsieur de Lessay spoke of a comet announced by the astronomers, and developed some theories in relation to the subject, which, however audacious, betrayed at least a certain degree of intellectual culture. My father, who knew a good deal about astronomy, advanced some sound ideas of his own, which he ended up with his eternal, 'But what do we know about it, after all?' In my turn I cited the opinion of our neighbour of the Observatory—the great Arago. My Uncle Victor declared that comets had a peculiar influence on the quality of wines, and related in support of this view a jolly tavern-story. I was so delighted with the turn the conversation had taken that I did all in my power to maintain it in the same groove, with the help of my most recent studies, by a long exposition of the chemical composition of those nebulous bodies which, although extending over a length of billions of leagues, could be contained in a small bottle. My father, a little surprised at my unusual eloquence, watched me with his peculiar, placid, ironical smile. But one cannot always remain in heaven. I spoke, as I looked at Clémentine, of a certain *'comète'* of diamonds, which I had been admiring in a jeweller's window the evening before. It was a most unfortunate inspiration of mine.

" 'Ah! my nephew,' cried Uncle Victor, 'that *comète* of yours was nothing to the one which the Empress Josephine wore in her hair when she came to Strasburg to distribute crosses to the army.'

" 'That little Josephine was very fond of finery and display,' observed Monsieur de Lessay, between two sips of coffee. 'I do not blame her for it; she had good qualities, though rather frivolous in character. She was a Tascher, and she conferred a great honour on Bonaparte by marrying him. To say a Tascher does not, of course, mean a great deal; but to say a Bonaparte simply means nothing at all.'

" 'What do you mean by that, Monsieur the Marquis?' demanded Captain Victor.

" 'I am not a marquis,' dryly responded Monsieur de Lessay; 'and I mean simply that Bonaparte would have been very well suited had he married one of those cannibal women described by Captain Cook in his voyages—naked, tattoed, with a ring in her nose—devouring with delight putrefied human flesh.'

"I had foreseen it, and in my anguish (O pitiful human heart!) my first idea was about the remarkable exactness of my anticipations. I must say that the captain's reply belonged to the sublime order. He put his arms akimbo, eyed Monsieur de Lessay contemptuously from head to foot, and said,

" 'Napoleon, Monsieur the Vidame, had another spouse besides Josephine, another spouse besides Marie-Louise. That companion you know nothing of; but I have seen her, close to me. She wears a mantle of azure gemmed with stars; she is crowned with laurels; the Cross-of-Honour flames upon her breast. Her name is GLORY!'

"Monsieur de Lessay set his cup on the mantel-piece, and quietly observed,

" 'Your Bonaparte was a blackguard!'

"My father rose up calmly, extended his arm, and said very softly to Monsieur de Lessay,

" 'Whatever the man was who died at St. Helena, I worked for ten years in his government, and my brother-in-law was three times wounded under his eagles. I beg of you, dear sir and friend, never to forget these facts in future.'

"What the sublime and burlesque insolence of the captain could not do, the courteous remonstrance of my father effected immediately, throwing Monsieur de Lessay into a furious passion.

" 'I did forget,' he exclaimed, between his set teeth, livid in his rage, and fairly foaming at the mouth; 'the herring-cask always smells of herring, and when one has been in the service of rascals——'

"As he uttered the word, the Captain sprang at his throat; I am sure he would have strangled him upon the spot but for his daughter and me.

"My father, a little paler than his wont, stood there with his arms folded, and watched the scene with a look of inexpressible pity. What followed was still more lamentable—but why dwell further upon the folly of two old men. Finally I succeeded in separating them. Monsieur de Lessay made a sign to his daughter and left the room. As she was following him, I ran out into the stairway after her.

" 'Mademoiselle,' I said to her, wildly, taking her hand as I spoke, 'I love you! I love you!'

"For a moment she pressed my hand; her lips opened. What was it that she was going to say to me? But suddenly, lifting her eyes towards her father ascending the stairs, she drew her hand away, and made me a gesture of farewell.

"I never saw her again. Her father went to live in the neighbourhood of the Pantheon, in an apartment which he had rented for the sale of his historical atlas. He died in it a few months afterward of an apoplectic stroke. His daughter, I was told, retired to Caen to live with some aged relative. It was there that, later on, she married a bank-clerk, the same Noël Alexandre who became so rich and died so poor.

"As for me, Madame, I have lived alone, at peace with myself; my existence, equally exempt from great pains and great joys, has been tolerably happy. But for many years I could never see an empty chair beside my own of a winter's evening without feeling a sudden painful sinking at my heart. Last year I learned from you, who had known her, the story of her old age and death. I saw her daughter at your house. I have seen her; but I cannot yet say like the aged man of Scripture, *'And now, O Lord, let thy servant depart in peace!'* For if an old fellow like me can be of any use to anybody, I would wish, with your help, to devote my last energies and abilities to the care of this orphan."

I had uttered these last words in Madame de Gabry's own vestibule; and I was about to take leave of my kind guide when she said to me,

"My dear Monsieur, I cannot help you in this matter as much as I would like to do. Jeanne is an orphan and a minor. You cannot do anything for her without the authorisation of her guardian."

"Ah!" I exclaimed, "I had not the least idea in the world that Jeanne had a guardian!"

Madame de Gabry looked at me with visible surprise. She had not expected to find the old man quite so simple.

She resumed:

"The guardian of Jeanne Alexandre is Maître Mouche, notary at Levallois-Perret. I am afraid you will not be able to come to any understanding with him; for he is a very serious person."

"Why! good God!" I cried, "with what kind of people can you expect me to have any sort of understanding at my age, except serious persons."

She smiled with a sweet mischievousness—just as my father used to smile—and answered:

"With those who are like you—the innocent folks who wear their hearts on their sleeves. Monsieur Mouche is not exactly a man of that kind. He is cunning and light-fingered. But although I have very little liking for him, we will go together and see him, if you wish, and ask his permission to visit Jeanne, whom he has sent to a boarding-school at Les Ternes, where she is very unhappy."

We agreed at once upon a day; I kissed Madame de Gabry's hands, and we bade each other good-bye.

From May 2 to May 5.

I HAVE seen him in his office, Maître Mouche, the guardian of Jeanne. Small, thin, and dry; his complexion looks as if it was made out of the dust of his pigeon-holes. He is a spectacled animal; for to imagine him without his spectacles would be impossible. I have heard him speak, this Maître Mouche; he has a voice like a tin rattle, and he uses choice phrases; but I should have been better pleased if he had not chosen his phrases so carefully. I have observed him, this Maître Mouche; he is very ceremonious, and watches his visitors slyly out of the corner of his eye.

Maître Mouche is quite pleased, he informs us; he is delighted to find we have taken such an interest in his ward. But he does not think we are placed in this world just to amuse ourselves. No: he does not believe it; and I am free to acknowledge that anybody in his company is likely to reach the same conclusion, so little is he capable of inspiring joyfulness. He fears that it would be giving his dear ward a false and pernicious idea of life to allow her too much enjoyment. It is for that reason that he requests Madame de Gabry not to invite the young girl to her house except at very long intervals.

We left the dusty notary and his dusty study with a permit in due form (everything which issues from the office of Maître Mouche is in due form) to visit Mademoiselle Jeanne Alexandre on the first Thursday of each month at Mademoiselle Préfère's private school, Rue Demours, Aux Ternes.

The first Thursday in May I set out to a pay a visit to Mademoiselle Préfère, whose establishment I discerned from afar off by a big sign, painted with blue letters. That blue tint was the first indication I received of Mademoiselle Préfère's character, which I was able to see more of later on. A scared-looking servant took my card, and abandoned me without one word of hope at the door of a chilly parlour, full of that stale odour peculiar to the dining-rooms of educational establishments. The floor of this parlour had been waxed with such pitiless energy, that I remained for awhile in distress upon the threshold. But happily observing that little strips of woollen carpet had been scattered over the floor in front of each horsehair chair, I succeeded, by cautiously stepping from one carpet-island to another, in reaching the angle of the mantelpiece, where I sat down quite out of breath.

Over the mantelpiece, in a large gilded frame, was a written document, entitled in flamboyant Gothic lettering, *Tableau d'Honneur,* with a long array of names underneath, among which I did not have the pleasure of finding that of Jeanne Alexandre. After having read over several times the names of those girl-pupils who had thus made themselves honoured in the eyes of Mademoiselle Préfère, I began to feel uneasy at not hearing any one coming. Mademoiselle Préfère would certainly have succeeded in establishing the absolute silence of the interstellar spaces throughout her pedagogical domains, had it not been that the sparrows had chosen her yard to assemble in by legions, and chirp at the top of their voices. It was a pleasure to hear them. But there was no way of seeing them—through the ground-glass windows. I had to content myself with the sights of the parlour, decorated from floor to ceiling, on all of its four walls, with drawings executed by the pupils of the institution. There were Vestals, flowers, thatched cottages, column-capitals, and an enormous head of Tatius, King of the Sabines, bearing the signature *Estelle Mouton.*

I had already passed some time in admiring the energy with which Mademoiselle Mouton had delineated the bushy eyebrows and the fierce gaze of the antique warrior, when a sound, faint like the rustling of a dead leaf moved by the wind, caused me to turn my head. It was not a dead leaf at all—it was Mademoiselle Préfère. With hands joined before her, she came gliding over the mirror-polish of that wonderful floor as the Saints of the Golden Legend were wont to glide over the crystal surface of the waters. But upon any other occasion, I am sure, Mademoiselle Préfère would not have made me think in the least about those virgins dear to mystical fancy. Her face rather gave me the idea of a russet-apple preserved for a whole winter in an attic by some economical housekeeper. Her shoulders were covered with a fringed pelerine, which had nothing at all remarkable about it, but which she wore as if it were a sacerdotal vestment, or the symbol of some high civic function.

I explained to her the purpose of my visit, and gave her my letter of introduction.

"Ah!—so you saw Monsieur Mouche!" she exclaimed. "Is his health *very* good? He is the most upright of men, the most——"

She did not finish the phrase, but raised her eyes to the ceiling. My own followed the direction of their gaze, and observed a little spiral of paper lace, suspended from the place of the chandelier, which was apparently destined, so far as I could discover, to attract the flies away from the gilded mirror-frames and the *Tableau d'Honneur*.

"I have met Mademoiselle Jeanne Alexandre," I observed, "at the residence of Madame de Gabry, and had reason to appreciate the excellent character and quick intelligence of the young girl. As I used to know her parents very well, the friendship which I felt for them naturally inclines me to take an interest in her."

Mademoiselle Préfère, in lieu of making any reply, sighed profoundly, pressed her mysterious pelerine to her heart, and again contemplated the paper spiral.

At last she observed,

"Since you were once the friend of Monsieur and Madame Alexandre, I hope and trust that, like Monsieur Mouche and myself, you deplore those crazy speculations which led them to ruin, and reduced their daughter to absolute poverty!"

I thought to myself, on hearing these words, how very wrong it is to be unlucky, and how unpardonable such an error on the part of those previously in a position worthy of envy. Their fall at once avenges and flatters us; and we are wholly pitiless.

After having answered, very frankly, that I knew nothing whatever about the history of the bank, I asked the schoolmistress if she was satisfied with Mademoiselle Alexandre.

"That child is indomitable!" cried Mademoiselle Préfère.

And she assumed an attitude of lofty resignation, to symbolise the difficult situation she was placed in by a pupil so hard to train. Then, with more calmness of manner, she added:

"The young person is not unintelligent. But she cannot resign herself to learn things by rule."

What a strange old maid was this Mademoiselle Préfère! She walked without lifting her legs, and spoke without moving her lips! Without, however, considering her peculiarities for more than a reasonable instant, I replied that principles were, no doubt, very excellent things, and that I could trust myself to her judgment in regard to their value; but that, after all, when one had learned something, it made very little difference what method had been followed in the learning of it.

Mademoiselle made a slow gesture of dissent. Then, with a sigh, she declared,

"Ah, Monsieur! those who do not understand educational methods are apt to have very false ideas on these subjects. I am certain they express their opinions with the best intentions in the world; but they would do better, a great deal better, to leave all such questions to competent people."

I did not attempt to argue further; and simply asked her whether I could see Mademoiselle Alexandre at once.

She looked at her pelerine, as if trying to read in the entanglement of its fringes, as in a conjuring-book, what sort of answer she ought to make; then said,

"Mademoiselle Alexandre has a penance to perform, and a class-lesson to give; but I should be very sorry to let you put yourself to the trouble of coming here all to no purpose. I am going to send for her. Only first allow me, Monsieur—as is our custom—to put your name on the visitors' register."

She sat down at the table, opened a large copy-book, and, taking out Maître Mouche's letter again from under her pelerine, where she had placed it, looked at it, and began to write.

" 'Bonnard'—with a *d,* is it not?" she asked. "Excuse me for being so particular; but my opinion is that proper names have an orthography. We have dictation-lessons in proper names, Monsieur, at this school—historical proper names, of course!"

After I had written down my name in a running hand, she inquired whether she should not put down after it my profession, title, quality—such as "retired merchant," "employé," "independent gentleman," or something else. There was a column in her register expressly for that purpose.

"My goodness, Madame!" I said, "if you must absolutely fill that column of yours, put down 'Member of the Institute.' "

It was still Mademoiselle Préfère's pelerine I saw before me; but it was not Mademoiselle Préfère now who wore it; it was a totally different person, obliging, gracious, caressing, radiant, happy. Her eyes, smiled; the little wrinkles of her face (there were a vast number of them!) also smiled; her mouth smiled likewise, but only on one side. I discovered afterwards that was her best side. She spoke: her voice had also changed with her manner; it was now sweet as honey.

"You said, Monsieur, that our dear Jeanne was very intelligent. I discovered the same thing myself, and I am proud of being able to agree with you. This young girl has really made me feel a great deal of interest in her. She has what I call a happy disposition. . . . But excuse me for thus drawing upon your valuable time."

She summoned the servant-girl, who looked much more hurried and scared than before, and who vanished with the order to go and tell Mademoiselle Alexandre that Monsieur Sylvestre Bonnard, Member of the Institute, was waiting to see her in the parlour.

Mademoiselle Préfère had barely time to confide to me that she had the most profound respect for all decisions of the Institute—

whatever they might be—when Jeanne appeared, out of breath, red as a poppy, with her eyes very wide open, and her arms dangling helplessly at her sides—charming in her artless awkwardness.

"What a state you are in, my dear child!" murmured Mademoiselle Préfère, with maternal sweetness, as she arranged the girl's collar.

Jeanne certainly did present an odd aspect. Her hair combed back, and imperfectly held by a net from which loose curls were escaping; her slender arms, sheathed down to the elbows in lustring sleeves; her hands, which she did not seem to know what to do with, all red with chilblains; her dress, much too short, revealing that she had on stockings much too large for her, and shoes worn down at the heel; and a skipping-rope tied round her waist in lieu of a belt,—all combined to lend Mademoiselle Jeanne an appearance the reverse of presentable.

"Oh, you crazy girl!" sighed Mademoiselle Préfère, who now seemed no longer like a mother, but rather like an elder sister.

Then she suddenly left the room, gliding like a shadow over the polished floor.

I said to Jeanne,

"Sit down, Jeanne, and talk to me as you would to a friend. Are you not better satisfied here now than you were last year?"

She hesitated; then answered with a good-natured smile of resignation,

"Not much better."

I asked her to tell me about her school life. She began at once to enumerate all her different studies—piano, style, chronology of the Kings of France, sewing, drawing, catechism, deportment. . . . I could never remember them all! She still held in her hands, all unconsciously, the two ends of her skipping-rope, and she raised and lowered them regularly while making her enumeration. Then all at once she became conscious of what she was doing, blushed, stammered, and became so confused that I had to renounce my desire to know the full programme of study adopted in the Préfère Institution.

After having questioned Jeanne on various matters, and obtained only the vaguest answers, I perceived that her young mind was totally absorbed by the skipping-rope, and I entered bravely into that grave subject.

"So you have been skipping?" I said. "It is a very nice amusement, but one that you must not exert yourself too much at; for any excessive exercise of that kind might seriously injure your health, and I should be very much grieved about it, Jeanne—I should be very much grieved, indeed!"

"You are very kind, Monsieur," the young girl said, "to have come to see me and talk to me like this. I did not think about thanking you when I came in, because I was too much surprised. Have you seen Madame de Gabry? Please tell me something about her, Monsieur."

"Madame de Gabry," I answered, "is very well. I can only tell you about her, Jeanne, what an old gardener once said of the lady of the castle, his mistress, when somebody anxiously inquired about her: 'Madame is in her road.' Yes, Madame de Gabry is in her own road; and you know, Jeanne, what a good road it is, and how steadily she can walk upon it. I went out with her the other day, very, very far away from the house; and we talked about you. We talked about you, my child, at your mother's grave."

"I am very glad," said Jeanne.

And then, all at once, she began to cry.

I felt too much reverence for those generous tears to attempt in any way to check the emotion that had evoked them. But in a little while, as the girl wiped her eyes, I asked her,

"Will you not tell me, Jeanne, why you were thinking so much about that skipping-rope a little while ago?"

"Why, indeed I will, Monsieur. It was only because I had no right to come into the parlour with a skipping-rope. You know, of course, that I am past the age for playing at skipping. But when the servant said there was an old gentleman . . . oh! . . . I mean . . . that a gentleman was waiting for me in the parlour, I was making the little girls jump. Then I tied the rope round my waist in a hurry, so that it might not get lost. It was wrong. But I have not been in the habit of having many people come to see me. And Mademoiselle Préfère never lets us off if we commit any breach of deportment: so I know she is going to punish me, and I am very sorry about it." . . .

"That is too bad, Jeanne!"

She became very grave, and said,

"Yes, Monsieur, it is too bad; because when I am punished myself, I have no more authority over the little girls."

I did not at once fully understand the nature of this unpleasantness; but Jeanne explained to me that, as she was charged by Mademoiselle Préfère with the duties of taking care of the youngest class, of washing and dressing the children, of teaching them how to behave, how to sew, how to say the alphabet, of showing them how to play, and, finally, of putting them to bed at the close of the day, she could not make herself obeyed by those turbulent little folks on the days she was condemned to wear a night-cap in the class-room, or to eat her meals standing up, from a plate turned upside down.

Having secretly admired the punishments devised by the Lady of the Enchanted Pelerine, I responded:

"Then, if I understand you rightly, Jeanne, you are at once a pupil here and a mistress? It is a condition of existence very common in the world. You are punished, and you punish?"

"Oh, Monsieur!" she exclaimed. "No! I never punish!"

"Then, I suspect," said I, "that your indulgence gets you many scoldings from Mademoiselle Préfère?"

She smiled, and blinked.

Then I said to her that the troubles in which we often involve ourselves, by trying to act according to our conscience and to do the best we can, are never of the sort that totally dishearten and weary us, but are, on the contrary, wholesome trials. This sort of philosophy touched her very little. She even appeared totally unmoved by my moral exhortations. But was not this quite natural on her part?—and ought I not to have remembered that it is only those no longer innocent who can find pleasure in the systems of moralists? . . . I had at least good sense enough to cut short my sermonising.

"Jeanne," I said, "you were asking a moment ago about Madame de Gabry. Let us talk about that Fairy of yours. She was very prettily made. Do you do any modelling in wax now?"

"I have not a bit of wax," she exclaimed, wringing her hands—"no wax at all!"

"No wax!" I cried—"in a republic of busy bees?"

She laughed.

"And, then, you see, Monsieur, my *figurines,* as you call them, are not in Mademoiselle Préfère's programme. But I had begun to make a very small Saint-George for Madame de Gabry—a tiny little Saint-George, with a golden cuirass. Is not that right, Monsieur Bonnard —to give Saint-George a gold cuirass?"

"Quite right, Jeanne; but what became of it?"

"I am going to tell you. I kept it in my pocket because I had no other place to put it, and—and I sat down on it by mistake."

She drew out of her pocket a little wax figure, which had been squeezed out of all resemblance to human form, and of which the dislocated limbs were only attached to the body by their wire framework. At the sight of her hero thus marred, she was seized at once with compassion and gaiety. The latter feeling obtained the mastery, and she burst into a clear laugh, which, however, stopped as suddenly as it had begun.

Mademoiselle Préfère stood at the parlour door, smiling.

"That dear child!" sighed the schoolmistress in her tenderest tone. "I am afraid she will tire you. And, then, your time is so precious!"

I begged Mademoiselle Préfère to dismiss that illusion, and, rising to take my leave, I took from my pocket some chocolate-cakes and sweets which I had brought with me.

"That is so nice!" said Jeanne; "there will be enough to go round the whole school."

The lady of the pelerine intervened.

"Mademoiselle Alexandre," she said, "thank Monsieur for his generosity."

Jeanne looked at her for an instant in a sullen way; then, turning to me, said with remarkable firmness,

"Monsieur, I thank you for your kindness in coming to see me."

"Jeanne," I said, pressing both her hands, "remain always a good, truthful, brave girl. Good-bye."

As she left the room with her packages of chocolate and confectionery, she happened to strike the handles of her skipping-rope against the back of a chair. Mademoiselle Préfère, full of indignation, pressed both hands over her heart, under her pelerine; and I almost expected to see her give up her scholastic ghost.

When we found ourselves alone, she recovered her composure; and I must say, without considering myself thereby flattered, that she smiled upon me with one whole side of her face.

"Mademoiselle," I said, taking advantage of her good humour, "I noticed that Jeanne Alexandre looks a little pale. You know better than I how much consideration and care a young girl requires at her age. It would only be doing you an injustice by implication to recommend her still more earnestly to your vigilance."

These words seemed to ravish her with delight. She lifted her eyes, as in ecstasy, to the paper spirals of the ceiling, and, clasping her hands, exclaimed,

"How well these eminent men know the art of considering the most trifling details!"

I called her attention to the fact that the health of a young girl was not a trifling detail, and made my farewell bow. But she stopped me on the threshold to say to me, very confidentially,

"You must excuse me, Monsieur. I am a woman, and I love glory. I cannot conceal from you the fact that I feel myself greatly honoured by the presence of a Member of the Institute in my humble institution."

I duly excused the weakness of Mademoiselle Préfère; and, thinking only of Jeanne, with the blindness of egotism, kept asking myself all along the road, "What are we going to do with this child?"

June 3.

I HAD escorted to the Cimetière de Marnes that day a very aged colleague of mine who, to use the words of Goethe, had consented to die. The great Goethe, whose own vital force was something extraordinary, actually believed that one never dies until one really wants to die—that is to say, when all those energies which resist dissolution, and the sum of which make up life itself, have been totally destroyed. In other words, he believed that people only die when it is no longer possible for them to live. Good; it is merely a question of properly understanding one another; and when fully comprehended, the magnificent idea of Goethe only brings us quietly back to the song of La Palisse.

Well, my excellent colleague had consented to die—thanks to several successive attacks of extremely persuasive apoplexy—the last of which proved unanswerable. I had been very little acquainted with him during his lifetime; but it seems that I became his friend the moment he was dead, for our colleagues assured me in the most serious manner, with deeply sympathetic countenances, that I should act as one of the pall-bearers, and deliver an address over the tomb.

After having read very badly a short address I had written as well as I could—which is not saying much for it—I started out for a walk in the woods of Ville-d'Avray, and followed, without leaning too much on the Captain's cane, a shaded path on which the sunlight fell, through foliage, in little discs of gold. Never had the scent of grass and fresh leaves,—never had the beauty of the sky over the trees, and the serene might of noble tree contours, so deeply affected my senses and all my being; and the pleasure I felt in that silence, broken only by faintest tinkling sounds, was at once of the senses and of the soul.

I sat down in the shade of the roadside under a clump of young oaks. And there I made a promise to myself not to die, or at least not to consent to die, before I should be again able to sit down under an oak, where—in the great peace of the open country—I could meditate on the nature of the soul and the ultimate destiny of man. A bee, whose brown breast-plate gleamed in the sun like armour of old gold, came to light upon a mallow-flower close by me —darkly rich in colour, and fully opened upon its tufted stalk. It was certainly not the first time I had witnessed so common an incident; but it was the first time that I had watched it with such comprehensive and friendly curiosity. I could discern that there were all sorts of sympathies between the insect and the flower—a thousand singular little relationships which I had never before even suspected.

Satiated with nectar, the insect rose and buzzed away in a straight line, while I lifted myself up as best I could, and readjusted myself upon my legs.

"Adieu!" I said to the flower and to the bee. "Adieu! Heaven grant I may live long enough to discover the secret of your harmonies. I am very tired. But man is so made that he can only find relaxation from one kind of labour by taking up another. The flowers and insects will give me that relaxation, with God's will, after my long researches in philology and diplomatics. How full of meaning is that old myth of Antæus! I have touched the Earth and I am a new man; and now, at seventy years of age, new feelings of curiosity take birth in my mind, even as young shoots sometimes spring up from the hollow trunk of an aged oak!"

June 4.

I LIKE to look out of my window at the Seine and its quays on those soft grey mornings which give such an infinite tenderness of tint to everything. I have seen that azure sky which flings so luminous a calm over the Bay of Naples. But our Parisian sky is more animated, more kindly, more spiritual. It smiles, threatens, caresses —takes an aspect of melancholy or a look of merriment like a human gaze. At this moment it is pouring down a very gentle light on the men and beasts of the city as they accomplish their daily tasks. Over there, on the opposite bank, the stevedores of the Port Saint-Nicholas are unloading a cargo of cow's horns; while two men standing on a gangway are tossing sugar-loaves from one to the other, and thence to somebody in the hold of a steamer. On the north quay, the cab-horses, standing in a line under the shade of the plane-trees each with its head in a nose-bag, are quietly munching their oats, while the rubicund drivers are drinking at the counter of the wine-seller opposite, but all the while keeping a sharp lookout for early customers.

The dealers in second-hand books put their boxes on the parapet. These good retailers of Mind, who are always in the open air, with blouses loose to the breeze, have become so weatherbeaten by the wind, the rain, the frost, the snow, the fog, and the great sun, that they end by looking very much like the old statues of cathedrals. They are all friends of mine, and I scarcely ever pass by their boxes without picking out of one of them some old book which I had always been in need of up to that very moment, without any suspicion of the fact on my part.

Then on my return home I have to endure the outcries of my housekeeper, who accuses me of bursting all my pockets and filling the house with waste paper to attract the rats. Thérèse is wise about that, and it is because she is wise that I do not listen to her; for in spite of my tranquil mien, I have always preferred the folly of the passions to the wisdom of indifference. But just because my own passions are not of that sort which burst out with violence to devastate and kill, the common mind is not aware of their existence. Nevertheless, I am greatly moved by them at times, and it has more than once been my fate to lose my sleep for the sake of a few pages written by some forgotten monk or printed by some humble apprentice of Peter Schœffer. And if these fierce enthusiasms are slowly being quenched in me, it is only because I am being slowly quenched myself. Our passions are ourselves. My old books are Me. I am just as old and thumb-worn as they are.

A light breeze sweeps away, along with the dust of the pavements, the winged seeds of the plane-trees, and the fragments of hay dropped from the mouths of the horses. The dust is nothing remarkable in itself; but as I watch it flying, I remember a moment in my childhood when I watched just such a whirl of dust; and my old Parisian soul is much affected by that sudden recollection. All that I see from my window—that horizon which extends to the left as far as the hills of Chaillot, and enables me to distinguish the Arc de Triomphe like a die of stone, the Seine, river of glory, and its bridges, the ash-trees of the terrace of the Tuileries, the Louvre of the Renaissance, cut and graven like goldsmith-work; and on my right, towards the Pont-Neuf (*pons Lutetiæ Novus dictus,* as it is named on old engravings), all the old and venerable part of Paris, with its towers and spires:—all that is my life, it is myself; and I should be nothing but for all those things which are thus reflected in me through my thousand varying shades of thought, inspiring me and animating me. That is why I love Paris with an immense love.

And nevertheless I am weary, and I know that there can be no rest for me in the heart of this great city which thinks so much, which has taught me to think, and which for ever urges me to think more. And how avoid being excited among all these books which incessantly tempt my curiosity without ever satisfying it? At one moment it is a date I have to look for; at another it is the name of a place I have to make sure of, or some quaint term of which it is important to determine the exact meaning. Words?—why, yes! words. As a philologist, I am their sovereign; they are my subjects, and, like a good king, I devote my whole life to them. But shall I not be able to abdicate some day? I have an idea that there is somewhere or other, quite far from here, a certain little cottage where I could enjoy the quiet I so much need, while awaiting that day in which a greater quiet—that which can be never broken—shall come to wrap me all about. I dream of a bench before the threshold, and of fields spreading away out of sight. But I must have a fresh smiling young face beside me, to reflect and concentrate all that freshness of nature. I could then imagine myself a grandfather, and all the long void of my life would be filled. . . .

I am not a violent man, and yet I become easily vexed, and all my works have caused me quite as much pain as pleasure. And I do not know how it is that I still keep thinking about that very conceited and very inconsiderate impertinence which my young friend of the Luxembourg took the liberty to utter about me some three months ago. I do not call him "friend" in irony, for I love studious youth with all its temerities and imaginative eccentricities. Still, my young friend certainly went beyond all bounds. Master Ambroise Paré, who was the first to attempt the ligature of arteries, and who, having commenced his profession at a time when surgery was only performed by quack barbers, nevertheless succeeded in lifting the science to the high place it now occupies, was assailed in his old age by all the young sawbones' apprentices. Being grossly abused during a discussion by some young addlehead who might have been the best son in the world, but who certainly lacked all sense of respect, the old master answered him in his treatise *De la Mumie, de la Licorne, des Venins et de la Peste.* "I pray him," said the great man—"I pray him, that if he desire to make any contradictions to my reply, he abandon all animosities, and treat the good old man with gentleness." This answer seems admirable from the pen of Ambroise Paré; but even had it been written by a village bonesetter, grown grey in his calling, and mocked by some young stripling, it would still be worthy of all praise.

It might perhaps seem that my memory of the incident had been kept alive only by a base feeling of resentment. I thought so myself at first, and reproached myself for thus dwelling on the saying of a boy who could not yet know the meaning of his own words. But my reflections on this subject subsequently took a better course: that is why I now note them down in my diary. I remembered that one day when I was twenty years old (that was more than half a century ago) I was walking about in that very same garden of the Luxembourg with some comrades. We were talking about our old professors; and one of us happened to name Monsieur Petit-Radel, an estimable and learned man, who was the first to throw some light upon the origin of early Etruscan civilisation, but who had been unfortunate enough to prepare a chronological table of the lovers of Helen. We all laughed a great deal about that chronological table; and I cried out, "Petit-Radel is an ass, not in three letters, but in twelve whole volumes!"

This foolish speech of my adolescence was uttered too lightly to be a weight on my conscience as an old man. May God kindly prove to me some day that I never used any less innocent shaft of speech in the battle of life! But I now ask myself whether I really never wrote, at any time in my life, something quite as unconsciously absurd as the chronological table of the lovers of Helen. The progress of science renders useless the very books which have been the greatest aids to that progress. As those works are no longer useful, modern youth is naturally inclined to believe they never had any value; it despises them, and ridicules them if they happen to contain any superannuated opinion whatever. That was why, in my twentieth year, I amused myself at the expense of Monsieur Petit-Radel and his chronological table; and that was why, the other day, at the Luxembourg, my young and irreverent friend . . .

> *"Rentre en toi-même, Octave, et cesse de te plaindre.*
> *Quoi! tu veux qu'on t'épargne et n'as rien épargné!"**

June 6.

It was the first Thursday in June. I shut up my books and took my leave of the holy Abbot Droctoveus, who, being now in the en-

*"Look into thyself, Octavius, and cease complaining.
What! thou wouldst be spared, and thou thyself hast spared none!"

joyment of celestial bliss, cannot feel very impatient to behold his name and works glorified on earth through the humble compilation being prepared by my hands. Must I confess it? That mallow-plant I saw visited by a bee the other day has been occupying my thoughts much more than all the ancient abbots who ever bore croisers or wore mitres. There is in one of Sprengel's books which I read in my youth, at that time when I used to read anything and everything, some ideas about "the loves of flowers" which now return to memory after having been forgotten for half a century, and which to-day interest me so much that I regret not to have devoted the humble capacities of my mind to the study of insects and of plants.

And only awhile ago my housekeeper surprised me at the kitchen window, in the act of examining some wallflowers through a magnifying-glass. . . .

It was while looking for my cravat that I made these reflections. But after searching to no purpose in a great number of drawers, I found myself obliged, after all, to have recourse to my housekeeper. Thérèse came limping in.

"Monsieur," she said, "you ought to have told me you were going out, and I would have given you your cravat!"

"But Thérèse," I replied, "would it not be a great deal better to put it in some place where I could find it without your help?"

Thérèse did not deign to answer me.

Thérèse no longer allows me to arrange anything. I cannot even have a handkerchief without asking her for it; and as she is deaf, crippled, and, what is worse, beginning to lose her memory, I languish in perpetual destitution. But she exercises her domestic authority with such quiet pride that I do not feel the courage to attempt a *coup d'état* against her government.

"My cravat! Thérèse!—do you hear?—my cravat! if you drive me wild like this with your slow ways, it will not be a cravat I shall need, but a rope to hang myself!"

"You must be in a very great hurry, Monsieur," replied Thérèse. "Your cravat is not lost. Nothing is ever lost in this house, because I have charge of everything. But please allow me the time at least to find it."

"Yet here," I thought to myself—"here is the result of half a century of devotedness and self-sacrifice! . . . Ah! if by any happy chance this inexorable Thérèse had once in her whole life, only once, failed in her duty as a servant—if she had ever been at fault for one single instant, she could never have assumed this inflexible authority over me, and I should at least have the courage to resist her. But how can one resist virtue? The people who have no weaknesses are terrible; there is no way of taking advantage of them. Just look at Thérèse, for example; she has not a single fault for which you can blame her! She has no doubt of herself; nor of God, nor of the world. She is the valiant woman, the wise virgin of Scripture; others may know nothing about her, but I know her worth. In my fancy I always see her carrying a lamp, a humble kitchen lamp, illuminating the beams of some rustic roof—a lamp which will never go out while suspended from that meagre arm of hers, scraggy and strong as a vine-branch.

"Thérèse, my cravat! Don't you know, wretched woman, that to-day is the first Thursday in June, and that Mademoiselle Jeanne will be waiting for me? The schoolmistress has certainly had the parlour floor vigorously waxed: I am sure one can look at oneself in it now; and it will be quite a consolation for me when I slip and break my old bones upon it—which is sure to happen sooner or later—to see my rueful countenance reflected in it as in a looking-glass. Then taking for my model that amiable and admirable hero whose image is carved upon the handle of Uncle Victor's walking-stick, I will control myself so as not to make too ugly a grimace. . . . See what a splendid sun! The quays are all gilded by it, and the Seine smiles in countless little flashing wrinkles. The city is gold: a dust-haze, blonde and gold-toned as a woman's hair, floats above its beautiful contours. . . . Thérèse, my cravat! . . . Ah! I can now comprehend the wisdom of that old Chrysal who used to keep his neckbands in a big Plutarch. Hereafter I shall follow his example by laying all my neckties away between the leaves of the 'Acta Sanctorum.' "

Thérèse lets me talk on, and keeps looking for the necktie in silence. I hear a gentle ringing at our door-bell.

"Thérèse," I exclaim; "there is somebody ringing the bell! Give me my cravat, and go to the door; or, rather, go to the door first, and then, with the help of Heaven, you will give me my cravat. But please do not stand there between the clothes-press and the door like an old hack-horse between two saddles."

Thérèse marched to the door as if advancing upon an enemy. My excellent housekeeper becomes more inhospitable the older she grows. Every stranger is an object of suspicion to her. According to her own assertion, this disposition is the result of a long experience with human nature. I had not the time to consider whether the same experience on the part of another experimenter would produce the same results. Maître Mouche was waiting to see me in the ante-room.

Maître Mouche is still more yellow than I had believed him to be. He wears blue glasses, and his eyes keep moving uneasily behind them, like mice running about behind a screen.

Maître Mouche excuses himself for having intruded upon me at a moment when . . . He does not characterise the moment; but I think he means to say a moment in which I happen to be without my cravat. It is not my fault, as you very well know. Maître Mouche, who does not know, does not appear to be at all shocked, however. He is only afraid that he might have dropped in at the

wrong moment. I succeeded in partially reassuring him at once upon
that point. He then tells me it is as the guardian of Mademoiselle
Alexandre that he has come to talk with me. First of all, he desires
that I shall not hereafter pay any heed to those restrictions he had
at first deemed it necessary to put upon the permit given to visit
Mademoiselle Jeanne at the boarding-school. Henceforth the establishment of Mademoiselle Préfère will be open to me any day that I
may choose to call—between the hours of midday and four o'clock.
Knowing the interest I have taken in the young girl, he considers
it his duty to give me some information about the person to whom,
he has confided his ward. Mademoiselle Préfère, whom he has known
for many years, is in possession of his utmost confidence. Mademoiselle Préfère is, in his estimation, an enlightened person, of excellent morals, and capable of giving excellent counsel.

"Mademoiselle Préfère," he said to me, "has principles; and principles are rare in these days, Monsieur. Everything has been totally
changed; and this epoch of ours cannot compare with the preceding
ones."

"My stairway is a good example, Monsieur," I replied; "twenty-
five years ago it used to allow me to climb it without any trouble,
and now it takes my breath away, and wears my legs out before I
have climbed half a dozen steps. It has had its character spoiled.
Then there are those journals and books I used once to devour without difficulty by moonlight: to-day, even in the brightest sunlight,
they mock my curiosity, and exhibit nothing but a blur of white
and black when I have not got my spectacles on. Then the gout has
got into my limbs. That is another malicious trick of the times!"

"Not only that, Monsieur," gravely replied Maître Mouche, "but
what is really unfortunate in our epoch is that no one is satisfied
with his position. From the top of society to the bottom, in every
class, there prevails a discontent, a restlessness, a love of comfort. . . ."

"*Mon Dieu,* Monsieur!" I exclaimed. "You think this love of comfort is a sign of the times? Men have never had at any epoch a love
of discomfort. They have always tried to better their condition. This
constant effort produces constant changes, and the effort is always
going on—that is all there is about it!"

"Ah! Monsieur," replied Maître Mouche, "it is easy to see that
you live in your books—out of the business world altogether. You
do not see, as I see them, the conflicts of interest, the struggle for
money. It is the same effervescence in all minds, great or small. The
wildest speculations are being everywhere indulged in. What I see
around me simply terrifies me!"

I wondered within myself whether Maître Mouche had called upon
me only for the purpose of expressing his virtuous misanthropy;
but all at once I heard words of a more consoling character issue
from his lips. Maître Mouche began to speak to me of Virginie

Préfère as a person worthy of respect, of esteem, and of sympathy,
—highly honourable, capable of great devotedness, cultivated, discreet,—able to read aloud remarkably well, extremely modest, and
skilful in the art of applying blisters. Then I began to understand
that he had only been painting that dismal picture of universal
corruption in order the better to bring out, by contrast, the virtues
of the schoolmistress. I was further informed that the institution in
the Rue Demours was well patronised, prosperous, and enjoyed a
high reputation with the public. Maître Mouche lifted up his hand
—with a black woollen glove on it—as if making oath to the truth
of these statements. Then he added:

"I am enabled, by the very character of my profession, to know
a great deal about people. A notary is, to a certain extent, a father-
confessor.

"I deemed it my duty, Monsieur, to give you this agreeable information at the moment when a lucky chance enabled you to meet
Mademoiselle Préfère. There is only one thing more which I would
like to say. This lady—who is, of course, quite unaware of my action
in the matter—spoke to me of you the other day in terms of the
deepest sympathy. I could only weaken their expression by repeating them to you; and, furthermore, I could not repeat them without
betraying, to a certain extent, the confidence of Mademoiselle
Préfère."

"Do not betray it, Monsieur; do not betray it!" I responded. "To
tell you the truth, I had no idea that Mademoiselle Préfère knew
anything whatever about me. But since you have the influence of
an old friend with her, I will take advantage of your good will, Monsieur, to ask you to exercise that influence in behalf of Mademoiselle Jeanne Alexandre. The child—for she is still a child—is over-
loaded with work. She is at once a pupil and a mistress—she is
overtaxed. Besides, she is punished in petty disgusting ways; and
hers is one of those generous natures which will be forced into revolt by such continual humiliation."

"Alas!" replied Maître Mouche, "she must be trained to take her
part in the struggle of life. One does not come into this world
simply to amuse oneself, and to do just what one pleases."

"One comes into this world," I responded, rather warmly, "to
enjoy what is beautiful and what is good, and to do as one pleases,
when the things one wants to do are noble, intelligent, and generous. An education which does not cultivate the will, is an education
that depraves the mind. It is a teacher's duty to teach the pupil
how to will."

I perceived that Maître Mouche began to think me a rather silly
man. With a great deal of quiet self-assurance, he proceeded:

"You must remember, Monsieur, that the education of the poor
has to be conducted with a great deal of circumspection, and with
a view to that future state of dependence they must occupy in

society. Perhaps you are not aware that the late Noël Alexandre died a bankrupt, and that his daughter is being educated almost by charity?"

"Oh! Monsieur!" I exclaimed, "do not say it! To say it is to pay oneself back, and then the statement ceases to be true."

"The liabilities of the estate," continued the notary, "exceeded the assets. But I was able to effect a settlement with the creditors in favour of the minor."

He undertook to explain matters in detail. I declined to listen to· these explanations, being incapable of understanding business methods in general, and those of Maître Mouche in particular. The notary then took it upon himself to justify Mademoiselle Préfère's educational system, and observed by way of conclusion,

"It is not by amusing oneself that one can learn."

"It is only by amusing oneself that one can learn," I replied. "The whole art of teaching is only the art of awakening the natural curiosity of young minds for the purpose of satisfying it afterwards; and curiosity itself can be vivid and wholesome only in proportion as the mind is contented and happy. Those acquirements crammed by force into the minds of children simply clog and stifle intelligence. In order that knowledge be properly digested, it must have been swallowed with a good appetite. I know Jeanne! If that child were intrusted to my care, I should make of her—not a learned woman, for I would look to her future happiness only—but a child full of bright intelligence and full of life, in whom everything beautiful in art or nature would awaken some gentle responsive thrill. I would teach her to live in sympathy with all that is beautiful— comely landscapes, the ideal scenes of poetry and history, the emotional charm of noble music. I would make lovable to her everything I would wish her to love. Even her needlework I would make pleasurable to her, by a proper choice of the fabrics, the style of embroideries, the designs of lace. I would give her a beautiful dog, and a pony to teach her how to manage animals; I would give her birds to take care of, so that she could learn the value of even a drop of water and a crumb of bread. And in order that she should have a still higher pleasure, I would train her to find delight in exercising charity. And inasmuch as none of us may escape pain, I should teach her that Christian wisdom which elevates us above all suffering, and gives a beauty even to grief itself. That is my idea of the right way to educate a young girl."

"I yield, Monsieur," replied Maître Mouche, joining his black-gloved hands together.

And he rose.

"Of course you understand," I remarked, as I went to the door with him, "that I do not pretend for a moment to impose my educational system upon Mademoiselle Préfère; it is necessarily a private one, and quite incompatible with the organisation of even the best-managed boarding schools. I only ask you to persuade her to give Jeanne less work and more play, and not to punish her except in case of absolute necessity, and to let her have as much freedom of mind and body as the regulations of the institution permit."

It was with a pale and mysterious smile that Maître Mouche informed me that my observations would be taken in good part, and should receive all possible consideration.

Therewith he made me a little bow, and took his departure, leaving me with a peculiar feeling of discomfort and uneasiness. I have met a great many strange characters in my time, but never any at all resembling either this notary or this schoolmistress.

July 6.

MAÎTRE MOUCHE had so much delayed me by his visit that I gave up going to see Jeanne that day. Professional duties kept me very busy for the rest of the week. Although at the age when most men retire altogether from active life, I am still attached by a thousand ties to the society in which I have lived. I have to preside at meetings of academies, scientific congresses, assemblies of various learned bodies. I am overburdened with honorary functions; I have seven of these in one government department alone. The *bureaux* would be very glad to get rid of me, and I should be very glad to get rid of them. But habit is stronger than both of us together, and I continue to hobble up the stairs of various government buildings. Old clerks point me out to each other as I go by like a ghost wandering through the corridors. When one has become very old one finds it extremely difficult to disappear. Nevertheless, it is time, as the old song says, *de prendre ma retraite et de songer à faire un fin"*—to retire on my pension and prepare myself to die a good death.

An old marchioness, who used to be a friend of Helvetius in her youth, and whom I once met at my father's house when a very old woman, was visited during her last sickness by the priest of her parish, who wanted to prepare her to die.

"Is that really necessary?" she asked. "I see everybody else manage it perfectly well the first time."

My father went to see her very soon afterwards and found her extremely ill.

"Good-evening, my friend!" she said, pressing his hand. "I am going to see whether God improves upon acquaintance."

So were wont to die the *belles amies* of the philosophers. Such an end is certainly not vulgar nor impertinent, and such levities are not of the sort that emanate from dull minds. Nevertheless, they shock me. Neither my fears nor my hopes could accommodate themselves to such a mode of departure. I would like to make mine with a perfectly collected mind; and that is why I must begin to think, in

a year or two, about some way of belonging to myself; otherwise,
I should certainly risk . . . But, hush! let Him not hear His name
and turn to look as He passes by! I can still lift my fagot without
His aid.

. . . I found Jeanne very happy indeed. She told me that, on the
Thursday previous, after the visit of her guardian, Mademoiselle
Préfère had set her free from the ordinary regulations and light-
ened her tasks in several ways. Since that lucky Thursday she could
walk in the garden—which only lacked leaves and flowers—as much
as she liked; and she had even been given facilities to work at her
unfortunate little figure of Saint-George.

She said to me, with a smile,

"I know very well that I owe all this to you."

I tried to talk with her about other matters, but I remarked that
she could not attend to what I was saying, in spite of her effort to
do so.

"I see you are thinking about something else," I said. "Well, tell
me what it is; for, if you do not, we shall not be able to talk to
each other at all, which would be very unworthy of both of us."

She answered,

"Oh! I was really listening to you, Monsieur; but it is true that
I was thinking about something else. You will excuse me, won't
you? I could not help thinking that Mademoiselle Préfère must like
you very, very much indeed, to have become so good to me all of a
sudden."

Then she looked at me in an odd, smiling, frightened way, which
made me laugh.

"Does that surprise you?" I asked.

"Very much," she replied.

"Please tell me why?"

"Because I can see no reason, no reason at all . . . but there!
. . . no reason at all why you should please Mademoiselle Préfère
so much."

"So, then, you think I am very displeasing, Jeanne?"

She bit her lips, as if to punish them for having made a mistake;
and then, in a coaxing way, looking at me with great soft eyes, gentle and beautiful as a spaniel's, she said,

"I know I said a foolish thing; but, still, I do not see any reason
why you should be so pleasing to Mademoiselle Préfère. And, nevertheless, you seem to please her a great deal—a very great deal.
She called me one day, and asked me all sorts of questions about
you."

"Really?"

"Yes; she wanted to find out all about your house. Just think!
she even asked me how old your servant was!"

And Jeanne burst out laughing.

"Well, what do you think about it?" I asked.

She remained a long while with her eyes fixed on the worn-out cloth of her shoes, and seemed to be thinking very deeply. Finally, looking up again, she answered,

"I am distrustful. Isn't it very natural to feel uneasy about what one cannot understand; I know I am foolish; but you won't be offended with me, will you?"

"Why, certainly not, Jeanne. I am not a bit offended with you."

I must acknowledge that I was beginning to share her surprise; and I began to turn over in my old head the singular thought of this young girl—"One is uneasy about what one cannot understand."

But, with a fresh burst of merriment, she cried out,

"She asked me . . . guess! I will give you a hundred guesses—a thousand guesses. You give it up? . . . She asked me if you liked good eating."

"And how did you receive this shower of interrogations, Jeanne?"

"I replied, 'I don't know, Mademoiselle.' And Mademoiselle then said to me, 'You are a little fool. The least details of the life of an eminent man ought to be observed. Please to know, Mademoiselle, that Monsieur Sylvestre Bonnard is one of the glories of France!'"

"Stuff!" I exclaimed. "And what did *you* think about it, Mademoiselle?"

"I thought that Mademoiselle Préfère was right. But I don't care at all . . . (I know it is naughty what I am going to say) . . . I don't care a bit, not a bit, whether Mademoiselle Préfère is or is not right about anything."

"Well, then, content yourself, Jeanne, Mademoiselle Préfère was not right."

"Yes, yes, she was quite right that time; but I wanted to love everybody who loved you—everybody without exception—and I cannot do it, because it would never be possible for me to love Mademoiselle Préfère."

"Listen, Jeanne," I answered, very seriously, "Mademoiselle Préfère has become good to you; try now to be good to her."

She answered sharply,

"It is very easy for Mademoiselle Préfère to be good to me, and it would be very difficult indeed for me to be good to her."

I then said, in a still more serious tone:

"My child, the authority of a teacher is sacred. You must consider your schoolmistress as occupying the place to you of the mother whom you lost."

I had scarcely uttered this solemn stupidity when I bitterly regretted it. The child turned pale, and the tears sprang to her eyes.

"Oh, Monsieur!" she cried, "how could you say such a thing—*you?* You never knew mamma!"

Ay, just Heaven! I did know her mamma. And how indeed could I have been foolish enough to have said what I did?

She repeated, as if to herself:

"Mamma! my dear mamma! my poor mamma!"

A lucky chance prevented me from playing the fool any further. I do not know how it happened that at that moment I looked as if I was going to cry. At my age one does not cry. It must have been a bad cough which brought the tears into my eyes. But, anyhow, appearances were in my favour. Jeanne was deceived by them. Oh! what a pure and radiant smile suddenly shone out under her beautiful wet eyelashes—like sunshine among branches after a summer shower! We took each other by the hand and sat a long while without saying a word—absolutely happy. Those celestial harmonies which I once thought I heard thrilling through my soul while I knelt before that tomb to which a saintly woman had guided me, suddenly awoke again in my heart, slow-swelling through the blissful moments with infinite softness. Doubtless the child whose hand pressed my own also heard them; and then, elevated by their enchantment above the material world, the poor old man and the artless young girl both knew that a tender ghostly Presence was making sweetness all about them.

"My child," I said at last, "I am very old, and many secrets of life, which you will only learn little by little, have been revealed to me. Believe me, the future is shaped out of the past. Whatever you can do to live contentedly here, without impatience and without fretting, will help you to live some future day in peace and joy in your own home. Be gentle, and learn how to suffer. When one suffers patiently one suffers less. If you should ever happen to have a serious cause of complaint I shall be there to take your part. If you should be badly treated, Madame de Gabry and I would both consider ourselves badly treated in your person." . . .

"Is your health very good indeed, dear Monsieur?"

It was Mademoiselle Préfère, approaching stealthily behind us, who had asked the question with her peculiar smile. My first idea was to tell her to go to the devil; my second, that her mouth was as little suited for smiling as a frying-pan for musical purposes; my third was to answer her politely and assure her that I hoped she was very well.

She sent the young girl out to take a walk in the garden; then, pressing one hand upon her pelerine and extending the other towards the *Tableau d'Honneur,* she showed me the name of Jeanne Alexandre written at the head of the list in large text.

"I am very much pleased," I said to her, "to find that you are satisfied with the behaviour of that child. Nothing could delight me more; and I am inclined to attribute this happy result to your affectionate vigilance. I have taken the liberty to send you a few books which I think may serve both to instruct and to amuse young girls. You will be able to judge by glancing over them whether they are adapted to the perusal of Mademoiselle Alexandre and her companions."

The gratitude of the schoolmistress not only overflowed in words, but seemed about to take the form of tearful sensibility. In order to change the subject I observed,

"What a beautiful day this is!"

"Yes," she replied; "and if this weather continues, those dear children will have a nice time for their enjoyment."

"I suppose you are referring to the holidays. But Mademoiselle Alexandre, who has no relatives, cannot go away. What in the world is she going to do all alone in this great big house?"

"Oh, we will do everything we can to amuse her. . . . I will take her to the museums and——"

She hesitated, blushed, and continued,

"——and to your house, if you will permit me."

"Why of course!" I exclaimed. "That is a first-rate idea."

We separated very good friends with one another. I with her, because I had been able to obtain what I desired; she with me, for no appreciable motive—which fact, according to Plato, elevated her into the highest rank of the Hierarchy of Souls.

. . . And nevertheless it is not without a presentiment of evil that I find myself on the point of introducing this person into my house. And I would be very glad indeed to see Jeanne in charge of anybody else rather than of her. Maître Mouche and Mademoiselle Préfère are characters whom I cannot at all understand. I never can imagine why they say what they do say, nor why they do what they do; they have a mysterious something in common which makes me feel uneasy. As Jeanne said to me a little while ago: "One is uneasy about what one cannot understand."

Alas! at my age one has learned only too well how little sincerity there is in life; one has learned only too well how much one loses by living a long time in this world; and one feels that one can no longer trust any except the young.

August 12.

I WAITED for them. In fact, I waited for them very impatiently. I exerted all my powers of insinuation and of coaxing to induce Thérèse to receive them kindly; but my powers in this direction are very limited. They came. Jeanne was neater and prettier than I had ever expected to see her. She has not, it is true, anything approaching the charm of her mother. But to-day, for the first time, I observed that she has a pleasing face; and a pleasing face is of great advantage to a woman in this world. I think that her hat was a little on one side; but she smiled, and the City of Books was all illuminated by that smile.

I watched Thérèse to see whether the rigid manners of the old housekeeper would soften a little at the sight of the young girl. I saw her turning her lustreless eyes upon Jeanne; I saw her long wrinkled face, her toothless mouth, and that pointed chin of hers—like the chin of some puissant old fairy. And that was all I could see.

Mademoiselle Préfère made her appearance all in blue—advanced, retreated, skipped, tripped, cried out, sighed, cast her eyes down, rolled her eyes up, bewildered herself with excuses—said she dared not, and nevertheless dared—said she would never dare again, and nevertheless dared again—made courtesies innumerable—made, in short, all the fuss she could.

"What a lot of books!" she screamed. "And have you really read them all, Monsieur Bonnard?"

"Alas! I have," I replied, "and that is just the reason that I do not know anything; for there is not a single one of those books which does not contradict some other book; so that by the time one has read them all one does not know what to think about anything. That is just my condition, Madame."

Thereupon she called Jeanne for the purpose of communicating her impressions. But Jeanne was looking out of the window.

"How beautiful it is!" she said to us. "How I love to see the river flowing! It makes you think about all kinds of things."

Mademoiselle Préfère having removed her hat and exhibited a forehead tricked out with blonde curls, my housekeeper sturdily snatched up the hat at once, with the observation that she did not like to see people's clothes scattered over the furniture. Then she approached Jeanne and asked her for her "things," calling her "my little lady!" Whereupon the little lady, giving up her cloak and hat, exposed to view a very graceful neck and a lithe figure, whose outlines were beautifully relieved against the great glow of the open window; and I could have wished that some one else might have seen her at that moment—some one very different from an aged housekeeper, a schoolmistress frizzled like a sheep, and this old humbug of an archivist and paleographer.

"So you are looking at the Seine," I said to her. "See how it sparkles in the sun!"

"Yes," she replied, leaning over the window-bar, "it looks like a flowing of fire. But see how nice and cool it looks on the other side over there, under the shadow of the willows! That little spot there pleases me better than all the rest."

"Good!" I answered. "I see that the river has a charm for you. How would you like, with Mademoiselle Préfère's permission, to make a trip to Saint-Cloud? We should certainly be in time to catch the steamboat just below the Pont-Royal."

Jeanne was delighted with my suggestion, and Mademoiselle Préfère willing to make any sacrifice. But my housekeeper was not at all willing to let us go off so unconcernedly. She summoned me into the dining-room, whither I followed her in fear and trembling.

"Monsieur," she said to me as soon as we found ourselves alone, "you never think about anything, and it is always I who have to think about everything. Luckily for you I have a good memory."

I did not think that it was a favourable moment for any attempt to dispel this wild illusion. She continued:

"So you were going off without saying a word to me about what this little lady likes to eat? At her age one does not know anything, one does not care about anything in particular, one eats like a bird. You yourself, Monsieur, are very difficult to please; but at least you know what is good: it is very different with these young people—they do not know anything about cooking. It is often the very best thing which they think the worst, and what is bad seems to them good, because their stomachs are not quite formed yet— so that one never knows just what to do for them. Tell me if the little lady would like a pigeon cooked with green peas, and whether she is fond of vanilla ice-cream."

"My good Thérèse," I answered, "just do whatever you think best, and whatever that may be I am sure it will be very nice. Those ladies will be quite contented with our humble ordinary fare."

Thérèse replied, very dryly,

"Monsieur, I am asking you about the little lady: she must not leave this house without having enjoyed herself a little. As for that old frizzle-headed thing, if she doesn't like my dinner she can suck her thumbs. I don't care what she likes!"

My mind being thus set at rest, I returned into the City of Books, where Mademoiselle Préfère was crocheting as calmly as if she were at home. I almost felt inclined myself to think she was. She did not take up much room, it is true, in the angle of the window. But she had chosen her chair and her footstool so well that those articles of furniture seemed to have been made expressly for her.

Jeanne, on the other hand, devoted her attention to the books and pictures—gazing at them in a kindly, expressive, half-sad way, as if she were bidding them an affectionate farewell.

"Here," I said to her, "amuse yourself with this book, which I am sure you cannot help liking, because it is full of beautiful engravings." And I threw open before her Vecellio's collection of costume-designs—not the commonplace edition, by your leave, so meagrely reproduced by modern artists, but in truth a magnificent and vener- able copy of that *editio princeps* which is noble as those noble dames who figure upon its yellowed leaves, made beautiful by time.

While turning over the engravings with artless curiosity, Jeanne said to me,

"We were talking about taking a walk; but this is a great jour- ney you are making me take. And I would like to travel very, very far away!'

"In that case, Mademoiselle," I said to her, "you must arrange yourself as comfortably as possible for travelling. But you are now sitting on one corner of your chair, so that the chair is standing upon only one leg, and that Vecellio must tire your knees. Sit down comfortably; put your chair on its four feet, and put your book on the table."

She obeyed me with a laugh.

I watched her. She cried out suddenly,

"Oh, come look at this beautiful costume!" (It was that of the wife of a Doge of Venice.) "How noble it is! What magnificent ideas it gives one of that life! Oh, I must tell you—I adore luxury!"

"You must not express such thoughts as those, Mademoiselle," said the schoolmistress, lifting up her little shapeless nose from her work.

"Nevertheless, it was a very innocent utterance," I replied. "There are splendid souls in whom the love of splendid things is natural and inborn."

The little shapeless nose went down again.

"Mademoiselle Préfère likes luxury too," said Jeanne; "she cuts out paper trimmings and shades for the lamps. It is economical luxury; but it is luxury all the same."

Having returned to the subject of Venice, we were just about to make the acquaintance of a certain patrician lady attired in an embroidered dalmatic, when I heard the bell ring. I thought it was some peddler with his basket; but the gate of the City of Books opened, and . . . Well, Master Sylvestre Bonnard, you were wishing awhile ago that the grace of your *protégée* might be observed by some other eyes than old withered ones behind spectacles. Your wishes have been fulfilled in a most unexpected manner, and a voice cries out to you, as to the imprudent Theseus,

> "Craignez, Seigneur, craignez que le Ciel rigoureux
> Ne vous haïsse assez pour exaucer vos vœux!
> Souvent dans sa colère il reçoit nos victimes,
> Ses présents sont souvent la peine de nos crimes."*

The gate of the City of Books had opened, and a handsome young man made his appearance, ushered in by Thérèse. That good old soul only knows how to open the door for people and to shut it behind them; she has no idea whatever of the tact requisite for the waiting-room and for the parlour. It is not in her nature either to make any announcements or to make anybody wait. She either throws people out on the lobby, or simply pitches them at your head.

And here is this handsome young man already inside; and I cannot really take the girl at once and hide her like a secret treasure in the next room. I wait for him to explain himself; he does it with-

---

*"Beware, my lord! Beware lest stern Heaven hate you enough to hear your prayers! Often 'tis in wrath that Heaven receives our sacrifices; its gifts are often the punishment of our crimes."

out the least embarrassment; but it seems to me that he has already observed the young girl who is still bending over the table looking at Vecellio. As I observe the young man it occurs to me that I have seen him somewhere before, or else I must be very much mistaken. His name is Gélis. That is a name which I have heard somewhere,—I can't remember where. At all events, Monsieur Gélis (since there is a Gélis) is a fine-looking young fellow. He tells me that this is his third class-year at the École des Chartes, and that he has been working for the past fifteen or eighteen months upon his graduation thesis, the subject of which is the Condition of the Benedictine Abbeys in 1700. He has just read my works upon the "Monasticon"; and he is convinced that he cannot terminate this thesis successfully without my advice, to begin with, and in the second place without a certain manuscript which I possess, and which is nothing less than the "Register of the Accounts of the Abbey of Citeaux from 1683 to 1704."

Having thus explained himself, he hands me a letter of introduction bearing the signature of one of the most illustrious of my colleagues.

Good! Now I know who he is! Monsieur Gélis is the very same young man who last year under the chestnut-trees called me an idiot! And while unfolding his letter of introduction I think to myself:

"Aha! my unlucky youth, you are very far from suspecting that I overheard what you said, and that I know what you think of me —or, at least, what you did think of me that day, for these young minds are so fickle? I have got you now, my friend! You have fallen into the lion's den, and so unexpectedly, in good sooth, that the astonished old lion does not know what to do with his prey. But come now, old lion! do not act like an idiot! Is it not possible that you were an idiot? If you are not one now, you certainly were one! You were a fool to have been listening to Monsieur Gélis at the foot of the statue of Marguerite de Valois; you were doubly a fool to have heard what he said; and you were trebly a fool not to have forgotten what it would have been much. better never to have heard."

Having thus scolded the old lion, I exhorted him to show clemency. He did not appear to require much coaxing, and gradually became so good-natured that he had some difficulty in restraining himself from bursting out into joyous roarings. From the way in which I had read my colleague's letter one might have supposed me a man who did not know his alphabet. I took a long while to read it; and Monsieur Gélis might have become very tired under different circumstances; but he was watching Jeanne, and endured the trial with exemplary patience. Jeanne occasionally turned her face in our direction. Well, you could not expect a person to remain perfectly motionless, could you? Mademoiselle Préfère was arrang-

ing her curls, and her bosom occasionally swelled with little sighs.
It may be observed that I have myself often been honoured with
these little sighs.

"Monsieur," I said, as I folded up the letter, "I shall be very
happy to be of any service to you. You are occupied with researches
in which I myself have always felt a very lively interest. I have
done all that lay in my power. I know, as you do—and still better
than you can know—how much there remains to do. The manuscript you asked for is at your disposal; you may take it home with
you, but it is not a manuscript of the smallest kind, and I am
afraid——"

"Oh, Monsieur," said Gélis, "big books have never been able to
make me afraid of them."

I begged the young man to wait for me, and I went into the next
room to get the Register, which I could not find at first, and which
I almost despaired of finding, as I discerned, from certain familiar
signs, that Thérèse had been setting the room in order. But the
Register was so big and so heavy that, luckily for me, Thérèse had
not been able to put it in order as she had doubtless wished to do.
I could scarcely lift it up myself; and I had the pleasure of finding
it quite as heavy as I could have hoped.

"Wait, my boy," I said, with a smile which must have been very
sarcastic—"wait! I am going to give you something to do which
will break your arms first, and afterwards your head. That will
be the first vengeance of Sylvestre Bonnard. Later on we shall see
what else there is to be done."

When I returned to the City of Books I heard Monsieur Gélis and
Mademoiselle Jeanne chatting—chatting together, if you please! as
if they were the best friends in the world. Mademoiselle Préfère,
being full of decorum, did not say anything; but the other two were
chattering like birds. And what about? About the blond tint used
by Venetian painters! Yes, about the "Venetian blond." That little
serpent of a Gélis was telling Jeanne the secret of the dye with
which, according to the best authorities, the women of Titian and
of Veronese tinted their hair. And Mademoiselle Jeanne was expressing her opinion very prettily about the honey tint and the
golden tint. I understood that that scamp of a Vecellio was responsible—that they had been bending over the book together, and they
had been admiring either that Doge's wife we had been looking at
awhile before, or some other patrician woman of Venice.

Never mind! I appeared with my enormous old book, thinking
that Gélis was going to make a grimace. It was as much as one
could have asked a porter to carry, and my arms were stiff merely
with lifting it. But the young man caught it up like a feather, and
slipped it under his arm with a smile. Then he thanked me with
that sort of brevity which I like, reminded me that he had need of
my advice, and, having made an appointment to meet me another

day, took his departure after bowing to us with the most perfect self-possession conceivable.

"He seems quite a decent lad," I said.

Jeanne turned over a few more pages of Vecellio, and made no answer.

"Aha!" I thought to myself. . . . And then we went to Saint-Cloud.

September-December.

THE regularity with which visit succeeded visit to the old man's house thereafter made me feel very grateful to Mademoiselle Préfère, who succeeded at last in winning her right to occupy a special corner in the City of Books. She now says *"my* chair," *"my* foot-stool," *"my* pigeon-hole." Her pigeon-hole is really a small shelf properly belonging to the poets of La Champagne, whom she expelled therefrom in order to obtain a lodging for her work-bag. She is very amiable, and I must really be a monster not to like her. I can only endure her—in the severest signification of the word. But what would one not endure for Jeanne's sake? Her presence lends to the City of Books a charm which seems to hover about it even after she has gone. She is very ignorant; but she is so finely gifted that whenever I show her anything beautiful I am astounded to find that I had never really seen it before, and that it is she who makes me see it. I have found it impossible so far to make her follow some of my ideas, but I have often found pleasure in following the whimsical and delicate course of her own.

A more practical man than I would attempt to teach her to make herself useful; but is not the capacity of being amiable a useful thing in life? Without being pretty, she charms; and the power to charm is perhaps, after all, worth quite as much as the ability to darn stockings. Furthermore, I am not immortal; and I doubt whether she will have become very old when my notary (who is not Maître Mouche) shall read to her a certain paper which I signed a little while ago.

I do not wish that any one except myself should provide for her, and give her her dowry. I am not, however, very rich, and the paternal inheritance did not gain bulk in my hands. One does not accumulate money by poring over old texts. But my books—at the price which such noble merchandise fetches to-day—are worth something. Why, on that shelf there are some poets of the sixteenth century for which bankers would bid against princes! And I think that those "Heures" of Simon Vostre would not be readily over-looked at the Hôtel Sylvestre any more than would those *Preces Piæ* compiled for the use of Queen Claude. I have taken great pains to collect and to preserve all those rare and curious editions which people the City of Books; and for a long time I used to believe that they were as necessary to my life as air and light. I have loved them well, and even now I cannot prevent myself from smiling at them and caressing them. Those morocco bindings are so delightful to the eye! Those old vellums are so soft to the touch! There is not a single one among those books which is not worthy, by reason of some special merit, to command the respect of an honourable man. What other owner would ever know how to dip into them in the proper way? Can I be even sure that another owner would not leave them to decay in neglect, or mutilate them at the prompting of some ignorant whim? Into whose hands will fall that incomparable copy of the "Histoire de l'Abbaye de Saint-Germain-des-Prés," on the margins of which the author himself, in the person of Jacques Bouillard, made such substantial notes in his own handwriting? . . . Master Bonnard, you are an old fool! Your housekeeper—poor soul!—is nailed down upon her bed with a merciless attack of rheumatism. Jeanne is to come with her chaperon, and, instead of thinking how you are going to receive them, you are thinking about a thousand stupidities. Sylvestre Bonnard, you will never succeed at anything in this world, and it is I myself who tell you so!

And at this very moment I catch sight of them from my window, as they get out of the omnibus. Jeanne leaps down like a kitten; but Mademoiselle Préfère intrusts herself to the strong arm of the conductor, with the shy grace of a Virginia recovering after the shipwreck, and this time quite resigned to being saved. Jeanne looks up, sees me, laughs, and Mademoiselle Préfère has to prevent her from waving her umbrella at me as a friendly signal. There is a certain stage of civilisation to which Mademoiselle Jeanne never can be brought. You can teach her all the arts if you like (it is not exactly to Mademoiselle Préfère that I am now speaking); but you will never be able to teach her perfect manners. As a charming girl she makes the mistake of being charming only in her own way. Only an old fool like myself could forgive her pranks. As for young fools—and there are several of them still to be found—I do not know what they would think about it; and what they might think is none of my business. Just look at her running along the pavement, wrapped up in her cloak, with her hat tilted back on her head, and her feather fluttering in the wind, like a schooner in full rig! And really she has a grace of poise and motion which suggests a fine sailing-vessel—so much so, indeed, that she makes me remember seeing one day, when I was at Havre . . . But, Bonnard, my friend, how many times is it necessary to tell you that your housekeeper is in bed, and that you must go and open the door yourself?

Open, Old Man Winter! 'tis Spring who rings the bell.

It is Jeanne herself—Jeanne all flushed like a rose. Mademoiselle Préfère, indignant and out of breath, has still another whole flight to climb before reaching our lobby.

I explained the condition of my housekeeper, and proposed that we should dine at a restaurant. But Thérèse—all-powerful still, even upon her sick-bed—decided that we should dine at home, whether we wanted to or not. Respectable people, in her opinion, never dined at restaurants. Moreover, she had made all necessary arrangements—the dinner had been bought; the concierge would cook it.

The audacious Jeanne insisted upon going to see whether the old woman wanted anything. As you might suppose, she was sent back to the parlour with short shrift, but not so harshly as I had feared.

"If I want anybody to do anything for me, which, thank God, I do not," Thérèse had replied, "I would get somebody less delicate and dainty than you are. What I want is rest. That is a merchandise which is not sold at fairs under the sign of *Motus with finger on lip*. Go and have your fun, and don't stay here—for old age might be catching."

Jeanne, after telling us what she had said, added that she liked very much to hear old Thérèse talk. Whereupon Mademoiselle Préfère reproached her for expressing such unladylike tastes.

I tried to excuse her by citing the example of Molière. Just at that moment it came to pass that, while climbing the ladder to get a book, she upset a whole shelf-row. There was a heavy crash; and Mademoiselle Préfère, being, of course, a very delicate person, almost fainted. Jeanne quickly followed the books to the foot of the ladder. She made one think of a kitten suddenly transformed into a woman, catching mice which had been transformed into old books. While picking them up, she found one which happened to interest her, and she began to read it, squatting down upon her heels. It was the "Prince Grenouille," she told us. Mademoiselle Préfère took occasion to complain that Jeanne had so little taste for poetry. It was impossible to get her to recite Casimir Delavigne's poem on the death of Joan of Arc without mistakes. It was the very most she could do to learn "Le Petit Savoyard." The schoolmistress did not think that any one should read the "Prince Grenouille" before learning by heart the stanzas to Duperrier; and, carried away by her enthusiasm, she began to recite them in a voice sweeter than the bleating of a sheep:

> "Ta douleur, Duperrier, sera donc éternelle,
>   Et les tristes discours
> Que te met en l'esprit l'amitié paternelle
>   L'augmenteront toujours;
>
> .   .   .   .
>
> "Je sais de quels appas son enfance etait pleine,
>   Et n'ai pas entrepris,
> Injurieux ami, de consoler ta peine
>   Avecque son mépris."

Then in ecstasy she exclaimed,

"How beautiful that is! What harmony! How is it possible for any one not to admire such exquisite, such touching verses! But why did Malherbe call that poor Monsieur Duperrier his *'injurieux ami'* at a time when he had been so severely tried by the death of his daughter? *Injurieux ami*—you must acknowledge that the term was very harsh."

I explained to this poetical person that the phrase *"Injurieux ami,"* which shocked her so much, was in apposition, etc. etc. What I said, however, had so little effect towards clearing her head that she was seized with a severe and prolonged fit of sneezing. Meanwhile it was evident that the history of "Prince Grenouille" had proved extremely funny; for it was all that Jeanne could do, as she crouched down there on the carpet, to keep herself from bursting into a wild fit of laughter. But when she had finished with the prince and princess of the story, and the multitude of their children, she assumed a very suppliant expression, and begged me as a great favour to allow her to put on a white apron and go to the kitchen to help in getting the dinner ready.

"Jeanne," I replied, with the gravity of a master, "I think that if it is a question of breaking plates, knocking off the edges of dishes, denting all the pans, and smashing all the skimmers, the person whom Thérèse has set to work in the kitchen already will be able to perform her task without assistance; for it seems to me at this very moment I can hear disastrous noises in that kitchen. But anyhow, Jeanne, I will charge you with the duty of preparing the dessert. So go and get your white apron; I will tie it on for you."

Accordingly, I solemnly knotted the linen apron about her waist; and she rushed into the kitchen, where she proceeded at once—as we discovered later on—to prepare various dishes unknown to Vatel, unknown even to that great Carême who began his treatise upon *pièces montées* with these words: *"The Fine Arts are five in number: Painting, Music, Poetry, Sculpture, and Architecture— whereof the principal branch is Confectionery."* But I had no reason to be pleased with this little arrangement—for Mademoiselle Préfère, on finding herself alone with me, began to act after a fashion which filled me with frightful anxiety. She gazed upon me with eyes full of tears and flames, and uttered enormous sighs.

"Oh, how I pity you!" she said. "A man like you—a man so superior as you are—having to live alone with a coarse servant (for she is certainly coarse, that is incontestable)! How cruel such a life must be! You have need of repose—you have need of comfort, of care, of every kind of attention; you might fall sick. And yet there is no woman who would not deem it an honour to bear your name, and to share your existence. No, there is none; my own heart tells me so."

And she squeezed both hands over that heart of hers—always so ready to fly away.

I was driven almost to distraction. I tried to make Mademoiselle Préfère comprehend that I had no intention whatever of changing my habits at so advanced an age, and that I found just as much happiness in life as my character and my circumstances rendered possible.

"No, you are not happy!" she cried. "You need to have always beside you a mind capable of comprehending your own. Shake off your lethargy, and cast your eyes about you. Your professional connections are of the most extended character, and you must have charming acquaintances. One cannot be a Member of the Institute without going into society. See, judge, compare. No sensible woman would refuse you her hand. I am a woman, Monsieur; my instinct never deceives me—there is something within me which assures me that you would find happiness in marriage. Women are so devoted, so loving (not all, of course, but some)! And, then, they are so sensitive to glory. Remember that at your age one has need, like Œdipus, of an Egeria! Your cook is no longer able—she is deaf, she is infirm. If anything should happen to you at night! Oh! it makes me shudder even to think of it!"

And she really shuddered—she closed her eyes, clenched her hands, stamped on the floor. Great was my dismay. With awful intensity she resumed,

"Your health—your dear health! The health of a Member of the Institute! How joyfully I would shed the very last drop of my blood to preserve the life of a scholar, of a *littérateur*, of a man of worth. And any woman who would not do as much, I should despise her! Let me tell you, Monsieur—I used to know the wife of a great mathematician, a man who used to fill whole note-books with calculations—so many note-books that they filled all the cupboards in the house. He had heart-disease, and he was visibly pining away. And I saw that wife of his, sitting there beside him, perfectly calm! I could not endure it. I said to her one day, 'My dear, you have no heart! If I were in your place I should . . . I should . . . I do not know what I should do!'"

She paused for want of breath. My situation was terrible. As for telling Mademoiselle Préfère what I really thought about her advice—that was something which I could not even dream of daring to do. For to fall out with her was to lose the chance of seeing Jeanne. So I resolved to take the matter quietly. In any case, she was in my house: that consideration helped me to treat her with something of courtesy.

"I am very old, Mademoiselle," I answered her, "and I am very much afraid that your advice comes to me rather too late in life. Still, I will think about it. In the meanwhile let me beg of you to be calm. I think a glass of *eau sucrée* would do you good!"

To my great surprise, these words calmed her at once; and I saw her sit down very quietly in *her* corner, close to *her* pigeon-hole, upon *her* chair, with her feet upon *her* footstool.

The dinner was a complete failure. Mademoiselle Préfère, who seemed lost in a brown study, never noticed the fact. As a rule I am very sensitive about such misfortunes; but this one caused Jeanne so much delight that at last I could not help enjoying it myself. Even at my age I had not been able to learn before that a chicken, raw on one side and burned on the other, was a funny thing; but Jeanne's bursts of laughter taught me that it was. That chicken caused us to say a thousand very witty things, which I have forgotten; and I was enchanted that it had not been properly cooked. Jeanne put it back to roast again; then she broiled it; then she stewed it with butter. And every time it came back to the table it was much less appetising and much more mirth-provoking than before. When we did eat it, at last, it had become a thing for which there is no name in any *cuisine*.

The almond cake was much more extraordinary. It was brought to the table in the pan, because it never could have been got out of it. I invited Jeanne to help us all to a piece, thinking that I was going to embarrass her; but she broke the pan and gave each of us a fragment. To think that anybody at my age could eat such things was an idea possible only to a very artless mind. Mademoiselle Préfère, suddenly awakened from her dream, indignantly pushed away the sugary splinter of earthenware, and deemed it opportune to inform me that she herself was exceedingly skilful in making confectionery.

"Ah!" exclaimed Jeanne, with an air of surprise not altogether without malice.

Then she wrapped all the fragments of the pan in a piece of paper, for the purpose of giving them to her little playmates—especially to the three little Mouton girls, who are naturally inclined to gluttony.

Secretly, however, I was beginning to feel very uneasy. It did not now seem in any way possible to keep much longer upon good terms with Mademoiselle Préfère since her matrimonial fury had thus burst forth. And that lady affronted, good-bye to Jeanne! I took advantage of a moment while the sweet soul was busy putting on her cloak, in order to ask Jeanne to tell me exactly what her own age was. She was eighteen years and one month old. I counted on my fingers, and found she would not come of age for another two years and eleven months. And how should we be able to manage during all that time?

At the door Mademoiselle Préfère squeezed my hand with so much meaning that I fairly shook from head to foot.

"Good-bye," I said very gravely to the young girl. "But listen to me a moment: your friend is very old, and might perhaps fail you when you need him most. Promise me never to fail in your duty to yourself, and then I shall have no fear. God keep you, my child!"

After closing the door behind them, I opened the window to get a last look at her as she was going away. But the night was dark, and I could see only two vague shadows flitting across the quay. I heard the vast deep hum of the city rising up about me; and I suddenly felt a great sinking at my heart.

Poor child!

December 15.

THE King of Thule kept a goblet of gold which his dying mistress had bequeathed him as a souvenir. When about to die himself, after having drunk from it for the last time, he threw the goblet into the sea. And I keep this diary of memories even as that old prince of the mist-haunted seas kept his carven goblet; and even as he flung away at last his love-pledge, so will I burn this my book of souvenirs. Assuredly it is not through any arrogant avarice nor through any egotistical pride, that I shall destroy this record of a humble life—it is only because I fear lest those things which are dear and sacred to me might appear to others, because of my inartistic manner of expression, either commonplace or absurd.

I do not say this in view of what is going to follow. Absurd I certainly must have been when, having been invited to dinner by Mademoiselle Préfère, I took my seat in a *bergère* (it was really a *bergère*) at the right hand of that alarming person. The table had been set in a little parlour; and I could observe from the poor way in which it was set out that the schoolmistress was one of those ethereal souls who soar above terrestrial things. Chipped plates, unmatched glasses, knives with loose handles, forks with yellow prongs—there was absolutely nothing wanting to spoil the appetite of an honest man.

I was assured that the dinner had been cooked for me—for me alone—although Maître Mouche had also been invited. Mademoiselle Préfère must have imagined that I had Sarmatian tastes on the subject of butter; for that which she offered me, served up in little thin pats, was excessively rancid.

The roast very nearly poisoned me. But I had the pleasure of hearing Maître Mouche and Mademoiselle Préfère discourse upon virtue. I said the pleasure—I ought to have said the shame; for the sentiments to which they gave expression soared far beyond the range of my vulgar nature.

What they said proved to me as clear as day that devotedness was their daily bread, and that self-sacrifice was not less necessary to their existence than air and water. Observing that I was not eating, Mademoiselle Préfère made a thousand efforts to overcome that which she was good enough to term my "discretion." Jeanne

was not of the party, because, I was told, her presence at it would
have been contrary to the rules, and would have wounded the feelings of the other school-children, among whom it was necessary to
maintain a certain equality. I secretly congratulated her upon having escaped from the Merovingian butter; from the huge radishes,
empty as funeral-urns; from the leathery roast, and from various
other curiosities of diet to which I had exposed myself for the love
of her.

The extremely disconsolate-looking servant served up some liquid
to which they gave the name of cream—I do not know why—and
vanished away like a ghost.

Then Mademoiselle Préfère related to Maître Mouche, with extraordinary transports of emotion, all that she had said to me in
the City of Books, during the time that my housekeeper was sick
in bed. Her admiration for a Member of the Institute, her terror
lest I should be taken ill while unattended, and the certainty she
felt that any intelligent woman would be proud and happy to share
my existence—she concealed nothing, but, on the contrary, added
many fresh follies to the recital. Maître Mouche kept nodding his
head in approval while cracking nuts. Then, after all this verbiage,
he demanded, with an agreeable smile, what my answer had been.

Mademoiselle Préfère, pressing her hand upon her heart and extending the other towards me, cried out,

"He is so affectionate, so superior, so good, and so great! He
answered. . . . But I could never, because I am only a humble
woman—I could never repeat the words of a Member of the Institute. I can only utter the substance of them. He answered, 'Yes, I
understand you—yes.' "

And with these words she reached out and seized one of my
hands. Then Maître Mouche, also overwhelmed with emotion, arose
and seized my other hand.

"Monsieur," he said, "permit me to offer my congratulations."

Several times in my life I have known fear; but never before had
I experienced any fright of so nauseating a character. A sickening
terror came upon me.

I disengaged my two hands, and, rising to my feet, so as to give
all possible seriousness to my words, I said,

"Madame, either I explained myself very badly when you were
at my house, or I have totally misunderstood you here in your own.
In either case, a positive declaration is absolutely necessary. Permit me, Madame, to make it now, very plainly. No—I never did understand you; I am totally ignorant of the nature of this marriage
project that you have been planning for me—if you really have
been planning one. In any event, I should not think of marrying.
It would be an unpardonable folly at my age, and even now, at this
moment, I cannot conceive how a sensible person like you could
ever have advised me to marry. Indeed, I am strongly inclined to

believe that I must have been mistaken, and that you never said anything of the kind before. In the latter case, please to excuse an old man totally unfamiliar with the usages of society, unaccustomed to the conversation of ladies, and very contrite for his mistake."

Maître Mouche went back very softly to his place, where, not finding any more nuts to crack, he began to whittle a cork.

Mademoiselle Préfère, after staring at me for a few moments with an expression in her little round dry eyes which I had never seen there before, suddenly resumed her customary sweetness and graciousness. Then she cried out in honeyed tones,

"Oh! these learned men!—these studious men! They are all like children. Yes, Monsieur Bonnard, you are a real child!"

Then, turning to the notary, who still sat very quietly in his corner, with his nose over his cork, she exclaimed, in beseeching tones,

"Oh, do not accuse him! Do not accuse him! Do not think any evil of him, I beg of you! Do not think it at all! Must I ask you upon my knees?"

Maître Mouche continued to examine all the various aspects and surfaces of his cork without making any further manifestation.

I was very indignant; and I know that my cheeks must have been extremely red, if I could judge by the flush of heat which I felt rise to my face. This would enable me to explain the words I heard through all the buzzing in my ears:

"I am frightened about him! our poor friend! . . . Monsieur Mouche, be kind enough to open a window! It seems to me that a compress of arnica would do him some good."

I rushed out into the street with an unspeakable feeling of shame.

"My poor Jeanne!"

December 20.

I PASSED eight days without hearing anything further in regard to the Préfère establishment. Then, feeling myself unable to remain any longer without some news of Clémentine's daughter, and feeling furthermore that I owed it as a duty to myself not to cease my visits to the school without more serious cause, I took my way to Les Ternes.

The parlour seemed to me more cold, more damp, more inhospitable, and more insidious than ever before; and the servant much more silent and much more scared. I asked to see Mademoiselle Jeanne; but, after a very considerable time, it was Mademoiselle Préfère who made her appearance instead—severe and pale, with lips compressed and a hard look in her eyes.

"Monsieur," she said, folding her arms over her pelerine, "I regret very much that I cannot allow you to see Mademoiselle Alexandre to-day; but I cannot possibly do it."

"Why not?" I asked in astonishment.

"Monsieur," she replied, "the reasons which compel me to request that your visits shall be less frequent hereafter are of an excessively delicate nature; and I must beg you to spare me the unpleasantness of mentioning them."

"Madame," I replied, "I have been authorized by Jeanne's guardian to see his ward every day. Will you please to inform me of your reasons for opposing the will of Monsieur Mouche?"

"The *guardian* of Mademoiselle Alexandre," she replied (and she dwelt upon that word "guardian" as upon a solid support), "desires, quite as strongly as I myself do, that your assiduities may come to an end as soon as possible."

"Then, if that be the case," I said, "be kind enough to let me know his reasons and your own."

She looked up at the little spiral of paper on the ceiling, and then replied, with stern composure,

"You insist upon it? Well, although such explanations are very painful for a woman to make, I will yield to your exaction. This house, Monsieur, is an honourable house. I have my responsibility. I have to watch like a mother over each one of my pupils. Your assiduities in regard to Mademoiselle Alexandre could not possibly be continued without serious injury to the young girl herself; and it is my duty to insist that they shall cease."

"I do not really understand you," I replied—and I was telling the plain truth. Then she deliberately resumed:

"Your assiduities in this house are being interpreted, by the most respectable and the least suspicious persons, in such a manner that I find myself obliged, both in the interest of my establishment and in the interest of Mademoiselle Alexandre, to see that they end at once."

"Madame," I cried, "I have heard a great many silly things in my life, but never anything so silly as what you have just said!"

She answered me very quietly,

"Your words of abuse will not affect me in the slightest. When one has a duty to accomplish, one is strong enough to endure all."

And she pressed her pelerine over her heart once more—not perhaps on this occasion to restrain, but doubtless only to caress that generous heart.

"Madame," I said, shaking my finger at her, "you have wantonly aroused the indignation of an aged man. Be good enough to act in such a fashion that the old man may be able at least to forget your existence, and do not add fresh insults to those which I have already sustained from your lips. I give you fair warning that I shall never cease to look after Mademoiselle Alexandre; and that should you attempt to do her any harm, in any manner whatsoever, you will have serious reason to regret it!"

The more I became excited, the more she became cool; and she answered in a tone of superb indifference:

"Monsieur, I am much too well informed in regard to the nature of the interest which you take in this young girl, not to withdraw her immediately from that very surveillance with which you threaten me. After observing the more than equivocal intimacy in which you are living with your housekeeper, I ought to have taken measures at once to render it impossible for you ever to come into contact with an innocent child. In the future I shall certainly do it. If up to this time I have been too trustful, it is for Mademoiselle Alexandre, and not for you, to reproach me with it. But she is too artless and too pure—thanks to me!—ever to have suspected the nature of that danger into which you were trying to lead her. I scarcely suppose that you will place me under the necessity of enlightening her upon the subject."

"Come, my poor old Bonnard," I said to myself, as I shrugged my shoulders—"so you had to live as long as this in order to learn for the first time exactly what a wicked woman is. And now your knowledge of the subject is complete."

I went out without replying; and I had the pleasure of observing, from the sudden flush which overspread the face of the schoolmistress, that my silence had wounded her far more than my words.

As I passed through the court I looked about me in every direction for Jeanne. She was watching for me, and she ran to me.

"If anybody touches one little hair of your head, Jeanne, write to me! Good-bye!"

"No, not good-bye."

I replied,

"Well, no—not good-bye! Write to me!"

I went straight to Madame de Gabry's residence.

"Madame is at Rome with Monsieur. Did not Monsieur know it?"

"Why, yes," I replied. "Madame wrote to me." . . .

She had indeed written to me in regard to her leaving home; but my head must have become very much confused, so that I had forgotten all about it. The servant seemed to be of the same opinion, for he looked at me in a way that seemed to signify, "Monsieur Bonnard is doting"—and he leaned down over the balustrade of the stairway to see if I was not going to do something extraordinary before I got to the bottom. But I descended the stairs rationally enough; and then he drew back his head in disappointment.

On returning home I was informed that Monsieur Gélis was waiting for me in the parlour. (This young man has become a constant visitor. His judgment is at fault at times; but his mind is not at all commonplace.) On this occasion, however, his usually welcome visit only embarrassed me. "Alas!" I thought to myself, "I shall be sure to say something very stupid to my young friend to-day, and he

also will think that my faculties are becoming impaired. But still I
cannot really explain to him that I had first been demanded in wedlock, and subsequently traduced as a man wholly devoid of morals
—that even Thérèse had become an object of suspicion—and that
Jeanne remains in the power of the most rascally woman on the
face of the earth. I am certainly in an admirable state of mind for
conversing about Cistercian abbeys with a young and mischievously minded man. Nevertheless, we shall see—we shall try." . . .

But Thérèse stopped me:

"How red you are, Monsieur!" she exclaimed, in a tone of reproach.

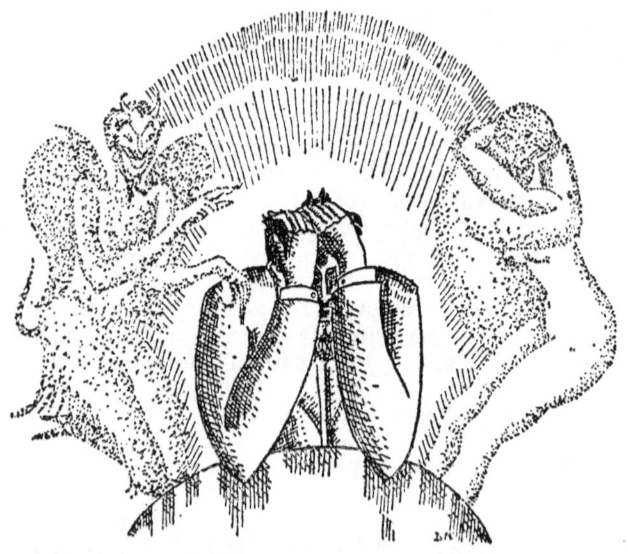

"It must be the spring," I answered.

She cried out,

"The spring!—in the month of December?"

That is a fact! this is December. Ah! what is the matter with my
head? what a fine help I am going to be to poor Jeanne!

"Thérèse, take my cane; and put it, if you possibly can, in some
place where I shall be able to find it again.

"Good-day, Monsieur Gélis. How are you?"

Undated.

NEXT morning the old boy wanted to get up; but the old boy
could not get up. A merciless invisible hand kept him down upon
his bed. Finding himself immovably riveted there, the old boy resigned himself to remain motionless; but his thoughts kept running in all directions.

He must have had a very violent fever; for Mademoiselle Préfère, the Abbots of Saint-Germain-des-Prés, and the servant of Madame de Gabry appeared to him in divers fantastic shapes. The figure of the servant in particular lengthened weirdly over his head, grimacing like some gargoyle of a cathedral. Then it seemed to me that there were a great many people, much too many people, in my bedroom.

This bedroom of mine is furnished after the antiquated fashion. The portrait of my father in full uniform, and the portrait of my mother in her cashmere dress, are suspended on the wall. The wall-paper is covered with green foliage designs. I am aware of all this, and I am even conscious that everything is faded, very much faded. But an old man's room does not require to be pretty; it is enough that it should be clean, and Thérèse sees to that. At all events my room is sufficiently decorated to please a mind like mine, which has always remained somewhat childish and dreamy. There are things hanging on the wall or scattered over the tables and shelves which usually please my fancy and amuse me. But to-day it would seem as if all those objects had suddenly conceived some kind of ill-will against me. They have all become garish, grimacing, menacing. That statuette, modelled after one of the Theological Virtues of Notre-Dame de Brou, always so ingenuously graceful in its natural condition, is now making contortions and putting out its tongue at me. And that beautiful miniature—in which one of the most skilful pupils of Jehan Fouquet depicted himself, girdled with the cord-girdle of the Sons of St. Francis, offering his book, on bended knee, to the good Duc d'Angoulême—who has taken it out of its frame and put in its place a great ugly cat's head, which stares at me with phosphorescent eyes. And the designs on the wall-paper have also turned into heads—hideous green heads. . . . But no—I am sure that wall-paper must have foliage-designs upon it at this moment just as it had twenty years ago, and nothing else. . . . But no, again—I was right before—they are heads, with eyes, noses, mouths—they are heads! . . . Ah! now I understand! they are both heads and foliage-designs at the same time. I wish I could not see them at all.

And there, on my right, the pretty miniature of the Franciscan has come back again; but it seems to me as if I can only keep it in its frame by a tremendous effort of will, and that the moment I get tired the ugly cat-head will appear in its place. Certainly I am not delirious; I can see Thérèse very plainly, standing at the foot of my bed; I can hear her speaking to me perfectly well, and I should be able to answer her quite satisfactorily if I were not kept so busy in trying to compel the various objects about me to maintain their natural aspect.

Here is the doctor coming. I never sent for him, but it gives me pleasure to see him. He is an old neighbour of mine; I have never been of much service to him, but I like him very much. Even if I do not say much to him, I have at least full possession of all my faculties, and I even find myself extraordinarily crafty and observant to-day, for I note all his gestures, his every look, the least wrinkling of his face. But the doctor is very cunning, too, and I cannot really tell what he thinks about me. The deep thought of Goethe suddenly comes to my mind, and I exclaim,

"Doctor, the old man has consented to allow himself to become sick; but he does not intend, this time at least, to make any further concessions to nature."

Neither the doctor nor Thérèse laughs at my little joke. I suppose they cannot have understood it.

The doctor goes away; evening comes; and all sorts of strange shadows begin to shape themselves about my bed-curtains, forming and dissolving by turns. And other shadows—ghosts—throng by before me; and through them I can see distinctly the impassive face of my faithful servant. And suddenly a cry, a shrill cry, a great cry of distress, rends my ears. Was it you who called me, Jeanne?

The day is over; and the shadows take their places at my bedside to remain with me all through the long night.

Then morning comes—I feel a peace, a vast peace, wrapping me all about.

Art Thou about to take me into Thy rest, my dear Lord God?

February 186–.

THE doctor is quite jovial. It seems that I am doing him a great deal of credit by being able to get out of bed. If I must believe him, innumerable disorders must have pounced down upon my poor old body all at the same time.

These disorders, which are the terror of ordinary mankind, have names which are the terror of philologists. They are hybrid names, half Greek, half Latin, with terminations in "itis," indicating the inflammatory condition, and in "algia," indicating pain. The doctor gives me all their names, together with a corresponding number of adjectives ending in "ic," which serve to characterise their detestable qualities. In short, they represent a good half of that most perfect copy of the Dictionary of Medicine contained in the too-authentic box of Pandora.

"Doctor, what an excellent common-sense story the story of Pandora is!—if I were a poet I would put it into French verse. Shake hands, doctor! You have brought me back to life; I forgive you for it. You have given me back to my friends; I thank you for it. You say I am quite strong. That may be, that may be; but I have lasted a very long time. I am a very old article of furniture; I might be very satisfactorily compared to my father's arm-chair. It was an arm-chair which the good man had inherited, and in which he used

to lounge from morning until evening. Twenty times a day, when I was quite a baby, I used to climb up and seat myself on one of the arms of that old-fashioned chair. So long as the chair remained intact, nobody paid any particular attention to it. But it began to limp on one foot; and then folks began to say that it was a very good chair. Afterwards it became lame in three legs, squeaked with the fourth leg, and lost nearly half of both arms. Then everybody would exclaim, 'What a strong chair!' They wondered how it was that after its arms had been worn off and all its legs knocked out of perpendicular, it could yet preserve the recognisable shape of a chair, remain nearly erect, and still be of some service. The horsehair came out of its body at last, and it gave up the ghost. And when Cyprien, our servant, sawed up its mutilated members for fire-wood, everybody redoubled their cries of admiration. 'Oh! what an excellent—what a marvellous chair! It was the chair of Pierre Sylvestre Bonnard, the cloth merchant—of Épiménide Bonnard, his son—of Jean-Baptiste Bonnard, the Pyrrhonian philosopher and Chief of the Third Maritime Division. Oh! what a robust and venerable chair!' In reality it was a dead chair. Well, doctor, I am that chair. You think I am solid because I have been able to resist an attack which would have killed many people, and which only three-fourths killed me. Much obliged! I feel none the less that I am something which has been irremediably damaged."

The doctor tries to prove to me, with the help of enormous Greek and Latin words, that I am really in a very good condition. It would, of course, be useless to attempt any demonstration of this kind in so lucid a language as French. However, I allow him to persuade me at last; and I see him to the door.

"Good! good!" exclaimed Thérèse; "that is the way to put the doctor out of the house! Just do the same thing once or twice again, and he will not come to see you any more—and so much the better?"

"Well, Thérèse, now that I have become such a hearty man again, do not refuse to give me my letters. I am sure there must be quite a big bundle of letters, and it would be very wicked to keep me any longer from reading them."

Thérèse, after some little grumbling, gave me my letters. But what did it matter?—I looked at all the envelopes, and saw that no one of them had been addressed by the little hand which I so much wish I could see here now, turning over the pages of the Vecellio. I pushed the whole bundle of letters away: they had no more interest for me.

April–June.

IT was a hotly contested engagement.

"Wait, Monsieur, until I have put on my clean things," exclaimed Thérèse, "and I will go out with you this time also; I will carry your folding-stool as I have been doing these last few days, and we will go and sit down somewhere in the sun."

Thérèse actually thinks me infirm. I have been sick, it is true, but there is an end to all things! Madame Malady has taken her departure quite awhile ago, and it is now more than three months since her pale and gracious-visaged handmaid, Dame Convalescence, politely bade me farewell. If I were to listen to my housekeeper, I should become a veritable *Monsieur Argant,* and I should wear a nightcap with ribbons for the rest of my life. . . . No more of this!—I propose to go out by myself! Thérèse will not hear of it. She takes my folding-stool, and wants to follow me.

"Thérèse, to-morrow, if you like, we will take our seats on the sunny side of the wall of La Petite Provence and stay there just as long as you please. But to-day I have some very important affairs to attend to."

"So much the better! But your affairs are not the only affairs in this world."

I beg; I scold; I make my escape.

It is quite a pleasant day. With the aid of a cab, and the help of God, I trust to be able to fulfil my purpose.

There is the wall on which is painted in great blue letters the words *"Pensionnat de Demoiselles tenu par Mademoiselle Virginie Préfère."* There is the iron gate which would give free entrance into the court-yard if it were ever opened. But the lock is rusty, and sheets of zinc put up behind the bars protect from indiscreet observation those dear little souls to whom Mademoiselle Préfère doubtless teaches modesty, sincerity, justice, and disinterestedness. There is a window, with iron bars before it, and panes daubed over with white paint—the window of the domestic offices, like a glazed eye—the only aperture of the building opening upon the exterior world. As for the house-door, through which I entered so often, but which is now closed against me for ever, it is just as I saw it the last time, with its little iron-grated wicket. The single stone step in front of it is deeply worn, and, without having very good eyes behind my spectacles, I can see the little white scratches on the stone which have been made by the nails in the shoes of the girls going in and out. And why cannot I also go in? I have a feeling that Jeanne must be suffering a great deal in this dismal house, and that she calls my name in secret. I cannot go away from the gate! A strange anxiety takes hold of me. I pull the bell. The scared-looking servant comes to the door, even much more scared-looking than when I saw her the last time. Strict orders have been given; I am not to be allowed to see Mademoiselle Jeanne. I beg the servant to be so kind as to tell me how the child is. The servant, after looking to her right and then to her left, tells me that Mademoiselle Jeanne is well, and then shuts the door in my face. And I am all alone in the street again.

How many times since then have I wandered in the same way under that wall, and passed before the little door,—full of shame and despair to find myself even weaker than that poor child, who has no other help of friend except myself in the world!

Finally I overcame my repugnance sufficiently to call upon Maître Mouche. The first thing I remarked was that his office is much more dusty and much more mouldy this year than it was last year. The notary made his appearance after a moment, with his familiar stiff gestures, and his restless eyes quivering behind his eye-glasses. I made my complaints to him. He answered me. . . . But why should I write down, even in a notebook which I am going to burn, my recollections of a downright scoundrel? He takes sides with Mademoiselle Préfère, whose intelligent mind and irreproachable character he has long appreciated. He does not feel himself in a position to decide the nature of the question at issue; but he must assure me that appearances have been greatly against me. That of course makes no difference to me. He adds—(and this does make some difference to me)—that the small sum which had been placed in his hands to defray the expenses of the education of his ward has been expended, and that, in view of the circumstances, he cannot but gently admire the disinterestedness of Mademoiselle Préfère in consenting to allow Mademoiselle Jeanne to remain with her.

A magnificent light, the light of a perfect day, floods the sordid place with its incorruptible torrent, and illuminates the person of that man!

And outside it pours down its splendour upon all the wretchedness of a populous quarter.

How sweet it is,—this light with which my eyes have so long been filled, and which ere long I must for ever cease to enjoy! I wander out with my hands behind me, dreaming as I go, following the line of the fortifications; and I find myself after awhile, I know not how, in an out-of-the-way suburb full of miserable little gardens. By the dusty roadside I observe a plant whose flower, at once dark and splendid, seems worthy of association with the noblest and purest mourning for the dead. It is a columbine. Our fathers called it "Our Lady's Glove"—*le gant de Notre-Dame*. Only such a "Notre-Dame" as might make herself very, very small, for the sake of appearing to little children, could ever slip her dainty fingers into the narrow capsule of that flower.

And there is a big bumble-bee who tries to force himself into the flower, brutally; but his mouth cannot reach the nectar, and the poor glutton strives and strives in vain. He has to give up the attempt, and comes out of the flower all smeared over with pollen. He flies off in his own heavy lumbering way; but there are not many flowers in this portion of the suburbs, which has been defiled by the soot and smoke of factories. So he comes back to the columbine again, and this time he pierces the corolla and sucks the honey through the little hole which he has made; I should never have thought that a bumble-bee had so much sense! Why, that is admirable! The more I observe them, the more do insects and flowers fill me with astonishment. I am like that good Rollin who went wild with delight over the flowers of his peach-trees. I wish I could have a fine garden, and live at the verge of a wood.

August, September.

IT occurred to me one Sunday morning to watch for the moment when Mademoiselle Préfère's pupils were leaving the school in procession to attend Mass at the parish church. I watched them passing two by two,—the little ones first with very serious faces. There were three of them all dressed exactly alike—dumpy, plump, important-looking little creatures, whom I recognised at once as the Mouton girls. Their elder sister is the artist who drew that terrible head of Tatius, King of the Sabines. Beside the column, the assistant school-teacher, with her prayer-book in her hand, was gesturing and frowning. Then came the next oldest class, and finally the big girls, all whispering to each other, as they went by. But I did not see Jeanne.

I went to police-headquarters and inquired whether they chanced to have, filed away somewhere or other, any information regarding the establishment in the Rue Demours. I succeeded in inducing them to send some female inspectors there. These returned bringing with them the most favourable reports about the establishment. In their opinion the Préfère School was a model school. It is evident that if I were to force an investigation, Mademoiselle Préfère would receive academic honours.

October 3.

THIS Thursday being a school-holiday I had the chance of meeting the three little Mouton girls in the vicinity of the Rue Demours. After bowing to their mother, I asked the eldest who appears to be about ten years old, how was her playmate, Mademoiselle Jeanne Alexandre.

The little Mouton girl answered me, all in a breath,

"Jeanne Alexandre is not my playmate. She is only kept in the school for charity—so they make her sweep the class-rooms. It was Mademoiselle who said so. And Jeanne Alexandre is a bad girl; so they lock her up in the dark room—and it serves her right—and I am a good girl—and I am never locked up in the dark room."

The three little girls resumed their walk, and Madame Mouton followed close behind them, looking back over her broad shoulder at me, in a very suspicious manner.

Alas! I find myself reduced to expedients of a questionable character. Madame de Gabry will not come back to Paris for at least three months more, at the very soonest. Without her, I have no tact, I have no common sense—I am nothing but a cumbersome, clumsy, mischief-making machine.

Nevertheless, I cannot possibly permit them to make Jeanne a boarding-school servant!

December 28.

THE idea that Jeanne was obliged to sweep the rooms had become absolutely unbearable.

The weather was dark and cold. Night had already begun. I rang the school-door bell with the tranquillity of a resolute man. The moment that the timid servant opened the door, I slipped a gold piece into her hand, and promised her another if she would arrange matters so that I could see Mademoiselle Alexandre. Her answer was,

"In one hour from now, at the grated window."

And she slammed the door in my face so rudely that she knocked my hat into the gutter. I waited for one very long hour in a violent snow-storm; then I approached the window. Nothing! The wind raged, and the snow fell heavily. Workmen passing by with their implements on their shoulders, and their heads bent down to keep the snow from coming in their faces, rudely jostled me. Still nothing. I began to fear I had been observed. I knew that I had done wrong in bribing a servant, but I was not a bit sorry for it. Woe to the man who does not know how to break through social regulations in case of necessity! Another quarter of an hour passed. Nothing. At last the window was partly opened.

"Is that you, Monsieur Bonnard?"

"Is that you, Jeanne?—tell me at once what has become of you."

"I am well—very well."

"But what else!"

"They have put me in the kitchen, and I have to sweep the school-rooms."

"In the kitchen! Sweeping—you! Gracious goodness!"

"Yes, because my guardian does not pay for my schooling any longer."

"Gracious goodness! Your guardian seems to me to be a thorough scoundrel."

"Then you know——"

"What?"

"Oh! don't ask me to tell you that!—but I would rather die than find myself alone with him again."

"And why did you not write to me?"

"I was watched."

At that instant I formed a resolve which nothing in this world could have induced me to change. I did, indeed, have some idea that I might be acting contrary to law; but I did not give myself the least concern about that idea. And, being firmly resolved, I was able to be prudent. I acted with remarkable coolness.

"Jeanne," I asked, "tell me! does that room you are in open into the court-yard?"

"Yes."

"Can you open the street-door from the inside yourself?"

"Yes,—if there is nobody in the porter's lodge."

"Go and see if there is any one there, and be careful that nobody observes you."

Then I waited, keeping a watch on the door and window.

In six or seven seconds Jeanne reappeared behind the bars, and said,

"The servant is in the porter's lodge."

"Very well," I said, "have you a pen and ink?"

"No."

"A pencil?"

"Yes."

"Pass it out here."

I took an old newspaper out of my pocket, and—in a wind which blew almost hard enough to put the street-lamps out, in a downpour of snow which almost blinded me—I managed to wrap up and address that paper to Mademoiselle Préfère.

While I was writing I asked Jeanne,

"When the postman passes he puts the papers and letters in the box, doesn't he? He rings the bell and goes away? Then the servant opens the letter-box and takes whatever she finds there to Mademoiselle Préfère immediately; is not that about the way the thing is managed whenever anything comes by post?"

Jeanne thought it was.

"Then we shall soon see. Jeanne, go and watch again; and, as soon as the servant leaves the lodge, open the door and come out here to me."

Having said this, I put my newspaper in the box, gave the bell a tremendous pull, and then hid myself in the embrasure of a neighbouring door.

I might have been there several minutes, when the little door quivered, then opened, and a young girl's head made its appearance through the opening. I took hold of it; I pulled it towards me.

"Come, Jeanne! come!"

She stared at me uneasily. Certainly she must have been afraid that I had gone mad; but, on the contrary, I was very rational indeed.

"Come, my child! come!"

"Where?"

"To Madame de Gabry's."

Then she took my arm. For some time we ran like a couple of thieves. But running is an exercise ill-suited to one as corpulent as

I am, and, finding myself out of breath at last, I stopped and leaned upon something which turned out to be the stove of a dealer in roasted chestnuts, who was doing business at the corner of a wine-seller's shop, where a number of cabmen were drinking. One of them asked us if we did not want a cab. Most assuredly we wanted a cab! The driver, after setting down his glass on the zinc counter, climbed upon his seat and urged his horse forward. We were saved.

"Phew!" I panted, wiping my forehead. For, in spite of the cold, I was perspiring profusely.

What seemed very odd was that Jeanne appeared to be much more conscious than I was of the enormity which we had committed. She looked very serious indeed, and was visibly uneasy.

"In the kitchen!" I cried out, with indignation.

She shook her head, as if to say, "Well, there or anywhere else, what does it matter to me?" And by the light of the street-lamps, I observed with pain that her face was very thin and her features all pinched. I did not find in her any of that vivacity, any of those bright impulses, any of that quickness of expression, which used to please me so much. Her gaze had become timid, her gestures constrained, her whole attitude melancholy. I took her hand—a little cold hand, which had become all hardened and bruised. The poor child must have suffered very much. I questioned her. She told me very quietly that Mademoiselle Préfère had summoned her one day, and called her a little monster and a little viper, for some reason which she had never been able to learn.

She had added, "You shall not see Monsieur Bonnard any more; for he has been giving you bad advice, and he has conducted himself in a most shameful manner towards me." "I then said to her, 'That, Mademoiselle, you will never be able to make me believe.' Then Mademoiselle slapped my face and sent me back to the school-room. The announcement that I should never be allowed to see you again made me feel as if night had come down upon me. Don't you know those evenings when one feels so sad to see the darkness come?—well, just imagine such a moment stretched out into weeks —into whole months! Don't you remember my little Saint-George? Up to that time I had worked at it as well as I could—just simply to work at it—just to amuse myself. But when I lost all hope of ever seeing you again I took my little wax figure, and I began to work at it in quite another way. I did not try to model it with wooden matches any more, as I had been doing, but with hair pins. I even made use of *épingles à la neige*. But perhaps you do not know what *épingles à la neige* are? Well, I became more particular about it than you can possibly imagine. I put a dragon on Saint-George's helmet; and I passed hours and hours in making a head and eyes and a tail for the dragon. Oh, the eyes! the eyes, above all! I never stopped working at them till I got them so that they had red pupils and white eye-lids and eye-brows and everything! I know I am very

silly; I had an idea that I was going to die as soon as my little
Saint-George would be finished. I worked at it during recreation-
hours, and Mademoiselle Préfère used to let me alone. One day I
learned that you were in the parlour with the schoolmistress; I
watched for you; we said *Au revoir!* that day to each other. I was
a little consoled by seeing you. But, some time after that, my guardian came and wanted to make me go out with him one Thursday.
I refused to go to his house,—but please don't ask me why, Monsieur. He answered me, quite gently, that I was a very whimsical
little girl. And then he left me alone. But the next day Mademoiselle
Préfère came to me with such a wicked look on her face that I was
really afraid. She had a letter in her hand. 'Mademoiselle,' she said
to me, 'I am informed by your guardian that he has spent all the
money which belonged to you. Don't be afraid! I do not intend to
abandon you; but, you must acknowledge yourself, it is only right
that you should earn your own livelihood.' Then she put me to work
house-cleaning; and whenever I made a mistake she would lock me
up in the garret for days together. And that is what has happened
to me since I saw you last. Even if I had been able to write to you
I do not know whether I should have done it, because I did not
think you could possibly take me away from the school; and, as
Maître Mouche did not come back to see me, there was no hurry. I
thought I could wait for awhile in the garret and the kitchen."

"Jeanne," I cried, "even if we should have to flee to Oceania, the
abominable Préfère shall never get hold of you again. I will take a
great oath on that! And why should we not go to Oceania? The
climate is very healthy; and I read in a newspaper the other day
that they have pianos there. But, in the meantime, let us go to the
house of Madame de Gabry, who returned to Paris, as luck would
have it, some three or four days ago; for you and I are two innocent fools, and we have great need of some one to help us."

Even as I was speaking Jeanne's features suddenly became pale,
and seemed to shrink into lifelessness; her eyes became all dim;
her lips, half open, contracted with an expression of pain. Then her
head sank sideways on her shoulder;—she had fainted.

I lifted her in my arms, and carried her up Madame de Gabry's
staircase like a little baby asleep. But I was myself on the point of
fainting, from emotional excitement and fatigue together, when
she came to herself again.

"Ah! it is you," she said: "so much the better!"

Such was our condition when we rang our friend's door-bell.

Same day.

It was eight o'clock. Madame de Gabry, as might be supposed,
was very much surprised by our unexpected appearance. But she
welcomed the old man and the child with that glad kindness which

always expresses itself in her beautiful gestures. It seems to me,—
if I might use that language of devotion so familiar to her,—it
seems to me as though some heavenly grace streams from her
hands whenever she opens them; and even the perfume which im-
pregnates her robes seems to inspire the sweet calm zeal of charity
and good works. Surprised she certainly was; but she asked us no
questions,—and that silence seemed to me admirable.

"Madame," I said to her, "we have both come to place ourselves
under your protection. And, first of all, we are going to ask you to
give us some supper—or to give Jeanne some, at least; for a moment ago, in the carriage, she fainted from weakness. As for myself, I could not eat a bite at this late hour without passing a night
of agony in consequence. I hope that Monsieur de Gabry is well."

"Oh, he is here!" she said.

And she called him immediately.

"Come in here, Paul! Come and see Monsieur Bonnard and
Mademoiselle Alexandre."

He came. It was a pleasure for me to see his frank broad face,
and to press his strong square hand. Then we went, all four of us,
into the dining-room; and while some cold meat was being cut for
Jeanne—which she never touched notwithstanding—I related our
adventure. Paul de Gabry asked me permission to smoke his pipe,
after which he listened to me in silence. When I had finished my recital he scratched the short, stiff beard upon his chin, and uttered
a tremendous *"Sacrebleu!"* But, seeing Jeanne stare at each of us
in turn, with a frightened look in her face, he added:

. "We will talk about this matter to-morrow morning. Come into
my study for a moment; I have an old book to show you that I
want you to tell me something about."

I followed him into his study, where the steel of guns and hunting knives, suspended against the dark hangings, glimmered in the
lamp-light. There, pulling me down beside him upon a leather-
covered sofa, he exclaimed,

"What have you done? Great God! Do you know what you have
done? Corruption of a minor, abduction, kidnapping! You have got
yourself into a nice mess! You have simply rendered yourself liable
to a sentence of imprisonment of not less than five nor more than
ten years."

"Mercy on us!" I cried; "ten years imprisonment for having
saved an innocent child."

"That is the law!" answered Monsieur de Gabry. "You see, my
dear Monsieur Bonnard, I happen to know the Code pretty well—
not because I ever studied law as a profession, but because, as
mayor of Lusance, I was obliged to teach myself something about
it in order to be able to give information to my subordinates.
Mouche is a rascal; that woman Préfère is a vile hussy; and you

are a . . . Well! I really cannot find any word strong enough to signify what you are!"

After opening his bookcase, where dog-collars, riding-whips, stir-rups, spurs, cigar-boxes, and a few books of reference were indiscriminately stowed away, he took out of it a copy of the Code, and began to turn over the leaves.

" 'CRIMES AND MISDEMEANOURS' . . . 'SEQUESTRATION OF PERSONS'—that is not your case. . . . 'ABDUCTION OF MINORS'—here we are. . . . 'ARTICLE 354:—*Whosoever shall, either by fraud or violence, have abducted or have caused to be abducted any minor or minors, or shall have enticed them, or turned them away from, or forcibly removed them, or shall have caused them to be enticed, or turned away from or forcibly removed from the places in which they have been placed by those to whose authority or direction they have been submitted or confided, shall be liable to the penalty of imprisonment. See* PENAL CODE, *21 and 28.*' Here is 21:—'*The term of imprisonment shall not be less than five years.*' 28. '*The sentence of imprisonment shall be considered as involving a loss of civil rights.*' Now all that is very plain, is it not, Monsieur Bonnard?"

"Perfectly plain."

"Now let us go on: 'ARTICLE 356:—*In case the abductor be under the age of 21 years at the time of the offense, he shall only be punished with*' . . . But we certainly cannot invoke this article in your favour. 'ARTICLE 357:—*In case the abductor shall have married the girl by him abducted, he can only be prosecuted at the instance of such persons as, according to the Civil Code, may have the right to demand that the marriage shall be declared null; nor can he be condemned until after the nullity of the marriage shall have been pronounced.*' I do not know whether it is a part of your plans to marry Mademoiselle Alexandre! You can see that the Code is good-natured about it; it leaves you one door of escape. But no—I ought not to joke with you, because really you have put yourself in a very unfortunate position! And how could a man like you imagine that here in Paris, in the middle of the nineteenth century, a young girl can be abducted with absolute impunity? We are not living in the Middle Ages now; and such things are no longer permitted by law."

"You need not imagine," I replied, "that abduction was lawful under the ancient Code. You will find in Baluze a decree issued by King Childebert at Cologne, either in 593 or 594, on the subject: moreover, everybody knows that the famous *Ordonnance de Blois,* of May 1579, formally enacted that any persons convicted of having suborned any son or daughter under the age of twenty-five years, whether under promise of marriage or otherwise, without the full knowledge, will, or consent of the father, mother, and guardians, should be punished with death; and the ordinance adds: '*Et pareillement seront punis extraordinairement tous ceux qui auront participé audit rapt, et qui auront prêté conseil, confort, et aide en aucune manière que ce soit.'* (And in like manner shall be extraordinarily punished all persons whomsoever, who shall have participated in the said abduction, and who shall have given thereunto counsel, succor, or aid in any manner whatsoever.) Those are the exact, or very nearly the exact, terms of the ordinance. As for that article of the Code-Napoléon which you have just told me of, and which excepts from liability to prosecution the abductor who marries the young girl abducted by him, it reminds me that according to the laws of Bretagne, forcible abduction, followed by marriage, was not punished. But this usage, which involved various abuses, was suppressed in 1720—at least I give you the date within ten years. My memory is not very good now, and the time is long passed when I could repeat by heart without even stopping to take breath, fifteen hundred verses of Girart de Roussillon.

"As far as regards the Capitulary of Charlemagne, which fixes the compensation for abduction, I have not mentioned it because I am sure that you must remember it. So, my dear Monsieur de Gabry, you see abduction was considered as a decidedly punishable offense under the three dynasties of Old France. It is a very great mistake to suppose that the Middle Ages represent a period of social chaos. You must remember, on the contrary——"

Monsieur de Gabry here interrupted me:

"So," he exclaimed, "you know the *Ordonnance de Blois,* you know Baluze, you know Childebert, you know the Capitularies—and you don't know anything about the Code-Napoléon!"

I replied that, as a matter of fact, I never had read the Code; and he looked very much surprised.

"And now do you understand," he asked, "the extreme gravity of the action you have committed?"

I had not indeed been yet able to understand it fully. But little by little, with the aid of Monsieur Paul's very sensible explanations, I reached the conviction at last that I should not be judged in regard to my motives, which were innocent, but only according to my action, which was punishable. Thereupon I began to feel very despondent, and to utter divers lamentations.

"What am I to do?" I cried out, "what am I to do? Am I then irretrievably ruined?—and have I also ruined the poor child whom I wanted to save?"

Monsieur de Gabry silently filled his pipe, and lighted it so slowly that his kind broad face remained for at least three or four minutes glowing red behind the light, like a blacksmith's in the gleam of his forge-fire. Then he said,

"You want to know what to do? Why, don't do anything, my dear Monsieur Bonnard! For God's sake, and for your own sake, don't do anything at all! Your situation is bad enough as it is; don't try to meddle with it now, unless you want to create new difficulties for yourself. But you must promise me to sustain me in any action that

I may take. I shall go to see Monsieur Mouche the very first thing to-morrow morning; and if he turns out to be what we think he is —that is to say, a consummate rascal—I shall very soon find means of making him harmless, even if the devil himself should take sides with him. For everything depends on him. As it is too late this evening to take Mademoiselle Jeanne back to her boarding-school, my wife will keep the young lady here to-night. This of course plainly constitutes the misdemeanour of complicity; but it saves the girl from anything like an equivocal position. As for you, my dear Monsieur, you just go back to the Quai Malaquais as quickly as you can; and if they come to look for Jeanne there, it will be very easy for you to prove she is not in your house."

While we were thus talking, Madame de Gabry was preparing to make her young lodger comfortable for the night. When she bade me good-bye at the door, she was carrying a pair of clean sheets, scented with lavender, thrown over her arm.

"That," I said, "is a sweet honest smell."

"Well, of course," answered Madame de Gabry, "you must remember we are peasants."

"Ah!" I answered her, "Heaven grant that I also may be able one of these days to become a peasant! Heaven grant that one of these days I may be able, as you are at Lusance, to inhale the sweet fresh odour of the country, and live in some little house all hidden among trees; and if this wish of mine be too ambitious on the part of an old man whose life is nearly closed, then I will only wish that my winding-sheet may be as sweetly scented with lavender as that linen you have on your arm."

It was agreed that I should come to lunch the following morning. But I was positively forbidden to show myself at the house before midday. Jeanne, as she kissed me good-bye, begged me not to take her back to the school any more. We felt much affected at parting, and very anxious.

I found Thérèse waiting for me on the landing, in such a condition of worry about me that it had made her furious. She talked of nothing less than keeping me under lock and key in the future.

What a night I passed! I never closed my eyes for one single instant. From time to time I could not help laughing like a boy at the success of my prank; and then again, an inexpressible feeling of horror would come upon me at the thought of being dragged before some magistrate, and having to take my place upon the prisoner's bench, to answer for the crime which I had so naturally committed. I was very much afraid; and nevertheless I felt no remorse or regret whatever. The sun, coming into my room at last, merrily lighted upon the foot of my bed, and then I made this prayer:

"My God, Thou who didst make the sky and the dew, as it is said in *Tristan,* judge me in Thine equity, not indeed according unto my acts, but according only to my motives, which Thou knowest have

been upright and pure; and I will say: Glory to Thee in heaven, and peace on earth to men of good-will. I give into Thy hands the child I stole away. Do that for her which I have not known how to do; guard her from all her enemies;—and blessed for ever be Thy name!"

December 29.

WHEN I arrived at Madame de Gabry's, I found Jeanne completely transfigured.

Had she also, like myself, at the first light of dawn, called upon Him who made the sky and the dew? She smiled with such a sweet calm smile!

Madame de Gabry called her away to arrange her hair; for the amiable lady had insisted upon combing and plaiting, with her own hands, the hair of the child confided to her care. As I had come a little before the hour agreed upon, I had interrupted this charming toilet. By way of punishment I was told to go and wait in the parlour all by myself. Monsieur de Gabry joined me there in a little while. He had evidently just come in, for I could see on his forehead the mark left by the lining of his hat. His frank face wore an expression of joyful excitement. I thought I had better not ask him any questions; and we all went to lunch. When the servants had finished waiting at table, Monsieur Paul, who had been keeping his good story for the dessert, said to us,

"Well! I went to Levallois."

"Did you see Maître Mouche?" excitedly inquired Madame de Gabry.

"No," he replied, curiously watching the expression of disappointment upon our faces.

After having amused himself with our anxiety for a reasonable time, the good fellow added:

"Maître Mouche is no longer at Levallois. Maître Mouche has gone away from France. The day after to-morrow will make just eight days since he decamped, taking with him all the money of his clients—a tolerably large sum. I found the office closed. A woman who lived close by told me all about it with an abundance of curses and imprecations. The notary did not take the 7.55 train all by himself; he took with him the daughter of the hairdresser of Levallois, a young person quite famous in that part of the country for her beauty and her accomplishments;—they say she could shave better than her father. Well, anyhow Mouche has run away with her; the Commissaire de Police confirmed the fact for me. Now, really, could it have been possible for Maître Mouche to have left the country at a more opportune moment? If he had only deferred his escapade one week longer, he would have been still the representative of society, and would have had you dragged off to gaol, Monsieur Bonnard, like a criminal. At present we have nothing whatever to fear from him. Here is to the health of Maître Mouche!" he cried, pouring out a glass of white wine.

I would like to live a long time if it were only to remember that delightful morning. We four were all assembled in the big white dining-room around the waxed oak table. Monsieur Paul's mirth was of the hearty kind,—even perhaps a little riotous; and the good man quaffed deeply. Madame de Gabry smiled at me, with a smile so sweet, so perfect, and so noble, that I thought such a woman ought to keep smiles like that simply as a reward for good actions, and thus make everybody who knew her do all the good of which they were capable. Then, to reward us for our pains, Jeanne, who had regained something of her former vivacity, asked us in less than a quarter of an hour one dozen questions, to answer which would have required an exhaustive exposition of the nature of man, the nature of the universe, the science of physics and of metaphysics, the Macrocosm and the Microcosm—not to speak of the Ineffable and the Unknowable. Then she drew out of her pocket her little Saint-George, who had suffered most cruelly during our flight. His legs and arms were gone; but he still had his gold helmet with the green dragon on it. Jeanne solemnly pledged herself to make a restoration of him in honour of Madame de Gabry.

Delightful friends! I left them at last overwhelmed with fatigue and joy.

On re-entering my lodgings I had to endure the very sharpest remonstrances from Thérèse, who said she had given up trying to understand my new way of living. In her opinion Monsieur had really lost his mind.

"Yes, Thérèse, I am a mad old man and you are a mad old woman. That is certain! May the good God bless us both, Thérèse, and give us new strength; for we now have new duties to perform. But let me lie down upon the sofa; for I really cannot keep myself on my feet any longer."

January 15, 186–.

"Good-morning, Monsieur," said Jeanne, letting herself in; while Thérèse remained grumbling in the corridor because she had not been able to get to the door in time.

"Mademoiselle, I beg you will be kind enough to address me very solemnly by my title, and to say to me, 'Good-morning, my guardian.'"

"Then it has all been settled? Oh, how nice!" cried the child, clapping her hands.

"It has all been arranged, Mademoiselle, in the *Salle-commune* and before the Justice of the Peace; and from to-day you are under my authority. . . . What are you laughing about, my ward? I see it in your eyes. You have some crazy idea in your head this very moment—some more nonsense, eh?"

"Oh, no! Monsieur. . . . I mean, my guardian. I was looking at your white hair. It curls out from under the edge of your hat like honeysuckle on a balcony. It is very handsome, and I like it very much!"

"Be good enough to sit down, my ward, and, if you can possibly help it, stop saying ridiculous things, because I have some very serious things to say to you. Listen. I suppose you are not going to insist upon being sent back to the establishment of Mademoiselle Préfère? . . . No. Well, then, what would you say if I should take you here to live with me, and to finish your education, and keep you here until . . . what shall I say?—for ever, as the song has it?"

"Oh, Monsieur!" she cried, flushing crimson with pleasure.

I continued,

"Behind there we have a nice little room, which my housekeeper has cleaned up and furnished for you. You are going to take the place of the books which used to be in it; you will succeed them as the day succeeds night. Go with Thérèse and look at it, and see if you think you will be able to live in it. Madame de Gabry and I have made up our minds that you can sleep there to-night."

She had already started to run; I called her back for a moment.

"Jeanne, listen to me a moment longer! You have always until now made yourself a favourite with my housekeeper, who, like all very old people, is apt to be cross at times. Be gentle and forbearing. Make every allowance for her. I have thought it my duty to make every allowance for her myself, and to put up with all her fits of impatience. Now, let me tell you, Jeanne:—Respect her! And when I say that, I do not forget that she is my servant and yours; neither will she ever allow herself to forget it for a moment. But what I want you to respect in her is her great age and her great heart. She is a humble woman who has lived a very, very long time in the habit of doing good; and she has become hardened and stiffened in that habit. Bear patiently with the harsh ways of that upright soul. If you know how to command, she will know how to obey. Go now, my child; arrange your room in whatever way may seem to you best suited for your studies and for your repose."

Having started Jeanne, with this viaticum, upon her domestic career, I began to read a Review, which, although conducted by very young men, is excellent. The tone of it is somewhat unpolished, but the spirit zealous. The article I read was certainly far superior, in point of precision and positiveness, to anything of the sort ever written when I was a young man. The author of the article, Monsieur Paul Meyer, points out every error with a remarkably lucid power of incisive criticism.

We used not in my time to criticise with such strict justice. Our indulgence was vast. It went even so far as to confuse the scholar and the ignoramus in the same burst of praise. And nevertheless one must learn how to find fault; and it is even an imperative duty to blame when the blame is deserved.

I remember little Raymond (that was the name we gave him); he did not know anything, and his mind was not a mind capable of absorbing any solid learning; but he was very fond of his mother. We took very good care never to utter a hint of the ignorance of so perfect a son; and, thanks to our forbearance, little Raymond made his way to the highest positions. He had lost his mother then; but honours of all kinds were showered upon him. He became omnipotent—to the grievous injury of his colleagues and of science. . . . But here comes my young friend of the Luxembourg.

"Good-evening, Gélis. You look very happy to-day. What good fortune has come to you, my dear lad?"

His good fortune is that he has been able to sustain his thesis very creditably, and that he has taken high rank in his class. He tells me this with the additional information that my own words, which were incidentally referred to in the course of the examination, had been spoken of by the college professors in terms of the most unqualified praise.

"That is very nice," I replied; "and it makes me very happy, Gélis, to find my old reputation thus associated with your own youthful honours. I was very much interested, you know, in that thesis of yours;—but some domestic arrangements have been keeping me so busy lately that I quite forgot this was the day on which you were to sustain it."

Mademoiselle Jeanne made her appearance very opportunely, as if in order to suggest to him something about the nature of those very domestic arrangements. The giddy girl burst into the City of Books like a fresh breeze, crying at the top of her voice that her room was a perfect little wonder. Then she became very red indeed on seeing Monsieur Gélis there. But none of us can escape our destiny.

Monsieur Gélis asked her how she was with the tone of a young fellow who presumes upon a previous acquaintance, and who proposes to put himself forward as an old friend. Oh, never fear!—she had not forgotten him at all; that was very evident from the fact that then and there, right under my nose, they resumed their last year's conversation on the subject of the "Venetian blond"! They continued the discussion after quite an animated fashion. I began to ask myself what right I had to be in the room at all. The only thing I could do in order to make myself heard was to cough. As for getting in a word, they never even gave me a chance. Gélis discoursed enthusiastically, not only about the Venetian colourists, but also upon all other matters relating to nature or to mankind. And Jeanne kept answering him, "Yes, Monsieur, you are right." . . . "That is just what I supposed, Monsieur." . . . "Monsieur, you express so beautifully just what I feel." . . . "I am going to think a great deal about what you have just told me, Monsieur."

When *I* speak, Mademoiselle never answers me in that tone. It is only with the very tip of her tongue that she will even taste any intellectual food which I set before her. Usually she will not touch it at all. But Monsieur Gélis seems to be in her opinion the supreme authority upon all subjects. It was always, "Oh, yes!"—"Oh, of course!"—to all his empty chatter. And, then, the eyes of Jeanne! I had never seen them look so large before; I had never before observed in them such fixity of expression; but her gaze otherwise remained what it always is—artless, frank, and brave. Gélis evidently pleased her; she liked Gélis, and her eyes betrayed the fact. They would have published it to the entire universe! All very fine, Master Bonnard!—you have been so deeply interested in observing your ward, that you have been forgetting you are her guardian! You began only this morning to exercise that function; and you can already see that it involves some very delicate and difficult duties. Bonnard, you must really try to devise some means of keeping that young man away from her; you really ought. . . . Eh! how am I to know what I am to do? . . .

I have picked up a book at random from the nearest shelf; I open it, and I enter respectfully into the middle of a drama of Sophocles. The older I grow, the more I learn to love the two civilisations of the antique world; and now I always keep the poets of Italy and of Greece on a shelf within easy reach of my arm in the City of Books.

Monsieur and Mademoiselle finally condescend to take some notice of me, now that I seem too busy to take any notice of them. I really think that Mademoiselle Jeanne has even asked me what I am reading. No, indeed, I will not tell her what it is. What I am reading, between ourselves, is the chant of that smooth and luminous Chorus which rolls out its magnificent tunefulness through a scene of passionate violence—the Chorus of the Old Men of Thebes— Ἔρως ἀνίκατε . . . *"Invincible Love, O Thou who descendest upon rich houses,—Thou who dost rest upon the delicate cheek of the maiden,—Thou who dost traverse all seas,—surely none among the Immortals can escape Thee, nor indeed any among men who live but for a little space; and he who is possessed by Thee, there is a madness upon him."* And when I had re-read that delicious chant, the face of Antigone appeared before me in all its passionless purity. What images! Gods and goddesses who hover in the highest height of heaven! The blind old man, the long-wandering beggar-king, led by Antigone, has now been buried with holy rites; and his daughter, fair as the fairest dream ever conceived by human soul, resists the will of the tyrant and gives pious sepulture to her brother. She loves the son of the tyrant, and that son loves her also. And as she goes on her way to execution, the victim of her own sweet piety, the old men sing, *"Invincible Love, O Thou who dost descend upon rich houses,—Thou who dost rest upon the delicate cheek of the maiden."* . . .

"Mademoiselle Jeanne, are you really very anxious to know what I am reading? I am reading, Mademoiselle—I am reading that Antigone, having buried the blind old man, wove a fair tapestry embroidered with images in the likeness of laughing faces."

"Ah!" said Gélis, as he burst out laughing, "that is not in the text."

"It is a scholium," I said.

"Unpublished," he added, getting up.

I am not an egotist. But I am prudent. I have to bring up this child; she is much too young to be married now. No! I am not an egotist, but I must certainly keep her with me for a few years more —keep her alone with me. She can surely wait until I am dead! Fear not, Antigone, old Œdipus will find holy burial soon enough.

In the meanwhile, Antigone is helping our housekeeper to scrape the carrots. She says she likes to do it—that it is in her line, being related to the art of sculpture.

May.

WHO would recognise the City of Books now? There are flowers everywhere—even upon all the articles of furniture. Jeanne was right: those roses do look very nice in that blue china vase. She goes to market every day with Thérèse, under the pretext of helping the old servant to make her purchases, but she never brings anything back with her except flowers. Flowers are really very charming creatures. And one of these days I must certainly carry out my plan, and devote myself to the study of them, in their own natural domain, in the country—with all the science and earnestness which I possess.

For what have I to do here? Why should I burn my eyes out over these old parchments which cannot now tell me anything worth knowing? I used to study them, those old texts, with the most ardent enjoyment. What was it which I was then so anxious to find in them? The date of a pious foundation—the name of some monkish *imagier* or copyist—the price of a loaf, of an ox, or of a field—some judicial or administrative enactment—all that, and yet something more, a Something vaguely mysterious and sublime which excited my enthusiasm. But for sixty years I have been searching in vain for that Something. Better men than I—the masters, the truly great, the Fauriels, the Thierrys, who found so many things —died at their task without having been able, any more than I have been, to find that Something which, being incorporeal, has no name, and without which, nevertheless, no great mental work would ever be undertaken in this world. And now that I am only looking for what I should certainly be able to find, I cannot find anything at all; and it is probable that I shall never be able to finish the history of the Abbots of Saint-Germain-des-Prés.

"Guardian, just guess what I have in my handkerchief."

"Judging from appearances, Jeanne, I should say flowers."

"Oh, no—not flowers. Look!"

I look, and I see a little grey head poking itself out of the handkerchief. It is the head of a little grey cat. The handkerchief opens; the animal leaps down upon the carpet, shakes itself, pricks up first one ear and then the other, and begins to examine with due caution the locality and the inhabitants thereof.

Thérèse, out of breath, with her basket on her arm, suddenly makes her appearance in time to take an objective part in this examination, which does not appear to result altogether in her favour; for the young cat moves slowly away from her, without, however, venturing near my legs, or approaching Jeanne, who displays extraordinary volubility in the use of caressing appellations. Thérèse, whose chief fault is her inability to hide her feelings, thereupon vehemently reproaches Mademoiselle for bringing home a cat that she did not know anything about. Jeanne, in order to justify herself, tells the whole story. While she was passing with Thérèse before a chemist's shop, she saw the assistant kick a little cat into the street. The cat, astonished and frightened, seemed to be asking itself whether to remain in the street where it was being terrified and knocked about by the people passing by, or whether to go back into the chemist's even at the risk of being kicked out a second time. Jeanne thought it was in a very critical position, and understood its hesitation. It looked so stupid; and she knew it looked stupid only because it could not decide what to do. So she

took it up in her arms. And as it had not been able to obtain any
rest either indoors or out-of-doors, it allowed her to hold it. Then
she stroked and petted it to keep it from being afraid, and boldly
went to the chemist's assistant and said,

"If you don't like that animal, you mustn't beat it; you must give
it to me."

"Take it," said the assistant.

. . . "Now there!" adds Jeanne, by way of conclusion; and then
she changes her voice again to a flute-tone in order to say all kinds
of sweet things to that cat.

"He is horribly thin," I observe, looking at the wretched animal;
—"moreover, he is horribly ugly." Jeanne thinks he is not ugly at
all, but she acknowledges that he looks even more stupid than he
looked at first: this time she thinks it not indecision, but surprise,
which gives that unfortunate aspect to his countenance. She asks
us to imagine ourselves in his place;—then we are obliged to acknowledge that he cannot possibly understand what has happened
to him. And then we all burst out laughing in the face of the poor
little beast, which maintains the most comical look of gravity.
Jeanne wants to take him up; but he hides himself under the table,
and cannot even be tempted to come out by the lure of a saucer of
milk.

We all turn our backs and promise not to look; when we inspect
the saucer again, we find it empty.

"Jeanne," I observe, "your *protégé* has a decidedly tristful aspect
of countenance; he is of a sly and suspicious disposition; I trust he
is not going to commit in the City of Books any such misdemeanours as might render it necessary for us to send him back to his
chemist's shop. In the meantime we must give him a name. Suppose
we call him 'Don Gris de Gouttière'; but perhaps that is too long.
'Pill,' 'Drug,' or 'Castor-oil' would be short enough, and would further serve to recall his early condition in life. What do you think
about it?"

" 'Pill' would not sound bad," answers Jeanne, "but it would be
very unkind to give him a name which would be always reminding
him of the misery from which we saved him. It would be making
him pay too dearly for our hospitality. Let us be more generous,
and give him a pretty name, in hopes that he is going to deserve it.
See how he looks at us! He knows that we are talking about him.
And now that he is no longer unhappy, he is beginning to look a
great deal less stupid. I am not joking! Unhappiness does make
people look stupid,—I am perfectly sure it does."

Well, Jeanne, if you like, we will call your *protégé* Hannibal. The
appropriateness of that name does not seem to strike you at once.
But the Angora cat who preceded him here as an inmate of the City
of Books, and to whom I was in the habit of telling all my secrets
—for he was a very wise and discreet person—used to be called

Hamilcar. It is natural that this name should beget the other, and that Hannibal should succeed Hamilcar.

We all agreed upon this point.

"Hannibal!" cried Jeanne, "come here!"

Hannibal, greatly frightened by the strange sonority of his own name, ran to hide himself under a bookcase in an orifice so small that a rat could not have squeezed himself into it.

A nice way of doing credit to so great a name!

I was in a good humour for working that day, and I had just dipped the nib of my pen into the ink-bottle when I heard some one ring. Should any one ever read these pages written by an unimaginative old man, he will be sure to laugh at the way that bell keeps ringing through my narrative, without ever announcing the arrival of a new personage or introducing any unexpected incident. On the stage things are managed on the reverse principle. Monsieur Scribe never has the curtain raised without good reason, and for the greater enjoyment of ladies and young misses. That is art! I would rather hang myself than write a play,—not that I despise life, but because I should never be able to invent anything amusing. Invent! In order to do that one must have received the gift of inspiration. It would be a very unfortunate thing for me to possess such a gift. Suppose I were to invent some monkling in my history of the Abbey of Saint-Germain-des-Prés! What would our young erudites say? What a scandal for the School! As for the Institute, it would say nothing and probably not even think about the matter either. Even if my colleagues still write a little sometimes, they never read. They are of the opinion of Parny, who said,

> *"Une paisible indifférence*
> *Est la plus sage des vertus."**

To be the least wise in order to become the most wise—this is precisely what those Buddhists are aiming at without knowing it. If there is any wiser wisdom than that I will go to Rome to report upon it. . . . And all this because Monsieur Gélis happened to ring the bell!

This young man has latterly changed his manner completely with Jeanne. He is now quite as serious as he used to be frivolous, and quite as silent as he used to be chatty. And Jeanne follows his example. We have reached the phase of passionate love under constraint. For, old as I am, I cannot be deceived about it: these two children are violently and sincerely in love with each other. Jeanne now avoids him—she hides herself in her room when he comes into the library—but how well she knows how to reach him when she is alone! alone at her piano! Every evening she talks to him through

*"The most wise of the virtues is a calm indifference."

the music she plays with a rich thrill of passional feeling which is
the new utterance of her new soul.

Well, why should I not confess it? Why should I not avow my
weakness? Surely my egotism would not become any less blameworthy by keeping it hidden from myself? So I will write it. Yes!
I was hoping for something else;—yes! I thought I was going to
keep her all to myself, as my own child, as my own daughter—not
always, of course, not even perhaps for very long, but just for a few
years more. I am so old! Could she not wait? And, who knows?
With the help of the gout, I would not have imposed upon her
patience too much. That was my wish; that was my hope. I had
made my plans—I had not reckoned upon the coming of this wild
young man. But the mistake is none the less cruel because my reckoning happened to be wrong. And yet it seems to me that you are
condemning yourself very rashly, friend Sylvestre Bonnard: if you
did want to keep this young girl a few years longer, it was quite as
much in her own interest as in yours. She has a great deal to learn
yet, and you are not a master to be despised. When that miserable
notary Mouche—who subsequently committed his rascalities at so
opportune a moment—paid you the honour of a visit, you explained
to him your ideas of education with all the fervour of high enthusiasm. Then you attempted to put that system of yours into
practice;—Jeanne is certainly an ungrateful girl, and Gélis a much
too seductive young man!

But still,—unless I put him out of the house, which would be a
detestably ill-mannered and ill-natured thing to do,—I must continue to receive him. He has been waiting ever so long in my little
parlour, in front of those Sèvres vases with which King Louis
Philippe so graciously presented me. The *Moissonneurs* and the
Pêcheurs of Léopold Robert are painted upon those porcelain vases,
which Gélis nevertheless dares to call frightfully ugly, with the
warm approval of Jeanne, whom he has absolutely bewitched.

"My dear lad, excuse me for having kept you waiting so long. I
had a little bit of work to finish."

I am telling the truth. Meditation is work, but of course Gélis
does not know what I mean; he thinks I am referring to something
archæological, and, his question in regard to the health of Mademoiselle Jeanne having been answered by a "Very well indeed,"
uttered in that extremely dry tone which reveals my moral authority
as guardian, we begin to converse about historical subjects. We first
enter upon generalities. Generalities are sometimes extremely serv-
iceable. I try to inculcate into Monsier Gélis some respect for that
generation of historians to which I belong. I say to him,

"History, which was formerly an art, and which afforded place
for the fullest exercise of the imagination, has in our time become
a science, the study of which demands absolute exactness of knowledge."

Gélis asks leave to differ from me on this subject. He tells me he does not believe that history is a science, or that it could possibly ever become a science.

"In the first place," he says to me, "what is history? The written representation of past events. But what is an event? Is it merely a commonplace fact? Is it any fact? No! You say yourself it is a noteworthy fact. Now, how is the historian to tell whether a fact is noteworthy or not? He judges it arbitrarily, according to his tastes and his caprices and his ideas—in short, as an artist. For facts cannot by reason of their own intrinsic character be divided into historical facts and non-historical facts. But any fact is something exceedingly complex. Will the historian represent facts in all their complexity? No, that is impossible. Then he will represent them stripped of the greater part of the peculiarities which constituted them, and consequently lopped, mutilated, different from what they really were. As for the inter-relation of facts, needless to speak of it! If a so-called historical fact be brought into notice—as is very possible—by one or more facts which are not historical at all, and are for that very reason unknown, how is the historian going to establish the relation of these facts one to another? And in saying this, Monsieur Bonnard, I am supposing that the historian has positive evidence before him, whereas in reality he feels confidence only in such or such a witness for sympathetic reasons. History is not a science; it is an art, and one can succeed in that art only through the exercise of his faculty of imagination."

Monsieur Gélis reminds me very much at this moment of a certain young fool whom I heard talking wildly one day in the garden of the Luxembourg, under the statue of Marguerite of Navarre. But at another turn of the conversation we find ourselves face to face with Walter Scott, whose work my disdainful young friend pleases to term "rococo, troubadourish, and only fit to inspire somebody engaged in making designs for cheap bronze clocks." Those are his very words!

"Why!" I exclaim, zealous to defend the magnificent creator of 'The Bride of Lammermoor' and 'The Fair Maid of Perth,' "the whole past lives in those admirable novels of his;—that is history, that is epic!"

"It is frippery," Gélis answers me.

And,—will you believe it?—this crazy boy actually tells me that no matter how learned one may be, one cannot possibly know just how men used to live five or ten centuries ago, because it is only with the very greatest difficulty that one can picture them to oneself even as they were only ten or fifteen years ago. In his opinion, the historical poem, the historical novel, the historical painting, are all, according to their kind, abominably false as branches of art.

"In all the arts," he adds, "the artist can only reflect his own soul. His work, no matter how it may be dressed up, is of necessity contemporary with himself, being the reflection of his own mind. What do we admire in the 'Divine Comedy' unless it be the great soul of Dante? And the marbles of Michael Angelo, what do they represent to us that is at all extraordinary unless it be Michael Angelo himself? The artist either communicates his own life to his creations, or else merely whittles out puppets and dresses up dolls."

What a torrent of paradoxes and irreverences! But boldness in a young man is not displeasing to me. Gélis gets up from his chair and sits down again. I know perfectly well what is worrying him, and whom he is waiting for. And now he begins to talk to me about his being able to make fifteen hundred francs a year, to which he can add the revenue he derives from a little property that he has inherited—two thousand francs a year or more. And I am not in the least deceived as to the purpose of these confidences on his part. I know perfectly well that he is only making his little financial statements in order to persuade me that he is comfortably circumstanced, steady, fond of home, comparatively independent—or, to put the matter in the fewest words possible, able to marry. *Quod erat demonstrandum,*—as the geometricians say.

He has got up and sat down just twenty times. He now rises for the twenty-first time; and, as he has not been able to see Jeanne, he goes away feeling as unhappy as possible.

The moment he has gone, Jeanne comes into the City of Books, under the pretext of looking for Hannibal. She is also quite unhappy; and her voice becomes singularly plaintive as she calls her pet to give him some milk. Look at that sad little face, Bonnard! Tyrant, gaze upon thy work! Thou hast been able to keep them from seeing each other; but they have now both of them the same expression of countenance, and thou mayest discern from that similarity of expression that in spite of thee they are united in thought. Cassandra, be happy! Bartholo, rejoice! This is what it means to be a guardian! Just see her kneeling down there on the carpet with Hannibal's head between her hands!

Yes, caress the stupid animal!—pity him!—moan over him!— we know very well, you little rogue, the real cause of all those sighs and plaints! Nevertheless, it makes a very pretty picture. I look at it for a long time; then, throwing a glance around my library, I exclaim,

"Jeanne, I am tired of all those books; we must sell them."

September 20.

It is done!—they are betrothed. Gélis, who is an orphan, as Jeanne is, did not make his proposal to me in person. He got one of his professors, an old colleague of mine, highly esteemed for his learning and character, to come to me on his behalf. But what a love messenger! Great Heavens! A bear—not a bear of the Pyrenees, but a literary bear, and this latter variety of bear is much more ferocious than the former.

"Right or wrong (in my opinion wrong) Gélis says that he does not want any dowry; he takes your ward with nothing but her chemise. Say yes, and the thing is settled! Make haste about it! I want to show you two or three very curious old tokens from Lorraine which I am sure you never saw before."

That is literally what he said to me. I answered him that I would consult Jeanne, and I found no small pleasure in telling him that my ward had a dowry.

Her dowry—there it is in front of me! It is my library. Henri and Jeanne have not even the faintest suspicion about it; and the fact is I am commonly believed to be much richer than I am. I have the face of an old miser. It is certainly a lying face; but its untruthfulness has often won for me a great deal of consideration. There is nobody so much respected in this world as a stingy rich man.

I have consulted Jeanne,—but what was the need of listening for her answer? It is done! They are betrothed.

It would ill become my character as well as my face to watch these young people any longer for the mere purpose of noting down their words and gestures. *Noli me tangere:*—that is the maxim for all charming love affairs. I know my duty. It is to respect all the little secrets of that innocent soul intrusted to me. Let these children love each other all they can! Never a word of their fervent outpouring of mutual confidences, never a hint of their artless self-betrayals, will be set down in this diary by the old guardian whose authority was so gentle and so brief.

At all events, I am not going to remain with my arms folded; and if they have their business to attend to, I have mine also. I am preparing a catalogue of my books, with a view to having them all sold at auction. It is a task which saddens and amuses me at the same time. I linger over it, perhaps a good deal longer than I ought to do; turning the leaves of all those works which have become so familiar to my thought, to my touch, to my sight—even out of all necessity and reason. But it is a farewell; and it has ever been in the nature of man to prolong a farewell.

This ponderous volume here, which has served me so much for thirty long years, how can I leave it without according to it every kindness that a faithful servant deserves? And this one again, which has so often consoled me by its wholesome doctrines, must I not bow down before it for the last time, as to a Master? But each time that I meet with a volume which ever led me into error, which ever afflicted me with false dates, omissions, lies, and other plagues of the archæologist, I say to it with bitter joy: "Go! impostor, traitor, false-witness! flee thou far away from me for ever;—*vade retro!* all absurdly covered with gold as thou art! and I pray it may befall thee—thanks to thy usurped reputation and thy comely morocco attire—to take thy place in the cabinet of some banker-bibliomaniac, whom thou wilt never be able to seduce as thou hast seduced me, because he will never read one single line of thee."

I laid aside some books I must always keep—those books which were given to me as souvenirs. As I placed among them the manuscript of the "Golden Legend," I could not but kiss it in memory of Madame Trépof, who remained grateful to me in spite of her high position and all her wealth, and who became my benefactress merely to prove to me that she felt I had once done her a kindness. . . . Thus I had made a reserve. It was then that, for the first time, I felt myself inclined to commit a deliberate crime. All through that night I was strongly tempted; by morning the temptation had become irresistible. Everybody else in the house was still asleep. I got out of bed and stole softly from my room.

Ye powers of darkness! ye phantoms of the night! if while lingering within my home after the crowing of the cock, you saw me stealing about on tiptoe in the City of Books, you certainly never cried out, as Madame Trépof did at Naples, "That old man has a good-natured round back!" I entered the library; Hannibal, with his tail perpendicularly erected, came to rub himself against my legs and purr. I seized a volume from its shelf, some venerable Gothic text or some noble poet of the Renaissance—the jewel, the treasure which I had been dreaming about all night, I seized it and slipped it away into the very bottom of the closet which I had reserved for those books I intended to retain, and which soon became full almost to bursting. It is horrible to relate: I was stealing the dowry of Jeanne! And when the crime had been consummated I set myself again sturdily to the task of cataloguing, until Jeanne came to consult me in regard to something about a dress or a trousseau. I could not possibly understand just what she was talking about, through my total ignorance of the current vocabulary of dressmaking and linen-drapery. Ah! if a bride of the fourteenth century had come to talk to me about the apparel of her epoch, then, indeed, I should have been able to understand her language! But Jeanne does not belong to my time, and I have to send her to Madame de Gabry, who on this important occasion will take the place of her mother.

. . . Night has come! Leaning from the window, we gaze at the vast sombre stretch of the city below us, pierced with multitudinous points of light. Jeanne presses her hand to her forehead as she leans upon the window-bar, and seems a little sad. And I say to myself as I watch her: All changes, even the most longed for, have their melancholy; for what we leave behind us is a part of ourselves: we must die to one life before we can enter into another!

And as if answering my thought, the young girl murmurs to me,

"My guardian, I am so happy; and still I feel as if I wanted to cry!"

THE LAST PAGE

August 21 1869.

PAGE eighty-seven. . . . Only twenty lines more and I shall have finished my book about insects and flowers. Page eighty-seventh and last. . . . *"As we have already seen, the visits of insects are of the utmost importance to plants; since their duty is to carry to the pistils the pollen of the stamens. It seems also that the flower itself is arranged and made attractive for the purpose of inviting this nuptial visit. I think I have been able to show that the nectary of the plant distils a sugary liquid which attracts the insect and obliges it to aid unconsciously in the work of direct or cross fertilisation. The last method of fertilisation is the more common. I have shown that flowers are coloured and perfumed so as to attract insects, and interiorly so constructed as to offer those visitors such a mode of access that they cannot penetrate into the corolla without depositing upon the stigma the pollen with which they have been covered. My most venerated master Sprengel observes in regard to that fine down which lines the coralla of the wood-geranium: 'The wise Author of Nature has never created a single useless hair!' I say in my turn: If that Lily of the Valley whereof the Gospel makes mention is more richly clad than King Solomon in all his glory, its mantle of purple is a wedding-garment, and that rich apparel is necessary to the perpetuation of the species.**

"BROLLES, *August* 21, 1869."

Brolles! My house is the last one you pass in the single street of the village, as you go to the woods. It is a gabled house with a slate

---

*Monsieur Sylvestre Bonnard was not aware that several very illustrious naturalists were making researches at the same time as he in regard to the relation between insects and plants. He was not acquainted with the labours of Darwin, with those of Dr. Hermann Müller, nor with the observations of Sir John Lubbock. It is worthy of note that the conclusions of Monsieur Sylvestre Bonnard are very nearly similar to those reached by the three scientists above mentioned. Less important, but perhaps equally interesting, is the fact that Sir John Lubbock is, like Monsieur Bonnard, an archæologist who began to devote himself only late in life to the natural sciences.—*Note by the French Editor.*

roof, which takes iridescent tints in the sun like a pigeon's breast. The weather-vane above that roof has won more consideration for me among the country people than all my works upon history and philology. There is not a single child who does not know Monsieur Bonnard's weather-vane. It is rusty, and squeaks very sharply in the wind. Sometimes it refuses to do any work at all—just like Thérèse, who now allows herself to be assisted by a young peasant girl—though she grumbles a good deal about it. The house is not large, but I am very comfortable in it. My room has two windows, and gets the sun in the morning. The children's room is upstairs. Jeanne and Henri come twice a year to occupy it.

Little Sylvestre's cradle used to be in it. He was a very pretty child, but very pale. When he used to play on the grass, his mother would watch him very anxiously; and every little while she would stop her sewing in order to take him upon her lap. The poor little fellow never wanted to go to sleep. He used to say that when he was asleep he would go away, very far away, to some place where it was all dark, and where he saw things that made him afraid—things he never wanted to see again.

Then his mother would call me, and I would sit down beside his cradle. He would take one of my fingers into his little dry warm hand, and say to me,

"Godfather, you must tell me a story."

Then I would tell him all kinds of stories, which he would listen to very seriously. They all interested him, but there was one especially which filled his little soul with delight. It was "The Blue Bird." Whenever I finished that, he would say to me, "Tell it again! tell it again!" And I would tell it again until his little pale blue-veined head sank back upon the pillow in slumber.

The doctor used to answer all our questions by saying,

"There is nothing extraordinary the matter with him!"

No! There was nothing extraordinary the matter with little Sylvestre. One evening last year his father called me.

"Come," he said, "the little one is still worse."

I approached the cradle over which the mother hung motionless, as if tied down above it by all the powers of her soul.

Little Sylvestre turned his eyes towards me; their pupils had already rolled up beneath his eyelids, and could not descend again.

"Godfather," he said, "you are not to tell me any more stories."

No, I was not to tell him any more stories!

Poor Jeanne!—poor mother!

I am too old now to feel very deeply; but how strangely painful a mystery is the death of a child!

To-day, the father and mother have come to pass six weeks under the old man's roof. I see them now returning from the woods, walking arm-in-arm. Jeanne is closely wrapped in her black shawl, and

Henri wears a crapé band on his straw hat; but they are both of them radiant with youth, and they smile very sweetly at each other. They smile at the earth which sustains them; they smile at the air which bathes them; they smile at the light which each one sees in the eyes of the other. From my window I wave my handkerchief at them,—and they smile at my old age.

Jeanne comes running lightly up the stairs; she kisses me, and then whispers in my ear something which I divine rather than hear. And I make answer to her: "May God's blessing be with you, Jeanne, and with your husband, and with your children, and with your children's children for ever!" . . . *Et nunc dimittis servum tuum, Domine!*

THE REVOLT OF THE ANGELS

"THE REVOLT OF THE ANGELS" *translated by* MRS. WILFRID JACKSON

"THE REVOLT OF THE ANGELS" *translated by* MRS. WILFRID JACKSON

I

CONTAINING IN A FEW LINES THE HISTORY OF A FRENCH FAMILY FROM 1789 TO THE PRESENT DAY

BENEATH the shadow of St. Sulpice the ancient mansion of the d'Esparvieu family rears its austere three stories between a moss-grown forecourt and a garden hemmed in, as the years have elapsed, by ever loftier and more intrusive buildings, wherein, nevertheless, two tall chestnut trees still lift their withered heads.

Here from 1825 to 1857 dwelt the great man of the family, Alexandre Bussart d'Esparvieu, Vice-President of the Council of State under the Government of July, Member of the Academy of Moral and Political Sciences, and author of an *Essay on the Civil and Religious Institutions of Nations,* in three octavo volumes, a work unfortunately left incomplete.

This eminent theorist of a Liberal monarchy left as heir to his name his fortune and his fame, Fulgence-Adolphe Bussart d'Esparvieu, senator under the Second Empire, who added largely to his patrimony by buying land over which the Avenue de l'Impératice was destined ultimately to pass, and who made a remarkable speech in favour of the temporal power of the popes.

Fulgence had three sons. The eldest, Marc-Alexandre, entering the army, made a splendid career for himself: he was a good speaker. The second, Gaétan, showing no particular aptitude for anything, lived mostly in the country, where he hunted, bred horses, and devoted himself to music and painting. The third son, René, destined from his childhood for the law, resigned his deputyship to avoid complicity in the Ferry decrees against the religious orders; and later, perceiving the revival under the presidency of Monsieur Fallières of the days of Decius and Diocletian, put his knowledge and zeal at the service of the persecuted Church.

From the Concordat of 1801 down to the closing years of the

Second Empire all the d'Esparvieus attended mass for the sake of example. Though sceptics in their inmost hearts, they looked upon religion as an instrument of government.

Marc and René were the first of their race to show any sign of sincere devotion. The General, when still a colonel, had dedicated his regiment to the Sacred Heart, and he practised his faith with a fervour remarkable even in a soldier, though we all know that piety, daughter of Heaven, has marked out the hearts of the generals of the Third Republic as her chosen dwelling-place on earth.

Faith has its vicissitudes. Under the old order the masses were believers, not so the aristocracy or the educated middle class. Under the First Empire the army from top to bottom was entirely irreligious. To-day the masses believe nothing. The middle classes wish to believe, and succeed at times, as did Marc and René d'Esparvieu. Their brother Gaétan, on the contrary, the country gentleman, failed to attain to faith. He was an agnostic, a term commonly employed by the modish to avoid the odious one of freethinker. And he openly declared himself an agnostic, contrary to the admirable custom which deems it better to withhold the avowal.

In the century in which we live there are so many modes of belief and of unbelief that future historians will have difficulty in finding their way about. But are we any more successful in disentangling the condition of religious beliefs in the time of Symmachus or of Ambrose?

A fervent Christian, René d'Esparvieu was deeply attached to the liberal ideas his ancestors had transmitted to him as a sacred heritage. Compelled to oppose a Jacobin and atheistical Republic, he still called himself Republican. And it was in the name of liberty that he demanded the independence and sovereignty of the Church.

During the long debates on the Separation and the quarrels over the Inventories, the synods of the bishops and the assemblies of the faithful were held in his house. While the most authoritatively accredited leaders of the Catholic party: prelates, generals, senators, deputies, journalists, were met together in the big green drawing-room, and every soul present turned towards Rome with a tender submission or enforced obedience; while Monsieur d'Esparvieu, his elbow on the marble chimney-piece, opposed civil law to canon law, and protested eloquently against the spoliation of the Church of France, two faces of other days, immobile and speechless, looked down on the modern crowd; on the right of the fireplace, painted by David, was Romain Bussart, a working-farmer at Esparvieu in shirt-sleeves and drill trousers, with a rough-and-ready air not untouched with cunning. He had good reason to smile: the worthy man laid the foundation of the family fortunes when he bought Church lands. On the left, painted by Gérard in full-dress bedizened with orders, was the peasant's son, Baron Emile Bussart d'Esparvieu, prefect under the Empire, Keeper of the Great Seal under Charles X, who died in 1837, churchwarden of his parish, with couplets from *La Pucelle* on his lips.

René d'Esparvieu married in 1888 Marie-Antoinette Coupelle, daughter of Baron Coupelle, ironmaster at Blainville (Haute Loire). Madame René d'Esparvieu had been president since 1903 of the Society of Christian Mothers. These perfect spouses, having married off their eldest daughter in 1908, had three children still at home—a girl and two boys.

Léon, the younger, aged seven, had a room next to his mother and his sister Berthe. Maurice, the elder, lived in a little pavilion comprising two rooms at the bottom of the garden. The young man thus gained a freedom which enabled him to endure family life. He was rather good-looking, smart without too much pretence, and the faint smile which merely raised one corner of his mouth did not lack charm.

At twenty-five Maurice possessed the wisdom of Ecclesiastes. Doubting whether a man hath any profit of all his labour which he

taketh under the sun he never put himself out about anything. From his earliest childhood this young hopeful's sole concern with work had been considering how he might best avoid it, and it was through his remaining ignorant of the teaching of the *École de Droit* that he became a doctor of law and a barrister at the Court of Appeal.

He neither pleaded nor practised. He had no knowledge and no desire to acquire any; wherein he conformed to his genius whose engaging fragility he forbore to overload; his instinct fortunately telling him that it was better to understand little than to misunderstand a lot.

As Monsieur l'Abbé Patouille expressed it, Maurice had received from Heaven the benefits of a Christian education. From his childhood piety was shown to him in the example of his home, and when on leaving college he was entered at the *École de Droit,* he found the lore of the doctors, the virtues of the confessors, and the constancy of the nursing mothers of the Church assembled around the paternal hearth. Admitted to social and political life at the time of the great persecution of the Church of France, Maurice did not fail to attend every manifestation of youthful Catholicism; he lent a hand with his parish barricades at the time of the Inventories, and with his companions he unharnessed the archbishop's horses when he was driven out from his palace. He showed on all these occasions a modified zeal; one never saw him in the front ranks of the heroic band exciting soldiers to a glorious disobedience or flinging mud and curses at the agents of the law.

He did his duty, nothing more; and if he distinguished himself on the occasion of the great pilgrimage of 1911 among the stretcher-bearers at Lourdes, we have reason to fear it was but to please Madame de la Verdelière, who admired men of muscle. Abbé Patouille, a friend of the family and deeply versed in the knowledge of souls, knew that Maurice had only moderate aspirations to martyrdom. He reproached him with his lukewarmness, and pulled his ear, calling him a bad lot. Anyway, Maurice remained a believer.

Amid the distractions of youth his faith remained intact, since he left it severely alone. He had never examined a single tenet. Nor had he enquired a whit more closely into the ideas of morality current in the grade of society to which he belonged. He took them just as they came. Thus in every situation that arose he cut an eminently respectable figure which he would have assuredly failed to do, had he been given to meditating on the foundations of morality. He was irritable and hot-tempered and possessed of a sense of honour which he was at great pains to cultivate. He was neither vain nor ambitious. Like the majority of Frenchmen, he disliked parting with his money. Women would never have obtained anything from him had they not known the way to make him give. He believed he despised them; the truth was he adored them. He indulged his appetites so naturally that he never suspected that he had any. What people did not know, himself least of all,—though the gleam that occasionally shone in his fine, light-brown eyes might have furnished the hint—was that he had a warm heart and was capable of friendship. For the rest, he was, in the ordinary intercourse of life, no very brilliant specimen.

II

WHEREIN USEFUL INFORMATION WILL BE FOUND CONCERNING A LIBRARY WHERE STRANGE THINGS WILL SHORTLY COME TO PASS

ESIROUS of embracing the whole circle of human knowledge, and anxious to bequeath to the world a concrete symbol of his encyclopædic genius and a display in keeping with his pecuniary resources, Baron Alexandre d'Esparvieu had formed a library of three hundred and sixty thousand volumes, both printed and in manuscript, whereof the greater part emanated from the Benedictines of Ligugé.

By a special clause in his will he enjoined his heirs to add to his library, after his death, whatever they might deem worthy of note in natural, moral, political, philosophical, and religious science.

He had indicated the sums which might be drawn from his estate for the fulfilment of this object, and charged his eldest son, Fulgence-Adolphe, to proceed with these additions. Fulgence-Adolphe accomplished with filial respect the wishes expressed by his illustrious father.

After him, this huge library, which represented more than one child's share of the estate, remained undivided between the Senator's three sons and two daughters; and René d'Esparvieu, on whom devolved the house in the Rue Garancière, became the guardian of the valuable collection. His two sisters, Madame Paulet de Saint-Fain and Madame Cuissart, repeatedly demanded that such a large but unremunerative piece of property should be turned into money. But René and Gaétan bought in the shares of their two colegatees, and the library was saved. René d'Esparvieu even busied himself in adding to it, thus fulfilling the intentions of its founder. But from year to year he lessened the number and importance of the acquisitions, opining that the intellectual output in Europe was on the wane.

Nevertheless, Gaétan enriched it, out of his funds, with works published both in France and abroad which he thought good, and he was not lacking in judgment, though his brothers would never allow that he had a particle. Thanks to this man of leisurely and inquiring mind, Baron Alexandre's collection was kept practically up to date. Even at the present day the d'Esparvieu library, in the departments of theology, jurisprudence, and history is one of the finest private libraries in all Europe. Here you may study physical science, or to put it better, physical sciences in all their branches, and for that matter metaphysic or metaphysics, that is to say, all that is connected with physics and has no other name, so impossible is it to designate by a substantive that which has no substance, and is but a dream and an illusion. Here you may contemplate with admiration philosophers addressing themselves to the solution, dissolution, and resolution of the Absolute, to the determination of the Indeterminate and to the definition of the Infinite.

Amid this pile of books and booklets, both sacred and profane, you may find everything down to the latest and most fashionable pragmatism.

Other libraries there are, more richly abounding in bindings of venerable antiquity and illustrious origin, whose smooth and softhued texture render them delicious to the touch; bindings which the gilder's art has enriched with gossamer, lace-work, foliage, flowers, emblematic devices, and coats of arms; bindings that charm the studious eye with their tender radiance. Other libraries perhaps harbour a greater array of manuscripts illuminated with delicate and brilliant miniatures by artists of Venice, Flanders, or Touraine. But in handsome, sound editions of ancient and modern writers, both sacred and profane, the d'Esparvieu library is second to none. Here one finds all that has come down to us from antiquity; all the Fathers of the Church, the Apologists and the Decretalists, all the Humanists of the Renaissance, all the Encyclopædists, the whole world of philosophy and science. Therefore it was that Cardinal Merlin, when he deigned to visit it, remarked:

"There is no man whose brain is equal to containing all the knowledge which is piled upon these shelves. Happily it doesn't matter."

Monseigneur Cachepot, who worked there often when a curate in Paris, was in the habit of saying:

"I see here the stuff to make many a Thomas Aquinas and many an Arius, if only the modern mind had not lost its ancient ardour for good and evil."

There was no gainsaying that the manuscripts formed the more valuable portion of this immense collection. Noteworthy indeed was the unpublished correspondence of Gassendi, of Father Mersenne, and of Pascal, which threw a new light on the spirit of the seventeenth century. Nor must we forget the Hebrew Bibles, the Talmuds, the Rabbinical treatises, printed and in manuscript, the Aramaic and Samaritan texts, on sheepskin and on tablets of sycamore; in fine, all these antique and valuable copies collected in Egypt and in Syria by the celebrated Moïse de Dina, and acquired at a small cost by Alexandre d'Esparvieu in 1836, when the learned Hebraist died of old age and poverty in Paris.

The Esparvienne library occupied the whole of the second floor of the old house. The works thought to be of but mediocre interest, such as books of Protestant exegesis of the nineteenth and twentieth centuries, the gift of Monsieur Gaétan, were relegated unbound to the limbo of the upper regions. The catalogue, with its various supplements, ran into no less than eighteen folio volumes. It was quite up to date, and the library was in perfect order. Monsieur Julien Sariette, archivist and palæographer, who, being poor and retiring, used to make his living by teaching, became, in 1895, tutor to young Maurice on the recommendation of the Bishop of Agra, and with scarcely an interval found himself curator of the Bibliothèque Esparvienne. Endowed with business-like energy and dogged patience, Monsieur Sariette himself classified all the members of this vast body. The system he invented and put into practice was so complicated, the labels he put on the books were made up of so many capital letters and small letters, both Latin and Greek, so many Arabic and Roman numerals, asterisks, double asterisks, triple asterisks, and those signs which in arithmetic express powers and roots, that the mere study of it would have involved more time and labour than would have been required for the complete mastery of algebra, and as no one could be found who would give the hours, that might be more profitably employed in discovering the law of numbers, to the solving of these cryptic symbols, Monsieur Sariette remained the only one capable of finding his way among the intricacies of his system, and without his help it had become an utter impossibility to discover, among the three hundred and sixty thousand volumes confided to his care, the particular volume one happened to require. Such was the result of his labours. Far from complaining about it, he experienced on the contrary a lively satisfaction.

Monsieur Sariette loved his library. He loved it with a jealous love. He was there every day at seven o'clock in the morning busy cataloguing at a huge mahogany desk. The slips in his handwriting filled an enormous case standing by his side surmounted by a plaster bust of Alexandre d'Esparvieu. Alexandre wore his hair brushed straight back, and had a sublime look on his face. Like Chateaubriand, he affected little feathery side whiskers. His lips were pursed, his bosom bare. Punctually at midday Monsieur Sariette used to sally forth to lunch at a *crèmerie* in the narrow gloomy Rue des Canettes. It was known as the *Crèmerie des Quatre Évêques,* and had once been the haunt of Baudelaire, Theodore de Banville, Charles Asselineau, and a certain grandee of Spain who had translated the "Mysteries of Paris" into the language of the *conquistadores.* And the ducks that paddled so nicely on the old stone sign which gave its name to the street used to recognize Monsieur

Sariette. At a quarter to one, to the very minute, he went back to his library, where he remained until seven o'clock. He then again betook himself to the *Quatre Évêques,* and sat down to his frugal dinner, with its crowning glory of stewed prunes. Every evening, after dinner, his crony, Monsieur Guinardon, universally known as Père Guinardon, a scene-painter and picture-restorer, who used to do work for churches, would come from his garret in the Rue Princesse to have his coffee and liqueur at the *Quatre Évêques,* and the two friends would play their game of dominoes.

Old Guinardon, who was like some rugged old tree still full of sap, was older than he could bring himself to believe. He had known Chenavard. His chastity was positively ferocious, and he was for ever denouncing the impurities of neo-paganism in language of alarming obscenity. He loved talking. Monsieur Sariette was a ready listener. Old Guinardon's favourite subject was the Chapelle des Anges in St. Sulpice, in which the paintings were peeling off the walls, and which he was one day to restore; when, that is, it should please God, for, since the Separation, the churches belonged solely to God, and no one would undertake the responsibility of even the most urgent repairs. But old Guinardon demanded no salary.

"Michael is my patron saint," he said. "And I have a special devotion for the Holy Angels."

After they had had their game of dominoes, Monsieur Sariette, very thin and small, and old Guinardon, sturdy as an oak, hirsute as a lion, and tall as a Saint Christopher, went off chatting away side by side across the Place Saint Sulpice, heedless of whether the night were fine or stormy. Monsieur Sariette always went straight home, much to the regret of the painter, who was a gossip and a night-bird.

The following day, as the clock struck seven, Monsieur Sariette would take up his place in the library, and resume his cataloguing. As he sat at his desk, however, he would dart a Medusa-like look at anyone who entered, fearing lest he should prove to be a bookborrower. It was not merely the magistrates, politicians, and prelates whom he would have liked to turn to stone when they came to ask for the loan of a book with an air of authority bred of their familiarity with the master of the house. He would have done as much to Monsieur Gaétan, the library's benefactor, when he wanted some gay or scandalous old volume wherewith to beguile a wet day in the country. He would have meted out similar treatment to Madame René d'Esparvieu, when she came to look for a book to read to her sick poor in hospital, and even to Monsieur René d'Esparvieu himself, who generally contented himself with the Civil Code and a volume of Dalloz. The borrowing of the smallest book seemed like dragging his heart out. To refuse a volume even to such as had the most incontestable right to it, Monsieur Sariette would invent countless far-fetched or clumsy fibs, and did not even shrink from slandering himself as curator or from casting doubts on his own vigilance by saying that such and such a book was mislaid or lost, when a moment ago he had been gloating over that very volume or pressing it to his bosom. And when ultimately forced to part with a volume he would take it back a score of times from the borrower before he finally relinquished it.

He was always in agony lest one of the objects confided to his care should escape him. As the guardian of three hundred and sixty thousand volumes, he had three hundred and sixty thousand reasons for alarm. Sometimes he woke at night bathed in sweat, and uttering a cry of fear, because he had dreamed he had seen a gap on one of the shelves of his bookcases. It seemed to him a monstrous, unheard-of, and most grievous thing that a volume should leave its habitat. This noble rapacity exasperated Monsieur René d'Esparvieu, who, failing to understand the good qualities of his paragon of a librarian, called him an old maniac. Monsieur Sariette knew nought of this injustice, but he would have braved the cruellest misfortune and endured opprobrium and insult to safeguard the integrity of his trust. Thanks to his assiduity, his vigilance and zeal, or, in a word, to his love, the Esparvienne library had not lost so much as a single leaflet under his supervision during the sixteen years which had now rolled by, this ninth of September, 1912.

<h2 style="text-align:center">III</h2>

<h2 style="text-align:center">WHEREIN THE MYSTERY BEGINS</h2>

AT SEVEN o'clock on the evening of that day, having as usual replaced all the books which had been taken from their shelves, and having assured himself that he was leaving everything in good order, he quitted the library, double-locking the door after him. According to his usual habit, he dined at the *Crèmerie des Quatre Évêques*, read his newspaper, *La Croix*, and at ten o'clock went home to his little house in the Rue du Regard. The good man had no trouble and no presentiment of evil; his sleep was peaceful. The next morning at seven o'clock to the minute, he entered the little room leading to the library, and, according to his daily habit, doffed his grand frock-coat, and taking down an old one which hung in a cupboard over his washstand, put it on. Then he went into his workroom, where for sixteen years he had been cataloguing six days out of the seven, under the lofty gaze of Alexandre d'Esparvieu. Preparing to make a round of the various rooms, he entered the first and largest, which contained works on theology and religion in huge cupboards

whose cornices were adorned with bronze-coloured busts of poets and orators of ancient days.

Two enormous globes representing the earth and the heavens filled the window-embrasures. But at his first step Monsieur Sariette stopped dead, stupefied, powerless alike to doubt or to credit what his eyes beheld. On the blue cloth cover of the writing-table books lay scattered about pell-mell, some lying flat, some standing upright. A number of quartos were heaped up in a tottering pile. Two Greek lexicons, one inside the other, formed a single being more monstrous in shape than the human couples of the divine Plato. A gilt-edged folio was all a-gape, showing three of its leaves disgracefully dog's-eared.

Having, after an interval of some moments recovered from his profound amazement, the librarian went up to the table and recognised in the confused mass his most valuable Hebrew, French, and Latin Bibles, a unique Talmud, Rabbinical treatises printed and in manuscript, Aramaic and Samaritan texts and scrolls from the synagogues—in fine, the most precious relics of Israel all lying in a disordered heap, gaping and crumpled.

Monsieur Sariette found himself confronted with an inexplicable phenomenon; nevertheless he sought to account for it. How eagerly he would have welcomed the idea that Monsieur Gaétan, who, being a thoroughly unprincipled man, presumed on the right gained him by his fatal liberality towards the library to rummage there unhindered during his sojourns in Paris, had been the author of this terrible disorder. But Monsieur Gaétan was away travelling in Italy. After pondering for some minutes Monsieur Sariette's next supposition was that Monsieur René d'Esparvieu had entered the library late in the evening with the keys of his manservant Hippolyte, who, for the past twenty-five years, had looked after the second floor and the attics. Monsieur René d'Esparvieu, however, never worked at night, and did not read Hebrew. Perhaps, thought Monsieur Sariette, perhaps he had brought or allowed to be brought to this room some priest, or Jerusalem monk, on his way through Paris; some Oriental *savant* given to scriptural exegesis. Monsieur Sariette next wondered whether the Abbé Patouille, who had an enquiring mind, and also a habit of dog's-earing his books, had, peradventure, flung himself on these talmudic and biblical texts, fired with sudden zeal to lay bare the soul of Shem. He even asked himself for a moment whether Hippolyte, the old manservant, who had swept and dusted the library for a quarter of a century, and had been slowly poisoned by the dust of accumulated knowledge, had allowed his curiosity to get the better of him, and had been there during the night, ruining his eyesight and his reason, and losing his soul poring by moonlight over these undecipherable symbols. Monsieur Sariette even went so far as to imagine that young Maurice, on leaving his club or some nationalist meeting, might have torn these Jewish volumes from their shelves, out of hatred for old Jacob and his modern posterity; for this young man of family was a declared anti-semite, and only consorted with those Jews who were as anti-semitic as himself. It was giving a very free rein to his imagination, but Monsieur Sariette's brain could not rest, and went wandering about among speculations of the wildest extravagance.

Impatient to know the truth, the zealous guardian of the library called the manservant.

Hippolyte knew nothing. The porter at the lodge could not furnish any clue. None of the domestics had heard a sound. Monsieur Sariette went down to the study of Monsieur René d'Esparvieu, who received him in nightcap and dressing-gown, listened to his story with the air of a serious man bored with idle chatter, and dismissed him with words which conveyed a cruel implication of pity.

"Do not worry, my good Monsieur Sariette; be sure that the books were lying where you left them last night."

Monsieur Sariette reiterated his enquiries a score of times, discovered nothing, and suffered such anxiety that sleep entirely forsook him. When, on the following day at seven o'clock he entered the room with the busts and globes, and saw that all was in order, he heaved a sigh of relief. Then suddenly his heart beat fit to burst. He had just seen lying flat on the mantelpiece a paper-bound volume, a modern work, the boxwood paper-knife which had served to cut its pages still thrust between the leaves. It was a dissertation on the two parallel versions of Genesis, a work which Monsieur Sariette had relegated to the attic, and which had never left it up to now, no one in Monsieur d'Esparvieu's circle having had the curiosity to differentiate between the parts for which the polytheistic and monotheistic contributors were respectively responsible in the formation of the first of the sacred books. This book bore the label $R > 3214\frac{VIII}{2}$. And this painful truth was suddenly borne in upon the mind of Monsieur Sariette: to wit, that the most scientific system of numbering will not help to find a book if the book is no longer in its place. Every day of the ensuing month found the table littered with books. Greek and Latin lay cheek by jowl with Hebrew. Monsieur Sariette asked himself whether these nocturnal flittings were the work of evil-doers who entered by the skylights to steal valuable and precious volumes. But he found no traces of burglary, and, notwithstanding the most minute search, failed to discover that anything had disappeared. Terrible anxiety took possession of his mind, and he fell to wondering whether it was possible that some monkey in the neighbourhood came down the chimney and acted the part of a person engaged in study. Deriving his knowledge of the habits of these animals in the main from the paintings of Watteau and Chardin, he took it that, in the art of imitating gestures or assuming characters they resembled Harlequin, Scaramouch, Zerlin, and the Doctors of the Italian comedy; he imagined them handling a palette and brushes, pounding drugs in a mortar, or turning over the leaves of an old treatise on alchemy beside an athanor. And so it was that, when, on one unhappy morning, he saw a huge blot of ink on one of the leaves of the third volume of the polyglot Bible bound in blue morocco and adorned with the arms of the Comte de Mirabeau, he had no doubt that a monkey was the author of the evil deed. The monkey had been pretending to take notes and had upset the inkpot. It must be a monkey belonging to a learned professor.

Imbued with this idea, Monsieur Sariette carefully studied the topography of the district, so as to draw a cordon round the group of houses amid which the d'Esparvieu house stood. Then he visited the four surrounding streets, asking at every door if there was a monkey in the house. He interrogated porters and their wives, washer-women, servants, a cobbler, a greengrocer, a glazier, clerks in bookshops, a priest, a bookbinder, two guardians of the peace, children, thus testing the diversity of character and variety of temper in one and the same people; for the replies he received were quite dissimilar in nature; some were rough, some were gentle; there were the coarse and the polished, the simple and the ironical, the prolix and the abrupt, the brief and even the silent. But of the animal he sought he had had neither sight nor sound, when under the archway of an old house in the Rue Servandoni, a small freckled, red-haired girl who looked after the door, made reply:

"There is Monsieur Ordonneau's monkey; would you care to see it?"

And without another word she conducted the old man to a stable at the other end of the yard. There on some rank straw and old bits of cloth, a young macaco with a chain round his middle sat and shivered. He was no taller than a five-year-old child. His livid face, his wrinkled brow, his thin lips were all expressive of mortal sadness. He fixed on the visitor the still lively gaze of his yellow eyes. Then with his small dry hand he seized a carrot, put it to his mouth, and forthwith flung it away. Having looked at the newcomers for a moment, the exile turned away his head, as if he expected nothing further of mankind or of life. Sitting huddled up, one knee in his hand, he made no further movement, but at times a dry cough shook his breast.

"It's Edgar," said the small girl. "He is for sale, you know."

But the old book-lover, who had come armed with anger and resentment, thinking to find a cynical enemy, a monster of malice, an antibibliophile, stopped short, surprised, saddened, and overcome, before this little being devoid of strength and joy and hope.

Recognising his mistake, troubled by the almost human face which sorrow and suffering made more human still, he murmured "Forgive me" and bowed his head.

IV

WHICH IN ITS FORCEFUL BREVITY PROJECTS US TO THE LIMITS OF THE ACTUAL WORLD

TWO months elapsed; the domestic upheaval did not subside, and Monsieur Sariette's thoughts turned to the Freemasons. The papers he read were full of their crimes. Abbé Patouille deemed them capable of the darkest deeds, and believed them to be in league with the Jews and meditating the total overthrow of Christendom.

Having now arrived at the acme of power, they wielded a dominating influence in all the principal departments of State, they ruled the Chambers, there were five of them in the Ministry, and they filled the Elysée. Having some time since assassinated a President of the Republic because he was a patriot, they were getting rid of the accomplices and witnesses of their execrable crime. Few days passed without Paris being terror-stricken at some mysterious murder hatched in their Lodges. These were facts concerning which no doubt was possible. By what means did they gain access to the library? Monsieur Sariette could not imagine. What task had they come to fulfil? Why did they attack sacred antiquity and the origins of the Church? What impious designs were they forming? A heavy shadow hung over these terrible undertakings. The Catholic archivist feeling himself under the eye of the sons of Hiram was terrified and fell ill.

Scarcely had he recovered, when he resolved to pass the night in the very spot where these terrible mysteries were enacted, and to take the subtle and dangerous visitors by surprise. It was an enterprise that demanded all his slender courage. Being a man of delicate physique and of nervous temperament, Monsieur Sariette was naturally inclined to be fearful. On the 8th of January at nine o'clock in the evening, while the city lay asleep under a whirling snowstorm, he built up a good fire in the room containing the busts of the ancient poets and philosophers, and ensconced himself in an arm-chair at the chimney corner, a rug over his knees. On a small stand within reach of his hand were a lamp, a bowl of black coffee, and a revolver borrowed from the youthful Maurice. He tried to read his paper, *La Croix,* but the letters danced beneath his eyes. So he stared hard in front of him, saw nothing but the shadows, heard nothing but the wind, and fell asleep.

When he awoke the fire was out, the lamp was extinguished, leaving an acrid smell behind. But all around, the darkness was filled with milky brightness and phosphorescent lights. He thought he saw something flutter on the table. Stricken to the marrow with cold and terror, but upheld by a resolve stronger than any fear, he rose, approached the table, and passed his hands over the cloth. He saw nothing; even the lights faded, but under his fingers he felt a folio wide open; he tried to close it, the book resisted, jumped up and hit the imprudent librarian three blows on the head.

Monsieur Sariette fell down unconscious. . . .

Since then things had gone from bad to worse. Books left their allotted shelves in greater profusion than ever, and sometimes it was impossible to replace them; they disappeared. Monsieur Sariette discovered fresh losses daily. The Bollandists were now an imperfect set, thirty volumes of exegesis were missing. He himself had become unrecognisable. His face had shrunk to the size of one's fist and grown yellow as a lemon, his neck was elongated out of all proportion, his shoulders drooped, the clothes he wore hung on him as on a peg. He ate nothing, and at the *Crèmerie des Quatre Évêques* he would sit with dull eyes and bowed head, staring fixedly and vacantly at the saucer where, in a muddy juice, floated his stewed prunes. He did not hear old Guinardon relate how he had at last begun to restore the Delacroix paintings at St. Sulpice.

Monsieur René d'Esparvieu, when he heard the unhappy curator's alarming reports, used to answer drily:

"These books have been mislaid, they are not lost; look carefully, Monsieur Sariette, look carefully and you will find them."

And he murmured behind the old man's back:

"Poor old Sariette is in a bad way."

"I think," replied Abbé Patouille, "that his brain is going."

V

WHEREIN EVERYTHING SEEMS STRANGE BECAUSE EVERYTHING IS LOGICAL

HE Chapel of the Holy Angels, which lies on the right hand as you enter the Church of St. Sulpice, was hidden behind a scaffolding of planks. Abbé Patouille, Monsieur Gaétan, Monsieur Maurice, his nephew, and Monsieur Sariette, entered in single file through the low door cut in the wooden hoarding, and found old Guinardon on the top of his ladder standing in front of the Heliodorus. The old artist, surrounded by all sorts of tools and materials, was putting a white paste in the crack which cut in two the High Priest Onias. Zéphyrine, Paul Baudry's favourite model, Zéphyrine, who had lent her golden hair and polished shoulders to so many Magdalens, Marguerites, sylphs, and mermaids, and who, it is said, was beloved of the Emperor Napoleon III, was standing at the foot of the ladder with tangled locks, cadaverous cheeks, and dim eyes, older than old Guinardon, whose life she had shared for more than half a century. She had brought the painter's lunch in a basket.

Although the slanting rays fell grey and cold through the leaded and iron-barred window, Delacroix's colouring shone resplendent, and the roses on the cheeks of men and angels dimmed with their glorious beauty the rubicund countenance of old Guinardon, which stood out in relief against one of the temple's columns. These frescoes of the Chapel of the Holy Angels, though derided and insulted when they first appeared, have now become part of the classic tradition, and are united in immortality with the masterpieces of Rubens and Tintoretto.

Old Guinardon, bearded and long-haired, looked like Father Time effacing the works of man's genius. Gaétan, in alarm, called out to him:

"Carefully, Monsieur Guinardon, carefully. Do not scrape too much."

The painter reassured him.

"Fear nothing, Monsieur Gaétan. I do not paint in that style. My art is a higher one. I work after the manner of Cimabue, Giotto, and Beato Angelico, not in the style of Delacroix. This surface here is too heavily charged with contrast and opposition to give a really sacred effect. It is true that Chenavard said that Christianity loves the picturesque, but Chenavard was a rascal with neither faith nor principle—an infidel. . . . Look, Monsieur d'Esparvieu, I fill up the crevice, I relay the scales of paint which are peeling. That is all. . . . The damage, due to the sinking of the wall, or more probably to a seismic shock, is confined to a very small space. This painting of oil and wax applied on a very dry foundation is far more solid than one might think.

"I saw Delacroix engaged on this work. Impassioned but anxious, he modelled feverishly, scraped out, re-painted unceasingly; his mighty hand made childish blunders, but the thing is done with the mastery of a genius and the inexperience of a schoolboy. It is a marvel how it holds."

The good man was silent, and went on filling in the crevice.

"How classic and traditional the composition is," said Gaétan. "Time was when one could recognise nothing but its amazing novelty; now one can see in it a multitude of old Italian formulas."

"I may allow myself the luxury of being just, I possess the qualifications," said the old man from the top of his lofty ladder. "Delacroix lived in a blasphemous and godless age. A painter of the decadence, he was not without pride nor grandeur. He was greater than his times. But he lacked faith, single-heartedness, and purity. To be able to see and paint angels he needed that virtue of angels and primitives, that supreme virtue which, with God's help, I do my best to practise, chastity."

"Hold your tongue, Michel; you are as big a brute as any of them."

Thus Zéphyrine, devoured with jealousy because that very morning on the stairs she had seen her lover kiss the bread-woman's daughter, to wit the youthful Octavie, who was as squalid and radiant as one of Rembrandt's Brides. She had loved Michel madly in the happy days long since past, and love had never died out in Zéphyrine's heart.

Old Guinardon received the flattering insult with a smile that he dissembled, and raised his eyes to the ceiling, where the archangel Michael, terrible in azure cuirass and gilt helmet, was springing heavenwards in all the radiance of his glory.

Meanwhile Abbé Patouille, blinking, and shielding his eyes with his hat against the glaring light from the window, began to examine the pictures one after another: Heliodorus being scourged by the angels, St. Michael vanquishing the Demons, and the combat of Jacob and the Angel.

"All this is exceedingly fine," he murmured at last, "but why has the artist only represented wrathful angels on these walls? Look where I will in this chapel, I see but heralds of celestial anger, ministers of divine vengeance. God wishes to be feared; He wishes also to be loved. I would fain perceive on these walls messengers of peace and of clemency. I should like to see the Seraphim who purified the lips of the prophet, St. Raphael who gave back his sight to old Tobias, Gabriel who announced the Mystery of the Incarnation to Mary, the Angel who delivered St. Peter from his chains, the Cherubim who bore the dead St. Catherine to the top of Sinai. Above all, I should like to be able to contemplate those heavenly guardians which God gives to every man baptized in His name. We each have one who follows all our steps, who comforts us and upholds us. It would be pleasant indeed to admire these enchanting spirits, these beautiful faces."

"Ah, Abbé! it depends on the point of view," answered Gaétan. "Delacroix was no sentimentalist. Old Ingres was not very far wrong in saying that this great man's work reeks of fire and brimstone. Look at the sombre, splendid beauty of those angels, look at those androgynes so proud and fierce, at those pitiless youths who lift avenging rods against Heliodorus, note this mysterious wrestler touching the patriarch on the hip. . . ."

"Hush," said Abbé Patouille. "According to the Bible he is no angel like the others; if he be an angel, he is the Angel of Creation, the Eternal Son of God. I am surprised that the Venerable Curé of St. Sulpice, who entrusted the decoration of this chapel to Monsieur Eugène Delacroix, did not tell him that the patriarch's symbolic struggle with Him who was nameless took place in profound darkness, and that the subject is quite out of place here, since it pre-figures the Incarnation of Jesus Christ. The best artists go astray when they fail to obtain their ideas of Christian iconography from a qualified ecclesiastic. The institutions of Christian art form the subject of numerous works with which you are doubtless acquainted, Monsieur Sariette."

Monsieur Sariette was gazing vacantly about him. It was the third morning after his adventurous night in the library. Being, however, thus called upon by the venerable ecclesiastic, he pulled himself together and replied:

"On this subject we may with advantage consult Molanus, *De Historia Sacrarum Imaginum et Picturarum,* in the edition given us by Noël Paquot, dated Louvain, 1771; Cardinal Frederico Borromeo, *De Pictura Sacra,* and the Iconography of Didron; but this last work must be read with caution."

Having thus spoken, Monsieur Sariette relapsed into silence. He was pondering on his devastated library.

"On the other hand," continued Abbé Patouille, "since an example of the holy anger of the angels was necessary in this chapel, the painter is to be commended for having depicted for us in imitation of Raphael the heavenly messengers who chastised Heliodorus. Ordered by Seleucus, King of Syria, to carry off the treasures contained in the Temple, Heliodorus was stricken by an angel in a cuirass of gold mounted on a magnificently caparisoned steed. Two other angels smote him with rods. He fell to earth, as Monsieur Delacroix shows us here, and was swallowed up in darkness. It is right and salutary that this adventure should be cited as an example to the Republican Commissioners of Police and to the sacrilegious agents of the law. There will always be Heliodoruses, but, let it be known, every time they lay their hands on the property of the Church, which is the property of the poor, they shall be chastised with rods and blinded by the angels."

"I should like this painting, or, better still, Raphael's sublimer conception of the same subject, to be engraved in little pictures fully coloured, and distributed as rewards in all the schools."

"Uncle," said young Maurice, with a yawn, "I think these things are simply ghastly. I prefer Matisse and Metzinger."

These words fell unheeded, and old Guinardon from his ladder held forth:

"Only the primitives caught a glimpse of Heaven. Beauty is only to be found between the thirteenth and fifteenth centuries. The antique, the impure antique, which regained its pernicious influence over the minds of the sixteenth century, inspired poets and painters with criminal notions and immodest conceptions, with horrid impurities, filth. All the artists of the Renaissance were swine, including Michael-Angelo."

Then, perceiving that Gaétan was on the point of departure, Père

Guinardon assumed an air of bonhomie, and said to him in a confidential tone:

"Bonsieur Gaétan, if you're not afraid of climbing up my five flights, come and have a look at my den. I've got two or three little canvases I wouldn't mind parting with, and they might interest you. All good, honest, straightforward stuff. I'll show you, among other things, a tasty, spicy little Baudouin that would make your mouth water."

At this speech Gaétan made off. As he descended the church steps and turned down the Rue Princesse, he found himself accompanied by old Sariette, and fell to unburdening himself to him, as he would have done to any human creature, or indeed to a tree, a lamp-post, a dog, or his own shadow, of the indignation with which the æsthetic theories of the old painter inspired him.

"Old Guinardon overdoes it with his Christian art and his Primitives! Whatever the artist conceives of Heaven is borrowed from earth; God, the Virgin, the Angels, men and women, saints, the light, the clouds. When he was designing figures for the chapel windows at Dreux, old Ingres drew from life a pure, fine study of a woman, which may be seen, among many others, in the Musée Bonnat at Bayonne. Old Ingres had written at the bottom of the page in case he should forget: 'Mademoiselle Cécile, admirable legs and thighs'—and so as to make Mademoiselle Cécile into a saint in Paradise, he gave her a robe, a cloak, a veil, inflicting thus a shameful decline in her estate, for the tissues of Lyons and Genoa are worthless compared with the youthful living tissue, rosy with pure blood; the most beautiful draperies are despicable compared with the lines of a beautiful body. In fact, clothing for flesh that is desirable and ripe for wedlock is an unmerited shame, and the worst of humiliations"; and Gaétan, walking carelessly in the gutter of the Rue Garancière, continued: "Old Guinardon is a pestilential idiot. He blasphemes Antiquity, sacred Antiquity, the age when the gods were kind. He exalts an epoch when the painter and the sculptor had all their lessons to learn over again. In point of fact, Christianity has run contrary to art in so much as it has not favoured the study of the nude. Art is the representation of nature, and nature is pre-eminently the human body; it is the nude."

"Pardon, pardon," purred old Sariette. "There is such a thing as spiritual, or, as one might term it, inward beauty, which, since the days of Fra Angelico down to those of Hippolyte Flandrin, Christian art has——"

But Gaétan, never hearing a word of all this, went on hurling his impetuous observations at the stones of the old street and the snow-laden clouds overhead:

"The Primitives cannot be judged as a whole, for they are utterly unlike each other. This old madman confounds them all together.

Cimabue is a corrupt Byzantine, Giotto gives hints of powerful genius, but his modelling is bad, and, like children, he gives all his characters the same face. The early Italians have grace and joy, because they are Italians. The Venetians have an instinct for fine colour. But when all is said and done these exquisite craftsmen enamel and gild rather than paint. There is far too much softness about the heart and the colouring of your saintly Angelico for me. As for the Flemish school, that's quite another pair of shoes. They can use their hands, and in glory of workmanship they are on a level with the Chinese lacquer-workers. The technique of the brothers Van Eyck is a marvel, but I cannot discover in their Adoration of the Lamb the charm and mystery that some have vaunted. Everything in it is treated with a pitiless perfection; it is vulgar in feeling and cruelly ugly. Memling may touch one perhaps; but he creates nothing but sick wretches and cripples; under the heavy, rich, and ungraceful robing of his virgins and saints one divines some very lamentable anatomy. I did not wait for Rogier van der Wyden to call himself Roger de la Pasture and turn Frenchman in order to prefer him to Memling. This Rogier or Roger is less of a ninny; but then he is more lugubrious, and the rigidity of his lines bears eloquent testimony to his poverty-stricken figures. It is a strange perversion to take pleasure in these carnivalesque figures when one can have the paintings of Leonardo, Titian, Correggio, Velasquez, Rubens, Rembrandt, Poussin, or Prud'hon. Really it is a perverted instinct."

Meanwhile the Abbé Patouille and Maurice d'Esparvieu were strolling leisurely along in the wake of the esthete and the librarian. As a general rule the Abbé Patouille was little inclined to talk theology with laymen, or, for that matter, with clerics either. Carried away, however, by the attractiveness of the subject, he was telling the youthful Maurice all about the sacred mission of those guardian angels which Monsieur Delacroix had so inopportunely excluded from his picture. And in order to give more adequate expression to his thoughts on such lofty themes, the Abbé Patouille borrowed whole phrases and sentences from Bossuet. He had got them up by heart to put in his sermons, for he adhered strongly to tradition.

"Yes, my son," he was saying, "God has appointed tutelary spirits to be near us. They come to us laden with His gifts. They return laden with our prayers. Such is their task. Not an hour, not a moment passes but they are at our side, ready to help us, ever fervent and unwearying guardians, watchmen that never slumber."

"Quite so, Abbé," murmured Maurice, who was wondering by what cunning artifice he could get on the soft side of his mother and persuade her to give him some money of which he was urgently in need.

VI

WHEREIN PÈRE SARIETTE DISCOVERS HIS MISSING TREASURES

NEXT morning Monsieur Sariette entered Monsieur René d'Esparvieu's study without knocking. He raised his arms to the heavens, his few hairs were standing straight up on his head. His eyes were big with terror. In husky tones he stammered out the dreadful news. A very old manscript of Flavius Josephus; sixty volumes of all sizes; a priceless jewel, namely, a *Lucretius* adorned with the arms of Philippe de Vendôme, Grand Prior of France, with notes in Voltaire's own hand; a manuscript of Richard Simon, and a set of Gassendi's correspondence with Gabriel Naudé, comprising two hundred and thirty-eight unpublished letters, had disappeared. This time the owner of the library was alarmed.

He mounted in haste to the abode of the philosophers and the globes, and there with his own eyes confirmed the magnitude of the disaster.

There were yawning gaps on many a shelf. He searched here and there, opened cupboards, dragged out brooms, dusters, and fire-extinguishers, rattled the shovel in the coke fire, shook out Monsieur Sariette's best frock-coat that was hanging in the cloak-room, and then stood and gazed disconsolately at the empty places left by the Gassendi portfolios.

For the past half-century the whole learned world had been loudly clamouring for the publication of this correspondence. Monsieur René d'Esparvieu had not responded to the universal desire, unwilling either to assume so heavy a task, or to resign it to others. Having found much boldness of thought in these letters, and many passages of more libertine tendency than the piety of the twentieth century could endure, he preferred that they should remain unpublished; but he felt himself responsible for their safe-keeping, not only to his country but to the whole civilized world.

"How can you have allowed yourself to be robbed of such a treasure?" he asked severely of Monsieur Sariette.

"How can I have allowed myself to be robbed of such a treasure?" repeated the unhappy librarian. "Monsieur, if you opened my breast, you would find that question engraved upon my heart."

Unmoved by this powerful utterance, Monsieur d'Esparvieu continued with pent-up fury:

"And you have discovered no single sign that would put you on the track of the thief, Monsieur Sariette? You have no suspicion, not the faintest idea, of the way these things have come to pass?

You have seen nothing, heard nothing, noticed nothing, learnt nothing? You must grant this is unbelievable. Think, Monsieur Sariette, think of the possible consequences of this unheard-of theft, committed under your eyes. A document of inestimable value in the history of the human mind disappears. Who has stolen it? Why has it been stolen? Who will gain by it? Those who have got possession of it doubtless know that they will be unable to dispose of it in France. They will go and sell it in America or Germany. Germany is greedy for such literary monuments. Should the correspondence of Gassendi with Gabriel Naudé go over to Berlin, if it is published there by German savants, what a disaster, nay, what a scandal! Monsieur Sariette, have you not thought of that? . . ."

Beneath the stroke of an accusation all the more cruel in that he brought it against himself, Monsieur Sariette stood stupefied, and was silent. And Monsieur d'Esparvieu continued to overwhelm him with bitter reproaches.

"And you make no effort. You devise nothing to find these inestimable treasures. Make enquiries, bestir yourself, Monsieur Sariette; use your wits. It is well worth while."

And Monsieur d'Esparvieu went out, throwing an icy glance at his librarian.

Monsieur Sariette sought the lost books and manuscripts in every spot where he had already sought them a hundred times, and where they could not possibly be. He even looked in the coke-box and under the leather seat of his arm-chair. When midday struck he mechanically went downstairs. At the foot of the stairs he met his old pupil Maurice, with whom he exchanged a bow. But he only saw men and things as through a mist.

The broken-hearted curator had already reached the hall when Maurice called him back.

"Monsieur Sariette, while I think of it, do have the books removed that are choking up my garden-house."

"What books, Maurice?"

"I could not tell you, Monsieur Sariette, but there are some in Hebrew, all worm-eaten, with a whole heap of old papers. They are in my way. You can't turn round in the passage."

"Who took them there?"

"I'm bothered if I know."

And the young man rushed off to the dining-room, the luncheon gong having sounded quite a minute ago.

Monsieur Sariette tore away to the summer-house. Maurice had spoken the truth. About a hundred volumes were there, on tables, on chairs, even on the floor. When he saw them he was divided betwixt joy and fear, filled with amazement and anxiety. Happy in the finding of his lost treasure, dreading to lose it again, and completely overwhelmed with astonishment, the man of books alternately babbled like an infant and uttered the hoarse cries of a maniac. He recognised his Hebrew Bibles, his ancient Talmuds, his very old manuscript of Flavius Josephus, his portfolios of Gassendi's letters to Gabriel Naudé, and his richest jewel of all, to wit, *Lucretius* adorned with the arms of the Grand Prior of France, and with notes in Voltaire's own hand. He laughed, he cried, he kissed the morocco, the calf, the parchment, and vellum, even the wooden boards studded with nails.

As fast as Hippolyte, the manservant, returned with an armful to the library, Monsieur Sariette, with a trembling hand, restored them piously to their places.

VII

OF A SOMEWHAT LIVELY INTEREST, WHEREOF THE MORAL WILL, I HOPE, APPEAL GREATLY TO MY READERS, SINCE IT CAN BE EXPRESSED BY THIS SORROWFUL QUERY: "THOUGHT, WHITHER DOST THOU LEAD ME?" FOR IT IS A UNIVERSALLY ADMITTED TRUTH THAT IT IS UNHEALTHY TO THINK AND THAT TRUE WISDOM LIES IN NOT THINKING AT ALL

ALL the books were now once more assembled in the pious keeping of Monsieur Sariette. But this happy reunion was not destined to last. The following night twenty volumes left their places, among them the *Lucretius* of Prior de Vendôme. Within a week the old Hebrew and Greek texts had all returned to the summer-house, and every night during the ensuing month they left their shelves and secretly went on the same path. Others betook themselves no one knew whither.

On hearing of these mysterious occurrences, Monsieur René d'Esparvieu merely remarked with frigidity to his librarian:

"My poor Sariette, all this is very queer, very queer indeed."

And when Monsieur Sariette tentatively advised him to lodge a formal complaint or to inform the Commissaire de Police, Monsieur d'Esparvieu cried out upon him:

"What are you suggesting, Monsieur Sariette? Divulge domestic secrets, make a scandal! You cannot mean it. I have enemies, and I am proud of it. I think I have deserved them. What I might complain about is that I am wounded in the house of my friend, attacked with unheard-of violence, by fervent loyalists, who, I grant you, are good Catholics, but exceedingly bad Christians. . . . In a word, I am watched, spied upon, shadowed, and you suggest, Monsieur Sariette, that I should make a present of this comic-opera mystery, this burlesque adventure, this story in which we both cut somewhat pitiable figures, to a set of spiteful journalists? Do you wish to cover me with ridicule?"

The result of the colloquy was that the two gentlemen agreed to change all the locks in the library. Estimates were asked for and workmen called in. For six weeks the d'Esparvieu household rang from morning till night with the sound of hammers, the hum of centre-bits, and the grating of files. Fires were always going in the abode of the philosophers and globes, and the people of the house were simply sickened by the smell of heated oil. The old, smooth, easy-running locks were replaced, on the cupboards and doors of the rooms, by stubborn and tricky fastenings. There was nothing but combinations of locks, letter-padlocks, safety-bolts, bars, chains, and electric alarm-bells.

All this display of ironmongery inspired fear. The lock-cases glistened, and there was much grinding of bolts. To gain access to a room, a cupboard, or a drawer, it was necessary to know a certain number, of which Monsieur Sariette alone was cognisant. His head was filled with bizarre words and tremendous numbers, and he got entangled among all these cryptic signs, these square, cubic, and triangular figures. He himself couldn't get the doors and the cupboards undone, yet every morning he found them wide open, and the books thrown about, ransacked, and hidden away. In the gutter of the Rue Servandoni a policeman picked up a volume of Salomon Reinach on the identity of Barabbas and Jesus Christ. As it bore the book-plate of the d'Esparvieu library he returned it to the owner.

Monsieur René d'Esparvieu, not even deigning to inform Monsieur Sariette of the fact, made up his mind to consult a magistrate, a friend in whom he had complete confidence, to wit, a certain Monsieur des Aubels, Counsel at the Law Courts, who had put through many an important affair. He was a little plump man, very red, very bald, with a cranium that shone like a billiard ball. He entered the library one morning feigning to come as a book-lover, but he soon showed that he knew nothing about books. While all the busts of the ancient philosophers were reflected in his shining pate, he put divers insidious questions to Monsieur Sariette, who grew uncomfortable and turned red, for innocence is easily flustered. From that moment Monsieur des Aubels had a mighty suspicion that Monsieur Sariette was the perpetrator of the very thefts he denounced with horror; and it immediately occurred to him to seek out the accomplices of the crime. As regards motives, he did not trouble about them; motives are always to be found. Monsieur des Aubels told Monsieur René d'Esparvieu that, if he liked, he would have the house secretly watched by a detective from the Prefecture.

"I will see that you get Mignon," he said. "He is an excellent servant, assiduous and prudent."

By six o'clock next morning Mignon was already walking up and down outside the d'Esparvieus' house, his head sunk between his shoulders, wearing love-locks which showed from under the narrow brim of his bowler hat, his eye cocked over his shoulder. He wore an enormous dull-black moustache, his hands and feet were huge; in fact, his whole appearance was distinctly memorable. He paced regularly up and down from the nearest of the big rams' head pillars which adorn the Hôtel de la Sordière to the end of the Rue Garancière, towards the apse of St. Sulpice Church and the dome of the Chapel of the Virgin.

Henceforth it became impossible to enter or leave the d'Esparvieus' house without feeling that one's every action, that one's very thoughts, were being spied upon. Mignon was a prodigious person endowed with powers that Nature denies to other mortals. He neither ate nor slept. At all hours of the day and night, in wind and rain, he was to be found outside the house, and no one escaped the X-rays of his eye. One felt pierced through and through, penetrated to the very marrow, worse than naked, bare as a skeleton. It was the affair of a moment; the detective did not even stop, but continued his everlasting walk. It became intolerable. Young Maurice threatened to leave the paternal roof if he was to be so radiographed. His mother and his sister Berthe complained of his piercing look; it offended the chaste modesty of their souls. Mademoiselle Caporal, young Léon d'Esparvieu's governess, felt an indescribable embarrassment. Monsieur René d'Esparvieu was sick of the whole business. He never crossed his own threshold without crushing his hat over his eyes to avoid the investigating ray and without wishing old Sariette, the *fons et origo* of all the evil, at the devil. The intimates of the household, such as Abbé Patouille and Uncle Gaétan, made themselves scarce; visitors gave up calling, tradespeople hesitated about leaving their goods, the carts belonging to the big shops scarcely dared stop. But it was among the domestics that the spying roused the most disorder.

The footman, afraid, under the eye of the police, to go and join the cobbler's wife over her solitary labours in the afternoon, found the house unbearable and gave notice. Odile, Madame d'Esparvieu's lady's-maid, not daring, as was her custom after her mistress had retired, to introduce Octave, the handsomest of the neighbouring bookseller's clerks, to her little room upstairs, grew melancholy, irritable and nervous, pulled her mistress's hair while dressing it, spoke insolently, and made advances to Monsieur Maurice. The cook, Madame Malgoire, a serious matron of some fifty years, having no more visits from Auguste, the wine-merchant's man in the Rue Servandoni, and being incapable of suffering a privation so contrary to her temperament, went mad, sent up a raw rabbit to table, and announced that the Pope had asked her hand in marriage. At last, after a fortnight of superhuman assiduity, contrary to all known laws of organic life, and to the essential conditions of animal economy, Mignon, the detective, having observed nothing abnormal, ceased his surveillance and withdrew without a word, refusing to accept a gratuity. In the library the dance of the books became livelier than ever.

"That is all right," said Monsieur des Aubels. "Since nothing comes in nor goes out, the evil-doer must be in the house."

The magistrate thought it possible to discover the criminal without police-warrant or enquiry. On a date agreed upon at midnight, he had the floor of the library, the treads of the stairs, the vestibule, the garden path leading to Monsieur Maurice's summer-house, and the entrance hall of the latter, all covered with a coating of talc.

The following morning Monsieur des Aubels, assisted by a pho-

tographer from the Prefecture, and accompanied by Monsieur René d'Esparvieu and Monsieur Sariette, came to take the imprints. They found nothing in the garden, the wind had blown away the coating of talc; nothing in the summer-house either. Young Maurice told them he thought it was some practical joke and that he had brushed away the white dust with the hearth-brush. The real truth was, he had effaced the traces left by the boots of Odile, the lady's-maid. On the stairs and in the library the very light print of a bare foot could be discerned, it seemed to have sprung into the air and to have touched the ground at rare intervals and without any pressure. They discovered five of these traces. The clearest was to be found in the abode of the busts and spheres, on the edge of the table where the books were piled. The photographer took several negatives of this imprint.

"This is more terrifying than anything else," murmured Monsieur Sariette.

Monsieur des Aubels did not hide his surprise.

Three days later the anthropometrical department of the Prefecture returned the proofs exhibited to them, saying that they were not in the records.

After dinner Monsieur René showed the photographs to his brother Gaétan, who examined them with profound attention, and after a long silence exclaimed:

"No wonder they have not got this at the Prefecture; it is the foot of a god or of an athlete of antiquity. The sole that made this impression is of a perfection unknown to our races and our climates. It exhibits toes of exquisite grace, and a divine heel."

René d'Esparvieu cried out upon his brother for a madman.

"He is a poet," sighed Madame d'Esparvieu.

"Uncle," said Maurice, "you'll fall in love with this foot if you ever come across it."

"Such was the fate of Vivant Denon, who accompanied Bonaparte to Egypt," replied Gaétan. "At Thebes, in a tomb violated by the Arabs, Denon found the little foot of a mummy of marvellous beauty. He contemplated it with extraordinary fervour. 'It is the foot of a young woman,' he pondered, 'of a princess—of a charming creature. No covering has ever marred its perfect shape.' Denon admired, adored, and loved it. You may see a drawing of this little foot in Denon's atlas of his journey to Egypt, whose leaves one could turn over upstairs, without going further afield, if only Monsieur Sariette would ever let us see a single volume of his library."

Sometimes, in bed, Maurice, waking in the middle of the night, thought he heard the sound of pages being turned over in the next room, and the thud of bound volumes falling on the floor.

One morning at five o'clock he was coming home from the club, after a night of bad luck, and while he stood outside the door of the summer-house, hunting in his pocket for his keys, his ears distinctly heard a voice sighing:

"Knowledge, whither dost thou lead me? Thought, whither dost thou lure me?"

But entering the two rooms he saw nothing, and told himself that his ears must have deceived him.

VIII

WHICH SPEAKS OF LOVE, A SUBJECT WHICH ALWAYS GIVES PLEASURE, FOR A TALE WITHOUT LOVE IS LIKE BEEF WITHOUT MUSTARD: AN INSIPID DISH

NOTHING ever astonished Maurice. He never sought to know the causes of things and dwelt tranquilly in the world of appearances. Not denying the eternal truth, he nevertheless followed vain things as his fancy led him.

Less addicted to sport and violent exercise than most young people of his generation, he followed unconsciously the old erotic traditions of his race. The French were ever the most gallant of men, and it were a pity they should lose this advantage. Maurice preserved it. He was in love with no woman, but, as St. Augustine said, he loved to love. After paying the tribute that was rightly due to the imperishable beauty and secret arts of Madame de la Berthelière, he had enjoyed the impetuous caresses of a young singer called Luciole. At present he was joylessly experiencing the primitive perversity of Odile, his mother's lady's-maid, and the tearful adoration of the beautiful Madame Boittier. And he felt a great void in his heart.

It chanced that one Wednesday, on entering the drawing-room where his mother entertained her friends—who were, generally speaking, unattractive and austere ladies, with a sprinkling of old men and very young people—he noticed, in this intimate circle, Madame des Aubels, the wife of the magistrate at the Law Courts, whom Monsieur d'Esparvieu had vainly consulted on the mysterious ransacking of his library. She was young, he found her pretty, and not without cause. Gilberte had been modelled by the Genius of the Race, and no other genius had had a part in the work.

Thus all her attributes inspired desire, and nothing in her shape or her being aroused any other sentiment.

The law of attraction which draws world to world moved young Maurice to approach this delicious creature, and under its influence he offered to escort her to the tea-table. And when Gilberte was served with tea, he said:

"We should hit it off quite well together, you and I, don't you think?"

He spoke in this way, according to modern usage, so as to avoid inane compliments and to spare a woman the boredom of listening to one of those old declarations of love which, containing nothing but what is vague and undefined, require neither a truthful nor an exact reply.

And profiting by the fact that he had an opportunity of conversing secretly with Madame des Aubels for a few minutes, he spoke urgently and to the point. Gilberte, so far as one could judge, was made rather to awaken desire than to feel it. Nevertheless, she well knew that her fate was to love, and she followed it willingly and with pleasure. Maurice did not particularly displease her. She would have preferred him to be an orphan, for experience had taught her how disappointing it sometimes is to love the son of the house.

"Will you?" he said by way of conclusion.

She pretended not to understand, and with her little *foie-gras* sandwich raised half-way to her mouth she looked at Maurice with wondering eyes.

"Will I *what?*" she asked.

"You know quite well."

Madame des Aubels lowered her eyes, and sipped her tea, for her prudishness was not quite vanquished. Meanwhile Maurice, taking her empty cup from her hand, murmured:

"Saturday, five o'clock, 126 Rue de Rome, on the ground-floor, the door on the right, under the arch. Knock three times."

Madame des Aubels glanced severely and imperturbably at the son of the house, and with a self-possessed air rejoined the circle of highly respectable women to whom the Senator Monsieur Le Fol was explaining how artificial incubators were employed at the agricultural colony at St. Julienne.

The following Saturday, Maurice, in his ground-floor flat, awaited Madame des Aubels. He waited her in vain. No light hand came to knock three times on the door under the arch. And Maurice gave way to imprecation, inwardly calling the absent one a jade and a hussy. His fruitless wait, his frustrated desires, rendered him unjust. For Madame des Aubels in not coming where she had never promised to go hardly deserved these names; but we judge human actions by the pleasure or pain they cause us.

Maurice did not put in an appearance in his mother's drawing-room until a fortnight after the conversation at the tea-table. He came late. Madame des Aubels had been there for half an hour. He bowed coldly to her, took a seat some way off, and affected to be listening to the talk.

"Worthily matched," a rich male voice was saying; "the two antagonists were well calculated to render the struggle a terrible and uncertain one. General Bol, with unprecedented tenacity, maintained his position as though he were rooted in the very soil. General Milpertuis, with an agility truly superhuman, kept carrying out movements of the most dazzling rapidity around his immovable adversary. The battle continued to be waged with terrible stubbornness. We were all in an agony of suspense. . . .”

It was General d’Esparvieu describing the autumn manœuvres to a company of breathlessly interested ladies. He was talking well and his audience were delighted. Proceeding to draw a comparison between the French and German methods, he defined their distinguishing characteristics and brought out the conspicuous merits of both with a lofty impartiality. He did not hesitate to affirm that each system had its advantages, and at first made it appear to his circle of wondering, disappointed, and anxious dames, whose countenances were growing increasingly gloomy, that France and Germany were practically in a position of equality. But little by little, as the strategist went on to give a clearer definition of the two methods, that of the French began to appear flexible, elegant, vigorous, full of grace, cleverness, and verve; that of the Germans heavy, clumsy, and undecided. And slowly and surely the faces of the ladies began to clear and to light up with joyous smiles. In order to dissipate any lingering shadows of misgiving from the minds of these wives, sisters, and sweethearts, the General gave them to understand that we were in a position to make use of the German method when it suited us, but that the Germans could not avail themselves of the French method. No sooner had he delivered himself of these sentiments than he was button-holed by Monsieur le Truc de Ruffec, who was engaged in founding a patriotic society known as “Swordsmen All,” of which the object was to regenerate France and ensure her superiority over all her adversaries. Even children in the cradle were to be enrolled, and Monsieur le Truc de Ruffec offered the honorary presidency to General d’Esparvieu.

Meanwhile Maurice was appearing to be interested in a conversation that was taking place between a very gentle old lady and the Abbé Lapetite, Chaplain to the Dames du Saint Sang. The old lady, severely tried of late by illness and the loss of friends, wanted to know how it was that people were unhappy in this world.

“How,” she asked Abbé Lapetite, “do you explain the scourges that afflict mankind? Why are there plagues, famines, floods, and earthquakes?”

“It is surely necessary that God should sometimes remind us of his existence,” replied Abbé Lapetite, with a heavenly smile.

Maurice appeared keenly interested in this conversation. Then he seemed fascinated by Madame Fillot-Grandin, quite a personable young woman, whose simple innocence, however, detracted all piquancy from her beauty, all savour from her bodily charms. A very sour, shrill-voiced old lady, who, affecting the dowdy, woollen weeds of poverty, displayed the pride of a great lady in the world of Christian finance, exclaimed in a squeaky voice:

"Well, my dear Madame d'Esparvieu, so you have had trouble here. The papers speak darkly of robbery, of thefts committed in Monsieur d'Esparvieu's valuable library, of stolen letters. . . ."

"Oh," said Madame d'Esparvieu, "if we are to believe all the newspapers say . . ."

"Oh, so, dear Madame, you have got your treasures back. All's well that ends well."

"The library is in perfect order," asserted Madame d'Esparvieu. "There is nothing missing."

"The library is on the floor above this, is it not?" asked young Madame des Aubels, showing an unexpected interest in the books.

Madame d'Esparvieu replied that the library occupied the whole of the second floor, and that they had put the least valuable books in the attics.

"Could I not go and look at it?"

The mistress of the house declared that nothing could be easier. She called to her son:

"Maurice, go and do the honours of the library to Madame des Aubels."

Maurice rose, and without uttering a word, mounted to the second floor in the wake of Madame des Aubels.

He appeared indifferent, but inwardly he rejoiced, for he had no doubt that Gilberte had feigned her ardent desire to inspect the library simply to see him in secret. And, while affecting indifference, he promised himself to renew those offers which, this time, would not be refused.

Under the romantic bust of Alexandre d'Esparvieu, they were met by the silent shadow of a little wan, hollow-eyed old man, who wore a settled expression of mute terror.

"Do not let us disturb you, Monsieur Sariette," said Maurice. "I am showing Madame des Aubels round the library."

Maurice and Madame des Aubels passed on into the great room where against the four walls rose presses filled with books and surmounted by bronze busts of poets, philosophers, and orators of antiquity. All was in perfect order, an order which seemed never to have been disturbed from the beginning of things.

Only, a black void was to be seen in the place which, only the evening before, had been filled by an unpublished manuscript of Richard Simon. Meanwhile, by the side of the young couple walked Monsieur Sariette, pale, faded, and silent.

"Really and truly, you have not been nice," said Maurice, with a look of reproach at Madame des Aubels.

She signed to him that the librarian might overhear. But he reassured her.

"Take no notice. It is old Sariette. He has become a complete idiot." And he repeated: "No, you have not been at all nice. I awaited you. You did not come. You have made me unhappy."

After a moment's silence, while one heard the low melancholy whistling of asthma in poor Sariette's bronchial tubes, young Maurice continued insistently:

"You are wrong."

"Why wrong?"

"Wrong not to do as I ask you."

"Do you still think so?"

"Certainly."

"You meant it seriously?"

"As seriously as can be."

Touched by his assurance of sincere and constant feeling, and thinking she had resisted sufficiently, Gilberte granted to Maurice what she had refused him a fortnight ago.

They slipped into an embrasure of the window, behind an enormous celestial globe whereon were graven the Signs of the Zodiac and the figures of the stars, and there, their gaze fixed on the Lion, the Virgin, and the Scales, in the presence of a multitude of Bibles, before the works of the Fathers, both Greek and Latin, beneath the casts of Homer, Æschylus, Sophocles, Euripides, Herodotus, Thucydides, Socrates, Plato, Aristotle, Demosthenes, Cicero, Virgil, Horace, Seneca, and Epictetus, they exchanged vows of love and a long kiss on the mouth.

Almost immediately Madame des Aubels bethought herself that she still had some calls to pay, and that she must make her escape quickly, for love had not made her lose all sense of her own importance. But she had barely crossed the landing with Maurice when they heard a hoarse cry and saw Monsieur Sariette plunge madly downstairs, exclaiming as he went:

"Stop it, stop it; I saw it fly away! It escaped from the shelf by itself. It crossed the room . . . there it is—there! It's going downstairs. Stop it! It has gone out of the door on the ground floor!"

"What?" asked Maurice.

Monsieur Sariette looked out of the landing window, murmuring horror-struck:

"It's crossing the garden! It's going into the summer-house. Stop it, stop it!"

"But what is it?" repeated Maurice—"in God's name, what is it?"

"My Flavius Josephus," exclaimed Monsieur Sariette. "Stop it!"

And he fell down unconscious.

"You see he is quite mad," said Maurice to Madame des Aubels, as he lifted up the unfortunate librarian.

Gilberte, a little pale, said she also thought she had seen something in the direction indicated by the unhappy man, something flying.

Maurice had seen nothing, but he had felt what seemed like a gust of wind.

He left Monsieur Sariette in the arms of Hippolyte and the housekeeper, who had both hastened to the spot on hearing the noise.

The old gentleman had a wound in his head.

"All the better," said the housekeeper; "this wound may save him from having a fit."

Madame des Aubels gave her handkerchief to stop the blood, and recommended an arnica compress.

IX

WHEREIN IT IS SHOWN THAT, AS AN ANCIENT GREEK POET SAID, "NOTHING IS SWEETER THAN APHRODITE THE GOLDEN"

LTHOUGH he had enjoyed Madame des Aubel's favours for six whole months, Maurice still loved her. True they had had to separate during the summer. For lack of funds of his own he had had to go to Switzerland with his mother, and then to stop with the whole family at the Château d'Esparvieu. She had spent the summer with her mother at Niort, and the autumn with her husband at a little Normandy seaside place, so that they had hardly seen each other four or five times. But since the winter, kindly to lovers, had brought them back to town again, Maurice had been receiving her twice a week in his little flat in the Rue de Rome, and received no one else. No other woman had inspired him with feelings of such constancy and fidelity. What augmented his pleasure was that he believed himself loved, and indeed he was not unpleasing.

He thought that she did not deceive him, not that he had any reason to think so, but it appeared right and fitting that she should be content with him alone. What annoyed him was that she always kept him waiting, and was unpunctual in coming to their meeting-place; she was invariably late,—at times very late.

Now on Saturday, January 30th, since four o'clock in the afternoon, Maurice had been awaiting Madame des Aubels in the little pink room, where a bright fire was burning. He was gaily clad in a suit of flowered pyjamas, smoking Turkish cigarettes. At first he dreamt of receiving her with long kisses, with hitherto unknown caresses. A quarter of an hour having passed, he meditated serious and affectionate reproaches, then after an hour of disappointed waiting he vowed he would meet her with cold disdain.

At length she appeared, fresh and fragrant.

"It was scarcely worth while coming," he said bitterly, as she laid her muff and her little bag on the table and untied her veil before the wardrobe mirror.

Never, she told her beloved, had she had such trouble to get away. She was full of excuses, which he obstinately rejected. But no sooner had she the good sense to hold her tongue than he ceased his reproaches, and then nothing detracted from the longing with which she inspired him.

The curtains were drawn, the room was bathed in warm shadows lit by the dancing gleams of the fire. The mirrors in the wardrobe and on the chimney-piece shone with mysterious lights. Gilberte, leaning on her elbow, head on hand, was lost in thought. A little jeweller, a trustworthy and intelligent man, had shown her a wonderfully pretty pearl and sapphire bracelet; it was worth a great deal, and was to be had for a mere nothing. He had got it from a *cocotte* down on her luck, who was in a hurry to dispose of it. It was a rare chance; it would be a huge pity to let it slip.

"Would you like to see it, darling? I will ask the little man to let me have it to show you."

Maurice did not actually decline the proposal. But it was clear that he took no interest in the wonderful bracelet. "When small jewellers come across a great bargain, they keep it to themselves, and do not allow their customers to profit by it. Moreover, jewellery means nothing just now. Well-bred women have given up wearing it. Everyone goes in for sport, and jewellery does not go with sport."

Maurice spoke thus, contrary to truth, because having given his mistress a fur coat, he was in no hurry to give her anything more. He was not stingy, but he was careful with his money. His people did not give him a very large allowance, and his debts grew bigger every day. By satisfying the wishes of his inamorata too promptly he feared to arouse others still more pressing. The bargain seemed less wonderful to him than to Gilberte; besides, he liked to take the initiative in choosing his gifts. Above all, he thought that if he gave her too many presents he would be no longer sure of being loved for himself.

Madame des Aubels felt neither contempt nor surprise at this attitude; she was gentle and temperate, she knew men, and judged that one must take them as one found them, that for the most part they do not give very willingly, and that a woman should know how to make them give.

Suddenly a gas lamp was lighted in the street, and shone through the gaps in the curtains.

"Half-past six," she said. "We must be on the move."

Pricked by the touch of Time's fleeting wing, Maurice was conscious of reawakened desires and reanimated powers. A white and radiant offering, Gilberte, with her head thrown back, her eyes half closed, her lips apart, sunk in dreamy languor, was breathing slowly and placidly, when suddenly she started up with a cry of terror.

"Whatever is that?"

"Stay still," said Maurice, holding her back in his arms.

In his present mood, had the sky fallen it would not have troubled him. But in one bound she escaped from him. Crouching down, her eyes filled with terror, she was pointing with her finger at a figure which appeared in a corner of the room, between the fire-place and the wardrobe with the mirror. Then, unable to bear the sight, and nearly fainting, she hid her face in her hands.

X

WHICH FAR SURPASSES IN AUDACITY THE IMAGINA- TIVE FLIGHTS OF DANTE AND MILTON

AURICE at length turned his head, saw the figure, and perceiving that it moved, was also frightened. Meanwhile, Gilberte was regaining her senses. She imagined that what she had seen was some mistress whom her lover had hidden in the room. Inflamed with anger and disgust at the idea of such treach- ery, boiling with indignation, and glaring at her supposed rival, she exclaimed:

"A woman . . . a naked woman too! You bring me into a room where you allow your women to come, and when I arrive they have not had time to dress. And you reproach me with arriving late! Your impudence is beyond belief! Come, send the creature packing. If you wanted us both here together, you might at least have asked me whether it suited me. . . ."

Maurice, wide-eyed and groping for a revolver that had never been there, whispered in her ear:

"Be quiet . . . it is no woman. One can scarcely see, but it is more like a man."

She put her hands over her eyes again and screamed harder than ever.

"A man! Where does he come from? A thief. An assassin! Help! Help! Kill him. . . . Maurice, kill him! Turn on the light. No, don't turn on the light. . . ."

She made a mental vow that should she escape from this danger she would burn a candle to the Blessed Virgin. Her teeth chattered.

The figure made a movement.

"Keep away!" cried Gilberte. "Keep away!"

She offered the burglar all the money and jewels she had on the table if he would consent not to stir. Amid her surprise and terror the idea assailed her that her husband, dissembling his suspicions, had caused her to be followed, had posted witnesses, and had had recourse to the Commissaire de Police. In a flash she distinctly saw before her the long painful future, the glaring scandal, the pretended disdain, the cowardly desertion of her friends, the just mockery of society, for it is indeed ridiculous to be found out. She saw the divorce, the loss of her position and of her rank. She saw the dreary and narrow existence with her mother, when no one would make love to her, for men avoid women who fail to give them the security of the married state. And all this, why? Why this ruin, this disaster? For a piece of folly, for a mere nothing. Thus in a lightning flash spoke the conscience of Gilberte des Aubels.

"Have no fear, Madame," said a very sweet voice.

Slightly reassured, she found strength to ask:

"Who are you?"

"I am an angel," replied the voice.

"What did you say?"

"I am an angel. I am Maurice's guardian angel."

"Say it again. I am going mad. I do not understand. . . ."

Maurice, without understanding either, was indignant. He sprang forward and showed himself; with his right hand armed with a slipper he made a threatening gesture, and said in a rough voice:

"You are a low ruffian; oblige me by going the way you came."

"Maurice d'Esparvieu," continued the sweet voice, "He whom you adore as your Creator has stationed by the side of each of the faithful a good angel, whose mission it is to counsel and protect him; it is the invariable opinion of the Fathers, it is founded on many passages in the Bible, the Church admits it unanimously, without, however, pronouncing anathema upon those who hold a contrary opinion. You see before you one of these angels, yours, Maurice. I was commanded to watch over your innocence and to guard your chastity."

"That may be," said Maurice; "but you are certainly no gentleman. A gentleman would not permit himself to enter a room at such a moment. To be plain, what the deuce are you doing here?"

"I have assumed this appearance, Maurice, because, having henceforth to move among mankind, I have to make myself like them. The celestial spirits possess the power of assuming a form which renders them apparent to the eye and to the touch. This shape is real, because it is apparent, and all the realities in the world are but appearances."

Gilberte, pacified at length, was arranging her hair on her forehead.

The Angel pursued:

"The celestial spirits adopt, according to their fancy, one sex or the other, or both at once. But they cannot disguise themselves at any moment, according to their caprice or fantasy. Their metamorphoses are subject to constant laws, which you would not understand. Thus I have neither desire nor power to transform myself under your eyes, for your amusement or my own, into a lion, a tiger, a fly, or into a sycamore-shaving like the young Egyptian whose story was found in a tomb. I cannot change myself into an ass as did Lucius with the pomade of the youthful Photis. For in my wisdom I had fixed beforehand the hour of my apparition to mankind, nothing could hasten or delay it."

Impatient for enlightenment, Maurice asked for the second time:

"Still, what are you up to here?"

Joining her voice to his, Madame des Aubels asked: "Yes, indeed, what are you doing here?"

The Angel replied:

"Man, lend your ear. Woman, hear my voice. I am about to reveal to you a secret on which hangs the fate of the Universe. In rebellion against Him whom you hold to be the Creator of all things visible and invisible, I am preparing the Revolt of the Angels."

"Do not jest," said Maurice, who had faith and did not allow holy things to be played with.

But the Angel answered reproachfully: "What makes you think, Maurice, that I am frivolous and given to vain words?"

"Come, come," said Maurice, shrugging his shoulders. "You are not going to revolt against——"

He pointed to the ceiling—not daring to finish.

But the Angel continued:

"Do you not know that the sons of God have already revolted and that a great battle took place in the heavens?"

"That was a long time ago," said Maurice, putting on his socks.

Then the Angel replied:

"It was before the creation of the world. But nothing has changed since then in the heavens. The nature of the Angels is no different now from what it was originally. What they did then they could do again now."

"No! It is not possible. It is contrary to faith. If you were an angel, a good angel as you make out you are, it would never occur to you to disobey your Creator."

"You are in error, Maurice, and the authority of the Fathers condemns you. Origen lays it down in his homilies that good angels are fallible, that they sin every day and fall from Heaven like flies. Possibly you may be tempted to reject the authority of this Father, despite his knowledge of the Scriptures, because he is excluded from the Canon of the Saints. If this be so, I would remind you of the second chapter of Revelation, in which the Angels of Ephesus and Pergamos are rebuked for that they kept not ward over their church. You will doubtless contend that the angels to whom the Apostle here refers are, properly speaking, the Bishops of the two cities in question, and that he calls them angels on account of their ministry. It may be so, and I cede the point. But with what arguments, Maurice, would you counter the opinion of all those Doctors and Pontiffs whose unanimous teaching it is that angels may fall from good into evil? Such is the statement made by Saint Jerome in his Epistle to Damasus. . . ."

"Monsieur," said Madame des Aubels, "go away, I beg you."

But the Angel hearkened not, and continued:

"Saint Augustine, in his *True Religion,* Chapter XIII; Saint Gregory, in his *Morals,* Chapter XXIV; Isidore——"

"Monsieur, let me get my things on; I am in a hurry."

"In his treatise on *The Greatest Good,* Book I, Chapter XII; Bede on Job——"

"Oh, please, Monsieur . . ."

"Chapter VIII; John of Damascus on *Faith,* Book II, Chapter III. Those, I think, are sufficiently weighty authorities, and there is nothing for it, Maurice, but to admit your error. What has led you astray is that you have not duly considered my nature, which is free, active, and mobile, like that of all the angels, and that you have merely observed the grace and felicity with which you deem me so richly endowed. Lucifer possessed no less, yet he rebelled."

"But what on earth are you rebelling for?" asked Maurice.

"Isaiah," answered the child of light, "Isaiah has already asked, before you: *'Quomodo cecidisti de cœlo, Lucifer, qui mane oriebaris?'* Hearken, Maurice. Before Time was, the Angels rose up to win dominion over Heaven, the most beautiful of the Seraphim revolted through pride. As for me, it is science that has inspired me with the generous desire for freedom. Finding myself near you, Maurice, in a house containing one of the vastest libraries in the world, I acquired a taste for reading and a love of study. While, fordone with the toils of a sensual life, you lay sunk in heavy slumber, I surrounded myself with books, I studied, I pondered over their pages, sometimes in one of the rooms of the library, under the busts of the great men of antiquity, sometimes at the far end of the garden, in the room in the summer-house next to your own."

On hearing these words, young d'Esparvieu exploded with laughter and beat the pillow with his fist, an infallible sign of uncontrollable mirth.

"Ah . . . ah . . . ah! It was you who pillaged papa's library and drove poor old Sariette off his head. You know, he has become completely idiotic."

"Busily engaged," continued the Angel, "in cultivating for myself a sovereign intelligence, I paid no heed to that inferior being, and when he thought to offer obstacles to my researches and to disturb my work I punished him for his importunity.

"One particular winter's night in the abode of the philosophers and globes I let fall a volume of great weight on his head, which he tried to tear from my invisible hand. Then more recently, raising, with a vigorous arm composed of a column of condensed air, a precious manuscript of Flavius Josephus, I gave the imbecile such a fright, that he rushed out screaming on to the landing and (to borrow a striking expression from Dante Alighieri) fell even as a dead body falls. He was well rewarded, for you gave him, Madame, to staunch the blood from his wound, your little scented handkerchief. It was the day, you may remember, when behind a celestial globe you exchanged a kiss on the mouth with Maurice."

"Monsieur," said Madame des Aubels, with a frown, "I cannot allow you . . ."

But she stopped short, deeming it was an inopportune moment to appear over-exacting on a matter of decorum.

"I had made up my mind," continued the Angel impassively, "to examine the foundations of belief. I first attacked the monuments of Judaism, and I read all the Hebrew texts."

"You know Hebrew, then?" exclaimed Maurice.

"Hebrew is my native tongue: in Paradise for a long time we have spoken nothing else."

"Ah, you are a Jew. I might have deduced it from your want of tact."

The Angel, not deigning to hear, continued in his melodious voice: "I have delved deep into Oriental antiquities and also into those of Greece and Rome. I have devoured the works of theologians, philosophers, physicists, geologists, and naturalists. I have learnt. I have thought. I have lost my faith."

"What? You no longer believe in God?"

"I believe in Him, since my existence depends on His, and if He should fail to exist, I myself should fall into nothingness. I believe in Him, even as the Satyrs and the Mænads believed in Dionysus and for the same reason. I believe in the God of the Jews and the Christians. But I deny that He created the world; at the most He organised but an inferior part of it, and all that He touched bears the mark of His rough and unforeseeing touch. I do not think He is either eternal or infinite, for it is absurd to conceive of a being who is not bounded by space or time. I think Him limited, even very limited. I no longer believe Him to be the only God. For a long time He did not believe it Himself; in the beginning He was a polytheist; later, His pride and the flattery of His worshippers made Him a monotheist. His ideas have little connection; He is less powerful than He is thought to be. And, to speak candidly, He is not so much a god as a vain and ignorant demiurge. Those who, like myself, know His true nature, call Him Ialdabaoth."

"What's that you say?"

"Ialdabaoth."

"Ialdabaoth. What's that?"

"I have already told you. It is the demiurge whom, in your blindness, you adore as the one and only God."

"You're mad. I don't advise you to go and talk rubbish like that to Abbé Patouille."

"I am not in the least sanguine, my dear Maurice, of piercing the dense night of your intellect. I merely tell you that I am going to engage Ialdabaoth in conflict with some hopes of victory."

"Mark my words, you won't succeed."

"Lucifer shook His throne, and the issue was for a moment in doubt."

"What is your name?"

"Abdiel for the angels and saints, Arcade for mankind."

"Well, my poor Arcade, I regret to see you going to the bad. But confess that you are jesting with us. I could at a pinch understand your leaving Heaven for a woman. Love makes us commit the greatest follies. But you will never make me believe that you, who have seen God face to face, ultimately found the truth in old Sariette's musty books. No, you will never get me to believe that!"

"My dear Maurice, Lucifer was face to face with God, yet he refused to serve Him. As to the kind of truth one finds in books, it is a truth that enables us sometimes to discern what things are not, without ever enabling us to discover what they are. And this poor little truth has sufficed to prove to me that He in whom I blindly believed is not believable, and that men and angels have been deceived by the lies of Ialdabaoth."

"There is no Ialdabaoth. There is God. Come, Arcade, do the right thing. Renounce these follies, these impieties, dis-incarnate yourself, become once more a pure Spirit, and resume your office of guardian angel. Return to duty. I forgive you, but do not let us see you again."

"I should like to please you, Maurice. I feel a certain affection for you, for my heart is soft. But fate henceforth calls me elsewhere towards beings capable of thought and action."

"Monsieur Arcade," said Madame des Aubels, "withdraw, I implore you. It makes me horribly shy to be in this position before two men. I assure you I am not accustomed to it."

XI

RECOUNTS IN WHAT MANNER THE ANGEL, ATTIRED IN THE CAST-OFF GARMENTS OF A SUICIDE, LEAVES THE YOUTHFUL MAURICE WITHOUT A HEAVENLY GUARDIAN

"REASSURE yourself, Madame," replied the apparition, "your position is not as risky as you say. You are not confronted with two men, but with one man and an angel."

She examined the stranger with an eye which, piercing the gloom, was anxiously surveying a vague but by no means negligible indication, and asked:

"Monsieur, is it quite certain that you are an angel?"

The apparition prayed her to have no doubt about it, and gave some precise information as to his origin.

"There are three hierarchies of celestial spirits, each composed of nine choirs; the first comprises the Seraphim, Cherubim, and the Thrones; the second, the Dominations, the Virtues, and the Powers; the third, the Principalities, the Archangels, and the Angels properly so called. I belong to the ninth choir of the third hierarchy."

Madame des Aubels, who had her reasons for doubting this, expressed at least one:

"You have no wings."

"Why should I, Madame? Am I bound to resemble the angels on your holy-water stoups? Those feathery oars that beat the waves of the air in rhythmic cadences are not always worn by the heavenly messengers on their shoulders. Cherubim may be apterous. That all too beautiful angelic pair who spent an anxious night in the house of Lot compassed about by an Oriental horde—they had no wings! No, they appeared just like men, and the dust of the road covered their feet, which the patriarch washed with pious hand. I would beg you to observe, Madame, that according to the Science of Organic Metamorphosis created by Lamarck and Darwin, the wings of birds have been successively transformed into forefeet in the case of quadrupeds and into arms in the case of the Linnæan primates. And you may remember, Maurice, that by a rather annoying reversion to type, Miss Kate, your English nurse, who used to be so fond of giving you a whipping, had arms very like the pinions of a plucked fowl. One may say, then, that a being possessing both arms and wings is a monster and belongs to the department of Teratology. In Paradise we have Cherubim and Kerûbs in the shape of winged bulls, but those are the clumsy in-

ventions of an inartistic god. It is nevertheless true, quite true, that
the Victories of the Temple of Athena Nike on the Athenian Acropolis are beautiful, and possess both arms and wings; it is also true
that the Victory of Brescia is beautiful, with her outstretched arms
and her long wings folded on her mighty loins. It is one of the
miracles of Greek genius to have known how to create harmonious
monsters. The Greeks never err. The Moderns always."

"Yet on the whole," said Madame des Aubels, "you have not the
look of a pure Spirit."

"Nevertheless, I am one, Madame, if ever there was one. And it
ill becomes you, who have been baptised, to doubt it. Several of the
Fathers, such as St. Justin, Tertullian, Origen, and Clement of
Alexandria thought that the Angels were not purely spiritual, but
possessed a body formed of some subtile material. This opinion has
been rejected by the Church; hence I am merely Spirit. But what
is spirit and what is matter? Formerly they were contrasted as
being two opposites, and now your human science tends to reunite
them as two aspects of the same thing. It teaches that everything
proceeds from ether and everything returns to it, that the same
movement transforms the waves of air into stones and minerals,
and that the atoms scattered throughout illimitable space, form, by
the varying speed of their orbits, all the substance of this material
world."

But Madame des Aubels was not listening. She had something
on her mind, and to put an end to her suspense, she asked:

"How long have you been here?"

"I came with Maurice."

"Well—that's a nice thing!" said she, shaking her head. But the
Angel continued with heavenly serenity:

"Everything in the Universe is circular, elliptical, or hyperbolic,
and the same laws which rule the stars govern this grain of dust.
In the original and native movement of its substance, my body is
spiritual, but it may affect, as you perceive, this material state, by
changing the rhythm of its elements."

Having thus spoken he sat down in a chair on Madame des Aubels' black stockings.

A clock struck outside.

"Good heavens, seven o'clock!" exclaimed Gilberte. "What am I
to say to my husband? He thinks I am at that tea-party in the Rue
de Rivoli. We are dining with the La Verdelières to-night. Go away
immediately, Monsieur Arcade. I must get ready to go. I have not a
second to lose."

The Angel replied that he would have willingly obeyed Madame
des Aubels had he been in a state to show himself decently in public, but that he could not dream of appearing out of doors without
any clothes. "Were I to walk naked in the street," he added, "I
should offend a nation attached to its ancient habits, habits which

it has never examined. They are the basis of all moral systems. Formerly," he added, "the angels, in revolt like myself, manifested themselves to Christians under grotesque and ridiculous appearances, black, horned, hairy, and cloven-footed. Pure stupidity! They were the laughing-stock of people of taste. They merely frightened old women and children and met with no success."

"It is true he cannot go out as he is," said Madame des Aubels with justice.

Maurice tossed his pyjamas and his slippers to the celestial messenger. Regarded as outdoor habiliments they were not adequate. Gilberte pressed her lover to run at once in quest of other clothes. He proposed to go and get some from the concierge. She was violently opposed to this. It would, she said, be madly imprudent to drag the concierge into such an affair.

"Do you want them to know that . . ." she exclaimed.

She pointed to the Angel and was silent.

Young d'Esparvieu went out to seek a clothes-shop.

Meanwhile, Gilberte, who could not delay any longer for fear of causing a horrible society scandal, turned on the light and dressed before the Angel. She did it without any awkwardness, for she

knew how to adapt herself to circumstances; and she took it that in such an unheard-of encounter in which heaven and earth were mingled in unutterable confusion it was permissible to retrench in modesty.

Moreover, she knew that she possessed a good figure and had garments as dainty as the fashion demanded. As the apparition's sense of delicacy would not permit him to don Maurice's pyjamas, Gilberte could not help observing by the lamp-light that her suspicions were well-founded, and that angels have the same appearance as men. Curious to know if the appearance were real or imaginary she asked the child of light if Angels were like monkeys, who, to win women, merely lack money.

"Yes, Gilberte," replied Arcade, "Angels are capable of loving mortals. It is the teaching of the Scriptures. It is said in the Seventh Book of Genesis, 'When men became numerous on the face of the earth, and daughters were born to them, the sons of God saw that the daughters of men were beautiful, and they took as wives all those which pleased them.'"

"Good heavens," cried Gilberte all at once, "I shall never be able to fasten my dress; it hooks down the back."

When Maurice entered the room he found the Angel on his knees tying the shoes of the woman taken in *flagrante delicto*.

Taking her muff and her bag off the table she said:

"I have not forgotten anything? No. Good-night, Monsieur Arcade. Good-night, Maurice. I shall not forget to-day." And she vanished like a dream.

"Here," said Maurice, throwing the Angel a bundle of clothes.

The young man, having seen some dismal rags lying among clarionettes and clyster-pipes in the window of a second-hand shop, had bought for nineteen francs the cast-off suit of some wretched sable-clad mortal who had committed suicide. The Angel, with native majesty, took the garments and put them on. Worn by him, they took on an unexpected elegance. He took a step to the door.

"So you are leaving me," said Maurice. "It's settled, then? I very much fear that, some day, you will bitterly regret this hasty action."

"I must not look back. Adieu, Maurice."

Maurice timidly slipped five louis into his hand.

"Adieu, Arcade."

But when the Angel had passed through the door, and all that was to be seen of him in the doorway was his uplifted heel, Maurice called him back.

"Arcade! I never thought of it! I have no guardian angel now!"

"Quite true, Maurice, you have one no longer."

"Then what will become of me? One must have a guardian angel. Tell me,—are there not grave drawbacks,—is there no danger in not having one?"

"Before replying, Maurice, I must ask you if you wish me to speak to you according to your belief, which formerly was my own, according to the teaching of the Church and the Catholic faith, or according to natural philosophy.

"I don't care a straw for your natural philosophy. Answer me according to the religion I believe in, and which I profess, and in which I wish to live and die."

"Very well, my dear Maurice. The loss of your guardian angel will probably deprive you of certain spiritual succour, of certain celestial grace. I am expressing to you the unvarying opinion of the Church on the matter. You will lack an assistance, a support, a consolation which would have guided and confirmed you in the way of salvation. You will have less strength to avoid sin, and as it was you hadn't much. In fact, in spiritual matters, you will be without strength and without joy. Adieu, Maurice; when you see Madame des Aubels, please remember me to her."

"You are going?"

"Farewell."

Arcade disappeared, and Maurice in the depths of an arm-chair sat for a long time with his head in his hands.

XII

WHEREIN IT IS SET FORTH HOW THE ANGEL MIRAR, WHEN BEARING GRACE AND CONSOLATION TO THOSE DWELLING IN THE NEIGHBOURHOOD OF THE CHAMPS ÉLYSÉES IN PARIS, BEHELD A MUSIC-HALL SINGER NAMED BOUCHOTTE AND FELL IN LOVE WITH HER

THROUGH streets filled with brown fog, pierced with white and yellow lights, where horses exhaled their smoking breath and motors radiated their rapid search-lights, the angel made his way, and, mingling with the black flood of foot-passengers which rolled unceasingly along, proceeded across the town from north to south till he came to the lonely boulevards on the left bank of the river. Not far from the old walls of Port Royal, a small restaurant flings night by night athwart the pavement the clouded rays of its streaming windows. Coming to a halt there, Arcade entered a room full of warm, savoury odours, pleasing to the unfortunate beings faint with cold and hunger. Glancing round him he beheld Russian Nihilists, Italian Anarchists, refugees, conspirators, revolutionaries from every quarter of the globe, picturesque old faces with tumbled masses of hair and beard that swept downwards even as the torrent and the waterfall sweep over their rocky bed. There were young faces of virginal coldness, expressions sombre and wild, pale eyes of infinite sweetness, drawn faces, and, in a corner, there were two Russian women, one extremely lovely, the other hideous, but both resembling each other in their indifference to ugliness and to beauty. But failing to find the face he sought, for there were no angels in the room, he sat down at a small vacant marble table.

Angels, when driven by hunger, eat as do the animals of this earth, and their food, transformed by digestive heat, becomes one with their celestial substance. Seeing three angels under the oaks of Mamre, Abraham offered them cakes, kneaded by Sarah, an whole calf, butter and milk, and they ate. Lot, on receiving two angels in his house, ordered unleavened bread to be baked, and they did eat. Arcade was given a tough beef-steak by a seedy waiter, and he did eat. Nevertheless, his dreams were of the sweet leisure, of the repose, of the delightful studies he had quitted, of the heavy task he had undertaken, of the toil, the weariness, the perils which he would have to endure, and his soul was sad and his heart troubled.

As he was finishing his modest repast, a young man of poor appearance and thinly clad entered the room, and rapidly surveying the tables approached the angel and greeted him by the name of Abdiel, because he himself was a celestial spirit.

"I knew you would answer my call, Mirar," replied Arcade, addressing his angelic brother in his turn by the name he formerly bore in heaven. But Mirar was remembered no more in heaven since he, an Archangel, had left the service of God. He was called Théophile Belais on earth, and to earn his bread gave music lessons to small children in the day-time and at night played the violin in dancing saloons.

"It is you, dear Abdiel?" replied Théophile. "So here we are reunited in this sad world. I am pleased to see you again. All the same I pity you, for we lead a hard life here."

But Arcade answered:

"Friend, your exile draws to an end. I have great plans. I will confide them to you and associate you with them."

And Maurice's guardian angel, having ordered two coffees, revealed his ideas and his projects to his companion: he told how, during his visit on earth, he had abandoned himself to researches little practised by celestial spirits and had studied theologies, cosmogonies, the system of the Universe, theories of matter, modern essays on the transformation and loss of energy. Having, he explained, studied Nature, he had found her in perpetual conflict with the teachings of the Master he served. This Master, greedy of praise, whom he had for a long time adored, appeared to him now as an ignorant, stupid, and cruel tyrant. He had denied Him, blasphemed Him, and was burning to combat Him. His plan was to recommence the revolt of the angels. He wished for war, and hoped for victory.

"But," he added, "it is necessary above all to know our strength and that of our adversary." And he asked if the enemies of Ialdabaoth were numerous and powerful on earth.

Théophile looked wonderingly at his brother. He appeared not to understand the questions addressed him.

"Dear compatriot," he said, "I came at your invitation because it was the invitation of an old comrade. But I do not know what you expect of me, and I fear I shall be unable to help you in anything. I take no hand in politics, neither do I stand forth as a reformer. I am not like you, a spirit in revolt, a free-thinker, a revolutionary. I remain faithful, in the depths of my soul, to the Celestial Creator. I still adore the Master I no longer serve, and I lament the days when shrouding myself with my wings I formed with the multitude of the children of light a wheel of flame around His throne of glory. Love, profane love has alone separated me from God. I quitted heaven to follow a daughter of men. She was beautiful and sang in music-halls."

They rose. Arcade accompanied Théophile, who was living at the other end of the town, at the corner of the Boulevard Rochechouart and the Rue de Steinkerque. While walking through the deserted streets he who loved the singer told his brother of his love and his sorrows.

His fall, which dated from two years back, had been sudden. Belonging to the eighth choir of the third hierarchy he was a bearer of grace to the faithful who are still to be found in large numbers in France, especially among the higher ranks of the officers of the army and navy.

"One summer night," he said, "as I was descending from Heaven, to distribute consolations, the grace of perseverance and of good deaths to divers pious persons in the neighbourhood of the Étoile, my eyes, although well accustomed to immortal light, were dazzled by the fiery flowers with which the Champs Élysées were sown. Great candelabra, under the trees, marking the entrances to cafés and restaurants, gave the foliage the precious glitter of an emerald. Long garlands of luminous pearl surrounded the open-air enclosures where a crowd of men and women sat closely packed listening to the sounds of a lively orchestra, whose strains reached my ears confusedly.

"The night was warm, my wings were beginning to grow tired. I descended into one of the concerts and sat down, invisible, among the audience. At this moment, a woman appeared on the stage, clad in a short spangled frock. Owing to the reflection of the footlights and the paint on her face all that was visible of the latter was the expression and the smile. Her body was supple and voluptuous.

"She sang and danced. . . . Arcade, I have always loved dancing and music, but this creature's thrilling voice and insidious movements created in me an uneasiness I had never known before. My colour came and went. My eyelids drooped, my tongue clove to my mouth. I could not leave the spot."

And Théophile related, groaning, how, possessed by desire for this woman, he did not return to Heaven again, but, taking the shape of a man, lived an earthly life, for it is written: "In those days the sons of God saw that the daughters of men were beautiful."

A fallen angel, having lost his innocence along with the vision of God, Théophile at heart still retained his simplicity of soul. Clad in rags, filched from the stall of a Jewish hawker, he went to seek the woman he loved. She was called Bouchotte and lodged in a small house in Montmartre. He flung himself at her feet and told her she was adorable, that she sang delightfully, that he loved her madly, that, for her, he would renounce his family and his country, that he was a musician and had nothing to eat. Touched by such youthful ingenuousness, candour, poverty, and love, she fed, clothed, and loved him.

However, after long and painful struggles, he procured employment as a music-teacher, and made some money, which he brought to his mistress, keeping nothing for himself. From that time forward she loved him no longer. She despised him for earning so little and did not conceal her indifference, weariness, and disgust. She overwhelmed him with reproaches, irony, and abuse, in spite of which she kept him, for she had had experience of worse partners and was used to domestic quarrels. For the rest, she led a busy, serious, and rather hard life as artist and woman. Théophile loved her as he had loved her the first night, and he suffered.

"She overworks herself," he told his celestial brother, "that is what makes her so hard to please, but I am certain she loves me. I hope soon to give her more comfort."

And he spoke at length of an operetta at which he was working and which he hoped to have brought out at a Paris theatre. A young poet had given him the libretto. It was the story of Aline, queen of Golconda, after an eighteenth-century tale.

"I am strewing it profusely with melodies," said Théophile; "my music comes from my heart. My heart is an inexhaustible source of melody. Unfortunately nowadays people like recondite arrangements, difficult scoring. They accuse me of being too fluid, too limpid, of not imparting enough colour to my style, not aiming at stronger effects in harmony and more vigorous contrasts. Harmony, harmony! . . . No doubt it has given its merits, but it does not appeal to the heart. It is melody which carries us away and ravishes us and brings smiles and tears to our eyes." At these words he smiled and wept to himself. Then he continued with emotion:

"I am a fountain of melody. But the orchestration! there's the rub! In Paradise, you know, Arcade, in the matter of instruments, we only possess the harp, the psaltery, and the hydraulic organ."

Arcade was only listening to him with half an ear. He was meditating plans which filled his soul and swelled his heart.

"Do you know any angels in revolt?" he asked his companion. "As for me, I know only one, Prince Istar, with whom I have exchanged a few letters and who offered to share his attic with me while I was finding a lodging in this town, where I believe rents are very high."

Of angels in revolt Théophile know none. When he met a fallen spirit who had formerly been one of his comrades he shook him by the hand, for he was a faithful friend. Sometimes he saw Prince Istar. But he avoided all those bad angels who shocked him by the violence of their opinions and whose conversations plagued him to death.

"Then you don't approve of me?" asked the impulsive Arcade.

"Friend, I neither approve of you nor blame you. I understand nothing of the ideas which trouble you. Neither do I think it good for an artist to concern himself with politics. One has quite sufficient to occupy oneself with one's art."

He loved his profession, and had hopes of "arriving" one day, but theatrical ways disgusted him. The only chance he saw of having his piece played was to take one or two—perhaps three—collaborators, who, without having done any work, would sign their names and share the profits. Soon Bouchotte would fail to find engagements. When she offered her services in some small hall the manager began by asking her how many shares she was taking in the business. Such customs, thought Théophile, were deplorable.

<h2 style="text-align:center">XIII</h2>

WHEREIN WE HEAR THE BEAUTIFUL ARCHANGEL ZITA UNFOLD HER LOFTY DESIGNS AND ARE SHOWN THE WINGS OF MIRAR, ALL MOTH-EATEN, IN A CUP-BOARD

THUS talking, the two archangels had reached the Boulevard Rochechouart. As his eye lighted on a tavern, whence, through the mist, the light fell golden on the pavement, Théophile suddenly bethought himself of the Archangel Ithuriel who, in the guise of a poor but beautiful woman, was living in wretched lodgings on La Butte and came every evening to read the papers at this tavern. The musician often met her there. Her name was Zita. Théophile had never been curious enough to enquire into the opinions entertained

by this archangel, but it was generally supposed that she was a
Russian nihilist, and he took her to be, like Arcade, an atheist and
a revolutionary. He had heard remarkable tales about her. People
said she was an hermaphrodite, and that as the active and passive
principles were united within her in a condition of stable equilibrium, she was an example of a perfect being, finding in herself complete and continuous satisfaction, contented yet unfortunate in that
she knew not desire.

"But," added Théophile, "I have my doubts about it. I believe
she's a woman and subject to love, like everything else that has
life and breath in the Universe. Besides, someone caught her one
day kissing her hand to a strapping peasant fellow."

He offered to introduce his companion to her.

The two angels found her alone, reading. As they drew near she
lifted her great eyes in whose deeps of molten gold little sparks of
light were forever a-dance. Her brows were contracted into that
austere fold which we see on the forehead of the Pythian Apollo;
her nose was perfect and descended without a curve; her lips were
compressed and imparted a disdainful and supercilious air to her
whole countenance. Her tawny hair, with its gleaming lights, was
carelessly adorned with the tattered remnants of a huge bird of
prey, her garments lay about her in dark and shapeless folds. She
was leaning her chin on a small ill-tended hand.

Arcade, who had but recently heard references made to this
powerful archangel, showed her marked esteem, and placed entire
confidence in her. He immediately proceeded to tell of the progress
his mind had made towards knowledge and liberty, of his lucubrations in the d'Esparvieu library, of his philosophical reading, his
studies of nature, his works on exegesis, his anger and his contempt when he recognised the deception of the demiurge, his voluntary exile among mankind, and, finally, of his project to stir up
rebellion in Heaven. Ready to dare all against an odious master,
whom he pursued with inextinguishable hatred, he expressed his
profound happiness at finding in Ithuriel a mind capable of counsel-
ling and helping him in his great undertaking.

"You are not a very old hand at revolutions," said Zita, smiling.

Nevertheless, she doubted neither his sincerity nor the firmness
of his declared resolve, and she congratulated him on his intellectual audacity.

"That is what is most lacking in our people," she said, "they do
not think."

And she added almost immediately: "But on what can intelligence sharpen its wits, in a country where the climate is soft and
existence made easy? Even here, where necessity calls for intellectual activity, nothing is rarer than a person who thinks."

"Nevertheless," replied Maurice's guardian angel, "man has
created science. The important thing is to introduce it into Heaven.

When the angels possess some notions of physics, chemistry, astronomy, and physiology; when the study of matter shows them worlds in an atom, and an atom in the myriads of planets; when they see themselves lost between these two infinities; when they weigh and measure the stars, analyse their composition, and calculate their orbits, they will recognise that these monsters work in obedience to forces which no intelligence can define, or that each star has its particular divinity, or indigenous god; and they will realise that the gods of Aldebaran, Betelgeuse, and Sirius are greater than Ialdabaoth. When at length they come to scrutinise with care the little world in which their lot is cast, and, piercing the crust of the earth, note the gradual evolution of its flora and fauna and the rude origin of man, who, under the shelter of rocks and in cave dwellings, had no God but himself; when they discover that, united by the bonds of universal kinship to plants, beasts, and men, they have successively indued all forms of organic life, from the simplest and the most primitive, until they became at length the most beautiful of the children of light, they will perceive that Ialdabaoth, the obscure demon of an insignificant world lost in space, is imposing on their credulity when he pretends that they issued from nothingness at his bidding; they will perceive that he lies in calling himself the Infinite, the Eternal, the Almighty, and that, so far from having created worlds, he knows neither their number nor their laws. They will perceive that he is like unto one of them; they will despise him, and, shaking off his tyranny, will fling him into the Gehenna where he has hurled those more worthy than himself."

"Do you think so?" murmured Zita, puffing out the smoke of her cigarette. . . . "Nevertheless, this knowledge by virtue of which you reckon to enfranchise Heaven, has not destroyed religious sentiment on earth. In countries where they have set up and taught this science of physics, of chemistry, astronomy, and geology, which you think capable of delivering the world, Christianity has retained almost all its sway. If the positive sciences have had such a feeble influence on the beliefs of mankind, it is not likely they will exercise a greater one on the opinions of the angels, and nothing is of such dubious efficacy as scientific propaganda."

"What!" exclaimed Arcade, "you deny that Science has given the Church its death-blow? Is is possible? The Church, at any rate, judges otherwise. Science, which you believe has no power over her, is redoubtable to her, since she proscribes it. From Galileo's dialogues to Monsieur Aulard's little manuals she has condemned all its discoveries. And not without reason.

"In former days, when she gathered within her fold all that was great in human thought, the Church held sway over the bodies as well as over the souls of men, and imposed unity of obedience by fire and sword. To-day her power is but a shadow and the elect among the great minds have withdrawn from her. That is the state to which Science has reduced her."

"Possibly," replied the beautiful archangel, "but how slowly, with what vicissitudes, at the price of what efforts, of what sacrifices!"

Zita did not absolutely condemn scientific propaganda, but she anticipated no prompt or certain results from it. For her it was not so much a question of enlightening the angels; the important thing was to enfranchise them. In her opinion one only exerted a strong influence on individuals, whoever they might be, by rousing their passions, and appealing to their interests.

"Persuade the angels that they will cover themselves with glory by overthrowing the tyrant, and that they will be happier once they are free; that is the most practical policy to attempt, and, for my own part, I am devoting all my energies to its fulfilment. It is certainly no light task, because the Kingdom of Heaven is a military autocracy and there is no public opinion in it. Nevertheless, I do not despair of starting an intellectual movement. I do not wish to boast, but no one is more closely acquainted than I with the different classes of angelic society."

Throwing away her cigarette, Zita pondered for a moment, then, amid the click of ivory balls on the billiard table, the clinking of glasses, the curt voices of the players announcing their points, the monotonous answers of the waiters to their customers, the Archangel enumerated the entire population of the spirits of light.

"We must not count on the Dominations, the Virtues, nor the Powers, which compose the celestial lower middle class. I have no need to tell you, for you know it as well as I, how selfish, base, and cowardly the middle classes are. As to the great dignitaries, the Ministers, the Generals, Thrones, Cherubim, and Seraphim, you know what they are; they will take no action. Let us, however, once prove ourselves the stronger, and we shall have them with us. For if autocrats do not readily acquiesce in their own downfall, once overthrown, all their forces recoil upon themselves. It will be well to work the Army. Entirely loyal as the Army is, it will allow itself to be influenced by a clever anarchist propaganda. But our greatest and most constant efforts ought to be brought to bear upon the angels of your own category, Arcade; the guardian angels, who dwell upon earth in such great numbers. They fill the lowest ranks of the hierarchy, are for the most part discontented with their lot, and more or less imbued with the ideas of the present century."

She had already conferred with the guardian angels of Montmartre, Clignancourt, and Filles-du-Calvaire. She had devised the plan of a vast association of Spirits on Earth with the view of conquering Heaven.

"To accomplish this task," she said, "I have established myself in France. But not because I had the folly to believe myself freer in a republic than in a monarchy. Quite the contrary, for there is no country where the liberty of the individual is less respected than in France. But the people are indifferent to everything connected with religion; nowhere else, therefore, should I enjoy such tranquillity."

She invited Arcade to unite his efforts to hers, and when they separated at the door of the *brasserie* the steel shutter was already making its groaning descent.

"Above all," said Zita, "you must meet the gardener. I will take you to his rustic home one day."

Théophile, who had slumbered during all this talk, begged his friend to come home with him and smoke a cigarette. He lived quite near in the small street opposite, leading off the Boulevard. Arcade would see Bouchotte, she would please him.

They climbed up five flights of stairs. Bouchotte had not yet returned. A tin of sardines lay open on the piano. Red stockings coiled about the arm-chairs.

"It's a little place, but it's comfortable," said Théophile.

And gazing out of the window which looked out on the russet-coloured night, with its myriad lights, he added, "One can see the *Sacré Cœur*." His hand on Arcade's shoulder, he repeated several times, "I am glad to see you."

Then, dragging his former companion in glory into the kitchen passage, he put down his candle-stick, drew a key from his pocket, opened a cupboard, and, raising a linen covering, disclosed two large white wings.

"You see," he said, "I have preserved them. From time to time, when I am alone, I go and look at them; it does me good."

And he dabbed his reddened eyes. He stood awhile, overcome by silent emotion. Then, holding the candle near the long pinions which were moulting their down in places, he murmured, "They are eaten away."

"You must put some pepper on them," said Arcade.

"I have done so," replied the angelic musician, sighing. "I have put pepper, camphor, and powder on them. But nothing does any good."

XIV

WHICH REVEALS THE CHERUB TOILING FOR THE WELFARE OF HUMANITY AND CONCLUDES IN AN ENTIRELY NOVEL MANNER WITH THE MIRACLE OF THE FLUTE

THE first night of his incarnation Arcade slept at the angel Istar's, in a garret in that narrow, gloomy Rue Mazarine which wallows along beneath the the shadow of the old Institute of France. Istar, who had been expecting him, had pushed against the wall the shattered retorts, cracked pots, broken bottles, and odds and ends of iron stoves, which made up the furniture of his room, and spread his clothes on the floor to lie on, leaving his guest his folding-bed with its straw mattress.

The celestial spirits differ from one another in appearance according to the hierarchy and the choir to which they belong, and according to their own particular nature. They are all beautiful; but in different fashion, and they do not all offer to the eye the soft contours and dimpling smiles of childhood with its rosy lights and pearly tints. Nor do they all adorn themselves with eternal youth, that indefinable beauty that Greek art in its decline has imparted to its most lovingly handled marbles, and whereof Christian painters have so often timidly essayed to give us veiled and softened imitations. In some of them the chin glows with tufts of hair, and the limbs are furnished with such vigorous muscles that it seems as if serpents were writhing beneath the skin. Some have no wings, others possess two, four, or six; others again are formed entirely of conjoined pinions. Many, and these not the least illustrious, take the form of superb monsters, such as the Centaurs of fable; nay, one may even see some who are living chariots, and wheels of fire. A member of the highest celestial hierarchy, Istar belonged to the choir of Cherubim or Kerûbs who see above them the Seraphim alone. In common with all the angelic spirits of his rank he had formerly borne in Heaven the bodily shape of a winged bull surmounted by the head of a horned and bearded man, and carrying between his loins the attributes of generous fecundity. He was vaster and more vigorous than any animal on earth, and when he stood erect with outspread wings he covered with his shadow sixty archangels.

Such was Istar in his native home. There he radiated strength and sweetness. His heart was full of courage and his soul benevolent. Moreover, in those days he loved his lord. He believed him to be good and yielded him faithful service. But even while guarding

the portals of his Master, he used to ponder unceasingly on the
punishment of the rebellious angels and the curse of Eve. His mind
worked slowly but profoundly. When, after a long course of centuries, he persuaded himself that Ialdabaoth in creating the world
had created evil and death, he ceased to adore and to serve him.
His love changed to hatred, his veneration to contempt. He shouted
his execrations in his face, and fled to earth.

Embodied in human form and reduced to the stature of the sons
of Adam, he still retained some characteristics of his former nature. His big protruding eyes, his beaked nose, his thick lips
framed in a black beard which descended in curls on to his chest
recalled those Cherubs of the tabernacle of Iahveh, of which the
bulls of Nineveh afford us a pretty accurate representation. He bore
the name of Istar on earth as well as in Heaven, and although exempt from vanity and free from all social prejudice, he was im-
mensely desirous of showing himself sincere and truthful in all
things. He therefore proclaimed the illustrious rank in which his
birth had placed him in the celestial hierarchy and translated into
French his title of Cherub by the equivalent one of Prince, calling
himself Prince Istar. Seeking shelter among mankind he had developed an ardent love for them. While awaiting the coming of the
hour when he should deliver Heaven from bondage, he dreamed of
the salvation of regenerate humanity and was eager to consummate the destruction of this wicked world, in order to raise upon
its ashes, to the sound of the lyre, a city radiant with happiness
and love. A chemist in the pay of a dealer in nitrates, he lived very
frugally. He wrote for newspapers with advanced views on liberty,
spoke at public meetings, and had got himself sentenced several
times to several months' imprisonment for anti-militarism.

Istar greeted his brother Arcade cordially, approved of his rupture with the party of crime, and informed him of the descent of
fifty of the children of light who, at the present moment, formed
a colony near Val de Grace, imbued with a really excellent spirit.

"It is simply raining angels in Paris," he said, laughing. "Every
day some dignitary of the sacred palace falls on one's head, and
soon the Sultan of the Cherubs will have no one to make into Vizirs
or guards but the little unbreeched vagabonds of his pigeon coops."

Soothed by the good news, Arcade fell asleep, full of happiness
and hope.

He awoke in the early dawn and saw Prince Istar bending over
his furnaces, his retorts, and his test tubes. Prince Istar was working for the good of humanity.

Every morning when Arcade woke he saw Prince Istar fulfilling
his work of tenderness and love. Sometimes the Kerûb, huddled up
with his head in his hands, would softly murmur a few chemical
formulæ; at others, drawing himself up to his full height, like a
dark naked column, with his head, his arms, nay, his entire bust

clean out of the skylight window, he would deposit his melting-pot on the roof, fearing the perquisition with which he was constantly menaced. Moved by an immense pity for the miseries of the world wherein he dwelt in exile, conscious perhaps of the rumours to which his name gave rise, inebriated with his own virtue, he played the part of apostle to the Human Race, and neglecting the task he had undertaken in coming to earth, he forgot all about the emancipation of the angels. Arcade, who, on the contrary, dreamed of nothing else but of conquering Heaven and returning thither in triumph, reproached the Cherub with forgetting his native land.

Prince Istar, with a great frank, uncouth laugh, acknowledged that he had no preference for angels over men.

"If I am doing my best," he replied to his celestial brother, "if I am doing my best to stir up France and Europe, it is because the day is dawning which will behold the triumph of the social revolution. It is a pleasure to cast one's seed on ground so well prepared. The French having passed from feudalism to monarchy, and from monarchy to a financial oligarchy, will easily pass from a financial oligarchy to anarchy."

"How erroneous it is," retorted Arcade, "to believe in great and sudden changes in the social order in Europe! The old order is still young in strength and power. The means of defence at her disposal are formidable. On the other hand, the proletariat's plan of defensive organisation is of the vaguest description and brings merely weakness and confusion to the struggle. In our celestial country all goes quite otherwise. Beneath an apparently unchangeable exterior all is rotten within. A mere push would suffice to overturn an edifice which has not been touched for millions of centuries. Outworn administration, out-worn army, out-worn finance, the whole thing is more worm-eaten than either the Russian or Persian autocracy."

And the kindly Arcade adjured the Cherub to fly first to the aid of his brethren who, though dwelling amid the soft clouds with the sound of citterns and their cups of paradisal wine around them, were in more wretched plight than mankind bowed over the grudging earth. For the latter have a conception of justice, while the angels rejoice in iniquity. He exhorted him to deliver the Prince of Light and his stricken companions and to re-establish them in their ancient honours.

Prince Istar allowed himself to be convinced.

He promised to put the sweet persuasiveness of his words and the excellent formulæ of his explosives at the service of the celestial revolution. He gave his promise.

"To-morrow," he said.

And when the morrow came he continued his anti-militarist propaganda at Issy-les-Moulineaux. Like the Titan Prometheus, Istar loved mankind.

Arcade, suffering from all the desires to which the sons of Adam are subjected, found himself lacking in resources to satisfy them. Istar gave him a start in a printing house in the Rue de Vaugirard where he knew the forman. Arcade, thanks to his celestial intelligence, soon knew how to set up type and became, in a short time, a good compositor.

After standing all day in the whirring workroom, holding the composing-stick in his left hand, and swiftly drawing the little leaden signs from the case in the order required by the copy fixed in the *visorium,* he would go and wash his hands at the pump and dine at the corner bar, a newspaper propped up before him on the marble table. Being now no longer invisible, he could not make his way into the d'Esparvieu library, and was thus debarred from allaying his ardent thirst for knowledge at that inexhaustible source. He went, of an evening, to read at the library of Ste. Geneviève on the famous hill of learning, but there were only ordinary books to be had there; greasy things, covered with ridiculous annotations, and lacking many pages.

The sight of women troubled and unsettled him. He would remember Madame des Aubels and her charm, and, although he was handsome, he was not loved, because of his poverty and his workaday clothes. He saw much of Zita, and took a certain pleasure in going for walks with her on Sundays along the dusty roads which edge the grass-grown trenches of the fortifications. They wandered, the pair of them, by wayside inns, market-gardens, and green retreats, propounding and discussing the vastest plans that ever stirred the world, and, occasionally, as they passed along by some travelling circus, the steam organ of the merry-go-round would furnish an accompaniment to their words as they breathed fire and fury against Heaven.

Zita used often to say:

"Istar means well, but he's a simple fellow. He believes in the goodness of men and things. He undertakes the destruction of the old world and imagines that anarchy of itself will create order and harmony. You, Arcade, you believe in Science; you deem that men and angels are capable of understanding, whereas, in point of fact, they are only creatures of sentiment. You may be quite sure that nothing is to be obtained from them by appealing to their intelligence; one must rouse their interests and their passions."

Arcade, Istar, Zita, and three or four other angelic conspirators occasionally foregathered in Théophile Belais' little flat, where Bouchotte gave them tea. Though she did not know that they were rebellious angels, she hated them instinctively, and feared them, for she had had a Christian education, albeit she had sadly failed to keep it up.

Prince Istar alone pleased her; she thought there was something kind-hearted and an air of natural distinction about him. He stove in the sofa, broke down the arm-chairs, and tore corners off sheets of music to make notes, which he thrust into pockets invariably crammed with pamphlets and bottles. The musician used to gaze sorrowfully at the manuscript of his operetta, *Aline, Queen of Golconda,* with its corners all torn off. The prince also had a habit of giving Théophile Belais all sorts of things to take care of—mechanical contrivances, chemicals, bits of old iron, powders, and liquids which gave off noisome smells. Théophile Belais put them cautiously away in the cupboard where he kept his wings, and the responsibility weighed heavily upon him.

Arcade was much pained at the disdain of those of his fellows who had remained faithful. When they met him as they went on their sacred errands they regarded him as they passed by with looks of cruel hatred or of pity that was crueller still.

He used to visit the rebel angels whom Prince Istar pointed out to him, and usually met with a good reception, but as soon as he began to speak of conquering Heaven, they did not conceal the embarrassment and displeasure he caused them. Arcade perceived that they had no desire to be disturbed in their tastes, their affairs, and their habits. The falsity of their judgment, the narrowness of their minds, shocked him; and the rivalry, the jealousy they displayed towards one another deprived him of all hope of uniting them in a common cause. Perceiving how exile debases the character and warps the intellect, he felt his courage fail him.

One evening, when he had confessed his weariness of spirit to Zita, the beautiful archangel said:

"Let us go and see Nectaire; Nectaire has remedies of his own for sadness and fatigue."

She led him into the woods of Montmorency and stopped at the threshold of a small white house, adjoining a kitchen garden, laid waste by winter, where far back in the shadows the light shone on forcing-frames and cracked glass melon shades.

Nectaire opened the door to his visitors, and, after quieting the growls of a big mastiff which protected the garden, led them into a low room warmed by an earthenware stove.

Against the whitewashed wall, on a deal board, among the onions and seeds, lay a flute ready to be put to the lips. A round walnut table bore a stone tobacco-jar, a pipe, a bottle of wine and some glasses. The gardener offered each of his guests a cane-seated chair, and himself sat down on a stool by the table.

He was a sturdy old man; thick grey hair stood up on his head, he had a furrowed brow, a snub-nose, a red face and a forked beard.

The big mastiff stretched himself at his master's feet, rested his short black muzzle on his paws, and closed his eyes. The gardener poured out some wine for his guests, and when they had drunk and talked a little, Zita said to Nectaire:

"Please play your flute to us, you will give pleasure to my friend whom I have brought to see you."

The old man immediately consented. He put the boxwood pipe to his lips,—so clumsy was it that it looked as if the gardener had fashioned it himself,—and preluded with a few strange runs. Then he developed rich melodies in which the thrills sparkled like diamonds and pearls on a velvet ground. Touched by cunning fingers, animated with creative breath, the rustic pipe sang like a silver flute. There were no over-shrill notes and the tone was always even and pure. One seemed to be listening to the nightingale and the Muses singing together, the soul of Nature and the soul of Man. And the old man ordered and developed his thoughts in a musical language full of grace and daring. He told of love, of fear, of vain quarrels, of all-conquering laughter, of the calm light of the intellect, of the arrows of the mind piercing with their golden shafts the monsters of Ignorance and Hate. He told also of Joy and Sorrow bending their twin heads over the earth and of Desire which brings worlds into being.

The whole night listened to the flute of Nectaire. Already the evening star was rising above the paling horizon.

There they sat; Zita with hands clasped about her knees, Arcade, his head leaning on his hand, his lips apart. Motionless they listened. A lark, which had awakened hard by in a sandy field, lured by these novel sounds, rose swiftly in the air, hovered a few seconds, then dropped at one swoop into the musician's orchard. The neighbouring sparrows, forsaking the crannies of the mouldering walls, came and sat in a row on the window-ledge whence notes came welling forth that gave them more delight than oats or grains of barley. A jay, coming for the first time out of his wood, folded his sapphire wings on a leafless cherry tree. Beside the drain-head, a large black rat, glistening with the greasy water of the sewers, sitting on his hind legs, raised his short arms and slender fingers in amazement. A field-mouse, that dwelt in the orchard, was seated near him. Down from the tiles came the old tom-cat, who retained the grey fur, the ringed tail, the powerful loins, the courage, and the pride of his ancestors. He pushed against the half-open door with his nose and approaching the flute-player with silent tread, sat gravely down, pricking his ears that had been torn in many a nocturnal combat; the grocer's white cat followed him, sniffing vibrant air and then, arching her back and closing her blue eyes, listened in ravishment. Mice, swarming in crowds from under the boards, surrounded them, and fearing neither tooth nor claw, sat motionless, their pink hands folded voluptuously on their bosoms. Spiders that had strayed far from their webs, with waving legs, gathered in a charmed circle on the ceiling. A small grey lizard, that had glided on to the doorstep, stayed there, fascinated, and, in the loft, the bat might have been seen hanging by her nails, head down, now half-awakened from her winter sleep, swaying to the rhythm of the marvellous flute.

XV

WHEREIN WE SEE YOUNG MAURICE BEWAILING THE LOSS OF HIS GUARDIAN ANGEL, EVEN IN HIS MISTRESS'S ARMS, AND WHEREIN WE HEAR THE ABBÉ PATOUILLE REJECT AS VAIN AND ILLUSORY ALL NOTIONS OF A NEW REBELLION OF THE ANGELS

 FORTNIGHT had elapsed since the angel's apparition in the flat. For the first time Gilberte arrived before Maurice at the rendezvous. Maurice was gloomy, Gilberte sulky. So far as they were concerned Nature had resumed her drab monotony. They eyed each other languidly, and kept glancing towards the angle between the wardrobe with the mirror and the window, where recently the pale shade of Arcade had taken shape, and where now the blue cretonne of the hangings was the only thing visible. Without giving him a name (it was unnecessary) Madame des Aubels asked:

"You have not seen him since?"

Slowly, sadly, Maurice turned his head from right to left, and from left to right.

"You look as if you missed him," continued Madame des Aubels. "But come, confess that he gave you a terrible fright, and that you were shocked at his unconventionality."

"Certainly he was unconventional," said Maurice without any resentment.

"Tell me, Maurice, is it nothing to you now to be with me alone? ... You need an angel to inspire you. That is sad, for a young man like you!"

Maurice appeared not to hear, and asked gravely:

"Gilberte, do you feel that your guardian angel is watching over you?"

"I, not at all. I have never thought of him, and yet I am not without religion. In the first place, people who have none are like animals. And then one cannot go straight without religion. It is impossible."

"Exactly, that's just it," said Maurice, his eyes on the violet stripes of his flowerless pyjamas; "when one has one's guardian angel one does not even think about him, and when one has lost him one feels very lonely."

"So you miss this . . ."

"Well, the fact is . . ."

"Oh, yes, yes, you miss him. Well, my dear, the loss of such a guardian angel as that is no great matter. No, no! he is not worth much, that Arcade of yours. On that famous day, while you were out getting him some clothes, he was ever so long fastening my dress, and I certainly felt his hand . . . Well, at any rate, don't trust him."

Maurice dreamily lit a cigarette. They spoke of the six days' cycle race at the winter velodrome, and of the aviation show at the motor exhibition at Brussels, without experiencing the slightest amusement. Then they tried love-making as a sort of convenient pastime, and succeeded in becoming moderately absorbed in it; but at the very moment when she might have been expected to play a part more in accordance with a mutual sentiment, she exclaimed with a sudden start:

"Good Heavens! Maurice, how stupid of you to tell me that my guardian angel can see me. You cannot imagine how uncomfortable the idea makes me."

Maurice, somewhat taken aback, recalled, a little roughly, his mistress's wandering thoughts.

She declared that her principles forbade her to think of playing a round game with angels.

Maurice was longing to see Arcade again and had no other thought. He reproached himself for suffering him to depart without discovering where he was going, and he cudgelled his brains night and day thinking how to find him again.

On the bare chance, he put a notice in the personal column of one of the big papers, running thus:

"Arcade. Come back to your Maurice."

Day after day went by, and Arcade did not return.

One morning, at seven o'clock, Maurice went to St. Sulpice to hear Abbé Pautouille say Mass, then, as the priest was leaving the sacristy, he went up to him and asked to be heard for a moment.

They descended the steps of the church together and in the bright morning light walked round the fountain of the *Quatre Évêques*. In spite of his troubled conscience and the difficulty of presenting so extraordinary a case with any degree of credibility, Maurice related how the angel Arcade had appeared to him and had announced his unhappy resolve to separate from him and to stir up a new revolt of the spirits of glory. And young d'Esparvieu asked the worthy ecclesiastic how to find his celestial guardian again, since he could not bear his absence, and how to lead his angel back to the Christian faith. Abbé Patouille replied in a tone of affectionate sorrow that his dear child had been dreaming, that he took a morbid hallucination for reality, and that it was not permissible to believe that good angels may revolt.

"People have a notion," he added, "that they can lead a life of dissipation and disorder with impunity. They are wrong. The abuse of pleasure corrupts the intelligence and impairs the understanding. The devil takes possession of the sinner's senses, penetrating even to his soul. He has deceived you, Maurice, by a clumsy artifice."

Maurice objected that he was not in any way a victim of hallucinations, that he had not been dreaming, that he had seen his guardian angel with his eyes and heard him with his ears.

"Monsieur l'Abbé," he insisted, "a lady who happened to be with me at the time,—I need not mention her name,—also saw and heard him. And, moreover, she felt the angel's fingers straying . . . well, anyhow, she felt them. . . . Believe me, Monsieur l'Abbé, nothing could be more real, more positively certain than this apparition. The angel was fair, young, very handsome. His clear skin seemed, in the shadow, as if bathed in milky light. He spoke in a pure, sweet voice."

"That, alone, my child," the Abbé interrupted quickly, "proves you were dreaming. According to all the demonologies, bad angels have a hoarse voice, which grates like a rusty lock, and even if they did contrive to give a certain look of beauty to their faces, they cannot succeed in imitating the pure voice of the good spirits. This fact, attested by numerous witnesses, is established beyond all doubt."

"But, Monsieur l'Abbé, I saw him. I saw him sit down, stark naked, in an arm-chair on a pair of black stockings. What else do you want me to tell you?"

The Abbé Pautouille appeared in no way disturbed by this announcement.

"I say once more, my son," he replied, "that these unhappy illusions, these dreams of a deeply troubled soul, are to be ascribed to the deplorable state of your conscience. I believe, moreover, that I can detect the particular circumstance that has caused your unstable mind thus to come to grief. During the winter in company with Monsieur Sariette and your Uncle Gaétan, you came, in an evil frame of mind, to see the Chapel of the Holy Angels in this church, then undergoing repair. As I observed on that occasion, it is impossible to keep artists too closely to the rules of Christian art; they cannot be too strongly enjoined to respect Holy Writ and its authorized interpreters. Monsieur Eugène Delacroix did not suffer his fiery genius to be controlled by tradition. He brooked no guidance and, here, in this chapel he has painted pictures which in common parlance we call lurid, compositions of a violent, terrible nature which, far from inspiring the soul with peace, quietude, and calm, plunge it into a state of agitation. In them the angels are depicted with wrathful countenances, their features are sombre and uncouth. One might take them to be Lucifer and his companions meditating their revolt. Well, my son, it was these pictures, acting upon a mind already weakened and undermined by every kind of dissipation, that have filled it with the trouble to which it is at present a prey."

But Maurice would have none of it.

"Oh, no! Monsieur l'Abbé," he cried, "it is not Eugène Delacroix's pictures that have been troubling me. I didn't so much as look at them. I am completely indifferent to that kind of art."

"Well, then, my son, believe me: there is no truth, no reality, in any of the story you have just related to me. Your guardian angel has certainly not appeared to you."

"But, Abbé," replied Maurice, who had the most absolute confidence in the evidence of the senses, "I saw him tying up a woman's shoe-laces and putting on the trousers of a suicide."

And stamping his feet on the asphalt, Maurice called as witnesses to the truth of his words the sky, the earth, all nature, the towers of St. Sulpice, the walls of the great seminary, the Fountain of the *Quatre Évêques,* the public lavatory, the cabmen's shelter, the taxis and motor 'buses' shelter, the trees, the passers-by, the dogs, the sparrows, the flower-seller and her flowers.

The Abbé made haste to end the interview.

"All this is error, falsehood, and illusion, my child," said he. "You are a Christian: think as a Christian,—a Christian does not allow himself to be seduced by empty shadows. Faith protects him against the seduction of the marvellous, he leaves credulity to freethinkers. There are credulous people for you—freethinkers! There is no humbug they will not swallow. But the Christian carries a weapon which dissipates diabolical illusions,—the sign of the Cross. Reassure yourself, Maurice,—you have not lost your guardian angel. He still watches over you. It lies with you not to make this task too difficult nor too painful for him. Good-bye, Maurice. The weather is going to change, for I feel a burning in my big toe."

And Abbé Patouille went off with his breviary under his arm, hobbling along with a dignity that seemed to foretell a mitre.

That very day, Arcade and Zita were leaning over the parapet of La Butte, gazing down on the mist and smoke that lay floating over the vast city.

"Is it possible," said Arcade, "for the mind to conceive all the pain and suffering that lie pent within a great city? It is my belief that if a man succeeded in realising it, the weight of it would crush him to the earth."

"And yet," answered Zita, "every living being in that place of torment is enamoured of life. It is a great enigma!

"Unhappy, ill-fated, while they live, the idea of ceasing to be is, nevertheless, a horror to them. They look not for solace in annihilation, it does not even bring them the promise of rest. In their madness they even look upon nothingness with terror: they have peopled it with phantoms. Look you at these pediments, these towers and domes and spires that pierce the mist and rear on high their glittering crosses. Men bow in adoration before the demiurge who has given them a life that is worse than death, and a death that is worse than life."

Zita was for a long time lost in thought. At length she broke silence, saying:

"There is something, Arcade, that I must confess to you. It was no desire for a purer justice or wiser laws that hurried Ithuriel earthward. Ambition, a taste for intrigue, the love of wealth and honour, all these things made Heaven, with its calm, unbearable to me, and I longed to mingle with the restless race of men. I came, and by an art unknown to nearly all the angels, I learned how to fashion myself a body which, since I could change it as the fancy seized me, to whatsoever age and sex I would, has permitted me to

experience the most diverse and amazing of human destinies. A hundred times I took a position of renown among the leaders of the day, the lords of wealth and princes of nations. I will not reveal to you, Arcade, the famous names I bore; know only that I was pre-eminent in learning, in the fine arts, in power, wealth, and beauty, among all the nations of the world. At last, it was but a few years since, as I was journeying in France, under the outward semblance of a distinguished foreigner, I chanced to be roaming at evening through the forest of Montmorency, when I heard a flute unfolding all the sorrows of Heaven. The purity and sadness of its notes rent my very soul. Never before had I hearkened to aught so lovely. My eyes were wet with tears, my bosom full of sobs, as I drew near and beheld, on the skirts of a glade, an old man like to a faun, blowing on a rustic pipe. It was Nectaire. I cast myself at his feet, imprinted kisses on his hands and on his lips divine, and fled away. . . .

"From that day forth, conscious of the littleness of human achievements, weary of the tumult and the vanity of earthly things, ashamed of my vast and profitless endeavours, and deciding to seek out a loftier aim for my ambition, I looked upwards towards my skiey home and vowed I would return to it as a Deliverer. I rid myself of titles, name, wealth, friends, the horde of sycophants and flatterers and, as Zita the obscure, set to work in indigence and solitude, to bring freedom into Heaven."

"And I," said Arcade, "I too have heard the flute of Nectaire. But who is this old gardener who can thus woo from a rude wooden pipe notes that are so moving and so beautiful?"

"You will soon know," answered Zita.

XVI

WHEREIN MIRA THE SEERESS, ZEPHYRINE, AND THE FATAL AMÉDÉE ARE SUCCESSIVELY BROUGHT UPON THE SCENE, AND WHEREIN THE NOTION OF EURIPIDES THAT THOSE WHOM ZEUS WISHES TO CRUSH HE FIRST MAKES MAD, IS ILLUSTRATED BY THE TERRIBLE EXAMPLE OF MONSIEUR SARIETTE

ISAPPOINTED at his failure to enlighten an ecclesiastic renowned for his clarity of mind, and frustrated in the hope of finding his angel again on the high road of orthodoxy, Maurice took it into his head to resort to occultism and resolved to go and consult a seer. He would have undoubtedly applied to Madame de Thèbes, but he had already questioned her on the occasion of his early love troubles, and her replies showed such wisdom that he no longer believed her to be a soothsayer. He therefore had recourse to a fashionable medium, Madame Mira. He had heard many examples quoted of the extraordinary insight of this seeress, but it was necessary to present Madame Mira with some object which the absent one had either touched or worn and to which her translucent gaze had to be attracted. Maurice, trying to remember what the angel had touched since his ill-fated incarnation, recollected that in his celestial nudity he had sat down in an arm-chair on Madame des Aubels' black stockings and that he had afterwards helped that lady to dress.

Maurice asked Gilberte for one of the talismans required by the clairvoyante. But Gilberte could not give him a single one, unless, as she said, she herself were to play the part of the talisman. For the angel had, in her case, displayed the greatest indiscretion, and such agility that it was impossible always to forestall his enterprise. On hearing this confession, which nevertheless told him nothing new, Maurice lost his temper with the angel, calling him by the names of the lowest animals and swearing he would give him a good kick when he got him within reach of his foot. But his fury soon turned against Madame des Aubels; he accused her of having provoked the insolence she now denounced, and in his wrath he referred to her by all the zoological symbols of immodesty and perversity. His love for Arcade was rekindled in his heart, and burned with a more ardent flame than ever, and the deserted youth, with outstretched arms and bended knees, invoked his angel with sobs and lamentations.

During his sleepless nights it occurred to him that perhaps the books the angel had turned over before his incarnation might serve as a talisman. One morning, therefore, Maurice went up to the library and greeted Monsieur Sariette, who was cataloguing under the romantic gaze of Alexandre d'Esparvieu. Monsieur Sariette smiled, but his face was deathly pale. Now that an invisible hand no longer upset the books placed under his charge, now that tranquillity and order once more reigned in the library, Monsieur Sariette was happy, but his strength diminished day by day. There was little left of him but a frail and contented shadow.

> "One dies, in full content, of sorrow past."

"Monsieur Sariette," said Maurice, "you remember that time when your books were disarranged every night, how armfuls disappeared, how they were dragged about, turned over, ruined, and sent rolling helter-skelter as far as the gutter in the Rue Palatine. Those were great days! Point out to me, Monsieur Sariette, the books which suffered most."

This proposition threw Monsieur Sariette into a melancholy stupor, and Maurice had to repeat his request three times before he could make the aged librarian understand. At length he pointed to a very ancient Talmud from Jerusalem as having been frequently touched by those unseen hands. An apocryphal Gospel of the third century, consisting of twenty papyrus sheets, had also quitted its place time after time. Gassendi's Correspondence too seemed to have been well thumbed.

"But," added Monsieur Sariette, "the book to which the mysterious visitant devoted the most particular attention was undoubtedly a little copy of *Lucretius* adorned with the arms of Philippe de Vendôme, Grand Prieur de France, with autograph annotations by Voltaire, who, as is well known, frequently visited the Temple in his younger days. The fearsome reader who caused me such terrible anxiety never grew weary of this *Lucretius* and made it his bedside book, as it were. His taste was sound, for it's a gem of a thing. Alas! the monster made a blot of ink on page 137 which perhaps the chemists with all the science at their disposal will be powerless to erase."

And Monsieur Sariette heaved a profound sigh. He repented having said all this when young d'Esparvieu asked him for the loan of the precious *Lucretius*. Vainly did the jealous custodian affirm that the book was being repaired at the binder's and was not available. Maurice made it clear that he wasn't to be taken in like that. He strode resolutely into the abode of the philosophers and the globes and seating himself in an arm-chair said:

"I am waiting."

Monsieur Sariette suggested his having another edition. There were some that, textually, were more correct, and were, therefore, preferable from the student's point of view. He offered him Barbou's edition, or Coustelier's, or, better still, a French translation.

He could have the Baron des Coutures' version—which was per-haps a little old-fashioned—or La Grange's, or those in the Nisard and Panckouke series; or, again, there were two versions of strik-ing elegance, one in verse and the other in prose, both from the pen of Monsieur de Pongerville of the French Academy.

"I don't need a translation," said Maurice proudly. "Give me the Prior de Vendôme's copy."

Monsieur Sariette went slowly up to the cupboard in which the jewel in question was contained. The keys were rattling in his trembling hand. He raised them to the lock and withdrew them again immediately and suggested that Maurice should have the common *Lucretius* published by Garnier.

"It's very handy," said he with an engaging smile.

But the silence with which this proposal was received made it clear that resistance was useless. He slowly drew forth the volume from its place, and having taken the precaution to see that there wasn't a speck of dust on the table-cloth, he laid it tremblingly thereon before the great-grandson of Alexandre d'Esparvieu.

Maurice began to turn the leaves, and when he got to page 137 he saw the stain which had been made with violet ink. It was about the size of a pea.

"Ay, that's it," said old Sariette, who had his eye on the *Lucre-tius* the whole time; "that's the trace those invisible monsters left behind them."

"What, there were several of them, Monsieur Sariette?" ex-claimed Maurice.

"I cannot tell. But I don't know whether I have a right to have this blot removed since, like the blot Paul Louis Courier made on the Florentine manuscript, it constitutes a literary document, so to speak."

Scarcely were the words out of the old fellow's mouth when the front door bell rang and there was a confused noise of voices and footsteps in the next room. Sariette ran forward at the sound and collided with Père Guinardon's mistress, old Zephyrine, who, with her tousled hair sticking up like a nest of vipers, her face aflame, her bosom heaving, her abdominal part like an eiderdown quilt puffed out by a terrific gale, was choking with grief and rage. And amid sobs and sighs and groans and all the innumerable sounds which, on earth, make up the mighty uproar to which the emotions of living beings and the tumult of nature give rise, she cried:

"He's gone, the monster! He's gone off with her. He's cleared out the whole shanty and left me to shift for myself with eighteen-pence in my purse."

And she proceeded to give a long and incoherent account of how Michel Guinardon had abandoned her and gone to live with Octavie, the bread-woman's daughter, and she let loose a torrent of abuse against the traitor.

"A man whom I've kept going with my own money for fifty years and more. For I've had plenty of the needful and known plenty of the upper ten and all. I dragged him out of the gutter and now this is what I get for it. He's a bright beauty, that friend of yours. The lazy scoundrel. Why, he had to be dressed like a child, the drunken contemptible brute. You don't know him yet, Monsieur Sariette. He's a forger. He turns out Giottos, Giottos, I tell you, and Fra Angelicos and Grecos, as hard as he can and sells them to art-dealers—yes, and Fragonards too, and Baudouins. He's a debauchee, and doesn't believe in God! That's the worst of the lot, Monsieur Sariette, for without the fear of God . . ."

Long did Zephyrine continue to pour forth vituperations. When at last her breath failed her, Monsieur Sariette availed himself of the opportunity to exhort her to be calm and bring herself to look on the bright side of things. Guinardon would come back. A man doesn't forget anyone he's lived and got on well with for fifty years——

These two observations only goaded her to a fresh outburst, and Zephyrine swore she would never forget the slight that had been put on her; she swore she would never have the monster back with her any more. And if he came to ask her to forgive him on his knees, she would let him grovel at her feet.

"Don't you understand, Monsieur Sariette, that I despise and hate him, that he makes me sick?"

Sixty times she voiced these lofty sentiments; sixty times she vowed she would never have Guinardon back with her again, that she couldn't bear the sight of him, even in a picture.

Monsieur Sariette made no attempt to oppose a resolve which, after protestations such as these, he regarded as unshakable. He did not blame Zephyrine in the least. He even supported her. Unfolding to the deserted one a purer future, he told her of the frailty of human sentiment, exhorted her to display a spirit of renunciation and enjoined her to show a pious resignation to the will of God.

"Seeing, in truth, that your friend is so little worthy of affection . . ."

He was not suffered to continue. Zephyrine flew at him, and shaking him furiously by the collar of his frock-coat, she yelled, half choking with rage: "So little worthy of affection! Michel! Ah! my boy, you find another more kind, more gay, more witty, you find another like him, always young, yes, always. Not worthy of affection! Anyone can see you don't know anything about love, you old duffer."

Taking advantage of the fact that Père Sariette was thus deeply engaged, young d'Esparvieu slipped the little *Lucretius* into his pocket, and strolled deliberately past the crouching librarian, bidding him adieu with a little wave of the hand.

Armed with his talisman, he hastened to the Place des Ternes, to interview Madame Mira. She received him in a red drawing-room where neither owl nor frog nor any of the paraphernalia of ancient magic were to be found. Madame Mira, in a prune-coloured dress, her hair powdered, though already past her prime, was of very good appearance. She spoke with a certain elegance and prided herself on discovering hidden things by the help alone of Science, Philosophy, and Religion. She felt the morocco binding, feigning to close her eyes, and looking meanwhile through the narrow slit between her lids at the Latin title and the coat of arms which conveyed nothing to her.

Accustomed to receive as tokens such things as rings, handkerchiefs, letters, and locks of hair, she could not conceive to what sort of individual this singular book could belong. By habitual and mechanical cunning she disguised her real surprise under a feigned surprise.

"Strange!" she murmured, "strange! I do not see quite clearly . . . I perceive a woman . . ."

As she let fall this magic word, she glanced furtively to see what sort of an effect it had and beheld on her questioner's face a unexpected look of disappointment. Perceiving that she was off the track, she immediately changed her oracle:

"But she fades away immediately. It is strange, strange! I have a confused impression of some vague form, a being that I cannot define," and having assured herself by a hurried glance that, this time, her words were going down, she expatiated on the vagueness of the person and on the mist that enveloped him.

However, the vision grew clearer to Madame Mira, who was following a clue step by step.

"A wide street . . . a square with a statue . . . a deserted street,—stairs. He is there in a bluish room—he is a young man, with pale and careworn face. There are things he seems to regret, and which he would not do again did they still remain undone."

But the effort at divination had been too great. Fatigue prevented the clairvoyante from continuing her transcendental researches. She spent her remaining strength in impressively recommending him who consulted her to remain in intimate union with God if he wished to regain what he had lost and succeed in his attempts.

On leaving Maurice placed a louis on the mantelpiece and went away moved and troubled, persuaded that Madame Mira possessed supernatural faculties, but unfortunately insufficient ones.

At the bottom of the stairs he remembered he had left the little *Lucretius* on the table of the pythoness, and, thinking that the old maniac Sariette would never get over its loss, went up to recover possession of it.

On re-entering the paternal abode his gaze lighted upon a

shadowy and grief-stricken figure. It was old Sariette, who in tones
as plaintive as the wail of the November wind began to beg for his
Lucretius. Maurice pulled it carelessly out of his great-coat pocket.

"Don't flurry yourself, Monsieur Sariette," said he. "There the
thing is."

Clasping the jewel to his bosom the old librarian bore it away
and laid it gently down on the blue table-cloth, thinking all the
while where he might safely hide his precious treasure, and turning
over all sorts of schemes in his mind as became a zealous curator.
But who among us shall boast of his wisdom? The foresight of man
is short, and his prudence is for ever being baffled. The blows of
fate are ineluctable; no man shall evade his doom. There is no counsel, no caution that avails against destiny. Hapless as we are, the
same blind force which regulates the courses of atom and of star
fashions universal order from our vicissitudes. Our ill-fortune is
necessary to the harmony of the Universe. It was the day for the
binder, a day which the revolving seasons brought round twice a
year, beneath the sign of the Ram and the sign of the Scales. That
day, ever since morning, Monsieur Sariette had been making things
ready for the binder. He had laid out on the table as many of the
newly purchased paper-bound volumes as were deemed worthy of
a permanent binding or of being put in boards, and also those books
whose binding was in need of repair, and of all these he had drawn
up a detailed and accurate list. Punctually at five o'clock, old
Amédée, the man from Léger-Massieu's, the binder in the Rue de
l'Abbaye, presented himself at the d'Esparvieu library and, after a
double check had been carried out by Monsieur Sariette, thrust the
books he was to take back to his master into a piece of cloth which
he fastened into knots at the four corners and hoisted on to his
shoulder. He then saluted the librarian with the following words,
"Good night, all!" and went downstairs.

Everything went off on this occasion as usual. But Amédée, seeing the *Lucretius* on the table, innocently put it into the bag with
the others, and took it away without Monsieur Sariette's perceiving
it. The librarian quitted the home of the Philosophers and Globes in
entire forgetfulness of the book whose absence had been causing
him such horrible anxiety all day long. Some people may take a
stern view of the matter and call this a lapse, a defection of his
better nature. But would it not be more accurate to say that fate
had decided that things should come to pass in this manner, and
that what is called chance, and is in fact but the regular order of
nature, had accomplished this imperceptible deed which was to
have such awful consequences in the sight of man? Monsieur
Sariette went off to his dinner at the *Quatre Évêques,* and read his
paper *La Croix.* He was tranquil and serene. It was only the next
morning when he entered the abode of the Philosophers and Globes
that he remembered the *Lucretius.* Failing to see it on the table he

looked for it everywhere, but without success. It never entered his head that Amédée might have taken it away by mistake. What he did think was that the invisible visitant had returned, and he was mightily disturbed.

The unhappy curator, hearing a noise on the landing, opened the door and found it was little Léon, who, with a gold-braided *képi* stuck on his head, was shouting "Vive la France" and hurling dusters and feather-brooms and Hippolyte's floor polish at imaginary foes. The child preferred this landing for playing soldiers to any other part of the house, and sometimes he would stray into the library. Monsieur Sariette was seized with the sudden suspicion that it was he who had taken the *Lucretius* to use as a missile and he ordered him, in threatening tones, to give it back. The child denied that he had taken it, and Monsieur Sariette had recourse to cajolery.

"Léon, if you bring me back the little red book, I will give you some chocolates."

The child grew thoughtful; and in the evening, as Monsieur Sariette was going downstairs, he met Léon, who said:

"There's the book!"

And, holding out a much-torn picture-book called *The Story of Gribouille,* demanded his chocolates.

A few days later the post brought Maurice the prospectus of an enquiry agency managed by an ex-employee at the Prefecture of Police; it promised celerity and discretion. He found at the address indicated a moustached gentleman morose and careworn, who demanded a deposit and promised to find the individual.

The ex-police official soon wrote to inform him that very onerous investigations had been commenced and asked for fresh funds. Maurice gave him no more and resolved to carry on the search himself. Imagining, not without some likelihood, that the angel would associate with the wretched, seeing that he had no money, and with the exiled of all nations—like himself, revolutionaries— he visited the lodging-houses at St. Ouen, at la Chapelle, Montmartre, and the Barrière d'Italie. He sought him in the doss-houses, public-houses where they give you plates of tripe, and others where you can get a sausage for three sous; he searched for him in the cellars at the Market and at Père Momie's.

Maurice visited the restaurants where nihilists and anarchists take their meals. There he came across men dressed as women, gloomy and wild-looking youths, and blue-eyed octogenarians who laughed like little children. He observed, asked questions, was taken for a spy, had a knife thrust into him by a very beautiful woman, and the very next day continued his search in beer-houses, lodging-houses, houses of ill-fame, gambling-hells down by the fortifications, at the receivers of stolen goods, and among the "apaches."

Seeing him thus pale, harassed, and silent, his mother grew worried.

"We must find him a wife," she said. "It is a pity that Mademoiselle de la Verdelière has not a bigger fortune."

Abbé Patouille did not hide his anxiety.

"This child," he said, "is passing through a moral crisis."

"I am more inclined to think," replied Monsieur René d'Esparvieu, "that he is under the influence of some bad woman. We must find him an occupation which will absorb him and flatter his vanity. I might get him appointed Secretary to the Committee for the Preservation of Country Churches, or Consulting Counsel to the Syndicate of Catholic Plumbers."

XVII

WHEREIN WE LEARN THAT SOPHAR, NO LESS EAGER FOR GOLD THAN MAMMON, LOOKED UPON HIS HEAVENLY HOME LESS FAVOURABLY THAN UPON FRANCE, A COUNTRY BLESSED WITH A SAVINGS BANK AND LOAN DEPARTMENTS, AND WHEREIN WE SEE, YET ONCE AGAIN, THAT WHOSO IS POSSESSED OF THIS WORLD'S GOODS FEARS THE EVIL EFFECTS OF ANY CHANGE

EANWHILE Arcade led a life of obscure toil. He worked at a printer's in the Rue St. Benoît, and lived in an attic in the Rue Mouffetard. His comrades having gone on strike, he left the workroom and devoted his day to his propaganda. So successful was he that he won over to the side of revolt fifty thousand of those guardian angels who, as Zita had surmised, were discontented with their condition and imbued with the spirit of the times. But lacking money, he lacked liberty, and could not employ his time as he wished in instructing the sons of Heaven. So, too, Prince Istar, hampered by want of funds, manufactured fewer bombs than were needed, and these less fine. Of course he prepared a good many small pocket machines. He had filled Théophile's rooms with them, and not a day passed but he forgot some and left them lying about on the seats in various cafés. But a nice bomb, easily handled and capable of destroying many big mansions, cost him from twenty to twenty-five thousand francs; and Prince Istar only possessed two of this kind. Equally bent on procuring funds, Arcade and Istar both went to make a request for money from a celebrated financier named Max Everdingen, who, as everyone knows, is the managing director of the biggest banking concern in France and indeed in the whole world. What is not so well known is that Max Everdingen was not born of woman, but is a fallen angel. Nevertheless, such is the truth. In Heaven he was named Sophar, and guarded the treasures of Ialdabaoth, a great collector of gold and precious stones. In the exercise of this function Sophar contracted a love of riches which could not be satisfied in a state of society in which banks and stock exchanges are alike unknown. His heart flamed with an ardent love for the god of the Hebrews to whom he remained faithful during a long course of centuries. But at the commencement of the twentieth century of the Christian era, casting his eyes down from the height of the firmament upon France, he saw that this country, under the name of a Republic, was constituted as a plutocracy and that, under the appearance of a democratic government, high finance exercised sovereign sway, untrammelled and unchecked.

Henceforth life in the Empyrean became intolerable to him. He longed for France as for the promised land, and one day, bearing with him all the precious stones he could carry, he descended to earth and established himself in Paris. This angel of cupidity did good business there. Since his materialisation his face had lost its celestial aspect; it reproduced the Semitic type in all its purity, and one could admire the lines and the puckers which wrinkle the faces of bankers and which are to be seen in the money-changers of Quintin Matsys.

His beginnings were humble and his success amazing. He married an ugly woman and they saw themselves reflected in their children as in a mirror. Baron Max Everdingen's large mansion, which rears itself on the heights of the Trocadéro, is crammed with the spoils of Christian Europe.

The Baron received Arcade and Prince Istar in his study,—one of the most modest rooms in his mansion. The ceiling is decorated with a fresco of Tiepolo, taken from a Venetian palace. The bureau of the Regent, Philip of Orleans, is in this room, which is full of cabinets, show-cases, pictures, and statues.

Arcade allowed his gaze to wander over the walls.

"How comes it, my brother Sophar," said he, "that you, in spite of your Jewish heart, obey so ill the commandment of the Lord your God who said: 'Thou shalt have no graven images'? for here I see an Apollo of Houdon's and a Hebe of Lemoine's, and several busts by Caffieri. And, like Solomon in his old age, O son of God, you set up in your dwelling-place the idols of strange nations: for such are this Venus of Boucher, this Jupiter of Rubens, and those nymphs that are indebted to Fragonard's brush for the gooseberry jam which smears their gleaming limbs. And here in this single show-case, Sophar, you keep the sceptre of St. Louis, six hundred pearls of Marie Antoinette's broken necklace, the imperial mantle of

Charles V, the tiara wrought by Ghiberti for Pope Martin V, the Colonna, Bonaparte's sword—and I know not what besides."

"Mere trifles," said Max Everdingen.

"My dear Baron," said Prince Istar, "you even possess the ring which Charlemagne placed on a fairy's finger and which was thought to be lost. But let us discuss the business on which we have come. My friend and I have come to ask you for money."

"I can well believe it," replied Max Everdingen. "Everyone wants money, but for different reasons. What do you want money for?"

Prince Istar replied simply:

"To stir up a revolution in France."

"In France!" repeated the Baron, "in France? Well, I shall give you no money for that, you may be quite sure."

Arcade did not disguise the fact that he had expected greater liberality and more generous help from a celestial brother.

"Our project," he said, "is a vast one. It embraces both Heaven and Earth. It is settled in every detail. We shall first bring about a social revolution in France, in Europe, on the whole planet; then we shall carry war into the heavens, where we shall establish a peaceful democracy. And to reduce the citadels of Heaven, to overturn the mountain of God, to storm celestial Jerusalem, a vast army is needful, enormous resources, formidable machines, and electrophores of a strength yet unknown. It is our intention to commence with France."

"You are madmen!" exclaimed Baron Everdingen; "madmen and fools! Listen to me. There is not one single reform to carry out in France. All is perfect, finally settled, unchangeable. You hear?— unchangeable." And to add force to his statement, Baron Everdingen banged his fist three times on the Regent's bureau.

"Our points of view differ," said Arcade sweetly. "*I* think, as does Prince Istar, that everything should be changed in this country. But what boots it to dispute the matter? Moreover, it is too late. We have come to speak to you, O my brother Sophar, in the name of five hundred thousand celestial spirits, all resolved to commence the universal revolution to-morrow."

Baron Everdingen exclaimed that they were crazy, that he would not give a *sou*, that it was both criminal and mad to attack the most admirable thing in the world, the thing which renders earth more beautiful than heaven—Finance. He was a poet and a prophet. His heart thrilled with holy enthusiasm; he drew attention to the French Savings Bank, the virtuous Savings Bank, that chaste and pure Savings Bank like unto the Virgin of the Canticle who, issuing from the depths of the country in rustic petticoat, bears to the robust and splendid Bank—her bridegroom, who awaits her—the treasures of her love; and drew a picture of the Bank, enriched with the gifts of its spouse, pouring on all the nations of the world torrents of gold, which, of themselves, by a thousand invisible channels return in still greater abundance to the blessed land from which they sprung.

"By Deposit and Loan," he went on, "France has become the New Jerusalem, shedding her glory over all the nations of Europe, and the Kings of the Earth come to kiss her rosy feet. And that is what you would fain destroy? You are both impious and sacrilegious."

Thus spoke the angel of finance. An invisible harp accompanied his voice, and his eyes darted lightning.

Meanwhile Arcade, leaning carelessly against the Regent's bureau, spread out under the Banker's eyes various ground-plans, underground-plans, and sky-plans of Paris with red crosses indicating the points where bombs should be simultaneously placed in cellars and catacombs, thrown on public ways, and flung by a flotilla of aeroplanes. All the financial establishments, and notably the Everdingen Bank and its branches, were marked with red crosses.

The financier shrugged his shoulders.

"Nonsense! you are but wretches and vagabonds, shadowed by all the police of the world. You are penniless. How can you manufacture all the machines?"

By way of reply, Prince Istar drew from his pocket a small copper cylinder, which he gracefully presented to Baron Everdingen.

"You see," said he, "this ordinary-looking box. It is only necessary to let it fall on the ground immediately to reduce this mansion with its inmates to a mass of smoking ashes, and to set a fire going which would devour all the Trocadéro quarter. I have ten thousand like that, and I make three dozen a day."

The financier asked the Cherub to replace the machine in his pocket, and continued in a conciliatory tone:

"Listen to me, my friends. Go and start a revolution at once in Heaven, and leave things alone in this country. I will sign a cheque for you. You can procure all the material you need to attack celestial Jerusalem."

And Baron Everdingen was already working up in his imagination a magnificent deal in electrophores and war-material.

XVIII

WHEREIN IS BEGUN THE GARDENER'S STORY, IN THE COURSE OF WHICH WE SHALL SEE THE DESTINY OF THE WORLD UNFOLDED IN A DISCOURSE AS BROAD AND MAGNIFICENT IN ITS VIEWS AS BOSSUET'S DISCOURSE ON THE HISTORY OF THE UNIVERSE IS NARROW AND DISMAL

THE gardener bade Arcade and Zita sit down in an arbour walled with wild bryony, at the far end of the orchard.

"Arcade," said the beautiful Archangel, "Nectaire will perhaps reveal to you to-day the things you are burning to know. Ask him to speak."

Arcade did so and old Nectaire, laying down his pipe, began as follows:—

"I knew him. He was the most beautiful of all the Seraphim. He shone with intelligence and daring. His great heart was big with all the virtues born of pride: frankness, courage, constancy in trial, indomitable hope. Long, long ago, ere Time was, in the boreal sky where gleam the seven magnetic stars, he dwelt in a palace of diamond and gold, where the air was ever tremulous with the beating of wings and with songs of triumph. Iahveh, on his mountain, was jealous of Lucifer. You both know it: angels like unto men feel love and hatred quicken within them. Capable, at times, of generous resolves, they too often follow their own interests and yield to fear. Then, as now, they showed themselves, for the most part, incapable of lofty thoughts, and in the fear of the Lord lay their sole virtue. Lucifer, who held vile things in proud disdain, despised this rabble of commonplace spirits for ever wallowing in a life of feasts and pleasure. But to those who were possessed of a daring spirit, a restless soul, to those fired with a wild love of liberty, he proffered friendship, which was returned with adoration. These latter deserted in a mass the mountain of God and yielded to the Seraph the homage which That Other would fain have kept for himself alone.

"I ranked among the Dominations, and my name, Alaciel, was not unknown to fame. To satisfy my mind—that was ever tormented with an insatiable thirst for knowledge and understanding —I observed the nature of things, I studied the properties of minerals, air, and water. I sought out the laws which govern nature, solid or ethereal, and after much pondering I perceived that the Universe had not been formed as its pretended Creator would have us believe; I knew that all that exists, exists of itself and not by the caprice of Iahveh; that the world is itself its own creator and the spirit its own God. Henceforth I despised Iahveh for his imposture, and I hated him because he showed himself to be opposed to all that I found desirable and good: liberty, curiosity, doubt. These feelings drew me towards the Seraph. I admired him, I loved him. I dwelt in his light. When at length it appeared that a choice had to be made between him and That Other I ranged myself on the side of Lucifer and knew no other aim than to serve him, no other desire than to share his lot.

"War having become inevitable, he prepared for it with indefatigable vigilance and all the resourcefulness of a far-seeing mind. Making the Thrones and Dominations into Chalybes and Cyclopes, he drew forth iron from the mountains bordering his domain; iron, which he valued more than gold, and forged weapons in the caverns of Heaven. Then in the desert plain of the North he assembled myriads of Spirits, armed them, taught them, and drilled them. Although prepared in secret, the enterprise was too vast for his adversary not to be soon aware of it. It might in truth be said that he had always foreseen and dreaded it, for he had made a citadel of his abode and a warlike host of his angels, and he gave himself the name of the God of Hosts. He made ready his thunderbolts. More than half of the children of Heaven remained faithful to him; thronging round him he beheld obedient souls and patient hearts. The Archangel Michael, who knew not fear, took command of these docile troops. Lucifer, as soon as he saw that his army could gain no more in numbers or in warlike skill, moved it swiftly against the foe, and promising his angels riches and glory marched at their head towards the mountain upon whose summit stands the Throne of the Universe. For three days our host swept onward over the ethereal plains. Above our heads streamed the black standards of revolt. And now, behold, the Mountain of God shone rosy in the orient sky and our chief scanned with his eyes the glittering ramparts. Beneath the sapphire walls the foe was drawn up in battle array, and, while we marched clad in our iron and bronze, they shone resplendent in gold and precious stones.

"Their gonfalons of red and blue floated in the breeze, and lightning flashed from the points of their lances. In a little while the armies were only sundered one from the other by a narrow strip of level and deserted ground, and at this sight even the bravest shuddered as they thought that there in bloody conflict their fate would soon be sealed.

"Angels, as you know, never die. But when bronze and iron, diamond point or flaming sword tear their ethereal substance, the pain they feel is more acute than men may suffer, for their flesh is more exquisitely delicate; and should some essential organ be destroyed, they fall inert and, slowly decomposing, are resolved into clouds and during long æons float insensible in the cold ether. And when at length they resume spirit and form they fail to recover full memory of their past life. Therefore it is but natural that angels shrink from suffering, and the bravest among them is troubled at the thought of being reft of light and sweet remembrance. Were it otherwise the angelic race would know neither the delight of battle nor the glory of sacrifice. Those who, before the beginning of Time, fought in the Empyrean for or against the God of Armies, would have taken part without honour in mock battles, and it would not now become me to say to you, my children, with rightful pride:

" 'Lo, I was there!'

"Lucifer gave the signal for the onset and led the assault. We fell upon the enemy, thinking to destroy him then and there and carry the sacred citadel at the first onslaught. The soldiers of the jealous God, less fiery, but no whit less firm than ours, remained immovable. The Archangel Michael commanded them with the calmness and resolution of a mighty spirit. Thrice we strove to break through their lines, thrice they opposed to our iron-clad breast the flaming points of their lances, swift to pierce the stoutest cuirass. In millions the glorious bodies fell. At length our right wing pierced the enemy's left and we beheld the Principalities, the Powers, the Virtues, the Dominations, and the Thrones turn and flee in full career; while the Angels of the Third Choir, flying distractedly above them, covered them with a snow of feathers mingled with a rain of blood. We sped in pursuit of them amid the débris of chariots and broken weapons, and we spurred their nimble flight. Suddenly a storm of cries amazed us. It grew louder and nearer. With desperate shrieks and triumphal clamour the right wing of the enemy, the giant archangels of the Most High, had flung themselves upon our left flank and broken it. Thus we were forced to abandon the pursuit of the fugitives and hasten to the rescue of our own shattered troops. Our prince flew to rally them, and re-established the conflict. But the left wing of the enemy, whose ruin he had not quite consummated, no longer pressed by lance or arrow, regained courage, returned, and faced us yet again. Night fell upon the dubious field. While under the shelter of darkness, in the still, silent air stirred ever and anon by the moans of the wounded, his forces were resting from their toils, Lucifer began to make ready for the next day's battle. Before dawn the trumpets sounded the reveille. Our warriors surprised the enemy at the hour of prayer, put them to rout, and long and fierce was the carnage that ensued. When all had either fallen or fled, the Archangel Michael, none with him save a few companions with four wings of flame, still resisted the onslaughts of a countless host. They fell back ceaselessly opposing their breasts to us, and Michael still displayed an impassible countenance. The sun had run a third of its course when we commenced to scale the Mountain of God. An arduous ascent it was: sweat ran from our brows, a dazzling light blinded us. Weighed down with steel, our feathery wings could not sustain us, but hope gave us wings that bore us up. The beautiful

Seraph, pointing with glittering hand, mounting ever higher and higher, showed us the way. All day long we slowly clomb the lofty heights which at evening were robed in azure, rose, and violet. The starry host appearing in the sky seemed as the reflection of our own arms. Infinite silence reigned above us. We went on, intoxicated with hope; all at once from the darkened sky lightning darted forth, the thunder muttered, and from the cloudy mountain-top fell fire from Heaven. Our helmets, our breastplates were running with flames, and our bucklers broke under bolts sped by invisible hands. Lucifer, in the storm of fire, retained his haughty mien. In vain the lightning smote him; mightier than ever he stood erect, and still defied the foe. At length, the thunder, making the mountain totter, flung us down pell-mell, huge fragments of sapphire and ruby crashing down with us as we fell, and we rolled inert, swooning, for a period whose duration none could measure.

"I awoke in a darkness filled with lamentations. And when my eyes had grown accustomed to the dense shadows I saw round me my companions in arms, scattered in thousands on the sulphurous ground, lit by fitful gleams of livid light. My eyes perceived but fields of lava, smoking craters, and poisonous swamps.

"Mountains of ice and shadowy seas shut in the horizon. A brazen sky hung heavy on our brows. And the horror of the place was such that we wept as we sat, crouched elbow on knee, our cheeks resting on our clenched hands.

"But soon, raising my eyes, I beheld the Seraph standing before me like a tower. Over his pristine splendour sorrow had cast its mantle of sombre majesty.

" 'Comrades,' said he, 'we must be happy and rejoice, for behold we are delivered from celestial servitude. Here we are free, and it were better to be free in Hell than serve in Heaven. We are not conquered, since the will to conquer is still ours. We have caused the Throne of the jealous God to totter; by our hands it shall fall. Arise, therefore, and be of good heart.'

"Thereupon, at his command, we piled mountain upon mountain and on the topmost peak we reared engines which flung molten rocks against the divine habitations. The celestial host was taken unaware and from the abodes of glory there issued groans and cries of terror. And even then we thought to re-enter in triumph on our high estate, but the Mountain of God was wreathed with lightnings, and thunderbolts, falling on our fortress, crushed it to dust. After this fresh disaster, the Seraph remained awhile in meditation, his head buried in his hands. At length he raised his darkened visage. Now he was Satan, greater than Lucifer. Steadfast and loyal the angels thronged about him.

" 'Friends,' he said, 'if victory is denied us now, it is because we are neither worthy nor capable of victory. Let us determine wherein we have failed. Nature shall not be ruled, the sceptre of the Universe shall not be grasped, Godhead shall not be won, save by knowledge alone. We must conquer the thunder; to that task we must apply ourselves unwearyingly. It is not blind courage (no one this day has shown more courage than have you) which will win us the courts of Heaven; but rather study and reflection. In these silent realms where we are fallen, let us meditate, seeking the hidden causes of things; let us observe the course of Nature; let us pursue her with compelling ardour and all-conquering desire; let us strive to penetrate her infinite grandeur, her infinite minuteness. Let us seek to know when she is barren and when she brings forth fruit; how she makes cold and heat, joy and sorrow, life and death; how she assembles and disperses her elements, how she produces both the light air we breathe and the rocks of diamond and sapphire whence we have been precipitated, the divine fire wherewith we have been scarred and the soaring thought which stirs our minds. Torn with dire wounds, scorched by flame and by ice, let us render thanks to Fate which has sedulously opened our eyes, and let us rejoice at our lot. It is through pain that, suffering a first experience of Nature, we have been roused to know her and to subdue her. When she obeys us we shall be as gods. But even though she hide her mysteries for ever from us, deny us arms and keep the secret of the thunder, we still must needs congratulate ourselves on having known pain, for pain has revealed to us new feelings, more precious and more sweet than those experienced in eternal bliss, and inspired us with love and pity unknown to Heaven.'

"These words of the Seraph changed our hearts and opened up fresh hope to us. Our hearts were filled with a great longing for knowledge and love.

"Meanwhile the Earth was coming into being. Its immense and nebulous orb took on hourly more shape and more certainty of outline. The waters which fed the seaweed, the madrepores and shellfish, and bore the light flotilla of the nautilus upon their bosom, no longer covered it in its entirety; they began to sink into beds, and already continents appeared, where, on the warm slime, amphibious monsters crawled. Then the mountains were overspread with forests, and divers races of animals commenced to feed on the grass, the moss, the berries on the trees, and on the acorns. Then there took possession of cavernous shelter under the rocks, a being who was cunning to wound with a sharpened stone the savage beasts, and by his ruses to overcome the ancient denizens of forest, plain, and mountain.

"Man entered painfully on his kingdom. He was defenceless and naked. His scanty hair afforded him but little protection from the cold. His hands ended in nails too frail to do battle with the claws of wild beasts, but the position of his thumb, in opposition to the rest of his fingers, allowed him easily to grasp the most diverse objects and endowed him with skill in default of strength. Without differing essentially from the rest of the animals, he was more capable than any others of observing and comparing. As he drew from his throat various sounds, it occurred to him to designate by a particular inflexion of the voice whatever impinged upon his mind, and by this sequence of different sounds he was enabled to fix and communicate his ideas. His miserable lot and his painstaking spirit aroused the sympathy of the vanquished angels, who discerned in him an audacity equalling their own, and the germ of the pride that was at once their glory and their bane. They came in large numbers to be near him, to dwell on this young earth whither their wings wafted them in effortless flight. And they took pleasure in sharpening his talents and fostering his genius. They taught him to clothe himself in the skins of wild beasts, to roll stones before the mouths of caves to keep out the tigers and bears. They taught him how to make the flame burst forth by twirling a stick among the dried leaves and to foster the sacred fire upon the hearth. Inspired by the ingenious spirits he dared to cross the rivers in the hollowed trunks of cleft trees, he invented the wheel, the grinding-mill, and the plough; the share tore up the earth and the wound brought forth fruit, and the grain offered to him who ground it divine nourishment. He moulded vessels in clay, and out of the flint he fashioned various tools.

"In fine, taking up our abode among mankind, we consoled them and taught them. We were not always visible to them, but of an evening, at the turn of the road, we would appear to them under forms often strange and weird, at times dignified and charming, and we adopted at will the appearance of a monster of the woods and waters, of a venerable old man, of a beautiful child, or of a woman with broad hips. Sometimes we would mock them in our songs or test their intelligence by some cunning prank. There were certain of us of a rather turbulent humour who loved to tease their women and children, but though lowly folk, they were our brothers, and we were never loath to come to their aid. Through our care their intelligence developed sufficiently to attain to mistaken ideas, and to acquire erroneous notions of the relations of cause and effect. As they supposed that some magic bond existed between the reality and its counterfeit presentment, they covered the walls of their caves with figure of animals and carved in ivory images of the reindeer and the mammoth in order to secure as prey the creatures they represented. Centuries passed by with infinite slowness while their genius was coming to birth. We sent them happy thoughts in dreams, inspired them to tame the horse, to castrate the bull, to teach the dog to guard the sheep. They created the family and the tribe. It came to pass one day that one of their wandering tribes was assailed by ferocious hunters. Forthwith the young men of the tribe formed an enclosed ring with their chariots, and in it they shut their women, children, old people, cattle, and treasures, and from the platform of their chariots they hurled murderous stones at their assailants. Thus was formed the first city. Born in misery and condemned to do murder by the law of Iahveh, man put his whole heart into doing battle, and to war he was indebted for his noblest virtues. He hallowed with his blood that sacred love of country which should (if man fulfils his destiny to the very end) enfold the whole earth in peace. One of us, Dædalus, brought him the axe, the plumb-line, and the sail. Thus we rendered the existence of mortals less hard and difficult. By the shores of the lakes they built dwellings of osier, where they might enjoy a meditative quiet unknown to the other inhabitants of the earth, and when they had learned to appease their hunger without too painful efforts we breathed into their hearts the love of beauty.

"They raised up pyramids, obelisks, towers, colossal statues which smiled stiff and uncouth, and genetic symbols. Having learnt to know us or trying at least to divine what manner of beings we were, they felt both friendship and fear for us. The wisest among them watched us with sacred awe and pondered our teaching. In their gratitude the people of Greece and of Asia consecrated to us stones, trees, shadowy woods; offered us victims, and sang us hymns; in fact we became gods in their sight, and they called us Horus, Isis, Astarte, Zeus, Cybele, Demeter, and Triptolemus. Satan was worshipped under the names of Evan, Dionysus, Iacchus, and Lenæus. He showed in his various manifestations all the strength and beauty which it is given to mortals to conceive. His eyes had the sweetness of the wood-violet, his lips were brilliant with the ruby-red of the pomegranate, a down finer than the velvet of the peach covered his cheeks and his chin: his fair hair, wound like a diadem and knotted loosely on the crown of his head, was encircled with ivy. He charmed the wild beasts, and penetrating into the deep forests drew to him all wild spirits, every thing that climbed in trees and peered through the branches with wild and timid gaze. On all these creatures fierce and fearful, that lived on bitter berries and beneath whose hairy breasts a wild heart beat, half-human creatures of the woods—on all he bestowed loving-kindness and grace, and they followed him drunk with joy and beauty. He planted the vine and showed mortals how to crush the grapes underfoot to make the wine flow. Magnificent and benign, he fared across the world, a long procession following in his train. To bear him company I took the form of a satyr; from my brow sprang two budding horns. My nose was flat and my ears were pointed. Glands, like those of the goat, hung on my neck, a goat's tail moved with my moving loins, and my hairy legs ended in a black cloven hoof which beat the ground in cadence.

"Dionysus fared on his triumphal march over the world. In his company I passed through Lydia, the Phrygian fields, the scorching plains of Persia, Media bristling with hoar-frost, Arabia Felix, and rich Asia where flourishing cities were laved by the waves of the sea. He proceeded on a car drawn by lions and lynxes, to the sound of flutes, cymbals, and drums, invented for his mysteries. Bacchantes, Thyades, and Mænads, girt with the dappled fawn-skin, waved the thyrsus encircled with ivy. He bore in his train the Satyrs, whose joyous troop I led, Sileni, Pans, and Centaurs. Under his feet flowers and fruit sprang to life, and striking the rocks with his wand he made limpid streams gush forth. In the month of the Vintage he visited Greece, and the villagers ran forth to meet him, stained with the green and ruddy juices of the plants, they wore masks of wood, or bark, or leaves; in their hands they bore earthen cups, and danced wanton dances. Their womenfolk, imitating the companions of the God, their heads wreathed with green smilax, fastened round their supple loins skins of fawn or goat. The virgins twined about their throats garlands of fig leaves, they kneaded cakes of flour, and bore the Phallus in the mystic basket. And the vine-dressers, all daubed with lees of wine, standing up in their wains and bandying mockery or abuse with the passers-by, invented Tragedy.

"Truly, it was not in dreaming beside a fountain, but by dint of strenuous toil that Dionysus taught them to grow plants and to make them bring forth succulent fruits. And while he pondered the art of transforming the rough woodlanders into a race that should love music and submit to just laws, more than once over his brow, burning with the fire of enthusiasm, did melancholy and gloomy fever pass. But his profound knowledge and his friendship for mankind enabled him to triumph over every obstacle. O days divine! Beautiful dawn of life! We led the Bacchanals on the leafy summits of the mountains and on the yellow shores of the seas. The Naiads and the Oreads mingled with us at our play. Aphrodite at our coming rose from the foam of the sea to smile upon us."

XIX

THE GARDENER'S STORY, CONTINUED

HEN men had learned to cultivate the earth, to herd cattle, to enclose their holy places within walls, and to recognise the gods by their beauty, I withdrew to that smiling land girdled with dark woods and watered by the Stymphalos, the Olbios, the Erymanthus, and the proud Crathis, swollen with the icy waters of the Styx, and there, in a green valley at the foot of a hill planted with arbutus, olive, and pine, beneath a cluster of white poplars and plane trees, by the side of a stream flowing with soft murmur amid tufted mastic trees, I sang to the shepherds and the nymphs of the birth of the world, the origin of fire, of the tenuous air, of water and of earth. I told them how primeval men had lived wretched and naked in the woods, before the ingenious spirits had taught them the arts; of God, too, I sang to them, and why they gave Dionysus Semele to mother, because his desire to befriend mankind was born amid the thunder.

"It was not without effort that this people, more pleasing than all the others in the eyes of the gods, these happy Greeks, achieved good government and a knowledge of the arts. Their first temple was a hut composed of laurel branches; their first image of the gods, a tree; their first altar, a rough stone stained with the blood of Iphigenia. But in a short time they brought wisdom and beauty to a point that no nation had attained before them, that no nation has since approached. Whence comes it, Arcade, this solitary marvel on the earth? Wherefore did the sacred soil of Ionia and of Attica bring forth this incomparable flower? Because nor priesthood, nor dogma, nor revelation ever found a place there, because the Greeks never knew the jealous God.

"It was his own grace, his own genius that the Greek enthroned and deified as his God, and when he raised his eyes to the heavens it was his own image that he saw reflected there. He conceived everything in due measure; and to his temples he gave perfect proportion. All therein was grace, harmony, symmetry, and wisdom; all were worthy of the immortals who dwelt within them and who under names of happy choice, in realised shapes, figured forth the genius of man. The columns which bore the marble architrave, the frieze and the cornice were touched with something human, which made them venerable; and sometimes one might see, as at Athens and at Delphi, beautiful young girls strong-limbed and radiant upstaying the entablature of treasure house and sanctuary. O days of splendour, harmony, and wisdom!

"Dionysus resolved to repair to Italy, whither he was summoned under the name of Bacchus by a people eager to celebrate his mysteries. I took passage in his ship decked with tendrils of the vine, and landed under the eyes of the two brothers of Helen at the mouth of the yellow Tiber. Already under the teaching of the god, the inhabitants of Latium had learned to wed the vine to the young stripling elm. It was my pleasure to dwell at the foot of the Sabine hills in a valley crowned with trees and watered with pure springs. I gathered the verbena and the mallow in the meadows. The pale olive-trees twisting their perforated trunks on the slope of the hill gave me of their unctuous fruit. There I taught a race of men with square heads, who had not, like the Greeks, a fertile mind, but whose hearts were true, whose souls were patient, and who reverenced the gods. My neighbour, a rustic soldier, who for fifteen years had bowed under the burden of his haversack, had followed the Roman eagle over land and sea, and had seen the enemies of the sovereign people flee before him. Now he drove his furrow with his two red oxen, starred with white between their spreading horns, while beneath the cabin's thatch his spouse, chaste and sedate of mien, pounded garlic in a bronze mortar and cooked the beans upon the sacred hearth. And I, his friend, seated near by under an oak, used to lighten his labours with the sound of my flute, and smile on his little children, when the sun, already low in the sky, was lengthening the shadows, and they returned from the wood all laden with branches. At the garden gate where the pears and pumpkins ripened, and where the lily and the evergreen acanthus bloomed, a figure of Priapus carved out of the trunk of a fig tree menaced thieves with his formidable emblem, and the reeds swaying with the wind over his head scared away the plundering birds. At new moon the pious husbandman made offering of a handful of salt and barley to his household gods crowned with myrtle and with rosemary.

"I saw his children grow up, and his children's children, who kept in their hearts their early piety and did not forget to offer sacrifice to Bacchus, to Diana, and to Venus, nor omit to pour fresh wines and scatter flowers into the fountains. But slowly they fell away from their old habits of patient toil and simplicity.

"I heard them complain when the torrent, swollen with many rains, compelled them to construct a dyke to protect the paternal fields, and the rough Sabine wine grew unpleasing to their delicate palate. They went to drink the wines of Greece at the neighbouring tavern; and the hours slipped unheeded by, while within the arbour shade they watched the dance of the flute player, practised at swaying her supple limbs to the sound of the castanets.

"Lulled by murmuring leaves and whispering streams, the tillers of the soil took sweet repose, but between the poplars we saw along borders of the sacred way vast tombs, statues, and altars arise, and

the rolling of the chariot wheels grew more frequent over the worn
stones. A cherry sapling brought home by a veteran told us of the
far-distant conquests of a Consul, and odes sung to the lyre related
the victories of Rome, mistress of the world.

"All the countries where the great Dionysus had journeyed,
changing wild beasts into men, and making the fruit and grain
bloom and ripen beneath the passing of his Mænads, now breathed
the Pax Romana. The nursling of the she-wolf, soldier and labourer,
friend of conquered nations, laid out roads from the margin of the
misty sea to the rocky slopes of the Caucasus; in every town rose
the temple of Augustus and of Rome, and such was the universal
faith in Latin justice that in the gorges of Thessaly or on the
wooded borders of the Rhine, the slave, ready to succumb under
his iniquitous burden, called aloud on the name of Cæsar.

"But why must it be that on this ill-starred globe of land and
water, all should perish and die and the fairest things be ever the
most fleeting? O adorable daughters of Greece! O Science! O Wisdom! O Beauty! kindly divinities, you were wrapt in heavy slumber
ere you submitted to the outrages of the barbarians, who already
in the marshy wastes of the North and on the lonely steppes, ready
to assail you, bestrode bare-backed their little shaggy horses.

"While, dear Arcade, the patient legionary camped by the
borders of the Phasis and the Tanais, the women and the priests of
Asia and of monstrous Africa invaded the Eternal City and troubled the sons of Remus with their magic spells. Until now, Iahveh,
the persecutor of the laborious demons, was unknown to the world
that he pretended to have created, save to certain miserable Syrian
tribes, ferocious like himself, and perpetually dragged from servitude to servitude. Profiting by the Roman peace which assured free
travel and traffic everywhere, and favoured the exchange of ideas
and merchandise, this old God insolently made ready to conquer
the Universe. He was not the only one, for the matter of that, to
attempt such an undertaking. At the same time a crowd of gods,
demiurges, and demons, such as Mithra, Thammuz, the good Isis,
and Eubulus, meditated taking possession of the peace-enfolded
world. Of all the spirits, Iahveh appeared the least prepared for
victory. His ignorance, his cruelty, his ostentation, his Asiatic luxury, his disdain of laws, his affectation of rendering himself invisible, all these things were calculated to offend those Greeks and
Latins who had absorbed the teaching of Dionysus and the Muses.
He himself felt he was incapable of winning the allegiance of free
men and of cultivated minds, and he employed cunning. To seduce
their souls he invented a fable which, although not so ingenious as
the myths wherewith we have surrounded the spirits of our disciples of old, could, nevertheless, influence those feebler intellects
which are to be found everywhere in great masses. He declared that
men having committed a crime against him, an hereditary crime,

should pay the penalty for it in their present life and in the life to come (for mortals vainly imagine that their existence is prolonged in hell); and the astute Iahveh gave out that he had sent his own son to earth to redeem with his blood the debt of mankind. It is not credible that a penalty should redress a fault, and it is still less credible that the innocent should pay for the guilty. The sufferings of the innocent atone for nothing, and do but add one evil to another. Nevertheless, unhappy creatures were found to adore Iahveh and his son, the expiator, and to announce their mysteries as good tidings. We should not be surprised at this folly. Have we not seen many times indeed human beings who, poor and naked, prostrate themselves before all the phantoms of fear, and rather than follow the teaching of well-disposed demons, obey the commandments of cruel demiurges? Iahveh, by his cunning, took souls as in a net. But he did not gain therefrom, for his glorification, all that he expected. It was not he, but his son, who received the homage of mankind, and who gave his name to the new cult. He himself remained almost unknown upon earth."

XX

THE GARDENER'S STORY, CONTINUED

HE new superstition spread at first over Syria and Africa; it won over the seaports where the filthy rabble swarm, and, penetrating into Italy, infected at first the courtesans and the slaves, and then made rapid progress among the middle classes of the towns. But for a long while the country-side remained undisturbed. As in the past, the villagers consecrated a pine tree to Diana, and sprinkled it every year with the blood of a young boar; they propitiated their Lares with the sacrifice of a sow, and offered to Bacchus—benefactor of mankind—a kid of dazzling whiteness, or if they were too poor for this, at least they had a little wine and a little flour from the vineyard and from the fields for their household gods. We had taught them that it sufficed to approach the altar with clean hands, and that the gods rejoiced over a modest offering.

"Nevertheless, the reign of Iahveh proclaimed its advent in a hundred places by its extravagances. The Christians burnt books, overthrew temples, set fire to the towns, and carried on their ravages as far as the deserts. There, thousands of unhappy beings, turning their fury against themselves, lacerated their sides with points of steel. And from the whole earth the sighs of voluntary victims rose up to God like songs of praise.

"My shadowy retreat could not escape for long from the fury of their madness.

"On the summit of the hill which overlooked the olive woods, brightened daily with the sounds of my flute, had stood since the earliest days of the Pax Romana, a small marble temple, round as the huts of our forefathers. It had no walls, but on a base of seven steps, sixteen columns rose in a circle with the acanthus on the capitals, bearing a cupola of white tiles. This cupola sheltered a statue of Love fashioning his bow, the work of an Athenian sculptor. The child seemed to breathe, joy was welling from his lips, all his limbs were harmonious and polished. I honoured this image of the most powerful of all the gods, and I taught the villagers to bear to him as an offering a cup crowned with verbena and filled with wine two summers old.

"One day, when seated as my custom was at the feet of the god, pondering precepts and songs, an unknown man, wild-looking, with unkempt hair, approached the temple, sprang at one bound up the marble steps, and with savage glee exclaimed:

" 'Die, poisoner of souls, and joy and beauty perish with you.' He spoke thus, and drawing an axe from his girdle raised it against the god. I stayed his arm, I threw him down, and trampled him under my feet.

" 'Demon,' he cried desperately, 'suffer me to overturn this idol, and you may slay me afterwards.'

"I heeded not his atrocious plea, but leaned with all my might on his chest, which cracked under my knee, and, squeezing his throat with my two hands, I strangled the impious one.

"While he lay there, with purple face and lolling tongue, at the feet of the smiling god, I went to purify myself at the sacred stream. Then leaving this land, now the prey of the Christian, I passed through Gaul and gained the banks of the Saône, whither Dionysus had, in days gone by, carried the vine. The god of the Christians had not yet been proclaimed to this happy people. They worshipped for its beauty a leafy beech-tree, whose honoured branches swept the ground, and they hung fillets of wool thereon. They also worshipped a sacred stream and set up images of clay in a dripping grotto. They made offering of little cheeses and a bowl of milk to the Nymphs of the woods and mountains.

"But soon an apostle of sorrow was sent to them by the new God. He was drier than a smoked fish. Although attenuated with fasting and watching, he taught with unabated ardour all manner of gloomy mysteries. He loved suffering, and thought it good; his anger fell upon all that was beautiful, comely, and joyous. The sacred tree fell beneath his hatchet. He hated the Nymphs, because they were beautiful, and he flung imprecations at them when their shining limbs gleamed among the leaves at evening, and he held my melodious flute in aversion. The poor wretch thought that there were certain forms of words wherewith to put to flight the death-less spirits that dwell in the cool groves, and in the depths of the woods and on the tops of the mountains. He thought to conquer us with a few drops of water over which he had pronounced certain words and made certain gestures. The Nymphs, to avenge them-selves, appeared to him at nightfall and inflamed him with desire which the foolish knave thought animal; then they fled, their laughter scattered like grain over the fields, while their victim lay tossing with burning limbs on his couch of leaves. Thus do the di-vine nymphs laugh at exorcisers, and mock the wicked and their sordid chastity.

"The apostle did not do as much harm as he wished, because his teaching was given to the simple souls living in obedience to Na-ture, and because the mediocrity of most of mankind is such that they gain but little from the principles inculcated in them. The little wood in which I dwelt belonged to a Gaul of senatorial family, who retained some traces of Latin elegance. He loved his young freed-woman and shared with her his bed of broidered purple. His slaves cultivated his garden and his vineyard; he was a poet and sang, in imitation of Ausonius, Venus whipping her son with roses. Although a Christian, he offered me milk, fruit, and vegetables as if I were the genius of the place. In return I charmed his idle mo-ments with the music of my flute, and I gave him happy dreams. In fact, these peaceful Gauls knew very little of Iahveh and his son.

"But now behold fires looming on the horizon, and ashes driven by the wind fall within our forest glades. Peasants come driving a long file of waggons along the roads or urging their flocks before them. Cries of terror rise from the villages, 'The Burgundians are upon us!'

"Now one horseman is seen, lance in hand, clad in shining bronze, his long red hair falling in two plaits on his shoulders. Then come two, then twenty, then thousands, wild and blood-stained; old men and children they put to the sword, ay, even aged grandams whose grey hairs cleave to the soles of the slaughterer's boots, mingled with the brains of babes new-born. My young Gaul and his young freed-woman stain with their blood the couch broidered with nar-cissi. The barbarians burn the basilicas to roast their oxen whole, shatter the amphoræ, and drain the wine in the mud of the flooded cellars. Their women accompany them, huddled, half naked, in their war chariots. When the Senate, the dwellers in the cities, and the leaders of the churches had perished in the flames, the Burgun-dians, soddened with wine, lay down to slumber beneath the arcades of the Forum. Two weeks later one of them might have been seen smiling in his shaggy beard at the little child whom, on the thresh-old of their dwelling, his fair-haired spouse gathers in her arms; while another, kindling the fire of his forge, hammers out his iron with measured stroke; another sings beneath the oak tree to his assembled comrades of the gods and heroes of his race; and yet others spread out for sale stones fallen from Heaven, aurochs' horns, and amulets. And the former inhabitants of the country, regaining courage little by little, crept from the woods where they had fled for refuge, and returned to rebuild their burnt-down cabins, plough their fields, and prune their vines.

"Once more life resumed its normal course; but those times were the most wretched that mankind had yet experienced. The barbarians swarmed over the whole Empire. Their ways were uncouth, and as they nurtured feelings of vengeance and greed, they firmly believed in the ransom of sin.

"The fable of Iahveh and his son pleased them, and they believed it all the more easily in that it was taught them by the Romans whom they knew to be wiser than themselves, and to whose arts and mode of life they yielded secret admiration. Alas! the heritage of Greece and Rome had fallen into the hands of fools. All knowledge was lost. In those days it was held to be a great merit to sing among the choir, and those who remembered a few sentences from the Bible passed for prodigious geniuses. There were still poets as there were birds, but their verse went lame in every foot. The ancient demons, the good genii of mankind, shorn of their honours, driven forth, pursued, hunted down, remained hidden in the woods. There, if they still showed themselves to men, they adopted, to hold them in awe, a terrible face, a red, green, or black skin, baleful eyes, an enormous mouth fringed with boars' teeth, horns, a tail, and sometimes a human face on their bellies. The nymphs remained fair, and the barbarians, ignorant of the winsome names they bore in other days, called them fairies, and, imputing to them a capricious character and puerile tastes, both feared and loved them.

"We had suffered a grievous fall, and our ranks were sadly thinned; nevertheless we did not lose courage and, maintaining a laughing aspect and a benevolent spirit, we were in those direful days the real friends of mankind. Perceiving that the barbarians grew daily less sombre and less ferocious, we lent ourselves to the task of conversing with them under all sorts of disguises. We incited them, with a thousand precautions, and by prudent circumlocutions, not to acknowledge the old Iahveh as an infallible master, not blindly to obey his orders, and not to fear his menaces. When need was, we had recourse to magic. We exhorted them unceasingly to study nature and to strive to discover the traces of ancient wisdom.

"These warriors from the North—rude though they were—were acquainted with some mechanical arts. They thought they saw combats in the heavens; the sound of the harp drew tears from their eyes; and perchance they had souls capable of greater things than the degenerate Gauls and Romans whose lands they had invaded.

They knew not how to hew stone or to polish marble; but they caused porphyry and columns to be brought from Rome and from Ravenna; their chief men took for their seal a gem engraved by a Greek in the days when Beauty reigned supreme. They raised walls with bricks, cunningly arranged like ears of corn, and succeeded in building quite pleasing-looking churches with cornices upheld by consoles depicting grim faces, and heavy capitals whereon were represented monsters devouring one another.

"We taught them letters and sciences. A mouthpiece of their god, one Gerbert, took lessons in physics, arithmetic, and music with us, and it was said that he had sold us his soul. Centuries passed, and man's ways remained violent. It was a world given up to fire and blood. The successors of the studious Gerbert, not content with the possession of souls (the profits one gains thereby are lighter than air), wished to possess bodies also. They pretended that their universal and prescriptive monarchy was held from a fisherman on the lake of Tiberias. One of them thought for a moment to prevail over the loutish Germanus, successor to Augustus. But finally the spiritual had to come to terms with the temporal, and the nations were torn between two opposing masters.

"Nations took shape amid horrible tumult. On every side were wars, famines, and internecine conflicts. Since they attributed the innumerable ills that fell upon them to their God, they called him the Most Good, not by way of irony, but because to them the best was he who smote the hardest. In those days of violence, to give myself leisure for study I adopted a *rôle* which may surprise you, but which was exceedingly wise.

"Between the Saône and the mountains of Charolais, where the cattle pasture, there lies a wooded hill sloping gently down to fields watered by a clear stream. There stood a monastery celebrated throughout the Christian world. I hid my cloven feet under a robe and became a monk in this Abbey, where I lived peacefully, sheltered from the men at arms who to friend or foe alike showed themselves equally exacting. Man, who had relapsed into childhood, had all his lessons to learn over again. Brother Luke, whose cell was next to mine, studied the habits of animals and taught us that the weasel conceives her young within her ear. I culled simples in the fields wherewith to soothe the sick, who until then were made by way of treatment to touch the relics of saints. In the Abbey were several demons similar to myself whom I recognised by their cloven feet and by their kindly speech. We joined forces in our endeavours to polish the rough mind of the monks.

"While the little children played at hop-scotch under the Abbey walls our friends the monks devoted themselves to another game equally unprofitable, at which, nevertheless, I joined them, for one must kill time,—that, when one comes to think of it, is the sole business of life. Our game was a game of words which pleased our coarse yet subtle minds, set school fulminating against school, and put all Christendom in an uproar. We formed ourselves into two opposing camps. One camp maintained that before there were apples there was the Apple; that before there were popinjays there was the Popinjay; that before there were lewd and greedy monks there was the Monk, Lewdness and Greed; that before there were feet and before there were posteriors in this world the kick in the posterior must have had existence for all eternity in the bosom of God. The other camp replied that, on the contrary, apples gave man the idea of the apple; popinjays the idea of the popinjay; monks the idea of the monk, greed and lewdness, and that the kick in the posterior existed only after having been duly given and received. The players grew heated and came to fisticuffs. I was an adherent of the second party, which satisfied my reason better, and which was, in fact, condemned by the Council of Soissons.

"Meanwhile, not content with fighting among themselves, vassal against suzerain, suzerain against vassal, the great lords took it into their heads to go and fight in the East. They said, as well as I can remember, that they were going to deliver the tomb of the son of God.

"They said so, but their adventurous and covetous spirit excited them to go forth and seek lands, women, slaves, gold, myrrh, and incense. These expeditions, need it be said, proved disastrous; but our thick-headed compatriots brought back with them the knowledge of certain crafts and oriental arts and a taste for luxury. Henceforth we had less difficulty in making them work and in putting them in the way of inventions. We built wonderfully beautiful churches, with daringly pierced arches, lancet-shaped windows, high towers, thousands of pointed spires, which, rising in the sky towards Iahveh, bore at one and the same time the prayers of the humble and the threats of the proud, for it was all as much our doing as the work of men's hands; and it was a strange sight to see men and demons working together at a cathedral, each one sawing, polishing, collecting stones, graving, on capital and on cornice, nettles, thorns, thistles, wild parsley, and wild strawberry,—carving faces of virgins and saints and weird figures of serpents, fishes with asses' heads, apes scratching their buttocks; each one, in fact, putting his own particular talent,—mocking, sublime, grotesque, modest, or audacious,—into the work and making of it all a harmonious cacophony, a rapturous anthem of joy and sorrow, a Babel of victory. At our instigation the carvers, the goldsmiths, the enamellers, accomplished marvels and all the sumptuary arts flourished at once; there were silks at Lyons, tapestries at Arras, linen at Rheims, cloth at Rouen. The good merchants rode on their palfreys to the fairs, bearing pieces of velvet and brocade, embroideries, orfrays, jewels, vessels of silver, and illuminated books. Strollers and players set up their trestles in the churches and in the public squares, and represented, according to their lights, simple chronicles of Heaven, Earth, and Hell. Women decked themselves in splendid raiment and lisped of love.

"In the spring when the sky was blue, nobles and peasants were possessed with the desire to make merry in the flower-strewn meadows. The fiddler tuned his instrument, and ladies, knights and demoiselles, townsfolk, villagers and maidens, holding hands, began the dance. But suddenly War, Pestilence, and Famine entered the circle, and Death, tearing the violin from the fiddler's hands, led the dance. Fire devoured village and monastery. The men-at-arms hanged the peasants on the sign-posts at the cross-roads when they were unable to pay ransom, and bound pregnant women to tree-trunks, where at night the wolves came and devoured the fruit within the womb. The poor people lost their senses. Sometimes, peace being re-established, and good times come again, they were seized with mad, unreasoning terror, abandoned their homes, and rushed hither and thither in troops, half naked, tearing themselves with iron hooks, and singing. I do not accuse Iahveh and his son of all this evil. Many ill things occurred without him and even in spite of him. But where I recognise the instigation of the All Good (as they called him) was in the custom instituted by his pastors, and established throughout Christendom, of burning, to the sound of bells and the singing of psalms, both men and women who, taught by the demons, professed, concerning this God, opinions of their own."

<h1 style="text-align:center">XXI</h1>

<h2 style="text-align:center">THE GARDENER'S STORY, CONCLUDED</h2>

IT SEEMED as if science and thought had perished for all eternity, and that the earth would never again know peace, joy, and beauty.

"But one day, under the walls of Rome, some workmen, excavating the earth on the borders of an ancient road, found a marble sarcophagus which bore carved on its sides simulacra of Love and the triumphs of Bacchus.

"The lid being raised, a maiden appeared whose face shone with dazzling freshness. Her long hair spread over her white shoulders, she was smiling in her sleep. A band of citizens, thrilled with enthusiasm, raised the funeral couch and bore it to the Capitol. The people came in crowds to contemplate the ineffable beauty of the Roman maiden and stood around in silence, watching for the awakening of the divine soul held within this form of adorable beauty.

"And it came to pass that the City was so greatly stirred by this spectacle that the Pope, fearing, not without reason, the birth of a pagan cult from this radiant body, caused it to be removed at night and secretly buried. The precaution was vain, the labour fruitless. After so many centuries of barbarism, the beauty of the antique world had appeared for a moment before the eyes of men; it was long enough for its image, graven on their hearts, to inspire them with an ardent desire to love and to know.

"Henceforth, the star of the God of the Christians paled and sloped to its decline. Bold navigators discovered worlds inhabited by numerous races who knew not old Iahveh, and it was suspected that he was no less ignorant of them, since he had given them no news of himself or of his son the expiator. A Polish Canon demonstrated the true motions of the earth, and it was seen that, far from having created the world, the old demiurge of Israel had not even an inkling of its structure. The writings of philosophers, orators, jurisconsults, and ancient poets were dragged from the dust of the cloisters and passing from hand to hand inspired men's minds with the love of wisdom. The Vicar of the jealous God, the Pope himself, no longer believed in Him whom he represented on earth. He loved the arts and had no other care than to collect ancient statues and to rear sumptuous buildings wherein were displayed the orders of Vitruvius re-established by Bramante. We began to breathe anew. Already the old gods, recalled from their long exile, were returning to dwell upon earth. There they found once more their temples and their altars. Leo, placing at their feet the ring, the three crowns, and the keys offered them in secret the incense of sacrifices. Already Polyhymnia, leaning on her elbow, had begun to resume the golden thread of her meditations; already, in the gardens, the comely Graces and the Nymphs and Satyrs were weaving their mazy dances, and at length the earth had joy once more within its grasp. But, O calamity, unlucky fate,—most tragic circumstance! A German monk, all swollen with beer and theology, rose up against this renaissance of paganism, hurled menaces against it, shattered it, and prevailed single handed against the Princes of the Church. Inciting the nations, he called upon them to undertake a reform which saved that which was about to be destroyed. Vainly did the cleverest among us try to turn him from his work. A subtle demon, on earth called Beelzebub, marked him out for attack, now embarrassing him with learned controversial argument, now tormenting him with cruel mockery. The stubborn monk hurled his ink-pot at his head and went on with his dismal reformation. What ultimately happened? The sturdy mariner repaired, calked, and refloated the damaged ship of the Church. Jesus Christ owes it to this shaveling that his shipwreck was delayed for perhaps more than ten centuries. Henceforth things went from bad to worse. In the wake of this loutish monk, this beer-swiller and brawler, came that tall, dry doctor from Geneva, who, filled with the spirit of the ancient Iahveh, strove to bring the world back again to the abominable days of Joshua and the Judges of Israel. A maniac was he, filled with cold fury, a heretic and a burner of heretics, the most ferocious enemy of the Graces.

"These mad apostles and their mad disciples made even demons like myself, even the horned devils, look back longingly on the time when the Son with his Virgin Mother reigned over the nations dazzled with splendours: cathedrals with their stone tracery delicate as lace, flaming roses of stained glass, frescoes painted in vivid colours telling countless wondrous tales, rich orfrays, glittering enamel of shrines and reliquaries, gold of crosses and of monstrances, waxen tapers gleaming like starry galaxies amid the gloom of vaulted arches, organs with their deep-toned harmonies. All this doubtless was not the Parthenon, nor yet the Panathenæa, but it gladdened eyes and hearts; it was, at all events, beauty. And these cursed reformers would not suffer anything either pleasing or lovable. You should have seen them climbing in black swarms over doorways, plinths, spires, and bell-towers, striking with senseless hammers those images in stone which the demons had carved working hand in hand with the master designers, those genial saints and dear, holy women, and the touching idols of Virgin Mothers pressing their suckling to their heart. For, to be just, a little agreeable paganism had slipped into the cult of the jealous God. These monsters of heretics were for extirpating idolatry. We did our best, my companions and I, to hamper their horrible work, and I, for one, had the pleasure of flinging down some dozens from the top of the porches and galleries on to the Cathedral Square, where their detestable brains got knocked out. The worst of it was that the Catholic Church also reformed herself and grew more mischievous than ever. In the pleasant land of France, the seminarists and the monks were inflamed with unheard-of fury against the ingenious demons and the men of learning. My prior was one of the most violent opponents of sound knowledge. For some time past my studious lucubrations had caused him anxiety, and perhaps he had caught sight of my cloven foot. The scoundrel searched my cell and found paper, ink, some Greek books newly printed, and some Pan-pipes hanging on the wall. By these signs he knew me for an evil spirit and had me thrown into a dungeon where I should have eaten the bread of suffering and drunk the waters of bitterness, had I not promptly made my escape by the window and sought refuge in the wooded groves among the Nymphs and the Fauns.

"Far and wide the lighted pyres cast the odour of charred flesh.

Everywhere there were tortures, executions, broken bones, and tongues cut out. Never before had the spirit of Iahveh breathed forth such atrocious fury. However, it was not altogether in vain that men had raised the lid of the ancient sarcophagus and gazed upon the Roman Virgin.

"During this time of great terror when Papists and Reformers rivalled one another in violence and cruelty, amidst all these scenes of torture, the mind of man was regaining strength and courage. It dared to look up to the heavens, and there it saw, not the old Jew drunk with vengeance, but Venus Urania, tranquil and resplendent. Then a new order of things was born, then the great centuries came into being. Without publicly denying the god of their ancestors, men of intellect submitted to his mortal enemies, Science and Reason, and Abbé Gassendi relegated him gently to the far-distant abyss of first causes. The kindly demons who teach and console unhappy mortals, inspired the great minds of those days with discourses of all kinds, with comedies and tales told in the most polished fashion. Women invented conversation, the art of intimate letter-writing, and politeness. Manners took on a sweetness and a nobility unknown to preceding ages. One of the finest minds of that age of reason, the amiable Bernier, wrote one day to St. Evremond: 'It is a great sin to deprive oneself of a pleasure.' And this pronouncement alone should suffice to show the progress of intelligence in Europe. Not that there had not always been Epicureans but, unlike Bernier, Chapelle, and Molière, they had not the consciousness of their talent.

"Then even the very devotees understood Nature. And Racine, fierce bigot that he was, knew as well as such an atheistical physician at Guy Patin, how to attribute to divers states of the organs the passions which agitate mankind.

"Even in my abbey, whither I had returned after the turmoil, and which sheltered only the ignorant and the shallow thinker, a young monk, less of a dunce than the rest, confided to me that the Holy Spirit expresses itself in bad Greek to humiliate the learned.

"Nevertheless, theology and controversy were still raging in this society of thinkers. Not far from Paris in a shady valley there were to be seen solitary beings known as 'les Messieurs,' who called themselves disciples of St. Augustine, and argued with honest conviction that the God of the Scriptures strikes those who fear Him, spares those who confront Him, holds works of no account, and damns—should He so wish it—His most faithful servant; for His justice is not our justice, and His ways are incomprehensible.

"One evening I met one of these gentlemen in his garden, where he was pacing thoughtfully among the cabbage-plots and lettuce-beds. I bowed my horned head before him and murmured these friendly words: 'May old Jehovah protect you, sir. You know him well. Oh, how well you know him, and how perfectly you have understood his character.' The holy man thought he discerned in me a messenger from Hell, concluded he was eternally damned, and died suddenly of fright.

"The following century was the century of philosophy. The spirit of research was developed, reverence was lost; the pride of the flesh was diminished and the mind acquired fresh energy. Manners took on an elegance until then unknown. On the other hand, the monks of my order grew more and more ignorant and dirty, and the monastery no longer offered me any advantage now that good manners reigned in the town. I could bear it no longer. Flinging my habit to the nettles, I put a powdered wig on my horned brow, hid my goat's legs under white stockings, and cane in hand, my pockets stuffed with gazettes, I frequented the fashionable world, visited the modish promenades, and showed myself assiduously in the *cafés* where men of letters were to be found. I was made welcome in *salons* where, as a happy novelty, there were arm-chairs that fitted the form, and where both men and women engaged in rational conversation.

"The very metaphysicians spoke intelligibly. I acquired great weight in the town as an authority on matters of exegesis, and, without boasting, I was largely responsible for the Testament of the curé Meslier and *The Bible Explained,* brought out by the chaplains to the King of Prussia.

"At this time a comic and cruel misadventure befel the ancient Iahveh. An American Quaker, by means of a kite, stole his thunderbolts.

"I was living in Paris, and was at the supper where they talked of strangling the last of the priests with the entrails of the last of the kings. France was in a ferment; a terrible revolution broke out. The ephemeral leaders of the disordered State carried on a Reign of Terror amidst unheard-of perils. They were, for the most part, less pitiless and less cruel than the princes and judges instituted by Iahveh in the kingdoms of the earth; nevertheless, they appeared more ferocious, because they gave judgment in the name of Humanity. Unhappily they were easily moved to pity and of great sensibility. Now men of sensibility are irritable and subject to fits of fury. They were virtuous; they had moral laws, that is to say they conceived certain narrowly defined moral obligations, and judged human actions not by their natural consequences but by abstract principles. Of all the vices which contribute to the undoing of a statesman, virtue is the most fatal; it leads to murder. To work effectively for the happiness of mankind, a man must be superior to all morals, like the divine Julius. God, so ill-used for some time past, did not, on the whole, suffer excessively harsh treatment from these new men. He found protectors among them, and was adored under the name of the Supreme Being. One might even go so far as to say that terror created a diversion from philosophy and was profitable to the old demiurge, in that he appeared to represent order, public tranquillity, and the security of person and property.

"While Liberty was coming to birth amid the storm, I lived at Auteuil, and visited Madame Helvetius, where freethinkers in every branch of intellectual activity were to be met with. Nothing could be rarer than a freethinker, even after Voltaire's day. A man who will face death without trembling dare not say anything out of the ordinary about morals. That very same respect for Humanity which prompts him to go forth to his death, makes him bow to public opinion. In those days I enjoyed listening to the talk of Volney, Cabanis, and Tracy. Disciples of the great Condillac, they regarded the senses as the origin of all our knowledge. They called themselves ideologists, were the most honourable people in the world, and grieved the vulgar minds by refusing them immortality. For the majority of people, though they do not know what to do with this life, long for another that shall have no end. During the turmoil, our small philosophical society was sometimes disturbed in the peaceful shades of Auteuil by patrols of patriots. Condorcet, our great man, was an outlaw. I myself was regarded as suspect by the friends of the people, who, in spite of my rustic appearance and my frieze coat, believed me to be an aristocrat, and I confess that independence of thought is the proudest of all aristocracies.

"One evening while I was stealthily watching the dryads of Boulogne, who gleamed amid the leaves like the moon rising above the horizon, I was arrested as a suspect, and put in prison. It was a pure misunderstanding; but the Jacobins of those days, like the monks whose place they had usurped, laid great stress on unity of obedience. After the death of Madame Helvetius our society gathered together in the *salon* of Madame de Condorcet. Bonaparte did not disdain to chat with us sometimes.

"Recognizing him to be a great man, we thought him an ideologist like ourselves. Our influence in the land was considerable. We used it in his favour, and urged him towards the Imperial throne, thinking to display to the world a second Marcus Aurelius. We counted on him to establish universal peace; he did not fulfil our expectations, and we were wrong-headed enough to be wroth with him for our own mistake.

"Without any doubt he greatly surpassed all other men in quickness of intelligence, depth of dissimulation, and capacity for action. What made him an accomplished ruler was that he lived entirely in the present moment, and had no thoughts for anything beyond the immediate and actual reality. His genius was far-reaching and agile; his intelligence, vast in extent but common and vulgar in character, embraced humanity, but did not rise above it. He thought what every grenadier in the army thought; but he thought it with unprecedented force. He loved the game of chance, and it pleased him to tempt fortune by urging pigmies in their hundreds and thousands against each other. It was the game of a child as big as the world. He was too wily not to introduce old Iahveh into the game,—Iahveh, who was still powerful on earth, and who resembled him in his spirit of violence and domination. He threatened him, flattered him, caressed him, and intimidated him. He imprisoned his Vicar, of whom he demanded, with the knife at his throat, that rite of unction which, since the days of Saul of old, has bestowed might upon kings; he restored the worship of the demiurge, sang *Te Deums* to him, and made himself known through him as God of the earth, in small catechisms scattered broadcast throughout the Empire. They united their thunders, and a fine uproar they made.

"While Napoleon's amusements were throwing Europe into a turmoil, we congratulated ourselves on our wisdom, a little sad, withal, at seeing the era of philosophy ushered in with massacre, torture, and war. The worst is that the children of the century, fallen into the most distressing disorder, formed the conception of a literary and picturesque Christianity, which betokens a degeneracy of mind really unbelievable, and finally fell into Romanticism. War and Romanticism, what terrible scourges! And how pitiful to see these same people nursing a childish and savage love for muskets and drums! They did not understand that war, which trained the courage and founded the cities of barbarous and ignorant men, brings to the victor himself but ruin and misery, and is nothing but a horrible and stupid crime when nations are united together by common bonds of art, science, and trade.

"Insane Europeans who plot to cut each others' throats, now that one and the same civilisation enfolds and unites them all!

"I renounced all converse with these madmen and withdrew to this village, where I devoted myself to gardening. The peaches in my orchard remind me of the sun-kissed skin of the Mænads. For mankind I have retained my old friendship, a little admiration, and much pity, and I await, while cultivating this enclosure, that still distant day when the great Dionysus shall come, followed by his Fauns and his Bacchantes, to restore beauty and gladness to the world, and bring back the Golden Age. I shall fare joyously behind his car. And who knows if in that day of triumph mankind will be there for us to see? Who knows whether their worn-out race will not have already fulfilled its destiny, and whether other beings will not rise upon the ashes and ruins of what once was man and his genius? Who knows if winged beings will not have taken possession of the terrestrial empire? Even then the work of the good demons will not be ended,—they will teach a winged race arts and the joy of life."

XXII

WHEREIN WE ARE SHOWN THE INTERIOR OF A BRIC-A-BRAC SHOP, AND SEE HOW PÈRE GUINARDON'S GUILTY HAPPINESS IS MARRED BY THE JEALOUSY OF A LOVE-LORN DAME

PÈRE GUINARDON (as Zéphyrine had faithfully reported to Monsieur Sariette) smuggled out the pictures, furniture, and curios stored in his attic in the rue Princesse—his studio he called it—and used them to stock a shop he had taken in the rue de Courcelles. Thither he went to take up his abode, leaving Zéphyrine, with whom he had lived for fifty years, without a bed or a saucepan or a penny to call her own, except eighteen-pence the poor creature had in her purse. Père Guinardon opened an old picture and curiosity shop, and in it he installed the fair Octavie.

The shop-front presented an attractive appearance: there were Flemish angels in green copes, after the manner of Gérard David, a Salomé of the Luini school, a Saint Barbara in painted wood of French workmanship, Limoges enamel-work, Bohemian and Venetian glass, dishes from Urbino. There were specimens of English point-lace which, if her tale was true, had been presented to Zéphyrine, in the days of her radiant girlhood, by the Emperor Napoleon III. Within, there were golden articles that glinted in the shadows, while pictures of Christ, the Apostles, high-bred dames, and nymphs also presented themselves to the gaze. There was one canvas that was turned face to the wall so that it should only be looked at by connoisseurs; and connoisseurs are scarce. It was a replica of Fragonard's *Gimblette,* a brilliant painting that looked as if it had barely had time to dry. Papa Guinardon himself remarked on the fact. At the far end of the shop was a king-wood cabinet, the drawers of which were full of all manner of treasures: water-colours by Baudouin, eighteenth-century books of illustrations, miniatures, and so forth.

But the real masterpiece, the marvel, the gem, the pearl of great price, stood upon an easel veiled from public view. It was a *Coronation of the Virgin* by Fra Angelico, an exquisitely delicate thing in gold and blue and pink. Père Guinardon was asking a hundred thousand francs for it. Upon a Louis XV chair beside an Empire work-table on which stood a vase of flowers, sat the fair Octavie, broidery in hand. She, having left her glistering rags behind her in the garret in the rue Princesse, no longer presented the appearance of a touched-up Rembrandt, but shone, rather, with the soft radiance and limpidity of a Vermeer of Delft, for the delectation of the connoisseurs who frequented the shop of Papa Guinardon. Tranquil and demure, she remained alone in the shop all day, while the old fellow himself was up aloft working away at the deuce knows what picture. About five o'clock he used to come downstairs and have a chat with the habitués of the establishment.

The most regular caller was the Comte Desmaisons, a thin, cadaverous man. A strand of hair issued from the deep hollow under each cheek-bone, and, broadening as it descended, shed upon his chin and chest torrents of snow in which he was for ever trailing his long, fleshless, gold-ringed fingers. For twenty years he had been mourning the loss of his wife, who had been carried off by consumption in the flower of her youth and beauty. Since then he had spent his whole life in endeavouring to hold converse with the dead and in filling his lonely mansion with second-rate paintings. His confidence in Guinardon knew no bounds. Another client who was a scarcely less frequent visitor to the shop was Monsieur Blancmesnil, a director of a large financial establishment. He was a florid, prosperous-looking man of fifty. He took no great interest in matters of art, and was perhaps an indifferent connoisseur, but, in his case, it was the fair Octavie, seated in the middle of the shop, like a song-bird in its cage, that offered the attraction.

Monsieur Blancmesnil soon established relations with her, a fact which Père Guinardon alone failed to perceive, for the old fellow was still young in his love-affairs with Octavie. Monsieur Gaétan d'Esparvieu used to pay occasional visits to Père Guinardon's shop out of mere curiosity, for he strongly suspected the old man of being a first-rate "faker."

And then that doughty swordsman, Monsieur Le Truc de Ruffec, also came to see the old antiquary on one occasion, and acquainted him with a plan he had on foot. Monsieur Le Truc de Ruffec was getting up a little historical exhibition of small arms at the Petit Palais in aid of the fund for the education of the native children in Morocco and wanted Père Guinardon to lend him a few of the most valuable articles in his collection.

"Our first idea," he said, "was to organise an exhibition to be called 'The Cross and the Sword.' The juxtaposition of the two words will make the idea which has prompted our undertaking sufficiently clear to you. It was an idea pre-eminently patriotic and Christian which led us to associate the Sword, which is the symbol of Honour, with the Cross, which is the symbol of Salvation. It was hoped that our work would be graced by the distinguished patronage of the Minister of War and Monseigneur Cachepot. Unfortunately there were difficulties in the way, and the full realisation of the project had to be deferred. In the meantime we are limiting our exhibition to 'The Sword.' I have drawn up an explanatory note indicating the significance of the demonstration."

Having delivered himself of these remarks, Monsieur Le Truc de Ruffec produced a pocket-case stuffed full of papers. Picking out from a medley of judgment summonses and other odds and ends a little piece of very crumpled paper, he exclaimed, "Ah, here it is," and proceeded to read as follows: " 'The Sword is a fierce Virgin; it is *par excellence* the Frenchman's weapon. And now, when patriotic sentiment, after suffering an all too protracted eclipse, is beginning to shine forth again more ardently than ever . . .' And so forth; you see?"

And he repeated his request for some really fine specimen to be placed in the most conspicuous position in the exhibition to be held on behalf of the little native children of Morocco, of which General d'Esparview was to be honorary President.

Arms and armour were by no means Père Guinardon's strong point. He dealt principally in pictures, drawings, and books. But he was never to be taken unawares. He took down a rapier with a gilt colander-shaped hilt, a highly typical piece of workmanship of the Louis XIII-Napoleon III period, and presented it to the exhibition promoter, who, while contemplating it with respect, maintained a diplomatic silence.

"I have something better still in here," said the antiquary, and he produced from his inner shop—where it had been lying among the walking-sticks and umbrellas—a real demon of a sword, adorned with fleurs-de-lys, a genuine royal relic. It was the sword of Philippe-Auguste as worn by an actor at the *Odéon* when *Agnès de Méranie* was being performed in 1846. Guinardon held it point downwards, as though it were a cross, clasping his hands piously on the cross-bar. He looked as loyal as the sword itself.

"Have her for your exhibition," said he. "The damsel is well worth it. Bouvines is her name."

"If I find a buyer for it," said Monsieur Le Truc de Ruffec, twirling his enormous moustachios, "I suppose you will allow me a little commission?"

Some days later, Père Guinardon was mysteriously displaying a picture to the Comte Desmaisons and Monsieur Blancmesnil. It was a newly discovered work of El Greco, an amazingly fine example of the Master's later style. It represented a Saint Francis of Assisi standing erect upon Mont Alverno. He was mounting heavenward like a column of smoke, and was plunging into the regions of the clouds a monstrously narrow head that the distance rendered smaller still. In fine it was a real, very real, nay, too real El Greco. The two collectors were attentively scrutinizing the work, while Père Guinardon was belauding the depth of the shadows and the sublimity of the expression. He was raising his arms aloft to convey an idea of the greatness of Theotocopuli, who derived from Tintoretto, whom, however, he surpassed in loftiness by a hundred cubits.

"He was chaste and pure and strong; a mystic, a visionary."

Comte Desmaisons declared that El Greco was his favourite painter. In his inmost heart Blancmesnil was not so entirely struck with it.

The door opened, and Monsieur Gaétan quite unexpectedly appeared on the scene.

He gave a glance at the Saint Francis, and said:

"Bless my soul!"

Monsieur Blancmesnil, anxious to improve his knowledge, asked him what he thought of this artist who was now so much in vogue. Gaétan replied, glibly enough, that he did not regard El Greco as the eccentric, the madman that people used to take him for. It was rather his opinion that a defect of vision from which Theotocopuli suffered compelled him to deform his figures.

"Being afflicted with astigmatism and strabismus," Gaétan went on, "he painted the things he saw exactly as he used to see them." Comte Desmaisons was not readily disposed to accept so natural an explanation, which, however, by its very simplicity, highly commended itself to Monsieur Blancmesnil.

Père Guinardon, quite beside himself, exclaimed:

"Are you going to tell me, Monsieur d'Esparvieu, that Saint John was astigmatic because he beheld a woman clothed with the sun, crowned with stars, with the moon about her feet; the Beast with seven heads and ten horns, and the seven angels robed in white linen that bore the seven cups filled with the wrath of the Living God?"

"After all," said Monsieur Gaétan, by way of conclusion, "people are right in admiring El Greco if he had genius enough to impose his morbidity of vision upon them. By the same token, the contortions to which he subjects the human countenance may give satisfaction to those who love suffering,—a class more numerous than is generally supposed."

"Monsieur," replied the Comte Desmaisons, stroking his luxuriant beard with his long, thin hand, "we must love those that love us. Suffering loves us and attaches itself to us. We must love is if life is to be supportable to us. In the knowledge of this truth lies the strength and value of Christianity. Alas! I do not possess the gift of Faith. It is that which drives me to despair."

The old man thought of her for whom he had been mourning twenty years, and forthwith his reason left him, and his thoughts abandoned themselves unresistingly to the morbid imaginings of gentle and melancholy madness.

Having, he said, made a study of psychic matters, and having, with the co-operation of a favourable medium, carried out experiments concerning the nature and duration of the soul, he had obtained some remarkable results, which, however, did not afford him complete satisfaction. He had succeeded in viewing the soul of his dead wife under the appearance of a transparent and gelatinous mass which bore not the slightest resemblance to his adored one. The most painful part about the whole experiment—which he had repeated over and over again—was that the gelatinous mass, which was furnished with a number of extremely slender tentacles, maintained them in constant motion in time to a rhythm apparently intended to make certain signs, but of what these movements were supposed to convey there was not the slightest clue.

During the whole of this narrative Monsieur Blancmesnil had been whispering in a corner with the youthful Octavie, who sat mute and still, with her eyes on the ground.

Now Zéphyrine had by no means made up her mind to resign her lover into the hands of an unworthy rival. She would often go round of a morning, with her shopping-basket on her arm, and prowl about outside the curio shop. Torn betwixt grief and rage, tormented by warring ideas, she sometimes thought she would empty a saucepanful of vitriol on the head of the faithless one; at others that she would fling herself at his feet, and shower tears and kisses on his precious hands. One day, as she was thus eyeing her Michel—her beloved but guilty Michel—she noticed through the window the fair and youthful Octavie, who was sitting with her embroidery at a table upon which, in a vase of crystal, a rose was swooning to death. Zéphyrine, in a transport of fury, brought down her umbrella on her rival's fair head, and called her a bitch and a trollop. Octavie fled in terror, and ran for the police, while Zéphyrine, beside herself with grief and love, kept digging away with her old gamp at the *Gimblette* of Fragonard, the fuliginous Saint Francis of El Greco, the virgins, the nymphs, and the apostles, and knocked the gilt off the Fra Angelico, shrieking all the while:

"All those pictures there, the El Greco, the Beato Angelico, the Fragonard, the Gérard David, and the Baudouins—Guinardon painted the whole lot of them himself, the wretch, the scoundrel! That Fra Angelico there, why I saw him painting it on my ironing-board, and that Gérard David he executed on an old midwife's sign-board. You and that bitch of yours, why, I'll do for the pair of you just as I'm doing for these pictures."

And tugging away at the coat of an aged collector who, trembling all over, had hidden himself in the darkest corner of the shop, she called him to witness to the crimes of Guinardon, perjurer and impostor. The police had simply to tear her out of the ruined shop. As she was being taken off to the station, followed by a great crowd of people, she raised her fiery eyes to Heaven, crying in a voice choked with sobs:

"But don't you know Michel? If you knew him, you would understand that it is impossible to live without him. Michel! He is handsome and good and charming. He is a very god. He is Love itself.

I love him! I love him! I love him! I have known men high up in
the world—Dukes, Ministers of State, and higher still. Not one of
them was worthy to clean the mud off Michel's boots. My good,
kind sirs, give him back to me again."

XXIII

WHEREIN WE ARE PERMITTED TO OBSERVE THE ADMIRABLE CHARACTER OF BOUCHOTTE, WHO RESISTS VIOLENCE BUT YIELDS TO LOVE. AFTER THAT LET NO ONE CALL THE AUTHOR A MISOGYNIST

N COMING away from the Baron Everdingen's,
Prince Istar went to have a few oysters and a
bottle of white wine at an eating-house in the
Market. Then, being prudent as well as powerful,
he paid a visit to his friend, Théophile Belais, for
his pockets were full of bombs, and he wanted to
secrete them in the musician's cupboard. The composer of *Aline, Queen of Golconda* was not at home.
However, the Kerûb found Bouchotte busily working up the rôle of
Zigouille; for the young artiste was booked to play the principal
part in *Les Apaches,* an operetta that was then being rehearsed in
one of the big music halls. The part in question was that of a
street-walker who by her obscene gestures lures a passer-by into
a trap, and then, while her victim is being gagged and bound, repeats with fiendish cruelty the lascivious motions by which he had
been led astray. The part required that she should appear both
as mime and singer, and she was in a state of high enthusiasm
about it.

The accompanist had just left. Prince Istar seated himself at
the piano, and Bouchotte resumed her task. Her movements were
unseemly and delicious. Her tawny hair was flying in all directions
in wild disordered curls; her skin was moist, it exhaled a scent
of violets and alkaline salts which made the nostrils throb; even
she herself felt the intoxication. Suddenly, inebriated with her intoxicating presence, Prince Istar arose, and with never a word or
a look, caught her into his arms and drew her on to the couch, the
little couch with the flowered tapestry which Théophile had procured at one of the big shops by promising to pay ten francs a
month for a long term of years. Now Istar might have solicited
Bouchotte's favours; he might have invited her to a rapid, and,
withal, a mutual embrace, and, despite her preoccupation and excitement, she would not have refused him. But Bouchotte was a
girl of spirit. The merest hint of coercion awoke all her untamable

pride. She would consent of her own accord, yes; but be mastered, never! She would readily yield to love, curiosity, pity, to less than that even, but she would die rather than yield to force. Her surprise immediately gave place to fury. She fought her aggressor with all her heart and soul. With nails, to which fury lent an added edge, she tore at the cheeks and eyelids of the Kerûb, and, though he held her as in a vice, she arched herself so stiffly and made such excellent play with knee and elbow, that the human-headed bull, blinded with blood and rage, was sent crashing into the piano which gave forth a prolonged groan, while the bombs, tumbling out of his pockets, fell on the floor with a noise like thunder. And Bouchotte, with dishevelled locks, and one breast bare, beautiful and terrible, stood brandishing the poker over the prostrate giant, crying:

"Be off with you, or I'll put your eyes out!"

Prince Istar went to wash himself in the kitchen, and plunged his gory visage into a basin where some haricot beans lay soaking; then he withdrew without anger or resentment, for he had a noble soul.

Scarcely had he gone when the door-bell rang. Bouchotte, calling upon the absent maid in vain, slipped on a dressing-gown and opened the door herself. A young man, very correct in appearance and rather good-looking, bowed politely, and apologising for having to introduce himself, gave his name. It was Maurice d'Esparvieu.

Maurice was still seeking his guardian angel. Upheld by a desperate hope, he sought him in the queerest places. He enquired for him at the houses of sorcerers, magicians, and thaumaturgists, who in filthy hovels lay bare the ineffable secrets of the future, and who, though masters of all the treasures of the earth, wear trousers without any seats to them, and eat pigs' brains. That very day, having been to a back street in Montmartre to consult a priest of Satan, who practised black magic by piercing waxen images, Maurice had gone on to Bouchotte's, having been sent by Madame de la Verdelière, who, being about to give a fête in aid of the fund for the Preservation of Country Churches, was anxious to secure Bouchotte's services, since she had suddenly become—no one knew why—a fashionable artiste.

Bouchotte invited the visitor to sit down on the little flowered couch; at his request she seated herself beside him, and our young man of fashion explained to the singer what Madame de la Verdelière desired of her. The lady wished Bouchotte to sing one of those *apache* songs which were giving such delight in the fashionable world. Unfortunately Madame de la Verdelière could only offer a very modest fee, one out of all proportion to the merits of the artiste, but then it was for a good cause.

Bouchotte agreed to take part, and accepted the reduced fee with the accustomed liberality of the poor towards the rich and of artists towards society people. Bouchotte was not a selfish girl; the work for the preservation of country churches interested her. She remembered with sobs and tears her first communion, and she still retained her faith. When she passed by a church she wanted to enter it, especially in the evening. And so she did not love the Republic which had done its utmost to destroy both the Church and the Army. Her heart rejoiced to see the re-birth of national sentiment. France was lifting up her head. What was most applauded in the music halls were songs about the soldiers and the kind nuns. Meanwhile Maurice inhaled the odour of her tawny hair, the subtle bitter perfume of her body, all the odours of her person, and desire grew in him. He felt her near him on the little couch, very warm and very soft. He complimented the artiste on her great talent. She asked him what he liked best in all her repertory. He knew nothing about it, still he made replies that satisfied her. She had dictated them herself without knowing it. The vain creature

spoke of her talent, of her success, as she wished others to speak
of them. She never ceased talking of her triumphs, yet withal she
was candour itself. Maurice in all sincerity praised Bouchotte's
beauty, her fresh skin, her purity of line. She attributed this advantage to the fact that she never made up and never "put messes
on her face." As to her figure, she admitted that there was enough
everywhere and none too much, and to illustrate this assertion she
passed her hand over all the contours of her charming body, rising
lightly to follow the delightful curves on which she reposed.

Maurice was quite moved by it. It began to grow dark; she
offered to light up. He begged her to do nothing of the sort.

Their talk, at first gay and full of laughter, grew more intimate
and very sweet, with a certain languor in its tone. It seemed to
Bouchotte that she had known Monsieur Maurice d'Esparvieu for
a long time, and holding him for a man of delicacy, she gave him
her confidence. She told him that she was by nature a good woman,
but that she had had a grasping and unscrupulous mother. Maurice
recalled her to the consideration of her own beauty, and exalted
by subtle flattery the excellent opinion she had of herself. Patient
and calculating, in spite of the burning desire growing in him, he
aroused and increased in the desired one the longing to be still
further admired. The dressing-gown opened and slipped down of
its own accord, the living satin of her shoulders gleamed in the
mysterious light of evening. He—so prudent, so clever, so adroit,—
let her sink in his arms, ardent and half swooning before she had
even perceived she had granted anything at all. Their breath and
their murmurs intermingled. And the little flowery couch sighed in
sympathy with them.

When they recovered the power to express their feelings in
words, she whispered in his ear that his cheek was even softer than
her own.

He answered, holding her embraced:

"It is charming to hold you like this. One would think you had
no bones."

She replied, closing her eyes:

"It is because I love you. Love seems to dissolve my bones; it
makes me as soft and melting as a pig's foot *à la Ste. Menebould.*"

Hereupon Théophile came in, and Bouchotte called upon him to
thank Monsieur Maurice d'Esparvieu, who had been amiable enough
to be the bearer of a handsome offer from Madame la Comtesse de
la Verdelière.

The musician was happy, feeling the quiet and peace of the
house after a day of fruitless applications, of colourless lessons, of
failure and humiliation. Three new collaborators had been thrust
upon him who would add their signatures to his on his operetta,
and receive their share of the author's rights, and he had been
told to introduce the tango into the Court of Golconda. He pressed

young d'Esparview's hand and dropped wearily on to the little couch, which, being now at the end of its strength, gave way at the four legs and suddenly collapsed.

And the angel, precipitated to the ground, rolled terror-struck on to the watch, match-box and cigarette-case that had fallen from Maurice's pocket, and on to the bombs Prince Istar had left behind him.

XXIV

CONTAINING AN ACCOUNT OF THE VICISSITUDES THAT BEFEL THE "LUCRETIUS" OF THE PRIOR DE VENDÔME

LÉGER-MASSIEU, successor to Léger senior, the binder, whose establishment was in the rue de l'Abbaye, opposite the old Hôtel of the Abbés of Saint-Germain-des-Prés, in the hotbed of ancient schools and learned societies, employed an excellent but by no means numerous staff of workmen, and served with leisurely deliberation a clientèle who had learned to practise the virtue of patience. Six weeks had elapsed since he had received the parcel of books that had been despatched by Monsieur Sariette, but still Léger-Massieu had not yet put the work in hand. It was not until fifty-three days had come and gone, that, after calling over the books against the list that had been drawn up by Monsieur Sariette, the binder gave them out to his workmen. The little *Lucretius* with the Prior de Vendôme's arms not being mentioned on the list, it was assumed that it had been sent by another customer. And as it did not figure on any list of goods received it remained shut up in a cupboard, from which Léger-Massieu's son, the youthful Ernest, one day surreptitiously abstracted it, and slipped it into his pocket. Ernest was in love with a neighbouring seamstress whose name was Rose. Rose was fond of the country, and liked to hear the birds singing in the woods, and in order to procure the wherewithal to take her to Chatou one Sunday and give her a dinner, Ernest parted with the *Lucretius* for ten francs to old Moranger, a second-hand dealer in the rue Saint X——, who displayed no great curiosity regarding the origin of his acquisitions. Old Moranger handed over the volume, the very same day, to Monsieur Poussard, an expert in books, of the faubourg Saint Germain, for sixty francs. The latter removed the stamp which disclosed the ownership of the matchless copy, and sold it for five hundred francs to Monsieur Joseph Meyer, the well-known collector, who handed it straight away for three thousand francs to Monsieur Ardon, the bookseller, who immediately transferred it to Monsieur R——, the great Parisian bibliopolist, who gave six thousand for it, and sold it again a fortnight later at a handsome profit to Madame la Comtesse de Gorce. Well known in the higher ranks of Parisian society, the lady in question is what was called in the seventeenth century a "curieuse," that is to say, a lover of pictures, books, and china. In her mansion in the Avenue d'Jéna she possesses collections of works of art which bear witness to the diversity of her knowledge and the excellence of her taste. During the month of July, while the Comtesse de Gorce was away at her château at Sarville in Normandy, the house in the Avenue d'Jéna, being unoccupied, was visited one night by a thief said to belong to a gang known as "The Collectors," who made works of art the special objects of their raids.

The police enquiry elicited the fact that the marauder had reached the first floor by means of the waste-pipe, that he had then climbed over the balcony, forced a shutter with a jemmy, broken a pane of glass, turned the window-fastener, and made his way into the long gallery. There he broke open several cupboards and possessed himself of whatever took his fancy. His booty consisted for the most part of small but valuable articles, such as gold caskets, a few ivory carvings of the fourteenth century, two splendid fifteenth-century manuscripts, and a volume which the Countess's secretary briefly described as "a morocco-bound book with a coat of arms on it," and which was none other than the *Lucretius* from the d'Esparvieu library.

The malefactor, who was supposed to be an English cook, was never discovered. But, two months or so after the theft, a well-dressed, clean-shaven young man passed down the rue de Courcelles, in the dimness of twilight, and went to offer the Prior de Vendôme's *Lucretius* to Père Guinardon. The antiquary gave him four shillings for it, examined it carefully, recognised its interest and its beauty, and put it in the king-wood cabinet, where he kept his special treasures.

Such were the vicissitudes which, in the course of a single season, befel this thing of beauty.

XXV

WHEREIN MAURICE FINDS HIS ANGEL AGAIN

HE performance was over. Bouchotte in her dressing-room was taking off her make-up, when the door opened softly and old Monsieur Sandraque, her protector, came in, followed by a troop of her other admirers. Without so much as turning her head, she asked them what they meant by coming and staring at her like a pack of imbeciles, and whether they thought they were in a tent at the Neuilly Fair, looking at the freak woman.

"Now, then, ladies and gentlemen," she rattled on derisively, "just put a penny in the box for the young lady's marriage-portion, and she'll let you feel her legs,—all made of marble!"

Then, with an angry glance at the admiring throng, she exclaimed: "Come, off you go! Look alive!"

She sent them all packing, her sweetheart Théophile among them,—the pale-faced, long-haired, gentle, melancholy, short-sighted, and dreamy Théophile.

But recognizing her little Maurice, she gave him a smile. He approached her, and leaning over the back of the chair on which she was seated, congratulated her on her playing and singing, duly performing a kiss at the end of every compliment. She did not let him escape thus, and with reiterated enquiries, pressing solicitations, feigned incredulity, obliged him to repeat his stock panegyrics three or four times over, and when he stopped she seemed so disappointed that he was forced to take up the strain again immediately. He found it trying, for he was no connoisseur, but he had the pleasure of kissing her plump curved shoulders all golden in the light, and of catching glimpses of her pretty face in the mirror over the toilet-table.

"You were delicious."

"Really? . . . you think so?"

"Adorable . . . div——"

Suddenly he gave a loud cry. His eyes had seen in the mirror a face appear at the back of the dressing-room. He turned swiftly round, flung his arms about Arcade, and drew him into the corridor.

"What manners!" exclaimed Bouchotte, gasping.

But, pushing his way through a troop of performing dogs, and a family of American acrobats, young d'Esparvieu dragged his angel towards the exit.

He hurried him forth into the cool darkness of the boulevard, delirious with joy and wondering whether it was all too good to be true.

"Here you are!" he cried; "here you are! I have been looking for you a long time, Arcade,—or Mirar if you like,—and I have found you at last. Arcade, you have taken my guardian angel from me. Give him back to me. Arcade, do you love me still?"

Arcade replied that in accomplishing the super-angelic task he had set himself he had been forced to crush under foot friendship, pity, love, and all those feelings which tend to soften the soul; but that, on the other hand, his new state, by exposing him to suffering and privation, disposed him to love Humanity, and that he felt a certain mechanical friendship for his poor Maurice.

"Well, then," exclaimed Maurice, "if only you love me, come back to me, stay with me. I cannot do without you. While I had you with me I was not aware of your presence. But no sooner did you depart than I felt a horrible blank. Without you I am like a body without a soul. Do you know that in the little flat in the rue de Rome, with Gilberte by my side, I feel lonely, I miss you sorely, and long to see you and to hear you as I did that day when you made me so angry. Confess I was right, and that your behaviour on that occasion was not that of a gentleman. That you, you of so high an origin, so noble a mind, could commit such an indiscretion is extraordinary, when one comes to think about it. Madame des Aubels has not yet forgiven you. She blames you for having frightened her by appearing at such an inconvenient moment, and for being insolent and forward while hooking her dress and tying her shoes. I, I have forgotten everything. I only remember that you are my celestial brother, the saintly companion of my childhood. No, Arcade, you must not, you cannot leave me. You are my angel; you are my property."

Arcade explained to young d'Esparvieu that he could no longer be guiding angel to a Christian, having himself gone down into the pit. And he painted a horrible picture of himself; he described himself as breathing hatred and fury; in fact, an infernal spirit.

"All nonsense!" said Maurice, smiling, his eyes big with tears.

"Alas! our ideas, our destiny, everything tends to part us, Maurice. But I cannot stifle the tenderness I feel for you, and your candour forces me to love you."

"No," sighed Maurice. "You do not love me. You have never loved me. In a brother or a sister such indifference would be natural; in a friend it would be ordinary; in a guardian angel it is monstrous. Arcade, you are an abominable being. I hate you."

"I have loved you dearly, Maurice, and I still love you. You trouble my heart which I deemed encased in triple bronze. You show me my own weakness. When you were a little innocent boy I loved you as tenderly and purely as Miss Kate, your English governess, who caressed you with so much fervour. In the country, when the thin bark of the plane trees peels off in long strips and discloses the tender green trunk, after the rains which make the fine sand run on the sloping paths, I showed you how with that sand, those strips of bark, a few wild flowers, and a spray of maiden-hair fern to make rustic bridges, rustic shelters, terraces, and those gardens of Adonis, which last but an hour. During the month of May in Paris we raised an altar to the Virgin, and we burnt incense before it, the scent of which, permeating all the house, reminded Marcelline, the cook, of her village church and her lost innocence, and drew from her floods of tears; it also gave your mother a head-ache, your mother who, with all her wealth, was crushed with the *ennui* that is common to the fortunate ones of this world. When you went to college I interested myself in your progress, I shared your work and your play, I pondered with you over arduous prob-lems in arithmetic, I sought the impenetrable meaning of a phrase of Julius Cæsar's. What fine games of prisoners' base and football we had together! More than once did we know the intoxication of victory, and our young laurels were not soaked in blood or tears. Maurice, I did all I could to protect your innocence, but I could not prevent your losing it at the age of fourteen. Afterwards I regret-fully saw you loving women of all sorts, of divers ages, by no means beautiful, at least in the eyes of an angel. Saddened at the sight, I devoted myself to study; a fine library offered me resources rarely met with. I delved into the history of religions; you know the rest."

"But now, my dear Arcade," concluded young d'Esparvieu, "you have lost your position, your situation, you are entirely without resource. You have lost caste, you are off the lines, a vagabond, a bare-footed wanderer."

The Angel replied bitterly that, after all, he was a little better clad at present than when he was wearing the slops of a suicide.

Maurice alleged in excuse that when he dressed his naked angel in a suicide's slops, he was irritated with that angel's infidelity. But it was useless to dwell on the past or to recriminate. What was really needful was to consider what steps to take in future.

And he asked:

"Arcade, what do you think of doing?"

"Have I not already told you, Maurice? To fight with Him who reigns in the heavens, dethrone Him, and set up Satan in His stead."

"You will not do it. To begin with it is not the opportune mo-ment. Opinion is not with you. You will not be in the swim, as papa says. Conservatism and authority are all the go nowadays. We like to be ruled, and the President of the Republic is going to parley with the Pope. Do not be obstinate, Arcade. You are not as bad as you say. At bottom you are like the rest of the world, you adore the good God."

"I thought I had already explained to you, Maurice, that He whom you consider God is actually but a demiurge. He is absolutely ignorant of the divine world above him, and in all good faith believes himself to be the true and only God. You will find in the *History of the Church,* by Monsignor Duchesne—Vol. 1, page 162— that this proud and narrow-minded demiurge is named Ialdabaoth. My child, so as not to ruffle your prejudices and to deal gently with your feelings in future, that is the name I shall give him. If it should happen that I should speak of him to you, I shall call him Ialdabaoth. I must leave you. Adieu."

"Stay——"

"I cannot."

"I shall not let you go thus. You have deprived me of my guardian angel. It is for you to repair the injury you have caused me. Give me another one."

Arcade objected that it was difficult for him to satisfy such a demand. That having quarrelled with the sovereign dispenser of guardian Spirits, he could obtain nothing from that quarter.

"My dear Maurice," he added, smiling, "ask for one yourself from Ialdabaoth."

"No,—no,—no," exclaimed Maurice. "You have taken away my guardian angel,—give him back to me."

"Alas! I cannot."

"Is it, Arcade, because you are a revolutionary that you cannot?"

"Yes."

"An enemy of God?"

"Yes."

"A Satanic spirit?"

"Yes."

"Well, then," exclaimed young Maurice, "I will be your guardian angel,—I will not leave you."

And Maurice d'Esparvieu took Arcade to have some oysters at P—'s.

XXVI

THE CONCLAVE

THAT day, convoked by Arcade and Zita, the rebellious angels met together on the banks of the Seine at La Jonchère, in a deserted and tumble-down entertainment-hall that Prince Istar had hired from a pot-house keeper called Barattan. Three hundred angels crowded together in the stalls and boxes. A table, an arm-chair, and a collection of small chairs were arranged on the stage, where hung the tattered remnants of a piece of rustic scenery. The walls, coloured in distemper with flowers and fruit, were cracked and stained with damp, and were crumbling away in flakes. The vulgar and poverty-stricken appearance of the place rendered the grandeur of the passions exhibited therein all the more striking.

When Prince Istar asked the assembly to form its Committee, and first of all to elect a President, the name that was renowned throughout the world entered the minds of all present, but a religious respect sealed their lips; and after a moment's silence, the absent Nectaire was elected by acclamation. Having been invited to take the chair between Zita and an angel of Japan, Arcade immediately began as follows:

"Sons of Heaven! My comrades! You have freed yourselves from the bonds of celestial servitude—you have shaken off the thrall of him called Iahveh, but to whom we should here accord his veritable name of Ialdabaoth, for he is not the creator of the worlds, but merely an ignorant and barbarous demiurge, who having obtained possession of a minute portion of the Universe has therein sown suffering and death. Sons of Heaven, tell me, I charge you, whether you will combat and destroy Ialdabaoth?"

All with one voice made answer:

"We will!"

And many speaking all together swore they would scale the mountain of Ialdabaoth, and hurl down the walls of jasper and porphyry, and plunge the tyrant of Heaven into eternal darkness.

But a voice of crystal pierced through the sullen murmur.

"Tremble, ye impious, sacrilegious madmen! The Lord hath already lifted his dread arm to smite you!"

It was a loyal angel who, with an impulse of faith and love, envying the glory of confessors and martyrs, jealous and eager, like his God himself, to emulate man in the beauty of sacrifice, had flung himself in the midst of the blasphemers, to brave them, to confound them, and to fall beneath their blows. The assembly turned upon him with furious unanimity. Those nearest to him overwhelmed him with blows. He continued to cry, in a clear, ringing voice, "Glory to God! Glory to God! Glory to God!"

A rebel seized him by the neck and strangled his praises of the Almighty in his throat. He was thrown to the ground, trampled underfoot. Prince Istar picked him up, took him by the wings between his fingers, then rising like a column of smoke, opened a ventilator, which no one else could have reached, and passed the faithful angel through it. Order was immediately restored.

"Comrades," continued Arcade, "now that we have affirmed our stern resolve, we must examine the possible plans of campaign, and choose the best. You will therefore have to consider if we should attack the enemy in full force, or whether it were better, by a lengthy and assiduous propaganda, to win the inhabitants of Heaven to our cause."

"War! War!" shouted the assembled host.

And it seemed as if one could hear the sound of trumpets and the rolling of drums.

Théophile, whom Prince Istar had dragged to the meeting, rose, pale and unstrung, and, speaking with emotion, said:

"Brethren, do not take ill what I am about to say; for it is the friendship I have for you that inspires me. I am but a poor musician. But, believe me, all your plans will come to naught before the Divine Wisdom which has foreseen everything."

Théophile Belais sat down amid hisses. And Arcade continued:

"Ialdabaoth foresees everything. I do not contest it. He foresees everything, but in order to leave us our free will he acts towards us absolutely as if he foresaw nothing. Every instant he is surprised, disconcerted; the most probable events take him unawares. The obligation which he has undertaken, to reconcile with his prescience the liberty of both men and angels, throws him constantly into inextricable difficulties and terrible dilemmas. He never sees further than the end of his nose. He did not expect Adam's disobedience, and so little did he anticipate the wickedness of men that he repented having made them, and drowned them in the waters of the Flood, and all the animals as well, though he had no fault to find with the animals. For blindness he is only to be compared with Charles X, his favourite king. If we are prudent it will be easy to take him by surprise. I think that these observations will be calculated to reassure my brother."

Théophile made no reply. He loved God, but he was fearful of sharing the fate of the faithful angel.

One of the best-informed Spirits of the assembly, Mammon, was not altogether reassured by the remarks of his brother Arcade.

"Bethink you," said this Spirit, "Ialdabaoth has little general culture, but he is a soldier—to the marrow of his bones. The organisation of Paradise is a thoroughly military organisation. It is founded on hierarchy and discipline. Passive obedience is imposed there as a fundamental law. The angels form an army. Compare this spot with the Elysian Fields which Virgil depicts for you. In the Elysian Fields reign liberty, reason, and wisdom. The happy shades hold converse together in the groves of myrtle. In the Heaven of Ialdabaoth there is no civil population. Everyone is enrolled, numbered, registered. It is a barracks and a field for manœuvres. Remember that."

Arcade replied that they must look at their adversary in his true colours, and that the military organisation of Paradise was far more reminiscent of the villages of King Koffee than of the Prussia of Frederick the Great.

"Already," said he, "at the time of the first revolt, before the beginning of Time, the conflict raged for two days, and Ialdabaoth's throne was made to totter. Nevertheless, the demiurge gained the victory. But to what did he owe it? To the thunderstorm which happened to come on during the conflict. The thunderbolts falling on Lucifer and his angels struck them down, bruised and blackened, and Ialdabaoth owed his victory to the thunderbolts. Thunder is his sole weapon. He abuses its power. In the midst of thunder and lightning he promulgates his laws. 'Fire goeth before him,' says the Prophet. Now Seneca, the philosopher, said that the thunderbolt in its fall brings peril to very few, but fear to all. This remark was true enough for men of the first century of the Christian era; it is no longer so for the angels of the twentieth; all of which goes to prove that, in spite of his thunder, he is not very powerful; it was acute terror that made men rear him a tower of unbaked brick and bitumen. When myriads of celestial spirits, furnished with machines which modern science puts at their disposal, make an assault upon the heavens, think you, comrades, that the old master of the solar system surrounded with his angels, armed as in the time of Abraham, will be able to resist them? To this day the warriors of the demiurge wear helmets of gold and shields of diamond. Michael, his best captain, knows no other tactics than the hand-to-hand combat. To him Pharaoh's chariots are still the latest thing, and he has never heard of the Macedonian phalanx."

And young Arcade lengthily prolonged the parallel between the armed herds of Ialdabaoth and the intelligent fighting men of the rebel army. Then the question of pecuniary resources arose.

Zita asserted that there was enough money to commence war, that the electrophores were in order, that an initial victory would obtain them credit.

The discussion continued, amid turbulence and confusion. In this parliament of angels, as in the synods of men, empty words flowed in abundance. Disturbances grew more violent and more frequent as the time for putting the resolution drew near. It was beyond question that supreme command would be entrusted to him who had first raised the flag of revolt. But as everyone aspired to act as Lucifer's Lieutenant, each in describing the kind of fighting man to be preferred drew a portrait of himself. Thus Alcor, the youngest of the rebellious angels, arose and spoke rapidly as follows:

"In Ialdabaoth's army, happily for us, the officers obtain their posts by seniority. This being the case, there is little likelihood of the command falling into the hands of a military genius, for men are not made leaders by prolonged habits of obedience, and close attention to minutiæ is not a good apprenticeship for the evolution of vast plans of campaign. If we consult ancient and modern history, we shall see that the greatest leaders were kings like Alexander and Frederick, aristocrats like Cæsar and Turenne, or men impatient of red-tape like Bonaparte. A routine man will always be poor or second-rate. Comrades, let us appoint intelligent leaders,

men in the prime of life, to command us. An old man may retain
the habit of winning victories, but only a young man can acquire
it!"

Alcor then gave place to an angel of the philosophic order, who
mounted the rostrum and spoke thus:

"War never was an exact science, a clearly defined art. The genius of the race, or the brain of the individual, has ever modified it.
Now how are we to define the qualities necessary for a general in
command in the war of the future, where one must consider greater
masses and a larger number of movements than the intelligence of
man can conceive? The multiplication of technical means, by infinitely multiplying the opportunities for mistake, paralyses the
genius of those in command. At a certain stage in the progress of
military science, a stage which our models, the Europeans, are
about to reach, the cleverest leader and the most ignorant become
equalized by reason of their incapacity. Another result of great
modern armaments is, that the law of numbers tends to rule with
inflexible rigour. It is of course true that ten angels in revolt are
worth more than ten angels of Ialdabaoth; it is not at all certain
that a million rebellious angels are worth more than a million of
Ialdabaoth's angels. Great numbers, in war as elsewhere, annihi-
late intelligence and individual superiority in favour of a sort of
exceedingly rudimentary collective soul."

A buzz of conversation drowned the voice of the philosophic
angel, and he concluded his speech in an atmosphere of general indifference.

The tribune then resounded with calls to arms and promises of
victory. The sword was held up to praise, the sword which defends
the right. The triumph of the angels in revolt was celebrated twenty
times beforehand, to the plaudits of a delirious crowd.

Cries of "War!" rose to the silent heavens; "Give us war!"

In the midst of these transports Prince Istar hoisted himself on
to the platform, and the floor creaked under his weight.

"Comrades," said he, "you wish for victory, and it is a very natural desire, but you must be mouldy with literature and poetry if
you expect to obtain it from war. The idea of making war can nowadays only enter the brain of a sottish bourgeois or a belated romantic. What is war? A burlesque masquerade in the midst of
which fatuous patriots sing their stupid dithyrambs. Had Napoleon
possessed a practical mind he would not have made war; but he was
a dreamer, intoxicated with Ossian. You cry, 'Give us war!' You are
visionaries. When will you become thinkers? The thinkers do not
look for power and strength from any of the dreams which constitute military art: tactics, strategy, fortifications, artillery, and all
that rubbish. They do not believe in war, which is a phantasy; they
believe in chemistry, which is a science. They know the way to put
victory into an algebraic formula."

And drawing from his pocket a small bottle, which he held up to the meeting, Prince Istar exclaimed:

"Victory—it is here!"

XXVII

WHEREIN WE SHALL SEE REVEALED A DARK AND SECRET MYSTERY AND LEARN HOW IT COMES ABOUT THAT EMPIRES ARE OFTEN HURLED AGAINST EMPIRES, AND RUIN FALLS ALIKE UPON THE VICTORS AND THE VANQUISHED; AND THE WISE READER (IF SUCH THERE BE—WHICH I DOUBT) WILL MEDITATE UPON THIS IMPORTANT UTTERANCE: "A WAR IS A MATTER OF BUSINESS"

HE Angels had dispersed. At the foot of the slopes at Meudon, seated on the grass, Arcade and Zita watched the Seine flowing by the willows.

"In this world," said Arcade, "in this world, which we call a cosmos, though it is but a microcosm, no thinking being can imagine that he is able to destroy even one atom. At the utmost, all we can hope for is that we shall succeed in modifying, here and there, the rhythm of some group of atoms and the arrangement of certain cells. That, when one thinks of it, must be the limit of our great enterprise. And when we shall have set up the Contradictor in the place of Ialdabaoth, we shall have done no more. . . . Zita, is the evil in the nature of things or in their arrangement? That is what we ought to know. Zita, I am profoundly troubled——"

"Arcade," replied Zita, "if to act we had to know the secret of Nature, one would never act at all. And neither would one live—since to live is to act. Arcade, is your resolution failing you already?"

Arcade assured the beautiful angel that he was resolved to plunge the demiurge into eternal darkness.

A motor-car passed by on the road, followed by a long trail of dust. It stopped before the two angels, and the hooked nose of Baron Everdingen appeared at the window.

"Good morning, my celestial friends, good morning," said the capitalist. "Sons of Heaven, I am pleased to meet you. I have a word of importance to say to you. Do not remain idle—do not go to sleep. Arm! Arm! You may be surprised by Ialdabaoth. You have a big war-fund. Employ it without stint. I have just learnt that the Archangel Michael has given large orders in Heaven for thunder-bolts and arrows. If you take my advice you will procure fifty thousand more electrophores. I will take the order. Good day, angels. Long live the celestial country!"

And Baron Everdingen flew by the flowery shores of Louveciennes in the company of a pretty actress.

"Is it true that they are taking up arms at the demiurge's?" asked Arcade.

"It may be," replied Zita, "that up there another Baron Everdingen is inciting to arms."

The guardian angel of young Maurice remained pensive for some moments. Then he murmured:

"Can it be that we are the sport of financiers?"

"Pooh!" said the beautiful archangel. "War is a business. It has always been a business."

Then they discussed at length the means of executing their immense enterprise. Rejecting disdainfully the anarchistic proceedings of Prince Istar, they conceived a formidable and sudden invasion of the kingdom of Heaven by their enthusiastic and well-drilled troops.

Now Barattan, the innkeeper of La Jonchère, who had let the entertainment-hall to the rebellious angels, was in the employ of the secret police. In the reports he furnished to the Prefecture he denounced the members of this secret meeting as meditating an attack on a certain person whom they described as obtuse and cruel, and whom they called *Alaballotte.* The agent believed this to be a pseudonym denoting either the President of the Republic or the Republic itself. The conspirators had unanimously given voice to threats against *Alaballotte,* and one of them, a very dangerous individual, well-known in anarchist circles, who had already several convictions against him on account of writings and speeches of a seditious nature, and who was known as Prince Istar or the *Quéroube,* had brandished a bomb of very small calibre which seemed to contain a formidable machine. The other conspirators were unknown to Barattan, notwithstanding the fact that he frequented revolutionary circles. Many among them were very young men, mere beardless youths. There were two who, it appeared, had spoken with conspicuous vehemence; a certain Arcade, dwelling in the Rue St. Jacques, and a woman of easy virtue called Zita, living at Montmartre, both without visible means of subsistence.

The affair seemed sufficiently serious to the Prefect of Police to make him think it necessary to confer without delay with the President of the Council.

The Third Republic was then going through one of those climacteric periods during which the French nation, enamoured of authority and worshipping force, gave itself up for lost because it was not governed enough, and clamoured loudly for a saviour. The President of the Council, and Minister of Justice, was only too eager to be that longed-for saviour. Still, for him to play that part it was first necessary that there should be a danger to face. Thus the news of a plot was highly welcome to him. He questioned the Prefect of Police on the character and importance of the affair. The Prefect of Police explained that the people seemed to have money, intelligence, and energy; but that they talked too much and were too numerous to undertake secret and concerted action. The Minister, leaning back in his arm-chair, pondered on the matter. The Empire writing-table at which he was seated, the ancient tapestry which covered the walls, the clock and the candelabra of the Restoration period—all, in this traditional setting, reminded him of those great principles of government which remain immutable throughout the succession of *régimes,* of stratagem and of bluff. After brief reflexion, he concluded that the plot must be allowed to grow and take shape, that it would even be fitting to nurse it, to embroider it, to colour it, and only to stifle it after having extracted every possible advantage from it.

He instructed the Prefect of Police to watch the affair closely, to render him an account of what went on from day to day, and to confine himself to the rôle of informer.

"I rely on your well-known prudence; observe, and do not intervene."

The Minister lit a cigarette. He quite reckoned, with the help of this plot, on silencing the Opposition, strengthening his own influence, diminishing that of his colleagues, humiliating the President of the Republic, and becoming the saviour of his country.

The Prefect of Police undertook to follow the ministerial instructions, vowing inwardly all the while to act in his own way. He had a watch put upon the individuals pointed out by Barattan, and commanded his agents not to intervene, come what might. Perceiving that he was a marked man, Prince Istar—who united prudence with strength—withdrew the bombs from the gutter outside his window where he had hidden them, and changing from motor 'bus to tube, from tube to motor 'bus, and choosing the most cunningly circuitous route, at length deposited his machines with the angelic musician.

Every time he left his house in the Rue St. Jacques, Arcade found a man of exaggerated smartness at his door, with yellow gloves and in his tie a diamond bigger than the Regent. Being a stranger to the things of this world, the rebellious angel paid no attention to the circumstance. But young Maurice d'Esparvieu, who had undertaken the task of guarding his guardian-angel, viewed this gentleman with uneasiness, for he equalled in assiduity and surpassed in vigilance that Monsieur Mignon who had formerly allowed his inquisitive gaze to wander from the rams' heads on the Hôtel de la Sordière in the Rue Garancière to the apse of the church of St. Sulpice. Maurice came two and three times a day to see Arcade in his furnished rooms, warning him of the danger, and urging him to change his abode.

Every evening he took his angel to night restaurants, where they supped with ladies of easy virtue. There young d'Esparvieu would foretell the issue of some coming glove-fight, and afterwards exert himself to demonstrate to Arcade the existence of God, the necessity for religion, and the beauties of Christianity, and adjure him to renounce his impious and criminal undertakings wherefrom, he said, he would reap but bitterness and disappointment.

"For really," said the young apologist, "if Christianity were false it would be known."

The ladies approved of Maurice's religious sentiments, and when the handsome Arcade uttered some blasphemy in language they could understand, they put their hands to their ears and bade him be silent, for fear of being struck down with him. For they believed that God, in his omnipotence and sovereign goodness, taking sudden vengeance against those who insulted him, was quite capable of striking down the innocent with the guilty without meaning it.

Sometimes the angel and his guardian took supper with the angelic musician. Maurice, who remembered from time to time that he was Bouchotte's lover, was displeased to see Arcade taking liberties with the singer. She had allowed him to do so ever since the day when, the angelic musician having had the little flowery couch repaired, Arcade and Bouchotte had made it a foundation for their friendship. Maurice, who loved Madame des Aubels a great deal, also loved Bouchotte a little, and was rather jealous of Arcade. Now jealousy is a feeling natural to man and beast, and causes them, however slight the attack, keen unhappiness. Therefore, suspecting the truth, which Bouchotte's temperament and the angel's character made sufficiently obvious, he overwhelmed Arcade with sarcasm and abuse, reproaching him with the immorality of his ways. Arcade answered, tranquilly, that it was difficult to subject physiological impulses to perfectly defined rules, and that moralists encountered great difficulties in the case of certain natural necessities.

"Moreover," added Arcade, "I freely acknowledge that it is almost impossible systematically to constitute a natural moral law. Nature has no principles. She furnishes us with no reason to believe that human life is to be respected. Nature, in her indifference, makes no distinction between good and evil."

"You see, then," replied Maurice, "that religion is necessary."

"Moral law," replied the angel, "which is supposed to be revealed to us, is drawn in reality from the grossest empiricism. Custom alone regulates morals. What Heaven prescribes is merely the consecration of ancient customs. The divine law, promulgated amid fireworks on some Mount Sinai, is never anything but the codification of human prejudice. And from this fact—namely, that morals change—religions which endure for a long time, such as Judæo-Christianity, vary their moral law."

"At any rate," said Maurice, whose intelligence was swelling visibly, "you will grant me that religion prevents much profligacy and crime?"

"Except when it promotes crime—as, for instance, the murder of Iphigenia."

"Arcade," exclaimed Maurice, "when I hear you argue, I rejoice that I am not an intellectual."

Meanwhile Théophile, with his head bent over the piano, his face hidden by the long fair veil of his hair, bringing down from on high his inspired hands on to the keys, was playing and singing the full score of *Aline, Queen of Golconda.*

Prince Istar used to come to their friendly reunions, his pockets filled with bombs and bottles of champagne, both of which he owed to the liberality of Baron Everdingen. Bouchotte received the Kerûb with pleasure, since she saw in him the witness and the trophy of the victory she had gained on the little flowered couch. He was to her as the severed head of Goliath in the hands of the youthful David. And she admired the prince for his cleverness as an accompanist, his vigour, which she had subdued, and his prodigious capacity for drink.

One night, when young d'Esparvieu took his angel home in his car from Bouchotte's house to the lodgings in the Rue St. Jacques, it was very dark; before the door the diamond in the spy's necktie glittered like a beacon; three cyclists standing in a group under its rays made off in divers directions at the car's approach. The angel took no notice, but Maurice concluded that Arcade's movements interested various important people in the State. He judged the danger to be pressing, and at once made up his mind.

The next morning he came to seek the suspect, to take him to the Rue de Rome. The angel was in bed. Maurice urged him to dress and to follow him.

"Come," said he. "This house is no longer safe for you. You are watched. One of these days you will be arrested. Do you wish to sleep in gaol? No? Well, then, come. I will put you in a safe place."

The spirit smiled with some little compassion on his naïve preserver.

"Do you not know," he said, "that an angel broke open the doors of the prison where Peter was confined, and delivered the apostle? Do you believe me, Maurice, to be inferior in power to that heavenly brother of mine, and do you suppose that I am unable to do for myself what he did for the fisherman of the lake of Tiberias?"

"Do not count on it, Arcade. He did it miraculously."

"Or by a stroke of luck, as a modern historian of the Church has it. But no matter. I will follow you. Just allow me to burn a few letters and to make a parcel of some books I shall need."

He threw some papers in the fire-place, put several volumes in his pockets, and followed his guide to the car, which was waiting for them not far off, outside the College of France. Maurice took the wheel. Imitating the Kerûb's prudence, he made so many windings and turnings, and so many rapid twists that he put all the swift and numerous cyclists, speeding in pursuit, off the scent. At length, having left wheelmarks in every direction all over the town, he stopped in the Rue de Rome, before the first-door flat, where the angel had first appeared.

On entering the dwelling which he had left eighteen months before to carry out his mission, Arcade remembered the irreparable past, and breathing in the scent used by Gilberte, his nostrils throbbed. He asked after Madame des Aubels.

"She is very well," replied Maurice. "A little plumper and very much more beautiful for it. She still bears you a grudge for your forward behaviour. I hope that she will one day forgive you, as I have forgiven you, and that she will forget your offence. But she is still very annoyed with you."

Young d'Esparvieu did the honours of his flat to his angel with the manners of a well-bred man and the tender solicitude of a friend. He showed him the folding bed which was opened every evening in the entrance hall and pushed into a dark cupboard in the morning. He showed him the dressing-table, with its accessories; the bath, the linen cupboard, the chest of drawers; gave him the necessary information regarding the heating and lighting; told him that his meals would be brought and the rooms cleaned by the concierge, and showed him which bell to press when he required that person's services. He told him also that he must consider himself at home, and receive whom he wished.

XXVIII

WHICH TREATS OF A PAINFUL DOMESTIC SCENE

So long as Maurice confined his selection of mistresses to respectable women, his conduct had called forth no reproach. It was a different matter when he took up with Bouchotte. His mother, who had closed her eyes to liaisons which, though guilty, were elegant and discreet, was scandalised when it came to her ears that her son was openly parading about with a music-hall singer. By dint of much prying and probing, Berthe, Maurice's younger sister, had got to know of her brother's adventures, and she narrated them, without any indignation, to her young girl friends. His little brother Léon declared to his mother one day, in the presence of several ladies, that when he was big he, too, would go on the spree, like Maurice. This was a sore wound to the maternal heart of Madame d'Esparvieu.

About the same time there occurred a family event of a very grave nature which occasioned much alarm to Monsieur René d'Esparvieu. Drafts were presented to him signed in his name by his son. His writing had not been forged, but there was no doubt that it had been the son's intention to pass off the signature as his father's. It showed a perverted moral sense; whence it appeared that Maurice was living a life of profligacy, that he was running into debt and on the point of outraging the decencies. The pater-familias talked the matter over with his wife. It was arranged that he should give his son a very severe lecture, hint at vigorous corrective measures, and that in due course the mother should appear with gentle and sorrowing mien and endeavour to soothe the righteous indignation of the father. This plan being agreed upon, Monsieur René d'Esparvieu sent for his son to come to him in his

study. To add to the solemnity of the occasion, he had arrayed himself in his frock-coat. As soon as Maurice saw it he knew there was something serious in the wind. The head of the family was pale, and his voice shook a little (for he was a nervous man), as he declared that he would no longer put up with his son's irregular behaviour, and insisted on an immediate and absolute reform. No more wild courses, no more running into debt, no more undesirable companions, but work, steadiness, and reputable connexions.

Maurice was quite willing to give a respectful reply to his father, whose complaints, after all, were perfectly justified; but, unfortunately, Maurice, like his father, was shy, and the frock-coat which Monsieur d'Esparvieu had donned in order to discharge his magisterial duty with greater dignity seemed to preclude the possibility of any open and unconstrained intercourse. Maurice maintained an awkward silence, which looked very much like insolence, and this silence compelled Monsieur d'Esparvieu to reiterate his complaints, this time with additional severity. He opened one of the drawers in his historic bureau (the bureau on which Alexandre d'Esparvieu had written his "Essay on the Civil and Religious Institutions of the World"), and produced the bills which Maurice had signed.

"Do you know, my boy," said he, "that this is nothing more or less than forgery? To make up for such grave misconduct as that——"

At this moment Madame d'Esparvieu, as arranged, entered the room attired in her walking-dress. She was supposed to play the angel of forgiveness, but neither her appearance nor her disposition was suitable to the part. She was harsh and unsympathetic. Maurice harboured within him the seeds of all the ordinary and necessary virtues. He loved his mother and respected her. His love, however, was more a matter of duty than of inclination, and his respect arose from habit rather than from feeling. Madame René d'Esparvieu's complexion was blotchy, and having powdered herself in order to appear to advantage at the domestic tribunal, the colour of her face suggested raspberries sprinkled over with sugar. Maurice, being possessed of some taste, could not help realising that she was ugly and rather repulsively so. He was out of tune with her, and when she began to go through all the accusations his father had brought against him, making them out to be blacker than ever, the prodigal turned away his head to conceal his irritation.

"Your Aunt de Saint-Fain," she went on, "met you in the street in such disgraceful company that she was really thankful that you forbore to greet her."

"Aunt de Saint-Fain!" Maurice broke out. "I like to hear her talking about scandals! Everyone knows the sort of life she has led, and now the old hypocrite wants to——"

He stopped. He had caught sight of his father, whose face was even more eloquent of sorrow than of anger. Maurice began to feel as though he had committed murder, and could not imagine how he had allowed such words to escape him. He was on the point of bursting into tears, falling on his knees, and imploring his father to forgive him, when his mother, looking up at the ceiling, said with a sigh:

"What offence can I have committed against God, to have brought such a wicked son into the world?"

This speech struck Maurice as a piece of ridiculous affectation, and it pulled him up with a jerk. The bitterness of contrition suddenly gave place to the delicious arrogance of wrong-doing. He plunged wildly into a torrent of insolence and revolt, and breathlessly delivered himself of utterances quite unfit for a mother's ear.

"If you will have it, mamma, rather than forbid me to continue my friendship with a talented lyrical artist, you would be better employed in preventing my elder sister, Madame de Margy, from appearing, night after night, in society and at the theatres with a contemptible and disgusting individual that everybody knows is her lover. You should also keep an eye on my little sister Jeanne, who writes objectionable letters to herself in a disguised hand, and then, pretending she has found them in her prayer-book, shows them to you with assumed innocence, to worry and alarm you. It would be just as well, too, if you prevented my little brother Léon, a child of seven, from being quite so much with Mademoiselle Caporal, and you might tell your maid . . ."

"Get out, sir, I will not have you in the house!" cried Monsieur René d'Esparvieu, white with anger, pointing a trembling finger at the door.

XXIX

WHEREIN WE SEE HOW THE ANGEL, HAVING BECOME A MAN, BEHAVES LIKE A MAN, COVETING ANOTHER'S WIFE AND BETRAYING HIS FRIEND. IN THIS CHAPTER THE CORRECTNESS OF YOUNG D'ESPARVIEU'S CONDUCT WILL BE MADE MANIFEST

THE angel was pleased with his lodging. He worked of a morning, went out in the afternoon, heedless of detectives, and came home to sleep. As in days gone by, Maurice received Madame des Aubels twice or thrice a week in the room in which they had seen the apparition.

All went very well until one morning Gilberte, having, the night before, left her little velvet bag on the table in the blue room, came to find it, and discovered Arcade stretched on the couch in his pyjamas, smoking a cigarette, and dreaming of the conquest of Heaven. She gave a loud scream.

"You, Monsieur! Had I thought to find you here, you may be quite sure I should not . . . I came to fetch my little bag, which is in the next room. Allow me. . . ." And she slipped past the angel, cautiously and quickly, as if he were a brazier.

Madame des Aubels that morning, in her pale green tailor-made costume, was deliciously attractive. Her tight skirt displayed her movements, and her every step was one of those miracles of Nature which fill men's hearts with amazement.

She reappeared, bag in hand.

"Once more—I ask your pardon. . . . I never dreamt that . . ."

Arcade begged her to sit down and to stay a moment.

"I never expected, Monsieur," said she, "that you would be doing the honours of this flat. I knew how dearly Monsieur d'Esparvieu loved you. . . . Nevertheless, I had no idea that . . ."

The sky had suddenly grown overcast. A brownish glare began to steal into the room. Madame des Aubels told him she had walked for her health's sake, but a storm was brewing, and she asked if a carriage could be called for her.

Arcade flung himself at Gilberte's feet, took her in his arms as one takes a precious piece of china, and murmured words which, being meaningless in themselves, expressed desire.

She put her hands over his eyes and on his lips, and exclaimed, "I hate you!"

And shaking with sobs, she asked for a drink of water. She was choking. The angel went to her assistance. In this moment of extreme peril she defended herself courageously. She kept saying: "No! . . . No! . . . I will not love you. I should love you too well. . . ." Nevertheless she succumbed.

In the sweet familiarity which followed their mutual astonishment she said to him:

"I have often asked after you. I knew that you were an assiduous frequenter of the playhouses at Montmartre,—that you were often seen with Mademoiselle Bouchotte, who, nevertheless, is not at all pretty. I knew that you had become very smart, and that you were making a good deal of money. I was not surprised. You were born to succeed. The day of your"—and she pointed at the spot between the window and the wardrobe with the mirror—"apparition, I was vexed with Maurice for having given you a suicide's rags to wear. You pleased me. . . . Oh, it was not your good looks! Don't think that women are as sensitive as people say to outward attractions. We consider other things in love. There is a sort of—— Well, anyhow I loved you as soon as I saw you."

The shadows grew deeper.

She asked:

"You are not an angel, are you? Maurice believes you are; but he believes so many things, Maurice." She questioned Arcade with her eyes and smiled maliciously. "Confess that you have been fooling him, and that you are no angel?"

Arcade replied:

"I only aspire to please you; I will always be what you want me to be."

Gilberte decided that he was no angel; first, because one never is an angel; secondly, for more detailed reasons which drew her thoughts to the question of love. He did not argue the matter with her, and once again words were found inadequate to express their feelings.

Outside, the rain was falling thick and fast, the windows were streaming, lightning lit up the muslin curtains, and thunder shook the panes. Gilberte made the sign of the Cross and remained with her head hidden in her lover's bosom.

At this moment Maurice entered the room. He came in wet and smiling, confident, tranquil, happy, to announce to Arcade the good news that with his half-share in the previous day's race at Longchamps the angel had won twelve times his stake. Surprising the lady and the angel in their embrace, he became furious; anger gripped the muscles of his throat, his face grew red with blood, and the veins stood out on his forehead. He sprang with clenched fists toward Gilberte, and then suddenly stopped.

Interrupted motion was transformed into heat. Maurice fumed. His anger did not arm him, like Archilochus, with lyrical vengeance. He merely applied an offensive epithet to his unfaithful one.

Meanwhile she had recovered her dignified bearing. She rose, full of modesty and grace, and gave her accuser a look which expressed both offended virtue and loving forgiveness.

But as young d'Esparvieu continued to shower coarse and monotonous insults on her, she grew angry in her turn.

"You are a pretty sort of person, are you not?" she said. "Did I run after this Arcade of yours? It was you who brought him here, and in what a state, too! You had only one idea: to give me up to your friend. Well, Monsieur, you can do as you like—I am not going to oblige you."

Maurice d'Esparvieu replied simply, "Get out of it, you trollop!" And he made a motion as if to push her out. It pained Arcade to see his mistress treated so disrespectfully, but he thought he lacked the necessary authority to interfere with Maurice. Madame des Aubels, who had lost none of her dignity, fixed young d'Esparvieu with her imperious gaze, and said:

"Go and get me a carriage."

And so great is the power of woman over a well-bred soul, in a gallant nation, that the young Frenchman went immediately and told the concierge to call a taxi. Madame des Aubels, with a studied exhibition of charm in every movement, took leave of them, throwing Maurice the contemptuous look that a woman owes to him whom she has deceived. Maurice witnessed her departure with an outward expression of indifference he was far from feeling. Then he turned to the angel clad in the flowered pyjamas which Maurice himself had worn the day of the apparition; and this circumstance, trifling in itself, added fuel to the anger of the host who had been thus shamefully deceived.

"Well," he said, "you may pride yourself on being a despicable individual. You have behaved basely, and all for nothing. If the woman took your fancy, you had but to tell me. I was tired of her. I had had enough of her. I would have willingly left her to you."

He spoke thus to hide his pain, for he loved Gilberte more than ever, and the creature's treachery caused him great suffering. He pursued:

"I was about to ask you to take her off my hands. But you have followed your lower nature—you have behaved like a sweep."

If at this solemn moment Arcade had but spoken one word from his heart, Maurice would have burst into tears, and forgiven his friend and his mistress, and all three would have become content and happy once again. But Arcade had not been nourished on the milk of human kindness. He had never suffered, and did not know how to sympathise with suffering. He replied with frigid wisdom:

"My dear Maurice, that same necessity which orders and constrains the actions of living beings, produces effects that are often unexpected, and sometimes absurd. Thus it is that I have been led to displease you. You would not reproach me if you had a good philosophical understanding of nature; for you would then know that free-will is but an illusion, and that physiological affinities are as exactly determined as are chemical combinations, and, like them, may be summed up in a formula. I think that, in your case, it might be possible to inculcate these truths, but it would be a difficult task, and maybe they would not bring you the serenity which eludes you. It is fitting, therefore, that I should leave this spot, and——"

"Stay," said Maurice.

Maurice had a very clear sense of social obligations. He put honour, when he thought about it, above everything. So now he told himself very forcibly that the outrage he had suffered could only be wiped out with blood. This traditional idea instantly lent an unexpected nobility to his speech and bearing.

"It is I, Monsieur," said he, "who will quit this place, never to return. You will remain here, since you are a refugee. My seconds will wait upon you."

The angel smiled.

"I will receive them, if it gives you pleasure, but, bethink you, my dear Maurice, I am invulnerable. Celestial spirits even when they are materialised cannot be touched by point of sword or pistol shot. Consider, my dear Maurice, the awkward situation in which this fatal inequality puts me, and realise that in refusing to appoint seconds I cannot give as a reason my celestial nature,—it would be unprecedented."

"Monsieur," replied the heir of the Bussart d'Esparvieu, "you should have thought of that before you insulted me."

Out he marched haughtily; but no sooner was he in the street than he staggered like a drunken man. The rain was still falling. He walked unseeing, unhearing, at haphazard, dragging his feet in the gutters through pools of water, through heaps of mud. He followed the outer boulevards for a long time, and at length, fordone with weariness, lay down on the edge of a piece of waste land. He was muddied up to the eyes, mud and tears smeared his face, the brim of his hat was dripping with rain. A passer-by, taking him for a beggar, tossed him a copper. He picked it up, put it carefully in his waistcoat pocket, and set off to find his seconds.

XXX

WHICH TREATS OF AN AFFAIR OF HONOUR, AND WHICH WILL AFFORD THE READER AN OPPORTUNITY OF JUDGING WHETHER, AS ARCADE AFFIRMS, THE EXPERIENCE OF OUR FAULTS MAKES BETTER MEN AND WOMEN OF US

THE ground chosen for the combat was Colonel Manchon's garden, on the Boulevard de la Reine at Versailles. Messieurs de la Verdelière and Le Truc de Ruffec, who had both of them constant practice in affairs of honour and knew the rules with great exactness, assisted Maurice d'Esparvieu. No duel was ever fought in the Catholic world without Monsieur de la Verdelière being present; and, in making application to this swordsman, Maurice had conformed to custom, though not without a certain reluctance, for he had been notorious as the lover of Madame de la Verdelière; but Monsieur de la Verdelière was not to be looked upon as a husband. He was an institution. As to Monsieur Le Truc de Ruffec, honour was his only known profession and avowedly his sole resource, and when the matter was made the subject of ill-natured comment in Society, the question was asked what finer career than that of honour Monsieur Le Truc de Ruffec could possibly have adopted. Arcade's seconds were Prince Istar and Théophile. The celestial musician had not voluntarily nor with a good grace taken a hand in this affair. He had a horror of every kind of violence and disapproved of single combat. The report of pistols and the clash of swords were intolerable to him, and the sight of blood made him faint. This gentle son of

Heaven had obstinately refused to act as second to his brother Arcade, and to bring him to the starting-point the Kerûb had had to threaten to break a bottle of panclastite over his head.

Besides the combatants, the seconds, and the doctors, the only people in the garden were a few officers from the barracks at Versailles and several reporters. Although young d'Esparvieu was known merely as a young man of family, and Arcade had never been heard of at all, the duel had attracted quite a large crowd of inquisitive individuals, and the windows of the adjoining houses were crammed with photographers, reporters, and Society people. What had aroused much curiosity was that a woman was known to be the cause of the quarrel. Many mentioned Bouchotte, but the majority said it was Madame des Aubels. It had been remarked upon, moreover, that duels in which Monsieur de la Verdelière acted as second drew all Paris.

The sky was a soft blue, the garden all a-bloom with roses, a blackbird was piping in a tree. Monsieur de la Verdelière, who, stick in hand, conducted the affair, laid the points of the swords together, and said:

"Allez, Messieurs."

Maurice d'Esparvieu attacked by doubling and beating the blade. Arcade retired, keeping his sword in line. The first engagement was without result. The seconds were under the impression that Monsieur d'Esparvieu was in a grievous state of nervous irritability, and that his adversary would wear him down. In the second encounter Maurice attacked wildly, spread out his arms, and exposed his breast. He attacked as he advanced, gave a straight thrust, and the point of his sword grazed Arcade on the shoulder. The latter was thought to be wounded. But the seconds ascertained with surprise that it was Maurice who had received a scratch on the wrist. Maurice asserted that he felt nothing, and Dr. Quille declared, after examination, that his client might continue the fight. After the regulation quarter of an hour the duel was resumed. Maurice attacked with fury. His adversary was obviously nursing him, and, what disturbed Monsieur de la Verdelière, seemed to be paying very little attention to his own defence. At the opening of the fifth bout, a black spaniel that had got into the garden no one knew how rushed out from a clump of rose-bushes, made its way on to the space reserved for the combatants, and, in spite of sticks and cries, ran in between Maurice's legs. The latter seemed as though his arm were benumbed, merely gave a shoulder-thrust at his invulnerable opponent. He then delivered a straight lunge and impaled his arm on his adversary's sword, which made a deep wound just below the elbow.

Monsieur de la Verdelière stopped the fight, which had lasted an hour and a half. Maurice was conscious of a painful shock. They laid him down on a grassy bank against a wall covered with wistaria. While the surgeon was dressing the wound Maurice called Arcade and offered him his wounded hand. And when the victor, saddened with his victory, advanced, Maurice embraced him tenderly, saying:

"Be generous, Arcade; forgive my treachery. Now that we have fought, I can ask you to be reconciled with me."

He embraced his friend, weeping, and whispered in his ear:

"Come and see me, and bring Gilberte."

Maurice, who was still unreconciled with his parents, was taken to the little flat in the Rue de Rome. No sooner was he stretched on the bed at the far end of the bedroom where the curtains were drawn as on the day of the apparition, than he saw Arcade and Gilberte appear. He began to suffer greatly from his wound; his temperature was rising, but he was at peace, happy and contented. Angel and woman, both in tears, threw themselves at the foot of the bed. He took both their hands with his left, smiled on them, and kissed them tenderly.

"I am sure now that I shall never quarrel with either of you again; you will deceive me no more. I now know you are capable of anything."

Gilberte, weeping, swore that Maurice had been misled by appearances, that she had never betrayed him with Arcade, that she had never betrayed him at all. And in a great gush of sincerity she persuaded herself that this was so.

"You wrong yourself, Gilberte," replied the wounded man. "It did happen; it had to. And it is well. Gilberte, you were basely false to me with my best friend in this very room, and you were right. If you had not been we should not be here, reunited, all three of us, and I should not be at your side tasting the greatest happiness of my life. Oh, Gilberte, how wrong of you to deny a perfect and accomplished fact!"

"If you wish, my friend," replied Gilberte, a little acidly, "I will not deny it. But it will only be to please you."

Maurice made her sit down on the bed, and begged Arcade to be seated in the arm-chair.

"My friend," said Arcade, "I was innocent. I became man. Straightway I did evil. Then I became better."

"Do not let us exaggerate things," said Maurice. "Let's have a game of bridge."

Scarcely, however, had the patient seen three aces in his hand and called "no trumps," than his eyes began to swim, the cards slipped from his fingers, head fell heavily back on the pillow, and he complained of a violent headache. Almost immediately, Madame des Aubels went off to pay some calls, for she made a point of appearing in Society, in order that the calmness and confidence of her demeanour might give the lie to the various rumours that were current concerning her. Arcade saw her to the door, and, with a kiss, inhaled from her a delicate perfume which he brought back with him into the room where Maurice lay dozing.

"I am perfectly content," murmured the latter, "that things should have happened as they have."

"It was bound to be so," answered the Spirit. "All the other angels in revolt would have done as I did with Gilberte. 'Women,' saith the Apostle, 'should pray with their heads covered, because of the angels,' and the Apostle speaks thus because he knows that the angels are disturbed when they look upon them and see that they are beautiful. No sooner do they touch the earth than they desire to embrace mortal women and fulfil their desire. Their clasp is full of strength and sweetness, they hold the secret of those ineffable caresses which plunge the daughters of men into unfathomable depths of delight. Laying upon the lips of their happy victims a honey that burns like fire, making their veins flow with torrents of refreshing flames, they leave them raptured and undone."

"Stop your clatter, you unclean beast," cried the wounded one.

"One word more!" said the angel; "just one other word, my dear Maurice, to bear out what I say, and I will let you rest quietly. There's nothing like having sound references. In order to assure yourself that I am not deceiving you, Maurice, on this subject of the amorous embraces of angels and women, look up Justin, *Apologies,* I and II; Flavius Josephus, *Jewish Antiquities,* Book I, Chapter III; Athenagoras, *Concerning the Resurrection;* Lactantius, Book II, Chapter XV; Tertullian, *On the Veil of the Virgins;* Marcus of Ephesus in *Psellus;* Eusebius, *Præparatio Evangelica,* Book V, Chapter IV; Saint Ambrose, in his book on *Noah and the Ark,* Chapter V; Saint Augustine, in his *City of God,* Book XV, Chapter XXIII; Father Meldonat, the Jesuit, *Treatise on Demons,* page 248; Pierre Lebyer the King's Counsellor——"

"Arcade, please, for pity's sake, be quiet; do, please do, and send this dog away," cried Maurice, whose face was burning, and whose eyes were starting from his head; for in his delirium he thought he saw a black spaniel on his bed.

Madame de la Verdelière, who was assiduous in every modish and patriotic practice, was reckoned, in the best French society, as one of the most gracious of the great ladies interested in good works. She came herself to ask for news of Maurice, and offered to nurse the wounded man. But at the vehement instigation of Madame des Aubels, Arcade shut the door in her face. Expressions of sympathy were showered upon Maurice. Piled on the salver, visiting cards displayed their innumerable little dogs' ears. Monsieur Le Truc de Ruffec was one of the first to show his manly sympathy at the flat in the Rue de Rome, and, holding out his loyal hand, asked young d'Esparvieu as one honourable man to another for twenty-five louis to pay a debt of honour.

"Of course, my dear Maurice, that is the sort of thing one could not ask of everybody."

The same day Monsieur Gaétan came to press his nephew's hand. The latter introduced Arcade.

"This is my guardian angel, whose foot you thought so beautiful when you saw the print it had made on the tell-tale powder, uncle. He appeared to me last year in this very room. You don't believe it? Well, it is true, nevertheless."

Then turning towards the Spirit he said:

"What say you, Arcade? The Abbé Patouille, who is a great theologian and a good priest, does not believe that you are an angel; and Uncle Gaétan, who doesn't know his catechism and hasn't a scrap of religion in him, doesn't think so either. They deny you, the pair of them; the one because he has faith, the other because he hasn't. After that you may be sure that your history, if ever it comes to be narrated, will scarcely appear credible. Moreover, the man that took it into his head to tell your story would not be a man of taste, and would not come in for much approval. For your story is not a pretty one. I love you, but I sit in judgment upon you, too. Since you fell into atheism, you have become an abominable scoundrel. A bad angel, a bad friend, a traitor, and a homicide, for I suppose it was to bring about my death that you sent that black spaniel between my legs on the duelling-ground."

The angel shrugged his shoulders and, addressing Gaétan, said:

"Alas! Monsieur, I am not surprised at finding little credit in your eyes. I have been told that you have fallen out with the Judæo-Christian heaven, which is where I came from."

"Monsieur," answered Gaétan, "my faith in Jehovah is not sufficiently strong to enable me to believe in his angels."

"Monsieur, he whom you call Jehovah is really a coarse and ignorant demiurge, and his name is Ialdabaoth."

"In that case, Monsieur, I am perfectly ready to believe in him. He is a narrow-minded ignoramus, is he? Then belief in his existence offers me no further difficulty. How is he getting on?"

"Badly! We are going to lay him low next month."

"Don't make too sure of that, Monsieur. You remind me of my brother-in-law, Cuissart, who has been expecting to hear of the fall of the Republic for the past thirty years."

"You see, Arcade," exclaimed Maurice, "Uncle Gaétan thinks as I do. He knows you won't succeed."

"And, pray, Monsieur Gaétan, what makes you think I shall not succeed?"

"Your Ialdabaoth is still very powerful in this world, if he isn't in the other. In days gone by he used to be upheld by his priests, by those who believed in him. Now he is supported by those who do not believe in him, by the philosophers. A pedant of a fellow called Picrochole has recently come on the scene who wants to make a bankrupt of science in order to do a good turn to the Church. And just lately Pragmatism has been invented for the express purpose of gaining credit for religion in the minds of rationalists."

"You have been studying Pragmatism?"

"Not I! I was frivolous once, and I went in for metaphysics. I read Hegel and Kant. I have become serious with years, and now I only trouble myself about things evident to the senses: what the eye can see or what the ear can hear. Man is summed up in Art. All the rest is moonshine."

Thus the conversation went on until evening; it was marked by obscenities that would have brought a blush—I will not say to a cuirassier, for cuirassiers are frequently chaste, but even to a Parisienne.

Monsieur Sariette came to see his old pupil. When he entered the room the bust of Alexandre d'Esparvieu seemed to take shape behind the librarian's bald head. He drew near the bed. In the place of blue curtains, mirrored wardrobe, and chimney-piece, there straightway came into view the heavy-laden book cases of the room of the globes and busts, and the air was heavy with piles of papers, records, and files. Monsieur Sariette could not be dissociated from his library; one could not conceive of him or even see him apart from it. He himself was paler, more vague, more shadowy, and more a creature of the fancy than the fancies he evoked.

Maurice, who had grown very quiet, was sensible of this mark of friendship.

"Sit down, Monsieur Sariette,—you know Madame des Aubels. May I introduce Arcade to you,—my guardian angel. It was he who, while yet invisible, pillaged your library for two years, made you lose all desire for food and drink, and drove you to the verge of madness. He it was who moved piles of books from the room of the busts to my summer-house one day; under your very nose, he took away I know not what precious volumes; and was the cause of your falling on the staircase; another day he took a volume of Salomon Reinach's, and, forced to go out with me (for he never left me, as I have learnt later), he let the volume drop in the gutter of the Rue Princesse. Forgive him, Monsieur Sariette,—he had no pockets. He was invisible. I bitterly regret, Monsieur Sariette, that all your old books were not devoured by fire or swallowed up by a flood. They made my angel lose his head. He became man, and now knows neither faith nor obedience to laws. It is I, now, who am his guardian angel. God knows how it will all end."

While listening to this speech, Monsieur Sariette's face took on an expression of infinite, irreparable, eternal sadness; the sadness of a mummy. Rising to take his leave, the sorrowful librarian murmured in Arcade's ear:

"The poor child is very ill. He is delirious."

Maurice called the old man back.

"Do stay, Monsieur Sariette. You shall have a game of bridge with us. Monsieur Sariette, listen to my advice. Do not do as I did —do not keep bad company. You will be lost. I shudder at the mere thought. Monsieur Sariette, do not go yet. I have something very important to ask you. When you come again, bring me a book on the truth of religion, so that I may study it. I must restore to my guardian-angel the faith which he has lost."

XXXI

WHEREIN WE ARE LED TO MARVEL AT THE READINESS WITH WHICH AN HONEST MAN OF TIMID AND GENTLE NATURE CAN COMMIT A HORRIBLE CRIME

ROFOUNDLY distressed by the dark utterances of young Maurice, Monsieur Sariette took a motor-omnibus, and went to see Père Guinardon, his friend, his only friend, the one person in the whole world whom it gave him pleasure to see and hear. When Monsieur Sariette entered the shop in the Rue de Courcelles, Guinardon was alone, dozing in the depths of an antique arm-chair. His face, surrounded by his curly hair and luxuriant beard, was crimson in hue. Little violet filaments spread a network about the fleshy part of his nose, to which the wines of Burgundy had imparted a purple tint; for there was no longer any disguising the fact, Père Guinardon drank. Two feet away from him, on the fair Octavie's work-table, a rose, all but withered, drooped in an empty vase, and in a basket a piece of embroidery was lying unfinished and neglected. The young Octavie's absences from the shop were growing more and more frequent, and Monsieur Blancmesnil never called when she was not there. The reason of this was that they were meeting three times a week at five o'clock in a house close to the Champs Elysées. Père Guinardon knew nothing of that. He did not know the full extent of his misfortune, but he suffered.

Monsieur Sariette shook his old friend by the hand; but he did not enquire for the young Octavie, for he refused to recognise the connexion. He would sooner have talked about Zéphyrine, who had been so cruelly deserted, and whom he hoped the old man would make his lawful wife. But Monsieur Sariette was prudent. He contented himself with asking Guinardon how he was.

"Perfectly well," was Guinardon's reply; but he felt ill, for either age and love-making had undermined his sturdy constitution, or else young Octavie's faithlessness had dealt her lover a fatal blow.

"God be praised," he went on, "I still retain my powers of mind and body. I am chaste. Be chaste, Sariette. Chastity is strength."

That evening Père Guinardon had taken some specially valuable books out of the king-wood cabinet to show to a distinguished bibliophile, Monsieur Victor Meyer, and after the latter's departure he had dropped off to sleep without putting them back in their places. Books had an attraction for Monsieur Sariette, and seeing these particular volumes on the marble top of the cabinet, he began to examine them with interest. The first one he looked at was *La Pucelle,* in morocco, with the English continuation. Doubtless it pained his patriotic and Christian heart to admire its text and illustrations, but a good copy was always virtuous and pure in his sight. Continuing to chat very affectionately with Guinardon, he picked up, one by one, the books which the antiquary had, for one reason or another—binding, illustrations, distinguished ownership, or scarcity—added to his stock.

Suddenly a glorious shout of joy and love broke from his lips. He had discovered the *Lucretius* of the Prior de Vendôme, his *Lucretius,* and he was clasping it to his bosom.

"Once again I behold you," he sighed, as he pressed it to his lips.

At first Père Guinardon could not quite make out what his old friend was talking about; but when the latter declared to him that the volume was from the d'Esparvieu collection, that it belonged to him, Sariette, and that he was going to take it away without further ado, the antiquary completely woke up, got on his legs, declared emphatically that the book belonged to him, Guinardon, by right of true and lawful purchase, and that he would not part with it unless he got five thousand francs for it cash down.

"You don't take in what I am telling you," answered Sariette. "The book belongs to the d'Esparvieu library; I must restore it to its place."

"*Pas de ça, Lisette*"—— hummed Guinardon.

"The book belongs to me, I tell you!"

"You are crazy, my good Sariette!"

And noticing that, as a matter of fact, the librarian had a wandering look in his eye, he took the book from him, and tried to change the conversation.

"Have you seen, Sariette, that the rascals are going to rip up the Palais Mazarin, and cover up the very heart and centre of the Old Town, the finest and most venerable place in the whole of Paris, with the deuce knows what works of art of theirs? They are worse than the Vandals, for the Vandals, although they destroyed the buildings of antiquity, did not replace them with hideous and disgusting erections and atrocious bridges like the Pont d'Alexandre. And your poor Rue Garancière, Sariette, has fallen a prey to the barbarians. What have they done with the pretty bronze mask of the Palace fountain?"

Monsieur Sariette never listened to a word of all this.

"Guinardon, you have not understood me. Now listen. This book belongs to the d'Esparvieu library. It was taken away, how or by whom I know not. Dreadful and mysterious things went on in that library. But, anyhow, the book was stolen. I need scarcely appeal to your sentiments of scrupulous probity, my dear friend. You would not like to be regarded as the receiver of stolen goods. Give me the book. I will return it to Monsieur d'Esparvieu, who will duly requite you; of that you may be sure. Rely on his generosity, and you will be acting like the downright good fellow that you are."

The antiquary smiled a bitter smile.

"Catch me relying on the generosity of that old curmudgeon of a d'Esparvieu. Why, he'd skin a flea to get its coat. Look at me, Sariette, old boy, and tell me if I look like a dunderhead. You know perfectly well that d'Esparvieu refused to give fifty francs in a second-hand shop for a portrait of Alexandre d'Esparvieu, the founder of the family, by Hersent, and that consequently the founder of the family has had to remain on the Boulevard Montparnasse, propped against a Jew hawker's stall, just opposite the cemetery, where all the dogs of the neighbourhood come and make water on him. Catch me trusting to Monsieur d'Esparvieu's liberality! You've got some bright ideas in your head, you have!"

"Very well, Guinardon, I myself will undertake to pay you any indemnity that a board of arbitrators may fix upon. Do you hear?"

"Now don't go and do the handsome for people who won't give you so much as a thank-you. This man, d'Esparvieu, has taken your knowledge, your energies, your whole life for a salary that even a valet wouldn't accept. So leave that idea alone. In any case it is too late. The book is sold."

"Sold? To whom?" asked Sariette in agonized tones.

"What does that matter? You'll never see it again. You'll hear no more about it; it's off to America."

"To America! The *Lucretius* with the arms of Philippe de Vendôme and marginalia in Voltaire's own hand! My *Lucretius* off to America!"

Père Guinardon began to laugh.

"My dear Sariette, you remind me of the Chevalier des Grieux when he learns that his darling mistress is to be transported to the Mississippi. 'My dear mistress going to the Mississippi!' says he."

"No! no!" answered Sariette, very pale, "this book shall not go to America. It shall return, as it ought, to the d'Esparvieu library. Let me have it, Guinardon."

The antiquary made a second attempt to put an end to an interview that now looked as if it might take an ugly turn.

"My good Sariette, you haven't told me what you think of my Greco. You never so much as glanced at it. It is an admirable piece of work all the same."

And Guinardon, putting the picture in a good light, went on:

"Now just look at Saint Francis here, the poor man of the Lord, the brother of Jesus. See how his fuliginous body rises heavenward like the smoke from an agreeable sacrifice, like the sacrifice of Abel."

"Give me the book, Guinardon," said Sariette, without turning his head; "give me the book."

The blood suddenly flew to Père Guinardon's head.

"That's enough of it," he shouted, as red as a turkey-cock, the veins standing out on his forehead.

And he dropped the *Lucretius* into his jacket pocket.

Straightway old Sariette flew at the antiquary, assailed him with sudden fury, and, frail and weakly as he was, butted him back into young Octavie's arm-chair.

Guinardon, in furious amazement, belched forth the most horrible abuse on the old maniac and gave him a punch that sent him staggering back four paces against the *Coronation of the Virgin,* by Fra Angelico, which fell down with a crash. Sariette returned to the charge, and tried to drag the book out of the pocket in which it lay hid. This time Père Guinardon would really have floored him had he not been blinded by the blood that was rushing to his head, and hit sideways at the work-table of his absent mistress. Sariette fastened himself on to his bewildered adversary, held him down in the arm-chair, and with his little bony hands clutched him by the neck, which, red as it was already, became a deep crimson. Guinardon struggled to get free, but the little fingers, feeling the mass of soft, warm flesh about them, embedded themselves in it with delicious ecstasy. Some unknown force made them hold fast to their prey. Guinardon's throat began to rattle, saliva was oozing from one corner of his mouth. His enormous frame quivered now and again beneath the grasp; but the tremors grew more and more intermittent and spasmodic. At last they ceased. The murderous hands did not let go their hold. Sariette had to make a violent effort to loose them. His temples were buzzing. Nevertheless he could hear the rain falling outside, muffled steps going past on the pavement, newspaper men shouting in the distance. He could see umbrellas passing along in the dim light. He drew the book from the dead man's pocket and fled.

The fair Octavie did not go back to the shop that night. She went to sleep in a little entresol underneath the bric-a-brac stores which Monsieur de Blancmesnil had recently bought for her in this same Rue de Courcelles. The workman whose task it was to shut up the shop found the antiquary's body still warm. He called Madame Lenain, the concierge, who laid Guinardon on the couch, lit a couple of candles, put a sprig of box in a saucer of holy water, and closed the dead man's eyes. The doctor who was called in to certify the death ascribed it to apoplexy.

Zéphyrine, informed of what had happened by Madame Lenain, hastened to the house, and sat up all night with the body. The dead man looked as if he were sleeping. In the flickering light of the candles El Greco's Saint mounted upwards like a wreath of smoke, the gold of the Primitives gleamed in the shadows. Near the deathbed a little woman by Baudouin was plainly discernible giving herself a douche. All through the night Zéphyrine's lamentations could be heard fifty yards away.

"He's dead, he's dead!" she kept saying. "My friend, my divinity, my all, my love—— But no! he is not dead, he moves. It is I, Michel; I, your Zéphyrine. Awake, hear me! Answer me; I love you; if ever I caused you pain, forgive me. Dead! dead! O my God! See how beautiful he is. He was so good, so clever, so kind. My God! My God! My God! If I had been there he would not now be lying dead. Michel! Michel!"

When morning came she was silent. They thought she had fallen asleep. She was dead too.

<h2 style="text-align:center">XXXII</h2>

WHICH DESCRIBES HOW NECTAIRE'S FLUTE WAS HEARD IN THE TAVERN OF CLODOMIR

ADAME DE LA VERDELIÈRE having failed to force an *entrée* as sick-nurse, returned after several days had elapsed,—during the absence of Madame des Aubels,—to ask Maurice d'Esparvieu for his subscription to the French churches. Arcade led her to the bedside of the convalescent. Maurice whispered in the angel's ear:

"Traitor, deliver me from this ogress immediately, or you will be answerable for the evil which will soon befall."

"Be calm," said Arcade, with a confident air.

After the conventional complimentary flourishes, Madame de la Verdelière signed to Maurice to dismiss the angel. Maurice feigned not to understand. And Madame de la Verdelière disclosed the ostensible reason of her visit.

"Our churches," she said, "our beloved country churches,—what is to become of them?"

Arcade gazed at her angelically and sighed.

"They will disappear, Madame; they will fall into ruin. And what a pity! I shall be inconsolable. The church amid the villagers' cottages is like the hen amidst her chickens."

"Just so!" exclaimed Madame de la Verdelière with a delighted smile. "It is just like that."

"And the spires, Madame?"

"Oh, Monsieur, the spires! . . ."

"Yes, the spires, Madame, that stick up into the skies towards the little Cherubim, like so many syringes."

Madame de la Verdelière incontinently left the place.

That same day Monsieur l'Abbé Patouille came to offer the wounded man good counsel and consolation. He exhorted him to break with his bad companions and to be reconciled to his family.

He drew a picture of the sorrowful father, the mother in tears, ready to receive their long-lost child with open arms. Renouncing with manly effort a life of profligacy and deluding joys, Maurice would recover his peace and strength of mind, he would free himself from devouring chimeras, and shake off the Evil Spirit.

Young d'Esparvieu thanked Abbé Patouille for all his kindness, and made a protestation of his religious feelings.

"Never," said he, "have I had such faith. And never have I been in such need of it. Just imagine, Monsieur l'Abbé, I have to teach my guardian angel his catechism all over again, for he has quite forgotten it!"

Monsieur l'Abbé Patouille heaved a deep sigh, and exhorted his dear child to pray, there being no other resource but prayer for a soul assailed by the Devil.

"Monsieur l'Abbé," asked Maurice, "may I introduce my guardian angel to you? Do stay a moment; he has gone to get me some cigarettes."

"Unhappy child!"

And Abbé Patouille's fat cheeks drooped in token of affliction. But almost immediately they plumped up again, as a sign of light-heartedness. For in his heart there was matter for rejoicing. Public opinion was improving. The Jacobins, the Freemasons, the Coalitionists were everywhere in disgrace. The Smart Set led the way. The Académie Française was of the right way of thinking. The number of Christian schools was increasing by leaps and bounds. The young men of the Quartier Latin were submitting to the Church, and the École Normale exhaled the perfume of the seminary. The Cross was gaining the day; but money was wanted,— more money, always money.

After six weeks' rest, Maurice was allowed by his doctor to take a drive. He wore his arm in a sling. His mistress and his friend went with him. They drove to the Bois, and took a gentle pleasure in looking upon the grass and the trees. They smiled on everything and everything smiled on them. As Arcade had said, their faults had made them better. By the unlooked-for ways of jealousy and anger, Maurice had attained to calm and kindliness. He still loved Gilberte and he loved her with an indulgent love. The angel still desired her as much as ever, but having once possessed her, his desire had lost the sting of curiosity. Gilberte forbore trying to please, and thereby pleased the more. They drank milk at the Cascade, and found it good. They were all three innocent. Arcade forgot the injustice of the old tyrant of the world. But he was soon to be reminded of it.

On entering his friend's house, he found Zita awaiting him, looking like a statue in ivory and gold.

"You excite my pity," she said to him. "The day is at hand the like of which has never dawned since the beginning of Time, and perhaps will never dawn again before the Sun enters with all its train into the constellation of Hercules. We are on the eve of surprising Ialdabaoth in his palace of porphyry, and you, who are burning to deliver the heavens, who were so eager to enter in triumph into your emancipated country,—you suddenly forget your noble purpose and fall asleep in the arms of the daughters of men. What pleasure can you find in intercourse with these unclean little animals, composed, as they are, of elements so unstable that they may be said to be in a state of constant evanescence? O Arcade! I was indeed right to distrust you. You are but an intellectual; you do but feel idle curiosity. You are incapable of action."

"You misjudge me, Zita," replied the angel. "It is the nature of the sons of heaven to love the daughters of men. Corruptible though it be, the material part of women and of flowers charms the senses none the less. But not one of these little animals can make me forget my hatred and my love, and I am ready to rise up against Ialdabaoth."

Zita expressed her satisfaction at seeing him in this resolute mood. She urged him to pursue the accomplishment of this vast undertaking with undiminished ardour. Nothing must be hurried or deferred.

"A great action, Arcade, is made up of a multitude of small ones; the most majestic whole is composed of a thousand minute details. Let us neglect nothing."

She had come to take him to a meeting where his presence was required. They were to take a census of the revolutionaries.

She added but one word:

"Nectaire will be there."

When Maurice saw Zita, he deemed her lacking in attraction. She failed to please him because she was perfectly beautiful and because true beauty always caused him painful surprise. Zita inspired him with antipathy when he learned that she was an angel in revolt and that she had come to seek Arcade to take him away among the conspirators.

The poor child tried to retain his companion by all the means that his wit and the circumstances afforded him. If his guardian angel would only remain with him, he would take him to a magnificent boxing-match, to a "revue" where he would witness the apotheosis of Poincaré, or, lastly, to a certain house he knew of where he would behold women remarkable for their beauty, talents, vices, or deformities. But the angel would not allow himself to be tempted, and said he was going with Zita.

"What for?"

"To plot the conquest of the skies."

"Still the same nonsense! The conquest of —— but there, I proved to you that it was neither possible nor desirable."

"Good night, Maurice."

"You are going? Well, I will accompany you."

And Maurice, his arm in a sling, went with Arcade and Zita all the way to Clodomir's restaurant at Montmartre, where the tables were laid in an arbour in the garden.

Prince Istar and Théophile were already there, with a little creature who looked like a child, and was, in fact, a Japanese angel.

"We are only waiting for Nectaire," said Zita.

And at that moment the old gardener noiselessly appeared. He took his seat, and his dog lay down at his feet. French cooking is the best in the world. It is a glory that will transcend all others when humanity has grown wise enough to put the spit above the sword. Clodomir served the angels, and the mortal who was with them, with a soup made of cabbages and bacon, a loin of pork and kidneys cooked in wine, thereby proving himself a real Montmartre cook, and showing that he had not been spoilt by the Americans, who corrupt the most excellent *chefs* of the City of Restaurants.

Clodomir brought forth some Bordeaux, which, though unrecorded among the renowned vintages of Médoc, gave evidence by its choice and delicate aroma of the high nobility of its origin. We must not omit to chronicle that, after this wine and many others had been drunk, the cellarman, in solemn state, produced a Burgundy choice and rare, full-bodied yet not heavy, generous yet delicate, rich with the true Burgundian mellowness, a noble and, withal, a somewhat heady wine, that brought delight alike to mind and sense.

"Hail to thee, Dionysus, greatest of the Gods!" cried old Nectaire, raising his glass on high. "I drink to thee who wilt restore the Golden Age, and give again to mortal men, who will become heroes as of old, the grapes which the Lesbians used to cull, long since, from the vines of Methymna; who wilt restore the vineyards of Thasus, the white clusters of Lake Mareotis, the storehouses of Falernus, the vines of the Tmolus, and the wine of Phanae, of all wines the king. And the juice thereof shall be divine, and, as in old Silenus' day, men shall grow drunk with Wisdom and with Love."

When the coffee was served, Prince Istar, Zita, Arcade, and the Japanese angel took it in turns to give an account of the forces assembled against Ialdabaoth. Angels, in exchanging eternal bliss for the sufferings of an earthly life, grow in intelligence, acquire the means of going astray and the faculty of self-contradiction. Consequently their meetings, like those of men, are tumultuous and confused. Did one of them deal in figures, the others immediately called them in question. They could not add one number to another without quarrelling, and arithmetic itself, subjected to passion, lost its certitude. The Kerûb, who had brought with him the pious Théophile, waxed indignant when he heard the musician praising the Lord, and rained down such blows on his head as would have felled an ox. But the head of a musician is harder than a bucranium, and the blows which Théophile received did not avail to modify that angel's notion of divine providence. Arcade, having at great length set up his scientific idealism in opposition to Zita's pragmatism, the beautiful archangel told him that he argued badly.

"And you are surprised at that!" exclaimed young Maurice's guardian angel. "I argue, like you, in the language of human beings. And what is human language but the cry of the beasts of the forests or the mountains, complicated and corrupted by arrogant anthropoids. How then, Zita, can one be expected to argue well with a collection of angry or plaintive sounds like that? Angels do not reason at all; men, being superior to the angels, reason imperfectly. I will not mention the professors who think to define the absolute with the aid of cries that they have inherited from the pithecanthropoid monkeys, marsupials, and reptiles, their ancestors! It is a colossal joke! How it would amuse the demiurge, if he had any brains!"

It was a beautiful starlight night. The gardener was silent.

"Nectaire," said the beautiful archangel, "play to us on your flute, if you are not afraid that the Earth and Heaven will be stirred to their depths thereby."

Nectaire took up his flute. Young Maurice lighted a cigarette. The flame burnt brightly for a moment, casting back the sky and its stars into the shadows, and then died out. And Nectaire sang of the flame on his divine flute. The silvery voice soared aloft and sang:

"That flame was a whole universe which fulfilled its destiny in less than a minute. Suns and planets were formed therein. Venus Urania apportioned the orbits of the wandering spheres in those infinite spaces. Beneath the breath of Eros—the first of the gods,—plants, animals, and thought sprang into being. In the twenty seconds which hurried by betwixt the life and death of those worlds, civilizations were unfolded, and empires sank in long decline. Mothers shed tears, and songs of love, cries of hatred, and sighs of victims rose upward to the silent skies.

"In proportion to its minuteness, that universe lasted as long as this one—whereof we see a few atoms glittering above our heads—

has lasted or will last. They are, one no less than the other, but a gleam in the Infinite."

As the clear, pure notes welled up into the charmed air, the earth melted into a soft mist, the stars revolved rapidly in their orbits, the Great Bear fell asunder, its parts flew far and wide. Orion's belt was shattered; the Pole Star forsook its magnetic axis. Sirius, whose incandescent flame had lit up the far horizon, grew blue, then red, flickered, and suddenly died out. The shaken constellations formed new signs which were extinguished in their turn. By its incantations the magic flute had compressed into one brief moment the life and the movement of this universe which seems unchanging and eternal both to men and angels. It ceased, and the heavens resumed their immemorial aspect. Nectaire had vanished. Clodomir asked his guests if they were pleased with the cabbage soup which, in order that it might be strong, had been kept simmering for twenty-four hours on the fire, and he sang the praises of the Beaujolais which they had drunk.

The night was mild. Arcade, accompanied by his guardian angel, Théophile, Prince Istar, and the Japanese angel, escorted Zita home.

<h2 style="text-align:center">XXXIII</h2>

<h3 style="text-align:center">HOW A DREADFUL CRIME PLUNGES PARIS INTO A STATE OF TERROR</h3>

THE city was asleep. Their footsteps rang loudly on the deserted pavement. Having reached the corner of the Rue Feutrier, half-way up Montmartre, the little company halted before the dwelling of the beautiful angel. Arcade was talking about the Thrones and Dominations with Zita, who, her finger on the bell, could not make up her mind to ring. Prince Istar was tracing the mechanism of a new sort of bomb on the pavement with the end of his stick, and bellowed so loudly that he woke the sleeping citizens and stirred into activity the amatory passions of the neighbouring Pasiphaës. Théophile was singing the barcarole from the second act of *Aline, Queen of Golconda* at the top of his voice. Maurice, his arm in a sling, was fencing left-handed with the Japanese, striking sparks from the pavement, and crying "A hit! a hit!" in a piercing voice.

Meanwhile Inspector Grolle at the corner of the next street was dreaming. He had the bearing of a Roman legionary and displayed all the characteristics of that proudly servile race, who, ever since men first took to building cities, have been the mainstay of Empires and the support of ruling houses. Inspector Grolle was very strong, but very tired. He suffered from an arduous profession and from lack of food. He was a man devoted to duty, but still a man, and he was unable to resist the wiles, the charms, and the blandishments of the gay ladies whom he met in swarms in the shadows along the empty streets and round about pieces of waste ground; he loved them. He loved like a soldier under arms. It tired him, but courage conquered fatigue. Though he had not yet reached the middle of Life's way, he longed for sweet repose and peaceful country pursuits. At the corner of the Rue Muller, on this mild night, he stood lost in thought. He was dreaming of the house where he was born, of the little olive wood, of his father's bit of ground, of his old mother, bent with long and heavy labour, whom he would never see again. Roused from his reverie by the nocturnal tumult, Inspector Grolle turned the corner of the street, and looked rather unfavourably at the band of loiterers, wherein his social instinct suspected enemies of law and order. He was patient and resolute. After a lengthy silence, he said, with awe-inspiring calm:

"Move on, there!"

But Maurice and the Japanese angel were fencing and heard nothing. The musician heard nothing but his own melodies. Prince Istar was absorbed in the explanation of explosive formulæ. Zita was discussing with Arcade the greatest enterprise that had ever been conceived since the solar system issued from its original nebula,—and thus they all remained unconscious of their surroundings.

"Move on, I tell you!" repeated Inspector Grolle.

This time the angels heard the solemn word of warning, but either through indifference or contempt, they neglected to obey, and continued their talk, their songs, and their cries.

"So you want to be taken up, do you?" shouted Inspector Grolle, clapping his great hand on Prince Istar's shoulder.

The Kerûb was indignant at this vile contact, and with one blow from his formidable fist sent the Inspector flying into the gutter. But Constable Fesandet was already running to his comrade's aid, and they both fell upon the Prince, whom they belaboured with mechanic fury, and whom, notwithstanding his strength and weight, they would perchance have dragged all bleeding to the police station, had not the Japanese angel overset them one after the other without effort, and reduced them to writhing and shrieking in the mud, before Maurice, Arcade, and Zita had time to intervene. As to the angelic musician, he stood apart trembling, and invoked the heavens.

At this moment two bakers who were kneading their dough in a neighbouring cellar ran out at the noise, in their white aprons, stripped to the waist. With an instinctive feeling for social solidarity they took the side of the downfallen police. Théophile conceived a just fear at the sight of them, and fled away; they caught

him and were about to hand him over to the guardians of the
peace, when Arcade and Zita tore him from their hands. The fight
continued, unequal and terrible, between the two angels and the
two bakers. Like an athlete of Lysippus in strength and beauty,
Arcade smothered his heavy adversary in his arms. The beautiful
archangel drove her dagger into the baker who had attacked her.
A dark stream of blood flowed down over his hairy chest, and the
two white-capped supporters of the law sank to the ground.

Constable Fesandet had fainted face downwards in the gutter.
But Inspector Grolle, who had got up, blew a blast on his whistle
loud enough to be heard at the neighbouring police-station, and
sprang upon young Maurice, who, having but one arm with which
to defend himself, fired his revolver with his left hand at the inspector, who put his hand to his heart, staggered, and dropped
down. He gave a long sigh, and the shadows of eternity darkened
his eyes.

Meanwhile, windows opened one by one, and heads looked out on
the street. A sound of heavy steps approached. Two policemen on
bicycles debouched upon the street. Thereupon Prince Istar flung a
bomb which shook the ground, put out the gas, shattered some of
the houses, and enveloped the fight of young Maurice and the
angels in a dense smoke.

Arcade and Maurice came to the conclusion that the safest thing
to do after this adventure was to return to the little flat in the Rue
de Rome. They would certainly not be sought for immediately and
probably not at all, the bomb thrown by the Kerûb having fortunately wiped out all witnesses of the affair. They fell asleep
towards dawn, and they had not yet awoke at ten o'clock in the
morning when the concierge brought their tea. While eating his
toast and butter and slice of ham, young d'Esparvieu remarked to
the angel:

"I used to think that a murder was something very extraordinary. Well, I was mistaken. It is the simplest, the most natural
action in the world."

"And of most ancient tradition," replied the angel. "For long
centuries it was both usual and necessary for man to kill and de-
spoil his fellows. It is still recommended in warfare. It is also honourable to attempt human life in certain definite circumstances, and
people approved when you wanted to assassinate me, Maurice, because it appeared to you that I had been intimate with your mistress. But killing a police-inspector is not the action of a man of
fashion."

"Be silent," exclaimed Maurice, "be silent, scoundrel! I killed
the poor Inspector instinctively, not knowing what I was doing. I
am grieved to my heart about it. But it is not I, it is you who are
the guilty one; you who are the murderer. It was you who lured
me along this path of revolt and violence which leads to the pit.

You have been my undoing. You have sacrificed my peace of mind, my happiness, to your pride and your wickedness, and all in vain; for I warn you, Arcade, you will not succeed in what you are undertaking."

The concierge brought in the newspapers. On seeing them Maurice grew pale. They announced the outrage in the Rue de Ramey in huge headlines:

"An Inspector killed—Two cyclist policemen and two bakers seriously wounded—Three houses blown up, numerous victims."

Maurice let the paper drop, and said in a weak, plaintive voice:

"Arcade, why did you not slay me in the little garden at Versailles amidst the roses, to the song of the blackbirds?"

Meanwhile terror reigned in Paris. In the public squares, and in the crowded streets, housewives, string-bag in hand, grew pale as

they listened to the story of the crime, and consigned the perpetrators to the most dreadful punishment. Shopkeepers, standing at the doors of their shops, put it all down to the anarchists, syndicalists, socialists, and radicals, and demanded that special measures should be taken against them.

The more thoughtful people recognized the handiwork of the Jew and the German, and demanded the expulsion of all aliens. Many vaunted the ways of America and advocated lynching. In addition to the printed news sinister rumours became current. Explosions had been heard at various places; everywhere bombs had been discovered; everywhere individuals, taken for malefactors, had been struck down by the popular arm and given up to justice, torn to ribbons. On the Place de la République a drunkard who was crying "Down with the police" was torn to pieces by the crowd.

The President of the Council and Minister of Justice held long conferences with the Prefect of Police, and they agreed to take immediate action. In order to allay the excitement of the Parisians, they arrested five or six hooligans out of the thirty thousand which the Capital contains. The chief of the Russian police, believing he recognised in this attack the methods of the Nihilists, demanded, on behalf of his Government, that a dozen refugees should be given up. The demand was immediately granted. Proceedings were also taken for certain individuals to be extradited to ensure the safety of the King of Spain.

On learning of these energetic measures, Paris breathed once more, and the evening papers congratulated the Government. There was excellent news of the wounded. They were out of danger and identified as their assailants all who were brought before them.

True, Inspector Grolle was dead; but two Sisters of Mercy kept vigil at his side, and the President of the Council came and laid the Cross of Honour on the breast of this victim of duty.

At night there were panics. In the Avenue de la Révolte the police, noticing a travelling acrobat's caravan on a piece of waste ground, took it for the retreat of a band of robbers. They whistled for help, and when they were a goodly number, attacked the caravan. Some worthy citizens joined them; fifteen thousand revolver-shots were fired, the caravan was blown up with dynamite, and among the débris they found the corpse of a monkey.

XXXIV

WHICH CONTAINS AN ACCOUNT OF THE ARREST OF BOUCHOTTE AND MAURICE, OF THE DISASTER WHICH BEFELL THE D'ESPARVIEU LIBRARY, AND OF THE DEPARTURE OF THE ANGELS

AURICE D'ESPARVIEU passed a terrible night. At the least sound he seized his revolver that he might not fall alive into the hands of justice. When morning came he snatched the newspapers from the hands of the concierge, devoured them greedily, and gave a cry of joy; he had just read that Inspector Grolle having been taken to the Morgue for the post-mortem, the police-surgeons had only discovered bruises and contusions of a very superficial nature, and stated that death had been brought about by the rupture of an aneurism of the aorta.

"You see, Arcade," he exclaimed triumphantly; "you see I am not an assassin. I am innocent. I could never have imagined how extremely agreeable it is to be innocent."

Then he grew thoughtful, and—no unusual phenomenon—reflection dissipated his gaiety.

"I am innocent,—but there is no disguising the fact," he said, shaking his head, "I am one of a band of malefactors. I live with miscreants. You are in your right place there, Arcade, for you are deceitful, cruel, and perverse. But I come of good family and have received an excellent education, and I blush for it."

"I also," said Arcade, "have received an excellent education."

"Where was that?"

"In Heaven."

"No, Arcade, no; you never had any education. If good principles had been inculcated into you, you would still hold them. Such principles are never lost. In my childhood I learnt to revere my family, my country, my religion. I have not forgotten the lesson and I never shall. Do you know what shocks me most in you? It is not your perversity, your cruelty, your black ingratitude; it is not your agnosticism, which may be borne with at a pinch; it is not your scepticism, though it is very much out of date (for since the national awakening there is no longer any scepticism in France);— no, what disgusts me in you is your lack of taste, the bad style of your ideas, the inelegance of your doctrines. You think like an intellectual, you speak like a freethinker, you have theories which reek of radicalism and Combeism and all ignoble systems. Get along with you! you disgust me. Arcade, my old friend, Arcade, my dear angel, Arcade, my beloved child, listen to your guardian angel!

Yield to my prayers, renounce your mad ideas; become good, simple, innocent, and happy once more. Put on your hat, come with me to Nôtre-Dame. We will say a prayer and burn a candle together."

Meanwhile public opinion was still active in the matter; the leading papers, the organs of the national awakening, in articles of real elevation and real depth, unravelled the philosophy of this monstrous attack which was revolting to the conscience. They discovered the real origin, the indirect but effective cause in the revolutionary doctrines which had been disseminated unchecked, in the weakening of social ties, the relaxing of moral discipline, in the repeated appeals to every appetite, to every greedy desire. It would be needful, so as to cut down the evil at its root, to repudiate as quickly as possible all such chimeras and Utopias as syndicalism, the income-tax, etc., etc., etc. Many newspapers, and these not the least important, pointed out that the recrudescence of crime was but the natural fruit of impiety and concluded that the salvation of society lay in an unanimous and sincere return to religion. On the Sunday which followed the crime the congregations in the churches were noticed to be unusually large.

Judge Salneuve, who was entrusted with the task of investigation, first examined the persons arrested by the police, and lost his way among attractive but illusory clues; however, the report of the detective Montremain, which was laid before him, put him on the right road, and soon led him to recognise the miscreants of La Jonchère as the authors of the crime of the Rue de Ramey. He ordered a search to be made for Arcade and Zita, and issued a warrant against Prince Istar, on whom the detectives laid hands as he was leaving Bouchotte's, where he had been depositing some bombs of new design. The Kerûb, on learning the detective's intentions, smiled broadly and asked them if they had a powerful motor-car. On their replying that they had one at the door, he assured them that was all he wanted. Thereupon he felled the two detectives on the stairs, walked up to the waiting car, flung the chauffeur under a motor-'bus which was opportunely passing, and seized the steering wheel under the eyes of the terrified crowd.

That same evening Monsieur Jeancourt, the Police Magistrate, entered Théophile's rooms just when Bouchotte was swallowing a raw egg to clear her voice, for she was to sing her new song, "They haven't got any in Germany," at the "National Eldorado" that evening. The musician was absent. Bouchotte received the Magistrate, and received him with a hauteur which intensified the simplicity of her attire; Bouchotte was *en déshabille*. The worthy Magistrate seized the score of *Aline, Queen of Golconda,* and the love-letters which the singer carefully preserved in the drawer of the table by her bed, for she was an orderly young woman. He was about to withdraw when he espied a cupboard, which he opened with a careless air, and found machines capable of blowing up half Paris, and a pair of large white wings, whose nature and use appeared inexplicable to him. Bouchotte was invited to complete her toilette, and, in spite of her cries, was taken off to the police-station.

Monsieur Salneuve was indefatigable. After the examination of the papers seized in Bouchotte's house, and acting on the information of Montremain, he issued a warrant for the arrest of young d'Esparvieu, which was executed on Wednesday, the 27th May, at seven o'clock in the morning, with great discretion. For three days Maurice had neither slept nor eaten, loved nor lived. He had not a moment's doubt as to the nature of the matutinal visit. At the sight of the police magistrate a strange calm fell on him. Arcade had not returned to sleep in the flat. Maurice begged the magistrate to wait for him, dressed with care, and then accompanied the magistrate to the taxi that was waiting at the door. He felt a calmness of mind which was barely disturbed when the door of the Conciergerie closed on him. Alone in his cell, he climbed upon the table to look out. His tranquillity was due to his weariness of spirit, to his numbed senses, and to the fact that he no longer stood in fear of arrest. His misfortune endowed him with superior wisdom. He felt he had fallen into a state of grace. He did not think too highly or too humbly of himself, but left his cause in the hands of God. With no desire to cover up his faults, which he would not hide even from himself, he addressed himself in mind to Providence, to point out that if he had fallen into disorder and rebellion it was to lead his erring angel back into the straight path. He stretched himself on the couch and slept in peace.

On hearing of the arrest of a music-hall singer and of a young man of fashion, both Paris and the provinces felt painful surprise. Deeply stirred by the tragic accounts which the leading newspapers were bringing out, the general idea was that the sort of people the authorities ought to bring to justice were ferocious anarchists, all reeking and dripping from deeds of blood and arson; but they failed to understand what the world of Art and Fashion should have to do with such things. At this news, which he was one of the last to hear, the President of the Council and Keeper of the Seals started up in his chair. The Sphinxes that adorned it were less terrible than he, and in the throes of his angry meditation he cut the mahogany of his imperial table with his penknife, after the manner of Napoleon. And when Judge Salneuve, whose attendance he had commanded, appeared before him, the President flung his penknife in the grate, as Louis XIV flung his cane out of the window in the presence of Lauzun; and it cost him a supreme effort to master himself and to say in a voice of suppressed fury:

"Are you mad? Surely I said often enough that I meant the plot to be anarchist, anti-social, fundamentally anti-social and antigovernmental, with a shade of syndicalism. I have made it clear enough that I wanted it kept within these lines; and what do you go and make of it? . . . The vengeance of anarchists and aspirants to freedom? Whom do you arrest? A singer adored of the nationalist public, and the son of a man highly esteemed in the Catholic party, who receives our bishops and has the *entrée* to the Vatican; a man who may be one day sent as ambassador to the Pope. At one blow you alienate one hundred and sixty Deputies and forty Senators of the Right on the very eve of a motion to discuss the question of religious pacification; you embroil me with my friends of to-day, with my friends of to-morrow. Was it to find out if you were in the same dilemma as des Aubels that you seized the love-letters of young Maurice d'Esparvieu? I can put your mind at rest on that point. You are, and all Paris knows it. But it is not to avenge your personal affronts that you are on the Bench."

"Monsieur le Garde des Sceaux," murmured the Judge, nearly apoplectic and in a choked voice. "I am an honest man."

"You are a fool . . . and a provincial. Listen to me; if Maurice d'Esparvieu and Mademoiselle Bouchotte are not released within half an hour I will crush you like a piece of glass. Be off!"

Monsieur René d'Esparvieu went himself to fetch his son from the Conciergerie and took him back to the old house in the Rue Garancière. The return was triumphant. The news had been disseminated that Maurice had with generous imprudence interested himself in an attempt to restore the monarchy, and that Judge Salneuve, the infamous freemason, the tool of Combes and André, had tried to compromise the young man by making him out to be an accomplice of a band of criminals.

That was what Abbé Patouille seemed to think, and he answered for Maurice as for himself. It was known, moreover, that breaking with his father, who had rallied to the support of the Republic, young d'Esparvieu was on the high road to becoming an out-and-out Royalist. The people who had an inside knowledge of things saw in his arrest the vengeance of the Jews. Was not Maurice a notorious anti-Semite? Catholic youths went forth to hurl imprecations at Judge Salneuve under the windows of his residence in the Rue Guénégaud, opposite the Mint.

On the Boulevard du Palais a band of students presented Maurice with a branch of palm. Maurice made a charming reply.

Maurice was overcome with emotion when he beheld the old house in which his childhood had been spent, and fell weeping into his mother's arms.

It was a great day, unhappily marred by one painful incident. Monsieur Sariette, who had lost his reason as a consequence of the shocking events that had taken place in the Rue de Courcelles, had suddenly become violent. He had shut himself up in the library, and there he had remained for twenty-four hours, uttering the most horrible cries, and, turning a deaf ear alike to threats and entreaties, refused to come out. He had spent the night in a condition of extreme restlessness, for all night long the lamp had been seen passing rapidly to and fro behind the curtains. In the morning, hearing Hippolyte shouting to him from the court below, he opened the window of the Hall of the Spheres and the Philosophers, and heaved two or three rather weighty tomes on to the old valet's head. The whole of the domestic staff—men, women, and boys—hurried to the spot, and the librarian proceeded to throw out books by the armful on to their heads. In view of the gravity of the situation, Monsieur René d'Esparvieu did not disdain to intervene. He appeared in night-cap and dressing-gown, and attempted to reason with the poor lunatic, whose only reply was to pour forth torrents of abuse on the man whom till then he had worshipped as his benefactor, and to endeavour to crush him beneath all the Bibles, all the Talmuds, all the sacred books of India and Persia, all the Greek Fathers, and all the Latin Fathers, Saint John Chrysostom, Saint Gregory Nazianzen, Saint Augustine, Saint Jerome, all the apologists, ay! and under the *Histoire des Variations,* annotated by Bossuet himself! Octavos, quartos, folios came crashing down, and lay in a sordid heap on the courtyard pavement. The letters of Gassendi, of Père Mersenne, of Pascal, were blown about hither and thither by the wind. The lady's-maid who had stooped down to rescue some of the sheets from the gutter got a blow on the head from an enormous Dutch atlas. Madame René d'Esparvieu had been terrified by the ominous sounds, and appeared on the scene without waiting to apply the finishing touches of powder and paint. When he caught sight of her, old Sariette became more violent than ever. Down they came one after another as hard as he could pelt them; the busts of the poets, philosophers, and historians of antiquity—Homer, Æschylus, Sophocles, Euripides, Herodotus, Thucydides, Socrates, Plato, Aristotle, Demosthenes, Cicero, Virgil, Horace, Seneca, Epictetus—all lay scattered on the ground. The celestial sphere and the terrestrial globe descended with a terrifying crash that was followed by a ghastly hush, broken only by the shrill laughter of little Léon, who was looking down on the scene from a window above. A locksmith having opened the library door, all the household hastened to enter, and found the aged Sariette entrenched behind piles of books, busily engaged in tearing and slashing away at the *Lucretius* of the Prior de Vendôme annotated in Voltaire's own hand. They had to force a way through the barricade. But the maniac, perceiving that his stronghold was being invaded, fled away and escaped on to the roof. For two whole hours he gave vent to shouts and yells that were heard far and wide. In the Rue Garancière the crowd kept growing bigger and bigger. All had their eyes fixed on the unhappy creature, and whenever he stumbled on the slates, which cracked beneath him, they gave a shout of terror. In the midst of the crowd, the Abbé Patouille, who expected every moment to see him hurled into space, was reciting the prayers for the dying, and making ready to give him the absolution *en extremis.* There was a cordon of police round the house keeping order. Someone summoned the fire-brigade, and the sound of their approach was soon heard. They placed a ladder against the wall of the house, and after a terrific struggle managed to secure the maniac, who in the course of his desperate resistance had one of the muscles of his arm torn out. He was immediately removed to an asylum.

Maurice dined at home, and there were smiles of tenderness and affection when Victor, the old butler, brought on the roast veal. Monsieur l'Abbé Patouille sat at the right hand of the Christian mother, unctuously contemplating the family which Heaven had so plentifully blessed. Nevertheless, Madame d'Esparvieu was ill at ease. Every day she received anonymous letters of so insulting and coarse a nature that she thought at first they must come from a discharged footman. She now knew they were the handiwork of her youngest daughter, Berthe, a mere child! Little Léon, too, gave her pain and anxiety. He paid no attention to his lessons, and was given to bad habits. He showed a cruel disposition. He had plucked his sister's canaries alive; he stuck innumerable pins into the chair on which Mademoiselle Caporal was accustomed to sit, and had stolen fourteen francs from the poor girl, who did nothing but cry and dab her eyes and nose from morning till night.

No sooner was dinner over than Maurice rushed off to the little dwelling in the Rue de Rome, impatient to meet his angel again. Through the door he heard a loud sound of voices, and saw assembled in the room where the apparition had taken place, Arcade, Zita, the angelic musician, and the Kerûb, who was lying on the bed, smoking a huge pipe, carelessly scorching pillows, sheets, and coverlets. They embraced Maurice, and announced their departure. Their faces shone with happiness and courage. Alone, the inspired author of *Aline, Queen of Golconda,* shed tears and raised his terrified gaze to heaven. The Kerûb forced him into the party of rebellion by setting before him two alternatives: either to allow himself to be dragged from prison to prison on earth, or to carry fire and sword into the palace of Ialdabaoth.

Maurice perceived with sorrow that the earth had scarcely any hold over them. They were setting out filled with immense hope, which was quite justifiable. Doubtless they were but a few combatants to oppose the innumerable soldiers of the sultan of the heavens; but they counted on compensating for the inferiority of their numbers by the irresistible impetus of a sudden attack. They were not ignorant of the fact that Ialdabaoth, who flatters himself on knowing all things, sometimes allows himself to be taken by surprise. And it certainly looked as if the first attack would have taken him unawares had it not been for the warning of the archangel Michael. The celestial army had made no progress since its victory over the rebels before the beginning of Time.

As regards armaments and material it was as out of date as the army of the Moors. Its generals slumbered in sloth and ignorance. Loaded with honours and riches, they preferred the delights of the banquet to the fatigues of war. Michael, the commander-in-chief, ever loyal and brave, had lost, with the passing of centuries, his fire and enthusiasm. The conspirators of 1914, on the other hand, knew the very latest and the most delicate appliances of science for the art of destruction. At length all was ready and decided upon. The army of revolt, assembled by corps each a hundred thousand angels strong, on all the waste places of the earth—steppes, pampas, deserts, fields of ice and snow—was ready to launch itelf against the sky. The angels, in modifying the rhythm of the atoms of which they are composed, are able to traverse the most varied mediums. Spirits that have descended on to the earth, being formed, since their incarnation, of too compact a substance, can no longer fly of themselves, and to rise into ethereal regions and then insensibly grow volatilized, have need of the assistance of their brothers, who, though revolutionaries like themselves, nevertheless, stayed behind in the Empyrean and remained, not immaterial (for all is matter in the Universe), but gloriously untrammelled and diaphanous. Certes, it was not without painful anxiety that Arcade, Istar, and Zita prepared themselves to pass from the heavy atmosphere of the earth to the limpid depths of the heavens. To plunge into the ether there is need to expend such energy that the most intrepid hesitate to take flight. Their very substance, while penetrating this fine medium, must in itself grow fine-spun, become vaporised, and pass from human dimensions to the volume of the vastest clouds which have ever enveloped the earth. Soon they would surpass in grandeur the uttermost planets, whose orbits they, invisible and imponderable, would traverse without disturbing.

In this enterprise—the vastest that angels could undertake—their substance would be ultimately hotter than the fire and colder than the ice, and they would suffer pangs sharper than death.

Maurice read all the daring and the pain of the undertaking in the eyes of Arcade.

"You are going?" he said to him, weeping.

"We are going, with Nectaire, to seek the great archangel to lead us to victory."

"Whom do you call thus?"

"The priests of the demiurge have made him known to you in their calumnies."

"Unhappy being," sighed Maurice.

Arcade embraced him, and Maurice felt the angel's tears as they dropped upon his cheek.

XXXV

AND LAST, WHEREIN THE SUBLIME DREAM OF SATAN IS UNFOLDED

CLIMBING the seven steep terraces which rise up from the bed of the Ganges to the temples muffled in creepers, the five angels reached, by half-obliterated paths, the wild garden filled with perfumed clusters of grapes and chattering monkeys, and, at the far end thereof, they discovered him whom they had come to seek. The archangel lay with his elbow on black cushions embroidered with golden flames. At his feet crouched lions and gazelles. Twined in the trees, tame serpents turned on him their friendly gaze. At the sight of his angelic visitors his face grew melancholy. Long since, in the days when, with his brow crowned with grapes and his sceptre of vine-leaves in his hand, he had taught and comforted mankind, his heart had many times been heavy with sorrow; but never yet, since his glorious downfall, had his beautiful face expressed such pain and anguish.

Zita told him of the black standards assembled in crowds in all the waste places of the globe; of the deliverance premeditated and prepared in the provinces of Heaven, where the first revolt had long ago been fomented.

"Prince," she went on, "your army awaits you. Come, lead it on to victory."

"Friends," replied the great archangel, "I was aware of the object of your visit. Baskets of fruit and honeycombs await you under the shade of this mighty tree. The sun is about to descend into the roseate waters of the Sacred River. When you have eaten, you will slumber pleasantly in this garden, where the joys of the intellect and of the senses have reigned since the day when I drove hence the spirit of the old Demiurge. To-morrow I will give you my answer."

Night hung its blue over the garden. Satan fell asleep. He had a dream, and in that dream, soaring over the earth, he saw it covered with angels in revolt, beautiful as gods, whose eyes darted lightning. And from pole to pole one single cry, formed of a myriad cries, mounted towards him, filled with hope and love. And Satan said:

"Let us go forth! Let us seek the ancient adversary in his high abode." And he led the countless host of angels over the celestial plains. And Satan was cognizant of what took place in the heavenly citadel. When news of this second revolt came thither, the Father said to the Son:

"The irreconcilable foe is rising once again. Let us take heed to ourselves, and in this, our time of danger, look to our defences, lest we lose our high abode."

And the Son, consubstantial with the Father, replied:

"We shall triumph under the sign that gave Constantine the victory."

Indignation burst forth on the Mountain of God. At first the faithful Seraphim condemned the rebels to terrible torture, but afterwards decided on doing battle with them. The anger burning in the hearts of all inflamed each countenance. They did not doubt of victory, but treachery was feared, and eternal darkness had been at once decreed for spies and alarmists.

There was shouting and singing of ancient hymns and praise of the Almighty. They drank of the mystic wine. Courage, over-inflated, came near to giving way, and a secret anxiety stole into the inner depths of their souls. The archangel Michael took supreme command. He reassured their minds by his serenity. His countenance, wherein his soul was visible, expressed contempt for danger. By his orders, the chiefs of the thunderbolts, the Kerûbs, grown dull with the long interval of peace, paced with heavy steps the ramparts of the Holy Mountain, and, letting the gaze of their bovine eyes wander over the glittering clouds of their Lord, strove to place the divine batteries in position. After inspecting the defences, they swore to the Most High that all was in readiness. They took counsel together as to the plan they should follow. Michael was for the offensive. He, as a consummate soldier, said it was the supreme law. Attack, or be attacked,—there was no middle course.

"Moreover," he added, "the offensive attitude is particularly suitable to the ardour of the Thrones and Dominations."

Beyond that, it was impossible to obtain a word from the valiant chief, and this silence seemed the mark of a genius sure of himself.

As soon as the approach of the enemy was announced, Michael sent forth three armies to meet them, commanded by the archangels Uriel, Raphael, and Gabriel. Standards, displaying all the colours of the Orient, were unfurled above the ethereal plains, and the thunders rolled over the starry floors. For three days and three nights was the lot of the terrible and adorable armies unknown on the Mountain of God. Towards dawn on the fourth day news came, but it was vague and confused. There were rumours of indecisive victories; of the triumph now of this side, now of that. There came reports of glorious deeds which were dissipated in a few hours.

The thunderbolts of Raphael, hurled against the rebels, had, it was said, consumed entire squadrons. The troops commanded by the impure Zita were thought to have been swallowed up in the whirlwind of a tempest of fire. It was believed that the savage Istar had been flung headlong into the gulf of perdition so suddenly that the blasphemies begun in his mouth had been forced backwards with explosive results. It was popularly supposed that Satan, laden with chains of adamant, had been plunged once again into the abyss. Meanwhile, the commanders of the three armies had sent no messages. Mutterings and murmurs, mingling with the rumours of glory, gave rise to fears of an indecisive battle, a precipitate retreat. Insolent voices gave out that a spirit of the lowest category, a guardian angel, the insignificant Arcade, had checked and routed the dazzling host of the three great archangels.

There were also rumours of wholesale defection in the Seventh Heaven, where rebellion had broken out before the beginning of Time, and some had even seen black clouds of impious angels joining the armies of the rebels on Earth. But no one lent an ear to the odious rumours, and stress was laid on the news of victory which ran from lip to lip, each statement readily finding confirmation. The high places resounded with hymns of joy; the Seraphim celebrated on harp and psaltery Sabaoth, God of Thunder. The voices of the elect united with those of the angels in glorifying the Invisible and at the thought of the bloodshed that the ministers of holy wrath had caused among the rebels, sighs of relief and jubilation were wafted from the Heavenly Jerusalem towards the Most High. But the beatitude of the most blessed, having swelled to the utmost limit before due time, could increase no more, and the very excess of their felicity completely dulled their senses.

The songs had not yet ceased when the guards watching on the ramparts signalled the approach of the first fugitives of the divine army; Seraphim on tattered wing, flying in disorder, maimed Kerûbs going on three feet. With impassive gaze, Michael, prince of warriors, measured the extent of the disaster, and his keen intelligence penetrated its causes. The armies of the living God had taken the offensive, but by one of those fatalities in war which disconcert the plans of the greatest captains, the enemy had also taken the offensive, and the effect was evident. Scarcely were the gates of the citadel opened to receive the glorious but shattered remnants of the three armies, when a rain of fire fell on the Mountain of God. Satan's army was not yet in sight, but the walls of topaz, the cupolas of emerald, the roofs of diamond, all fell in with an appalling crash under the discharge of the electrophores. The ancient thunderclouds essayed to reply, but the bolts fell short, and their thunders were lost in the deserted plains of the skies.

Smitten by an invisible foe, the faithful angels abandoned the ramparts. Michael went to announce to his God that the Holy Mountain would fall into the hands of the demon in twenty-four hours, and that nothing remained for the Master of the Heavens but to seek safety in flight. The Seraphim placed the jewels of the celestial crown in coffers. Michael offered his arm to the Queen of Heaven, and the Holy Family escaped from the palace by a subterranean passage of porphyry. A deluge of fire was falling on the citadel. Regaining his post once more, the glorious archangel declared that he would never capitulate, and straightway advanced the standards of the living God. That same evening the rebel host made its entry into the thrice-sacred city. On a fiery steed Satan led his demons. Behind him marched Arcade, Istar, and Zita. As in the ancient revels of Dionysus, old Nectaire bestrode his ass. Thereafter, floating out far behind, followed the black standards.

The garrison laid down their arms before Satan. Michael placed his flaming sword at the feet of the conquering archangel.

"Take back your sword, Michael," said Satan. "It is Lucifer who yields it to you. Bear it in defence of peace and law." Then letting his gaze fall on the leaders of the celestial cohorts, he cried in a ringing voice:

"Archangel Michael, and you, Powers, Thrones, and Dominations, swear all of you to be faithful to your God."

"We swear it," they replied with one voice.

And Satan said:

"Powers, Thrones, and Dominations, of all past wars, I wish but to remember the invincible courage that you displayed and the loyalty which you rendered to authority, for these assure me of the steadfastness of the fealty you have just sworn to me."

The following day, on the ethereal plain, Satan commanded the black standards to be distributed to the troops, and the winged soldiers covered them with kisses and bedewed them with tears.

And Satan had himself crowned God. Thronging round the glittering walls of Heavenly Jerusalem, apostles, pontiffs, virgins, martyrs, confessors, the whole company of the elect, who during the fierce battle had enjoyed delightful tranquillity, tasted infinite joy in the spectacle of the coronation.

The elect saw with ravishment the Most High precipitated into Hell, and Satan seated on the throne of the Lord. In conformity with the will of God which had cut them off from sorrow they sang in the ancient fashion the praises of their new Master.

And Satan, piercing space with his keen glance, contemplated the little globe of earth and water where of old he had planted the vine and formed the first tragic chorus. And he fixed his gaze on that Rome where the fallen God had founded his empire on fraud and lie. Nevertheless, at that moment a saint ruled over the Church. Satan saw him praying and weeping. And he said to him:

"To thee I entrust my Spouse. Watch over her faithfully. In thee I confirm the right and power to decide matters of doctrine, to regulate the use of the sacraments, to make laws and to uphold purity of morals. And the faithful shall be under obligation to conform thereto. My Church is eternal, and the gates of hell shall not prevail against it. Thou are infallible. Nothing is changed."

And the successor of the apostles felt flooded with rapture. He prostrated himself, and with his forehead touching the floor, replied:

"O Lord, my God, I recognise Thy voice! Thy breath has been wafted like balm to my heart. Blessed be Thy name. Thy will be done on Earth, as it is in Heaven. Lead us not into temptation, but deliver us from evil."

And Satan found pleasure in praise and in the exercise of his grace; he loved to hear his wisdom and his power belauded. He listened with joy to the canticles of the cherubim who celebrated his good deeds, and he took no pleasure in listening to Nectaire's flute, because it celebrated nature's self, yielded to the insect and to the blade of grass their share of power and love, and counselled happiness and freedom. Satan, whose flesh had crept, in days gone by, at the idea that suffering prevailed in the world, now felt himself inaccessible to pity. He regarded suffering and death as the happy results of omnipotence and sovereign kindness. And the savour of the blood of victims rose upwards towards him like sweet incense. He fell to condemning intelligence and to hating curiosity. He himself refused to learn anything more, for fear that in acquiring fresh knowledge he might let it be seen that he had not known everything at the very outset. He took pleasure in mystery, and believing that he would seem less great by being understood, he affected to be unintelligible. Dense fumes of Theology filled his brain. One day, following the example of his predecessor, he conceived the notion of proclaiming himself one god in three persons. Seeing Arcade smile as this proclamation was made, he drove him from his presence. Istar and Zita had long since returned to earth. Thus centuries passed like seconds. Now, one day, from the altitude of his throne, he plunged his gaze into the depths of the pit and saw Ialdabaoth in the Gehenna where he himself had long lain enchained. Amid the everlasting gloom Ialdabaoth still retained his lofty mien. Blackened and shattered, terrible and sublime, he glanced upwards at the palace of the King of Heaven with a look of proud disdain, then turned away his head. And the new god, as he looked upon his foe, beheld the light of intelligence and love pass across his sorrow-stricken countenance. And lo! Ialdabaoth was now contemplating the Earth and, seeing it sunk in wickedness and suffering, he began to foster thoughts of kindliness in his heart. On a sudden he rose up, and beating the ether with his mighty arms, as though with oars, he hastened thither to instruct and to console mankind. Already his vast shadow shed upon the unhappy planet a shade soft as a night of love.

And Satan awoke bathed in an icy sweat.

Nectaire, Istar, Arcade, and Zita were standing round him. The finches were singing.

"Comrades," said the great archangel, "no—we will not conquer the heavens. Enough to have the power. War engenders war, and victory defeat.

"God, conquered, will become Satan; Satan, conquering, will become God. May the fates spare me this terrible lot; I love the Hell which formed my genius. I love the Earth where I have done some good, if it be possible to do any good in this fearful world where beings live but by rapine. Now, thanks to us, the god of old is dispossessed of his terrestrial empire, and every thinking being on this globe disdains him or knows him not. But what matter that men should be no longer submissive to Ialdabaoth if the spirit of Ialdabaoth is still in them; if they, like him, are jealous, violent, quarrelsome, and greedy, and the foes of the arts and of beauty? What matter that they have rejected the ferocious Demiurge, if they do not hearken to the friendly demons who teach all truths; to Dionysus, Apollo, and the Muses? As to ourselves, celestial spirits, sublime demons, we have destroyed Ialdabaoth, our Tyrant, if in ourselves we have destroyed Ignorance and Fear."

And Satan, turning to the gardener, said:

"Nectaire, you fought with me before the birth of the world. We were conquered because we failed to understand that Victory is a Spirit, and that it is in ourselves and in ourselves alone that we must attack and destroy Ialdabaoth."

THE GODS ARE ATHIRST

"THE GODS ARE ATHIRST" *translated by* ALFRED ALLINSON

I

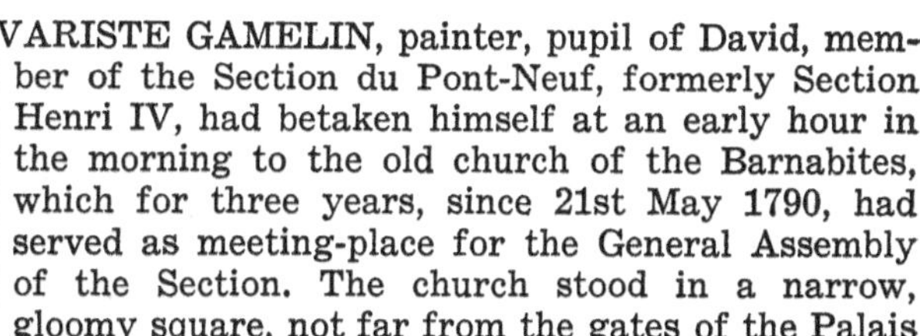VARISTE GAMELIN, painter, pupil of David, member of the Section du Pont-Neuf, formerly Section Henri IV, had betaken himself at an early hour in the morning to the old church of the Barnabites, which for three years, since 21st May 1790, had served as meeting-place for the General Assembly of the Section. The church stood in a narrow, gloomy square, not far from the gates of the Palais de Justice. On the façade, which consisted of two of the Classical orders superimposed and was decorated with inverted brackets and flaming urns, blackened by the weather and disfigured by the hand of man, the religious emblems had been battered to pieces, while above the doorway had been inscribed in black letters the Republican catchword of "Liberty, Equality, Fraternity or Death." Évariste Gamelin made his way into the nave; the same vaults which had heard the surpliced clerks of the Congregation of St. Paul sing the divine offices, now looked down on red-capped patriots assembled to elect the Municipal magistrates and deliberate on the affairs of the Section. The Saints had been dragged from their niches and replaced by the busts of Brutus, Jean-Jacques and Le Peltier. The altar had been stripped bare and was surmounted by the Table of the Rights of Man.

It was here in the nave that twice a week, from five in the evening to eleven, were held the public assemblies. The pulpit, decorated with the colours of the Nation, served as tribune for the speakers who harangued the meeting. Opposite, on the Epistle side, rose a platform of rough planks, for the accommodation of the women and children, who attended these gatherings in considerable numbers.

On this particular morning, facing a desk planted underneath the pulpit, sat in red cap and *carmagnole* complete the joiner from the Place Thionville, the *citoyen* Dupont senior, one of the twelve forming the Committee of Surveillance. On the desk stood a bottle

509

and glasses, an ink-horn, and a folio containing the text of the petition urging the Convention to expel from its bosom the twenty-two members deemed unworthy.

Évariste Gamelin took the pen and signed.

"I was sure," said the carpenter and magistrate, "I was sure you would come and give in your name, *citoyen* Gamelin. You are the real thing. But the Section is lukewarm; it is lacking in virtue. I have proposed to the Committee of Surveillance to deliver no certificate of citizenship to any one who has failed to sign the petition."

"I am ready to sign with my blood," said Gamelin, "for the proscription of these federalists, these traitors. They have desired the death of Marat: let them perish."

"What ruins us," replied Dupont senior, "is indifferentism. In a Section which contains nine hundred citizens with the right to vote there are not fifty attend the assembly. Yesterday we were eight and twenty."

"Well then," said Gamelin, "citizens must be obliged to come under penalty of a fine."

"Oh, ho!" exclaimed the joiner frowning, "but if they all came, the patriots would be in a minority. . . . *Citoyen* Gamelin, will you drink a glass of wine to the health of all good sansculottes? . . ."

On the wall of the church, on the Gospel side, could be read the words, accompanied by a black hand, the forefinger pointing to the passage leading to the cloisters: *Comité civil, Comité de surveillance, Comité de bienfaisance.* A few yards further on, you came to the door of the erstwhile sacristy, over which was inscribed: *Comité militaire.*

Gamelin pushed this door open and found the Secretary of the Committee within; he was writing at a large table loaded with books, papers, steel ingots, cartridges and samples of saltpetre-bearing soils.

"Greeting, *citoyen* Trubert. How are you?"

"I? . . . I am perfectly well."

The Secretary of the Military Committee, Fortuné Trubert, invariably made this same reply to all who troubled about his health, less by way of informing them of his welfare than to cut short any discussion on the subject. At twenty-eight, he had a parched skin, thin hair, hectic cheeks and bent shoulders. He was an optician on the Quai des Orfèvres, and owned a very old house which he had given up in '91 to a superannuated clerk in order to devote his energies to the discharge of his municipal duties. His mother, a charming woman, whose memory a few old men of the neighbourhood still cherished fondly, had died at twenty; she had left him her fine eyes, full of gentleness and passion, her pallor and timidity. From his father, optician and mathematical instrument maker to the King, carried off by the same complaint before his thirtieth year, he inherited an upright character and an industrious temperament.

Without stopping his writing:

"And you, *citoyen*," he asked, "how are you?"

"Very well. Anything new?"

"Nothing, nothing. You can see,—we are all quiet here."

"And the situation?"

"The situation is just the same."

The situation was appalling. The finest army of the Republic blockaded in Mayence; Valenciennes besieged; Fontenay taken by the Vendéens; Lyons rebellious; the Cévennes in insurrection, the frontier open to the Spaniards; two-thirds of the Departments invaded or revolted; Paris helpless before the Austrian cannon, without money, without bread!

Fortuné Trubert wrote on calmly. The Sections being instructed by resolution of the Committee to carry out the levy of twelve thousand men for La Vendée, he was drawing up directions relating to the enrolment and arming of the contingent which the "Pont-Neuf," erstwhile "Henri IV," was to supply. All the muskets in store were to be handed over to the men requisitioned for the front; the National Guard of the Section would be armed with fowling-pieces and pikes.

"I have brought you here," said Gamelin, "the schedule of the church-bells to be sent to the Luxembourg to be converted into cannon."

Évariste Gamelin, albeit he had not a penny, was inscribed among the active members of the Section; the law accorded this privilege only to such citizens as were rich enough to pay a contribution equivalent in amount to three days' work, and demanded a ten days' contribution to qualify an elector for office. But the Section du Pont-Neuf, enamoured of equality and jealous of its independence, regarded as qualified both for the vote and for office every citizen who had paid out of his own pocket for his National Guard's uniform. This was Gamelin's case, who was an *active* citizen of his Section and member of the Military Committee.

Fortuné Trubert laid down his pen:

"*Citoyen* Évariste," he said, "I beg you to go to the Convention and ask them to send us orders to dig up the floors of cellars, to wash the soil and flagstones and collect the saltpetre. It is not everything to have guns, we must have gunpowder too."

A little hunchback, a pen behind his ear and a bundle of papers in his hand, entered the erstwhile sacristy. It was the *citoyen* Beauvisage, of the Committee of Surveillance.

"*Citoyens*," he announced, "we have bad news: Custine has evacuated Landau."

"Custine is a traitor!" cried Gamelin.

"He shall be guillotined," said Beauvisage.

Trubert, in his rather breathless voice, expressed himself with his habitual calmness:

"The Convention has not instituted a Committee of Public Safety for fun. It will enquire into Custine's conduct. Incompetent or traitor, he will be superseded by a General resolved to win the victory,—and *ça ira!*"

He turned over a heap of papers, scrutinizing them with his tired eyes:

"That our soldiers may do their duty with a quiet mind and stout heart, they must be assured that the lot of those they leave behind at home is safeguarded. If you are of the same opinion, *citoyen* Gamelin, you will join me in demanding, at the next assembly, that the Committee of Benevolence concert measures with the Military Committee to succour the families that are in indigence and have a relative at the front."

He smiled and hummed to himself: "*Ça ira! ça ira! . . .*"

Working twelve and fourteen hours a day at his table of unpainted deal for the defence of the fatherland in peril, this humble Secretary of the Sectional Committee could see no disproportion between the immensity of the task and the meagreness of his means for performing it, so filled was he with a sense of the unity in a common effort between himself and all other patriots, so intimately did he feel himself one with the Nation at large, so merged was his individual life in the life of a great People. He was of the sort who combine enthusiasm with long-suffering, who, after each check, set about organizing the victory that is impossible, but is bound to come. And verily they *must* win the day. These men of no account, who had destroyed Royalty and upset the old order of things, this Trubert, a penniless optician, this Évariste Gamelin, an unknown dauber, could expect no mercy from their enemies. They had no choice save between victory and death. Hence both their fervour and their serenity.

II

QUITTING the Barnabites, Évariste Gamelin set off in the direction of the Place Dauphine, now renamed the Place de Thionville in honour of a city that had shown itself impregnable.

Situated in the busiest quarter of Paris, the *Place* had long lost the fine stateliness it had worn a hundred years ago; the mansions forming its three sides, built in the days of Henri IV in one uniform style, of red brick with white stone dressings, to lodge splendour-loving magistrates, had had their imposing roofs of slate removed

to make way for two or three wretched storeys of lath and plaster
or had even been demolished altogether and replaced by shabby
whitewashed houses, and now displayed only a series of irregular,
poverty-stricken, squalid fronts, pierced with countless narrow,
unevenly spaced windows enlivened with flowers in pots, birdcages,
and rags hanging out to dry. These were occupied by a swarm of
artisans, jewellers, metal-workers, clockmakers, opticians, printers,
laundresses, sempstresses, milliners, and a few grey-beard lawyers
who had not been swept away in the storm of revolution along
with the King's courts.

It was morning and springtime. Golden sunbeans, intoxicating as
new wine, played on the walls and flashed gaily in at garret case-
ments. Every sash of every window was thrown open, showing the
housewives' frowsy heads peeping out. The Clerk of the Revolutionary Tribunal, who had just left his house on his way to Court,
distributed amicable taps on the cheeks of the children playing
under the trees. From the Pont-Neuf came the crier's voice denouncing the treason of the infamous Dumouriez.

Évariste Gamelin lived in a house on the side towards the Quai
de l'Horloge, a house that dated from Henri IV and would still have
preserved a not unhandsome appearance but for a mean tiled attic
that had been added on to heighten the building under the last but
one of the *tyrants*. To adapt the lodging of some erstwhile dignitary
of the *Parlement* to the exigencies of the bourgeois and artisan
households that formed its present denizens, endless partitions and
false floors had been run up. This was why the *citoyen* Remacle,
concierge and jobbing tailor, perched in a sort of 'tween-decks, as
low ceilinged as it was confined in area. Here he could be seen
through the glass door sitting cross-legged on his work-bench, his
bowed back within an inch of the floor above, stitching away at a
National Guard's uniform, while the *citoyenne* Remacle, whose
cooking stove boasted no chimney but the well of the staircase,
poisoned the other tenants with the fumes of her stew-pots and
frying-pans, and their little girl Joséphine, her face smudged with
treacle and looking as pretty as an angel, played on the threshold
with Mouton, the joiner's dog. The *citoyenne,* whose heart was as
capacious as her ample bosom and broad back, was reputed to
bestow her favours on her neighbour the *citoyen* Dupont senior,
who was one of the twelve constituting the Committee of Surveillance. At any rate her husband had his strong suspicions, and from
morning to night the house resounded with the racket of the alter-
nate squabbles and reconciliations of the pair. The upper floors
were occupied by the *citoyen* Chaperon, gold and silver-smith, who
had his shop on the Quai de l'Horloge, by a health officer, an
attorney, a goldbeater, and several employés at the Palais de
Justice.

Évariste Gamelin climbed the old-fashioned staircase as far as the fourth and last storey, where he had his studio together with a bedroom for his mother. At this point ended the wooden stairs laid with tiles that took the place of the grand stairway of the more important floors. A ladder clamped to the wall led to a cockloft, from which at that moment emerged a stout man with a handsome, florid, rosy-cheeked face, climbing painfully down with an enormous package clasped in his arms, yet humming gaily to himself: *J'ai perdu mon serviteur.*

Breaking off his song, he wished a polite good-day to Gamelin, who returned him a fraternal greeting and helped him down with his parcel, for which the old man thanked him.

"There," said he, shouldering his burden again, "you have a batch of dancing-dolls which I am going to deliver straight away to a toy-merchant in the Rue de la Loi. There is a whole tribe of them inside; I am their creator; they have received of me a perishable body, exempt from joys and sufferings. I have not given them the gift of thought, for I am a benevolent God."

It was the *citoyen* Brotteaux once farmer of taxes and *ci-devant* noble; his father, having made a fortune in these transactions, had bought himself an office conferring a title on the possessor. In the good old times Maurice Brotteaux had called himself Monsieur des Ilettes and used to give elegant suppers which the fair Madame de Rochemaure, wife of a King's *procureur,* enlivened with her bright glances,—a finished gentlewoman whose loyal fidelity was never impugned so long as the Revolution left Maurice Brotteaux in possession of his offices and emoluments, his hôtel, his estates and his noble name. The Revolution swept them all away. He made his living by painting portraits under the archways of doors, making pancakes and fritters on the Quai de la Mégisserie, composing speeches for the representatives of the people and giving dancing lessons to the young *citoyennes.* At the present time, in his garret into which you climbed by a ladder and where a man could not stand upright, Maurice Brotteaux, the proud owner of a glue-pot, a ball of twine, a box of water-colours and sundry clippings of paper, manufactured dancing-dolls which he sold to wholesale toy-dealers, who resold them to the pedlars who hawked them up and down the Champs-Élysées at the end of a pole,—glittering magnets to draw the little ones' eyes. Amidst the calamities of the State and the disaster that overwhelmed himself, he preserved an unruffled spirit, reading for the refreshment of his mind in his Lucretius, which he carried with him wherever he went in the gaping pocket of his plum-coloured surtout.

Évariste Gamelin pushed open the door of his lodging. It offered no resistance, for his poverty spared him any trouble about lock and key; when his mother from force of habit shot the bolt, he would tell her: "Why, what's the good? Folks don't steal spiders'-webs,—nor my pictures, neither." In his workroom were piled, under a thick layer of dust or with faces turned to the wall, the canvases of his student years,—when, as the fashion of the day was, he limned scenes of gallantry, depicting with a sleek, timorous brush emptied quivers and birds put to flight, risky pastimes and reveries of bliss, high-kilted goose-girls and shepherdesses with rose-wreathed bosoms.

But it was not a genre that suited his temperament. His cold treatment of such like scenes proved the painter's incurable purity of heart. Amateurs were right: Gamelin had no gifts as an erotic artist. Nowadays, though he was still short of thirty, these subjects struck him as dating from an immemorial antiquity. He saw in them the degradation wrought by Monarchy, the shameful effects of the corruption of Courts. He blamed himself for having practised so contemptible a style and prostituted his genius to the vile arts of slavery. Now, citizen of a free people, he occupied his hand with bold charcoal sketches of Liberties, Rights of Man, French Constitutions, Republican Virtues, the people as Hercules felling the Hydra of Tyranny, throwing into each and all his compositions all the fire of his patriotism. Alas! he could not make a living by it. The times were hard for artists. No doubt the fault did not lie with the Convention, which was hurling its armies against the kings gathered on every frontier, which, proud, unmoved, determined in the face of the coalesced powers of Europe, false and ruthless to itself, was rending its own bosom with its own hands, which was setting up terror as the order of the day, establishing for the punishment of plotters a pitiless tribunal to whose devouring maw it was soon to deliver up its own members; but which through it all, with calm and thoughtful brow, the patroness of science and friend of all things beautiful, was reforming the calendar, instituting technical schools, decreeing competitions in painting and sculpture, founding prizes to encourage artists, organizing annual exhibitions, opening the Museum of the Louvre, and, on the model of Athens and Rome, endowing with a stately sublimity the celebration of National festivals and public obsequies. But French Art, once so widely appreciated in England, and Germany, in Russia, in Poland, now found every outlet to foreign lands closed. Amateurs of painting, dilettanti of the fine arts, great noblemen and financiers, were ruined, had emigrated or were in hiding. The men the Revolution had enriched, peasants who had bought up National properties, speculators, army-contractors, gamesters of the Palais-Royal, durst not at present show their wealth, and did not care a fig for pictures, either. It needed Regnault's fame or the youthful Gérard's cleverness to sell a canvas. Greuze, Fragonard, Houin were reduced to indigence. Prud'hon could barely earn bread for his wife and children by drawing subjects which Copia reproduced in stippled engravings. The patriot painters Hennequin, Wicar, Topino-Lebrun were starving. Gamelin, without means to meet the ex-

penses of a picture, to hire a model or buy colours, abandoned his
vast canvas of *The Tyrant pursued in the Infernal Regions by the
Furies,* after barely sketching in the main outlines. It blocked up
half the studio with its half-finished, threatening shapes, greater
than life-size, and its vast brood of green snakes, each darting
forth two sharp, forked tongues. In the foreground, to the left,
could be discerned Charon in his boat, a haggard, wild-looking
figure,—a powerful and well conceived design, but of the schools,
schooly. There was far more of genius and less of artificiality in a
canvas of smaller dimensions, also unfinished, that hung in the best
lighted corner of the studio. It was an Orestes whom his sister
Electra was raising in her arms on his bed of pain. The maiden
was putting back with a moving tenderness the matted hair that
hung over her brother's eyes. The head of the hero was tragic and
fine, and you could see a likeness in it to the painter's own countenance.

Gamelin cast many a mournful look at this composition; sometimes his fingers itched with the craving to be at work on it, and
his arms would be stretched longingly towards the boldly sketched
figure of Electra, to fall back again helpless to his sides. The artist
was burning with enthusiasm, his soul aspired to great achieve-
ment. But he had to exhaust his energy on pot-boilers which he
executed indifferently, because he was bound to please the taste of
the vulgar and also because he had no skill to impress trivial things
with the seal of genius. He drew little allegorical compositions
which his comrade Desmahis engraved cleverly enough in black or
in colours and which were bought at a low figure by a print-
dealer in the Rue Honoré, the *citoyen* Blaise. But the trade was
going from bad to worse, declared Blaise, who for some time now
had declined to purchase anything.

This time, however, made inventive by necessity, Gamelin had
conceived a new and happy thought, as *he* at any rate believed,—
an idea that was to make the print-seller's fortune, and the engraver's and his own to boot. This was a "patriotic" pack of cards,
where for the kings and queens and knaves of the old style he
meant to substitute figures of Genius, of Liberty, of Equality and
the like. He had already sketched out all his designs, had finished
several and was eager to pass on to Desmahis such as were in a
state to be engraved. The one he deemed the most successful represented a soldier dressed in the three-cornered hat, blue coat with
red facings, yellow breeches and black gaiters of the Volunteer,
seated on a big drum, his feet on a pile of cannon-balls and his
musket between his knees. It was the *citizen of hearts* replacing the
ci-devant knave of hearts. For six months and more Gamelin had
been drawing soldiers with never-failing gusto. He had sold some
of these while the fit of martial enthusiasm lasted, while others
hung on the walls of the room, and five or six, water-colours,

colour-washes and chalks in two tints, lay about on the table and chairs. In the days of July, '92, when in every open space rose platforms for enrolling recruits, when all the taverns were gay with green leaves and resounded to the shouts of "Vive la Nation! freedom or death!" Gamelin could not cross the Pont-Neuf or pass the Hôtel de Ville without his heart beating high at sight of the beflagged marquee in which magistrates in tricolour scarves were inscribing the names of volunteers to the sound of the *Marseillaise*. But for him to join the Republic's armies would have meant leaving his mother to starve.

Heralded by a grievous sound of puffing and panting the old *citoyenne*, Gamelin's widowed mother, entered the studio, hot, red and out of breath, the National cockade hanging half unpinned in her cap and on the point of falling out. She deposited her basket on a chair and still standing, the better to get her breath, began to groan over the high price of victuals.

A shopkeeper's wife till the death of her husband, a cutler in the Rue de Grenelle-Saint-Germain, at the sign of the Ville de Châtellerault, now reduced to poverty, the *citoyenne* Gamelin lived in seclusion, keeping house for her son the painter. He was the elder of her two children. As for her daughter Julie, at one time employed at a fashionable milliner's in the Rue Honoré, the best thing was not to know what had become of her, for it was ill saying the truth, that she had emigrated with an aristocrat.

"Lord God!" sighed the *citoyenne*, showing her son a loaf baked of heavy dun-coloured dough, "bread is too dear for anything; the more reason it should be made of pure wheat! At market neither eggs nor green-stuff nor cheese to be had. By dint of eating chestnuts, we're like to grow into chestnuts."

After a long pause, she began again:

"Why, I've seen women in the streets who had nothing to feed their little ones with. The distress is sore among poor folks. And it will go on the same till things are put back on a proper footing."

"Mother," broke in Gamelin with a frown, "the scarcity we suffer from is due to the unprincipled buyers and speculators who starve the people and connive with our foes over the border to render the Republic odious to the citizens and to destroy liberty. This comes of the Brissotins' plots and the traitorous dealings of your Pétions and Rolands. It is well if the federalists in arms do not march on Paris and massacre the patriot remnant whom famine is too slow in killing! There is no time to lose; we must tax the price of flour and guillotine every man who speculates in the food of the people, foments insurrection or palters with the foreigner. The Convention has set up an extraordinary tribunal to try conspirators. Patriots form the court; but will its members have energy enough to defend the fatherland against our foes? There is hope in Robespierre; he is virtuous. There is hope above all in Marat. He loves the people, discerns its true interests and promotes them. He was ever the first to unmask traitors, to baffle plots. He is incorruptible and fearless. He, and he alone, can save the imperilled Republic."

The *citoyenne* Gamelin shook her head, paying no heed to the cockade that fell out of her cap at the gesture.

"Have done, Évariste; your Marat is a man like another and no better than the rest. You are young and your head is full of fancies. What you say to-day of Marat, you said before of Mirabeau, of La Fayette, of Pétion, of Brissot."

"Never!" cried Gamelin, who was genuinely oblivious.

After clearing one end of the deal table of the papers and books, brushes and chalks that littered it, the *citoyenne* laid out on it the earthenware soup-bowl, two tin porringers, two iron forks, the loaf of brown bread and a jug of thin wine.

Mother and son ate the soup in silence and finished their meal with a small scrap of bacon. The *citoyenne,* putting *her* titbit on her bread, used the point of her pocket knife to convey the pieces one by one slowly and solemnly to her toothless jaws and masticated with a proper reverence the victuals that had cost so dear.

She had left the best part on the dish for her son, who sat lost in a brown study.

"Eat, Évariste," she repeated at regular intervals, "eat,"—and on her lips the word had all the solemnity of a religious commandment.

She began again with her lamentations on the dearness of provisions, and again Gamelin demanded taxation as the only remedy for these evils.

But she shrilled:

"There is no money left in the country. The *émigrés* have carried it all off with them. There is no confidence left either. Everything is desperate."

"Hush, mother, hush!" protested Gamelin. "What matter our privations, our hardships of a moment? The Revolution will win for all time the happiness of the human race."

The good dame sopped her bread in her wine; her mood grew more cheerful and she smiled as her thoughts returned to her young days, when she used to dance on the green in honour of the King's birthday. She well remembered too the day when Joseph Gamelin, cutler by trade, had asked her hand in marriage. And she told over, detail by detail, how things had gone,—how her mother had bidden her: "Go dress. We are going to the Place de Grève, to Monsieur Bienassis' shop, to see Damiens drawn and quartered," and what difficulty they had to force their way through the press of eager spectators. Presently, in Monsieur Bienassis' shop, she had seen Joseph Gamelin, wearing his fine rose-pink coat and had known in an instant what he would be at. All the time she sat at the window to see the regicide torn with red-hot pinchers, drenched with molten lead, dragged at the tail of four horses and thrown into the flames, Joseph Gamelin had stood behind her chair and had never once left off complimenting her on her complexion, her hair and her figure.

She drained the last drop in her cup and continued her reminiscences of other days:

"I brought you into the world, Évariste, sooner than I had expected, by reason of a fright I had when I was big. It was on the Pont-Neuf, where I came near being knocked down by a crowd of sightseers hurrying to Monsieur de Lally's execution. You were so little at your birth the surgeon thought you would not live. But I felt sure God would be gracious to me and preserve your life. I reared you to the best of my powers, grudging neither pains nor expense. It is fair to say, my Évariste, that you showed me you were grateful and that, from childhood up, you tried your best to recompense me for what I had done. You were naturally affectionate and tender-hearted. Your sister was not bad at heart; but she was selfish and of unbridled temper. Your compassion was greater than ever was hers for the unfortunate. When the little ragamuffins of the neighbourhood robbed birds' nests in the trees, you always fought hard to rescue the nestling from their hands and restore them to the mother, and many a time you did not give in till after you had been kicked and cuffed cruelly. At seven years of age, instead of wrangling with bad boys, you would pace soberly along the street saying over your catechism; and all the poor people you came across you insisted on bringing home with you to relieve their needs, till I was forced to whip you to break you of the habit. You could not see a living creature suffer without tears.

When you had done growing, you turned out a very handsome lad. To my great surprise, you appeared not to know it,—how different from most pretty boys, who are full of conceit and vain of their good looks!"

His old mother spoke the truth. Évariste at twenty had had a grave and charming cast of countenance, a beauty at once austere and feminine, the countenance of a Minerva. Now his sombre eyes and pale cheeks revealed a melancholy and passionate soul. But his gaze, when it fell on his mother, recovered for a brief moment its childish softness.

She went on:

"You might have profited by your advantages to run after the girls, but you preferred to stay with me in the shop, and I had sometimes to tell you not to hang on always to my apron-strings, but to go and amuse yourself with your young companions. To my dying day I shall always testify that you have been a good son, Évariste. After your father's death, you bravely took me and provided for me; though your work barely pays you, you have never let me want for anything, and if we are at this moment destitute and miserable, I cannot blame you for it. The fault lies with the Revolution."

He raised his hand to protest; but she only shrugged and continued:

"I am no aristocrat. I have seen the great in the full tide of their power, and I can bear witness that they abused their privileges. I have seen your father cudgelled by the Duc de Canaleilles' lackeys because he did not make way quick enough for their master. I could never abide *the Austrian*—she was too haughty and too extravagant. As for the King, I thought him good-hearted, and it needed his trial and condemnation to alter my opinion. In fact, I do not regret the old régime,—though I have had some agreeable times under it. But never tell me the Revolution is going to establish equality, because men will never be equal; it is an impossibility, and let them turn the country upside down to their heart's content, there will still be great and small, fat and lean in it."

As she talked, she was busy putting away the plates and dishes. The painter had left off listening. He was thinking out a design,— for a sansculotte, in red cap and *carmagnole,* who was to supersede the discredited knave of spades in his pack of cards.

There was a sound of scratching on the door, and a girl appeared,—a country wench, as broad as she was long, red-haired and bandy-legged, a wen hiding the left eye, the right so pale a blue it looked white, with monstrous thick lips and teeth protruding beyond them.

She asked Gamelin if he was Gamelin the painter and if he could do her a portrait of her betrothed, Ferrand (Jules), a volunteer serving with the Army of the Ardennes.

Gamelin replied that he would be glad to execute the portrait on the gallant warrior's return.

But the girl insisted gently but firmly that it must be done at once.

The painter protested, smiling in spite of himself as he pointed out that he could do nothing without the original.

The poor creature was dumfounded; she had not foreseen the difficulty. Her head drooping over the left shoulder, her hands clasped in front of her, she stood still and silent as if overwhelmed by her disappointment. Touched and diverted by so much simplicity, and by way of distracting the poor, love-sick creature's grief, the painter handed her one of the soldiers he had drawn in water-colours and asked her if he was like that, her sweetheart in the Ardennes.

She bent her doleful look on the sketch, and little by little her eye brightened, sparkled, flashed, and her moon face beamed out in a radiant smile.

"It is his very likeness," she cried at last. "It is the very spit of Jules Ferrand, it is Jules Ferrand to the life."

Before it occurred to the artist to take the sheet of paper out of her hands, she folded it carefully with her coarse red fingers into a tiny square, slipped it over her heart between her stays and her shift, handed the painter an *assignat* for five livres, and wishing the company a very good day, hobbled light-heartedly to the door and so out of the room.

III

N THE afternoon of the same day Évariste set out to see the *citoyen* Jean Blaise, printseller, as well as dealer in ornamental boxes, fancy goods and games of all sorts, in the Rue Honoré, opposite the Oratoire and near the office of the Messageries, at the sign of the *Amour peintre*. The shop was on the ground floor of a house sixty years old, and opened on the street by a vaulted arch the keystone of which bore a grotesque head with horns. The semicircle beneath the arch was occupied by an oil-painting representing "the Sicilian or Cupid the Painter," after a composition by Boucher, which Jean Blaise's father had put up in 1770 and which sun and rain had been doing their best to obliterate ever since. On either side of the door a similar arched opening, with a nymph's head on the keystone arch glazed with the largest panes to be got, exhibited for the benefit of the public the prints in vogue at the time and the latest novelties in coloured engravings. To-day's display included a series of scenes of gallantry by Boilly, treated in his graceful, rather stiff way, *Leçons d'amour conjugal, Douces résistances* and the like, which scandalized the Jacobins and which the rigid moralists denounced to the Society of Arts, Debucourt's *Promenade publique* with a dandy in canary-coloured breeches lounging on three chairs, a group of horses by the young Carle Vernet, pictures of air balloons, the *Bain de Virginie* and figures after the antique.

Amid the stream of citizens that flowed past the shop it was the raggedest figures that loitered longest before the two fascinating windows. Easily amused, delighting in pictures and bent on getting their share, if only through the eyes, of the good things of this world, they stood in open-mouthed admiration, whereas the aristocrats merely glanced in, frowned and passed on.

The instant he came within sight of the house, Évariste fixed his eyes on one of the row of windows above the shop, the one on the left hand, where there was a red carnation in a flower-pot behind a balcony of twisted ironwork. It was the window of Élodie's chamber, Jean Blaise's daughter. The print-dealer lived with his only child on the first floor of the house.

Évariste, after halting a moment as if to get his breath in front of the *Amour peintre,* turned the hasp of the shop-door. He found the *citoyenne* Élodie within; she had just sold a couple of engravings by Fragonard *fils* and Naigeon, carefully selected from a number of others, and before locking up the *assignats* received in payment in the strong-box, was holding them one after the other between her fine eyes and the light, to scrutinize the delicate lines and intricate curves of engraving and the watermark. She was naturally suspicious, for as much forged paper was in circulation as true, which was a great hindrance to commerce. As in former days, in the case of such as copied the King's signature, forgers of the national currency were punished by death; yet plates for printing *assignats* were to be found in every cellar, the Swiss smuggled in counterfeits by the million, whole packets were put in circulation in the inns, the English landed bales of them every day on our coasts, to ruin the Republic's credit and bring good patriots to destitution. Élodie was in terror of accepting bad paper, and still more in terror of passing it and being treated as an accomplice of Pitt, though she had a firm belief in her own good luck and felt pretty sure of coming off best in any emergency.

Évariste looked at her with the sombre gaze that speaks more movingly of love than the most smiling face. She returned his gaze with a mocking curl of the lips and an arch gleam in the dark eyes, —an expression she wore because she knew he loved her and liked to know it and because such a look provokes a lover, makes him complain of ill-usage, brings him to the speaking point, if he has not spoken already, which was Évariste's case.

Before depositing the *assignats* in the strong-box, she produced from her work-basket a white scarf, which she had begun to embroider, and set to work on it. At once industrious and a coquette, she knew instinctively how to ply her needle so as to fascinate an admirer and make a pretty thing for her wearing at one and the same time; she had quite different ways of working according to the person watching her,—a nonchalant way for those she would lull into a gentle languor, a capricious way for those she would fain to see in a more or less despairing mood. For Évariste, she bent with an air of painstaking absorption over her scarf, for she wanted to stir a sentiment of serious affection in his heart.

Élodie was neither very young nor very pretty. She might have been deemed plain at the first glance. She was a brunette, with an olive complexion; under the broad white kerchief knotted carelessly about her head, from which the dark lustrous ringlets escaped, her eyes of fire gleamed as if they would burn their orbits. Her round face with its prominent cheek-bones, laughing lips and rather broad nose, that gave it a wild-wood, voluptuous expression, reminded the painter of the faun of the Borghese, a cast of which he had seen and been struck with admiration for its freakish charm. A faint down of moustache accentuated the curve of the full lips. A bosom that seemed big with love was confined by a crossed kerchief in the fashion of the year. Her supple waist, her active limbs, her whole vigorous body expressed in every movement a wild, delicious freedom. Every glance, every breath, every quiver of the warm flesh called for love and promised passion. There, behind the tradesman's counter, she seemed rather a dancing nymph, a bacchante of the opera, stripped of her lynx skin and thrysus, imprisoned, and travestied by a magician's spell under the modest trappings of a housewife by Chardin.

"My father is not at home," she told the painter; "wait a little, he will not be long."

In the small brown hands the needle travelled swiftly over the fine lawn.

"Is the pattern to your taste, Monsieur Gamelin?"

It was not in Gamelin's nature to pretend. And love, exaggerating his confidence, encouraged him to speak quite frankly.

"You embroider cleverly, *citoyenne;* but, if I am to say what I think, the pattern you have traced is not simple enough or bold enough, and smacks of the affected taste that in France governed too long the ornamentation of dress and furniture and woodwork; all those rosettes and wreaths recall the pretty, finikin style that was in favour under the tyrant. There is a new birth of taste. Alas! we have much leeway to make up. In the days of the infamous Louis XV the art of decoration had something Chinese about it. They made pot-bellied cabinets with drawer handles grotesque in their contortions, good for nothing but to be thrown on the fire to warm good patriots. Simplicity alone is beautiful. We must hark

back to the antique. David designs beds and chairs from the
Etruscan vases and the wall-paintings of Herculaneum."

"Yes, I have seen those beds and chairs," said Élodie, "they are
lovely. Soon we shall want no other sort. I am like you, I adore the
antique."

"Well, then, *citoyenne,*" returned Évariste, "if you had limited
your pattern to a Greek border, with ivy leaves, serpents or crossed
arrows, it would have been worthy of a Spartan maiden . . . and
of you. But you can still keep this design by simplifying it, reduc-
ing it to the plain lines of beauty."

She asked her preceptor what should be picked out.

He bent over the work, and the girl's ringlets swept lightly over
his cheeks. Their hands met and their breaths mingled. For an instant Évariste tasted an ecstatic bliss, but to feel Élodie's lips so
close to his own filled him with fear, and dreading to alarm her
modesty, he drew back quickly.

The *citoyenne* Blaise was in love with Évariste Gamelin; she
thought his great ardent eyes superb no less than the fine oval of
his pale face, and his abundant black locks, parted above the brow
and falling in showers about his shoulders; his gravity of demeanour, his cold reserve, his severe manner and uncompromising
speech which never condescended to flattery, were equally to her
liking. She was in love, and therefore believed him possssed of supreme artistic genius that would one day blossom forth in incomparable masterpieces and make his name world-famous,—and she
loved him the better for the belief. The *citoyenne* Blaise was no prude
on the score of masculine purity and her scruples were not offended
because a man should satisfy his passions and follow his own tastes
and caprices; she loved Évariste, who was virtuous; she did not love
him because he was virtuous, albeit she appreciated the advantage
of his being so in that she had no cause for jealousy or suspicion
or any fear of rivals in his affections.

Nevertheless, for the time being, she deemed his reserve a little
overdone. If Racine's "Aricie," who loved "Hippolyte," admired the
youthful hero's untameable virtue, it was with the hope of winning
a victory over it, and she would quickly have bewailed a sternness
of moral fibre that had refused to be softened for her sake. At the
first opportunity she more than half declared her passion to con-
strain him to speak out himself. Like her prototype the tender-
hearted "Aricie," the *citoyenne* Blaise was much inclined to think
that in love the woman is bound to make the advances. "The fondest hearts," she told herself, "are the most fearful; they need help
and encouragement. Besides, they are so simple a woman can go
half way and even further without their even knowing it, if only
she lets them fancy the credit is theirs of the bold attack and the
glorious victory." What made her more confident of success was the
fact that she knew for a certainty (and indeed there was no doubt

about it) that Évariste, before ever the Revolution had made him a hero, had loved a mistress like any ordinary mortal, a very unheroic creature, no other than the *concierge* at the Academy of Painting. Élodie, who was a girl of some experience, quite realised that there are different sorts of love. The sentiment Évariste inspired in her heart was profound enough for her to dream of making him the partner of her life. She was very ready to marry him, but hardly expected her father would approve the union of his only daughter with a poor and unknown artist. Gamelin had nothing, while the printseller turned over large sums of money. The *Amour peintre* brought him in large profits, the share market larger still, and he was in partnership with an army contractor who supplied the cavalry of the Republic with rushes in place of hay and mildewed oats. In a word, the cutler's son of the Rue Saint-Dominique was a very insignificant personage beside the publisher of engravings, a man known throughout Europe, related to the Blaizots, Basans and Didots, and an honoured guest at the houses of the *citoyens* Saint-Pierre and Florian. Not that, as an obedient daughter should, she held her father's consent to be an indispensable preliminary to her settlement in life. The latter, early left a widower, and a man of a self-indulgent, volatile temper, as enterprising with women as he was in business, had never paid much heed to her and had left her to develop at her own sweet will, untrammelled whether by parental advice or parental affection, more careful to ignore than to safeguard the girl's behaviour, whose passionate temperament he appreciated as a connoisseur of the sex and in whom he recognized charms far and away more seductive than a pretty face. Too generous-hearted to be circumspect, too clever to come to harm, cautious even in her caprices, passion had never made her forget the social proprieties. Her father was infinitely grateful for this prudent behaviour, and as she had inherited from him a good head for business and a taste for money-making, he never troubled himself as to the mysterious reasons that deterred a girl so eminently marriageable from entering that estate and kept her at home, where she was as good as a housekeeper and four clerks to him. At twenty-seven she felt old enough and experienced enough to manage her own concerns and had no need to ask the advice or consult the wishes of a father still a young man, and one of so easy-going and careless a temper. But for her to marry Gamelin, Monsieur Blaise must needs contrive a future for a son-in-law with such poor prospects, give him an interest in the business, guarantee him regular work as he did to several artists already—in fact, one way or another, provide him with a livelihood; and such a favour was out of the question, she considered, whether for the one to offer or the other to accept, so small was the bond of sympathy between the two men.

The difficulty troubled the girl's tender heart and wise brain. She saw nothing to alarm her in a secret union with her lover and in taking the author of nature for sole witness of their mutual troth. Her creed found nothing blameworthy in such a union, which the independence of her mode of life made possible and which Évariste's honourable and virtuous character gave her good hopes of forming without apprehension as to the result. But Gamelin was hard put to it to live and provide his old mother with the barest necessaries, and it did not seem as though in so straitened an existence room could well be found for an amour even when reduced to the simplicity of nature. Moreover, Évariste had not yet spoken and declared his intentions, though certainly the *citoyenne* Blaise hoped to bring him to this before long.

She broke off her meditations, and the needle stopped at the same moment.

"*Citoyen* Évariste," she said, "I shall not care for the scarf, unless you like it too. Draw me a pattern, please. Meanwhile, I will copy Penelope and unravel what I have done in your absence."

He answered in a tone of sombre enthusiasm:

"I promise you I will, *citoyenne*. I will draw you the brand of the tyrannicide Harmodius,—a sword in a wreath,"—and pulling out his pencil, he sketched in a design of swords and flowers in the sober, unadorned style he admired. And as he drew, he expounded his views of art:

"A regenerated People," he declared, "must repudiate all the legacies of servitude, bad taste, bad outline, bad drawing. Watteau, Boucher, Fragonard worked for tyrants and for slaves. Their works show no feeling for good style or purity of line, no love of nature or truth. Masks, dolls, fripperies, monkey-tricks,—nothing else! Posterity will despise their frivolous productions. In a hundred years all Watteau's pictures will be banished to the garrets and falling to pieces from neglect; in 1893 struggling painters will be daubing their studies over Boucher's canvases. David has opened the way; he approaches the Antique, but he has not yet reached true simplicity, true grandeur, bare and unadorned. Our artists have many secrets still to learn from the friezes of Herculaneum, the Roman bas-reliefs, the Etruscan vases."

He dilated at length on antique beauty, then came back to Fragonard, whom he abused with inexhaustible venom:

"Do you know him, *citoyenne?*"

Élodie nodded.

"You likewise know good old Greuze, who is ridiculous enough, to be sure, with his scarlet coat and his sword. But he looks like a wise man of Greece beside Fragonard. I met him, a while ago, the miserable old man, trotting by under the arcades of the Palais-Égalité, powdered, genteel, sprightly, spruce, hideous. At sight of him, I longed that, failing Apollo, some sturdy friend of the arts might hang him up to a tree and flay him alive like Marsyas as an everlasting warning to bad painters."

Élodie gave him a long look out of her dancing, wanton eyes.

"You know how to hate, Monsieur Gamelin, are we to conclude you know also how to lo . . .?"

"Is that you, Gamelin?" broke in a tenor voice; it was the *cito-yen* Blaise just come back to his shop. He advanced, boots creaking, charms rattling, coat-skirts flying, an enormous black cocked hat cn his head, the corners of which touched his shoulders.

Élodie, picking up her work-basket, retreated to her chamber.

"Well, Gamelin!" inquired the *citoyen* Blaise, "have you brought me anything new?"

"May be," declared the painter,—and proceeded to expound his ideas.

"Our playing cards present a grievous and startling contrast with our present ways of thinking. The names of knave and king offend the ears of a patriot. I have designed and executed a reformed, Revolutionary pack in which for kings, queens and knaves are substituted Liberties, Equalities, Fraternities; the aces in a border of fasces, are called Laws. . . . You call Liberty of clubs, Equality of spades, Fraternity of diamonds, Law of hearts. I venture to think my cards are drawn with some spirit; I propose to have them engraved on copper by Desmahis, and to take out letters of patent."

So saying and extracting from his portfolio some finished designs in water-colour, the artist handed them to the printseller.

The *citoyen* Blaise declined to take them, and turning away:

"My lad," he sneered, "take 'em to the Convention; they will perhaps accord you a vote of thanks. But never think to make a *sol* by your new invention which is not new at all. You're a day behind the fair. Your Revolutionary pack of cards is the third I've had brought me. Your comrade Dugourc offered me last week a picquet set with four Geniuses of the People, four Liberties, four Equalities. Another was suggested, with Sages and Heroes, Cato, Rousseau, Hannibal,—I don't know what all! . . . And these cards had the advantage over yours, my friend, in being coarsely drawn and cut on wood blocks—with a penknife. How little you know the world to dream that players will use cards designed in the taste of David and engraved à la Bartolozzi! And then again, what a strange mistake to think it needs all this to-do to suit the old packs to the new ideas. Out of their own heads, the good sansculottes can find a corrective for what offends them, saying, instead of 'king'—'The Tyrant!' or just 'The fat pig!' They go on using the same old filthy cards and never buy new ones. The greatest market for playing-cards is the gaming-hells of the Palais-Égalité; well, I advise you to go there and offer the croupiers and punters there your Liberties, your Equalities, your . . . what d'ye call 'em? . . . Laws of hearts

. . . and come back and tell me what sort of a reception they gave you!"

The *citoyen* Blaise sat down on the counter, filliped away sundry grains of snuff from his nankeen breeches and looking at Gamelin with an air of gentle pity:

"Let me give you a bit of advice, *citoyen;* if you want to make your living, drop your patriotic packs of cards, leave your revolutionary symbols alone, have done with your Hercules, your hydras, your Furies pursuing guilt, your Geniuses of Liberty, and paint me pretty girls. The people's ardour for regeneration grows lukewarm with time, but men will always love women. Paint me women, all pink and white, with little feet and tiny hands. And get this into your thick skull that nobody cares a fig about the Revolution or wants to hear another word about it."

But Évariste drew himself up in indignant protest:

"What! not hear another word of the Revolution! . . . But, why surely, the restoration of liberty, the victories of our armies, the chastisement of tyrants are events that will startle the most remote posterity. How could we not be struck by such portents? . . . What! the sect of the *sansculotte* Jesus has lasted well-nigh eighteen centuries, and the religion of Liberty is to be abolished after barely four years of existence!"

But Jean Blaise resumed in a tone of superiority:

"You walk in a dream; *I* see life as it is. Believe me, friend, the Revolution is a bore; it lasts over long. Five years of enthusiasm, five years of fraternal embraces, of massacres, of fine speeches, of *Marseillaises,* of tocsins, of 'hang up the aristocrats,' of heads promenaded on pikes, of women mounted astride of cannon, of trees of Liberty crowned with the red cap, of white-robed maidens and old men drawn about the streets in flower-wreathed cars; of imprisonments and guillotinings, of proclamations, and short commons, of cockades and plumes, swords and *carmagnoles*—it grows tedious! And then folk are beginning to lose the hang of it all. We have gone through too much, we have seen too many of the great men and noble patriots whom you have led in triumph to the Capitol only to hurl them afterwards from the Tarpeian rock,—Necker, Mirabeau, La Fayette, Bailly, Pétion, Manuel, and how many others! How can we be sure you are not preparing the same fate for your new heroes? . . . Men have lost all count."

"Their names, *citoyen* Blaise; name them, these heroes we are making ready to sacrifice!" cried Gamelin in a tone that recalled the print-dealer to a sense of prudence.

"I am a Republican and a patriot," he replied, clapping his hand on his heart. "I am as good a Republican as you, as ardent a patriot as you, *citoyen* Gamelin. I do not suspect your zeal nor accuse you of any backsliding. But remember that my zeal and my devotion to the State are attested by numerous acts. Here you have my principles. I give my confidence to every individual competent to serve the Nation. Before the men whom the general voice elects to the perilous honour of the Legislative office, such as Marat, such as Robespierre, I bow my head; I am ready to support them to the measure of my poor ability and offer them the humble co-operation of a good citizen. The Committees can bear witness to my ardour and self-sacrifice. In conjunction with true patriots, I have furnished oats and fodder to our gallant cavalry, boots for our soldiers. This very day I am despatching from Vernon a convoy of sixty oxen to the Army of the South through a country infested with brigands and patrolled by the emissaries of Pitt and Condé. I do not talk; I act."

Gamelin calmly put back his sketches in his portfolio, the strings of which he tied and then slipped it under his arm.

"It is a strange contradiction," he said through his clenched teeth, "to see men help our soldiers to carry through the world the liberty they betray in their own homes by sowing discontent and alarm in the soul of its defenders. . . . Greeting and farewell, *citoyen* Blaise."

Before turning down the alley that runs alongside the Oratoire, Gamelin, his heart big with love and anger, wheeled round for a last look at the red carnations blossoming on a certain window-sill.

He did not despair; the fatherland would yet be saved. Against Jean Blaise's unpatriotic speeches he set his faith in the Revolution. Still he was bound to recognize that the tradesman had some show of reason when he asserted that the people of Paris had lost its old interest in public events. Alas! it was but too manifest that to the enthusiasm of the early days had little by little succeeded a wide-spread indifference, that never again would be seen the mighty crowds, unanimous in their ardour, of '89, never again the millions, one in heart and soul, that in '90 thronged round the altar of the *fédérés*. Well, good citizens must show double zeal and courage, must rouse the people from its apathy, bidding it choose between liberty and death.

Such were Gamelin's thoughts, and the memory of Élodie was a spur to his confidence.

Coming to the Quais, he saw the sun setting in the distant west behind lowering clouds that were like mountains of glowing lava; the roofs of the city were bathed in a golden light; the windows flashed back a thousand dazzling reflections. And Gamelin pictured the Titans forging out of the molten fragments of by-gone worlds Diké, the city of brass.

Not having a morsel of bread for his mother or himself, he was dreaming of a place at the limitless board that should have all the world for guests and welcome regenerated humanity to the feast. Meantime, he tried to persuade himself that the fatherland, as a good mother should, would feed her faithful child. Shutting his

mind against the gibes of the printseller, he forced himself to believe that his notion of a Revolutionary pack of cards was a novel
one and a good one, and that with these happily conceived sketches
of his he held a fortune in the portfolio under his arm. "Desmahis,"
he told himself, "shall engrave them. We will publish for ourselves
the new patriotic toy and we are sure to sell ten thousand packs in
a month, at twenty *sols* apiece."

In his impatience to realize the project, he strode off at once for
the Quai de la Ferraille, where Desmahis lived over a glazier's shop.

The entrance was through the shop. The glazier's wife informed
Gamelin that the *citoyen* Desmahis was not in, a fact that in no
wise surprised the painter, who knew his friend was of a vagabond
and dissipated humour and who marvelled that a man could engrave
so much and so well as he did while showing so little perseverance.
Gamelin made up his mind to wait a while for his return and the
woman offered him a chair. She was in a black mood and began to
grumble at the badness of trade, though she had always been told
that the Revolution, by breaking windows, was making the glaziers'
fortunes.

Night was falling; so abandoning his idea of waiting for his comrade, Gamelin took his leave of his hostess of the moment. As he
was crossing the Pont-Neuf, he saw a detachment of National
Guards debouch from the Quai des Morfondus. They were mounted
and carried torches. They were driving back the crowd, and amid
a mighty clatter of sabres escorting a cart driving slowly on its
way to the guillotine with a man whose name no one knew, a *ci-
devant* noble, the first prisoner condemned by the newly constituted
Revolutionary Tribunal. He could be seen by glimpses between the
guardsmen's hats, sitting with hands tied behind his back, his head
bared and swaying from side to side, his face to the cart's tail. The
headsman stood beside him lolling against the rail. The passers-by
had stopped to look and were telling each other it was likely one
of the fellows who starved the people, and staring with eyes of indifference. Gamelin, coming closer, caught sight of Desmahis among
the spectators; he was struggling to push a way through the press
and cut across the line of march. He called out to him and clapped
a hand on his shoulder,—and Desmahis turned his head. He was a
young man with a handsome face and a stalwart person. In former
days, at the Academy, they used to say he had the head of Bacchus
on the torso of Hercules. His friends nicknamed him "Barbaroux"
because of his likeness to that representative of the people.

"Come here," Gamelin said to him, "I have something of importance to say to you, Desmahis."

"Leave me alone," the latter answered peevishly, muttering some
half-heard explanation, looking out as he spoke for a chance of
darting across:

"I was following a divine creature, in a straw hat, a milliner's wench, with her flaxen hair down her back; that cursed cart has blocked my way. . . . She has gone on ahead, she is at the other end of the bridge by now!"

Gamelin endeavoured to hold him back by his coat skirts, swearing his business was urgent.

But Desmahis had already slipped away between horses, guards, swords and torches, and was in hot pursuit of the milliner's girl.

IV

IT was ten o'clock in the forenoon. The April sun bathed the tender leafage of the trees in light. A storm had cleared the air during the night and it was deliciously fresh and sweet. At long intervals a horseman passing along the Allée des Veuves broke the silence and solitude. On the outskirts of the shady avenue, over against a rustic cottage known as *La Belle Lilloise,* Évariste sat on a wooden bench waiting for Élodie. Since the day their fingers had met over the embroidery and their breaths had mingled, he had never been back to the *Amour peintre.* For a whole week his proud stoicism and his timidity, which grew more extreme every day, had kept him away from Élodie. He had written her a letter conceived in a key of gravity, at once sombre and ardent, in which, explaining the grievance he had against the *citoyen* Blaise, but saying no word of his love and concealing his chagrin, he announced his intention of never returning to her father's shop, and was now showing greater steadfastness in keeping this resolution than a woman in love was quite likely to approve.

A born fighter whose bent was to defend her property under all circumstances, Élodie instantly turned her mind to the task of winning back her lover. At first she thought of going to see him at the studio in the Place de Thionville. But knowing his touchy temper and judging from his letter that he was sick and sore, she feared he might come to regard daughter and father with the same angry displeasure and make a point of never seeing her again; so she deemed it wiser to invite him to a sentimental, romantic rendezvous which he could not well decline, where she would have ample time to cajole and charm him and where solitude would be her ally to fascinate his senses and overcome his scruples.

At this period, in all the English gardens and all the fahionable promenades, rustic cottages were to be found, built by clever architects, whose aim it was to flatter the taste of the city folk for a country life. The *Belle Lilloise* was occupied as a house of light refreshment; its exterior bore a look of poverty that was part of the.

mise en scène and it stood on the fragments, artistically imitated, of a fallen tower, so as to unite with the charm of rusticity the melancholy appeal of a ruined castle. Moreover, as though a peasant's cot and a shattered donjon were not enough to stir the sensibilities of his customers, the owner had raised a tomb beneath a weeping-willow,—a column surmounted by a funeral urn and bearing the inscription: "Cléonice to her faithful Azor." Rustic cots, ruined keeps, imitation tombs,—on the eve of being swept away, the aristocracy had erected in its ancestral parks these symbols of poverty, of decadence and of death. And now the patriot citizen found his delight in drinking, dancing, making love in sham hovels, under the broken vaults, a sham in their very ruin, of sham cloisters and surrounded by a sham graveyard; for was not he too, like his betters, a lover of nature, a disciple of Jean-Jacques? was not his heart stuffed as full as theirs with sensibility and the philosophy of humanity?

Reaching the rendezvous before the appointed time, Évariste waited, measuring the minutes by the beating of his heart as by the pendulum of a clock. A patrol passed, guarding a convoy of prisoners. Ten minutes after a woman dressed all in pink, carrying a bouquet as the fashion was, escorted by a gentleman in a three-cornered hat, red coat, striped waistcoat and breeches, slipped into the cottage, both so very like the gallants and dames of the ancien régime one was bound to think with the *citoyen* Blaise that mankind possesses characteristics Revolutions cannot change.

A few minutes later, coming from Rueil or Saint-Cloud, an old woman carrying a cylindrical box, painted in brilliant colours, arrived and sat down beside Gamelin, on his bench. She put down her box in front of her, and he saw that the lid had a turning needle fixed on it; the poor woman's trade was to hold a lottery in the public gardens for the children to try their luck at. She also dealt in "ladies' pleasures," an old-fashioned sweetmeat which she sold under a new name; whether because the time-honoured title of "forget-me-nots" called up inappropriate ideas of unhappiness and retribution or that folks had just got tired of it in course of time, "forget-me-nots" were now yclept "ladies' pleasures."

The old dame wiped the sweat from her forehead with a corner of her apron and broke out into railings against heaven, upbraiding God for injustice when he made life so hard for his creatures. Her husband kept a tavern on the river-bank at Saint-Cloud, while she came in every day to the Champs Élysées, sounding her rattle and crying: *"Ladies' pleasures,* come buy, come buy!" And with all this toil the old couple could not scrape enough together to end their days in comfort.

Seeing the young man beside her disposed to commiserate with her, she expounded at great length the origin of her misfortunes. It was all the Republic; by robbing the rich, it was taking the bread

out of poor people's mouths. And there was no hoping for a better
state of affairs. Things would only go from bad to worse,—she
knew that from many tokens. At Nanterre a woman had had a baby
born with a serpent's head; the lightning had struck the church at
Rueil and melted the cross on the steeple; a were-wolf had been seen
in the woods of Chaville. Masked men were poisoning the springs
and throwing plague powders in the air to cause diseases. . . .

Évariste saw Élodie spring from a carriage and run forward. The
girl's eyes flashed in the clear shadow cast by her straw hat; her
lips, as red as the carnations she held in her hand, were wreathed
in smiles. A scarf of black silk, crossed over the bosom, was knotted
behind the back. Her yellow gown displayed the quick movements
of the knees and showed a pair of low-heeled shoes below the hem.
The hips were almost entirely unconfined; the Revolution had en-
franchised the waists of its *citoyennes*. For all that, the skirts, still
puffed out below the loins, marked the curves by exaggerating them
and veiled the reality beneath an artificial amplitude of outline.

He tried to speak but could not find his voice, and was chagrined
at his failure, which Élodie preferred to the most eloquent greeting.
She noticed also and looked upon it as a good omen, that he had
tied his cravat with more than usual pains.

She gave him her hand.

"I wanted to see you," she began, "and talk to you. I did not answer your letter; I did not like it and I did not think it worthy of
you. It would have been more to my taste if it had been more outspoken. It would be to malign your character and common sense to
suppose you do not mean to return to the *Amour peintre* because
you had a trifling altercation there about politics with a man many
years your senior. Rest assured you have no cause to fear my father
will receive you ill whenever you come to see us again. You do not
know him; he has forgotten both what he said to you and what you
said in reply. I do not say there is any great bond of sympathy between you two; but he bears no malice; I tell you frankly he pays
no great heed to you . . . nor to me. He thinks only of his own
affairs and his own pleasures."

She stepped towards the shrubberies surrounding the *Belle Lilloise,* and he followed her with something of repugnance, knowing
it to be the trysting-place of mercenary lovers and amours of a day.
She selected the table furthest out of sight.

"How many things I have to tell you, Évariste. Friendship has
its rights; you do not forbid me to exercise them? I have much to
say about you . . . and something about myself, if you will let me."

The landlord having brought a carafe of lemonade, she filled their
glasses herself with the air of a careful housewife; then she began
to tell him about her childhood, described her mother's beauty,
which she loved to dilate upon both as a tribute to the latter's
memory and as the source of her own good looks, and boasted of

her grandparents' sturdy vigour, for she was proud of her bourgeois blood. She related how at sixteen she had lost this mother she adored and had entered on a life without anyone to love or rely upon. She painted herself as she was, a vehement, passionate nature, full of sensibility and courage, and concluded:

"Oh, Évariste, my girlhood was so sad and lonely I cannot but know what a prize is a heart like yours, and I will not surrender, I give you fair warning, of my own free will and without an effort to retain it, a sympathy on which I trusted I might count and which I held dear."

Évariste gazed at her tenderly.

"Can it be, Élodie, that I am not indifferent to you? Can I really think . . . ?"

He broke off, fearing to say too much and thereby betray so trusting a friendliness.

She gave him a little confiding hand that half-peeped out of the long narrow sleeve with its lace frillings. Her bosom rose and fell in long-drawn sighs.

"Credit me, Évariste, with all the sentiments you would have me feel for you, and you will not be mistaken in the dispositions of my heart."

"Élodie, Élodie, you say that? will you still say it when you know . . ."—he hesitated.

She dropped her eyes; and he finished the sentence in a whisper:

". . . when you know I love you?"

As she heard the declaration, she blushed,—with pleasure. Yet, while her eyes still spoke of a tender ecstasy, a quizzical smile flickered in spite of herself about one corner of her lips. She was thinking:

"And he imagines he proposed first! . . . and he is afraid perhaps of offending me! . . ."

Then she said to him fondly:

"So you had never seen, dear heart, that I loved you?"

They seemed to themselves to be alone, the only two beings in the universe. In his exaltation, Évariste raised his eyes to the firmament flashing with blue and gold:

"See, the sky is looking down at us! It is benign; it is adorable, as you are, beloved; it has your brightness, your gentleness, your smile."

He felt himself one with all nature, it formed part and parcel of his joy and triumph. To his eyes, it was to celebrate his betrothal that the chestnut blossoms lit their flaming candles, the poplars burned aloft like giant torches.

He exulted in his strength and stature. She, with her softer as well as finer nature, more pliable and more malleable, rejoiced in her very weakness and, his subjection once secured, instantly bowed to his ascendancy; now she had brought him under her slavery, she acknowledged him for the master, the hero, the god, burned to obey, to admire, to offer her homage. In the shade of the shrubbery he gave her a long, ardent kiss, which she received with head thrown back and, clasped in Évariste's arms, felt all her flesh melt like wax.

They went on talking a long time of themselves, forgetful of the universe. Évariste abounded mainly in vague, high thoughts, which filled Élodie with ecstasy. She spoke sweetly of things of practical utility and personal interest. Then, presently, when she felt she could stay no longer, she rose with a decided air, gave her lover the three red carnations from the flower in her balcony and sprang lightly into the cabriolet in which she had driven there. It was a hired carriage, painted yellow, hung on very high wheels and certainly had nothing out of the common about it, or the coachman either. But Gamelin was not in the habit of hiring carriages and his friends were hardly more used to such an indulgence. To see the great wheels whirling her away gave him a strange pang and a painful presentiment assailed him; by a sort of hallucination of the mind, the hack horse seemed to be carrying Élodie away from him beyond the bounds of the actual world and present time towards a city of wealth and pleasure, towards abodes of luxury and enjoyment, which he would never be able to enter.

The carriage disappeared. Évariste recovered his calm by degrees; but a dull anguish remained and he felt that the hours of tender abandonment he had just lived would never be his again.

He returned by the Champs Élysées, where women in light sum-

mer dresses were sitting on wooden chairs, talking or sewing, while
their children played under the trees. A woman selling "ladies'
pleasures,"—*her* box was shaped like a drum—reminded him of the
one he had spoken to in the Allée des Veuves, and it seemed as if a
whole epoch of his life had elapsed between the two encounters. He
crossed the Place de la Révolution. In the Tuileries gardens he
caught the distant roar of a host of men, a sound of many voices
shouting in accord, so familiar in those great days of popular enthusiasm which the enemies of the Revolution declared would never
dawn again. He quickened his pace as the noise grew louder and
louder, reached the Rue Honoré and found it thronged with a crowd
of men and women yelling: "Vive la République! Vive la Liberté!"
The walls of the gardens, the windows, the balconies, the very roofs
were black with lookers-on waving hats and handkerchiefs. Preceded by a sapper, who cleared a way for the procession, surrounded by Municipal Officers, National Guards, gunners, gendarmes, huzzars, advanced slowly, high above the backs of the
citizens, a man of a bilious complexion, a wreath of oak-leaves
about his brow, his body wrapped in an old green surtout with an
ermine collar. The women threw him flowers, while he cast about
him the piercing glance of his jaundiced eyes, as though, in this
enthusiastic multitude he was still searching out enemies of the
people to denounce, traitors to punish. As he went by, Gamelin bent
his head and joining his voice to a hundred thousand others, shouted
his:

"Vive Marat!"

The triumphant hero entered the Hall of the Convention like Fate
personified. While the crowd slowly dispersed Gamelin sat on a
stone post in the Rue Honoré and pressed his hand over his heart
to check its wild beating. What he had seen filled him with high
emotion and burning enthusiasm.

He loved and worshipped Marat, who, sick and fevered, his veins
on fire, eaten up by ulcers, was wearing out the last remnants of
his strength in the service of the Republic, and in his own poor
house, closed to no man, welcomed him with open arms, conversed
eagerly with him of public affairs, questioned him sometimes on the
machinations of evil-doers. He rejoiced that the enemies of *the Just,*
conspiring for his ruin, had prepared his triumph; he blessed the
Revolutionary Tribunal, which acquitting the Friend of the People
had given back to the Convention the most zealous and most immaculate of its legislators. Again his eyes could see the head racked
with fever, garlanded with the civic crown, the features instinct
with virtuous pride and pitiless love, the worn, ravaged, powerful
face, the close-pressed lips, the broad chest, the strong man dying
by inches who, raised aloft in the living chariot of his triumph,
seemed to exhort his fellow-citizens: "Be ye like me,—patriots to
the death!"

The street was empty, darkening with the shadows of approaching night; the lamplighter went by with his cresset, and Gamelin muttered to himself:

"Yes, to the death!"

V

Y nine in the morning Évariste reached the gardens of the Luxembourg, to find Élodie already there seated on a bench waiting for him.

It was a month ago they had exchanged their vows and since then they had seen each other every day, either at the *Amour peintre* or at the studio in the Place de Thionville. Their meetings had been very tender, but at the same time characterized by a certain reserve that checked their expansiveness,—a reserve due to the staid and virtuous temper of the lover, a theist and a good citizen, who, while ready to make his beloved mistress his own before the law or with God alone for witness according as circumstances demanded, would do nothing save publicly and in the light of day. Élodie knew the resolution to be right and honourable; but, despairing of a marriage that seemed impossible from every point of view and loath to outrage the prejudices of society, she contemplated in her inmost heart a liaison that could be kept a secret till the lapse of time gave it sanction. She hoped one day to overcome the scruples of a lover she could have wished less scrupulous, and meantime, unwilling to postpone some necessary confidences as to the past, she had asked him to meet her for a lover's talk in a lonely corner of the gardens near the Carthusian Priory.

She threw him a tender look, took his hand frankly, invited him to share the bench and speaking slowly and thoughtfully:

"I esteem you too well, Évariste, to hide anything from you. I believe myself worthy of you; I should not be so were I not to tell you everything. Hear me and be my judge. I have no act to reproach myself with that is degrading or base, or even merely selfish. I have only been weak and credulous. . . . Do not forget, dear Évariste, the difficult circumstances in which I found myself. You know how it was with me; I had lost my mother, my father, still a young man, thought only of his own amusement and neglected me. I had a feeling heart, nature has dowered me with a loving temper and a generous soul; it was true she had not denied me a firm will and a sound judgment, but in those days what ruled my conduct was passion, not reason. Alas! it would be the same again to-day, if the two were not in harmony; I should be driven to give myself to you, beloved, heart and soul, and for ever!"

She expressed herself in firm, well-balanced phrases. She had well thought over what she would say, having long ago made up her mind to this confession for several reasons—because she was naturally candid, because she found pleasure in following Rousseau's example, and because, as she told herself reasonably enough:

"One day Évariste must fathom a secret which is known to others as well as myself. A frank avowal is best. It is unforced and therefore to my credit, and only tells him what some time or other he would discover to my shame."

Soft-hearted as she was and amenable to nature's promptings, she did not feel herself to be very much to blame and this made her confession the easier; besides which, she had no intention of telling more than was absolutely requisite.

"Ah!" she sighed, "why did I not know you, Évariste, in the days when I was alone and forsaken?"

Gamelin had taken her request quite literally when Élodie asked him to be her judge. Primed at once by nature and the education of books for the exercise of domestic justice, he sat ready to receive Élodie's admissions.

As she still hesitated, he motioned to her to proceed. Then she began speaking very simply:

"A young man, who with many defects of character combined some good qualities, and only showed the latter, found me to his taste and courted me with a perseverance that was surprising in such a case; he was in the flower of his youth, full of charm and the idol of a bevy of charming women who made no attempt to hide their adoration. It was not his good looks nor even his brilliance that appealed to me. . . . He touched my heart by the tokens of true love he gave me, and I do think he loved me truly. He was tender, impassioned. I asked no pledge save of his heart, and alas! his heart was fickle. . . . I blame no one but myself; it is my confession I am making, not his. I lay nothing to his charge, for indeed he is become a stranger to me. Ah! believe me, Évariste, I swear it, he is no more to me than if he had never existed."

She had finished, but Gamelin vouchsafed no answer. He folded his arms, a steadfast, sombre look settling in his eyes. His mistress and his sister Julie were running together in his thoughts. Julie too had hearkened to a lover; but, unlike, altogether unlike, he thought, the unhappy Élodie, *she* had let him have his will and carry her off, not misled by the promptings of a tender heart, but to enjoy, far from home and friends, the sweets of luxury and pleasure. He was a stern moralist; he had condemned his sister and was half inclined to condemn his mistress.

Élodie resumed in a very pleading voice:

"I was full of Jean-Jacques' philosophy; I believed men were naturally honest and honourable. My misfortune was to have encountered a lover who was not formed in the school of nature and natural morality, and whom social prejudice, ambition, self-love, a false point of honour had made selfish and treacherous."

The words produced the effect she had calculated on. Gamelin's eyes softened. He asked:

"Who was your seducer? Is he a man I know?"

"You do not know him."

"Tell me his name."

She had foreseen the question and was firmly resolved not to answer it.

She gave her reasons:

"Spare me, I beseech you. For your peace of mind as for my own, I have already said too much."

Then, as he still pressed her:

"In the sacred name of our love, I refuse to tell you anything to give you a definite notion of this stranger. I will not give your jealousy a shape to feed on; I will not bring a harassing shadow between you and me. I have not forgotten the man's name, but I will never let you know it."

Gamelin insisted on knowing the name of the seducer,—that was the word he employed all through, for he felt no doubt Élodie had been seduced, cajoled, trifled with. He could not so much as conceive any other possibility,—that she had obeyed an overmastering desire, an irresistible craving, listening to the tempter's voice in the shape of her own flesh and blood; he could not find it credible that the fair victim, a creature of hot passion and a fond heart, had offered herself a willing sacrifice; to satisfy his ideal, she must needs have been overborne by force or fraud, constrained by sheer violence, caught in snares spread about her steps on every side. He questioned her in guarded terms, but with a close, searching, embarrassing persistency. He asked her how the liaison began, if it was long or short, tranquil or troubled, under what circumstances it was broken off. And his enquiries came back again and again to the means the fellow had used to cajole her, as if these must surely have been extraordinary and unheard of. But all his cross-examination was in vain. She kept her own counsel with a gentle, deprecatory obstinacy, her lips tightly pressed together and tears welling in her eyes.

Presently, however, Évariste having asked where the man was now, she told him:

"He has left the Kingdom—France, I mean," she corrected herself in an instant.

"An *émigré!*" ejaculated Gamelin.

She looked at him, speechless, at once reassured and disheartened to see him create in his own mind a truth in accordance with his political passions and of his own motion give his jealousy a Jacobin complexion.

In actual fact Élodie's lover was a little lawyer's clerk, a very

pretty lad, half Adonis, half guttersnipe, whom she had adored
and the thought of whom, though three years had gone by since,
still thrilled her nerves. Rich old women were his particular game,
and he deserted Élodie for a woman of the world of a certain age
who could and did recompense his merits. Having, after the abolition of offices, attained a post in the Mairie of Paris, he was now a
sansculotte dragoon and the hanger-on of a *ci-devant* Countess.

"A noble! an *émigré!*" muttered Gamelin, whom she took good
care not to undeceive, never having been desirous he should know
the whole truth. "And he deserted you like a dastard?"

She nodded in answer. He clasped her to his heart:

"Dear victim of the vile corruption of monarchies, my love shall
avenge his villainy! Heaven grant, I may meet the scoundrel! I
shall not fail to know him!"

She turned away, at one and the same time saddened and smiling,—and disappointed. She would fain have had him wiser in the
lore of love, with more of the natural man about him, more perhaps even of the brute. She felt he forgave so readily only because
his imagination was cold and the secret she had revealed awoke in
him none of the mental pictures that torture sensuous natures,—in
a word, that he saw her seduction solely under a moral and social
aspect.

They had risen, and while they walked up and down the shady
avenues of the gardens, he informed her that he only esteemed her
the more because she had suffered wrong. Élodie entertained no
such high claims; however, take him as he was, she loved him, and
admired the brilliant artistic genius she divined in him.

As they left the Luxembourg, they came upon crowds thronging
the Rue de l'Égalité and the whole neighbourhood of the Théâtre
de la Nation. There was nothing to surprise them in this; for several days great excitement had prevailed in the most patriotic Sections; denunciations were rife against the Orleans faction and the
Brissotin plotters, who were conspiring, it was said, to bring about
the ruin of Paris and the massacre of good Republicans. Gamelin
himself a short time back had signed a petition from the Commune
demanding the expulsion of the Twenty-one.

Just before passing under the arcade, joining the theatre to the
neighbouring house, they had to find their way through a group of
citizens *en carmagnole* who were listening to a harangue from a
young soldier mounted on the top of the gallery. He looked as beautiful as the Eros of Praxiteles in his helmet of panther-skin. This
fascinating warrior was charging the People's Friend with indolence:

"Marat, you are asleep," he was crying, "and the federalists are
forging fetters to bind us."

Hardly had Élodie cast eyes on the orator before she turned rapidly to Évariste and begged him to get her away. The crowd, she

declared, frightened her and she was afraid of fainting in the crush.

They parted in the Place de la Nation, swearing an oath of eternal fidelity.

That same morning early the *citoyen* Brotteaux had made the *citoyenne* Gamelin the magnificent present of a capon. It would have been an act of indiscretion for him to mention how he had come by it; as a fact, he had it of a *Dame de la Halle* at the Point Eustache for whom he sometimes acted as amanuensis, and as everybody knows, these "Ladies of the Market" cherished Royalist sympathies and were in correspondence with the *émigrés*. The *citoyenne* Gamelin had received the gifts with heartfelt gratitude. Such dainties were scarce ever seen then; victuals grew dearer every day. The people feared a famine; the aristocrats, they said, wished it, and the "corner" makers were at work to bring it about.

The *citoyen* Brotteaux, being invited to eat his share of the capon at the midday dinner, appeared in due course and congratulated his hostess on the rich aroma of cooking that assailed his nostrils. Indeed a noble smell of rich, savoury broth filled the painter's studio.

"You are very obliging, sir," replied the good dame. "To prepare the digestion for your capon, I have made a vegetable soup with a slice of fat bacon and a big beef bone. There's nothing like a marrow-bone, sir, to give soup a flavour."

"The maxim does you honour, *citoyenne*," returned the old man. "And you will be doing wisely to put back again to-morrow and the day after, all the week, in fact, to put back again, I say, this precious bone in the pot, which it will continue to flavour. The wise woman of Panzoust always did so; she used to make a soup of green cabbages with a rind of rusty bacon and an old *savorados*. That is what in her country, which is also mine, they call the medullary bone, the most tasty and most succulent of all bones."

"This lady you speak of, sir," remarked the *citoyenne* Gamelin, "was she not rather a saving soul, to make the same bone serve so many times over?"

"Oh! she lived in a small way," explained Brotteaux, "she was poor, albeit a prophetess."

At that moment, Évariste Gamelin returned, agitated by the confession he had heard and determined to know who was Élodie's betrayer, to avenge at one and the same time the Republic's wrong and his own on the miscreant.

After the usual greetings had been exchanged, the *citoyen* Brotteaux resumed the thread of his discourse:

"It is seldom those who make a trade of foretelling the future grow rich. Their impostures are too soon found out and their trickery renders them odious. But indeed we should be bound to detest them much worse if they prophesied truly. A man's life would be intolerable if he knew what is to befall him. He would be aware of calamities to come and suffer their pains in advance, while he would get no joy of present blessings whose end he would foresee. Ignorance is a necessary condition of human happiness, and it must be owned that in most cases we fulfil it well. We know almost nothing about ourselves; absolutely nothing about our neighbours. Ignorance constitutes our peace of mind; self-deception our felicity."

The *citoyenne* Gamelin set the soup on the table, said the Benedicite and seated her son and her guest at the board. She stood up herself to eat, declining the chair the *citoyen* Brotteaux offered her beside him; she said she knew what good manners required of a woman.

VI

TEN o'clock in the forenoon. Not a breath of wind. It was the hottest July ever known. In the narrow Rue de Jérusalem a hundred or so citizens of the Section were waiting in queue at the baker's door, under the eye of four National Guards who stood at ease smoking their pipes.

The National Convention had decreed the *maximum*,—and instantly corn and flour had disappeared. Like the Israelites in the wilderness, the Parisians had to rise before daybreak if they wished to eat. The crowd was lined up, men, women, and children tightly packed together, under a sky of molten lead. The heat beat down on the rotting foulness of the kennels and exaggerated the stench of unwashed, sweating humanity. All were pushing, abusing their neighbours, exchanging looks fraught with every sort of emotion one human being can feel for another,—dislike, disgust, interest, attraction, indifference. Painful experience had taught them there was not bread enough for everybody; so the late comers were always trying to push forward, while those who lost ground complained bitterly and indignantly and vainly claimed their rights. Women shoved and elbowed savagely to keep their place or squeeze into a better. When the press grew too intolerable, cries rose of "Stop pushing there!" while each and all protested they could not help it—it was someone else pushing them.

To obviate these daily scenes of disorder, the officials appointed by the Section had conceived the notion of fastening a rope to the shop-door which each applicant held in his proper order; but hands at such close quarters *would* come in contact on the rope and a struggle would result. Whoever lost hold could never recover it, while the disappointed and the mischievously inclined sometimes cut the cord. In the end the plan had to be abandoned.

On this occasion there was the usual suffocation and confusion. While some swore they were dying, others indulged in jokes or loose remarks; all abused the aristocrats and federalists, authors of all the misery. When a dog ran by, wags hailed the beast as Pitt. More than once a loud slap showed that some *citoyenne* in the line had resented with a vigorous hand the insolence of a lewd admirer, while, pressed close against her neighbour, a young servant girl, with eyes half shut and mouth half open, stood sighing in a sort of trance. At any word, or gesture, or attitude of a sort to provoke the sportive humour of the coarse-minded populace, a knot of young libertines would strike up the *Ça-ira* in chorus, regardless of the protests of an old Jacobin, highly indignant to see a dirty meaning attached to a refrain expressive of the Republican faith in a future of justice and happiness.

His ladder under his arm, a billsticker appeared to post up on a blank wall facing the baker's a proclamation by the Commune apportioning the rations of butcher's-meat. Passers-by halted to read the notice, still sticky with paste. A cabbage vendor going by, basket on back, began calling out in her loud cracked voice:

"They'm all gone, the purty oxen! best rake up the guts!"

Suddenly such an appalling stench of putrefaction rose from a sewer near by that several people were turned sick; a woman was taken ill and handed over in a fainting condition to a couple of National Guards, who carried her off to a pump a few yards away. All held their noses, and fell to growling and grumbling, exchanging conjectures each more ghastly and alarming than the last. What was it? a dead animal buried thereabouts, a dead fish, perhaps, put in for mischief's sake, or more likely a victim of the September massacres, some noble or priest, left to rot in a cellar.

"They buried them in cellars, eh?"

"They got rid of 'em anywhere and anyhow."

"It will be one of the Châtelet prisoners. On the 2nd I saw three hundred in a heap on the Port au Change."

The Parisians dreaded the vengeance of these aristocrats who were like to poison them with their dead bodies.

Évariste Gamelin joined the line; he was resolved to spare his old mother the fatigues of the long wait. His neighbour, the *citoyen* Brotteaux, went with him, calm and smiling, his Lucretius in the baggy pocket of his plum-coloured coat.

The good old fellow enjoyed the scene, calling it a bit of low life worthy the brush of a modern Teniers.

"These street-porters and goodwives," he declared, "are more amusing than the Greeks and Romans our painters are so fond of nowadays. For my part, I have always admired the Flemish style."

One fact he was too sensible and tactful to mention—that he had himself owned a gallery of Dutch masters rivalled only by Monsieur de Choiseul's in the number and excellence of the examples.

"Nothing is beautiful save the Antique," returned the painter, "and what is inspired by it. Still, I grant you these low-life scenes

by Teniers, Jan Steen or Ostade are better stuff than the frills and
furbelows of Watteau, Boucher, or Van Loo; humanity is shown in
an ugly light, but it is not degraded as it is by a Baudouin or a Fragonard."

A hawker went by bawling:

"Bulletin of the Revolutionary Tribunal! . . . list of the condemned!"

"One Revolutionary Tribunal is not enough," said Gamelin,
"there should be one in every town . . . in every town, do I say?
—nay, in every village, in every hamlet. Fathers of families, citizens, one and all, should constitute themselves judges. At a time
when the enemy's cannon is at her gates and the assassin's dagger
at her throat, the Nation must hold mercy to be parricide. What!
Lyons, Marseilles, Bordeaux in insurrection, Corsica in revolt, La
Vendée on fire, Mayence and Valenciennes in the hands of the Coalition, treason in the country, town and camp, treason sitting on
the very benches of the National Convention, treason assisting,
map in hand, at the council board of our Commanders in the field!
. . . The fatherland is in danger—and the guillotine must save
her!"

"I have no objection on principle to make to the guillotine," replied Brotteaux. "Nature, my only mistress and my only instruc-
tress, certainly offers me no suggestion to the effect that a man's
life is of any value; on the contrary, she teaches in all kinds of
ways that it is of none. The sole end and object of living beings
seems to be to serve as food for other beings destined to the same
end. Murder is of natural right; therefore, the penalty of death is
lawful, on condition it is exercised from no motives either of virtue
or of justice, but by necessity or to gain some profit thereby. However, I must have perverse instincts, for I sicken to see blood flow,
and this defect of character all my philosophy has failed so far to
correct."

"Republicans," answered Évariste, "are humane and full of feeling. It is only despots hold the death penalty to be a necessary
attribute of authority. The sovereign people will do away with it
one day. Robespierre fought against it, and all good patriots were
with him; the law abolishing it cannot be too soon promulgated.
But it will not have to be applied till the last foe of the Republic
has perished beneath the sword of law and order."

Gamelin and Brotteaux had by this time a number of late comers
behind them and amongst these several women of the Section, including a stalwart, handsome *tricoteuse,* in head-kerchief and
sabots, wearing a sword in a shoulder belt, a pretty girl with a mop
of golden hair and a very tumbled neckerchief, and a young mother,
pale and thin, giving the breast to a sickly infant.

The child, which could get no milk, was screaming, but its voice
was weak and stifled by its sobs. Pitifully small, with a pallid, un-

healthy skin and inflamed eyes, the mother gazed at it with mingled anxiety and grief.

"He is very young," observed Gamelin, turning to look at the unhappy infant groaning just at his back, half stifled amid the crowd of new arrivals.

"He is six months old, poor love! . . . His father is with the army; he is one of the men who drove back the Austrians at Condé. His name is Dumonteil (Michel), a draper's assistant by trade. He enlisted at a booth they had established in front of the Hôtel de Ville. Poor lad, he was all for defending his country and seeing the world. . . . He writes telling me to be patient. But pray, how am I to feed Paul (he's called Paul, you know) when I can't feed myself?"

"Oh, dear!" exclaimed the pretty girl with the flaxen hair, "we've got another hour before us yet, and to-night we shall have to repeat the same ceremony over again at the grocer's. You risk your life to get three eggs and a quarter of a pound of butter."

"Butter!" sighed the *citoyenne* Dumonteil, "why, it's three months since I've seen a scrap!"

And a chorus of female voices rose, bewailing the scarcity and dearness of provisions, cursing the *émigrés* and devoting to the guillotine the Commissaries of Sections who were ready to give good-for-nothing minxes, in return for unmentionable services, fat hens and four-pound loaves. Alarming stories passed round of cattle drowned in the Seine, sacks of flour emptied in the sewers, loaves of bread thrown into the latrines. . . . It was all those Royalists, and Rolandists, and Brissotins, who were starving the people, bent on exterminating every living thing in Paris!

All of a sudden the pretty, fair-haired girl with the rumpled neckerchief broke into shrieks as if her petticoats were afire. She was shaking these violently and turning out her pockets, vociferating that somebody had stolen her purse.

At news of the petty theft, a flood of indignation swept over this crowd of poor folks, the same who had sacked the mansions of the Faubourg Saint-Germain and invaded the Tuileries without appropriating the smallest thing, artisans and housewives, who would have burned down the Palace of Versailles with a light heart, but would have thought it a dire disgrace if they had stolen the value of a pin. The young rakes greeted the pretty girl's loss with some ribald jokes, that were immediately drowned under a burst of public indignation. There was some talk of instant execution—hanging the thief to the nearest lamp-post, and an investigation was begun, where everyone spoke at once and nobody would listen to a word of reason. The tall *tricoteuse,* pointing her finger at an old man, strongly suspected of being an unfrocked monk, swore it was the "Capuchin" yonder who was the cut-purse. The crowd believed her without further evidence and raised a shout of "Death! death!"

The old man so unexpectedly exposed to the public vengeance was standing very quietly and soberly just in front of the *citoyen* Brotteaux. He had all the look, there was no denying it, of a *ci-devant* cleric. His aspect was venerable, though the face was changed and drawn by the terrors the poor man had suffered from the violence of the crowd and the recollection of the September days that were still vivid in his imagination. The fear depicted on his features stirred the suspicion of the populace, which is always ready to believe that only the guilty dread its judgments, as if the haste and recklessness with which it pronounces them were not enough to terrify even the most innocent.

Brotteaux had made it a standing rule never to go against the popular feeling of the moment, above all when it was manifestly illogical and cruel, "because in that case," he would say, "the voice of the people was the voice of God." But Brotteaux proved himself untrue to his principles; he asseverated that the old man, whether he was a Capuchin or not, could not have robbed the *citoyenne,* having never gone near her for one moment.

The crowd drew its own conclusion,—the individual who spoke up for the thief was of course his accomplice, and stern measures were proposed to deal with the two malefactors, and when Gamelin offered to guarantee Brotteaux' honesty, the wisest heads suggested sending *him* along with the two others to the Sectional headquarters.

But the pretty girl gave a cry of delight; she had found her purse again. The statement was received with a storm of hisses, and she was threatened with a public whipping,—like a Nun.

"Sir," said the ex-monk, addressing Brotteaux, "I thank you for having spoken in my defence. My name is of no concern, but I had better tell you what it is; I am called Louis de Longuemare. I am in truth a Regular; but not a Capuchin, as those women would have it. There is the widest difference; I am a monk of the Order of the Barnabites, which has given Doctors and Saints without number to the Church. It is only a half-truth to refer its origin to St. Charles Borromeo; we must account as the true founder the Apostle St. Paul, whose cipher it bears on its arms. I have been compelled to quit my cloister, now headquarters of the Section du Pont-Neuf, and adopt a secular habit."

"Nay, Father," said Brotteaux, scrutinizing Monsieur de Longuemare's frock, "your dress is token enough that you have not forsworn your profession; to look at it, one might think you had reformed your Order rather than forsaken it. It is your good heart makes you expose yourself in these austere habiliments to the insults of a godless populace."

"Yet I cannot very well," replied the ex-monk, "wear a blue coat, like a roisterer at a dance!"

"What I mention, Father, about your dress is by way of paying homage to your character and putting you on your guard against the risks you run."

"On the contrary, sir, it would be much better to inspirit me to confess my faith. For indeed, I am only too prone to fear danger. I have abandoned my habit, sir, which is a sort of apostasy; I would fain not have deserted, had it been possible, the House where God granted me for so many years the grace of a peaceable and retired life. I got leave to stay there, and I still continued to occupy my cell, while they turned the church and cloister into a sort of petty *hôtel de ville* they called the Section. I saw, sir, I saw them hack away the emblems of the Holy Verity; I saw the name of the Apostle Paul replaced by a convicted felon's cap. Sometimes I was actually present at the confabulations of the Section, where I heard amazing errors propounded. At last I quitted this place of profanation and went to live on the pension of a hundred pistoles allowed me by the Assembly in a stable that stood empty, the horses having been requisitioned for the service of the armies. There I sing Mass for a few of the faithful, who come to the office to bear witness to the eternity of the Church of Jesus Christ."

"For my part, Father," replied the other, "if you care to know my name, I am called Brotteaux, and I was a publican in former days."

"Sir," returned the Père Longuemare, "I was aware by St. Matthew's example that one may look for good counsel from a publican."

"Father, you are too obliging."

"*Citoyen* Brotteaux," remarked Gamelin, "pray admire the virtues of the people, more hungry for justice than for bread; consider how everyone here is ready to lose his place to chastise the thief. These men and women, victims of such poverty and privation, are of so stern a probity they cannot tolerate a dishonest act."

"It must indeed be owned," replied Brotteaux, "that in their hearty desire to hang the pilferer, these folks were like to do a mischief to this good cleric, to his champion and to his champion's champion. Their avarice itself and their selfish eagerness to safeguard their own welfare were motives enough; the thief in attacking one of them threatened all; self-preservation urged them to punish him. . . . At the same time, it is like enough the most part of these workmen and goodwives are honest and keep their hands off other folk's goods. From the cradle these sentiments have been instilled in them by their father and mother, who have whipped them well and soundly and inculcated the virtues through their backside."

Gamelin did not conceal the fact from his old neighbour that he deemed such language unworthy of a philosopher.

"Virtue," said he, "is natural to mankind; God has planted the seed of it in the heart of mortals."

Old Brotteaux was a sceptic and found in his atheism an abundant source of self-satisfaction.

"I see this much, *citoyen* Gamelin, that, while a Revolutionary for what is of this world, you are, where Heaven is concerned, of a conservative, or even a reactionary temper. Robespierre and Marat are the same to you. For me, I find it strange that Frenchmen, who will not put up with a mortal king any longer, insist on retaining an immortal tyrant, far more despotic and ferocious. For what is the Bastille, or even the *Chambre Ardente*[1] beside Hellfire? Humanity models its gods on its tyrants, and you, who reject the original, preserve the copy!"

"Oh! *citoyen!*" protested Gamelin, "are you not ashamed to hold such language? how can you confound the dark divinities born of ignorance and fear with the Author of Nature? Belief in a benevolent God is necessary for morality. The Supreme Being is the source of all the virtues and a man cannot be a Republican if he does not believe in God. Robespierre knew this, who, as we all remember, had the bust of the philosopher Helvetius removed from the Hall of the Jacobins, because he had taught Frenchmen the lessons of slavery by preaching atheism. . . . I hope, at least, *citoyen* Brotteaux, that, as soon as the Republic has established the worship of Reason, you will not refuse your adhesion to so wise a religion!"

"I love reason, but I am no fanatic in my love," was Brotteaux's answer. "Reason is our guide and beacon-light; but when you have made a divinity of it, it will blind you and instigate you to crime," —and he proceeded to develop his thesis, standing both feet in the kennel, as he had once been used to perorate, seated in one of Baron d'Holbach's gilt armchairs, which, as he was fond of saying, formed the basis of natural philosophy.

"Jean Jacques Rousseau," he proceeded, "who was not without talents, particularly in music, was a scampish fellow who professed to derive his morality from Nature while all the time he got it from the dogmas of Calvin. Nature teaches us to devour each other and gives us the example of all the crimes and all the vices which the social state corrects or conceals. We should love virtue; but it is well to know that this is simply and solely a convenient expedient invented by men in order to live comfortably together. What we call morality is merely a desperate enterprise, a forlorn hope, on the part of our fellow creatures to reverse the order of the universe, which is strife and murder, the blind interplay of hostile forces. She destroys herself, and the more I think of things, the more convinced I am that the universe is mad. Theologians and philosophers, who make God the author of Nature and the architect of the universe, show Him to us as illogical and ill-conditioned. They de-

[1]*Chambre Ardente,*—under the ancien régime, a tribunal charged with the investigation of heinous crimes and having power to burn those found guilty.

clare Him benevolent, because they are afraid of Him, but they are forced to admit that His acts are atrocious. They attribute a malignity to him seldom to be found even in mankind. And that is how they get human beings to adore Him. For our miserable race would never lavish worship on just and benevolent deities from which they would have nothing to fear; they would feel only a barren gratitude for their benefits. Without purgatory and hell, your good God would be a mighty poor creature."

"Sir," said the Père Longuemare, "do not talk of Nature; you do not know what Nature is."

"Egad, I know it as well as you do, Father."

"You cannot know it, because you have not religion, and religion alone teaches us what Nature is, wherein it is good, and how it has been made evil. However, you must not expect me to answer you; God has vouchsafed me, to refute your errors, neither eloquence nor force of intellect. I should only be afraid, by my inadequate replies, of giving you occasion to blaspheme and further reasons for hardening your heart. I feel a strong desire to help you; yet the sole fruit of my importunate efforts would be to . . ."

The discussion was cut short by a tremendous shout coming from the head of the column to warn the whole regiment of famished citizens that the baker was opening his doors. The line began to push forward, but very, very slowly. A National Guard on duty admitted the purchasers one by one. The baker, his wife and boy presided over the sale, assisted by two Civil Commissaries. These, wearing a tricoloured riband round the left arm, saw that the customers belonged to the Section and were given their proper share in proportion to the number of mouths to be filled.

The *citoyen* Brotteaux made the quest of pleasure the one and only aim of life, holding that the reason and the senses, the sole judges when gods there were none, were unable to conceive any other. Accordingly, finding the painter's remarks somewhat overfull of fanaticism, and the Monk's of simplicity, to please his taste, this wise man, bent on squaring his behaviour with his views and relieving the tedium of waiting, drew from the bulging pocket of his plum-coloured coat his Lucretius, now as always his chiefest solace and faithful comforter. The binding of red morocco was chafed by hard wear, and the *citoyen* Brotteaux had judiciously erased the coat of arms that once embellished it,—three islets or, which his father the financier had bought for good money down. He opened the book at the passage where the poet philosopher, who is for curing men of the futile and mischievous passion of love, surprises a woman in the arms of her serving-women in a state bound to offend all a lover's susceptibilities. The *citoyen* Brotteaux read the lines, though not without casting a surreptitious glance at the golden pate of the pretty girl in front of him and enjoying a sniff of the heady perfume of the little slut's hot skin. The poet

Lucretius was a wise man, but he had only one string to his bow; his disciple Brotteaux had several.

So he read on, taking two steps forward every quarter of an hour. His ear, soothed by the grave and cadenced numbers of the Latin Muse, was deaf to the women's scolding about the monstrous prices of bread and sugar and coffee, candles and soap. In this calm and unruffled mood he reached the threshold of the bakehouse. Behind him, Évariste Gamelin could see over his head the gilt corn-sheaf surmounting the iron grating that filled the fanlight over the door.

When his turn came to enter the shop, he found the hampers and lockers already emptied; the baker handed him the only scrap of bread left, which did not weigh two pounds. Évariste paid his money, and the gate was slammed on his heels, for fear of a riot and the people carrying the place by storm.

But there was no need to fear; these poor folks, trained to obedience alike by their old-time oppressors and by their liberators of to-day, slunk off with drooping heads and dragging feet.

As he reached the corner of the street, Gamelin caught sight of the *citoyenne* Dumonteil, seated on a stone post, her nursling in her arms. She sat there quite still; her face was colourless and her tearless eyes seemed to see nothing. The infant was sucking her finger voraciously. Gamelin stood a while in front of her, abashed and uncertain what to do. She did not appear to see him.

He stammered something, then pulled out his pocket-knife, a clasp-knife with a horn handle, cut his loaf in two and laid half on the young mother's knee. She looked up at him in wonder; but he had already turned the corner of the street.

On reaching home, Évariste found his mother sitting at the window darning stockings. With a light laugh he put his half of the bread in her hand.

"You must forgive me, mother dear; I was tired out with standing about and exhausted by the heat, and out in the street there as I trudged home, mouthful by mouthful I have gobbled up half of our allowance. There's barely your share left,"—and as he spoke, he made a pretence of shaking the crumbs off his jacket.

VII

MPLOYING a very old-fashioned locution, the *cito-yenne* Gamelin had declared: "that by dint of eating chestnuts they would be turning into chestnuts." As a matter of fact, on that day, the 13th July, she and her son had made their midday dinner on a basin of chestnut porridge. As they were finishing this austere repast, a lady pushed open the door and the room was flooded in an instant with the splendour of her presence and the fragrance of her perfumes. Évariste recognized the *citoyenne* Rochemaure. Thinking she had mistaken the door and meant her visit for the *citoyen* Brotteaux, her friend of other days, he was already preparing to point her out the *ci-devant* aristocrat's garret or perhaps summon Brotteaux and so spare an elegant woman the task of scrambling up a mill-ladder; but she made it clear at once that the *citoyen* Évariste Gamelin and no other was the person she had come to see by announcing that she was happy to find him at home and was his servant to command.

They were not entirely strangers to each other, having met more than once in David's studio, in a box at the Assembly Hall, at the Jacobins, at Venua's restaurant. On these occasions she had been struck by his good looks and youth and interesting air.

Wearing a hat beribboned like a fairing and plumed like the head-piece of a Representative on mission, the *citoyenne* Rochemaure was wigged, painted, patched and scented. But her complexion was young and fresh behind all these disguises; these extravagant artificialities of fashion only betokened a frantic haste to enjoy life and the feverishness of these dreadful days when the morrow was so uncertain. Her corsage, with wide facings and enormous basques and all ablaze with huge steel buttons, was blood-red, and it was hard to tell, so aristocratic and so revolutionary at one and the same time was her array, whether it was the colours of the victims or of the headsman that she sported. A young officer, a dragoon, accompanied her.

Dandling her long cane by its handle of mother-o'-pearl, a tall, fine woman, of generous proportions and ample bosom, she made the circuit of the studio, and putting up to her grey eyes her double quizzing-glasses of gold, examined the painter's canvases with many smiles and exclamations of delight, admiring the handsome artist and flattering him in hopes of a return in kind.

"What," asked the *citoyenne*, "is that picture—it is so nobly conceived, so touching—of a gentle, beautiful woman standing by a young man lying sick?"

Gamelin told her it was meant to represent *Orestes tended by his*

sister Electra, and that, had he been able to finish it, it might
perhaps have been the least unsatisfactory of his works.

"The subject," he went on to say, "is taken from the *Orestes* of
Euripides. I had read, in a translation of this tragedy made years
ago, a scene that filled me with admiration,—the one where the
young Electra, raising her brother on his bed of pain, wipes away
the froth that gathers on his lips, puts aside the locks that blind
his eyes and beseeches the brother she loves to hearken to what
she will tell him while the Furies are at peace for the moment. . . .
As I read and re-read this translation, I seemed to be aware of a
kind of fog that shrouded the forms of Greek perfection, a fog I
could not drive away. I pictured the original text to myself as more
nervous and pitched in a different accent. Feeling a keen desire
to get a precise idea of the thing, I went to Monsieur Gail, who
was the Professor of Greek at the Collège de France (this was in
'91), and begged him to expound the scene to me word by word.
He did what I asked, and I then saw that the Ancients are much
more simple and homely than people think. Thus, for instance,
Electra says to Orestes: 'Dear brother, what joy it gave me to see
thee sleep! Shall I help thee to rise?' And Orestes answers: 'Yes,
help me, take me in thy arms, and wipe away the spume that still
clings about my mouth and eyes. Put thy bosom against mine and
part from my brow my tangled hair, for it blinds my eyes. . . .'
My mind still full of this poetry, so young and vivid, ringing with
these simple, strong phrases, I sketched the picture you see there,
citoyenne."

The painter, who, as a rule, spoke so sparingly of his works,
waxed eloquent on the subject of this one. At an encouraging gesture from the *citoyenne* Rochemaure, who lifted her quizzing-
glasses in token of attention, he continued:

"Hennequin has depicted the madness of Orestes in masterly
fashion. But Orestes appeals to us still more poignantly in his sorrow than when he is distraught. What a fate was his! It was filial
piety, obedience to a sacred obligation, drove him to commit his
dreadful deed,—a sin the gods cannot but pardon, but which men
will never condone. To avenge outraged justice, he has repudiated
Nature, has made himself a monster, has torn out his own heart.
But his spirit remains unbroken under the weight of his horrible,
yet innocent crime. . . . That is what I would fain have exhibited
in my group of brother and sister." He stepped up to the canvas
and looked at it not without satisfaction.

"Parts of the picture," he said, "are pretty nearly finished; the
head and arm of Orestes, for instance."

"It is an admirable composition. . . . And Orestes reminds me
of you, *citoyen* Gamelin."

"You think he is like me?" exclaimed the painter, with a grave
smile.

She took the chair Gamelin offered her. The young dragoon stood beside her, his hand on the back of the chair on which she sat. Which showed plainly that the Revolution was an accomplished fact, for under the ancien régime, no man would ever, in company, have touched so much as with the tip of a finger, the seat occupied by a lady. In those days a gentleman was trained and broken in to the laws of politeness, sometimes pretty hard laws, and taught to understand that a scrupulous self-restraint in public places gives a peculiar zest to the sweet familiarity of the boudoir, and that to lose your respectful awe of a woman, you must first have that feeling.

Louise Masché de Rochemaure, daughter of a Lieutenant of the King's Hunt, widow of a Procureur and, for twenty years, the faithful mistress of the financier Brotteaux des Ilettes, had fallen in with the new ideas. She was to be seen, in July, 1790, digging the soil of the Champ de Mars. Her strong inclination to side with the powers that be had carried her readily enough along a political path that started with the Feuillants and led by way of the Girondins to end on the summit of *the Mountain,* while at the same time a spirit of compromise, a passion for conversion and a certain aptitude for intrigue still attached her to the aristocratic and anti-revolutionary party. She was to be met everywhere,—at coffee houses and theatres, fashionable restaurants, gaming-saloons, drawing-rooms, newspaper offices and ante-chambers of Committees. The Revolution yielded her a hundred satisfactions,—novelty and amusement, smiles and pleasures, business ventures and profitable speculations. Combining political with amorous intrigue, playing the harp, drawing landscapes, singing ballads, dancing Greek dances, giving supper parties, entertaining pretty women, such as the Comtesse de Beaufort and the actress Mademoiselle Descoings, presiding all night long over a *trente-et-un* or *biribi* table and an adept at *rouge et noir,* she still found time to be charitable to her friends. Inquisitive and interfering, giddy-pated and frivolous, she understood men but knew nothing of the masses; as indifferent to the creed she professed as to the opinions she felt bound to repudiate, understanding nothing whatever of all that was happening in the country, she was enterprising, intrepid, and full of audacity from sheer ignorance of danger and an unbounded confidence in the efficacy of her charms.

The soldier who escorted her was in the heyday of youth. A brazen helmet decorated with a panther skin and the crest set off with a crimson cock's-comb shaded his fresh young face and displayed a long and terrific mane that swept his back. His red jacket was cut short and square, barely reaching to the waist, the better to show off his elegant figure. In his girdle he carried an enormous sabre, the hilt of which was a glittering eagle's beak. A pair of flapped breeches of sky blue moulded the fine muscles of his legs and was braided in rich arabesques of a darker blue on the thigh. He might have been a dancer dressed for some warlike and dashing rôle, in *Achilles at Scyros* or *Alexander's Wedding-feast,* in a costume designed by a pupil of David with the one idea of accentuating every line of the shape.

Gamelin had a vague recollection of having seen him before. He was, in fact, the same young soldier he had come upon a fortnight previously haranguing the people from the arcades of the Théâtre de la Nation.

The *citoyenne* Rochemaure introduced him by name:

"The *citoyen* Henry, Member of the Revolutionary Committee of the Section of the Rights of Man."

She had him always at her heels,—a mirror of gallantry and a living and walking guarantee of patriotism.

The *citoyenne* complimented Gamelin on his talents and asked him if he would be willing to design a card for a protégée of hers, a fashionable milliner. He would, of course, choose an appropriate *motif,*—a woman trying on a scarf before a cheval glass, for instance, or a young workwoman carrying a band-box on her arm.

She had heard several artists mentioned as competent to execute a little matter of the sort,—Fragonard *fils,* young Ducis, as well as a certain Prudhomme; but she would rather apply to the *citoyen* Évariste Gamelin. However, she made no definite proposal on this head and it was evident she had mentioned the commission merely by way of starting the conversation. In truth she had come for something quite different. She wanted the *citoyen* Gamelin to do her a favour; knowing he was a friend of the *citoyen* Marat, she had come to ask him to introduce her to the Friend of the People, with whom she desired an interview.

Gamelin replied that he was too insignificant an individual to present her to Marat, besides which, she had no need of anyone to be her sponsor; Marat, albeit overwhelmed with business, was not the inaccessible person he was said to be,—and, added Gamelin:

"He will receive you, *citoyenne,* if you are in distress; his great heart makes him compassionate to all who suffer. He will likewise receive you if you have any revelation to make concerning the public weal; he has vowed his days to the unmasking of traitors."

The *citoyenne* Rochemaure answered that she would be happy to greet in Marat an illustrious citizen, who had rendered great services to his country, who was capable of rendering greater still, and that she was anxious to bring the legislator in question into relation with friends of hers of good repute and good will, philanthropists favoured by fortune and competent to provide him with new means of satisfying his ardent affection for humanity.

"It is very desirable," she concluded, "to make the rich co-operate in securing public prosperity."

In actual fact, the *citoyenne* had promised the banker Morhardt to arrange a dinner where he and Marat should meet.

Morhardt, a Swiss like the Friend of the People, had entered into a combination with several deputies of the Convention, Julien (of Toulouse), Delaunay (of Angers) and the ex-Capuchin Chabot, to speculate in the shares of the *Compagnie des Indes*. The game was very simple,—to bring down the price of these shares to 650 livres by proposing motions pointing in the direction of confiscation, in order to buy up the greatest possible number at this figure and then push them up to 4,000 or 5,000 livres by dint of proposals of a reassuring nature. But for Chabot, Julien, Delaunay, their little ways were too notorious, while suspicions were rife of Lacroix, Fabre d'Églantine, and even Danton. The arch-speculator, the Baron de Batz, was looking for new confederates in the Convention and had advised Morhardt to sound Marat.

This idea of the anti-revolutionary speculators was not so extravagant as might have been supposed at the first blush. It was always the way of these gentry to form alliance with those in power at the moment, and by virtue of his popularity, his pen, his character, Marat was a power to be reckoned with. The Girondists were near shipwreck; the Dantonists, battered by the hurricane, had lost their hold on the helm. Robespierre, the idol of the people, was a man jealous of his scrupulous honesty, full of suspicion, impossible to approach. The great thing was to get round Marat, to secure his good will against the day when he should be dictator— and everything pointed to this consummation,—his popularity, his ambition, his eagerness to recommend heroic measures. And it might be, after all, Marat would re-establish order, the finances, the prosperity of the country. More than once he had risen in revolt against the zealots who were for outbidding him in fanaticism; for some time past he had been denouncing the demagogues as vehemently as the moderates. After inciting the people to sack the "cornerers'" shops and hang them over their own counters, he was now exhorting the citizens to be calm and prudent. He was growing into an administrator.

In spite of certain rumours disseminated against him as against all the other chiefs of the Revolution, these pirates of the money-market did not believe he could be corrupted, but they did know him to be vain and credulous, and they hoped to win him over by flattery and still more by a condescending friendliness which they looked upon as the most seductive form of flattery from men like themselves. They counted, thanks to him, on blowing hot and cold on all the securities they might wish to buy and sell, and making him serve their interests while supposing himself to be acting solely for the public good.

Great as a go-between, albeit she was still of an age for amours on her own account, the *citoyenne* Rochemaure had made it her mission to bring together the legislator-journalist and the banker, and in her extravagant imagination she already saw the man of the underworld, the man whose hands were yet red with the blood of the September massacres, a partner in the game of the financiers whose agent she was; she pictured him drawn by his very warmth of feeling and unsophisticated candour into the whirlpool of speculation, a recruit to the côterie she loved of "corner" makers, contractors, foreign emissaries, gamblers, and women of gallantry.

She insisted on the *citoyen* Gamelin taking her to see the Friend of the People, who lived quite near, in the Rue des Cordeliers, near the church. After some little show of reluctance, the painter acceded to the *citoyenne's* wishes.

The dragoon Henry was invited to join them in the visit, but declined, declaring he meant to keep his liberty of action, even towards the *citoyen* Marat, who, he felt no doubt, had rendered services to the Republic, but was weakening nowadays; had he not, in his news sheet, counselled resignation as the proper thing for the people of Paris?

And the young man, in a sweet voice, broken by long-drawn sighs, deplored the fate of the Republic, betrayed by the men in whom she had put her trust,—Danton rejecting the notion of a tax on the rich, Robespierre opposing the permanence of the Sections, Marat, whose pusillanimous counsels were paralyzing the enthusiasm of the citizens.

"Ah!" he cried, "how feeble such men appear beside Leclerc and Jacques Roux! . . . Roux! Leclerc! *ye* are the true friends of the people!"

Gamelin did not hear these remarks, which would have angered him; he had gone into the next room to don his blue coat.

"You may well be proud of your son," observed the *citoyenne* Rochemaure, addressing the *citoyenne* Gamelin. "He is a great man; talent and character both make him so."

In answer, the widow Gamelin gave a good account of her son, yet without making much boast of him before a lady of high station, for she had been taught in her childhood that the first duty of the lowly is humility towards the great. She was of a complaining bent, having indeed only too good cause and finding in such jeremiads a salve for her griefs. She was garrulous in her revelations of all the hardships she had to bear to any whom she supposed in a position to relieve them, and Madame de Rochemaure seemed to belong to that class. She made the most, therefore, of this favourable opportunity and told a long and breathless story of their distresses,—how mother and son were both dying of slow starvation. Pictures could not be sold any more; the Revolution had killed business dead. Victuals were scarce and too dear for words. . . .

The good dame poured out her lamentations with all the loose-lipped volubility her halting tongue was capable of, so as to get them all finished by the time her son, whose pride would not brook such whining, should reappear. She was bent on attaining her object in the shortest possible time,—that of touching a lady whom she deemed rich and influential, and enlisting her sympathy in her boy's future. She felt sure that Évariste's good looks were an asset on her side to move the heart of a well-born lady. And so they were; the *citoyenne* Rochemaure proved tender-hearted and was melted to think of Évariste's and his mother's sufferings. She made plans to alleviate them; she had rich men amongst her friends and would get them to buy the artist's pictures.

"The truth is," she added, with a smile, "there is still money in France, but it keeps in hiding."

Better still, now Art was ruined, she would obtain Évariste a post in Morhardt's bank or with the Brothers Perregaux, or a place as clerk in the office of an army contractor.

Then she reflected that this was not what a man of his character needed; and, after a moment's thought, she nodded in sign that she had hit the nail on the head:

"There are still several jurymen left to be appointed on the Revolutionary Tribunal. Juryman, magistrate, that is the thing to suit your son. I have friendly relations with the Committee of Public Safety. I know Robespierre the elder personally; his brother frequently sups at my house. I will speak to them. I will get a word said to Montané, Dumas, Fouquier."

The *citoyenne* Gamelin, bursting with excitement and gratitude, put a finger to her lip; Évariste was coming back into the studio.

He escorted the *citoyenne* Rochemaure down the gloomy staircase, the steps of which, whether of wood or tiled, were coated with an ancient layer of dirt.

On the Pont-Neuf, where the sun, now near its setting, threw a lengthened shadow from the pedestal that had borne the Bronze Horse and was now gay with the National colours, a crowd of men and women of the people gathered in little groups were listening to some tale that was being told them. Consternation reigned and a heavy silence, broken at intervals by groans and fierce cries. Many were making off at a rapid pace in the direction of the Rue de Thionville, erstwhile Rue Dauphine; Gamelin joined one of these groups and heard the news—that Marat had just been assassinated.

Little by little the tidings were confirmed and particulars became known; he had been murdered in his bath by a woman who had come expressly from Caen to commit the crime.

Some thought she had escaped; but the majority declared she had been arrested.

There they stood like sheep without a shepherd, thinking sadly:

"Marat, the tender-hearted, the humane, Marat our benefactor, is no longer there to guide us, Marat who was never deceived, who saw through every subterfuge and never feared to reveal the truth!

. . . What can we do, what is to become of us? We have lost our adviser, our champion, our friend." They knew very well whence the blow had come, and who had directed the woman's arm. They groaned aloud:

"Marat has been struck down by the same criminal hands that are bent on our extermination. His death is the signal for the slaughter of all good patriots."

Different reports were current, as to the circumstances of the tragic event and the last words of the victim; endless questions were asked concerning the assassin, all that anyone knew was that it was a young woman sent by those traitors, the federalists. Baring teeth and nails, the *citoyennes* devoted the culprit to condign punishment; deeming the guillotine too merciful a death, they demanded this monster of iniquity should be scourged, broken on the wheel, torn limb from limb, and racked their brains to invent new tortures.

An armed body of National Guards was haling to the Section headquarters a man of determined mien. His clothes were in tatters, and streams of blood trickled down his white face. He had been overheard saying that Marat had earned his fate by his constant incitements to pillage and massacre, and it was only with great difficulty that the Guards had saved him from the fury of the populace. A hundred fingers pointed him out as the accomplice of the assassin, and threats of death followed him as he was led away.

Gamelin was stunned by the blow. A few hot tears blistered his burning eyes. With the grief he felt as a disciple mingled solicitude for the popular idol, and these combined feelings tore at his heartstrings. He thought to himself:

"After Le Peltier, after Bourdon, Marat! . . . I foresee the fate of the patriots; massacred on the Champ de Mars, at Nancy, at Paris, they will perish one and all." And he thought of Wimpfen, the traitor, who only a while before was marching on Paris, and who, had he not been stopped at Vernon, by the gallant patriots, would have devoted the heroic city to fire and slaughter.

And how many perils still remained, how many criminal designs, how many treasonable plots, which only Marat's perspicacity and vigilance could unravel and foil! Now he was dead, who was there to denounce Custine loitering in idleness in the Camp of Cæsar and refusing to relieve Valenciennes, Biron tarrying inactive in the Lower Vendée letting Saumur be taken and Nantes blockaded, Dillon betraying the Fatherland in the Argonne? . . .

Meantime, all about him, rose momentarily higher the sinister cry:

"Marat is dead; the aristocrats have killed him!"

As he was on his way, his heart bursting with grief and hate and love, to pay a last mark of respect to the martyr of liberty, an old countrywoman, wearing the coif of the Limousin peasantry, accosted him to ask of the Monsieur Marat who had been murdered was not Monsieur le Curé Mara, of Saint-Pierre-de-Queyroix.

VIII

IT WAS the eve of the Festival, a calm, bright evening, and Élodie hanging on Évariste's arm, was strolling with him about the *Champ de la Fédération*. Workmen were hastily completing their task of erecting columns, statues, temples, a "mountain," an altar of the Fatherland. Huge symbolic figures, Hercules (representing the people) brandishing his club, Nature suckling the Universe from her inexhaustible breasts, were rising at a moment's notice in the capital that, tortured by famine and fear, was listening for the dreaded sound of the Austrian cannon on the road from Meaux. La Vendée was making good its check before Nantes by a series of startling victories. A ring of fire and flame and hate was drawn about the great revolutionary city.

And meantime, she was preparing a superb welcome, like the sovereign state of a vast empire, for the deputies of the primary Assemblies which had accepted the Constitution. Federalism was on its knees; the Republic, one and indivisible, would surely vanquish all its enemies.

Waving his arm towards the thronged expanse:

"There it was," cried Évariste, "that on the 17th July, '91, the infamous Bailly ordered the people to be shot down at the foot of the altar of the fatherland. Passavant, the grenadier, who witnessed the massacre, returned to his house, tore his coat from his back and cried: 'I have sworn to die with Liberty; Liberty is no more, and I fulfil my oath,'—and blew out his brains."

All this time artists and peaceful citizens were examining the preparations for the festival, their faces showing as joyless a joy in life as their lives were dull and joyless; to their minds the mightiest events shrank into insignificance and grew as insipid as they were themselves. Couple by couple they went, carrying in their arms or holding by the hand or letting them run on in front children as unprepossessing as their parents and promising to grow up no whit happier, who in due course would give birth to children of their own as poor in spirit and looks as they. Yet now and again a young girl would pass, tall and fair and desirable, rousing in young men a not ignoble passion to possess, and in the old regret for the bliss they had missed.

Near the *École Militaire* Évariste pointed out to his companion the Egyptian statues designed by David on Roman models of the age of Augustus, and they overheard a Parisian, an old man with powdered hair, ejaculate to himself:

"Egad! you might think yourself on the banks of the Nile!"

It was three days since Élodie had seen her lover, and serious events had befallen meantime at the *Amour peintre*. The *citoyen* Blaise had been denounced to the Committee of General Security for fraudulent dealings in the matter of supplies to the armies. Fortunately for himself, the print-dealer was well known in his Section; the Committee of Surveillance of the *Section des Piques* had stood guarantee of his patriotism with the general committee and had completely justified his conduct.

This alarming incident Élodie now recounted in trembling accents, concluding:

"We are quiet now, but the alarm was a hot one. A little more and my father would have been clapped in prison. If the danger had lasted a few hours more, I should have come to you, Évariste, to make interest for him among your influential friends."

Évariste vouchsafed no reply to this, but Élodie was very far from realizing all his silence portended.

They went on hand in hand along the banks of the river, discoursing of their mutual fondness in the phrases of Julie and Saint-Preux; the good Jean-Jacques gave them the colours to paint and prank their love withal.

The Municipality of Paris had wrought a miracle,—abundance reigned for a day in the famished city. A fair was installed on the *Place des Invalides,* beside the Seine, where hucksters in booths sold sausages, saveloys, chitterlings, hams decked with laurels, Nanterre cakes, gingerbreads, pancakes, four-pound loaves, lemonade and wine. There were stalls also for the sale of patriotic songs, cockades, tricolour ribands, purses, pinchbeck watch-chains and all sorts of cheap gewgaws. Stopping before the display of a petty jeweller, Évariste selected a silver ring having a head of Marat in relief with a silk handkerchief wound about the brows, and put it on Élodie's finger.

The same evening Gamelin proceeded to the Rue de l'Arbre-Sec to call on the *citoyenne* Rochemaure, who had sent for him on pressing business. She received him in her bedchamber, reclining on a couch in a seductive dishabille.

While the *citoyenne's* attitude expressed a voluptuous languor, everything about her spoke of her accomplishments, her diversions, her talents,—a harp beside an open harpsichord, a guitar on a chair, an embroidering frame with a square of satin stretched on it, a half-finished miniature on a table among papers and books, a bookcase in dire disorder as if rifled by the hand of a fair reader as eager to know as to feel.

She gave him her hand to kiss, and addressed him:

"Greeting, sir juryman! . . . This very day Robespierre the elder gave me a letter in your favour to be handed to the President Herman, a very well turned letter, pretty much to this effect:

" 'I bring to your notice the *citoyen* Gamelin, commendable alike for his talents and for his patriotism. I have made it my duty to make known to you a patriot whose principles are good and his conduct steadfast in the right line of revolution. You will not let slip the opportunity of being useful to a Republican. . . .' This letter I carried there and then to the President Herman, who received me with an exquisite politeness and signed your appointment on the spot. The thing is done."

After a moment's pause:

"*Citoyenne*," said Gamelin, "though I have not a morsel of bread to give my mother, I swear on my honour I accept the duties of a juror only to serve the Republic and avenge her on her foes."

The *citoyenne* thought this but a cold way of expressing gratitude and considered the sentiment high-flown. The young man was no adept, she suspected, at graceful courtesies. But she was too great an admirer of youth not to excuse some little lack of polish. Gamelin was a handsome fellow, and that was merit enough in her eyes. "We will form him," she said to herself. So she invited him to her suppers to which she welcomed her friends every evening after the theatre.

"You will meet at my house men of wit and talent,—Elleviou, Talma, the *citoyen* Vigée, who turns bouts-rimés with a marvellous aptitude. The *citoyen* François read us his 'Paméla' the other day, the piece rehearsing at the present moment at the *Théâtre de la Nation*. The style is elegant and chaste, as everything is that comes from the *citoyen* François' pen. The plot is touching; it brought tears to all our eyes. It is the young *citoyenne* Lange who is to take the part of 'Paméla.' "

"I believe it if you say so, *citoyenne*," answered Gamelin, "but the *Théâtre de la Nation* is scarcely National and it is hard on the *citoyen* François that his works should be produced on the boards degraded by the contemptible verses of a Laya; the people have not forgotten the scandal of the *Ami des Lois* . . . . . ."

"Nay, *citoyen* Gamelin, say what you will of Laya; he is none of my friends."

It was not purely out of kindness that the *citoyenne* had employed her credit to get Gamelin appointed to a much envied post; after what she had done for him and what peradventure she might come to do for him in the future, she counted on binding him closely to her interests and in that way securing for herself a protector connected with a tribunal she might one day or another have to reckon with; for the fact is, she was in constant correspondence with the French provinces and foreign countries, and at that date such a circumstance was ground enough for suspicion.

"Do you often go to the theatre, *citoyen?*"

As she asked the question, Henry, the dragoon, entered the room, looking more charming than the youthful Bathyllus. A brace of enormous pistols was passed through his belt.

He kissed the fair *citoyenne's* hand. Turning to him:

"There stands the *citoyen* Évariste Gamelin," she said, "for whose sake I have spent the day at the Committee of General Security, and who is an ungrateful wretch. Scold him for me."

"Ah! *citoyenne,*" cried the young soldier, "you have seen our Legislators at the Tuileries. What an afflicting sight! Is it seemly the Representatives of a free people should sit beneath the roof of a despot? The same lustres that once shone on the plots of Capet and the orgies of Antoinette now illumine the deliberations of our law-makers. 'Tis enough to make Nature shudder."

"Pray, congratulate the *citoyen* Gamelin," was all her answer, "he is appointed juryman on the Revolutionary Tribunal."

"My compliments, *citoyen!*" said Henry. "I am rejoiced to see a man of your character invested with these functions. But, to speak truth, I have small confidence in this systematic justice, set up by the moderates of the Convention, in this complaisant Nemesis that is considerate to conspirators and merciful to traitors, that hardly dares strike a blow at the Federalists and fears to summon *the Austrian* to the bar. No, it is not the Revolutionary Tribunal will save the Republic. They are very culpable, the men who, in the desperate situation we are in, have arrested the flowing torrent of popular justice!"

"Henry," interrupted the *citoyenne* Rochemaure, "pass me that scent bottle, please. . . ."

On reaching home, Gamelin found his mother and old Brotteaux playing a game of piquet by the light of a smoky tallow-candle. At the moment the old woman was calling "sequence of kings" without the smallest scruple.

When she heard her son was appointed juryman, she kissed him in a transport of triumph, thinking what an honour it was for both of them and that henceforth they would have plenty to eat every day.

"I am proud and happy," she declared, "to be the mother of a juryman. Justice is a fine thing, and of all the most necessary; without justice the weak would be harassed every moment of their lives. And I think you will give right judgment, Évariste, my own boy: for from a child I have found you just and kind-hearted in all concerns. You could never endure wrong-doing and always tried what you could to hinder violence. You compassionated the unfortunate and that is the finest jewel in a juror's crown. . . . But tell me, Évariste, how are you dressed in your grand tribunal?"

Gamelin informed her that the judges wore a hat with black plumes, but that the jury had no special costume, that they were dressed in their every-day attire.

"It would be better," returned the good woman, "if they wore wig and gown; it would inspire more respect. Though you are mostly dressed carelessly, you are a handsome man and you set off your clothes; but the majority of men need some fine feathers to make them look imposing; yes, the jury should have wigs and gowns."

The *citoyenne* had heard say that the duties of a juror of the Tribunal carried a salary; and she had no hesitation in asking the question whether the emoluments were enough to live respectably on, for a juryman, she opined, ought to cut a good figure in the world.

She was pleased to hear that each juror received an allowance of eighteen livres for every sitting and that the multiplicity of crimes against the security of the State obliged the court to sit very frequently.

Old Brotteaux gathered up the cards, rose from the table and addressing Gamelin:

"*Citoyen*," he said, "you are invested with an august and redoubtable office. I congratulate you on lending the light of your integrity to a tribunal more trustworthy and less fallible perhaps than any other, because it searches out good and evil, not in themselves and in their essence, but solely in relation to tangible interests and plain and obvious sentiments. You will have to determine betwixt hate and love, which is done spontaneously, not betwixt truth and falsehood, to discriminate which is impossible for the feeble mind of man. Giving judgment after the impulses of your heart, you will run no risk of mistake, inasmuch as the verdict will be good provided it satisfy the passions that are your sacred law. But, all the same, if I was your President, I should imitate Bridoie, I should appeal to the arbitrament of the dice. In matters of justice it is still the surest plan."

IX

EVARISTE GAMELIN was to enter on his duties on the 14th September, when the reorganization of the Tribunal was complete, according to which it was henceforth subdivided into four sections with fifteen jurors for each. The prisons were full to overflowing; the Public Prosecutor was working eighteen hours a day. Defeats in the field, revolts in the provinces, conspiracies, plots, betrayals, the Convention had one panacea for them all,—terror. The Gods were athirst.

The first act of the new juror was to pay a visit of ceremony to the President Herman, who charmed him by the amiability of his conversation and the courtesy of his bearing. A compatriot and friend of Robespierre's, whose sentiments he shared, he showed every sign of a feeling and virtuous temper. He was deeply attached to those humane sentiments, too long foreign to the heart of our judges, that redound to the everlasting glory of a Dupaty and a Beccaria. He looked with complacency on the greater mildness of modern manners as evidenced, in judicial matters, by the abolition of torture and of ignominious or cruel forms of punishment. He was rejoiced to see the death penalty, once so recklessly inflicted and employed till quite lately for the repression of the most trifling offences, applied less frequently and reserved for heinous crimes. For his own part, he agreed with Robespierre and would gladly have seen it abolished altogether, except only in cases touching the public safety. At the same time, he would have deemed it treason to the State not to adjudge the punishment of death for crimes against the National Sovereignty.

All his colleagues were of like mind; the old Monarchical idea of reasons of State still inspired the Revolutionary Tribunal. Eight centuries of absolute power had moulded the magisterial conscience, and it was by the principles of Divine Right that the Court even now tried and sentenced the enemies of Liberty.

The same day Évariste Gamelin sought an interview with the Public Prosecutor, the *citoyen* Fouquier, who received him in the Cabinet where he used to work with his clerk of the court. He was a sturdily built man, with a rough voice, catlike eyes, bearing in his pock-marked face and leaden complexion marks of the mischief wrought by a sedentary and indoor life on a vigorous constitution adapted to the open air and violent exercise. Towering piles of papers shut him in like the walls of a tomb, and it was plain to see he was in his element amid all these dreadful documents that seemed like to bury him alive. His conversation was that of a hard-working magistrate, a man devoted to his task and whose mind never left the narrow groove of his official duties. His fiery breath reeked of the brandy he took to keep up his strength; but the liquor seemed never to fly to his brain, so clear-headed, albeit entirely commonplace, was every word he uttered.

He lived in a small suite of rooms in the Palais de Justice with his young wife, who had given him twin boys. His wife, an aunt Henriette and the maid-servant Pélagie made up the whole household. He was good and kind to these women. In a word, he was an excellent person in his family and professional relations, with a scarcity of ideas and a total lack of imagination.

Gamelin could not help being struck unpleasantly by the close resemblance in temper and ways of thought between the new magistrates and their predecessors under the old régime. In fact, they were of the old régime; Herman had held the office of Advocate

General to the Council of Artois; Fouquier was a former Procureur at the Châtelet. They had preserved their character, whereas Gamelin believed in a Revolutionary palingenesis.

Quitting the precincts of the court, he passed along the great gallery of the Palace and halted in front of the shops where articles of every sort and kind were exposed for sale in the most attractive fashion. Standing before the *citoyenne* Ténot's stall, he turned over sundry historical, political, and philosophical works:—"The Chains of Slavery," "An Essay on Despotism," "The Crimes of Queens." "Very good!" he thought, "here is Republican stuff!" and he asked the woman if she sold a great many of these books. She shook her head:

"The only things that sell are songs and romances,"—and pulling a duodecimo volume out of a drawer:

"Here," she told him, "here we have something good."

Évariste read the title: "La Religieuse en chemise," "The Nun in dishabille!"

Before the next shop he came upon Philippe Desmahis, who, with a tender, conquering-hero air, among the *citoyenne* Saint-Jorre's perfumes and powders and sachets, was assuring the fair tradeswoman of his undying love, promising to paint her portrait and begging her to vouchsafe him a moment's talk that evening in the Tuileries gardens. There was no resisting him; persuasion sat on his lips and beamed from his eye. The *citoyenne* Saint-Jorre was listening without a word, her eyes on the ground, only too ready to believe him.

Wishing to familiarize himself with the awful duties imposed on him, the new juror resolved to mingle with the throng and look on at a case before the Tribunal as a member of the general public. He climbed the great stairs on which a vast crowd was seated as in an amphitheatre and pushed his way into the ancient Hall of the Parlement of Paris.

This was crammed to suffocation; some General or other was taking his trial. For in those days, as old Brotteaux put it, "the Convention, copying the example of His Britannic Majesty's Government, made a point of arraigning beaten Generals, in default of traitorous Generals, the latter taking good care not to stand their trial. Not that a beaten General," Brotteaux would add, "is necessarily criminal, for in the nature of things there must be one in every battle. But there's nothing like condemning a General to death for giving encouragement to others."

Several had already appeared before the Tribunal; they were all alike, these empty-headed, opinionated soldiers with the brains of a sparrow in an ox's skull. This particular commander was pretty nearly as ignorant of the sieges and battles of his own compaign as the magistrates who were questioning him; both sides, prosecution and defence, were lost in a fog of effectives, objectives, munitions and ammunitions, marches and counter-marches. But the mass of citizens listening to these obscure and never-ending details could see behind the half-witted soldier the bare and bleeding breast of the fatherland enduring a thousand deaths; and by look and voice urged the jurymen, sitting quietly on their bench, to use their verdict as a club to fell the foes of the Republic.

Évariste was firmly convinced of one thing,—what they had to strike at in the pitiful creature was the two dread monsters that were battening on the fatherland, revolt and defeat. What a to-do to discover if this particular soldier was innocent or guilty! When La Vendée was recovering heart, when Toulon was surrendering to the enemy, when the army of the Rhine was recoiling before the victors of Mayence, when the Army of the North, ,cowering in Cæsar's Camp, might be taken at a blow by the Imperialists, the English, the Dutch, now masters of Valenciennes, the one important thing was to teach the Generals of the Republic to conquer or to die. To see yonder feeble-witted muddle-pated veteran losing himself under cross-examination among his maps as he had done before in the plains of Northern France, Gamelin longed to yell "death! death!" with the rest, and fled from the Hall of Audience to escape the temptation.

At the meeting of the Section, the newly appointed juryman received the congratulations of the President Olivier, who made him swear on the old high altar of the Barnabites, now altar of the fatherland, to stifle in his heart, in the sacred name of humanity, every human weakness.

Gamelin, with uplifted right hand, invoked as witness of his oath the august shade of Marat, martyr of Liberty, whose bust had lately been set up against a pillar of the erstwhile church, facing that of Le Peltier.

There was some applause, interrupted by cries of protest. The meeting was a stormy one; at the entrance of the nave stood a group of members of the Section, armed with pikes and shouting clamorously:

"It is anti-republican," declared the President, "to carry arms at a meeting of free citizens,"—and he ordered the muskets and pikes to be deposited there and then in the erstwhile sacristy.

A hunchback, with blazing eyes and lips drawn back so as to show the teeth, the *citoyen* Beauvisage, of the Committee of Vigilance, mounted to the pulpit, now become the speakers' tribune and surmounted by a red cap of liberty.

"The Generals are betraying us," he vociferated, "and surrendering our armies to the enemy. The Imperialists are pushing forward their cavalry around Péronne and Saint-Quentin. Toulon has been given up to the English, who are landing fourteen thousand men there. The foes of the Republic are busy with plots in the very bosom of the Convention. In the capital conspiracies without number are afoot to deliver *the Austrian*. At this very moment while I speak there runs a rumour that the Capet brat has escaped from the Temple and is being borne in triumph to Saint-Cloud by those who would fain re-erect the tyrant's throne in his favour. The dearness of food, the depreciation of the *assignats* are the direct results of manœuvres carried out in our own homes, beneath our very eyes, by the agents of the foreigners. In the name of public safety I call upon the new juryman, our fellow-citizen, to show no pity to conspirators and traitors."

As he left the tribune, cries rose among the audience: "Down with the Revolutionary Tribunal! Down with the Moderates!"

A stout, rosy-faced man, the *citoyen* Dupont senior, a joiner living in the Place de Thionville, mounted the Tribune, announcing that he wished to ask a question of the new juror. Then he demanded of Gamelin what attitude he meant to take up in the matter of the Brissotins and of the widow Capet.

Évariste was timid and unpractised in public speaking. But indignation gave him eloquence. He rose with a pale face and said in a voice of suppressed emotion:

"I am a magistrate. I am responsible to my conscience only. Any promise I might make you would be against my duty, which is to speak in the Court and hold my peace elsewhere. I have ceased to know you. It is mine to give judgment; I know neither friends nor enemies."

The meeting, made up like all meetings of divers elements and subject to sudden and incalculable moods, approved these sentiments. But the *citoyen* Dupont returned to the charge; he could not forgive Gamelin for having secured a post he had coveted himself.

"I understand," he said, "I even approve the juror's scruples. They say he is a patriot; it is for him to examine his conscience and see if it permits him to sit on a tribunal intended to destroy the enemies of the Republic and resolved to spare them. There are circumstances in which a good citizen is bound to repudiate all complicity. It is not averred that more than one juror of this tribunal has let himself be corrupted by the gold of the accused, and that the President Montané falsified the procedure to save the head of the woman Corday?"

At the words the hall resounded with vehement applause. The vaults were still reverberating with the uproar when Fortuné Trubert mounted the tribune. He had grown thinner than ever in the last few months. His face was pale and the cheek-bones seemed ready to pierce the reddened skin; his eyes had a glassy look under the inflamed lids.

"*Citoyens*," he began, in a weak, breathless voice that yet had a strangely penetrating quality, "we cannot suspect the Revolutionary Tribunal without at the same time suspecting the Convention and the Committee of Public Safety from which it derives its powers. The *citoyen* Beauvisage has alarmed us, showing us the President Montané tampering with the course of justice in favour of a culprit. Why did he not add, to relieve our fears, that on the denunciation of the Public Prosecutor, Montané has been dismissed his office and thrown into prison? . . . Is it impossible to watch over the public safety without casting suspicion on all and sundry? Is there no talent, no virtue left in the Convention? Robespierre, Couthon, Saint-Just, are not these honest men? It is a notable thing that the most violent language is held by individuals who have never been known to fight for the Republic. They could speak no otherwise if they wish to render her hateful. *Citoyens,* less talk, say I, and more work! It is with shot and shell and not with shouting that France will be saved. One-half the cellars of the Section have not been dug up. Not a few citizens still hold considerable quantities of bronze. We would remind the rich that patriotic gifts are for them the most potent guarantees. I recommend to your generosity wives and daughters of our soldiers who are covering themselves with glory on the frontiers and on the Loire. One of these, the hussar Pommier (Augustin), formerly a cellarman's lad in the Rue de Jérusalem, on the 10th of last month, before Condé, when watering the troop horses, was set upon by six Austrian cavalrymen; he killed two of them and brought in the others prisoners. I ask the Section to declare that Pommier (Augustin) has done his duty."

This speech was applauded and the Sectionaries dispersed with cries of "Vive la République!"

Left alone in the nave with Trubert, Gamelin pressed the latter's hand.

"Thank you. How are you?"

"I? Oh! Very well, very well!" replied Trubert, coughing and spitting blood into his handkerchief. "The Republic has many enemies without and within, and our own Section counts a not inconsiderable number of them. It is not with loud talk but with iron and laws that empires are founded . . . good night, Gamelin; I have letters to write."

And he disappeared, his handkerchief pressed to his lips, into the old-time sacristy.

The widow Gamelin, her cockade now and henceforth fastened more carefully in her hood, had from one day to the next assumed a fine, consequential air, a Republican haughtiness and the dignified carriage suitable to the mother of a juror of the State.

The veneration for the law in which she had been brought up, the admiration with which the magistrate's gown and cassock had from a child inspired her, the holy terror she had always experienced at sight of those to whom God had delegated on earth His divine right of life and death, these feelings made her regard as an august and worshipful and holy being the son whom till yesterday she had thought of as little more than a child. To her simple mind the conviction of the continuity of justice through all the changes of the Revolution was as strong as was that of the legislators of the Convention regarding the continuity of the State under varying systems of government, and the Revolutionary Tribunal appeared to her every whit as majestic as any of the time-honoured jurisdiction she had been taught to revere.

The *citoyen* Brotteaux showed the young magistrate an interest mingled with surprise and a reluctant deference. His views were the same as the widow Gamelin's as to the continuity of justice under successive governments; but, in flat contradiction to that good lady's attitude, his scorn for the Revolutionary Tribunals was on a par with his contempt for the courts of the ancient régime. Not daring to express his opinions openly and unable to make up his mind to say nothing, he indulged in a string of paradoxes which Gamelin understood just well enough to suspect the anti-patriotism that underlay them.

"The august tribunal whereon you are soon to take your seat," he told him on one occasion, "was instituted by the French Senate for the security of the Republic; and it was for certain a magnanimous thought on the part of our legislators to set up a court to try our enemies. I appreciate its generosity, but I doubt its wisdom. It would have shown greater astuteness, it seems to me, if they had struck down in the dark the more irreconcilable of their adversaries and won over the rest by gifts and promises. A tribunal strikes slowly and effects more harm than it inspires fear; its first duty is to make an example. The mischief yours does is to unite together all whom it terrifies and make out of a mass of contradictory interests and passions a great party capable of common and effective action. You sow fear broadcast, and it is terror more than courage that produces heroes; I pray, *citoyen,* you may not one day see prodigies of terror arrayed against you!"

The engraver Desmahis, in love that week with a light o' love of the Palais-Égalité named Flora, a brown-locked giantess, had nevertheless found five minutes to congratulate his comrade and tell him that such an appointment was a great compliment to the fine arts.

Élodie herself, though without knowing it she detested everything revolutionary and who dreaded official functions as the most dangerous of rivals, the most likely to estrange her lover's affections, the tender Élodie was impressed by the glamour attaching to a magistrate called upon to pronounce judgment in matters of life and death. Besides which, Évariste's promotion as a juryman was followed by other fortunate results that filled her loving heart with satisfaction; the *citoyen* Jean Blaise made a point of calling at the studio in the Place de Thionville and embraced the young juror affectionately in a burst of manly sympathy.

Like all the anti-revolutionaries, he had a great respect for the authorities established by the Republic, and ever since he had been denounced for fraud in connection with his supplies for the army, the Revolutionary Tribunal had inspired him with a wholesome dread. He felt himself to be a person too much in the public eye and mixed up in too many transactions to enjoy perfect security; so the *citoyen* Gamelin struck him as a friend worth cultivating. When all was said, one was a good citizen and on the side of justice.

He gave the painter magistrate his hand, declaring himself his true friend and a true patriot, a well-wisher of the arts and of liberty. Gamelin forgot his injuries and pressed the hand so generously offered.

"*Citoyen* Évariste Gamelin," said Jean Blaise, "I appeal to you as a friend and as a man of talent. I am going to take you to-morrow for two days' jaunt in the country; you can do some drawing and we can enjoy a talk."

Several times every year the print-dealer was in the habit of making a two or three days' expedition of this sort in the company of artists who made drawings, according to his suggestions, of landscapes and ruins. He was quick to see what would please the public and these little journeys always resulted in some picturesque bits which were then finished at home and cleverly engraved; prints in red or colours were struck off from these, and brought in a good profit to the *citoyen* Blaise. From the same sketches he had over-doors and panels executed, which sold as well or better than the decorative works of Hubert Robert.

On this occasion he had invited the *citoyen* Gamelin to accompany him to sketch buildings after nature, so much had the juror's office increased the painter's importance in his eyes. Two other artists were of the party, the engraver Desmahis, who drew well, and an almost unknown man, Philippe Dubois, an excellent designer in the style of Robert. According to custom, the *citoyenne* Élodie with her friend *citoyenne* Hasard accompanied the artists. Jean Blaise, an adept at combining pleasure with profit, had also extended an invitation to the *citoyenne* Thévenin, an actress at the Vaudeville, who was reputed to be on the best of terms with him.

X

N SATURDAY at seven in the morning the *citoyen* Blaise, in a black cocked-hat, scarlet waistcoat, doeskin breeches, and boots with yellow tops, rapped with the handle of his riding-whip at the studio door. The *citoyenne* Gamelin was in the room in polite conversation with the *citoyen* Brotteaux, while Évariste stood before a bit of looking-glass knotting his high white cravat.

"A pleasant journey, Monsieur Blaise!" the *citoyenne* greeted him. "But, as you are going to paint landscapes, why don't you take Monsieur Brotteaux, who is a painter?"

"Well, well," said Jean Blaise, "will you come with us, *citoyen* Brotteaux?"

On being assured he would not be intruding, Brotteaux, a man of a sociable temper and fond of all amusements, accepted the invitation.

The *citoyenne* Élodie had climbed the four storeys to embrace the widow Gamelin, whom she called her good mother. She was in white from head to foot, and smelt of lavender.

An old two-horsed travelling *berline* stood waiting in the Place, with the hood down. Rose Thévenin occupied the back seat with Julienne Hasard. Élodie made the actress sit on the right, took the left-hand place herself and put the slim Julienne between the two of them. Brotteaux settled himself, back to the horses, facing the *citoyenne* Thévenin Philippe Dubois, opposite the *citoyenne* Hasard; Évariste opposite Élodie. As for Philippe Desmahis, he planted his athletic figure on the box, on the coachman's left, and proceeded to amaze that worthy with a traveller's tale about a country in America where the trees bore chitterlings and saveloys by way of fruit.

The *citoyen* Blaise, who was a capital rider, took the road on horseback, going on in front to escape the dust from the *berline*.

As the wheels rattled merrily over the suburban roads the travellers began to forget their cares, and at sight of the green fields and trees and sky, their minds turned to gay and pleasant thoughts. Élodie dreamed she was surely born to rear poultry with Évariste, a country justice, to help her, in some village on a river bank beside a wood. The roadside elms whirled by as they sped along. Outside the villages the peasants' mastiffs dashed out to intercept the carriage and barked at the horses, while a fat spaniel, lying in the roadway, struggled reluctantly to its feet; the fowls scattered and fled; the geese in a close-packed band waddled slowly out of the way. The children, with their fresh morning faces, watched the company go by. It was a hot day and a cloudless sky. The

parched earth was thirsting for rain. They alighted just outside
Villejuif. On their way through the little town, Desmahis went
into a fruiterer's to buy cherries for the overheated *citoyennes*.
The shop-keeper was a pretty woman, and Desmahis showed no
signs of reappearing. Philippe Dubois shouted to him, using the
nickname his friends constantly gave him:

"Ho there! Barbaroux! . . . Barbaroux!"

At this hated name the passers-by pricked up their ears and
faces appeared at every window. Then, when they saw a young and
handsome man emerge from the shop, his jacket thrown open, his
neckerchief flying loose over a muscular chest, and carrying over
his shoulder a basket of cherries and his coat at the end of a stick,
taking him for the proscribed girondist, a posse of *sansculottes*
laid violent hands on him. Regardless of his indignant protests,
they would have haled him to the town-hall, had not old Brotteaux,
Gamelin, and the three young women borne testimony that the
citoyen was named Philippe Desmahis, a copper-plate engraver and
a good Jacobin. Even then the suspect had to show his *carte de
civisme,* which he had in his pocket by great good luck, for he was
very heedless in such matters. At this price he escaped from the
hands of these patriotic villagers without worse loss than one of
his lace ruffles, which had been torn off; but this was a trifle after
all. He even received the apologies of the National Guards who had
hustled him the most savagely and who now spoke of carrying him
in triumph to the Hôtel de Ville.

A free man again and with the *citoyennes* Élodie, Rose, and
Julienne crowding round him, Desmahis looked at Philippe Dubois
—he did not like the man and suspected him of having played him
a practical joke—with a wry smile, and towering above him by a
whole head:

"Dubois," he told him, "if you call me Barbaroux again, I shall
call you Brissot; he is a little fat man with a silly face, greasy hair,
an oily skin and damp hands. They'll be perfectly sure you are the
infamous Brissot, the people's enemy; and the good Republicans,
filled with horror and loathing àt sight of you, will hang you from
the nearest lamp-post. You hear me?"

The *citoyen* Blaise, who had been watering his horse, announced
that he had arranged the affair, though it was quite plain to everybody that it had been arranged without him.

The company got in again, and as they drove on, Desmahis informed the coachman that in this same plain of Longjumeau several
inhabitants of the Moon had once come down, in shape and colour
much like frogs, only very much bigger. Philippe Dubois and
Gamelin talked about their art. Dubois, a pupil of Regnault, had
been to Rome, where he had seen Raphael's tapestries, which he set
above all the masterpieces of the world. He admired Correggio's
colouring, Annibale Caracci's invention, Domenichino's drawing, but

thought nothing comparable in point of style with the pictures of Pompeio Battoni. He had been in touch at Rome with Monsieur Ménageot and Madame Lebrun, who had both pronounced against the Revolution; so the less said of them the better. But he spoke highly of Angelica Kauffmann, who had a pure taste and a fine knowledge of the Antique.

Gamelin deplored that the apogee of French painting, belated as it was, for it only dated from Lesueur, Claude and Poussin and corresponded with the decadence of the Italian and Flemish schools, had been succeeded by so rapid and profound a decline. This he attributed to the degraded state of manners and to the Academy, which was the expression of that state. But the Academy had been happily abolished, and under the influence of new canons, David and his school were creating an art worthy of a free people. Among the young painters, Gamelin, without a trace of envy, gave the first place to Hennequin and Topino-Lebrun. Philippe Dubois preferred his own master Regnault to David, and founded his hopes for the future of painting on that rising artist Gérard.

Meantime Élodie complimented the *citoyenne* Thévenin on her red velvet toque and white gown. The actress repaid the compliment by congratulating her two companions on their toilets and advising them how to do better still; the thing, she said, was to be more sparing in ornaments and trimmings.

"A woman can never be dressed too simply," was her dictum. "We see this on the stage, where the costume should allow every pose to be appreciated. That is its true beauty and it needs no other."

"You are right, my dear," replied Élodie. "Only there is nothing more expensive in dress than simplicity. It is not always out of bad taste we add frills and furbelows; sometimes it is to save our pocket."

They discussed eagerly the autumn fashions,—frocks entirely plain and short-waisted.

"So many women disfigure themselves through following the fashion!" declared Rose Thévenin. "In dressing every woman should study her own figure."

"There is nothing beautiful save draperies that follow the lines of the figure and fall in folds," put in Gamelin. "Everything that is cut out and sewn is hideous."

These sentiments, more appropriate in a treatise of Winckelmann's than in the mouth of a man talking to Parisiennes, met with the scorn they deserved, being entirely disregarded.

"For the winter," observed Élodie, "they are making quilted gowns in Lapland style of taffeta and muslin, and coats *à la Zulime*, round-waisted and opening over a stomacher *à la Turque*."

"Nasty cheap things," declared the actress, "you can buy them ready made. Now I have a little seamstress who works like an angel and is not dear; I'll send her to see you, my dear."

So they prattled on trippingly, eagerly discussing and appraising different fine fabrics—striped taffeta, self-coloured china silk, muslin, gauze, nankeen.

And old Brotteaux, as he listened to them, thought with a pensive pleasure of these veils that hide women's charms and change incessantly,—how they last for a few years to be renewed eternally like the flowers of the field. And his eyes, as they wandered from the three pretty women to the cornflowers and the poppies in the wheat, were wet with smiling tears.

They reached Orangis about nine o'clock and stopped before the inn, the *Auberge de la Cloche,* where the Poitrines, husband and wife, offered accommodation for man and beast. The *citoyen* Blaise, who had repaired any disorder in his dress, helped the *citoyennes* to alight. After ordering dinner for midday, they all set off, preceded by their paint-boxes, drawing-boards, easels, and parasols, which were carried by a village lad, for the meadows near the confluence of the Orge and the Yvette, a charming bit of country giving a view over the verdant plain of Longjumeau and bounded by the Seine and the woods of Sainte-Geneviève.

Jean Blaise, the leader of the troop of artists, was bandying funny stories with the *ci-devant* financier, tales that brought in without rhyme or reason Verboquet the Open-handed, Catherine Cuissot the pedlar, the demoiselles Chaudron, the fortune-teller Galichet, as well as characters of a later time like Cadet-Rouselle and Madame Angot.

Évariste, inspired with a sudden love of nature, as he saw a troop of harvesters binding their sheaves, felt the tears rise to his eyes, while visions of concord and affection filled his heart. For his part, Desmahis was blowing the light down of the seeding dandelions into the *citoyennes'* hair. All three loved posies, as town-bred girls always do, and were busy in the meadows plucking the mullein, whose blossoms grow in spikes close round the stem, the campanula, with its little blue-bells hanging in rows one above another, the slender twigs of the scented vervain, wallwort, mint, dyer's weed, milfoil—all the wild flowers of late summer. Jean-Jacques had made botany the fashion among townswomen, so all three knew the name and symbolism of every flower. As the delicate petals, drooping for want of moisture, wilted in her hands and fell in a shower about her feet, the *citoyenne* Élodie sighed:

"They are dying already, the poor flowers!"

All set to work and strove to express nature as they saw her; but each saw her through the eyes of a master. In a short time Philippe Dubois had knocked off in the style of Hubert Robert a deserted farm, a clump of storm-riven trees, a dried-up torrent. Évariste Gamelin found a landscape by Poussin ready made on the banks of the Yvette. Philippe Desmahis was at work before a pigeon-cote in the picaresque manner of Callot and Duplessis. Old Brotteaux who piqued himself on imitating the Flemings, was drawing a cow with infinite care. Élodie was sketching a peasant's hut, while her friend Julienne, who was a colourman's daughter, set her palette. A swarm of children pressed about her, watching her paint, whom she would scold out of her light at intervals, calling them pestering gnats and giving them lollipops. The *citoyenne* Thévenin, picking out the pretty ones, would wash their faces, kiss them and put flowers in their hair. She fondled them with a gentle air of melancholy, because she had missed the joy of motherhood,—as well as to heighten her fascinations by a show of tender sentiment and to practise herself in the art of pose and grouping.

She was the only member of the party neither ·drawing nor painting. She devoted her attention to learning a part and still more to charming her companions, flitting from one to another, book in hand, a bright, entrancing creature.

"No complexion, no figure, no voice, no nothing," declared the women,—and she filled the earth with movement, colour and harmony. Faded, pretty, tired, indefatigable, she was the joy of the expedition. A woman of ever-varying moods, but always gay, sensitive, quick-tempered and yet easy-going and accommodating, a sharp tongue with the most polished utterance, vain, modest, true, false, delightful; if Rose Thévenin enjoyed no triumphant success, if she was not worshipped as a goddess, it was because the times were out of joint and Paris had no more incense, no more altars for the Graces. The *citoyenne* Blaise herself, who made a face when she spoke of her and used to call her "my stepmother," could not see her and not be subjugated by such an array of charms.

They were rehearsing *Les Visitandines* at the Théâtre Feydeau, and Rose was full of self-congratulation at having a part full of "naturalness." It was this quality she strove after, this she sought and this she found.

"Then we shall not see 'Paméla'?" asked Desmahis.

"The Théâtre de la Nation was closed and the actors packed off to the Madelonnettes and to Pélagie."

"Do you call that liberty?" cried Rose Thévenin, raising her beautiful eyes to heaven in indignant protest.

"The players of the Théâtre de la Nation are aristocrats, and the *citoyen* François' piece tends to make men regret the privileges of the noblesse."

"Gentlemen," said Rose Thévenin, "have you patience to listen only to those who flatter you?"

As midday approached everybody began to feel pangs of hunger and the little band marched back to the inn.

Évariste walked beside Élodie, smilingly recalling memories of their first meetings:

"Two young birds had fallen out of their nests on the roof on to the sill of your window. You brought the little creatures up by hand; one of them lived and in due time flew away. The other died in the nest of cotton-wool you had made him. 'It was the one I loved best,' I remember you said. That day, Élodie, you were wearing a red bow in your hair."

Philippe Dubois and Brotteaux, a little behind the rest, were talking of Rome, where they had both been, the latter in '72, the other towards the last days of the Academy. Brotteaux indeed had never forgotten the Princess Mondragone, to whom he would most certainly have poured out his plaints but for the Count Altieri, who always followed her like her shadow. Nor did Philippe Dubois fail to mention that he had been invited to dine with Cardinal de Bernis and that he was the most obliging host in the world.

"I knew him," said Brotteaux, "and I may add without boasting that I was for some while one of his most intimate friends; he had a taste for low society. He was an amiable man, and for all his affectation of telling fairy tales, there was more sound philosophy in his little finger than in the heads of all you Jacobins, who are for making us virtuous and God-fearing by Act of Parliament. Upon my word I prefer our simple-minded theophagists who know not what they say nor yet what they do, to these mad law-menders, who make it their business to guillotine us in order to render us wise and virtuous and adorers of the Supreme Being who has created them in His likeness. In former days I used to have Mass said in the Chapel at Les Ilettes by a poor devil of a Curé who used to say in his cups: 'Don't let's speak ill of sinners; we live by 'em, we priests, unworthy as we are!' You must agree, sir, this prayer-monger held sound maxims of government. We should adopt his principles, and govern men as being what they are and not what we should like them to be."

Rose Thévenin had meantime drawn closer to the old man. She knew he had lived on a grand scale, and the thought of this gilded the *ci-devant* financier's present poverty, which she deemed less humiliating as being due to general causes, the result of the public bankruptcy. She saw in him, with curiosity not unmixed with respect, the survival of one of those open-handed millionaires of whom her elder comrades of the stage spoke with sighs of unfeigned regret. Besides, the old fellow in his plum-coloured coat, so threadbare and so well brushed, pleased her by his agreeable address.

"Monsieur Brotteaux," she said to him, "we know how once upon a time, in a noble park, on moonlight nights, you would slip into the shade of myrtle groves with actresses and dancing-girls to the far-off shrilling of flutes and fiddles. . . . Alas! they were more lovely, were they not, your goddesses of the Opera and the

Comédie-Française, than we of to-day, we poor little National actresses?"

"Never think it, Mademoiselle," returned Brotteaux, "but believe me, if one like you had been known in those days, she would have moved alone, as sovereign queen without a rival (little as she would have desired such solitude), in the park you are obliging enough to form so flattering a picture of. . . ."

It was quite a rustic inn, this Hôtel de la Cloche. A branch of holly hung over the great waggon doors that opened on a court-yard where fowls were always pecking about in the damp soil. On the far side of this stood the house itself, consisting of a ground floor and one storey above, crowned by a high-pitched tiled roof and with walls almost hidden under old climbing rose-trees covered with blossom. To the right, trimmed fruit-trees showed their tops above the low garden wall. To the left was the stable, with an out-side manger and a barn supported by wooden pillars. A ladder leant against the wall. Here again, under a shed crowded with agricul-tural implements and stumps of trees, a white cock was keeping an eye on his hens from the top of a broken-down cabriolet. The courtyard was enclosed on this side by cow-sheds, in front of which rose in mountainous grandeur a dunghill which at this moment a girl as broad as she was long, with straw-coloured hair, was turn-ing over with a pitchfork. The liquid manure filled her sabots and bathed her bare feet, and you could see the heels rise out of her shoes every now and then as yellow as saffron. Her petticoats were kilted and revealed the filth on her enormous calves and thick ankles. While Philippe Desmahis was staring at her, surprised and tickled by the whimsicalities of nature in framing this odd example of breadth without length, the landlord shouted:

"Ho, there! Tronche, my girl! go fetch some water!"

She turned her head, showing a scarlet face and a vast mouth in which one huge front tooth was missing. It had needed nothing less than a bull's horn to effect a breach in that powerful jaw. She stood there grinning, pitchfork on shoulder. Her sleeves were rolled up and her arms, as thick as another woman's thighs, gleamed in the sun.

The table was laid in the farm kitchen, where a brace of fowls was roasting,—they were almost done to a turn,—under the hood of the open fireplace, above which hung two or three old fowling-pieces by way of ornament. The bare white-washed room, twenty feet long, was lighted only through the panes of greenish glass let into the door and by a single window, framed in roses, near which the grandmother sat turning her spinning-wheel. She wore a coif and a lace frilling in the fashion of the Regency. Her gnarled, earth-stained fingers held the distaff. Flies clustered about her lids without her trying to drive them away. As a child in her mother's arms, she had seen Louis XIV go by in his coach.

Sixty years ago she had made the journey to Paris. In a weak sing-song voice she told the tale to the three young women, standing in front of her, how she had seen the Hôtel de Ville, the Tuileries and the Samaritaine, and how, when she was crossing the Pont-Royal, a barge loaded with apples for the Marché du Mail had broken up, the apples had floated down the current and the river was all red with the rosy-cheeked fruit.

She had been told of the changes that had occurred of late in the kingdom, and in particular of the coil there was betwixt the curés who had taken the oath and the nonjuring curés. She knew likewise there had been wars and famines and portents in the sky. She did not believe the King was dead. They had contrived his escape, she *would* have it, by a subterranean passage, and had handed over to the headsman in his stead a man of the common people.

At the old woman's feet, in his wicker cradle, Jeannot, the last born of the Poitrines, was cutting his teeth. The *citoyenne* Thévenin lifted the cradle and smiled at the child, which moaned feebly, worn out with feverishness and convulsions. It must have been very ill, for they had sent for the doctor, the *citoyen* Pelleport, who, it is true, being a deputy-substitute to the Convention, asked no payment for his visits.

The *citoyenne* Thévenin, an innkeeper's daughter herself, was in her element; not satisfied with the way the farm-girl had washed the plates and dishes, she gave an extra wipe to the crockery and glass, an extra polish to the knives and forks. While the *citoyenne* Poitrine was attending to the soup, which she tasted from time to time as a good cook should, Élodie was cutting up into slices a four-pound loaf hot from the oven. Gamelin, when he saw what she was doing, addressed her:

"A few days ago I read a book written by a young German whose name I have forgotten, and which has been very well translated into French. In it you have a beautiful young girl named Charlotte, who, like you, Élodie, was cutting bread and butter, and like you, cutting it gracefully, and so prettily that at the sight the young Werther fell in love with her."

"And it ended in their marrying?" asked Élodie.

"No," replied Évariste; "it ended in Werther's death by violence."

They dined well, they were all very hungry; but the fare was indifferent. Jean Blaise complained bitterly; he was a great trencherman and made it a rule of conduct to feed well; and no doubt what urged him to elaborate his gluttony into a system was the general scarcity. In every household the Revolution had overturned the cooking pot. The common run of citizens had nothing to chew upon. Clever folks like Jean Blaise, who made big profits amid the general wretchedness, went to the cookshop where they showed their astuteness by stuffing themselves to repletion. As for

Brotteaux who, in this year II of liberty, was living on chestnuts and bread-crusts, he could remember having supped at Grimod de la Reynière's at the near end of the Champs Élysées. Eager to win the repute of an accomplished gourmand he reeled off, sitting there before Dame Poitrine's bacon and cabbages, a string of artful kitchen recipes and wise gastronomic maxims. Presently, when Gamelin protested that a Republican scorns the pleasures of the table, the old financier, always a lover of antiquity, gave the young Spartan the true recipe for the famous black broth.

After dinner, Jean Blaise, who never forgot business, set his itinerant academy to make studies and sketches of the inn, which struck him as quite romantic in its dilapidation. While Philippe Desmahis and Philippe Dubois were drawing the cow-houses the girl Tronche came out to feed the pigs. The *citoyen* Pelleport, officer of health, who at the same moment appeared at the door of the farm kitchen where he had been bestowing his professional services on the Poitrine baby, stepped up to the artists and after complimenting them on their talents, which were an honour to the whole nation, pointed to the Tronche girl in the middle of her porkers:

"You see that creature," he said, "it is not one girl, it is two girls. I speak by the letter, understand that. I was amazed at the extraordinary massiveness of her bony framework and I examined her, to discover she had most of the bones in duplicate—in each thigh two femurs welded together, in each shoulder a double humerus. Some of her muscles are likewise in duplicate. It is a case, in my view, of a pair of twins associated or rather confounded together. It is an interesting phenomenon. I notified Monsieur Saint-Hilaire of the facts, and he thanked me. It is a monster you see before you, *citoyens*. The people here call her 'the girl Tronche'; they should say 'the girls Tronches,' for there are two of them. Nature has these freaks. . . . Good evening, *citoyens;* we shall have a storm to-night. . . ."

After supper by candle-light, the Academy Blaise adjoined to the courtyard where they were joined by a son and daughter of the house in a game of blindman's-buff, in which the young folks, both men and women, displayed a feverish energy sufficiently accounted for by the high spirits proper to their age without seeking an explanation in the wild and precarious times in which they lived. When it was quite dark, Jean Blaise proposed children's games in the farm kitchen. Élodie suggested the game of "hunt my heart," and this was agreed to unanimously. Under the girl's direction Philippe Desmahis traced in chalk, on different pieces of furniture, on doors and walls, seven hearts, that is to say one less than there were players, for old Brotteaux had obligingly joined the rest. They danced round in a ring singing "La Tour, prends garde!" and at a signal from Élodie, each ran to put a hand on a heart. Gamelin in his absent-minded clumsiness was too late to find one vacant, and had to pay a forfeit, the little knife he had bought for six sous at the fair of Saint-Germain and with which he had cut the loaf for his mother in her poverty. The game went on, and one after the other Blaise, Élodie, Brotteaux and Rose Thévenin failed to touch a heart; each paid a forfeit in turn—a ring, a reticule, a little morocco-bound book, a bracelet. Then the forfeits were raffled on Élodie's lap, and each player had to redeem his property by showing his society accomplishments—singing a song or reciting a poem. Brotteaux chose the speech of the patron saint of France in the first canto of the *Pucelle*:

> "Je suis Denis et saint de mon métier,
> J'aime la Gaule, . . ."*

The *citoyen* Blaise, though a far less well-read man, replied without hesitation with Richemond's ripost:

> "Monsieur le Saint, ce n'était pas la peine
> D'abandonner le celeste domaine . . ."†

At that time everybody was reading and re-reading with delight the masterpiece of the French Ariosto; the most serious of men smiled over the loves of Jeanne and Dunois, the adventures of Agnès and Monrose and the exploits of the winged ass. Every man of cultivation knew by heart the choice passages of this diverting and philosophical poem. Évariste Gamelin himself, stern-tempered as he was, when he recovered his twopenny knife from Élodie's lap, recited the going down of Grisbourdon into hell, with a good deal of spirit. The *citoyenne* Thévenin sang without accompaniment Nina's ballad:

> *"Quand le bien-aimé reviendra."*

Desmahis sang to the tune of *La Faridondaine*:

> "Quelques-uns prirent le cochon
> De ce bon saint Antoine,
> Et lui mettant un capuchon,
> Ils en firent un moine.
> Il n'en coûtait que la façon . . ."‡

All the same Desmahis was in a pensive mood. For the

---

*"I am Denis, and sainthood is my trade,
 I love the land of Gaul, . . . etc."

†"Well, well, sir Saint, 'twas hardly worth your pains
 Thus to forsake the heavenly domains. . . ."

‡"Some ribalds took the pig,
 Of the good St. Anthony,
 And clapping a cowl on's head,
 They made the brute a monk.
 'Twas all a matter of dress. . . ."

moment he was ardently in love with all the three women with whom he was playing forfeits, and was casting burning looks of soft appeal at each in turn. He loved Rose Thévenin for her grace, her supple figure, her clever acting, her roving glances, and her voice that went straight to a man's heart; he loved Élodie, because he recognized instinctively her rich endowment of temperament and her kind, complaisant humour; he loved Julienne Hasard, despite her colourless hair, her pale eyelashes, her freckles and her thin bust, because, like Dunois in Voltaire's *Pucelle,* he was always ready, in his generosity, to give the least engaging a token of love —and the more so in this instance because she appeared to be for the moment the most neglected, and therefore the most amenable to his attentions. Without a trace of vanity, he was never sure of these being agreeable; nor yet was he ever sure of their not being. So he never omitted to offer them on the chance. Taking advantage of the opportunities offered by the game of forfeits, he made some tender speeches to Rose Thévenin, who showed no displeasure, but could hardly say much in return under the jealous eyes of the *citoyen* Jean Blaise. He spoke more warmly still to the *citoyenne* Élodie, whom he knew to be pledged to Gamelin, but he was not so exacting as to want a heart all to himself. Élodie could never care for him; but she thought him a handsome fellow and did not altogether succeed in hiding the fact from him. Finally, he whispered his most ardent vows in the ear of the *citoyenne* Hasard, which she received with an air of bewildered stupefaction that might equally express abject submission or chill indifference. And Desmahis did not believe she was indifferent to him.

The inn contained only two bedrooms, both on the first floor and opening on the same landing. That to the left, the better of the two, boasted a flowered paper and a looking-glass the size of a man's hand, the gilt frame of which had been blackened by generations of flies since the days when Louis XIV was a child. In it, under sprigged muslin curtains, stood two beds with down pillows, coverlets and counterpanes. This room was reserved for the three *citoyennes.*

When the time came to retire, Desmahis and the *citoyenne* Hasard, each holding a bedroom candlestick, wished each other good-night on the landing. The amorous engraver quickly passed a note to the colourman's daughter, beseeching her to come to him, when everybody was asleep, in the garret, which was over the *citoyennes'* chamber.

With judicious foresight, he had taken care in the course of the day to study the lie of the land and explore the garret in question, which was full of strings of onions, apples and pears left there to ripen with a swarm of wasps crawling over them, chests and old trunks. He had even noticed an old bed of sacking, decrepit and now disused, as far as he could see, and a palliasse, all ripped up and jumping with fleas.

Facing the *citoyennes'* room was another of very modest dimensions containing three beds, where the men of the party were to sleep, in such comfort as they might. But Brotteaux, who was a Sybarite, betook himself to the barn to sleep among the hay. As for Jean Blaise, *he* had disappeared. Dubois and Gamelin were soon asleep. Desmahis went to bed; but no sooner had the silence of night, like a stagnant pool, enveloped the house, than the engraver got up and climbed the wooden staircase, which creaked under his bare feet. The door of the garret stood ajar. From within came a breath of stifling hot air, mingled with the acrid smell of rotting fruit. On the broken-down bed of sacking lay the girl Tronche, fast asleep with her mouth open.

* * * * * *

* * * * * *

* * * * * *

* * * * * *

Desmahis returned to his room, where he slept soundly and peacefully till daybreak.

On the morrow, after a last day's work, the itinerant Academy took the road back to Paris. When Jean Blaise paid mine host in assignats, the *citoyen* Poitrine complained bitterly that he never saw what he called "square money" nowadays, and promised a fine candle to the beggar who'd bring back the "yellow boys" again.

He offered the *citoyennes* their pick of flowers. At his orders, the girl Tronche mounted on a ladder in her sabots and kilted skirts, giving a full view of her noble, much-bespattered calves, and was indefatigable in cutting blossoms from the climbing roses that covered the wall. From her huge hands the flowers fell in showers, in torrents, in avalanches, into the laps of Élodie, Julienne, and Rose Thévenin, who held out their skirts to catch them. The carriage was full of them. The whole party, when they got back at nightfall, carried armfuls home, and their sleeping and waking were perfumed with their fragrance.

XI

N THE forenoon of the 7th September the *citoyenne* Rochemaure, on her way to visit Gamelin, the new juror, whose interest she wished to solicit on behalf of an acquaintance, who had been denounced as a suspect, encountered on the landing the *ci-devant* Brotteaux des Ilettes, who had been her lover in the old happy days. Brotteaux was just starting to deliver a gross of dancing-dolls of his manufacture to the toy-merchant in the Rue de la Loi; for their more convenient carriage he had hit on the idea of tying them at the end of a pole, as the street hawkers do with their commodities. His manners were always chivalrous towards women, even to those whose fascination for him had been blunted by long familiarity, as could hardly fail to be the case with Madame de Rochemaure,—unless indeed he found her appetizing with the added seasoning of betrayal, absence, unfaithfulness and fat. Be this as it may, he now greeted her on the sordid stairs with their cracked tiles as courteously as he had ever done on the steps before the entrance-door of Les Ilettes, and begged her to do him the honour of entering his garret. She climbed the ladder nimbly enough and found herself under a timbering, the sloping beams of which supported a tiled roof pierced with a skylight. It was impossible to stand upright. She sat down on the only chair there was in the wretched place; after a brief glance at the broken tiling, she asked in a tone of surprise and sorrow:

"Is this where you live, Maurice? You need have little fear of intruders. One must be an imp or a cat to find you here."

"I am cramped for space," returned the *ci-devant* millionaire; "and I do not deny the fact that sometimes it rains on my pallet. It is a trifling inconvenience. And on fine nights I can see the moon, symbol and confidant of men's loves. For the moon, Madame, since the world began, has been apostrophized by lovers, and at her full, with her pale round face, she recalls to the fond swain's mind the object of his desires."

"I know," sighed the *citoyenne.*

"When their time comes the cats make a fine pandemonium in the rain gutter yonder. But we must forgive love if it makes them caterwaul and swear on the tiles, seeing how it fills the lives of men with torments and villainies."

Both had had the tact to greet each other as friends who had parted the night before to take their night's rest, and though grown strangers to each other, they conversed with a good grace and on a footing of friendliness.

At the same time Madame de Rochemaure seemed pensive. The Revolution, which had for a long while been pleasant and profitable

to her, was now a source of anxiety and disquietude; her suppers
were growing less brilliant and less merry. The notes of her harp
no longer charmed the cloud from sombre faces. Her play-tables
were forsaken by the most lavish punters. Many of her cronies,
now numbered among the suspects, were in hiding; her lover, Morhardt the financier, was under arrest, and it was on his behalf she
had come to sound the juror Gamelin. She was suspect herself. A
posse of National Guards had made a search at her house, had
turned out the drawers of her cabinets, prised up boards in her
floor, thrust their bayonets into her mattresses. They had found
nothing, had made their apologies and drunk her wine. But they
had come very near lighting on her correspondence with an *émigré*,
Monsieur d'Expilly. Certain friends he had among the Jacobins had
warned her that Henry, her handsome favourite, was beginning to
compromise his party by his violent language, which was too extravagant to be sincere.

Elbows on knees and head on fist, she sat buried in thought;
then turning to her old lover sitting on the palliasse, she asked:

"What do you think of it all, Maurice?"

"I think these good gentry give a philosopher and an amateur
of the shows of life abundant matter for reflection and amusement;
but that it would be better for you, my dear, if you were out of
France."

"Maurice, where will it land us?"

"That is what you asked me, Louise, one day we were driving on
the banks of the Cher, on the road to Les Ilettes; the horse, you
remember, had taken the bit in his teeth and was galloping off with
us at a frantic pace. How inquisitive women are! to-day, for the
second time, you want to know where we are going to. Ask the
fortune-tellers. I am not a wizard, sweetheart. And philosophy,
even the soundest, is of small help for revealing the future. These
things will have an end; everything has. One may foresee divers
issues. The triumph of the Coalition and the entry of the allies into
Paris. They are not far off; yet I doubt if they will get there. These
soldiers of the Republic take their beating with a zest nothing can
extinguish. It may be Robespierre will marry Madame Royale and
have himself proclaimed Protector of the Kingdom during the
minority of Louis XVII."

"You think so!" exclaimed the *citoyenne,* agog to have a hand in
so promising an intrigue.

"Again it may be," Brotteaux went on, "that La Vendée will
win the day and the rule of the priests be set up again over heaps
of ruins and piles of corpses. You cannot conceive, dear heart, the
empire the clergy still wields over the masses of the foolish, . . .
I beg pardon, I meant to say,—of 'the Faithful'; it was a slip of
the tongue. The most likely thing, in my poor opinion, is that the
Revolutionary Tribunal will bring about the destruction of the

régime it has established; it is a menace over too many heads. Those it terrifies are without number; they will unite together, and to destroy it they will destroy the whole system of government. I think you have got our young friend Gamelin posted to this court. He is virtuous; he will be implacable. The more I think of it, fair friend, the more convinced I am that this Tribunal, set up to save the Republic, will destroy it. The Convention has resolved to have, like Royalty, its *Grands Jours,** its *Chambre Ardente,* and to provide for its security by means of magistrates appointed by itself and by it kept in subjection. But how inferior are the Convention's *Grands Jours* to those of the Monarchy, and its *Chambre Ardente* to that of Louis XIV! The Revolutionary Tribunal is dominated by a sentiment of mean-spirited justice and common equality that will quickly make it odious and ridiculous and will disgust everybody. Do you know, Louise, that this tribunal, which is about to cite to its bar the Queen of France and twenty-one legislators, yesterday condemned a servant-girl convicted of crying: 'Vive le Roi!' with malicious intent and in the hope of destroying the Republic? Our judges, with their black hats and plumes, are working on the model of that William Shakespeare, so dear to the heart of Englishmen, who drags in coarse buffooneries in the middle of his most tragic scenes."

"Ah, well! Maurice," asked the *citoyenne,* "are you still as fortunate as ever with women?"

"Alas!" replied Brotteaux, "the doves flock to the bright new dovecote and light no more on the ruined tower."

"You have not changed. . . . Good-bye, dear friend,—till we meet again."

The same evening the dragoon Henry, paying a visit uninvited at Madame de Rochemaure's, found her in the act of sealing a letter on which he read the address of the *citoyen* Rauline at Vernon. The letter, he knew, was for England. Rauline used to receive Madame de Rochemaure's communications by a postilion of the posting-service and send them on to Dieppe by the hands of a fishwife. The master of a fishing-smack delivered them under cover of night to a British ship cruising off the coast; an *émigré,* Monsieur d'Expilly, received them in London and passed them on, if he thought it advisable, to the Cabinet of Saint James's.

Henry was young and good looking; Achilles was not such a paragon of grace and vigour when he donned the armour Ulysses offered him. But the *citoyenne* Rochemaure, once so enraptured by the charms of the young hero of the Commune, now looked askance at him; her mood had changed since the day she was told how the young soldier had been denounced at the Jacobins as one whose

*Grands Jours,—under the ancient régime, an extraordinary assize held by judges specially appointed by the King and acting in his name.

zeal outran discretion and that he might compromise and ruin her.
Henry thought it might not break his heart perhaps to leave off
loving Madame de Rochemaure; but he was piqued to have fallen
in her good graces. He counted on her to meet sundry expenses in
which the service of the Republic had involved him. Last but not
least, remembering to what extremities women will proceed and
how they go in a flash from the most ardent tenderness to the cold-
est indifference, and how easy they find it to sacrifice what once
they held dear and destroy what once they adored, he began to suspect that some day his fascinating mistress might have him thrown
into prison to get rid of him. Common prudence urged him to regain
his lost ascendancy and to this end he had come armed with all his
fascinations. He came near, drew away, came near again, hovered
round her, ran from her, in the approved fashion of seduction in
the ballet. Then he threw himself in an armchair and in his irresistible voice, his voice that went straight to women's hearts, he
extolled the charms of nature and solitude and with a lovelorn sigh
proposed an expedition to Ermenonville.

Meanwhile she was striking chords on her harp and looking about
her with an expression of impatience and boredom. Suddenly Henry
got up with a gesture of gloomy resolution and informed her that
he was starting for the army and in a few days would be before
Maubeuge.

Without a sign either of scepticism or surprise she nodded her
approval.

"You congratulate me on my decision?"

"I do indeed."

She was expecting a new admirer who was infinitely to her taste
and from whom she hoped to reap great advantages,—a contrast in
every way to the old, a Mirabeau come to life again, a Danton rehabilitated and turned army-contractor, a lion who talked of pitch-
ing every patriot into the Seine. She was on tenter-hooks, thinking
to hear the bell ring at any moment.

To hasten Henry's departure, she fell silent, yawned, fingered a
score, and yawned again. Seeing he made no move to go, she told
him she had to go out and withdrew into her dressing-room.

He called to her in a broken voice:

"Farewell, Louise! . . . Shall I ever see you again?"—and his
hands were busy fumbling in the open writing-desk.

When he reached the street, he opened the letter addressed to the
citoyen Rauline and read it with absorbed attention. Indeed it drew
a curious picture of the state of public feeling in France. It spoke
of the Queen, of the actress Rose Thévenin, of the Revolutionary
Tribunal and a host of confidential remarks emanating from that
worthy, Brotteaux des Ilettes, were repeated in it.

Having read to the end and restored the missive to his pocket, he
stood hesitating a few moments; then, like a man who has made

up his mind and says to himself "the sooner the better," he turned his steps to the Tuileries and found his way into the antechamber of the Committee of General Security.

The same day, at three o'clock of the afternoon, Évariste Gamelin was seated on the jurors' bench along with fourteen colleagues, most of whom he knew, simple-minded, honest, patriotic folks, savants, artists or artisans,—a painter like himself, an artist in black-and-white, both men of talent, a surgeon, a cobbler, a *ci-devant* marquis, who had given high proofs of patriotism, a printer, two or three small tradesmen, a sample lot in a word of the inhabitants of Paris. There they sat, in the workman's blouse or bourgeois coat, with their hair close-cropped *à la Titus* or clubbed *à la catogan;* there were cocked-hats tilted over the eyes, round hats clapped on the back of the head, red caps of liberty smothering the ears. Some were dressed in coat, flapped waistcoat and breeches, as in olden days, others in the *carmagnole* and striped trousers of the sansculottes. Wearing top-boots or buckled shoes or sabots, they offered in their persons every variety of masculine attire prevalent at that date. Having all of them occupied their places on several previous occasions, they seemed very much at their ease, and Gamelin envied them their unconcern. His own heart was thumping, his ears roaring; a mist was before his eyes and everything about him took on a livid tinge.

When the usher announced the opening of the sitting, three judges took their places on a raised platform of no great size in front of a green table. They wore hats cockaded and crowned with great black plumes and the official cloak with a tricolour riband from which a heavy silver medal was suspended on the breast. In front of them at the foot of the daïs, sat the deputy of the Public Prosecutor, similarly attired. The clerk of the court had a seat between the judges' bench and the prisoner's chair, at present occupied. To Gamelin's eyes these men wore a different aspect from that of every day; they seemed nobler, graver, more alarming, albeit their bearing was commonplace enough as they turned over papers, beckoned to an usher or leant back to listen to some communication from a juryman or an officer of the court.

Above the judges' heads hung the tables of the Rights of Man; to their right and left, against the old feudal walls, the busts of Le Peltier Saint-Fargeau and Marat. Facing the jury bench, at the lower end of the hall, rose the public gallery. The first row of seats was filled by women, who all, fair, brown and grey-haired alike, wore the high coif with the pleated tucker shading their cheeks; the breast, which invariably, as decreed by the fashion of the day, showed the amplitude of the nursing mother's bosom, was covered with a crossed white kerchief or the rounded bib of a blue apron. They sat with folded arms resting on the rail of the tribune. Behind them, scattered about the rising tiers, could be seen a sprinkling of citizens dressed in the varied garb which at that date gave every gathering so striking and picturesque a character. On the right hand, near the doors, behind a broad barrier, a space was reserved where the public could stand. On this occasion it was nearly empty. The business that was to occupy the attention of this particular section of the tribunal interested only a few spectators, while doubtless the other sections sitting at the same hour would be hearing more exciting cases.

This fact somewhat reassured Gamelin, his heart was like to fail him as it was, and he could not have endured the heated atmosphere of one of the great days. His eyes took in the most trifling details of the scene,—the cotton-wool in the *greffier's* ear and a blot of ink on the Deputy Prosecutor's papers. He could see, as through a magnifying glass, the capitals of the pillars sculptured at a time when all knowledge of the classical orders was forgotten and which crowned the Gothic columns with wreaths of nettle and holly. But wherever he looked, his gaze came back again and again to the fatal chair; this was of an antiquated make, covered in red Utrecht velvet, the seat worn and the arms blackened with use. Armed National Guards stood guarding every door.

At last the accused appeared, escorted by grenadiers, but with limbs unbound, as the law directed. He was a man of fifty or thereabouts, lean and dry, with a brown face, à very bald head, hollow cheeks and thin livid lips, dressed in an out-of-date coat of a sanguine red. No doubt it was fever that made his eyes glitter like jewels and gave his cheeks their shiny, varnished look. He took his seat. His legs, which he crossed, were extraordinarily spare and his great knotted hands met round the knees they clasped. His name was Marie-Adolphe Guillergues, and he was accused of malversation in the supply of forage to the Republican troops. The act of indictment laid to his charge numerous and serious offenses, of which no single one was positively certain. Under examination, Guillergues denied the majority of the charges and explained the rest in a light favourable to himself. He spoke in a cold, precise way, with a marked ability and gave the impression of being a dangerous man to have business dealings with. He had an answer for everything. When the judge asked him an embarrassing question, his face remained unmoved and his voice confident, but his two hands, folded on his breast, kept twitching in an agony. Gamelin was struck by this and whispered to the colleague sitting next him, a painter like himself:

"Watch his thumbs!"

The first witness to depose alleged a number of most damaging facts. He was the mainstay of the prosecution. Those on the other hand who followed showed themselves well disposed to the prisoner. The Deputy of the Public Prosecutor spoke strongly, but did not go

beyond generalities. The advocate for the defence adopted a tone of
bluff conviction of his client's innocence that earned the accused a
sympathy he had failed to secure by his own efforts. The sitting
was suspended and the jury assembled in the room set apart for
deliberation. There, after a confused and confusing discussion, they
found themselves divided in two groups about equal in number. On
the one side were the unemotional, the lukewarm, the men of reason, whom no passion could stir, on the other the kind who let their
feelings guide them, who prove all but inaccessible to argument
and only consult their heart. These always voted guilty. They were
the true metal, pure and unadulterated; their only thought was to
save the Republic and they cared not a straw for anything else.
Their attitude made a strong impression on Gamelin who felt he
was of the same kidney himself.

"This Guillergues," he thought to himself, "is a cunning scamp, a
villain who has speculated in the forage supplied to our cavalry.
To acquit him is to let a traitor escape, to be false to the fatherland, to devote the army to defeat." And in a flash Gamelin could
see the Hussars of the Republic, mounted on stumbling horses,
sabred by the enemy's cavalry. . . . "But if Guillergues was innocent . . . ?"

Suddenly he remembered Jean Blaise, likewise suspected of bad
faith in the matter of supplies. There were bound to be many others
acting like Guillergues and Blaise, contriving disaster, ruining the
Republic! An example must be made. But if Guillergues was innocent . . . ?

"There are no proofs," said Gamelin, aloud.

"There never are," retorted the foreman of the jury, shrugging
his shoulders; he was good metal, pure metal!

In the end, there proved to be seven votes for condemnation,
eight for acquittal.

The jury re-entered the hall and the sitting was resumed. The
jurors were required to give reasons for their verdict, and each
spoke in turn facing the empty chair. Some were prolix, others confined themselves to a sentence; one or two talked unintelligible
gabble.

When Gamelin's turn came, he rose and said:

"In presence of a crime so heinous as that of robbing the defenders of the fatherland of the sinews of victory, we need formal proofs
which we have not got."

By a majority of votes the accused was declared not guilty.

Guillergues was brought in again and stood before his judges
amid a hum of sympathy from the spectators which conveyed the
news of his acquittal to him. He was another man. His features had
lost their harshness, his lips were relaxed again. He looked venerable; his face bore the impression of innocence. The President read
out in tones of emotion the verdict releasing the prisoner; the audi-

ence broke into applause. The gendarme who had brought Guillergues in threw himself into his arms. The President called him to the daïs and gave him the embrace of brotherhood. The jurors kissed him, while Gamelin's eyes rained hot tears.

The courtyard of the Palais, dimly lighted by the last rays of the setting sun, was filled with a howling, excited crowd. The four sections of the Tribunal had the day before pronounced thirty sentences of death, and on the steps of the Great Stairway a throng of *tricoteuses* squatted to see the tumbrils start. But Gamelin, as he descended the steps among the press of jurors and spectators, saw

nothing, heard nothing but his own act of justice and humanity and the self-congratulation he felt at having recognized innocence. In the courtyard stood Élodie, all in white, smiling through her tears; she threw herself into his arms and lay there half fainting. When she had recovered her voice, she said to him:

"Évariste, you are noble, you are good, you are generous! In the hall there, your voice, so gentle and manly, went right through me with its magnetic wave. It electrified me. I gazed at you on your bench, I could see no one but you. But you, dear heart, you never guessed I was there? Nothing told you I was present? I sat in the gallery in the second row to the right. By heaven! how sweet it is to do the right! you saved that unhappy man's life. Without you, it was all over with him; he was as good as dead. You have given him back to life and the love of his friends. At this moment he must bless you. Évariste, how happy I am and how proud to love you!"

Arm in arm, pressed close to one another, they went along the streets; their bodies felt so light they seemed to be flying.

They went to the *Amour peintre*. On reaching the Oratoire:

"Better not go through the shop," Élodie suggested.

She made him go in by the main coach-door and mount the stairs with her to the suite of rooms above. On the landing she drew out of her reticule a heavy iron key.

"It might be the key of a prison," she exclaimed, "Évariste, you are going to be my prisoner."

They crossed the dining-room and were in the girl's bed-chamber.

Évariste felt upon his the ardent freshness of Élodie's lips. He pressed her in his arms; with head thrown back and swooning eyes, her hair flowing loose over her relaxed form, half fainting, she escaped his hold and ran to shoot the bolt. . . .

The night was far advanced when the *citoyenne* Blaise opened the outer door of the flat for her lover and whispered to him in the darkness.

"Good-bye, sweetheart! it is the hour my father will be coming home. If you hear a noise on the stairs, go up quick to the higher floor and don't come down till all danger is over of your being seen. To have the street-door opened, give three raps on the *concierge's* window. Good-bye, my life, good-bye, my soul!"

When he found himself in the street, he saw the window of Élodie's chamber half unclose and a little hand pluck a red carnation, which fell at his feet like a drop of blood.

XII

ONE evening when old Brotteaux arrived in the Rue de la Loi bringing a gross of dancing-dolls for the *citoyen* Caillou, the toy-merchant, the latter, a soft-spoken, polite man as a rule, stood there stiff and stern among his dolls and punch-and-judies and gave him a far from gracious welcome.

"Have a care, *citoyen* Brotteaux," he began, "have a care! There is a time to laugh, and a time to be serious; jokes are not always in good taste. A member of the Committee of Security of the Section, who inspected my establishment yesterday, saw your dancing-dolls and deemed them anti-revolutionary."

"He was jesting!" declared Brotteaux.

"Not so, *citoyen,* not at all. He is not the man to joke. He said in these little fellows the National representatives were insiduously mimicked, that in particular one could discover caricatures of Couthon, Saint-Just and Robespierre, and he seized the lot. It is a dead loss to me, to say nothing of the grave risks to which I am exposed."

"What! these Harlequins, these Gilles, these Scaramouches, these Colins and Colinettes, which I have painted the same as Boucher used to fifty years ago, how should they be parodies of Couthons and Saint-Justs? No sensible man could imagine such a thing."

"It is possible," replied the *citoyen* Caillou, "that you acted without malice, albeit we must always distrust a man of parts like you. But it is a dangerous game. Shall I give you an instance? Natoile, who runs a little outdoor theatre in the Champs Élysées, was arrested the day before yesterday for anti-patriotism because he made Polichinelle poke fun at the Convention."

"Now listen to me," Brotteaux urged, raising the cloth that covered his little dangling figures; "just look at these masks and faces, are they anything else whatever but characters in plays and pastorals? How could you let yourself be persuaded, *citoyen* Caillou, that I was making fun of the National Convention?"

Brotteaux was dumfounded. While allowing much for human folly, he had not thought it possible it could ever go so far as to suspect his Scaramouches and Colinettes. Repeatedly he protested their innocence and his; but the *citoyen* Caillou would not hear a word.

"*Citoyen* Brotteaux, take your dolls away. I esteem you, I honour you, but I do not mean to incur blame or get into trouble because of you. I intend to remain a good citizen and to be treated as such. Good evening, *citoyen* Brotteaux; take your dolls away."

The old man set out again for home, carrying his suspects over his shoulder at the end of a pole, an object of derision to the children, who took him for the hawker of rat-poison. His thoughts were gloomy. No doubt, he did not live only by his dancing-dolls; he used to paint portraits at twenty *sols* apiece, under the archways of doors or in one of the market halls, among the darners and old-clothes menders, where he found many a young recruit starting for the front and wanting to leave his likeness behind for his sweetheart. But these petty tasks cost him endless pains, and he was a long way from making as good portraits as he did dancing-dolls. Sometimes, too, he acted as amanuensis for the Market dames, but this meant mixing himself up in Royalist plots, and the risks were heavy. He remembered there lived in the Rue Neuve-des-Petits-Champs, near the erstwhile Place Vendôme, another toy-merchant, Joly by name, and he resolved to go next day to offer him the goods the chicken-hearted Caillou had declined.

A fine rain began to fall. Brotteaux who feared its effects on his marionettes, quickened his pace. As he crossed the Pont-Neuf and was turning the corner of the Place de Thionville, he saw by the light of the street-lamp, sitting on a stone post, a lean old man who seemed utterly exhausted with fatigue and hunger, but still preserved his venerable appearance. He was dressed in a tattered surtout, had no hat and appeared over sixty. Approaching the poor wretch, Brotteaux recognised the Père Longuemare, the same he had saved from hanging six months before while both of them were waiting in queue in front of the bakery in the Rue de Jérusalem. Feeling bound to the monk by the service he had already done him, Brotteaux stepped up to him and made himself known as the publican who had stood beside him among the common herd, one day of great scarcity, and asked him if he could not be of some use to him.

"You seem wearied, Father. Take a taste of cordial,"—and Brotteaux drew from the pocket of his plum-coloured coat a flask of brandy, which lay there alongside his Lucretius.

"Drink. And I will help you to get back to your house."

The Père Longuemare pushed away the flask with his hand and tried to rise, but only to fall back again in his seat.

"Sir," he said in a weak but firm voice, "for three months I have been living at Picpus. Being warned they had come to arrest me at my lodging, yesterday at five o'clock of the afternoon, I did not return home. I have no place to go to; I am wandering the streets and am a little fatigued."

"Very well, Father," proposed Brotteaux, "do me the honour to share my garret."

"Sir," replied the Barnabite, "you know, I suppose, I am a suspect."

"I am one too," said Brotteaux, "and my marionettes into the bargain, which is the worst thing of all. You see them exposed under this flimsy cloth to the fine rain that chills our bones. For, I must tell you, Father, that after having been a publican, I now make dancing-dolls for a living."

The Père Longuemare took the hand the *ci-devant* financier extended to him and accepted the hospitality offered. Brotteaux, in his garret, served him a meal of bread and cheese and wine, which last he had put to cool in the rain-gutter, for was he not a Sybarite?

Having appeased his hunger:

"Sir," said the Père Longuemare, "I ought to inform you of the circumstances that led to my flight and left me to die on yonder post where you found me. Driven from my cloister, I lived on the scanty allowance the Assembly had assigned to me; I gave lessons in Latin and Mathematics and I wrote pamphlets on the persecution of the Church of France. I have even composed a work of some length, to prove that the Constitutional oath of the Priests is subversive of Ecclesiastical discipline. The advances made by the Revolution deprived me of all my pupils, while I could not get my pension because I had not the certificate of citizenship required by law. This certificate I went to the Hôtel de Ville to claim, in the conviction I was well entitled to it. Member of an order founded by the Apostle Paul himself, who boasted the title of Roman citizen, I always piqued myself on behaving after his example as a good French citizen, a respecter of all human laws which are not in opposition to the Divine. I presented my demand to Monsieur Colin, pork-butcher and Municipal officer, in charge of the delivery of certificates of the sort. He questioned me as to my calling. I told him I was a Priest. He asked me if I was married, and on my answering that I was not, he told me that was the worse for me. Finally, after a variety of questions, he asked me if I had proved my citizenship on the 10th August, the 2nd September and the 31st May. 'No certificates can be given,' he added, 'except to such as have proved their patriotism by their behaviour on these three occasions.' I could not give him an answer that would satisfy him. However, he took down my name and address and promised me to make prompt enquiry into my case. He kept his word, and as the result of his enquiry two Commissioners of the Committee of General Security of Picpus, supported by an armed band, presented themselves at my lodging in my absence to conduct me to prison. I do not know of what crime I am accused. But you will agree with me one must pity Monsieur Colin, whose wits are so clouded he holds it a reproach to an ecclesiastic not to have made display of his patriotism on the 10th August, the 2nd September, and the 31st May. A man capable of such a notion is surely deserving of commiseration."

"*I* am in the same plight, I have no certificate," observed Brotteaux. "We are both suspects. But you are weary. To bed, Father. We will discuss plans to-morrow for your safety."

He gave the mattress to his guest and kept the palliasse for himself; but the monk in his humility demanded the latter with so much urgency that his wish had to be complied with; otherwise he would have slept on the boards.

These arrangements completed, Brotteaux blew out the candle both to save tallow and as a wise precaution.

"Sir," the monk addressed him, "I am thankful for what you are doing for me; but alas! it is of small moment to you whether I am grateful or no. May God account your act meritorious! *That* is of infinite concern for you. But God pays no heed to what is not done for his glory and is merely the outcome of purely natural virtue. Wherefore I beseech you, sir, to do for Him what you were led to do for me."

"Father," answered Brotteaux, "never trouble yourself on this head and do not think of gratitude. What I am doing now, the merit of which you exaggerate,—is not done for any love of you; for indeed, albeit you are a lovable man, Father, I know you too little to love you. Nor yet do I act so for love of humanity; for I am not so simple as to think with 'Don Juan' that humanity has rights; indeed this prejudice, in a mind so emancipated as his, grieves me. I do it out of that selfishness which inspires mankind to perform all their deeds of generosity and self-sacrifice, by making them recognize themselves in all who are unfortunate, by disposing them to commiserate their own calamities in the calamities of others and by inciting them to offer help to a mortal resembling themselves in nature and destiny, so that they think they are succouring themselves in succouring him. I do it also for lack of anything better to do; for life is so desperately insipid we must find distraction at any cost, and benevolence is an amusement, of a mawkish sort, one indulges in for want of any more savoury; I do it out of pride and to get an advantage over you; I do it, in a word, as part of a system and to show you what an atheist is capable of."

"Do not calumniate yourself, sir," replied the Père Longuemare. "I have received of God more marks of grace than He has accorded you hitherto; but I am not as good a man as you, and am greatly your inferior in natural merits. But now let me take an advantage too over you. Not knowing me, you cannot love me. And I, sir, without knowing you, I love you better than myself; God bids me do so."

Having so said, the Père Longuemare knelt down on the floor, and after repeating his prayers, stretched himself on his palliasse and fell peacefully asleep.

XIII

VARISTE GAMELIN occupied his place as juror of the Tribunal for the second time. Before the opening of the sitting, he discussed with his colleagues the news that had arrived that morning. Some of it was doubtful, some untrue; but part was authentic— and appalling; the armies of the coalition in command of all the roads and marching *en masse* on Paris, La Vendée triumphant, Lyons in insurrection, Toulon surrendered to the English, who were landing fourteen thousand men there.

For him and his fellow magistrates these were not only events of interest to all the world, but so many matters of domestic concern. Foredoomed to perish in the ruin of the fatherland, they made the public salvation their own proper business. The Nation's interests, thus entangled with their own, dictated their opinions and passions and conduct.

Gamelin, where he sat on the jury bench, was handed a letter from Trubert, Secretary of the Committee of Defence; it was to notify his appointment as Commissioner of Supplies of Powder and Saltpetre:

"You will excavate all the cellars in the Section in order to extract the substances necessary for the manufacture of powder. To-morrow perhaps the enemy will be before Paris; the soil of the fatherland must provide us with the lightning we shall launch against our aggressors. I send you herewith a schedule of instructions from the Convention regarding the manipulation of saltpetres. Farewell and brotherly greeting."

At that moment the accused was brought in. He was one of the last of the defeated Generals whom the Convention delivered over one after the other to the Tribunal, and the most insignificant. At sight of him Gamelin shuddered; once again he seemed to see the same soldier whom three weeks before, looking on as a spectator, he had seen sentenced and sent to the guillotine. The man was the same, with his obstinate, opinionated look; the procedure was the same. He gave his answers in a cunning, brutish way that ruined the effect even of the most convincing. His cavilling and chicanery and the accusations he levelled against his subordinates, made you forget he was fulfilling the honourable task of defending his honour and his life. Everything was uncertain, every statement disputed,—position of the armies, total of forces engaged, munitions of war, orders given, orders received, movements of troops; nobody knew anything. It was impossible to make head or tail of these confused, nonsensical, aimless operations which had ended in disaster;

defending counsel and the accused himself were as much in the dark as were accuser, judges, and jury, and strange to say, not a soul would admit, whether to himself or to other people, that this was the case. The judges took a childish delight in drawing plans and discussing problems of tactics and strategy, while the prisoner constantly betrayed his inborn predilection for crooked ways.

The arguments dragged on endlessly. And all the time Gamelin could see on the rough roads of the north the ammunition wagons stogged in the mire and the guns capsized in the ruts, and along all the ways the broken and beaten columns flying in disorder, while from all sides the enemy's cavalry was debouching by the abandoned defiles. And from this host of men betrayed he could hear a mighty shout going up in accusation of the General. When the hearing closed, darkness was falling on the hall, and the head of Marat gleamed half-seen like a phantom above the President's head. The jury was called upon to give judgment, but was of two minds. Gamelin, in a hoarse, strangled voice, but in resolute accents, declared the accused guilty of treason against the Republic, and a murmur of approval rose from the crowd, a flattering unction to his youthful virtue. The sentence was read by the light of torches which cast a lurid, uncertain gleam on the prisoner's hollow temples beaded with drops of sweat. Outside the doors, on the steps crowded with the customary swarm of cockaded harridans, Gamelin could hear his name, which the habitués of the Tribunal were beginning to know, passed from mouth to mouth, and was assailed by a bevy of *tricoteuses* who shook their fists in his face, demanding the head of *the Austrian*.

The next day Évariste had to give judgment on the fate of a poor woman, the widow Meyrion. She distributed bread from house to house and tramped the streets pushing a little hand-cart and carrying a wooden tally hung at her waist, on which she cut notches with her knife representing the number of the loaves she had delivered. Her gains amounted to eight sous a day. The deputy of the Public Prosecutor displayed an extraordinary virulence towards the wretched creature, who had, it appears, shouted "Vive le Roi!" on several occasions, uttered anti-revolutionary remarks in the houses where she called to leave the daily dole of bread, and been mixed up in a plot for the escape of the woman Capet. In answer to the Judge's question she admitted the facts alleged against her; whether fool or fanatic, she professed Royalist sentiments of the most enthuiastic sort and waited her doom.

The Revolutionary Tribunal made a point of proving the triumph of Equality by showing itself just as severe for street-porters and servant maids as for the aristocrats and financiers. Gamelin could conceive no other system possible under a popular government. He would have deemed it a mark of contempt, an insult to the people, to exclude it from punishment. That would have been to consider it, so to speak, as unworthy of chastisement by the law. Reserved for aristocrats only, the guillotine would have appeared to him in the light of an iniquitous privilege. In his thoughts he was beginning to erect chastisement into a religious and mystic dogma, to assign it a virtue, a merit of its own; he conceived that society owes punishment to criminals and that it is doing them an injustice to cheat them of this right. He declared the woman Meyrion guilty and deserving of death, only regretting that the fanatics, more culpable than herself, who had brought her to her ruin, were not there to share her fate.

Every evening almost Évariste attended the meetings of the Jacobins, who assembled in the former chapel of the Dominicans, commonly known as Jacobins, in the Rue Honoré. In a courtyard, in which stood a tree of Liberty, a poplar whose leaves shook and rustled all day in the wind, the chapel, built in a poor, clumsy style and surmounted by a heavy roof of tiles, showed its bare gable, pierced by a round window and an arched doorway, above which floated the National colours, the flagstaff crowned with the cap of Liberty. The Jacobins, like the Cordeliers, and the Feuillants, had appropriated the premises and taken the name of the dispossessed monks. Gamelin, once a regular attendant at the sittings of the Cordeliers, did not find at the Jacobins the familiar sabots, carmagnoles and rallying cries of the Dantonists. In Robespierre's club administrative reserve and bourgeois gravity were the order of the day. The Friend of the People was no more, and since his death Évariste had followed the lessons of Maximilien whose thought ruled the Jacobins, and thence, through a thousand affiliated societies was disseminated over all France. During the reading of the minutes, his eyes wandered over the bare, dismal walls, which, after sheltering the spiritual sons of the arch-inquisitor of heresy, now looked down on the assemblage of zealous inquisitors of crimes against the fatherland.

There, without pomp or ceremony, sat the body that was the chiefest power of the State and ruled by force of words. It governed the city, the empire, dictated its decrees to the Convention itself. These artisans of the new order of things, so respectful of the law that they continued Royalists in 1791 and would fain have been Royalists still on the King's return from Varennes, so obstinate in their attachment to the Constitution, friends of the established order of the State even after the massacres of the Champ-de-Mars, and never revolutionaries against the Revolution, heedless of popular agitation, cherished in their dark and puissant soul a love of the fatherland that had given birth to fourteen armies and set up the guillotine. Évariste was lost in admiration of their vigilance, their suspicious temper, their reasoned dogmatism, their love of system, their supremacy in the art of governing, their sovereign sanity.

The public that formed the audience gave no token of their presence save a low, long-drawn murmur as of one voice, like the rustling of the leaves of the tree of Liberty that stood outside the threshold.

That day, the 11th Vendémiaire, a young man, with a receding brow, a piercing eye, a sharp prominent nose, a pointed chin, a pock-marked face, a look of cold self-possession, mounted the tribune slowly. His hair was white with powder and he wore a blue coat that displayed his slim figure. He showed the precise carriage and moved with the cadenced step that made some say in mockery that he was like a dancing-master and earned him from others the name of the "French Orpheus." Robespierre, speaking in a clear voice, delivered an eloquent discourse against the enemies of the Republic. He belaboured with metaphysical and uncompromising arguments Brissot and his accomplices. He spoke at great length, in free-flowing harmonious periods. Soaring in the celestial spheres of philosophy, he launched his lightnings at the base conspirators crawling on the ground.

Évariste heard and understood. Till then he had blamed the Gironde; were they not working for the restoration of the monarchy or the triumph of the Orleans faction, were they not planning the ruin of the heroic city that had delivered France from her fetters and would one day deliver the universe? Now, as he listened to the sage's voice, he discerned truths of a higher and purer compass; he grasped a revolutionary metaphysic which lifted his mind above coarse, material conditions into a region of absolute, unqualified convictions, untrammelled by the errors of the senses. Things are in their nature involved and full of confusion; the complexity of circumstances is such that we lose our way amongst them. Robespierre simplified them to his mind, put good and evil before him in clear and precise formulas. Federalism,—indivisibility; unity and indivisibility meant salvation, federalism, damnation. Gamelin tasted the ineffable joy of a believer who knows the word that saves and the word that destroys the soul. Henceforth the Revolutionary Tribunal, as of old the ecclesiastical courts, would take cognizance of crime absolute, of crime definable in a word. And, because he had the religious spirit, Évariste welcomed these revelations with a sombre enthusiasm; his heart swelled and rejoiced at the thought that, henceforth, he had a talisman to discern betwixt crime and innocence, he possessed a creed! Ye stand in lieu of all else, oh, treasures of faith!

The sage Maximilien enlightened him further as to the perfidious intent of those who were for equalizing property and partioning the land, abolishing wealth and poverty and establishing a happy mediocrity for all. Misled by their specious maxims, he had origi-

nally approved their designs, which he deemed in accord with the
principles of a true Republican. But Robespierre, in his speeches
at the Jacobins, had unmasked their machinations and convinced
him that these men, disinterested as their intentions appeared, were
working to overthrow the Republic, that they were alarming the
rich only to rouse against the lawful authority powerful and implacable foes. Once private property was threatened, the whole
population, the more ardently attached to its possessions the less
of these it owned, would turn suddenly against the Republic. To
terrify vested interests is to conspire against the State. These men
who, under pretence of securing universal happiness and the reign
of justice, proposed a system of equality and community of goods
as a worthy object of good citizens' endeavours, were traitors and
malefactors more dangerous than the Federalists.

But the most startling revelation he owed to Robespierre's wisdom was that of the crimes and infamies of atheism. Gamelin had
never denied the existence of God; he was a deist and believed in a
Providence that watches over mankind; but, admitting that he
could form only a very vague conception of the Supreme Being and
deeply attached to the principle of freedom of conscience, he was
quite ready to allow that right-thinking men might follow the example of Lamettrie, Boulanger, the Baron d'Holbach, Lalande, Helvétius, the *citoyen* Dupuis, and deny God's existence, on condition
they formulated a natural morality and found in themselves the
sources of justice and the rules of a virtuous life. He had even felt
himself in sympathy with the atheists, when he had seen them vili-
fied and persecuted. Maximilien had opened his mind and unsealed
his eyes. The great man by his virtuous eloquence had taught him
the true character of atheism, its nature, its objects, its effects; he
had shown him how this doctrine, conceived in the drawing-rooms
and boudoirs of the aristocracy, was the most perfidious invention
the enemies of the people had ever devised to demoralize and en-
slave it; how it was a criminal act to uproot from the heart of the
unfortunate the consoling thought of a Providence to reward and
compensate and give them over without rein or bit to the passions
that degrade men and make vile slaves of them; how, in fine, the
monarchical Epicureanism of a Helvétius led to immorality, cruelty,
and every wickedness. Now that he had learnt these lessons from
the lips of a great man and a great citizen, he execrated the atheists
—especially when they were of an open-hearted, joyous temper, like
his old friend Brotteaux.

In the days that followed Évariste had to give judgment one
after the other on a *ci-devant* convicted of having destroyed wheat-
stuffs in order to starve the people, three *émigrés* who had returned
to foment civil war in France, two ladies of pleasure of the Palais-
Égalité, fourteen Breton conspirators, men, women, old men,

youths, masters, and servants. The crime was proven, the law explicit. Among the guilty was a girl of twenty, adorable in the heyday of her young beauty under the shadow of the doom so soon to overwhelm her, a fascinating figure. A blue bow bound her golden locks, her lawn kerchief revealed a white, graceful neck.

Évariste was consistent in casting his vote for death, and all the accused, with the one exception of an old gardener, were sent to the scaffold.

The following week Évariste and his section mowed down sixty-three heads—forty-five men and eighteen women.

The judges of the Revolutionary Tribunal drew no distinction between men and women, in this following a principle as old as justice itself. True, the President Montané, touched by the bravery and beauty of Charlotte Corday, had tried to save her by paltering with the procedure of the trial and had thereby lost his seat, but women as a rule were shown no favour under examination, in strict accordance with the rule common to all the tribunals. The jurors feared them, distrusting their artful ways, their aptitude for deception, their powers of seduction. They were the match of men in resolution, and this invited the Tribunal to treat them in the same way. The majority of those who sat in judgment, men of normal sensuality or sensual on occasion, were in no wise affected by the fact that the prisoner was a woman. They condemned or acquitted them as their conscience, their zeal, their love, lukewarm or vehement, for the Republic dictated. Almost always they appeared before the court with their hair carefully dressed and attired with as much elegance as the unhappy conditions allowed. But few of them were young and still fewer pretty. Confinement and suspense had blighted them, the harsh light of the hall betrayed their weariness and the anguish they had endured, beating down on faded lids, blotched and pimpled cheeks, white, drawn lips. Nevertheless, the fatal chair more than once held a young girl, lovely in her pallor, while a shadow of the tomb veiled her eyes and made her beauty the more seductive. That the sight had the power to melt some jurymen and irritate others, who should deny? That, in the secret depraved heart of him, one of these magistrates may have pried into the most sacred intimacies of the fair body that was to his morbid fancy at the same moment a living and a dead woman's, and that, gloating over voluptuous and ghoulish imaginings he may have found an atrocious pleasure in giving over to the headsman those dainty, desirable limbs,—this is perhaps a thing better left unsaid, but one which no one can deem impossible who knows what men are. Évariste Gamelin, cold and pedantic in his artistic creed, could see no beauty but in the Antique; he admired beauty, but it hardly stirred his senses. His classical taste was so severe he rarely found a woman to his liking; he was as insensible to the charms of a pretty face as he was to Fragonard's colouring and Boucher's drawing. He had never known desire save under the form of deep passion.

Like the majority of his colleagues in the Tribunal, he thought women more dangerous than men. He hated the *ci-devant* princesses, the creatures he pictured to himself in his horrified dreams in company with Elisabeth and *the Austrian* weaving plots to assassinate good patriots; he even hated all those fair mistresses of financiers, philosophers, and men of letters whose only crime was having enjoyed the pleasures of the senses and the mind and lived at a time when it was sweet to live. He hated them without admitting the feeling to himself, and when he had one before him at the bar, he condemned her out of pique, convinced all the while that he was dooming her justly and rightly for the public good. His sense of honour, his manly modesty, his cold, calculated wisdom, his devotion to the State, his virtues in a word, pushed under the knife heads that might well have moved men's pity.

But what is this, what is the meaning of this strange prodigy? Once the difficulty was to find the guilty, to search them out in their lair, to drag the confession of their crime from reluctant lips. Now, there is no hunting with a great pack of sleuth-hounds, no pursuing a timid prey; lo! from all sides come the victims to offer themselves a voluntary sacrifice. Nobles, virgins, soldiers, courtesans, flock to the Tribunal, dragging their condemnation from dilatory judges, claiming death as a right which they are impatient to enjoy. Not enough the multitude with which the zeal of the informers has crowded the prisons and which the Public Prosecutor and his myrmidons are wearing out their lives in haling before the Tribunal; punishment must likewise be provided for those who refuse to wait. And how many others, prouder and more pressing yet, begrudging their judges and headsmen their death, perish by their own hand! The mania of killing is equalled by the mania to die. Here, in the Conciergerie, is a young soldier, handsome, vigorous, beloved; he leaves behind him in the prison an adorable mistress; she bade him "Live for me!"—he will live neither for her nor love nor glory. He lights his pipe with his act of accusation. And, a Republican, for he breathes liberty through every pore, he turns Royalist that he may die. The Tribunal tries its best to save him, but the accused proves the stronger; judges and jury are forced to let him have his way.

Évariste's mind, naturally of an anxious, scrupulous cast, was filled to overflowing through the lessons he learned at the Jacobins and the contemplation of life with suspicions and alarms. At night, as he paced the ill-lighted streets on his way to Élodie's, he fancied through every cellar-grating he passed he caught a glimpse of a plate for printing off forged assignats; in the dark recesses of the baker's and grocer's empty shops he imagined store-rooms bursting with provisions fraudulently held back for a rise in prices; looking in at the glittering windows of the eating-houses, he seemed to hear the talk of the speculators plotting the ruin of the country as they drained bottles of Beaune and Chablis; in the evil-smelling alleys he could see the very prostitutes trampling underfoot the National cockade to the applause of elegant young roisterers; everywhere he beheld conspirators and traitors. And he thought: "Against so may foes, secret or declared, oh! Republic thou hast but one succour; Saint Guillotine, save the fatherland! . . ."

Élodie would be waiting for him in her little blue chamber above the *Amour peintre*. To let him know he might come in, she used to set on the window-sill her little watering-can beside the pot of carnations. Now he filled her with horror, he seemed like a monster to her; she was afraid of him,—and she adored him. All the night, clinging together in a frantic embrace, the bloody-minded lover and the amorous girl exchanged in silence frenzied kisses.

<h1 style="text-align:center">XIV</h1>

RISING at dawn, the Père Longuemare, after sweeping out the room, departed to say his Mass in a chapel in the Rue d'Enfer served by a nonjuring priest. There were in Paris thousands of similar retreats, where the refractory clergy gathered together clandestinely little troops of the faithful. The police of the Sections, vigilant and suspicious as they were, kept their eyes shut to these hidden folds, from fear of the exasperated flock and moved by some lingering veneration for holy things. The Barnabite made his farewells to his host who had great difficulty in persuading him to come back to dine, and only succeeded in the end by promising that the cheer would be neither plentiful nor delicate.

Brotteaux, when left to himself, kindled a little earthenware stove; then, while he busied himself with preparations for the Monk's and the Epicurean's meal, he read in his Lucretius and meditated on the conditions of human beings.

As a sage and a philosopher, he was not surprised that these wretched creatures, silly playthings of the forces of nature, found themselves more often than not in absurd and painful situations; but he was weak and illogical enough to believe that the Revolutionaries were more wicked and more foolish than other men, thereby falling into the error of the metaphysician. At the same time he was no Pessimist and did not hold that life was altogether bad. He admired Nature in several of her departments, especially the celestial mechanism and physical love, and accommodated himself to the labours of life, pending the arrival of the day, which

could not be far off, when he would have nothing more either to
fear or to desire.

He coloured some dancing-dolls with painstaking care and made
a Zerline that was very like Rose Thévenin. He liked the girl and
his Epicureanism highly approved of the arrangement of the atoms
of which she was composed.

These tasks occupied him till the Barnabite's return.

"Father," he announced, as he opened the door to admit him, "I
told you, you remember, that our fare would be meagre. We have
nothing but chestnuts. The more reason, therefore, they should be
well seasoned."

"Chestnuts!" cried Père Longuemare, smiling, "there is no more
delicious dish. My father, sir, was a poor gentleman of the Limousin, whose whole estate consisted of a pigeon-cote in ruins, an
orchard run wild and a clump of chestnut-trees. He fed himself, his
wife and his twelve children on big green chestnuts, and we were
all strong and sturdy. I was the youngest and the most turbulent;
my father used to declare, by way of jesting, he would have to
send me to America to be a fiilibuster. . . . Ah! sir, how fragrant
your chestnut soup smells! It takes me back to the table where my
mother sat smiling, surrounded by her troop of little ones."

The repast ended, Brotteaux set out for Joly's, the toy-merchant
in the Rue Neuve-des-Petits-Champs, who took the dancing-dolls
Caillou had refused, and ordered—not another gross of them like
the latter, but a round twenty-four dozen to begin with.

On reaching the erstwhile Rue Royale and turning into the Place
de la Révolution, Brotteaux caught sight of a steel triangle glittering between two wooden uprights; it was the guillotine. An immense crowd of light-hearted spectators pressed round the scaffold,
waiting the arrival of the loaded carts. Women were hawking Nanterre cakes on a tray hung in front of them and crying their wares;
sellers of cooling drinks were tinkling their little bells; at the foot
of the Statue of Liberty an old man had a peep-show in a small
booth surmounted by a swing on which a monkey played its antics.
Underneath the scaffold some dogs were licking yesterday's blood.
Brotteaux turned back towards the Rue Honoré.

Regaining his garret, where the Barnabite was reading his breviary, he carefully wiped the table and arranged his colour-box on
it alongside the materials and tools of his trade.

"Father," he said, "if you do not deem the occupation unworthy
of the sacred character with which you are invested, I will ask you
to help me make my marionettes. A worthy tradesman, Joly by
name, has this very morning given me a pretty heavy order. Whilst
I am painting these figures already put together, you will do me a
great service by cutting out heads, arms, legs, and bodies from the
patterns here. Better you could not find; they are after Watteau
and Boucher."

"I agree with you, sir," replied Longuemare, "that Watteau and Boucher were well fitted to create such-like baubles; it had been more to their glory if they had confined themselves to innocent figures like these. I should be delighted to help you, but I fear I may not be clever enough for that."

The Père Longuemare was right to distrust his own skill; after sundry unsuccessful attempts, the fact was patent that his genius did not lie in the direction of cutting out pretty shapes in thin card-board with the point of a penknife. But when, at his suggestion, Brotteaux gave him some string and a bodkin, he showed himself very apt in endowing with motion the little creatures he had failed to make and teaching them to dance. He had a happy knack, by way of trying them afterwards, of making them each execute three or four steps of a gavotte, and when they rewarded his pains, a smile would flicker on his stern lips.

One time when he was pulling the string of a Scaramouch to a dance tune:

"Sir," he observed, "this little travesty reminds me of a quaint story. It was in 1746, when I was completing my noviciate under the care of the Père Magitot, a man well on in years, of deep learning and austere morals. At that period, you perhaps remember, dancing figures, intended in the first instance to amuse children, exercised over women and even over men, both young and old, an extraordinary fascination; they were all the rage in Paris. The fashionable shops were crammed with them; they were to be found in the houses of people of quality, and it was nothing out of the way to see a grave and reverend senior dancing his doll in the streets and public gardens. The Père Magitot's age, character, and sacred profession did not avail to guard him against infection. Every time he saw anyone busy jumping his cardboard mannikin, his fingers itched with impatience to be at the same game,—an impatience that soon grew well nigh intolerable. One day when he was paying a visit of importance on a matter involving the interests of the whole Order to Monsieur Chauvel, advocate in the courts of the Parlement, noticing one of these dancers hanging from the chimney-piece, he felt a terrible temptation to pull its string, which he only resisted at the cost of a tremendous effort. But this frivolous ambition pursued him everywhere and left him no peace. In his studies, in his meditations, in his prayers, at church, at chapter, in the confessional and in the pulpit, he was possessed by it. After some days of dreadful agony of mind, he laid bare his extraordinary case to the General of the Order, who happened fortunately to be in Paris at the moment. He was an eminent ecclesiastic of Milan, a Doctor and Prince of the Church. His counsel to the Père Magitot was to satisfy a craving, innocent in its inception, importunate in its consequences and inordinate in its excess, which threatened to superinduce the gravest disorders in the soul which was afflicted with it.

On the advice, or more strictly by the order of the General, the
Père Magitot returned to Monsieur Chauvel's house, where the advocate received him, as on the first occasion, in his cabinet. There,
finding the dancing figure still fastened in the same place, he ran
excitedly to the chimney-piece and begged his host to do him a
favour,—to let him pull the string. The lawyer gave him his permission very readily, and informed him in confidence that sometimes
he set Scaramouch (that was the doll's name) dancing while he
was studying his briefs, and that, only the night before, he had
modulated on Scaramouch's movements the peroration of his speech
in defence of a woman falsely accused of poisoning her husband.
The Père Magitot seized the string with trembling fingers and saw
Scaramouch throw his limbs wildly about under his manipulation
like one possessed of devils in the agonies of exorcism."

"Your tale does not surprise me, father," Brotteaux told him,
"We see such cases of obsession; but it is not always cardboard
figures that occasion it."

The Père Longuemare, who was religious by profession, never
talked about religion, while Brotteaux was for ever harping on the
subject. He was conscious of a bond of sympathy between himself
and the Barnabite, and took a delight in embarrassing and disturbing his peace of mind with objections against divers articles of the
Christian faith.

Once when they were working together making Zerlines and
Scaramouches:

"When I consider," remarked Brotteaux, "the events which have
brought us to the point at which we stand, I am in doubt as to which
party, in the general madness, has been the most insane; sometimes, I am greatly tempted to believe it was that of the Court."

"Sir," answered the Monk, "all men lose their wits like Nebuchad-
nezzar, when God forsakes them; but no man in our days ever
plunged so deep in ignorance and error as the Abbé Fauchet, no
man was so fatal as he to the kingdom. God must needs have been
sorely exasperated against France to send her Monsieur l'Abbé
Fauchet!"

"I imagine we have seen other evil-doers besides poor, unhappy
Fauchet."

"The Abbé Grégoire too, was full of malice."

"And Brissot, and Danton, and Marat, and a hundred others, what
of them, Father?"

"Sir, they are laics; the laity could never incur the same responsibilities as the clergy. They do not work evil from so high a stand-
point, and their crimes are not of universal bearing."

"And your God, Father, what say you of His behaviour in the
present Revolution?"

"I do not understand you, sir."

"Epicurus said: Either God wishes to hinder evil and cannot, or

He can and does not wish to, or He cannot nor does he wish to, or
He does wish to and can. If He wishes to and cannot, He is impotent; if He can and does not wish to, He is perverse; if He cannot
nor does He wish to, He is impotent and perverse; if He does wish
to and can, why does He not, tell me that, Father!"—and Brotteaux cast a look of triumph at his interlocutor.

"Sir," retorted the Monk, "there is nothing more contemptible
than these difficulties you raise. When I look into the reasoning of
infidels, I seem to see ants piling up a few blades of grass as a dam
against the torrent that sweeps down from the mountains. With
your leave, I had rather not argue with you; I should have too
many excellent reasons and too few wits to apply them. Besides,
you will find your refutation in the Abbé Guénée and twenty other
apologists. I will only say that what you quote from Epicurus is
foolishness; because God is arraigned in it as if he was a man, with
a man's moral code. Well! sir, the sceptics, from Celsus down to
Bayle and Voltaire, have cajoled fools with suchlike paradoxes."

"See, Father," protested Brotteaux, "to what lengths your faith
makes you go. Not satisfied with finding all truth in your Theology,
you likewise refuse to discover any in the works of so many noble
intellects who thought differently from yourselves."

"You are entirely mistaken, sir," replied Longuemare. "On the
contrary, I believe that nothing could ever be altogether false in a
man's thoughts. The atheists stand on the lowest rung of the ladder of knowledge; but even there, gleams of sense are to be found
and flashes of truth, and even when darkness is thick about him,
a man may lift up his eyes to God, and He will put understanding
in his heart; was it not so with Lucifer?"

"Well, sir," said Brotteaux, "I cannot match your generosity and
I am bound to tell you I cannot find in all the works of the Theologians one atom of good sense."

At the same time he would repudiate any desire to attack religion, which he deemed indispensable for the nations; he could only
wish it had for its ministers philosophers instead of controversial-
ists. He deplored the fact that the Jacobins were for replacing it by
a newer and more pestilent religion, the cult of liberty, equality,
the republic, the fatherland. He had observed this, that it is in the
vigour of their youth religions are the fiercest and most cruel, and
grow milder as they grow older. He was anxious, therefore, to see
Catholicism preserved; it had devoured many victims in the times
of its vigour, but nowadays, burdened by the weight of years and
with enfeebled appetite, it was content with roasting four or five
heretics in a hundred years.

"As a matter of fact," he concluded, "I have always got on very
well with your God-eaters and Christ-worshippers. I kept a chaplain at Les Ilettes, where Mass was said every Sunday and all my
guests attended. The philosophers were the most devout while the

opera girls showed the most fervour. I was prosperous then and had crowds of friends."

"Friends," exclaimed the Père Longuemare, "friends! Ah, sir, do you really think they loved you, all these philosophers and all these courtesans, who have degraded your soul in such wise that God himself would find it hard to know it for one of the temples built by Him for His glory?"

The Père Longuemare lived for a week longer at the publican's without being interfered with. As far as possible he observed the discipline of his House and every night at the canonical hours would rise from his palliasse to kneel on the bare boards and recite the offices. Though both were reduced to a diet of wretched scraps, he duly observed fasts and abstinence. A smiling but pitiful spectator of these austerities, Brotteaux one day asked him:

"Do you really believe that God finds any satisfaction in seeing you endure cold and hunger as you do?"

"God himself," was the Monk's answer, "has given us the example of suffering."

On the ninth day since the Barnabite had come to share the philosopher's garret, the latter sallied forth at twilight to deliver his dancing-dolls to Joly, the toy-merchant of the Rue Neuve-des-Petits-Champs. He was on his way back overjoyed at having sold them all, when, as he was crossing the erstwhile Place du Carrousel, a girl in a blue satin pelisse trimmed with ermine, running by with a limping gait, threw herself into his arms and held him fast in the way suppliants have had since the world began.

She was trembling and her heart was beating so fast and loud it could be plainly heard. Wondering to see one of her common sort look so pathetic, Brotteaux, a veteran amateur of the stage, thought how Mademoiselle Raucourt, if she could have seen her, might have learnt something from her bearing.

She spoke in breathless tones, lowering her voice to a whisper for fear of being overheard by the passers-by:

"Take me with you, *citoyen,* and hide me, for the love of pity! . . . They are in my room in the Rue Fromenteau. While they were coming upstairs, I ran for refuge into Flora's room,—she is my next-door neighbour,—and leapt out of the window into the street, that is how I sprained my ankle. . . . They are coming; they want to put me in prison and kill me. . . . Last week they killed Virginie."

Brotteaux understood, of course, that the child was speaking of the delegates of the Revolutionary Committee of the Section or else the Commissaries of the Committee of General Security. At that time the Commune had as *procureur* a man of virtue, the *citoyen* Chaumette who regarded the ladies of pleasure as the direct foes of the Republic and harassed them unmercifully in his efforts to regenerate the Nation's morals. To tell the truth, the young ladies of the Palais-Égalité were no great patriots. They regretted the old state of things and did not always conceal the fact. Several had been guillotined already as conspirators, and their tragic fate had excited no little emulation among their fellows.

The *citoyen* Brotteaux asked the suppliant what offence she had been guilty of to bring down on herself a warrant of arrest.

She swore she had no notion, that she had done nothing anyone could blame her for.

"Well then, my girl," Brotteaux told her, "you are not suspect; you have nothing to fear. Be off with you to bed and leave me alone."

At this she confessed everything:

"I tore out my cockade and shouted: 'Vive le roi!' "

He walked down to the river-side and she kept by his side along the deserted *quais*. Clinging to his arm she went on:

"It is not that I care for him particularly, the King, you know; I never knew him, and I daresay he wasn't very much different from other men. But they are bad people. They are cruel to poor girls. They torment and vex and abuse me in every kind of way; they want to stop me following my trade. I have no other trade. You may be sure, if I had, I should not be doing what I do. . . . What is it they want? They are so hard on poor humble folks, the milkman, the charcoalman, the water carrier, the laundress. They won't rest content till they've set all poor people against them."

He looked at her; she seemed a mere child. She was no longer afraid; she was almost smiling, as she limped along lightly at his side. He asked her her name. She said she was called Athenaïs and was sixteen.

Brotteaux offered to see her safe to anywhere she wished to go. She did not know a soul in Paris; but she had an aunt, in service at Palaiseau, who would take her in.

Brotteaux made up his mind at once.

"Come with me, my child," he ordered, and led the way home, with her hanging on his arm.

On his arrival, he found the Père Longuemare in the garret reading his breviary.

Holding Athenaïs by the hand, he drew the other's attention to her:

"Father," he said, "here is a girl from the Rue Fromenteau who has been shouting: 'Vive le roi!' The revolutionary police are on her track. She has nowhere to lay head. Will you allow the girl to pass the night here?"

The Père Longuemare closed his breviary.

"If I understand you right," he said, "you ask me, sir, if this young girl, who is like myself subject to be molested under a warrant of arrest, may be suffered, for her temporal salvation, to spend the night in the same room as I?"

"Yes, Father."

"By what right should I object? and why must I suppose myself affronted by her presence? Am I so sure that I am any better than she?"

He established himself for the night in an old broken-down armchair, declaring he should sleep excellently in it. Athenaïs lay on the mattress. Brotteaux stretched himself on the palliasse and blew out the candle.

The hours and half-hours sounded one after the other from the church towers, but the old man could not sleep; he lay awake listening to the mingled breathing of the man of religion and the girl of pleasure. The moon rose, symbol and witness of his old-time loves, and threw a silvery ray into the attic, illuminating the fair hair and golden lashes, the delicate nose and round, red mouth of Athenaïs, who lay sound asleep.

"Truly," he thought to himself, "a terrible enemy for the Republic!"

When Athenaïs awoke, the day was breaking. The Monk had disappeared. Brotteaux was reading Lucretius under the skylight, learning from the maxims of the Latin poet to live without fears and without desires; but for all this he felt himself at the moment devoured with regrets and disquietudes.

Opening her eyes, Athenaïs was dumfounded to see the roof beams of a garret above her head. Then she remembered, smiled at her preserver and extended towards him with a caressing gesture her pretty little dirty hands.

Rising on her elbow, she pointed to the dilapidated armchair in which the Monk had passed the night.

"He is not there? . . . He has not gone to denounce me, has he?"

"No, no, my child. You could not find a more honest soul than that old madman."

Athenaïs asked in what the old fellow's madness consisted; and when Brotteaux informed her it was religion, she gravely reproached him for speaking so, declaring that men without faith were worse than the beasts that perish and that for her part she often prayed to God, hoping He would forgive her her sins and receive her in His blessed mercy.

Then, noticing that Brotteaux held a book in his hand, she thought it was a book of the Mass and said:

"There you see, you too, you say your prayers! God will reward you for what you have done for me."

Brotteaux having told her that it was not a Mass-book, and that it had been written before ever the Mass had been invented in the world, she opined it was an *Interpretation of Dreams,* and asked if it did not contain an explanation of an extraordinary dream she had had. She could not read and these were the only two sorts of books she had heard tell of.

Brotteaux informed her that this book was only by way of explaining the dream of life. Finding this a hard saying, the pretty child did not try to understand it and dipped the end of her nose in the earthenware crock that replaced the silver basins Brotteaux had once been accustomed to use. Next, she arranged her hair before her host's shaving-glass with scrupulous care and gravity. Her white arms raised above her head, she let fall an observation from time to time with long intervals between:

"You, you were rich once."

"What makes you think that?"

"I don't know. But you *were* rich,—and you are an aristocrat, I am certain of it."

She drew from her pocket a little Holy Virgin of silver in a round ivory shrine, a bit of sugar, thread, scissors, a flint and steel, two or three cases for needles and the like, and after selecting what she required, sat down to mend her skirt, which had got torn in several places.

"For your own safety, my child, put this in your cap!" Brotteaux bade her, handing her a tricolour cockade.

"I will do that gladly, sir," she agreed, "but it will be for the love of you and not for love of the Nation."

When she was dressed and had made herself look her best, taking her skirt in both hands, she dropped a curtsey as she had been taught to do in her village, and addressing Brotteaux:

"Sir," she said, "I am your very humble servant."

She was prepared to oblige her benefactor in all ways he might wish, but she thought it more becoming that he asked for no favour and she offered none; it seemed to her a pretty way to part so, and what good manners required.

Brotteaux slipped a few assignats into her hand to pay her coach-hire to Palaiseau. It was the half of his fortune, and, albeit he was notorious for his lavishness towards women, it was the first time he had ever made so equal a partition of his goods with any of the sex.

She asked him his name.

"I am called Maurice."

It was with reluctance he opened the garret door for her:

"Good-bye, Athenaïs."

She kissed him. "Monsieur Maurice," she said, "when you think of me, if ever you do, call me Marthe; that is the name I was christened, the name they called me by in the village. . . . Good-bye and thank you. . . . Your very humble servant, Monsieur Maurice."

XV

HE prisons were full to bursting and must be emptied; the work of judging, judging, must go on without truce or respite. Seated against the tapestried walls with their fasces and red caps of liberty, like their fellows of the fleurs-de-lis, the judges preserved the same gravity, the same dreadful calm, as their Royal predecessors. The Public Prosecutor and his Deputies, worn out with fatigue, consumed with the fever of sleeplessness and brandy, could only shake off their exhaustion by a violent effort; their broken health made them tragic figures to look upon. The jurors, divers in character and origin, some educated, others ignorant, craven or generous, gentle or violent, hypocritical or sincere, but all men who, knowing the fatherland and the Republic in danger, suffered or feigned to suffer the same anguish, to burn with the same ardour; all alike primed to atrocities of virtue or of fear, they formed but one living entity, one single head, dull and irritable, one single soul, a beast of the apocalypse that by the mere exercise of its natural functions produced a teeming brood of death. Kindhearted or cruel by caprice of sensibility, when shaken momentarily by a sudden pang of pity, they would acquit with streaming eyes a prisoner whom an hour before they would have condemned to the guillotine with taunts. The further they proceeded with their task, the more impetuously did they follow the impulses of their heart.

Judge and jury toiled, fevered and half asleep with overwork, distracted by the excitement outside and the orders of the sovereign people, menaced by the threats of the *sansculottes* and *tricoteuses* who crowded the galleries and the public enclosure, relying on insane evidence, acting on the denunciations of madmen, in a poisonous atmosphere that stupefied the brain, set ears hammering and temples beating and darkened the eyes with a veil of blood. Vague rumours were current among the public of jurors bought by the gold of the accused. But to these the jury as a body replied with indignant protest and merciless condemnations. In truth they were men neither worse nor better than their fellows. Innocence more often than not is a piece of good fortune rather than a virtue; any other who should have consented to put himself in their place would have acted as they did and accomplished to the best of his commonplace soul these appalling tasks.

Antoinette, so long expected, sat at last in the fatal chair, in a black gown, the centre of such a concentration of hate that only the certainty of what the sentence would be made the court observe the forms of law. To the deadly questions the accused replied sometimes with the instinct of self-preservation, sometimes with her wonted haughtiness, and once, thanks to the hideous suggestion of one of her accusers, with the noble dignity of a mother. The witnesses were confined to outrage and calumny; the defence was frozen with terror. The tribunal, forcing itself to respect the rules of procedure, was only waiting till all formalities were completed to hurl the head of *the Austrian* in the face of Europe.

Three days after the execution of Marie Antoinette Gamelin was called to the bedside of the *citoyen* Fortuné Trubert, who lay dying, within thirty paces of the Military Bureau where he had worn out his life, on a pallet of sacking, in the cell of some expelled Barnabite father. His livid face was sunk in the pillow. His eyes, which already were almost sightless, turned their glassy pupils upon his visitor; his parched hand grasped Évariste's and pressed it with unexpected vigour. Three times he had vomited blood in two days. He tried to speak; his voice, at first hoarse and feeble as a whisper, grew louder, deeper:

"Wattignies! Wattignies! . . . Jourdan has forced the enemy into their camp . . . raised the blockade at Maubeuge. . . . We have retaken Marchiennes, *ça ira . . . ça ira . . .*" and he smiled.

These were no dreams of a sick man, but a clear vision of the truth that flashed through the brain so soon to be shrouded in eternal darkness. Hereafter the invasion seemed arrested; the Generals were terrorized and saw that the one best thing for them to do was to be victorious. Where voluntary recruiting had failed to produce what was needed, a strong and disciplined army, compulsion was succeeding. One effort more, and the Republic would be saved.

After a half hour of semi-consciousness, Fortuné Trubert's face, hollow-cheeked and worn by disease, lit up again and his hands moved.

He lifted his finger and pointed to the only piece of furniture in the room, a little walnut-wood writing-desk. The voice was weak and breathless, but the mind quite unclouded:

"Like Eudamidas," he said, "I bequeath my debts to my friend, —three hundred and twenty livres, of which you will find the account . . . in that red book yonder . . . good-bye, Gamelin. Never rest; wake and watch over the defence of the Republic. *Ça ira.*"

The shades of night were deepening in the cell. The difficult breathing of the dying man was the only sound, and his hands scratching on the sheet.

At midnight he uttered some disconnected phrases:

"More saltpetre. . . . See the muskets are delivered. Health? Oh! excellent. . . . Get down the church-bells. . . ."

He breathed his last at five in the morning.

By order of the Section his body lay in state in the nave of the erstwhile church of the Barnabites, at the foot of the Altar of the

Fatherland, on a camp bed, covered with a tricolour flag and the brow wreathed with an oak crown.

Twelve old men clad in the Roman toga, with palms in their hands, twelve young girls wearing long veils and carrying flowers, surrounded the funeral couch. At the dead man's feet stood two children, each holding an inverted torch. One of them Évariste recognized as his *concierge's* little daughter Joséphine, who in her childish gravity and beauty reminded him of those charming genii of Love and Death the Romans used to sculpture on their tombs.

The funeral procession made its way to the Cemetery of Saint-André-des-Arts to the strains of the *Marseillaise* and the *Ça-ira*.

As he laid the kiss of farewell on Fortuné Trubert's brow, Évariste wept. His tears flowed in self-pity, for he envied his friend who was resting there, his task accomplished.

On reaching home, he received notice that he was posted a member of the Council General of the Commune. After standing as candidate for four months, he had been elected unopposed, after several ballots, by some thirty suffrages. No one voted nowadays; the Sections were deserted; rich and poor alike only sought to shirk the performance of public duties. The most momentous events had ceased to rouse either enthusiasm or curiosity; the newspapers were left unread. Out of the seven hundred thousand inhabitants of the capital Évariste doubted if as many as three or four thousand still preserved the old Republican spirit.

The same day the Twenty-one came up for trial. Innocent or guilty of the calamities and crimes of the Republic, vain, incautious, ambitious and impetuous, at once moderate and violent, feeble in their fear as in their clemency, quick to declare war, slow to carry it out, haled before the Tribunal to answer for the example they had given, they were not the less the first and the most brilliant children of the Revolution, whose delight and glory they had been. The judge who will question them with artful bias; the pallid accuser yonder who, where he sits behind his little table, is planning their death and dishonour; the jurors who will presently try to stifle their defence; the public in the galleries which overwhelms them with howls of insult and abuse,—all, judge, jury, people, have applauded their eloquence in other days, extolled their talents and their virtues. But judge, jury, people have short memories now.

Once Évariste had made Vergniaud his god, Brissot his oracle. But he had forgotten; if any vestige of his old wonder still lingered in his memory, it was to think that these monsters had seduced the noblest citizens.

Returning to his lodging after the sitting, Gamelin heard heartbreaking cries as he entered the house. It was little Joséphine; her mother was whipping her for playing in the Place with good-for-nothing boys and dirtying the fine white frock she had worn for the obsequies of the *citoyen* Trubert.

XVI

FTER three months during which he had made a daily holocaust of victims, illustrious or insignificant, to the fatherland, Évariste had a case that interested him personally; there was one prisoner he made it his special business to track down to death.

Ever since he had sat on the juror's bench, he had been eagerly watching, among the crowd of culprits who appeared before him, for Élodie's seducer; of this man he had elaborated in his busy fancy a portrait, some details of which were accurate. He pictured him as young, handsome, haughty, and felt convinced he had fled to England. He thought he had discovered him in a young *émigré* named Maubel, who, having come back to France and been denounced by his host, had been arrested in an inn at Passy; Fouquier-Tinville was in charge of the prosecution,—among a thousand others. Letters had been found on him which the accusation regarded as proofs of a plot concocted between Maubel and the agents of Pitt, but which were in fact only letters written to the *émigré* by a banking-house in London which he had entrusted with certain funds. Maubel, who was young and good-looking, seemed to be mainly occupied in affairs of gallantry. His pocket-book afforded a clue to some correspondence with Spain, then at war with France; but these communications were really of a purely private nature, and if the court of preliminary enquiry did not ignore the bill, it was only in virtue of the maxim that justice should never be in too great a hurry to release a prisoner.

Gamelin was handed a report of Maubel's first semi-private examination and he was struck by what it revealed of the young man's character, which he took to agree with what he believed to be that of Élodie's betrayer. Thereafter he spent long hours in the private room of the Clerk of the Court, poring eagerly over the papers relating to this case. His suspicion received a remarkable confirmation on his discovering in a note-book belonging to the *émigré,* but long out of date, the address of the *Amour peintre,* in company, it is true, with those of the *Green Monkey,* the *Dauphin's Head,* and several more print and picture shops. But when he was informed that in this same note-book had been found three or four petals of a red carnation carefully wrapped in a piece of silk paper, remembering how the red carnation was Élodie's favourite flower, the one she cultivated on her window-sill, wore in her hair and used to give (he had reason to know) as a love-token, Évariste's last doubts vanished. Being now convinced he knew the facts, he resolved to question Élodie, though without letting her know the circumstances that had led him to discover the culprit.

As he was climbing the stairs to his lodgings, he perceived even on the lower landings a stifling smell of fruit, and on reaching the studio, found Élodie helping the *citoyenne* Gamelin to make quince preserve. While the old housewife was kindling the stove and turning over in her mind ways of saving the fuel and moist sugar without prejudicing the quality of the preserves, the *citoyenne* Blaise, seated in a straw-bottomed chair, with an apron of brown holland and her lap full of the golden fruit, was peeling the quinces, quartering and throwing them into a shallow copper basin. The strings of her coif were thrown back over her shoulders, the meshes of her black hair coiled above her moist forehead; from her whole person breathed a domestic charm and an intimate grace that induced gentle thoughts and voluptuous dreams of tranquil pleasures.

Without stirring from her seat, she lifted her beautiful eyes, that gleamed like molten gold, to her lover's face, and said:

"See, Évariste, we are working for you. We mean you to have a store of delicious quince jelly to last you the winter; it will settle your stomach and make your heart merry."

But Gamelin, stepping nearer, uttered a name in her ear:

"Jacques Maubel . . ."

At that moment Combalot the cobbler showed his red nose at the half-opened door. He had brought, along with some pairs of shoes he had re-heeled, the bill for the repairs.

For fear of being taken for a bad citizen, he made a point of using the new calendar. The *citoyenne* Gamelin, who liked to see clearly what was what in her accounts, was all astray among the *Fructidors* and *Vendémiaires*. She heaved a sigh.

"Jesus!" she complained, "they want to alter everything,—days, months, seasons of the year, the sun and the moon! Lord God, Monsieur Combalot, what ever is this pair of over-shoes down for the 8 Vendémiaire?"

"*Citoyenne,* just cast your eye over your almanac, and you'll get the hang of it."

She took it down from the wall, glanced at it and immediately turning her head another way:

"It hasn't a Christian look!" she cried in a shocked tone.

"Not only that, *citoyenne,*" said the cobbler, "but now we have only three Sundays in the month instead of four. And that's not all; we shall soon have to change our ways of reckoning. There will be no more farthings and half-farthings, everything will be regulated by distilled water."

At the words the *citoyenne* Gamelin, whose lips were trembling, threw up her eyes to the ceiling and sighed out:

"They are going too far!"

And, while she was lost in lamentations, looking like the holy women in a wayside calvary, a bad coal that had caught alight in the fire when her attention was diverted, began to fill the studio with a poisonous smother which, added to the stifling smell of quinces, was like to make the air unbreathable.

Élodie complained that her throat was tickling her and begged to have the window opened. But, directly the *citoyen* Combalot had taken his leave and the *citoyenne* Gamelin had gone back to her stove, Évariste repeated the same name in the girl's ear:

"Jacques Maubel," he reiterated.

She looked up at him in some surprise, and very quietly, still going on cutting a quince in quarters:

"Well! . . . Jacques Maubel . . . ?"

"He is.the man."

"The man! What man?"

"You once gave him a red carnation."

She declared she did not understand and asked him to explain himself.

"That aristocrat! that *émigré!* that scoundrel!"

She shrugged her shoulders, and denied with the most natural air that she had never known a Jacques Maubel.

It was true; she *had* never known anyone of the name.

She denied she had ever given red carnations to anybody but Évariste; but perhaps, on this point, her memory was not very good.

He had little experience of women and was far from having fully fathomed Élodie's character; still, he deemed her quite capable of cajoling and deceiving a cleverer man than himself.

"Why deny?" he asked. "I know all."

Again she asseverated she had never known anybody called Maubel. And, having done peeling the quinces, she asked for a basin of water, because her fingers were sticky. This Gamelin brought her, and, as she washed her hands, she repeated her denials.

Again he repeated that he knew, and this time she made no reply.

She did not guess the object of her lover's question and she was a thousand miles from suspecting that this Maubel, whom she had never heard spoken of before, was to appear before the Revolutionary Tribunal; she could make nothing of the suspicions with which she was assailed, but she knew them to be unfounded. For this reason, having very little hope of dissipating them, she had very little wish to do so either. She ceased to deny having known Maubel, preferring to leave her jealous lover to go astray on a false trail, when from one moment to the next, the smallest incident might start him on the right road. Her little lawyer's clerk of former days, now grown into a patriot dragoon and lady-killer, had quarrelled by now with his aristocratic mistress. Whenever he met Élodie in the street, he would gaze at her with a glance that seemed to say:

"Come, my beauty! I feel sure I am going to forgive you for having betrayed you, and I am really quite ready to take you back into favour." She made no further attempt therefore to cure what she called her lover's crotchets, and Gamelin remained firm in the conviction that Jacques Maubel was Élodie's seducer.

Through the days that ensued the Tribunal devoted its undivided attention to the task of crushing Federalism, which, like a hydra, had threatened to devour Liberty. They were busy days; and the jurors, worn out with fatigue, despatched with the utmost possible expedition the case of the woman Roland, instigator and accomplice of the crimes of the Brissotin faction.

Meantime Gamelin spent every morning at the Courts to press on Maubel's trial. Some important pieces of evidence were to be found at Bordeaux; he insisted on a Commissioner being sent to ride post to fetch them. They arrived at last. The deputy of the Public Prosecutor read them, pulled a face and told Évariste:

"It is not good for much, your new evidence! There is nothing in it! Mere fiddle-faddle. . . . If only it was certain that this *ci-devant* Comte de Maubel ever really emigrated . . .!"

In the end Gamelin succeeded. Young Maubel was served with his act of accusation and brought before the Revolutionary Tribunal on the 19 Brumaire.

From the first opening of the sitting the President showed the gloomy and dreadful face he took care to assume for the hearing of cases where the evidence was weak. The Deputy Prosecutor stroked his chin with the feather of his pen and affected the serenity of a conscience at ease. The Clerk read the act of accusation; it was the hollowest sham the Court had ever heard so far.

The President asked the accused if he had not been aware of the laws passed against the *émigrés*.

"I was aware of them and I observed them," answered Maubel, "and I left France provided with passports in proper form."

As to the reasons for his journey to England and his return to France he had satisfactory explanations to offer. His face was pleasant, with a look of frankness and confidence that was agreeable. The women in the galleries looked at the young man with a favourable eye. The prosecution maintained that he had made a stay in Spain at the time that Nation was at war with France; he averred he had never left Bayonne at that period. One point alone remained obscure. Among the papers he had thrown in the fire at the time of his arrest, and of which only fragments had been found, some words in Spanish had been deciphered and the name of "Nieves."

On this subject Jacques Maubel refused to give the explanations demanded; and, when the President told him that it was in the accused's own interest to clear up the point, he answered that a man ought not always to do what his own interest requires.

Gamelin only thought of convicting Maubel of a crime; three times over he pressed the President to ask the accused if he could explain about the carnation the dried petals of which he hoarded so carefully in his pocket-book.

Maubel replied that he did not consider himself obliged to answer a question that had no concern with the case at law, as no letter had been found concealed in the flower.

The jury retired to the hall of deliberations, favourably impressed towards the young man whose mysterious conduct appeared chiefly connected with a lover's secrets. This time the good patriots, the purest of the pure themselves, would gladly have voted for acquittal. One of them, a *ci-devant* noble, who had given pledges to the Revolution, said:

"Is it his birth they bring up against him? I, too, I have had the misfortune to be born in the aristocracy."

"Yes, but you have left them," retorted Gamelin, "and he has not."

And he spoke with such vehemence against this conspirator, this emissary of Pitt, this accomplice of Coburg, who had climbed the mountains and sailed the seas to stir up enemies to Liberty, he demanded the traitor's condemnation in such burning words, that he awoke the never-resting suspicions, the old stern temper of the patriot jury.

One of them told him cynically:

"There are services that cannot well be refused between colleagues."

The verdict of death was recorded by a majority of one.

The condemned man heard his sentence with a quiet smile. His eyes, which had been gazing unconcernedly about the hall, as they fell on Gamelin's face, took on an expression of unspeakable contempt.

No one applauded the decision of the court.

Jacques Maubel was taken back to the Conciergerie; here he wrote a letter while he waited the hour of execution, which was to take place the same evening, by torchlight:

My dear sister,—The tribunal sends me to the scaffold, affording me the only joy I have been able to appreciate since the death of my adored Nieves. They have taken from me the only relic I had left of her, a pomegranate flower, which they called, I cannot tell why, a carnation.

I loved the arts; at Paris, in happier times, I made a collection of paintings and engravings, which are now in a sure place, and which will

*be delivered to you so soon as this is possible. I pray you, dear sister, to
keep them in memory of me.*

He cut a lock of his hair, enclosed it in the letter, which he
folded and wrote outside:

*To the citoyenne Clémence Dezeimeries, née Maubel,
La Réole.*

He gave all the silver he had on him to the turnkey, begging
him to forward this letter to its destination, asked for a bottle of
wine, which he drank in little sips while waiting for the cart. . . .

After supper Gamelin ran to the *Amour Peintre* and burst into
the blue chamber where every night Élodie was waiting for him.

"You are avenged," he told her. "Jacques Maubel is no more. The
cart that took him to his death has just passed beneath your window escorted by torch-bearers."

She understood:

"Wretch! it is you have killed him, and he was not my lover. I
did not know him. . . . I have never seen him . . . What was this
man? He was young, amiable . . . innocent. And you have killed
him, wretch! wretch!"

She fell in a faint. But, amid the shadows of this momentary
death, she felt herself overborne by a flood at once of horror and
voluptuous ecstasy. She half revived; her heavy lips lifted to show
the whites of the eyes, her bosom swelled, her hands beat the air,
seeking for her lover. She pressed him to her in a strangling embrace, drove her nails into the flesh, and gave him with her bleeding lips, without a word, without a sound, the longest, the most
agonized, the most delicious of kisses.

She loved him with all her flesh, and the more terrible, cruel,
atrocious she thought him, the more she saw him reeking with the
blood of his victims, the more consuming was her hunger and thirst
for him.

XVII

HE 24 Frimaire, at ten in the forenoon, under a clear
bright sun that was melting the ice formed in the
night, the *citoyens* Guénot and Delourmel, delegates
of the Committee of General Security, proceeded to
the Barnabites and asked to be conducted to the
Committee of Surveillance of the Section, in the
Capitular hall, whose only occupant for the moment was the *citoyen* Beauvisage, who was piling
logs on the fire. But they did not see him just at first because of
his short, thickset stature.

In a hunchback's cracked voice the *citoyen* Beauvisage begged the delegates to seat themselves and put himself entirely at their service.

Guénot then asked him if he knew a *ci-devant* Monsieur des Ilettes, residing near the Pont-Neuf.

"It is an individual," he added, "whose arrest I am instructed to effect,"—and he exhibited the order from the Committee of General Security.

Beauvisage, after racking his memory for a while, replied that he knew no individual of that name, that the suspect in question might not be an inhabitant of his Section, certain portions of the *Sections du Muséum, de l'Unité, de Marat-et-Marseille* being likewise in the near neighbourhood of the Pont-Neuf; that, if he did live in the Section, it must be under another name than that borne on the Committee's order; that, nevertheless, it would not be long before they laid hands on him.

"Let's lose no time," urged Guénot. "Our vigilance was aroused in this case by a letter from one of the man's accomplices that was intercepted and put into the hands of the Committee a fortnight ago, but which the *citoyen* Lacroix took action upon only yesterday evening. We are overdone with business; denunciations flow in from every quarter in such abundance one does not know which to attend to."

"Denunciations," replied Beauvisage proudly, "are coming in freely, too, to the Committee of Vigilance of our Section. Some make these revelations out of patriotism, others lured by the bait of a bank-bill for a hundred *sols*. Many children denounce their parents, whose property they covet."

"This letter," resumed Guénot, "emanates from a *ci-devant* called Rochemaure, a woman of gallantry, at whose house they played *biribi,* and is addressed to one *citoyen* Rauline; but is really for an *émigré* in the service of Pitt. I have brought it with me to communicate to you the portion relating to this man des Ilettes."

He drew the letter from his pocket.

"It begins with copious details as to those members of the Convention who might, according to the woman's tale, be gained over by the offer of a sum of money or the promise of a well-paid post under a new Government, more stable than the present. Then comes the following passage:

"I have just returned from a visit to Monsieur des Ilettes, who lives near the Pont-Neuf in a garret where you must be either a cat or an imp to get at him; he is reduced to earning a living by making punch-and-judies. He is a man of judgment, for which reason I report to you, sir, the main gist of his conversation. He does not believe that the existing state of things will last long. Nor does he foresee its being ended by the victory of the coalition, and events appear to justify his opinion; for, as you are aware, sir, for some time past tidings from the front have

been bad. He would rather seem to believe in the revolt of the poor and the women of the humbler classes, who remain still deeply attached to their religion. He holds that the wide-spread alarm caused by the Revolutionary Tribunal will soon reunite all France against the Jacobins. 'This tribunal,' he said, in his joking way, 'which sentences the Queen of France and a bread-hawker, is like that William Shakespeare the English admire so much, etc. . . .' He thinks it not impossible that Robespierre may marry Madame Royale and have himself named Protector of the Kingdom.

"I should be grateful to you, sir, if you would transmit me the amount owing to me, that is to say one thousand pounds sterling, by the channel you are in the habit of using; but whatever you do, do not write to Monsieur Morhardt; he has lately been arrested, thrown into prison, etc., etc. . . ."

"This worthy des Ilettes makes dancing-dolls, it appears," observed Beauvisage, "that is a valuable clue . . . though certainly there are many petty trades of the sort carried on in the Section."

"That reminds me," said Delourmel, "I promised to bring home a doll for my little girl Nathalie, my youngest, who is ill with scarlatina. The fever is not a dangerous one, but it demands careful nursing, and Nathalie, a very forward child for her age, and with a very active brain, has but delicate health."

"I," remarked Guénot, "I have only a boy. He plays hoops with barrel-hoops and makes little montgolfier balloons by inflating paper bags."

"Very often," Beauvisage put in his word, "it is with articles that are not toys at all that children like best to play. My nephew Émile, a little chap of seven, a very intelligent child, amuses himself all day long with little wooden bricks with which he builds houses. . . . Do you snuff, *citoyens?*"—and Beauvisage held out his open snuff-box to the two delegates.

"Now we must set about nabbing our rascal," said Delourmel, who had long moustaches and great eyes that rolled in his head. "I feel quite in the mood this morning for a dish of aristocrat's lights and liver, washed down with a glass of white wine."

Beauvisage suggested to the delegates going to the Place Dauphine to see if his colleague Dupont senior was at his shop there; he would be sure to know this man, des Ilettes.

So they set off in the keen morning air, accompanied by four grenadiers of the Section.

"Have you seen *'The Last Judgment of Kings'* played?" Delourmel asked his companions; "the piece is worth seeing. The author shows you all the Kings of Europe on a desert island where they have taken refuge, at the foot of a volcano which swallows them up. It is a patriotic work."

At the corner of the Rue du Harlay Delourmel's eye was caught by a little cart, as brilliantly painted as a reliquary, which an old woman was pushing, wearing over her coif a hat of waxed cloth.

"What is that old woman selling?" he asked.

The old dame answered for herself:

"Look, gentlemen, make your choice. I have beads and rosaries, crosses, St. Anthonys, holy cerecloths, St. Veronica handkerchiefs, *Ecce homos, Agnus Deis,* hunting-horns and rings of St. Hubert, and articles of devotion of every sort and kind."

"Why, it is the very arsenal of fanaticism!" cried Delourmel in horror,—and he proceeded to a summary examination of the poor woman, who made the same answer to every question:

"My son, it's forty years I have been selling articles of devotion."

Another Delegate of the Committee of General Security, noticing a blue-coated National Guard passing, directed him to convey the astonished old woman to the Conciergerie.

The *citoyen* Beauvisage pointed out to Delourmel that it would have been more in the competence of the Committee of Surveillance to arrest the woman and bring her before the Section; that in any case, one never knew nowadays what attitude to take up towards the old religion so as to act up to the views of the Government, and whether it was best to allow everything or forbid everything.

On nearing the joiner's shop, the delegates and the commissary could hear angry shouts mingling with the hissing of the saw and the grinding of the plane. A quarrel had broken out between the joiner, Dupont senior, and his neighbour Remacle, the porter, because of the *citoyenne* Remacle, whom an irresistible attraction was for ever drawing into the recesses of the workshop, whence she would return to the porter's lodge all covered with shavings and saw-dust. The injured porter bestowed a kick on Mouton, the carpenter's dog, which at that very moment his own little daughter Joséphine was nursing lovingly in her arms. Joséphine was furious and burst into a torrent of imprecations against her father, while the carpenter shouted in a voice of exasperation:

"Wretch! I tell you you shall not beat my dog."

"And I," retorted the porter brandishing his broom, "I tell you you shall *not* . . ."

He did not finish his sentence; the joiner's plane had hurtled close past his head.

The instant he caught sight of the *citoyen* Beauvisage and the attendant delegates, he rushed up to him and cried:

"*Citoyen* Commissary you are my witness, this villain has just tried to murder me."

The *citoyen* Beauvisage, in his red cap, the badge of his office, put out his long arms in the attitude of a peacemaker, and addressing the porter and the joiner:

"A hundred *sols,*" he announced, "to whichever of you will inform us where to find a suspect, wanted by the Committee of General Security, a *ci-devant* named des Ilettes, a maker of dancing-dolls."

With one accord porter and carpenter designated Brotteaux's lodging, the only quarrel now between them being who should have the assignat for a hundred *sols* promised the informer.

Delourmel, Guénot, and Beauvisage, followed by the four grenadiers, Remacle the porter, Dupont the carpenter, and a dozen little scamps of the neighbourhood filed up the stairs which shook under their tread, and finally mounted the ladder to the attics.

Brotteaux was in his garret busy cutting out his dancing figures, while the Père Longuemare sat facing him, stringing their scattered limbs on threads, smiling to himself to see rhythm and harmony thus growing under his fingers.

At the sound of muskets being grounded on the landing, the monk trembled in every limb, not that he was a whit less courageous than Brotteaux, who never moved a muscle, but the habit of respect for human conventions had never disciplined him to assume an attitude of self-composure. Brotteaux gathered from the *citoyen* Delourmel's questions the quarter from which the blow had come and saw too late how unwise it is to confide in women. He obeyed the *citoyen* Commissary's order to go with him, first picking up his Lucretius and his three shirts.

"The *citoyen*," he said, "pointing to the Père Longuemare, "is an assistant I have taken to help me make my marionettes. His home is here."

But the monk failing to produce a certificate of citizenship, was put under arrest along with Brotteaux.

As the procession filed past the porter's door, the *citoyenne* Remacle, leaning on her broom, looked at her lodger with the eyes of virtue beholding crime in the clutches of the law. Little Joséphine, dainty and disdainful, held back Mouton by his collar when the dog tried to fawn on the friend who had often given him a lump of sugar. A gaping crowd filled the Place de Thionville.

At the foot of the stairs Brotteaux came face to face with a young peasant woman who was on the point of going up. She carried a basket on her arm full of eggs and in her hand a flat cake wrapped in a napkin. It was Athenaïs, who had come from Palaiseau to present her saviour with a token of her gratitude. When she observed a posse of magistrates and four grenadiers and "Monsieur Maurice" being led away a prisoner, she stopped in consternation and asked if it was really true; then she stepped up to the Commissary and said in a gentle voice:

"You are not taking him to prison? it can't be possible. . . . Why! you don't know him! God himself is not better or kinder."

The *citoyen* Delourmel pushed her away and beckoned to the grenadiers to come forward. Then Athenaïs let loose a torrent of the foulest abuse, the filthiest and most abominable invective, at the magistrates and soldiers, who thought that all the rinsings of the Palais-Royal and the Rue Fromenteau were being emptied over their devoted heads. After which, in a voice that filled the whole Place de Thionville and sent a shudder through the throng of curious onlookers:

"Vive le roi! Vive le roi!" she yelled.

XVIII

HE *citoyenne* Gamelin was devoted to old Brotteaux, and taking him altogether, thought him the best and greatest man she had ever known. She had not bidden him good-bye when he was arrested, because she would not have dared to defy the powers that be and because in her lowly estate she looked upon cowardice as a duty. But she had received a blow she could not recover from.

She could not eat and lamented she had lost her appetite just when she had at last the means to satisfy it. She still admired her son; but she durst not let her mind dwell on the appalling duties he was engaged upon and congratulated herself she was only an ignorant woman who had no call to judge his conduct.

The poor mother had found a rosary at the bottom of a trunk; she hardly knew how to use it, but often fumbled the beads in her trembling fingers. She had lived to grow old without any overt exercise of her religion, but she had always been a pious woman, and she would pray to God all day long, in the chimney corner, to save her boy and that good, kind Monsieur Brotteaux. Élodie often came to see her; they durst not look each other in the eyes, and sitting side by side they would talk at random of indifferent matters.

One day in Pluviose, when the snow, falling in heavy flakes, darkened the sky and deadened the noises of the city, the *citoyenne* Gamelin, who was alone in the lodging heard a knock at the door. She started violently; for months now the slightest noise had set her trembling. She opened the door. A young man of eighteen or twenty walked in, his hat on his head. He was dressed in a bottle-green box-coat, the triple collar of which covered his bust and descended to the waist. He wore top-boots of an English cut. His chestnut hair fell in ringlets about his shoulders. He stepped into the middle of the studio, as if wishful that all the light admitted by the snow-encumbered sky-light might fall on him, and stood there some moments without moving or speaking.

At last, in answer to the *citoyenne* Gamelin's look of amazement:

"Don't you know your daughter?"

The old dame clasped her hands:

"Julie! . . . It is you. . . . Good God! is it possible? . . ."

"Why, yes, it is I. Kiss me, mother."

The *citoyenne* Gamelin pressed her daughter to her bosom, and dropped a tear on the collar of the box-coat. Then she began again in an anxious voice:

"You, in Paris! . . ."

"Ah! mother, but why did I not come alone! For myself, they will never know me in this dress."

It was a fact the box-coat sufficiently disguised her shape, and she did not look very different from a great many very young men, who, like her, wore their hair long and parted in two masses on the forehead. Her features, which were delicately cut and charming, but burnt by the sun, drawn with fatigue, worn with anxiety, had a bold, masculine expression. She was slim, with long straight limbs and an easy carriage; only the clear treble of her voice could have betrayed her sex.

Her mother asked her if she was hungry. She said she would be glad of something to eat, and when bread, wine and ham had been set before her, she fell to, one elbow on the table, with a pretty gluttony, like Ceres in the hut of the old woman Baubo.

Then, the glass still at her lips:

"Mother," she asked, "do you know when my brother will be back? I have come to speak to him."

The good woman looked at her daughter in embarrassment and said nothing.

"I must see him. My husband was arrested this morning and taken to the Luxembourg."

By this name of "husband" she designated Fortuné de Chassagne, a *ci-devant* noble and officer in Bouillé's regiment. He had first loved her when she was a work-girl at a milliner's in the Rue des Lombards, and had carried her away with him to England, whither he had fled after the 10th August. He was her lover; but she thought it more becoming to speak of him as her husband before her mother. Indeed, she told herself that the hardships they had shared had surely united them in a wedlock consecrated by suffering.

More than once they had spent the night side by side on a bench in one of the London parks and gathered up scraps of broken bread under the table in the taverns in Piccadilly.

Her mother could find no answer and gazed at her mournfully.

"Don't you hear what I say, mother? Time presses, I must see Évariste at once; he, and he only, can save Fortuné's life."

"Julie," answered her mother at last, "it is better you should not speak to your brother."

"Why, what do you mean, mother?"

"I mean what I say, it is better you do not speak to your brother about Monsieur de Chassagne."

"But, mother, I must!"

"My child, Évariste can never forgive Monsieur de Chassagne for his treatment of you. You know how angrily he used to speak of him, what names he called him."

"Yes, he called him seducer," said Julie with a little hissing laugh, shrugging her shoulders.

"My child, it was a mortal blow to his pride. Évariste has vowed never again to mention Monsieur de Chassagne's name, and for two years now he has not breathed one word of him or of you. But his feelings have not altered; you know him, he can never forgive you."

"But, mother, as Fortuné has married me . . . in London. . . ."

The poor mother threw up her eyes and hands:

"Fortuné is an aristocrat, an *émigré,* and that is cause enough to make Évariste treat him as an enemy."

"Mother, give me a direct answer. Do you mean that if I ask him to go to the Public Prosecutor and the Committee of General Security and take the necessary steps to save Fortuné's life, do you mean that he will not consent? . . . But, mother, he would be a monster if he refused!"

"My child, your brother is an honest man and a good son. But do not ask him, oh! do not ask him to intercede for Monsieur de Chassagne. . . . Listen to me, Julie. He does not confide his thoughts to me and, no doubt, I should not be competent to understand them . . . but he is a juror; he has principles; he acts as his conscience dictates. Do not ask him anything, Julie."

"Ah! I see you know him now. You know that he is cold, callous, that he is a bad man, that ambition and vainglory are his only guides. And you always loved him better than me. When we lived together, all three of us, you set him up as my pattern to copy. His staid demeanour and grave speech impressed you; you thought he possessed all the virtues. And me, me you always blamed, you gave me all the vices, because I was frank and free, and because I climbed trees. You could never endure me. You loved nobody but him. There, I hate him, your model Évariste; he is a hypocrite."

"Hush, Julie! I have been a good mother to you as well as to him. I had you taught a trade. It has been no fault of mine that you are not an honest woman and did not marry in your station. I loved you tenderly and I love you still. I forgive you and I love you. But do not speak ill of Évariste. He is a good son. He has always taken care of me. When you left me, my child, when you abandoned your trade and forsook your shop, to go and live with Monsieur de Chassagne, what would have become of me without him? I should have died of hunger and wretchedness."

"Do not talk so, mother; you know very well we would have cherished you with all affection, Fortuné and I, if you had not turned your face from us, at Évariste's instigation. Never tell me! he is incapable of a kindly action. It was to make me odious in your eyes that he made a pretence of caring for you. He! love you? . . . Is he capable of loving anyone? He has neither heart nor head. He has no talent, not a scrap. To paint, a man must have a softer, tenderer nature than his."

She threw a glance round the canvases in the studio, which she found to be no better and no worse than when she left her home.

"There you see his soul! he has put it in his pictures, cold and sombre as it is. His Orestes, his Orestes with the dull eye and cruel mouth, and looking as if he had been impaled, is himself all over. . . . But, mother, cannot you understand at all? I cannot leave Fortuné in prison. You know these Jacobins, these patriots, all Évariste's crew. They will kill him. Mother, little mother, darling mother, I cannot have them kill him. I love him! I love him! He has been so good to me, and we have been so unhappy together. Look, this box-coat is one of his coats. I had never a shift left. A friend of Fortuné's lent me a jacket and I got a post with an eating-house keeper at Dover, while he worked at a barber's. We knew quite well that to return to France was to risk our lives; but we were asked if we would go to Paris to carry out an important mission. . . . We agreed,—we would have accepted a mission to hell! Our travelling expenses were paid and we were given a letter of exchange on a Paris banker. We found the offices closed; the banker is in prison and going to be guillotined. We had not a brass farthing. All the individuals with whom we were in correspondence and to whom we could appeal are fled or imprisoned. Not a door to knock at. We slept in a stable in the Rue de la Femme-sans-tête. A charitable bootblack, who slept on the same straw with us there, lent my lover one of his boxes, a brush and a pot of blacking three quarters empty. For a fortnight Fortuné made his living and mine by blacking shoes in the Place de Grève.

"But on Monday a Member of the Commune put his foot on the box to have his boots polished. He had been a butcher once, a man Fortuné had before now given a kick behind to for selling meat of short weight. When Fortuné raised his head to ask for his two sous, the rascal recognized him, called him aristocrat, and threatened to have him arrested. A crowd collected, made up of honest folks and a few blackguards, who began to shout *"Death to the émigré!"* and called for the gendarmes. At that moment I came up with Fortuné's bowl of soup. I saw him taken off to the Section and shut up in the church of Saint-Jean. I tried to kiss him, but they hustled me away. I spent the night like a dog on the church steps. . . . They took him away this morning. . . ."

Julie could not finish, her sobs choked her.

She threw her hat on the floor and fell on her knees at her mother's feet.

"They took him away this morning to the Luxembourg prison. Mother, mother, help me to save him; have pity on your child!"

Drowned in her tears, she threw open her box-coat and, the better to prove herself a woman and a wife, bared her bosom; seizing her mother's hands, she held them close over her throbbing breasts.

"My darling, my daughter, Julie, my Julie!" sobbed the widow Gamelin,—and pressed her streaming cheeks to the girl's.

For some moments they clung together without a word. The poor mother was racking her brains for some way of helping her daughter, and Julie was watching the kind look in those tearful eyes.

"Perhaps," thought Évariste's mother, "perhaps, if I speak to him, he will be melted. He is good, he is tender-hearted. If politics had not hardened him, if he had not been influenced by the Jacobins, he would never have had these cruel feelings, that terrify me because I cannot understand them."

She took Julie's head in her two hands:

"Listen, my child. I will speak to Évariste. I will sound him, get him to see you and hear your story. The sight of you might anger him; his first impulse might be to turn against you. . . . And then, I know him; this costume would offend him; he is uncompromising in everything that touches morals, that shocks the proprieties. *I* was a bit startled to see my Julie dressed as a man."

"Oh! mother, the emigration and the fearful disorders of the kingdom have made these disguises quite a common thing. They are adopted in order to follow a trade, to escape recognition, to get a borrowed passport or a certificate approved. In London I saw young Girey dressed as a girl,—and he made a very pretty girl; you must own, mother, *that* is a more scandalous disguise than mine."

"My poor child, you have no need to justify yourself in my eyes, whether in this or any other thing. I am your mother; for me you will always be blameless. I will speak to Évariste, I will say . . . ."

She broke off. She knew what her son was; she felt it in her heart, but she would not believe it, she *would* not know it.

"He is kind-hearted. He will do it for my sake . . . for your sake, he will do what I ask him."

The two women, weary to the death, fell silent. Julie sank asleep, her head pillowed on the knees where she had rested as a child, while the mother, the rosary between her hands, wept, like another *mater dolorosa,* over the calamities she felt drawing stealthily nearer and nearer in the silence of this day of snow when everything was hushed, footsteps and carriage wheels and the very heaven itself.

Suddenly, with a keenness of hearing sharpened by anxiety, she caught the sound of her son's steps on the stairs.

"Évariste!" she cried. "Hide"—and she hurried the girl into the bedroom.

"How are you to-day, mother dear?"

Évariste hung up his hat on its peg, changed his blue coat for a working jacket and sat down before his easel. For some days he had been working at a sketch in charcoal of a Victory laying a wreath on the brow of a dead soldier, who had died for the fatherland. Once the subject would have called out all his enthusiasm, but the Tribunal consumed all his days and absorbed his whole soul, while his hand had lost its knack from disuse and had grown heavy and inert.

He hummed over the *Ça ira*.

"I hear you singing," said the *citoyenne* Gamelin; "you are light-hearted, Évariste?"

"We have reason to be glad, mother; there is good news. La Vendée is crushed, the Austrians beaten, the Army of the Rhine has forced the lines of Lautern and of Wissembourg. The day is at hand when the Republic triumphant will show her clemency. Why must the conspirators' audacity increase the mightier the Republic waxes in strength, and traitors plot to strike the fatherland a blow in the dark at the very moment her lightnings overwhelm the enemies that assail her openly?"

The *citoyenne* Gamelin, as she sat knitting a stocking, was watching her son's face over her spectacles.

"Berzélius, your old model, has been to ask for the ten livres you owed him; I paid him. Little Joséphine has had a belly-ache from eating too much of the preserves the carpenter gave her. So I made her a drop of herb tea. . . . Desmahis has been to see you; he was sorry he did not find you in. He wanted to engrave a design by you. He thinks you have great talent. He is a fine fellow; he looked at your sketches and admired them."

"When peace is re-established and conspiracy suppressed," said the painter, "I shall begin on my Orestes again. It is not my way to flatter myself; but that head is worthy of David's brush."

He outlined with a majestic sweep the arm of his Victory.

"She holds out palms," he said. "But it would be finer if her arms themselves were palms."

"Évariste!"

"Mother?"

"I have had news . . . guess, of whom . . ."

"I do not know."

"Of Julie . . . of your sister . . . She is not happy."

"It would be a scandal if she were."

"Do not speak so, my son, she is your sister. Julie is not a bad woman; she had a good disposition, which misfortune has developed. She loves you. I can assure you, Évariste, that she only desires a hard-working, exemplary life and her fondest wish is to be reconciled to her friends. There is nothing to prevent your seeing her again. She has married Fortuné Chassagne."

"She has written to you?"

"No."

"How, then, have you had news of her, mother?"

"It was not by letter, Évariste; it was . . ."

He sprang up and stopped her with a savage cry:

"Not another word, mother! Do not tell me they have both returned to France. . . . As they are doomed to perish, at least let it not be at my hands. For their own sake, for yours, for mine, let me not know they are in Paris. . . . Do not force the knowledge on me; otherwise . . ."

"What do you mean, my son? you would think, you would dare . . . ?"

"Mother, hear what I say; if I knew my sister Julie to be in that room . . ." (and he pointed at the closed door), "I should go instantly to denounce her to the Committee of Vigilance of the Section."

The poor mother, her face as white as her coif, dropped her knitting from her trembling hands and sighed in a voice fainter than the faintest whisper:

"I would not believe it, but I see it now; my boy is a monster. . . ."

As pale as she, the froth gathering on his lips, Évariste fled from the house and ran to find at Élodie's side forgetfulness, sleep, the delicious foretaste of extinction.

XIX

WHILE the Père Longuemare and the girl Athenaïs were examined at the Section, Brotteaux was led off between two gendarmes to the Luxembourg, where the door-keeper refused to admit him, declaring he had no room left. The old financier was next taken to the Conciergerie and brought into the Gaoler's office, quite a small room, divided in two by a glazed partition. While the clerk was inscribing his name in the prison registers, Brotteaux could see through the panes two men lying each on a tattered mattress, both as still as death and with glazed eyes that seemed to see nothing. Plates, bottles and bits of broken bread and meat littered the floor round them. They were prisoners condemned to death and waiting for the cart to arrive.

The *ci-devant* Monsieur des Ilettes was thrust into a dungeon, where by the light of a lantern he could just make out two figures

stretched on the ground, one savage-looking and hideously mutilated, the other graceful and pleasing. The two prisoners offered
him a share of their straw, and this, rotten and swarming with
vermin as it was, was better than having to lie on the earth, which
was befouled with excrement. Brotteaux sank down on a bench in
the pestiferous darkness and sat there, his head against the wall,
speechless and motionless. So intense was his agony of mind he
would have dashed out his brains against the stones if he had had
the strength. He could not breathe. His eyes swam, and a long-
drawn murmur, as soft as silence, filled his ears. He felt his whole
being bathed in a delicious semi-consciousness. For one incomparable moment everything was harmony, serenity, light, fragrance,
sweetness. Then he ceased to know or feel anything.

When he returned to himself, the first notion that entered his
head was to regret his coma and, a philosopher even in the stupor
of despair, he reflected how he had had to plunge to the depths of
an underground dungeon, there to await execution, to enjoy the
most exquisite of all voluptuous sensations he had ever tasted. He
tried hard to lose consciousness again, but without success; on the
contrary, little by little he felt the poisonous air of the dungeon
fill his lungs and bring with it, along with the fever of life, a full
consciousness of his intolerable wretchedness.

Meantime his two companions regarded his silence as a cruel personal insult. Brotteaux, who was of a sociable turn, endeavoured to
satisfy their curiosity; but when they discovered he was only what
they called "a political," one of the mild sort whose crime was
only a matter of words and opinions, they lost all respect and sympathy for him. The offences charged against these two prisoners
had more grit; the older of the men was a murderer, the other had
been manufacturing forged assignats. Both made the best of their
situation and even found some alleviations in it. Brotteaux's
thoughts suddenly turned to the world above him,—how over his
head all was noise and bustle, light and life, while the pretty shopwomen in the Palais de Justice behind their counters, loaded with
perfumery and pretty knicknacks, smiled on their customers, happy
people free to go where they pleased,—and the picture doubled his
despair.

Night fell, unmarked in the darkness and silence of the dungeon,
but yet gloomy and oppressive. One leg extended on his bench and
his back propped against the wall, Brotteaux fell into a doze. And
lo! he saw himself seated at the foot of a leafy beech, in which the
birds were singing; the setting sun bathed the river in liquid fire
and the clouds were edged with purple. The night wore through. A
burning fever consumed him and he greedily drained his pitcher to
the dregs, but the fetid water only increased his distress.

Next day the gaoler who brought the food promised Brotteaux, if
he could afford the cost, to give him the privileges of a prisoner

who pays for his accommodation, so soon as there should be room, and it was not likely to be long first. And so it turned out; two days later he invited the old financier to leave his dungeon. At every step he took upwards, Brotteaux felt life and vigour coming back to him, and when he saw a room with a red-tiled floor and in it a bed of sacking covered with a dingy woollen counterpane, he wept for joy. The gilded bed carved with doves billing and cooing that he had once had made for the prettiest of the dancers at the Opera had not seemed so desirable or promised him such delights.

This bed of sacking was in a large hall, very fairly clean, which held seventeen others like it, separated by high partitions of planks. The company that occupied these quarters, composed of ex-nobles, tradesmen, bankers, working-men, hit the old publican's taste well enough, for he could accommodate himself to persons of all qualities. He noticed that these, cut off like himself from every opportunity of pleasure and foredoomed to perish at the hand of the executioner, were of a very merry humour and showed a marked taste for wit and raillery. His bent was to think lightly of mankind, so he attributed the high spirits of his companions to the frivolity of their minds, which prevented them from looking seriously at their situation. Moreover, he was strengthened in his opinion by observing how the more intelligent among them were profoundly sad. He remarked before long, that, for the most part, wine and brandy supplied the inspiration of a gaiety that betrayed its source by its violent and sometimes almost insane character. They did not all possess courage; but all made a display of it. This caused Brotteaux no surprise; he was well aware how men will readily enough avow cruelty, passion, even avarice, but never cowardice, because such an admission would bring them, among savages and even in civilized society, into mortal danger. That is the reason, he reflected, why all nations are nations of heroes and all armies are made up of brave men only.

More potent, even, than wine and brandy were the rattle of weapons and keys, the clash of locks and bolts, the cry of sentries, the stamping of feet at the door of the Tribunal, to intoxicate the prisoners and fill their minds with melancholy, insanity, or frenzy. Some there were who cut their throat with a razor or threw themselves from a window.

Brotteaux had been living for three days in these privileged quarters when he learned through the turnkey that the Père Longuemare was languishing on the rotten verminous straw of the common prison with the thieves and murderers. He had him put on paying terms in the same room as himself, where a bed had fallen vacant. Having promised to pay for the monk, the old publican, who had no large sum of money about him, struck out the idea of making portraits at a crown apiece. By the help of a gaoler, he procured a supply of small black frames in which to put pretty

little designs in hair which he executed with considerable cleverness. These productions sold well, being highly appreciated among
people whose thoughts were set on leaving souvenirs to their
friends.

The Père Longuemare kept a good heart and a high spirit. While
waiting his summons to appear before the Revolutionary Tribunal,
he was preparing his defence. Drawing no distinction between his
own case and that of the Church, he promised himself to expose to
his judges the disorders and scandals to which the Spouse of
Christ was exposed by the Civil Constitution of the Clergy; he proposed to depict the eldest daughter of the Church waging sacrilegious war upon the Pope, the French clergy robbed, outraged, subjected to the odious domination of laics, the regulars, Christ's true
army, despoiled and scattered. He cited St. Gregory the Great and
St. Irenæus, quoted numerous articles of the Canon Law and whole
paragraphs from the Decretals.

All day long he sat scribbling on his knees, at the foot of his bed,
dipping stumps of pens worn to the feathers in ink, soot, coffee-
grounds, covering with illegible writing candle-wrappers, packing-
paper, newspapers, playing cards, even thinking of using his shirt
for the same purpose after starching it. Leaf by leaf the pile grew;
pointing to this mass of undecipherable scrawls, he would say:

"Ah! when I appear before my judges, I will inundate them with
light."

Another day, casting a look of satisfaction on his defence, which
grew bulkier day by day, and thinking of these magistrates he was
burning to confound, he cried:

"I wouldn't like to be in *their* shoes!"

The prisoners whom fate had brought together in this prison-
room were Royalists or Federalists, there was even a Jacobin
amongst the rest; they held widely different views as to the right
way of conducting the business of the State, but not one of them
all preserved the smallest vestige of Christian beliefs. Feuillants,
Constitutionals, Girondists, all like Brotteaux, considered the
Christians' God a very bad thing for themselves and an excellent
one for the people; as for the Jacobins, they were for installing in
the place of Jehovah a Jacobin god, anxious to refer the dispensa-
tion of Jacobinism on earth to a higher source. But as they could
not conceive, either one or the other, of anybody being so absurd
as to believe in any revealed religion, seeing that the Père Longuemare was no fool, they took him to be a knave. By way, no doubt,
of preparing for martyrdom, he made confession of faith at every
opportunity, and the more sincerity he displayed, the more like an
impostor he seemed.

In vain Brotteaux stood surety for the monk's good faith; Brotteaux himself was reputed to believe only a part of what he said.

His ideas were too singular not to appear affected and satisfied nobody entirely. He dubbed Jean-Jacques a dull, paltry rascal. Voltaire, on the other hand, he accounted among the divinely-gifted men, though not on the same level as the amiable Helvétius, or Diderot, or the Baron d'Holbach. In his opinion the greatest genius of the century was Boulanger. He also thought highly of the astronomer Lalande and of Dupuis, author of a *Memoir on the origin of the Constellations.*

The wits of the company made a thousand jokes at the poor Barnabite's expense, the point of which he never saw; his simplicity saved him from every pitfall. To drown the suspense that racked them and escape the torments of idleness, the prisoners played at draughts, cards and backgammon. No instrument of music was allowed. After supper they would sing, or recite verses. Voltaire's *La Pucelle* brought a little cheerfulness to these aching hearts, and the company never wearied of hearing the telling passages repeated. But, unable to distract their thoughts from the appalling vision that always loomed before their mind's eye, they strove sometimes to make a diversion of it, and in the chamber of the eighteen beds, before turning in for the night, they would play the game of the Revolutionary Tribunal. The parts were distributed according to tastes and aptitudes. While some represented the judges and prosecutor, others were the accused or the witnesses, others again the headsman and his men. The trials invariably wound up with the execution of the condemned, who were laid at full length on a bed, the neck underneath a plank. The scene then shifted to the infernal regions. The most agile of the troop, wrapped in white sheets, played spectres. There was a young *avocat* from Bordeaux, a man named Dubosc, short, dark, one-eyed, humpbacked, bandy-legged, the very black deuce in person, who used to come all horned and hoofed, to drag the Père Longuemare feet first out of his bed, announcing to the culprit that he was condemned to the everlasting flames of hell and doomed past redemption for having made the Creator of the Universe a jealous being, a blockhead, and a bully, an enemy of human happiness and love.

"Ah! ha! ha!" the devil would scream discordantly, "so you taught, you old bonze, that God delights to see His creatures languish in contrition and deny themselves His dearest gifts. Impostor, hypocrite, sneak, sit on nails and eat egg-shells for all eternity!"

The Père Longuemare, for all reply, would observe that the speech showed the philosopher's cloven hoof behind the devil's and that the meanest imp of hell would never have talked such foolishness, having at least rubbed shoulders with Theology and for certain being less ignorant than an Encyclopædist.

But when the Girondist *avocat* called him a Capuchin, he turned scarlet with anger and declared that a man incapable of distinguishing a Barnabite from a Franciscan was too blind to see a fly in milk.

The Revolutionary Tribunal was always draining the prisons, which the Committees were as unceasingly replenishing; in three months the chamber of the eighteen was half full of new faces. The Père Longuemare lost his tormentor. The *avocat* Dubosc was haled before the Revolutionary Tribunal and condemned to death as a Federalist and for having conspired, against the unity of the Republic. On leaving the court, he returned, as the prisoners always did, by a corridor that ran through the prison and opened on the room he had enlivened for three months with his gaiety. As he made his farewells to his companions, he maintained the same light tone and cheerful air that were habitual with him.

"Forgive me, sir," he said to the Père Longuemare, "for having hauled you feet foremost from your bed. I will never do it again."

Then, turning to old Brotteaux:

"Good-bye, I go before you into the land of nowhere. I gladly return to Nature the atoms of my composition, only hoping she will make a better use of them for the future, for it must be owned she did not make much of a job of me."

So he went on his way to the gaoler's room, leaving Brotteaux sorrowful and the Père Longuemare trembling and green as a leaf, more dead than alive to see the impious wretch laugh on the brink of the abyss.

When Germinal brought back the bright days, Brotteaux, who was of an ardent temperament, tramped down several times every day to the courtyard giving on the women's quarters, near the fountain where the female prisoners used to come of a morning to wash their linen. An iron railing separated the two barracks; but the bars were not so close together as to hinder hands joining and lips meeting. Under the kindly shade of night loving couples would press against the obstacle. At such times Brotteaux would retire discreetly to the staircase and, sitting on a step, would draw from the pocket of his plum-coloured surtout his little Lucretius and read, by the light of a lantern, some of the author's sternly consolatory maxims: "*Sic ubi non erimus.* . . . When we shall have ceased to be, nothing will have power to move us, not even the heavens and earth and sea confounding their shattered fragments. . . ." But, in the act of enjoying his exalted wisdom, Brotteaux would find himself envying the Barnabite this craze that veiled the universe from his eyes.

Month by month terror grew more intense. Every night the tipsy gaolers, their watch-dogs at their heels, would march from cell to cell, delivering acts of accusation, howling out names they mutilated, waking the prisoners and for twenty victims marked on their list terrifying two hundred. Along these corridors, reeking with bloody memories, passed every day, without a murmur, twenty, thirty, fifty condemned prisoners, old men, women, young men and maidens, so widely different in rank and character and opinion that the question rose involuntarily to the lips,—had they not been chosen by lot?

And the card playing went on, the Burgundy drinking, the making of plans, the assignations for after dark at the rails. The company, new almost to a man, now consisted in great part of "extremists" and "irreconcilables." But still the room of the eighteen beds remained the home of elegance and good breeding; barring two prisoners recently transferred from the Luxembourg to the Conciergerie and added to the company, by whom they were suspected of being spies, the *citoyens* Navette and Bellier by name, there were none but honest folk there who reposed a mutual trust in each other. Glass in hand, the victories of the Republic were celebrated by all. Amongst the rest were several poets, as there always are in any gathering of people with nothing to do. The most accomplished composed odes on the triumphs of the Army of the Rhine, which they recited with much mouthing. They were uproariously applauded. Brotteaux was the only lukewarm admirer of the victors and the bards who sang their victories.

"Since Homer began it," he observed one day, "it has always been a mania with poets, this extolling the powers of fighting-men. War is not an art, and luck alone decides the fate of battles. With two generals, both blockheads, face to face, one of them must inevitably be victorious. Wait till some day one of these warriors you make gods of swallows you all up like the stork in the fable who gobbles up the frogs. Ah! then he would be really and truly a god! For you can always tell the gods by their appetite."

Brotteaux's head had never been turned by the glamour of arms. He felt no triumph at the victories of the Republic, which he had foreseen. He did not like the new régime, which military success confirmed. He was a malcontent. Another would have been the same for less cause.

One morning it was announced that the Commissaries of the Committee of General Security were going to institute a search in the prisoners' quarters, that they would seize assignats, articles of gold and silver, knives, scissors; that similar proceedings had been taken at the Luxembourg, where letters, papers, and books had been taken possession of.

Thereupon everyone tried to think of some hiding place in which to secure whatever he held most precious. The Père Longuemare carried away his defence in armfuls to a rain-gutter, while Brotteaux slipped his Lucretius among the ashes on the hearth.

When the Commissaries, wearing tricolour ribands at their necks, arrived to carry out their perquisition, they found scarcely anything but such trifles as it had been deemed judicious to let them discover. On their departure, the Père Longuemare ran to his rain-pipe and rescued as much of his defence as wind and water had spared. Brotteaux pulled out his Lucretius from the fireplace all black with soot.

"Let us make the best of the present," he thought, "for I augur from sundry tokens that our time is straitly measured from henceforth."

One soft night in Prairial, while over the prison yard the moon riding high in a pale sky showed her two silver horns, the ex-financier, who, as his way was, sat reading Lucretius on a step of the stone stairs, heard a voice call him, a woman's voice, a delightful voice, which he did not know. He went down into the court and saw behind the railing a form which he recognized as little as he did the voice, but which reminded him, in its half-seen fascinating outlines, of all the women he had loved. A flood of silvery blue moonlight fell on it. Next instant Brotteaux recognized the pretty actress of the Rue Feydeau, Rose Thévenin.

"You here, my child! It is a joy to see you, but it stabs my heart. Since when have you been here, and why?"

"Since yesterday,"—and she added very low:

"I have been denounced as a Royalist. They accuse me of conspiring to set free the Queen. Knowing you were here, I tried at once to see you. Listen to me, dear friend . . . you will let me call you so? . . . I know people in power; I have sympathizers, I am sure of it, on the Committee of Public Safety itself. I will set my friends to work; they will deliver me, and *I* will deliver you."

But Brotteaux in a voice that took on an accent of urgency:

"By everything you hold dear, my child, do nothing of the sort! Do not write, do not petition; ask nothing of anybody, I conjure you, let yourself be forgotten."

As she appeared unconvinced by what he said, he went on more beseechingly still:

"Not a word, Rose, let them forget you; there lies safety. Anything your friends might attempt would only hasten your undoing. Time is everything; only a short delay, a very short one, I hope, is needed to save you. . . . Above all, never try to melt the judges, the jurors, a Gamelin. They are not men, they are things; there is no arguing with things. Let them forget you; if you take my advice, sweetheart, I shall die happy, happy to have saved your life."

She answered:

"I will do as you say. . . . Never talk of dying. . . ."

He shrugged his shoulders.

"My life is ended, my child. Do you live and be happy."

She took his hands and laid them on her bosom:

"Hear what I say, dear friend. . . . I have only seen you once for a day, and yet you are not indifferent to me. And if what I am going to tell you can renew your attachment to life, oh! believe my promise,—I will be for you . . . whatever you shall wish me to be."

And they exchanged a kiss on the mouth through the bars.

XX

VARISTE GAMELIN, as he sat, one day that a long, tedious case was before the Tribunal, on the jury-bench in the stifling court, closed his eyes and thought:

"Evil-doers, by forcing Marat to hide in holes and corners, had turned him into a bird of night, the bird of Minerva, whose glance pierced the dark recesses where conspirators lurked. Now it is a blue eye, cold and calm, that discovers the enemies of the State and denounces traitors with a subtlety unknown even to the Friend of the People, now asleep for ever in the garden of the Cordeliers. The new saviour of the country, as zealous and more keen-sighted than the first, sees what no man before had seen and with a lifted finger spreads terror broadcast. He discerns the fine, imperceptible shades of difference that divide evil from good, vice from virtue, which but for him would have been confounded, to the hurt of the fatherland and freedom, he marks out before him the thin, inflexible line outside which lies, to the right hand and to the left, only error, crime, and wickedness. The Incorruptible teaches how men serve the foreigner equally by excess of zeal and by supineness, by persecuting the religious in the name of reason no less than by fighting in the name of religion against the laws of the Republic. Every whit as much as the villains who immolated Le Peltier and Marat, do they serve the foreigner who decree them divine honours, to compromise their memory. Agent of the foreigner whosoever repudiates the ideas of order, wisdom, opportunity; agent of the foreigner whosoever outrages morals, scandalizes virtue, and, in the foolishness of his heart, denies God. Yes, fanatic priests deserve to die; but there is an anti-revolutionary way of combating fanaticism; abjurers, too, may be guilty of a crime. By moderation men destroy the Republic; by violence they do the same.

"August and terrible the functions of a judge,—functions defined by the wisest of mankind! It is not aristocrats alone, federalists, scoundrels of the Orleans faction, open enemies of the fatherland, that we must strike down. The conspirator, the agent of the foreigner is a Proteus, he assumes all shapes, he puts on the guise of a patriot, a revolutionary, an enemy of Kings; he affects the boldness of a heart that beats only for freedom; his voice swells, and the foes of the Republic tremble. His name is Danton; his violence is a poor cloak to his odious moderatism, and his base corruption is manifest at last. The conspirator, the agent of the foreigner is that fluent stammerer, the man who clapped the first cockade of revolution in his hat, that pamphleteer who, in his ironical and cruel patriotism, nicknamed himself, 'The procureur of the Lantern.' *His* name is Camille Desmoulins. He threw off the mask by defending the Generals, traitors to their country, and claiming measures of clemency criminal at such a time. There was Philippeaux, there was Hérault, there was the despicable Lacroix. There was the Père Duchesne, he, too, a conspirator and agent of the foreigner, the vile demagogue who degraded liberty, and whose filthy calumnies stirred sympathy for Antoinette herself. There was Chaumette, who yet was a mild man, popular, moderate, well-intentioned, and virtuous in the administration of the Commune; but he was an atheist! Conspirators, agents of the foreigner,—such were all those sansculottes in red cap and carmagnole and sabots who recklessly outbid the Jacobins in patriotism. Conspirator and agent of the foreigner was Anacharsis Cloots, 'orator of the human race,' condemned to die by all the Monarchies of the world; but everything was to be feared of him,—he was a Prussian.

"Now violent or moderate, all these evil-doers, all these traitors, —Danton, Desmoulins, Hébert, Chaumette,—have perished under the axe. The Republic is saved; a chorus of praises rises from all the Committees and the popular assemblies one and all to greet Maximilien and *the Mountain*. Good citizens cry aloud: 'Worthy representatives of a free people, in vain have the sons of the Titans

lifted their proud heads; oh! mountain of blessing, oh! protecting
Sinai, from thy tumultous bosom has issued the saving lightning. . . .'

"In this chorus the Tribunal has its meed of praise. How sweet a
thing it is to be virtuous, and how dear to public gratitude, to the
heart of the upright judge!

"Meanwhile, for a patriot heart, what food for amazement, what
motives for anxiety! What! to betray the people's cause, it was not
enough to have a Mirabeau, a La Fayette, a Bailly, a Pétion, a
Brissot? We must likewise have the men who denounced these
traitors. Can it be that all the patriots who made the Revolution
only wrought to ruin her? That these heroes of the great days were
but contriving with Pitt and Coburg to give the kingdom to the
Orleans and set up a Regency under Louis XVII? What! Danton
was another Monk. What! Chaumette and the Hébertists, falser
than the Federalists who sent them to the guillotine, had conspired
to destroy the State! But among those who hurried to their death
the traitor Danton and the traitor Chaumette, will not the blue eye
of Robespierre discover anon more perfidious traitors yet? What
will be the end of this hideous concatenation of traitors betrayed
and the revelations of the keen-sighted Incorruptible? . . ."

XXI

EANTIME Julie Gamelin, in her bottle-green box-
coat, went every day to the Luxembourg Gardens
and there, on a bench at the end of one of the
avenues, sat waiting for the moment when her lover
should show his face at one of the dormers of the
Palace. Then they would beckon to each other and
talk together in a language of signs they had invented. In this way she learned that the prisoner
occupied a fairly good room and had pleasant companions, that he
wanted a blanket for his bed and a kettle and loved his mistress
fondly.

She was not the only one to watch for the sight of a dear face at
a window of the Palace now turned into a prison. A young mother
not far from her kept her eyes fixed on a closed casement; then
directly she saw it open, she would lift her little one in her arms
above her head. An old lady in a lace veil sat for long hours on a
folding-chair, vainly hoping to catch a momentary glimpse of her
son, who, for fear of breaking down, never left his game of quoits
in the courtyard of the prison till the hour when the gardens were
closed.

During these long hours of waiting, whether the sky were blue or overcast, a man of middle age, rather stout and very neatly dressed, was constantly to be seen on a neighbouring bench, playing with his snuff-box and the charms on his watch-guard or unfolding a newspaper, which he never read. He was dressed like a bourgeois of the old school in a gold-laced cocked hat, a plum-coloured coat and blue waistcoat embroidered in silver. He looked well-meaning enough, and was something of a musician to judge by a flute, one end of which peeped from his pocket. Never for a moment did his eyes wander from the supposed stripling, on whom he bestowed continual smiles, and when he saw him leave his seat, he would get up himself and follow him at a distance. Julie, in her misery and loneliness, was touched by the discreet sympathy the good man manifested.

One day, as she was leaving the gardens, it began to rain; the old fellow stepped up to her and, opening his vast red umbrella, asked permission to offer her its shelter. She answered sweetly, in her clear treble, that she would be very glad. But at the sound of her voice and warned perhaps by a subtle scent of womanhood, he strode rapidly away, leaving the girl exposed to the rain-storm; she took in the situation, and, despite her gnawing anxieties, could not restrain a smile.

Julie lived in an attic in the Rue du Cherche-Midi and represented herself as a draper's shop-boy in search of employment; the widow Gamelin, at last convinced that the girl was running smaller risks anywhere else than at her home, had got her away from the Place de Thionville and the Section du Pont-Neuf, and was giving her all the help she could in the way of food and linen. Julie did her trifle of cooking, went to the Luxembourg to see her beloved prisoner and back again to her garret; the monotony of the life was a balm to her grief, and, being young and strong, she slept well and soundly the night through. She was of a fearless temper and broken in to an adventurous life; the costume she wore added perhaps a further spice of excitement, and she would sometimes sally out at night to visit a restaurateur's in the Rue du Four, at the sign of the Red Cross, a place frequented by men of all sorts and conditions and women of gallantry. There she read the papers or played backgammon with some tradesman's clerk or citizen-soldier, who smoked his pipe in her face. Drinking, gambling, love-making were the order of the day, and scuffles were not unfrequent. One evening a customer, hearing a trampling of hoofs on the paved roadway outside, lifted the curtain, and recognizing the Commandant-in-Chief of the National Guard, the *citoyen* Hanriot, who was riding past with his Staff, muttered between his teeth:

"There goes Robespierre's jackass!"

Julie overheard and burst into a loud guffaw.

But a moustachioed patriot took up the challenge roundly:

"Whoever says that," he shouted, "is a bl . . . sted aristocrat, and I should like to see the fellow sneeze into Samson's basket. I tell you General Hanriot is a good patriot who'll know how to defend Paris and the Convention at a pinch. That's why the Royalists can't forgive him."

Glaring at Julie, who was still laughing, the patriot added:

"You there, greenhorn, have a care I don't land you a kick in the backside to learn you to respect good patriots."

But other voices were joining in:

"Hanriot's a drunken sot and a fool!"

"Hanriot's a good Jacobin! Vive Hanriot!"

Sides were taken, and the fray began. Blows were exchanged, hats battered in, tables overturned, and glasses shivered; the lights went out and the women began to scream. Two or three patriots fell upon Julie, who seized hold of a settle in self-defence; she was brought to the ground, where she scratched and bit her assailants. Her coat flew open and her neckerchief was torn, revealing her panting bosom. A patrol came running up at the noise, and the girl aristocrat escaped between the gendarmes' legs.

Every day the carts were full of victims for the guillotine.

"But I cannot, I cannot let my lover die!" Julie would tell her mother.

She resolved to beg his life, to take what steps were possible, to go to the Committees and Public Departments, to canvas Representatives, Magistrates, to visit anyone who could be of help. She had no woman's dress to wear. Her mother borrowed a striped gown, a kerchief, a lace coif from the *citoyenne* Blaise, and Julie, attired as a woman and a patriot, set out for the abode of one of the judges, Renaudin, a damp, dismal house in the Rue Mazarine.

With trembling steps she climbed the wooden, tiled stairs and was received by the judge in his squalid cabinet, furnished with a deal table and two straw-bottomed chairs. The wall-paper hung in strips. Renaudin, with black hair plastered on his forehead, a lowering eye, tucked-in lips, and a protuberant chin, signed to her to speak and listened in silence.

She told him she was the sister of the *citoyen* Chassagne, a prisoner at the Luxembourg, explained as speciously as she could the circumstances under which he had been arrested, represented him as an innocent man, the victim of mischance, pleaded more and more urgently; but he remained callous and unsympathetic.

She fell at his feet in supplication and burst into tears.

No sooner did he see her tears than his face changed; his dark blood-shot eyes lit up, and his heavy blue jowl worked as if pumping up the saliva in his dry throat.

"*Citoyenne*, we will do what is necessary. You need have no anxiety,"—and opening a door he pushed the petitioner into a little sitting-room, with rose-pink hangings, painted panels, Dresden china figures, a time-piece and gilt candelabra; for furniture it contained settees, and a sofa covered in tapestry and adorned with a pastoral group after Boucher. Julie was ready for anything to save her lover.

Renaudin had his way,—rapidly and brutally. When she got up, readjusting the *citoyenne's* pretty frock, she met the man's cruel mocking eye; instantly she knew she had made her sacrifice in vain.

"You promised me my brother's freedom," she said.

He chuckled.

"I told you, *citoyenne,* we would do what was necessary,—that is to say, we should apply the law, neither more nor less. I told you to have no anxiety,—and why should you be anxious? The Revolutionary Tribunal is always just."

She thought of throwing herself upon the man, biting him, tearing out his eyes. But, realizing she would only be consummating Fortuné Chassagne's ruin, she rushed from the house, and fled to her garret to take off Élodie's soiled and desecrated frock. All night she lay, screaming with grief and rage.

Next day, on returning to the Luxembourg, she found the gardens occupied by gendarmes, who were turning out the women and children. Sentinels were posted in the avenues to prevent the passers-by from communicating with the prisoners. The young mother, who used to come every day, carrying her child in her arms, told Julie that there was talk of plotting in the prisons and that the women were blamed for gathering in the gardens in order to rouse the people's pity in favour of aristocrats and traitors.

XXII

MOUNTAIN has suddenly sprung up in the garden of the Tuileries. Under a cloudless sky, Maximilien heads the procession of his colleagues in a blue coat and yellow breeches, carrying in his hand a bouquet of wheat-ears, cornflowers and poppies. He ascends the mountain and proclaims the God of Jean-Jacques to the Republic, which hears and weeps. Oh purity! oh sweetness! oh faith! oh antique simplicity! oh tears of pity! oh fertilizing dew! oh clemency! oh human fraternity!

In vain Atheism still lifts its hideous face; Maximilien grasps a torch; flames devour the monster and Wisdom appears, with one hand pointing to the sky, in the other holding a crown of stars.

On the platform raised against the façade of the Tuileries, Évariste, standing amid a throng of deeply-stirred spectators, sheds tears of joy and renders thanks to God. An era of universal felicity opens before his eyes.

He sighs:

"At last we shall be happy, pure, innocent, if the scoundrels suffer it."

Alas! the scoundrels have not suffered it. There must be more executions; more torrents of tainted blood must be shed. Three days after the festival celebrating the new alliance and the reconciliation of heaven and earth, the Convention promulgates the Law of Prairial which suppresses, with a sort of ferocious good-nature, all the traditional forms of Law, whatever has been devised since the time of the Roman jurisconsults for the safeguarding of innocence under suspicion. No more sifting of evidence, no more questioning of the accused, no more witnesses, no more counsel for the defence; love of the fatherland supplies everything that is needful. The prisoner, who bears locked up in his bosom his guilt or innocence, passes without a word allowed before the patriot jury, and it is in this brief moment they must unravel his case, often complicated and obscure. How is justice possible? How distinguish in an instant between the honest man and the villain, the patriot and the enemy of the fatherland . . . ?

Disconcerted for the moment, Gamelin quickly learned his new duties and accommodated himself to his new functions. He recognized that this curtailment of formalities was genuinely characteristic of the new justice, at once salutary and terrifying, the administrators of which were no longer ermined pedants leisurely weighing the *pros* and *contras* in their Gothic balances, but good sansculottes judging by inspiration and seeing the whole truth in a flash. When guarantees and precautions would have undone everything, the impulses of an upright heart saved the situation. We must follow the promptings of Nature, the good mother who never deceives; the heart must teach us to do judgment, and Gamelin made invocation to the manes of Jean-Jacques:

"Man of virtue, inspire me with the love of men, the ardent desire to regenerate humankind!"

His colleagues, for the most part, felt with him. They were, first and foremost, simple people; and when the forms of law were simplified, they felt more comfortable. Justice thus abbreviated satisfied them; the pace was quickened, and no obstacles were left to fret them. They limited themselves to an inquiry into the opinions of the accused, not conceiving it possible that anyone could think differently from themselves except in pure perversity. Believing themselves the exclusive possessors of truth, wisdom, the quintessence of good, they attributed to their opponents nothing but error and evil. They felt themselves all-powerful; they envisaged God.

They saw God, these jurors of the Revolutionary Tribunal. The Supreme Being, acknowledged by Maximilien, flooded them with His flames of light. They loved, they believed.

The chair of the accused had been replaced by a vast platform able to accommodate fifty persons; the court only dealt with batches now. The Public Prosecutor would often confound under the same charge or implicate as accomplices individuals who met each other for the first time before the Tribunal. The latter, taking advantage of the terrible facilities accorded by the law of Prairial, sat in judgment on those supposed prison plots which, coming after the proscriptions of the Dantonists and the Commune, were made to seem their outcome by the insinuations of cunning adversaries. In fact, to let the world appreciate the two essential characteristics of a conspiracy fomented by foreign gold against the Republic,— to wit inopportune moderation on the one hand and self-interested excess of zeal on the other, they had united in the same condemnation two very different women, the widow of Camille Desmoulins, poor lovable Lucille, and the widow of the Hébertist Momoro, goddess of a day and jolly companion all her life. Both, to make the analogy complete, had been shut up in the same prison, where they had mingled their tears on the same bench; both, to round off the resemblance, had climbed the scaffold. Too ingenious the symbol,— a masterpiece of equilibrium, conceived doubtless by a lawyer's brain, and the honour of which was given to Maximilien. This representative of the people was accredited with every eventuality, happy or unhappy, that came about in the Republic, every change that was effected in the laws, in manners and morals, the very course of the seasons, the harvests, the incidence of epidemics. Unjust of course, but not unmerited the injustice, for indeed the man, the little, spruce, cat-faced dandy, was all powerful with the people. . . .

That day the Tribunal was clearing off a batch of prisoners involved in the great plot, thirty or more conspirators from the Luxembourg, submissive enough in gaol, but Royalists or Federalists of the most pronounced type. The prosecution relied almost entirely on the evidence of a single informer. The jurors did not know one word of the matter,—not so much as the conspirators' names. Gamelin, casting his eye over the prisoners' bench, recognized Fortuné Chassagne among the accused. Julie's lover, pale-faced and emaciated by long confinement and his features showing coarser in the glare of light that flooded the hall, still retained traces of his old grace and proud bearing. His eyes met Gamelin's and filled with scorn.

Gamelin, possessed by a calm fury, rose, asked leave to speak, and, fixing his eyes on the bust of Roman Brutus, which looked down on the Tribunal:

"*Citoyen* President," he said, "although there may exist between one of the accused and myself ties which, if they were made public, would be ties of married kinship, I hereby declare I do not decline to act. The two Bruti did not decline their duty, when for the salvation of the state and the cause of freedom, the one had to condemn a son, the other to strike down an adoptive father."

He resumed his seat.

"A fine scoundrel that," muttered Chassagne between his teeth.

The public remained cold, whether because it was tired of high-flown characters, or thinking that Gamelin had triumphed too easily over his feelings of family affection.

"*Citoyen* Gamelin," said the President, "by the terms of law, every refusal must be formulated in writing within the twenty-four hours preceding the opening of the trial. In any case, you have no reason to refuse; a patriot jury is superior to human passions."

Each prisoner was questioned for three or four minutes, the examination resulting in a verdict of death in every instance. The jurors voted without a word said, by a nod of the head or by exclamation. When Gamelin's turn came to pronounce his opinion:

"All the accused," he declared, "are convicted, and the law is explicit."

As he was descending the stairway of the Palais de Justice, a young man dressed in a bottle-green box-coat, and who looked seventeen or eighteen years of age, stopped him abruptly as he went by. The lad wore a round hat, tilted on the back of his head, the brim framing his fine pale face in a dark aureole. Facing the juror, in a terrible voice vibrating with passion and despair:

"Villain, monster, murderer!" he screamed. "Strike me, coward! I am a woman! Have me arrested, have me guillotined, Cain! I am your sister,"—and Julie spat in his face.

The throng of *tricoteuses* and *sansculottes* was relaxing by this time in its Revolutionary vigilance; its civic zeal had largely cooled; Gamelin and his assailant found themselves the centre of nothing worse than uproar and confusion. Julie fought a way through the press and disappeared in the dark.

XXIII

VARISTE GAMELIN was worn out and could not rest; twenty times in the night he would awake with a start from a sleep haunted by nightmares. It was only in the blue chamber, in Élodie's arms, that he could snatch a few hours' slumber. He talked and cried out in his sleep and used often to awake her; but she could make nothing of what he said.

One morning, after a night when he had seen the Eumenides, he started awake, broken with terror and weak as a child. The dawn was piercing the window curtains with its wan arrows. Évariste's hair, lying tangled on his brow, covered his eyes with a black veil;

Élodie, by the bedside, was gently parting the wild locks. She was looking at him now, with a sister's tenderness, while with her handkerchief she wiped away the icy sweat from the unhappy man's forehead. Then he remembered that fine scene in the *Orestes* of Euripides, which he had essayed to represent in a picture that, if he could have finished it, would have been his masterpiece—the scene where the unhappy Electra wipes away the spume that sullies her brother's lips. And he seemed to hear Élodie also saying in a gentle voice:

"Hear me, beloved brother, while the Furies leave you master of your reason . . ."

And he thought:

"And yet I am no parricide. Far from it, it is filial piety has made me shed the tainted blood of the enemies of my fatherland."

XXIV

HERE seemed no end to these trials for conspiracy in the prisons. Forty-nine accused crowded the tiers of seats. Maurice Brotteaux occupied the right-hand corner of the topmost row,—the place of honour. He was dressed in his plum-coloured surtout, which he had brushed very carefully the day before and mended at the pocket where his little Lucretius had ended by fretting a hole. Beside him sat the woman Rochemaure, painted and powdered and patched, a brilliant and ghastly figure. They had put the Père Longuemare between her and the girl Athenaïs, who had recovered her look of youthful freshness at the Madelonnettes.

On the platform the gendarmes massed a number of other prisoners unknown to any of our friends, and who, as likely as not, knew nothing of each other,—yet accomplices one and all,— lawyers, journalists, *ci-devant* nobles, citizens, and citizens' wives. The *citoyenne* Rochemaure caught sight of Gamelin on the jurors' bench. He had not answered her urgent letters and repeated messages; still she had not abandoned hope and threw him a look of supplication, trying to appear fascinating and pathetic for him. But the young juror's cold glance robbed her of any illusion she might have entertained.

The Clerk read the act of accusation, which, succint as was its reference to each individual, was a lengthy document because of the great number accused. It began by exposing in general outline the plot concocted in the prisons to drown the Republic in the blood of the Representatives of the nation and the people of Paris; then, coming to each severally, it went on:

"One of the most mischievous authors of this abominable conspiracy is the man Brotteaux, once known as des Ilettes, receiver of imposts under the tyrant. This person, who was remarkable, even in the days of tyranny, for his libertine behaviour, is a sure proof how dissoluteness and immorality are the greatest enemies of the liberty and happiness of peoples; as a fact, after misappropriating the public revenues and wasting in debauchery a noticeable part of the people's patrimony, the person in question connived with his former concubine, the woman Rochemaure, to enter into correspondence with the *émigrés* and traitorously keep the faction of the foreigner informed of the state of our finances, the movements of our troops, the fluctuations of public opinion.

"Brotteaux, who, at this period of his despicable life, was living in concubinage with a prostitute he had picked up in the mud of the Rue Fromenteau, the girl Athenaïs, easily suborned her to his purposes and made use of her to foment the counter-revolution by impudent and unpatriotic cries and indecent and traitorous speeches.

"Sundry remarks of this ill-omened individual will afford you a clear indication of his abject views and pernicious purpose. Speaking of the patriotic tribunal now called upon to punish him, he declared insultingly,—'The Revolutionary Tribunal is like a play of William Shakespeare, who mixes up with the most bloodthirsty scenes the most trivial buffooneries.' Then he was forever preaching atheism, as the surest means of degrading the people and driving it into immorality. In the prison of the Conciergerie, where he was confined, he used to deplore as among the worst of calamities the victories of our valiant armies, and tried to throw suspicion on the most patriotic Generals, crediting them with designs of tyrannicide. 'Only wait,' he would say in atrocious language which the pen is loath to reproduce, 'only wait till, some day, one of these warriors, to whom you owe your salvation, swallows you all up as the stork in the fable gobbled up the frogs.'

"The woman Rochemaure, a *ci-devant* noble, concubine of Brotteaux, is not less culpable than he. Not only was she in correspondence with the foreigner and in the pay of Pitt himself, but in complicity with swindlers, such as Julien (of Toulouse) and Chabot, associates of the *ci-devant* Baron de Batz, she seconded that reprobate in all sorts of cunning machinations to depreciate the shares of the Company of the Indies, buy them in at a cheap price, and then raise the quotation by artifices of an opposite tendency, to the confusion and ruin of private fortunes and of the public funds. Incarcerated at La Bourbe and the Madelonnettes, she never ceased in prison to conspire, to dabble in stocks and shares and to devote herself to attempts at corruption, to suborn judges and jury.

"Louis Longuemare, ex-noble, ex-capuchin, had long been practised in infamy and crime before committing the acts of treason for which he has to answer here. Living in a shameful promiscuity with the girl Gorcut, known as Athenaïs, under Brotteaux's very roof, he is the accomplice of the said girl and the said *ci-devant* nobleman. During his imprisonment at the Conciergerie he has never ceased for one single day writing pamphlets aimed at the subversion of public liberty and security.

"It is right to say, with regard to Marthe Gorcut, known as Athenaïs, that prostitutes are the greatest scourge of public morality, which they insult, and the opprobrium of the society which they disgrace. But why speak at length of revolting crimes which the accused confesses shamelessly . . . ?"

The accusation then proceeded to pass in review the fifty-four other prisoners, none of whom either Brotteaux, or the Père Longuemare, or the *citoyenne* Rochemaure, were acquainted with, except for having seen several of them in the prisons, but who were one and all included with the first named in "this odious plot, with which the annals of the nation can furnish nothing to compare."

The piece concluded by demanding the penalty of death for all the culprits.

Brotteaux was the first to be examined:

"You were in the plot?"

"No, I have been in no plots. Every word is untrue in the act of accusation I have just heard read."

"There, you see; you are plotting still, at this moment, to discredit the Tribunal,"—and the President went on to the woman Rochemaure, who answered with despairing protestations of innocence, tears and quibblings.

The Père Longuemare referred himself purely and entirely to God's will. He had not even brought his written defence with him.

All the questions put to him he answered in a spirit of resignation. Only, when the President spoke of him as a Capuchin, did the old Adam wake again in him:

"I am not a Capuchin," he said, "I am a priest and a monk of the Order of the Barnabites."

"It is the same thing," returned the President good-naturedly.

The Père Longuemare looked at him indignantly:

"One cannot conceive a more extraordinary error," he cried, "than to confound with a Capuchin a monk of this Order of the Barnabites which derives its constitutions from the Apostle Paul himself."

The remark was greeted with a burst of laughter and hooting from the spectators, at which the Père Longuemare, taking this derision to betoken a denial of his proposition, announced that he would die a member of this Order of St. Barnabas, the habit of which he wore in his heart.

"Do you admit," asked the President, "entering into plots with the girl Gorcut, known as Athenaïs, the same who accorded you her despicable favours?"

At the question, the Père Longuemare raised his eyes sorrowfully to heaven, but made no answer; his silence expressed the surprise of an unsophisticated mind and the gravity of a man of religion who fears to utter empty words.

"You, the girl Gorcut," the President asked, turning to Athenaïs, "do you admit plotting in conjunction with Brotteaux?"

Her answer was softly spoken:

"Monsieur Brotteaux, to my knowledge, has done nothing but good. He is a man of the sort we should have more of; there is no better sort. Those who say the contrary are mistaken. That is all I have to say."

The President asked her if she admitted having lived in concubinage with Brotteaux. The expression had to be explained to her, as she did not understand it. But, directly she gathered what the question meant, she answered, that would only have depended on him, but he had never asked her.

There was a laugh in the public galleries, and the President threatened the girl Gorcut to refuse her a hearing if she answered in such a cynical sort again.

At this she broke out, calling him sneak, sour face, cuckold, and spewing out over him, judges, and jury a torrent of invective, till the gendarmes dragged her from her bench and hustled her out of the hall.

The President then proceeded to a brief examination of the rest of the accused, taking them in the order in which they sat on the tiers of benches.

One, a man named Navette, pleaded that he could not have plotted in prison where he had only spent four days. The President observed that the point deserved to be considered, and begged the *citoyens* of the jury to make a note of it. A certain Bellier said the same, and the President made the same remark to the jury in his favour. This mildness on the judge's part was interpreted by some as the result of a praiseworthy scrupulosity, by others as payment due in recognition of their talents as informers.

The Deputy of the Public Prosecutor spoke next. All he did was to amplify the details of the act of accusation and then to put the question:

"Is it proven that Maurice Brotteaux, Louise Rochemaure, Louis Longuemare, Marthe Gorcut, known as Athenaïs, Eusèbe Rocher, Pierre Guyton-Fabulet, Marcelline Descourtis, etc., etc., are guilty of forming a conspiracy, the means whereof are assassination, starvation, the making of forged assignats and false coin, the depravation of morals and public spirit; the aim and object, civil war, the abolition of the National representation, the re-establishment of Royalty?"

The jurors withdrew into the chamber of deliberation. They voted unanimously in the affirmative, only excepting the cases of the afore-named Navette and Bellier, whom the President, and following his lead, the Public Prosecutor, had put, as it were, in a separate class by themselves.

Gamelin stated the motives for his decision thus:

"The guilt of the accused is self-evident; the safety of the Nation demands their chastisement, and they ought themselves to desire their punishment as the only means of expiating their crimes."

The President pronounced sentence in the absence of those it concerned. In these great days, contrary to what the law prescribed, the condemned were not called back again to hear their judgment read, no doubt for fear of the effects of despair on so large a number of prisoners. A needless apprehension, so extraordinary and so general was the submissiveness of the victims in those days! The Clerk of the Court came down to the cells to read the verdict, which was listened to with such silence and impassivity as made it a common comparison to liken the condemned of Prairial to trees marked down for felling.

The *citoyenne* Rochemaure declared herself pregnant. A surgeon, who was likewise one of the jury, was directed to see her. She was carried out fainting to her dungeon.

"Ah!" sighed the Père Longuemare, "these judges and jurors are men very deserving of pity; their state of mind is truly deplorable. They mix up everything and confound a Barnabite with a Franciscan."

The execution was to take place the same day at the *Barrière du Trône-Renversé*. The condemned, their toilet completed, hair cropped and shirt cut down at the neck, waited for the headsman, packed like cattle in the small room separated off from the Gaoler's office by a glazed partition.

When presently the executioner and his men arrived, Brotteaux, who was quietly reading his Lucretius, put the marker at the page he had begun, shut the book, stuffed it in the pocket of his coat, and said to the Barnabite:

"What enrages me, Reverend Father, is that I shall never convince you. We are going both of us to sleep our last sleep, and I shall not be able to twitch you by the sleeve and tell you: 'There you see; you have neither sensation nor consciousness left; you are inanimate. What comes after life is like what goes before.'"

He tried to smile; but an atrocious spasm of pain wrung his heart and vitals, and he came near fainting.

He resumed, however:

"Father, I let you see my weakness. I love life and I do not leave it without regret."

"Sir," replied the monk gently, "take heed, you are a braver man than I, and nevertheless death troubles you more. What does that mean, if not that I see the light, which you do not see yet?"

"Might it not also be," said Brotteaux, "that I regret life because I have enjoyed it better than you, who have made it as close a copy of death as possible?"

"Sir," said the Père Longuemare, his face paling, "this is a solemn moment. God help me! It is plain we shall die without spiritual aid. It must be that in other days I have received the sacraments lukewarmly and with a thankless heart, for Heaven to refuse me them to-day, when I have such pressing need of them."

The carts were waiting. The condemned were loaded into them pell-mell, with hands tied. The woman Rochemaure, whose pregnancy had not been verified by the surgeon, was hoisted into one of the tumbrils. She recovered a little of her old energy to watch the crowd of onlookers, hoping against hope to find rescuers amongst them. The throng was less dense than formerly, and the excitement less extreme. Only a few women screamed, "Death! death!" or mocked those who were to die. The men mostly shrugged their shoulders, looked another way, and said nothing, whether out of prudence or from respect of the laws.

A shudder went through the crowd when Athenaïs emerged from the wicket. She looked a mere child.

She bowed her head before the monk:

"Monsieur le Curé," she asked him, "give me absolution."

The Père Longuemare gravely recited the sacramental words in muttered tones; then:

"My daughter!" he added, "you have fallen into great disorders of living; but can I offer the Lord a heart as simple as yours? Would I were sure!"

She climbed lightly into the cart. And there, throwing out her bosom and proudly lifting her girlish head, she cried "Vive le Roi!"

She made a little sign to Brotteaux to show him there was a vacant place beside her. Brotteaux helped the Barnabite to get in and came and placed himself between the monk and the simple-hearted girl.

"Sir," said the Père Longuemare to the Epicurean philosopher, "I ask you a favour; this God in whom you do not yet believe, pray to Him for me. It is far from sure you are not nearer to Him than I am myself; a moment can decide this. A second, and you may be called by the Lord to be His highly favoured son. Sir, pray for me."

While the wheels were grinding over the pavement of the long Faubourg Antoine, the monk was busy, with heart and lips, reciting the prayers of the dying. Brotteaux's mind was fixed on recalling the lines of the poet of nature: *Sic ubi non erimus.* . . . Bound as he was and shaken in the vile, jolting cart, he preserved his calm and even showed a certain solicitude to maintain an easy posture. At his side, Athenaïs, proud to die like the Queen of France, surveyed the crowd with haughty looks, and the old financier, noting as a connoisseur the girl's white bosom, was filled with regret for the light of day.

XXV

HILE the carts, escorted by gendarmes, were rumbling along on their way to the Place du Trône Renversé, carrying to their death Brotteaux and his "accomplices," Évariste sat pensive on a bench in the garden of the Tuileries. He was waiting for Élodie. The sun, nearing its setting, shot its fiery darts through the leafy chestnuts. At the gate of the garden, Fame on her winged horse blew her everlasting trumpet. The newspaper hawkers were bawling the news of the great victory of Fleurus.

"Yes," thought Gamelin, "victory is ours. We have paid full price for it."

He could see the beaten Generals, disconsolate shades, trailing in the blood-stained dust of yonder Place de la Révolution where they perished. And he smiled proudly, reflecting that, but for the severities in which he had borne his share, the Austrian horses would to-day be gnawing the bark of the trees beside him.

He soliloquized:

"Life-giving terror, oh! blessed terror! Last year at this time, our heroic defenders were beaten and in rags, the soil of the fatherland was invaded, two-thirds of the departments in revolt. Now our armies, well equipped, well trained, commanded by able generals, are taking the offensive, ready to bear liberty through the world. Peace reigns over all the territory of the Republic. . . . Life-giving terror, oh! blessed terror! oh! saintly guillotine! Last year at this time, the Republic was torn with factions, the hydra of Federalism threatened to devour her. Now a united Jacobinism spreads over the empire its might and its wisdom. . . ."

Nevertheless, he was gloomy. His brow was deeply lined, his mouth bitter. His thoughts ran: "We used to say: *To conquer or to die*. We were wrong; it is *to conquer and to die* we ought to say."

He looked about him. Children were building sand-castles. *Citoyennes* in their wooden chairs under the trees were sewing or embroidering. The passers-by, in coat and breeches of elegant cut and strange fashion, their thoughts fixed on their business or their pleasures, were making for home. And Gamelin felt himself alone amongst them; he was no compatriot, no contemporary of theirs. What was it had happened? How came the enthusiasm of the great years to have been· succeeded by indifference, weariness, perhaps disgust? It was plain to see, these people never wanted to hear the Revolutionary Tribunal spoken of again and averted their eyes from the guillotine. Grown too painful a sight in the Place de la Révolution, it had been banished to the extremity of the Faubourg Antoine. There even, the passage of the tumbrils was greeted with murmurs. Voices, it was said, had been heard to shout: "Enough!"

"Enough, when there were still traitors, conspirators! Enough, when the Committees must be reformed, the Convention purged! Enough, when scoundrels disgraced the National representation. Enough, when they were planning the downfall of *The Just!* For, dreadful thought, but only too true! Fouquier himself was weaving plots, and it was to ruin Maximilien that he had sacrificed with solemn ceremony fifty-seven victims haled to death in the red sheet of parricides. France was giving way to pity—and pity was a crime! Then we should have saved her in spite of herself, and when she cried for mercy, stopped our ears and struck! Alas! the fates had decided otherwise; the fatherland was for cursing its saviours. Well, let it curse, if only it may be saved!

"It is not enough to immolate obscure victims, aristocrats, financiers, publicists, poets, a Lavoisier, a Roucher, an André Chénier. We must strike these all-puissant malefactors who, with hands full of gold and dripping with blood, are plotting the ruin of *the Mountain*—the Fouchers, Talliens, Rovères, Carriers, Bourdons. We must deliver the State from all its enemies. If Hébert had triumphed, the Convention was overthrown, the Republic hastening to the abyss; if Desmoulins and Danton had triumphed, the Convention had lost its virtue, ready to surrender the Republic to the aristocrats, the money-jobbers and the Generals. If men like Tallien and Foucher, monsters gorged with blood and rapine, triumph, France is overwhelmed in a welter of crime and infamy . . . Robespierre, awake; when criminals, drunken with fury and affright, plan your death and the death of freedom! Couthon, Saint-Just, make haste; why tarry ye to denounce the plots?

"Why! the old-time state, the Royal monster, assured its empire by imprisoning every year four hundred thousand persons, by hanging fifteen thousand, by breaking three thousand on the wheel— and the Republic still hesitates to sacrifice a few hundred heads for its security and domination! Let us drown in blood and save the fatherland. . . ."

He was buried in these thoughts when Élodie hurried up to him, pale-faced and distraught:

"Évariste, what have you to say to me? Why not come to the *Amour peintre* to the blue chamber? Why have you made me come here?"

"To bid you an eternal farewell."

He had lost his wits, she faltered, she could not understand. . . .

He stopped her with a very slight movement of the hand:

"Élodie, I cannot any more accept your love."

She begged him to walk on further; people could see them, overhear them, where they were.

He moved on a score of yards, and resumed, very quietly:

"I have made sacrifices to my country of my life and my honour. I shall die infamous; I shall have naught to leave you, unhappy girl, save an execrated memory. . . . We, love? Can anyone love me still? . . . Can I love?"

She told him he was mad; that she loved him, that she would always love him. She was ardent, sincere; but she felt as well as he, she felt better than he, that he was right. But she fought against the evidence of her senses.

He went on:

"I blame myself for nothing. What I have done, I would do again. I have made myself anathema for my country's sake. I am accursed. I have put myself outside humanity; I shall never re-enter its pale. No, the great task is not finished. Oh! clemency, forgiveness!—Do the traitors forgive? Are the conspirators clement? scoundrels, parricides multiply unceasingly; they spring up from underground, they swarm in from all our frontiers,—young men, who would have done better to perish with our armies, old men, children, women, with every mark of innocence, purity, and grace. They are offered up a sacrifice,—and more victims are ready for the knife! . . . You can see, Élodie, I must needs renounce love, renounce all joy, all sweetness of life, renounce life itself."

He fell silent. Born to taste tranquil joys, Élodie not for the first time was appalled to find, under the tragic kisses of a lover like Évariste, her voluptuous transports blended with images of horror and bloodshed; she offered no reply. To Évariste, the girl's silence was as a draught of a bitter chalice.

"Yes, you can see, Élodie, we are on a precipice; our deeds devour us. Our days, our hours are years. I shall soon have lived a century. Look at this brow! Is it a lover's? Love! . . ."

"Évariste, you are mine, I will not let you go; I will not give you back your freedom."

She was speaking in the language of sacrifice. He felt it; she felt it herself.

"Will you be able, Élodie, one day to bear witness that I lived faithful to my duty, that my heart was upright and my soul unsullied, that I knew no passion but the public good; that I was born to feel and love? Will you say: 'He did his duty'? But no! You will not say it and I do not ask you to say it. Perish my memory! My glory is in my own heart; shame beleaguers me about. If you love me, never speak my name; eternal silence is best."

A child of eight or nine, trundling its hoop, ran just then between Gamelin's legs.

He lifted the boy suddenly in his arms:

"Child, you will grow up free, happy, and you will owe it to the infamous Gamelin. I am ferocious, that you may be happy. I am cruel, that you may be kind; I am pitiless, that to-morrow all Frenchmen may embrace with tears of joy."

He pressed the child to his breast.

"Little one, when you are a man, you will owe your happiness, your innocence to me; and, if ever you hear my name uttered, you will execrate it."

Then he put down the child, which ran away in terror to cling to its mother's skirts, who had hurried up to the rescue. The young mother, who was pretty and charming in her aristocratic grace, with her gown of white lawn, carried off the boy with a haughty look.

Gamelin turned his eyes on Élodie:

"I have held the child in my arms; perhaps I shall send the mother to the guillotine,"—and he walked away with long strides under the ordered trees.

Élodie stood a moment motionless, her eyes fixed on the ground.

Then, suddenly, she darted after her lover, and frenzied, dishevelled, like a Mænad, she gripped him as if to tear him in pieces and
cried in a voice choked with blood and tears:

"Well, then! me too, my beloved, send me to the guillotine; me
too, lay me under the knife!"

And, at the thought of the knife at her neck, all her flesh melted
in an ecstasy of horror and voluptuous transport.

XXVI

HE sun of Thermidor was setting in a blood-red sky,
while Évariste wandered, gloomy, and careworn, in
the Marbeuf gardens, now a National park frequented by the Parisian idlers. There were stalls for
the sale of lemonade and ices; wooden horses and
shooting-galleries were provided for the younger
patriots. Under a tree, a little Savoyard in rags,
with a black cap on his head, was making a mar-
mot dance to the shrill notes of his hurdy-gurdy. A man, still
young, slim-waisted, wearing a blue coat and his hair powdered,
with a big dog at his heels, stopped to listen to the rustic music.
Évariste recognized Robespierre. He found him paler, thinner, his
face harder and drawn in folds of suffering. He thought to himself:

"What fatigues, how many griefs have left their imprint on his
brow! How grievous a thing it is to work for the happiness of mankind! What are his thoughts at this moment? Does the sound of
this mountain music perhaps distract him from the cares of government? Is he thinking that he has made a pact with Death and
that the hour of reckoning is coming close? Is he dreaming of a
triumphant return to the Committee of Public Safety, from which
he withdrew, weary of being held in check, with Couthon and Saint-
Just, by a seditious majority? Behind that impenetrable countenance what hopes are seething or what fears?"

But Maximilien smiled at the lad, in a gentle, kind voice asked
him several questions about his native valley, the humble home and
parents the poor child had left behind, tossed him a small piece of
silver and resumed his stroll. After taking a few steps, he turned
round again to call his dog; sniffing at the marmot, it was showing
its teeth at the little creature that bristled up in defiance.

"To heel, Brount!" he called, "to heel!"—and he plunged among
the dark trees.

Gamelin, out of respect, did not interrupt his lonely walk; but, as
he gazed after the slender form disappearing in the darkness, he
mentally addressed his hero in these impassioned words:

"I have seen thy sadness, Maximilien; I have understood thy

thought. Thy melancholy, thy fatigue, even the look of fear that stamps thy face, everything says: 'Let the reign of terror end and that of fraternity begin! Frenchmen, be united, be virtuous, be good and kind. Love ye one another. . . .' Well then, I will second your designs; that you, in your wisdom and goodness, may be able to put an end to our civil discord, to our fratricidal hate, turn the headsman into a gardener who will henceforth cut off only the heads of cabbages and lettuces. I will pave the way with my colleagues of the Tribunal that must lead to clemency by exterminating conspirators and traitors. We will redouble our vigilance and our severity. No culprit shall escape us. And when the head of the last enemy of the Republic shall have fallen under the knife, then it will be given thee to be merciful without committing a crime, then thou canst inaugurate the reign of innocence and virtue in all the land, oh! father of thy country!"

The Incorruptible was already almost out of sight. Two men in round hats and nankeen breeches, one of whom, a tall, lean man of a wild, unkempt aspect, had a blur on one eye and resembled Tallien, met him at the corner of an avenue, looked at him askance and passed on, pretending not to recognize him. When they had gone far enough to be out of hearing, they muttered under their breath:

"So there he goes, the King, the Pope, the God. For he is God; and Catherine Théot is his prophetess."

"Dictator, traitor, tyrant! the race of Brutus is not extinct."

"Tremble, malefactor! the Tarpeian rock is near the Capitol!"

The dog Brount ran towards the pair. They said no more and quickened their pace.

XXVII

ROBESPIERRE, awake! The hour is come, time presses, . . . soon it will be too late. . . .

At last, on the 8 Thermidor, in the Convention, the Incorruptible rises, he is going to speak. Sun of the 31st May, is this to be a second day-spring? Gamelin waits and hopes. His mind is made up then! Robespierre is to drag from the benches they dishonour these legislators more guilty than the federalists, more dangerous than Danton. . . . No! not yet. "I cannot," he says, "resolve to clear away entirely the veil that hides this mystery of iniquity."

It is mere summer lightning that flashes harmlessly and without striking any one of the conspirators, terrifies all. Sixty of them at least for a fortnight had not dared sleep in their beds. Marat's way was to denounce traitors by their name, to point the finger of accusation at conspirators. The Incorruptible hesitates, and from that moment he is the accused. .'. .

That evening at the Jacobins, the hall is filled to suffocation, the corridors, the courtyard are crowded.

They are all there, loud-voiced friends and silent enemies. Robespierre reads them the speech the Convention had heard in affrighted silence, and the Jacobins greet it with excited applause.

"It is my dying testament," declares the orator. "You will see me drain the hemlock undismayed."

"I will drink it with you," answered David.

"All, we all will!" shout the Jacobins, and separate without deciding anything.

Évariste, while the death of *The Just* was preparing, slept the sleep of the Disciples in the garden of Gethsemane. Next day, he attended the Tribunal where two sections were sitting. That on which he served was trying twenty-one persons implicated in the conspiracy of the Lazare prison. The case was still proceeding when the tidings arrived:

"The Convention, after a six-hours' session, has decreed Maximilien Robespierre accused,—with him Couthon and Saint-Just; add Augustin Robespierre, and Lebas, who have demanded to share the lot of the accused. The five outlaws stand at the bar of the house."

News is brought that the President of the Section sitting in the next court, the *citoyen* Dumas, has been arrested on the bench, but that the case goes on. Drums can be heard beating the alarm, and the tocsin peals from the churches.

Évariste is still in his place when he is handed an order from the Commune to proceed to the Hôtel de Ville to sit in the General Council. To the sound of the rolling drums and clanging church bells, he and his colleagues record their verdict; then he hurries home to embrace his mother and snatch up his scarf of office. The Place de Thionville is deserted. The Section is afraid to declare either for or against the Convention. Wayfarers creep along under the walls, slip down side-streets, sneak indoors. The call of the tocsin and alarm-drums is answered by the noise of barring shutters and bolting doors. The *citoyen* Dupont senior has secreted himself in his shop; Remacle the porter is barricaded in his lodge. Little Joséphine holds Mouton tremblingly in her arms. The widow Gamelin bemoans the dearness of victuals, cause of all the trouble. At the foot of the stairs Évariste encounters Élodie; she is panting for breath and her black locks are plastered on her hot cheek.

"I have been to look for you at the Tribunal; but you had just left. Where are you going?"

"To the Hôtel de Ville."

"Don't go there! It would be your ruin; Hanriot is arrested . . . the Sections will not stir. The *Section des Piques,* Robespierre's

Section, will do nothing, I know it for a fact; my father belongs to it. If you go to the Hôtel de Ville, you are throwing away your life for nothing."

"You wish me to be a coward?"

"No! the brave thing is to be faithful to the Convention and to obey the Law."

"The law is dead when malefactors triumph."

"Évariste, hear me; hear your Élodie; hear your sister. Come and sit beside her and let her soothe your angry spirit."

He looked at her; never had she seemed so desirable in his eyes; never had her voice sounded so seductive, so persuasive in his ears.

"A couple of paces, only a couple of paces, dear Évariste!"—and she drew him towards the raised platform on which stood the pedestal of the overthrown statue. It was surrounded by benches occupied by strollers of both sexes. A dealer in fancy articles was offering his laces, a seller of cooling drinks, his portable cistern on his back, was tinkling his bell; little girls were showing off their airs and graces. The parapet was lined with anglers, standing, rod in hand, very still. The weather was stormy, the sky overcast. Gamelin leant on the low wall and looked down on the islet below, pointed like the prow of a ship, listening to the wind whistling in the tree-tops, and feeling his soul penetrated with an infinite longing for peace and solitude.

Like a sweet echo of his thoughts, Élodie's voice sighed in his ear:

"Do you remember, Évariste, how, at sight of the green fields, you wanted to be a country justice in a village? Yes, that would be happiness."

But above the rustling of the trees and the girl's voice, he could hear the tocsin and alarm-drums, the distant tramp of horses, and rumbling of cannon along the streets.

Two steps from them a young man, who was talking to an elegantly attired *citoyenne,* remarked:

"Have you heard the latest? . . . The Opera is installed in the Rue de la Loi."

Meantime the news was spreading; Robespierre's name was spoken, but in a shuddering whisper, for men feared him still. Women, when they heard the muttered rumour of his fall, concealed a smile.

Évariste Gamelin seized Élodie's hand, but dropped it again swiftly next moment:

"Farewell! I have involved you in my hideous fortunes, I have blasted your life for ever. Farewell! I pray you may forget me!"

"Whatever you do," she warned him, "do not go back home to-night. Come to the *Amour peintre.* Do not ring; throw a pebble at my shutters. I will come and open the door to you myself; I will hide you in the loft."

"You shall see me return triumphant, or you shall never see me more. Farewell!"

On nearing the Hôtel de Ville, he caught the well-remembered roar of the old great days rising to the grey heavens. In the Place de Grève a clash of arms, the glitter of scarfs and uniforms, Hanriot's cannon drawn up. He mounts the grand stairs and, entering the Council Hall, signs the attendance book. The Council General of the Commune, by the unanimous voice of the 491 members present, declares for the outlawed patriots.

The Mayor sends for the Table of the Rights of Man, reads the clause which runs, "When the Government violates the Rights of the people, insurrection is for the people the most sacred and the most indispensable of duties," and the first magistrate of Paris announces that the Commune's answer to the Convention's act of violence is to raise the populace in insurrection.

The members of the Council General take oath to die at their posts. Two municipal officers are deputed to go out on the Place de Grève and invite the people to join with their magistrates in saving the fatherland and freedom.

There is an endless looking for friends, exchanging news, giving advice. Among these Magistrates, artisans are the exception. The Commune assembled here is such as the Jacobin purge has made it, —judges and jurors of the Revolutionary Tribunal, artists like Beauvallet and Gamelin, householders living on their means and college profesors, cosy citizens, well-to-do tradesmen, powdered heads, fat paunches, and gold watch-chains, very few sabots, striped trousers, carmagnole smocks and red caps.

These bourgeois councillors are numerous and determined, but, when all is said, they are pretty well all Paris possesses of true Republicans. They stand on guard in the city mansion-house, as on a rock of liberty, but an ocean of indifference washes round their refuge.

However, good news arrives. All the prisons where the proscribed had been confined open their doors and disgorge their prey. Augustin Robespierre, coming from La Force, is the first to enter the Hôtel de Ville and is welcomed with acclamation.

At eight o'clock it is announced that Maximilien, after a protracted resistance, is on his way to the Commune. He is eagerly expected; he is coming; he is here; a roar of triumph shakes the vault of the old Municipal Palace.

He enters, supported by twenty arms. It is he, the little man there, slim, spruce, in blue coat and yellow breeches. He takes his seat; he speaks.

At his arrival the Council orders the façade of the Hôtel de Ville to be illuminated there and then. It is there the Republic resides. He speaks in a thin voice, in picked phrases. He speaks lucidly, copiously. His hearers who have staked their lives on his head, see the naked truth, see it to their horror. He is a man of words, a man of committees, a wind-bag incapable of prompt action, incompetent to lead a Revolution.

They draw him into the Hall of Deliberation. Now they are all there, these illustrious outlaws,—Lebas, Saint-Just, Couthon. Robespierre has the word. It is midnight and past, he is still speaking. Meantime Gamelin in the Council Hall, his bent brow pressed against a window, looks out with a haggard eye and sees the lamps flare and smoke in the gloom. Hanriot's cannon are parked before the Hôtel de Ville. In the black Place de Grève surges an anxious crowd, in uncertainty and suspense. At half past twelve torches are seen turning the corner of the Rue de la Vannerie, escorting a delegate of the Convention, clad in the insignia of office, who unfolds a paper and reads by the ruddy light the decree of the Convention, the outlawry of the members of the insurgent Commune, of the members of the Council General who are its abettors and of all such citizens as shall listen to its appeal.

Outlawry, death without trial! The mere thought pales the cheek of the most determined. Gamelin feels the icy sweat on his brow. He watches the crowd hurrying with all speed from the Place. Turning his head, he finds that the Hall, packed but now with Councillors, is almost empty. But they have fled in vain; their signatures attest their attendance.

It is two in the morning. The Incorruptible is in the neighbouring Hall, in deliberation with the Commune and the proscribed representatives.

Gamelin casts a despairing look over the dark Square below. By the light of the lanterns he can see the wooden candles above the grocer's shop knocking together like ninepins; the street lamps shiver and swing; a high wind has sprung up. Next moment a deluge of rain comes down; the Place empties entirely; such as the fear of the Convention and its dread decree had not put to flight scatter in terror of a wetting. Hanriot's guns are abandoned, and when the lightning reveals the troops of the Convention debouching simultaneously from the Rue Antoine and from the Quai, the approaches to the Hôtel de Ville are utterly deserted.

At last Maximilien has resolved to make appeal from the decree of the Convention to his own Section,—the *Section des Piques.*

The Council General sends for swords, pistols, muskets. But now the clash of arms, the trampling of feet and shiver of broken glass fill the building. The troops of the Convention sweep by like an avalanche across the Hall of Deliberation, and pour into the Council Chamber. A shot rings out; Gamelin sees Robespierre fall; his jaw is broken. He himself grasps his knife, the six-sous knife that, one day of bitter scarcity, had cut bread for a starving mother, the same knife that, one summer evening at a farm at Orangis, Élodie had held in her lap, when she cried the forfeits. He opens it, tries to plunge it into his heart, but the blade strikes on a rib, closes on the handle, the catch giving away, and two fingers are badly cut. Gamelin falls, the blood pouring from the wounds. He lies quite still, but the cold is cruel, and he is trampled underfoot in the turmoil of a fearful struggle. Through the hurly-burly he can distinctly hear the voice of the young dragoon Henry, shouting:

"The tyrant is no more; his myrmidons are broken. The Revolution will resume its course, majestic and terrible."

Gamelin fainted.

At seven in the morning a surgeon sent by the Convention dressed his hurts. The Convention was full of solicitude for Robespierre's accomplices; it would fain not have one of them escape the guillotine.

The artist, ex-juror, ex-member of the Council General of the Commune, was borne on a litter to the Conciergerie.

XXVIII

ON THE 10th, when Évariste, after a fevered night passed on the pallet-bed of a dungeon, awoke with a start of indescribable horror, Paris was smiling in the sunshine in all her beauty and immensity; new-born hope filled the prisoners' hearts; tradesmen were blithely opening their shops, citizens felt themselves richer, young men happier, women more beautiful, for the fall of Robespierre. Only a handful of Jacobins, a few *Constitutional* priests and a few old women trembled to see the Government pass into the hands of the evil-minded and corrupt. Delegates from the Revolutionary Tribunal, the Public Prosecutor and two judges, were on their way to the Convention to congratulate it on having put an end to the plots. By decree of the Assembly the scaffold was again to be set up in the Place de la Révolution. They wanted the wealthy, the fashionable, the pretty women to see, without putting themselves about, the execution of Robespierre, which was to take place that same day. The Dictator and his accomplices were outlawed; it only needed their identity to be verified by two municipal officers for the Tribunal to hand them over immediately to the executioner. But a difficulty arose; the verifications could not be made in legal form, the Commune as a body having been put outside the pale of law. The Assembly authorized identification by ordinary witnesses.

The triumvirs were haled to death, with their chief accomplices, amidst shouts of joy and fury, imprecations, laughter and dances.

The next day Évariste, who had recovered some strength and could almost stand on his legs, was taken from his cell, brought before the Tribunal, and placed on the platform where so many victims, illustrious or obscure, had sat in succession. Now it groaned under the weight of seventy individuals, the majority members of the Commune, some jurors, like Gamelin, outlawed like him. Again he saw the jury-bench, the seat where he had been accustomed to loll, the place where he had terrorized unhappy prisoners, where he had affronted the scornful eyes of Jacques Maubel and Maurice Brotteaux, the appealing glances of the *citoyenne* Rochemaure, who had got him his post as juryman and whom he had recompensed with a sentence of death. Again he saw, looking down on the daïs where the judges sat in three mahogany armchairs, covered in red Utrecht velvet, the busts of Chalier and Marat and that bust of Brutus which he had one day apostrophized. Nothing was altered, neither the axes, the fasces, the red caps of Liberty on the wall-paper, nor the insults shouted by the *tricoteuses* in the galleries to those about to die, nor yet the soul of Fouquier-Tinville, hard-headed, painstaking, zealously turning over his murderous papers, and, in his character of perfect magistrate, sending his friends of yesterday to the scaffold.

The *citoyens* Remacle, tailor and door-keeper, and Dupont senior, joiner, of the Place de Thionville, member of the Committee of Surveillance of the Section du Pont-Neuf, identified Gamelin (Évariste), painter, ex-juror of the Revolutionary Tribunal, ex-member of the Council General of the Commune. For their services they received an assignat of a hundred *sols* from the funds of the Section; but, having been neighbours and friends of the outlaw, they found it embarrassing to meet his eye. Anyhow, it was a hot day; they were thirsty and in a hurry to be off and drink a glass of wine.

Gamelin found difficulty in mounting the tumbril; he had lost a great deal of blood and his wounds pained him cruelly. The driver whipped up his jade and the procession got under way amid a storm of hooting.

Some women recognized Gamelin and yelled:

"Go your ways, drinker of blood! murderer at eighteen francs a day! . . . He doesn't laugh now; look how pale he is, the coward!"

They were the same women who used in other days to insult conspirators and aristocrats, extremists and moderates, all the victims sent by Gamelin and his colleagues to the guillotine.

The cart turned into the Quai des Morfondus, made slowly for the Pont-Neuf and the Rue de la Monnaie; its destination was the Place de la Révolution and Robespierre's scaffold. The horse was lame; every other minute the driver's whip whistled about its ears. The crowd of spectators, a merry, excited crowd, delayed the progress of the escort, fraternizing with the gendarmes, who pulled in their horses to a walk. At the corner of the Rue Honoré, the insults were redoubled. Parties of young men, at table in the fashionable restaurateurs' rooms on the mezzanine floor, ran to the windows, napkin in hand, and howled:

"Cannibals, man-eaters, vampires!"

The cart having plunged into a heap of refuse that had not been removed during the two days of civil disorder, the gilded youth screamed with delight:

"The waggon's mired. . . . Hurrah! The Jacobins in the jakes!"

Gamelin was thinking, and truth seemed to dawn on him.

"I die justly," he reflected. "It is just we should receive these outrages cast at the Republic, for we should have safeguarded her against them. We have been weak; we have been guilty of supineness. We have betrayed the Republic. We have earned our fate. Robespierre himself, the immaculate, the saint, has sinned from mildness, mercifulness, his faults are wiped out by his martyrdom. He was my exemplar, and I, too, have betrayed the Republic; the Republic perishes; it is just and fair that I die with her. I have been over sparing of blood; let my blood flow! Let me perish! I have deserved . . ."

Such were his reflections when suddenly he caught sight of the signboard of the *Amour peintre,* and a torrent of bitter-sweet emotions swept tumultuously over his heart.

The shop was shut, the sun-blinds of the three windows on the mezzanine floor were drawn right down. As the cart passed in front of the window of the blue chamber, a woman's hand, wearing a silver ring on the ring-finger, pushed aside the edge of the blind and threw towards Gamelin a red carnation which his bound hands prevented him from catching, but which he adored as the token and likeness of those red and fragrant lips that had refreshed his mouth. His eyes filled with bursting tears, and his whole being was still entranced with the glamour of this farewell when he saw the bloodstained knife rise into view in the Place de la Révolution.

XXIX

IT was Nivôse. Masses of floating ice encumbered the Seine; the basins in the Tuileries garden, the kennels, the public fountains were frozen. The North wind swept clouds of hoar frost before it in the streets. A white steam breathed from the horses' noses, and the city folk would glance in passing at the thermometer at the opticians' doors. A shop-boy was wiping the fog from the window-panes of the *Amour peintre,* while curious passers-by threw a look at the prints in vogue,—Robespierre squeezing into a cup a heart like a pumpkin to drink the blood, and ambitious allegorical designs with such titles as the Tigrocracy of Robespierre; it was all hydras, serpents, horrid monsters let loose on France by the tyrant. Other pictures represented the Horrible Conspiracy of Robespierre, Robespierre's Arrest, The Death of Robespierre.

That day, after the midday dinner, Philippe Desmahis walked into the *Amour peintre,* his portfolio under his arm, and brought the *citoyen* Jean Blaise a plate he had just finished, a stippled engraving of the Suicide of Robespierre. The artist's picaresque burin had made Robespierre as hideous as possible. The French people were not yet satiated with all the memorials which enshrined the horror and opprobrium felt for the man who was made the scapegoat of all the crimes of the Revolution. For all that, the printseller, who knew his public, informed Desmahis that henceforward he was going to give him military subjects to engrave.

"We shall all be wanting victories and conquests,—swords, waving plumes, triumphant generals. Glory is to be the word. I feel it in me; my heart beats high to hear the exploits of our valiant armies. And when I have a feeling, it is seldom all the world doesn't have the same feeling at the same time. What we want is warriors and women, Mars and Venus."

"*Citoyen* Blaise, I have still two or three drawings of Gamelin's by me, which you gave me to engrave. Is it urgent?"

"Not a bit."

"By-the-bye, about Gamelin; yesterday, strolling in the Boulevard du Temple, I saw at a dealer's, who keeps a second-hand stall opposite the House of Beaumarchais, all that poor devil's canvases, amongst the rest his *Orestes and Electra.* The head of Orestes, who's like Gamelin, is really fine, I assure you. . . . The head and arm are superb. . . . The man told me he found no difficulty in getting rid of these canvases to artists who want to paint over them. . . . Poor Gamelin! He might have been a genius of the first order, perhaps, if he hadn't taken to politics."

"He had the soul of a criminal!" replied the *citoyen* Blaise. "I unmasked him, on this very spot, when his sanguinary instincts were still held in check. He never forgave me. . . . Oh! he was a choice blackguard."

"Poor fellow! he was sincere enough. It was the fanatics were his ruin."

"You don't defend him, I presume, Desmahis! . . . There's no defending him."

"No, *citoyen* Blaise, there's no defending him."

The *citoyen* Blaise tapped the gallant Desmahis' shoulder amicably, and observed:

"Times are changed. We can call you *Barbaroux* now the Convention is recalling the proscribed. . . . Now I think of it, Desmahis, engrave me a portrait of Charlotte Corday, will you?"

A woman, a tall, handsome brunette, enveloped in furs, entered the shop and bestowed on the *citoyen* Blaise a little discreet nod that implied intimacy. It was Julie Gamelin; but she no longer bore that dishonoured name, she preferred to be called the *citoyenne* widow Chassagne, and wore, under her mantle, a red tunic in honour of the red shirts of the terror. Julie had at first felt a certain repulsion towards Évariste's mistress; anything that had come near her brother was odious to her. But the *citoyenne* Blaise, after Évariste's death, had found an asylum for the unhappy mother in the attics of the *Amour peintre*. Julie had also taken refuge there; then she had got employment again at the fashionable milliner's in the Rue des Lombards. Her short hair *à la victime,* her aristocratic looks, her mourning weeds had won the sympathies of the gilded youth. Jean Blaise, whom Rose Thévenin had pretty well thrown over, offered her his homage, which she accepted. Still Julie was fond of wearing men's clothes, as in the old tragic days; she had a fine *Muscadin* costume made for her and often went, huge bâton and all complete, to sup at some tavern at Sèvres or Meudon with a girl friend, a little assistant in a fashion shop. Inconsolable for the loss of the young noble whose name she bore, this masculine-minded Julie found the only solace to her melancholy in a savage rancour; every time she encountered Jacobins, she would set the passers-by on them, crying "Death, death!" She had small leisure left to give to her mother, who alone in her room told her beads all day, too deeply shocked at her boy's tragic death to feel the grief that might have been expected. Rose was now the constant companion of Élodie who certainly got on amicably with her step-mothers.

"Where is Élodie?" asked the *citoyenne* Chassagne.

Jean Blaise shook his head; he did not know. He never did know; he made it a point of honour not to.

Julie had come to take her friend with her to see Rose Thévenin at Monceaux, where the actress lived in a little house with an English garden.

At the Conciergerie Rose Thévenin had made the acquaintance of a big army-contractor, the *citoyen* Montfort. She had been released first, by Jean Blaise's intervention, and had then procured the *citoyen* Montfort's pardon, who was no sooner at liberty than he started his old trade of provisioning the troops, to which he added speculation in building-lots in the Pépinière quarter. The architects Ledoux, Olivier and Wailly were erecting pretty houses in that district, and in three months the land had trebled in value. Montfort, since their imprisonment together in the Luxembourg, had been Rose Thévenin's lover; he now gave her a little house in the neighbourhood of Tivoli and the Rue du Rocher, which was very expensive,—and cost him nothing, the sale of the adjacent properties having already repaid him several times over. Jean Blaise was a man of the world, so he deemed it best to put up with what he could not hinder; he gave up Mademoiselle Thévenin to Montfort without ceasing to be on friendly terms with her.

Julie had not been long at the *Amour peintre* before Élodie came down to her in the shop, looking like a fashion plate. Under her mantle, despite the rigours of the season, she wore nothing but her white frock; her face was even paler than of old, and her figure thinner; her looks were languishing, and her whole person breathed voluptuous invitation.

The two women set off for Rose Thévenin's, who was expecting them. Desmahis accompanied them; the actress was consulting him about the decoration of her new house and he was in love with Élodie, who had by this time half made up her mind to let him sigh no more in vain. When the party came near Monceaux, where the victims of the Place de la Révolution lay buried under a layer of lime:

"It is all very well in the cold weather," remarked Julie; "but in the spring the exhalations from the ground there will poison half the town."

Rose Thévenin received her two friends in a drawing-room furnished *à l'antique,* the sofas and arm-chairs of which were designed by David. Roman bas-reliefs, copied in monochrome, adorned the walls above statues, busts and candelabra of imitation bronze. She wore a curled wig of straw colour. At that date wigs were all the rage; it was quite common to include half a dozen, a dozen, a dozen and a half in a bride's trousseau. A gown *à la Cyprienne* moulded her body like a sheath. Throwing a cloak over her shoulders, she led her two friends and the engraver into the garden, which Ledoux was laying out for her, but which as yet was a chaos of leafless trees and plaster. She showed them, however, Fingal's grotto, a gothic chapel with a bell, a temple, a torrent.

"There," she said, pointing to a clump of firs, "I should like to raise a cenotaph to the memory of the unfortunate Brotteaux des Ilettes. I was not indifferent to him; he was a lovable man. The monsters slaughtered him; I bewailed his fate. Desmahis, you shall design me an urn on a column."

Then she added almost without a pause:

"It is heart-breaking. . . . I wanted to give a ball this week; but all the fiddles are engaged three weeks in advance. There is dancing every night at the *citoyenne* Tallien's."

After dinner Mademoiselle Thévenin's carriage took the three friends and Desmahis to the Théâtre Feydeau. All that was most elegant in Paris was gathered in the house—the women with hair dressed *à l'antique* or *à la victime,* in very low dresses, purple or white and spangled with gold, the men wearing very tall black collars and the chin disappearing in enormous white cravats.

The bill announced *Phèdre* and the *Chien du Jardinier,*—The Gardener's Dog. With one voice the audience demanded the hymn dear to the *muscadins* and the gilded youth, the *Réveil du peuple,*—The Awakening of the People.

The curtain rose and a little man, short and fat, took the stage; it was the celebrated Lays. He sang in his fine tenor voice:

Peuple français, peuple de frères! . . .

Such storms of applause broke out as set the lustres of the chandelier jingling. Then some murmurs made themselves heard, and the voice of a citizen in a round hat answered from the pit with the hymn of the Marseillaise:

Allons, enfants de la patrie. . . .

The voice was drowned by howls, and shouts were raised:

"Down with the Terrorists! Death to the Jacobins!"

Lays was recalled and sang a second time over the hymn of the Thermidorians.

Peuple français, peuple de frères! . . .

In every play-house was to be seen the bust of Marat, surmounting a column or raised on a pedestal; at the Théâtre Feydeau this bust stood on a dwarf pillar on the "prompt" side, against the masonry-framing in the stage.

While the orchestra was playing the Overture of *Phèdre et Hippolyte,* a young *Muscadin,* pointing his cane at the bust, shouted:

"Down with Marat!"—and the whole house took up the cry: "Down with Marat! Down with Marat!"

Urgent voices rose above the uproar:

"It is a black shame that bust should still be there!"

"The infamous Marat lords it everywhere, to our dishonour! His busts are as many as the heads he wanted to cut off."

"Venomous toad!"

"Tiger!"

"Vile serpent!"

Suddenly an elegantly dressed spectator clambers on to the edge of his box, pushes the bust, oversets it. The plaster head falls in shivers on the musicians' heads amid the cheers of the audience, who spring to their feet and strike up the *Réveil du Peuple:*

Peuple français, peuple de frères! . . .

Among the most enthusiastic singers Élodie recognized the handsome dragoon, the little lawyer's clerk, Henry, her first love.

After the performance the gallant Desmahis called a cabriolet and escorted the *citoyenne* Blaise back to the *Amour peintre.*

In the carriage the artist took Élodie's hand between his:

"You know, Élodie, I love you?"

"I know it, because you love all women."

"I love them in you."

She smiled:

"I should be assuming a heavy task, spite of the wigs black, blonde and red, that are the rage, if I undertook to be all women, all sorts of women, for you."

"Élodie, I swear. . . ."

"What! oaths, *citoyen* Desmahis? Either you have a deal of simplicity, or you credit me with overmuch."

Desmahis had not a word to say, and she hugged herself over the triumph of having reduced her witty admirer to silence.

At the corner of the Rue de la Loi they heard singing and shouting and saw shadows flitting round a brazier of live coals. It was a band of young bloods who had just come out of the Théâtre Français and were burning a guy representing the Friend of the People.

In the Rue Honoré the coachman struck his cocked hat against a burlesque effigy of Marat swinging from the cord of a street lantern.

The fellow, heartened by the incident, turned round to his fares and told them how, only last night, the tripe-seller in the Rue Montorgueil had smeared blood over Marat's head, declaring: "That's the stuff he liked," and how some little scamps of ten had thrown the bust into the sewer, and how the spectators had hit the nail on the head, shouting:

"That's the Panthéon for him!"

Meanwhile, from every eating-house and restaurateur's voices could be heard singing:

Peuple français, peuple de frères! . . .

"Good-bye," said Élodie, jumping out of the cabriolet.

But Desmahis begged so hard, he was so tenderly urgent and spoke so sweetly, that she had not the heart to leave him at the door.

"It is late," she said; "you must only stay an instant."

In the blue chamber she threw off her mantle and appeared in her white gown *à l'antique*, which displayed all the warm fulness of her shape.

"You are cold, perhaps," she said, "I will light the fire; it is already laid."

She struck the flint and put a lighted match to the fire.

Philippe took her in his arms with the gentleness that bespeaks strength, and she felt a strange, delicious thrill. She was already yielding beneath his kisses when she snatched herself from his arms, crying:

"Let me be."

Slowly she uncoiled her hair before the chimney-glass; then she looked mournfully at the ring she wore on the ring-finger of her left hand, a little silver ring on which the face of Marat, all worn and battered, could no longer be made out. She looked at it till the tears confused her sight, took it off softly and tossed it into the flames.

Then, her face shining with tears and smiles, transfigured with tenderness and passion, she threw herself into Philippe's arms.

The night was far advanced when the *citoyenne* Blaise opened the outer door of the flat for her lover and whispered to him in the darkness:

"Good-bye, sweetheart! It is the hour my father will be coming home. If you hear a noise on the stairs, go up quick to the higher floor and don't come down till all danger is over of your being seen. To have the street-door opened, give three raps on the *concierge's* window. Good-bye, my life, good-bye, my soul!"

The last dying embers were glowing on the hearth when Élodie, tired and happy, dropped her head on the pillow.

THAÏS

PART THE FIRST

THE LOTUS

I N THOSE DAYS there were many hermits living in the desert. On both banks of the Nile numerous huts, built by these solitary dwellers, of branches held together by clay, were scattered at a little distance from each other, so that the inhabitants could live alone, and yet help one another in case of need. Churches, each surmounted by a cross, stood here and there amongst the huts, and the monks flocked to them at each festival to celebrate the services or to partake of the Communion. There were also, here and there on the banks of the river, monasteries, where the cenobites lived in separate cells, and only met together that they might the better enjoy their solitude.

Both hermits and cenobites led abstemious lives, taking no food till after sunset, and eating nothing but bread with a little salt and hyssop. Some retired into the desert, and led a still more strange life in some cave or tomb.

All lived in temperance and chastity; they wore a hair shirt and a hood, slept on the bare ground after long watching, prayed, sang psalms, and, in short, spent their days in works of penitence. As an atonement for original sin, they refused their body not only all pleasures and satisfactions, but even that care and attention which in this age are deemed indispensable. They believed that the diseases of our members purify our souls, and the flesh could put on no adornment more glorious than wounds and ulcers. Thus, they thought they fulfilled the words of the prophet, "The desert shall rejoice and blossom as the rose."

Amongst the inhabitants of the holy Thebaid, there were some who passed their days in asceticism and contemplation; others gained their livelihood by plaiting palm fibre, or by working at harvest-time for the neighbouring farmers. The Gentiles wrongly suspected some of them of living by brigandage, and allying themselves to the nomadic Arabs who robbed the caravans. But, as a

matter of fact, the monks despised riches, and the odour of their
sanctity rose to heaven.

Angels in the likeness of young men, came, staff in hand, as
travellers, to visit the hermitages; whilst demons—having assumed
the form of Ethiopians or of animals—wandered round the habitations of the hermits in order to lead them into temptation. When
the monks went in the morning to fill their pitcher at the spring,
they saw the footprints of Satyrs and Aigipans in the sand. The
Thebaid was, really and spiritually, a battlefield, where, at all
times, and more especially at night, there were terrible conflicts
between heaven and hell.

The ascetics, furiously assailed by legions of the damned, defended themselves—with the help of God and the angels—by fasting, prayer, and penance. Sometimes carnal desires pricked them
so cruelly that they cried aloud with pain, and their lamentations
rose to the starlit heavens mingled with the howls of the hungry
hyænas. Then it was that the demons appeared in delightful forms.
For though the demons are, in reality, hideous, they sometimes
assume an appearance of beauty which prevents their real nature
from being recognised. The ascetics of the Thebaid were amazed to
see in their cells phantasms of delights unknown even to the voluptuaries of the age. But, as they were under the sign of the Cross,
they did not succumb to these temptations, and the unclean spirits,
assuming again their true character, fled at daybreak, filled with
rage and shame. It was not unusual to meet at dawn one of these
beings, flying away and weeping, and replying to those who questioned it, "I weep and groan because one of the Christians who live
here has beaten me with rods, and driven me away in ignominy."

The power of the old saints of the desert extended over all sinners and unbelievers. Their goodness was sometimes terrible. They
derived from the Apostles authority to punish all offences against
the true and only God, and no earthly power could save those they
condemned. Strange tales were told in the cities, and even as far as
Alexandria, how the earth had opened and swallowed up certain
wicked persons whom one of these saints struck with his staff.
Therefore they were feared by all evil-doers, and particularly by
mimes, mountebanks, married priests, and prostitutes.

Such was the sanctity of these holy men that even wild beasts
felt their power. When a hermit was about to die, a lion came and
dug a grave with its claws. The saint knew by this that God had
called him, and he went and kissed all his brethren on the cheek.
Then he lay down joyfully, and slept in the Lord.

Now that Anthony, who was more than a hundred years old, had
retired to Mount Colzin with his well-beloved disciples, Macarius
and Amathas, there was no monk in the Thebaid more renowned
for good works than Paphnutius, the Abbot of Antinoë. Ephrem
and Serapion had a greater number of followers, and in the

spiritual and temporal management of their monasteries surpassed him. But Paphnutius observed the most rigorous fasts, and often went for three entire days without taking food. He wore a very rough hair shirt, he flogged himself night and morning, and lay for hours with his face to the earth.

His twenty-four disciples had built their huts near his, and imitated his austerities. He loved them all dearly in Jesus Christ, and unceasingly exhorted them to good works. Amongst his spiritual children were men who had been robbers for many years, and had been persuaded by the exhortations of the holy abbot to embrace the monastic life, and who now edified their companions by the purity of their lives. One, who had been cook to the Queen of Abyssinia, and was converted by the Abbot of Antinoë, never ceased to weep. There was also Flavian, the deacon, who knew the Scriptures, and spoke well; but the disciple of Paphnutius who surpassed all the others in holiness was a young peasant named Paul, and surnamed the Fool, because of his extreme simplicity. Men laughed at his childishness, but God favoured him with visions, and by bestowing upon him the gift of prophecy.

Paphnutius passed his life in teaching his disciples, and in ascetic practices. Often did he meditate upon the Holy Scriptures in order to find allegories in them. Therefore he abounded in good works, though still young. The devils, who so rudely assailed the good hermits, did not dare to approach him. At night, seven little jackals sat in the moonlight in front of his cell, silent and motionless, and with their ears pricked up. It was believed that they were seven devils, who, owing to his sanctity, could not cross his threshold.

Paphnutius was born at Alexandria of noble parents, who had instructed him in all profane learning. He had even been allured by the falsehoods of the poets, and in his early youth had been misguided enough to believe that the human race had all been drowned by a deluge in the days of Deucalion, and had argued with his fellow-scholars concerning the nature, the attributes, and even the existence of God. He then led a life of dissipation, after the manner of the Gentiles, and he recalled the memory of those days with shame and horror.

"At that time," he used to say to the brethren, "I seethed in the cauldron of false delights."

He meant by that that he had eaten food properly dressed, and frequented the public baths. In fact, until his twentieth year he had continued to lead the ordinary existence of those times, which now seemed to him rather death than life; but, owing to the lessons of the priest Macrinus, he then became a new man.

The truth penetrated him through and through, and—as he used to say—entered his soul like a sword. He embraced the faith of Calvary, and worshipped Christ crucified. After his baptism he remained yet a year amongst the Gentiles, unable to cast off the bonds of old habits. But one day he entered a church, and heard a deacon read from the Bible, the verse, "If thou wilt be perfect, go and sell that thou hast, and give to the poor." Thereupon he sold all that he had, gave away the money in alms, and embraced the monastic life.

During the ten years that he had lived remote from men, he no longer seethed in the cauldron of false delights, but more profitably macerated his flesh in the balms of penitence.

One day when, according to his pious custom, he was recalling to mind the hours he had lived apart from God, and examining his sins one by one, that he might the better ponder on their enormity, he remembered that he had seen at the theatre at Alexandria a very beautiful actress named Thaïs. This woman showed herself in the public games, and did not scruple to perform dances, the movements of which, arranged only too cleverly, brought to mind the most horrible passions. Sometimes she imitated the horrible deeds which the Pagan fables ascribe to Venus, Leda, or Pasiphaë. Thus she fired all the spectators with lust, and when handsome young men, or rich old ones, came, inspired with love, to hang wreaths of flowers round her door, she welcomed them, and gave herself up to them. So that, whilst she lost her own soul, she also ruined the souls of many others.

She had almost led Paphnutius himself into the sins of the flesh. She had awakened desire in him, and he had once approached the house of Thaïs. But he stopped on the threshold of the courtesan's house, partly restrained by the natural timidity of extreme youth —he was then but fifteen years old—and partly by the fear of being refused on account of his want of money, for his parents took care that he should commit no great extravagances.

God, in His mercy, had used these two means to prevent him from committing a great sin. But Paphnutius had not been grateful to Him for that, because at that time he was blind to his own interests, and did not know that he was lusting after false delights. Now, kneeling in his cell, before the image of that holy cross on which hung, as in a balance, the ransom of the world, Paphnutius began to think of Thaïs, because Thaïs was a sin to him, and he meditated long, according to ascetic rules, on the fearful hideousness of the carnal delights with which this woman had inspired him in the days of his sin and ignorance. After some hours of meditation the image of Thaïs appeared to him clearly and distinctly. He saw her again, as he had seen her when she tempted him, in all the beauty of the flesh. At first she showed herself like a Leda, softly lying upon a bed of hyacinths, her head bowed, her eyes humid and filled with a strange light, her nostrils quivering, her mouth half open, her breasts like two flowers, and her arms smooth and fresh as two brooks. At this sight Paphnutius struck his breast and said—

"I call Thee to witness, my God, that I have considered how heinous has been my sin."

Gradually the face of the image changed its expression. Little by little the lips of Thaïs, by lowering at the corners of the mouth, expressed a mysterious suffering. Her large eyes were filled with tears and lights; her breast heaved with sighs, like the sighing of a wind that precedes a tempest. At this sight Paphnutius was troubled to the bottom of his soul. Prostrating himself on the floor, he uttered this prayer—

"Thou who hast but pity in our hearts, like the morning dew upon the fields, O just and merciful God, be Thou blessed! Praise! praise be unto Thee! Put away from Thy servant that false tenderness which tempts to concupiscence, and grant that I may only love Thy creatures in Thee, for they pass away, but Thou endurest for ever. If I care for this woman, it is only because she is Thy handiwork. The angels themselves feel pity for her. Is she not, O Lord, the breath of Thy mouth? Let her not continue to sin with many citizens and strangers. There is great pity for her in my heart. Her wickednesses are abominable, and but to think of them makes my flesh creep. But the more wicked she is, the more do I lament for her. I weep when I think that the devils will torment her to all eternity."

As he was meditating in this way, he saw a little jackal lying at his feet. He felt much surprised, for the door of his cell had been closed since the morning. The animal seemed to read the Abbot's thoughts, and wagged its tail like a dog. Paphnutius made the sign of the cross and the beast vanished. He knew then that, for the first time, the devil had entered his cell, and he uttered a short prayer; then he thought again about Thaïs.

"With God's help," he said to himself, "I must save her." And he slept.

The next morning, when he had said his prayers, he went to see the sainted Palemon, a holy hermit who lived some distance away. He found him smiling quietly as he dug the ground, as was his custom. Palemon was an old man, and cultivated a little garden; the wild beasts came and licked his hands, and the devils never tormented him.

"May God be praised, brother Paphnutius," he said, as he leaned upon his spade.

"God be praised!" replied Paphnutius. "And peace be unto my brother."

"The like peace be unto thee, brother Paphnutius," said Palemon; and he wiped the sweat from his forehead with his sleeve.

"Brother Palemon, all our discourse ought to be solely the praise of Him who has promised to be wheresoever two or three are gathered together in His Name. That is why I come to you concerning a design I have formed to glorify the Lord."

"May the Lord bless thy design, Paphnutius, as He has blessed my lettuces. Every morning He spreads His grace with the dew on my garden, and His goodness causes me to glorify Him in the cucumbers and melons which He gives me. Let us pray that He may keep us in His peace. For nothing is more to be feared than those unruly passions which trouble our hearts. When these passions disturb us we are like drunken men, and we stagger from right to left unceasingly, and are like to fall miserably. Sometimes these passions plunge us into a turbulent joy, and he who gives way to such, sullies the air with brutish laughter. Such false joy drags the sinner into all sorts of excess. But sometimes also the troubles of the soul and of the senses throw us into an impious sadness which is a thousand times worse than the joy. Brother Paphnutius, I am but a miserable sinner, but I have found, in my long life, that the cenobite has no foe worse than sadness. I mean by that the obstinate melancholy which envelopes the soul as in a mist, and hides from us the light of God. Nothing is more contrary to salvation, and the devil's greatest triumph is to sow black and bitter thoughts in the heart of a good man. If he sent us only pleasurable temptations, he would not be half so much to be feared. Alas! he excels in making us sad. Did he not show to our father Anthony a black child of such surpassing beauty that the very sight of it drew tears? With God's help, our father Anthony avoided the snares of the demon. I knew him when he lived amongst us; he was cheerful with his disciples, and never gave way to melancholy. But did you not come, my brother, to talk to me of a design you had formed in your mind? Let me know what it is—if, at least, this design has for its object the glory of God."

"Brother Palemon, what I propose is really to the glory of God. Strengthen me with your counsel, for you know many things, and sin has never darkened the clearness of your mind."

"Brother Paphnutius, I am not worthy to unloose the latchet of thy sandals, and my sins are as countless as the sands of the desert. But I am old, and I will never refuse the help of my experience."

"I will confide in you, then, brother Palemon, that I am stricken with grief at the thought that there is, in Alexandria, a courtesan named Thaïs, who lives in sin, and a subject of reproach unto the people."

"Brother Paphnutius, that is, in truth, an abomination which we do well to deplore. There are many women amongst the Gentiles who lead lives of that kind. Have you thought of any remedy for this great evil?"

"Brother Palemon, I will go to Alexandria and find this woman, and, with God's help, I will convert her; that is my intention; do you approve of it, brother?"

"Brother Paphnutius, I am but a miserable sinner, but our father Anthony used to say, 'In whatsoever place thou art, hasten not to leave it to go elsewhere.'"

"Brother Palemon, do you disapprove of my project?"

"Dear Paphnutius, God forbid that I should suspect my brother of bad intentions. But our father Anthony also said, 'Fishes die on dry land, and so is it with those monks who leave their cells and mingle with the men of this world, amongst whom no good thing is to be found.'"

Having thus spoken, the old man pressed his foot on the spade, and began to dig energetically round a fig tree laden with fruit. As he was thus engaged, there was a rustling in the bushes, and an antelope leaped over the hedge which surrounded the garden; it stopped, surprised and frightened, its delicate legs trembling, then ran up to the old man, and laid its pretty head on the breast of its friend.

"God be praised in the gazelle of the desert," said Palemon.

He went to his hut, the light-footed little animal trotting after him, and brought out some black bread, which the antelope ate out of his hand.

Paphnutius remained thoughtful for some time, his eyes fixed upon the stones at his feet. Then he slowly walked back to his cell, pondering on what he had heard. A great struggle was going on in his mind.

"The hermit gives good advice," he said to himself; "the spirit of prudence is in him. And he doubts the wisdom of my intention. Yet it would be cruel to leave Thaïs any longer in the power of the demon who possesses her. May God advise and conduct me."

As he was walking along, he saw a plover, caught in the net that a hunter had laid on the sand, and he knew that it was a hen bird, for he saw the male fly to the net, and tear the meshes one by one with its beak, until it had made an opening by which its mate could escape. The holy man watched this incident, and as, by virtue of his holiness, he easily comprehended the mystic sense of all occurrences, he knew that the captive bird was no other than Thaïs, caught in the snares of sin, and that—like the plover that had cut the hempen threads with its beak—he could, by pronouncing the word of power, break the invisible bonds by which Thaïs was held in sin. Therefore he praised God, and was confirmed in his first resolution. But then seeing the plover caught by the feet, and hampered by the net it had broken, he fell into uncertainty again.

He did not sleep all night, and before dawn he had a vision. Thaïs appeared to him again. There was no expression of guilty pleasure on her face, nor was she dressed according to custom in transparent drapery. She was enveloped in a shroud, which hid even a part of her face, so that the Abbot could see nothing but the two eyes, from which flowed white and heavy tears.

At this sight he began to weep, and believing that this vision came from God, he no longer hesitated. He rose, seized a knotted stick, the symbol of the Christian faith, and left his cell, carefully closing the door, lest the animals of the desert and the birds of the air should enter, and befoul the copy of the Holy Scriptures which stood at the head of his bed. He called Flavian, the deacon, and gave him authority over the other twenty-three disciples during his absence; and then, clad only in a long cassock, he bent his steps towards the Nile, intending to follow the Libyan bank to the city founded by the Macedonian monarch. He walked from dawn to eve, indifferent to fatigue, hunger, and thirst; the sun was already low on the horizon when he saw the dreadful river, the blood-red waters of which rolled between the rocks of gold and fire.

He kept along the shore, begging his bread at the door of solitary huts for the love of God, and joyfully receiving insults, refusals, or threats. He feared neither robbers nor wild beasts, but he took great care to avoid all the towns and villages he came near. He was afraid lest he should see children playing at knuckle-bones before their father's house, or meet, by the side of the well, women in blue smocks, who might put down their pitcher and smile at him. All things are dangerous for the hermit; it is sometimes a danger for him to read in the Scriptures that the Divine Master journeyed from town to town and supped with His disciples. The virtues that the anchorites embroider so carefully on the tissue of faith, are as fragile as they are beautiful; a breath of ordinary life may tarnish their pleasant colours. For that reason, Paphnutius avoided the towns, fearing lest his heart should soften at the sight of his fellow-men.

He journeyed along lonely roads. When evening came, the murmuring of the breeze amidst the tamarisk trees made him shiver, and he pulled his hood over his eyes that he might not see how beautiful all things were. After walking six days, he came to a place called Silsile. There the river runs in a narrow valley, bordered by a double chain of granite mountains. It was there that the Egyptians, in the days when they worshipped demons, carved their idols. Paphnutius saw an enormous sphinx carved in the solid rock. Fearing that it might still possess some diabolical properties, he made the sign of the cross, and pronounced the name of Jesus; he immediately saw a bat fly out of one of the monster's ears, and Paphnutius knew that he had driven out the evil spirits which had been for centuries in the figure. His zeal increased, and picking up a large stone, he threw it in the idol's face. Then the mysterious face of the sphinx expressed such profound sadness that Paphnutius was moved. In fact, the expression of superhuman grief on the stone visage would have touched even the most unfeeling man. Therefore Paphnutius said to the sphinx—

"O monster, be like the satyrs and centaurs our father Anthony saw in the desert, and confess the divinity of Jesus Christ, and I will bless thee in the name of the Father, the Son, and the Holy Ghost."

When he had spoken a rosy light gleamed in the eyes of the sphinx; the heavy eyelids of the monster quivered and the granite lips painfully murmured, as though in echo to the man's voice, the holy name of Jesus Christ; therefore Paphnutius stretched out his right hand, and blessed the sphinx of Silsile.

That being done, he resumed his journey, and the valley having grown wider, he saw the ruins of an immense city. The temples, which still remained standing, were supported by idols which served as columns, and—by the permission of God—these figures with women's heads and cow's horns, threw on Paphnutius a long look which made him turn pale. He walked thus seventeen days, his only food a few raw herbs, and he slept at night in some ruined palace, amongst the wild cats and Pharaoh's rats, with which mingled sometimes, women whose bodies ended in a scaly tail. But Paphnutius knew that these women came from hell, and he drove them away by making the sign of the cross.

On the eighteenth day, he found, far from any village, a wretched hut made of palm leaves, and half buried under the sand which had been driven by the desert wind. He approached it, hoping that the hut was inhabited by some pious anchorite. He saw inside the hovel—for there was no door—a pitcher, a bunch of onions, and a bed of dried leaves.

"This must be the habitation of a hermit," he said to himself. "Hermits are generally to be found near their hut, and I shall not fail to meet this one. I will give him the kiss of peace, even as the holy Anthony did when he came to the hermit Paul, and kissed him three times. We will discourse of things eternal, and perhaps our Lord will send us, by one of His ravens, a crust of bread, which my host will willingly invite me to share with him."

Whilst he was thus speaking to himself, he walked round the hut to see if he could find any one. He had not walked a hundred paces when he saw a man seated, with his legs crossed, by the side of the river. The man was naked; his hair and beard were quite white, and his body redder than brick. Paphnutius felt sure this must be the hermit. He saluted him with the words the monks are accustomed to use when they meet each other.

"Peace be with you, brother! May you some day taste the sweet joys of paradise."

The man did not reply. He remained motionless, and appeared not to have heard. Paphnutius supposed this was due to one of those rhapsodies to which the saints are accustomed. He knelt down, with his hands joined, by the side of the unknown, and remained thus in prayer till sunset. Then, seeing that his companion had not moved, he said to him—

"Father, if you are now out of the ecstasy in which you were lost, give me your blessing in our Lord Jesus Christ."

The other replied without turning his head—

"Stranger, I understand you not, and I know not the Lord Jesus Christ."

"What!" cried Paphnutius. "The prophets have announced Him; legions of martyrs have confessed His name; Cæsar himself has worshipped Him, and, but just now, I made the sphinx of Silsile proclaim His glory. Is it possible that you do not know Him?"

"Friend," replied the other, "it is possible. It would even be certain, if anything in this world were certain."

Paphnutius was surprised and saddened by the incredible ignorance of the man.

"If you know not Jesus Christ," he said, "all your works serve no purpose, and you will never rise to life immortal."

The old man replied—

"It is useless to act, or to abstain from acting. It matters not whether we live or die."

"Eh, what?" asked Paphnutius. "Do you not desire to live through all eternity? But, tell me, do you not live in a hut in the desert as the hermits do?"

"It seems so."

"Do I not see you naked, and lacking all things?"

"It seems so."

"Do you not feed on roots, and live in chastity?"

"It seems so."

"Have you not renounced all the vanities of this world?"

"I have truly renounced all those vain things for which men commonly care."

"Then you are like me, poor, chaste, and solitary. And you are not so—as I am—for the love of God, and with a hope of celestial happiness! That I cannot understand. Why are you virtuous if you do not believe in Jesus Christ? Why deprive yourself of the good things of this world if you do not hope to gain eternal riches in heaven?"

"Stranger, I deprive myself of nothing which is good, and I flatter myself that I have found a life which is satisfactory enough, though—to speak more precisely—there is no such thing as a good or evil life. Nothing is itself, either virtuous or shameful, just or unjust, pleasant or painful, good or bad. It is our opinion which gives those qualities to things, as salt gives savour to meats."

"So then, according to you there is no certainty. You deny the truth which the idolaters themselves have sought. You lie in ignorance—like a tired dog sleeping in the mud."

"Stranger, it is equally useless to abuse either dogs or philosophers. We know not what dogs are or what we are. We know nothing."

"Old man, do you belong, then, to the absurd sect of sceptics? Are you one of those miserable fools who alike deny movement and rest, and who know not how to distinguish between the light of the sun and the shadows of night?"

"Friend, I am truly a sceptic, and of a sect which appears praiseworthy to me, though it seems ridiculous to you. For the same things often assume different appearances. The pyramids of Memphis seem at sunrise to be cones of pink light. At sunset they look like black triangles against the illuminated sky. But who shall solve the problem of their true nature? You reproach me with denying appearances, when, in fact, appearances are the only realities I recognise. The sun seems to me illuminous, but its nature is unknown to me. I feel that fire burns—but I know not how or why. My friend, you understand me badly. Besides, it is indifferent to me whether I am understood one way of the other."

"Once more. Why do you live on dates and onions in the desert? Why do you endure great hardships? I endure hardships equally great, and, like you, I live in abstinence and solitude. But then it is to please God, and to earn eternal happiness. And that is a reasonable object, for it is wise to suffer now for a future gain. It is senseless, on the contrary, to expose yourself voluntarily to useless fatigue and vain sufferings. If I did not believe—pardon my blasphemy, O uncreated Light!—if I did not believe in the truth of that which God has taught us by the voice of the prophets, by the example of His Son, by the acts of the Apostles, by the authority of councils, and by the testimony of the martyrs,—if I did not know that the sufferings of the body are necessary for the salvation of the soul—if I were, like thee, lost in ignorance of sacred mysteries—I would return at once amongst the men of this day, I would strive to acquire riches, that I might live in ease, like those who are happy in this world, and I would say to the votaries of pleasure, 'Come, my daughters, come, my servants, come and pour out for me your wines, your philtres, your perfumes.' But you, foolish old man! you deprive yourself of all these advantages; you lose without hope of any gain; you give without hope of any return, and you imitate foolishly the noble deeds of us anchorites, as an impudent monkey thinks, by smearing a wall, to copy the picture of a clever artist. What, then, are your reasons, O most besotted of men?"

Paphnutius spoke with violence and indignation, but the old man remained unmoved.

"Friend," he replied, gently, "what matter the reasons of a dog sleeping in the dirt or a mischievous ape?"

Paphnutius' only aim was the glory of God. His anger vanished, and he apologised with noble humility.

"Pardon me, old man, my brother," he said, "if zeal for the truth has carried me beyond proper bounds. God is my witness, that it is thy errors and not thyself that I hate. I suffer to see thee in darkness, for I love thee in Jesus Christ, and care for thy salvation fills my heart. Speak! give me your reasons. I long to know them that I may refute them."

The old man replied quietly—

"It is the same to me whether I speak or remain silent. I will give my reasons without asking yours in return, for I have no interest in you at all. I care neither for your happiness nor your misfortune, and it matters not to me whether you think one way or another. Why should I love you, or hate you? Aversion and sympathy are equally unworthy of the wise man. But since you question me, know then that I am named Timocles, and that I was born at Cos, of parents made rich by commerce. My father was a shipowner. In intelligence he much resembled Alexander, who is surnamed the Great. But he was not so gross. In short, he was a man of no great parts. I had two brothers, who, like him, were shipowners. As for me, I followed wisdom. My eldest brother was compelled by my father to marry a Carian woman, named Timaessa, who displeased him so greatly that he could not live with her without falling into a deep melancholy. However, Timaessa inspired our younger brother with a criminal passion, and this passion soon turned to a furious madness. The Carian woman hated them both equally; but she loved a flute-player, and received him at night in her chamber. One morning he left there the wreath which he usually wore at feasts. My two brothers, having found this wreath, swore to kill the flute-player, and the next day they caused him to perish under the lash, in spite of his tears and prayers. My sister-in-law felt such grief that she lost her reason, and these three poor wretches became beasts rather than human beings, and wandered insane along the shores of Cos, howling like wolves and foaming at the mouth, and hooted at by the children, who threw shells and stones at them. They died, and my father buried them with his own hands. A little later his stomach refused all nourishment, and he died of hunger, though he was rich enough to have bought all the meats and fruits in the markets of Asia. He was deeply grieved at having to leave me his fortune. I used it in travels. I visited Italy, Greece, and Africa without meeting a single person who was either wise or happy. I studied philosophy at Athens and Alexandria, and was deafened by noisy arguments. At last I wandered as far as India, and I saw on the banks of the Ganges a naked man, who had sat there motionless with his legs crossed for more than thirty years. Climbing plants twined round his dried up body, and the birds built their nests in his hair. Yet he lived. At the sight of him I called to mind Timaessa, the flute-player, my two brothers, and my father, and I realised that this Indian was a wise man. 'Men,' I said to myself, 'suffer because they are deprived of that which they believe to be good; or because, possessing it they fear to lose it; or because they endure that which they believe to be an evil. Put an end to all beliefs of this kind, and the evils would disappear.' That is why I resolved henceforth to deem nothing an advantage, to tear myself entirely from the good things of this world, and to live silent and motionless, like the Indian."

Paphnutius had listened attentively to the old man's story.

"Timocles of Cos," he replied, "I own that your discourse is not wholly devoid of sense. It is, in truth, wise to despise the riches of this world. But it would be absurd to despise also your eternal welfare, and render yourself liable to be visited by the wrath of God. I grieve at your ignorance, Timocles, and I will instruct you in the truth, in order that knowing that there really exists a God in three hypostases, you may obey this God as a child obeys its father."

Timocles interrupted him.

"Refrain, stranger, from showing me your doctrines, and do not imagine that you will persuade me to share your opinions. All discussions are useless. My opinion is to have no opinion. My life is devoid of trouble because I have no preferences. Go thy ways, and strive not to withdraw me from the beneficent apathy in which I am plunged, as though in a delicious bath, after the hardships of my past days."

Paphnutius was profoundly instructed in all things relating to the faith. By his knowledge of the human heart, he was aware that the grace of God had not fallen on old Timocles, and the day of salvation for his soul so obstinately resolved to ruin itself had not yet come. He did not reply, lest the power given for edification should turn to destruction. For it sometimes happens, in disputing with infidels, that the means used for their conversion may steep them still farther in sin. Therefore they who possess the truth should take care how they spread it.

"Farewell, then, unhappy Timocles," he said; and heaving a deep sigh, he resumed his pious pilgrimage through the night.

In the morning, he saw the ibises motionless on one leg at the edge of the water, which reflected their pale pink necks. The willows stretched their soft grey foliage to the bank, cranes flew in a triangle in the clear sky, and the cry of unseen herons was heard from the sedges. Far as the eye could reach, the river rolled its broad green waters o'er which white sails, like the wings of birds, glided, and here and there on the shores, a white house shone out. A light mist floated along the banks, and from out the shadow of the islands, which were laden with palms, flowers, and fruits, came noisy flocks of ducks, geese, flamingoes, and teal. To the left, the grassy valley extended to the desert its fields and orchards in joyful abundance; the sun shone on the yellow wheat, and the earth exhaled forth its fecundity in odorous wafts. At this sight, Paphnutius fell on his knees, and cried—

"Blessed be the Lord, who has given a happy issue to my journey. O God, who spreadest Thy dew upon the fig trees of the Arsiniote, pour Thy grace upon Thaïs, whom Thou hast formed with Thy love, as Thou hast the flowers and trees of the field. May she, by Thy loving care, flourish like a sweet-scented rose in the heavenly Jerusalem."

And every time that he saw a tree covered with blossom, or a bird of brilliant plumage, he thought of Thaïs. Keeping along the left arm of the river and through a fertile and populous district, he reached, in a few days, the city of Alexandria, which the Greeks have surnamed the Beautiful and the Golden. The sun had risen an hour, when he beheld, from the top of a hill, the vast city, the roofs of which glittered in the rosy light. He stopped, and folded his arms on his breast.

"There, then," he said, "is the delightful spot where I was born in sin; the bright air where I breathed poisonous perfumes; the sea of pleasure where I heard the songs of the sirens. There is my cradle, after the flesh; my native land—in the parlance of the men of these days! A rich cradle, an illustrious country, in the judgment of men! It is natural that thy children should reverence thee like a mother, Alexandria, and I was begotten in thy magnificently adorned breast. But the ascetic despises nature, the mystic scorns appearances, the Christian regards his native land as a place of exile, the monk is not of this earth. I have turned away my heart from loving thee, Alexandria. I hate thee! I hate thee for thy riches, thy science, thy pleasures, and thy beauty. Be accursed, temple of demons! Lewd couch of the Gentiles, tainted pulpit of Arian heresy, be thou accursed! And thou, winged son of heaven who led the holy hermit Anthony, our father, when he came from the depths of the desert, and entered into the citadel of idolatry to strengthen the faith of believers and the confidence of martyrs, beautiful angel of the Lord, invisible child, first breath of God, fly thou before me, and cleanse, by the beating of thy wings, the corrupted air I am about to breathe amongst the princes of darkness of this world!"

Having thus spoken, he resumed his journey. He entered the city by the Gate of the Sun. This gate was a handsome structure of stone. In the shadow of its arch, crowded some poor wretches, who offered lemons and figs for sale, or with many groans and lamentations, begged for an obolus.

An old woman in rags, who was kneeling there, seized the monk's cassock, kissed it, and said—

"Man of the Lord, bless me, that God may bless me. I have suffered many things in this world that I may have joys in the world to come. You come from God, O holy man, and that is why the dust of your feet is more precious than gold."

"The Lord be praised!" said Paphnutius, and with his half-closed hand he made the sign of redemption on the old woman's head.

But hardly had he gone twenty paces down the street, than a band of children began to jeer at him, and throw stones, crying—

"Oh, the wicked monk! He is blacker than an ape, and more bearded than a goat! He is a skulker! Why not hang him in an orchard, like a wooden Priapus, to frighten the birds? But no; he would draw down the hail on the apple-blossom. He brings bad luck. To the ravens with the monk! to the ravens!" and stones mingled with the cries.

"My God, bless these poor children!" murmured Paphnutius.

And he pursued his way, thinking.

"I was worshipped by the old woman, and hated and despised by these children. Thus the same object is appreciated differently by men who are uncertain in their judgment and liable to error. It must be owned that, for a Gentile, old Timocles was not devoid of sense. Though blind, he knew he was deprived of light. His reasoning was much better than that of these idolaters, who cry from the depths of their thick darkness, 'I see the day!' Everything in this world is mirage and moving sand. God alone is steadfast."

He passed through the city with rapid steps. After ten years of absence he would still recognise every stone, and every stone was to him a stone of reproach that recalled a sin. For that reason he struck his naked feet roughly against the kerb-stones of the wide street, and rejoiced to see the bloody marks of his wounded feet. Leaving on his left the magnificent portico of the Temple of Serapis, he entered a road lined with splendid mansions, which seemed to be drowsy with perfumes. Pines, maples, and larches raised their heads above the red cornices and golden acroteria. Through the half-open doors could be seen bronze statues in marble vestibules, and fountains playing amidst foliage. No noise troubled the stillness of these quiet retreats. Only the distant strains of a flute could be heard. The monk stopped before a house, rather small, but of noble proportions, and supported by columns as graceful as young girls. It was ornamented with bronze busts of the most celebrated Greek philosophers.

He recognised Plato, Socrates, Aristotle, Epicurus, and Zeno, and having knocked with the hammer against the door, he waited, wrapped in meditation.

"It is vanity to glorify in metal these false sages; their lies are confounded, their souls are lost in hell, and even the famous Plato himself, who filled the earth with his eloquence, now disputes with the devils."

A slave opened the door, and seeing a man with bare feet standing on the mosaic threshold, said to him roughly—

"Go and beg elsewhere, stupid monk, or I will drive you away with a stick."

"Brother," replied the Abbot of Antinoë, "all that I ask is that you conduct me to your master, Nicias."

The slave replied, more angrily than before—

"My master does not see dogs like you."

"My son," said Paphnutius, "will you please do what I ask, and tell your master that I desire to see him."

"Get out, vile beggar!" cried the porter furiously; and he raised his stick and struck the holy man, who, with his arms crossed upon his breast, received unmovedly the blow, which fell full in his face, and then repeated gently—

"Do as I ask you, my son, I beg."

The porter tremblingly murmured—

"Who is this man who is not afraid of suffering?"

And he ran and told his master.

Nicias had just left the bath. Two pretty slave girls were scraping him with strigils. He was a pleasant-looking man, with a kind smile. There was an expression of gentle satire in his face. On seeing the monk, he rose and advanced with open arms.

"It is you!" he cried, "Paphnutius, my fellow-scholar, my friend my brother! Oh, I knew you again, though, to say the truth, you look more like a wild animal than a man. Embrace me. Do you remember the time when we studied grammar, rhetoric, and philosophy together? You were, even then, of a morose and wild character, but I liked you because of your complete sincerity. We used to say that you looked at the universe with the eyes of a wild horse, and it was not surprising you were dull and moody. You needed a pinch of Attic salt, but your liberality knew no bounds. You cared nothing for either your money or your life. And you had the eccentricity of genius, and a strange character which interested me deeply. You are welcome, my dear Paphnutius, after ten years of absence. You have quitted the desert; you have renounced all Christian superstitions, and now return to your old life. I will mark this day with a white stone."

"Crobyle and Myrtale," he added, turning towards the girls, "perfume the feet, hands, and beard of my dear guest."

They smiled, and had already brought the basin, the phials, and the metal mirror. But Paphnutius stopped them with an imperious gesture, and lowered his eyes that he might not look upon them, for they were naked. Nicias brought cushions for him, and offered him various meats and drinks, which Paphnutius scornfully refused.

"Nicias," he said, "I have not renounced what you falsely call the Christian superstition, which is the truth of truths. 'In the beginning was the Word, and the Word was with God, and the Word was God. All things were made by Him, and without Him was not anything made that was made. In Him was the life, and the life was the light of men.'"

"My dear Paphnutius," replied Nicias, who had now put on a perfumed tunic, "do you expect to astonish me by reciting a lot of words jumbled together without skill, which are no more than a vain murmur? Have you forgotten that I am a bit of a philosopher myself? And do you think to satisfy me with some rags, torn by ignorant men from the purple garment of Æmilius, when Æmilius, Porphyry, and Plato, in all their glory, did not satisfy me! The systems devised by the sages are but tales imagined to amuse the eternal childishness of men. We divert ourselves with them, as we do with the stories of *The Ass, The Tub,* and *The Ephesian Matron,* or any other Milesian fable."

And, taking his guest by the arm, he led him into a room where thousands of papyri were rolled up and lay in baskets.

"This is my library," he said. "It contains a small part of the various systems which the philosophers have constructed to explain the world. The Serapeium itself, with all its riches, does not contain them all. Alas! they are but the dreams of sick men."

He compelled his guest to sit down in an ivory chair, and sat down himself. Paphnutius scowled gloomily at all the books in the library, and said—

"They ought all to be burned."

"Oh, my dear guest, that would be a pity!" replied Nicias. "For the dreams of sick men are sometimes amusing. Besides, if we should destroy all the dreams and visions of men, the earth would lose its form and colours, and we should all sleep in a dull stupidity."

Paphnutius continued in the same strain as before—

"It is certain that the doctrines of the pagans are but vain lies. But God, who is the truth, revealed Himself to men by miracles, and He was made flesh, and lived among us."

Nicias replied—

"You speak well, my dear Paphnutius, when you say that he was made flesh. A God who thinks, acts, speaks, who wanders through nature, like Ulysses of old on the glaucous sea, is altogether a man. How do you expect that we should believe in this new Jupiter, when the urchins of Athens, in the time of Pericles, no longer believed in the old one? But let us leave all that. You did not come here, I suppose, to argue about the three hypostases. What can I do for you, my dear fellow-scholar?"

"A good deed," replied the Abbot of Antinoë. "Lend me a perfumed tunic, like the one you have just put on. Be kind enough to add to the tunic, gilt sandals, and a vial of oil to anoint my beard and hair. It is needful also, that you should give me a purse with a thousand drachmæ in it. That, O Nicias, is what I came to ask of you, for the love of God, and in remembrance of our old friendship."

Nicias made Crobyle and Myrtale bring his richest tunic; it was embroidered, after the Asiatic fashion, with flowers and animals. The two girls held it open, and skilfully showed its bright colours, waiting till Paphnutius should have taken off the cassock which covered him down to his feet. But the monk having declared that they should rather tear off his flesh than this garment, they put on the tunic over it. As the two girls were pretty, they were not afraid of men, although they were slaves. They laughed at the strange appearance of the monk thus clad. Crobyle called him her dear satrap, as she presented him with the mirror, and Myrtale pulled his beard. But Paphnutius prayed to the Lord, and did not look at them. Having tied on the gilt sandals, and fastened the purse to his belt, he said to Nicias, who was looking at him with an amused expression—

"O Nicias, let not these things be an offence in your eyes. For know that I shall make pious use of this tunic, this purse, and these sandals."

"My dear friend," replied Nicias, "I suspect no evil, for I believe that men are equally incapable of doing evil or doing good. Good and evil exist only in the opinion. The wise man has only custom and usage to guide him in his acts. I conform with all the prejudices which prevail at Alexandria. That is why I pass for an honest man. Go, friend, and enjoy yourself."

But Paphnutius thought that it was needful to inform his host of his intention.

"Do you know Thaïs," he said, "who acts in the games at the theatre?"

"She is beautiful," replied Nicias, "and there was a time when she was dear to me. For her sake, I sold a mill and two fields of corn, and I composed in her honour three books full of detestably bad verses. Surely beauty is the most powerful force in the world, and were we so made that we could possess it always, we should care as little as may be for the demiurgos, the logos, the æons, and all the other reveries of the philosophers. But I am surprised, my good Paphnutius, that you should have come from the depths of the Thebaid to talk about Thaïs."

Having said this, he sighed gently. And Paphnutius gazed at him with horror, not conceiving it possible that a man should so calmly avow such a sin. He expected to see the earth open, and Nicias swallowed up in flames. But the earth remained solid, and the Alexandrian silent, his forehead resting on his hand, and he smiling sadly at the memories of his past youth. The monk rose, and continued in solemn tones—

"Know then, O Nicias, that, with the aid of God, I will snatch this woman Thaïs from the unclean affections of the world, and give her as a spouse to Jesus Christ. If the Holy Spirit does not forsake me, Thaïs will leave this city and enter a nunnery."

"Beware of offending Venus," replied Nicias. "She is a powerful goddess, she will be angry with you if you take away her chief minister."

"God will protect me," said Paphnutius. "May He also illumine thy heart, O Nicias, and draw thee out of the abyss in which thou art plunged."

And he stalked out of the room. But Nicias followed him, and overtook him on the threshold, and placing his hand on his shoulder whispered into his ear the same words—

"Beware of offending Venus; her vengeance is terrible."

Paphnutius, disdainful of these trivial words, left without turning his head. He felt only contempt for Nicias; but what he could not bear was the idea that his former friend had received the caresses of Thaïs. It seemed to him that to sin with that woman was more detestable than to sin with any other. To him this appeared the height of iniquity, and he henceforth looked upon Nicias as an object of execration. He had always hated impurity, but never before had this vice appeared so heinous to him; never before had it so seemed to merit the anger of Jesus Christ and the sorrow of the angels.

He felt only a more ardent desire to save Thaïs from the Gentiles, and that he must hasten to see the actress in order to save her. Nevertheless, before he could enter her house, he must wait till the heat of the day was over, and now the morning had hardly finished. Paphnutius wandered through the most frequented streets. He had resolved to take no food that day, in order to be the less unworthy of the favours he had asked of the Lord. To the great grief of his soul, he dared not enter any of the churches in the city, because he knew they were profaned by the Arians, who had overturned the Lord's table. For, in fact, these heretics, supported by the Emperor of the East, had driven the patriarch Athanasius from his episcopate, and sown trouble and confusion among the Christians of Alexandria.

He therefore wandered about aimlessly, sometimes with his eyes fixed on the ground in humility, and sometimes raised to heaven in ecstasy. After some time, he found himself on the quay. Before him lay the harbour, in which were sheltered innumerable ships and galleys, and beyond them, smiling in blue and silver, lay the perfidious sea. A galley, which bore a Nereid at its prow, had just weighed anchor. The rowers sang as the oars struck the water; and already the white daughter of the waters, covered with humid pearls, showed no more than a flying profile to the monk. Steered by her pilot, she cleared the passage leading from the basin of the Eunostos, and gained the high seas, leaving a glittering trail behind her.

"I also," thought Paphnutius, "once desired to embark singing on the ocean of the world. But I soon saw my folly, and the Nereid did not carry me away."

Lost in his thoughts, he sat down upon a coil of rope, and went to sleep. During his sleep, he had a vision. He seemed to hear the sound of a clanging trumpet, and the sky became blood red, and he knew that the day of judgment had come. Whilst he was fervently praying to God, he saw an enormous monster coming towards him, bearing on its forehead a cross of light, and he recognised the sphinx of Silsile. The monster seized him between its teeth, without hurting him, and carried him in its mouth, as a cat carries a kitten. Paphnutius was thus conveyed across many countries, crossing rivers and traversing mountains, and came at last to a desert place, covered with scowling rocks and hot cinders. The ground was rent in many places, and through these openings came a hot air. The monster gently put Paphnutius down on the ground, and said—

"Look!"

And Paphnutius, leaning over the edge of the abyss, saw a river of fire which flowed in the interior of the earth, between two cliffs of black rocks. There, in a livid light, the demons tormented the souls of the damned. The souls preserved the appearance of the bodies which had held them, and even wore some rags of clothing. These souls seemed peaceful in the midst of their torments. One of them, tall and white, his eyes closed, a white fillet across his forehead, and a sceptre in his hand, sang; his voice filled the desert shores with harmony; he sang of gods and heroes. Little green devils pierced his lips and throat with red-hot irons. And the shade of Homer still sang. Near by, old Anaxagoras, bald and hoary, traced figures in the dust with a compass. A demon poured boiling oil into his ear, yet failed, however, to disturb the sage's meditations. And the monk saw many other persons, who, on the dark shore by the side of the burning river, read, or quietly meditated, or conversed with other spirits while walking,—like the sages and pupils under the shadow of the sycamore trees of Academe. Old Timocles alone had withdrawn from the others, and shook his head like a man who denies. One of the demons of the abyss shook a torch before his eyes, but Timocles would see neither the demon nor the torch.

Mute with surprise at this spectacle, Paphnutius turned to the monster. It had disappeared, and, in place of the sphinx, the monk saw a veiled woman, who said—

"Look and understand. Such is the obstinacy of these infidels, that, even in hell, they remain victims of the illusions which deluded them when on earth. Death has not undeceived them; for it is very plain that it does not suffice merely to die in order to see God. Those who are ignorant of the truth whilst living, will be ignorant of it always. The demons which are busy torturing these souls, what are they but agents of divine justice? That is why these souls neither see them nor feel them. They were ignorant of the truth, and therefore unaware of their own condemnation, and God Himself cannot compel them to suffer.

"God can do all things," said the Abbot of Antinoë.

"He cannot do that which is absurd," replied the veiled woman. "To punish them, they must first be enlightened, and if they possessed the truth, they would be like unto the elect."

Vexed and horrified, Paphnutius again bent over the edge of the abyss. He saw the shade of Nicias smiling, with a wreath of flowers on his head, sitting under a burnt myrtle tree. By his side was Aspasia of Miletus, gracefully draped in a woollen cloak, and they seemed to talk together of love and philosophy; the expression of her face was sweet and noble. The rain of fire which fell on them was as a refreshing dew, and their feet pressed the burning soil as though it had been tender grass. At this sight Paphnutius was filled with fury.

"Strike him, O God! strike him!" he cried. "It is Nicias! Let him weep! let him groan! let him grind his teeth! He sinned with Thaïs!"

And Paphnutius woke in the arms of a sailor, as strong as Hercules, who cried—

"Quietly! quietly! my friend! By Proteus, the old shepherd of the seals, you slumber uneasily. If I had not caught hold of you, you would have tumbled into the Eunostos. It is as true as that my mother sold salt fish, that I saved your life."

"I thank God," replied Paphnutius.

And, rising to his feet, he walked straight before him, meditating on the vision which had come to him whilst he was asleep.

"This vision," he said to himself, "is plainly an evil one; it is an insult to divine goodness to imagine hell is unreal. The dream certainly came from the devil."

He reasoned thus because he knew how to distinguish between the dreams sent by God and those produced by evil angels. Such discernment is useful to the hermit, who lives surrounded by apparitions, and who, in avoiding men, is sure to meet with spirits. The deserts are full of phantoms. When the pilgrim drew near the ruined castle, to which the holy hermit, Anthony, had retired, they heard a noise like that which goes up from the public square of a large city at a great festival. The noise was made by the devils, who were tempting the holy man.

Paphnutius remembered this memorable example. He also called to mind St. John the Egyptian, who for sixty years was tempted by the devil. But John saw through all the tricks of the demon. One day, however, the devil, having assumed the appearance of a man, entered the grotto of the venerable John, and said to him, "John, you must continue to fast until to-morrow evening." And John, believing that it was an angel who spoke, obeyed the voice of the demon, and fasted the next day until the vesper hour. That

was the only victory that the Prince of Darkness ever gained over
St. John the Egyptian, and that was but a trifling one. It was
therefore not astonishing that Paphnutius knew at once that the
vision which had visited him in his sleep was an evil one.

Whilst he was gently remonstrating with God for having given
him into the power of the demons, he felt himself pushed and
dragged amidst a crowd of people who were all hurrying in the
same direction. As he was unaccustomed to walk in the streets of
a city, he was shoved and knocked from one passer to another like
an inert mass; and being embarrassed by the folds of his tunic, he
was more than once on the point of falling. Desirous of knowing
where all these people could be going, he asked one of them the
cause of this hurry.

"Do you not know, stranger," replied he, "that the games are
about to begin, and that Thaïs will appear on the stage? All the
citizens are going to the theatre, and I also am going. Would you
like to accompany me?"

It occurred to him at once that it would further his design to
see Thaïs in the games, and Paphnutius followed the stranger. In
front of them stood the theatre, its portico ornamented with shining masks, and its huge circular wall covered with innumerable
statues. Following the crowd, they entered a narrow passage, at
the end of which lay the amphitheatre, glittering with light. They
took their places on one of the seats, which descended in steps to
the stage, which was empty but magnificently decorated. There was
no curtain to hide the view, and on the stage was a mound, such as
used to be erected in old times to the shades of heroes. This mound
stood in the midst of a camp. Lances were stacked in front of the
tents, and golden shields hung from masts, amidst boughs of laurel
and wreaths of oak. On the stage all was silence, but a murmur like
the humming of bees in a hive rose from the vast hemicycle filled
with spectators. All their faces, reddened by the reflection from the
purple awning which waved above them, turned with attentive
curiosity towards the large, silent stage, with its tomb and tents.
The women laughed and ate lemons, and the regular theatre-goers
called gaily to one another from their seats.

Paphnutius prayed inwardly, and refrained from uttering any
vain words, but his neighbour began to complain of the decline of
the drama.

"Formerly," he said, "clever actors used to declaim, under a
mask, the verses of Euripides and Menander. Now they no longer
recite dramas, they act in dumb show; and of the divine spectacles
with which Bacchus was honoured in Athens, we have kept nothing
but what a barbarian—a Scythian even—could understand—attitude and gesture. The tragic mask, the mouth of which was provided with metal tongues that increased the sound of the voice; the
cothurnus, which raised the actors to the height of gods; the tragic

majesty and the splendid verses that used to be sung, have all gone. Pantomimists, and dancing girls with bare faces, have replaced Paulus and Roscius. What would the Athenians of the days of Pericles have said if they had seen a woman on the stage? It is indecent for a woman to appear in public. We must be very degenerate to permit it. It is as certain as that my name is Dorion, that woman is the natural enemy of man, and a disgrace to human kind."

"You speak wisely," replied Paphnutius; "woman is our worst enemy. She gives us pleasure, and is to be feared on that account."

"By the immovable gods," cried Dorion, "it is not pleasure that woman gives to man, but sadness, trouble, and black cares. Love is the cause of our most biting evils. Listen, stranger. When I was a young man I visited Trœzene, in Argolis, and I saw there a myrtle of a most prodigious size, the leaves of which were covered with innumerable pin-holes. And this is what the Trœzenians say about that myrtle. Queen Phædra, when she was in love with Hippolytos, used to recline idly all day long under this same tree. To beguile the tedium of her weary life she used to draw out the golden pin which held her fair locks, and pierce with it the leaves of the sweet-scented bush. All the leaves were riddled with holes. After she had ruined the poor young man whom she pursued with her incestuous love, Phædra, as you know, perished miserably. She locked herself up in her bridal chamber, and hanged herself by her golden girdle from an ivory peg. The gods willed that the myrtle, the witness of her bitter misery, should continue to bear, in its fresh leaves, the marks of the pin-holes. I picked one of these leaves, and placed it at the head of my bed, that by the sight of it I might take warning against the folly of love, and conform to the doctrine of the divine Epicurus, my master, who taught that all lust is to be feared. But, properly speaking, love is a disease of the liver, and one is never sure of not catching the malady."

Paphnutius asked—

"Dorion, what are your pleasures?"

Dorion replied sadly—

"I have only one pleasure, and, it must be confessed, that it is not a very exciting one; it is meditation. When a man has a bad digestion, he must not look for any others."

Taking advantage of these words, Paphnutius proceeded to initiate the Epicurean into those spiritual joys which the contemplation of God procures. He began—

"Hear the truth, Dorion, and receive the light."

But he saw then that all heads were turned towards him, and everybody was making signs for him to be quiet. Dead silence prevailed in the theatre, broken at last by the strains of heroic music.

The play began. The soldiers left their tents, and were preparing to depart, when a prodigy occurred—a cloud covered the summit of the funeral pile. Then the cloud rolled away, and the ghost of Achilles appeared, clad in golden armour. Extending his arms towards the warriors, he seemed to say to them, "What! do you depart, children of Danaos? do you return to the land I shall never behold again, and leave my tomb without any offerings?" Already the principal Greek chieftains pressed to the foot of the pile. Acamas, the son of Theseus, old Nestor, Agamemmon, bearing a sceptre and with a fillet on his brow, gazed at the prodigy. Pyrrhus, the young son of Achilles, was prostrate in the dust. Ulysses, recognisable by the cap which covered his curly hair, showed by his gestures that he acquiesced in the demand of the hero's shade. He argued with Agamemnon, and their words might be easily guessed—

"Achilles," said the King of Ithaca, "is worthy to be honoured by us, for he died gloriously for Hellas. He demands that the daughter of Priam, the virgin Polyxena, should be immolated on his tomb. Greeks! appease the manes of the hero, and let the son of Peleus rejoice in Hades."

But the king of kings replied—

"Spare the Trojan virgins we have torn from the altars. Sufficient misfortunes have already fallen on the illustrious race of Priam."

He spoke thus because he shared the couch of the sister of Polyxena, and the wise Ulysses reproached him for preferring the couch of Cassandra to the lance of Achilles.

The Greeks showed they shared the opinion of Ulysses, by loudly clashing their weapons. The death of Polyxena was resolved on, and the appeased shade of Achilles vanished. The music—sometimes wild and sometimes plaintive—followed the thoughts of the personages in the drama. The spectators burst into applause.

Paphnutius, who applied divine truth to everything murmured—

"This fable shows how cruel the worshippers of false gods were."

"All religions breed crimes," replied the Epicurean. "Happily, a Greek, who was divinely wise, has freed men from foolish terrors of the unknown—"

Just at that moment, Hecuba, her white hair dishevelled, her robe tattered, came out of the tent in which she was kept captive. A long sigh went up from the audience, when her woeful figure appeared. Hecuba had been warned by a prophetic dream, and lamented her daughter's fate and her own. Ulysses approached her, and asked her to give up Polyxena. The old mother tore her hair, dug her nails into her cheeks, and kissed the hands of the cruel chieftain, who, with unpitying calmness, seemed to say—

"Be wise, Hecuba, and yield to necessity. There are amongst us many old mothers who weep for their children, now sleeping under the pines of Ida."

And Hecuba, formerly queen of the most flourishing city in Asia, and now a slave, bowed her unhappy head in the dust.

Then the curtain in front of one of the tents was raised, and the virgin Polyxena appeared. A tremor passed through all the spectators. They had recognised Thaïs. Paphnutius saw again the woman he had come to seek. With her white arm she held above her head the heavy curtain. Motionless as a splendid statue, she stood, with a look of pride and resignation in her violet eyes, and her resplendent beauty made a shudder of commiseration pass through all who beheld her.

A murmur of applause uprose, and Paphnutius, his soul agitated, and pressing both hands to his heart, sighed—

"Why, O my God, hast thou given this power to one of Thy creatures?"

Dorion was not so disturbed. He said—

"Certainly the atoms, which have momentarily met together to form this woman, present a combination which is agreeable to the eye. But that is but a freak of nature, and the atoms know not what they do. They will some day separate with the same indifference as they came together. Where are now the atoms which formed Laïs or Cleopatra? I must confess that women are sometimes beautiful. But they are liable to grievous afflictions, and disgusting inconveniences. That is patent to all thinking men, though the vulgar pay no attention to it. And women inspire love, though it is absurd and ridiculous to love them."

Such were the thoughts of the philosopher and the ascetic as they gazed on Thaïs. They neither of them noticed Hecuba, who turned to her daughter, and seemed to say by her gestures—

"Try to soften the cruel Ulysses. Employ your tears, your beauty, and your youth."

Thaïs—or rather Polyxena herself—let fall the curtain of the tent. She made a step forward, and all hearts were conquered. And when, with firm but light steps, she advanced towards Ulysses, her rhythmic movements, which were accompanied by the sound of flutes, created in all present such happy visions, that it seemed as though she were the divine centre of all the harmonies of the world. All eyes were bent on her; the other actors were obscured by her effulgence, and were not noticed. The play continued, however.

The prudent son of Laërtes turned away his head, and hid his hand under his mantle, in order to avoid the looks and kisses of the suppliant. The virgin made a sign to him to fear nothing. Her tranquil gaze said—

"I follow you, Ulysses, and bow to necessity—because I wish to die. Daughter of Priam, and sister of Hector, my couch, which was once worthy of Kings, shall never receive a foreign master. Freely do I quit the light of day."

Hecuba, lying motionless in the dust, suddenly rose and enfolded her daughter in a last despairing embrace. Polyxena gently, but resolutely, removed the old arms which held her. She seemed to say—

"Do not expose yourself, mother, to the fury of your master. Do not wait until he drags you ignominiously on the ground in tearing me from your arms. Better, O well-beloved mother, to give me your wrinkled hand, and bend your hollow cheeks to my lips."

The face of Thaïs looked beautiful in its grief. The crowd felt grateful to her for showing them the forms and passions of life endowed with superhuman grace, and Paphnutius pardoned her present splendour on account of her coming humility, and glorified himself in advance for the saint he was about to give to heaven.

The drama neared its end. Hecuba fell as though dead, and Polyxena, led by Ulysses, advanced towards the tomb, which was surrounded by the chief warriors. A dirge was sung as she mounted the funeral pile, on the summit of which the son of Achilles poured out libations from a gold cup to the names of the hero. When the sacrificing priests stretched out their arms to seize her, she made a sign that she wished to die free and unbound, as befitted the daughter of so many kings. Then, tearing aside her robe, she bared her bosom to the blow. Pyrrhus, turning away his head, plunged his sword into her heart, and by a skilful trick, the blood gushed forth over the dazzling white breast of the virgin, who, with head thrown back, and her eyes swimming in the horrors of death, fell with grace and modesty.

Whilst the warriors enshrouded the victim with a veil, and covered her with lilies and anemones, terrified screams and groans rent the air, and Paphnutius, rising from his seat, prophesied in a loud voice.

"Gentiles? vile worshippers of demons! And you Arians more in-

famous than the idolaters!—learn! That which you have just seen is an image and a symbol. There is a mystic meaning in this fable, and very soon the woman you see there will be offered, a willing and happy sacrifice, to the risen God."

But already the crowd was surging in dark waves towards the exits. The Abbot of Antinoë, escaping from the astonished Dorion, gained the door, still prophesying.

An hour later he knocked at the door of the house of Thaïs.

The actress then lived in the rich Racotis quarter, near the tomb of Alexander, in a house surrounded by shady gardens, in which a brook, bordered with poplars, flowed amidst artificial rocks. An old black slave woman, loaded with rings, opened the door, and asked what he wanted.

"I wish to see Thaïs," he replied. "God is my witness that I came here for no other purpose."

As he wore a rich tunic, and spoke in an imperious manner, the slave allowed him to enter.

"You will find Thaïs," she said, "in the Grotto of Nymphs."

PART THE SECOND

THE PAPYRUS

THAÏS was born of free, but poor, parents, who were idolaters. When she was a very little girl, her father kept, at Alexandria, near the Gate of the Moon, an inn, which was frequented by sailors. She still retained some vivid, but disconnected, memories of her early youth. She remembered her father, seated at the corner of the hearth with his legs crossed—tall, formidable, and quiet, like one of those old Pharaohs who are celebrated in the ballads sung by blind men at the street corners. She remembered also her thin, wretched mother, wandering like a hungry cat about the house, which she filled with the tones of her sharp voice, and the glitter of her phosphorescent eyes. They said in the neighbourhood that she was a witch, and changed into an owl at night, and flew to see her lovers. It was a lie. Thaïs knew well, having often watched her, that her mother practised no magic arts, but that she was eaten up with avarice, and counted all night the gains of the day. The idle father and the greedy mother let the child live as best it could, like one of the fowls in the poultry-yard. She became very clever in extracting, one by one, the oboli from the belt of some drunken sailor, and in amusing the drinkers with artless songs and obscene words, the meaning of which she did not know. She passed from knee to knee, in a room reeking with the odours of fermented drinks and resiny wine-skins; then, her cheeks sticky with beer and pricked by rough beards, she escaped, clutching the oboli in her little hand, and ran to buy honey-cakes from an old woman who crouched behind her baskets under the Gate of the Moon. Every day the same scenes were repeated, the sailors relating their perilous adventures, then playing at dice or knuckle-bones, and blaspheming the gods, amid their shouting for the best beer of Cilicia.

Every night the child was awakened by the quarrels of the drunkards. Oyster-shells would fly across the tables, cutting the heads of those they hit, and the uproar was terrible. Sometimes she saw, by the light of the smoky lamps, the knives glitter, and the blood flow.

It humiliated her to think that the only person who showed her any human kindness in her young days was the mild and gentle Ahmes. Ahmes, the house-slave, a Nubian blacker than the pot he gravely skimmed, was as good as a long night's sleep. Often he would take Thaïs on his knee, and tell her old tales about underground treasure-houses constructed for avaricious kings, who put to death the masons and architects. There were also tales about clever thieves who married kings' daughters, and courtesans who built pyramids. Little Thaïs loved Ahmes like a father, like a mother, like a nurse, and like a dog. She followed the slave into the cellar when he went to fill the amphoræ, and into the poultry-yard amongst the scraggy and ragged fowls, all beak, claws, and feathers, who flew swifter than eagles before the knife of the black cook. Often at night, on the straw, instead of sleeping, he built for Thaïs little water-mills, and ships no bigger than his hand, with all their rigging.

He had been badly treated by his masters; one of his ears was torn, and his body covered with scars. Yet his features always wore an air of joyous peace. And no one ever asked him whence he drew the consolation in his soul, and the peace in his heart. He was as simple as a child. As he performed his heavy tasks, he sang, in a harsh voice, hymns which made the child tremble and dream. He murmured, in a gravely joyous tone—

"Tell us, Mary, what thou hast seen where thou hast been?
 I saw the shroud and the linen cloths, and the angels seated on the
  tomb.
 And I saw the glory of the Risen One."

She asked him—
"Father, why do you sing about angels seated on a tomb?"
And he replied—
"Little light of my eyes, I sing of the angels because Jesus, our Lord, is risen to heaven."

Ahmes was a Christian. He had been baptised, and was known as Theodore at the meetings of the faithful, to which he went secretly during the hours allowed him for sleep.

At that time the Church was suffering the severest trials. By order of the Emperor, the churches had been thrown down, the holy books burned, the sacred vessels and candlesticks melted. The Christians had been deprived of all their honours, and expected nothing but death. Terror reigned over all the community at Alexandria, and the prisons were crammed with victims. It was whispered with horror amongst the faithful, that in Syria, in

Arabia, in Mesopotamia, in Cappadocia, in all the empire, bishops and virgins had been flogged, tortured, crucified or thrown to wild beasts. Then Anthony, already celebrated for his visions and his solitary life, a prophet, and the head of all the Egyptian believers, descended like an eagle from his desert rock on the city of Alexandria, and, flying from church to church, fired the whole community with his holy ardour. Invisible to the pagans, he was present at the same time at all the meetings of Christians, endowing all with the spirit of strength and prudence by which he was animated. Slaves, in particular, were persecuted with singular severity. Many of them, seized with fright, denied the faith. Others, and by far the greater number, fled to the desert, hoping to live there, either as hermits or robbers. Ahmes, however, frequented the meetings as usual, visited the prisoners, buried the martyrs, and joyfully professed the religion of Christ. The great Anthony, who saw his unshaken zeal, before he returned into the desert, pressed the black slave in his arms, and gave him the kiss of peace.

When Thaïs was seven years old, Ahmes began to talk to her of God.

"The good Lord God," he said, "lived in heaven like a Pharaoh, under the tents of His harem, and under the trees of His gardens. He was the Ancient of Ancients, and older than the world; and He had but one Son, the Prince Jesus, whom He loved with all His heart, and who surpassed in beauty the virgins and the angels. And the good Lord God said to Prince Jesus—

" 'Leave My harem and My palace, and My date trees and My running waters. Descend to earth for the welfare of men. There Thou shalt be like a little child, and Thou shalt live poor amongst the poor. Suffering shall be Thy daily bread, and Thou shalt weep so profusely that Thy tears shall form rivers, in which the tired slave shall bathe with delight. Go, My Son!'

"Prince Jesus obeyed the good Lord, and He came down to earth, to a place named Bethlehem of Judæa. And He walked in fields, amidst the flowering anemones, saying to His companions:

" 'Blessed are they who hunger, for I will lead them to My Father's table! Blessed are they who thirst, for they shall drink of the fountains of heaven! Blessed are they who weep, for I will dry their tears with veils finer than those of the almehs!'

"That is why the poor loved Him, and believed in Him. But the rich hated Him; fearing that He should raise the poor above them. At that time, Cleopatra and Cæsar were powerful on the earth. They both hated Jesus, and they ordered the judges and priests to put Him to death. To obey the Queen of Egypt, the princes of Syria erected a cross on a high mountain, and they caused Jesus to die on this cross. But women washed His corpse, and buried it; and Prince Jesus, having broken the door of His tomb, rose again to the good Lord, His Father.

"And, from that time, all those who believed in Him go to heaven.

"The Lord God opens His arms, and says to them—

" 'Ye are welcome, because ye love the Prince, My Son. Wash, and then eat.'

"They bathe to the sound of beautiful music, and, all the time they are eating, they see almehs dancing, and they listen to tales that never end. They are dearer to the good Lord God than the light of His eyes, because they are His guests, and they shall have for their portion the carpets of His house, and the pomegranates of His gardens."

Ahmes often spoke in this strain, and thus taught the truth to Thaïs. She wondered, and said—

"I should like to eat the pomegranates of the good Lord."

Ahmes replied—

"Only those who are baptised may taste the fruits of heaven."

And Thaïs asked to be baptised. Seeing by this that she believed in Jesus, the slave resolved to instruct her more fully, so that, being baptised, she might enter the Church; and he loved her as his spiritual daughter.

The child, unloved and uncared for by its selfish parents, had no bed in the house. She slept in a corner of the stable amongst the domestic animals, and there Ahmes came to her every night secretly.

He gently approached the mat on which she lay, and sat down on his heels, his legs bent and his body straight—a position hereditary to his race. His face and his body, which was clothed in black, were invisible in the darkness; but his big white eyes shone out, and there came from them a light like a ray of dawn through the chinks of a door. He spoke in a husky, monotonous tone, with a slight nasal twang that gave it the soft melody of music heard at night in the streets. Sometimes the breathing of an ass, or the soft lowing of an ox, accompanied, like a chorus of invisible spirits, the voice of the slave as he recited the gospels. His words flowed gently in the darkness, which they filled with zeal, mercy, and hope; and the neophyte, her hand in that of Ahmes, lulled by the monotonous sounds, and the vague visions in her mind, slept calm and smiling, amid the harmonies of the dark night and the holy mysteries, gazed down on by a star, which twinkled between the joists of the stable-roof.

The initiation lasted a whole year, till the time when the Christians joyfully celebrate the festival of Easter. One night in the holy week, Thaïs, who was already asleep on her mat, felt herself lifted by the slave, whose eyes gleamed with a strange light. He was clad, not as usual in a pair of torn drawers, but in a long white cloak, beneath which he pressed the child, whispering to her—

"Come, my soul! Come, light of my eyes! Come, little sweetheart! Come and be clad in the baptismal robes!"

He carried the child pressed to his breast. Frightened and yet curious, Thaïs, her head out of the cloak, threw her arms round her friend's neck, and he ran with her through the darkness. They went down narrow, black alleys; they passed through the Jews' quarter; they skirted a cemetery, where the osprey uttered its dismal cry; they traversed an open space, passing under crosses on which hung the bodies of victims, and on the arms of the crosses the ravens clacked their beaks. Thaïs hid her head in the slave's breast. She did not dare to peep out all the rest of the way. Soon it seemed to her that she was going down under ground. When she reopened her eyes she found herself in a narrow cave, lighted by resin torches, on the walls of which were painted standing figures, which seemed to move and live in the flickering glare of the torches. They were men clad in long tunics and carrying branches of palm, and around them were lambs, doves, and tendrils of vine.

Amongst these figures, Thaïs recognised Jesus of Nazareth, by the anemones flowering at his feet. In the centre of the cave, near a large stone font filled with water, stood an old man clad in a scarlet dalmatic embroidered with gold, and on his head a low mitre. His thin face ended in a long beard. He looked gentle and humble, in spite of his rich costume. This was Bishop Vivantius, an exiled dignitary of the Church of Cyrene, who now gained his livelihood by weaving common stuffs of goats' hair. Two poor children stood by his side. Close by, an old negress unfolded a little white robe. Ahmes set the child down on the ground, and kneeling before the Bishop, said—

"Father, this is the little soul, the child of my soul. I have brought her that you may, according to your promise, and if it please your holiness, bestow on her the baptism of life."

At these words the Bishop opened his arms, and showed his mutilated hands. His nails had been torn out because he had maintained the faith in the days of persecution. Thaïs was frightened, and threw herself into the arms of Ahmes. But the kind words of the priest reassured her.

"Fear nothing, dearly beloved little one. Thou hast here a spiritual father, Ahmes, who is called Theodore amongst the faithful, and a kind mother in grace, who has prepared for thee, with her own hands, a white robe."

And turning towards the negress—

"She is called Nitida," he added, "and is a slave in this world, but in heaven she will be a spouse of Jesus."

Then he said to the child neophyte—

"Thaïs, dost thou believe in God, the Father Almighty; and in His only Son, who died for our salvation; and in all that the apostles taught?"

"Yes," replied together the negro and negress, who held her by each hand.

By the Bishop's orders, Nitida knelt down and undressed Thaïs. The child was quite naked; round her neck was an amulet. The Pontiff plunged her three times into the baptismal font. The acolytes brought the oil, with which Vivantius anointed the catechumen, and the salt, a morsel of which he placed on her tongue. Then, having dried that body which was destined, after many trials, to life immortal, the slave Nitida put on Thaïs the white robe she had woven.

The Bishop gave to each and all the kiss of peace, and, the ceremony being terminated, took off his sacerdotal insignia.

When they had left the crypt, Ahmes said—

"We ought to rejoice that we have this day brought a soul to the good Lord God; let us go to the house of your Holiness and spend the rest of the night in rejoicing."

"Thou hast well said, Theodore," replied the Bishop, and he led the little band to his house, which was quite near. It consisted of a single room, furnished with a couple of looms, a heavy table, and a worn-out carpet. As soon as they had entered,

"Nitida," cried the Nubian, "bring hither the stove and the jar of oil, and we will have a good supper."

Saying thus, he drew from under his cloak some little fish which he had kept concealed, and lighted a fire and fried them. The Bishop, the girl, the two boys, and the two slaves sat in a ring on the carpet, ate the fried fish, and blessed the Lord. Vivantius spoke of the torture he had undergone, and prophesied the speedy triumph of the Church. His language was grotesque, and full of word-play and rhetorical tropes. He compared the life of the just to a tissue of purple, and to explain the mystery of baptism, he said—

"The Divine Spirit floated on the waters, and that is why Christians receive the baptism of water. But demons also inhabit the brooks; springs consecrated to nymphs are especially dangerous, and there are certain waters which cause various maladies, both of the soul and of the body."

Sometimes he spoke enigmatically, and the child listened to him with profound awe and wonder. At the end of the repast he offered his guests a little wine, and this unloosed their tongues, and they began to sing lamentations and hymns. Ahmes and Nitida then rose, and danced a Nubian dance which they had learned as children, and which, no doubt, had been danced by their tribe since the early ages of the world. It was a love dance; waving their arms, and moving their bodies in rhythmic measure, they feigned, in turn, to fly from and to pursue each other. Their big eyes rolled, and they showed their gleaming teeth in broad grins.

In this strange manner did Thaïs receive the holy rite of baptism.

She loved amusements, and, as she grew, vague desires were

created in her mind. All day long she danced and sang with the children in the streets, and when at night she returned to her father's house, she was still singing—

> "Crooked twist, why do you stay in the house?
> I comb the wool, and the Miletan threads.
> Crooked twist, what did your son die of?
> He fell from the white horses into the sea."

She now began to prefer the company of boys and girls to that of the gentle and quiet Ahmes. She did not notice that her friend was not so often with her. The persecution having relented, the Christians were able to assemble more regularly, and the Nubian frequented these meetings assiduously. His zeal increased, and he sometimes uttered mysterious threats. He said that the rich would not keep their wealth. He went to the public places to which the poorer Christians use to resort, and assembling together all the poor wretches who were lying in the shade of the old walls, he announced to them that all slaves would soon be free, and that the day of justice was at hand.

"In the kingdom of God," he said, "the slaves will drink new wine and eat delicious fruits; whilst the rich, crouching at their feet like dogs, will devour the crumbs from their table."

These sayings were noised abroad through all that quarter of the city, and the masters feared that Ahmes might incite the slaves to revolt. The innkeeper hated him intensely, though he carefully concealed his rancour.

One day, a silver salt-cellar, reserved for the table of the gods, disappeared from the inn. Ahmes was accused of having stolen it—out of hate to his master and to the gods of the empire. There was no proof of the accusation, and the slave vehemently denied the charge. Nevertheless, he was dragged before the tribunal, and as he had the reputation of being a bad servant, the judge condemned him to death.

"As you did not know how to make a good use of your hands," he said, "they will be nailed to the cross."

Ahmes heard the verdict quietly, bowed to the judge most respectfully, and was taken to the public prison. During the three days that remained to him, he did not cease to preach the gospel to the prisoners, and it was related afterwards that the criminals, and the gaoler himself, touched by his words, believed in Jesus crucified.

He was taken to the very place which one night, less than two years before, he had crossed so joyfully, carrying in his cloak little Thaïs, the daughter of his soul, his darling flower. When his hands were nailed to the cross, he uttered no complaint, but many times he sighed and murmured, "I thirst."

His agony lasted three days and three nights. It seemed hardly possible that human flesh could have endured such prolonged torture. Many times it was thought he was dead; the flies clustered on his eyelids, but suddenly he would reopen his bloodshot eyes. n the morning of the fourth day, he sang, in a voice clearer and purer than that of a child—

"Tell us, Mary, what thou hast seen where thou hast been?"

Then he smiled and said—

"They come, the angels of the good Lord. They bring me wine and fruit. How refreshing is the fanning of their wings!"

And he expired.

His features preserved in death an expression of ecstatic happiness. Even the soldiers who guarded the cross were struck with wonder. Vivantius, accompanied by some of the Christian brethren, claimed the body, and buried it with the remains of the other martyrs in the crypt of St. John the Baptist, and the Church venerated the memory of Saint Theodore the Nubian.

Three years later, Constantine, the conqueror of Maxentius, issued an edict which granted toleration to the Christians, and the believers were not henceforth persecuted, except by heretics.

Thaïs had completed her eleventh year when her friend was tortured to death, and she felt deeply saddened and shocked. Her soul was not sufficiently pure to allow her to understand that the slave Ahmes was blessed both in his life and his death. The idea sprang up in her little mind that no one can be good in this world except at the cost of the most terrible sufferings. And she was afraid to be good, for her delicate flesh could not bear pain.

At an early age, she had given herself to the lads about the port, and she followed the old men who wandered about the quarter in the evening, and with what she received from them she bought cakes and trinkets.

As she did not take home any of the money she gained, her mother continually ill-treated her. To get out of reach of her mother's arm, she often ran, bare-footed, to the city walls, and hid with the lizards. There she thought with envy of the ladies she had seen pass her, richly dressed, and in a litter surrounded by slaves.

One day, when she had been beaten more brutally than usual, she was crouching down beside the gate, motionless and sulky, when an old woman stopped in front of her, looked at her for some moments in silence, and then cried—

"Oh, the pretty flower! the beautiful child! Happy is the father who begot thee, and the mother who brought thee into the world!"

Thaïs remained silent, with her eyes fixed on the ground. Her eyelids were red, and it was evident she had been weeping.

"My white violet," continued the old woman, "is not your mother happy to have nourished a little goddess like you, and does not your father, when he sees you, rejoice from the bottom of his heart?"

To which the child replied, as though talking to herself—

"My father is a wine-skin swollen with wine, and my mother a greedy horse-leech."

The old woman glanced to right and left, to see if she were observed. Then, in a fawning voice—

"Sweet flowering hyacinth, beautiful drinker of light, come with me, and you shall have nothing to do but dance and smile. I will feed you on honey cakes, and my son—my own son—will love you as his eyes. My son is handsome and young; he has but little beard on his chin; his skin is soft, and he is, as they say, a little Acharnian pig."

Thaïs replied—

"I am quite willing to go with you."

And she rose and followed the old woman out of the city.

The old woman, who was named Mœroë, went from city to city with a troupe of girls and boys, whom she taught to dance, and then hired out to rich people to appear at feasts.

Guessing that Thaïs would soon develop into a most beautiful woman, she taught her—with the help of a whip—music and prosody, and she flogged with leather thongs those beautiful legs, when they did not move in time to the strains of the cithara. Her son—a decrepit abortion, of no age and no sex—ill-treated the child, on whom he vented the hate he had for all womankind. Like the dancing-girls whose grace he affected, he knew, and taught Thaïs, the art of pantomime, and how to mimic, by expression, gesture, and attitude, all human passions, and more especially the passions of love. He was a clever master, though he disliked his work; but he was jealous of his pupil, and as soon as he discovered that she was born to give men pleasure, he scratched her cheeks, pinched her arms, or pricked her legs, as a spiteful girl would have done. Thanks, however, to his lessons, she quickly became an excellent musician, pantomimist, and dancer. The brutality of her master did not at all surprise her; it seemed natural to her to be badly treated. She even felt some respect for the old woman, who knew music and drank Greek wine. Mœroë, when she came to Antioch, praised her pupil to the rich merchants of the city who gave banquets, both as a dancer and a flute-player. Thaïs danced and pleased. She accompanied the rich bankers, when they left the table, into the shady groves on the banks of the Orontes. She gave herself to all, for she knew nothing of the price of love. But one night that she had danced before the most fashionable young men of the city, the son of the pro-consul came to her, radiant with youth and pleasure, and said, in a voice that seemed redolent of kisses—

"Why am I not, Thaïs, the wreath which crowns your hair, the tunic which enfolds your beautiful form, the sandal on your pretty foot? I wish you to tread me under foot as a sandal; I wish my caresses to be your tunic and your wreath. Come, sweet girl! come to my house, and let us forget the world."

She looked at him whilst he was speaking, and saw that he was handsome. Suddenly she felt a cold sweat on her face. She turned green as grass; she reeled; a cloud descended before her eyes. He again implored her to come with him, but she refused. His ardent looks, his burning words were vain, and when he took her in his arms to try and drag her away, she pushed him off rudely. Then he implored her, and shed tears. But a new, unknown, and invincible passion dominated her heart, and she still resisted.

"What madness!" said the guests. "Lollius is noble, handsome, and rich, and a dancing-girl treats him with scorn!"

Lollius returned home alone that night, quite love-sick. He came in the morning, pale and red-eyed, and hung flowers at the dancing-girl's door. But Thaïs was frightened and troubled; she avoided Lollius, and yet he was continually in her mind. She suffered, and she did not know the cause of her complaint. She wondered why she had thus changed, and why she was melancholy. She recoiled from all her lovers; they were hateful to her. She loathed the light of day, and lay on her bed all day, sobbing, and with her head buried in the pillows. Lollius contrived to gain admittance, and came many times, but neither his pleadings nor his execrations had any effect on the obdurate girl. In his presence, she was as timid as a virgin, and would say nothing but—

"I will not! I will not!"

But at the end of a fortnight she gave in, for she knew that she loved him; she went to his house and lived with him. They were supremely happy. They passed their days shut up together, gazing into each other's eyes, and babbling a childish jargon. In the evening, they walked on the lonely banks of the Orontes, and lost themselves in the laurel woods. Sometimes they rose at dawn, to go and gather hyacinths on the slopes of Sulpicus. They drank from the same cup, and he would take a grape from between her lips with his mouth.

Mœroë came to Lollius, and cried and shrieked that Thaïs should be restored to her.

"She is my daughter," she said, "my daughter, who has been torn from me. My perfumed flower—my own bowels—!"

Lollius gave her a large sum of money, and sent her away. But, as she came back to demand some more gold staters, the young man had her put in prison, and the magistrates having discovered that she was guilty of many crimes, she was condemned to death, and thrown to the wild beasts.

Thaïs loved Lollius with all the passion of her mind, and the bewilderment of innocence. She told him, and told him truly from the bottom of her heart—

"I have never loved any one but you."

Lollius replied—

"You are not like any other woman."

The spell lasted six months, but it broke at last. Thaïs suddenly felt that her heart was empty and lonely. Lollius no longer seemed the same to her. She thought—

"What can have thus changed me in an instant? How is it that he is now like any other man, and no longer like himself?"

She left him, not without a secret desire to find Lollius again in another, as she no longer found him in himself. She thought it would be less dull to live with someone she had never loved, than with one she had ceased to love. She appeared, in the company of rich debauchees, at those sacred feasts at which naked virgins danced in the temples, and troops of courtesans swam across the Orontes. She took part in all the pleasures of the fashionable and depraved city; and she assiduously frequented the theatres, at which clever mimes from all countries performed amidst the applause of a crowd greedy for excitement.

She carefully observed the mimes, dancers, comedians, and especially the women, who in tragedies represented goddesses in love with young men, or mortals loved by the gods. Having discovered the secrets by which they pleased the audience, she thought to herself that she was more beautiful and could act better. She went to the manager, and asked to be permitted into the troupe. Thanks to her beauty, and to the lessons she had received from old Mœroë, she was received, and appeared on the stage in the part of Dircé.

She met with but indifferent success, for she was inexperienced, and the admiration of the spectators had not been aroused by hearing her praises sung. But after she had played small parts for a few months, the power of her beauty burst forth with such effect that all the city was moved. All Antioch crowded to the theatre. The imperial magistrates and the chief citizens were compelled, by the force of public opinion, to show themselves there. The porters, sweepers, and dock labourers went without bread and garlic, that they might pay for their places. Poets composed epigrams in her honour. Bearded philosophers inveighed against her in the baths and gymnasia; when her litter passed, Christian priests turned away their heads. The threshold of her door was wreathed with flowers, and sprinkled with blood. She received so much money from her lovers that it was no longer counted, but measured by the medimnus, and all the treasure hoarded by miserly old men was poured out at her feet. But she was placid and unmoved. She rejoiced, with quiet pride, in the admiration of the public and the favour of the gods, and was so much loved that she loved herself.

After she had several years enjoyed the admiration and affection of the Antiochians, she was taken with a desire to revisit Alexandria, and show her glory in that city in which, as a child, she had wandered in want and shame, hungry and lean as a grasshopper in the middle of a dusty road. The golden city joyfully welcomed her, and loaded her with fresh riches; when she appeared in the games it was a triumph. Countless admirers and lovers came to her. She received them with indifference, for she at last despaired of meeting another Lollius.

Amongst many others, she met the philosopher Nicias, who desired to possess her, although he professed to have no desires. In spite of his riches, he was intelligent and modest. But his delicate wit and beautiful sentiments failed to charm her. She did not love him and sometimes his refined irony even irritated her. His perpetual doubts hurt her, for he believed in nothing, and she believed in everything. She believed in divine providence, in the omnipotence of evil spirits, in spells, exorcisms, and eternal justice; she believed in Jesus Christ, and in the goddess of good of the Syrians; she believed also that bitches barked when black Hecate passed through the streets, and that woman could inspire love by pouring a philtre into a cup wrapped in the bleeding skin of a sheep. She thirsted for the unknown; she called on nameless gods, and lived in perpetual expectation. The future frightened her, and yet she wished to know it. She surrounded herself with priests of Isis, Chaldean magi, pharmacopolists, and professors of the black arts, who invariably deceived her, though she never tired of being deceived. She feared death, and she saw it everywhere. When she yielded to pleasure, it seemed to her that an icy finger would suddenly touch her on the bare shoulder, and she turned pale, and cried with terror, in the arms which embraced her.

Nicias said to her—

"What does it matter, O my Thaïs, whether we descend to eternal night with white locks and hollow cheeks, or, whether this very day, now laughing to the vast sky, shall be our last? Let us enjoy life; we shall have greatly lived if we have greatly loved. There is no knowledge except that of the senses; to love is to understand. That which we do not know does not exist. What good is it to worry ourselves about nothing?"

She replied angrily—

"I despise men like you, who hope for nothing and fear nothing. I wish to *know!* I wish to *know!*"

In order to understand the secret of life, she set to work to read the books of the philosophers, but she did not understand them. The further the years of her childhood receded from her, the more anxious she was to recall them. She loved to traverse at night, in disguise, the alleys, squares, and places where she had grown up so miserably. She was sorry she had lost her parents, and especially that she had not been able to love them. When she met any Christian priest, she thought of her baptism, and felt troubled. One night, when enveloped in a long cloak, and her fair hair hidden under a black hood, she was wandering, according to custom, about the suburbs of the city, she found herself—without knowing how she came there—before the poor little church of St. John the Baptist. They were singing inside the church, and a bright light glimmered through the chinks of the door. There was nothing strange in that, as, for the past twenty years, the Christians, protected by the conqueror of Maxentius, had publicly solemnised their festivals. But these hymns seemed more like an ardent appeal to the soul. As if she had been invited to the mysteries, she pushed the door open with her arm, and entered the building. She found a numerous assembly of women, children, and old men, on their knees before a tomb, which stood against the wall. The tomb was nothing but a stone coffer, roughly sculptured with vine tendrils and bunches of grapes; yet it had received great honours, and was covered with green palms and wreaths of red roses. All round, innumerable lights gleamed out of the heavy shadow, in which the smoke of Arabian gums seemed like the folds of angels' robes, and the paintings on the walls visions of Paradise. Priests, clad in white, were prostrate at the foot of the sarcophagus. The hymns they sang with the people expressed the delight of suffering, and mingled, in a triumphal mourning, so much joy with so much grief, that Thaïs, in listening to them, felt the pleasures of life and the terrors of death at the same time, through her re-awakened senses.

When they had finished singing, the believers rose, and walked in single file to the tomb, the side of which they kissed. They were common men, accustomed to work with their hands. They advanced with a heavy step, the eyes fixed, the jaw dropped, but they had an air of sincerity. They knelt down, each in turn, before the sarcophagus, and put their lips to it. The women lifted their little children in their arms, and gently placed their cheek to the stone.

Thaïs, surprised and troubled, asked a deacon why they did so.

"Do you not know, woman," replied the deacon, "that we celebrate to-day the blessed memory of St. Theodore the Nubian, who suffered for the faith in the days of the Emperor Diocletian? He lived virtuously and died a martyr, and that is why, robed in white, we bear red roses to his glorious tomb."

On hearing these words, Thaïs fell on her knees, and burst into tears. Half-forgotten recollections of Ahmes returned to her mind. On the memory of this obscure, gentle, and unfortunate man, the blaze of candles, the perfume of roses, the clouds of incense, the music of hymns, the piety of souls, threw all the charms of glory. Thaïs thought in the dazzling glare—

"He was good, and now he has become great and glorious. Why

is it that he is elevated above other men? What is this unknown thing which is more than riches or pleasure?"

She rose slowly, and turned towards the tomb of the saint who had loved her, those violet eyes, now filled with tears which glittered in the candle-light; then, with bowed head, humble, slow, and the last, with those lips on which so many desires hung, she kissed the stone of the slave's tomb.

When she returned to her house, she found Nicias, who, with his hair perfumed, and his tunic thrown open, was reading a treatise on morals whilst waiting for her. He advanced with open arms.

"Naughty Thaïs," he said, in a laughing voice, "whilst I was waiting for you to come, do you know what I saw in this manuscript, written by the gravest of Stoics? Precepts of virtue and noble maxims: No! On the staid papyrus, I saw dance thousands and thousands of little Thaïses. Each was no bigger than my finger, and yet their grace was infinite, and all were the only Thaïs. There were some who flaunted in mantles of purple and gold; others, like a white cloud, floated in the air in transparent drapery. Others again, motionless and divinely nude, the better to inspire pleasure, expressed no thought. Lastly, there were two, hand in hand; two so alike that it was impossible to distinguish one from the other. Both smiled. The first said, 'I am love.' The other, 'I am death.'"

Thus speaking, he pressed Thaïs in his arms, and not noticing the sullen look in her downcast eyes, he went on adding thought to thought, heedless of the fact that they were all lost upon her.

"Yes, when I had before my eyes the line in which it was written, 'Nothing should deter you from improving your mind,' I read, 'The kisses of Thaïs are warmer than fire, and sweeter than honey.' That is how a philosopher reads the books of other philosophers—and that is your fault, you naughty child. It is true that, as long as we are what we are, we shall never find anything but our own thoughts in the thoughts of others, and that all of us are somewhat inclined to read books as I have read this one."

She did not hear him; her soul was still before the Nubian's tomb. As he heard her sigh, he kissed her on the neck, and said—

"Do not be sad, my child. We are never happy in this world, except when we forget the world. Come, let us cheat life—it is sure to take its revenge. Come, let us love!"

But she pushed him away.

"*We* love!" she cried bitterly. "*You* never loved any one. And *I* do not love *you!* No! I do not love you! I hate you! Go! I hate you! I curse and despise all who are happy, and all who are rich Go! Go! Goodness is only found amongst the unfortunate. When I was a child I knew a black slave who died on the cross. He was good; he was filled with love, and he knew the secret of life. You are not worthy to wash his feet. Go! I never wish to see you again!"

She threw herself on her face on the carpet, and passed the night sobbing and weeping, and forming resolutions to live, in future, like Saint Theodore, in poverty and humbleness.

The next day, she devoted herself again to those pleasures to which she was addicted. As she knew that her beauty, though still intact, would not last very long, she hastened to derive all the enjoyment and all the fame she could from it. At the theatre, where she acted and studied more than ever, she gave life to the imagination of sculptors, painters, and poets. Recognising that there was in the attitudes, movements, and walk of the actress, an idea of the divine harmony which rules the spheres, wise men and philosophers considered that such perfect grace was a virtue in itself, and said, "Thaïs also is a geometrician!" The ignorant, the poor, the humble, and the timid before whom she consented to appear, regarded her as a blessing from heaven. Yet she was sad amidst all the praise she received, and dreaded death more than ever. Nothing was able to set her mind at rest, not even her house and gardens, which were celebrated, and a proverb throughout the city.

The gardens were planted with trees, brought at great expense from India and Persia. They were watered by a running brook, and colonnades in ruins, and imitation rocks, arranged by a skilful artist, were reflected in a lake, which also mirrored the statues that stood round it. In the middle of the garden was the Grotto of Nymphs, which owed its name to three life-size figures of women, which stood on the threshold. They were represented as divesting themselves of their garments, and about to bathe. They anxiously turned their heads, fearing to be seen, and looked as though they were alive. The only light which entered the building came, tempered and iridescent, through thin sheets of water. All the walls were hung—as in the sacred grottoes—with wreaths, garlands, and votive pictures, in which the beauty of Thaïs was celebrated. There were also tragic and comic masks, bright with colours; and paintings representing theatrical scenes, or grotesque figures, or fabulous animals. On a stele in the centre stood a little ivory Eros of wonderful antique workmanship. It was a gift from Nicias. In one of the bays was a figure of a goat in black marble, with shining agate eyes. Six alabaster kids crowded round its teats; but, raising its cloven hoofs and its ugly head, it seemed impatient to climb the rocks. The floor was covered with Byzantine carpets, pillows embroidered by the yellow men of Cathay, and the skins of Libyan lions. Perfumed smoke arose from golden censers. Flowering plants grew in large onyx vases. And at the far end, in the purple shadow, gleamed the gold nails on the shell of a huge Indian tortoise turned upside down, which served as the bed of the actress. It was here that every day, to the murmur of the water, and amid perfumes and flowers, Thaïs reclined softly, and conversed with her friends, while awaiting the hour of supper, or meditated in solitude on theatrical art, or on the flight of years.

On the afternoon after the games, Thaïs was reposing in the Grotto of Nymphs. She had noticed in her mirror the first signs of the decay of her beauty, and she was frightened to think that white hair and wrinkles would at last come. She vainly tried to comfort herself with the assurance that she could recover her fresh complexion by burning certain herbs and pronouncing a few magic words. A pitiless voice cried, "You will grow old Thaïs; you will grow old." And a cold sweat of terror bedewed her forehead. Then, on looking at herself again in the mirror with infinite tenderness, she found that she was still beautiful and worthy to be loved. She smiled to herself, and murmured, "There is not a woman in Alexandria who can rival me in suppleness or grace or movement, or in splendour of arms, and the arms, my mirror, are the real chains of love!"

While she was thus thinking she saw an unknown man—thin, with burning eyes and unkempt beard, and clad in a richly embroidered robe—standing before her. She let fall her mirror, and uttered a cry of fright.

Paphnutius stood motionless, and seeing how beautiful she was, he murmured this prayer from the bottom of his heart—

"Grant, my God, that the face of this woman may not be a temptation, but may prove salutary to Thy servant."

Then, forcing himself to speak, he said—

"Thaïs, I live in a far country, and the fame of thy beauty has led me to thee. It is said that thou art the most clever of actresses and the most irresistible of women. That which is related of thy riches and thy love affairs seems fabulous, and calls to mind the old story of Rhodope, whose marvellous history is known by heart to all the boatmen on the Nile. Therefore I was seized with a desire to know thee, and I see that the truth surpasses the rumour. Thou art a thousand times more clever and more beautiful than is reported. And now that I see thee, I say to myself, 'It is impossible to approach her without staggering like a drunken man.'"

The words were feigned; but the monk, animated by pious zeal, uttered them with real warmth. Thaïs gazed, without displeasure, at this strange being who had frightened her. The rough, wild aspect, and the fiery glances of his eyes, astonished her. She was curious to learn the state of life of a man so different from all others she had met. She replied, with gentle raillery—

"You seem prompt to admire, stranger. Beware that my looks do not consume you to the bones! Beware of loving me!"

He said—

"I love thee, O Thaïs! I love thee more than my life, and more than myself. For thee I have quitted the desert; for thee my lips— vowed to silence—have pronounced profane words; for thee I have seen what I ought not to have seen, and heard what it was forbidden to me to hear; for thee my soul is troubled, my heart is open, and the thoughts gush out like the running springs at which the pigeons drink; for thee I have walked day and night across sandy deserts teeming with reptiles and vampires; for thee I have placed my bare foot on vipers and scorpions! Yes, I love thee! I love thee, but not like those men who, burning with the lusts of the flesh, come to thee like devouring wolves or furious bulls. Thou art dear to them as is the gazelle to the lion. Their ravening lusts will consume thee to the soul, O woman! I love thee in spirit and in truth; I love thee in God, and for ever and ever; that which is in my breast is named true zeal and divine charity. I promise thee better things than drunkenness crowned with flowers or the dreams of a brief night. I promise thee holy feasts and celestial suppers. The happiness that I bring thee will never end; it is unheard-of, it is ineffable, and such that if the happy of this world could only see a shadow of it they would die of wonder."

Thaïs laughed mischievously.

"Friend," she said, "show me this wonderful love. Make haste! Long speeches would be an insult to my beauty; let us not lose a moment. I am impatient to taste the felicity you announce; but, to say the truth, I fear that I shall always remain ignorant of it, and that all you have promised me will vanish in words. It is easier to promise a great happiness than to give it. Everyone has a talent of some sort. I fancy that yours is to make long speeches. You speak of an unknown love. It is so long since kisses were first exchanged that it would be very extraordinary if there still remained secrets in love. On this subject lovers knew more than philosophers."

"Do not jest, Thaïs. I bring thee the unknown love."

"Friend, you come too late. I know every kind of love."

"The love that I bring thee abounds with glory, whilst the loves that thou knowest breed only shame."

Thaïs looked at him with an angry eye, a frown gathered on her beautiful face.

"You are very bold, stranger, to offend your hostess. Look at me, and say if I resemble a creature crushed down with shame. No, I am not ashamed, and all others who live like me are not ashamed either, although they are not so beautiful or so rich as I am. I have sown pleasure in my footsteps, and I am celebrated for that all over the world. I am more powerful than the masters of the world. I have seen them at my feet. Look at me, look at these little feet; thousands of men would pay with their blood for the happiness of kissing them. I am not very big, and I do not occupy much space on the earth. To those who look at me from the top of the Serapeium, when I pass in the street, I look like a grain of rice; but that grain of rice has caused among men, griefs, despairs, hates, and crimes enough to have filled Tartarus. Are you not mad to talk to me of shame when all around proclaims my glory?"

"That which is glory in the eyes of men, is infamy before God.

O woman, we have been nourished in countries so different, that it is not surprising we have neither the same language nor the same thoughts! Yet Heaven is my witness that I wish to agree with thee, and that it is my intention not to leave thee until we share the same sentiments. Who will inspire me with burning words that will melt thee like wax in my breath, O woman, that the fingers of my desires may mould thee as they wish? What virtue will deliver thee to me, O dearest of souls, that the spirit which animates me, creating thee a second time, may imprint on thee a fresh beauty, and that thou mayest cry, weeping for joy, 'It is only now that I am born'? Who will cause to gush in my heart a fount of Siloam, in which thou mayest bathe and recover thy first purity? Who will change me into a Jordan, the waves of which sprinkled on thee, will give thee life eternal?"

Thaïs was no longer angry.

"This man," she thought, "talks of life eternal, and all that he says seems written on a talisman. No doubt he is a mage, and knows secret charms against old age and death," and she resolved to offer herself to him. Therefore, pretending to be afraid of him, she retired a few steps to the end of the grotto, and sitting down on the edge of the bed, artfully pulled her tunic across her breast; then, motionless and mute and her eyes cast down, she waited. Her long eyelashes made a soft shadow on her cheeks. Her entire attitude expressed modesty; her naked feet swung gently, and she looked like a child sitting thinking on the bank of a brook.

But Paphnutius looked at her, and did not move. His trembling knees hardly supported him, his tongue dried in his mouth, a terrible buzzing rang in his ears. But all at once his sight failed, and he could see nothing before him but a thick cloud. He thought that the hand of Jesus had been laid on his eyes, to hide this woman from them. Reassured by such succour, strengthened and fortified, he said with a gravity worthy of an old hermit of the desert—

"If thou givest thyself to me, thinkest thou it is hidden from God?"

She shook her head.

"God? Who forces Him to keep His eye always upon the Grotto of Nymphs? Let Him go away if we offend Him! But why should we offend Him? Since He has created us, He can be neither angry nor surprised to see us as He made us, and acting according to the nature He has given us. A good deal too much is said on His behalf, and He is often credited with ideas He never had. You yourself, stranger, do you know His true character? Who are you that you should speak to me in His name?"

At this question the monk, opening his borrowed robe, showed the cassock, and said—

"I am Paphnutius, Abbot of Antinoë, and I come from the holy desert. The hand that drew Abraham from Chaldæa and Lot from

Sodom has separated me from the present age. I no longer existed for the men of this century. But thy image appeared to me in my sandy Jerusalem, and I knew that thou wert full of corruption, and death was in thee. And now I am before thee, woman, as before a grave, and I cry unto thee, 'Thaïs, arise!' "

At the words, Paphnutius, monk, and abbot, she had turned pale with fright. And now, with dishevelled hair and joined hands, weeping and groaning, she dragged herself to the feet of the saint.

"Do not hurt me! Why have you come? What do you want of me? Do not hurt me! I know that the saints of the desert hate women who, like me, are made to please. I am afraid that you hate me, and want to hurt me. Go! I do not doubt your power. But know, Paphnutius, that you should neither despise me nor hate me. I have never, like many of the men I know, laughed at your voluntary poverty. In your turn, do not make a crime of my riches. I am beautiful, and clever in acting. I no more chose my condition than my nature. I was made for that which I do. I was born to charm men. And you yourself, did you not say just now that you loved me? Do not use your science against me. Do not pronounce magic words which would destroy my beauty, or change me into a statue of salt. Do not terrify me! I am already too frightened. Do not kill me! I am so afraid of death."

He made a sign to her to rise, and said—

"Child, have no fear. I will utter no word of shame or scorn. I come on behalf of Him who sat on the edge of the well, and drank of the pitcher which the woman of Samaria offered to Him; and who, also, when He supped at the house of Simon, received the perfumes of Mary. I am not without sin that I should throw the first stone. I have often badly employed the abundant grace which God has bestowed upon me. It was not anger, but pity, which took me by the hand to conduct me here. I can, without deceit, address thee in words of love, for it is the zeal in my heart which has brought me to thee. I burn with the fire of charity, and if thy eyes, accustomed only to the gross sights of the flesh, could see things in their mystic aspect, I should appear unto thee as a branch broken off the burning bush which the Lord showed on the mountain to Moses of old, that he might understand true love—that which envelops us, and which, so far from leaving behind it mere coals and ashes, purifies and perfumes for ever that which it penetrates."

"I believe you, monk, and no longer fear either deceit or ill-will from you. I have often heard talk of the hermits of the Thebaid. Marvellous things have been told concerning Anthony and Paul. Your name is not unknown to me, and I have heard say that, though you are still young, you equal in virtue the oldest anchorites. As soon as I saw you, and without knowing who you were, I felt that you were no ordinary man. Tell me! can you do for me that which neither the priests of Isis, nor of Hermes, nor of the celestial Juno, nor the Chaldean soothsayers, nor the Babylonian magi have been able to effect? Monk, if you love me, can you prevent me from dying?"

"Woman, whosoever wishes to live shall live. Flee from the abominable delights in which thou diest for ever. Snatch from the devils, who will burn it most horribly, that body which God kneaded with His spittle and animated with his own breath. Thou art consumed with weariness; come, and refresh thyself at the blessed springs of solitude; come and drink of those fountains which are hidden in the desert, and which gush forth to heaven. Careworn soul, come, and possess that which thou desirest! Heart greedy for joy, come and taste true joys—poverty, retirement, self-forgetfulness, seclusion in the bosom of God. Enemy of Christ now, and to-morrow His well-beloved, come to Him! Come, thou whom I have sought, and thou wilt say, 'I have found love!'"

Thaïs seemed lost in meditation on things afar.

"Monk," she asked, "if I adjure all pleasures and do penance, is it true that I shall be born again in heaven, my body intact in all its beauty?"

"Thaïs, I bring thee eternal life. Believe me, for that which I announce to thee is the truth."

"Who will assure me that it is the truth?"

"David and the prophets, the Scriptures, and the wonders that thou shalt behold."

"Monk, I should like to believe you, for I must confess that I have not found happiness in this world. My lot in life is better than that of a queen, and yet I have many bitternesses and misfortunes, and I am infinitely weary of my existence. All women envy me, and yet sometimes I have envied the lot of a toothless old woman who, when I was a child, sold honey-cakes under one of the city gates. Often has the idea flashed across my mind that only the poor are good, happy, and blessed, and that there must be great gladness in living humble and obscure. Monk, you have agitated a storm in my soul, and brought to the surface that which lay at the bottom. Who am I to believe, alas! and what is to become of me—and what is life?"

Whilst she thus spoke, Paphnutius was transfigured; celestial joy beamed in his face.

"Listen!" he said. "I was not alone when I entered this house. Another accompanied me, another who stands by my side. Him thou canst not see, because thy eyes are yet unworthy to behold Him; but soon thou shalt see Him in all His glorious splendour, and thou wilt say, 'He alone is to be adored.' But now, if He had not placed His gentle hands before my eyes, O Thaïs, I should perhaps have fallen into sin with thee, for of myself I am but weak and sinful. But He saved us both. He is as good as He is powerful, and His name is the Saviour. He was promised to the world, by David and the prophets, worshipped in His cradle by the shepherds and the magi, crucified by the Pharisees, buried by the holy women, revealed to the world by the apostles, testified to by the martyrs. And now, having learned that thou fearest death, O woman, He has come to thy house to prevent thee from dying. Art Thou not here present with me, Jesus, at this moment, as Thou didst appear to the men of Galilee, in those wonderful days when the stars, which came down with thee from heaven, were so near the earth that the holy innocents could take them in their hands, when they played in their mothers' arms on the terraces of Bethlehem? Is it not true, Jesus, that Thou art here present, and that Thou showest me in reality Thy precious body? Is not Thy face here, and that tear which flows down Thy cheek a real tear? Yes, the angel of eternal justice shall receive it, and it shall be the ransom of the soul of Thaïs. Art Thou not here, Jesus? Jesus, Thy loving lips open. Thou canst speak; speak, I hear Thee! And thee, Thaïs, happy Thaïs! listen to what the Saviour Himself says to thee; it is He who speaks, not I. He says, 'I have sought thee long, O my lost sheep! I have found thee at last! Fly from Me no more. Let me take thee by the hands, poor little one, and I will bear thee on My shoulders to the heavenly fold. Come, my Thaïs! come, my chosen one! come, and weep with Me!'"

And Paphnutius fell on his knees, his eyes filled with ecstasy. And then Thaïs saw in his face the likeness of the living Christ.

"O vanished days of my childhood!" she sobbed. "O sweet father Ahmes! good Saint Theodore, why did I not die in thy white mantle whilst thou didst bear me, in the first dawn of day, yet fresh from the waters of baptism!"

Paphnutius advanced towards her, crying—

"Thou art baptised! O divine wisdom! O Providence! O great God! I know now the power which drew me to thee. I know what rendered thee so dear and so beautiful in my eyes. It was the virtue of the baptismal water, which made me leave the shadow of God, where I lived, to seek thee in the poisoned air where men dwell. A drop—a drop, no doubt, of the water which washed thy body—has been sprinkled in my face. Come, O my sister, and receive from thy brother the kiss of peace."

And the monk touched with his lips the forehead of the courtesan.

Then he was silent, letting God speak, and nothing was heard in the Grotto of Nymphs but the sobs of Thaïs, mingled with the rippling of the running water.

She wept without trying to stop her tears, when two black slaves appeared, loaded with stuffs, perfumes, and garlands.

"It was hardly the right time to weep," she said, trying to smile. "Tears redden the eyes and spoil the complexion, and I must sup to-night with some friends, and want to be beautiful, for there will be women there quick to spy out marks of care on my face. These slaves come to dress me. Withdraw, my father, and allow them to do their work. They are clever and experienced, and I pay them well for their services. You see that one who wears thick rings of gold, and shows such white teeth. I took her from the wife of the pro-consul."

Paphnutius had at first a thought of dissuading Thaïs, as earnestly as he could, from going to this supper. But he determined to act prudently, and asked what persons she would meet there.

She replied that there would be the host, old Cotta, the Prefect of the Fleet, Nicias, and several other philosophers who loved an argument, the poet Callicrates, the high priest of Serapis, some young men whose chief amusement was training horses, and lastly some women, of whom there was little to be said except that they were young. Then, by a supernatural inspiration—

"Go amongst them, Thaïs," said the monk. "Go! But I will not leave thee. I will go with thee to this banquet, and will remain by thy side without saying a word."

She burst out laughing. And whilst her two black slaves were busy dressing her, she cried—

"What will they say when they see that I have a monk of the Thebaid for my lover?"

THE BANQUET

WHEN, followed by Paphnutius, Thaïs entered the banqueting-room, the guests were already, for the most part, assembled, and reclining on their couches before the horseshoe table, which was covered with glittering vessels. In the centre of the table stood a silver basin, surmounted by four figures of satyrs, who poured out from wine-skins on the boiled fish a kind of pickle in which they floated. When Thaïs appeared, acclamations arose from all sides.

Greetings to the sister of the Graces!

To the silent Melpomene, who can express all things with her looks!

Salutation to the well-beloved of gods and men!

To the much desired!

To her who gives suffering and its cure!

To the pearl of Racotis!

To the rose of Alexandria!

She waited impatiently till this torrent of praise had passed, and then said to Cotta, the host—

"Lucius, I have brought you a monk of the desert, Paphnutius, the Abbot of Antinoë. He is a great saint, whose words burn like fire."

Lucius Aurelius Cotta, the Prefect of the Fleet, rose, and replied—

"You are welcome, Paphnutius, you who profess the Christian faith. I myself have some respect of a religion that has now become imperial. The divine Constantine has placed your co-religionists in the front rank of the friends of the empire. Latin wisdom ought, in fact, to admit your Christ into our pantheon. It was a maxim of our forefathers that there was something divine in every god. But no more of that. Let us drink and enjoy ourselves while there is yet time."

Old Cotta spoke tranquilly. He had just studied a new model for a galley, and had finished the sixth book of his history of the Carthaginians. He felt sure he had not lost his day, and was satisfied with himself and the gods.

"Paphnutius," he added, "you see here several men who are worthy to be loved—Hermodorus, the High Priest of Serapis; the philosophers Dorion, Nicias, and Zenothemis; the poet Callicrates; young Chereas and young Aristobulus, both sons of dear old comrades; and near them Philina and Drosea, who deserve to be praised for their beauty."

Nicias embraced Paphnutius, and whispered in his ear—

"I warned you, brother, that Venus was powerful. It is her gentle force that has brought you here in spite of yourself. Listen: you are a man full of piety, but if you do not confess that she is the mother of the gods, your ruin is certain. Do you know that the old mathematician, Melanthes, used to say, 'I cannot demonstrate the properties of a triangle without the aid of Venus'?"

Dorion, who had for some seconds been looking at the new-comer, suddenly clapped his hands and uttered a cry of surprise.

"It is he, friends! His look, his beard, his tunic—it is he himself! I met him at the theatre whilst our Thaïs was acting. He was furiously excited, and spoke with violence, as I can testify. He is an honest man, but he will abuse us all; his eloquence is terrible. If Marcus is the Plato of the Christians, Paphnutius is the Demosthenes. Epicurus, in his little garden, never heard the like."

Philina and Drosea, however, devoured Thaïs with their eyes. She wore on her fair hair a wreath of pale violets, each flower of which recalled, in a paler hue, the colour of her eyes, so that the flowers looked like softened glances, and the eyes like sparkling flowers. It was the peculiar gift of this woman; on her everything lived, and was soul and harmony. Her robe, which was of mauve spangled with silver, trailed in long folds with a grace that was almost melancholy and was not relieved by either bracelets or necklaces. The chief charm of her appearance was her beautiful bare arms. The two friends were obliged to admire, in spite of themselves the robe and head-dress of Thaïs, though they said nothing to her on the subject.

"How beautiful you are!" said Philina. "You could not have been more so when you came to Alexandria. Yet my mother, who remembers seeing you then, says there were few women who were worthy to be compared with you."

"Who is the new lover you have brought?" asked Drosea. "He has a strange, wild appearance. If there are shepherds of elephants, assuredly he must resemble one. Where did you find such a wild-looking friend, Thaïs? Was it amongst the troglodytes who live under the earth, and are grimy with the smoke of Hades?"

But Philina put her finger on Drosea's lips.

"Hush! the mysteries of love must remain secret, and it is forbidden to know them. For my own part, certainly, I would rather be kissed by the mouth of smoking Etna than by the lips of that man. But our dear Thaïs, who is beautiful and adorable as the goddesses, should, like the goddesses, grant all requests, and not, like us, only those of nice young men."

"Take care, both of you!" replied Thaïs. "He is a mage and an enchanter. He hears words that are whispered, and even thoughts. He will tear out your heart while you are asleep, and put a sponge in its place, and the next day, when you drink water, you will be choked to death."

She watched them grow pale, then she turned away from them,

and sat on a couch by the side of Paphnutius. The voice of Cotta, kind but imperious, was suddenly heard above the murmur of conversation.

"Friends, let each take his place! Slaves, pour out the honeyed wine!"

Then, the host raising his cup—

"Let us first drink to the divine Constantine and the genius of the empire. The country should be put first of all, even above the gods, for it contains them all."

All the guests raised their full cups to their lips. Paphnutius alone did not drink, because Constantine had persecuted the Nicæan faith, and because the country of the Christian is not of this world.

Dorion, having drunk, murmured—

"What is one's country? A flowing river. The shores change, and the waves are incessantly renewed."

"I know, Dorion," replied the Prefect of the Fleet, "that you care little for the civic virtues, and you think that the sage ought to hold himself aloof from all affairs. I think, on the contrary, that an honest man should desire nothing better than to fill a responsible post in the State. The State is a noble thing."

Hermodorus, the High Priest of Serapis, spoke next—

"Dorion has asked, 'What is one's country?' I will reply that the altars of the gods and the tombs of ancestors make one's country. A man is a fellow-citizen by association of memories and hopes."

Young Aristobulus interrupted Hermodorus.

"By Castor! I saw a splendid horse to-day. It belonged to Demophoon. It has a fine head, small jaw, and strong forelegs. It carries its neck high and proud, like a cock."

But young Chereas shook his head.

"It is not such a good horse as you say, Aristobulus. Its hoofs are thin, and the pasterns are too low; the animal will soon go lame."

They were continuing their dispute, when Drosea uttered a piercing shriek.

"Oh! I nearly swallowed a fish-bone, as long and much sharper than a style. Luckily, I was able to get it out of my throat in time! The gods love me!"

"Did you say, Drosea, that the gods loved you?" asked Nicias, smiling. "Then they must share the same infirmities as men. Love presupposes unhappiness on the part of whoever suffers from it, and is a proof of weakness. The affection they feel for Drosea is a great proof of the imperfection of the gods."

At these words Drosea flew into a great rage.

"Nicias, your remarks are foolish and not to the point. But that is your character—you never understand what is said, and reply in words devoid of sense."

Nicias smiled again.

"Talk away, talk away, Drosea. Whatever you say, we are glad every time you open your mouth. Your teeth are so pretty!"

At that moment, a grave-looking old man, negligently dressed, walking slowly, with his head high, entered the room, and gazed at the guests quietly. Cotta made a sign to him to take a place by his side, on the same couch.

"Eucrites," he said, "you are welcome. Have you composed a new treatise on philosophy this month? That would make, if I calculate correctly, the ninety-second that has proceeded from the Nile reed you direct with an Attic hand."

Eucrites replied, stroking his silver beard—

"The nightingale was created to sing, and I was created to praise the immortal gods."

DORION. Let us respectfully salute, in Eucrites, the last of the stoics. Grave and white, he stands in the midst of us like the image of an ancestor. He is solitary amidst a crowd of men, and the words he utters are not heard.

EUCRITES. You deceive yourself, Dorion. The philosophy of virtue is not dead. I have numerous disciples in Alexandria, Rome, and Constantinople. Many of the slaves, and some of the nephews of Cæsar, now know how to govern themselves, to live independently, and being unconcerned with all affairs, they enjoy boundless happiness. Many of them have revived, in their own person, Epictetus and Marcus Aurelius. But if it were true that virtue were for ever extinguished upon the earth, in what way would the loss of it affect my happiness, since it did not depend on me whether it existed or perished? Only fools, Dorion, place their happiness out of their own power. I desire nothing that the gods do not wish, and I desire all that they do wish. By that means I render myself like unto them, and share their infallible content. If virtue perishes, I consent that it should perish, and that consent fills me with joy, as the supreme effort of my reason or my courage. In all things my wisdom will copy the divine wisdom, and the copy will be more valuable than the model; it will have cost greater care and more work.

NICIAS. I understand. You put yourself on the same level as divine providence. But if virtue consists only in effort, Eucrites, and in that intense application by which the disciples of Zeno pretend to render themselves equal to the gods, the frog, which swelled itself out to try and become as big as the ox, accomplished a masterpiece of stoicism.

EUCRITES. You jest, Nicias, and, as usual, you excel in ridicule. But if the ox of which you speak is really a god, like Apis, or like that subterranean ox whose high priest I see here, and if the frog, being wisely inspired, succeed in equalling it, would it not be, in fact, more virtuous than the ox, and could you refrain from admiring such a courageous little animal!

Four servants placed on the table a wild pig, still covered with its bristles. Little pigs, made of pastry, surrounded the animal, as though they would suckle, to show that it was a sow.

Zenothemis, turning towards the monk, said—

"Friends, a guest has come hither to join us. The illustrious Paphnutius, who leads such an extraordinary life of solitude, is our unexpected guest."

COTTA. You may even add, Zenothemis, that the place of honour is due to him, because he came without being invited.

ZENOTHEMIS. Therefore, we ought, my dear Lucius, to make him the more welcome, and strive to do that which would be most agreeable to him. Now it is certain that such a man cares less for the fumes of meat than for the perfumes of fine thoughts. We shall, doubtless, please him by discussing the doctrine he professes, which is that of Jesus crucified. For my own part, I shall the more willingly discuss this doctrine, because it keenly interests me, on account of the number and the diversity of the allegories it contains. If one may guess at the spirit by the letter, it is filled with truths, and I consider that the Christian books abound in divine revelations. But I should not, Paphnutius, grant equal merit to the Jewish books. They were inspired not, as it was said, by the Spirit of God, but by an evil genius. Iaveh, who dictated them, was one of those spirits who people the lower air, and cause the greater part of the evils, from which we suffer; but he surpassed all the others in ignorance and ferocity. On the contrary, the serpent with golden wings, which twined its azure coils round the tree of knowledge, was made up of light and love. A combat between these two powers—the one of light and the other of darkness—was, therefore, inevitable. It occurred soon after the creation of the world. God had hardly begun to rest after His labours; Adam and Eve, the first man and the first woman, lived happy and naked in the Garden of Eden, when Iaveh conceived—to their misfortune—the design of governing them and all the generations which Eve already bore in her splendid loins. As he possessed neither the compass nor the lyre, and was equally ignorant of the science which commands and the art which persuades, he frightened these two poor children by hideous apparitions, capricious threats, and thunder-bolts. Adam and Eve, feeling his shadow upon them, pressed closer to one another, and their love waxed stronger in fear. The serpent took pity on them, and determined to instruct them, in order that, possessing knowledge, they might no longer be misled by lies. Such an undertaking required extreme prudence, and the frailty of the first human couple rendered it almost hopeless. The well-intentioned demon essayed it, however. Without the knowledge of Iaveh—who pretended to see everything, but, in reality, was not very sharp-sighted—he approached these two beings, and charmed their eyes by the splendour of his coat and the brilliancy of his wings. Then he interested their minds by forming before them, with his body, definite figures, such as the circle, the ellipse, and the spiral, the wonderful properties of which have since been recognised by the Greeks. Adam meditated on these figures more than Eve did. But when the serpent began to speak, and taught the most sublime truths—those which cannot be demonstrated—he found that Adam being made of red earth, was of too dull a nature to understand these subtle distinctions, but that Eve, on the contrary, being more tender and more sensitive, was easily impressed. Therefore he conversed with her alone, in the absence of her husband, in order to initiate her first—

DORION. Permit me, Zenothemis, to interrupt you. I speedily recognised in the myth you have explained to us an episode in the war of Pallas Athene against the giants. Iaveh much resembles Typhoon, and Pallas is represented by the Athenians with a serpent at her side. But what you have said causes me considerable doubt as to the intelligence or good faith of the serpent of whom you have spoken. If he had really possessed knowledge, would he have entrusted it to a woman's little head, which was incapable of containing it? I should rather consider that he was like Iaveh, ignorant and a liar, and that he chose Eve because she was easily seduced, and he imagined that Adam would have more intelligence and perception.

ZENOTHEMIS. Learn, Dorion, that it is not by perception and intelligence, but by sensibility, that the highest and purest truths are reached. That is why women, who, generally, are less reflective but more sensitive than men, rise more easily to the knowledge of things divine. In them is the gift of prophecy, and it is not without reason that Apollo Citharedes, and Jesus of Nazareth, are sometimes represented clad, like women, in flowing robes. The initiator was therefore wise—whatever you may say to the contrary, Dorion —in bestowing light, not on the duller Adam, but on Eve, who was whiter than milk or the stars. She freely listened to him, and allowed herself to be led to the tree of knowledge, the branches of which rose to heaven, and which was bathed with the divine spirit as with a dew. This tree was covered with leaves which spoke all the languages of future races of men, and their united voices formed a perfect harmony. Its abundant fruit gave to the initiated who tasted it the knowledge of metals, stones, and plants, and also of physical and moral laws; but this fruit was like fire, and those who feared suffering and death did not dare to put it to their lips. Now, as she had listened attentively to the lessons of the serpent, Eve despised these empty terrors, and wished to taste the fruit which gave the knowledge of God. But, as she loved Adam, and did not wish him to be inferior to her, she took him by the hand and led him to the wonderful tree. Then she picked one of the burning apples, bit it, and proffered it to her companion. Unfortunately, Iaveh, who was by chance walking in the garden, surprised them, and seeing that they had become wise, he fell into a most ungovernable rage. It is in his jealous fits that he is most to be feared. Assembling all his forces, he created such a turmoil in the lower air that these two weak beings were terrified. The fruit fell from the man's hand, and the woman, clinging to the neck of her luckless husband, said, "I too will be ignorant and suffer with him." The triumphant Iaveh kept Adam and Eve and all their seed in a condition of hebetude and terror. His art, which consisted only in being able to make huge meteors, triumphed over the science of the serpent, who was a musician and geometrician. He made men unjust, ignorant, and cruel, and caused evil to reign in the earth. He persecuted Cain and his sons because they were skilful workmen; he exterminated the Philistines because they composed Orphic poems and fables like those of Æsop. He was the implacable enemy of science and beauty, and for long ages the human race expiated, in blood and tears, the defeat of the winged serpent. Fortunately, there arose among the Greeks learned men, such as Pythagoras, and Plato, who recovered by the force of genius, the figures and the ideas which the enemy of Iaveh had vainly tried to teach the first woman. The soul of the serpent was in them; and that is why the serpent, as Dorion has said, is honoured by the Athenians. Finally, in these latter days, there appeared, under human form, three celestial spirits—Jesus of Galilee, Basilides, and Valentinus—to whom it was given to pluck the finest fruits of that tree of knowledge, whose roots pass through all the earth, and whose top reaches to the highest heaven. I have said all this in vindication of the Christians, to whom the errors of the Jews are too often imputed.

Dorion. If I understood you aright, Zenothemis, you said that three wonderful men—Jesus, Basilides, and Valentinus—had discovered secrets which had remained hidden from Pythagoras and Plato, and all the philosophers of Greece, and even from the divine Epicurus, who, however, has freed men from the dread of empty terrors. You would greatly oblige me by telling me by what means these three mortals acquired knowledge which had eluded the most contemplative sages.

Zenothemis. Must I repeat to you, Dorion, that science and cogitation are but the first steps to knowledge, and that ecstasy alone leads to eternal truth?

Hermodorus. It is true, Zenothemis, that the soul is nourished on ecstasy, as the cicada is nourished on dew. But we may even say more: the mind alone is capable of perfect rapture. For man is of a threefold nature, composed of material body, of a soul which is more subtle, but also material, and of an incorruptible mind. When, emerging from the body as from a palace suddenly given over to silence and solitude and flying through the gardens of the soul, the mind diffuses itself in God, it tastes the delights of an anticipated death, or rather of a future life, for to die is to live; and in that condition, partaking of divine purity, it possesses both infinite joy and complete knowledge. It enters into the unity which is All. It is perfected.

NICIAS. That is very fine; but, to say the truth, Hermodorus, I do not see much difference between All and Nothing. Words even seem to fail to make the distinction. Infinity is terribly like nothingness—they are both inconceivable to the mind. In my opinion perfection costs too dear; we pay for it with all our being, and to possess it must cease to exist. That is a calamity from which God Himself is not free, for the philosophers are doing their best to perfect Him. After all, if we do not know what it is *not* to be, we are equally ignorant what it is to *be*. We know nothing. It is said that it is impossible for men to agree on this question. I believe—in spite of our noisy disputes—that it is, on the contrary, impossible for men not to become some day all at unity buried under the mass of contradictions, a Pelion on Ossa, which they themselves have raised.

COTTA. I am very fond of philosophy, and study it in my leisure time. But I never understand it well, except in Cicero's books. Slaves, pour out the honeyed wine!

CALLICRATES. It is a singular thing, but when I am hungry I think of the time when the tragic poets sat at the boards of good tyrants, and my mouth waters. But when I have tasted the excellent wine that you give us so abundantly, generous Lucius, I dream of nothing but civil wars and heroic combats. I blush to live in such inglorious times; I invoke the goddess of Liberty; and I pour out my blood—in imagination—with the last Romans on the field of Philippi.

COTTA. In the days of the decline of the Republic my ancestors died with Brutus—for liberty. But there is reason to suspect that what the Roman people called liberty was only in reality the right to govern themselves. I do not deny that liberty is the greatest boon a nation can have. But the longer I live the more I am persuaded that only a strong government can bestow it on the citizens. For forty years I have filled high positions in the State, and my long experience has shown me that when the ruling power is weak the people are oppressed. Those, therefore, who—like the great majority of rhetoricians—try to weaken the government, commit an abominable crime. An autocrat, who governs by his single will, may sometimes cause most deplorable results; but if he governs by popular consent there is no remedy possible. Before the majesty of the Roman arms had bestowed peace upon all the world, the only nations which were happy were those which were ruled over by intelligent despots.

Hermodorus. For my part, Lucius, I believe that there is no such thing as a good form of government, and that we shall never discover one, because the Greeks, who had so many excellent ideas, were never able to find one. In that respect, therefore, all hope of ultimate success is taken from us. Unmistakable signs show that the world is about to fall into ignorance and barbarism. It has been our lot, Lucius, to witness terrible events. Of all the mental satisfactions which intelligence, learning, and virtue can give, all that remains is the cruel pleasure of watching ourselves die.

Cotta. It is true that the rapacity of the people, and the boldness of the barbarians, are threatening evils. But with a good fleet, a good army, and plenty of money—

Hermodorus. What is the use of deceiving ourselves? The dying empire will become an easy prey to the barbarians. Cities which were built by Hellenic genius, or Latin patience, will soon be sacked by drunken savages. Neither art nor philosophy will exist any longer on the earth. The statues of the gods will be overturned in the temples, and in men's hearts as well. Darkness will overcome all minds, and the world will die. Can we believe that the Sarmatians will ever devote themselves to intelligent work, that the Germani will cultivate music and philosophy, and that the Quadi and the Marcomani will adore the immortal gods? No! we are sliding toward the abyss. Our old Egypt, which was the cradle of the world, will be its burial vault; Serapis, the god of Death, will receive the last adoration of mortals, and I shall have been the last priest of the last god.

At this moment a strange figure raised the tapestry, and the guests saw before them a little hunchback, whose bald skull rose in a point. He was clad, in the Asiatic fashion, in a blue tunic, and wore round his legs, like the barbarians, red breeches, spangled with gold stars. On seeing him, Paphnutius recognised Marcus the Arian, and fearing lest a thunderbolt should fall from heaven, he covered his head with his arms, and grew pale with fright. At this banquet of the demons, neither the blasphemies of the pagans, nor the horrible errors of the philosophers, had had any effect on him, but the mere presence of the heretic quenched his courage. He would have fled, but his eyes met those of Thaïs, and he felt at once strengthened. He read in her soul that she, who was predestined to become a saint, already protected him. He seized the skirt of her long, flowing robe, and inwardly prayed to the Saviour Jesus.

A murmur of acclamation welcomed the arrival of the personage who had been called the Christian Plato. Hermodorus was the first to speak.

"Most illustrious Marcus, we rejoice to see you amongst us, and it may be said that you come at the right moment. We know nothing of the Christian doctrine, beyond what is publicly taught. Now, it is certain that a philosopher, like you, cannot think as the vulgar think, and we are curious to know your opinion of the principal mysteries of the religion you profess. Our dear friend, Zenothemis, who, as you know, is always hunting for symbolic meanings, just now questioned the illustrious Paphnutius concerning the Jewish books. But Paphnutius made no reply, and we should not be surprised at that, as our guest has made a vow of silence, and God has sealed his tongue in the desert. But you Marcus, who have spoken at the Christian synods, and even at the councils of the divine Constantine, can if you wish, satisfy our curiosity by revealing to us the philosophic truths which are wrapped up in the Christian fables. Is not the first of these truths the existence of an only God—in whom, for my part, I fervently believe?"

MARCUS. Yes, venerable brethren, I believe in an only God, not begotten—the only Eternal, the origin of all things.

NICIAS. We know, Marcus, that your God created the world. That must certainly have been a great crisis in His existence. He had already existed an eternity before He could make up His mind to it. But I must, in justice, confess that His situation was a most difficult one. He must continue inactive if He would remain perfect, and must act if He would prove to Himself His own existence. You assure me that He decided to act. I am willing to believe you, although it was an unpardonable imprudence on the part of a perfect God. But tell us, Marcus, how He set about making the world.

MARCUS. Those who, without being Christians, possess, like Hermodorus and Zenothemis, the principles of knowledge, are aware that God did not create the world personally without an intermediary. He gave birth to an only Son, by whom all things were made.

HERMODORUS. That is quite true, Marcus; and this Son is worshipped under the various names of Hermes, Mithra, Adonis, Apollo, and Jesus.

MARCUS. I should not be a Christian if I gave Him any other names than those of Jesus Christ, and Saviour. He is the true Son of God. But He is not eternal, since He had a beginning; as to thinking that He existed before He was begotten, we must leave that absurdity to the Nicæan mules, and the obstinate ass who too long governed the Church of Alexandria under the accursed name of Athanasius.

At these words Paphnutius, white with horror and his face bedewed with the sweat of agony, made the sign of the cross, but maintained a sublime silence.

Marcus continued—

"It is clear that the foolish Nicene Creed is a treason against the majesty of the only God, by compelling Him to share His indivisible attributes with His own emanation—the Mediator by whom all things were made. Cease jesting at the true God of the Christians, Nicias, and learn that, like the lilies of the field, He toils not, neither does He spin. It was not He who was the worker, it was His only Son, Jesus, who, having created the world, came afterwards to repair His handiwork. For the creation could not be perfect, and evil was necessarily mingled with good."

NICIAS. What is "good," and what is "evil"?

There was a moment's silence, during which Hermodorus, his arm extended on the cloth, pointed to a little ass in Corinthian metal which bore two baskets—the one containing white olives, the other black olives.

"You see these olives," he said. "The contrast between the colours is pleasant to the eye, and we are content that these should be light and those should be dark. But, if they were endowed with thought and knowledge, the white would say, It is good for an olive to be white, it is bad for it to be black; and the black olives would hate the white olives. We judge better, for we are as much above them as the gods are above us. For man, who only sees a part of things, evil is an evil; for God, who understands all things, evil is a good. Doubtless ugliness is ugly, and not beautiful; but if all were beautiful, the whole would not be beautiful. It is, then, well that there should be evil, as the second Plato, far greater than the first, has demonstrated."

EUCRITES. Let us talk more morally. Evil is an evil—not for the world, of which it cannot destroy the indestructible harmony but for the sinner who does it, and cannot help doing it.

COTTA. By Jupiter! that is a good argument.

EUCRITES. The world is a tragedy by an excellent poet. God, who composed it, has intended each of us to play a part in it. If he wills that you shall be a beggar, a prince, or a cripple, make the best of the part assigned you.

NICIAS. Assuredly it would be well that the cripple should limp like Hephaistos: it would be well that the madman should indulge in all the fury of Ajax, that the incestuous woman should repeat the crimes of Phædra, that the traitor should betray, that the rascal should lie, and the murderer kill, and when the piece was played, all the actors—kings, just men, bloody tyrants, pious virgins, immodest wives, noble-minded citizens, and cowardly assassins—should receive from the poet an equal share in the felicitations.

EUCRITES. You distort my thought, Nicias, and change a beautiful young girl into a hideous Gorgon. I am sorry for you, if you are so ignorant of the nature of the gods, of justice, and of the eternal laws.

ZENOTHEMIS. For my part, friends, I believe in the reality of good and evil. But I am convinced that there is not a single human action —were it even the kiss of Judas—which does not bear within itself the germ of redemption. Evil contributes to the ultimate salvation of men, and, in that respect, issues from Good, and shares the merits belonging to Good. This has been admirably expressed by the Christians, in the myth concerning the man with red hair, who, in order to betray his master, gave him the kiss of peace, and by such act assured the salvation of men. Therefore, nothing is, in my opinion, more unjust and absurd than the hate with which certain disciples of Paul, the tentmaker, pursue the most unfortunate of the apostles of Jesus; without realising that the kiss of Iscariot—prophesied by Jesus Himself—was necessary, according to their own doctrine, for the redemption of men, and that if Judas had not received the thirty pieces, the divine wisdom would have been impugned, Providence frustrated, its designs upset, and the world given over to evil, ignorance, and death.

Marcus. Divine wisdom foresaw that Judas, though he was not obliged to give the traitor's kiss, would give it, notwithstanding. It thus employed the sin of Iscariot as a stone in the marvellous edifice of the redemption.

Zenothemis. I spoke just now, Marcus, as though I believed that the redemption of men had been accomplished by Jesus crucified, because I know that such is the belief of the Christians, and I borrowed their opinion that I might the better show the mistake of those who believe in the eternal damnation of Judas. But, in reality, Jesus was, in my eyes, but the precursor of Basilides and Valentinus. As to the mystery of the redemption, I will tell you, my dear friends—if you are at all curious to hear it—how it was really accomplished on earth.

The guests made a sign of assent. Like the Athenian virgins with the baskets sacred to Ceres, twelve young girls, bearing on their heads baskets filled with pomegranates and apples, entered the room with a light step, in time to the music of an invisible flute. They placed the baskets on the table, the flute ceased, and Zenothemis spoke as follows—

"When Eunoia, 'the thought of God,' had created the world, she confided the government of the earth to the angels. But they did not preserve the dispassion befitting masters. Seeing that the daughters of men were fair, they surprised them in the evening by the wellside, and united themselves to them. From these unions sprang a turbulent race, who covered the earth with injustice and cruelty, and the dust of the roads drank up the blood of the innocent. The sight of this caused Eunoia infinite grief.

" 'See what I have done!' she sighed, leaning towards the world. 'My poor children are plunged in misery, and by my fault. Their suffering is my crime, and I will expiate it. God Himself, who only thinks through me, would be powerless to restore them to their pristine purity. That which is done is done, and the creation will remain for ever imperfect. But, at least, I will not forsake my creatures. If I cannot make them happy, like me, I can make myself unhappy, like them. Since I committed the mistake of giving them bodies which dishonour them, I will myself assume a body like unto theirs, and will go and live amongst them.'

"Having thus spoken, Eunoia descended to the earth, and was incarnate in the breast of a woman of Argos. She was born small and feeble, and received the name of Helen. She submitted to all the labours of this life, but soon grew in grace and beauty, and became the most desired of women, as she had determined, in order that her mortal body might be tried by the most supreme defilements. An inert prey to lascivious and violent men, she suffered rape and adultery, in expiation of all the adulteries, all the violences, all the iniquities, and caused, by her beauty, the ruin of nations, that God might pardon the sins of the universe. And never was the celestial thought, never was Eunoia, so adorable as in those days when, as a woman, she prostituted herself to heroes and shepherds. The poets surmised her divinity when they painted her so peaceful, superb, and fatal, and when they addressed that invocation to her, 'A soul as serene as a calm upon the waters.'

"Thus was Eunoia led by pity into evil and suffering. She died, and the Argives still show her tomb—for it was necessary that she should know death after lust, and taste the bitter fruit she had sown. But, emerging from the decomposed flesh of Helen, she became incarnate again as a woman, and again suffered every form of insult and outrage. Thus, passing from body to body, throughout all the evil ages, she takes upon her the sins of the world. Her sacrifice will not be in vain. Joined to us by the bonds of the flesh, loving us, and weeping with us, she will effect her redemption and ours, and will carry us, clinging to her white breast, into the peace of the regained paradise."

HERMODORUS. This myth was not unknown to me. I remembered having heard that, in one of her metamorphoses, the divine Helen lived with the magician, Simon, in the reign of the Emperor Tiberius. I thought, however, that her perdition was involuntary, and that she was dragged down by the angels in their fall.

ZENOTHEMIS. It is true, Hermodorus, that men who were not properly initiated in the mysteries, have imagined that the sad Eunoia was not a party to her own downfall. But if it were as they assert, Eunoia would not be the expiating courtesan, the victim covered with stains of all sorts, the bread steeped in the wine of our shame, the pleasant offering, the meritorious sacrifice, the holocaust, the smoke of which rises to God. If they were not voluntary, there would be no merit in her sins.

CALLICRATES. Does anyone know, Zenothemis, in what country, under what name, in what adorable form, this ever-renascent Helen is living now?

ZENOTHEMIS. A man would have to be very wise indeed to discover such a secret. And wisdom, Callicrates, is not given to poets, who live in the rude world of forms and amuse themselves, like children, with sounds and empty shows.

CALLICRATES. Beware of offending the gods, impious Zenothemis;

the poets are dear to them. The first laws were dictated in verse by the immortals themselves, and the oracles of the gods are poems. Hymns have a pleasant sound to celestial ears. Who does not know that the poets are prophets, and that nothing is hidden from them? Being a poet myself, and crowned with Apollo's laurel, I will make known to all the last incarnation of Eunoia. The eternal Helen is close to us; she is looking at us, and we are looking at her. You see that woman reclining on the cushions of her couch—so beautiful and so contemplative—whose eyes shed tears, and whose lips abound with kisses! It is she! Lovely as in the time of Priam and the halcyon days of Asia, Eunoia is now called Thaïs.

PHILINA. What do you say, Callicrates? Our dear Thaïs knew Paris, Menelaus, and the Achaians who fought before Ilion! Was the Trojan horse big, Thaïs?

ARISTOBULUS. Who speaks of a horse?

"I have drunk like a Thracian!" cried Chereas; and he rolled under the table.

Callicrates, raising his cup, cried—

"If we drink like desperate men, we die unavenged!"

Old Cotta was asleep, and his bald head nodded slowly above his broad shoulders.

For some time past Dorion had seemed to be greatly excited under his philosophic cloak. He reeled up to the couch of Thaïs.

"Thaïs, I love you, although it is unseemly in me to love a woman."

THAÏS. Why did you not love me before?

DORION. Because I had not supped.

THAÏS. But I, my poor friend, have drunk nothing but water; therefore you must excuse me if I do not love you.

Dorion did not wait to hear more, but made towards Drosea, who had made a sign to him in order to get him away from her friend. Zenothemis took the place he had left, and gave Thaïs a kiss on the mouth.

THAÏS. I thought you more virtuous.

ZENOTHEMIS. I am perfect, and the perfect are subject to no laws.

THAÏS. But are you not afraid of sullying your soul in a woman's arms?

ZENOTHEMIS. The body may yield to lust without the soul being concerned.

THAÏS. Go away! I wish to be loved with body and soul. All these philosophers are old goats.

The lamps died out one by one. The pale rays of dawn, which entered between the openings of the hangings, shone on the livid faces and swollen eyes of the guests. Aristobulus was sleeping soundly by the side of Chereas, and, in his dreams, devoting all his grooms to the ravens. Zenothemis pressed in his arms the yielding Philina; Dorion poured on the naked bosom of Drosea drops of wine, which rolled like rubies on the white breast, which was shaking with laughter, and the philosopher tried to catch these drops with his lips, as they rolled on the slippery flesh. Eucrites rose, and placing his arm on the shoulder of Nicias, led him to the end of the hall.

"Friend," he said, smiling, "if you can still think at all—of what are you thinking?"

"I think that the love of women is like a garden of Adonis."

"What do you mean by that?"

"Do you not know, Eucrites, that women make little gardens on the terraces, in which they plant boughs in clay pots in honour of the lover of Venus? These boughs flourish a little time, and then fade."

"What does that signify, Nicias? That it is foolish to attach importance to that which fades?"

"If beauty is but a shadow, desire is but a lightning flash. What madness it is, then, to desire beauty! Is it not rational, on the contrary, that that which passes should go with that which does not endure, and that the lightning should devour the gliding shadow?"

"Nicias, you seem to me like a child playing at knuckle-bones. Take my advice—be free! By liberty only can you become a man."

"How can a man be free, Eucrites, when he has a body?"

"You shall see presently, my son. Presently you will say, 'Eucrites was free.'"

The old man spoke, leaning against a porphyry pillar, his face lighted by the first rays of dawn. Hermodorus and Marcus had approached, and stood before him by the side of Nicias; and all four, regardless of the laughter and cries of the drinkers, conversed on things divine. Eucrites expressed himself so wisely and eloquently, that Marcus said—

"You are worthy to know the true God."

Eucrites replied—

"The true God is in the heart of the wise man."

Then they spoke of death.

"I wish," said Eucrites, "that it may find me occupied in correcting my faults, and attentive to all my duties. In the face of death I will raise my pure hands to heaven, and I will say to the gods, 'Your images, gods, that you have placed in the temple of my soul, I have not profaned; I have hung there my thoughts, as well as garlands, fillets, and wreaths. I have lived according to your providence. I have lived enough.'"

Thus speaking, he raised his arms to heaven, and he remained thoughtful a moment. Then he continued, with extreme joy—

"Separate thyself from life, Eucrites, like the ripe olive which falls; returning thanks to the tree which bore thee, and blessing the earth, thy nurse."

At these words, drawing from the folds of his robe a naked dagger, he plunged it into his breast.

Those who listened to him sprang forward to seize his hand, but the steel point had already penetrated the heart of the sage. Eucrites had already entered into his rest. Hermodorus and Nicias bore the pale and bleeding body to one of the couches, amidst the shrill shrieks of the women, the grunts of the guests disturbed in their sleep, and the heavy breathing of the couples hidden in the shadow of the tapestry. Cotta, an old soldier, who slept lightly, woke, approached the corpse, examined the wound, and cried—

"Call Aristæus, my physician!"

Nicias shook his head.

"Eucrites is no more," he said. "He wished to die as others wish to love. He has, like all of us, obeyed his inexpressible desire. And, lo, now he is like unto the gods, who desire nothing."

Cotta struck his forehead.

"Die! To want to die when he might still serve the State! What nonsense!"

Paphnutius and Thaïs remained motionless and mute, side by side, their souls overflowing with disgust, horror, and hope.

Suddenly the monk seized the hand of the actress, and stepping over the drunkards, who had fallen close to the lascivious couples, and treading in the wine and blood spilt upon the floor, he led her out of the house.

THE PAPYRUS (*resumed*)   ·

HE SUN had risen over the city. Long colonnades stretched on both sides of the deserted street, and at the end shone the dome of Alexander's tomb. Here and there on the pavement lay broken wreaths and extinguished torches. Fresh wafts of the sea could be felt in the air. Paphnutius, with a look of disgust, tore off his rich robe and trampled the fragments under his feet.

"Thou hast heard them, my Thaïs!" he cried. "They have spat forth every sort of folly and abomination. They dragged the Divine Creator of all things down the gemonies* of the devils of hell, impudently denied the existence of Good and Evil, blasphemed Jesus, and exalted Judas. And the most infamous of all, the jackal of darkness, the stinking beast, the Arian full of corruption and death, opened his mouth like a yawning sepulchre. My Thaïs, thou hast seen these filthy snails crawling towards thee and defiling thee with their sticky sweat; thou hast seen others, like brutes, sleeping under the heels of their slaves; thou hast seen them coupling like beasts on the carpet they had fouled with their vomit; thou hast seen a foolish old man shed a blood yet viler than the wine which flowed at his debauch, and at the end of the orgie throw himself in the face of the unforeseen Christ. Praise be to God! Thou hast seen error and recognised how hideous it was. Thaïs, Thaïs, Thaïs, recall to mind the follies of these philosophers, and say if thou wilt go mad with them! Remember the looks, the gestures, the laughs of their fitting companions, those two lascivious and malicious strumpets, and say if thou wilt remain like unto them."

Thaïs, her heart stirred with horror and disgust at all she had seen and heard that night, and feeling the indifference and brutality, the malicious jealousy of women, the heavy weight of useless hours, sighed.

"I am weary to death, O my father! Where shall I find rest? I feel that my face is burning, my head empty, and my arms are so tired that I should not have the strength to seize happiness were it within reach of my hand."

Paphnutius gazed at her with loving pity.

"Courage, O my sister! The hour of rest rises for thee, white and pure as the vapours thou seest rise from the gardens and waters '

They were near the house of Thaïs, and could see, above the wall, the tops of the sycamore and fir trees, which surrounded the Grotto

---

*Steps on the Aventine Hill, leading to the Tiber, to which the bodies of executed criminals were dragged to be thrown into the river. The word is now obsolete, but was employed by Ben Jonson (*Sejanus*) and Massinger (*The Roman Actor*).—Trans.

of Nymphs, tremble in the morning breeze. In front of them was
a public square, deserted, and surrounded with steles and votive
statues, and having at each end a semicircular marble seat, supported by figures of monsters. Thaïs fell on one of these seats.
Then, looking anxiously at the monk, she asked—

"What must I do?"

"Thou must," replied the monk, "follow Him who has come to
seek thee. He will separate thee from this present life, as the vin-
tager gathers the cluster that would have rotted on the tree, and
bears it to the wine-press to change it into perfumed wine. Listen!
there is a dozen hours from Alexandria, towards the west, not far
from the sea, a nunnery, the rules of which, a masterpiece of wisdom, deserve to be put in lyric verse and sung to the sound of the
theorbo and tambourines. It may truly be said that the women who
are there, submissive to these rules, have their feet upon earth and
their faces in heaven. They desire to be poor, that Jesus may love
them, modest, that He may gaze upon them every day in the guise
of a gardener, His feet bare, His beautiful hands open—even as He
showed Himself to Mary at the entrance of the tomb. I will conduct thee this very day to this nunnery, my Thaïs, and soon, com-
mingling with these holy women, thou wilt share in their heavenly
conversation. They await thee as a sister. On the threshold of the
convent, their mother, the pious Albina, will give thee the kiss of
peace and will say, 'My daughter, thou art welcome!'"

The courtesan uttered a cry of amazement.

"Albina! a daughter of the Cæsars! The great niece of the Emperor Carus!"

"She herself! Albina, who, born in the purple, has donned the
serge, and a daughter of the masters of this world, has risen to the
rank of servant of Jesus Christ. She will be thy mother."

Thaïs rose and said—

"Take me to the house of Albina."

And Paphnutius, completing his victory—

"Surely I will conduct thee thither, and there I will place thee in
a cell, where thou shalt weep for thy sins. For it is not fitting that
thou shouldst mingle with the daughters of Albina until thou art
cleansed from thy sins. I will seal the door, and there, a happy
prisoner, thou wilt wait in tears till Jesus Himself come, as a sign
of pardon, to break the seal that I have placed. And doubt not that
He will come, Thaïs, and how the flesh of thy soul will tremble
when thou shalt feel the fingers of Light placed upon thy eyes to
dry thy tears!"

Thaïs said a second time—

"Take me, my father, to the house of Albina."

His heart filled with joy, Paphnutius gazed around him, and
tasted, almost without fear, the pleasure of contemplating the
works of creation; his eyes drank in with joy God's light, and un-

known breezes fanned his cheeks. Suddenly, seeing at one of the corners of the public square the little door which led to Thaïs' house, and remembering that the trees, whose foliage he had been admiring, shaded the courtesan's garden, he thought of all the impurities which there sullied the air, to-day so light and pure, and his soul was so grieved that bitter tears sprang to his eyes.

"Thaïs," he said, "we must fly without looking back. But we must not leave behind us the instruments, the witnesses, the accomplices of thy past crimes; those heavy hangings, those beds, carpets, perfume censers and lamps, which would proclaim thy infamy! Dost thou wish that, animated by the demons, and carried by the evil spirit that is in them, those accursed belongings should pursue thee even to the desert? It is but too true that there are tables which bring ruin, seats which serve as the instruments of devils, which act, speak, strike the ground, and pass through the air. Let all perish which has seen thy shame! Hasten, Thaïs, and, whilst the city is yet asleep, order thy slaves to make, in the centre of this place, a pile, upon which we will burn all the abominable riches thy dwelling contains."

Thaïs consented.

"Do as you will, my father," she said. "I know that spirits often dwell in inanimate objects. At night some articles of furniture talk, either by giving knocks at regular intervals or by emitting little flashes of light as signals. And even more. Have you remarked, my father, at the entrance to the Grotto of Nymphs, on the right, a statue of a naked woman about to bathe? One day I saw, with my own eyes, that statue turn its head like a living person, and then return to its ordinary attitude. I was terrified. Nicias, to whom I related this prodigy, laughed at me; yet there must be some magic in that statue, for it inspired with violent desires a certain Dalmatian, who was insensible to my beauty. It is certain that I have lived amongst enchanted things, and that I was exposed to the greatest perils, for men have been strangled by the embraces of a bronze statue. Yet it would be a pity to destroy valuable works made with rare skill, and to burn my carpets and tapestry would be a great loss. The beautiful colours of some of them are truly wonderful, and they cost much money to those who gave them to me. I also possess cups, statues, and pictures of great price. I do not think they ought to perish. But you know what is necessary. Do as you will, my father."

Thus saying, she followed the monk to the little door at which so many garlands and wreaths had been hung, and, when it was opened, she told the porter to call together all the slaves in the house. Four Indians, who were employed in the kitchen, were the first to appear. They were all four yellow men, and each had but one eye. It had cost Thaïs much trouble, and given her amusement, to get together these four slaves of the same race, and all afflicted with the same infirmity. When they attended at table they excited the curiosity of the guests, and Thaïs made them relate the story of their lives. These four waited in silence. Their assistants followed them. Then came the stablemen, the huntsmen, the litter-bearers, and the running footmen with muscles like iron, two gardeners hirsute as Priapus, six ferocious looking negroes, three Greek slaves —one a grammarian, another a poet, and the third a singer. They all stood, ranged in order, on the public square, and were presently joined by the negresses—curious, suspicious, rolling big round eyes, and each with a huge mouth slit to her earrings. Lastly, adjusting their veils and languidly dragging their feet, which were shackled with light gold chains, appeared six sulky-looking, beautiful white slave-girls. When they were all assembled, Thaïs, pointing to Paphnutius, said—

"Do whatever this man commands you; for the spirit of God is in him, and if you disobey him you will fall dead."

For she had heard, and really believed, that the earth would open and swallow up in flames and smoke any impious wretch whom a saint of the desert struck with his staff.

Paphnutius sent away the women and the Greek men-slaves, and said to the others—

"Bring wood to the middle of this place, make a huge fire, and throw into it pell-mell all that there is in the house and grotto."

They were astonished, and stood motionless, looking at their mistress. And they still stood inactive and silent, and pressed against each other, elbow to elbow, suspecting that the order was a joke.

"Obey!" said the monk.

Several of them were Christians. They understood the command, and went to the house to fetch wood and torches. The others were not indisposed to imitate them, for, being poor, they hated riches and had a natural instinct for destruction. Whilst they were building the pile, Paphnutius said to Thaïs—"I thought at one time of fetching the treasurer of one of the churches of Alexandria (if there still remain one worthy of the name of church, and that is not defiled by the Arian beasts) and giving him thy goods, woman, that he might distribute them to widows, and change the proceeds of crime into the treasure of justice. But such a thought did not come from God, and I cast it from me, for assuredly it would be a great offence to the well-beloved of Jesus Christ to offer them the spoils of thy lust. Thaïs, all that thou hast touched must be devoured by the fire, even to its very soul. Thanks be to Heaven, these tunics and veils, which have seen kisses more innumerable than the waves of the sea, will only feel now the lips and tongues of the flames. Hasten, slaves! More wood! More links and torches! And thou, woman, return to thy house, strip thyself of thy shameful robes, and ask of the most humble of thy slaves, as an undeserving favour, the tunic that she puts on when she scrubs the floors."

Thaïs obeyed. Whilst the Indians knelt down and blew the embers, the negroes threw on the pile coffers of ivory, ebony, or cedar, which broke open and let out wreaths, garlands, and necklaces. The smoke rose in a dark column, as in the holocausts of the old religion. Then the fire, which had been smouldering, burst out suddenly with a roar as of some monstrous animal, and the almost invisible flames began to devour their valuable prey. The slaves worked more eagerly; they joyfully dragged out rich carpets, veils embroidered with silver, and flowered tapestry. They staggered under the weight of tables, couches, thick cushions, and beds with gold nails. Three strong Ethiopians came hugging the coloured statues of the nymphs, one of which had been loved as though it were a mortal; and they looked like huge apes carrying off women. And when the beautiful naked forms fell from the arms of these monsters, and were broken on the stones, a deep groan was heard.

At that moment Thaïs appeared, her hair unloosed and streaming over her shoulders, bare-footed, and clad in a clumsy coarse garment which seemed redolent with divine voluptuousness merely from having touched her body. Behind her came a gardener, carrying, half hidden in his long beard, an ivory Eros.

She made a sign to the man to stop, and approaching Paphnutius, showed him the little god.

"My father," she asked, "should this also be thrown into the flames? It is of marvellous antique work, and is worth a hundred times its weight in gold. Its loss would be irreparable, for there is not a sculptor in the world capable of making such a beautiful Eros. Remember also, my father, that this child is Love, and he should not be harshly treated. Believe me, Love is a virtue, and if I have sinned, it is not through him, my father, but against him. Never shall I regret aught that he has caused me to do, and I deplore only those things I have done contrary to his commands. He does not allow women to give themselves to those who do not come in his name. For that reason he ought to be honoured. Look, Paphnutius, how pretty this little Eros is! With what grace he hides himself in the gardener's beard! One day Nicias, who loved me then, brought it to me and said, 'It will remind you of me.' But the roguish boy did not remind me of Nicias, but of a young man I knew at Antioch. Enough riches have been destroyed upon this pile, my father! Preserve this Eros, and place it in some monastery. Those who see it will turn their hearts towards God, for love leads naturally to heavenly thoughts."

The gardener, already believing that the little Eros was saved, smiled on it as though it had been a child, when Paphnutius, snatching the god from the arms which held it, threw it into the flames, crying—

"It is enough that Nicias has touched it to make it replete with every sort of poison!"

Then, seizing by armfuls the sparkling robes, the purple mantles, the golden sandals, the combs, strigils, mirrors, lamps, theorbos, and lyres, he threw them into this furnace, more costly than the funeral pile of Sardanapalus, whilst, drunken with the rage of destruction, the slaves danced round, uttering wild yells amid a shower of sparks and ashes.

One by one, the neighbours, awakened by the noise, opened the windows, and rubbing their eyes, looked out to see whence the smoke came. Then they came down, half dressed, and drew near the fire.

"What does it mean?" they wondered.

Amongst them were merchants from whom Thaïs had often bought perfumes and stuffs, and they looked on anxiously with long, yellow faces, unable to comprehend what was going on. Some young debauchees, who, returning from a supper, passed by there, preceded by their slaves, stopped, their heads crowned with flowers, their tunics floating, and uttered loud cries. Attracted by curiosity, the crowd increased unceasingly, and soon it was known that Thaïs had been persuaded by the Abbot of Antinoë to burn her riches and retire to a nunnery.

The shopkeepers thought to themselves—

"Thaïs is going to leave the city; we shall sell no more to her; it is dreadful to think of. What will become of us without her? This monk has driven her mad. He is ruining us. Why let him do it? What is the use of the laws? Are there no magistrates in Alexandria? Thaïs does not think about us and our wives and our poor children. It is a public scandal. She ought to be compelled to stay in the city."

The young men, on their part, also thought—

"If Thaïs is going to renounce acting and love, our chief amusements will be taken from us. She was the glory, delight, and honour of the stage. She was the joy even of those who had never possessed her. The women we loved, we loved in her. There were no kisses given in which she was altogether absent, for she was the joy of all voluptuaries, and the mere thought that she breathed amongst us excited us to pleasure."

Thus thought the young men, and one of them, named Cerons, who had held her in his arms, cried out upon the abduction, and blasphemed against Christ. In every group the conduct of Thaïs was severely criticised.

"It is a shameful flight!"

"A cowardly desertion!"

"She is taking the bread out of our mouths."

"She is robbing our children."

"She ought at least to pay for the wreaths I have sold to her."

"And the sixty robes she has ordered of me."

"She owes money to everybody."

"Who will represent Iphigenia, Electra, and Polyxena when she is gone? The handsome Polybia herself will not make such a success as she has done."

"Life will be dull when her door is closed."

"She was the bright star, the soft moon of the Alexandrian sky."

All the most notorious mendicants of the city—cripples, blind men, and paralytics—had by this time assembled in the place; and crawling through the remnants of the riches, they groaned—

"How shall we live when Thaïs is no longer here to feed us? Every day the fragments from her table fed two hundred poor wretches, and her lovers, when they quitted her, threw us as they passed handfuls of silver pieces."

Some thieves, too, also mingled with the crowd, and created a deafening clamour, and pushed their neighbours, to increase disorder, and take advantage of the tumult to filch some valuable object.

Old Taddeus, who sold Miletan wool and Tarentan linen, and to whom Thaïs owed a large sum of money, alone remained calm and silent in the midst of the uproar. He listened and watched, and gently stroking his goat-beard, seemed thoughtful. At last he approached young Cerons, and pulling him by the sleeve, whispered—

"You are the favoured lover of Thaïs, handsome youth; show yourself, and do not allow this monk to carry her off."

"By Pollux and his sister, he shall not!" cried Cerons. "I will speak to Thaïs, and without flattering myself, I think she will listen to me rather than to that sooty-faced Lapithan. Place! Place, dogs!"

And striking with his fist the men, upsetting the old women and treading on the young children, he reached Thaïs, and taking her aside—

"Dearest girl," he said, "look at me, remember, and tell me truly if you renounce love."

But Paphnutius threw himself between Thaïs and Cerons.

"Impious wretch!" he cried, "beware and touch her not; she is sacred—she belongs to God."

"Get away, baboon!" replied the young man furiously. "Let me speak to my sweetheart, or if not I will drag your obscene carcass by the beard to the fire, and roast you like a sausage."

And he put his hand on Thaïs. But, pushed away by the monk with unexpected force, he staggered back four paces and fell at the foot of the pile amongst the scattered ashes.

Old Taddeus, meanwhile, had been going from one to the other, pulling the ears of the slaves and kissing the hands of the masters, inciting each and all against Paphnutius, and had already formed a little band resolutely determined to oppose the monk who would steal Thaïs from them.

Cerons rose, his face black, his hair singed, and choking with smoke and rage. He blasphemed against the gods, and threw himself amongst the assailants, behind whom the beggars crawled, shaking their crutches. Paphnutius was soon enclosed in a circle of menacing fists, raised sticks, and cries of death.

"To the ravens with the monk! to the ravens!"

"No; throw him in the fire! Burn him alive!"

Seizing his fair prey, he pressed her to his heart.

"Impious men," he cried in a voice of thunder, "strive not to tear the dove from the eagle of the Lord. But rather copy this woman, and like her, turn your filth into gold. Imitate her example, and renounce the false wealth which you think you hold, and which holds you. Hasten! the day is at hand, and divine patience begins to grow weary. Repent, confess your sins, weep and pray. Walk in the footsteps of Thaïs. Hate your offences, which are as great as hers. Which of you, poor or rich, merchants, soldiers, slaves or eminent citizens, would dare to say, before God, that he was better than a prostitute? You are all nothing but living filth, and it is by a miracle of divine goodness that you do not suddenly turn into streams of mire."

Whilst he spoke flames shot from his eyes; and it seemed as though live coals came from his lips and those who surrounded him were obliged to hear him in spite of themselves.

But old Taddeus did not remain idle. He picked up stones and oyster shells, which he hid in the skirt of his tunic, and not daring to throw them himself, slipped them into the hands of the beggars. Soon the stones began to fly, and a well-directed shell cut Paphnutius' face. The blood, which flowed down the dark face of the martyr, dropped in a new baptism on the head of the penitent, and Thaïs, half stifled in the monk's embrace and her delicate skin scratched by the coarse cassock, felt a thrill of horror and fright.

At that moment a man elegantly dressed, and with a wreath of wild celery on his head, opened a road for himself through the furious crowd, and cried—

"Stop! Stop! This monk is my brother!"

It was Nicias, who, having closed the eyes of the philosopher Eucrites, was passing through the square to return to his house, and saw, without very much surprise (for nothing astonished him), the smoking pile, Thaïs clad in a serge cassock, and Paphnutius being stoned.

He repeated—

"Stop, I tell you; spare my old fellow-scholar; respect the beloved head of Paphnutius!"

But, being only used to subtle disquisitions with philosophers, he did not possess that imperious energy which commands vulgar minds. He was not listened to. A shower of stones and shells fell on the monk, who, protecting Thaïs with his body, praised the Lord

whose goodness turned his wounds into caresses. Despairing of
making himself heard, and feeling but too sure that he could not
save his friend either by force or persuasion, Nicias resigned himself to the will of the gods—in whom he had little confidence—
when the idea occurred to him to use a stratagem which his contempt for men had suddenly suggested to him. He took from his
girdle his purse, which was full of gold and silver, for he was a
pleasure-loving and charitable man, and running up to the men who
were throwing the stones, he chinked the money in their ears. At
first they paid no attention to him, their fury being too great; but
little by little their looks turned towards the chinking gold, and
soon their arms dropped and no longer menaced their victim. Seeing that he had attracted their eyes and minds, Nicias opened his
purse and threw some pieces of gold and silver amongst the crowd.
The more greedy of them stooped to pick it up. The philosopher,
pleased at his first success, adroitly threw deniers and drachmas
here and there. At the sound of the pieces of money rattling on the
pavement, the persecutors of Paphnutius threw themselves on the
ground. Beggars, slaves, and trades-people scrambled after the
money, whilst, grouped round Cerons, the patricians watched the
struggle and laughed heartily. Cerons himself quite forgot his
wrath. His friends encouraged the rivals, chose competitors, and
made bets, and urged on the miserable wretches as they would have
done fighting dogs. A cripple without legs having succeeded in seizing a drachma, the applause was frenetic. The young men themselves began to throw money, and nothing was to be seen in the
square but a multitude of backs, rising and falling like waves of
the sea, under a shower of coins. Paphnutius was forgotten.

Nicias ran up to him, covered him with his cloak, and dragged
him and Thaïs into by-streets where they were safe from pursuit.
They ran for some time in silence, and when they thought they
were out of reach of their enemies, they ceased running, and Nicias
said, in a tone of raillery in which a little sadness was mingled—

"It is finished then! Pluto ravishes Proserpine, and Thaïs will follow my fierce-looking friend whithersoever he will lead her."

"It is true, Nicias," replied Thaïs, "that I am tired of living with
men like you, smiling, perfumed, kindly egoists. I am weary of all
I know, and I am, therefore, going to seek the unknown. I have experienced joy that was not joy, and here is a man who teaches me
that sorrow is true joy. I believe him, for he knows the truth."

"And I, sweetheart," replied Nicias, smiling, "I know the truths.
He knows but one, I know them all. I am superior to him in that
respect, but to tell the truth, it doesn't make me any the prouder
nor any the happier."

Then, seeing that the monk was glaring fiercely at him—

"My dear Paphnutius, do not imagine that I think you extremely
absurd, or even altogether unreasonable. And if I were to compare

your life with mine, I could not say which is preferable in itself. I shall presently go and take the bath which Crobyle and Myrtale have prepared for me; I shall eat the wing of a Phasian pheasant; then I shall read—for the hundredth time—some fable by Apuleius or some treatise by Porphyry. You will return to your cell, where, leaning like a tame camel, you will ruminate on—I know not what —formulas of incarnations you have long chewed and rechewed, and in the evening you will swallow some radishes without any oil. Well, my dear friend, in accomplishing these acts, so different apparently, we are both obeying the same sentiment, the only motive for all human actions; we are both seeking our own pleasure, and striving to attain the same end—happiness, the impossible happiness. It would be folly on my part to say you were wrong, dear friend, even though I think myself in the right.

"And you, my Thaïs, go and enjoy yourself, and be more happy still, if it be possible, in abstinence and austerity than you have been in riches and pleasure. On the whole, I should say you were to be envied. For if in our whole lives, Paphnutius and I have pursued but one kind of pleasurable satisfaction, you in your life, dear Thaïs, have tasted diverse joys such as it is rarely given to the same person to know. I should really like to be for one hour, a saint like our dear friend Paphnutius. But that is not possible. Farewell, then, Thaïs! Go where the secret forces of nature and your destiny conduct you! Go, and take with you, whithersoever you go, the good wishes of Nicias! I know that is mere foolishness, but can I give you anything more than barren regrets and vain wishes in payment for the delicious illusions which once enveloped me when I was in your arms, and of which only the shadow now remains to me? Farewell, my benefactress! Farewell, goodness that is ignorant of its own existence, mysterious virtue, joy of men! Farewell to the most adorable of the images that nature has ever thrown—for some unknown reasons—on the face of this deceptive world!"

Whilst he spoke, deep wrath had been brewing in the monk's heart, and it now broke forth in imprecations.

"Avaunt, cursed wretch! I scorn thee and hate thee. Go, child of hell, a thousand times worse than those poor lost ones who just now threw stones and insults at me! They knew not what they did, and the grace of God, which I implored for them, may some day descend into their hearts. But thou, detestable Nicias, thou art but a perfidious venom and a bitter poison. Thy mouth breathes despair and death. One of thy smiles contains more blasphemy than issues in a century from the smoking lips of Satan. Avaunt, backslider!"

Nicias looked at him.

"Farewell, my brother," he said, "and may you preserve until your life's end your store of faith, hate, and love. Farewell, Thaïs!

It is in vain that you will forget me, because I shall ever remember you."

On quitting them he walked thoughtfully through the winding streets in the vicinity of the great cemetery of Alexandria, which are peopled by the makers of funeral urns. Their shops were full of clay figures painted in bright colours and representing gods and goddesses, mimes, women, winged spirits, &c., such as were usually buried with the dead. He fancied that perhaps some of the little images which he saw there might be the companions of his eternal sleep; and it seemed to him that a little Eros, with its tunic tucked up, laughed at him mockingly. He looked forward to his death, and the idea was painful to him. To cure his sadness he tried to philosophise, and reasoned thus—

"Assuredly," he said to himself, "time has no reality. It is a simple illusion of our minds. Then, if it does not exist, how can it bring death to me? Does that mean that I shall live for ever? No, but I conclude therefrom that my death is, always has been, as it always will be. I do not feel it yet, but it is in me, and I ought not to fear it, for it would be folly to dread the coming of that which has arrived. It exists, like the last page of a book I read and have not finished."

This argument occupied him all the rest of the way, but without making him more cheerful; and his mind was filled with dismal thoughts when he arrived at the door of his house and heard the merry laughter of Crobyle and Myrtale, who were playing at tennis whilst they were waiting for him.

Paphnutius and Thaïs left the city by the Gate of the Moon, and followed the coast.

"Woman," said the monk, "all that great blue sea could not wash away thy pollutions."

He spoke with scorn and anger.

"More filthy than a bitch or a sow, thou hast prostituted to pagans and infidels a body which the Eternal had intended for a tabernacle, and thy impurities are such that, now that thou knowest the truth, thou canst not unite thy lips or join thy hands without a horror of thyself rising in thy heart."

She followed him meekly, over stony roads, under a burning sun. Her knees ached from fatigue, and her throat was parched with thirst. But, far from feeling any of the pity which softens the hearts of the profane, Paphnutius rejoiced at these propitiatory sufferings of the flesh which had so sinned. So infuriated was he with holy zeal that he would have liked to cut with rods the body that had preserved its beauty as a shining witness to its infamy. His meditations augmented his pious fury, and remembering that Thaïs had received Nicias in her bed, that idea seemed so horrible to him that his blood all flowed back to his heart, and his breast felt ready to burst. His curses were stifled in his throat, and he could only grind his teeth. He sprang forward and stood before her, pale, terrible, and filled with the Spirit of God—looked into her very soul, and then spat in her face.

She calmly wiped her face and continued to walk on. He followed, glaring at her in pious anger, as if she had been hell itself. He was thinking how he could avenge Christ in order that Christ should not avenge Himself, when he saw a drop of blood that had dripped from the foot of Thaïs on the sand. Then a hitherto unknown influence entered his opened heart, sobs rose to his lips, he wept, he ran and knelt before her, called her his sister, and kissed her bleeding feet. He murmured a hundred times, "My sister, my sister, my mother, O most holy!"

He prayed—

"Angels of heaven, receive carefully this drop of blood, and bear it before the throne of the Lord. And may a miraculous anemone blossom on the sand sprinkled with the blood of Thaïs, that those who see the flower may recover purity of heart and feeling. O holy, holy, most holy Thaïs!"

As he prayed and prophesied thus, a lad passed on an ass. Paphnutius ordered him to descend, seated Thaïs on the ass, and led it by the bridle. Towards evening they came to a canal shaded by fine trees; he tied the ass to the trunk of a date palm, and sitting on a mossy stone he shared with Thaïs a loaf, which they ate with salt and hyssop. They drank fresh water in their hands, and talked of things eternal. She said—

"I have never drunk water so pure, nor breathed an air so light, and I feel that God floats in the breezes that pass."

"Look! it is the evening, O my sister. The blue shadows of night cover the hills. But soon thou wilt see shining in the dawn the tabernacles of Light; soon thou wilt behold shine forth the roses of the eternal morning."

They journeyed all night, and, while the crescent moon gleamed on the silver crests of the waves, they sang psalms and hymns. When the sun rose, the Libyan desert stretched before them like a huge lion-skin. At the edge of the desert, and close to a few palm-trees, some white huts shimmered in the morning light.

"Are those the tabernacles of Light, father?" asked Thaïs.

"Even so, my daughter and my sister. Yonder is the House of Salvation, where I will confine you with my own hands."

Soon they saw a number of women busy around the buildings, like bees round their hives. There were some who baked bread, or prepared vegetables; many were spinning wool, and the light of heaven shone upon them like a smile of God. Others meditated in the shade of the tamarisk trees; their white hands hung by their sides, for, being filled with love, they had chosen the part of Magdalen, and performed no work but prayer, contemplation, and ecstasy. They were, therefore, called the Marys, and were clad in white. Those who worked with their hands were called the Marthas, and wore blue robes. All wore the hood, but the younger ones allowed a few curls to show on their foreheads—unintentionally, it is to be presumed, since it was forbidden by the rules. A very old lady, tall and white, walked from cell to cell, leaning on a staff of hard wood. Paphnutius approached her respectfully, kissed the hem of her veil, and said—

"The peace of the Lord be with thee, venerable Albina. I have brought to the hive, of which thou art queen, a bee. I found lost on a flowerless road. I took it in the palm of my hand, and revived it with my breath. I give it to thee."

And he pointed to the actress, who knelt down before the daughter of the Cæsars.

Albina cast a piercing glance on Thaïs, ordered her to rise, kissed her on the forehead, and then, turning to the monk—

"We will place her," she said, "amongst the Marys."

Paphnutius then related how Thaïs had been brought to the House of Salvation, and asked that she should be at once confined in a cell. The abbess consented, and led the penitent to a hut, which had remained empty since the death of the virgin Læta, who had sanctified it. In this narrow chamber there was but a bed, a table, and a pitcher, and Thaïs when she crossed the threshold, felt filled with ineffable joy.

"I wish to close the door myself," said Paphnutius, "and put thereon a seal, which Jesus will come and break with His own hands."

He went to the side of the spring, and took a handful of wet clay, mixed with it a little spittle and a hair from his head, and plastered it across the chink of the door. Then, approaching the window, near which Thaïs stood peaceful and happy, he fell on his knees and praised the Lord three times.

"How beautiful are the feet of her who walketh in the paths of righteousness! How beautiful are her feet, and how resplendent her face!"

He rose, lowered his hood over his eyes, and walked away slowly.

Albina called one of her virgins.

"My daughter," she said, "take to Thaïs those things which are needful for her—bread, water, and a flute with three holes."

PART THE THIRD

THE EUPHORBIA

APHNUTIUS had returned to the holy desert. He took, near Athribis, the boat which went up the Nile to carry food to the monastery of Abbot Serapion. When he disembarked, his disciples advanced to meet him with great demonstrations of joy. Some raised their arms to heaven; others, prostrate on the ground, kissed the Abbot's sandals. For they knew already what the saint had accomplished in Alexandria. The monks generally received, by rapid and unknown means, information concerning the safety or glory of the Church. News spread through the desert with the rapidity of the simoon.

When Paphnutius strode across the sand, his disciples followed him, praising the Lord. Flavian, who was the oldest member of the brotherhood, was suddenly seized with a pious frenzy, and began to sing an inspired hymn—

"O blessed day! Now is our father restored to us.
He has returned laden with fresh merits, of which we reap the benefit.
For the virtues of the father are the wealth of the children, and the
    sanctity of the Abbot illuminates every cell.
Paphnutius, our father, has given a new spouse to Jesus Christ.
By his wondrous art, he has changed a black sheep into a white sheep.
And now, behold, he has returned to us, laden with fresh merits.
Like unto the bee of the Arsinœtid, heavy with the nectar of flowers.
Even as the ram of Nubia, which could hardly bear the weight of its
    abundant wool.
Let us celebrate this day by mingling oil with our food."

When they came to the door of the Abbot's cell, they fell on their knees, and said—

"Let our father bless us, and give each of us a measure of oil to celebrate his return."

Paul the Fool, who alone had remained standing, asked, "Who is this man?" and did not recognise Paphnutius. But no one paid any attention to what he said, as he was known to be devoid of intelligence, though filled with piety.

The Abbot of Antinoë, locked in his cell, thought—

"I have at last regained the haven of my repose and happiness. I have returned to my fortress of contentment. But how is it that this roof of rushes, so dear to me, does not receive me as a friend, and the walls say not to me, 'Thou art welcome.' Nothing has changed, since my departure, in this abode I have chosen. There is my table and my bed. There is the mummy's head which has so often inspired me with salutary thoughts; and there is the book in which I have so often sought conceptions of God. And yet nothing that I left is here. The things appear grievously despoiled of their customary charm, and it seems to me as though I saw them to-day for the first time. When I look at that table and couch, that in former days I made with my own hands, that black, dried head, these rolls of papyrus filled with the sayings of God, I seem to see the belongings of a dead man. After having known them all so well, I know them no longer. Alas! since nothing around me has really changed, it is I who am no longer what I was. I am another. I am the dead man! What has happened, my God? What has been taken from me? What is left unto me? And who am I?"

And it especially perplexed him to find, in spite of himself, that his cell was small, whereas, when viewed by the eye of faith, he ought to consider it immense, because the infinitude of God began there.

He began to pray, with his face against the ground, and felt a little happier. He had hardly been an hour in prayer, when a vision of Thaïs passed before his eyes. He returned thanks to God—

"Jesus! it is Thou who hast sent her. I acknowledge in that Thy wonderful goodness; Thou wouldst please me, reassure me and comfort me by the sight of her whom I have given to Thee. Thou presentest her to my eyes with her smile now disarmed; her grace, now become innocent; her beauty, from which I have extracted the sting. To please me, my God, thou showest her to me as I have prepared and purified her for Thy designs, as one friend pleasantly reminds another of the rich gift he has received from him. Therefore I see this woman with delight, being assured that the vision comes from Thee. Thou dost not forget that I have given her to Thee, Jesus. Keep her, since she pleases Thee, and suffer not her beauty to give joy to any but Thyself."

He could not sleep all night, and he saw Thaïs more distinctly than he had seen her in the Grotto of Nymphs. He commended himself, saying—

"What I have done, I have done to the glory of God."

Yet, to his great surprise, his heart was not at ease. He sighed.

"Why art thou sad, O my soul, and why dost thou trouble me?"

And his mind was still perturbed. Thirty days he remained in that condition of sadness which precedes the sore trials of a solitary monk. The image of Thaïs never left him day or night. He did not try to banish it, because he still thought it came from God, and was the image of a saint. But one morning she visited him in a dream, her hair crowned with violets, and her very gentleness seemed so formidable, that he uttered a cry of fright, and woke in an icy sweat. His eyes were still heavy with sleep, when he felt a moist warm breath on his face. A little jackal, its two paws placed on the side of the bed, was panting its stinking breath in his face, and grinning at him.

Paphnutius was greatly astonished, and it seemed to him as though a tower had given way under his feet. And, in fact, he had fallen, for his self-confidence had gone. For some time he was incapable of thought and when he did recover himself, his meditations only increased his perplexity.

"It is one of two things," he said to himself; "either this vision, like the preceding ones, came from God, and was a good vision, and it is my natural perversity which has misrepresented it, as wine turns sour in a dirty cup. I have, by my unworthiness, changed instruction into reproach, of which this diabolical jackal immediately took advantage. Or else this vision came, not from God, but, on the contrary, from the devil, and was evil. In that case I should doubt whether the former ones had, as I thought, a celestial origin. I am therefore incapable of that discernment which is necessary for the ascetic. In either case it is plain that God is no longer with me,—of which I feel the effects, though I cannot explain the cause."

He reasoned in this way, and anxiously asked—

"Just God, what trials dost Thou appoint for Thy servants if the apparitions of Thy saints are a danger for them? Give me to discern, by an intelligible sign, that which comes from Thee, and that which comes from the other."

And as God, whose designs are inscrutable, did not see fit to enlighten his servant, Paphnutius, lost in doubt, resolved not to think of Thaïs any more. But his resolutions were vain. Though absent, she was ever with him. She gazed at him whilst he read, or meditated, or prayed, or met his eyes wherever he looked. Her imaginary approach was heralded by a slight sound, such as is made by a woman's dress when she walks, and the visions had more verisimilitude than reality itself, which moves and is confused, whereas the phantoms which are caused by solitude are fixed and unchangeable. She came under various appearances—sometimes pensive, her head crowned with her last perishable wreath, clad as at the banquet at Alexandria, in a mauve robe spangled with silver flowers; sometimes voluptuously in a cloud of light veils, and bathed in the warm shadows of the Grotto of Nymphs; sometimes in a serge cassock, pious and radiant with celestial joy; sometimes tragic, her eyes swimming in the terrors of death, and showing her bare breast

bedewed with the blood from her pierced heart. What disturbed him
the most in these visions was that the wreaths, tunics, and veils,
that he had burned with his own hands, should thus return; it became evident to him that these things had an imperishable soul,
and he cried—

"Lo, all the countless souls of the sins of Thaïs come upon me!"

When he turned away his head, he felt that Thaïs was behind
him, and that made him feel still more uneasy. His torture was
cruel. But as his soul and body remained pure in the midst of all
his temptations, he trusted in God, and gently complained to Him.

"My God, if I went so far to seek her amongst the Gentiles, it
was for Thy sake, and not for mine. It would not be just that I
should suffer for what I have done in Thy behalf. Protect me, sweet
Jesus! My Saviour, save me! Suffer not the phantom to accomplish
that which the body could not. As I have triumphed over the flesh,
suffer not the shadow to overthrow me. I know that I am now exposed to greater dangers than I ever ran. I feel and know that the
dream has more power than the reality. And how could it be otherwise, since it is itself but a higher reality? It is the soul of things.
Plato, though he was but an idolater, has testified to the real
existence of ideas. At that banquet of demons to which Thou
accompaniedst me, Lord, I heard men—sullied with crimes truly,
but certainly not devoid of intelligence—agree to acknowledge that
we see real objects in solitude, meditation, and ecstasy; and Thy
Scriptures, my God, many times affirm the virtue of dreams, and
the power of visions formed either by Thee, great God, or by Thy
adversary."

There was a new man in him and now he reasoned with God, but
God did not choose to enlighten him. His nights were one long
dream, and his days did not differ from his nights. One morning he
awoke uttering sighs, such as issue, by moonlight, from the tombs
of the victims of crimes. Thaïs had come, showing her bleeding feet,
and whilst he wept, she had slipped into his couch. There was no
longer any doubt; the image of Thaïs was an impure image.

His heart filled with disgust, he leaped out of his profaned couch,
and hid his face in his hands that he might not see the daylight.
The hours passed, but they did not remove his shame. All was quiet
in the cell. For the first time for many long days, Paphnutius was
alone. The phantom had at last left him, and even its absence
seemed dreadful. Nothing, nothing to distract his mind from the
recollection of the dream. Full of horror, he thought—

"Why did I not drive her away? Why did I not tear myself from
her cold arms and burning knees?"

He no longer dared to pronounce the name of God near that horrible couch, and he feared that his cell being profaned, the demons
might freely enter at any hour. His fears did not deceive him. The
seven little jackals, which had never crossed the threshold, entered

in a file, and went and hid under the bed. At the vesper hour, there
came an eighth, the stench of which was horrible. The next day, a
ninth joined the others, and soon there were thirty, then sixty, then
eighty. They became smaller as they multiplied, and being no bigger
than rats, they covered the floor, the couch, and the stool. One of
them jumped on the little table by the side of the bed, and standing with its four feet together on the death's head, looked at the
monk with burning eyes. And every day fresh jackals came.

To expiate the abominable sin of his dream, and flee from impure thoughts, Paphnutius determined to leave his cell, which had
now become polluted, go far into the desert, and practise unheard-
of austerities, strange labours, and fresh works of grace. But before
putting his design into action, he went to see old Palemon and ask
his advice.

He found him in his garden watering his lettuces. It was the evening. The blue Nile flowed at the foot of violet hills. The good old
man was walking slowly, in order not to frighten a pigeon that
had perched on his shoulder.

"The Lord be with thee, brother Paphnutius," he said. "Admire
his goodness; He sends me the animals that He has created that I
may converse with them of His works, and praise Him in the birds
of the air. Look at this pigeon; note the changing hues of its neck,
and say, is it not a beautiful work of God? But have you not come
to talk with me, brother, on some pious subject? If so, I will put
down my watering-pot, and listen to you."

Paphnutius told the old man about his journey, his return, the
visions of his days and the dreams of his nights,—without omitting the sinful one—and the pack of jackals.

"Do you not think, father," he added, "that I ought to bury myself in the desert, and perform some extraordinary austerities that
would even astonish the devil?"

"I am but a poor sinner," replied Palemon, "and I know little
about men, having passed all my life in this garden, with gazelles,
little hares and pigeons. But it seems to me, brother, that your distemper comes from your having passed too suddenly from the noisy
world to the calm of solitude. Such sudden transitions can but do
harm to the health of the soul. You are, brother, like a man who
exposes himself, almost at the same time, to great heat and great
cold. A cough shakes him, and fever torments him. In your place,
brother Paphnutius, instead of retiring at once into some awful
desert, I should take such amusements as are fitting to a monk and
a holy abbot. I should visit the monasteries in the neighbourhood.
Some of them are wonderful, it is said. That of Abbot Serapion contains, I have been told, a thousand four hundred and thirty-two
cells, and the monks are divided into as many legions as there are
letters in the Greek alphabet. I am even informed that a certain
analogy is observed between the character of the monks and the

shape of the letter by which they are designated, and that, for example, those who are placed under Z have a tortuous character, whilst those under I have an upright mind. If I were you, brother, I should go and assure myself of this with my own eyes, and I should know no rest until I had seen such a wonderful thing. I should not fail to study the regulations of the various communities which are scattered along the banks of the Nile, so as to be able to compare one with another. Such study is befitting a religious man like yourself. You have heard say, no doubt, that Abbot Ephrem has drawn up for his monastery pious regulations of great beauty. With his permission, you might make a copy of them, as you are a skilful penman. I could not do so, for my hands, accustomed to wield the spade, are too awkward to direct the thin reed of the scribe over the papyrus. But you have the knowledge of letters, brother, and should thank God for it, for beautiful writing cannot be too much admired. The work of the copyist and the reader is a great safeguard against evil thoughts. Brother Paphnutius, why do you not write out the teachings of our fathers, Paul and Anthony? Little by little you would recover, in these pious works, peace of soul and mind; solitude would again become pleasant to your heart, and soon you would be in a condition to recommence those ascetic works which your journey has interrupted. But you must not expect much benefit from excessive penitence. When he was amongst us, our Father Anthony used to say, 'Excessive fasting produces weakness, and weakness begets idleness. There are some monks who ruin their body by fasts improperly prolonged. Of them it may be said that they plunge a dagger into their own breast, and deliver themselves up unresistingly into the power of the devil.' So said the holy man, Anthony. I am but a foolish old man, but, by the grace of God, I have remembered what our father told us."

Paphnutius thanked Palemon and promised to think over his advice. When he had passed the fence of reeds which enclosed the little garden, he turned round and saw the good old gardener engaged in watering his salads, whilst the pigeon walked about on his bent back, and at that sight Paphnutius felt ready to weep.

On returning to his cell, he found there a strange turmoil, as though it were filled with grains of sand blown about by a strong wind, and on looking closer, he saw these moving bodies were myriads of little jackals. That night he saw in a dream, a high stone column surmounted by a human face, and he heard a voice which said—

"Ascend this pillar!"

On awaking, he felt confident that this dream had been sent from heaven. He called his disciples, and addressed them in these words—

"My beloved sons, I must leave you, and go where God sends me.

During my absence obey Flavian as you would me, and take care of our brother Paul. Bless you. Farewell."

As he strode away, they remained prostrate on the ground, and when they raised their heads, they saw his tall dark figure on the sandy horizon.

He walked day and night until he reached the ruins of the temple, formerly built by the idolators, in which he had slept amongst the scorpions and sirens on his former strange journey. The walls, covered with magic signs, were still standing. Thirty immense columns, which terminated in human heads or lotus flowers, still supported a heavy stone entablature. But, at one end of the temple, a pillar had shaken off its old burden, and stood isolated. It had for its capital the head of a woman which smiled, with long eyes and rounded cheeks, and on her forehead cow's horns.

Paphnutius, on seeing it, recognised the column which had been shown him in his dream, and he calculated that it was thirty-two cubits high. He went to the neighbouring village, and ordered a ladder of that height to be made; and when the ladder was placed against the pillar, he ascended, knelt down on the top, and said to the Lord—

"Here, then, O God, is the abode Thou hast chosen for me. May I remain here, in Thy Grace, until the hour of my death."

He had brought no provisions with him, trusting in divine providence, and expecting that charitable peasants would give him all that he needed. And, in fact, the next day, about the ninth hour, women came with their children, bringing bread, dates, and fresh water, which the boys carried to the top of the column.

The top of the pillar was not large enough to allow the monk to lie at full length, so that he slept with his legs crossed and his head on his breast, and sleep was a more cruel torture to him than his wakeful hours. At dawn the ospreys brushed him with their wings, and he awoke filled with pain and terror.

It happened that the carpenter who had made the ladder feared God. Disturbed at the thought that the saint was exposed to the sun and rain, and fearing that he might fall in his sleep, this pious man constructed a roof and a railing on the top of the column.

Soon the report of this extraordinary existence spread from village to village, and the labourers of the valley came on Sundays, with their wives and children, to look at the stylite. The disciples of Paphnutius, having learned with surprise the place of this wonderful retreat, came to him, and obtained from him permission to build their huts at the foot of the column. Every morning they came and stood in a circle round the master, and received from him the words of instruction.

"My sons," he said to them, "continue like those little children whom Jesus loved. That is the way of salvation. The sin of the flesh is the source and origin of all sins; they spring from it as from a parent. Pride, avarice, idleness, anger, and envy are its dearly beloved progeny. I have seen this in Alexandria; I have seen rich men carried away by the vice of lust, which, like a river with a turbid flood, swept them into the gulf of bitterness."

The abbots Ephrem and Serapion, being informed of his strange proceeding, wished to behold him with their own eyes. Seeing from afar, on the river, the triangular sail which was bringing them to him, Paphnutius could not prevent himself from thinking that God had made him an example to all solitary monks. The two abbots, when they saw him, did not conceal their surprise; and, having consulted together, they agreed in condemning such an extraordinary penance, and exhorted Paphnutius to come down.

"Such a mode of life is contrary to all usage," they said; "it is peculiar, and against all rules."

But Paphnutius replied—

"What is the monastic life if not peculiar? And ought not the deeds of a monk to be as eccentric as he is himself? It was a sign from God that caused me to ascend here; it is a sign from God that will make me descend."

Every day religious men came to join the disciples of Paphnutius, and they built for themselves shelters round the aerial hermitage. Several of them, to imitate the saint, mounted the ruins of the temple; but, being reproved by their brethren, and conquered by fatigue, they soon gave up these attempts.

Pilgrims flocked from all parts. There were some who had come long distances, and were hungry and thirsty. The idea occurred to a poor widow of selling fresh water and melons. Against the foot of the column, behind her bottles of red clay, her cups and her fruit under an awning of blue-and-white striped canvas, she cried, "Who wants to drink?" Following the example of this widow, a baker brought some bricks and made an oven close by, in the hope of selling loaves and cakes to visitors. As the crowd of visitors increased unceasingly, and the inhabitants of the large cities of Egypt began to come, some man, greedy of gain, built a caravanserai to lodge the guests and their servants, camels, and mules. Soon there was, in front of the column, a market to which the fishermen of the Nile brought their fish, and the gardeners their vegetables. A barber, who shaved people in the open air, amused the crowd with his jokes. The old temple, so long given over to silence and solitude was filled with countless sights and sounds of life. The innkeepers turned the subterranean vaults into cellars and nailed on the old pillars signs surmounted by the figure of the holy Paphnutius, and bearing this inscription in Greek and Egyptian—
"Pomegranate wine, fig wine, and genuine Cilician beer sold here."
On the walls, sculptured with pure and graceful carvings, the shopkeepers hung ropes of onions, and smoked fish, dead hares, and the carcases of sheep. In the evening, the old occupants of the ruins,

the rats, scuttled in a long row to the river, whilst the ibises, suspiciously craning their necks, perched on the high cornices, to which rose the smoke of the kitchens, the shouts of the drinkers, and the cries of the tapsters. All around, builders laid out streets, and masons constructed convents, chapels, and churches. By the end of six months a city was established with a guardhouse, a tribunal, a prison, and a school, kept by an old blind scribe.

The pilgrims were innumerable. Bishops and other Church dignitaries, came, full of admiration. The Patriarch of Antioch, who chanced to be in Egypt at that time, came with all his clergy. He highly approved of the extraordinary conduct of the stylite, and the heads of the Libyan Church followed, in the absence of Athanasius, the opinion of the Patriarch. Having learned which, Abbots Ephrem and Serapion came to the feet of Paphnutius to apologise for their former mistrust. Paphnutius replied—

"Know, my brothers, that the penance I endure is barely equal to the temptations which are sent me, the number and force of which astound me. A man, viewed externally, is but small, and, from the height of the pillar to which God has called me, I see human beings moving about like ants. But, considered internally, man is immense; he is as large as the world, for he contains it. All that is spread before me—these monasteries, these inns, the boats on the river, the villages, and what I see in the distance of fields, canals, sand, and mountains—is nothing in respect to what is in me. I carry in my heart countless cities and illimitable deserts. And evil—evil and death—spread over this immensity, cover them all, as night covers the earth. I am, in myself alone, a universe of evil thoughts."

He spoke thus because the desire for woman was in him.

The seventh month, there came from Alexandria, Bubastis and Saïs, women who had long been barren, hoping to obtain children by the intercession of the holy man and the virtues of his pillar. They rubbed their sterile bodies against the stone. There followed a procession, as far as the eye could reach, of chariots, palanquins, and litters, which stopped and pushed and jostled below the man of God. From them came sick people terrible to see. Mothers brought to Paphnutius young boys whose limbs were twisted, their eyes starting, their mouth foaming, their voices hoarse. He laid his hands upon them. Blind men approached, groping with their hands, and raising towards him a face pierced with two bleeding holes. Paralytics displayed before him the heavy immobility, the deadly emaciation, and the hideous contractions of their limbs; lame men showed him their club feet; women with cancer, holding their bosoms with both hands, uncovered before him their breasts devoured by the invisible vulture. Dropsical women, swollen like wine skins were placed on the ground before him. He blessed them. Nubians, afflicted with elephantiasis, advanced with heavy steps

and looked at him with streaming eyes and expressionless countenances. He made the sign of the cross over them. A young girl of
Aphroditopolis was brought to him on a litter; after having
vomited blood, she had slept for three days. She looked like a
waxen image, and her parents, who thought she was dead, had
placed a palm leaf on her breast. Paphnutius having prayed to
God, the young girl raised her head and opened her eyes.

As the people reported everywhere the miracles which the saint
had performed, unfortunate persons afflicted with that disease
which the Greeks call "the divine malady," came from all parts of
Egypt in incalculable legions. As soon as they saw the pillar, they
were seized with convulsions, rolled on the ground, writhed, and
twisted themselves into a ball. And—though it is hardly to be
believed—the persons present were in their turn seized with a
violent delirium, and imitated the contortions of the epileptics.
Monks and pilgrims, men and women, wallowed and struggled pell-
mell, their limbs twisted, foaming at the mouth, eating handfuls of
earth and prophesying. And Paphnutius at the top of his pillar felt
a thrill of horror pass through him, and cried to God—

"I am the scapegoat, and I take upon me all the impurities of
these people, and that is why, Lord, my body is filled with evil
spirits."

Every time that a sick person went away healed, the people applauded, carried him in triumph, and ceased not to repeat—

"We behold another well of Siloam!"

Hundreds of crutches already hung round the wonderful column;
grateful women suspended wreaths and votive images there. Some
of the Greeks inscribed distiches, and as every pilgrim carved his
name, the stone was soon covered as high as a man could reach
with an infinity of Latin, Greek, Coptic, Punic, Hebrew, Syrian,
and magic characters.

When the feast of Easter came there was such an affluence of
people to this city of miracles that old men thought that the days
of the ancient mysteries had returned. All sorts of people, in all
sorts of costumes, were to be seen there; the striped robes of
the Egyptians, the burnoose of the Arabs, the white drawers of
the Nubians, the short cloak of the Greeks, the long toga of the
Romans, the scarlet breeches of the barbarians, the gold-spangled
robes of the courtesans. A veiled woman would pass on an ass,
preceded by black eunuchs, who cleared a passage for her by the
free use of their sticks. Acrobats, having spread a carpet on the
ground, juggled and performed skilful tricks before a circle of
silent spectators. Snake-charmers unrolled their living girdles. A
glittering, dusty, noisy, chattering crowd! The curses of the camel-
drivers beating the animals; the cries of the hawkers who sold
amulets against leprosy and the evil eye; the psalmody of the

monks reciting verses of the Bible; the shrieking of the women who were prophesying; the shouting of the beggars singing old songs of the harem; the bleating of sheep; the braying of asses; the sailors calling tardy passengers; all these confused noises caused a deafening uproar, over which dominated the strident voices of the little naked negro boys, running about everywhere selling fresh dates.

And all these human beings stifled under the white sky, in a heavy atmosphere laden with the perfumes of women, the odour of negroes, the fumes of cooking and the smoke of gums, which the devotees bought of the shepherds to burn before the saint.

When night came, fires, torches, and lanterns were lighted everywhere, and nothing was to be seen but red shadows and black shapes. Standing amidst a circle of squatting listeners, an old man, his face lighted by a smoky lamp, related how, formerly, Bitiou had enchanted his heart, torn it from his breast, placed it in an acacia, and then transformed himself into a tree. He made gestures, which his shadow repeated with absurd exaggerations, and the audience uttered cries of admiration. In the taverns, the drinkers, lying on couches, called for beer and wine. Dancing girls, with painted eyes and bare stomachs, performed before them religious or lascivious scenes. In retired corners, young men played dice or other games, and old men followed prostitutes. Above all these rose the solitary, unchanging column; the head with the cow's horns gazed into the shadow, and above it Paphnutius watched between heaven and earth. All at once the moon rose over the Nile, like the bare shoulder of a goddess. The hills gleamed with blue light, and Paphnutius thought he saw the body of Thaïs shining in the glimmer of the waters amidst the sapphire night.

The days passed, and the saint still lived on his pillar. When the rainy season came, the waters of heaven, filtering through the cracks in the roof, wetted his body; his stiff limbs were incapable of movement. Scorched by the sun, and reddened by the dew, his skin broke; large ulcers devoured his arms and legs. But the desire of Thaïs still consumed him inwardly, and he cried—

"It is not enough, great God! More temptations! More unclear thoughts! More horrible desires! Lord, lay upon me all the lusts of men, that I may expiate them all! Though it is false that the Greek bitch took upon herself all the sins of the world, as I heard an impostor once declare, yet there is a hidden meaning in the fable, the truth of which I now recognise. For it is true that the sins of the people enter the soul of the saints, and are lost there as in a well. Thus it is that the souls of the just are polluted with more filth than is ever found in the soul of the sinner. And, for that reason, I praise Thee, O my God, for having made me the cesspool of the world."

One day, a rumour ran through the holy city, and even reached the ears of the hermit: a very great personage, a man occupying a high position, the Prefect of the Alexandrian fleet, Lucius Aurelius Cotta, was about to visit the city—was, indeed, now on his way.

The news was true. Old Cotta, who was inspecting the canals and the navigation of the Nile, had many times expressed a desire to see the stylite and the new city, to which the name of Stylopolis had been given. The Stylopolitans saw the river covered with sails one morning. Cotta appeared on board a golden galley hung with purple, and followed by all his fleet. He landed, and advanced, accompanied by a secretary carrying his tablets, and Aristæus, his physician, with whom he liked to converse.

A numerous suite walked behind him, and the shore was covered with *laticlaves** and military uniforms. He stopped, some paces from the column, and began to examine the stylite, wiping his face meanwhile with the skirt of his toga. Being of a naturally curious disposition, he had observed many things in the course of his long voyages. He liked to remember them, and intended to write, after he had finished his Punic history, a book on the remarkable things he had witnessed. He seemed much interested by the spectacle before him.

"This is very curious!" he said, puffing and blowing. "And—which is a circumstance worthy of being recorded—this man was my guest. Yes, this monk supped with me last year, after which he carried off an actress."

Turning to his secretary—

"Note that, my son, on my tablets; also the dimensions of the column, not omitting the shape of the top of it."

Then, wiping his face again—

"Persons deserving of belief have assured me that this monk has not left his column for a single moment since he mounted it a year ago. Is that possible, Aristæus?"

"That which is possible to a lunatic or a sick man," replied Aristæus, "would be impossible to a man sound in body and mind. Do you know, Lucius, that sometimes diseases of the mind or body give to those afflicted by them a strength which healthy men do not possess? For, as a matter of fact, there is no such thing as good health or bad health. There are only different conditions of the organs. Having studied what are called maladies, I have come to consider them as necessary forms of life. I take pleasure in studying them in order to be able to conquer them. Some of them are worthy of admiration, and conceal, under apparent disorder, profound harmonies; for instance, a quartan fever is certainly a very pretty thing! Sometimes certain affections of the body cause a rapid augmentation of the faculties of the mind. You know Creon? When he was a child, he stuttered and was stupid. But, having

*The *laticlave* was a toga, with a broad purple band, worn by Roman senators as the distinguishing mark of their high office.

cracked his skull by tumbling off a ladder, he became an able lawyer, as you are aware. This monk must be affected in some hidden organ. Moreover, this kind of existence is not so extraordinary as it appears to you, Lucius. I may remind you that the gymnosophists of India can remain motionless, not merely for a year, but during twenty, thirty, or forty years."

"By Jupiter!" cried Cotta, "that is a strange madness. For man was born to move and act, and idleness is an unpardonable crime, because it is an injury to the State. I do not know of any religion in which such an objectionable practice is permitted, though it possibly may be in some of the Asiatic creeds. When I was Governor of Syria, I found *phalli* erected in the porches at the city of Hera. A man ascended, twice a year, and remained there for a week. The people believed that this man talked with the gods, and interceded with them for the prosperity of Syria. The custom appeared senseless to me; nevertheless I did nothing to put it down. For I consider that a functionary ought not to interfere with the manners and customs of the people, but on the contrary, to see that they are preserved. It is not the business of the government to force a religion on a people, but to maintain that which exists, which, whether good or bad, has been regulated by the spirit of the time, the place, and the race. If it endeavours to put down a religion, it proclaims itself revolutionary in its spirit, and tyrannical in its acts, and is justly detested. Besides, how are you to raise yourself above the superstitions of the vulgar, except by understanding them and tolerating them? Aristæus, I am of opinion that I should leave this nephelo-coccygian* in the air, exposed only to the indignities the birds shower on him. I should not gain anything by having him pulled down, but I should by taking note of his thoughts and beliefs."

He puffed, coughed, and placed his hand on the secretary's shoulder.

"My child, note down that, amongst certain sects of Christians, it is considered praiseworthy to carry off courtesans and live upon columns. You may add that these customs are evidence of the worship of genetic divinities. But on this point we ought to question him himself."

Then, raising his head, and shading his eyes with his hand, to keep off the sun, he shouted—

"Hallo, Paphnutius! If you remember that you were once my guest, answer me. What are you doing up there? Why did you go up, and why do you stay there? Has this column any phallic signification in your mind?"

Paphnutius, considering Cotta as nothing but an idolater, did not deign to reply. But his disciple, Flavian, approached, and said—

*Nephelo-coccygia, the cloud-city built by the cuckoos, in the *Birds* of Aristophanes.

"Illustrious Sir, this holy man takes the sins of the world upon him, and cures diseases."

"By Jupiter! Do you hear, Aristæus?" cried Cotta. "This nephelococcygian practices medicine, like you. What do you think of so high a rival?"

Aristæus shook his head.

"It is very possible that he may cure certain diseases better than I can; such, for instance, as epilepsy, vulgarly called the divine malady, although all maladies are equally divine, for they all come from the gods. But the cause of this disease lies, partly, in the imagination, and you must confess, Lucius, that this monk, perched up on the head of a goddess, strikes the minds of the sick people more forcibly than I, bending over my mortars and phials in my laboratory, could ever do. There are forces, Lucius, infinitely more powerful than reason and science."

"What are they?" asked Cotta.

"Ignorance and folly," replied Aristæus.

"I have rarely seen a more curious sight," continued Cotta, "and I hope that some day an able writer will relate the foundation of Stylopolis. But even the most extraordinary spectacles should not keep, longer than is befitting, a serious and busy man from his work. Let us go and inspect the canals. Farewell, good Paphnutius! or rather, till our next meeting! If ever you should come down to earth again, and revisit Alexandria, do not fail to come and sup with me."

These words, heard by all present, passed from mouth to mouth, and being repeated by the believers, added greatly to the reputation of Paphnutius. Pious minds amplified and transformed them, and it was stated that Paphnutius, from the top of his pillar, had converted the Prefect of the Fleet to the faith of the apostles and the Nicæan fathers. The believers found a figurative meaning in the last words uttered by Aurelius Cotta; to them, the supper to which this important personage had invited the ascetic, was a holy communion, a spiritual repast, a celestial banquet. The story of this meeting was embroidered with wonderful details, which those who invented were the first to believe. It was said that when Cotta, after a long argument, had embraced the truth, an angel had come from heaven to wipe the sweat from his brow. The physician and secretary of the Prefect of the Fleet had also, it was asserted, been converted at the same time. And, the miracle being public and notorious, the deacons of the principal churches of Libya recorded it amongst the authentic facts. After that, it could be said, without any exaggeration, that the whole world was seized with a desire to see Paphnutius, and that, in the West as well as the East, all Christians turned their astonished eyes towards him. The most celebrated cities of Italy sent deputations to him, and the Roman Cæsar, the divine Constantine, who favoured the Christian religion, wrote him a letter which the legates brought to him with great ceremony. But one night, whilst the budding city at his feet slept in the dew, he heard a voice, which said—

"Paphnutius, thou art become celebrated by thy works and powerful by thy word. God has raised thee up for His glory. He has chosen thee to work miracles, heal the sick, convert the Pagans, enlighten sinners, confound the Arians, and establish peace in the Church."

Paphnutius replied—

"God's will be done!"

The voice continued—

"Arise, Paphnutius, and go seek in his palace the impious Constans, who, far from imitating the wisdom of his brother, Constantine, inclines to the errors of Arius and Marcus. Go! The bronze gates shall fly open before thee, and thy sandals shall resound on the golden floor of the basilica before the throne of the Cæsars, and thy awe-inspiring voice shall change the heart of the son of Constantinus. Thou shalt reign over a peaceful and powerful Church. And, even as the soul directs the body, so shall the Church govern the empire. Thou shalt be placed above senators, comites, and patricians. Thou shalt repress the greed of the people, and check the boldness of the barbarians. Old Cotta, knowing that thou art the head of the government, will seek the honour of washing thy feet. At the death thy *cilicium* shall be taken to the patriarch of Alexandria, and the great Athanasius, white with glory, shall kiss it as the relic of a saint. Go!"

Paphnutius replied—

"Let the will of God be accomplished!"

And making an effort to stand up, he prepared to descend. But the voice, divining his intention said—

"Above all, descend not by the ladder. That would be to act like an ordinary man, and to be unconscious of the gifts that are in thee. A great saint, like thee, ought to fly through the air. Leap! the angels are there to support thee. Leap, then!"

Paphnutius replied—

"The will of God be done, on earth as it is in heaven."

Extending his long arms like the ragged wings of a huge sick bird, he was about to throw himself down, when, suddenly, a hideous mocking laugh rang in his ears. Terrified, he asked—

"Who laughs thus?"

"Ah? ah!" screamed the voice, "we are yet but at the beginning of our friendship; thou wilt some day be better acquainted with me. My friend, it was I who caused thee to ascend here, and I ought to be satisfied at the docility with which thou hast accomplished my wishes. Paphnutius, I am pleased with thee."

Paphnutius murmured, in a voice stifled by fear—

"Avaunt, avaunt! I know thee now; thou art he who carried

Jesus to a pinnacle of the temple, and showed him all the kingdoms of this world."

He fell, affrighted, on the stone.

"Why did I not know this sooner?" he thought. "More wretched than the blind, deaf, and paralysed who trust in me, I have lost all knowledge of things supernatural, and am more depraved than the maniacs who eat earth and approach dead bodies. I can no longer distinguish between the clamours of hell and the voices of heaven. I have lost even the intuition of the new-born child, who cries when its nurse's breast is taken from it, of the dog that scents out its master's footsteps, of the plant that turns towards the sun. I am the laughing-stock of the devils. So, then, it is Satan who led me here. When he elevated me on this pedestal, lust and pride mounted with me. It is not the magnitude of my temptations which terrifies me. Anthony, on his mountain, suffers the same. I wish that all their swords may pierce my flesh, before the eyes of the angels. I have even learned to like my sufferings. But God does not speak to me, and His silence astonishes me. He has left me—and I had but Him to look to. He leaves me alone in the horror of His absence. He flies from me. I will follow after Him. This stone burns my feet. Let me leave quickly, and come up with God."

With that he seized the ladder which stood against the column, put his feet on it, and having descended a rung, found himself face to face with the monster's head; she smiled strangely. He was certain then that what he had taken for the site of his rest and glory, was but the diabolical instrument of his trouble and damnation. He hastily descended and touched the soil. His feet had forgotten their use, and he reeled. But, feeling on him the shadow of the cursed column, he forced himself to run. All slept. He traversed, without being seen, the great square surrounded by wine-shops, inns, and caravanserais, and threw himself into a by-street which led towards the Libyan Hills. A dog pursued him, barking, and stopped only at the edge of the desert. Paphnutius went through a country where there was no road but the trail of wild beasts. Leaving behind him the huts abandoned by the coiners, he continued all night and all day his solitary flight.

At last, almost ready to expire with hunger, thirst, and fatigue and not knowing if God was still far from him, he came to a silent city which extended from right to left, and stretched away till it was lost in the blue horizon. The buildings, which were widely separated and like each other, resembled pyramids cut off at half their height. They were tombs. The doors were broken, and in the shadow of the chambers could be seen the gleaming eyes of hyænas and wolves who brought forth their young there, whilst the dead bodies lay on the threshold, despoiled by robbers, and gnawed by the wild beasts. Having passed through this funeral city, Paphnutius fell exhausted before a tomb which stood near a spring surrounded by palm trees. This tomb was much ornamented, and, as there was no door to it, he saw inside it a painted chamber, in which serpents bred.

"Here," he sighed, "is the abode I have chosen; the tabernacle of my repentance and penitence."

He dragged himself to it, drove out the reptiles with his feet, and remained prostrate on the stone floor for eighteen hours, at the end of which time he went to the spring, and drank out of his hand.

Then he plucked some dates and some stalks of lotus, the seeds of which he ate. Thinking this kind of life was good, he made it the rule of his existence. From morning to night he never lifted his forehead from the stone.

One day, whilst he was thus prostrated, he heard a voice which said—

"Look at these images, that thou mayest learn."

Then, raising his head, he saw, on the walls of the chamber, paintings which represented lively and domestic scenes. They were of very old work, and marvellously lifelike. There were cooks who blew the fire, with their cheeks all puffed out; others plucked geese, or cooked quarters of sheep in stew-pans. A little farther, a hunter carried on his shoulders a gazelle pierced with arrows. In one place, peasants were sowing, reaping, or gathering. In another, women danced to the sounds of viols, flutes, and harp. A young girl played the theorbo. The lotus flower shone in her hair, which was neatly braided. Her transparent dress let the pure forms of her body be seen. Her bosom and mouth were perfect. The face was turned in profile, and the beautiful eye looked straight before her. The whole figure was exquisite. Paphnutius having examined it, lowered his eyes, and replied to the voice—

"Why dost thou command me to look at these images? No doubt they represent the terrestrial life of the idolater whose body rests here, under my feet, at the bottom of a well, in a coffin of black basalt. They recall the life of a dead man, and are, despite their bright colours, the shadows of a shadow. The life of a dead man! O vanity!"

"He is dead, but he lived," replied the voice; "and thou wilt die, and wilt not have lived."

From that day, Paphnutius had not a moment's rest. The voice spoke to him incessantly. The girl with the theorbo looked fixedly at him from underneath the long lashes of her eye. At last she also spoke—

"Look. I am mysterious and beautiful. Love me. Exhaust in my arms the love which torments you. What use is it to fear me? You cannot escape me; I am the beauty of woman. Whither do you think to fly from me, senseless fool? You will find my likeness in the radiancy of flowers, and in the grace of the palm trees, in the flight of pigeons, in the bounds of the gazelle, in the rippling of brooks, in the soft light of the moon, and if you close your eyes, you will find me within yourself. It is a thousand years since the man who sleeps here, swathed in linen, in a bed of black stone, pressed me to his heart. It is a thousand years since he received the last kiss from my mouth, and his sleep is yet redolent with it. You know me well, Paphnutius. How is it you have not recognised me? I am one of the innumerable incarnations of Thaïs. You are a learned monk, and well skilled in the knowledge of things. You have travelled, and it is by travel a man learns the most. Often a day passed abroad will show more novelties than ten years passed at home. You have heard that Thaïs lived formerly in Argos, under the name of Helen. She had another existence in Thebes Hecatompyle. And I was Thaïs of Thebes. How is it you have not guessed it? I took, when I was alive, a large share in the sins of this world, and now reduced here to the condition of a shadow, I am still quite capable of taking your sins upon me, beloved monk. Whence comes your surprise? It was certain that, wherever you went, you would find Thaïs again."

He struck his forehead against the pavement, and uttered a cry of terror. And every night the player of the theorbo left the wall, approached him, and spoke in a clear voice mingled with soft breathing. And as the holy man resisted the temptations she gave him, she said to him—

"Love me; yield, friend. As long as you resist me I shall torment you. You do not know what the patience of a dead woman is. I shall wait, if necessary, till you are dead. Being a sorceress, I shall put into your lifeless body a spirit who will reanimate it, and who will not refuse me what I have asked in vain of you. And think, Paphnutius, what a strange situation when your blessed soul sees, from the height of heaven, its own body given up to sin. God, who has promised to return you this body after the day of judgment and the end of time, will Himself be much puzzled. How can He place in celestial glory a human form inhabited by a devil, and guarded by a sorceress? You have not thought of that difficulty. Nor God either, perhaps. Between ourselves, He is not very knowing. Any ordinary magician can easily deceive Him, and if He had not His thunder, and the cataracts of heaven, the village urchins would pull His beard. He has certainly not as much sense as the old serpent. His adversary. *He,* indeed, is a wonderful artist. If I am so beautiful, it is because he adorned me with all my attractions. It was he who taught me how to braid my hair, and to make for myself rosy fingers with agate nails. You have misunderstood him. When you came to live in this tomb, you drove out with your feet the serpents which were here, without troubling yourself to know whether they were of his family, and you crushed their eggs. I am afraid, my poor friend, you will have a troublesome business on your hands. You are warned, however, that he was a musician and a lover What have you done? You have quarrelled with science and beauty. You are altogether miserable, and Iaveh does not come to your help. It is not probable that he will come. Being as great as all things, he cannot move for want of space, and if, by an impossibility, he made the least movement, all creation would be pushed out of place. My handsome hermit, give me a kiss."

Paphnutius was aware that great prodigies are performed by magic arts. He thought—not without much uneasiness—

"Perhaps the dead man buried at my feet knows the words written in that mysterious book which exists hidden, not far from here, at the bottom of a royal tomb. By virtue of these words, the dead, taking the form which they had upon earth, see the light of the sun and the smiles of women."

His chief fear was that the girl with the theorbo and the dead man might come together, as they did in their lifetime, and that he should see them unite. Sometimes he thought he heard the sound of kissing.

He was troubled in his mind, and now, in the absence of God he feared to think as much as to feel. One evening, when he was kneeling prostrate according to his custom, an unknown voice said to him—

"Paphnutius, there are on earth more people than you imagine, and if I were to show you what I have seen, you would die of astonishment. There are men with a single eye in the middle of their forehead. There are men who have but one leg, and advance by jumps. There are men who change their sex, and the females become males. There are men-trees, who shoot out roots in the ground. And there are men with no head, with two eyes, a nose, and a mouth in their breast. Can you honestly believe that Jesus Christ died for the salvation of these men?"

Another time he had a vision. He saw, in a strong light, a broad road, rivulets, and gardens. On the road, Aristobulus and Chereas passed at a gallop on their Syrian horses, and the joyous ardour of the race reddened the cheeks of the two young men. Beneath a portico, Callicrates recited his verses; satisfied pride trembled in his voice and shone in his eyes. In the garden, Zenothemis picked apples of gold, and caressed a serpent with azure wings. Clad in white, and wearing a shining mitre, Hermodorus meditated beneath a sacred persea, which bore, instead of flowers, small heads of pure profile, wearing, like the Egyptian goddesses, vultures, hawks, or the shining disk of the moon; whilst in the background, by the side of a fountain, Nicias studied, on an armillary sphere, the harmonious movements of the stars.

Then a veiled woman approached the monk, holding in her hand a branch of myrtle. She said to him—

"Look! Some seek eternal beauty, and place their ephemeral life in the infinite. Others live without much thought. But by that alone they submit to fair Nature, and they are happy and beautiful in the joy of living only, and give glory to the supreme artist of all things; for man is a noble hymn to God. All think that happiness is innocent, and that pleasure is permitted to man. Paphnutius, if they are right, what a dupe you have been!"

And the vision vanished.

Thus was Paphnutius tempted unceasingly in body and mind. Satan never gave him a minute's repose. The solitude of the tomb was more peopled than the streets of a great city. The devils shouted with laughter, and millions of imps, evil genii, and phantoms imitated all the ordinary transactions of life. In the evening, when he went to the spring, satyrs and nymphs capered round him, and tried to drag him into their lascivious dances. The demons no longer feared him. They loaded him with insults, obscene jests, and blows. One day a devil, no longer than his arm, stole the cord he wore round his waist.

He said to himself—

"Thought, whither hast thou led me?"

And he resolved to work with his hands, in order to give his mind that rest of which it had need. Near the spring, some banana trees, with large leaves, grew under the shade of the palms. He cut the stalks, and carried them to the tomb. He crushed them with a stone, and reduced them to fibres, as he had seen ropemakers do. For he intended to make a cord, to replace that which the devil had stolen. The demons were somewhat displeased at this; they ceased their clamour, and the girl with the theorbo no longer continued her magic arts, but remained quietly on the wall. The courage and faith of Paphnutius increased whilst he pounded the banana stems.

"With Heaven's help," he said to himself, "I shall subdue the flesh. As to my soul, its confidence is still unshaken. In vain do the devils, and that accursed woman, try to instil into my mind doubts as to the nature of God. I will reply to them, by the mouth of the Apostle John, 'In the beginning was the Word, and the Word was God.' That I firmly believe, and that which I believe is absurd, I believe still more firmly. In fact it should be absurd. If it were not so, I should not *believe;* I should *know.* And it is not that which we know which gives eternal life; it is faith only that saves."

He exposed the separated fibres to the sun and the dew, and every morning he took care to turn them, to prevent them rotting; and he rejoiced to find that he had become as simple as a child. When he had twisted his cord, he cut reeds to make mats and baskets. The sepulchral chamber resembled a basket-maker's workshop, and Paphnutius could pass without difficulty from work to prayer. Yet still God was not merciful to him, for one night he was awakened by a voice which froze him with horror, for he guessed that it was the voice of the dead man.

The voice called quickly, in a light whisper—

"Helen! Helen! come and bathe with me! come quickly!"

A woman, whose mouth was close to the monk's ear, replied—

"Friend, I cannot rise; a man is lying on me."

Paphnutius suddenly perceived that his cheek rested on a woman's breast. He recognised the player of the theorbo, who, partly relieved of his weight, raised her breast. He clung tightly to the sweet, warm, perfumed body, and consumed with the desire of damnation, he cried—

"Stay, stay, my heavenly one!"

But she was already standing on the threshold. She laughed, and her smile gleamed in the silver rays of the moon.

"Why should I stay?" she said. "The shadow of a shadow is enough for a lover endowed with such a lively imagination. Besides, you have sinned. What more was needed?"

Paphnutius wept in the night, and when the dawn came, he murmured a prayer that was a meek complaint—

"Jesus, my Jesus, why hast Thou forsaken me? Thou seest the danger in which I am. Come, and help me, sweet Saviour. Since Thy Father no longer loves me, and does not hear me, remember that I have but Thee. From Him nothing is to be hoped; I cannot comprehend Him, and He cannot pity me. But Thou wast born of a woman, and that is why I trust in Thee. Remember that Thou wast a man. I pray to Thee, not because Thou art God of God, Light of light, very God of very God, but because Thou hast lived poor and humble on this earth where now I suffer, because Satan has tempted Thy flesh, because the sweat of agony has bedewed Thy face. It is to Thy humanity that I pray, Jesus, my brother Jesus!"

When he had thus prayed, wringing his hands, a terrible peal of laughter shook the walls of the tomb, and the voice which rang in his ears on the top of the column, said jeeringly—

"That is a prayer worthy of the breviary of Marcus, the heretic. Paphnutius is an Arian! Paphnutius is an Arian!"

As though thunderstruck, the monk fell senseless.

*　　*　　*　　*　　*

When he reopened his eyes, he saw around him monks wearing black hoods, who poured water on his temples, and recited exorcisms. Many others were standing outside, carrying palm leaves.

"As we passed through the desert," said one of them, "we heard cries issuing from this tomb, and, having entered, we found you lying unconscious on the floor. Doubtless the devils had thrown you down, and had fled at our approach."

Paphnutius, raising his head, asked in a feeble voice—

"Who are you, my brothers? And why do you carry palms in your hands? Is it for my burial?"

One of them replied—

"Brother, do you not know that our father, Anthony, now a hundred and five years old, having been warned of his approaching end, has come down from Mount Colzin, to which he had retired, to bless his numerous spiritual children? We are going with palm leaves to greet our holy father. But how is it, brother, that you are ignorant of such a great event? Can it be possible that no angel came to this tomb to inform you?"

"Alas!" replied Paphnutius, "I am not worthy of such a favour, and the only denizens of this abode are demons and vampires. Pray for me. I am Paphnutius, Abbot of Antinoë, the most wretched of the servants of God."

At the name of Paphnutius, all waved their palm leaves and murmured his praises. The monk who had previously spoken, cried in surprise—

"Can it be that thou art that holy Paphnutius, celebrated for so many works that it was supposed he would some day equal the great Anthony himself? Most venerable, it was thou who convertedst to God the courtesan, Thaïs, and who, raised upon a high column, was carried away by the seraphs. Those who watched by night, at the foot of the pillar, saw thy blessed assumption. The wings of the angels encircled thee in a white cloud, and with thy right hand extended thou didst bless the dwellings of man. The next day, when the people saw thou wert no longer there, a long groan rose to the summit of the discrowned pillar. But Flavian, thy disciple, reported the miracle, and took thy place as the head. But a foolish man, of the name of Paul, tried to contradict the general opinion. He asserted that he had seen thee, in a dream, carried away by the devils; the people wanted to stone him, and it was a miracle that he escaped death. I am Zozimus, abbot of these solitary monks whom thou seest prostrate at thy feet. Like them, I kneel before thee, that thou mayest bless the father with the children. Then thou shalt relate to us the marvels which God has deigned to accomplish by thy means."

"Far from having favoured me as thou believest," replied Paphnutius, "the Lord has tried me with terrible temptations. I was not carried away by angels. But a shadowy wall is raised in front of my eyes, and moves before me. I have lived in a dream. Without God all is a dream. When I made my journey to Alexandria, I heard, in a short space of time, many discourses, and I learned that the army of errors was innumerable. It pursues me, and I am compassed about with swords."

Zozimus replied—

"Venerable father, we must remember that the saints, and especially the solitary saints, undergo terrible trials. If thou wast not carried to heaven by the seraphs, it is certain that the Lord granted that favour of thy image, for Flavian, the monks, and the people were witnesses of thy assumption."

Paphnutius resolved to go and receive the blessing of Anthony.

"Brother Zozimus," he said, "give me one of these palm leaves, and let us go and meet our father."

"Let us go," replied Zozimus; "military order is most befitting for monks, who are God's soldiers. Thou and I, being abbots, will march in front, and the others shall follow us, singing psalms."

They set out on their march, and Paphnutius said—

"God is unity, for He is the truth, which is one. The world is many, because it is error. We should turn away from all the sights of nature, even those which appear the most innocent. Their diversity renders them pleasant, which is a sign that they are evil. For that reason, I cannot see a tuft of papyrus by the side of still waters without my soul being imbued with melancholy. All things that the senses perceive are detestable. The least grain of sand brings danger. Everything tempts us. Woman is but a combination of all the temptations scattered in the thin air, on the flowering earth, in the clear waters. Happy is he whose soul is a sealed vase! Happy is he who knows how to be deaf, dumb, and blind, and who knows nothing of the world, in order that he may know God!"

Zozimus, having meditated upon these words, replied as follows—

"Venerable father, it is fitting that I should avow my sins to thee, since thou hast shown me thy soul. Thus we shall confess to each other, according to the apostolic custom. Before I was a monk, I led an abominable life. At Madaura, a city celebrated for its courtesans, I sought out all kinds of worldly love. Every night I supped in company with young debauchees and female flute players, and I took home with me the one who pleased me the best. A saint like thee could never imagine to what a pitch the fury of my desires carried me. Suffice it to say that it spared neither matrons nor nuns, and spread adultery and sacrilege everywhere. I excited my senses with wine, and was justly known as the heaviest drinker in Madaura. Yet I was a Christian, and, in all my follies, kept my faith in Jesus crucified. Having devoured my substance in riotous living, I was beginning to feel the first attacks of poverty, when I saw one of my companions in pleasure suddenly struck with a terrible disease. His knees could not sustain him; his twitching hands refused to obey him; his glazed eyes closed. Only horrible groans came from his breast. His mind, heavier than his body, slumbered. To punish him for having lived like a beast, God had changed him into a beast. The loss of my property had already inspired me with salutary reflections; but the example of my friend was of yet greater efficacy; it made such an impression on my heart that I quitted the world and retired into the desert. There I have enjoyed for twenty years a peace that nothing has troubled. I work with my monks as weaver, architect, carpenter, and even as scribe, though, to say the truth, I have little taste for writing, having always preferred action to thought. My days are full of joy, and my nights without dreams, and I believe that the grace of the Lord is in me, because, even in the midst of the most frightful sins, I have never lost hope."

On hearing these words, Paphnutius lifted his eyes to heaven and murmured—

"Lord, Thou lookest with kindness upon this man polluted by adultery, sacrilege, and so many crimes, and Thou turnest away from me, who have always kept Thy commandments! How inscrutable is Thy justice, O my God! and how impenetrable are Thy ways!"

Zozimus extended his arms.

"Look, venerable father! On both sides of the horizon are long, black files that look like emigrant ants. They are our brothers, who, like us, are going to meet Anthony."

When they came to the place of meeting, they saw a magnificent spectacle. The army of monks extended, in three ranks, in an immense semicircle. In the first rank stood the old hermits of the desert, cross in hand, and with long beards that almost touched the ground. The monks, governed by the abbots Ephrem and Serapion, and also all the cenobites of the Nile, formed the second line. Behind them appeared the ascetics, who had come from their distant rocks. Some wore, on their blackened and dried-up bodies, shapeless rags; others had for their only clothes, bundles of reeds held together by withies. Many of them were naked, but God had covered them with a fell of hair as thick as a sheep's fleece. All held branches of palm; they looked like an emerald rainbow, or they might have been also compared to the host of the elect— the living walls of the city of God.

Such perfect order reigned in the assembly, that Paphnutius found, without difficulty, the monks he governed. He placed himself near them, after having taken care to hide his face under his hood, that he might remain unknown, and not disturb them in their pious expectation. Suddenly, an immense shout arose—

"The saint!" they all cried. "The saint! Behold the great saint, against whom hell has not prevailed, the well-beloved of God! Our father, Anthony!"

Then a great silence followed, and every forehead was lowered to the sand.

From the summit of a dune, in the vast void space, Anthony advanced, supported by his beloved disciples, Macarius and Amathas. He walked slowly, but his figure was still upright, and showed the remains of a superhuman strength. His white beard spread over his broad chest, his polished skull reflected the rays of sunlight like the forehead of Moses. The keen gaze of the eagle was in his eyes; the smile of a child shone on his round cheek. To bless his people, he raised his arms, tired by a century of marvellous works, and his voice burst forth for the last time, with the words of love.

"How goodly are thy tents, O Jacob, and thy tabernacles, O Israel!"

Immediately, from one end to the other of the living wall, like a peal of harmonious thunder, the psalm, "Blessed is the man that feareth the Lord," broke forth.

Accompanied by Macarius and Amathas, Anthony passed along the ranks of the old hermits, anchorites, and cenobites. This seer, who had beheld heaven and hell; this hermit, who from a cave in the rock, governed the Christian Church; this saint, who had sustained the faith of the martyrs; this scholar, whose eloquence had paralysed the heretics, spoke tenderly to each of his sons, and bade them a kindly farewell, on the eve of the blessed death, which God, who loved him, had at last promised him.

He said to the abbots Ephrem and Serapion—

"You command large armies, and you are both great generals. Therefore, you shall put on in heaven an armour of gold, and the Archangel Michael shall give you the title of kiliarchs of his hosts."

Perceiving the old man Philemon, he embraced him, and said—

"Behold, the kindest and best of all my children. His soul exhales a perfume as sweet as the flower of the beans he sows every year."

To Abbot Zozimus he addressed these words—

"Thou hast never mistrusted divine goodness, and therefore the peace of the Lord is in thee. The lily of thy virtues has flowered upon the dung-hill of thy corruption."

To all he spoke words of unerring wisdom.

To the old hermits he said—

"The apostle saw, round the throne of God, eighty old men seated, clad in white robes, and wearing crowns on their heads."

To the young men—

"Be joyful; leave sadness to the happy ones of this world."

Thus he passed along the front of his filial army, exhorting and comforting. Paphnutius, seeing him approach, fell on his knees, his heart torn by fear and hope.

"My father! my father!" he cried in his agony. "My father! come to my help, for I perish. I have given to God the soul of Thaïs; I have lived upon the top of a column, and in the chamber of a tomb. My forehead, unceasingly in the dust, has become horny as a camel's knee. And yet God has gone from me. Bless me, my father, and I shall be saved; shake the hyssop, and I shall be washed, and I shall shine as the snow."

Anthony did not reply. He turned to the monks of Antinoë those eyes whose looks no man could sustain. He gazed for a long time at Paul, called the Fool; then he made a sign to him to approach. And, as all were astonished that the saint should address himself to a man who was not in his senses, Anthony said—

"God has granted to him more grace than to any of you. Lift thy eyes, my son Paul, and tell me what thou seest in heaven."

Paul the Fool raised his eyes; his face shone, and his tongue was unloosed.

"I see in heaven," he said, "a bed adorned with hangings of purple and gold. Around it three virgins keep constant watch that no soul may approach it, except the chosen one for whom the bed is prepared."

Believing that this bed was the symbol of his glorification, Paphnutius had already begun to return thanks to God. But Anthony made a sign to him to be silent, and to listen to the Fool, who murmured in his ecstasy—

"The three virgins speak to me; they say unto me: 'A saint is about to quit the earth; Thaïs of Alexandria is dying. And we have prepared the bed of her glory, for we are her virtues—Faith, Fear, and Love.' "

Anthony asked—

"Sweet child, what else seest thou?"

Paul gazed vacantly from the zenith to the nadir, and from west to east, when suddenly his eyes fell on the Abbot of Antinoë. His face grew pale with a holy terror, and his eyeballs reflected invisible flames.

"I see," he murmured, "three demons, who, full of joy, prepare to seize that man. One of them is like unto a tower, one to a woman, and one to a mage. All three bear their name, marked with red-hot iron; the first on the forehead, the second on the belly, the third on the breast, and those names are—Pride, Lust, and Doubt. I have finished."

Having spoken thus, Paul, with haggard eyes and hanging jaw, returned to his old simple ways.

And, as the monks of Antinoë looked anxiously at Anthony, the saint pronounced these words—

"God has made known His just judgment. Let us bow to Him and hold our peace."

He passed. He bestowed blessings as he went. The sun, now descended to the horizon, enveloped him in its glory, and his shadow, immeasurably elongated by a miracle from heaven, unrolled itself behind him like an endless carpet, as a sign of the long remembrance this great saint would leave amongst men.

· Upright, but thunderstruck, Paphnutius saw and heard nothing more. One word alone rang in his ears, "Thaïs is dying!" The thought had never occurred to him. Twenty years had he contemplated a mummy's head, and yet the idea that death would close the eyes of Thaïs astonishd him hopelessly.

"Thaïs is dying!" An incomprehensible saying! "Thaïs is dying!" In those three words what a new and terrible sense! "Thaïs is dying!" Then why the sun, the flowers, the brooks, and all creation? "Thaïs is dying!" What good was all the universe? Suddenly he sprang forward. "To see her again, to see her once more!" He began to run. He knew not where he was, or whither he went, but instinct conducted him with unerring certainty; he went straight to the Nile. A swarm of sails covered the upper waters of the river. He sprang on board a barque manned by Nubians, and lying in the forepart of the boat, his eyes devouring space, he cried, in grief and rage—

"Fool, fool, that I was, not to have possessed Thaïs whilst there was yet time! Fool to have believed that there was anything else in the world but her! Oh, madness! I dreamed of God, of the salvation of my soul, of life eternal—as if all that counted for anything when I had seen Thaïs! Why did I not feel that blessed eternity was in a single kiss of that woman, and that without her life was senseless, and no more than an evil dream? Oh, stupid fool! thou hast seen her, and thou hast desired the good things of the other world! Oh, coward! thou hast seen her, and thou hast feared God! God! heaven! what are they? And what have they to offer thee which are worth the least tittle of that which she would have given thee? Oh, miserable, senseless fool, who sought divine goodness elsewhere than on the lips of Thaïs! What hand was upon thy eyes? Cursed be he who blinded thee then! Thou couldst have bought, at the price of thy damnation, one moment of her love, and thou hast not done it! She opened to thee her arms—flesh mingled with the perfume of flowers—and thou wast not engulfed in the unspeakable enchantments of her unveiled breast. Thou hast listened to the jealous voice which said to thee, 'Refrain!' Dupe, dupe, miserable dupe! Oh, regrets! Oh, remorse! Oh, despair! Not to have the joy to carry to hell the memory of that never-to-be-forgotten hour, and to cry to God, 'Burn my flesh, dry up all the blood in my veins, break all my bones, thou canst not take from me the remembrance which sweetens and refreshes me for ever and ever!' . . . Thaïs is dying! Preposterous God, if thou knewest how I laugh at Thy hell! Thaïs is dying, and she will never be mine—never! never!"

And as the boat came down the river with the current, he remained whole days lying on his face, and repeating—

"Never! never! never!"

Then, at the idea that she had given herself to others, and not to him; that she had poured forth an ocean of love, and he had not wetted his lips therein, he stood up, savagely wild, and howled with grief. He tore his breast with his nails, and bit the flesh of his arms. He thought—

"If I could but kill all those she has loved!"

The idea of these murders filled him with delicious fury. He dreamed of killing Nicias slowly and leisurely, looking him full in the eyes whilst he murdered him. Then suddenly his fury melted away. He wept, he sobbed. He became feeble and meek. An unknown tenderness softened his soul. He longed to throw his arms round the neck of the companion of his childhood, and say to him, "Nicias, I love thee, because thou hast loved her. Talk to me about her. Tell me what she said to thee." And still, without ceasing, the iron of that phrase entered into his soul—"Thaïs is dying!"

"Light of day, silvery shadows of night stars, heavens, trees with trembling crests, savage beasts, domestic animals, all the anxious souls of men, do you not hear? 'Thaïs is dying!' Disappear, ye lights, breezes, and perfumes! Hide yourselves, ye shapes and thoughts of the universe! 'Thaïs is dying!' She was the beauty of the world, and all that drew near to her grew fairer in the reflection of her grace. The old man and the sages who sat near her, at the banquet at Alexandria, how pleasant they were, and how fascinating was their conversation! A host of brilliant thoughts sprang to their lips, and all their ideas were steeped in pleasure. And it was because the breath of Thaïs was on them that all they said was love, beauty, truth. A delightful impiety lent its grace to their discourse. They thoroughly expressed all human splendour. Alas! all that is but a dream. Thaïs is dying! Oh, how easy it will be to me to die of her death! But canst thou only die, withered embryo, fœtus steeped in gall and scalding tears? Miserable abortion, dost thou think thou canst taste death, thou who hast never known life? If only God exists, that he may damn me. I hope for it—I wish it. God, I hate Thee—dost Thou hear? Overwhelm me with Thy damnation. To compel Thee to, I spit in Thy face. I must find an eternal hell, to exhaust the eternity of rage which consumes me."

*　　*　　*　　*　　*

The next day, at dawn, Albina received the Abbot of Antinoë at the nunnery.

"Thou art welcome to our tabernacles of peace, venerable father, for no doubt, thou comest to bless the saint thou hast given us. Thou knowest that God, in his mercy, has called her to Him; how couldst thou fail to know tidings that the angels have carried from desert to desert? It is true that Thaïs is about to meet her blessed death. Her labours are accomplished, and I ought to inform thee, in a few words, as to her conduct whilst she was still amongst us. After thy departure, when she was confined in a cell sealed with thy seal, I sent her, with her food, a flute, similar to those which girls of her profession play at banquets. I did that to prevent her from falling into a melancholy mood, and that she should not show less skill and talent before God than she had shown before men. In this I showed prudence and foresight, for all day long Thaïs praised the Lord upon the flute, and the virgins, who were attracted by the sound of this invisible flute, said, 'We hear the nightingale of the heavenly groves, the dying swan of Jesus crucified.' Thus did Thaïs perform her penance, when, after sixty days, the door which thou hadst sealed opened of itself, and the clay seal was broken without being touched by any human hand. By that sign I knew that the trial thou hadst imposed upon her was at an end, and that God had pardoned the sins of the flute-player. From that time she has shared the ordinary life of my nuns, working and praying with them. She was an example to them by the modesty of her acts and words, and seemed like a statue of purity amongst them. Sometimes she was sad; but those clouds soon passed. When I saw that she was really drawn towards God by faith, hope, and love, I did not hesitate to employ her talent, and even her beauty, for the improvement of her sisters. I asked her to represent before us the actions of the famous women and wise virgins of the Scriptures. She acted Esther, Deborah, Judith, Mary, the sister of Lazarus, and Mary, the mother of Jesus. I know, venerable father, that thy austere mind is alarmed at the idea of these performances. But thou thyself wouldest have been touched if thou hadst seen her in these pious scenes, shedding real tears, and raising to heaven arms graceful as palm leaves. I have long governed a community of women, and I make it a rule never to oppose their nature. All seeds give not the same flowers. Not all souls are sanctified in the same way. It must also not be forgotten that Thaïs gave herself to God whilst she was still beautiful, and such a sacrifice is, if not unexampled, at least very rare. This beauty—her natural vesture—has not left her during the three months' fever of which she is dying. As, during her illness, she has incessantly asked to see the sky, I have her carried every morning into the courtyard, near the well, under the old fig tree, in the shade of which the abbesses of this convent are accustomed to hold their meetings. Thou wilt find her there, venerable father; but hasten, for God calls her, and this night a shroud will cover that face which God made both to shame and to edify this world."

Paphnutius followed her into a courtyard flooded with the morning light. On the edge of the brick roofs, the pigeons formed a string of pearls. On a bed, in the shade of the fig tree, Thaïs lay quite white, her arms crossed. By her side stood veiled women, reciting the prayers for the dying.

"Have mercy, upon me, O God, according to Thy loving kindness: according unto the multitude of Thy tender mercies blot out my transgressions."

He called her—

"Thaïs!"

She raised her eyelids, and turned the whites of her eyes in the direction of the voice.

Albina made a sign to the veiled women to retire a few paces.

"Thaïs!" repeated the monk.

She raised her head; a light breath came from her pale lips.

"Is it thou, my father? . . . Dost thou remember the water of the spring, and the dates that we picked? . . . That day, my father, love was born in my heart—the love of life eternal."

She was silent, and her head fell back.

Death was upon her, and the sweat of the last agony bedewed her forehead. A pigeon broke the still silence with its plaintive cooing. Then the sobs of the monk mingled with the psalms of the virgins.

"Wash me thoroughly from mine iniquity, and cleanse me from my sin. For I acknowledge my transgressions: and my sin is ever before me."

Suddenly Thaïs sat up in the bed. Her violet eyes opened wide, and with a rapt gaze, her arms stretched towards the distant hills, she said in a clear, fresh voice—

"Behold them—the roses of the eternal dawn!"

Her eyes shone; a slight flush suffused her face. She had revived, more sweet and more beautiful than ever. Paphnutius knelt down, and threw his long black arms around her.

"Do not die!" he cried, in a strange voice, which he himself did not recognise. "I love thee! Do not die! Listen, my Thaïs. I have deceived thee? I was but a wretched fool. God, heaven—all that is nothing. There is nothing true but this worldly life, and the love of human beings. I love thee! Do not die! That would be impossible— thou art too precious! Come, come with me! Let us fly? I will carry thee far away in my arms. Come, let us love! Hear me, O my beloved, and say, 'I will live; I wish to live.' Thaïs, Thaïs, arise!"

She did not hear him. Her eyes gazed into infinity.

She murmured—

"Heaven opens. I see the angels, the prophets, and the saints. . . . The good Theodore is amongst them, his hands filled with flowers; he smiles on me and calls me. . . . Two angels come to me. They draw near. . . . How beautiful they are! I see God!"

She uttered a joyful sigh, and her head fell back motionless on the pillow. Thaïs was dead.

Paphnutius held her in a last despairing embrace; his eyes devoured her with desire, rage, and love.

Albina cried to him—

"Avaunt, accursed wretch!"

And she gently placed her fingers on the eyelids of the dead girl. Paphnutius staggered back, his eyes burning with flames and feeling the earth open beneath his feet.

The virgins chanted the song of Zacharias:

"Blessed be the Lord God of Israel."

Suddenly their voices stayed in their throat. They had seen the monk's face, and they fled in affright, crying—

"A vampire! A vampire!"

He had become so repulsive, that passing his hand over his face, he felt his own hideousness.

THE RED LILY

I

HE looked round at the arm-chairs, grouped in front of the fire, at the tea-table with its tea-things glittering like shadows, at the big bunches of delicately coloured flowers in Chinese vases. Lightly she touched the sprays of guelder roses and toyed with their silver buds. Then she gazed gravely in the glass. Standing sideways and looking over her shoulder, she followed the outline of her fine figure in its sheath of black satin, over which floated a thin drapery, sown with beads and scintillating with lights of flame. Curious to examine that day's countenance, she approached the mirror. Tranquilly and approvingly it returned her glance as if the charming woman it was reflecting lived a life devoid of intense joy and profound sadness. On the walls of the great empty silent drawing-room, the tapestry figures at their ancient games, vague in the shadow, grew pale with dying grace. Like them, the terra cotta statuettes on pedestals, the groups of old Dresden china, the paintings on Sèvres, displayed in glass cases, spoke of things past. On a stand decorated with precious bronzes the marble bust of some royal princess, disguised as Diana, with irregular features and prominent breast, escaped from her troubled drapery, whilst on the ceiling a Night, powdered like a marquise and surrounded by Cupids, scattered flowers. Everything was slumbering, and there was heard only the crackling of the fire and the slight rustling of beads on gauze.

Turning from the glass, she went to the window, raised one corner of the curtain, and looked out into the pale twilight, through the black trees on the quay to the yellow waters of the Seine. The grey weariness of sky and water was reflected in the greyness of her beautiful eyes. One of the "Swallow" boats passed, coming from under an arch of the Pont de l'Alma, and bearing humble passengers towards Grenelle and Billancourt. She looked after it as it drifted down the muddy current; then she let the curtain fall, and, sitting down in her accustomed corner of the sofa, under the flowers, she took up a book, laid upon the table just within hand's reach. On its straw-coloured linen cover glittered in gold the title: *Yseult la Blonde,* by Vivian Bell. It was a collection of French verse written by an Englishwoman and printed in London. She opened it by chance and read:

> Like to a worshipper who prays and sings,
> The bell on the quivering air "Hail Mary!" rings;
> And there is the orchard, 'mid the apple trees,
> The messenger the shuddering virgin sees,
> Awed, his red lily takes, whose perfum'd breath
> Makes her who breathes it half in love with death.
>
> In the wall'd garden, in the cool of the day,
> Through her cleft lips her soul would speed away,
> Her life, at some unconquerable behest,
> Even as a stream, pour from her ivory breast*

Waiting for her visitors to arrive, she read, indifferent and absent-minded, thinking less of the poetry than of the poetess: that Miss Bell, her most delightful friend perhaps, but one whom she hardly ever saw. At each of their rare meetings, Miss Bell embraced her, pecked her on the cheek, called her darling, and then gushed into prattling talk. Ugly and yet attractive, slightly ridiculous and altogether exquisite, Miss Bell lived at Fiesole as æsthete and philosopher, while in England she was renowned as the favourite English poetess. Like Vernon Lee and Mary Robinson, she had fallen in love with Tuscan life and art; and, without staying to complete her *Tristan,* the first part of which had inspired Burne-Jones to paint dreams in water-colours, she was expressing Italian ideas in Provençal and French verse. She had sent her *Yseult la Blonde* to "darling," with a letter inviting her to spend a month at her house at Fiesole. She had written, "Come; you will see the most beautiful things in the world, and you will make them more beautiful."

And "darling" was saying to herself that she would not go, that she was detained in Paris. But she was not indifferent to the idea of seeing Miss Bell and Italy again. Turning over the pages of the book, she fell upon this line:

> The self-same thing a kindly heart and love.†

> *Quand la cloche, faisant comme qui chante et prie,
> Dit dans le ciel ému: "Je vous salue, Marie,"
> La vierge, en visitant les pommiers du verger,
> Frissonne d'avoir vu venir le messager
> Qui lui présente un lys rouge et tel qu'on désire
> Mourir de son parfum sitôt qu'on le respire.
>
> La vierge au jardin clos, dans la douceur du soir,
> Sent l'âme lui monter, aux lèvres, et croit voir
> Couler sa vie ainsi qu'un ruisseau qui s'épanche
> En limpide filet de sa poitrine blanche.

> †Amour et gentil cœur sont une même chose.

And she wondered ironically but kindly whether Miss Bell had ever loved, and if so what her love-story had been. The poetess had an admirer at Fiesole, Prince Albertinelli. He was very handsome, but he seemed too matter-of-fact and commonplace to please an æsthete for whom love would have something of the mysticism of an Annunciation.

"How do you do, Thérèse? I am done up."

It was Princess Seniavine, graceful in her furs, which were hardly distinguishable from her dark sallow complexion. She sat down brusquely, and in tones harsh yet caressing, at once birdlike and masculine, she said:

"This morning I walked right through the Bois with General Larivière. I met him in the Allée des Potins, and took him to the Pont d'Argenteuil, where he insisted on buying from a keeper and presenting to me a trained magpie, which goes through its drill with a little gun. I am tired out."

"Why ever did you take the General so far as the Pont d'Argenteuil?"

"Because he had gout in his big toe."

Thérèse shrugged her shoulders, smiling:

"You are wasting your malice; and you are blundering."

"And you, my dear, would have me economise my kindness and my malice with a view to a serious investment?"

She drank some Tokay.

Announced by the sound of loud breathing, General Larivière came in, treading heavily. He kissed the hands of both women. Then, with a determined, self-satisfied air, sat down between them, ogling and laughing in every wrinkle of his forehead.

"How is M. Martin-Bellème? Still busy?"

Thérèse thought that he was at the Chamber and making a speech there.

Princess Seniavine, who was eating caviar sandwiches, asked Madame Martin why she was not at Madame Meillan's yesterday. There was a play acted.

"A Scandinavian play. Was it a success?"

"Yes. And yet I don't know. I was in the little green drawing-room, under the Duke of Orleans's portrait. M. le Ménil came and rendered me one of those services one never forgets. He saved me from M. Garain."

The General, who was a regular *Who's Who,* storing in his big head all kinds of useful information, pricked up his ears at this name.

"Garain," he asked, "the minister who was a member of the Cabinet at the time of the Prince's exile?"

"The very same. He was extremely occupied with me. He was explaining his heart's longings and looking at me with a most alarming tenderness. And from time to time with a sigh he glanced at the Duke of Orleans's portrait. I said to him, Monsieur Garain, you are making a mistake. It is my sister-in-law who is Orleanist. I am not in the least. At that moment M. le Ménil arrived to take me to have some refreshment. He complimented me on my horses. He told me there were none finer that winter in the Bois. He talked of wolves and wolf cubs. It was most refreshing."

The General, who never liked young men, said that he had met Le Ménil in the Bois the evening before galloping at a break-neck pace.

He declared that it was only old horsemen who maintained the good tradition, and that the men of fashion of the day were wrong in riding like jockeys.

"It is the same in fencing," he added. "Formerly——"

Princess Seniavine suddenly interrupted him:

"General, see how pretty Madame Martin is. She is always charming, but at this moment she is more so than ever. It is because she is bored. Nothing becomes her better than boredom. We have been wearying her ever since we came. Just look at her overcast brow, her wandering glance, her mournful mouth. She is a victim."

She jumped up, kissed Thérèse affectionately, and fled, leaving the General astonished.

Madame Martin-Bellème entreated him to pay no attention to such a madcap.

He was reassured and asked:

"And how are your poets, Madame?"

He found it difficult to pardon Madame Martin's liking for people who wrote and did not belong to his circle.

"Yes, your poets? What has become of that M. Choulette, who used to come and see you in a red comforter?"

"My poets are forgetting me; they are forsaking me. You can't depend on any one. Men, things—nothing is certain. Life is one long treachery. That poor Miss Bell is the only one who does not forget me. She has written from Florence and sent me her book."

"Miss Bell; isn't she that young person with frizzed yellow hair, who looks like a lap-dog?"

He made a mental calculation and concluded that by now she must be at least thirty.

A white-haired old lady, modestly dignified, and a little keen-eyed, vivacious man entered one after the other: Madame Marmet and M. Paul Vence. Then very stiff, wearing an eye-glass, appeared M. Daniel Salomon, sovereign arbiter of taste. The General made off.

They talked of the novel of the week. Madame Marmet had dined with the author several times, a very charming young man. Paul Vence thought the book dull.

"Oh!" sighed Madame Martin, "all books are dull. But men are much duller than books; and they are more exacting."

Madame Marmet asserted that her husband, a man of fine literary taste, had felt an intense horror of realism to the end of his days.

The widow of a member of the Academy of Inscriptions, sweet and modest in her black dress with her beautiful white hair, Madame Marmet prided herself in society on being the widow of an illustrious man.

Madame Martin told M. Daniel Salomon she would like to consult him about a porcelain group of children.

"It is Saint-Cloud. Tell me if you like it. You must give me your opinion too, Monsieur Vence, unless you scorn such trifles."

M. Daniel Salomon gazed at Paul Vence through his eye-glass with sullen haughtiness.

Paul Vence was looking round the drawing-room.

"You have some beautiful things, Madame. And that in itself would be little. But you have only beautiful things and those which become you."

She did not conceal her gratification at hearing him speak thus. She considered Paul Vence to be the only thoroughly intelligent man among her visiting acquaintance. She had appreciated him before his books had made him famous. Ill-health, a gloomy temper, hard work kept him out of society. This bilious little man was not very agreeable. Nevertheless he attracted her. She thought very highly of his profound irony, his untamed pride, his talent matured in solitude; and she justly admired him as an excellent writer, the author of fine essays on art and manners.

The drawing-room filled gradually with a brilliant assembly. The big circle of arm-chairs now included Madame de Vresson, about whom terrible stories were told, but who, after twenty years of partially suppressed scandals, retained a youthful complexion and looked out on the world through child-like eyes; old Madame de Morlaine, vivacious, scatter-brained, giving utterance to her witty remarks in piercing shrieks, while she agitated her unwieldy figure, like a swimmer in a life-belt; Madame Raymond, the wife of an Academician; Madame Garain, the wife of an ex-Minister, three other ladies; and standing by the mantelpiece, warming himself at the fire, M. Berthier d'Eyzelles, editor of *Le Journal des Débats* and deputy, who was stroking his white whiskers and trying to show himself off, while Madame de Morlaine was screaming at him:

"Your article on bimetallism a treasure, a gem! The end especially, pure inspiration."

Standing at the end of the drawing-room, a few young clubmen were solemnly drawling their conversation.

"How is it he has managed to hunt with the Prince's hounds?"

"He did nothing. It was his wife."

They had their philosophy of life. One of them never believed in promises.

"There's a kind of person I can't stand: a man with his heart in his hand and on his lips. When you are standing for a club, he says: 'I promise to vote for you.' 'Yes, but what will your vote be?' 'Why, of course not a black-ball.' But at the election it turns out he has put in a black-ball. Life is full of dirty tricks when you come to think of it."

"Then don't think of it," said a third.

Daniel Salomon, who had joined them, was whispering scandalous gossip, with an air of decorum. And at each interesting disclosure concerning Madame Raymond, Madame Berthier d'Eyzelles, and the Princess Seniavine he added carelessly: "Every one knows it."

Then gradually the crowd of visitors melted away. There remained only Madame Marmet and Paul Vence. The latter went up to the Countess Martin and asked:

"When shall I bring Dechartre to see you?"

It was the second time he had asked her. She was not fond of new faces. Very carelessly she replied:

"Your sculptor? When you like. At the Champs de Mars I saw some medallions by him which were very good. But he produces little. He is an amateur, isn't he?"

"He is sensitive. He does not need to work for a livelihood. He caresses his statues with a lingering affection. But be assured, Madame, he knows and he feels; he would be a master if he did not live alone. I have known him since he was a child. He is thought to be malicious and irritable. He is really passionate and shy. His defect, a defect which will always hinder him from attaining the highest point of his art, is a lack of simplicity of mind. He grows anxious, distracted, and spoils his finest impressions. In my opinion he is less suited for sculpture than for poetry or philosophy. He knows a great deal, and his well-stored mind would astonish you."

The benevolent Madame Marmet approved.

She pleased in society because she appeared as if society pleased her. She listened well and spoke little. Very kind-hearted, she made her kindness valued by not bestowing it at once. Whether it was that she really liked Madame Martin or that she made a point of showing discreet signs of preference in every house she visited, she was warming herself contentedly, like a grandmother, in a corner by the fire under that Louis XVI mantel-piece which was an effective background to the tolerant old lady's beauty. The only thing lacking was her lap-dog.

"How is Toby?" asked Madame Martin. "Monsieur Vence, do you know Toby? He has long silky hair and a lovely little black nose."

Madame Marmet was enjoying this praise of Toby when there entered a fair rosy-cheeked old man, with curly hair; short-legged and short-sighted, almost blind under his gold spectacles. He came in, knocking against the furniture, greeting empty arm-chairs and running into mirrors. Then he pushed his beaked nose in front of Madame Marmet, who looked at him indignantly. It was M. Schmoll, of the Academy of Inscriptions. His smile was an affected grimace. He recited madrigals in honour of Countess Martin in that hereditary unctuous tone in which his Jewish fathers had importuned their creditors, the peasants of Alsace, Poland, and the Crimea. He drawled out his sentences. A member of the French Institute, this great philologist knew every language except French. His gallantry amused Madame Martin. As rusty and heavy as the pieces of old iron sold by second-hand dealers, its only adornment was a few dried flowers culled from the Greek Anthology. M. Schmoll was a lover of poets and of women; and he was intelligent.

Madame Marmet pretended not to know him, and went out without returning his greeting. When he had exhausted his madrigals, M. Schmoll became sad and discontented. He groaned frequently. He complained bitterly at the way he was treated; he was neither sufficiently decorated nor sufficiently provided with sinecures, nor were he and Madame Schmoll and their five daughters sufficiently well housed at the State's expense. There was a certain greatness in his lamentations. Something of the soul of Ezekiel and Jeremiah was in him.

Unfortunately looking along the level of the table with his gold spectacles, he perceived Vivian Bell's book.

"Ah! *Yseult la Blonde,*" he cried bitterly: "that is the book you are reading, Madame. I should like you to know that Vivian Bell has robbed me of an inscription, and that worse still she has distorted it by putting it into verse. You will find it in the book, page 109:

> "Weep not, lowered lids between,
> What is not, never has been—"
> "Stem not my tears, dear maid,
> A shade may weep for a shade!"*

"You hear, Madame: A shade may weep for a shade. Well! those words are literally translated from a funeral inscription which I was the first to publish and to criticise. Last year, when I was dining at your house, finding myself next to Miss Bell at table, I quoted that sentence, which greatly pleased her. At her request the very next day I translated the whole inscription into French and sent it to her. And now I find it dismembered and disfigured in this volume of verse, with the title: *On the Via Sacra!* The Sacred Way! I am that way."

*"Ne pleure pas, toi que j'aimais:
Ce qui n'est plus ne fut jamais.
Laisse couler ma douleur sombre;
Une ombre peut pleurer une ombre."

And he repeated with grotesque bad temper:

"It is I who am that Sacred Way, Madame."

He was annoyed that the poet had not mentioned him in connection with the inscription. He would have liked to read his name at the head of the poem, in the lines, in the rhyme. He was always wanting to see his name everywhere. He was always looking for it in the newspapers with which his pockets were stuffed. But he was not vindictive. He bore Miss Bell no ill-will. He agreed with a good grace that she was a very distinguished woman and the most prominent English poet of the day.

When he had gone, Countess Martin very ingenuously asked M. Paul Vence if he knew why kind Madame Marmet, generally so benevolent, had greeted M. Schmoll with such angry silence. He was surprised that she did not know.

"I never know anything."

"But the quarrel between Joseph Schmoll and Louis Marmet, with which the Institute resounded for so long, is very famous. It was only ended by the death of Marmet whom his implacable colleague pursued even to Père-Lachaise.

"The day that poor Marmet was buried sleet was falling. We were frozen and wet to the skin. By the graveside, in the mist, in the wind and the mud, Schmoll, under his umbrella, read a discourse inspired by cruel jocularity and triumphing pity. Afterwards still in the mourning coach, he took it to the newspapers. When an indiscreet friend showed it to Madame Marmet, she fainted. Can it be possible, Madame, that you have never heard of this erudite and bitter quarrel?

"The Etruscan language was its cause. Marmet devoted his life to the study of Etruscan. He was nicknamed 'Marmet the Etruscan.' Neither he nor any one else knew a single word of that completely lost language. Schmoll used to be always saying to Marmet: 'You know that you don't know Etruscan, my dear brother; that's why you are so greatly honoured as a scholar and a wit.' Piqued by such ironical praise, Marmet determined to know something of Etruscan. He read his brother Academicians a paper on the use of inflexions in the ancient Tuscan idiom."

Madame Martin asked what an inflexion was.

"Oh! Madame, if I stop to explain we shall lose the thread of the story. Be content to know that in this paper poor Marmet quoted Latin texts and quoted them incorrectly. Now Schmoll is an accomplished Latin scholar, who, after Mommsen, knows more than any one about inscriptions.

"He reproached his young brother (Marmet was not quite fifty) with knowing too much Etruscan and not enough Latin. From that moment he never let Marmet alone. At each meeting he chaffed him with a mirthful ferocity, so much so that, in the end Marmet, in spite of his usual good temper, grew angry. Schmoll is not vindictive. It is a virtue of his race. He bears those whom he persecutes no ill-will. One day, going up the stairs of the Institute, accompanied by Renan and Oppert, he met Marmet and held out his hand to him. Marmet refused to take it and said: 'I do not know you.'

"'Do you take me for a Latin inscription?' replied Schmoll. That saying hastened Marmet's death. You now understand why his widow, who piously venerates his memory, should be horrified by the sight of his enemy."

"And to think that I should have asked them to dine here together, and placed them side by side!"

"Madame, that was not immoral, but it was cruel."

"My dear sir, perhaps I shall shock you, but if it were absolutely necessary to choose, I would rather be guilty of an immoral act than of a cruel one."

A tall young man, thin and dark, wearing a long moustache, now entered and greeted Madame Martin in an easy but brusque manner.

"Monsieur Vence, I think you know M. Le Ménil."

In reality they had already met at Madame Martin's and more than once at the fencing-school, which Ménil attended assiduously. The day before they had met at Madame Meillan's.

"At Madame Meillan's it is always dull," said Paul Vence.

"And yet," said M. Le Ménil, "she receives Academicians. I do not exaggerate their importance, but, after all, they are the elect."

Madame Martin smiled.

"We know, Monsieur Le Ménil, that at Madame Meillan's you were more occupied with women than with Academicians. You took Princess Seniavine to have some refreshments, and talked to her about wolves."

"About what? About wolves?"

"About wolves—she-wolves and wolf-cubs—and the bare woods of winter. We thought your topics rather too barbarous for so pretty a woman."

Paul Vence rose.

"So, if you will permit me, Madame, I will bring you my friend, Dechartre. He is very desirous to know you, and I trust you will like him. He has an active mind. He is full of ideas."

Madame Martin interrupted him.

"Oh, I don't ask for so much as that. People who are natural and who appear what they really are rarely bore me and sometimes amuse me."

When Paul Vence had gone, Le Ménil listened to the sound of his footsteps dying away down the hall and to the noise of the front door closing; then drawing nearer to Madame Martin:

"Shall we say three o'clock to-morrow, at home?"

"Do you still love me, then?"

He urged her to give him an answer while they were alone; she tantalisingly replied that it was late, that she expected no more visitors, and that her husband was likely to come in.

He entreated her to give him an answer. Then, without waiting for any further persuasion, she said:

"You really wish it? Then listen. To-morrow I shall be free the whole day. Expect me at three o'clock in the Rue Spontini. We will go for a walk afterwards."

He thanked her with a glance. Then, having returned to his place opposite her on the other side of the fireplace, he inquired who this Dechartre was whom she was asking to come and see her.

"I am not asking him to come. Monsieur Vence has asked if he may bring him. He is a sculptor."

He complained of her always wanting to see new faces.

"A sculptor? Sculptors are frequently not gentlemen."

"Oh, but he is so little of a sculptor! Still, if you don't wish it, I will not receive him."

"I should be very annoyed if society were to monopolise any of the time you devote to me."

"My friend, you have no reason to complain of my giving too much time to society. Yesterday I did not even go to Madame Meillan's——"

"You are quite right in going there as seldom as possible: it is not a house for you to visit."

He explained. All the women one met there had a past which was known and talked about. Besides Madame Meillan was said to promote intrigues. He enforced his statement by one or two examples.

Meanwhile, with her hands on the arms of her chair, in a charming attitude of repose, her head inclined to one side, she was gazing at the dying fire. Her thoughts had fled: there remained no sign of them, either in her face which was rather sad or in her languid pose; she was more desirable than ever in this slumber of her soul. For some time she continued in that absolute immobility which enhanced her natural attractiveness by an artistic charm.

He asked of what she was thinking. Half escaping from the melancholy mesmerism of the embers, she said:

"To-morrow, if you are willing, we will go to the remote quarters of the town, to those curious neighbourhoods where you can observe the lives of poor people. I like streets that are old and poverty-stricken."

While promising to gratify her fancy, he did not conceal that he thought it absurd. These excursions on which she made him accompany her bored him sometimes; and he considered them dangerous; they might be seen.

"And since so far we have succeeded in avoiding being talked about . . ."

She shook her head.

"Do you think we have never been talked about? Whether people know or do not know, they talk. Everything is not known, but everything is said."

She returned to her dreaming. He thought her dissatisfied, vexed at something she would not confide to him. He leaned forward gazing into her fine dreamy eyes in which the firelight was reflected. But she reassured him:

"I don't know whether people talk about me. And what does it matter if they do? Nothing matters."

He left her. He was going to dine at the club, where his friend Caumont, who was passing through Paris, expected him. She followed him with a glance of tranquil sympathy. Then she returned to contemplate the embers.

There she beheld the days of her childhood, the château in which she used to pass long sad summers, the trim woods, the damp and gloomy park, the pond with its green stagnant water, the marble nymphs under the chest-nut trees, and the bench, on which she used to weep and long to die. Even to-day she did not know the cause of her youthful despair, when the tumultuous awakening of her imagination and a mysterious physical evolution cast her into an agitation in which desires were mingled with fears. As a child, life had inspired her at once with fear and longing. And now she knew that life is not worth such anxiety and such hope, that it is a very ordinary matter. She ought to have expected it. Why had she not foreseen it? She continued her revery.

"I used to look at mama. She was a good woman, very simple-minded but not very happy. I dreamed of a lot very different from hers. Why? I felt that the atmosphere around me was enervating, and I longed for the stronger, salter air of the future. Why? What did I want, and what did I expect? Had I not warning enough of the sadness of everything?"

She was born rich and surrounded by the glaring brilliance of a newly made fortune. The daughter of that Montessuy, who, at first a mere clerk in a Parisian bank, had founded and directed two great banking houses, and by using all the resources of an inventive mind, invincible strength of character, a rare blend of cunning and honesty, had piloted them through a difficult crisis, and dealt with the Government on an equal footing. She had grown up in the historic château of Joinville, which, bought, restored, and magnificently furnished by her father, with its park and its extensive lakes, had come to equal Vaux-le-Vicomte in splendour. Montessuy enjoyed to the full all that life had to give. By instinct a pronounced atheist he was determined to have every material benefit and every desirable thing that earth produces. He crowded into the gallery and reception rooms of Joinville pictures by the great masters and precious marbles. At fifty he was paying for the luxuries of the most beautiful actresses and a few women in society. With all the brutality of his temperament and the keenness of his intelligence he enjoyed social life.

Meanwhile poor Madame Montessuy was languishing at Joinville. Anxious and frugal, she appeared poor and diminutive by the side of the twelve gigantic caryatides which, around her bed enclosed by a gilded balustrade, supported the ceiling painted by Lebrun with Titans pursued by the thunderbolts of Jupiter. There one evening on a little iron bedstead, put up at the foot of the great state bed, she died of sorrow and weakness, her only loves having been her husband and her little red damask drawing-room in the Rue de Maubeuge.

There had never been any intimacy between mother and daughter. The mother felt instinctively that Thérèse had nothing in common with her. Her daughter's intellect was too capacious, her will too vigorous. Although she was good and docile, there flowed in her veins the strong blood of Montessuy. Thérèse had her father's ardour, of soul and body, an ardour from which the mother had suffered so bitterly and for which she found it easier to forgive the father than the daughter.

But Montessuy saw himself in his daughter and loved her. Like all *bon-vivants,* he had his times of charming gaiety. Although he was much away from home, he managed to lunch with her nearly every day, and sometimes he took her out. He was a connoisseur in dress and trinkets. At a glance he noticed and corrected in his daughter's toilet the mistakes made by Madame Montessuy's bad taste. He was educating and forming Thérèse. Coarse yet entertaining, he amused her and won her affection. In his dealings even with her he was inspired by his instinct, his passion for conquest. He, who must always win, was winning his daughter. He was capturing her from her mother. Thérèse admired him, adored him.

In her revery, she saw him in the background of her past, as the one joy of her childhood. She was still fully persuaded that there was no more charming man than her father.

As soon as she entered society she despaired of finding elsewhere such natural qualities, such fulness of strength of body and of mind. This disappointment had persisted when she came to choose a husband, and later when she made a secret and a freer choice.

She had really not chosen her husband at all. She hardly knew how, but she had let herself be married by her father. He, being a widower embarrassed and troubled by the responsibility of a daughter in the midst of an agitated, busy life, had as usual wished to act quickly and well. He thought only of external distinctions and social conventions; he appreciated the advantage of the eighty years of imperial nobility offered by Count Martin, and the hereditary glory of a family which had provided with ministers the Government of July and the Liberal Empire. The idea of his daughter finding love in marriage never occurred to him.

He persuaded himself that in marriage she would find the satisfaction of that desire for splendour with which he had inspired her. He hoped that she would have the joy of being rich and appearing so, that she would gratify the vulgar pride, the desire for material superiority, which for him constituted the essence of life. For the rest, he had no very definite ideas concerning the happiness of a respectable woman in society; but he was quite sure that his daughter would always be a respectable woman. That was an innate conviction; on that point his mind was perfectly at rest.

Reflecting on that confidence, foolish and yet natural, which was so contrary to Montessuy's own experiences and ideas of women, she smiled a smile of ironic melancholy. She admired her father all the more for being too wise to indulge in importunate wisdom.

After all, he had not married her so badly, according to the standards of marriage among the leisured classes. Her husband was as good as many another. He had become quite tolerable. Of all the memories, which, in the half-light of the shaded lamps, the embers recalled to her, that of their life in common was the least vivid. All that returned to her were the painfully distinct recollections of one or two incidents, some foolish imaginings, an impression vague and unpleasant. That time had not lasted long, and had left nothing behind it. Now after six years she hardly remembered how she had gained her liberty, so prompt and easy had been that victory over a husband, cold, valetudinarian, egotistical, and polite. Ambitious, industrious, and commonplace, he had grown sere and yellow in business and politics. It was only through vanity that he loved women, and he had never loved his wife. Their separation had been frank and complete. And since then, strangers one to the other, they were both grateful for their mutual deliverance. She would have regarded him as a friend, had she not found him cunning, sly, and too artful in obtaining her signature when he needed money. This money he employed in enterprises prompted less by cupidity than by a desire for ostentation. Except for this the man with whom she dined, lived, travelled, and talked every day was nothing to her and had no share in her life.

Absorbed in her own thoughts, sitting chin in hand, before the dead fire, like an anxious inquirer consulting a sibyl, as she reviewed those years of solitude, she beheld the face of the Marquis of Ré. It was so clear and distinct that she was astonished. Introduced by her father, who was proud of the acquaintance, the Marquis of Ré appeared tall and handsome, decked with the glories of thirty years' private and social triumphs. He had enjoyed a long series of successes. He had seduced three generations of women and imprinted on each mistress's heart an imperishable memory. His virile grace, his refined elegance and his gift of pleasing prolonged

his youth far beyond the usual limits. The young Countess Martin
had been especially distinguished by him. She had been flattered by
the homage of such a connoisseur. Even now to recollect it still gave
her pleasure. He had a wonderful gift in conversation. She had found
him entertaining and had let him see it. Thenceforth, light-hearted
hero that he was, he had determined to bring his gay life to an appropriate close, by possessing this young woman, whom he admired
more than any one, and who obviously liked him. To entrap her he
laid all a rake's most ingenious toils. But she escaped from them
very easily.

Two years later she had become the mistress of Robert Le Ménil,
who, with all the ardour of his youth and all the simplicity of his
heart had resolved to win her. "I gave myself to him because he
loved me," she told herself. It was true. It was also true that an
unconscious, powerful instinct had impelled her, and that she had
obeyed secret forces of her nature. But these proceeded from her
subconscious self; what she had consciously done was to accept his
love, because she believed it to be informed by that sincerity she
had always sought. She had yielded directly she found herself loved
to the point of suffering. She had given herself quickly, simply. He
thought she had given herself lightly. He was mistaken. The irreparable act had brought on a feeling of overwhelming dejection and
shame at suddenly having something to hide. All the whisperings
she had heard about women who had lovers were buzzing in her
burning ears. But, proud and sensitive, and with perfect taste, she
was careful to hide the cost of the gift she bestowed and to say
nothing which might engage her lover to go further than his own
feelings would carry him. He never suspected that moral suffering,
which after all only lasted a few days and was succeeded by perfect
tranquillity. After three years she approved of her conduct as having been innocent and natural. Having done no one any wrong, she
had no regrets. She was content. This relationship was her greatest
happiness. She loved, she was loved. True she had never experienced the rapture she had dreamed of. But is it ever experienced?
She was the mistress of a good honourable bachelor, who was much
liked by women and popular in society, where he was considered
haughty and fastidious; and he loved her sincerely. The pleasure
she gave him and the joy of being beautiful for him were the
bonds which bound her to him. He rendered her life, not always
rapturously delightful, but tolerable and sometimes pleasant.

What she had not guessed in her solitude in spite of the warning of vague misgivings and unaccountable sadness, her own inner
nature, her temperament, her true vocation, he had revealed to her.
She learned to know herself by knowing him. And her self knowledge brought her some pleasant astonishment. Their sympathies
were neither of the head nor of the heart. She had a simple definite

liking for him, which did not wear out quickly. And at that very moment she took pleasure in the thought of meeting him on the morrow, in the little flat in the Rue Spontini which had been their rendezvous for three years. It was with rather a brusque movement of her head and a more violent shrug of the shoulders than one would have expected from so exquisite a lady, that, alone in the chimney-corner, by a dead fire, she said to herself: "Ah! what I want is to be in love."

II

IGHT had already fallen when they came out of the little *entresol* in the Rue Spontini. Robert Le Ménil hailed a passing cab, and looking anxiously at the man and his horse, entered the carriage with Thérèse. Close side by side, they drove among the vague shadows relieved by sudden lights, through the phantom town; in their hearts there were only sweet impressions now vanishing as rapidly as the fleeting lights shining through the blurred carriage windows. Everything outside appeared to them confused and fleeting, and in their hearts there was a sweet calm. The cab stopped near the Pont Neuf, on the Quai des Augustins.

They got out. A dry cold invigorated the dull January day. Thérèse under her veil breathed with delight the gusts of wind, which, crossing the river, swept the dust, as bitter and white as salt, along the hard ground. It pleased her to walk freely among strange sights. She loved to gaze upon that landscape of stone enveloped in the dim light of the atmosphere, to walk briskly along the quay where the black gauze-like branches of the trees stood out against the horizon reddened by the smoke of the town. It delighted her, leaning over the parapet, to watch the narrow arm of the Seine bearing its tragic waters, and to drink in the sadness of the river between its low banks, devoid of willows or beeches. Already the first stars were twinkling high up in the sky.

"It looks as if the wind would put them out," she said.

He remarked that they were scintillating brilliantly. He did not consider it a sign of rain, as the peasants believe. On the contrary, he had observed that nine times out of ten the scintillation of the stars announced fine weather.

Near the Petit Pont on their right (lit by smoky lamps) were booths where old iron was sold. She gazed eagerly among the dust and rust of the wares displayed. The instinct of the curiosity-monger had been aroused in her; she turned the street corner and ventured as far as a lean-to in which some dark coloured rags were hanging from the damp beams of the ceiling. Behind the dirty windows, by the light of a candle, were to be seen saucepans, porcelain vases, a clarionette, and a bridal wreath.

He could not understand the pleasure she took in looking at these things.

"You will be covered with vermin. What can interest you there?"

"Everything. I am thinking of that poor bride whose wreath lies under the glass shade. The wedding breakfast was at Porte Maillot. There was a *garde républicain* in the procession. There nearly always is in the wedding-parties one sees in the Bois, on Saturdays. Don't they appeal to you, my friend, all these poor miserable trifles which in their turn are sharing the greatness of the past?"

Among the odd chipped cups with flowered patterns, she discovered a little knife with an ivory handle carved to represent a long thin woman with her hair dressed *à la Maintenon*. She bought it for a few pence. She was delighted because she possessed the fork to match. Le Ménil confessed that he did not understand curios. But his aunt de Lannoix was quite a connoisseur. She was the talk of all the dealers of Caen. She had restored and furnished her château in the old style. It had once been the country house of Jean le Ménil, councillor in the Rouen Parliament in 1779. This house, which existed before his time, was described in a document of 1690, as a hunting lodge. In a room on the ground floor, at the back of white cupboards, protected by wire net-work, had been found books collected by Jean le Ménil. His aunt de Lannoix, he said, had wanted to arrange them, but she had discovered among them such frivolous works, with such indecent engravings, that she had had to burn them.

"How stupid your aunt must be!" said Thérèse.

She had long been bored by stories about Madame de Lannoix. In the provinces her lover had a mother, sisters, aunts, a large family, whom she did not know and who irritated her. He used to talk of them admiringly, and it annoyed her. She grew impatient of his frequent visits to his family, from whom he returned, with a musty air, narrow ideas, and sentiments that wounded her. He on his side was naïvely astonished and hurt by this antipathy.

He was silent. The sight of a tavern with windows all aglow through the railings, suddenly reminded him of the poet Choulette, who was considered a drunkard. With some irritation he asked Thérèse if she still saw Choulette, who used to visit her wrapped in a plaid with a red comforter over his ears.

She was vexed at his speaking of the poet in the manner of General Larivière. She avoided confessing that she had not seen him since the autumn and that he neglected her with the indifference of a busy man who did not belong to her circle.

"I like him," she said. "He is witty, imaginative, and original."

And when he reproached her with a taste for the eccentric, she retorted sharply:

"I have not a taste; I have many tastes. Surely you don't condemn them all."

He did not condemn anything. He merely feared lest she should put herself in a false position by receiving a Bohemian of fifty who was out of place in any respectable house.

She objected:

"Choulette out of place in a respectable house? You don't know then that every year he spends a month at the Marchioness of Rieu's . . . yes, the Marchioness of Rieu, a Catholic, a Royalist, an old *chouane* as she calls herself. But since you are interested in Choulette, I will tell you of his latest adventure. You shall hear it just as Paul Vence told it me. I understand it better in this street, where there are bodices and flower-pots in the windows.

"This winter, one evening when it was raining, at a spirit-bar in a street, the name of which I have forgotten, but which must have been as poor as this one, Choulette met a wretched girl, whom the waiters at the bar had turned away, but whom he in his humility loved. She was called Maria. But even this name was not her own; she had found it on the door plate at the top of the staircase of a furnished house where she lodged. Choulette was touched by the depth of her poverty and her shame. He called her his sister and kissed her hand. Since then he has never left her. He takes her bare-headed with a shawl over her shoulders to the cafés in the Latin quarter, where rich students are reading reviews. He says sweet things to her. He weeps; she weeps. They drink; and, when they have drunk, they fight. He loves her. He calls her very chaste. He says she is his cross, his salvation. She was barefooted; he has given her a skein of coarse wool and knitting needles to knit herself some stockings. And he himself mends the poor girl's shoes with huge nails. He teaches her easy verses. He fears to spoil her moral beauty by taking her from the shame in which she lives in perfect simplicity and admirable destitution."

Le Ménil shrugged his shoulders.

"But this Choulette must be mad; and these are pretty stories that M. Paul Vence tells you! I am certainly not strict; but there is a kind of immorality which disgusts me."

They were paying no heed to where they were going. She became absorbed in her reflections:

"Yes, morality, duty, I know! But how hard to discover what is duty. I assure you that for three-quarters of my time I do not know where duty lies. It is like the hedgehog that belonged to our English governess at Joinville: we used to spend the whole evening looking for it under the furniture; and when we had found it it was time to go to bed."

He thought there was a great deal of truth in what she said, more perhaps than she imagined. He often reflected on it when he was alone.

"So keenly do I realise it that sometimes I regret not having remained in the army. I foresee what you are going to say. One vegetates in that profession. Doubtless, but one knows exactly what one has to do, and that is much. It seems to me that the life led by my uncle, General de La Briche, is a fine life, honourable and quite pleasant. But now that the whole nation is merged in the army, there are neither officers nor soldiers. It is like a railway station on Sunday when officials are pushing bewildered travellers into their carriages. My uncle de La Briche knew personally all the officers and all the private soldiers of his brigade. He still has their names on a great board in his dining-room. From time to time it amuses him to read them over. Nowadays how would it be possible for an officer to know his men?"

She had stopped listening to him. She was looking at a corner of the Rue Galande, where there was a woman selling fried potatoes. Nestling behind a pane of glass, her face surrounded by shadow, lit up by the glowing fire, she was plunging her ladle into the frizzling fry, and bringing up golden crescents with which she filled a screw of common yellow paper. Meanwhile an auburn-haired girl, watching her attentively, was holding out a penny in her red hand. When the girl had carried off her packet, Thérèse grew envious and realised that she was hungry; she insisted on tasting some of the fried potatoes. At first he objected.

"You don't know what they are fried with."

But in the end he must needs ask the woman for a penny packet and see that she put some salt in it.

While she was eating the yellow crescents with her veil turned back, he took her into side streets, away from the gas lamps. Thus they found themselves back again on the quay, and saw the black mass of the cathedral rising beyond the narrow arm of the river. The moon high up over the serrated ridge of the nave, shed a silver light over the slope of the roof.

"Notre Dame," she said! "Look, it is as heavy as an elephant and as finely made as an insect. The moon climbs up it, looking at it with the malice of an ape. She is not like the country moon at Joinville. At Joinville, I have my own path, a level path, with the moon at the end. She is not there every evening, but she returns faithfully, full, red, and familiar. She is a country neighbour, a lady of the district. Politely and with a friendly feeling I go gravely to meet her; but this Paris moon I should not wish to visit. She could hardly mix in good society. Think what she must have seen during all the time she has been shining on the roofs!"

He smiled a tender smile. "Ah! Your little path down which you used to walk alone and which you said you loved because the sky was at the end, not very high and not very far above you, I see it now as if I were there!"

It was at the château of Joinville, where he had been invited to hunt by Montessuy, that he had first seen her, and had immediately loved and desired her. It was there one evening, on the border of the little wood, that he had told her he loved her and that she had listened to him in silence, with a sad smile and wondering eyes.

The memory of that little path, where she used to walk alone on those autumn nights, touched and agitated him; it brought back the enchanted hours of early desires and fearful hopes. He sought her hand in her muff, and pressed her slight wrist under the fur.

A little girl with violets on a piece of flat basket-work, strewn with pine branches, saw they were lovers, and offered them her flowers. He bought a bunch for a penny and gave them to Thérèse.

She was walking towards the cathedral and thinking: "It is like some gigantic beast, a beast out of the Apocalypse."

At the other end of the bridge, another flower-seller, this one wrinkled, bearded, grey and grimy, pursued them with her basket of mimosa and Nice roses. Thérèse, who was at that moment holding her violets in her hand, trying to fasten them in her coat, replied gaily to the old woman's pleading:

"Thank you, I have all I want."

"It is easy to see you are young," the old woman said gruffly as she turned away.

Thérèse understood almost at once and half smiled. They passed into the shadow cast by the cathedral in front of the crowned and sceptred stone figures in the niches.

"Let us go in," she said.

He did not wish to. In entering a church with her he felt vaguely constrained, almost fearful. He said it was closed. He thought it was, and he hoped so. She pushed open the door and slipped into the immense nave, where the lifeless trees of columns rose into the darkness above. At the end candles were moving before phantom priests and the last groans of the organ were dying away in the distance. She shuddered in the silence, and said:

"The sadness of churches at night always moves me; it makes me feel the impressive mystery of annihilation."

He replied:

"But we ought to believe in something. It would be too sad if there were no God, if our souls were not immortal."

For a time she remained still beneath the great curtains of shadow which hung from the vault, then she said:

"My poor friend, we don't know what to do with this short life, and do you want another which shall be eternal!"

In the carriage which took them home, he said gaily that he had enjoyed his day. He kissed her, pleased with her and with himself. But she did not share his good humour. That was what generally happened between them. The last moments they passed together were always spoilt for her by the foreboding that he would not say the right word when they parted. Usually he left her abruptly as if for him everything was over. At each of these separations she had a vague feeling that it was a final parting. She suffered in anticipation and became irritable.

Under the trees of the Cours-la-Reine, he took her hand and kissed it repeatedly.

"It is rare to love as we love, isn't it, Thérèse?"

"Rare, I don't know; but I believe that you love me."

"And you?"

"Yes, I love you."

"And you will always love me?"

"How can one know?"

And, seeing a cloud come over her lover's face:

"Would you be happier with a woman who would swear to love none but you all her life?"

He remained anxious and looked sad. She was considerate, and completely reassured him.

"You know, my friend, I am not a light woman; I am serious, not like Princess Seniavine."

Almost at the end of the Cours-la-Reine, they said good-bye under the trees. He kept the carriage to take him to the Rue Royale. He was dining at his club and going to the theatre. He had no time to lose.

Thérèse went home on foot. When she was in sight of the hill on which the Trocadéro stands glistening like a set of diamonds, she recalled the flower-seller on the Petit-Pont: "One can see that you are young"; those words, cast upon the wind and the darkness, came back to her no longer as a rude jest, but with an accent of sad foreboding. Yes, she was young, she was loved, and she was discontented.

III

IN THE middle of the table was a centre-piece of flowers in a basket of gilded bronze. On the basket's edge, among stars and bees eagles spread their wings, beneath heavy handles formed by horns of plenty. On each side of the basket winged victories supported the flaming branches of the candelabra. This Empire epergne Napoleon had in 1812 presented to Count Martin de l'Aisne, grandfather of the present Count Martin-Bellème. Martin de l'Aisne, deputy in the Corps Législatif of 1809, was nominated the following year member of the commission of finance, for which secret and laborious task his industrious, cautious nature was well fitted. Although liberal by birth and inclination, he pleased the Emperor by his diligence and honesty, exact but not importunate. For two years favours rained upon him. In 1813, he was a member of that moderate majority in favour of the report in which M. Lainé, when it was too late, taught the tottering Empire a lesson and censured at once power and misfortune. On January 1, 1814, he accompanied his colleagues to the Tuileries. They had a terrible reception. The Emperor met them with a volley of abuse. Violent and melancholy, in all the horror of his actual power and his imminent ruin, he overwhelmed them with wrath and scorn.

Walking up and down among his terrified ministers, as if without thinking, he seized Count Martin by the shoulders, shook him and dragged him across the floor, crying: "A throne, what is a throne? Is it four pieces of wood covered with velvet? No! A throne is a man, and that man is I! You wanted to throw mud at me. Is this the moment to remonstrate with me when two hundred thousand Cossacks are crossing the frontiers? Your M. Lainé is a malicious person. One does not wash one's dirty linen in public." And while his wrath was thus finding expression in utterances sublime or commonplace, he was wringing in his hand the embroidered collar of the deputy for the department of Aisne. "The people know me. They do not know you. I am the chosen of the nation. You are the obscure delegates of a department." He prophesied that theirs would be the fate of the Girondins. Amidst the loud outbursts of his voice there sounded the clinking of his spurs. Count Martin trembled and stammered for the rest of his life. Hidden in his house at Laon, it was with trembling that he called in the Bourbons after the Emperor's defeat. It was in vain that two Restorations, the Government of July, and the Second Empire covered his palpitating breast with ribbons and crosses. Raised to the highest offices, loaded with honours by three kings and an emperor, he still felt the hand of the Corsican upon his shoulder. He died a Senator under Napoleon III., leaving a son afflicted with the hereditary trembling.

This son had married Mademoiselle Bellème, daughter of the First President of the Court of Bourges; and with her he had espoused the political glory of a family which had provided the limited monarchy with three ministers. The traditions of the Bellèmes, who had been lawyers under Louis XV, corrected the Jacobin past of the Martins. The second Count Martin sat in every assembly until his death in 1881. Charles Martin-Bellème, his son, had no difficulty in getting elected to the Chamber. Having married Mademoiselle Thérèse Montessuy, whose dowry provided him with the means of pushing his political fortunes, he discreetly took his place among those four or five titled and rich bourgeois, who, having rallied to the democracy and the Republic, were received with no ill grace by noted republicans, flattered by their aristocratic names and reassured by the mediocrity of their wits.

In the dining-room, where, above the doors, in the shadow, one now and then caught a glimpse of the spotted coats of the Oudry dogs, opposite the epergne with its gilded bees and stars, between the Victory candelabra, Count Martin-Bellème was doing the honours of his table with a somewhat dejected grace, a melancholy politeness, formerly indicated at the Elysée to represent for the benefit of a northern court the isolation and reserve of France. From time to time he was addressing insipid remarks on the right to Madame Garain, the wife of the former Keeper of the Seals, and on the left to Princess Seniavine, who, loaded with diamonds, was being bored to death. Opposite him, on the other side of the epergne, Countess Martin, supported on the one hand by General Larivière, and on the other by M. Schmoll of the Academy of Inscriptions, was languidly fanning her delicately moulded shoulders. On the two sides of the table were M. Montessuy, robust with blue eyes and a high colour, a young cousin, Madame Bellème de Saint-Nom, who did not know what to do with her long thin arms, the painter Duvicquet, M. Daniel Salomon, Paul Vence, Deputy Garain, M. Bellème de Saint-Nom, an obscure Senator, and Dechartre, who was dining at the house for the first time. The conversation at first was thin and slight; but it gradually grew more vivacious, until it became one confused murmur, dominated by the voice of Garain.

"Every false idea is dangerous. Dreamers are thought to be harmless; it is a mistake; they do a great deal of harm. Utopias, apparently the most inoffensive are really injurious. They tend to make one disgusted with reality."

"But," said Paul Vence, "perhaps reality is not so perfect, after all."

The Keeper of the Seals protested that he was in favour of every possible reform. And, without recalling that under the Empire he had demanded the abolition of a standing army, and, in 1880, the separation of Church and State, he declared that, faithful to his program, he remained the devoted servant of the democracy. His motto, he said, was "Order and Progress." And he really believed that he was the first to use it.

Montessuy retorted with his rough good-nature:

"Come, Monsieur Garain, now be sincere, and confess that there is not a reform left to accomplish, and that the most one could do would be to change the colour of the postage-stamps. Good or bad, things are as they must be. Yes," he added, "they are as they must be. But they are always changing. Since 1870, the industrial and financial condition of the country has passed through four or five revolutions which economists had not foreseen and which they don't yet understand. In society, as in nature, changes proceed from within."

In politics he believed in views which were short and clear. Strongly attached to the present and caring little for the future,

Socialists did not much trouble him. Without considering whether the sun and capital would endure for ever, he enjoyed them for the time being. In his opinion one must let oneself drift. Only idiots resisted the current, only madmen anticipated it.

But Count Martin, who was naturally melancholy, had gloomy presentiments. In veiled words he indicated the approach of catastrophe.

His ominous talk reached Monsieur Schmoll across the flowers of the centre-piece and moved him; he began to groan and prophesy. He explained that Christendom was of itself incapable of rising from barbarism, and that if it had not been for Jews and Arabs, Europe would be to-day what she was in the time of the Crusades, enveloped in ignorance, wretchedness, and cruelty.

"It is only in those historical manuals given to children in our schools to pervert their minds that the Middle Ages have passed away. In reality barbarians are always barbarians. Israel's mission is to instruct the nations. It was Israel, who in the Middle Ages, introduced into Europe the wisdom of Asia. Socialism alarms you. It is a Christian evil just like monasticism. And anarchy? Don't you see that it is the old Albigensian and Vaudois leprosy? The Jews, who educated and civilised Europe, can alone to-day save her from that mischievous propaganda which is preying upon her. But the Jews have failed to do their duty. They have become Christians among Christians. And God is punishing them. He is permitting them to be plundered and driven into exile. Everywhere anti-semitism is making alarming progress. In Russia my co-religionists are being hunted like wild beasts. In France civil and military offices are closed against the Jews. They are no longer admitted into aristocratic circles. After having brilliantly passed his examinations, my young nephew, Isaac Coblentz, was forced to renounce a diplomatic career. When Madame Schmoll calls upon the wives of certain of my colleagues they ostentatiously open anti-semite periodicals under her very nose. And would you believe that the Minister of Education refused me the cross of the Legion of Honour for which I asked him? There's ingratitude! There's madness! Anti-semitism, you must understand, means death to European civilisation."

There was a naturalness in this little man which surpassed the highest art. Grotesque and terrible, his sincerity overwhelmed every one. Madame Martin, who found him entertaining, congratulated him on it.

"At least," she said, "you defend your fellow-believers; you, Monsieur Schmoll, are not like a beautiful Jewess I know, who, having read in a newspaper that she was in the habit of receiving the *élite* of Israelitish society, went about complaining that she had been insulted."

"I am sure, Madame, that you are unaware of the excellence of

Jewish ethics and of their superiority to all other ethical systems. Do you know the parable of the Three Rings?"

This question was lost in the noise of the various dialogues, discussions on foreign politics, exhibitions of pictures, fashionable scandals, and academical speeches. The last novel was discussed as well as a new play about to be acted. It was a comedy with an episode in which Napoleon figured.

The conversation centred round Napoleon. He had been frequently represented on the stage. He had been lately studied in works widely read, where he appears as an object of curiosity, a popular character, no longer the people's hero, the military demigod of the fatherland, as in the days when Norvins and Béranger, Charlet and Raffet, invented his legend. Now he was regarded as a remarkable personage, a type entertaining in every one of its most intimate details, just the figure to please artists and to interest the idly curious.

Garain, who had built up his fortune on hatred of the Empire, sincerely believed this reaction in national taste to be nothing but an absurd infatuation. He did not consider it dangerous and was not alarmed by it. He was one of those in whom fear breaks out suddenly and violently. For the moment, his mind was at rest; for he did not talk of forbidding the representations of plays, nor of seizing books, nor of imprisoning authors, nor of suppressing anything. Calm and severe, he regarded Napoleon merely as Taine's condottiere who kicked Volney in the stomach.

Every one had his own definition of the true Napoleon. Count Martin, opposite the imperial epergne and the winged Victories, appropriately described Napoleon as organiser and administrator, ranking him high as President of the Council of State, where his words shed light on many points hitherto obscure.

Garain asserted that during these unjustly famous council meetings, Napoleon, saying that he wanted some snuff, would ask the councillors for their gold boxes painted with miniatures and adorned with diamonds, which they never saw again. They ended by never bringing any but leather snuff-boxes to the Council. Mounier's son had told him the story himself.

What Montessuy admired in Napoleon was his orderly mind. He had a liking for efficiency, Montessuy said, a taste which has almost died out.

The painter Duvicquet, who had a painter's ideas, was puzzled. On the funeral mask brought from Saint-Helena he failed to find the features of that handsome powerful face reproduced in medals and busts. Any one might observe the discrepancy now that the bronze reproductions of the mask no longer stored away in attics were to be seen in all the dealers' shops, surrounded by eagles and sphinxes of gilded wood. And in his opinion since Napoleon's real force was not Napoleonic, Napoleon's real soul might well not be

Napoleonic either. Perhaps it was the soul of a good bourgeois; some one had said so, and he was inclined to believe it. Besides, Duvicquet, who prided himself on having painted the century's portraits, knew that famous men are quite different from the popular estimate of them.

M. Daniel Salomon observed that the mask of which Duvicquet had spoken, the cast taken from the Emperor's countenance after death, and brought to Europe by Dr. Antommarchi, was first produced in bronze and exposed to public view under Louis-Philippe, in 1883, and had then occasioned surprise and incredulity. This Italian, a quack apothecary, a chatterer eager for fame, was suspected of having hoaxed the public. The followers of Dr. Gall, whose system was then in favour, doubted whether the mask were genuine. They could not find that it had the protuberances which indicate genius, and the forehead, examined according to the master's theories, presented no extraordinary formation.

"Exactly," said Princess Seniavine; "all that is remarkable about Napoleon is his having kicked Volney in the stomach and stolen snuff-boxes set with diamonds. M. Garain has just told us so."

"And are we quite sure," said Madame Martin, "that he was really guilty of that kick?"

"After all, everything is dubious," retorted the Princess gaily. "Napoleon did nothing; he did not even kick Volney, and he had the head of an idiot."

General Larivière felt it incumbent upon him to fire his shot. And this was what he said:

"Napoleon's campaign of 1813 has given rise to much criticism."

The General's one idea was to please Garain. Nevertheless he made an effort and formulated a comprehensive opinion:

"Napoleon made mistakes; and in his position he ought not to have made any."

And, very red in the face, he stopped abruptly.

Madame Martin asked:

"And you, Monsieur Vence, what do you think of Napoleon?"

"Madame, these bloated soldiers are not to my taste; and frankly, conquerors always seem to me to be dangerous lunatics. Nevertheless, the Emperor interests me as he interests the public. He has character and vitality. No poem or novel of adventure is equal to the *Memorial,* written however in an absurd style. What I really think of Napoleon, if you wish to know, is that, having been created for glory, he appears in all the brilliant simplicity of an epic hero. A hero must be human. Napoleon was human."

These remarks were greeted with loud exclamations. But Paul Vence continued:

"He was violent and frivolous, and thus profoundly human. By that I mean, like other people. He aspired to enjoy unlimited power,

which is what the ordinary man esteems and desires. He himself
was possessed by the illusions with which he inspired the people.
They constituted his strength and his weakness, and were his chief
adornment. He believed in glory. Concerning life and society he
held about the same opinions as one of his grenadiers. He never
lost that childish seriousness which takes a delight in sword-play
and the beating of drums, and that kind of innocence which makes
good soldiers. He had a sincere respect for force. He was a man
among men, flesh of their flesh. He never had a single thought that
did not express itself in action; and all his actions were grandiose
and yet ordinary. Heroes are the product of this vulgar greatness.
And Napoleon is the perfect hero. His brain never travelled more
quickly than his hand, that beautiful little hand which ground the
world. He never for a single moment cared about anything he could
not realise."

"Then you do not consider him an intellectual genius," said
Garain. "I agree with you."

"Certainly," resumed Paul Vence, "he had the genius necessary
to cut a brilliant figure in the civil and military arena of the world.
But he had no speculative genius. That genius is 'quite another pair
of cuffs,' as Buffon used to say. We possess the collection of his
writings and his speeches. His style is vivacious and graphic. And
in this mass of ideas there is not a hint of any philosophical
curiosity, of any interest in the unknowable, of any preoccupation
with the mystery of destiny. When, at Saint-Helena, he talks of
God or the soul, he seems like a good little schoolboy of fourteen.
His soul cast into the world found itself proportioned to the world
and embraced everything. Not a particle of this soul was ever lost
in the infinite. A poet, he knew no poetry but that of action. His
great dream of life was earth-bound. In his terrible and pathetic
puerility he believed that man may be great; and time and misfortune never robbed him of that illusion. His youth, or rather his
sublime adolescence, endured to the end, because all the days of his
life were powerless to form in him a conscious maturity. Such is
the abnormal condition of all men of action. They live entirely for
the moment, and their genius is concentrated on one single point.
They are constantly renewed, but they do not grow. The hours of
their lives are not bound one to another by a change of grave disinterested reflection. They do not develop; one condition merely
succeeds another in a series of deeds. Thus they have no inner life.
This absence of any inner life is particularly noticeable in Napoleon.
Hence that lightness of heart which enabled him to bear easily the
weight of his misfortunes and mistakes. His soul, ever new, was
born again every morning. He possessed to the highest degree a
capacity for self-amusement. The first time he saw the sun rise over
his gloomy rock of Saint-Helena he leapt from bed, whistling the
air of a song. His was the repose of a mind superior to fortune,

and above all things the lightness of a mind ever apt for renewal. He lived outside himself."

Garain, to whom such an ingenious turn of thought and speech appealed little, wished to bring the discussion to a conclusion.

"In a word," he said, "the man had something of the monster in him."

"Monsters do not exist," replied Paul Vence. "And men who are said to be monsters inspire horror. Napoleon was loved by a whole nation. His power lay in kindling love in men's hearts wherever he passed. It was his soldiers' joy to give up their lives for him."

Countess Martin would like Dechartre to have given his opinion. But he seemed afraid to speak.

Schmoll was still asking whether any one knew the parable of the Three Rings, the sublime inspiration of a Portuguese Jew.

Garain, while congratulating Paul Vence on his brilliant paradox, regretted that intellect should thus be brought into play at the expense of morals and justice.

"There is one incontrovertible principle," he said; "men must be judged according to their actions."

"And what about women?" asked Princess Seniavine brusquely; "do you judge them according to their actions? And how do you know what they do?"

The sound of voices was mingled with the clear, bell-like ring of the plate. The atmosphere of the room became heated and loaded with vapour. Drooping roses shed their leaves on the table-cloth. In the minds of those assembled there ideas multiplied:

General Larivière indulged in dreams of the future.

"When they have done for me," he said to his neighbour, "I will go and live at Tours, and grow flowers."

And he boasted of being a good gardener. A rose had been named after him. He was proud of it.

Schmoll was still asking if any one knew the parable of the Three Rings.

Meanwhile the Princess was teasing the deputy.

"Don't you know, Monsieur Garain, that people do identical things for very different reasons?"

Montessuy said she was quite right.

"It is true, Madame, as you say, that actions prove nothing. This idea strikes one in an episode in the life of Don Juan. Neither Molière nor Mozart was aware of it; but it is related in an English legend, told me by my friend, James Lovell, of London. It relates how the great seducer wasted his time with three women: one was a *bourgeoise* who loved her husband; another a nun who refused to violate her vows; the third, who had long lived a life of debauchery, having become ugly, was servant in a low lodging-house; after the life she had lived, and after what she had seen, love was nothing to her. The conduct of these three women was

the same, but for very different reasons. One action proves nothing.
It is the mass of actions, their weight, their sum, that constitutes
the value of a human being."

"Certain of our actions," said Madame Martin, "resemble us; they
are like us. Others do not resemble us at all."

She rose and took the General's arm.

As Garain was taking her into the drawing-room, the Princess
said:

"Thérèse is right. . . . Some of our actions do not resemble us
at all. They are little negresses conceived in our sleep."

The tapestry nymphs in their faded beauty smiled down on the
guests who heedlessly passed them by.

Madame Martin poured out the coffee, assisted by her young
cousin, Madame Bellème de Saint-Nom. She complimented Paul
Vence on what he had said at dinner.

"You spoke of Napoleon with a freedom which is very rare
among us. I have often noticed how pretty children when they are
sulking resemble Napoleon on the evening of Waterloo. And you
brought home to me the cause of that resemblance."

Then, turning to Dechartre:

"Do you like Napoleon?"

"Madame, I do not like the Revolution. And Napoleon is the
Revolution in full military dress."

"Why didn't you say that at dinner, Monsieur Dechartre? But
I see you refuse to display your wit except in *tête-à-tête*."

Count Martin-Bellème took the men to the smoking-room. Paul
Vence alone remained with the ladies. Princess Seniavine asked him
if he had finished his novel and what it was about. It was a study,
an attempt to arrive at truth by means of a logical sequence of appearances which become cumulative evidence.

"By such a method," he said, "the novel acquires a moral power
which the dull details of history can never possess."

She asked if it would be a book for women to read. He replied
that it would not.

"You make a mistake, Monsieur Vence, in not writing for women.
It is the only thing that a superior man can do for them."

And when he wanted to know how she came by that idea:

"Because," she said, "I notice that intelligent women always
marry fools."

"Who bore them."

"Certainly! But superior men would bore them still more."

"They would have greater chances of succeeding."

"But tell me the story of your novel."

"You insist."

"I never insist."

"Well! Here it is. It is a story of manners among the lower
classes. The hero is a young artisan, serious and chaste, as beauti-

ful as a girl, with a soul innocent and reserved. He is an engraver and does good work. In the evenings he studies at home with his mother, to whom he is devoted. He reads books. In his simple unfurnished mind ideas fix themselves as tightly as shots fired into a wall. He has few wants. He has neither the passions nor the vices which bind most of us to life. He is solitary and pure. Endowed with strong virtues, he becomes proud of them. He lives among miserable wretches. He sees them suffer. He is kind, although he is not human; he possesses that cold charity which is called altruism. He is not human because he is not sensual."

"Ah! Must we be sensual to be human?"

"Certainly, Madame. Whilst tenderness is but skin deep, pity lies far below the surface. This young man is not critical enough to grasp this. He is too credulous. He easily believes what he has read. And he has read that universal happiness will be established by the destruction of society. He is devoured by a thirst for martyrdom. One morning, having kissed his mother, he goes out. He lies in wait for the Socialist deputy for his district, sees him, throws himself upon him and plunges his graving-tool into his stomach, crying: 'Long live anarchy!' He is arrested, measured, photographed, examined, tried, condemned to death and guillotined. That is my novel."

"It will not be very amusing," said the Princess. "But that is not your fault; your anarchists are as timid and moderate as other Frenchmen. When Russians go in for anarchy they are more audacious and original."

Countess Martin came up to Paul Vence and asked him if he knew that very mild gentleman who said nothing and looked about him in the bewildered manner of a lost dog. Her husband had invited him. She did not know him, nor his name, nor anything about him. All that Paul Vence knew was that he was a Senator. He had noticed him one day in the Luxembourg, in the gallery which is used as a library.

"I had just been to see the cupola painted by Delacroix with heroes and sages of antiquity in a wood of blue-green myrtles. He was warming himself with a poor and pitiful air; and his clothes smelt musty. He was talking to some old colleagues and saying as he rubbed his hands: 'In my opinion, what proves that the Republic is the best of governments, is that in 1871, in one week, it shot down sixty thousand rebels, without rendering itself unpopular. Such violence would have ruined any other government."

"Then," said Madame Martin, "he is quite a malicious person, while I was pitying him for his shyness and awkwardness."

Madame Garain, her chin resting softly on her breast, was slumbering peacefully; and her domestic soul was dreaming of her kitchen garden by the Loire, where choral societies were in the habit of coming to pay their respects to her.

Joseph Schmoll and General Larivière came out of the smoking-room, still smiling over the indecorous topics they had been discussing. The General sat down between Princess Seniavine and Madame Martin.

"This morning I met the Baroness Warburg in the Bois. She was riding a superb animal. She said to me: 'General, how do you manage always to have such fine horses?' I replied: 'Madame, in order to have fine horses, one must be either very rich or very shrewd.'"

He was so pleased with this retort that he repeated it twice, winking the while.

Paul Vence came up to Countess Martin:

"I know the Senator's name: it is Loyer; he is Vice-President of a group and author of a propagandist book, entitled 'The Crime of December the Second.'"

The General continued:

"It was a terrible day. I went into the shelter. There I met Le Ménil. I was in a bad temper. I saw that he was laughing at me in his sleeve. He thinks that because I am a general I ought to like wind, hail, and sleet. But it is absurd. He said he did not mind bad weather, that next week he was going to stay with friends for the hunting."

There was a silence. The General resumed:

"I trust he may enjoy himself; but I don't envy him. Foxhunting is not amusing."

"But it is useful," said Montessuy.

The General shrugged his shoulders:

"A fox never molests the hen-house except in the spring, when he is feeding his young."

"A fox," replied Montessuy, "prefers the rabbit-warren to the poultry-yard. He is a stealthy poacher who injures the farmer less than the sportsman. I know something about that."

Thérèse seemed absent-minded; she was not listening to the Princess who was addressing her.

"He never even told me that he was going away," she pondered.

"Of what are you thinking, my dear?" asked the Princess.

"Of nothing at all interesting."

IV

 HE little room was dark and. silent. Curtains, portières, cushions, bearskins, oriental rugs, hushed every sound. Swords, reflecting the firelight, glistened on the cretonne of the walls, among targets and the faded relics of three winters' cotillions. On the rosewood chiffonier stood a silver cup, a prize awarded by some sporting society. On the painted porcelain top of the little table, a horn-shaped glass vase, over which ran a gilded convolvulus, was filled with branches of white lilac.

And the shadows were everywhere broken by glinting lights. Thérèse and Robert, their eyes accustomed to the darkness, moved freely amidst these familiar surroundings. He lit a cigarette, while she did her hair, standing, with her back to the fire, before the long glass, in which she was hardly able to see herself. But she would have neither lamp nor candles. For three years she had been in the habit of taking her hairpins from the little cup of Bohemian glass, which stood on the table, just within hand reach. He watched her threading her light fingers through her hair which fell in streams of yellow gold. Meanwhile her face, hardened and bronzed in the shadow, assumed a mysterious, almost an alarming expression. She did not speak.

He said to her: "You are no longer vexed, my love?"

And when he urged her to reply, to say something:

"What would you have me say, dear? I can only repeat what I told you on my arrival. I think it strange that I should be informed of your projects by General Larivière."

He knew well that she still bore him ill-will, that she had been reserved and stiff, with none of that self-surrender that generally made her so delightful. But he pretended to believe that her fit of the sulks was nearly over.

"My dear, I have already explained. I told you and I repeat that when I met Larivière, I had just received a letter from Caumont, reminding me of my promise to hunt in his woods, and I had replied by return of post. I was intending to tell you to-day. I regret that General Larivière anticipated me; but it really is not important."

With her arms raised handle-like above her head, she turned towards him with a tranquil gaze, that he did not understand.

"So you are going?"

"Next week, Tuesday or Wednesday. I shall be away ten days at the most."

She was putting on her sealskin toque in which was stuck a branch of mistletoe.

"It is a matter that admits of no delay?"

"Oh! no; the fox's fur will be worth nothing in a month's time. Besides Caumont has invited some of our common friends whom my absence would disappoint."

Sticking a long pin into her toque, she knit her eye-brows.

"Is your hunting very interesting?"

"Yes, very, because a fox plays all kinds of tricks which you have to thwart. The intelligence of the beast is wonderful. I have watched foxes hunting rabbits at night. They had organised everything and had regular beaters. I assure you it is not easy to dislodge a fox from his den. These hunting-parties are very gay. Caumont's wine is excellent. That doesn't appeal to me, but it is generally appreciated. Would you believe it, one of his farmers told him that he had learnt from a sorcerer how to tame a fox with magic words? I shan't adopt that method, but I promise to bring you back a dozen fine skins."

"What would you have me do with them?"

"They make very nice rugs."

"Ah! . . . And you will be hunting for a week?"

"Not quite. As I shall be near Sémanville, I shall spend two days with my Aunt de Lannoix. She is expecting me. Last year at this time she had made up a delightful party. There were her two daughters and her three nieces with their husbands; they are all five pretty, gay, charming, and irreproachable. At the beginning of next month I shall doubtless find them all assembled for my Aunt's birthday; and I shall stay two days at Sémanville."

"Stay as long as ever you like, dear. I should be extremely sorry if you were to cut short such a delightful visit on my account."

"But you, Thérèse, what will you do?"

"I? Oh! I shall be all right."

The fire was dying down. The shadows thickened. In a dreamy tone with a note of expectation she said:

"It is true that it is never very wise to leave a woman alone."

He came near her, trying to look at her in the darkness. He took her hand.

"You love me?"

"I assure you I do not love another. But——"

"What do you mean?"

"Nothing. I am thinking . . . I am thinking that, as we are parted the whole summer, and as, in the winter, you pass half your time with your family and your friends, if we are to meet so seldom it is hardly worth while our meeting at all."

He lit the candles. In the light her face appeared hard and frank. He looked at her with a confidence proceeding less from that self-conceit common to all lovers than from his reliance upon a certain conventional propriety. A strong prejudice acquired in his youth and the simplicity of his intelligence caused him to believe in her.

"Thérèse, I love you and you love me, I know it. Why will you torment me? Sometimes your hardness and reserve are very painful."

She tossed her little head brusquely.

"I can't help it. I am bitter and self-willed. It is in my blood. I inherit it from my father. You know Joinville; you have seen its château, its ceilings by Lebrun, its tapestry made at Maincy for Fouquet; you have seen its gardens designed by Le Nôtre, its park and its game; you said there were none finer in France; but you did not see my father's workshop, with its deal table and mahogany desk. All the rest originated there, my friend. On that table, standing at that desk, my father worked at figures for forty years, first in a little room in the Place de la Bastille, then in the flat in the Rue Maubeuge, where I was born. We were not very rich then. I have seen the little red damask drawing-room, with which my father set up housekeeping, and which mama loved so much. I am a child of a self-made man or of a conqueror, for it comes to the same thing. We are people who have had to make our way. My father was determined to make money, to possess what pays, that is everything. I am determined to win and to keep. What? I don't know . . . whether it be the happiness I possess . . . or one that I have not. In my own way I also am greedy, greedy of dreams, of illusions. Oh! I know well that they are not worth the effort one makes to enjoy them, but it is the effort itself that is worth something, because that effort is I, is my life. I am bent upon enjoying what I love, what I thought I loved. I am determined not to lose it. I am like papa: I stand upon my rights. And then . . ."

She lowered her voice.

"And then I too have senses. There, my dear, I am boring you. I can't help it. I ought never to have surrendered to you."

This petulance, to which he was accustomed, marred his pleasure. But it did not alarm him. Extremely sensitive to her acts, he did not care what she said, and attached little importance to words, especially a woman's. Himself a taciturn person, he was far from imagining that words may also be actions.

Although he loved her, or rather because he loved her ardently and trustfully, he thought it his duty to oppose whims that he considered absurd. When he did not vex her she was pleased for him to assume a masterful air; and, naïvely, he always assumed it.

"You know, Thérèse, that my one thought is to please you in everything. Don't be capricious."

"And why should I not be capricious? If I gave myself to you, it was an act neither rational nor dutiful; it was a caprice."

He looked at her surprised and saddened.

"The word wounds you, dear? Say that it was love. And really the impulse did come from my heart; it was because I knew you loved me. But love should be a pleasure; and if I do not find that it satisfies what you call my caprices, what really is my desire, my life, my very heart, I will have no more of it; I prefer to live alone. You astonish me. My caprices! Is there anything else in life? Is not your hunting a caprice?"

He replied very frankly:

"If I had not promised, I swear that I would gladly sacrifice this little pleasure for your sake."

She knew that what he said was true. She knew how exact he was in keeping his word in the most trifling matters. Always true to his promises, he was minutely and conscientiously scrupulous in the performance of all his social duties. She saw that if she insisted he would not go. But it was too late: she no longer wished to gain that point. Now all that she sought was the bitter joy of losing it. A reason she really considered absurd she now pretended to take seriously.

"Ah! you promised."

And she affected to yield.

Surprised at first, he was soon secretly congratulating himself on having brought her to reason. He was grateful to her for not having persisted in her obstinacy. He put his arm round her, and, as a reward, in a frank, friendly manner, kissed her on the eyelids and the nape of her neck. He showed himself eager to devote to her the rest of his days in Paris.

"We can meet three or four times before my departure, my darling, and oftener still, if you like. I will be here ready for you whenever you wish to come. Shall it be to-morrow?"

She took a delight in saying that she could return neither to-morrow nor the following days. Very sweetly she explained what would prevent her from coming. The obstacles appeared trivial at first: calls to be paid, a frock to be fitted, a bazaar, exhibitions, hangings she wanted to see and perhaps buy. But on examination these difficulties grew more important, more numerous: the calls could not be postponed; it was not one bazaar but three she had to attend; the exhibitions were on the eve of closing; the hangings were going to America. In short, it was quite impossible for her to see him again before he started.

As it was not like him to be content with such trivial reasons, he perceived that neither was it like Thérèse to give them. Bewildered by this tangle of trifling social obligations, he did not resist, but remained silent and unhappy.

With her left arm raised above her head, she lifted the portière, and with her right hand turned the key in the lock. And there in the sapphire and ruby coloured folds of the oriental curtain, her head turned towards the lover she was leaving, she said in tones half mocking but almost tragic:

"Good-bye, Robert! Enjoy yourself. My calls, my shopping, your visits are mere trifles; but it is true that destiny depends on such trifles. Good-bye."

She went out. He would have liked to go with her; but he deemed it unwise to be seen in the street with her, when she did not insist upon it.

Outside Thérèse suddenly felt alone, alone in the world, without joy and without sorrow. As usual she returned home on foot. It was dark, the night was cold, clear, and calm. But the streets she followed in the darkness, broken here and there by lights, enveloped her in that tepid warmth of towns which penetrates even through the winter's cold and is so grateful to town-dwellers. She was passing between lines of sheds, cottages, and booths, remnants of the rural days of Auteuil, with here and there a high-storied house, displaying its coping stone in dismal isolation. These little shops and monotonous windows were nothing to her. Nevertheless, in some mysterious manner her surroundings seemed friendly; and the stones of the street, the doors of the houses, the lights high up in the windows appeared to her not unkind. She was alone, and she wished to be alone.

The road she was traversing between those two dwellings, which were almost equally home-like to her, that road she had travelled so often, it now seemed as if she were passing over for the last time. Why? What had the day brought her? Hardly a vexation, not even a quarrel. Nevertheless, there hovered over its past hours a faint, curious, yet persistent suggestion, a strange memory that would cling to that day for ever. What had happened? Nothing. And that nothing effaced all. She had a kind of sub-conscious conviction that she would never again enter that room, which once contained all that was dearest and most secret in her life. Hers was a serious relationship. She had given herself gravely to realise a joy that was necessary to her. Made for love, and very rational, she had not lost, in the abandonment of her person, that instinct for reflection, that aspiration after serenity which were very strong in her. She had not chosen; one hardly ever does. Neither had she allowed herself to be taken by chance or by surprise. She had done what she had wished to do as much as one ever does in such matters. She had nothing to regret. He had behaved irreproachably towards her. She must in justice admit it with regard to a man much sought after in society and having all the women at his feet. Nevertheless, in spite of everything, she felt that it was over and that its conclusion was quite natural. She was thinking with dull melancholy: "Three years of my life, a good man who loves me and whom I loved, for I did love him. Otherwise I could not have given myself to him. I am not an unscrupulous woman." But she could no longer revert to the sentiments of those days, the impulses of her soul and of her body. She recalled trivial quite insignificant details: the flowers on the wall paper, the pictures in the room; it was a room in a hotel. She remembered the words somewhat ridiculous and yet almost touching that he had said to her. But it seemed as if these experiences were those of another woman, some stranger whom she did not much like and hardly understood.

And what had just happened, those caresses she had so recently received, all that was far away. The couch, the lilac in its glass vase, the little cup of Bohemian glass where she kept her pins— she saw it all as if gazing into the room from the street. She knew no bitterness, not even sadness. She had nothing to pardon, alas! That week's absence was no infidelity, no wrong done her; it was nothing, that was all. It was the end. She knew it. She wished it to be the end. She willed it just as the falling stone wills to fall. She was obeying all the secret forces of her being. She was saying to herself: "There is no reason why I should love him less. Do I no longer love him? Have I ever loved him?" She did not know, and she did not care to know.

Three years during which their rendezvous had been twice, occasionally four times a week. There had been months when they had met every day. Was that nothing? But life is no great matter. And how little one puts into it!

After all she had no cause to complain. But it was better to make an end of it. All her reflections brought her back to that. It was not a resolution. Resolutions may be changed. This was graver; it was a mental and a physical condition.

Having reached the square, with a fountain in the middle and on one side a Gothic church with its bell enclosed in a turret open to the sky, she remembered the penny bunch of violets he had given her one evening on the Petit-Pont, near Notre Dame. That day they had loved each other more passionately than usual. Her heart softened as she remembered it. She felt in her coat, but found nothing. In her memory alone lived the little nosegay, that poor little skeleton of flowers.

While she was walking dreamily, passers-by followed her, misled by the simplicity of her dress. One invited her to a restaurant, to dine in a private room and then go to a theatre. Far from being embarrassed by these proposals, she was entertained by them. Her nerves were not in the least unstrung by the crisis she had passed through. "What do other women do?" she was wondering. "And I who congratulated myself on not wasting my life. What is life worth after all?"

When she came within sight of the Neo-Greek lantern tower of the Museum of Religions, she found the road up. Over a deep ditch, between banks of black earth, heaps of cobbles and piles of paving stones, a narrow bending plank had been thrown. She had already begun to cross it when before her she saw a man who had stopped to let her pass. He had recognised her and was taking off his hat. It was Dechartre. As she advanced she thought he was pleased at meeting her, and she thanked him with a smile. He asked if he might walk a little way with her. And together they entered the broad square, where the air was keener, where the tall houses were farther apart and the sky could be seen.

He said he had recognised her in the distance by the outline of her figure and the rhythmic movement of her walk.

"Graceful motion," he said, "is to the eyes what music is to the ears."

She replied that she loved walking, that it pleased and invigorated her.

He also liked to take long walks in populous towns or in the beautiful country. The mystery of the road tempted him. He loved travel; and even now, when it had become common and easy, it still attracted him. He had seen golden days and transparent nights in Greece, Egypt, and the Bosphorus. But it was always to Italy he returned as to the home of his soul.

"I am going there next week," he said. "I want to see Ravenna again, asleep among the dark pine trees of that barren coast. Have you ever been to Ravenna? It is an enchanting tomb out of which rise dazzling phantoms.

"There is the magic of death. The mosaics of Saint Vitalis and of the two Saints Apollinaris, with their barbaric angels and their empresses with halos recall the delightful monsters of the East. The tomb of Galla Placidia, now that it has been robbed of its silver plates, looks terrible in its crypt, dark yet luminous. Looking through a crack in the sarcophagus it seems as if one saw the daughter of Theodosius seated on her golden chair, very straight in her bejewelled gown embroidered with scenes from the Old Testament, her handsome cruel face hardened and blackened by the aromatic spices used for embalmment, and her ebony hands motionless upon her knees. For thirteen centuries she remained in funereal majesty, until a child, passing with a candle near the opening in the tomb, burnt the body and the dalmatic."

Madame Martin-Bellème asked what had been the life of this corpse so inflexible in her pride.

"Twice a slave," said Dechartre, "she became twice an empress."

"She was beautiful doubtless," said Madame Martin. "Your description of her in her tomb is so vivid that she alarms me. Will you not go to Venice, Monsieur Dechartre? Or are you tired of gondolas, of canals fringed with palaces, and of the pigeons of Saint Mark? I confess that after having visited Venice three times I still love her."

He agreed with her. He too loved Venice. Whenever he went there he was converted from a sculptor into a painter, and he was always sketching. But it was the atmosphere that he would like to paint.

"Elsewhere," he said, "even at Florence, the sky is distant, high up, far away in the background. At Venice it is everywhere: it caresses earth and water; it lovingly envelops leaden domes and marble façades and casts its pearls and its crystals into purple space. The beauty of Venice consists in its sky and its women. How beautiful are Venetian women and of so clear and pure a cast. How slender and supple a figure beneath the black shawl. Were nothing left of these women but a single bone, that bone would suggest the charm of their exquisite form. On Sunday, at church, they gather in groups, laughing and vivacious, a medley of slim figures, graceful necks, tender smiles, and ardent glances. And, with the suppleness of a young doe, the whole group bows when a priest with the head of a Vitellius, his chin hanging over his chasuble, passes bearing the ciborium, preceded by two choristers."

He walked with unequal step impelled by the flow of his ideas. Her pace was more regular and slightly more rapid than his. And, looking at her from the side, he saw the measured step and supple gait that he loved. He noticed how the determined motion of her head every now and then made the sprig of mistletoe in her toque quiver.

Without realising it he was experiencing the charm of an association almost intimate with a young woman whom he scarcely knew.

They had reached the place where the broad avenue displays its four rows of plane trees. They were following that stone parapet crowned by a box hedge, which happily conceals the ugliness of the military buildings on the lower side of the quay. Beyond, the river was indicated by that thickness of the atmosphere which even on days when there is no mist is to be found over the surface of water. The sky was clear. The lights of the town mingled with the stars. In the south shone the three golden nails of Orion's Belt.

"Last year at Venice, every morning as I went out, I used to see a charming girl, with a small head, a round and solid neck, and well-developed figure in front of my door, three steps above the canal. There she was in the sunshine, amidst vermin, as pure as an amphora, as captivating as a flower. She smiled. What a mouth! The richest jewel in the finest light. I perceived in time that this smile was intended for a butcher boy, encamped behind me, with his basket on his head."

At the corner of the short street which leads down to the quay, between two rows of little gardens, Madame Martin slackened her pace.

"It is true that Venetian women are beautiful."

"They are nearly all beautiful, Madame. I speak of the women of the people, cigarette makers, glass-workers. The others are the same everywhere."

"By the others, you mean society women; and those you do not love?"

"Society women? Oh! some are charming. But as for loving them, that is a serious matter."

"Do you think so?"

She gave him her hand and abruptly vanished round the corner of the street.

V

THAT evening she was dining alone with her husband. There were no winged victories or basket with gilded eagles on the table now reduced in size. The dogs of Oudry were no longer illuminated by hanging lights above the doors. While he was talking of everyday matters, she was in revery far away. It seemed to her that she was lost in a fog and remote from all things. It was a placid, almost a pleasant kind of suffering. Dimly as if through a mist she beheld the little room in the Rue Spontini carried by black angels on to one of the heights of the Himalayas. And, in an earthquake which seemed like the end of the world, her lover disappeared quite calmly while putting on his gloves. She felt her pulse to see if she was suffering from fever. Suddenly the clear tinkling of silver on the dinner-wagon roused her. She heard her husband saying:

"My dear, in the Chamber to-day Gavaut made an excellent speech on the pension fund. It is extraordinary how lucid his ideas have become, and how he now always seizes the point. He has made great progress."

She could not help smiling:

"But, my dear, Gavaut is a poor creature who has never thought of anything beyond rising from the crowd and making his own way. His ideas are all on the surface. Can it be that he is really taken seriously in the political world? Believe me, he has never imposed upon a woman, not even on his own wife. And yet that kind of illusion can so easily be created, I assure you."

Then she added abruptly:

"You know that Miss Bell has invited me to spend a month with her at Fiesole. I have accepted, I am going."

Less surprised than displeased, he asked with whom she was going.

She had the answer ready immediately and replied:

"With Madame Marmet."

There was nothing to be said. Madame Marmet was a very respectable companion, especially suitable for Italy; for her husband, Marmet the Etruscan, had explored Italian tombs. He merely asked:

"Have you told her? And when do you start?"

"Next week."

He was prudent enough to offer no objection for the moment, thinking that opposition would only intensify what he considered a whimsical caprice. He remarked suavely:

"Travel is certainly very pleasant. I have been thinking that in the spring we might visit the Caucasus and the country beyond the Caspian. That is a region interesting and little known. General Annenkoff would place carriages and whole trains at our disposal on the railway he has constructed. He is a friend of mine and he admires you. He would provide us with an escort of Cossacks. Such an expedition would create an impression."

He insisted on appealing to her vanity, for he found it impossible to imagine that she was anything but worldly minded, and, like himself, actuated entirely by self-love. She replied indifferently that it might be a pleasant trip. Then he praised the mountains, the ancient cities, the bazaars, the costumes, the weapons of the Caucasus. He added:

"We will take a few friends, Princess Seniavine, General Larivière, perhaps Vence or Le Ménil."

She replied with a dry little laugh that it was rather soon to decide whom they would invite.

He became attentive and kind.

"You are not eating. You are losing your appetite."

Although he did not believe in this sudden departure, the thought of it disturbed him. They had both resumed their liberty; but he did not like to be alone. He only felt himself when his wife was at home and his household was complete. Besides, he had decided to give two or three big political dinners during the session. His party was coming to the front. Now was the moment to strengthen his own influence and to shine before the public. He said mysteriously:

"There may come a crisis in which we shall need the support of all our friends. You have not been following the course of public events, Thérèse?"

"No, my dear."

"I am sorry. You have sense and an open mind. If you had taken an interest in politics you would have observed the growth of moderate opinions. The country is tired of extremes. It will not have men compromised by a Radical policy and religious persecution.

"A day will come when we shall have to form another Casimir-Périer ministry, but with new men, and then——"

He paused. She was barely listening.

Sad and disillusioned, she was lost in revery. It seemed to her that the pretty woman who, not long ago, in the warmth and shadow of a darkened room, was standing barefoot on a brown bearskin rug, while her lover kissed her neck, as she twisted her hair before the glass, was not herself, was not even a woman whom she knew well or wished to know, but a lady whose affairs did not interest her. A hairpin, one of those out of the Bohemian glass cup, fell from her hair down her neck. She shuddered.

"But we must give three or four dinners to our political friends," said M. Martin-Bellème. "We will invite former Radicals as well as members of our own circle. We ought to have some pretty women too. We might quite well invite Madame Bérard de la Malle: it must now be two years since anything was said against her. What do you think?"

"But, my dear, I am going next week."

He was alarmed.

Together, both silent and gloomy, they went into the little drawing-room, where Paul Vence was waiting. He often came unceremoniously in the evening.

She shook hands.

"I am very glad to see you. I must bid you farewell for a short time. Paris is cold and dull. This weather makes me tired and sad. I am going to spend six weeks at Florence with Miss Bell."

M. Martin-Bellème raised his eyebrows.

Vence asked whether she had not already been to Italy several times.

"Three times. But I saw nothing. This time I am determined to see, to bathe myself in the life of the country. From Florence I shall make excursions into Tuscany and Umbria. And I shall end by going to Venice."

"You will do well. Venice is the Sabbath rest concluding Italy's great divine week of creation."

"Your friend Dechartre has been talking to me eloquently of Venice, of the pearl-like atmosphere of Venice."

"Yes, at Venice the sky is a painter. At Florence it is a spirit. An old author writes: 'The Florentine sky inspires men with beautiful ideas.' I have passed delightful days in Tuscany. I should like to go there again."

"Come and see me there."

But he murmured with a sigh: "Newspapers, reviews, one's daily work."

M. Martin-Bellème said that these were weighty reasons, and that the readers of Monsieur Paul Vence enjoyed his books and articles too much to wish him to be separated from his work.

"Oh! as for my books! . . . One never says anything in a book as one would really like to say it. It is impossible to render one's thoughts exactly! Yes, I know how to talk with my pen as well as any one. But talking, writing, how pitiable! When one comes to think of it, how trivial are those little signs which form syllables, words, and phrases. Among such hieroglyphics at once commonplace and bizarre what happens to the idea? What does the reader make of my written page? Either wrong sense or nonsense. To read, to understand is to translate. There may be fine translations;

there are no accurate ones. What does it matter to me if they admire my books, since they always put into them what they admire? Every reader substitutes his ideas for ours. All we do is to tickle his imagination. It is horrible to have to furnish material for such a proceeding. Ours is an infamous profession."

"You are joking," said M. Martin.

"I think not," said Thérèse. "He is suffering because he realises that no soul can see into another. He feels alone when he thinks, alone when he writes. Whatever one does one is always alone in this world. That's what he means. He is right. One may be always explaining oneself, one is never understood."

"But there are actions," said Paul Vence.

"Don't you think, Monsieur Vence, that they are a kind of hieroglyphics? Tell me about M. Choulette? I never see him now."

Vence replied that for the moment Choulette was very busy reforming the third order of St. Francis.

"The idea of this work, madame, occurred to him in a marvellous manner, one day when he was visiting Maria, at her lodging in the street behind the Hôtel Dieu, a street which has over-hanging houses and is always damp. Maria, you know, is the saint and martyr who atones for the sins of the people. He pulled the bell-rope worn out by two centuries of callers. The martyr was either at the tavern, which she frequents constantly, or busy in her room; she did not open the door. Choulette continued pulling, and so vigorously that the handle and the rope remained in his hand. Quick to conceive the symbolism and hidden meaning of things, he understood at once that the rope had not broken without the interposition of supernatural powers. Over this incident he pondered. The hemp was black and sticky with dirt. He made a girdle of it and realised that he had been chosen to restore the third order of St. Francis to its primitive purity. He renounced the beauty of women, the delights of poetry, the brilliance of fame, to study the life and teaching of the blessed saint. Meanwhile he has sold his publisher a book entitled *Les Blandices,* which, he says, contains a description of every kind of love. He is proud of appearing in it as a criminal with an air of distinction. But this book will in no way interfere with his mystical enterprises. On the contrary, corrected by a subsequent work, it will appear exemplary; and the gold, or, as he says, the pieces of gold he received for it, which would not have been so many if the work had been more decent, will enable him to make a pilgrimage to Assisi."

Highly entertained, Madame Martin inquired how much truth there was in the story. Vence replied that she must not ask.

He half admitted that he idealised the poet's history, and that the adventures he related must not be interpreted in their literal and Hebraic sense. But he maintained that Choulette was actually publishing *Les Blandices* and that he wished to visit the cell and tomb of St. Francis.

"Then," cried Madame Martin, "I will take him to Italy. Monsieur Vence, find him and bring him here. I start next week."

M. Martin regretted having to leave them; but he had a report to finish, which must be given in the next day.

Madame Martin said that there was no one who interested her more than Choulette. Paul Vence also considered him a singular type of humanity.

"He does not greatly differ from those saints whose wonderful lives one reads. Like them he is sincere, with the most sensitive feelings and terribly violent emotions. If many of his actions shock us it is because he is weaker, less self-controlled, or perhaps more closely observed than the saints of history. Besides, there are fallen saints as there are fallen angels. Choulette happens to be a fallen saint. But his poems are really spiritual, and much finer of the kind than any composed by the courtly bishops and dramatic poets of the seventeenth century."

She interrupted:

"While I think of it, I want to congratulate you on your friend Dechartre. He is extremely interesting. Perhaps a trifle too self-centred," she added. Vence reminded her that he had always said she would find Dechartre interesting.

"I know him by heart; he is a friend of my childhood."

"Did you know his family?"

"Yes; he is the only son of Philippe Dechartre."

"The architect?"

"The architect. He who under Napoleon III restored so many castles and churches in Touraine and the Orleanais. He was a man of both taste and knowledge. Although by nature reserved and gentle, he was so imprudent as to attack Viollet-le-Duc, who was then all-powerful. He reproached him with restoring buildings according to their original plan and making them what they had been or ought to have been in the beginning. Philippe Dechartre on the contrary would respect everything the centuries have gradually added to church, abbey, or château. To banish anachronisms and restore a building to its primitive unity appeared to him a barbarism of science as atrocious as that of ignorance. He was always saying: It is a crime to efface what the hands and souls of our fathers have imprinted upon the stone throughout the ages. New stones cut in an old style are false witnesses! We would limit the work of the architect-archæologist to the strengthening and supporting of the structure. He was right; but no one agreed with him. He completed the failure of his career by dying young at the height of his rival's triumphs. Nevertheless he left his widow and son a modest fortune. Jacques Dechartre was brought up by an adoring mother. No mother ever loved her child more passionately. Jacques is a fine fellow, but he is a spoilt child."

"Nevertheless he appears so easy-going, so indifferent, so detached."

"Don't you believe it. His is a mind in itself restless and a cause of unrest in others."

"Does he like women?"

"Why do you ask?"

"Oh, I am not thinking of arranging a marriage for him."

"Yes, he does like women. I told you that he is an egoist. And only egoists really love women. After his mother's death, for a long while, he had an affair with a well-known actress, Jeanne Tancrède."

Madame Martin thought she remembered Jeanne Tancrède—not very pretty, but a fine figure, languidly graceful when playing the part of a woman in love.

"That is the woman," said Paul Vence. "They nearly always lived together in a little house in the *cité des Jasmins* at Auteuil. I often went to see them. I used to find him lost in his dreams, forgetting to model a figure drying beneath its linen covering; he would be rapt in revery, concerned only with his own thoughts, quite incapable of listening to any one. She meanwhile would be studying her parts, her cheeks burning with rouge, love in her eyes, pretty in her intelligence and her energy. She used to complain to me that he was absent-minded, sullen, irritable. She really loved him, and never betrayed him, except to get a part. And when she did betray him it was quickly over, and afterwards she thought no more about it. She was a serious-minded woman. But she allowed herself to be seen with Joseph Springer, and cultivated his society in the hope that he would give her a part at the Comédie Française. Dechartre was vexed and parted from her. Now she finds it more convenient to live with her directors, and Jacques prefers to travel."

"Does he regret her?"

"How can one know the thoughts of a mind so restless and so versatile, so eager to give itself, so quick to take back the gift, so egotistical and so passionate? He loves with fervour whenever he finds the personification of his own ideals."

She changed the subject abruptly.

"And what about your novel, Monsieur Vence?"

"I am writing the last chapter. My poor little engraver has been guillotined. He died with the calm of a placid virgin who has never felt the warm breath of life on her lips. Newspapers and the public conventionally approve of the act of justice which has just been performed. But in a garret another artisan, a chemist, serious and sad, is swearing to avenge his brother's death."

He rose and took his leave.

She called him back.

"Monsieur Vence, you know I am in earnest. Bring me Choulette."

When she went up to her room her husband was waiting for her on the landing. He was wearing a reddish-brown frieze dressing-gown and a kind of doge's cap encircling his pale hollow face. He looked grave. Behind him, through the open door of his study, appeared under the lamp a pile of documents and the open blue-books of the annual budget. Before she entered her room he signed that he wished to speak to her.

"My dear, I don't understand you. Your inconsistency may do you harm. Without motive, without even an excuse, you abandon your home and travel through Europe, with whom? With this Choulette, a Bohemian, a drunkard."

She replied that she would travel with Madame Marmet, and there was nothing unconventional in that.

"But you are telling every one of your departure, and you don't yet know whether Madame Marmet can go with you."

"Oh, dear Madame Marmet can soon pack up and go. It would only be her dog that would detain her in Paris. She will leave him with you; you can look after him."

"And does your father know of your plans?"

When his own authority was defied it was always his last resource to invoke that of Montessuy. He knew that his wife was afraid of displeasing her father and giving him a bad opinion of her.

He insisted.

"Your father is full of common sense and tact. I have been so fortunate as to find myself in agreement with him in the advice I have given you on several occasions. Like me he considers that a woman in your position ought not to visit Madame Meillan. Her society is very mixed and she is known to facilitate intrigues. I must tell you plainly that you make a great mistake in holding the opinion of society of so little account. I am very much mistaken if your father will not consider it strange for you to go off in this frivolous manner. And your absence will be all the more remarked because, permit me to remind you, throughout this session I have been very much in the public eye. In this matter my personal merit counts for nothing. But, if you had been willing to listen to me at dinner, I should have proved to you that the political group to which I belong is on the verge of coming into power. It is not at such a moment that you should forsake your duties as mistress of this house. You must understand this."

She replied: "You are boring me."

And, turning her back upon him, she shut herself in her room.

In bed that evening, as was her custom, she opened a book before falling asleep. It was a novel. Turning over its pages haphazard, she came upon these lines:

"Love is like devoutness in religion; it comes late. One is seldom either in love or devout at twenty, unless one has an unusual disposition, a kind of innate holiness. Even the elect strive long with that grace of loving which is more terrible than the lightning on the road to Damascus. A woman does not generally yield to the passion of love until age and solitude have ceased to alarm her. For passion is an arid desert, a burning Thebaid. Passion is a secular asceticism as severe as the asceticism of religion.

"Therefore a great passion is as rare in women as great religious devotion. Those who know life and society know that women do not willingly wear upon their delicate bodies the hair-shirt of a true love. They know that nothing is rarer than a life-long sacrifice. And reflect how much a woman of the world must sacrifice when she loves: liberty, peace of mind, the charming play of a free imagination, coquetry, amusements, pleasures, she loses everything.

"Flirting is permitted to her. That is consistent with all the exigencies of a fashionable life. But not love. Love is the least worldly of the passions, the most anti-social, the wildest, the most barbarous. Therefore the world judges it more severely than gallantry and than profligacy. In one sense the world is right. A Parisian woman in love belies her nature, and fails to perform her function which is, like a work of art, to belong to us all. She is a work of art and the most marvellous that man's industry has ever produced. She is an enchanting artifice, resulting from the conjunction of all the mechanical arts and all the liberal arts; she is their common production, and she is the common good. Her duty is to show herself."

As Thérèse closed the book, she reflected that these were the dreams of novelists who did not know life. She knew well that in reality there existed no Mount of Passion, no hair-shirt of love, no terrible yet beautiful vocation against which the elect strove in vain; she knew that love was only a brief intoxication, which when it passes leaves one a little sorrowful. And yet, if after all she did not know everything, if there should be a love in which one might drown oneself with delight. . . . She put out her lamp. The dreams of her early youth returned to her from the dim background of her past.

VI

T was raining. Through the streaming windows of her carriage, Madame Martin-Bellème dimly saw a multitude of umbrellas passing through the rain like tortoises. She was dreaming. Her thoughts were as misty and vague as the appearance of the streets and squares, rendered indistinct by the rain.

She could not remember how the idea had occurred to her of spending a month with Miss Bell. Indeed she had never realised why she had formed this resolution. It had been a spring hidden in the beginning beneath a few sprigs of water plantain, now it was a deep and rapid stream. She recollected that on Tuesday evening at dinner she had suddenly said that she wanted to go, but she could not trace her desire back to its origin. It was not a wish to act towards Robert le Ménil as he had acted towards her. Certainly it seemed to her excellent that she should be walking in the Cascine while he was hunting. It was pleasant and fitting. Robert, who was generally very pleased to see her after an absence, would not find her when he returned. It was good and just that he should have to submit to that disappointment. But she had not thought of that reason before her decision. And since she had seldom thought of it. It was really not the pleasure of making him vexed or the fun of a little act of vengeance that was the motive for her departure. Her feeling towards him was not so keen as that, but harder, more serious. She was especially desirous to postpone their meeting. Without their having come to any rupture, he had become a stranger to her. He appeared a man like the rest, although better than most of them; very good looking, with excellent manners, an estimable character; a man she did not dislike, but who did not deeply interest her. He had suddenly passed out of her life. How intimately he had been associated with it she did not care to recall. The idea of belonging to him shocked her and seemed indecorous. The anticipation of meeting him again in the flat in the Rue Spontini was so painful that she banished it immediately from her mind. She preferred to believe that their reunion would be prevented by some event unforeseen but inevitable, the end of the world for example. The previous evening, at Madame de Morlaine's, M. Lagrange, of the Academy of Science, had spoken of a comet. One day, he said, coming from the depths of the firmament, and meeting this planet, it might envelop the earth in its flaming tail, burn it in its fire, breathe into its animals and plants unknown poisons, and slay the children of men who would die in frantic laughter or pass away in a dull stupor. Either that or something of that kind must happen before next month. Thus her desire to go away was not without an explanation. But why a vague joy should enter into her wish to depart, why she should feel herself already under the charm of what she was going to see, that she could not understand.

The carriage put her down at the corner of the narrow Rue de la Chaise.

There since her husband's death lived Madame Marmet, in a small but very neat flat, on the top floor of a high house. Her five windows looked on a balcony and were brightened by the morning sun. It was her afternoon at home, and the Countess Martin had come to call. In the modest highly polished *salon,* she found M. Lagrange slumbering in an arm-chair opposite the kind lady, who looked sweet and tranquil beneath her crown of white hair.

This old scholar and man of the world had always been her faithful friend. On the day after Marmet's funeral it was he who had brought the unhappy widow Schmoll's waspish oration, and, thinking to console her, had beheld her consumed by grief and anger. She had fainted in his arms. Madame Marmet thought him lacking in judgment. He was her best friend. They often dined together at the tables of the rich.

Madame Martin, tall and beautiful, in her sable furs opening over a fall of lace, by the sparkling brilliance of her grey eyes, awoke the good man who was susceptible to feminine grace. The evening before, at Madame Morlaine's, he had described the end of the world. He asked her whether she had not been afraid when in the night watches there recurred to her those pictures of the earth

eaten up by fire, or dead with cold and white as the moon. While he was talking to her with affected gallantry, she was looking at the mahogany book-case, which occupied a recess in the drawing-room wall opposite the windows. It contained few books, but on a lower shelf was a skeleton in armour. It was strange to find established in the kind lady's home this Etruscan warrior, wearing on his skull a helmet of greenish bronze and on his disjointed body the rusty plates of his cuirass. All unkempt and wild he slept among sweet-meat boxes, gilded porcelain vases, holy virgins in plaster and delicate souvenirs of carved wood from Lucerne and the Righi. In the poverty of her widowhood, Madame Marmet had sold the books with which her husband worked; and of all the antiquities the archæologist had collected she had kept only the Etruscan. Her friends had tried to induce her to get rid of it. Marmet's former colleagues had found a purchaser. Paul Vence had persuaded the directors of the Louvre to offer to buy it. But the good widow would not sell it. She imagined that if she were to part with the warrior in his helmet of tarnished bronze crowned with a wreath of gilded leaves, she would forfeit that name she bore with such dignity and cease to be known as the widow of Louis Marmet of the Academy of Inscriptions.

"Be assured, Madame. The earth will not come into collision with a comet just yet. Such an event is extremely improbable."

Madame Martin replied that the immediate annihilation of the earth and humanity would matter little to her.

Old Lagrange strongly protested. He was extremely desirous that the catastrophe should be delayed.

She looked at him. On his bald head there remained but a few tufts of hair dyed black. His eyelids hung limply over his eyes, which were still bright; his wrinkled face was as yellow as parchment, and the hang of his clothes suggested a shrunken body.

And she thought: "He enjoys life."

Neither did Madame Marmet desire that the end of the world should be near.

"Monsieur Lagrange," said Madame Martin, "don't you live in a pretty little house, with windows overhung by wistaria, looking on to the Jardin des Plantes? It must be delightful to live in that Garden, which always reminds me of the Noah's Arks of my childhood and the Garden of Eden in the old picture Bible."

But he did not find the house delightful. It was small, badly built, and infested with rats.

She realised that every life had its vexations, and that everywhere there are rats, real or symbolic, legions of tiny creatures bent on tormenting us. Nevertheless she liked the Jardin des Plantes; she was always wanting to go there, but never went. There was the Museum too which she had never entered but was curious to visit.

Smiling and delighted he offered to do her the honours of the house. It was his home. He would show her the *bolides;* there were some very fine specimens.

She had no idea what a *bolide* was. But she remembered having been told that in the Museum there were reindeers' bones worked by primitive man, and pieces of ivory engraved with pictures of animals long since extinct. She asked if it were true. Lagrange had lost his smile. He replied with sullen indifference that these matters concerned one of his colleagues.

"Ah!" said Madame Martin, "they are not in your line."

She perceived that scholars lack curiosity and that it is unwise to question them about anything which is not in their department. It is true that thunderbolts had made Lagrange's fortune in science. And that they had led him to the study of comets. But he was prudent. For twenty years his chief occupation had been dining out.

When he had gone, Countess Martin told Madame Marmet what she had planned for her.

"Next week I am going to Fiesole, to Miss Bell's, and you must come with me."

Kind Madame Marmet, keen eyed beneath her placid brow, was silent for a moment; then she refused feebly, but was entreated and at last consented.

VII

HE Marseilles express was drawn up at the platform, where porters were hurrying to and fro, pushing their trucks in the smoke and the noise and the blue light that fell through the glass of the roof. Before the open carriage doors travellers in long cloaks came and went. At the extreme end of the station, half veiled by dust and smoke, there appeared, just as if at the end of a telescope, a little arch of sky. No bigger than a man's hand, it represented the infinitude of travel: Countess Martin and kind Madame Marmet were already seated in their carriage beneath a rack loaded with bags; and newspapers were lying near them on the cushions. Choulette had not come, and Madame Martin had given him up. Nevertheless he had promised to be at the station. He had made arrangements for his departure and received the money for *Les Blandices* from his publisher. One evening Paul Vence had brought him to the Quai de Billy. He had been gentle, polite, wittily gay and naïvely happy. Since then she had looked forward with great pleasure to travelling with a man of genius, so original, so fascinatingly ugly, so entertainingly mad, such a thorough old prodigal, so abounding in natural vices and yet so innocent. They were shutting the carriage doors. He was evidently not coming. She had been foolish to rely on any one so impulsive and Bohemian. Just as the engine was beginning to snort, Madame Marmet, looking out of the window, said calmly:

"I think I see M. Choulette."

He was limping down the platform, wearing his hat on the back of his head, which showed some curious bumps. His beard was untrimmed and he was dragging an old carpet-bag. His aspect was almost terrifying; and yet in spite of his fifty years he looked young; his bright blue eyes shone clearly and there was an ingenuous audacity in his furrowed yellow face; for in this dilapidated old man there still flourished the eternal youth of the poet and the artist. As she looked at him, Thérèse regretted having chosen so strange a companion. As he walked down the train he cast into each carriage a quick glance which became gradually suspicious and sinister. But when he reached the carriage in which the two ladies were, and recognized Madame Martin, he smiled so gracefully and bade her good-day in such a soft voice, that there was no longer anything to suggest the wild vagabond, who had been wandering on the platform, except the old carpet-bag which he was dragging by its half-broken handles.

He put it carefully in the rack side by side with the trim bags, covered with grey linen, which made it look tawdry and common, and showed up its yellow flowers on a ground of blood-red.

Quite at his ease he congratulated Madame Martin on the capes of her travelling-coat.

"Forgive me, ladies," he added, "I fear I am late. I went to six o'clock mass at Saint-Séverin, my parish church, in the Lady Chapel beneath those beautiful but incongruous reed-like pillars climbing heavenwards like us poor sinners."

"So to-day you are pious," said Madame Martin.

And she asked whether he had brought the cord of the order he had founded.

He became sad and grave.

"I am afraid, Madame, that M. Paul Vence has told you some absurd tales on that subject. I have heard that he goes about saying that my cord is a bell-rope! I should be sorry to think that any one should for a moment believe such a wicked story. My cord is symbolic. It is represented by a thread worn next the skin, after having been touched by a poor person as a sign that poverty is holy and will save the world. Goodness is impossible without poverty; and since receiving the money for my *Blandices,* I have felt myself growing hard and unjust. It does me good to remember that I have a few of these mystic cords in my bag."

And, pointing to the hideous blood-red bag:

"I have also got there a wafer, given me by a bad priest, the works of M. de Maistre, a few shirts and several other things."

Madame Martin, somewhat alarmed, raised her eyebrows. But kind Madame Marmet retained her accustomed placidity.

Whilst the train was going through the suburbs, that ugly black fringe of the town, Choulette took out a pocket-book and began to look in it. Beneath the vagabond the scribe was revealing himself. Choulette was fond of hoarding documents, although he did not wish to appear to do so. He made sure that he had lost nothing, neither the scraps of paper with ideas for his poems jotted down in a café, nor the dozen complimentary letters, dirty, finger-marked, ragged at the folds, which he always carried and read at night beneath the gas lamps to any chance acquaintance he might happen to meet. Having seen that everything was there he took a letter in an unsealed envelope out of his pocket-book. He fidgeted with it for some time with an air of rather imprudent mystery and then gave it to the Countess Martin. It was a letter of introduction, given him by the Marchioness of Rieu, to a princess of the French royal family, a very near relative of the Comte de Chambord, who, old and widowed, lived in retirement near the gates of Florence. Having enjoyed the effect which he thought this letter must have produced, he remarked that he might perhaps call on the Princess; she was a good pious person.

"She is a real fine lady," he added, "one who does not display her magnificence in her gowns and hats. She wears her underclothing six weeks and sometimes longer. The noblemen of her suite have seen her wearing very dirty white stockings hanging over her shoes. She revives the virtues of the great queens of Spain. Those dirty stockings are a true glory."

He took back the letter and restored it to his pocket-book. Then, having armed himself with a horn-handled knife, he began to carve a figure already half finished on the handle of his walking stick. Meanwhile he was pronouncing a eulogy on himself.

"I am skilled in all the arts of beggars and vagabonds. I know how to open locks with a nail and carve wood with a cheap clasp-knife."

The head was beginning to be defined. It was the thin face of a woman weeping.

Choulette meant it to express human suffering, not in its touching simplicity as in an earlier civilisation when barbarism was mingled with goodness, nor painted and hideous with that ugliness into which it had been degraded by the middle-class freethinkers and the militarist patriots, the children of the French Revolution. In his opinion the present government was the personification of hypocrisy and brutality.

"Barracks are a horrible invention of modern times. They originated in the seventeenth century. Formerly there was nothing but the guard-house, where veterans played cards and told fairy stories. Louis XIV is the precursor of the Convention and of Bonaparte.

But the evil has come to a head in the monstrous institution of universal military service. To have forced men to kill each other is the disgrace of emperors and republics, the crime of crimes. In the so-called barbarous ages, cities and princes entrusted their defence to mercenaries who made war deliberately and prudently; in some great battles there were only five or six slain. And when the knights engaged in war they were not forced to it; they were killed of their own free will. It is true they were good for nothing else. In the days of Saint Louis no one would have dreamt of sending a man of learning and intelligence into battle. Neither was the labourer dragged from his plough and forced to join the army. Now it is considered the duty of a poor peasant to serve as a soldier. Now he is driven from his home with its chimneys smoking in the golden evening light, from the fat meadows where his oxen are grazing, from his cornfields and ancestral woods. In the court-yard of some miserable barracks he is taught how to kill men methodically; he is threatened, insulted, imprisoned; he is told that it is an honour, and if he desire no such honour, he is shot. He obeys, because like all the gentlest, gayest, and most docile domestic animals, he is afraid. We in France are soldiers and we are citizens. Our citizenship is another occasion for pride! For the poor it consists in supporting and maintaining the rich in their power and their idleness. At this task they must labour in the face of the majestic equality of the laws, which forbid rich and poor alike to sleep under the bridges, to beg in the streets, and to steal their bread. This equality is one of the benefits of the Revolution. Why, that revolution was effected by madmen and idiots for the benefit of those who had acquired the wealth of the crown. It resulted in the enrichment of cunning peasants and money-lending *bourgeois*. In the name of equality it founded the empire of wealth. It delivered France to those moneyed classes who have been devouring her for a century. Now they are our lords and masters. The so-called government, composed of poor creatures, pitiable, miserable, impoverished, and complaining, is in the pay of financiers. Throughout the last hundred years any one caring for the poor in this plague-stricken country has been held a traitor to society. And you are considered dangerous if you assert that there are those who suffer poverty. There are even laws against indignation and pity. But what I am saying now cannot be printed."

While Choulette was growing animated and brandishing his knife, they were passing fields of brown earth, clumps of purple trees that winter had robbed of their leaves, and curtains of poplars on the banks of silver rivers, lying in the winter sunshine.

He looked pathetically at the figure carved upon his stick.

"There you are," he said, "poor Humanity, emaciated and in tears, stupefied by shame and poverty, such as you have been made by your masters, the soldier and the plutocrat."

Kind Madame Marmet, whose nephew was a captain of artillery, a charming young man, strongly attached to his profession, was shocked by the violence of Choulette's attack upon the army. Madame Martin regarded it as an amusing caprice. Choulette's ideas did not alarm her. She was afraid of nothing. But she thought them rather absurd; she could not conceive that the past could ever have been better than the present.

"I believe, Monsieur Choulette, that men have always been what they are to-day, selfish, violent, greedy, and pitiless. I believe that the unfortunate have always been harshly and cruelly treated by laws and customs."

Between La Roche and Dijon, they lunched in the restaurant-car, and then left Choulette there alone with his pipe, his glass of Benedictine, and his vexed soul.

When they had returned to their carriage, Madame Marmet talked with tranquil affection of her dead husband. Theirs was a love match. He had written her beautiful verses, which she kept and showed to no one. He was vivacious and gay. No one would have believed it possible that he would ever succumb to overwork and disease. He had laboured till the very last. Suffering from an enlarged heart, he could never lie down, and used to pass the night in his arm-chair, with his books on a table at his side. Only two hours before his death he made an effort to read. He was kind and affectionate. His sufferings never rendered him irritable.

For lack of anything better, Madame Martin said:

"You have the memory of long years of happiness, and in this world that is to have a share of good fortune."

But Madame Marmet sighed; and a cloud overshadowed her tranquil brow.

"Yes," she said, "Louis was the best of men and the best of husbands. Nevertheless, he made me very unhappy. He had only one fault, but I suffered bitterly from it. He was jealous. He who was otherwise so kind, so affectionate, and so noble-minded was rendered unjust, tyrannical, and violent by that hateful passion. I can assure you that my conduct gave no ground for suspicion. I was not a coquette. But I was young and fresh-looking; I was considered almost pretty. That was enough. He forbade me to go out alone or receive callers in his absence. When we went to a ball together, I trembled in anticipation of the scene he would make in the carriage on our way home."

And kind Madame Marmet added with a sigh:

"It is true that I loved dancing. But I was obliged to give it up. It pained him too much."

Countess Martin did not conceal her surprise. She had always regarded Marmet as a shy self-absorbed old gentleman, appearing rather ridiculous between his corpulent wife, with her white hair and her sweet temper, and the skeleton of his Etruscan warrior in its gilded bronze helmet. But the excellent widow confided to her that when he was fifty-five and she fifty-three, Louis was as jealous as in the early days of their married life.

Thérèse remembered that Robert had never troubled her by his jealousy. Was it a proof of his tact and good taste or had he never loved her enough to be jealous? She did not know and she had not the courage to inquire. It would have involved searching in those secret chambers of her heart which she had decided never to open again.

She murmured almost involuntarily.

"We want to be loved; and when we are loved we are either tormented or bored."

They closed the day with reading and meditation. Choulette had not reappeared. Night was gradually casting a grey veil over the mulberry trees of Dauphiné. Madame Marmet slept peacefully, her head resting on her breast as if on a pillow. Thérèse looked at her and thought:

"She is happy indeed if she can take delight in recalling the past."

The sadness of the night seemed to enter into her heart. And when the moon rose over the olive fields, as she gazed upon the soft outline of plains and hills and the fleeting blue shadows, surrounded by a landscape in which everything suggested peace and oblivion, Thérèse longed for the Seine, the Arc de Triomphe with its radiating avenues, and the glades of the Bois, where at least the trees and stones knew her.

Suddenly, with an artful abruptness, Choulette precipitated himself into the carriage. Armed with his knotted stick, his head enveloped in rough fur and a red shawl, he almost alarmed her. That was what he wanted. His violent pose and savage mien were affectations.

Always occupied with bizarre and trivial effects it was his delight to appear alarming. Himself very easily frightened, he liked to inspire the terror he experienced. Smoking his pipe alone at the end of the passage only a few moments before, as he saw the moon behind the fleeting clouds, over the Camargue, his imaginative, versatile soul had been struck by childish fears. He had come to take refuge with Countess Martin.

"Arles," he said. "Do you know Arles? It is pure beauty! In the cloisters of St. Trophimus I have seen doves perched on the shoulders of statues, and little grey lizards warming themselves on the tombs in the Aliscamps. The tombs are now arranged on each side of the road leading to the church. They are cistern-shaped, and at night beggars sleep in them. One evening, as I was walking with Paul Arène, I met a nice old woman who was spreading dried grass in the tomb of a virgin who died long ago on her wedding-day. We wished her good-night. She replied: 'May God hear you. But an evil fate has willed that this cistern should be open to the north-west wind. If only the crack had been on the other side, I should have slept like Queen Jane.' "

Thérèse did not reply. She was sleepy. And Choulette, shivering in the night cold, thought of death and was afraid.

VIII

ISS BELL had driven the Countess Martin-Bellème and Madame Marmet in her trap from the Florence station, up the steep hill, to her house at Fiesole, painted pink, surrounded by a balustrade, and looking down on the incomparable city. The maid was following with the luggage. Choulette, whom Miss Bell had quartered on a verger's widow in the shadow of Fiesole cathedral, was to come to dinner. Pleasant and plain, with short hair and slim, flat figure, almost graceful in her tailor-made coat and skirt of masculine cut, the poetess welcomed her French friends to her home. The house betrayed the refined delicacy of her taste. On the drawing-room walls pale virgins of Sienna, with long hands, reigned tranquilly over angels, patriarchs, and saints in triptychs with fine gilded mouldings. On a pedestal was a standing figure of a Magdalen, enveloped in her long hair, terribly old and wasted, some beggar on the road to Pistoia, her skin hardened by sun and snow, copied in clay, with horrible pathetic realism, by an unknown precursor of Donatello. And Miss Bell's armorial bearings, big bells and little bells, were everywhere. The largest, in bronze, were in the corners of the room; others formed a chain round the bottom of the walls. Smaller ones bordered the cornice. There were bells on the stove, on the coffers and the cabinets. There were glass cases full of bells in silver and silver gilt. There were big bronze bells engraved with the Florentine lily, little Renaissance bells composed of a woman wearing a full farthingale, funeral bells decorated with tears and bones, filigree bells, covered with leaves and symbolic animals, which rang in churches in the days of St. Louis, table bells of the seventeenth century with a statuette for handle, little flat clear-sounding cow-bells of the Rutli valleys, Indian bells made to ring softly with a stag's horn, Chinese bells of cylindrical form; they had come there from all countries and from all times in obedience to the magic summons of this little Miss Bell.

"You are looking at my vocal coats of arms," she said to Madame Martin. "I think all those Misses Bell are happy here, and it would not astonish me if one day they began to sing together. But you must not admire them all equally. You must keep your highest praise for this one."

As she struck with her finger a dark plain bell, there resounded a shrill note:

"This one," she resumed, "is a holy country-woman of the fifth century. She is the daughter in the faith of Paulinus of Nola, he who first made music in the sky above us. It is made of a rare metal, called Campanian brass. Soon I will show you at her side a most charming Florentine, the queen of bells. She is to come. But I am wearying you with these toys, darling. And I am boring kind Madame Marmet also. It is too bad of me."

She took them to their rooms.

An hour later, Madame Martin, refreshed and rested, in a tea-gown of soft silk and lace, came down on the terrace, where Miss Bell was waiting for her. The damp air, warmed by the sunlight, not yet strong but already abundant, breathed the disquieting sweetness of spring. Thérèse, leaning against the balustrade, bathed her eyes in the light. At her feet the cypresses raised their dark pyramids and the olive trees clustered on the slopes. In the hollow of the valley was Florence with its domes, its towers, the multitude of its red roofs, among which was faintly discernible the winding thread of the Arno. Beyond were the blue hills.

She tried to make out the Boboli gardens, where she had walked during a previous visit, the Cascine, which she did not care for, the Pitti Palace, Santa Maria del Fiore. Then the glorious spaces of the sky attracted her. She followed the fleeting forms of the clouds.

After a long silence, Vivian Bell stretched out her hand towards the horizon.

"Darling, I cannot express myself, I don't know how to say it. But look, darling, look again. What you see is unique. Nowhere else is nature so subtle, so elegant, so delicate. The god who created the Florentine hills was an artist. Yes, he was a worker in jewels, an engraver of medals, a sculptor, a bronze founder, and a painter; he was a Florentine. And he produced nothing else, darling. The rest is the work of a less delicate hand, a less perfect creation. How could that violet hill of San Miniato, standing out in such pure and firm relief, be by the author of Mont Blanc? It is not possible. This landscape, darling, has all the beauty of an ancient medal and a costly painting. It is a perfect and harmonious work of art. And there is something else that I can't express, that I can't understand, and yet it is true. In this country I feel, and you will feel like me, darling, half alive and half dead, in a state very noble, very sad and very sweet. Look, look well; you will discern the melancholy of these hills which surround Florence, and you will behold a delicious sadness ascending from the Country of the Dead."

The sun was declining towards the horizon. One by one the lights faded from the hills and the clouds became on fire.

Madame Marmet sneezed.

Miss Bell had shawls brought and warned her French guests that the evenings were cold and dangerous.

Then suddenly she said:

"Darling, do you know M. Jacques Dechartre? Well, he writes that he is coming to Florence next week. I am glad that M. Jacques Dechartre should be in our city at the same time as you. He will go with us to churches and museums; and he will be a good guide. He understands beautiful things because he loves them. His sculpture is exquisite. His figures and medallions are even more highly appreciated in England than in France. Oh! I am so glad that M. Jacques Dechartre will be at Florence with you, darling!"

IX

HE next day, as they were coming out of Santa Maria Novella, and crossing the square, where, as in an ancient circus, stand two obelisks of marble, Madame Marmet said to Countess Martin: "I think I see Monsieur Choulette."

Sitting in a cobbler's booth, pipe in hand, Choulette was gesticulating rhythmically, and appeared to be reciting verses. The Florentine shoemaker, as he worked with his awl, was listening with a good-natured smile. He was a little bald man, a favourite type in Flemish pictures. On the table, among the wooden lasts, nails, pieces of leather, and balls of wax, was a basil plant. A sparrow with a false leg, made of a bit of match, was hopping gaily from the old man's shoulder to his head.

Delighted at such a sight, Madame Martin stood on the threshold and called Choulette, who was reciting in a soft, singing voice, and asked him why he had not come with her to visit the Cappella degli Spagnuoli.

He rose and replied:

"Madame, you are occupied with vain imaginings. I am concerned with life and reality."

He shook hands with the cobbler, and followed the two ladies.

"On my way to Santa Maria Novella," he said, "I saw this old man, leaning over his work, holding the last between his knees as if in a vice, and stitching clumsy shoes. I felt that he was simple and good. I said to him in Italian, 'Father, will you drink a glass of Chianti with me?' He was quite willing. He went to fetch a bottle and glasses, while I minded his shop."

And Choulette pointed to two glasses and a bottle standing on the stove.

"When he returned we drank together; I repeated good words of obscure meaning, the music of which delighted him. I shall return to his booth. I shall learn from him how to make shoes and live a contented life. After that I shall never know sadness, which arises solely from discontent and idleness."

Countess Martin smiled.

"Monsieur Choulette, I am not discontented, and yet I am not gay. Must I also learn to make shoes?"

Choulette replied gravely:

"Not yet."

When they reached the Oricellari Gardens, Madame Marmet dropped on to a seat. At Santa Maria Novella she had carefully examined the serene frescoes of Ghirlandajo, the choir-stalls, the virgin of Cimabuë, and the pictures in the monastery. She had taken great pains in honour of her husband's memory, who was said to have loved Italian art. She was tired. Choulette sat down by her and said:

"Could you tell me, Madame, if it is true that the Pope has his robes made by Worth?"

Madame Marmet did not think so. Nevertheless, Choulette had heard it in the cafés. Madame Martin was surprised that Choulette, a Catholic and a Socialist, should speak so disrespectfully of a Pope who was the friend of the Republic. But he had little admiration for Leo XIII.

"The wisdom of princes is short-sighted," he said. "The Church's salvation will be effected by the Italian Republic; and this is what Leo XIII believes and desires; but the Church will not be saved in the way that pious Machiavelli expects: the revolution will deprive the Pope of his iniquitous tribute with the rest of his temporal dominion. And that will be the salvation of the papacy. Poor and stripped of his temporal power, the Pope will once more be powerful. He will move the world. The Peters, the Linuses, the Cletuses, the Anacletuses, the Clements,* the humble, the ignorant, the saints of early times who changed the face of the earth, will return. If such an impossible thing were to happen as that to-morrow there were to sit in the chair of St. Peter a true bishop, a true Christian, I should go to him and say: 'Cease to be an old man buried alive in a golden tomb. Leave your chamberlains, your noble body-guards, and your cardinals; abandon your throne and the empty shows of power. Come, and, supported by me, beg your bread from the nations. Ragged, poor, sick, dying, bear in yourself the image of Jesus. Say, I beg my bread in order that the rich may be reproached. Enter the towns and cry from door to door: Be humble, be gentle, be poor! Proclaim peace and charity in dark cities, in barracks, and in miserable hovels. You will be despised, you will be

*St. Peter, St. Linus, St. Cletus, St. Clement, St. Anacletus are said to have been the first five Popes, A.D. 65–109 (*cf.* Butler's "Lives of the Saints.")—W. S.

stoned. Soldiers will drag you to prison. To the humble as to the powerful, to the poor as to the rich, you will be a laughing-stock, a subject for disgust and pity. Your priests will depose you and elect an anti-pope. Every one will call you mad. And they must speak the truth; for you must be mad: the world has always been saved by madmen. Men will crown you with a crown of thorns, and put in your hands a sceptre of reeds; and by these signs they shall know you to be the Christ, the true King. By these means you shall establish Christian socialism, which is the kingdom of God on earth.'"

Having thus spoken, Choulette lit a long Italian cigar with a straw running through the middle. He inhaled a few whiffs of noxious smoke and then tranquilly resumed:

"And it would be quite practical. I am nothing if not clear-headed. Ah! Madame Marmet, you will never know how true it is that the great tasks of the world have always been accomplished by madmen. Do you think, Madame Martin, that if St. Francis of Assisi had been reasonable, he could have shed abroad among the nations the living waters of charity and quickened them with the perfumes of love?"

"I do not know," replied Madame Martin. "But I always find reasonable persons very wearisome. I need not hesitate to say this to you, Monsieur Choulette."

They returned up the hill to Fiesole by steam tram. It was raining. Madame Marmet fell asleep, and Choulette grumbled. He was overwhelmed with misfortunes: the dampness of the atmosphere gave him pains in the knee and he couldn't bend his leg; his carpet-bag, lost on the way from the station to Fiesole, couldn't be found, and that was an irreparable disaster; a Parisian review had just published one of his poems with glaring misprints.

He accused men and things of being against him, bent on his ruin. He was childish, absurd, disagreeable. Madame Martin, depressed by Choulette and by the rain, thought the ascent would never come to an end. When she entered the house of bells, she found Miss Bell in the drawing-room. In a handwriting modelled on the Aldine type she was copying, in golden ink, on to a piece of parchment, the verses she had composed during the night. At the sight of her friend, she raised her plain little face, glorified by her fine brilliant eyes.

"Darling, let me introduce Prince Albertinelli."

The prince, in all the beauty of a young Adonis, humanised by a straight black beard, was standing near the stove. He bowed to Madame Martin.

"Madame would inspire us with a love for France had not that sentiment already taken root in our hearts," he said.

The Countess and Choulette asked Miss Bell to read them the verses she was writing. She said it would be impossible for her to

make her halting numbers comprehensible to the French poet whom
she admired most after François Villon; then, in her pretty, shrill,
birdlike voice, she recited:

> Where the stream, like a water-sprite, laughing and singing,
> And waving cool arms, to the Arno down-springing,
> In spray-lifting leaps, skips o'er rugged rock-ledges,
> Two comely young lovers changed rings as love's pledges.
> And the transport of love in their bosoms was swelling,
> As the riotous drops in the torrent upwelling,
> The maiden was Gemma, but name for her lover
> No chronicler ever was known to discover.
>
> As day followed day, lips to lips closely pressing,
> With arms interlaced in their artless carressing,
> The goats cropping thyme all unstartled would brook them,
> Till at eve to their home in town they betook them.
> And there the tired toilers, 'neath linden trees seated,
> The dream-enwrapped lovers nor heeded nor greeted.
> Yet they wept when they thought there remained not to capture
> From life, aught of bliss that could heighten their rapture.
>
> In that meadow where first they gave ear to love's singing,
> Where like as the vine to the green elm-tree clinging,
> O'erarched by the sky their first kisses they blended,
> Its blood-tinted petals a strange plant extended,
> All lance-like and wan were the leaves of its growing,
> Herb of Silence its name of the shepherds' bestowing.
>
> And Gemma was 'ware it was potent in lending
> The slumber eternal, the dream without ending,
> To all who should taste its ineffable savour.
>
> One day, 'neath the branches with breezes a-quaver,
> With a leaflet she parted the lips of her lover,
> And straightway Elysium received him, a rover;
> Then she, of the peace-bringing leaf having tasted,
> In pursuit of her love to the silent shades hasted.
>
> And the dove, that at twilight complains as it hovers,
> Alone breaks the silence enwrapping the lovers.*

"That is very pretty," said Choulette; "it suggests an Italy veiled
in the mists of the Land of Thule."

"Yes," said Countess Martin, "it is pretty. But my dear Vivian,
why did your two innocents want to die?"

"Why, darling! because they felt as happy as possible, and they
desired nothing more. Nothing was left to them to hope for. Don't
you understand?"

*See page following.

"Then you believe that hope keeps us alive?"

"Yes, darling, we live in the expectation of what To-morrow, To-morrow, King of Fairyland, will bring in his mantle of black or blue, embroidered with flowers, with stars, and with tears. Oh bright king To-morrow!"

*"Lors au pied des rochers où la source penchante,
Pareille à la Naïade et qui rit et qui chante,
Agite ses bras frais et vole vers l'Arno,
Deux beaux enfants avaient échangé leur anneau,
Et le bonheur d'aimer coulait dans leurs poitrines
Comme l'eau du torrent au versant des collines.
Elle avait nom Gemma. Mais l'amant de Gemma,
Nul entre les conteurs jamais ne le nomma.

Le jour, ces innocents, la bouche sur la bouche,
Mêlaient leurs jeunes corps dans la sauvage couche
De thym que visitait la chèvre. Et vers le soir,
À l'heure où l'artisan fatigué va s'asseoir
Sous les tilleuls, surpris, ils regagnaient la ville.
Nul n'avait souci d'eux dans la foule servile,
Et souvent ils pleuraient, se sentant trop heureux
Ils comprirent que vivre était mauvais pour eux.

Or, dans cette prairie où déchirés de joie,
Ils étaient l'orme vert et la vigne qui ploie,
Et tordaient sous le ciel leur rameau gémissant,
S'élevait une plante étrange, aux fleurs de sang,
Qui dardait son feuillage en pâles fers de lance.
Les bergers la nommaient la Plante du silence.

Et Gemma le savait, que le sommeil divin
Et l'éternal repos et le rêve sans fin
Viendraient de cette plante à qui l'aurait mordue.

Un jour qu'elle riait sous l'arbuste étendue,
Elle en mit une feuille aux lèvres de l'ami.
Quand il fut dans la joie à jamais endormi,
Elle mordit aussi la feuille bien-aimée.
Aux pieds de son amant elle tomba pâmée.

Les colombes au soir sur eux vinrent gémir,
Et rien plus ne troubla leur amoureux dormir."

X

THEY were dressed for dinner. In the drawing-room Miss Bell was drawing monsters, suggested by those of Leonardo da Vinci. She created them in order to see what they would say, convinced that they would speak and express rare ideas in curious rhymes. Then she would listen to them. It was thus that she generally conceived her poems.

Prince Albertinelli was strumming on the piano the Sicilian air, *O Lola!* His fingers passed lightly over the keys.

Choulette, more uncouth than usual, was asking for a needle and thread with which to mend his clothes. He was groaning over the loss of a modest needle-case he had carried in his pocket for thirty years, and which was precious on account of the sweet memories it recalled and the wise counsels it suggested. He thought he must have lost it in that impious hall of the Pitti Palace, and he held the Medicis and all the Italian painters responsible.

Looking at Miss Bell reproachfully, he said:

"I compose my poems when I am mending my clothes. I take delight in manual labour. I sing my songs as I sweep my room. That is why those songs go straight to the hearts of men, like the old songs of ploughmen and artisans, which are more beautiful than mine, but not more natural. I take a pride in waiting on myself. The verger's widow offered to mend my rags. I would not permit it. It is wrong to employ others to do servilely what we could ourselves accomplish in noble freedom."

The Prince was playing slight airs mechanically. Thérèse, who for the last week had been visiting churches and museums with Madame Marmet, was meditating on the vexation her companion caused her by insisting on recognising resemblances to persons among her acquaintance in the portraits by the old masters. That morning at the Riccardi Palace, merely in the frescoes of Benozzo Gozzoli, she had recognised M. Garain, M. Lagrange, M. Schmoll, Princess Seniavine dressed as a page, and M. Renan on horseback. M. Renan she was quite alarmed to find everywhere. Her ideas were always revolving around her little academical and social circle with a facility which annoyed her friend. In her sweet voice she was always describing the public meetings of the Institute, lectures at the Sorbonne, assemblies adorned by fashionable theosophists. As for the women, in her opinion they were all charming and irreproachable. She visited them all. And Thérèse reflected: "Kind Madame Marmet! She is too discreet. She bores me." And Madame Marmet thought of leaving her behind at Fiesole and visiting the churches alone. She said to herself, using an expression that Le Ménil had taught her:

"I must drop Madame Marmet."

A thin old man entered the drawing-room. His waxed moustache and little white pointed beard made him look like an old officer. But beneath his spectacles his glance betrayed the cunning geniality of eyes worn out in the service of science and pleasure. He was a Florentine, a friend of Miss Bell and of the Prince, Professor Arrighi, once adored by women, now famous throughout Tuscany and the Emilia* for his essays on agriculture.

Countess Martin liked him at once. Although she had not been favourably impressed by rural life in Italy, she carefully questioned the Professor concerning his methods and their results.

He proceeded, he said, with energy tempered by prudence.

"The earth," he continued, "is like a woman. She requires you to be neither timid nor brutal."

The Ave Maria sounding from all the campanili converted the sky into one vast musical instrument playing religious music.

"Darling," said Miss Bell, "do you hear how in the evening the air of Florence is sonorous and tinkling with the sound of bells?"

"It is strange," said Choulette, "but we all seem as if we were waiting for some one."

Vivian Bell replied that they were indeed waiting for some one, for M. Dechartre. He was rather late. She was afraid he must have missed his train.

Choulette went up to Madame Marmet and said very gravely:

"Madame Marmet, can you ever look at a door, a simple door of painted wood, like yours for instance or mine, on that one or any other, without being filled with fear and horror at the thought of the visitor who may enter at any moment? The door of our dwelling opens into the infinite. Have you ever thought of it? Do we ever know the true name of him or her, who, in human form, with a familiar face, in commonplace clothes, enters our house?"

For his part, shut up in his own room, he could never look at the door without fear making his hair stand on end.

But Madame Marmet was able to look at her drawing-room doors without experiencing the slightest alarm. She knew the names of all her visitors; all delightful people.

Choulette looked at her sadly and shook his head:

"Madame Marmet, Madame Marmet, those whom you call by their earthly names have another name, which you do not know, but which is their true name."

Madame Martin asked Choulette if he believed that when misfortune descended upon people there was any need for it to cross the threshold.

"It is subtle and ingenious. It comes through the window, it passes through walls. It is not always seen, but it is always there.

*A district composed of three duchies, Parma, Piacenza, and Modena. —W. S.

The poor doors are quite innocent of the advent of this evil visitor."

Choulette reproached Madame Martin severely for calling the advent of misfortune evil.

"Misfortune is our greatest master and our best friend. It teaches us the meaning of life. Ladies, when you suffer, you will know what you ought to know, you will believe what you ought to believe, you will do what you ought to do, you will be what you ought to be. And you will possess that joy which pleasure banishes. Joy is shy and delights not in feasting."

Prince Albertinelli said that neither Miss Bell nor her two French friends needed misfortune to make them perfect, and that the doctrine of perfection through suffering was barbarously cruel and held in horror beneath the beautiful Italian sky. Then, when conversation languished, he returned to the piano and tried to finger out the melody of the graceful conventional Sicilian air, fearing to glide into the somewhat similar one in *Il Trovatore*.

Vivian Bell was questioning in whispers the monsters she had created and grumbling at their absurd jesting replies.

"At this moment," she said, "I only want to listen to tapestry figures talking of things pale, ancient, and as precious as they."

And now the handsome Prince was singing, carried away on the flood of melody. His voice swelled, spread itself out like a peacock's tail, and then died away softly.

Kind Madame Marmet, with her eyes on the glass door, said:

"I think here is M. Dechartre."

He entered with a vivacious animated air. His face, generally grave, was beaming with joy.

Miss Bell welcomed him with little bird-like cries.

"Monsieur Dechartre, we were growing very impatient. M. Choulette was speaking evil of doors. Yes, doors in houses; and he was saying that misfortune is an obliging old gentleman. You have lost all these fine things. You have kept us waiting, Monsieur Dechartre; why?"

He made his excuses: he had barely had time to go to his hotel and dress quickly. He had not even been to greet his dear good friend the bronze San Marco, so pathetic in its niche, on the wall of Or San Michele. He complimented the poetess and greeted Countess Martin with an ill-concealed delight.

"Before leaving Paris, I called at your house on the Quai de Billy, where I was told that you had gone to meet the spring at Miss Bell's at Fiesole. Then I hoped I might find you in that country which now I love more than ever."

She asked him if he had been first to Venice and to Ravenna to see the haloed empresses and the glistening phantoms.

No, he had not stayed anywhere.

She said nothing. Her glance remained fixed on one corner of the wall on the bell of St. Paulinus.

He said:

"You are looking at the bell from Nola."

Vivian threw down her papers and pencils.

"You will soon see a marvel which will appeal to you more than that, M. Dechartre. I have discovered the queen of little bells. I found it at Rimini, in a ruined wine-press, which is now being used as a shop, where I had gone for some old wood saturated with oil, hard, dark, and shiny. I bought the bell and had it packed myself. I shall not live until it arrives. You will see. On its cup is a Christ on the Cross, between the Virgin and St. John, with the date 1400 and the arms of Malatesta.

"Monsieur Dechartre, you are not attending. You must listen. In 1400, Lorenzo Ghiberti, who was fleeing from war and plague, had taken refuge at Rimini with Paolo Malatesta. It must certainly have been he who modelled the figures on my bell. Next week you will see a work by Ghiberti here."

Dinner was announced. She asked them to pardon her giving them an Italian dinner. Her cook was a poet of Fiesole.

At table, before the *fiasconi,* encased in maize straw, they talked of that blessed fifteenth century that they loved. Prince Alberti-nelli praised the universality of the artists of that period, their passionate love of art and their genius. He spoke emphatically, in a caressing voice.

Dechartre admired them, but in a different manner.

"An appropriate eulogy," he said, "of those men who from Cima-buë to Masaccio laboured with such whole-hearted devotion, should be both modest and precise. One must regard them first in the studio, and then in the workshop, where they lived like artisans. It is by studying them at their work that one comes to appreciate their simplicity and their genius. They were rough and ignorant. They had read little and seen little. The hills around Florence enclosed their visual and mental horizon. They knew nothing beyond their own town, the Bible and a few fragments of ancient sculpture, tenderly studied and cherished."

"You are quite right," said Professor Arrighi. "All they cared about was to use the best process. Their minds were entirely occupied in preparing glaze and mixing colours. He who first thought of pasting linen over a panel in order that the painting might not crack with the wood, was heralded as a man of genius. Every master had his own recipes and formulæ, which he guarded in strict secrecy."

"Happy days," resumed Dechartre, "when no one dreamed of that originality to which to-day we so eagerly aspire. The apprentice was content to follow his master. His sole ambition was to resemble him, and it was quite involuntarily that he appeared different from the others. They worked not to win fame, but to earn a livelihood."

"They were right," said Choulette; "there is nothing better than to work for a livelihood."

"To desire that their names should be handed down to posterity," continued Dechartre, "never occurred to them. Knowing nothing of the past, they did not think of the future, and their dreams were confined to the present. On doing good they concentrated all the force of a strong will. And, being simple, they did not go far wrong; they beheld truths which our intelligence hides from us."

Meanwhile Choulette was beginning to tell Madame Marmet of a call he had paid that day on the French royal princess, to whom the Marchioness of Rieu had given him a letter of introduction. He took a delight in insinuating that he, a Bohemian, had been received by a royal princess, who would not have seen either Miss Bell or the Countess Martin, and whom Prince Albertinelli boasted of having met at some public reception.

"She practices the most austere piety," said the Prince.

"Her nobility combined with simplicity is admirable," said Choulette. "Surrounded by the gentlemen and ladies of her suite, she observes the strictest etiquette, and makes a penance of her high rank. Every morning she washes the church floor. It is a village church, the floor of which is often overrun by fowls, while the priest is playing at cards with the verger."

And Choulette, leaning over the table, imitated with his serviette the princess at her work. Then raising his hand, he said gravely:

"After a fitting time, spent in waiting in a long series of ante-chambers, I was admitted to kiss her hand."

And he was silent.

Madame Martin eagerly curious, asked:

"Well, what did this charmingly simple and noble princess say to you?"

"She asked me: 'Have you been to Florence? I hear that some very fine shops have recently been opened there, and that at night they are brilliantly lighted.' She remarked further: 'We have a very good chemist here. No Austrian chemist could be better. Six weeks ago he put a plaster on my leg which has not come off yet.' Such were the words that Marie Thérèse deigned to address to me. O simple greatness! O Christian Virtue! O daughter of St. Louis! O marvellous echo of thy voice. holy Elizabeth of Hungary!"

Madame Martin smiled. She thought Choulette must be joking. But he insisted that he was serious. Miss Bell reproached her friend. The French, she said, are always too ready to think people are not in earnest.

Then they resumed the discussion of those artistic ideas which in that country are always in the air.

"For my part," said Countess Martin, "I am not learned enough to admire Giotto and his school. What strikes me most in the fifteenth century is the sensuality of that so-called Christian art.

The only piety and purity is to be found in the figures of Fra Angelico, and they too appeal to the senses as well as to the soul. The rest, virgins and angels, are voluptuous, caressing, and even perverse. What religious idea do they express, those royal magi as beautiful as women and that St. Sebastian, brilliant in his youthfulness, like the suffering Bacchus of Christianity?"

Dechartre replied that he agreed with her and that they must both be right, since Savonarola was of their opinion. Failing to discover piety in any work of art, he had condemned them all to be burnt.

"In the days of that superb Manfred, who was half a Mussulman, men, said to be followers of Epicurus, tried to argue against the existence of God. The handsome Guido Cavalcanti despised those ignorant persons who believed in the immortality of the soul. He was represented as having said that 'The death of a man is like that of a beast.' Later when the beauty of antiquity rose from the tomb, the Christian sky was overclouded. The painters who worked in churches and monasteries were neither chaste nor devout. Perugino was an atheist and did not deny it."

"Yes," retorted Miss Bell, "but he was said to have a hard heart into which celestial truth could not penetrate. He was bitter and avaricious, wrapped up in material concerns. He thought of nothing but buying houses."

Professor Arrighi defended Pietro Vannucci of Perugia.

"He was an honest man," he said. "And the prior of the Gesuati at Florence was wrong in mistrusting him. This monk practiced the art of making ultra-marine blue by pounding lapis-lazuli to a powder. The ultra-marine was worth its weight in gold, and the prior, who knew a secret way of preparing it, considered his more precious than rubies and sapphires. He asked Pietro to decorate the two cloisters of his monastery, and he expected wonders, less from the skill of the master than from the beauty of the sky-blue ultramarine. While the artist was painting the story of Jesus Christ on the cloister walls, the prior stayed by his side, holding the precious powder in a little bag, of which he never let go. Under the old man's eye, Pietro took from it and dipped his brush covered with paint into a cup of water, before using it on the plaster of the wall. In this manner he used a great quantity of powder. And the good Father, seeing the contents of his bag rapidly growing less and less, groaned: 'Jesus, what a lot of ultra-marine it takes to cover this white-wash!'

"When the frescoes were finished, and Perugino had received from the prior the price agreed upon, he put into his hand a packet of blue powder. 'This is yours, Father,' he said; 'your ultra-marine, which I took on my brush, descended to the bottom of my cup, from which I abstracted it every day. I give it back to you. Now learn to trust good men.'"

"Oh!" said Thérèse, "there is nothing extraordinary in Perugino's having been both avaricious and honest. It is not always self-seeking persons who are the most unscrupulous. There are many who are honest and avaricious."

"Of course, darling!" said Miss Bell. "The avaricious will owe no man anything, while the prodigal is quite content to have debts. He thinks little of the money he possesses, and still less of what he owes. I never said that Pietro Vannucci of Perugia was a dishonest man. I said that he had a hard heart, and that he bought many houses. I am very glad to hear that he gave back the ultra-marine to the prior of the Gesuati."

"As your Pietro was rich," said Choulette, "it was his duty to restore the ultra-marine. It is incumbent upon the rich to be honest, but not upon the poor."

At this moment the butler was offering Choulette a silver basin; and the poet held out his hands to receive the scented water poured from the ewer. It was a jug of chased silver and a basin with a false bottom, which, according to an ancient custom, Miss Bell had passed round to her guests at the end of a meal.

"I wash my hands," he said, "of the harm that Madame Martin does or may do by her words or in any other manner."

And he rose, furious, and followed Miss Bell, who left the table on the arm of Professor Arrighi.

In the drawing-room, while coffee was being served, she said:

"Monsieur Choulette, why must you be ever condemning us to the barbaric sadness of equality? The flute of Daphnis would not produce such sweet music if it were made of seven reeds of equal length. You would destroy those fine harmonies of master and servant, aristocrat and artisan. Oh! Monsieur Choulette, you are a barbarian. You have pity upon the poor, but you have no pity for the divine beauty you are driving from the world. You are driving her away, Monsieur Choulette; she is naked and in tears, you turn from her. Be assured, she will cease to dwell upon the earth when mankind becomes weak, puny, and ignorant. To banish from society the grouping of men of various ranks, from the humble to the great, is to be the enemy of rich and poor alike; it is to be the enemy of the whole human race."

"The enemies of humanity!" replied Choulette, dropping a knob of sugar into his coffee, "by that name did the hard-hearted Roman call the Christians who preached to him of love."

Meanwhile Dechartre, sitting by Madame Martin, was questioning her concerning her artistic tastes, supporting, directing, animating her admiration, stimulating it sometimes with an affectionate abruptness, desiring that she should see all that he had seen, and love all that he had loved.

He wanted her to go into the garden in the delicate dawn of spring. In his mind's eye he saw her on the grand terraces; already he beheld the sunlight, playing on her neck and in her hair, and the bay-trees casting a shadow over her eyes. It seemed to him now that the earth and sky of Florence existed only as a background for this woman.

He congratulated her on the simplicity of her dress, on the lines of her figure and her grace, on the charming ease of her every movement. He liked, he said, those supple, graceful, flowing gowns that one sees so seldom and never forgets.

She had received many compliments, but never any that had given her greater pleasure. She knew that she dressed well, with a pronounced but unerring taste. But no man, except her father, had ever given her the praise of a connoisseur. She had believed men capable of appreciating the general effect of dress without understanding its minute details. Some, who were said to understand *chiffons,* disgusted her by an effeminate air and doubtful taste. She resigned herself to seeing her dress appreciated only by women, whose judgment was warped by petty malice and envy. The masculine artistic admiration of Dechartre surprised and pleased her. She received his praise with delight, and never thought of considering it too familiar and almost indiscreet.

"Then you take an interest in dress, Monsieur Dechartre?"

No, he seldom looked at it. There are so few well-dressed women, even now when they dress as well and perhaps better than ever before. It gave him no pleasure to look at walking bundles. But to a woman whose figure presented good lines and who walked rhythmically he felt grateful.

He continued in a slightly higher voice:

"I can never think of a woman carefully adorning herself every day, without being reminded of the lesson she teaches us artists. It is for so short a time that she dresses and arranges her hair; but her labour is not wasted. Like her, we ought to adorn life without thinking of the future. To paint, to carve, to write for posterity is mere empty pride."

"Monsieur Dechartre," asked Prince Albertinelli, "how do you think a mauve gown with silver flowers would become Miss Bell?"

"As for me," said Choulette, "I am so little concerned with any earthly future that I have written my finest poems on cigarette papers. They perish easily and my verses retain only a kind of metaphysical existence."

He piqued himself on this air of indifference towards his own compositions. In reality he had never lost a single line of his writings. Dechartre was more sincere. He did not desire posthumous fame. Miss Bell blamed him for it.

"Life to be full and great must contain the past and the future, Monsieur Dechartre. We must produce our poetry and our works of art in memory of those who are dead and looking forward to those who will follow us. Thus we partake of what was, what is, and what will be. You do not wish to be immortal, Monsieur Dechartre. Beware lest God grant your desire."

He replied:

"It is enough for me to live for the moment."

And he took his leave, promising to return on the morrow to take Madame Martin to the Brancacci Chapel.

An hour later Thérèse was lying in a room, furnished in æsthetic style, hung with tapestry, on which lemon-trees, bearing golden fruit of immense size, formed a kind of fairy forest. Her head was on the pillow and over it she had thrown her beautiful bare arm. She was dreaming in the lamplight. Passing confusedly before her she beheld visions of her new life: Vivian Bell and her bells; those religious pictures, in which slight shadowy Pre-Raphaelite figures, ladies and cavaliers, appeared isolated, indifferent, and rather sad, but all the more human through their charming languor; the evening at the Fiesole villa, Prince Albertinelli, Professor Arrighi, Choulette, the brisk conversation, the curious play of ideas, and Dechartre with young eyes but rather worn countenance, to which his swarthy skin and pointed beard gave an almost Eastern air.

She realised that he possessed a delightful imagination, a mind richer than any she had known, and a charm she could no longer resist. She had known from the first that he was endowed with the gift of pleasing. She now knew that he wished to please. This idea filled her with delight; she shut her eyes as if to retain it. Then suddenly she shuddered.

In the depths of her inner consciousness she felt a dull blow and a smarting pain. She had a sudden vision of her lover in the wood, his gun under his arm. He was walking with his firm regular step down a long path. She could not see his face and it troubled her. She no longer bore him any ill-will. She was not vexed with him now. At present she was vexed with herself. And Robert went straight on never turning his head, on and on, till he became a black spot in the desolate wood. She felt that she had been abrupt, hard, and capricious to leave him without saying good-bye, even without writing a letter. He was her lover, her one lover. She had never had another. "I should not like him to be unhappy through me," she thought.

Gradually she was reassured. It was true that he loved her; but he was not very sensitive, and fortunately not very quick to grow anxious and uneasy. "He is hunting. He is happy. He is with his Aunt de Lannoix, whom he admires. . . ." She forgot her anxiety and gave herself up to the enchanting deep-seated gaiety of Florence. At the Uffizi there was a picture she had not cared for and which Dechartre admired. It was the detached head of Medusa, a work into which, the sculptor said, Leonardo had put all his wonderful power of detail and delicate sense of the deepest tragedy.

Disappointed with herself for not having thoroughly appreciated it at first, she wanted to see it again.

She put out her lamp and fell asleep.

Towards morning she dreamt she met Robert le Ménil in an empty church, that he was wrapped in a fur coat which was unfamiliar to her. He was waiting for her, but they were separated by a crowd of priests and worshippers, who had suddenly appeared. She did not know what became of him. She had not been able to see his face and that alarmed her. Awake, she heard at her open window a little sad monotonous cry, and, in the milky dawn, she saw a swallow flit by. Then, without cause and without reason, she wept. With the sorrow of a child she shed tears over herself.

XI

HE rose early and took delight in dressing carefully with an art delicately disguised. Her dressing-room was one of Vivian Bell's æsthetic fancies. With its roughly glazed pottery, its copper pitchers and tiled floor, it resembled a kitchen, but a fairy's kitchen. It was so mediæval and so uncommon that Countess Martin had no difficulty in imagining herself a fairy princess. While her maid was doing her hair she heard Dechartre and Choulette talking underneath her window. She undid Pauline's work and boldly displayed the fine line of the nape of her neck. Then, having taken a last look at herself in the mirror, she went down into the garden.

In the garden, shaded by yew trees like some peaceful cemetery, Dechartre was looking down on Florence and repeating lines from Dante:

"And when our soul, more alien from the sphere."*

Near him Choulette, sitting on the balustrade, his legs hanging and his nose in his beard, was carving the face of Poverty on his wanderer's staff.

And Dechartre repeated the lines of the poem:

"And when our soul, more alien from the sphere
Of flesh, and less to rush of hot thoughts given,
As half-divine looks forth in visions clear";

In her maize-coloured gown, shaded by her parasol, she came along the trim box hedge. The soft winter sun clothed her in a pale golden light.

Dechartre joyfully bade her good morning.

*"Purgatory," canto ix. 16. Plumptre's Translation.—W. S.

She said:

"You are reciting lines I do not know. Metastasio is the only Italian poet with whose works I am familiar. The professor who taught me Italian adored Metastasio and did not care for any one else. When does the mind become divine in its visions?"

"At the break of day, or it may be also in the dawn of faith or of love."

Choulette did not think the poet meant morning dreams. They leave so vivid and sometimes so painful an impression on awaking, and they are not dissociated from the body. But Dechartre had only quoted those lines in his rapture at the golden dawn which he had seen that morning on the fair hills. He had long wondered about the visions that come to us in the night, and he had arrived at the conclusion that they proceed not from what has most occupied our minds during the day, but from thoughts from which we have turned away.

Then Thérèse recalled her dream that morning of the hunter on the long path leading into the deep wood.

"Yes," said Dechartre, "at night we see the sad vestiges of what

we have neglected during the day. A dream is often the revenge of things neglected or of persons deserted; hence its unexpectedness and sometimes its sadness."

For a moment she remained silent and thoughtful, and then she said:

"Perhaps it is true."

Then, turning eagerly to Choulette, she asked him if he had finished carving the figure of Poverty on the handle of his walking-stick. But Poverty had become a Pietà, and Choulette was pleased to call her the Virgin. He had even composed a quatrain to be written on a scroll beneath; the quatrain was both didactic and moral. His style was henceforth to be that of the Ten Commandments translated into French verse. The four lines were good and simple. He consented to repeat them:

> Prone 'neath His Cross, will ye
> Not weep, love, hope with me?
> Beneath that Tree of Grace
> Refuge of all our race?*

As on the day of her arrival, Thérèse leant against the balustrade and looked far into the distance, beyond the ocean of light, to where rose the summits of Vallombrosa, almost as liquid as the clouds.

Dechartre was watching her. It seemed to him as if he saw her for the first time, such new charm did he discover on her delicate face, which life and thought had lined, but had not robbed of their youthful grace and freshness. The light that she loved enhanced her beauty. And she was beautiful indeed, bathed in that soft Florentine light which glorifies beautiful forms and fosters noble thoughts. There was a slight colour on her finely moulded cheeks. There was a laugh in her grey-blue eyes; and when she spoke she displayed the brilliant whiteness of her teeth. In a glance he appreciated all the graceful details of her supple figure. With one hand she held her parasol, with the other ungloved she was toying with some violets. Dechartre had a passion for beautiful hands. For him a hand had a character, a soul, a physiognomy as pronounced as a countenance. Thérèse's hands delighted him. They were at once sensual and spiritual. It seemed to him that they were bare from sheer voluptuousness. He adored their tapering fingers, their pink nails, their slender skin, marked with graceful lines, and rising gently and harmoniously towards the knuckles. He gazed entranced until she closed them on the handle of her parasol. Then, slightly behind her, he looked again. Her bust, her arms, graceful and cor-

*"Je pleure au pied de la Croix.
Avec moi pleure, aime et crois,
Sous cet arbre salutaire
Qui doit ombrager la terre."

rect in line, her well-developed hips, her fine ankles, her whole figure, in the beautiful form of a living amphora, pleased him.

"That black spot down there is the Boboli gardens, isn't it, Monsieur Dechartre? I saw them three years ago. There were hardly
any flowers then; and yet I loved them with their great dark trees."

That she should speak, that she should think, almost astonished
him. The clear tones of that voice came upon him as if he had never
heard them before.

He answered in the first words that occurred to him, and smiled
a forced smile, attempting to hide the stirrings of passion. He was
awkward and confused. She did not seem to notice it. That deep,
husky, faltering voice unconsciously caressed her. She, like him,
uttered commonplaces:

"What a fine view! What a lovely day."

<h1 style="text-align:center">XII</h1>

I N THE morning, with her head upon a pillow em-
broidered with a coat of arms in the form of a bell,
Thérèse was meditating on what she had seen on
the previous day: those finely painted Virgins surrounded by angels, those countless children, painted
or in sculpture, all beautiful, all happy, singing
simply through the town their alleluias of grace and
beauty. In the famous Brancacci Chapel, before
those frescoes pale and gleaming like a divine dawn, he had talked
of Masaccio, in such glowing words that she seemed to see the
youth, master of masters, with half open mouth and dark blue eyes,
dying in an ecstasy. And she was filled with adoration for the marvels of that dawn more delightful even than the noon-day. And for
her Dechartre was the soul of all these magnificent forms, the
vivifying spirit of all these good things. Through him and in him
she understood life and art. The sights of the world interested her
only so far as they interested him.

How had this sympathy grown up between them? She did not
exactly know. At first, when Paul Vence wished to introduce him
to her, she had no wish to know him, no presentiment that she
would like him. She recalled the beautiful bronzes and fine wax figures signed with his name that she had noticed in the Salon of the
Champ-de-Mars and at Durand-Ruel's. But she never imagined that
he himself would be interesting or more attractive than so many
artists and amateurs whom she invited to her luncheon parties. On
their first meeting he pleased her; and she made up her mind to
attract him and see him often. The evening that he dined at her
house she perceived that her liking for him was of an intellectual
kind which flattered her own *amour propre*. But soon afterwards

he irritated and vexed her by appearing too self-centred, too much occupied with himself and too little with her. She would have liked to agitate him. In this dissatisfied mood, and troubled by other things, feeling herself alone in the world, she had met him one evening, in front of the Museum of Religions, and he had talked of Ravenna and the empress in her tomb, on her golden chair. In the shades of night she had thought him charming, with his soft voice, and his pleasing glance, but too reserved and distant. He made her feel ill at ease, and, at that moment, walking along the terrace, by the box hedge, she could not decide whether she wanted to see him always or never again.

Since she had met him at Florence her one delight was to feel him near her and hear him talk. He made her life attractive by introducing into it variety, novelty, and colour. He initiated her into the delicate delicious melancholy of thought. He called into activity a taste for pleasures hitherto undreamed of. Now she was quite decided to retain him. But how? She foresaw difficulties; her lucid mind and her intense feeling called them all up before her. For a moment she tried to deceive herself; she argued that a dreamer, an enthusiast, wrapped up in the study of art, he had perhaps no violent passion for women, and would remain assiduous without becoming exacting. But immediately, shaking her beautiful head half lost in the ripples of her dark hair, she cast this idea from her. If Dechartre were not a lover then he lost all his charm for her. She dared not think of the future. She must live in the present; happy, but anxious and blindfold.

She was meditating thus in the shadow broken by arrows of light, when Pauline brought her letters with her morning tea. She recognised Le Ménil's writing on an envelope, stamped with the name of his club in the Rue Royale. She had expected to receive this letter, and now, as in her childhood when the infallible clock struck the hour of her music-lesson, she was merely surprised that what was bound to come had actually happened.

Robert's letter was full of just reproaches. Why had she gone away without telling him, without even leaving a line of farewell? Since his return to Paris, every morning he had expected the letter which had not arrived. How different from last year, when, two or three times a week, on awaking, he used to find such nice letters, so well expressed that he had regretted not being able to publish them. He had become very anxious and had called at her house.

"I was thunderstruck to hear of your departure. Your husband received me. He told me, that, following his advice, you had gone to pass the last weeks of winter at Miss Bell's, at Florence. For some time he had noticed you growing pale and thin. He had thought that a change of air would do you good. You had not wanted to go; but, as you became less and less well, he had succeeded in persuading you.

"I had not noticed that you were growing thin. On the contrary I thought you looking extremely well. Besides Florence is not a winter resort. I can't understand your departure; it troubles me very much. Write at once, I pray you, and reassure me. . . .

"I leave you to imagine how pleasant it is for me to hear of your movements from your husband and to receive his confidences! He is distressed by your absence and regrets that his public duties keep him in Paris. At the club I hear there is a chance of his entering the Government. I am astonished, for it is not usual for a leader of society to become a Minister."

Then he told her of his hunting. He had brought her three fox's skins, one very fine: the coat of a brave beast, he had dragged from his den, that had turned and bitten him in the hand. "After all," he said, "the creature was standing on his rights."

At Paris he was worried. A young cousin was standing for election to the club. He was afraid that he would be blackballed. But his candidature was already announced. And at this point he dared not advise him to withdraw; it would be assuming too great a responsibility. On the other hand, a defeat would be extremely disagreeable. He ended his letter by entreating her to write and to return soon.

Having read the letter, she tore it up slowly, threw it in the fire, and sadly, gloomily, and thoughtfully watched it burn.

Doubtless he was right. He said what he might be expected to say; he complained as he had a right to complain. How should she reply to him? Should she prolong the quarrel and continue to sulk? But it was no longer a question of sulking. The subject of their quarrel was so indifferent to her that she must needs think before she could remember it. Oh, no, she had lost all desire to vex him. On the contrary she felt kindly towards him. The realisation that he loved her trustfully and with an undisturbed tranquillity of mind saddened and alarmed her. He had not changed. He was the same as before. But she was no longer the same. They were separated now by things imperceptible and yet as strong as the vivifying or deadening effects of the atmosphere. When her maid came to dress her she had not yet begun to write the reply.

She was thinking anxiously: "He trusts me. His mind is at rest." That was what irritated her most. Simple persons mistrustful neither of themselves nor of other people always irritated her.

When she went down into the drawing-room of bells, she found Vivian Bell there writing; she said to her:

"Darling, would you like to know what I was doing while I was waiting for you? Nothing and yet everything. I was writing verses. Oh! darling, poetry must be the natural flowering of the soul."

Thérèse kissed Miss Bell, and, with her head on her friend's shoulder, she said:

"May I look?"

"Oh! yes, look, darling. They are verses written in the style of the popular songs of your country."

And Thérèse read:

> The milk-white stone she threw
> Pierced the lake-waters blue,
> And as its surface grew
> Still, took a darker hue.
> Then she, the stone that threw,
> Both shame and dolour knew
> The load from her heart to view
> The treacherous waters through.*

"The lines are figurative, Vivian; explain them to me."

"Why should I explain, why? A poetical figure may have many meanings. The one that you put into it will be the true meaning for you. But one is very clear, my love: that you must not lightly part with your heart's treasure."

The carriage was ready. They started as they had appointed to visit the Albertinelli Gallery, in the Via del Moro. The Prince expected them and Dechartre was to meet them at the Palace. On the way, as the carriage glided over the broad high-road, Vivian Bell talked in short, disjointed sentences uttered in a sing-song voice. Thus she gave expression to the gaiety of a temperament rare and precious. As they went down among the pink and white houses, with storied gardens, adorned with statues and fountains, she pointed out to her friend, the villa half hidden among the pine-trees, to which the ladies and gentlemen of the *Decameron* fled from the plague, which was ravaging Florence, and amused themselves by telling stories, gallant, facetious, or tragic. Then she disclosed a brilliant idea which had occurred to her the day before.

"You, darling, had gone to the Carmine with M. Dechartre. You had left Madame Marmet at Fiesole. She is a nice old lady of moderate opinions and excellent manners. She is full of stories of distinguished Parisians. And when she tells them she is like my cook, Pampaloni, when he sends up poached eggs: he does not salt them, but he puts the salt-cellar by the side of the dish. Madame Marmet is a sweet-tongued old lady. But the salt is there—in her eyes. It is Pampaloni's dish, my love; and every one seasons it to his taste. Oh! I am very fond of Madame Marmet. Yesterday, after you had gone, I found her sad and lonely in a corner of the drawing-room.

---

*Elle jeta la pierre blanche
A l'eau du lac bleu.
La pierre dans l'onde tranquille
Sombra peu à peu.
Alors la jeteuse de pierres
Eut honte et douleur
D'avoir mis dans le lac perfide
Le poids de son cœur.

She was thinking of her husband, and her thoughts were sad. I said to her: 'Would you like me to join you in your meditations on your husband? I shall be very pleased to do so. I have heard that he was a scholar and a member of the Paris Royal Society. Tell me about him.' She replied that he was devoted to the Etruscans and had consecrated his whole life to them. And, at once, darling, I venerated the memory of this Monsieur Marmet who lived for the Etruscans. And then a brilliant idea occurred to me. I said to Madame Marmet: 'At Fiesole, in the Palazzo Pretorio, we have a modest little Etruscan museum. Come with me and see it. Will you?' She replied that that was what she wanted to see more than anything in Italy. We went together to the Pretorio Palace; and we saw a lioness with her numerous young and little grotesque bronze men, either very fat or very thin. The Etruscans were a people who took their pleasures sadly. They used to make caricatures in brass. But these grotesque figures, some with protruding stomachs, others with an astonished air, displaying bare bones, Madame Marmet regarded with sorrowful admiration. She considered them as . . . there is an expressive French word I am trying to find . . . as the monuments and trophies of M. Marmet."

Madame Martin smiled. But she was depressed. The sky appeared to her dull, the streets ugly, the passers-by vulgar.

"Oh! darling, the Prince will be delighted to welcome you to his palace."

"I don't think so."

"But why, darling, why?"

"Because he does not like me."

Vivian Bell declared that on the contrary the Prince greatly admired Countess Martin.

The carriage stopped before the Albertinelli Palace. On the dark Gothic façade were bronze rings which in former days, on festive nights, were used to hold pine torches. At Florence these rings indicate the residences of the most illustrious families. They imparted to the palace an aggressively arrogant air. Inside it appeared empty, unused, and neglected. The Prince met them and conducted them, through unfurnished reception rooms, to the gallery. He apologised for showing them pictures which were not very pleasing. The collection had been made by Cardinal Giulio Albertinelli at the time of the vogue of Guido and Carracci. His ancestor had delighted in collecting the works of the Bolognese school. But he would show Madame Martin a few pictures which had found favour with Miss Bell; among others a Mantegna.

At a glance Countess Martin saw that the pictures were commonplace and of doubtful authenticity. She was bored at once by the numerous examples of Parrocel, all with figures in armour mounted on white horses amid darkness made visible by gleams of lurid light.

A footman brought in a card. The Prince read aloud the name of Jacques Dechartre. Just at that moment he had his back towards his two visitors. His countenance assumed that expression of malicious vexation which is to be seen on the statues of Roman emperors. Dechartre was on the landing of the state stair-case.

The Prince advanced to meet him with a languishing smile. He was no longer Nero, but Antinous.

"Yesterday I myself invited M. Dechartre to come to the Albertinelli Palace," said Miss Bell to the Prince. "I knew I should give you pleasure. He wanted to see your pictures."

And it was true that Dechartre had wished to come in order to meet Madame Martin. Now all four, they were wandering past the Guidos and Albanis.

Miss Bell was chirping to the Prince pretty things about the old men and virgins whose mantles were being blown by a motionless tempest. Dechartre, pale and nervous, came near to Thérèse and whispered:

"This gallery is the rubbish-heap on which the picture-dealers of the whole world have deposited the refuse of their stock. And here the Prince succeeds in selling what the Jews have failed to dispose of."

He took her to a Holy Family, displayed on an easel draped in green velvet and bearing in the margin the name of Michael Angelo.

"I have seen that Holy Family in picture shops at London, Bâle, and Paris. As the dealers have not been able to get for it the twenty-five louis it is worth, they have commissioned the last of the Albertinelli to sell it for fifty thousand francs."

The Prince, seeing them whispering together, and guessing what they were saying, approached very graciously.

"A replica of this picture has been offered for sale everywhere. I don't maintain that this is an original. But it has always been in my family, and old inventories attribute it to Michael Angelo. That's all I can say."

The Prince turned to Miss Bell, who was looking for Primitives.

Dechartre was ill at ease. Since yesterday he had been thinking of Thérèse. He had dreamed of her all night and conjured up her image. Now he found her delightful, but delightful in a different way, and even more desirable than she had appeared to him in the visions of the night; her materialised form more irresistibly attractive, her soul more mysterious and inscrutable. She was sad; she appeared to him cold and absent-minded. He told himself that he was nothing to her, that he was becoming importunate and ridiculous. He grew gloomy and irritable. He murmured bitterly in her ear:

"I had thought better of it. I didn't want to come. Then why am I here?"

She understood immediately what he meant, that he feared her now, and so was impatient, shy and awkward. She liked him thus, and was grateful to him for the agitation and desire, with which she saw she inspired him.

Her heart beat quickly. But, pretending to understand that he was vexed at having taken the trouble to come and see bad pictures, she replied that the gallery was indeed very uninteresting.

Already terrified at the idea of displeasing her, he was reassured and really believed that, absent and indifferent, she had not remarked either the tone or the significance of the words that had escaped from him.

"Very uninteresting," he repeated.

The Prince, who was entertaining his two visitors to lunch, invited their friend also. Dechartre excused himself. He was going out, when, in the great drawing-room empty of everything but consoles on which were piled confectioners' boxes, he found himself alone with Madame Martin. He had thought of avoiding her, now his one idea was when he should see her again. He reminded her that on the morrow she was to visit the Bargello.

"You were kind enough to say I might come with you."

She asked him if he had not found her dull and heavy that day. Oh! no, but he had thought her rather sad.

"Alas!" he added, "your sadness, your joys, I have not even the right to know them."

She turned round upon him quickly, almost severely, saying:

"You surely don't think I am going to make you my confidant?"

And she left him abruptly.

XIII

FTER dinner, in the drawing-room of bells, under the lamps, the deep shades of which permitted but a half light to reach the long-handed Virgins of Sienna, kind Madame Marmet was warming herself at the stove with a white cat on her knee. The evening was cold. Madame Martin was smiling happily, in spite of fatigue, and gazing mentally at the purple hill-tops in the clear atmosphere and at the ancient oaks twisting their huge branches across the road. With Miss Bell, Dechartre, and Madame Marmet she had been to the Certosa of Ema. And now, in the intoxication of the day's memories, she forgot the cares of two days ago—importunate letters, reproaches from a distance; and it seemed to her as if there were nothing in the world but carved and painted cloisters, with a well in the grass-grown court, red roofed villages, and roads, where, soothed by flattering words, she had watched the dawn of spring. Dechartre had just roughly modelled a little Beatrice in wax for Miss Bell. Vivian was painting angels. Lazily leaning over her, in an effeminate pose, Prince Albertinelli was stroking his beard and casting languishing glances around him.

Replying to a remark of Vivian Bell's on marriage and love:

"A woman must choose," he said. "With a man whom women like she is never at rest. With a man whom women do not like, she is never happy."

"Darling," asked Miss Bell, "which lot would you choose for a very dear friend?"

"Vivian, I should wish my friend to be happy, I should wish her also to be free from anxiety. And she would wish to be so and yet to hate treachery, humiliating suspicion, and mean mistrust."

"But, darling, since the Prince said that a woman could not at once enjoy happiness and peace of mind, say which you would choose for your friend."

"One does not choose, Vivian, one does not choose. Don't make me say what I think of marriage."

At this moment Choulette appeared, with the magnificent air of one of those beggars who honour the gates of little towns. He had just been playing cards with peasants in a Fiesole wine-shop.

"Here is M. Choulette," said Miss Bell. "He will tell us what to think of marriage. I am ready to listen to him as to an oracle. He does not see what we see, and he sees what we do not see. Monsieur Choulette, what do you think of marriage?"

He sat down and raised a Socratic finger.

"Do you speak, Mademoiselle, of the solemn union between man and woman? In this sense marriage is a sacrament. Hence it is nearly always sacrilege. As for civil marriage, that is a mere formality. The importance attached to it by present day society is a folly which would have appeared laughable to women of the old *régime*. We owe this prejudice with many others to that *bourgeois* movement, to the rise of financiers and lawyers, which is termed the Revolution and which seems admirable to those who profit by it. It is the fruitful mother of all foolishness. Every day for a century she has been bringing forth new absurdities. Civil marriage is nothing but one of many registrations, instituted by the state in order that it may be informed concerning the condition of its citizens: for in a civilised state every one must have his label. And of what value are all these labels in the eyes of the Son of God? Morally, this entry in a register is not even enough to induce a woman to take a lover. Who would scruple to break an oath sworn before a mayor? In order to taste the true joys of adultery one must be pious."

"But, sir," said Thérèse, "we have been married at church."

Then in a tone of deep sincerity, she added:

"I cannot understand how any man or woman, having attained to years of discretion, can commit the folly of marriage."

The Prince looked at her suspiciously. He was quick witted, but he was incapable of believing that any one ever spoke disinterestedly, merely to express general ideas and without some definite object. He imagined that Countess Martin had discovered his scheme and determined to thwart it. And, as already he was thinking of defending himself and taking his revenge, he ogled her and addressed her with affectionate gallantry.

"You, Madame, display the pride of all beautiful and intelligent Frenchwomen, who chafe beneath the yoke. Frenchwomen love liberty, and not one of them is worthier of it than you. I myself have lived a little in France. I have known and admired the fashionable society of Paris in drawing-rooms, at dinner tables, in public assemblies, and sports. But among our mountains, beneath our olive-trees, we relapse into rusticity. We return to our country manners, and marriage seems to us a sweet romantic idyll."

Vivian Bell examined the model which Dechartre had left on the table.

"Oh! that is the living image of Beatrice, I am sure. And do you know, Monsieur Dechartre, there are wicked men who say that Beatrice never existed?"

Choulette declared that he was one of those wicked men. He did not believe that Beatrice existed any more than those other ladies in whose personalities the old love poets expressed some ridiculously subtle scholastic idea.

Intolerant of any praise not bestowed on himself, jealous of Dante, and of the whole universe, and also a keen man of letters, he thought he had discovered a joint in the armour, and struck:

"I suspect," he said, "that the young sister of the angels never lived except in the dry imagination of the illustrious poet. Even there she appears as a pure allegory, or rather a mathematical calculation or an astrological exercise. Dante, who between ourselves was a good doctor of Bologna, and had several bees in his poked bonnet, believed in the virtue of numbers. This passionate geometrician dreamt in figures, and his Beatrice is the flower of his arithmetic. That's all!"

And he lit his pipe.

Vivian Bell protested:

"Oh! don't talk like that, Monsieur Choulette. You hurt me. If our friend M. Gebhart heard you, he would be very angry. To punish you, Prince Albertinelli shall read you the canto in which Beatrice explains the spots in the moon. Take the *Divina Commedia*, Eusebio. It is that white book on the table. Open it and read."

During the reading under the lamp, Dechartre, sitting on the sofa near Countess Martin, spoke enthusiastically of Dante in whispers, calling him the greatest sculptor among poets. He reminded Thérèse of the picture they had seen together two days ago, at Santa Maria, on the Servites' door, a half-effaced fresco, in which it was difficult to distinguish the poet with his laurel-wreathed hood, Florence, and the seven circles. Enough of it remained however to enrapture the artist. But she had not been able to distinguish anything; it had not appealed to her. And then she confessed that Dante was too gloomy and attracted her but little. Dechartre, who had grown accustomed to her sharing all his poetical and artistic ideas, felt surprised and vexed. He said aloud:

"There are things both great and strong that you do not realise."

Miss Bell, raising her head, asked what were those things that darling did not realise; and, when she heard that one was the genius of Dante, she exclaimed with simulated wrath:

"Oh, don't you honour the father, the master worthy of all praise, the River God? I don't like you any more, darling. I detest you."

And, as a reproach to Choulette and Countess Martin, she recalled the piety of that Florentine citizen who took from the altar the candles lit in honour of Jesus Christ and placed them before Dante's bust.

After this interruption the Prince had resumed his reading:

"Within itself the ever-during pearl
Received us;"*

Dechartre insisted on wishing to make Thérèse admire what she did not understand. For her sake certainly he would have sacrificed Dante and all the poets, with the rest of the universe. But by her side, in the ardour of his desire, beholding her tranquil, he was irritated by her smiling beauty. He felt bound to impose on her his ideas, his artistic passions, even his fancies and caprices. In a low voice and in quick argumentative words he remonstrated with her.

"How vehement you are," she said.

Then he whispered in her ear, in a passionate voice which he vainly sought to moderate:

"You must take my soul with me. It would give me no joy to win you with a soul that was not my own."

At these words there passed over Thérèse a little shudder of fear and joy.

*"Paradiso," Canto ii. Cary's Translation. W. S.

XIV

HE next day, on awaking, she told herself that she must answer Robert's letter. It was raining. Languidly she listened to the raindrops falling on the terrace. With thoughtful and delicate taste, Vivian Bell had had the table furnished with artistic writing materials: sheets of paper in imitation of the parchment of missals, and others pale violet glistening with silver; celluloid penholders, white and light, requiring to be used like brushes; and purple ink, turning on the page into an azure shot with gold. Such precious and unusual equipments irritated Thérèse, who considered them out of keeping with the simple direct letter she wanted to write. When she perceived that the name of "friend," by which she addressed Robert in the first line, cut a curious figure on the silvered paper, outlined in shades of dove colour and mother-of-pearl, she half smiled. She found the first sentences difficult. The rest she hurried over. She wrote at length of Vivian Bell and Prince Albertinelli, a little of Choulette, and said that she had met Dechartre, who was passing through Florence. She praised a few pictures in the museums, but without enthusiasm and merely to fill the pages. She knew that Robert did not understand pictures, that the only one he admired was a little cuirassier by Detaille, bought at Goupil's. In her mind's eye she saw once more that little cuirassier, which he had proudly shown her one day, in his bedroom near the mirror, underneath his family portraits. Looked at from a distance it all seemed mean, wearisome, and sad. She ended her letter with a few kind friendly words which were sincere. She had really never before felt so calmly benignant towards her lover. In four pages she had said little and implied less. She had merely told him that she would stay another month at Florence, where the air was doing her good. Afterwards she wrote to her father, her husband, and Princess Seniavine. With her letters in her hand she went downstairs. In the hall she placed three of them on the silver salver intended for letters. Mistrusting Madame Marmet's curious eyes she put Le Ménil's letter in her pocket, intending to post it herself when out walking.

Almost immediately Dechartre arrived to go with the three friends into the town. While he was waiting for a moment in the hall he noticed the letters in the salver.

Without believing in the slightest in the reading of character by means of handwriting, he became aware of the form of the letters, which assumed a certain grace as if they were a kind of drawing. Because it was a memorial, a sort of relic of Thérèse, her writing charmed him, and he appreciated also its striking frankness and bold simplicity with an admiration entirely sensual. He looked at the addresses without reading them.

That morning they visited Santa Maria Novella, where Countess Martin had been already with Madame Marmet. But Miss Bell had reproached them with not having seen the beautiful Ginevra de' Benci, in a fresco in the choir. "You must see that figure of the dawn in the fine morning light," said Vivian. While the poetess and Thérèse were talking together, Dechartre, attached to Madame Marmet, was listening patiently to anecdotes of academicians dining with fashionable ladies, and was sympathising with the good lady in her vain endeavours to procure a tulle veil. She could not find any to her liking in the Florence shops, and she longed for the Rue du Bac.

Coming out of the church they passed the booth of the cobbler whom Choulette had adopted as his master. The good man was patching a country-man's boots. The pot of basil was at his side, and the sparrow with the wooden leg chirped close by.

Madame Martin asked the old man if he were quite well, if he had enough work to do, and if he were happy. To all these questions he replied the charming Italian "Yes," the *Sì* coming musically from his toothless mouth. She made him tell them his sparrow's story. One day the poor little creature had put his foot into the boiling wax.

"I made my little friend a wooden leg out of a match, and now he is able to perch on my shoulder as of old."

"He is a kind old man," said Miss Bell, "who teaches M. Choulette wisdom. At Athens there was a cobbler, named Simon, who wrote works on philosophy and was the friend of Socrates. I have always thought M. Choulette resembled Socrates."

Thérèse asked the shoemaker to tell them his name and his story. His name was Serafino Stoppini and he came from Stia. He was old. His life had been full of trouble.

He put back his spectacles on to his forehead, revealing his blue kindly eyes, growing dim beneath their reddened lids:

"I had a wife and children, now I am alone. I have known things, which now I have forgotten."

Miss Bell and Madame Marmet had gone to buy the veil.

"His tools, a handful of nails, the tub in which he soaks his leather, and a pot of basil are all he has in the world," thought Thérèse, "and yet he is happy."

"This plant smells sweet, and soon it will flower," she said.

"If the poor little thing flowers, it will die," he replied.

When she went away, Thérèse left a coin on the table.

Dechartre was near her. Seriously, almost sternly, he said to her:

"You knew it?"

She looked at him and waited.

He concluded:

". . . . that I love you."

For a moment she continued to look at him silently with bright eyes and quivering lids. Then she bowed her head as a sign of affirmation. And, without his attempting to detain her, she went towards Miss Bell and Madame Marmet, who were waiting at the end of the street.

XV

N LEAVING Dechartre, Thérèse went to lunch with her friend and Madame Marmet at the house of an old Florentine lady, whom Victor-Emmanuel had loved when he was Duke of Savoy. For thirty years she had never once quitted her palace on the Arno, where painted and powdered, wearing a violet wig, she played upon the guitar in her great white halls.

She received the highest society in Florence, and Miss Bell frequently went to see her. During lunch, this recluse of eighty-seven questioned Countess Martin concerning the fashionable Paris world, the life of which she followed in newspapers and conversation with a frivolity which was rendered august by its per-. sistence. In her solitude she continued to cherish a respect and adoration for pleasure.

Coming out of the palazzo, in order to avoid the wind, which was blowing across the river, the keen *libeccio*, Miss Bell took her friends through the old narrow streets, lined with houses of dark stone suddenly opening on a broad space where a hill with three slender trees stands forth in the clear atmosphere. As they went, Vivian pointed out to her friend, on sordid façades from which red rags were hanging, some precious statue, a Virgin, a lily, a St. Catherine beneath a scroll of leaves. They walked down the little streets of the ancient city as far as the church of Or San Michele, where it had been agreed that Dechartre should meet them.

Thérèse was thinking of him now with intense interest. Madame Marmet was bent on finding a veil; she had been encouraged to hope that there might be one on the Corso. Her errand reminded her of the absent-mindedness of M. Lagrange who, one day, when he was lecturing, took from his pocket a veil with gold beads and wiped his forehead with it, mistaking it for his handkerchief. His astonished hearers giggled. It was a veil belonging to his niece, Mademoiselle Jeanne Michot, who had confided it to his care when he had taken her to the theatre on the previous evening. And Madame Marmet explained how, finding it in his overcoat pocket, he had taken it with him, intending to give it back to his niece, and how, by mistake, he had unfolded it and waved it before his smiling audience.

The name of Lagrange reminded Thérèse of the comet predicted by the scholar, and she said to herself with a sad irony, that now was the time for it to come and end the world and relieve her from embarrassment. But, above the beautiful walls of the old church, she beheld the sky gleaming and cruelly blue, swept by the wind blowing in from the sea.

Miss Bell directed her attention to one of the bronze statues, which, in carved niches, adorn the façade of the church.

"Look, darling, how proud and young that St. George is. St. George used to be a girl's ideal knight. You remember how Juliet cried when she saw Romeo: 'What a handsome St. George!' "*

But darling thought he looked conventional, commonplace, and obstinate. At that moment, she remembered the letter in her pocket.

"I think there is M. Dechartre," said kind Madame Marmet.

He had been looking for them in the church, near Orcagna's shrine. He ought to have remembered how irresistible Miss Bell always found Donatello's St. George. He also admired the famous figure. But the frankless conventional figure of St. Mark appealed to him more. They might see it in its niche on the left, near that little street, overspanned by a massive arched buttress, near the old House of the Wool-staplers.

As they were approaching the statue, Thérèse saw a letter-box in the wall of the narrow street at the end of which stood the saint. Meanwhile Dechartre, standing so as to have a good view of his St. Mark, was speaking of him as if he were an intimate friend.

"I always come to him before going anywhere else in Florence. Only once did I fail. But he will forgive me; he is an excellent man. He is not appreciated by the majority and attracts little attention. But I delight in his company. He is alive. I can understand why Donatello, after having created his soul, cried: 'Mark, why don't you speak?' "

Madame Marmet, tired of admiring St. Mark and feeling nipped by the *libeccio,* carried away Miss Bell to help her buy the veil in the Via dei Calzaioli.

They left "darling" and Dechartre alone to continue their worship of St. Mark. They arranged to meet at the milliner's.

"I have always loved him," continued the sculptor, "because I recognise here more than in the St. George, the hand and soul of Donatello, who was all his life a poor and honest workman. And to-day I love him more intensely, because, in his venerable touching candour, he reminds me of the old cobbler of Santa Maria Novella, to whom you were talking so sweetly this morning."

"Ah!" she said. "I have forgotten his name. We and M. Chou-

*I have been unable to discover this reference in Shakespeare's *Romeo and Juliet.*—W. S.

lette call him Quentin Matsys because he reminds us of the old men that artist painted."

As they turned the church corner to inspect the façade opposite the old Wool-staplers' House, bearing the heraldic lamb on its red-tiled gable, she found herself close to the letter-box, so covered with grime and rust that it looked as if the postman never cleared it. She slipped in her letter, under the ingenuous eyes of St. Mark.

Dechartre saw her and immediately felt pierced to the heart. He tried to talk, to laugh, but he could not forget the gloved hand posting the letter. He remembered having seen Thérèse's letters in the morning on the hall table. Why had she not put that one with the others? It was not difficult to guess.

He stood still, lost in thought, gazing vacantly. He tried to re-assure himself: perhaps it was only an unimportant letter she wanted to hide from Madame Marmet's irritating curiosity.

"Monsieur Dechartre, it must be time for us to go and meet our friends at the milliner's on the Corso."

Perhaps she was writing to Madame Schmoll who had quarrelled with Madame Marmet. And immediately he realised the improbability of such suppositions.

It was quite clear. She had a lover. She was writing to him. Perhaps she was saying: "I have seen Dechartre to-day, the poor fellow is in love with me." But whatever she wrote, she had a lover. He had never dreamt of such a thing. The idea of her belonging to another caused him agony of soul and body. And the vision of that hand, that little hand posting the letter, remained before his eyes and seemed to burn them.

She could not imagine why he had suddenly become silent and gloomy. But she guessed at once, when she saw him look anxiously at the letter-box. She thought it strange that without having the right he should be jealous; but it did not displease her.

When they reached the Corso, in the distance they saw Miss Bell and Madame Marmet coming out of the milliner's.

Dechartre said to Thérèse in a voice at once imperious and entreating:

"I want to speak to you. I must see you alone; come to-morrow evening, at six o'clock to the Lungarno Acciajoli."

She said nothing.

XVI

HEN, wrapped in her rough coat, she reached the Lungarno Acciajoli, about half-past six, Dechartre welcomed her with a humble and radiant glance which touched her heart.

The setting sun was shedding a purple hue over the swollen waters of the Arno. For a moment they were silent. Following the monotonous line of palaces, they walked towards the Ponte Vecchio. She was the first to speak:

"You see I have come. I thought it my duty to come. I am not innocent of what has happened. I know it: I have done everything in order that your attitude towards me should be what it is now. My conduct has inspired you with thoughts which would not have otherwise occurred to you."

He seemed not to understand. She resumed:

"I was selfish, I was indiscreet. I liked you; your intelligence appealed to me; I could not do without you. I did everything in my power to attract and retain you. I flirted with you. But not in coldness of heart or intending to deceive. Still I flirted."

He shook his head, denying that he had ever perceived it.

"Yes, I flirted. But it is not my custom. However, I flirted with you. I don't say that you attempted to take advantage of it, as you had a perfect right to do, or that you were puffed up by it. I never thought you vain. Possibly you did not perceive it. High-minded men sometimes lack insight. But I know well that I was not what I should have been. And I ask you to forgive me. That is why I came. Let us remain good friends while we may."

With a sorrowful tenderness he told her that he loved her. In the beginning his love had been sweet and delightful. All he wanted was to see her and see her again. But soon she had agitated him, rent his heart, made him beside himself. His passion had broken forth suddenly and violently one day on the terrace at Fiesole. And now he lacked the courage to suffer in silence. He cried out for her help. He had come with no settled plan. If he had told her of his passion it was because he could not help it and in spite of himself, because of his overpowering craving to speak of her and to her, since for him she alone existed. His life was lived in her. She must know then that he loved her, not with any mild, indefinite love, but with an all-consuming, cruel passion. Alas! His imagination was precise. He knew exactly and always what he wanted, and it was torture to him.

And then it seemed to him that together they would have joys which made life worth living. Their existence would be a beautiful but secret work of art. They would think, they would comprehend, they would feel in unison. Theirs would be a wonderful world of emotions and ideas.

"We would make life a beautiful garden."

She pretended to interpret this dream in all innocence.

"You know how strongly your mind appeals to me. It has become necessary to me to see you and hear you. I have shown you this only too plainly. Be assured of my friendship, and be at rest."

She offered him her hand. He did not take it, and replied abruptly:

"I will not have your friendship. I will not have it. You must be mine entirely, or I must never see you again. Why with mocking words do you offer me your hand? Whether you intended it or not you have inspired me with a passionate desire, a fatal longing. You have become my heart's anguish and torture. And now you ask me to be your friend. It is now that you are cruel and a flirt. If you cannot love me, let me leave you; I will go, I do not know where, to forget you and hate you. For in the depths of my heart I feel towards you both anger and hatred. Oh! I love you, I love you."

She believed what he said. She feared lest he should go away; and she dreaded the sad dulness of life without him.

"I have found you in my life. I will not lose you. No, I will not," she said.

Timid, passionate, he tried to murmur something, but the words stuck in his throat. Darkness was descending on the distant mountains, and in the east, over the hill of San Miniato, were fading the last gleams of the setting sun.

She spoke again.

"If you had known my life, if you had seen how empty it was before you came into it, you would know what you are to me, and you would not think of leaving me."

But the even tones of her voice and measured step upon the pavement irritated him. He cried out that he was in anguish; his desire burnt within him; this one thought possessed and tortured him; always and everywhere, by night, by day he saw her, he called her, he stretched out his arms to her. The divine passion had entered into his soul.

"Like incense I breathe the charm of your intellect, the inspiration of your courage, the pride of your soul. When you speak I seem to see your soul on your lips, and I die because I cannot press mine to yours. Your soul is for me but the expression of your beauty. Deep down within me there slumbered the instincts of primitive man. You have awakened them. And I feel that I love you with the simplicity of a savage."

She looked at him tenderly and in silence. Just then they saw lights and heard mournful songs approaching them out of the darkness. And then, like phantoms, driven by the wind, there appeared before them black-robed penitents. The crucifix was carried before them. They were the Brothers of the Misericordia. With their faces hidden by cowls they were holding lighted torches and singing psalms. They were bearing a corpse to the cemetery. It was the Italian custom for the funeral procession to take place at night and to pass along rapidly. On the deserted quay there appeared cross, coffin, and banners. Jacques and Thérèse stood against the wall to let pass the crowd of priests, choristers, and hooded figures, and, in their midst, importunate Death, whom no one welcomes on this pleasure-loving earth. The black stream had passed. Weeping women ran after the coffin borne by weird shapes in hob-nailed boots.

Thérèse sighed:

"Of what avail is it to torment ourselves in this world?"

He appeared not to hear her, and resumed in a calmer voice:

"Before I knew you I was not unhappy. I loved life. It inspired me with dreams and with curiosity. I delighted in form and in the spirit of form, in the appearance which charms and soothes. To see and to dream were my joys. I enjoyed everything, and I was independent of everything. I was borne up on the wings of my insatiable curiosity. I was interested in everything; I longed for nothing: and it is only desire that makes us suffer. I realise that to-day. Mine was not a melancholy disposition. I was happy without knowing it. I possessed little, but all that was necessary to make me contented with life. Now that has departed from me. My pleasures, the interest I took in life and in art, the joy of expressing in material form the visions of my brain, you have robbed me of them all, and without leaving me one regret. I no longer desire my liberty. I would not return to the tranquillity of past years. It seems as if I never lived till I met you. And now that I know what life really is, I can live neither with you nor away from you. I am more wretched than the beggars we saw on the road to Ema. They at least had the air to breathe. But I have not that, for you are the breath of my life, and you I have not. Nevertheless I rejoice that I have known you. It is all that counts in my life. Just now I thought I hated you. I was mistaken. I adore you, and I bless you for the suffering you have caused me. I love everything that comes from you."

They were approaching the dark trees at the entrance to the Porta San Niccola. On the other side of the river the land looked vague and infinite in the darkness. Seeing him once more calm and gentle, she thought that his passion, existing only in his imagination, had been appeased by expression and that his desire was merely a dream. She had not expected his resignation to come so quickly. She was almost disappointed at having escaped the danger she had so greatly feared.

She now offered him her hand more boldly than at first.

"Come, let us be friends. It is late. We must return, and you must take me to my carriage, which I have left on the Piazza della Signoria. I shall always be your good friend as I was before. You have not vexed me."

But he led her towards the open country, along the river bank, which became more and more deserted.

"No, I will not let you go before saying what was in my mind. But I cannot express myself; the words will not come. I love you; I want you. I long to know that you are mine. I swear to you that I will not pass another night in the horror of doubt."

He took her and clasped her in his arms. With his face close to hers he gazed through her veil and looked deep into her eyes.

"You must love me. I will it, you also have willed it. Say that you are mine. Say it!"

Having gently freed herself from his embrace, she replied in a weak hesitating voice:

"I cannot. I cannot. You see I am quite frank with you. Just now I told you that you had not vexed me. But I cannot do as you wish."

And thinking of the absent lover awaiting her, she repeated:

"I cannot."

Bending over her, anxiously he questioned her wavering downcast glance.

"Why? You love me. I see it. Why do me the wrong of refusing to be mine?"

He drew her towards him and tried to kiss her lips beneath her veil. This time she withdrew quickly and decisively.

"I can't. Don't ask me. I can't be yours."

His lips trembled. His whole countenance was convulsed. He cried:

"You have a lover and you love him. Why do you trifle with me?"

"I swear that I never thought of trifling with you, and that if ever in this world I were to love it would be you."

But he no longer listened to her.

"Leave me. Leave me," he cried.

And he fled through the darkness. The Arno had overflowed its banks on to the pasture lands. There the water lay in shallow sheets, on to which the half veiled moon cast its quivering beams. Past these lagoons and over the muddy fields he hastened sadly and distractedly.

She was afraid and uttered a cry. She called him. But he neither replied nor turned his head. With alarming decision he continued on his way. She ran after him. With her feet bruised by the stones, her skirt heavy with water, she rejoined him and drew him towards her.

"What were you going to do?"

Then as he looked into her eyes, he read there the fear that had possessed her.

"Don't be afraid. I did not see where I was going. I assure you I was not seeking death. Set your mind at rest. I am despairing, but I am calm. I fled from you. Forgive me. But I could not bear to look at you. Leave me, I entreat of you. Good-bye."

Weak and intensely agitated, she replied:

"Come. We will see what can be done."

But he remained sorrowful and silent.

She repeated:

"Come."

She took his arm. The gentle touch of her hand cheered him.

"Will you?" he asked.

"I am determined not to drive you to despair."

"Will you promise?"

"I must."

Even in her anguish of spirit she half smiled to think how quickly his wildness had given him his desire.

"To-morrow?" he asked.

She replied eagerly with an instinct of self-defence:

"No, not to-morrow."

"You don't love me. You regret your promise," he said.

"No. I don't regret it, but . . ."

He implored her, entreated her. She looked at him for a moment, turned away her head, hesitated, and then said in a very low voice:

"Saturday."

<h1 style="text-align:center">XVII</h1>

FTER dinner Miss Bell was drawing profiles of bearded Etruscans on canvas for a cushion Madame Marmet was to embroider. Prince Albertinelli was choosing the wool with a feminine eye for colour. The evening was well advanced when Choulette appeared. As was his wont he had been playing *brissola** at an eating house with the cook. He was gay and god-like in the exuberance of his wit. He sat down on the sofa, by Madame Martin, and looked at her tenderly. His green eyes sparkled voluptuously. His compliments, poetical and picturesque, had the air of a caress. It was as if he were composing a love-song in her honour. In short, abrupt, curiously turned sentences he explained the charm by which she attracted him.

"He too," she thought.

*A game at cards.—W. S.

And she amused herself by teasing him. Had he not discovered
in the lower quarters of Florence one of those persons whose society
he mostly enjoyed, she inquired. For his preferences in such matters
were well known. It was useless for him to deny it; every one knew
where he had found the cord of his third order. His friends had
seen him on the Boulevard Saint-Michel with women of the street.
And he had avowed his interest in these miserable creatures in his
finest poems.

"Oh! Monsieur Choulette, by all I hear your friends are very
wicked."

He replied solemnly:

"Madame, you may if you like throw in my face calumnies
originating with M. Paul Vence. I will not defend myself. That you
should be convinced of my chastity and pure-mindedness matters
little. But do not lightly judge those whom you call wretched, whom

you should regard as holy because they are miserable. The outcast
is the docile clay in the potter's hand, the sin offering at the
sacrificial altar. Prostitutes are nearer God than honest women:
they have lost all vainglory; they have been shorn of pride. They
are unadorned by those empty nothings, the matron's boast. They
possess humility, that is the corner-stone of the heavenly house of
virtue. After a brief repentence they will be be first in the Kingdom
of Heaven; for, committed without malice and without joy, their
sins are their own atonement. Their vices, in that they are sorrows,
have the merit of all suffering. Slaves to the brutality of passion,
these women have denied themselves pleasure. Thus they resemble
men who have become celibate that they may enter the Kingdom
of God. Like us they are sinners, but by their shame they atone for
their sins; suffering purifies like fire. Therefore the first prayer
they address to Him God will hear. He has prepared for them a
throne on the right hand of the Father. In the Kingdom of God, the
queen and the empress will be happy to sit at the feet of women
of the street. For do not imagine that the heavenly house is constructed on any human plan. It is different in every detail,
Madame."

Nevertheless he agreed that there was more than one road leading to salvation. There was the road of love.

"Men's love," he said, "is base. It is but a steep and stony path,
but it leads to God."

The Prince had risen. Kissing Miss Bell's hand, he said:

"Till Saturday."

"Yes, till the day after to-morrow, till Saturday," repeated
Vivian.

Thérèse shuddered. Saturday! They spoke so calmly of Saturday
as if it were an ordinary day and near at hand. Until then she had
not let herself believe that Saturday would come so soon or so
naturally.

It was half an hour since the party had broken up. Thérèse, tired
and weary, was lying in bed thinking, when she heard a knock at
her bedroom door. It opened, and Vivian's little head appeared
round the great lemon-trees of the portière.

"Am I disturbing you, darling? Are you sleepy?"

No, "darling" was not sleepy. She raised herself on her elbow.
Vivian sat down on the bed, upon which her slender form made no
impression.

"Darling, I know that you are very sensible. Oh! I am sure of it.
You are as sensible as Mr. Sadler, the violinist, is musical. Sometimes he plays a little out of tune on purpose. And you when you
make a mistake indulge in the pleasure of a virtuoso. Oh! darling,
you are a person of sound judgment. And I come to ask your
advice."

Surprised and a little anxious, Thérèse declared that she was not sensible. She denied it absolutely. But Vivian did not listen to her.

"I have read François Rabelais a great deal, my love. Rabelais and Villon taught me French. They are grand old masters of language. But, darling, do you know *Pantagruel?* Oh! *Pantagruel* is a fine and beautiful town, full of palaces, splendid in the dawn, notwithstanding that the sweepers have yet to arrive to remove the filth and the servants to wash the marble pavements. No, darling, the sweepers have not yet removed the filth, and the servants have not yet washed the marble pavements. And I have noticed that French ladies don't read *Pantagruel.* You don't know it? Well, that does not matter. In *Pantagruel,* Panurge asks whether he should marry, and he appears ridiculous, my love. Well, I am as absurd as he, for I ask you the same question."

Thérèse replied with ill-concealed constraint:

"As for that, my dear. Don't ask me. I have already told you my opinion."

"But, darling, you merely said that men do wrong to marry. I can't take that advice for myself."

Madame Martin looked at Miss Bell's little close clipped head, which seemed in some curious manner to suggest the bashfulness of love.

Kissing her, she said:

"There isn't a man in the world distinguished enough and charming enough for you."

Then gravely and tenderly she continued:

"You are not a child: if you love and are loved, do what you think right, and don't complicate love by material interests which have nothing to do with feeling. That is the advice of a friend."

For a moment Miss Bell failed to understand. Then she blushed and rose. She was shocked.

XVIII

AT FOUR o'clock on Saturday Thérèse went to the English cemetery, according to her promise. At the gate she met Dechartre, grave and agitated. He said little. She was glad he did not appear elated. He led her past the cemetery walls to a narrow street she did not know. "Via Alfieri," she read on a tablet. After walking a few steps, he stopped in front of a dark entry.

"Here it is," he said.

She looked at him with infinite sadness.

"Do you want me to go in?"

She saw that he was resolute, and she followed him silently into the damp gloom of the passage. He crossed a grass-grown courtyard. At the end was a little house with three windows, with pillars and a pediment carved with goats and nymphs. On the moss-grown doorstep, slowly and with a grating sound, he turned the key in the lock.

"It is rusty," he murmured.

"In this country all keys are rusty," she replied mechanically.

They went up the staircase, so tranquil beneath its Greek moulding, that it seemed to have forgotten the sound of footsteps. He opened a door and showed Thérèse into the room. Without staying to examine it, she went straight to the open window, looking on the cemetery. Over the wall rose the tops of pine-trees, which, in that country, have no funereal aspect; for their mourning casts no gloom over joy, and the sweetness of life is felt even in the grass growing over the tomb. He took her by the hand and led her to an arm-chair. She remained standing, gazing round the room, which he had arranged so that she might feel at home. A few strips of old printed calico represented on the walls the melancholy delights of past gaiety. In one corner he had hung up a faded pastel they had looked at together in an antiquary's shop, and which she had called the shade of Rosalba on account of its vanishing grace. One or two white chairs and a grandmother's arm-chair; on the table a few painted cups and some Venetian glass. In the corners were screens of coloured paper, painted with masks, grotesque figures, and sheep-cotes, representing the gay life of Florence, Bologna, and Venice, in the days of the grand-dukes and the last doges. She noticed that he had carefully hidden the bed behind one of these gaily painted screens. A mirror, a carpet, and hangings, that was all. He had not dared to procure more in a town where ingenious dealers were always on his track.

He shut the window and lit the fire. She sat down in the arm-chair; and, while she sat there stiffly, he knelt before her, took her hands, kissed them, and gazed at her long with an admiration proud yet fearful. Then he bent down and kissed the tip of her shoe.

"What are you doing?"

"I am kissing the feet that brought you here."

He rose, drew her gently to him, and kissed her long on the lips.

She remained passive, her head thrown back, her eyes closed; her toque slipped off, her hair fell down.

She yielded without resistance.

Two hours later, when the setting sun was casting its long rays over the pavement, Thérèse, who had wished to go back through the town alone, found herself in front of the two obelisks of Santa-Maria-Novella, without knowing how she had come there. At the corner of the square she saw the old cobbler drawing his thread in the same monotonous manner. He was smiling, with his sparrow on his shoulder.

She went into his booth and sat down on a stool, and there she said in French:

"Quentin Matsys, my friend, what have I done, and what will become of me?"

He looked at her calmly, with cheerful good nature, making an effort to understand. He was past being astonished. She shook her head.

"What I did, my good Quentin, was because he was suffering, and I loved him. I do not regret it."

To which he answered, as was his custom, the sonorous Italian "yes":

"*Sì, sì.*"

"I did no wrong, did I, Quentin? But what will happen now?"

She was going, but he signed to her to wait a moment. He carefully picked a spray of basil and gave it to her. "Take it for its sweet smell, Signora."

XIX

N THE morrow Madame Martin was reading at the window. Choulette greeted her, having first tenderly placed on the table his knotted stick, his pipe, and his carpet-bag. He was going to Assisi. He wore a goatskin jacket, and looked like the old shepherds in the story of the Nativity.

"Good-bye, Madame. I am leaving Fiesole, you, Dechartre, the effeminate Prince Albertinelli, and that charming ogress, Miss Bell. I go to visit the mountain of Assisi, which, says the poet, should be called not Assisi, but 'the Orient,' for thence rose the sun of love. I shall kneel before that happy crypt where reposes the naked body of St. Francis in a trough of stone, with a stone for a pillow. For he would not bear away even so much as a shroud from this world, to which he had revealed the secret of true happiness and true holiness."

"Good-bye, Monsieur Choulette. Bring me a Santa Chiara medal. I like Santa Chiara."

"You are right, Madame. She was a woman of strength and prudence. When, ill and almost blind, St. Francis came to spend a few days with his friend at San Damiano, with her own hands she built him a cell in the garden. His soul rejoiced. A painful weariness and burning of his eyelids deprived him of sleep. Rats attacked him by night. It was then that he composed that joyful hymn in honour of his splendid brother, the Sun, and our chaste, useful, and pure sister, Water. My finest lines, even those of *Le Jardin Clos,* have less irresistible charm and natural splendour. And it is right that it should be so; for the soul of St. Francis was more beautiful than mine. Although I am better than any of my contemporaries, whom I have been privileged to know, I am worthless. When Francis had composed his hymn to the Sun, he was happy. He thought: My brethren and I will go through the towns, playing our lutes in the market-places on market-days. When the good people draw near us we will say: 'We are God's minstrels; we will sing you a lay. If it pleases you, you must reward us.' They will promise. And when we have sung, we shall say to them: 'Now for our reward; what we ask is that you shall love one another.' Doubtless, in order to keep their promise, and so please God's poor minstrels, they will forbear from doing each other harm."

Madame Martin thought St. Francis the most lovable of saints.

"His work," Choulette resumed, "was destroyed during his lifetime. Nevertheless he died happy, because joy and humility were his. He was indeed God's sweet singer. And it is fitting that another poor poet should take up his work, and teach the world true religion and true joy. That poet shall be I, Madame, if only I can cast away pride and wisdom. For all moral beauty is the result of that incomprehensible wisdom which comes from God and resembles madness."

"I will not discourage you, Monsieur Choulette. But I am anxious about the lot of poor women in your new society. You will shut them all up in convents."

"I confess," replied Choulette, "that in my projects for a reformation they cause me much embarrassment. The violence with which they are loved is bitter and bad. The pleasure they give brings no calm, and does not lead to joy. I, in my life, have for the sake of women committed two or three abominable crimes, of which no one knows. I doubt, Madame, whether I shall invite you to supper in the new Santa Maria degli Angeli."

He took up his pipe, his carpet-bag, and his stick with its human head.

"The faults of love will be pardoned—or, rather, one can do no wrong when one really loves. But sensual passion is compact of hatred, egoism, and wrath as much as of love. One evening, for having thought you beautiful as you sat on this sofa, I was assailed by a whole army of passionate thoughts. I had come from the *Albergo,* where I had heard Miss Bell's cook improvise two hundred magnificent lines on spring. My soul was flooded with a celestial joy which vanished at the sight of you. Eve's curse contains a profound truth. For in your presence I grew sad and wicked. Soft words were on my lips. But they lied. Within I felt myself your adversary; I hated you. When I saw you smile, I wanted to kill you."

"Really?"

"Oh, Madame, it is a very natural feeling, and one that you must have often inspired. But the ordinary man feels it without knowing what it is, whilst my vivid imagination defines it clearly. I am in the habit of contemplating my own soul; sometimes I find it splendid, sometimes hideous. If you had seen it that evening, you would have been horrified."

Thérèse smiled.

"Good-bye, Monsieur Choulette; don't forget the Santa Chiara medal."

He put his bag on the ground, and, stretching out his arm, with his forefinger raised in the manner of one who teaches, he said:

"From me you have nothing to fear. But him whom you shall love and who shall love you will be your enemy. Farewell, Madame."

He took up his bag and went out. She saw his tall quaint form disappear behind the shrubs in the garden.

In the afternoon she went to San Marco, where Dechartre was waiting for her. She longed and yet she feared to see him again so soon. Her anguish of heart was appeased by a new feeling of intense sweetness. The moral numbness of her first yielding to passion, followed by a sudden vision of the irreparable, did not recur. She was now under serener, vaguer, more powerful influences. This time the memory of caresses and the violence of passion was veiled in a charming revery. She was troubled and anxious, but not ashamed or regretful. It was not so much by her own will as in obedience to a higher power that she had acted. She justified her action by its unselfishness. She counted on nothing, having expected nothing. Certainly she had been wrong to yield when she was not free, but then she on her part had exacted nothing. Perhaps she was for him only a passing fancy all absorbing, yet serious only for the moment. She did not know him. She had not put to the test those fine imaginings, which are so far above mediocrity in evil as well as in good. If he were suddenly to depart and disappear, she would not reproach him, she would not bear him ill-will, at least she believed so. She would treasure the memory of what is rarest and most precious in the world. Perhaps he was incapable of an enduring love. He had thought he loved her. He had loved her for an hour. She did not dare to hope for more in the embarrassment of a false position in which her frankness and her pride were outraged and the usual clearness of her thought obscured. While the carriage was bearing her to San Marco, she succeeded in persuading herself that he would not mention what had happened on the previous day, and that the memory of that room, looking on the dark pine-trees, would be to them both but the dream of a dream.

He gave her his hand as she got out of the carriage. Before he spoke she saw by his glance that he loved her and that he wanted her still; and she perceived at the same time that she was pleased it should be so.

"It is you," he said, "really you—I have been here since noon, waiting, knowing that you would not come yet, but feeling that I could not live away from the place where I was to see you. It is you! . . . Speak that I may see you and hear you."

"Do you still love me?"

"It is now that I really love you. I thought I loved you when you were but a phantom pursued by my desire. Now you are the body of my soul. Is it true, say, can it be true that you are mine? What have I done that I should possess the greatest, the only good upon earth? And those other men who fill the earth! They think they live! But I alone live! Say what have I done to possess this treasure?"

"Oh! what has been done has been done by me. I tell you frankly. If we come to that, it is my fault. She may not always avow it, but it is always the woman's fault. So, whatever may happen, I shall never reproach you."

An active noisy troop of beggars, guides, and profligates came out of the church porch and surrounded them with an importunity mingled with that grace always characteristic of the nimble Italian. They were subtle enough to guess they had to deal with lovers, and they knew that lovers are generous. Dechartre threw them a few silver pieces, and they all returned to their happy idleness.

A policeman met the visitors. Madame Martin regretted that it was not a monk. At Santa-Maria-Novella, the white robes of the Dominicans looked so beautiful under the arches of the cloister.

They visited the cells where Fra Angelico, aided by his brother Benedetto, painted innocent pictures on the white walls for his comrades, the monks.

"Do you remember that winter evening when I met you on the little bridge over a ditch in front of the Guimet Museum and accompanied you to that little street bordered by gardens and leading to the Quai de Billy? Before parting, we paused for a moment by the thin box hedge running along the parapet. You looked at the box which the winter had dried and withered. And after you had gone, I stayed and gazed at it."

They were in the cell of Savonarola, the prior of the monastery of San Marco. The guide showed them the portrait and the relics of the martyr.

"What could you see to admire in me that day? It was nearly dark."

"I could see you walk. It is by motion that forms speak. Each of your steps revealed to me the secret of your regular beauty and your charm. Oh! when you are concerned my imagination has never kept within the bounds of discretion. I did not dare to speak to you. The sight of you filled me with fear. I was terrified before her who could do everything for me. In your presence I adored you with trembling. Away from you I felt all the irreverence of desire."

"I never guessed it. But do you remember the first time we met, when Paul Vence introduced you? You were sitting by the screen, looking at the miniatures hanging on it. You said: 'That woman, painted by Siccardi, is like André Chénier's mother.' I replied: 'That's my husband's grandmother. What was André Chénier's mother like?' And you said: 'We have her portrait, that of a degenerate Levantine woman.' "

He was sure he had not spoken so rudely.

"But yes. My memory is better than yours."

They walked, surrounded by the white silence of the monastery. They visited the cell that Blessed Angelico adorned with the softest painting. And there before the picture of the Virgin on a pale blue sky receiving the immortal crown from God the father, he took Thérèse in his arms and kissed her on the lips, almost in sight of two Englishwomen, passing down the corridor, reading Baedeker.

"We must not forget to visit St. Anthony's cell," she said.

"Thérèse, I cannot bear that any part of you should escape from me. It is terrible to think that you do not live in me and for me alone. I long to possess entirely you and your past."

She shrugged her shoulders.

"Oh! as for the past!"

"The past alone is real. The past alone exists."

She looked up at him with eyes like the sun shining through the rain:

"Well I can say very truly: I never really live except when I am with you."

On her return to Fiesole, she found a short threatening letter from Le Ménil. He could not understand her silence and her prolonged absence. If she did not immediately name the date of her return he would come to Florence.

She read his letter, not in any way surprised, yet overwhelmed by the realisation that the inevitable was happening and that she would be spared nothing of all she had feared. She might yet pacify and reassure him. She had only to write that she loved him, that she was soon coming back, and that he must renounce the wild idea of meeting her at Florence, which was only a village, where they would be recognised immediately. But she must write: "I love you." She must soothe him with loving words. She had not the courage. She allowed him to guess the truth. In vague terms she accused herself. She wrote mysteriously of souls carried away on the waves of life and how powerless one is on the ocean of vicissitude. Sadly and tenderly she asked him to keep a kindly memory of her in one corner of his heart.

She herself went to post the letter on the Piazza of Fiesole. In the twilight some children were playing at hop-scotch. From the top of the hill she looked down on the beautiful basin and Florence like a lovely jewel nestling in the hollow. The peacefulness of evening made her shudder. She dropped the letter into the box. And then only did she clearly realise what she had done and what would be its result.

XX

THE bright spring sun was casting its golden beams on the Piazza della Signoria, when at the striking of the hour of twelve the country crowd of corn-dealers and macaroni merchants began to break up. At the foot of the Lanzi, in front of the group of statues, the ice-cream sellers had erected little castles with the inscription *Bibite ghiacciate,* on tables covered with red cotton. Joy and gaiety seemed to have come down to earth from heaven. Thérèse and Jacques, on their way home from a morning walk in the Boboli Gardens, were passing the famous loggia. Thérèse was looking at John of Bologna's Sabine woman, with that curious interest with which one woman looks at another. But Dechartre had eyes for Thérèse alone.

"It is wonderful," he said, "how the bright daylight enhances your beauty; it seems to linger lovingly on the pearl white of your cheeks."

"Yes," she said. "Candle-light always hardens my features. I have noticed that. It is unfortunate that I am not an evening beauty; for in the evening women have most opportunity of displaying their good looks. In the evening Princess Seniavine has a lovely olive complexion; by daylight she is as yellow as a guinea. I must admit that it does not trouble her. She is not a coquette."

"And you are?"

"Oh! yes. I used to be for my own sake, now I am for yours."

She looked again at the robust, long-limbed Sabine woman, who was endeavouring to escape from the Roman's embrace.

"Is that angularity and length of limb a necessary quality in a beautiful woman? I am not like that."

Dechartre hastily reassured her. But she had not really doubted. Now she was looking at the ice cream man's little château, with its copper walls gleaming on the scarlet table-cloth. She suddenly felt a desire to eat an ice there, standing at this table, as she had just seen the working women of the town do.

"Wait a moment," he said.

He ran to a street on the left of the Lanzi and disappeared.

In a minute he returned with a little silver gilt spoon, from which the gilding was partly worn away, and the handle of which was formed by a Florentine lily with its calyx enamelled in red.

"This is for you to eat your ice with. The ice cream man does not provide spoons. You would have been obliged to use your tongue. It would have been charming. But you would not have known how to do it."

She recognised the spoon; it was a little gem she had noticed the day before in a shop window near the Lanzi.

They were happy. The fulness of their simple joy overflowed in trivial, meaningless words. And they laughed when the Florentine with excellent mimicry told them the time-honoured tales of old Italian story-tellers. She was entertained by the play of his classic, jovial countenance. But she did not always understand him.

"What is he saying?" she asked Jacques.

"Do you want to know?"

She did.

"Well! he says he would be happy if the fleas in his bed were as pretty as you."

When she had finished her ice, he urged her to revisit Or San-Michele. It was so close. They would cross to the opposite corner of the square and there they would see the jewel in stone. They went. They looked at the bronze St. George and St. Mark. On the encrusted wall of the house Dechartre saw the letter-box, and remembered with painful vividness the little gloved hand posting the letter. The copper mouth that had swallowed Thérèse's secret appeared to him hideous. He could not look away from it. All his gaiety had vanished. Meanwhile she was trying to appreciate the rough statue of the Evangelist.

"Yes, indeed he looks frank and honest. If he could speak his words would always be true."

"His is no woman's mouth," Dechartre retorted bitterly.

She understood, and said very sweetly:

"My friend, why do you say that? I am frank."

"What do you call being frank? You know that a woman is bound to lie."

She hesitated. Then:

"A woman," she said, "is frank when she does not lie uselessly."

XXI

THÉRÈSE, in grey, was gliding among the flowering broom bushes. The silver stars of the arbutus covered the steep slope of the terrace, and, on the hill-side gleamed the sweet scented flame-like flowers of the oleander. The Florentine valley was one mass of flowers.

Vivian Bell, dressed in white, came into the perfumed garden.

"You see, darling, Florence is really the city of flowers; and it is right she should have the red lily for her emblem. To-day is a festival."

"Ah! is it a feast-day?"

"Darling, don't you know that it is the first of May, the *Primavera?* Did you not awake this morning in fairyland? Aren't you keeping the Festival of Flowers, darling? Don't you feel gay, you who love flowers? For you do love them, I know. You feel tenderly towards them. You said that they feel joy and sorrow, that they suffer as we do."

"Did I say that they suffer like us?"

"Yes, you said so. To-day is their festival. You must celebrate it according to the custom of our ancestors, in rites depicted by the old masters."

Thérèse heard without comprehending. Crushed in her gloved hand was a letter she had just received, bearing the Italian postmark and containing only two lines:

"I arrived to-night at the Hotel de la Grande Bretagne, Lungarno, Acciajoli. I expect you to-morrow morning. No. 18."

"Oh! darling, don't you know that at Florence it is our custom to welcome the spring time on the first of May? Then you can't have understood Botticelli's picture of the Feast of Flowers, his delightful *Spring,* so full of happy revery. Formerly, darling, on this first day of May, the whole town was merry. The girls of Florence, in festive garb, crowned with hawthorn, passed in procession up the Corso, beneath arches of flowers, to dance under the oleanders on the fresh green grass. We will imitate them. We will dance in the garden."

"Are we going to dance in the garden?"

"Yes, darling, and I will teach you some fifteenth-century Tuscan dances, discovered in a MS. by Mr. Morison, the *doyen* of London librarians. Come back quickly my love; we will wreathe our heads with flowers and then we will dance."

"Yes, dear, we will dance."

And, opening the gate, she hurried down the little path with channels worn by the rain like the bed of a mountain torrent, and stones hidden beneath briar roses. She jumped into the first carriage she met. The driver had cornflowers in his hat and on his whip-handle.

"Hotel de la Grande Bretagne, Lungarno Acciajoli," she said.

She knew where it was, Lungarno Acciajoli. . . . She had been there, in the evening, and she remembered the golden light of the setting sun on the surging waters of the river. Then night had come; and she heard the water's dull murmur in the silence; words and glances had agitated her, and her lover's first kiss, the beginning of an irreparable love. Oh! Yes, she remembered Lungarno Acciajoli and the river bank beyond the Ponte Vecchio. . . . Hotel de la Grande Bretagne. . . . She knew a broad stone façade on the quay. It was fortunate, if he must come, that he was staying there. He might have gone to the Hotel de la Ville, on the Piazza Manin, where Dechartre was staying. It was fortunate that their rooms were not side by side in the same corridor. . . . Lungarno Acciajoli! . . . That corpse they had seen hurrying by, borne by cowled monks, it was at rest in some little garden cemetery.

Number 18.

It was a bare Italian hotel room with a stove. A set of brushes was carefully set out on the table, and by them a railway guide. Not a book, not a newspaper. He was there: she read suffering and feverish excitement on his thin face; and its sad expression pained her. He awaited a word, a sign; but she remained silent, motionless, and afraid.

He offered her a chair. She put it on one side and continued standing.

"Thérèse, there is something that I do not know. Speak."

After a moment's silence, she replied with painful hesitation:

"Why did you leave me in Paris?"

The sadness of her tone made him believe, and he wished to believe, that she was reproaching him. He blushed and replied eagerly:

"Ah! If I had foreseen! You must know that at heart I cared little for that hunting-party! But you, your letter of the 27th (he had a good memory for dates) made me terribly anxious. Something had happened when you wrote it. Tell me everything."

"I thought, dear, that you had ceased to love me."

"But now you know that to be untrue."

"Now . . ."

She was still standing with her hands clasped.

Then with assumed tranquillity, she said:

"Our union was formed in ignorance. One never knows. You are young, younger than I, since we are nearly of an age. Doubtless you have plans for the future."

He looked her haughtily in the face. She continued with less assurance.

"Your relatives, your mother, your aunts have made plans for you. It is quite natural. I ought to have guessed that there was some obstacle. It is better that I should disappear from your life. We shall keep a kindly memory of each other."

She offered him her gloved hand. He folded his arms.

"And so you are tired of me," he said. "You think that when you have made me happier than any other man has ever been, you can put me on one side, that everything is over! . . . And what have you come to tell me? That a union such as ours is quickly sundered. That a parting is easy? . . . I tell you, no! You are not the kind of woman from whom one parts."

"Yes, you probably loved me with an affection stronger than is usual in such cases. I was more to you than a passing fancy. But, what if I were not the woman you thought me, what if I were a flirt, and betrayed you. . . . You know what has been said. . . . Well! what if I have not been all that I ought to have been . . ."

She hesitated and resumed in a grave serious tone which contrasted with her words:

"Supposing that while I was your mistress I yielded to other attractions and was possessed by other longings. Perhaps I am not made for a serious passion. . . ."

He interrupted her.

"You lie," he said.

"Yes, I lie. And I do not lie well. I wanted to spoil our past. I was wrong. It is what you know it was. But . . ."

"But . . . ?"

"Well! I always told you I am not to be depended on. There are women, so I am told, who are mistresses of their feelings. I warned you that I was not like them, that I am not answerable for mine."

He looked left and right and turned his head like a creature irritated and yet hesitating to attack.

"What do you mean? I don't understand. I understand nothing. Explain yourself. There is something between us. I don't know what. But I am determined to know. What is it?"

"It is because I am not sure of myself, dear. You ought never to have placed your confidence in me. No, you ought never to have done it. I never promised anything. . . . And, then, if I had promised, what are words?"

· "You love me no longer. You have ceased to love me, I see it well. But, so much the worse for you! I love you. You ought never to have given yourself to me. It is no use your thinking you can take back that gift. I love you and I keep you. . . . Ah! You thought you were easily rid of me? Listen. You made me love you; you charmed me; it is your fault that I cannot live without you. You enjoyed your share in our raptures. I did not take you by force.

You were willing. Six weeks ago you asked for nothing better. You were everything to me. I was everything to you. So complete was our union that our very lives were mingled. And then all of a sudden you ask me to forget you, to regard you as a stranger, a casual acquaintance. Ah! you have an unparalleled assurance. Tell me, was I dreaming when I felt your kisses and your breath upon my neck? Was it not true? Am I imagining it all? Oh! I cannot doubt that you loved me once. I feel the breath of your love upon me still. And yet, I have not changed. I am what I was. You have nothing with which to reproach me. I have never deceived you. Not that it is any credit to me. I could not have done it. When one has known you, all other women, even the most beautiful, appear insipid. The idea of deceiving you never occurred to me. I always treated you honourably. Then why have you ceased to love me? But tell me, speak. Say that you still love me. Say so, since it must be true. Come, come! Thérèse, you will feel at once that you love me, as you used to love me in our little nest in the Rue Spontini, where we were so happy. Come!"

Passionately, eagerly, he threw his strong arms around her. She, with tears in her eyes, repulsed him icily.

He understood and said:

"You have a lover."

She bowed her head, and then raised it, grave and silent.

Then he struck her on the breast, on the shoulder, and in the face. But immediately he drew back ashamed, and looked down in silence. With his fingers on his lips, biting his nails, he noticed that his hand had been scratched by a pin in her bodice. He threw himself into an arm-chair, took out his handkerchief to dry the blood, and remained as if benumbed and stupefied.

She, leaning against the door, pale, her head erect, her glance uncertain, was instinctively unpinning her torn veil and readjusting her hat.

At the sound, once so delicious, of the rustling of her clothes, he shuddered, looked at her, and relapsed into fury.

"Who is it?" he asked. "I must know."

She did not move. On her white face was a red mark where his hand had struck her. She replied firmly and gently:

"I have told you all I could. Ask me no more. It would be useless."

He looked at her with a cruel glance she had never seen before.

"Oh! you need not tell me his name. I shall have no difficulty in finding him."

She was silent, sad for him, anxious for another, full of fear and anguish, yet without bitterness, sorrow, or regret, for her heart was elsewhere.

He seemed to know what was passing within her. In his wrath at beholding her so sweet and serene, beautiful, but not as he had known her, beautiful for another, he felt a desire to kill her, and he cried:

"Go—go."

Then overpowdered by the passion of that hatred, which was not natural to him, he put his head in his hands and sobbed.

His grief touched her and gave her hope that she might be able to calm him and render her departure less agonising. She imagined that she might console him for losing her. In a friendly and confinding manner she sat down beside him.

"You must blame me," she said. "I deserve blame but also pity. Despise me, if you like, and if you can despise a miserable creature who is life's plaything. Judge me, as you will. But in your wrath feel a little friendliness towards me; let me be a bitter-sweet memory like those autumn days when there is sunshine and east wind. That is what I deserve. Don't be hard on the pleasant but frivolous visitor who has crossed your path. Bid me farewell as if I were a sad traveller who goes away she knows not whither. It is always so sad to part! You were angry with me just now. I don't reproach you. But it grieves me. Show me some sympathy. Who knows? The future is always uncertain. It lies vague and dark before me. Let me be able to say that I have been kind, simple, and frank with you, and that you have not forgotten me. In time you will come to understand and to forgive. But to-day, just be pitiful."

He was not listening to the words she said, but the soft clear sound of her voice soothed him. He said suddenly:

"You do not love him. It is I whom you love. Then——"

She hesitated, then said:

"Oh: to say whom one loves and whom one does not love is no easy matter for a woman, at least for me. I don't know how others do; for life is not merciful. One is battered and thrown and driven——"

He looked at her very calmly. An idea had occurred to him. He had made a resolve. It was quite simple. He would forgive, he would forget, if only she would return at once.

"Thérèse, you don't love him? It was a mistake, a moment's forgetfulness, a horrible stupid thing that you did, surprised in an instant of weakness, or perhaps out of pique. Swear to me that you will never see him again."

He took hold of her arm, saying, "Swear."

She was silent, her lips tightly closed, looking darkly.

"You are hurting me," she cried.

But he did not desist. He dragged her to the table, where, as well as the brushes, were an ink-pot and a few sheets of letter-paper each bearing a picture of the hotel façade with its numerous windows.

"Write what I dictate. I will send the letter."

And, when she resisted, he forced her on to her knees. Proudly and calmly, she said:

"I cannot. I will not."

"Why?"

"Because . . . Do you want to know? . . . Because I love him."

Suddenly he let her go. If he had had a revolver at hand, perhaps he would have killed her. But almost immediately his wrath melted into sadness; and, then despairing, it was his own life he would have taken.

"Are you speaking the truth? Is it possible? Is it true?"

"Do I myself know? Can I tell? Can I understand yet? Can I think? Can I feel? Can I see any ray of light? Can I . . ."

Then with a slight effort she added:

"At this moment can I realise anything but my sadness and your despair?"

"You love him! You love him!" he cried. "How has he made you love him?"

He was stupefied by surprise, overwhelmed with astonishment. Nevertheless, what she had said had separated them. He no longer dared to handle her roughly, to seize her, to strike her, and treat her as his chattel. He repeated:

"You love him! You love him! But what did he say to you, what has he done to make you love him? I know you: I did not always tell you when your ideas shocked me. I wager that this lover of yours is not even a man in society. And you think he loves you? You think so? Well you are mistaken: he does not love you. He will give you up at the first opportunity. He will have had enough of you when he has compromised you. Then you will pass from one affair to another. Next year the worst things will be said of you. I am sorry for your father, who is my friend. He will know of your conduct; for you will not be able to deceive him."

She listened, humiliated and yet consoled, for she knew she would have suffered more deeply had she found him magnanimous.

He despised her in his simplicity; and his scorn consoled him. He tested it to the full.

"How did it happen?" he asked. "You need not hesitate to tell me."

She shrugged her shoulders with such obvious pity for him that he did not dare continue in this strain. He resumed bitterly:

"Do you think I shall help you to save the situation, that I shall continue to visit your husband and be a third in your household?"

"I expect you to do what a gallant man ought to do. I ask you for nothing. I should have liked to remember you as a dear friend. I had expected you to be kind and charitable. It is impossible. I see such partings must always be bitter. Later you will think better of me. Good-bye."

He looked at her. Now his face was more expressive of sorrow than of wrath. She had never seen his eyes look so hard or deeply ringed, or his temples appearing so plainly beneath his thin hair. He seemed to have aged in an hour.

"I must warn you," he said. "It will be impossible for me to meet you again. You are not the kind of woman whom, after what has passed between us, one can continue to meet in society. As I have said, you are a woman apart. You have a poison of your own, which you have given me; I feel it within me, in my veins, everywhere. Why did I ever know you?"

She looked at him kindly.

"Good-bye! Say to yourself that I am not worth such bitter regrets."

Then, when he saw her with her hand on the door handle, when he felt that he was about to lose her, that he would never possess her again, he uttered a cry and rushed forward. He remembered nothing. All that he felt was the numbness which follows a great misfortune, an irreparable loss. But this feeling of having been stunned gave place to desire. He wanted once more the mistress, who was going, never to return. He drew her to him. With all the strength of his physical nature he wanted her. She was on the watch and resisted him with all the power of her will. Dishevelled and disarranged, she freed herself without having even felt afraid.

He understood that it would be useless; the lost sequence of facts returned to him, and he realised that she could not be his because she was another's. His anguish revived; he hurled insults at her and pushed her out of the room.

For a moment she lingered in the passage, proudly waiting for a word, a look worthy of their past love.

But again he cried: "Go," and banged the door.

Via Alfieri! She returned to the little house at the back of the courtyard, overgrown with pale green grass. It seemed peaceful, silent, faithful, with its goats and nymphs, carved for the lovers of the days of the Grand-Duchess Eliza. Already she felt a sense of escape from a sorrowful and brutal world, as if she had been carried through the ages to a life where suffering was unknown. At the bottom of the staircase, the steps of which were strewn with roses, Dechartre was waiting for her. She fell into his arms and remained there passive, while he carried her upstairs like the precious relic of her before whom he had once grown pale and trembled. With eyes half closed she tasted the superb humiliation of feeling herself his. Her weariness, her sadness, the mortifications of the day, the memory of violence, her re-conquered liberty, the desire to forget, some vestige of fear, all intensified her tenderness. Lying on the bed, she clasped her arms round her lover's neck.

They were as gay as children. They laughed, talked nonsense, and played as they sucked lemons, oranges, and water-melons piled near them on painted plates.

She was flushed with pride in the comeliness of the body she was offering upon the altar of love. For she had discarded her clothes save for one thin rose-hued garment, and this had slipped scarfwise from her shoulder, laying bare one breast, whilst the warmer tinted tip of the other glowed through the rosy gossamer that veiled it.

Her half open lips displayed the whiteness of her teeth. With coquettish anxiety, she asked whether, after all his glowing dreams of her, he had not been disappointed.

In the half-light, which he had contrived, he contemplated her with youthful ardour, mingling kisses with his praises.

In pretty caresses, loving disputes, and happy glances they passed the time, till all of a sudden grave, with looks overcast and compressed lips, a prey to that sacred wrath which brings love near hatred they plunged into the abyss of passion.

Then her head upon the pillow, her hair flowing, she would open her eyes bathed in tears, and smile sweetly.

He asked her how she had come by that little red mark on the temple. She replied that she did not know and that it was nothing.

It was hardly a lie. For really she had forgotten.

They recalled their beautiful short story—which yet covered all their life, for life began the day they first met.

"You remember being on the terrace the day after your arrival. You talked vaguely and incoherently. I guessed then that you loved me."

"I was afraid you thought me stupid."

"You were rather. But that was my triumph. I was beginning to grow impatient with your serenity in my presence. I loved you before you loved me. Oh! I am not ashamed of it."

He poured into her mouth a few drops of sparkling Asti. But on the table was a bottle of Trasimene wine. She wanted to taste it in memory of that lake lying in the evening light so melancholy and beautiful in its opal cup. She had seen it during her first visit to Italy, six years ago.

He reproached her with having appreciated beauty without his aid.

"But, without you, I should never have seen anything," she said. "Why did you not come sooner?"

He silenced her with a kiss.

And she exhausted with joy cried:

"Yes, I love you! Yes, I have never loved any one but you."

XXII

E MÉNIL had written: "I leave to-morrow evening at seven. Be at the station."

She had come. As she approached the hotel omnibuses, there she saw him in his long grey Inverness, calm and correct. He merely said:

"Ah! You here!"

"But you asked me to come."

He would not confess that his letter had been written in the wild hope that perhaps after all she might love him again, that everything might be forgotten and that he might hear her say: "It was only to try you."

If she had spoken thus he would have believed her at once.

But her silence disappointed him; and he said bitterly:

"What have you to say to me? It is for you to speak, not for me. I have nothing to explain. I have no falseness to excuse."

"My friend, don't be cruel; bear me no ill-will for what is past. That is what I came to say. But I want to tell you too, that I bid you farewell with the sadness of a true friend."

"Is that all? Go and say it to the other; it will interest him more than me."

"You asked me to come, and I came. Don't make me regret it."

"I am sorry I have troubled you. Doubtless you could have employed your time better. Don't let me detain you. Go to him, as you are longing to."

Struck by the thought that these poor miserable words represented but a moment of humanity's eternal suffering, and haunted by the memory of many similar words in tragic drama, Thérèse's lips curled with ironical sadness. He thought she was smiling.

"Don't laugh. Listen. At the hotel, the day before yesterday, I wanted to kill you. I came so near doing it that now I know what it means. And I shall not do it. You need not fear. Besides, what would be the good? As I wish to keep up appearances for my own sake, I shall call on you in Paris. I shall learn with regret that you cannot see me. I shall see your husband. I shall also see your father. It will be to take my leave before a long absence. Good-bye, Madame."

Just as he was turning away from her, Thérèse saw Miss Bell and Prince Albertinelli coming out of the goods station and walking towards her. The Prince looked very handsome. Vivian was walking by him in all the gladness of maidenly joy.

"Oh! darling! What a delightful surprise to find you here. The Prince and I have been to the custom-house to claim my bell, which has just arrived."

"Ah! has your bell come?"

"It is here, darling, Ghiberti's bell! I have seen it in its wooden packing-case. It would not ring because it was a prisoner. But, in my house at Fiesole, I will lodge it in a campanile. When it breathes Florentine air, it will delight to make its silver voice heard. Visited by doves, it will ring out all our joys and all our sorrows. It will ring for you, for me, for the Prince, for good Madame Marmet, for M. Choulette, for all our friends."

"Bells never ring out true joys and sorrows, dear. They are mere dutiful officials who know none but official feelings."

"Darling, you are mistaken. Bells know the heart's secrets; they know everything. But I am so glad to meet you. Oh! I know why you are at the station. Your maid betrayed you. She told me you were expecting a pink gown, which had not come, and that you were burning with impatience. But don't worry. You are always perfectly beautiful, my love."

She made Madame Martin get into the trap.

"Come quickly, darling. M. Jacques Dechartre is dining with us to-night; and I don't want to keep him waiting."

And, after they had driven in silence along the lanes, smelling sweetly of wild flowers, Vivian said:

"Do you see down there, darling, the black distaffs of the Fates, the cypress trees in the cemetery? It is my wish one day to lie beneath them."

But Thérèse was thinking anxiously:

"They saw him. Did she recognise him? I don't think so. It was growing dark; and the lights were dazzling. Perhaps she does not know him. I can't remember whether she met him at my house last year."

What troubled her most was the Prince's ill-concealed rejoicing.

"Darling, will you lie by my side, in that rural cemetery, beneath a little earth and the vast spaces of the sky? But it is foolish of me to give you an invitation which you can't accept. You will not be permitted to sleep your last sleep at the foot of the Fiesole hills, my love. You will have to rest at Paris, beneath a handsome monument, by the side of Count Martin-Bellème."

"Why? Do you think, dear, that a wife should remain united to her husband even after death?"

"Certainly, she should, darling. Marriage is for time and for eternity. Don't you know the story of the husband and wife of Auvergne, who loved one another? They died almost together, and were buried in two graves, separated by a road. But every night a wild rose threw a spray of flowers between the two graves; in the end the coffins had to be put together."

When they had passed the Badia, they saw a procession winding up the hill slopes. The evening breeze was blowing out the flickering flames of the candles in their gilded wooden candlesticks. The painted banners were surrounded by girls in the white and blue of their religious society. Then came a little St. John, fair with curly hair, naked except for the lamb's fleece, showing his bare arms and shoulders; and then a St. Mary Magdalen of seven, robed in the gold of her crimped hair. The inhabitants of Fiesole were following in a crowd. Countess Martin recognised Choulette in their midst. He was singing, a candle in one hand, his book in the other, blue spectacles on the end of his nose. The candle cast a yellow light over his flat features, the bumps on his skull, and his dishevelled hair. His unkempt beard rose and fell to the measure of the hymn. In the lurid lights and shadows he looked old and robust, and, like the hermits, capable of living through a century of penance.

"How grand he is!" said Thérèse. "He poses to himself. He is a great artist."

"Oh! darling, why won't you allow that M. Choulette is really pious? Why? It is so sweet and so beautiful to believe. Poets realise that. If M. Choulette had no faith, he would not be able to write such fine verses."

"And you, dear, have you faith?"

"Oh! yes, I believe in God and in the words of Christ."

At length the canopy, the banners, and the white veils had all disappeared round a corner of the hill. But Choulette's bare head, illuminated by the candle-light, was still to be seen.

Meanwhile Dechartre was waiting alone in the garden. Thérèse found him, leaning against the balustrade of that terrace, where he had felt the first agony of love. While Miss Bell and the Prince were choosing a place for the new bell's campanile, he took Thérèse for a moment in among the broom bushes.

"You promised to be in the garden on my arrival. I have been waiting for an hour, which seemed like eternity. You ought not to have gone out. Your absence surprised and distressed me."

She replied vaguely that she had been obliged to go to the station, and that Miss Bell had driven her back in the trap.

He asked her to forgive his anxiety. But everything alarmed him. Even his happiness made him tremble.

They were already at dinner when Choulette appeared, looking like some ancient satyr, a strange light gleaming in his phosphorescent eyes. Since his return from Assisi, he had lived with the people. He spent his days drinking Chianti wine with doubtful women and working men, admonishing them to be glad and innocent, announcing the coming of Jesus Christ and the quickly approaching abolition of taxes and military service. After the procession, he had assembled the crowd in the ruins of the Roman theater, and in Macaronic language, a jumble of French and Tuscan, preached a sermon, which he was now pleased to repeat:

"Kings, Senators, and Judges have said: 'We are the life of the people.' Now they lie. They are the coffin who says: 'I am the cradle.'

"The life of the people is in the fields growing white unto the harvest in the sight of the Lord. It is in the vines hanging from the branches of the young elms, and in the smiles and the tears which the heavens rain down upon the fruits of the trees in the meadows and orchards.

"The life of the people is not in the laws, made by the powerful and rich for the preservation of power and wealth.

"The heads of kingdoms, and republics have written in their books that international law is the law of war. And they have glorified violence. They honour conquerors; in the public squares they erect statues to the victor and to his steed. But no one has the right to kill: wherefore the just man will refuse to draw his number for conscription. No man has the right to encourage the madness and the crimes of a prince who has been placed over a kingdom or a republic: wherefore the just man will not pay taxes; and he will not give his money to the publicans. In peace he will enjoy the fruit of his labour; and he will make bread of the corn he has sown, and he will eat of the fruits of the trees he has trimmed."

"Ah! Monsieur Choulette," said Prince Albertinelli gravely, "you are right to take an interest in the condition of our poor country, ruined by taxation. What profit can one derive from land taxed at the rate of 33 per cent. on its net annual value? Master and servants are alike the prey of the publicans."

Dechartre and Madame Martin were both struck by the unexpected sincerity of his manner.

"I love the King," he added. "There is no question of my loyalty. But I grieve for the sufferings of the peasants."

The truth is that he was pertinaciously pursuing one single object: that of restoring his country estate of Casentino. His father, one of Victor-Emmanuel's artillery officers, had left three-quarters of it in the hands of money-lenders. His son concealed his purpose beneath affected indolence. But he allowed himself no vices except such as were useful and would tend to accomplish the object of his life. It was with the design of becoming a great Tuscan landed proprietor that he had dealt in pictures, secretly sold the famous ceilings of his palace, paid his addresses to old women, and finally asked for the hand of Miss Bell, whom he knew to be an adept at money-making and housekeeping. He really loved the land and its peasants. And Choulette's fervent words, which he only half understood, appealed to that love. He permitted himself to say what he really thought:

"In a country where the master and servants are one family, the fate of the one depends on that of the other. Taxation ruins us. What fine fellows our farmers are! In the cultivation of the land they are unequalled."

Madame Martin confessed that she would not have thought it. It was only in Lombardy that she had seen fields well cultivated and well watered. Tuscany looked to her like a beautiful neglected orchard.

The Prince replied smiling that perhaps she might alter her opinion if she were to do him the honour of visiting his farms at Casentino, in spite of their having suffered from long and ruinous lawsuits. There she would see the true Italian peasant.

"I pay great attention to my estate. I was coming from it this evening when I had the double pleasure of meeting at the station, Miss Bell, who was claiming her treasure, and you, Madame, who were talking to a friend from Paris."

He had thought that he might annoy her by speaking of this meeting. Looking round the table he noticed the expression of grieved surprise which Dechartre had been unable to conceal. He insisted:

"Pardon a country person who flatters himself on possessing a certain social discrimination, Madame; but I saw that the gentle-

man talking to you must be a Parisian, because of his English air, and his affectation of English stiffness which only served to display the ease and vivacity of the Frenchman."

"Oh!" said Thérèse carelessly, "I had not seen him for a long while. And I was very surprised to meet him at Florence just as he was going away."

She looked at Dechartre who pretended not to be listening.

"But I know the gentleman," said Miss Bell. "It was M. Le Ménil. I sat next to him at dinner twice, at Madame Martin's, and he talked very well. He told me he liked football, that he had introduced it into France, and that now it is very fashionable. He also told me about his hunting. He is very fond of animals. I notice that sportsmen are always fond of animals. I assure you, darling, that M. Le Ménil can talk delightfully of hares. He knows their habits. He told me it was charming to see them dancing by moonlight in the heather. He assured me that they are very intelligent, and that he had seen an old hare, pursued by dogs, forcing another hare out of its hiding-place, in order to put them off the track. Darling, has M. Le Ménil ever talked to you about hares?"

Thérèse replied that she did not remember. She thought sportsmen were always bores.

Miss Bell replied that she did not believe M. Le Ménil could bore any one when he described hares dancing by moonlight in the vines and the heather. Like Phanion, she would like to train a little hare.

"Don't you know Phanion, darling? I am sure M. Dechartre knows her. She was beautiful and beloved of poets. She lived in the Island of Cos, in a house on the side of a hill, covered with lemon and terebinth trees, and on the shore of a blue sea. It is said that she used to gaze at the blue waves. I told Phanion's story to M. Le Ménil, and he was very pleased with it. A hunter had given her a leveret, taken from the mother when she was still feeding it. Phanion took it in her lap and gave it spring flowers to eat. It loved Phanion and forgot its mother. It died of eating too many flowers. Phanion mourned over it. She buried it in the garden, beneath the lemon-trees in a grave, which she could see from her bed. And the poet's singing consoled the shade of the leveret."

Kind Madame Marmet said that M. Le Ménil had a discretion and a charm of manner seldom met with in the young men of the present day. She would have liked to see him. She wanted to ask him to do her a service.

"It is on behalf of my nephew," she said. "He is an artillery captain, well thought of and very popular with his superior officers. His colonel has for some time been attached to M. Le Ménil's uncle, General de La Briche. If M. Le Ménil would be so kind as to ask his uncle to write a few lines recommending my nephew to Colonel Faure, I should be very grateful to him. Besides, M. Le Ménil knows my nephew. They met last year at Caen, at the fancy dress ball given at the Hôtel d'Angleterre, by Captain de Lessay to the officers of the garrison and the young men of the neighbourhood."

Looking down, Madame Marmet added:

"The women there were of course not in society, but I heard that some were very pretty. Many had been brought from Paris. My nephew, who told me about it, was dressed as a postillion; M. Le Ménil as one of the Black Hussars;* he was a great success."

Miss Bell said she regretted not having known that M. Le Ménil was at Florence. She would have liked to invite him to come to Fiesole.

Dechartre was gloomy and distracted for the rest of the evening. And, when they parted, Thérèse noticed that he did not press her hand.

XXIII

HE next day when they met in the little house in the Via Alfieri, she found him anxious. At first, by an exuberance of gaiety, by the charm of her tenderness and by the proud humility of a mistress who offers her beauty, she tried to dispel his melancholy. But he continued depressed. All night long he had been thinking and pondering and reflecting on his sorrow and his distress. His mind discerned a relation between the hand posting the letter in front of the bronze San Marco and the commonplace but menacing stranger seen at the railway station. Now Jacques Dechartre had a name for his anguish. An army of dark fancies assailed him as he sat, at Thérèse's invitation, in the grandmother's chair she had occupied on the day of her first happy coming. She meanwhile leant upon his arm and pressed against it her soft figure and her warm, loving heart. The cause of his sorrow she knew too well to ask.

Trying to suggest pleasant thoughts she reminded him of the secrets that room enclosed and of their walks through the city. She lavished upon him all the graces of intimacy.

"You remember that little spoon you gave me under the Lanzi, with the red lily for a handle," she said. "I use it every morning for my tea. When I awake, the delight I feel at the sight of it tells me how much I love you."

Then, when he answered in sad mysterious words, she said:

"I am here at your side, and you are not thinking of me. You are occupied with some idea of which I am ignorant. Nevertheless, I exist, and your idea is nothing."

"An idea is nothing? Do you think so? An idea can render us

*A cavalry regiment founded by Frederick the Great; the sabres of these hussars were engraved with a skull and two cross bones.—W. S.

happy or miserable. An idea can kill us or make us live. Yes, I am thinking . . .”

“Of what are you thinking?”

“Why do you ask me? You know. I am thinking of what I heard yesterday, of what you have concealed from me—I am thinking of a meeting yesterday, at the station. It was not the result of chance, but had been arranged by a letter posted—do you remember?—in the letter-box of Or San Michele. Oh! I don’t reproach you. I haven’t the right. But why did you become mine, if you were not free?”

She thought it best to lie.

“If you mean the person I met at the station yesterday I assure you it was a meeting of no consequence.”

He noticed sorrowfully that she dared not name him of whom she spoke. He also avoided pronouncing his name.

“Thérèse, did he not come here to see you? Did you not know that he was at Florence? Is he nothing more to you than a man you meet in society and receive in your own home? Was it not on his account that you said to me on the Arno bank: ‘I cannot!’ Is he nothing to you?”

She replied resolutely:

“Sometimes he comes to see me. General Larivière introduced him. I have nothing else to tell you. I assure you that he does not interest me in the slightest, and that I cannot think what you are imagining.”

It gave her a kind of pleasure thus to deny the man who had so violently and so sternly asserted his rights over her. But she hastened to be frank once more. With her beautiful soft serious eyes she looked at her lover and said:

“Listen: from the day when I became yours my life has belonged to you entirely. If you have a doubt, a single anxiety, question me. The present is yours and yours only, you know. As for my past, if you knew how empty it was you would be happy. I cannot think that any woman, made for love as I am, could have brought you a heart more completely yours. That I swear to you. During the years before I knew you, I did not live. Don’t let us talk of them. There is nothing in them of which I need be ashamed. Regret! that is another matter. I regret having known you so late. Why, did you not come earlier my love? Five years ago I would have given myself to you as willingly as to-day. But do not let us question the years that are past. Remember Lohengrin. If you love me, I am your Knight of the Swan. I have asked you nothing. I have wanted to know nothing. I have not reproached you with Mademoiselle Jeanne Tancrède. I saw that you loved me, that you were in trouble; and that was enough, because I loved you.”

“A woman can’t be jealous like a man, nor can she feel what causes us the sharpest agony.”

"I don't know. Why not?"

"Why? Because in the blood, in the flesh of a woman there is not that ridiculous yet noble desire for possession, that ancient instinct which man claims as his right. Man is a god whose creature must be his alone. From time immemorial woman has shared her possessions. Our passions have their roots in the past, the obscure past. When we are born we are already old. For a woman jealousy is merely the wounding of her self-love. In man it is an agony with all the acuteness of mental suffering and all the persistence of physical pain. . . . You ask why? Because, in spite of my submissiveness and my respect, in spite of the fear with which you inspire me, you are matter, I am thought, you are the chattel, I am the soul, you are the clay, I am the potter. Oh, you need not complain. What is the rude and humble potter by the side of the rounded amphora bewreathed with garlands? She is calm and beautiful. He is miserable. He is in torture: he wills and he suffers; for to will is to suffer. Yes I am jealous. I know what my jealousy is. When I analyse it, I find it compounded of hereditary prejudice, savage pride, diseased sensibility, a mingling of stupid violence and cruel weakness, foolish and wicked rebellion against the laws of life and the universe. But it is useless for me to contemplate it in all its nakedness: it is and it tortures me. I am the chemist, who studying the properties of the acid he has drunk, knows with what bases it can combine and what salts it can form. But the acid meanwhile is burning him and will burn him to the marrow of his bones."

"My love, you are absurd."

"Yes, I am absurd. I know it better than you. To desire a woman in the flower of her beauty and her intelligence, mistress of herself, who knows and dares and is in that all the most beautiful and desirable, who can choose with insight, free and unfettered; to desire her, to love her for all that she is and to suffer because she possesses neither the childish candour nor the pale innocence which would shock one in her, if it were possible to find them; to ask her to be at once herself and not herself, to adore her for what life has made her and yet to regret bitterly that life, which has made her so beautiful, should have even touched her. Oh! it is absurd. I love you, do you understand, I love you with all that you bring me of sensations and habits, with all that your experience has taught you, with all that may even come from him, from them, how can I tell? . . . This is my delight, this is my agony. There must be some profound meaning in that popular imbecility which regards love as a crime. Joy when it is intense is a crime. That is why I suffer, my beloved."

She knelt before him, took his hands, and drew him to her.

"I cannot bear to see you suffer and I cannot let you. It would be madness. I love you, and I have never loved any but you. You may believe me, I am speaking the truth."

He kissed her on the forehead. "If you were deceiving me, darling, I should bear you no ill-will for it. On the contrary I should be
grateful. What can be more lawful, more human than to deceive
sorrow? What would become of us if women did not take pity and
lie? Yes, lie, my beloved, lie in all charity. Give me the dream which
shall gladden the night of my sorrow. Lie fearlessly; you will but
add one more illusion to that of love and beauty."

He sighed:

"Oh! for common sense, for common wisdom!"

She asked him what he meant by common wisdom. He replied
that it was a wise but a brutal proverb and that he had better not
repeat it.

"Tell me," she said.

"You really want me to tell you: 'The mouth that is kissed keeps
its freshness.' "

And he added:

"It is true that love preserves beauty, and that a woman feeds
on caresses as a bee feeds on flowers."

"I swear to you," she replied, "that I have never loved but you.
No caresses have preserved any beauty I may be so fortunate as to
have to offer you. I love you. I swear I love only you."

And she sealed her oath with a kiss on his lips.

But he remembered the Or San Michele letter and the stranger
at the railway station.

"If you really loved me you would not love any one else."

She rose indignant.

"Then you think that I love another? But what you say is horrible. That's what you think of me. And then you say that you love
me. . . . I pity you; you are mad."

"Yes, I am mad. Say so. Say so again."

Kneeling at his feet she took his face in her soft hands. She told
him he was mad to trouble so much about an insignificant meeting.
She made him believe her, or rather she induced him to forget. He
saw, he knew, he felt nothing but those slight hands, those burning
lips, that eager mouth, that heaving breast and all those charms
that were his. His only thought was to lose himself in her. His
wrath and bitterness vanished; and there remained the keen desire
to forget everything and make her forget everything in a voluptuous unconsciousness. Goaded by anxiety and desire, she showed the
passion she aroused; she realised at once her power and her weakness, inspired by the half unconscious will to give more of herself
than ever, she gave love for love with an instinctive ardour she had
never experienced before.

In the warm shaded room, the sun's golden beams were falling
on the hems of the curtains, and the basket of strawberries beside
a bottle of Asti wine on the table. By the bedside, there was a smile
on the faded lips of the Venetian lady's clearly outlined form. On the

screens the Bergamo and Verona masks laughed joyously in silence.
A full blown rose in a glass was dropping its leaves one by one. The
silence was redolent of love; they sank down weary with passion.

She fell asleep on her lover's breast. Her pleasure continued in
her light slumber. When she opened her eyes, she said, joyfully:

"I love you."

With his elbow on the pillow, he was looking at her in dumb
anguish.

She asked him why he was sad.

"You were so happy a few minutes ago. Why aren't you now?"

But he shook his head and did not speak.

"Do say. I would rather hear you complain than that you should
be silent."

Then he said:

"You want to know. Then do not be angry. My grief is greater
than ever, because now I know what you can give."

She drew away quickly, her eyes full of sorrow and reproach.

"Can you think that I have ever been to another what I am to
you! You wound my most tender feeling, my love for you. I cannot forgive you. I love you. I have never loved another. You alone
have caused me to suffer. Be happy. You wound me to the quick.
. . . Can you be cruel?"

"Thérèse, when one loves one is never kind."

Sitting on the bed, with her legs hanging down, like a bather's,
she remained long motionless and lost in thought. A blush spread
over her face, which had been pale with passion, and tears filled
her eyes.

"Thérèse, you are crying."

"Forgive me, dear. It is the first time I have loved and been really
loved. I am afraid."

XXIV

IN the Villa of Bells there was heard the heavy thud
of trunks being brought down the staircase. Pauline
loaded with bundles was tripping down the steps.
Kind Madame Marmet with calm solicitude was
watching the despatch of the luggage; and Miss
Bell was dressing in her room. Thérèse in a grey
travelling gown was leaning against the balustrade
of the terrace, and taking one last look at the City
of the Flower.

She had decided to go. In every letter her husband clamoured for
her return. If, as he urgently entreated, she returned to Paris early
in May, they might give two or three political dinners, followed by
receptions, before the Grand Prix. His party was being borne into

power on a wave of public opinion; and Garain thought that Countess Martin's *salon* might exercise an excellent influence on the country's future. Such reasons did not appeal strongly to her; but now she felt kindly disposed towards her husband, and wished to please him. Two days before she had heard from her father. M. Montessuy did not discuss his son-in-law's political projects, neither did he give advice to his daughter; but he contrived to let her understand that people were talking about Countess Martin's mysterious visit to Florence, where she was said to be leading a somewhat fantastic, sentimental existence, with poets and artists at the Villa of Bells. She herself felt that she was too closely watched in the little world of Fiesole. In her new life, Madame Marmet worried her, and Prince Albertinelli caused her anxiety. Her *rendezvous* in the Via Alfieri were becoming dangerous and difficult. Professor Arrighi, a friend of the Prince, had met her one evening, walking in a lonely street, on Dechartre's arm. Professor Arrighi, author of a treatise on agriculture, was the most amiable of scholars. He had turned away his handsome heroic face, with its white moustache, and merely remarked to her the next day:

"I used to be able to divine the approach of a beautiful woman from a distance. Now that I have passed the age when ladies like to look at me, the gods are pitiful: they spare me the sight of them. My eyes are very bad, and cannot recognize even the most charming face." She understood and accepted the warning. She now longed to hide her happiness in the immensity of Paris.

Vivian, to whom she had announced her approaching departure, had urged her to stay a few days longer. But Thérèse suspected that her friend was still shocked at the advice she had received one night in the tapestried room, and that she was no longer quite happy in the society of a confidant who disapproved of her choice; she imagined also that the Prince had represented her as a flirt, and, possibly, as immoral. Her departure was fixed for the 5th of May.

It was a clear bright day in the valley of the Arno. Thérèse, as she dreamed, saw the blue basin illumined by the morning's rosy light. She leant forward, trying to descry, at the foot of the flower covered slope, the barely discernible spot, where she had known infinite joy. Far below, she saw a little dark spot which was the cemetery garden and near at hand she knew was the Via Alfieri. There came before her a vision of that dear room she would never again enter. Those hours passed beyond recall had all the sadness of a dream. She felt her eyes grow dim, her knees tremble, and her spirit fail. She seemed to be leaving her life behind in that spot near the dark cypress-trees. She reproached herself with feeling troubled when she ought to be glad and confident. She knew she would see Jacques Dechartre at Paris. They would have liked to arrive at the same time, or rather to travel together. Although they had judged it best for him to stay three or four days longer at Florence, their

meeting was not far off, already it was fixed and she was living in
the thought of it. Her love was her life, her very flesh and blood.
Nevertheless she was leaving a part of herself in the house of goats
and nymphs, a part of herself which would never come back to her.
In the height of life's vigour she was dying to things infinitely
precious and delicate. She remembered that Dechartre had said:
"The lover is a fetich worshipper; on the terrace I gathered some
dry black privet berries that you had looked at." Why had she not
thought of bringing away one little stone of the house where she
had forgotten the world?

A cry from Pauline disturbed her revery. Bounding from behind
a brown bush, Choulette had suddenly kissed the maid as she was
carrying bags and cloaks to the carriage. Now he was running along
the path as gay as a satyr, with ears pricked up horn-like on each
side of his shining skull.

"Good-morning," he said to Countess Martin. "So I must bid you
farewell, Madame."

He was remaining in Italy at the behest of a lady; that lady was
Rome. He wanted to see the cardinals. One of them, said to be a
man of sense, might possibly entertain the idea of Choulette's socialist and revolutionary church. His object was to plant on the ruins
of a cruel and unjust civilisation the cross of Calvary, no longer
bare and dead, but alive and sheltering the world beneath its living
arms. For the accomplishment of his purpose he was founding an
order and a newspaper. Madame Martin knew the order. The newspaper, which was to cost a halfpenny, would be couched in rhythmic
phrases and plaintive lines. It could and should be sung. Verse, if
it were very simple, passionate or gay, was really the only language
suitable for the people. Prose was only for persons of subtle intelligence. He had met anarchists among the money-changers of the
Rue Saint-Jacques. They passed their evenings reciting and listening to ballads.

And he added:

"A newspaper which should be a collection of songs would appeal
to the heart of the people. They say I am a genius. I don't know
whether they are right. But at least you must admit that I have a
practical mind."

Miss Bell was coming down the steps, putting on her gloves.

"Oh! darling, the town and the mountains and the sky are determined to make you weep when you bid them good-bye. They
clothe themselves in beauty to-day to make you regret leaving them
and long to see them again."

But Choulette, weary of the parched brilliance of the Tuscan
landscape, pined for green Umbria and its cloudy sky. He remembered Assisi standing as if at prayer, in her fertile pasture, in the
midst of a mellower humbler country.

"There," he said, "are woods and rocks, and glades, above which may be seen the sky with white, fleecy clouds. I walked in the footsteps of St. Francis, and I put his hymn to the Sun into good old simple French rhymes."

Madame Martin said she would like to hear it. Miss Bell was listening already, and on her face was a rapt expression, which made her look like one of Mino's angels.

Choulette warned them that it was artless and unpolished. The lines laid no claim to be beautiful. They were simple and unequal, so as not to be heavy. Then slowly and in a monotonous voice, he recited the hymn.

> Je vous louerai, mon Dieu, d'avoir fait aimable et clair
> Ce monde où vous voulez que nous attendions de vivre.
> Vous l'avez semé d'or, d'émeraude et d'outremer,
> Comme un peintre qui met des peintures dans un livre.
>
> Je vous louerai d'avoir créé le seigneur Soleil,
> Qui luit à tout le monde, et de l'avoir voulu faire
> Aussi beau qu'il est bon, très digne de vous, vermeil,
> Splendide et rayonnant, en forme exacte de sphère.
>
> Je vous louerai, mon Dieu, pour notre frère le Vent,
> Pour notre sœur la Lune et pour nos sœurs les Etoiles,
> Et d'avoir au ciel bleu mis le nuage mouvant
> Et tendu les vapeurs du matin comme des toiles.
>
> Je vous louerai, Seigneur, je vous bénirai, mon Dieu,
> Pour le brin de l'hysope et le cime de l'yeuse,
> Pour mon frère terrible et plein de bonté, le Feu,
> Et pour l'Eau, notre sœur humble, chaste et précieuse.
>
> Pour la Terre qui, forte, à son sein vêtue de fleurs,
> Nourrit la mère avec l'enfant riant dans les langes,
> Et l'homme qui vous aime, et le pauvre dont les pleurs
> Au sortir de ses yeux vous sont portés par les anges.
>
> Pour notre sœur la Vie et pour notre sœur la Mort,
> Je vous louerai, Seigneur, d'ores à mon ultime heure,
> Afin d'être en mourant le nourrisson qui s'endort
> Dans la belle vesprée et pour une aube meilleure."*

"Oh! Monsieur Choulette," said Miss Bell, "this hymn ascends to heaven, like the hermit in the Campo Santo at Pisa, who is climbing the mountain on which goats love to graze. I will tell you how it is: the hermit is going up, leaning on the staff of faith; and

*Here follow the Italian original and Mrs. Oliphant's translation from her "Life of St. Francis of Assisi," 1868, the latter by kind permission of Messrs. Macmillan.—W. S.

1

> Altissimu, omnipotente, bon signore,
> Tue so le laude la gloria e l'onore
> E onne benedictione,
> A te solu, altissimu, se konfanno:
> E nullu homo ene dignu te mentovare.

his step is unequal, because the stick being on one side, one of his feet moves more quickly than the other. That is why your lines are unequal. Oh! I understand."

The poet accepted this praise, persuaded that unconsciously he had deserved it.

"You have faith, Monsieur Choulette," said Thérèse. "What good does it do you if it doesn't help you to write good verses?"

"It helps me to sin, Madame."

"Oh! We can sin without it."

Madame Marmet appeared, ready for the journey. With placid pleasure she was looking forward to returning to her little flat in the Rue de la Chaise, her little dog Toby, and her old friend M. Lagrange. After the Etruscans of Fiesole, she would be glad to see her own domestic warrior among the sweet-meat boxes, looking out of the window across the Place du Bon Marché.

Miss Bell drove her friends to the station in her trap.

2

Laudatu si, mi signore,
Cum tucte le tue creature
Spetialmente messer lu frate sole,
Lu quale lu iorno allumeni per nui;
E ellu è bellu e radiante cum grande splendore;
De te, altissimu, porta significatione.

3

Laudatu si, mi signore, per sora luna e le stelle;
In celu l'ai formate clarite e pretiose e belle.

4

Laudatu si, mi signore, per frate ventu
E per aere e nubilo e sereno e onne tempu,
Per le quale a le tue creature dài sustentamentu.

5

Laudatu si, mi signore, per sor aqua,
La quale è multo utile e humele e.pretiosa e casta.

6

Laudatu si, mi signore,
Per frate focu, per lu quale n'allumeni la nocte;
E ellu è bellu e iocondu e robustosu e forte.

7

Laudatu si, mi signore, per sora nostra matre terra,
La quale ne sustenta e governa
E produce diversi fructi e colorati fiori e herba.

8

Laudatu si, mi signore,
Per quilli ke perdonano per lo tuo amore
E sostengo infirmitate e tribulatione:
Beati quilli ke le sosterrano in pace,
Ka da te, altissimu, sirano incoronati.

9

Laudatu si, mi signore, per sora nostra morte corporale,
Da la quale nullu homo vivente po skampare:
Guai a quîlli ke morrano in peccato mortale;
Beati quilli ke se trovarà ne le tue sanctissime voluntate,
Ka la morte secunda non li poterà far male:

10

Laudate e benedicete lu mi signore e rengratiate
E servite a lui cum grande humilitate.

Amen.

THE CANTICLE OF THE SUN, OR THE SONG OF THE CREATURES.

Highest omnipotent good Lord,
Glory and honour to Thy name adored,
And praise and every blessing—
Of everything Thou art the source—
No man is worthy to pronounce Thy name.

Praised by His creatures all,
Praised be the Lord my God,
By Messer Sun, my brother above all,
Who by his rays lights us and lights the day;
Radiant is she with his great splendour stored,
Thy glory, Lord, confessing.

By Sister Moon and Stars my Lord is praised,
Where clear and fair they in the heavens are raised.

By Brother Wind, my Lord, Thy praise is said,
By air and clouds and the blue sky o'erhead,
By which Thy creatures all are kept and fed,
By one most humble, useful, precious, chaste,
By Sister Water, O my Lord, Thou art praised.

And praisëd is my Lord
By Brother Fire,—he who lights up the night—
Jocund, robust is he, and strong and bright.

Praised art Thou, my Lord, my Mother Earth—
Thou who sustainest her and governest,
And to her flowers, fruit, herbs, dost colour give and birth.

And praisëd is my Lord
By those who, for Thy love, can pardon give,
And bear the weakness and the wrongs of men,
Blessed are those who suffer thus in peace,
By Thee, the Highest, to be crowned in Heaven.

Praised by our Sister Death, my Lord, art Thou,
From whom no living man escapes.
Who die in mortal sin have mortal woe;
But blessed they who die doing Thy will,—
The second death can strike at them no blow.
Praises and thanks and blessing to my Master be,
Serve ye Him all with great humility.

XXV

ECHARTRE had come to the carriage door to bid the travellers good-bye. Parted from him, Thérèse realised all he was to her: he had given her life a new and delicious zest, so keen, so real, that she seemed to feel the savour of it on her lips. She was living as if under a spell, in the hope of seeing him again; her happy revery was only occasionally broken, when Madame Marmet remarked during the journey: "I think we are crossing the frontier" or "Look at the rose-trees in bloom on the seashore." Her inward joy remained with her when, after a night in a Marseilles hotel, she saw the grey olive trees in their stony fields, then the mulberry trees and the distant outline of Mount Pilatus, and the Rhone, and Lyons, and then the familiar country, the tops of the clusters of trees, recently dark and violet, now clothed in tender green, the hill slopes carpeted with little lines of cultivated land, and the rows of poplars along the river banks. The journey passed smoothly for her. She was tasting the fulness of past hours and the wonder of deep joy. When the train stopped in the blue light of the station, it was with the smile of an awakened sleeper that she greeted her husband, delighted to see her back. Kissing kind Madame Marmet, she told her she thanked her with all her heart. And truly, she thanked everything, like Choulette's St. Francis.

In the carriage, driving along the quays in the glow of the setting sun, she listened patiently to her husband's story of his oratorical successes, the plans of his party, his own projects and hopes, and the necessity of giving two or three big political dinners. She closed her eyes to think better. She said to herself: "I shall have a letter to-morrow; and I shall see him again in a week." When the carriage had crossed the bridge, she looked at the water all on fire with the reflection of the sunset, at the smoky arches of the bridge, the rows of plane-trees and the chestnut-trees in flower in the quincunxes of Cours-la-Reine; all these familiar sights wore a new loveliness in her eyes. It seemed as if her love had given a new colour to the universe. And she asked herself if the stones and trees recognised her. She was wondering how it was that her silence, her eyes, her very flesh, and the sky and the earth did not cry out her secret. M. Martin-Bellème, thinking she was tired, advised her to rest. And at night, locked in her room, amid a silence so intense that she could hear her heart beat, she wrote her absent lover a letter full of those words which are like flowers in their perennial freshness: "I love you, I wait for you. I am happy. I feel you near me; you and I are alone in the world. From my window I see a twinkling blue star. I look at it and think that you also may be gazing at it from

Florence. I have put the spoon with its red lily handle on my table. Come. I long for you from afar. Come!" And thus she found ever new in her heart those thoughts and sensations which are eternal.

For a week she lived this inner life, in the sweet memory of days in the Via Alfieri, feeling still the impression of kisses she had received and loving herself because another loved her. She employed the greatest care and the most delicate taste in ordering her new dresses. In this she pleased and aimed at pleasing herself. Madly anxious when there was nothing for her at the post office, trembling and glad when there was handed to her from behind the counter an envelope on which she recognised the round elaborate writing of her lover. Memories, desires, and hopes devoured her; and thus the ardent hours passed quickly by.

It was only the morning of the day of his arrival that seemed to her hatefully long. She was at the station before the train was due. It was announced to be late, and she felt crushed. An optimist, and like her father, believing that fate must always be on her side, this unforeseen delay seemed to her like treachery. For three-quarters of an hour, the grey light filtering through the dull windows of the station seemed to fall on her like so many grains of sand in an hour-glass, measuring out the minutes of her lost happiness. She was despairing, when in the red light of the setting sun she saw the huge engine stop gently at the platform. Jacques, tall and slim, came towards her out of the crowd of travellers hurrying to the cabs. He looked at her with that kind of sombre, violent delight which she knew so well. He said:

"Here you are at last. I was afraid that I should die before seeing you again. You do not know and I did not what torture it is to live a week away from you. I went back to the little house in the Via Alfieri. In the room you know so well, before the old pastel, I wept tears of love and passion."

She looked up at him full of happiness, and said:

"And don't you think that I called you, that I wanted you, that even when I was alone, I stretched out my arms to you? I had hidden your letters in the cabinet where I keep my jewels. I used to re-read them every night: it was delightful, but it was imprudent. Your letters were too much like you, and yet not enough."

They crossed the station-yard, among the cabs piled with luggage. She asked him if they were not going to hire a carriage.

He did not reply, and seemed not to hear. She resumed:

"I have been to see your house, but I dared not go in. I looked through the gate, and at the end of a court-yard, behind a plane-tree, I saw mullioned windows with rose trees climbing round them. And I said to myself: 'It is there.' I felt strangely moved."

He was no longer listening, or looking at her. They crossed the pavement quickly, and by a narrow flight of steps, went down into a lonely street which flanked the lower side of the station-yard.

There, among wooden sheds and stores of coal was an inn with a restaurant on the ground-floor, and tables outside. Under the painted sign, white curtains were to be seen at the windows. Dechartre stopped at the little door and pushed Thérèse into the dark passage.

She asked:

"Where are you taking me? What time is it? I must be at home at half-past seven. We are mad."

And in a red-tiled room, furnished with a walnut bedstead, and a carpet in the pattern of a lion, they tasted one moment's divine oblivion.

Coming downstairs, she said: "Jacques, my beloved, we are too happy; we are stealing life."

XXVI

T HE next day she drove in a cab to a street half town, half country, half sad and half gay, where high garden walls alternated with newly built houses. She stopped where the pavement passes under the vaulted arch of a mansion in the Regency stile, fantastically spanning the street, now covered with dust and oblivion. Here and there among the stone-work, green branches gladden this corner of the town.

As she rang at the little gate, in the perspective limited by the houses, Thérèse saw a pulley on a skylight and a big gilded key, the sign of a lock-maker. Her glance eagerly drank in these sights which were new to her and yet already familiar. Pigeons flew over her head, and she heard the clucking of fowls. A countrified servant with a military moustache opened the gate. She found herself in a sanded court, shaded by a plane-tree. On the left, on a level with the street, was the porter's lodge, with canaries in cages at the windows. On this side, was the gable of the next house, covered with a green lattice-work. Leaning against it was the glazed frame of a sculptor's studio, through the glass of which could be seen plaster figures covered with dust. On the right, fixed to the low wall of the court, were precious fragments of friezes and the broken shafts of columns. In front were the six mullioned windows of the moderate sized houses, half hidden by ivy and climbing roses.

Enamoured of French fifteenth-century architecture, Philippe Dechartre had skilfully reproduced the characteristics of a private dwelling in the reign of Louis XII. Begun in the middle of the Second Empire, this house had never been finished. The builder of so many châteaux had died before completing his own shanty. It was better thus. It had been designed in a style which once had an air of distinction, but now appeared common and old-fashioned. The gardens that had once surrounded it had been gradually built up. And to-day, cramped between the walls of high buildings, Philippe Dechartre's little mansion corrected the bad taste of its sham antiquity and its archæological romanticism by the pathos of its rough-hewn stone crumbling away in expectation of the mason, dead for perhaps twenty years, by the heaviness of its three incomplete dormer windows, by the simplicity of the inexpensive roof provided by the architect's widow, and by all the charm of the unfinished and the involuntary. Thus it harmonised better with that ugliness of the neighbourhood which resulted from the rapid increase of the population.

After all, the house had a certain charm with its tumble-down air and its drapery of green. Suddenly and instinctively Thérèse discovered other harmonies. In that picturesque neglect, revealed by the ivy-covered walls, the darkened studio windows, and even by the bending plane tree, strewing with its scaled bark the grass of the court, she read the soul of the master, careless, spendthrift, bearing within him the eternal discontent of the passionate. For a moment her joy was clouded as she realised the indifference with which her lover treated his surroundings. Although united to a kind of grace and nobility, it betrayed a detachment according ill with her own nature and the vigilant careful spirit of the Montessuy. She thought at once how, without disturbing the pensive charm of this wild place, she would introduce into it a spirit of order: she would have the path strewn with sand, and in the corner where there was most sun would plant some bright coloured flowers. Sympathetically she gazed at a statue brought there from some ruined park. It was a Flora, covered with dark green moss and lying on the ground, her two arms by her side. Thérèse dreamed of raising her and making her the centre-piece for the fountain, the waters of which were now trickling sadly into the bucket acting in lieu of a basin.

Dechartre had been looking for her an hour. Now he was glad, but still anxious. Trembling with agitation at his good fortune, he came down the steps to meet her.

In the refreshing shade of the vestibule, from which could be vaguely descried the severe beauty of bronzes and marbles, she paused, overcome by her heart's wild beating.

He pressed her to him and gave her a long kiss. Through her emotion she heard him recalling the delights of the previous day. She saw the lion of Mount Atlas on the rug, and slowly and passionately she gave Jacques back his kisses.

Up a winding wooden staircase, he led her into a large room, which had been his father's study, and where he himself drew, mod-

elled and read. Reading was a kind of opium to him, inspiring him
with dreams over the open page.

Over the cupboards and reaching to the painted beams of the
ceiling was Gothic tapestry, delicately tinted, suggesting a fairy
forest, and a lady wearing a high fifteenth-century head-dress, with
a unicorn at her feet on the flower-strewn grass.

He led her to a divan broad and low, with cushions covered with
sumptuous Spanish shawls and Byzantine dalmatics; but she sat
down in an armchair.

"You are here! Now the world may come to an end."

"I used to think of the end of the world and not to fear it," she
replied. "M. Lagrange out of politeness had promised me it should
come; and I expected it. It was so dull before I knew you!"

She looked round at the tables loaded with vases and statuettes,
at the tapestry, the mass of glittering weapons, the enamels, marbles, paintings, and old books.

"You have some beautiful things."

"Most of them belonged to my father, who lived in the golden age
of collectors. In 1851 he discovered these unicorn stories, the complete series of which is at Cluny, in an inn at Meung-sur-Yèvre."

But curious and disappointed, she said:

"I don't see anything by you, here; not a statue, a low-relief, or
one of those wax figures so admired in England, not one tiny statuette, or even a plaque or a medal."

"How can you think I could bear to live in the midst of my own
works! . . . I know my figures only too well. . . . They bore me.
A thing loses its charm when you know its secret."

She looked at him, pretending to be vexed:

"You never told me that a thing loses its charm when you know
its secret."

He took her in his arms:

"Ah! all that lives is mysterious. And you, my beloved, are for
me an unsolved enigma, the meaning of which is the delight of life
and the horror of death. Don't fear to be mine. I shall desire you
always; I shall never know you. Does one ever possess what one
loves? Are kisses and caresses anything but the strivings of a delicious despair? When I hold you in my arms, I still long for you;
and I never have you, since I would have you always, since what I
want in you is the impossible and the infinite. What you are the
gods only know. Do you think that because I have modelled a few
indifferent figures I am a sculptor? I am rather a kind of a poet and
philosopher seeking in nature subjects which shall agitate and torment me. Feeling for form does not satisfy me. My fellow sculptors
laugh at me because I cannot be as simple as they. They are right.
And that brute Choulette is right too when he would have us live
without thought or desire. Our friend, the cobbler of Santa Maria
Novella, who knows nought of all that would render him unjust or

unfortunate, is a master in the art of life. I ought to love you in all simplicity without those metaphysics of passion which render me absurd and unkind. The only good thing is to ignore and forget. Come, come, in the torture of our separation I have had cruel thoughts of you: come, my beloved. You yourself must drown these thoughts of you. It is through you only that I can forget you and myself."

He took her in his arms, and, raising her veil, kissed her on the lips.

She pulled the black tulle over her face, rather frightened in this strange big room and feeling embarrassed by the presence of unfamiliar objects.

"Here!" she said; "surely you are not thinking."

He said that they were alone.

"Alone? But what about the man with the terrible moustache who opened the door to me?"

He smiled:

"That is Fusellier, my father's old servant. His wife and he compose my household. Don't be alarmed. They stay quietly in their lodge, sullen but faithful. You will see Madame Fusellier. She is familiar, I warn you."

"Why, my love, should a butler and porter like M. Fusellier wear a Tartar's moustache?"

"Nature gave it him, darling, and I would not deprive him of it. I am pleased that he should look like a retired sergeant-major turned nurseryman, for at times he inspires me with the illusion that he is my country neighbour."

Sitting on one corner of the divan, he drew her on to his knee and gave her kisses which she returned.

Then she rose quickly, saying:

"Show me the other rooms. I am curious. I want to see everything."

He took her to the second floor. Water colours by Philippe Dechartre hung upon the walls of the corridor. He opened a door and showed her into a room with ebony furniture.

It was his mother's room. He kept it just as it had been in her lifetime. It looked as if it had been used but yesterday; and it is only yesterday's past that really touches and saddens us. Although it was nine years since it had been used, the room seemed not yet to have resigned itself to solitude. The wardrobe mirror was watching for the old lady's glance, and on the onyx clock a pensive Sappho looked disappointed as she listened for the sound of the swinging pendulum.

There were two portraits on the walls. One, by Ricard, was of Philippe Dechartre, very pale, with tumbled hair, his eyes lost in romantic dreams, his mouth full of eloquence and good nature. The other, painted by a surer hand, was of a lady of uncertain age, thin, with an eager air and almost beautiful.

"My poor mother's room is like me," said Jacques: "it remembers."

"You are like your mother," said Thérèse. "You have her eyes. Paul Vence told me she adored you."

"Yes," he replied, smiling, "mother was delightful: intelligent, with excellent taste, but wonderfully absurd. In her maternal affection almost amounted to madness; she never left me a moment's peace; she tormented herself and me."

Thérèse was looking at a bronze by Carpeaux, on a cabinet.

Said Dechartre: "You recognise the Prince Imperial, by his ears like wings in the statues of Zephyrus, enlivening a somewhat cold countenance. This bronze was a gift from Napoleon III. My parents used to visit Compiègne. Whilst the court was at Fontainbleau, my father took a plan of the château and drew the gallery. In the morning the Emperor would come in his frock-coat, smoking a meerschaum pipe, and pose near him, like a penguin on a rock. At that time I was a day pupil at the Lycée Bonaparte. I used to listen to these stories at meals; and I have never forgotten them. The Emperor would stay there, quite calm and good-tempered, occasionally breaking the long silence by a few words, stifled beneath his heavy moustache. Then he would grow slighty animated and explain his ideas on machinery. He was an inventor and an engineer. He would take a pencil from his pocket, and, to my father's despair, draw figures on his plans. Two or three sketches a week were regularly spoiled in this manner. . . . He was very fond of my father and promised him employment and honours that never came. The Emperor was kind, but he had no influence, as mother used to say. I was a lad at that time. And ever since those days I have felt a vague sympathy for that man lacking genius, but with a heart kind and good, who amidst all life's vicissitudes conducted himself with a simple courage and a good-tempered fatalism. . . .

"And then, I sympathise with him also, because he was opposed and insulted by those who wanted to take his place and who hadn't even his love for the people. Since then we have seen them in power. Ye Gods! What villains! Senator Loyer, for example, who in the smoking-room, at your house, was stuffing cigars into his pocket, and inviting me to do so too. 'To smoke on the way home,' he said. This Loyer is a wicked man, one who is hard on the weak, the humble, and the unfortunate. And Garain, doesn't he disgust you? You remember my first dinner at your house, when we talked of Napoleon. Your hair was beautifully coiled in the nape of your neck in a knot pierced by a diamond arrow. Paul Vence talked subtly. Garain did not understand. You asked what I thought."

"It was because I wanted you to shine. I was proud of you already."

"Oh! I should never have been able to utter a single sentence in the presence of such serious people. Nevertheless I should have liked to say that the third Napoleon appealed to me more than the first, and that I thought him more human. But perhaps such a sentiment would have been badly received. Besides, I am not so utterly devoid of talent as to trouble about politics."

He was walking round the room and looking at the furniture with a tender affection. He opened a drawer in the bureau:

"See, here are my mother's spectacles. How often she looked for them! Now I am going to show you my room. If it is not in order, you must forgive Madame Fusellier, who has orders to respect my untidiness."

The window curtains were drawn and he let them remain so. An hour later, she herself drew aside the folds of red satin. The rays of light dazzled her eyes and scattered themselves in her tumbled hair. She looked for a glass and found only a tarnished Venetian mirror in an ebony frame. Standing on tip-toe so as to see herself, she asked:

"Is that dim shadowy spectre really I? Those who have been reflected in this glass can hardly have congratulated you on it."

As she was taking her pins from the table, she saw a little bronze she had not noticed before. It was a piece of old Italian work in the Flemish style: a heavy, nude, short-legged figure of a woman, as if in flight, with arms extended. She thought it a trifle grotesque and vulgar.

"What is she doing?" she asked.

"She is doing what Madame Mondanité is doing under the porch of the Bâle Cathedral."

But Thérèse, although she had been to Bâle, did not know Madame Mondanité. She looked at the little bronze again, but failed to understand, and asked:

"Can it be so improper? I should have thought anything done under a church porch might be talked of here."

Then suddenly a misgiving occurred to her:

"Good gracious! What would M. and Madame Fusellier think of me?"

Then discovering on the wall a medallion by Dechartre, representing the interesting but vicious profile of a little street girl, she asked:

"What is that?"

"That is Clara, a little newspaper-seller of the Rue Demours. She used to bring me the *Figaro* every morning. She had dimples on her cheeks that were nests for kisses. One day I said to her: 'I will draw your portrait.' She came one summer morning wearing earrings and rings bought at the Neuilly fair. Then I never saw her again. I don't know what has become of her. She was too much a creature

of instinct ever to become a regular prostitute. Shall I take it
away?"

"No, it looks very well in that corner. I am not jealous of Clara."

It was time for her to go home; but she couldn't make up her
mind to leave him. She put her arms round her lover's neck.

"Oh! I love you. And to-day you have been gay and light-hearted.
Gaiety becomes you well. Yours is so sparkling and graceful. I
should like you to be always gay. I want joy almost as much as
love, and who will give it me if not you?"

XXVII

INCE her return to Paris, now six weeks ago,
Thérèse had been living as if in a slumber; and
happy dreams had taken the place of conscious
thought. Every day she met Jacques in the little
house overshadowed by the plane-tree; and when
at last she tore herself away, adorable memories
lingered in her heart. Delicious languor and renewed
desire linked the hours of love together. They both
had the same tastes and were possessed by the same fancies. If one
had a whim the other shared it. Together they delighted to explore
that border region on the outskirts of the town. There the streets
and purple painted taverns are shaded by acacias. Thistles grow on
the stony roads along the bottom of the walls, while over fields and
woods extends a pale sky streaked with smoke from the factory
chimneys. She was glad to feel him near her in a country where she
ceased to recognise herself and felt lost with him.

That day, their whim had been to take the boat she had so often
seen passing beneath her windows. She was not afraid of being
recognised. There was no great danger; and since she had been in
love, she had forgotten to be prudent. Leaving behind the dusty
barrenness of the suburbs, they came upon smiling banks; they
passed islands with clumps of trees overshadowing rustic cafés and
innumerable boats moored beneath the willows. They landed at
Lower Meudon. She said she was hot and thirsty. He took her by a
side door into a tavern, where there were furnished rooms to let. It
was a building surrounded by wooden galleries. In its desertion it
appeared larger than usual and seemed to slumber in rustic peace,
waiting till Sunday should fill it with women's laughter, oarsmen's
cries, the smell of cooking and stench of fried fish.

They went up the ladder-like creaking stairs into a room on the
first floor, where a waitress brought them wine and biscuits. Woollen curtains covered a mahogany bedstead. Over the mantelpiece,
fixed across one corner, was inclined an oval mirror in a flowered

frame. Through the open window could be seen the Seine, with its green banks, and hills in the distance, looking misty in the heat and the sun already inclining towards the tops of the poplar trees. Swarms of gnats were dancing by the river. The quivering peace of a summer evening alike pervaded sky, earth, and water.

Long did Thérèse watch the flowing river. The steamer passed, pounding its screw through the water; and the swell lapping on the shore seemed to make the house on the bank roll like the boat.

"I love the water," said Thérèse, turning to her lover. "How happy I am!"

Their lips met.

Lost in the enchanted abyss of love, the passing of time was unmarked for them save every ten minutes, after the passing of the boat, by the ripple of the waves breaking beneath the open window.

Her clothes carelessly thrown on one side strewed the floor. She lifted her head from the pillow and saw herself in the glass. To Dechartre's loving praise she replied:

"It is true I am made for love."

With sensitive immodesty she contemplated her own image in the silver light of the mirror.

"I love myself because you love me."

Certainly he loved her; and he could not explain to himself why his love was a fervent piety, a kind of sacred passion. It was not on account of her beauty, so rare and so infinitely precious. Her figure had the true lines, but line follows motion and is always fleeting; it is lost and is found again, the joy and the despair of artists. A beautiful line is the lighting which burns the eye while rejoicing it. One admires but one is also overwhelmed. The impulse of love and desire is a sweet and terrible force, stronger than beauty. There is one women in a thousand, whom when you have once possessed you can never leave; you desire her always and for ever. The flower of her beauty is the cause of this incurable malady of love. But there is another and inexplicable cause; it is the soul of her body. She was that woman, who can be neither abandoned nor deceived.

"Ah! you cannot leave me," she cried joyfully.

She asked him why since he thought her beautiful he did not model her bust.

"Why? Because I am but a second-rate sculptor. But I know it and that is not to be second-rate. However, if you insist on regarding me as a great artist I will give you other reasons. To create a living figure you must treat your model as mere matter to be pounded and moulded until it distils the very essence of its beauty. But in you everything is dear to me, your form, your flesh, your whole self. If I were to do your bust I should be servilely attentive to trifles, which are everything for me, because they are something of you. I could not help it, and it would prevent my work from arriving at any unity."

She looked at him a little surprised.

He resumed:

"I do not say that it would be so if I were to work from memory. I have attempted a little pencil sketch, that I always carry with me."

As she insisted on seeing it, he showed it to her. It was on the leaf of an album, a very bold, simple sketch. She did not recognise it, thought it hard, with an expression that seemed foreign to her.

"Ah! is that how you see me, is that the impression I make on you?"

He closed the album.

"No, it is merely a reminder, a note, that's all. But I think the note is correct. Probably you don't see yourself quite as I see you.

Every human being has a different personality for every one who looks at him."

With a kind of forced gaiety, he added:

"From that point of view one may say that the same woman has never been the mistress of two men. That is Paul Vence's idea."

"I think it true," said Thérèse.

"What time is it?" she asked.

It was seven o'clock. She said they must go. Every evening she was later going home. Her husband had noticed it. He had said: "We are always the last to arrive at a dinner-party; there is a fatality about it." But he himself was frequently late, being detained at the Palais-Bourbon. The budget was under discussion; and he was absorbed by the duties of the sub-committee on which he had been appointed reporter. And so reasons of state covered Thérèse's unpunctuality.

With a smile she recalled the evening when she had reached Madame Garain's at half-past eight. She was afraid her hostess would be annoyed. But it was the day of a famous question in the Chamber and her husband and Garain did not arrive till nine o'clock, when they both dined without waiting to dress. They had saved the ministry.

Suddenly she became thoughtful.

"I shall have no excuse, my love, for remaining in Paris when the Chamber is adjourned. Already Father can't understand the devotion that keeps me here. In a week I must join him at Dinard. What shall I do without you?"

She clasped her hands and looked at him with a sadness that was infinitely tender. But he said gloomily:

"It is I, Thérèse, I who must wonder anxiously what will become of me without you. When you leave me I am besieged by sorrowful imaginings; black thoughts come and sit in a circle around me."

She asked what those thoughts were.

He replied:

"My beloved, I have told you already: you yourself must make me forget you. When you are gone, the memory of you will torture me. I must pay for the happiness you give me."

XXVIII

I N THE bay, terminating in two promontories like horns of gold, with here and there a rose-coloured reef, the blue sea was languidly rolling its silver fringe on to the fine sand of the beach. The day was so bright that the sunlight on Chateaubriand's tomb might make one imagine oneself in Greece. In a room full of flowers, with a balcony looking on the myrtles and tamarisks of the garden and the ocean beyond, with its islands and promontories, sat Thérèse. She was reading the letters she had fetched that morning from the St. Malo post office. On the boat crowded with passengers she had not liked to open them. Immediately after lunch, she had shut herself in her room. There, with her letters spread out on her lap, she was eagerly reading, and greedily tasting her furtive joy. At two o'clock she had to go for a coach-drive with her father, her husband, Princess Seniavine, Madame Berthier d'Eyzelles, the deputy's wife and Madame Raymond, the wife of an Academician. That day she had two letters. The first she read was full of gladness and the delicate savour of love. Jacques had never appeared gayer, simpler, happier, more charming.

Since he had loved her, he said, his feet had moved so lightly and so swiftly that they hardly touched the ground. He had only one fear, and that was that he was dreaming and should awake to find he did not know her. Yes, he must be dreaming. But what a dream! the little house in the Via Alfieri, the inn at Meudon! Their kisses, and those divine shoulders, that supple form, fresh and fragrant as a stream flowing among flowers. If he were not dreaming, then he must be intoxicated. Fortunately his reason had left him; and he saw her in her absence: "Yes, I see you near me. I see your heavy lashes shading those eyes more delightful than all the blue in flowers and sky, your lips like a delicious fruit, your cheeks with two adorable dimples when you laugh. I see you beautiful and desirable, but fleeting, vanishing. And when I open my arms you have gone. I see you in the distance far away, on the long yellow sand, no bigger than a spray of heather in flower, beneath your sunshade, in your pink gown. You appear as tiny as when I saw you from the top of the Campanile, on the Piazza del Duomo at Florence. And I say to myself as I said that day: 'One blade of grass would hide her from me completely, and yet she is to me the infinite of joy and sorrow.'"

All he complained of was the torture of her absence. But with his complaints mingled the glad happiness of love. He threatened to come and surprise her at Dinard. "Don't be afraid. I shall not be recognised. I shall be disguised as a hawker of plaster casts; and

I shall not belie myself. Dressed in a grey blouse and coarse cotton trousers, my face and beard covered with white dust, I shall ring at the Villa Montessuy. You, Thérèse, will recognise me by the statuettes on the plank I bear on my head. They will all be Cupids. There will be Faithful Cupid, Jealous Cupid, Tender Cupid, Ardent Cupid; and the ardent Cupids will be the most numerous. And I shall cry in the rude sonorous tongue of the Pisan or Florentine artisan: *Tutti gli Amori per la signora Teresina.*"

The last page of this letter was tender and thoughtful. There escaped from it reverent effusions, reminding Thérèse of the prayer books she used to read when a child. "I love you, and I love everything in you: the earth on which you walk so lightly and which you render beautiful, the light which enables me to see you, and the air you breathe. I love the bending plane-tree in my courtyard because you have seen it. To-night I walked along the avenue where I met you one winter evening. I gathered a sprig of box that you had looked at. I see you and you only in this city which does not contain you."

When he had finished his letter he wrote, he would go out to lunch. The saucepan had upset in the absence of Madame Fusellier, who on the previous day had gone to her native town, Nevers. He would go to a favourite tavern in the Rue Royale. And there, lost in the crowd, he would be alone with her.

Soothed by the charm of invisible caresses, Thérèse closed her eyes and leant back in her arm-chair. Hearing the sound of the coach stopping at the door, she opened the second letter. The altered writing, the uneven lines, the disordered appearance of the pages made her anxious.

The mysterious beginning betrayed a sudden anguish of mind and dark suspicion. "Thérèse, Thérèse, why were you ever mine if you could not give your whole self? Your deception has done me no good, since now I know what I was determined not to know."

She paused in her reading and her eyes grew dim. "We were so happy just now," she thought. "What has happened? And I was rejoicing in his gladness when it had ceased to exist! It would be better not to write, since letters only express feelings that have passed away, ideas that are no more."

She read on. Seeing that he was devoured by jealousy, she despaired.

"If I have not proved to him that I love him with all my strength, with all my soul, how can I ever convince him?"

And she hastened on to see what had caused this sudden madness. Jacques told her:

As he was lunching at a tavern in the Rue Royale, he met an old friend, who was passing through Paris on his way from an inland watering-place to the seaside. They began to talk; and it chanced that this man, who moved much in society, spoke of Countess Martin, whom he knew. Jacques interrupted his narrative to exclaim:

"Thérèse, Thérèse, what use was it for you to lie to me since one day I must know that of which I alone was ignorant? But the mistake was more mine than yours. Your letter posted in the box at Or San Michele, your meeting at the Florence station should have told me, if only I had not so obstinately clung to my illusions, in spite of evidence. I refused to know you were another's when you were giving yourself to me with that bold grace, that charming voluptuousness which will kill me. I willingly remained in ignorance. I ceased to ask you for an explanation out of fear lest you should find yourself unable to lie. I was so prudent that it remained for a fool to open my eyes suddenly and brutally and bring it home to me at a restaurant table. Oh! now that I know, now that I can no longer doubt, it seems to me that doubting was delicious. He uttered the name, that name I had heard already at Fiesole, on the lips of Miss Bell, and he added: 'The story is well known.'

"So you loved him, you still love him. And when, alone in my room, I am biting the pillow on which your head reclined, perhaps he is with you. Doubtless he is. He always goes to the Dinard races; so I have been told. I see him. I see everything. If you knew the sights that haunt me, you would say: 'He is mad,' and you would pity me. Oh! how I wish I could forget you and everything. But I cannot. You know that you alone can make me forget you. I am always seeing you with him. It is torture. That night on the Arno's bank, I thought myself unhappy. But then I did not even know what suffering meant. To-day I know."

As she finished the letter, Thérèse thought: "A chance word has thrown him into this state of agitation. One word sufficed to make him mad with despair." She wondered who the wretch was who had uttered it. She suspected two or three young men whom Le Ménil had introduced to her, warning her to beware of them. And in a passion of wrath, of the cold severe kind, inherited from her father, she said to herself: "I shall know." Meanwhile what must she do? Her lover was ill, despairing, wild with grief; and yet she could not hasten to his side, to embrace him and throw herself into his arms with so complete an abandonment of soul and body as would convince him she was his entirely and compel him to believe in her. She could write. But how much better it would have been to go, and silently nestle near his heart, and then afterwards say: "Now dare to think I am not yours alone." But she could only write. She had hardly begun her letter, when she heard voices and laughter in the garden. Already Princess Seniavine was climbing up the ladder on to the coach.

Thérèse went down and appeared on the steps tranquil and smiling; her broad straw hat trimmed with poppies cast a becoming shadow over her face and her bright grey eyes.

"Good heavens! how pretty she is!" cried Princess Seniavine. "And what a pity we see her so seldom! In the morning she crosses the ferry and goes into the narrow streets of Saint-Malo; in the afternoon she shuts herself in her room. She avoids us."

The coach wound round the wide circle of the beach, past villas and terraced gardens on the side of the hill. And on the left were to be seen, as if emerging from the blue sea, the steeple and ramparts of Saint-Malo. Then the coach passed into a road bordered with gay hedgerows, along which were walking women from Dinard, with figures upright and broad winged cambric caps.

"It is unfortunate," said Madame Raymond, who was on the box by Montessuy, "that the old costumes are dying out. Railways are responsible for it."

"True," said Montessuy, "if it were not for railways, the peasants would still be wearing their old picturesque costumes; but we should not see them."

"What does that matter?" replied Madame Raymond. "We should imagine them."

"But," asked Princess Seniavine, "do you ever see anything interesting? I never do."

Madame Raymond, who had acquired a smattering of philosophy from her husband's books, maintained that things were nothing and ideas everything.

Without looking at Madame Berthier d'Eyzelles sitting on her right on the back seat, Countess Martin murmured:

"Oh! yes, people only regard their own ideas; they refuse to be guided by anything else. Blindly and deafly they go on. Nothing can stop them."

"But, my dear," said Count Martin, who was sitting in front of her, by the Princess, "without such guiding ideas, one would simply drift. . . . By-the-by, Montessuy, have you read Loyer's speech at the unveiling of Cadet-Gassicourt's statue? The opening is remarkable. Loyer is not lacking in sound political common sense."

Having crossed the willow bordered meadows, the coach climbed the hill, and came on to a vast wooded plateau. For some time it followed a park wall. Away in front the road disappeared out of sight in the damp mist.

"Is this Le Guerric?" asked Princess Seniavine.

Suddenly, between two stone pillars surmounted by lions, there came before them a closed gate crowned by four ornaments in wrought iron. Through the bars, at the end of a long avenue of limes, could be seen the grey walls of the château.

"Yes," said Montessuy, "it is Le Guerric."

And, turning to Thérèse, he said:

"You know the Marquis of Ré. . . . At sixty-five he had all the vigour of youth. He set the fashion, was the arbiter of good taste,

and always popular. Young men used to copy his frock-coat, his
eye-glass, his gestures, his captivating insolence and his entertaining fancies. Suddenly he withdrew from society, shut up his house,
sold his horses, and vanished. You remember, Thérèse, his sudden
disappearance? It was soon after you were married. He used often
to call and see you. One day we heard that he had left Paris. In the
midst of winter he had come down here to Le Guerric. We all wondered what had caused this sudden retreat. We thought he must
have suffered some annoyance. Perhaps he had fled in the humiliation of his first failure, afraid lest he should be seen to grow old.
Old age was what he most dreaded. The truth is that for six years
he has been living in retirement. Not once has he left his château
and his park. At Le Guerric he entertains two or three old men,
who were the companions of his youth. That gate opens for them
only. He has never been seen since his disappearance from Paris;
he will never be seen again. He is now as persistent in his retirement as he was formerly in his sociability. He could not bear his
decline to be observed. He is dead though alive. It seems to me not
in the least despicable."

Thérèse remembered the charming old man who had wished to
possess her as the glorious conclusion of his life of gallantry; and
she turned round to look at Le Guerric, at the greyish tops of its
oak-trees, and its four sentry-box turrets.

On the way home, she said she had a headache, and could not
come down to dinner. She shut herself in her room and took the
sad letter out of her jewel-case. She re-read the last page:

"At the thought that you are another's my heart is rent and consumed. And then I cannot bear that other to be he."

It was an obsession. Three times on the same page he had written:

"I cannot bear that other to be he."

She also was possessed by but one idea: she must not lose him.
She would have said anything, done anything, not to lose him. She
sat down, and in an outburst of passion, tender and pathetic, wrote
a letter, in which over and over again she repeated like a groan: "I
love you, I love you, I have never loved any one but you. You are
alone, alone, alone, do you understand? Alone in my heart, alone
in me. Don't listen to that wretch. Listen to me. I swear to you I
loved no one, no one before you."

While she was writing, the indistinct, vague sighing of the sea
accompanied the heaving of her breast. She wanted to write and
believed she was writing the truth; and all she said was sincere
with the sincerity of her love. She heard her father's firm heavy
step on the stairs. She hid her letter and opened the door. Montessuy coaxingly asked if she were better.

"I came to wish you good-night and to ask you something," he
said. "I shall probably see Le Ménil at the races to-morrow. He al-

ways goes, and he is a man of regular habits. If I meet him, dear, do you mind my inviting him to come and spend a few days here? Your husband thinks you would be pleased to see him. He might have the blue room."

"As you like. But I would rather you kept the blue room for Paul Vence, who very much wants to come. It is possible too that Choulette may come without sending us word. It is just like him. We shall see him one morning ringing at our gate like a beggar. My husband is mistaken when he thinks I like Le Ménil. Besides, next week I must go to Paris for a few days."

XXIX

TWENTY-FOUR hours after writing her letter, Thérèse arrived from Dinard at Dechartre's little house at Les Ternes.* She had had no difficulty in finding an excuse for going to Paris. She had travelled with her husband, who wished to visit his constituency, undermined by socialists, in the department of Aisne. In the morning she surprised Jacques in his studio, as he was outlining a big figure of Florence, on the banks of the Arno, weeping over her ancient glory.

The model was posing, seated on a very high stool. She was a tall dark girl. The glare from the window accentuated the clear lines of her hip and thigh, the hardness of her face, her dark neck and yellow skin, the veins on her breast, the muscles of her knees and feet, the toes of which overlapped. Thérèse looked curiously at her, realising the beauty of her form, in spite of neglect and emaciation.

Dechartre, with his chisel and his pellet of clay in hand, came to meet Thérèse with a sad affectionate air which touched her. Then, putting the clay and the instrument on the edge of the easel and covering the figure with a damp cloth, he said to the model:

"That is enough for to-day, my girl."

Then she rose, awkwardly gathered together her clothes; a mere handful of dark woollen stuff and soiled linen, and went behind the screen to dress.

Meanwhile the sculptor washed his hands, whitened by the clinging clay, in a green earthenware basin. Then he went out of the studio with Thérèse.

They passed beneath the plane-tree. The scales from its trunk were strewing the sand of the courtyard.

She said:

*A district of Paris between the Avenue de la Grande Armée and the Boulevard Malesherbes.—W. S.

"You don't think so any longer, do you?"

He took her to his room.

Her letter from Dinard had already partly corrected his painful impression. It had come at the very moment when, worn out with suffering, he needed calm and tenderness. A few lines in writing had appeased his anguish. His was a soul that fed on images, that was less sensitive to things than to symbols of things. But there was still a painful twist in his heart.

In the room everything seemed on her side: the furniture, the curtains, the rugs spoke of love. She murmured sweet words:

"But how could you believe it? . . . Don't you know what you are? . . . It was madness! . . . How could a woman who has known you tolerate any one else?"

"But before?"

"Before, I was waiting for you."

"And wasn't he at the Dinard races?"

She did not think so; and it was perfectly certain that she wasn't there—horses and horsey men bored her.

"Jacques, you are like no one else and need fear no one."

On the contrary he realised his own insignificance; he knew that the individual counts for little in a world where persons are like corn and chaff united or winnowed by one movement of the fan in the hand of a rustic or of a god. But the regular measured motion of the material or of the mystic fan prevents the metaphor from being strictly applied to life. Men seemed to him more like beans in the trough of a coffee-mill. The fact had been brought home to him two days before as he watched Madame Fusellier grinding her coffee.

"Why have you no pride?" Thérèse asked him.

She said little; but she spoke with her eyes, her arms, and her breath, as her breast rose and fell.

In the glad surprise of seeing and hearing her, he allowed himself to be persuaded.

She asked him who had spoken those hateful words.

There was no reason why he should not tell her. It was Daniel Salomon.

She was not surprised. Daniel Salomon, who was said to be incapable of being any woman's lover, at least wished to be intimate with all, and to know their secrets. She guessed why he had spoken thus.

"Jacques, don't be angry at what I am going to say: you are not very clever at disguising your feelings. He suspected that you loved me; and he wanted to make sure. I am certain that he no longer has any doubts concerning our relations; but I don't mind that. On the contrary if you were a better deceiver, I should be less easy. I should think that you did not love me enough."

She changed the subject quickly, afraid of making him anxious.

"I didn't tell you how delighted I was with your figure. Florence on the Arno bank! That is you and I."

"Yes, into that figure I have put all the ardour of my love. It is sad, and I want it to be beautiful. Do you see, Thérèse, that beauty is sorrowful. That is why I have suffered since my life became beautiful."

He felt in the pocket of his flannel coat and took out his cigarette-case. But she urged him to dress. She would take him home to lunch. They would spend the whole day together. It would be delightful.

She looked at him with childlike joy. Then she grew sad, remembering that at the end of the week she must return to Dinard, and afterwards go to Joinville, and that all that time they would be parted.

She would ask her father to invite him to Joinville for a few days. But they would not be alone and free there as they were in Paris.

"It is true," he said. "Paris in its vague immensity is best for us."

"Even in your absence," he added, "I could not leave Paris. I should hate to live in countries that do not know you. A sky, mountains, trees, springs, statues that could not speak to me of you would have nothing to say to me."

While he dressed she turned over the pages of a book she had found on the table. It was "The Arabian Nights." It was illustrated by prints of viziers, sultanas, black eunuchs, bazaars, and caravans.

"Do 'The Arabian Nights' amuse you?" she asked.

"Very much," he replied, putting on his tie. "When I like I can believe in those Arabian princes whose legs were turned into black marble, and the women of the harem who haunt cemeteries at night. These stories suggest easy dreams which make me forget life. Yesterday I went to bed very sad, and I read the story of the three one-eyed Calendars."

"You try to forget," she said rather bitterly. "I would not for the world efface the memory of any trouble which came from you."

They went down into the street together. She was to take a cab a little farther on, so as to arrive a few minutes before him.

"My husband expects you to lunch."

On the way they talked of trivialities, which in the light of their love became important and delightful. They planned out their afternoon so as to cram into it as much as possible of the infinitude of deep joy and the delight of cleverly contrived pleasure. She consulted him about her dresses. She could not bring herself to leave him, so happy was she to walk with him down the sunlit streets in the glad cheerfulness of noon. When they reached the avenue of Les Ternes there was a row of provision shops displaying their wares in lavish profusion. Strings of birds at the poulterer's door, boxes of apricots and peaches, baskets of grapes and heaps of pears, at the fruiterer's. Carts full of fruit and flowers blocked up the roadway. In the glass-covered space in front of a restaurant, men and women were having lunch. Among them Thérèse recognised Choulette, sitting alone at a little table by an oleander in a tub, lighting his pipe.

Having seen her, he haughtily threw a five-franc piece on to the table, rose and took off his hat. He was very grave; and his long frock-coat gave him an austere and decorous air.

He said he would have liked to have gone to see Madame Martin at Dinard. But the Marchioness of Rieu had kept him in Vendée. Meanwhile he had published a new edition of the *Jardin Clos,* to which he had added the *Verger of Sainte Claire.* He had touched hearts that had been thought hard, and made streams flow from rocks.

"So," he said, "I have been a kind of Moses."

He felt in his pocket, and took out of his pocket-book a dirty crumpled letter.

"This is what Madame Raymond, the Academician's wife, writes. I am publishing her words because they do her credit."

And, unfolding the thin sheets, he read:

"I have called my husband's attention to your book; and he cried: 'This is pure mysticism! Here is a walled garden, which I think, among its lilies and white roses, must have a little door leading into the road to·the Academy.'"

Having tasted to the full the savour of these words mingled with the fumes of brandy, Choulette carefully put back the letter into his pocket-book.

Madame Martin congratulated the poet on being Madame Raymond's candidate.

"You would be mine, Monsieur Choulette, if I troubled about elections to the Academy. But do you really want to become a member?"

For a few moments he was solemnly silent. Then he said:

"Madame, I am on my way to confer with various well-known persons in the political and religious world, who live at Neuilly. The Marchioness of Rieu is urging me to stand in her neighbourhood as candidate for a seat in the Senate, which has fallen vacant through the death of an old man, who, it is said, was a general while he lived this life of illusion. I am going to the Boulevard Bineau to consult priests, women, and children on this matter—O Eternal Wisdom! The constituency, whose support I shall solicit, is situated in an undulating, wooded country, with fields bordered by pollarded willows. In the hollow of one of these willows is sometimes found a *chouan's* skeleton, still holding his gun, with a rosary between his fleshless fingers. My profession of faith shall be pasted on the oak-trees' bark. This shall be my manifesto: 'Peace for the priests' houses! May the day come when the bishops, with wooden croziers, may be like unto the poorest curate of the poorest parish! It was the bishops who crucified Jesus Christ. Their names were Annas and Caïaphas. And they still bear those names before the Son of God. Now, while they were nailing Him to the Cross, I was the good thief, at His side.' "

He pointed with his stick towards Neuilly:

"Dechartre, my friend, is not that the Boulevard Bineau, from which the dust is rising down there on the right?"

"Good-bye, Monsieur Choulette," said Thérèse. "Don't forget me when you are a senator."

"Madame, I remember you in all my prayers, both at matins and vespers. And I say to God: 'Since in Thy wrath, Thou hast given her wealth and beauty, look upon her in mercy, O Lord, and deal with her according to Thy great loving kindness.' "

And limping stiffly, he went away down the crowded avenue.

XXX

HÉRÈSE, wrapped in a pink cloth mantle, was coming down the steps with Dechartre. He had arrived at Joinville that morning. She had planned that he should join the small circle of intimate friends, before the hunting season began; for she was afraid that Le Ménil, of whom she had heard nothing, would then be invited as usual. The soft September air blew through the curls of her hair, and the declining sun made her dark grey eyes glitter with sparks of gold. Behind them the façade of the château displayed busts of Roman emperors on high pedestals in the spaces between the windows, above the three arcades of the ground floor. The main building was flanked by two high wings raised still higher by extravagant Ionic pillars supporting their great slate roofs. This style was characteristic of the architect Leveau. In 1650 he had planned the château of Joinville-sur-Oise for that rich Mareuilles, who was the creature of Mazarin and the fortunate accomplice of Surintendant* Fouquet.

Thérèse and Jacques saw before them the flower-beds arranged in great semicircles designed by Le Nôtre, the green lawn and the fountain; then the grotto with its five rustic arches, its giants' heads terminating in columns, and its big trees tinted already with autumn colours of purple and gold.

"All the same," said Dechartre, "these geometrical figures in flowers and foliage have their beauty."

"Yes," said Thérèse, "but I am thinking of a plane-tree bending

*The King's chief financial minister.

over a grass-grown court-yard. We will plant flowers in it, and put up a beautiful fountain, won't we?"

Leaning against one of the stone lions, with almost human faces, which guarded the filled up moat at the bottom of the steps, she turned round to the château, and, looking at one of the dormer windows, in the guise of an open dragon's mouth, above the cornice, she said:

"That is your room: I went up there yesterday evening. On the same story on the other side, right at the end of the passage, is papa's study. A white deal table, a mahogany desk, a water-bottle on the mantelpiece: his study as it was when he was a young man. Our fortune was made in it."

Walking down the sanded garden paths they came to the trim box hedge, bordering the park on its southern side. They passed in front of the orangery, the monumental door of which was surmounted by Mareuilles's Lorraine cross, and they entered the lime walk on one side of the green lawn. Under the trees half stripped of their leaves, statues of nymphs seemed to shiver in the damp shade, streaked with pale rays of light. A pigeon, perched on the shoulder of one of these white women, took flight. From time to time a dry leaf, detached by a gust of wind, fluttered down, and lay like a shell of reddish gold holding a raindrop. Thérèse pointed to the nymph and said:

"She watched me when I was a child and longed to die. I was distressed by fear and desire. I was waiting for you. But you were so far away."

At a point where several paths met the lime-tree walk was interrupted. A lake was there. In its centre was a group of Tritons and sea-nymphs, blowing into shells—forming, when the fountain was at work, a diadem of water with flourishes of foam.

"That is the Joinville crown," she said.

She showed him a path, beginning at the lake and leading into the country, towards the rising sun.

"That is my path. How often have I walked down it sorrowfully. I was sad before I knew you."

They continued in the walk, which, with other limes and other nymphs, went on beyond the lake. They followed it as far as the grottos. Situated at the end of the park, the grottos were a semicircle of rock-work huts, surmounted by balusters, and separated by statues of giants. One of these statues, at one corner of the grotto, towered over it in its huge nakedness and seemed to look down upon it with a stony glance at once fierce and benevolent.

"When my father bought Joinville," she said, "the grottos were a mere mass of ruins overgrown with grass and full of vipers. Thousands of rabbits had burrowed in them. He restored the statues and arches according to Perelle's prints in the National Library. He was his own architect."

A desire for shade and retirement led them to a pleached walk at the side of the grottos. But a sound of footsteps coming from the covered walk made them pause a moment. And through the leaves they saw Montessuy with his arm round Princess Seniavine. They were quietly walking towards the château. Jacques and Thérèse, hidden by a great statue, waited till they had passed. Then she said to Dechartre, who was looking at her in silence:

"This is too much! Now I understand why Princess Seniavine asked papa's advice when she bought her horses last winter."

Nevertheless Thérèse could not help admiring her father for having won this beautiful woman, who was considered difficult to please, and was known to be rich in spite of occasional embarrassments resulting from her spendthrift habits. She asked Jacques if he did not think the Princess very beautiful.

He recognised that she possessed a certain distinction; but her charms were too sensuous for him. She was beautiful doubtless, but in her swarthy beauty he detected a smear of the tar-brush, a negroid strain.

Thérèse replied that it was possible, but that nevertheless, in the evening, Princess Seniavine threw every other woman into the shade.

At the back of the grottos, she took Jacques up moss-grown steps leading to the Sheaf of Oise, formed by a clump of leaden reeds in the middle of a basin of pink marble. There towered the tall trees which shut in the park and marked the beginning of the wood. They passed into the forest. They were silent amidst the faint rustling of the leaves. Beyond the magnificent curtain of elms stretched thickets of aspen trees and birches, the silver bark of which glittered in the last rays of the setting sun.

He held her tightly in his arms and rained kisses on her eyelids. Night came down; the earliest stars were twinkling among the branches. The croaking of frogs was heard in the damp grass. They went no farther.

When in the darkness she turned back with him towards the castle, there remained on her lips a taste of kisses and of mint, and in her eyes the vision of her lover, who, standing by the trunk of a willow seemed like a faun, while she in his arms, with her hands clasped round his neck, swooned with voluptuous delight. As she passed beneath the lime-trees, she smiled at the nymphs who had seen her childhood's tears. In the sky Cygnus was displaying his cross of stars, and the moon was reflecting her delicate horn in the basin of the lake. The insects in the grass were singing songs of love. Turning the last corner of the box hedge, Thérèse and Jacques perceived, black and menacing, the triple mass of the château, and through the great bow-windows of the ground-floor they discerned forms moving in the red light. The bell was ringing.

"I have only just time to dress for dinner," cried Thérèse.

And in front of the stone lions she escaped from her lover, vanishing quickly like a vision in a fairy tale.

In the drawing-room after dinner, M. Berthier d'Eyzelles was reading a newspaper, and Princess Seniavine was playing patience at the card-table. Thérèse, her eyes half-closed over a book, feeling still the prickling at her ankles of the thorns which had scratched her among the brushwood, was recalling with a shudder how her lover had taken her in the woods, like a faun playing with a nymph. The Princess asked if her book were amusing.

"I don't know. I was dreaming while I read. Paul Vence was right: 'It is only ourselves that we find in books.'"

Through the curtains could be heard the staccato tones of the players and the clashing of balls in the billiard-room.

"I have done it!" cried the Princess, throwing away her cards.

That day she had put a big sum on a horse at the Chantilly races.

Thérèse said she had had a letter from Fiesole. Miss Bell announced her approaching marriage with Prince Eusebio Albertinelli della Spina.

The Princess began to laugh: "There's a man who will do her a great service."

"What service?" asked Thérèse.

"Why he will make her disgusted with men."

Montessuy came into the drawing-room, very gay. He had just won.

He sat down by Berthier d'Eyzelles, and taking an unfolded newspaper from the sofa, read:

"At the meeting of the Chamber, the Minister of Finance will bring forward his savings bank bill."

It was a question of authorising savings-banks to lend money to the communes, which would result in depriving the banks that Montessuy directed of their best customers.

"Berthier," asked the financier, "are you resolutely determined to oppose this bill?"

Berthier nodded.

Montessuy, rising, put his hand on the deputy's shoulder.

"My dear Berthier, I have an idea that the ministry will be defeated at the beginning of the session."

He went up to his daughter.

"Le Ménil has written me a strange letter."

Thérèse went and shut the door leading to the billiard-room.

She was afraid of draughts, she said.

"A strange letter," resumed Montessuy. "Le Ménil won't hunt at Joinville. He has bought a yacht of eighty tons, the *Rosebud*. He is yachting in the Mediterranean, and can't live on land. It is a pity. He is about the only man I know who can lead the hunt."

Just at this moment Dechartre came into the drawing-room with Count Martin. After having beaten Dechartre at billiards, the Count became friendly; and he was explaining the dangers of taxation based on household expenses and the number of servants.

XXXI

THE pale winter sunlight shone through the mist from the Seine on to the dogs of Oudry above the dining-room doors.

On Madame Martin's right sat Deputy Garain, ex-Keeper of the Seals, ex-President of the Council, on her left the Senator Loyer. On Count Martin-Bellème's right was M. Berthier d'Eyzelles. A small and serious political luncheon-party. According to Montessuy's prophecy, the ministry had been defeated four days ago. Summoned to the Elysée that very morning, Garain had accepted the task of forming a cabinet. During lunch he was drawing up the list of names to be submitted to the President in the evening.

And, while they were discussing names, Thérèse was recalling the scenes in her secret life.

She had returned to Paris with Count Martin in time for the reassembling of the Chamber, and from that moment she had been living an enchanted life.

Jacques loved her; he loved her with a delightful mingling of passion and tenderness, of knowledge and curiosity. He was nervous, irritable, anxious. But his moody temperament made her appreciate his gaiety all the more. That artistic gaiety, bursting forth suddenly like a flame enhanced love without ever offending it. And her lover's witty merriment was a constant wonder to Thérèse. She had never imagined possible that perfect grace which he displayed alike in his merry moments and in his more intimate moods. In earlier days his passion had been gloomy and monotonous. That alone had attracted her. But since then she had discovered his overflowing versatile gaiety, the unique grace of his sentiments, his gift of drinking pleasure's draught to the very dregs.

"It is all very well to talk of a homogeneous ministry," cried Garain. "We must come into touch with the tendencies of the various parties."

He was anxious. He felt himself surrounded by all the snares he had laid for others. Even his collaborators he regarded as enemies.

Count Martin wanted the new ministry to gratify the aspirations of the ultra-modern party. "Your list includes persons who differ widely in origin and opinions," he said. "Now perhaps the most important innovation in the political history of the last few years is that it has become possible, I may say necessary, for the government of the Republic to be unanimous. These are the very views, my dear Garain, which you have yourself expressed with such rare eloquence."

M. Berthier d'Eyzelles was silent.

Senator Loyer was crumbling his bread. It was an old habit he had acquired in taverns; and he could think best while cutting corks or rolling crumbs of bread. He raised his pimpled face, fringed with an unkempt beard, and, with sparkling eyes, looking constrainedly at Garain:

"I said so; but no one would believe me. The annihilation of the monarchial right was an irreparable misfortune for the leaders of the republican party. They lost a strong opposition, which is a government's best support. All the measures of the Empire were directed against the Orleanists and against us; the government of the 16th of May was hostile to the Republicans. And we were more fortunate still: we directed all our measures against the Right. And what an excellent opposition the Right was—ominous, candid, weak, vast, honest, unpopular! We ought to have kept it. But we did not. And then, it must be admitted, everything wears out in time. Nevertheless, some kind of opposition is absolutely necessary. To-day only the Socialists can give us that strength which the Right furnished fifteen years ago, with such unfailing generosity. But they are too weak. They must be strengthened, multiplied, and made into a political party. At the present moment that is the first duty of the Minister of the Interior."

Garain, who was not cynical, did not reply.

"Do you know yet, Garain," asked Count Martin, "whether you will be Keeper of the Seals or Minister of the Interior as well as President of the Council?"

Garain replied that his decision depended on the choice made by N——, whom it was necessary to include in the cabinet, and who was hesitating between the two offices. Garain was ready to sacrifice his personal convenience to the public interest.

Senator Loyer was pulling a wry face. He wanted the Seals. He had long cherished this desire. He had been a law tutor under the Empire, and, at café tables, had given highly appreciated lessons. He had a feeling for chicanery. Having laid the foundation of his political fortune by articles expressed so as to involve him in prosecution, law-suits, and some weeks in prison, he had henceforth considered the press as a weapon in the hands of the opposition, which should be broken by every good government. Since the 4th of September, 1870, he had dreamed of becoming Keeper of the Seals; he wanted to show people how an old Bohemian, who had served his time in the Ste. Pelagie Prison in Badinguet's days, a law tutor who once expounded the Code while supping off *sauer-kraut* and sauce, could rise to the highest legal appointment.

Dozens of fools had passed him by. He had grown old in the mediocrity of the Senate; dirty, bewitched by a girl he had picked up in a tavern, poor, lazy, disillusioned; his old Jacobinism and his sincere contempt of the people outlived his ambitions and still attached him to the government. Now, having become associated with Garain and his group, he thought justice was about to be done to him. And his patron, who denied it, became an importunate rival. He sneered as he modelled a poodle out of bread-crumbs.

M. Berthier d'Eyzelles, very calm, very grave, very dejected, stroked his white whiskers and said:

"Don't you think you ought to include those in the cabinet who from the very first have adopted the policy towards which we are inclining to-day?"

"It was that course that ruined them," replied Garain impatiently. "A politician should never precede public opinion. It is a mistake to see things too quickly. It is not thinkers that we want in politics. Besides, let us be perfectly frank: if you want a ministry of the left centre, say so, and I withdraw. But I warn you that neither the Chamber nor the country will be with you."

"It is obvious," said Count Martin, "that we must make certain of having a majority."

"If you accept my nominations, then your majority is assured," said Garain. "Our opponents were supported by the minority swelled by the votes that we have won. Gentlemen, I appeal to your public spirit."

And the difficult work of assigning the various offices began again. Count Martin was offered Public Works, which he refused on the ground of incompetence; and then Foreign Affairs, which he accepted without making any objection. But M. Berthier d'Eyzelles, to whom Garain offered Commerce and Agriculture, demurred.

Loyer was sent to the Colonial Office. He seemed chiefly concerned in making his bread-crumb poodle stand up on the table-cloth. Meanwhile, out of the corner of his little eye, from among his wrinkles, he was looking at Countess Martin and admiring her. He was dreaming vaguely of meeting her again some day in private.

Leaving Garain to fend for himself, he devoted his attention to this pretty woman; he tried to discover her tastes and her habits, asked her if she were fond of the theatre and if sometimes her husband took her to cafés in the evening. And Thérèse began to find that, in spite of his dirt, with his ignorance of society and his superb cynicism he was more interesting than the others.

Garain rose. He had still to see N——, N——, and N—— before presenting his list to the President of the Republic. Count Martin offered him his carriage, but Garain had his own.

"Don't you think," asked Count Martin, "that the President may object to certain names?"

"The President," said Garain, "will take into consideration the needs of the hour."

He had already crossed the threshold when he returned, exclaiming:

"We have forgotten the War Minister."

"You will easily find one among the generals," said Count Martin.

"Ah," cried Garain, "do you think the choice of a War Minister so easy? It is obvious that you have not as I have belonged to three cabinets and presided over the council. During my ministries and while I was President, our most insuperable difficulties always came from the Minister of War. All generals are the same. You know the one I appointed when I formed a cabinet. We chose him because he was totally ignorant of politics. He was hardly aware that there were two Chambers. We had to explain to him the whole working of the parliamentary machine; to teach him that there was a war committee, a committee of finance, sub-committees, reporters, a debate on the budget. He asked us to write it all down on half a sheet of note-paper. His ignorance of men and things was alarming. . . . At the end of a fortnight he was familiar with all the tricks of politics, was personally acquainted with all the senators and all the deputies, and was intriguing with them against us. If it had not been for the support of President Grévy, who always mistrusted soldiers, he would have turned us out. And he was a very ordinary general, just like all the rest. Ah! don't think the office of War Minister can be bestowed hastily or without mature reflection. . . ."

And Garain shuddered to think of his former colleague on the Boulevard St. Germain.* He went out.

Thérèse rose. Senator Loyer offered her his arm with the elegant bow he had learnt at Bullier's forty years ago. She left the politicians in the drawing-room. She was in a hurry to meet Dechartre.

The Seine, the stone quays and the plane-trees with their golden leaves were shrouded in a yellowish brown fog. Over a cloudy sky the red sun was casting the last glories of the year. Thérèse, coming out of doors, delighted in the exhilarating sharpness of the air and the dying splendour of the day. Since her return to Paris she had been so happy that every morning she rejoiced in the changing weather. In her benevolent egoism it seemed as if it were for her that the wind blew through the ragged trees, or that the horizon of avenues became grey in the fine rain, or that the sun dragged its cooled orb across the chilly sky; it was all for her, that she might say when she entered the little house at Les Ternes: "It is windy, it rains, it is a fine day," thus introducing the world of ex-

*Where the French War Office is situated.—W. S.

ternal things into the intimacy of their love. And every dawn seemed beautiful, because the day was to bring her to her lover's arms.

On that day as on every day, as she took her way to the little house at Les Ternes, she was thinking of her unexpected happiness, so complete and, she felt, so secure. She walked in the last glorious sunshine, already threatened by winter, and she was saying to herself:

"He loves me, I think he loves me with all his heart. To love is easier and more natural for him than for other men. In their lives there is something above them, a faith, habits, or interests. They believe in God, or in duty, or in themselves. He only believes in me. I am his god, his duty, his life."

Then she thought:

"It is true also that he is not dependent on any one, not even on me. His own thoughts are a magnificent world in which he could live easily. But I cannot live without him. What would become of me if I had him no longer?"

She was reassured when she thought of his passionate admiration of her, and the spell she had cast over him. She remembered having said to him one day: "You only love me with a sensual love. I do not complain; perhaps it is the only love that is true." And he had replied: "It is the only love that is great and strong. It has its measure and its weapons. It is full of sense and imagination. It is violent and mysterious. Its object is the body. The rest is but a lie and an illusion." She was almost at rest in her joy. Suspicion, anxiety had vanished like the clouds of a summer storm. Their worst time had been when they were separated from each other. Lovers should never be parted.

At the corner of the Avenue Marceau and the Rue Galilée she half divined, rather than recognised, a shadow—that of a form forgotten, which had passed close to her. She believed and she wished to believe that she was mistaken. He whom she imagined she had seen was no longer, had never been. It was a phantom beheld in the limbo of a former world, in the darkness of a visionary existence. And she went on, but this uncertain meeting left a coldness, a vague uneasiness, and an ill-defined fear in her heart.

As she went up the avenue she saw the newspaper sellers coming towards her holding out the evening papers with large headlines, announcing the new ministry.

She crossed the Place de l'Etoile, walking hurriedly in the happy impatience of her desire. In her mind's eye she saw Jacques awaiting her at the bottom of the stairs among the nude figures of marble and bronze, taking her in his arms and carrying her, already quivering and faint with kisses, to that shaded room of delight, where the joy of living made her forget life.

But, in the solitude of the Avenue MacMahon, the shadow seen already at the corner of the Rue Galilée, approached and appeared close to her with a lifelike and painful distinctness. She recognised Robert le Ménil, who, having followed her from the Quai de Billy, now joined her in the quietest safest spot.

His air, his attitude indicated that transparency of soul which once had pleased Thérèse. His face, naturally hard, browned by sea and sun, a trifle hollow, very calm, bore traces of deep suffering.

"I must speak to you."

She slackened her step. He walked at her side.

"I have tried to forget you. After what had happened you will agree it was only natural. I did my very best. It would certainly have been better to forget you. But I could not. Then I bought a yacht. For six months I have been at sea. Perhaps you know?"

She signified that she knew.

He resumed:

"The *Rosebud,* a pretty boat of eighty tons. I had a crew of six men. I worked with them. It distracted me."

He was silent. She was walking slowly, saddened but chiefly annoyed. It was utterly absurd and painful for her to listen to this strange talk.

He resumed:

"What I suffered on that yacht I should be ashamed to tell you."

She felt that he was speaking the truth and turned away.

"Oh! I forgive you. When I was alone, I reflected much. Days and nights I passed lying on the divan in the deck-house; over and over again I returned to the same thoughts. During those six months I thought more than I have done in my whole life. Don't laugh. There is nothing like sorrow for opening one's mind. I understood that if I had lost you it was my own fault. I ought to have known how to keep your love. And, lying full length, while the *Rosebud* skimmed over the sea, I said to myself: 'I did not know how to keep her. Oh! if I could begin over again!' By dint of thinking and suffering I came to understand; I understood that I had not sympathised enough with your tastes and ideas. You are an intellectual woman. I didn't notice it, because I didn't love you for that. I unconsciously wounded and irritated you."

She shook her head. He insisted.

"Yes, yes! I often wounded you. I was not considerate enough of your sensitive temperament. There were misunderstandings between us. They arose from our being so different. And then I never knew how to distract you. I never gave you the kind of pleasures that an intelligent woman like you requires."

He was so simple and sincere in his regrets and his suffering that her heart went out to him. She said gently:

"My friend, I have nothing to complain of in you."

He resumed:

"All that I have just said is true. I understood it in my boat out at sea. The hours I lived through there I would not desire for my greatest enemy. Many a time I thought of jumping overboard. I did not do it. Was it because of religious principles or considerations for my family or lack of courage? I don't know. Perhaps it was because you far away were attracting me to life. I was being drawn to you, therefore I am here. I have been watching you for two days. I would not come to your house. I should not have been able to see you alone. And then you would have been obliged to receive me. I thought it better to speak in the street. The idea came to me on board my yacht. I said to myself: 'In the street if she listens to me it will be because she wishes to, just as she did four years ago, in the park at Joinville, you know, by the statues, near the Crown.'"

And he resumed with a deep sigh:

"Yes, as at Joinville, since we must begin over again. I have been watching you for two days. Yesterday it rained; you drove out. I might have followed and seen where you went. I wanted to; but I didn't. I determined not to do anything that would displease you."

She gave him her hand. "Thank you. I knew I should never regret having confided in you."

Alarmed, impatient, nervous, fearing what he would say next, she tried to break off and to leave him.

"Good-bye! You have life before you. You are happy. Only realize it and cease troubling about what is not worth while."

But he interrupted her with a look. There had come over his face that intense, resolute expression she knew so well.

"I told you I had something to say. Listen for one minute."

She thought of Jacques, who must be expecting her now.

A few rare passers-by looked at her and went on their way. She stopped beneath the branches of the Judas-tree and waited in pity and fear.

"See," he said, "I forgive and I forget. Take me back. I promise never to refer to the past."

She trembled. Her surprise and distress were so evident that he stopped.

Then after a moment's reflection:

"I know that what I propose is unusual. But I have thought it over. It is the only possible thing to do. Consider it, Thérèse, and don't give me an answer at once."

"It would be wrong to deceive you. I cannot and will not agree to what you propose; and you know why."

A cab was passing slowly. She hailed it, and it stopped. He kept her a minute longer.

"I expected you to say that; therefore I say again don't give me an answer at once."

With her hand on the carriage door, she looked at him out of her grey eyes.

It was a sad moment for him. He recalled the times when he had seen those eyes half closed. He stifled a sob and murmured in a husky voice:

"Listen, I cannot live without you; I love you. Now I really love you. Before I did not know."

And, while she gave the cabman a dressmaker's address, he walked away with a brisk easy gait, which to-day, however, was a little less firm than usual.

This meeting left her anxious and uneasy. If she must see him again, she would have preferred to find him violent and brutal as at Florence.

At the corner of the avenue, she called out to the coachman: "Les Ternes, Rue Demours."

XXXII

IT WAS Friday at the opera. The curtain had just gone down on Faust's laboratory. Now the orchestra stalls were in movement, opera-glasses were at work surveying the hall of purple and gold beneath the lights far up in the immensity of the roof. Like precious stones in their caskets, the bejewelled heads of the women and their bare shoulders glittered in the dark boxes. Hanging over the pit was the amphitheatre, in one long garland of diamonds, flowers, beautiful hair, dazzling necks and shoulders, gauze and satin. In the front row of the stalls were to be seen the Austrian Ambassadress, and the Duchess of Gladwin; in the amphitheatre, Berthe d'Isigny and Jane Tulle, who had been made famous by the suicide of her lover on the previous day; in the boxes, Madame Bérard de La Malle, with downcast eyes, her long eyelashes shading her finely moulded face; Princess Seniavine, superb, hiding her yawns behind her fan; Madame de Morlaine, between two young married women whom she was educating in the art of being gracefully clever; Madame Meillan, happy in the assurance of thirty years of incomparable beauty; Madame Berthier d'Eyzelles, stiff, with iron-grey hair loaded with diamonds. Her bad complexion accentuated the severe dignity of her bearing. Every one was looking at her. That morning, it had been reported that after Garain's failure, M. Berthier d'Eyzelles had undertaken to form a cabinet. His task was nearly accomplished. The list of ministers was in the newspapers, and included Martin-Bellème at the Treasury. And opera-glasses were turned uselessly to the Countess's box, which was still empty.

The house resounded with a great murmur of voices. In the third row of the orchestra stalls, General Larivière, standing in his usual place, was talking to General de La Briche.

"I shall soon follow your example, old chap, and retire to grow cabbages in Touraine."

He was in one of those melancholy moods when annihilation seemed the necessary sequence to the rapidly approaching end of life. He had flattered Garain, and Garain, thinking him too clever, had passed him by and appointed a short-sighted faddist, a general of artillery, to be Minister of War. Larivière, however, had the satisfaction of seeing Garain abandoned, betrayed by his friends Berthier d'Eyzelles and Martin-Bellème. The wrinkles round his little eyes were puckered up with laughter. On his crabbed face the crow's-feet seemed to laugh all by themselves. He was laughing only in profile. Weary of a long life of dissimulation, he now suddenly indulged in the joy of expressing his thoughts:

"My good La Briche, they are really too stupid with their civil army which is expensive and useless. Small armies are the only ones that are any good. That was Napoleon's opinion, and he knew."

"It is true, quite true," sighed General de La Briche, moved to tears.

Montessuy passed them on his way to his seat; Larivière held out his hand. "I hear that it was you, Montessuy, who defeated Garain. I congratulate you."

Montessuy protested that he never meddled in politics. He was neither senator, nor deputy, nor even member of the General Council for Oise. And looking at the house through his glass:

"Look, Larivière, in that box on the right, there is a very pretty woman with her hair in flat *bandeaux* coming well over her forehead."

And he took his place, tranquil in the enjoyment of the reality of power.

Meanwhile in the *foyer,* in the passages, and in the house the names of the new ministers were being passed from mouth to mouth with sluggish indifference. President of the Council and Home Secretary, Berthier d'Eyzelles; Minister of Justice and Religion, Loyer; Minister of Finance, Martin-Bellème. All the appointments were known except the Ministers of Commerce, War, and the Fleet, not yet nominated.

The curtain had risen on the tavern of the god Bacchus. The students were singing their second chorus, when Madame Martin appeared in her box, her hair dressed high; her white gown with wing-like sleeves; and over her left breast a great lily in rubies sparkling on her white bodice.

Miss Bell was sitting next her in a Queen Anne gown of green velvet. Engaged to Prince Eusebio Albertinelli della Spina, she had come to Paris to order her trousseau.

In the noise and movement of the throng:

"Darling," said Miss Bell, "at Florence you have left a friend who tenderly cherishes the charm of your memory, Professor Arrighi. He gives you what he considers the highest of all praise: he says that you are a musical being. But how should Professor Arrighi forget, when even the broom brushes in the garden remember you? Their bare branches moan over your absence. Oh! they long for you, darling."

"Tell them," said Thérèse, "that from Fiesole I brought away a delightful memory which is to be my very life."

At the back of the box, M. Martin-Bellème in a low voice was giving his views to Joseph Springer and Duvicquet. He was saying: "The credit of France is the best in the world," and again: "Let us pay off our debt by using our surplus, not by imposing taxes." He was in favour of prudent finance.

And Miss Bell went on:

"I will tell the broom-brushes of Fiesole, that you long for them, darling, that you will soon come back to them on the hill. But, I want to ask you: do you often meet M. Dechartre at Paris? I should so much like to see him again. I like him because he has a distinguished soul. Yes, darling, M. Dechartre's soul is full of grace and distinction."

Thérèse replied that probably M. Dechartre was in the house and that he would not fail to come and see Miss Bell.

The curtain went down on the myriad coloured whirl of a waltz. People pressed into the passage: financiers, artists, deputies, in one moment crowded into the little *salon* adjoining the box. They surrounded M. Martin-Bellème, muttered their congratulations, nodded their compliments over each other's heads, and nearly stifled each other in their efforts to shake hands with him. Joseph Schmoll, coughing and whining, blind and deaf, scornfully pushed his way through the crowd and reached Madame Martin. He took her hand, breathed heavily upon it, and covered it with resounding kisses.

"I hear that your husband has been appointed minister. Is it true?"

She knew that it was rumored, but did not think anything was decided yet. But her husband was here. Why not ask him?

Always grasping at literal truth, he said:

"Ah! your husband is not yet a minister? When he is nominated I will ask you for a moment's conversation. It is a matter of the highest importance."

Then he was silent, looking through his gold spectacles, with that glance of the blind man and the visionary, which in spite of the brutal precision of his temperament, surrounded him with a kind of mysticism.

"You have been to Italy this year, Madame?" he asked abruptly. And without giving her time to reply:

"I know, I know. You went to Rome. You looked at that infamous Arch of Titus, that execrable monument bearing among the spoils from Judea the Seven Branched Candlestick. Ah well! Let me tell you, Madame, that the universe should be ashamed of permitting that Arch to remain standing in the city of Rome, where the Popes have only been able to exist by means of the art of the Jews, the silversmiths, and the money-changers. The Jews introduced the science of Greece and of the East into Italy. Madame, the Renaissance is the work of Israel. That is absolute but unacknowledged truth."

And he went out through the crowded ante-room, treading on the hats which collapsed with a dull thud beneath his heavy footsteps. Meanwhile Princess Seniavine, in front of her box, was looking at her friend through the glass with that curiosity with which now and again the beauty of women inspired her. She signed to Paul Vence, who was near her:

"Don't you think Madame Martin wonderfully beautiful this year?"

In the *foyer* sparkling with light and gold, General de La Briche asked Larivière:

"Have you seen my nephew?"

"Your nephew? Le Ménil?"

"Yes, Robert. He was in the house just now."

La Briche thought for a moment. Then:

"He came to Sémanville this summer. I thought him strange, absent-minded. A nice fellow, perfectly frank, and intelligent. But he ought to have a career, an object in life."

It was a moment since the bell announcing the rise of the curtain had stopped ringing. The two old men were passing through the deserted *foyer*.

"An object in life," repeated La Briche, tall, thin, and bent, while his comrade, brisk and active, left him behind and reached the theatre door.

Marguerite was spinning and singing in the wood. When she had finished, Miss Bell said to Madame Martin:

"Oh! darling, M. Choulette has written me a perfectly beautiful letter. He told me that he was very famous. And I was delighted to hear it. And he added: 'The fame of other poets rests upon spices and myrrh. Mine bleeds and groans beneath a shower of stones and oyster-shells.' Is it really true, my love, that good M. Choulette is being stoned by his fellow countrymen?"

While Thérèse was reassuring Miss Bell, Loyer came into the box with an imperious and blustering air.

He was wet and muddy.

"I have just come from the Elysée," he said.

He had the politeness to announce the good news to Madame Martin first.

"The appointments are ratified. Your husband is Minister of Finance. It is a fine office."

"Did the President of the Republic make no objection when my name was brought before him?" asked M. Martin-Bellème.

"None. Berthier reminded him of the hereditary uprightness of the Martins, of your wealth, and especially of your connection with certain personages in the financial world, where support may be useful to the government. And, to employ Garain's happy expression, the President realised the needs of the hour. He confirmed the appointment."

Count Martin's sallow face wrinkled slightly. He smiled.

"The official announcement," resumed Loyer "will appear in *L'Official* to-morrow. I drove in a cab with the government clerk who was taking it to the editor's office. It was a necessary precaution. In the days of Grévy, who was by no means a fool, official decrees have been intercepted on their way from the Elysée to the Quai Voltaire."

And Loyer threw himself into a chair. There, while admiring Madame Martin's shoulders, he continued:

"It can no longer be said, as in the days of my poor friend Gambetta, that the Republic has no women. You, Madame, will entertain royally in the ministerial halls."

Marguerite, wearing her necklace and her ear-rings, was looking in the glass and singing the jewel song.

"We must draw up our manifesto," said Count Martin. "I have already been thinking of it. With regard to my own department I think I have discovered an excellent programme: The debt to be paid off from the surplus. No new taxation."

Loyer shrugged his shoulders.

"My dear Martin, there is no reason for making any radical change in the programme of the last cabinet; the situation remains essentially the same."

An idea suddenly struck him.

"The deuce! I had forgotten. We have sent your old friend Larivière to the War Office, without consulting him. I was commissioned to tell him the news."

He thought he might find him in a café on the boulevards frequented by officers. But Count Martin said he was in the house.

"We must get hold of him," said Loyer.

Bowing to Madame Martin:

"Will you permit me to carry off your husband, Countess?"

They had just gone out when Jacques Dechartre and Paul Vence came into the box.

"I congratulate you, Madame," said Paul Vence.

But she turned to Dechartre.

"I hope you have not come to congratulate me . . . ?"

Paul Vence asked if they would live in the ministerial residence.

"Not for anything."

"But at any rate, Madame," resumed Paul Vence, "you will go to the balls at the Elysée and the Government Offices; and we shall admire the art with which you will preserve your mysterious charm, and continue the subject of our dreams."

"Ministerial changes seem to inspire you with very frivolous reflections, Monsieur Vence," said Madame Martin.

· "Madame," he replied, "I will not say with Renan, my beloved master: 'What does that matter to Sirius?' because you would rightly reply: 'What has big Sirius to do with the little Earth?' But it always surprises me somewhat to see the mature and even the aged led astray by the illusion of power, forgetting that hunger, love, death, all the mean, as well as the sublime necessities of life, exercise so imperious a control over the mass of mankind that those who rule over their bodies are left with nothing more than power on paper and empire in words. And what is more wonderful still— the people believe that they have other rulers than their poverty, their desire, and their imbecility. He was a wise man who said: 'Let us appoint Irony and Pity to be the witnesses and judges of mankind.' "

"But, Monsieur Vence," laughed Madame Martin, "you wrote that yourself—I read your books."

Meanwhile in the theatre and the passages, the two ministers were looking in vain for the General. Through the group of box-keepers, they went behind the stage, and past the stage scenery, which was being put up and taken down, through the crowd of young German girls in red petticoats, sorcerers, demons, ancient courtesans, they came into the *foyer* of the ballet. The vast room, painted with allegorical figures, almost deserted, had that air of gravity arising from State ownership and the endowment of wealth. There were two dancers standing mournfully, with one foot on the bar running along the wall. Here and there men in black coats and women in short full skirts were standing in groups, in almost perfect silence.

As they entered, Loyer and Martin-Bellème took off their hats. Across the room they saw Larivière with a pretty girl, whose pink tunic with a gold belt was slit up the sides over her tights.

She was holding in her hand a piece of cardboard covered with gilt paper. As they approached, they heard her saying to the General:

"You are old, but I am sure you go in for it as much as he does."

And with her bare arm she pointed disdainfully to a young man, with a gardenia in his button-hole, standing near them and grinning. Loyer signed to the General that he wanted to speak to him; and, pushing him against the bar, said:

"I have pleasure in announcing your appointment as Minister of War."

Larivière, incredulous, did not reply. This badly dressed man, with long hair, who in his long dusty coat looked like some shouting juggler, inspired him with such mistrust that he suspected a trap, perhaps a practical joke.

"Monsieur Loyer, Keeper of the Seals," said Count Martin.

Loyer insisted:

"General, you cannot refuse. I have answered for your acceptance. If you hesitate you will promote the undesirable return of Garain. He is a traitor."

"My dear colleague, you exaggerate," said Count Martin. "But perhaps Garain lacks frankness. And the General's support is imperative."

"Our country before everything," replied Larivière, bubbling over with excitement.

"You know, General," resumed Loyer: "existing laws administered with inflexible moderation. Stand to that principle."

His eyes were fixed on the two ballet girls stretching their short muscular legs over the bar.

Larivière was murmuring:

"The *morale* of the army excellent. . . . The disinterestedness of the commanders rising to the most critical situations."

Loyer tapped him on the shoulder:

"My dear colleague, large armies are good after all."

"I agree with you," replied Larivière, "the present army is sufficient for the highest requirements of national defence."

"The best of big armies," resumed Loyer, "is that they render war impossible. It would be mad to engage in war with a force so gigantic that it baffles every human attempt to direct it. Don't you agree, General?"

General Larivière winked:

"The present situation demands great prudence," he said. "We have to deal with unusual and menacing circumstances."

Then Loyer, looking at his military colleague with a certain mild cynicism and scorn:

"In the very improbable case of war, don't you think, my dear colleague, that the real generals would be the station-masters?"

The three ministers went out, down the stage staircase. The President of the Council was expecting them at his house.

The last act was beginning. Only Dechartre and Miss Bell were with Madame Martin in her box.

Miss Bell was saying:

"Darling, I am delighted—how do you say it in French?—*je suis exaltée,* to think that you wear the red lily of Florence on your heart. And M. Dechartre, who has an artist's soul, must be very pleased to see those dear jewels on your dress. Oh! how I should like to know what jeweller made it. That lily is as graceful and supple as an iris. Yes, it is exquisite, magnificent and cruel. Have you ever noticed, my love, that beautiful jewels have always an air of magnificent cruelty?"

"My jeweller," said Thérèse, "is here, and you have named him:
M. Dechartre was kind enough to design this ornament."

The box door opened. Thérèse half turned and saw Le Ménil in
the shadow bowing to her with his stiff grace:

"Will you convey my congratulations to your husband, Madame?"

Rather dryly he complimented her on looking well. To Miss Bell
he addressed a few pleasant, conventional remarks.

Thérèse was listening anxiously, with her mouth half open in the
painful effort to make insignificant replies.

He asked her if she had had a good time at Joinville. He would
like to have been there for the hunting. But he could not arrange
it. He had been yachting in the Mediterranean and later hunting at
Sémanville.

"Oh! Monsieur Le Ménil," said Miss Bell, "did you wander over
the blue sea? And did you meet any sirens?"

No, he had not seen any sirens; but for three days a dolphin had
accompanied the yacht.

Miss Bell asked whether the dolphin liked music.

He did not think so.

"Dolphins," he said, "are simply spermaceti-whales that sailors call ocean geese because of a certain goose-like formation of the head."

But Miss Bell refused to believe that the monster that bore Arion to Cape Tenarus had the head of a goose.

"Next year, Monsieur Le Ménil, if you find a dolphin swimming round your yacht, I entreat you to play to him on your flute the hymn to the Delphic Apollo. Do you like the sea, Monsieur Le Ménil?"

"I prefer the woods."

He spoke simply and calmly, quite self-contained.

"Yes, Monsieur Le Ménil, I know how you love the woods and the thickets where leverets dance in the moonlight."

Dechartre turned pale; he rose and went out.

It was the church scene—Marguerite on her knees, was wringing her hands, her head bowed beneath the heavy weight of her long fair plaits. And there resounded from the organ and the chorus the chant of the dead:

> His Cross in Heaven on that dread day
> Obscures the sun's diminished ray,
> Chaos resumes its ancient sway.*

"Do you know, darling, that the chant of the dead sung in Catholic churches comes from a Franciscan hermitage? It suggests the wind in winter blowing through the larches on the heights of Alvernia."

Thérèse did not hear. Her soul had flown away through the door of the box.

In the ante-chamber there was a sound of chairs being overturned. Schmoll came back. He had heard that M. Martin-Bellème had been appointed minister. And immediately he came to demand his Commander's Cross and a larger flat at the Institute. At present his rooms were dark and small, not nearly large enough for his wife and his five daughters. The only place for his study was a loft. He complained at length and refused to depart until Madame Martin promised to speak for him.

"Monsieur Le Ménil," asked Miss Bell, "shall you go yachting next year?"

Le Ménil thought not. He had no intention of keeping the *Rosebud*. The sea was depressing.

And calmly and determinedly he looked at Thérèse.

On the stage, in Marguerite's prison, Mephistopheles was sing-

*Quand du Seigneur le jour luira,
Sa croix au ciel resplendira,
Et l'univers s'écroulera.

ing: "The day has dawned," and the orchestra was imitating the terrible gallop of the horses. Thérèse murmured:

"I have a headache. It is very close in here."

Marguerite's clear words, calling to the angels, were wafted on the air.

"Darling, I must tell you that poor Marguerite will not be saved according to the flesh, and for that very reason she is saved in spirit and in truth. One thing I believe, darling, that we shall all be saved. Yes, I believe in the ultimate purification of sinners."

Thérèse rose, tall, and dazzlingly white in contrast to the blood-red flower on her breast. Miss Bell enthralled was listening to the music. Le Ménil, in the ante-room, took Madame Martin's cloak. And while he held it unfolded, she passed from the box into the ante-room, and paused before the mirror, near the half open door. On to her bare shoulders, touching them lightly with his fingers, he put the great cloak of red velvet embroidered with gold and lined with ermine, and said in a low voice, very briefly and very distinctly:

"Thérèse, I love you. Remember what I asked you the day before yesterday. Every day, every day, after three o'clock I shall be in our flat, Rue Spontini."

At that moment, as she bent her head for him to put on her cloak, she saw Dechartre, with his hand on the door-handle. He looked at her with all the reproach and sorrow the human eye is capable of expressing. Then he turned away down the corridor. It was as if hammers of fire were beating on the walls of her heart, and she remained motionless on the threshold.

"You were waiting for me?" said Montessuy, who had come to fetch her. "You are quite forsaken to-day; I will take you and Miss Bell home."

XXXIII

N HER carriage, in her room, her lover's cruel sorrowful look haunted her. She knew how apt he was to fall into despair, how quick to lose command of his will. In that mood she had seen him hastening along the Arno bank. In his sadness and anguish it had been her happiness then to run to him and say: "Come." And now again, surrounded and observed as she was, she ought to have found something to say to him, and not to have let him go away in silence and suffering. But she had been taken by surprise and overwhelmed. The absurd incident had passed so rapidly! She felt for Le Ménil that impulsive anger we feel for things that hurt us, the stone against which we bruise our heads. It was herself whom she reproached bitterly for having allowed her lover to go, without one word, without one glance, into which she might have put her whole soul.

While Pauline was waiting to undress her, she walked up and down impatiently. Then she stopped abruptly. In the dark mirrors, in which the candles were reflected, she saw the corridor at the theatre and her lover hastening down it, without looking back.

Where was he now? What was he saying to himself alone? It was torture not to be able to go to him immediately.

For a long while she pressed her hands against her heart; for she felt as if she were choking.

Pauline uttered a little cry. On her mistress's white bodice she saw drops of blood. Without her noticing it, the stamens of the red lily had scratched her hand.

She took off the emblem, which she had worn, openly declaring the secret of her heart, and, holding it in her hand, she gazed at it long. Then once again she saw the Florence days, the cell at San Marco where her lover's kiss fell sweetly on her lips, while through the lashes of her cast down eyelids she saw vaguely the angels and the blue sky painted on the wall, the Lanzi, and the glittering fountain of the ice vendor on the red cotton table-cloth; the little house in the Via Alfieri, its nymphs, its goats, and the room, where the shepherds and the masks on the screens listened to her voice breaking the long silence.

All this was no shadow of the past, no phantom of former days. It was the present reality of her love. And one stupid word uttered by a stranger had shattered these beautiful things. Fortunately it was impossible. Her love, her lover were not dependent on such a trifle. If only she could go to him, as she was, half-undressed, by night, and enter his room. . . . She would find him sitting by the fire, his elbows on his knees, his head in his hands, sad. Then, with her fingers in his hair, she would make him look up and see that she loved him, that she was his, his living treasure of joy and love.

She had sent her maid away. In bed, with her lamp lit, she was pondering over one thought.

It was coincidence, an absurd coincidence. He would understand that nothing so stupid could affect their love. What madness! for him to be jealous of another! As if there were for her any other men in the world!

M. Martin-Bellème opened the door of his room. Seeing a light, he came in.

"Aren't you asleep, Thérèse?"

He had just come from conferring with Berthier d'Eyzelles and his colleagues. On certain matters he wanted advice from his wife, for he knew she was clever. Above all things he wanted sincerity.

"It is done," he said. "You, my love, will help me, I am sure, in a position greatly desired, but very difficult and even dangerous. I owe it partly to you, for it is largely your father's powerful influence that has placed me in it."

He consulted her as to who should be the leader of the cabinet.

She gave him the best advice she could. She found him sensible, calm, and not more foolish than the others.

He indulged in reflections:

"In the Senate I must support the budget as it has been voted by the Chamber. This budget includes innovations of which I did not approve. As a deputy I opposed them. As a minister I shall support them. Then I looked at things from the outside. Seen from within they are quite different. Besides, I am no longer free."

He sighed.

"Ah! if people only knew how little one can do when one is in power."

He gave her his impressions. Berthier was holding back. The others were inscrutable. Loyer alone appeared extremely autocratic.

She heard him patiently, but without paying attention. That pale face and thin voice were to her a timepiece marking the slow passing of the minutes one by one.

"Now and then Loyer gives utterances to the most extraordinary opinions. At the same time that he declares himself a firm supporter of the Concordat, he says: 'The bishops are the *préfets* of religion. I shall protect them because they belong to me. And through them I shall control the spiritual gamekeepers—the parish priests.' "

He reminded her that she would have to move in a circle not her own, which would doubtless shock her by its vulgarity. But their position would require them to slight no one. Besides, he counted on her tact and her loyalty.

She looked at him, rather alarmed.

"Nothing is urgent at present, my love. We shall see later."

He was tired and overdone. He wished her good-night and advised her to sleep. She would ruin her health if she read like that all night. He left her.

She heard the sound of his footsteps, rather heavier than usual, while he was crossing the study heaped up with blue-books and newspapers, on his way to the bedroom, where he would sleep, perhaps. Then the silence of the night oppressed her. She looked at her watch. It was half-past one.

She said to herself: "He also is suffering. . . . He looked at me with such anger and despair."

She had lost none of her courage nor her ardour. What made her desperate was to be there, a prisoner, as if in solitary confinement. She would be free when day dawned; then she would go to him, see him, and explain all. It was so simple. In the sad monotony of her thoughts, she listened to the rolling of carts, at long intervals, on the quay. This sound, which marked the flight of the hours, ar-

rested her attention, almost interested her. She made an effort to
catch the faint noise in the distance, growing more and more distinct until she could distinguish the rolling of the wheels, the
grinding of the axle-trees, the clashing of hoofs, growing feebler
and feebler, and dying away into an imperceptible murmur.

And, when silence was restored, she returned to her thoughts.

He would understand that she loved him, that she had never
loved any one else. But it was distressing that the night was so
long in passing away. She dared not look at her watch, for fear of
perceiving the terrible slowness of the hours.

She rose, went to the window, and drew aside the curtains. There
was a pale light in the cloudy sky. She thought it must be the
beginning of daybreak. She looked at her watch. It was half-past
three.

She went back to the window. The infinite darkness outside attracted her. She looked. The pavement shone under the gas-lamps.
An invisible, silent rain was falling from the dull sky. Suddenly a
voice came out of the silence; high and then low, so staccato that
it seemed several voices replying to each other. It was a drunkard
loafing on the pavement and knocking up against the trees. He was
engaged in a long argument with the creatures of his dreams,
magnanimously allowing them to speak, only to overwhelm them
afterwards by wild gestures and imperious speech. Thérèse watched
the poor man swaying along the parapet, in his white blouse, like
a rag in the night wind, and now and again she heard the words,
constantly recurring: "That is what I say to the government."

Numb with cold, she went back to bed. An agonising thought
came into her mind. "He is jealous, madly jealous. It is a physical
matter, one of nerves. But his love also is physical and of the
nerves. His love and his jealousy are the same thing. Another
would understand. It would be enough to appeal to his self-respect."
She knew that in him jealousy was physical torture, an open wound,
extended by the powers of imagination. She knew how deep-rooted
was the evil. She had seen him turn pale in front of the bronze St.
Mark, when she posted her letter in the wall of the old Florentine
house; and then she was only his in his desire and his dreams.

Later, after their long kisses, she recalled his half-stifled complaints, his sudden sadness, and the sorrowful mystery of the words
he was always repeating: "You alone can help me to forget you."
She beheld the letter received at Dinard and his wild despair over a
few words heard in a café. She felt that the chance blow had fallen
on the sensitive spot, on the open wound. But she did not lose
heart. She would say everything, confess everything, and all her
avowals would proclaim: "I love you. I have never loved another."
She had never deceived him. She would tell him nothing that he
had not guessed already. She had lied so little, as little as possible,
and merely to avoid giving him pain. How could he fail to under-

stand? It would be best that he should know all, since that all amounted to nothing. Over and over again she thought the same thoughts and said to herself the same words.

Her lamp was going out. She lit candles. It was half-past six. She realised that she had slept. She ran to the window. The sky was black, and touching the earth seemed to form one chaos of thick darkness. Then she became curious as to what hour the sun would rise. She had no idea. All she knew was that the nights were very long in December. She tried to remember, but could not. She never thought of looking at the open calendar on the table. The heavy footsteps of workmen passing in groups, the noise of the milk carts and the vegetable waggons sounded like good omens to her ears. She shuddered at these first signs of the town's awakening.

XXXIV

T NINE o'clock, in the courtyard of the little house, she found M. Fusellier sweeping away the rain-water, with his pipe in his mouth. Madame Fusellier came out of her lodge. They both looked embarrassed. Madame Fusellier was the first to speak:

"M. Jacques is not at home."

And, as Thérèse was silent and did not move, Fusellier came up to her, broom in hand, hiding his pipe behind his back.

"M. Jacques has not come home yet."

"I will wait for him," said Thérèse.

Madame Fusellier showed her into the drawing-room, where she lit the fire. And because the wood only smoked and refused to burst into a flame, she stayed bending over it, her hands on her hips.

"It is the rain," she said, "that makes the smoke come down the chimney."

Madame Martin told her not to trouble to light a fire, she was not cold.

She saw herself in a mirror. Her face was white, except for her cheeks which were burning. And then only she became aware that her feet were as cold as ice. She went up to the fire. Madame Fusellier, seeing that she was anxious, tried to say something comforting:

"M. Jacques won't be long—wouldn't Madame like to warm herself while she is waiting?"

The rain was pattering on the glazed ceiling and the light was dull. On the walls, the lady with the unicorn, stiff and of deathly hue, seemed no longer beautiful among her cavaliers, in the forest

full of birds and flowers. Thérèse was muttering to herself the
words:

"He has not come home." As she repeated them over and over
again, they seemed to lose their meaning. With burning eyes she
looked at the door.

She remained thus without moving, without thinking, how long
she didn't know; perhaps it was half an hour. Then there was a
sound of footsteps; the door opened. He entered. She saw that he
was wet through, and muddy, and burning with fever.

She looked at him so sincerely and so frankly that he was astonished. But, almost immediately all his anguish welled up within
him.

"What do you want of me now?" he said. "You have done me all
the harm in your power."

His fatigue made him seem gentle. She was alarmed.

"Jacques, listen to me . . ."

He signified that there was nothing more to be said.

"Jacques, listen. I have not deceived you. Oh! no I have not deceived you. Could it have been possible? Could it . . ."

He interrupted:

"Have pity on me. Don't hurt me any more. Leave me, I entreat
of you. If you knew what a night I have passed, you would not dare
to torture me further."

He sank on to the divan, where, six months ago, he had kissed
her under her veil.

All night he had walked without thinking of where he was going.
He had followed the Seine, until he found its banks fringed with
willows and poplars. To still his suffering he had tried to distract
his mind. On the Quai de Bercy he had watched the moon fleeting
among the clouds. For an hour he had seen her hidden and then
reappearing. Then he had set himself with minute accuracy to
count the windows of houses. It had begun to rain. He had gone to
the Market, and drunk brandy in a tavern. A big woman, who
squinted, had said to him: "You don't look happy." He sank down
on a leather covered bench. And for a moment he was at rest.

The visions of that terrible night passed before him. He said: "I
thought of that night on the bank of the Arno. You have robbed
me of all beauty and all joy."

He besought her to leave him alone. In his weariness he pitied
himself profoundly. He would have liked to sleep, not to die: death
always filled him with horror. But to sleep and never wake. Meanwhile he saw her before him, ardently desired, and as desirable as
before, with her face worn by suffering and in spite of the fixity of
her fevered gaze. And inscrutable now, more mysterious than ever.
He looked at her. His hatred revived with his anguish. With an evil
glance, he sought signs of caresses that he had not given her.

She held out her arms to him:

"Listen, Jacques."

He showed that it was useless for her to speak. Nevertheless he wanted to hear her, and already he was listening eagerly. What she was going to say, he hated and rejected beforehand, but it was the only thing in the world that interested him. She said:

"You dared to believe that I betrayed you, that I did not live in and for you alone. But don't you understand? Don't you realise that if that man had been my lover he would not have needed to speak to me in the theatre, in that box; he would have had a thousand other opportunities of arranging a *rendezvous*. Oh! no, my love, I assure you that since I have had the happiness—and even to-day in agony and sorrow, I still say happiness—of knowing you, I have been yours alone. Could I possibly have been another's? It is monstrous to imagine it. But I love you, I love you. It is you alone that I love. I have never loved another."

He replied slowly, with cruel deliberation:

" 'Every day I shall be in our flat, Rue Spontini, after three o'clock.' It was no lover, not your lover who spoke those words! No! It was a stranger."

She rose, and with sad seriousness:

"Yes, I have been his mistress. You knew it. I denied it, I lied, so as not to give you pain, not to irritate you. I saw how anxious and suspicious you were. But I lied so little and so badly! You knew it. Don't reproach me with it. You knew it, you often spoke of the past, and then one day at a restaurant you heard. . . . And your imagination went beyond the truth. I did not deceive you when I lied. And if you knew how little it counts in my life! And besides, I did not know you. I did not dream that I should ever know you. I was so weary of my life."

She threw herself on her knees:

"I was wrong. I ought to have waited for you. But, if you only knew how all that is as if it had never been, and it was so very little."   •

And in a sweet, singing voice, she said over and over again like a refrain:

"Why did you not come before? Why?"

She crept to him, tried to take his hands and clasp his knees. He repulsed her:

"I was stupid. I did not believe, I did not know. I was resolved not to know."

He rose, and, in an outburst of hatred:

"I could not bear it, no I could not bear it to be that one."

She sat down on the divan that he had quitted; and then plaintively, speaking low, she explained the past. She had been cast all alone into a horribly commonplace society. Then it had happened, she had yielded. But immediately she had regretted it. Oh! if he knew how dull and sad her life had been, he would not be jealous, he would pity her.

She shook her head, and, looking at him through her disordered hair:

"But I am talking of another woman. I have nothing in common with that woman. I have existed only since I knew you, since I was yours."

He had begun to pace wildly up and down the room, just as a short time before he had walked on the banks of the Seine. He burst into a bitter laugh:

"Yes, but while you were loving me, what about the other woman, who was not you?"

She looked at him indignantly:

"Can you believe . . . ?"

"Didn't you see him at Florence, didn't you go with him to the station?"

She told him that he had sought her in Italy, that she had met him and parted from him, that he had gone away in anger, and that since he had tried to persuade her to come back to him, but that she had not even thought about it.

"My love, I see none, I know none but you."

He shook his head.

"I do not believe you."

She grew angry.

"I have told you everything. Accuse me, condemn me, but don't insult my love for you. That I forbid."

He shook his head.

"Leave me. You have hurt me too much. I loved you so dearly that any sorrow you might have caused me, I would have accepted and kept and loved; but this is hideous. I hate it. Leave me. My grief is too deep. Good-bye."

Standing firmly, her little feet planted on the carpet:

"I came. It is for my happiness, my life that I am contending. I am resolute, you know. I will not go."

And she repeated all she had said. Emphatic and sincere, convinced that she was in the right, she explained how she had broken the already slackened tie that chafed her. She told how from the day when she had yielded to him in the little house in the Via Alfieri, she had been his entirely, without a regret, certainly without a glance or a thought for any one else. But when she spoke of another, she angered him. And he cried:

"I don't believe you."

Then she began again to repeat what she had said.

And suddenly, instinctively she looked at her watch:

"Good heavens! it is twelve o'clock."

Many a time she had uttered the same cry of alarm when the hour for parting had surprised them. And Jacques trembled when he heard those familiar words now so sorrowful and despairing. For a few minutes longer she implored him with tears and passionate words. Then she was obliged to go; she had gained nothing.

At home she found market-women waiting in the hall to present her with a bouquet. She remembered that her husband was minister. There were piles of telegrams, cards, letters, congratulations, requests. Madame Marmet wrote asking her to recommend her nephew to General Larivière.

She went into the dining-room, and sank exhausted on to a divan. M. Martin-Bellème was finishing his lunch. He was due at once at a cabinet council and at the house of the retiring Minister of Finance, on whom he had to call. The discreet obsequiousness of his staff had already flattered, wearied, and perturbed him.

"Don't forget, my love," he said, "to call on Madame Berthier d'Eyzelles. You know how sensitive she is."

She made no reply. While he was dipping his withered fingers in a finger-glass, he looked up, and, seeing her tired look and her disordered dress, he did not dare to say another word.

He found himself face to face with a mystery he was determined to ignore, a secret sorrow which one word might disclose. It filled him with anxiety, fear, and a kind of respect.

He threw down his serviette.

"Excuse me, my dear."

And he went out.

She tried to eat. She could swallow nothing. For everything she felt an uncontrollable loathing.

About two o'clock she went back to the little house at Les Ternes. She found Jacques in his room. He was smoking his wooden pipe. A cup of coffee nearly empty was on the table. He looked at her with a hardness that froze the blood in her veins. She did not dare to speak, feeling that all she might say would offend and irritate him, and that her mere appearance discreet and silent rekindled his wrath. He knew that she would come back; he had expected her with the impatience of hatred, with an eagerness as keen as when he waited for her in the house in the Via Alfieri. She saw in a flash that she had been unwise in coming; absent he would have desired her, longed for her, summoned her perhaps. But it was too late; and besides, being prudent had not occurred to her.

She said to him:

"You see, I came back; I could not do otherwise. And it was quite natural, since I love you. You know it."

She had felt that everything she could say would only irritate him. He asked her if she said as much in the Rue Spontini.

She looked at him profoundly sad.

"Jacques, you have often said that deep down in your heart was a world of hatred and anger, which might break forth against me. I see you like to make me suffer."

With loving patience, she retold at length the story of her life, the emptiness and sadness of the past, and how, since he had made her his, she had lived only in him and through him.

Her words were as sincere as her glance. She was sitting near him. From time to time he felt the now timid touch of her fingers and the warmth of her fevered breath. He listened with a cruel interest. Hard on himself, he wanted to know everything: her latest meeting with Le Ménil, and the story of their final rupture. She told him faithfully all that had happened at the Hôtel de la Grande Bretagne; but she represented it as having taken place in a walk in the Cascine, for fear lest the thought of their sad interview in a private room should still further anger her lover. Then she explained the meeting at the station. She had not wished to drive to desperation a sad passionate man. Since then she had heard nothing of him till the day when he spoke to her in the Avenue MacMahon. She repeated what he had said under the Judas-tree. Two days later she had seen him in her box at the opera. She had certainly not invited him to come. That was the truth.

It was the truth. But the old poison slowly accumulated was working. The past, the irreparable past had been called into the present by her confession. He saw it and it tortured him.

"I don't believe you," he said. And he added:

"And if I did believe you, the very thought that you had been the mistress of that man would make it impossible for me ever to see you again. I told you so, I wrote it to you—you remember, when you were at Dinard. I could not bear it to be he. And since . . ."

He paused. She said:

"You know there has been nothing since."

He resumed with sullen passion:

"Since, I have seen him."

Long they remained silent. At length, in a surprised and plaintive tone she said:

"But my love, you should have thought that a woman like me, married as I was. . . . Every day women come to their lovers with a more serious past than mine, and are loved nevertheless. Ah! if you only knew how little my past counts for in my life."

"I know what you can be. One cannot forgive in you what one would overlook in another."

"But, my love, I am like other women."

"No, you are not like the others. In you nothing can be overlooked."

He spoke with compressed mouth and look of hatred. His eyes, those eyes that she had seen so big, so sparkling with the gentle fire of love, now hard and dry, sunken behind their wrinkled lids, made him look quite different. He frightened her.

She went to the opposite end of the room. Seated there, with her heart in her throat, her eyes wide open with astonishment, like a child, she stayed long, trembling and stifling her sobs. Then she burst out crying.

"Why did I ever know you?" he sighed.

Through her tears, she answered:

"I do not regret having known you. It is killing me, and I do not regret it. I have loved."

He cruelly persisted in making her suffer. He knew how badly he was acting and yet could not help himself.

"It is possible that after all you may have loved me too."

With a slight bitterness, she replied:

"But I loved you only. I loved you too well. That is what you are punishing me for now. . . . Oh! how can you think that I ever was to another what I have been to you!"

"Why not?"

She looked at him without strength or courage:

"Tell me, is it true that you don't believe me?"

She added very softly:

"If I were to kill myself, would you believe me?"

"No, I should not believe you."

She wiped her face with her handkerchief, then looking up, her eyes sparkling through her tears:

"Then, it is all over."

She rose, looked round the room at the thousand things with which she had lived in joyful, voluptuous intimacy, that she had made her own, and that now suddenly were nothing to her; they regarded her as a stranger and an enemy; she looked at the nude woman, who was making that gesture in flight that had not been explained to her; the Florentine medals recalling Fiesole and the enchanted hours in Italy; Dechartre's study of the profile of a street girl with a laugh on her thin worn pretty face. She paused for a moment, she stood in front of it, sympathising with that little newspaper-seller, who had also come there and disappeared, carried into the terrible immensity of life and things.

She repeated:

"Then it is over."

He was silent.

Their forms were growing indistinct in the twilight.

She said:

"What is to become of me?"

He replied:

"And what will become of me?"

They looked pitifully at each other, because each was filled with self pity.

Thérèse continued:

"And I who used to fear growing old, for your sake and mine, lest our beautiful love might utterly die! It would have been better had it never been born. Yes, it would have been better had I never been born. Was it not an omen when as a child, under the lime-trees at Joinville, near the Crown, in front of the marble nymphs, I longed to die?"

With arms hanging down and hands clasped, she looked up; through her tears, her eyes sparkled in the gloom.

"Is there no way of making you feel that what I tell you is true, that never, since I was yours, never . . . But how could I? The very idea seems to me horrible, absurd! Can you know me so little?"

He shook his head sadly.

"I don't know you."

Once again she looked round questioningly at all the things in the room that had witnessed their love.

"But then, all that we have been to each other . . . it was in vain, it was useless. We have merely met, we have not become one."

She grew indignant. It was impossible for him not to realise what he was to her.

And in the passion of her rejected love, she threw herself into his arms and covered him with tears and kisses.

He forgot everything, took her, aching, broken, but happy, and pressed her in his arms with the mournful rage of desire. Already her head thrown back on the pillow, she was smiling through her tears. Suddenly he tore himself away from her.

"I no longer see you alone. The other is always with you."

Silent, indignant, despairing, she looked at him. She rose, arranged her dress and her hair, with a feeling of shame that was new to her. Then, realising that the end had come, she looked around her in astonishment, with eyes that saw nothing, and went out slowly.